The Rose of the Prophet

TRILOGY

Margaret Weis and Tracy Hickman

The Will of the Wanderer

The Paladin of the Night

The Prophet of Akhran

Cover art by Larry Elmore
Interior art by Paul Bielaczyc and Mike Bielaczyc
Maps by Sean Macdonald

margaret weis
productions, ltd.

THE ROSE OF THE PROPHET TRILOGY

Cover art by Larry Elmore
Trade Paperback Edition First Printing: October 2006

ISBN-10: 1-931567-43-3
ISBN-13: 978-1-931567-43-5

Margaret Weis Productions, Ltd.
253 Center St #126
Lake Geneva, WI 53147
Tel 262-725-3518
Fax 262-725-3521

Visit our website at **www.margaretweis.com**

Introduction
by Margaret Weis
April 2006

Tracy and I had just finished the *Darksword* books—an introspective, brooding series about one man's struggle to rise from darkness into the light. We were considering what to do for our next work and the idea came to us that we wanted to have some fun, not be quite so serious. We would do a "wahoo" adventurous story that would be very different from anything we'd done before.

At the time, Tracy and his wife, Laura, were reading the *Arabian Nights* stories and enjoying them immesensely. Tracy suggested it would be fun to do a series with an Arabian-like fantasy setting and thus the idea for this series, the *Rose of the Prophet*, came about.

We did research on all things Arabian, from the food to the clothing to the history to the language, names, and the layout of the cities. Tracy developed a unique perspective on the gods and religion (and any relationship to a twenty-sided die is purely coincidental!). He came up with the idea that magic would be the province of women in this setting, which would give the women a power base and would also provide for interesting conflict when a medieval-era, Western-type male magic-user suddenly finds himself in what to him is a strange and bewildering environment.

As usual, we had lots of fun working on this project. I remember one incident in particular. I'm accustomed, when working with Tracy, to write the characters into all sorts of terrible situations and then turning to him for help to save them. In this series, I had come to a part in which the wizard, Mathew, is captured by the enemy (I'll be vague so as not to ruin the suspense for you!) and it occurred to me that these people would simply kill him. There was no reason for them to allow him to live. And, Mathew had to survive at this point!

So I called Tracy and explained the problem. I suggested that perhaps Mathew knew something or he had something in his possession that would be so important to these people that they would not only let him live, but even help keep him alive. I had no idea what that could be, however.

Tracy knew. He said that Mathew was carrying a crystal globe filled with water and inside were two fish. (Now, mind you, this fish bowl is in the desert!) I said, fine, what's so special about these fish?

Tracy refused to tell me. "Just make certain that nothing happens to them!" he warned me.

So Mathew and I carried these fish through the desert for a good many chapters with neither of us having the slightest idea who or what they were, just both of us knowing they were crucial to the plot and that we couldn't allow anything to happen to them.

Both Tracy and I enjoyed working on the *Rose of the Prophet*. We gained insight into a culture vastly different from our own, an ancient culture with a proud heritage and tradition and one for which we both came to have a great respect.

The Will of the Wanderer

FOREWORD

Look where you will, bold adventurer, for as far as the eye can see, there is nothing.

You stand near the Well of Akhran, a large oasis located in the center of the great Pagrah Desert. This is the last water you will find between here and the Kurdin Sea, which lies to the east. The rest of the party, delighting in the first signs of life they have seen after two days of travel through rolling, empty dunes, revels in the shady greenness, lounging beneath the date palms, dabbling their feet and hands in the cool water that bubbles up from somewhere underground. You, however—by nature restless and wandering—are already tired of this place and pace about, eager to leave and continue your journey. The sun is dipping down in the west and your guide has decreed that you must spend the night riding, for no one crosses the stretch of desert to the east, known as the Sun's Anvil, during the hours of daylight.

You look to the south. The landscape unfolds before you, an endless expanse of windswept granite whose broad, brownish, reddish monotony is occasionally relieved by touches of green: the feathery-limbed tamarisk, the tall acacia, manshaped cacti, scrub pine, thorn trees, and clumps of a silvery-green grass (which your camels love to eat) that springs up in odd and unexpected places. Continue traveling to the southwest and you will enter the land of Bas, a land of contrast, a land of huge cities of vast wealth and primitive tribes, skulking on the plains.

Glancing to the north, you see more of the same monotonous windswept land. But well-traveled as you are, you know that if you journey several hundred miles north, you will eventually leave the desert behind. Entering into the foothills of the Idrith Mountains, you follow a pass between the Idrith and the Kich ranges and arrive at a well-traveled highway built of wood over which rolls innumerable wagons and carts, all heading still farther north for the magnificent *Kasbah* of Khandar, the once-great capital city of the land known as Tara-kan.

Irritably slapping your camel stick against your leg, you glance about to see that your guides are loading the *girba*, the waterskins, onto the camels. It is nearly time to leave. Turning to the east, you look in the direction you are to travel. The patches of green grow less and less, for that way lies the eerily singing, shifting white sands, known appropriately as the Sun's Anvil. Beyond those dunes to the east, so it is told, is a vast and locked ocean-the Kurdin Sea.

Your guide has informed you that it has another name. Among the desert nomads it was once known scornfully as the Water of the Kafir—the unbeliever—since they had never seen it and therefore assumed that it existed only in the minds of the city-dwellers. Any statement made within the hearing of a nomad that he believes to be a lie is received with the caustic remark, "No doubt you drink the Water of the Kafir as well!"

You are sorry not to have seen any of these fierce *spahi*—the nomadic desert horse riders—for you have heard many tales of their daring and courage. When you mention this to your guide, he coolly replies that though you do not see them, they see you, for this is their oasis and they know who comes to its banks and who goes.

"You have paid well for the privilege of using their water, *Effendi*." Your guide gestures to where the servants are spreading out a fine blanket upon the sand near the banks of the lake, heaping it with gold and semiprecious gems, baskets of dates and melons brought from the cool lands to the north. "There," he says in a low voice, pointing. "You see?"

You turn swiftly. A tall sand dune to the east marks the beginning of the Sun's Anvil. Standing upon that dune, silhouetted against the emptiness of the sky behind them, are four figures. They ride horses—even from this distance you can appreciate the magnificence of their animals. Their *haiks*—or head cloths—are black, their faces are shrouded in black masks. You wave to them, but they neither move nor respond.

"What would have happened had we not paid their tribute?" you ask.

"Ah, *Effendi,* instead of *you* drinking the blood of the desert, it is the desert who would be drinking your blood."

Nodding, you look back, only to see the dune is once more barren and empty. The nomads have vanished.

Your guide hurries off, shouting at the servants, the sight obviously having disquieted him. Your eyes-aching from the glare of the sun off the sand-turn westward to find rest.

Here a line of red rock hills thrusts abruptly out of the desert, looking as if some gigantic hand had reached down and dragged them up out of the ground. This is country you left two days ago and you think back on it fondly. Icy-cold streams meander through the hills, to finally lose their way in the hot sand. Grass grows in abundance on the hillsides, as do juniper trees, tall pines, cedar, willows, and bushes and shrubs of all description. Entering the hills was, at first, a welcome relief after traversing the desert land that lies between these foothills and the mountains of Kich. But you soon found that the hills are—in their way—every bit as eerie and forbidding as the desert.

Jagged cliffs of red rock, whose very redness is enhanced by the contrasting green of the trees, soar into the overcast skies. Gray-white clouds hang over them, trailing long wisps of rain that drag across the hilltops. The wind howls among the crags and crevices, the chill streams rush wildly over smooth rocks as though they know their destination is the desert and are trying in vain to escape their destiny. Occasionally, upon a hillside, you can see a patch of white that moves across the green grass in an odd, undulating, flowing motion-a flock of sheep being driven to new pasture by the sheepherding nomads who dwell in this region; nomads who—you understand—are distantly related to those you have just seen.

Your guide hastens back with word that all is ready. You cast a final look about your surroundings and notice—not for the first time—the most unusual phenomenon in this strange landscape. Immediately behind you stands a small hill. It has no business being in the desert; it is sadly out of place and appears to have been left behind when the bigger hills ran off to play in the west. As if to further emphasize the hill's incongruity, your guide has told you that a plant growing on this hill grows nowhere else in the desert, or in the world for that matter.

Before you leave, you walk over to examine the plant. It is an ugly, lethal-looking species of cactus. Squat, with fat, bulbous, pointed-tip leaves, it sprouts slender needles that must leap out at their victim, for you swear that you do not go near the plant, yet you find—when you look down—the wicked-looking thorns sticking in the tops of your boots.

"What is the name of this abhorrent cactus?" you ask, plucking out thorns.

"It is called the Rose of the Prophet, *Effendi*."

"What a beautiful name for something so hideous!" you remark, astonished.

Your guide shrugs and says nothing. He is a city-dweller, uncomfortable in this place and impatient to leave. You look again at the strange hill in the middle of the desert and at the even stranger plant growing on the hill—the ugly plant with the beautiful, romantic name.

The Rose of the Prophet.

There must be a story here, you think as you rejoin the waiting caravan.

There is, fellow wanderer, and I—the *meddah*—*will* tell it to you.

The Book
of the Gods

The universe, as everyone knows, is a huge twenty-faceted jewel that revolves around Sul, Truth, the center. The Jewel rotates on an axis that has Good at the top and Evil at the bottom. The twenty facets of the Jewel are made up of connecting triangles, each triangle sharing sides with four other triangles. The nexus of their sides—the points on the Jewel—number twelve and represent the twelve philosophies of Sul. The positive philosophies—Good (at the top), Mercy, Faith, Charity, Patience and Law—are balanced by the negative—Evil (at the bottom), Intolerance, Reality, Greed, Impatience, and Chaos. Each of the twenty Gods combines three of these philosophies to make up one facet of Sul. Thus each God reflects a different facet of the Center's Truth.

Five Gods at the top touch the axis of Good. These are the Gods of Light. Five Gods at the bottom touch the axis of Evil. These are the Gods of Darkness. Ten Gods exist in the middle, touching both Light and Darkness. These are the Neutral Gods.

When the world of Sularin was first created, it glowed brightly in the universe because each God remained joined to his fellows and Truth's Jewel shone as a single, brilliant planet in the heavens. Man worshiped all the Gods equally, speaking to them directly, and there was peace in the world and in the universe.

But as time went by, each God began to focus only on his or her facet of the Truth, coming to see that particular facet as *The* Truth and pulling away from the others. The light of the Jewel became fragmented, starting to shift and vary among the Gods as they fought with each other.

In order to increase his power, each God sought to outdo the others by showering blessings down upon his mortal worshipers. As mortals will, the more blessings they received, the more they sought. Men began to call upon the Gods day and night, demanding favors, boons, gifts, long life, wealth, fair daughters, strong sons, fast horses, more rain, less rain, and so forth and so on.

The Gods became deeply involved in the petty, day-to-day affairs of mortal men on Sularin, and the universe began to suffer, for it is written in Sul that the Gods must look not upon the light of one sun as it rises and the darkness of one night as it falls but must see the rise of an eternity of suns and the fall of an eternity of nights. Because the Gods looked increasingly at the world and less at the heavens, the Jewel of Truth began to totter and wobble.

The Gods were at a loss. They dared not offend their followers, or it would mean losing their own existence. Yet they had to get back to the business of keeping the universe in motion. To help with this problem, the Gods summoned forth the immortals. A gift from Sul to the Gods, the immortals were beings created in the image of the Gods and given eternal life, but not unlimited power. Divided up equally among the Gods, these immortal beings had originally been performing the task of greeting the deceased after their departure from Sularin and escorting them to the Realms of the Dead.

"From now on, however," said the Gods to the immortals, "*you* will be the ones who must listen to the bleating and whining and incessant 'I want's of mortal man. You will deal with those wants that are within your power to provide—gold, jewels, horses, assassinations, and so forth. Other matters more difficult to arrange, such as marriages, babies, and rainfall, you will continue to bring to us."

The immortals were delighted with this new service; the Realm of the Dead being, as one might imagine, an extremely dull and boring place. The Gods, in vast relief, began to distribute their share of immortals as each God thought best.

As the nature of the Gods differed, so did the nature of the immortals and their workings among men. Some of the Gods feared that the immortals might become as great a nuisance as man himself, while others desired to protect their immortals from the follies and vagaries of man. These Gods established a hierarchy of immortals, assigning the lower echelon to act as emissaries to ones above.

For example, the immortals of Promenthas—God of Goodness, Charity, and Faith—instructed his immortals, whom he called angels, to speak to only the most holy and pious of mankind. These men became—in time—priests of Promenthas.

The worshipers of Promenthas brought their wants and needs to the priests, who brought them to the angels, who brought them to the archangels, who brought them to the cherubim, who brought them to the seraphim, who brought them finally—if the wants and needs were truly important—to the attention of the God. This arrangement proved a satisfactory one, providing a well-ordered and structured society of humans who dwelt primarily in large cities on the continent of Tirish Aranth. Promenthas's priests grew in power, religion became the center of the lives of the people, and the Promenthas himself became one of the most powerful Gods.

Other Gods differed in their ways of utilizing the immortals, however, just as they differed in their ways of looking at Truth. Akhran—the God of Faith, Chaos, and Impatience—was also known as the Wandering God, for He could never stay in one place for any length of time but was constantly roaming the universe, seeking out new ideas, new scenes, new lands. His followers, being like their God, were nomads who roamed the desert lands of Pagrah on the continent of Sardish Jardan. Not wanting to be bothered with his faithful—who returned the favor by not wanting to be much bothered with their God—Akhran turned over almost all his power to his followers. Known as djinn, these immortals lived among men and worked with them on a day-to-day basis.

Quar, God of Reality, Greed, and Law, took his time and studied the various methods of deploying immortals—from Promenthas's hierarchy of angels to Akhran's jumble of djinn. While Quar admired the firm grip Promenthas's priests kept on the people with their highly structured system of rules and regulations, Quar found the bureaucratic stratification of the angels cumbersome and unwieldy. Messages were often garbled in translation, it took endless amounts of time to get anything done, and—as Quar watched closely—he saw that in small matters mankind was starting to depend upon himself instead of bringing matters to the attention of Promenthas.

Promenthas was, so Quar thought, unreasonably proud of this freedom of thought among his followers. The God of Light enjoyed the philosophical and theological discussions carried on among his people. A studious lot, the people of Tirish Aranth never tired of probing into the mysteries of life, death, and the hereafter. They relied on themselves to find gold and jewels and marry off their sons and daughters. Quar did not like to see man assuming such responsibilities; it gave him grandiose ideas.

But neither did Quar ascribe to Akhran's heedless casting away of all responsibility into the increasingly fat laps of the djinn, who were meddling in the mortal world with lively enthusiasm.

Quar chose a middle ground. He established priests or *Imams* who ruled over the people of his realm, Tara-kan, on the continent of Sardish Jardan. The Imams were each given djinn of a lower nature who, in turn, reported to higher djinn known as 'efreets. Quar also distributed djinn to certain people in power: Emperors, Empresses, Sultans, Sultanas, their viceroys—the Wazirs—and the generals of the armies—the Amirs. Thus the Imams did not become too powerful. . . and neither did the Emperors, the Sultans, the Wazirs, or the Amirs.

Mankind fared well, all things considered, as each God acting through his immortals—sought to outdo the others in terms of blessings.

Thus began the Cycle of Faith that is set forth in the Book of the Gods:

"As a man waters a bed of flowers, so the Gods pour down streams of blessings from the heavens. The immortals catch the streams in their hands. Walking upon the world, the immortals let fall the blessings from their fingers like drops of gentle rain. Man drinks the blessing of the Gods and gives the Gods his faithful following in return. As the numbers of the faithful increase, their faith in one God becomes vast and wide as an ocean. The God drinks from the water of the ocean and in turn grows stronger and stronger. Thus is the Cycle of Faith."

The Gods were well-pleased with the Cycle, and once each God had his affairs in order, he was able to return to performing Godlike works—that is, bickering and fighting with the other Gods about the nature of Truth. Because of the Cycle of Faith, the Jewel of One and Twenty became more or less stabilized and continued revolving through the centuries. Until now the time had come for a meeting of the Gods of Sularin. The Cycle of Faith had been broken. Two of their number were dying.

It was Quar who summoned the Twenty. During past centuries Quar had worked untiringly to try to mend the rift between

Evren, Goddess of Goodness, Charity, and Faith, and Zhakrin, God of Evil, Intolerance, and Reality. It was the constant strife between these two that had disrupted the Cycle of Faith.

Due to their strife, the blessings of the two Gods were falling on mortal man not as a steady stream but as an intermittent drizzle. Their immortals, all vying for the meager drops of blessings, were forced to resort to trickery and scheming—each immortal determined to grab a cupful of blessing for his particular master.

Such blessings, doled out in miserly portions like coppers to a beggar, did not satisfy the wants and needs of mortal man, who turned from the immortals in anger. Those among mortal men who remained loyal to their Gods withdrew into secret societies-living, working, and meeting in secret places throughout the world; writing volumes of secret texts; fighting bitter, secret, and deadly battles with their enemies. The oceans of faith of the two Gods dwindled to a trickle, leaving Evren and Zhakrin nothing to drink. And so these two Gods grew weaker, their blessings grew less, and now it was feared that their oceans of faith might dry up completely.

All of the Gods and Goddesses were upset and naturally took steps to protect themselves. The turmoil and strife spread quickly to the plane of the immortals. The djinn snubbed the angels, whom the djinn considered a snobbish, prudish band of elitists. The angels, on the other hand, looked upon the djinn as boorish, hedonistic barbarians and refused to have anything to do with them. Two entire civilizations of humans-those on the continent of Sardish Jardan and those on the continent of Tirish Aranth—eventually refused even to acknowledge the other's existence.

To make matters worse, the rumor began to spread that the immortals of certain Gods were disappearing.

At the urgent behest of Quar, therefore, the Twenty came together. Or perhaps we should say nineteen came together. Akhran the Wanderer—to the surprise of no one—did not make an appearance.

In order to facilitate matters during the meeting, each God assumed a mortal form and took mortal voice for ease of communication—speaking mind-to-mind becoming a bit confused when twenty minds are all endeavoring to talk at once as was usually the case when the Gods came together.

The Gods met in the fabled Jewel Pavilion located on top

of the highest mountain peak on the very bottom of the world in a barren, snow-covered land that has no name. A mortal who climbs that mountain would see nothing but snow and rock, for the Jewel Pavilion exists only in the minds of the Gods. Its look varies, therefore, according to the mind of each God, just as everything else varies according to the minds of the Gods on Sularin.

Quar viewed the Pavilion as a lush pleasure garden in one of his turreted palaces in one of his walled cities. Promenthas saw it as a cathedral made of marble with spires and flying buttresses, stained-glass windows, and gargoyles. Akhran, if he had been there, would have ridden his white steed into a desert oasis, pitching his tent among the cedars and junipers. Hurishta saw it as a grotto of coral beneath the sea where she dwelt. To Benario, God of Faith, Chaos, and Greed (Thieves), it was a dark cavern filled with the possessions of all the other Gods. Benario's opposite, Kharmani, God of Faith, Mercy and Greed (Wealth) viewed it as an opulent palace filled with every material possession coveted by man.

Each God sees the other nineteen entering *his* particular surroundings. Thus, the dark-eyed Quar, attired in a *burnoose* and silk turban, looked barbaric and exotic to Promenthas in his cathedral. The white-bearded Promenthas, dressed in his surplice and cassock, appeared equally ridiculous, lounging beneath the eucalyptus in Quar's pleasure garden. Hammah, a fierce warrior God who dressed in animal skins and wore a horned metal helm, stomped about the cherry trees of a tea garden belonging to Shistar, the monk Chu-lin sat in a cross-legged meditative pose on the freezing steppes of Hammah's home in Tara-kan. Naturally this gave each God—comfortable in his own surroundings— good reason to feel superior to the other nineteen.

At any other time a meeting of the Twenty would have been a form of discussion and argument that might have gone on for generations of mortal man had not the situation been of such severity that—for one—petty differences were put aside. Each God, glancing about the sea or the cavern or the garden or wherever he happened to be, noticed uneasily that in addition to Akhran (whom no one counted) two other Gods were missing. These were two of the major Gods—Evren, Goddess of Goodness, Charity and Faith, and Zhakrin, God of Evil, Intolerance, and Reality.

Promenthas was just about to question their whereabouts when he saw a decrepit and wasted man enter the Pavilion. The steps of this man were feeble. His ragged clothes were falling off, exposing his limbs, which were covered with sores and scabs; he seemed afflicted by every disease known to mortal man. The Gods started in shock as this wretched being crept down the red-carpeted aisle of the cathedral or among the splashing fountains of the pleasure garden, or through the waters of the sea, for the Gods recognized him as one of their own—Zhakrin. And it was obvious, from his cadaverous face and emaciated body, that the God was dying of starvation.

His eyes dull and glazed, Zhakrin looked around the assembled multitude, most of whom could not hide the signs of appalled horror on their human faces. Zhakrin's feverish gaze skipped over his fellows, however, obviously searching intently for one he did not, at first see.

Then she entered—the Goddess, Evren.

The Gods of Light cried out in anger and pity, many averting their gaze from the ghastly sight. The once beautiful face of the Goddess was wasted and skull-like. Her hair was white and hung from her shriveled head in ragged wisps. Her teeth were gone, her limbs twisted, her form bent. It seemed she could barely walk, and Quar hastened forward to catch hold of the poor woman and aid her faltering steps.

At sight of her, Zhakrin sneered and spit out a curse.

Evren, with a strength unimaginable in her thin and wasted body, shoved Quar away from her and threw herself at Zhakrin. Her clawlike hands closed around his neck. He grappled with her, the two falling to the red carpet of the cathedral or to the mosaic tile of the garden or the bottom of the ocean floor. Shrieking and howling in hatred, the battling Gods rolled and writhed in what seemed a hideous parody of lovemaking—a bitter struggle to the death.

So frightful was this that the other Gods could do nothing but watch helplessly. Even Quar appeared so sickened and stunned by the sight of these two dying Gods—each attempting with his or her last strength to murder the other—that he stood staring at the twisting bodies and did nothing.

And then, slowly, Zhakrin began to fade away.

Evren, screaming in triumph, scratched at his vanishing face with her nails. But she was too weak to do him further injury. Falling backward, she lay gasping for breath. Quar, moved by pity, knelt down beside her and took the Goddess in his arms. All could see that she, too, was beginning to disappear.

"Evren!" Quar called to her. "Do not let this happen! You are strong! You have defeated your enemy! Remain with us!"

But it was useless. As she shook her head feebly, the Goddess's image grew fainter and fainter. Zhakrin could no longer be seen at all, and within moments Quar found himself kneeling on the tile of his perfumed garden, holding nothing in his arms but the wind.

The other Gods cried out in anger and fear, wondering what would happen now that the order of the universe was thrown completely out of balance. They began taking sides, the Gods of Darkness blaming Evren; the Gods of Light blaming Zhakrin. Quar—one of the Neutral Gods—ignored them all. He remained on his knees, his head bowed in profound sorrow. Several of the other Neutral Gods moved to his side, offering condolences and adding their praise for his unrelenting attempts to mediate between the two.

At that moment the air whispering through the eucalyptus, the silence of the cathedral, the murmuring of ocean water was broken by a harsh sound, a shocking sound, a sound that caused all argument and conversation to suddenly cease. It was the sound of hands clapping, the sound of applause.

"Well done, Quar!" boomed a loud baritone voice. "Well done! By Sul, I have been standing here weeping until it is a wonder my eyes didn't run from my head."

"What irreverence is this?" Promenthas said severely. His long white beard falling in shining waves over his gold-embroidered surplice, the hem of his cassock rustling around his ankles, the God strode down the cathedral aisle to confront the figure who had entered. "Be off with you, Akhran the Wanderer! This is a serious matter. You are not needed here."

Folding his arms across his chest, Akhran gazed around him loftily, not at all disconcerted by this distinct lack of welcome. He was not attired in robes of honor as were the other Gods. Akhran the Wanderer wore the traditional dress of the *spahi*, a desert rider—a tunic of white over white woolen trousers, cut full for comfort and tucked into the tops of shiny black leather riding boots. Over the tunic and trousers he wore long black robes that brushed the floor, their flowing sleeves covering his arms to the elbow. A white woolen sash girdled his waist. When he gracefully tossed the folds of his robes over his arm, the blade of the scimitar and the jeweled hilt of a dagger could be seen, flashing in the light of Sul.

As he stared coldly at Promenthas, Akhran's bearded upper lip—barely visible above his black face mask worn with the black turbanlike *haik*—curled in a sneer, his teeth showing gleaming white against his brown, weather-lined skin.

"What is the meaning of this outburst?" Promenthas demanded sternly. "Did you not witness the tragedy that has occurred here this terrible day?"

"I witnessed it," Akhran said grimly. His smoldering black eyes went from Promenthas to Quar, who—with the help of his fellows—was rising slowly to his feet, his pious face drawn with grief and sorrow. Lifting a brown, weathered hand, Akhran pointed at the pallid, slender, and elegant Quar. "I have seen it and I see the cause of it!"

"Fie! What are you saying?" Indignation rustled among all the Gods, many of whom gathered about Quar, reaching out to touch him in respect and regard (Benario managing at the same time to acquire a fine ruby pendant).

At Akhran's speech, Promenthas's beard quivered with suppressed anger, his stern face grew sterner still. "For many, many decades," he began, his low voice sounding magnificently through the cathedral, less magnificently in the pleasure garden, where it was competing with the shrill screams of peacocks and the splashing of the fountains. In the oasis, where Akhran stood, regarding the Gods with cynical amusement, the whitebearded Promenthas's sonorous tones could barely be heard at all above the clicking of the palm fronds, the bleating of sheep, the neighing of horses, and the grumbling of camels. "For many decades, we have watched the untiring efforts of Quar the Lawful"—Promenthas nodded respectfully to the God, who received the accolade with a humble bow—"to end this bitter fight between two of our number. He has failed"—Promenthas shook his head—"and now we are left in a state of turmoil and chaos—"

"—That is of his making," Akhran said succinctly. "Oh, I know all about Quar's 'peace efforts.' How many times have you seen Evren and Zhakrin on the verge of burying their differences when our friend Quar here brought the skeletons of their past grievances dancing out of the tombs again. How many times have you heard Quar the Lawful say, 'Let us forget the time when Evren did such and such to Zhakrin, who in turn did so and so to Evren.' Fresh wood tossed on dying coals. The fire always flamed up again while friend Quar stood looking on, biding his time.

"Quar the Lawful!" Akhran spit upon the floor. Then, amid outraged silence, the Wandering God pointed at the place where Evren and Zhakrin had breathed their last. "Mark my words, for I speak them over the bodies of the dead. Trust this Quar the Lawful and the rest of you will suffer the same fate as Evren and Zhakrin. You have heard the rumors. You have heard of the disappearance of the immortals of Evren and Zhakrin. Some of you others have lost immortals as well." The accusatory finger rose again, pointing at Quar. "Ask this God! Ask him where your immortals are!"

"Alas, Akhran the Wanderer," Quar said in his soft, gentle voice, spreading his delicate hands. "I am grieved beyond telling at this misunderstanding between us. It is through no fault of my own. It takes two to make a quarrel, and I, for my part, have never been angered with you, my Brother of the Desert. As for the disappearance of the immortals, I wish with all my heart I could solve this mystery, especially"—Quar added sadly—"as mine are among those who have vanished!"

This was shocking news. The Gods sucked in a collective breath, exchanging glances that were now fearful and wary. The news appeared to take Akhran by surprise; his tanned face flushed, his bushy black brows came together beneath his *haik,* and he fingered the hilt of his favorite dagger.

Promenthas, perhaps slightly unnerved by the sight of Akhran running his broad thumb over the jeweled hilt of the weapon, took advantage of the sudden silence to inform the Wandering God once again that his presence was not wanted. It was obvious he was doing nothing but breeding discord and discontent among the Gods.

At this, Akhran cast a dark glance at Quar. Stroking his black beard, he gazed at the other Gods, who were glaring at him disapprovingly. "Very well," he said abruptly. "I will leave. But I will be back, and when I return, it will be to prove to those of you who still survive"—his voice was tinged with irony—"that this Quar the Lawful intends to become Quar the Law. Farewell, my brothers and sisters."

Turning on his heel, his scimitar clashing against the wooden pews with a ringing sound, Akhran stalked out of the doors of the cathedral of Promenthas, trampled the flowers of the pleasure garden of Quar. The other Gods watched him go, muttering among themselves and shaking their heads.

Fuming, Akhran paced the silvery-green grass of his own oasis. After many hours of walking back and forth, staring at the bright light of Sul that burned above him hotter than the desert sun, Akhran finally knew what to do. His plan formed, he summoned two of his immortals.

It took some time for these immortals to answer the summons of their God. Neither had been contacted by Akhran in eons, and both were more than a little startled to hear the words of their Eternal Master booming in their ears.

The djinn Sond, hunting gazelle with his mortal master, Sheykh Majiid al Fakhar, blinked in astonishment at the sound and glanced around, wondering why there was thunder in a perfectly sunny sky. The djinn Fedj, tending to sheep with his mortal master, Sheykh Jaafar al Widjar, was thoroughly unnerved that he leaped out of his bottle with a shrill yell, causing the herdsmen to start up in panic.

Both djinn repaired immediately to the plane of their God, finding him pacing back and forth beneath a towering fan palm, muttering imprecations on the heads of each of the other nineteen—now unfortunately seventeen—Gods. The two djinn, prostrating themselves humbly before their Master, kissed the ground between their hands. Had Akhran been more observant and less absorbed in his own anger, he would have noted that each djinn—while appearing to have eyes only for his Eternal Master—was in reality keeping one eye upon his Deity and one eye—a wary, unfriendly eye—upon his fellow djinn.

Akhran the Omnipercipient did not notice, however.

"Stop that nonsense!" he commanded, irritably kicking at the djinn groveling on their bellies before him. "Get up and face me."

Hurriedly the djinn scrambled to their feet. Taking the forms of mortal men, they were both tall, handsome, and well-built. Muscles rippled across their bare chests; gold bracelets encircled their strong arms; silken *pantalons* covered their powerful, shapely legs; silk turbans set with jewels adorned their heads.

"It is my pleasure to serve you, 0 *Hazrat* Akhran the Omnipotent," said Sond, bowing three times from the waist.

"It is an honor to stand before you once again, 0 *Hazrat* Akhran the Omnibenevolent," said Fedj, bowing four times from the waist.

"I am highly displeased with you both!" Akhran stated, his black brows coming together over his hawklike nose. "Why didn't you inform me that Quar's djinn were disappearing?"

Sond and Fedj—enemies suddenly drawn together to face a common foe—exchanged startled glances.

"Well?" growled Akhran impatiently.

"Are you testing us in some way, *Effendi?* Surely you who are All-Knowing know this," said Sond, thinking quickly.

"If this is a test to see if we are remaining alert, 0 Wise Wanderer," added Fedj, taking up the reins of his companion's horse, as the adage goes, "I can answer any question concerning this tragedy which you care to put to me."

"Not as many questions as I can answer, *Effendi,*" interposed Sond. "I would obviously know more about this important matter than one who spends his time with sheep."

"I am the more knowledgeable, *Effendi,*" countered Fedj angrily. "I do not waste my time in mindless gallopings and *thieving!*"

"*Thieving!*" Sond turned upon Fedj.

"You cannot deny it!" Fedj turned upon Sond.

"If your grass-killing beasts stray upon our land, consuming the sustenance which is meant for our noble steeds, then it is the will of Akhran that we in turn consume your beasts!" "*Your* land! All the world is Your Land, according to your four-legged master, who was born thus because his father visited his horse in the night instead of the tent of his wife!"

Daggers flashed in the hands of the djinn.

"*Andak!*" thundered Akhran. "Stop this! Attend to me."

Breathing heavily, glaring at each other, both djinn reluctantly thrust their weapons into the sashes around their slim waists and turned once again to face their God. A final exchange of looks, however, promised that the quarrel would be continued at a more convenient time in more private surroundings.

Akhran—who was all-knowing when he cared to be—saw and understood this exchange. He smiled grimly.

"Very well," he said, "I will 'test' you both. Are the disappearances of Quar's djinn similar in nature to the disappearance of the immortals of Evren and Zhakrin?"

"No, O Ominiprevelant One," said Sond sullenly, still rankling at the insult to his master. "The immortals of the Two Dead—Evren and Zhakrin—dwindled away even as the faith in their Gods dwindled away."

"Quar's power is not lessening, O Omniparent," added Fedj, fingering the hilt of his dagger with a vicious, sidelong glance at his companion. "Rather, it grows, which makes the disappearance of his djinn all the more mysterious."

"Is he dealing with mortals directly?" Akhran asked in astonishment and some disgust. "Oh, no, *Effendi!*" Both djinn—seeing once again the dull and boring Realms of the Dead loom in their vision—hastened to reassure their God. "In place of the many djinn who once dwelt with Quar's people, the God is consolidating more and more power in the hands of one Kaug—an 'efreet.

Sond's lip curled in anger as he spoke this name. Fedj's hand closed tightly about the hilt of his dagger.

Akhran noted this reaction, and obviously disturbed at this news, which shouldn't have been news had he been paying attention to what was transpiring in the world and in heaven, he stroked his beard thoughtfully. "An ingenious move," Akhran muttered. "I wonder. . ." He bowed his head in deep thought, the folds of the *haik* falling forward to hide his face in shadow.

Fedj and Sond stood before their Master in silence, their tension growing with each passing moment. Though each djinn had been somewhat disturbed at the strange disappearances and the increasing turmoil among the immortals, these djinn—like their God—had considered themselves above the fray. They were lucky, in fact, that they knew anything about it at all. Though neither admitted it, both had received their information from Pukah—an inquisitive, meddling young djinn belonging to the Calif, Khardan, son of Sheykh Majiid al Fakhar.

Sensitive to the feelings and desires of their mortal masters, the djinn were also sensitive to the moods of their Eternal Master.

Danger clung to him like a heady perfume. Catching a whiff of it now, the djinn felt their skin prickle and twitch like dogs who scent an enemy. They knew suddenly that they were no longer going to be above the fray, but in it.

Finally Akhran stirred. Lifting his head, he fixed each djinn with a piercing, black-eyed gaze. "You will take a message to my people."

"Your wish is my command, *Effendi*," said Sond, bowing. "To hear is to obey, *Effendi*," said Fedj, bowing lower than Sond.

Akhran gave them the message.

As they listened to it, Sond's mouth fell open so wide that a swarm of bats might have taken up residence within the cavernous opening. Fedj's eyes bulged from his head. When the God had completed relaying his instructions, each djinn glanced at the other, as if to ascertain from the face of his companion that he had heard the words of his Master correctly.

There was no doubt. Fedj had gone three shades paler. Sond was slightly green around the nose and lips. Both djinn, swallowing, attempted to speak. Sond, the quickerthinking, as usual put a voice to his opinion first. But his throat thickened and he was forced to cough several times before he could get the words out.

"O *Almost* Ominiscient Akhran, this plan of yours is a good. . . I may truthfully say a *great* plan. . . to discomfit our enemies. There is just one small detail you *may*, in your vast genius, have overlooked. It is, I hasten to add, a very *small* matter. . ."

"*Very* small," interjected Fedj.

"And that is?" Akhran glared impatiently at the djinn. Nearby, the God's noble white steed was pawing the ground, wanting to be off and riding with the winds of heaven once more. It was obvious that Akhran, who had been in one place longer than he liked, shared his horse's desire.

The two djinn stared at their bare feet, shuffling in the sand, one thinking with longing of retreating to his golden bottle, the other to his golden ring. The great horse neighed and shook his white mane. Akhran made a rumbling sound, deep in his chest.

"Master," began Sond, the words bursting from him, "for the last five hundred years our two families have killed each other on sight!"

"*Arghhh!*" Akhran's hand clenched around the hilt of his scimitar. Drawing it forth from its metal scabbard with a ringing sound, he brandished it threateningly. Both djinn dropped to their knees, cowering before his rage. "Petty human frailties! This childish quarreling among my people must end or Quar will take advantage of it and devour us one by one as so many seeds in a pomegranate!"

"Yes, *Hazrat* Akhran!" cried the quivering djinn.

"You will undertake what I have told you," continued Akhran in a towering fury, slashing recklessly about him with the scimitar, "or I swear by Sul that I will cut off your ears, your hands, and your feet, seal you up in your vessels, and hurl you into the deepest part of the Kurdin Sea! Is that understood?"

"Yes, O Most Gentle and Merciful Master," wailed the djinn, their heads nearly buried in the sand.

With a final "*Humphf!*" Akhran put his leather-booted foot on the posterior of each djinn and with a kick, sent each sprawling on his belly in the sand. Stalking off without another word, the God mounted his horse. The animal leaped into the starlit sky and the two were gone.

Picking themselves up, spitting sand from their mouths, the djinn looked at each other, suspiciously, warily.

"*Akhran* be praised," said one.

"All praise to His name," said the other quickly, not to be outdone.

And may He find *qarakurt* in his booth this night, added both silently as they reluctantly returned to the world of mortals and bring their people a startling message from their Wandering God.

The Book
of Akhran

CHAPTER 1

*i*t is the will of Akhran, *sidi*," said Fedj.

Sheykh Jaafar al Widjar groaned. "What have I done that *Hazrat* Akhran brings this curse upon me?" he wailed, flinging his arms wide, questioning the heavens through the hole in the roof. "Explain this to me, Fedj!"

The two, djinn and master, sat in the Sheykh's spacious yurt, set up in the Hrana tribe's winter camp. The sheepherding Hrana lived among the red rock hills that thrust up out of the western edge of the Pagrah desert. In the summer the sheep were pastured up in the higher elevations. Winter forced the nomads down into the desert, where their flocks lived off the sparse vegetation found there until the snow receded and they could move back to the hills in the spring.

It was a difficult life, every day proving a constant struggle to survive. The sheep were the tribe's lifeblood—their wool providing clothing and shelter, their milk and their flesh providing sustenance. If *Hazrat* Akhran was good to the Hrana and the herds grew large, sheep and lambs could be taken to the city of Kich and sold in the *souks*—the bazaars—providing money for such luxuries as silk, perfume, tea, and tobacco. If *Hazrat* Akhran forgot his people, their herds dwindled and no one thought of perfume, only of surviving the winter in the desert.

Fortunately the last few years had been prosperous—no thanks to Akhran, Fedj thought angrily, though he did not dare say such a sacrilege aloud. How could the djinn answer his Sheykh's plea for understanding? Fedj could not very well reveal the turmoil among the Gods to the mortals who looked up to them. And he didn't see how this crazed scheme of his Eternal Master was going to help matters in that direction anyhow. Crouched on his knees before his mortal master, the djinn glanced about the yurt helplessly, seeking inspiration from the designs in the many-colored carpets that covered the felt walls.

Fedj had known Jaafar would take this badly. His master took everything so personally! Let a lamb be born dead, a tarantula bite a child—the Sheykh was certain to blame the catastrophes on himself and wander about in a state of gloom for days. Now this blow. Fedj heaved a sigh. Jaafar might well never recover.

"Cursed! Cursed!"

The Sheykh rocked back and forth on the bench among his cushions. Certainly it seemed the fates were conspiring against the Sheykh, beginning with his appearance. Although only in his late forties, Jaafar appeared older. His hair was almost completely gray. His skin was deeply tanned and lined from years spent in the hills. He was short and thin, with scrawny, sinewy limbs that resembled the legs of a bustard. The long, flowing robes of the shepherds enhanced his short stature. Two streaks of gray in his beard trailed from the corners of his mouth in a perpetual frown that was not fierce—only sad. His black eyes, almost hidden in the shadows of his *haik*—long folds of white cloth bound around the head with an *agal*, a golden cord—were large and liquid and always slightly red around the rims, giving the impression that he was about to burst into tears at any moment. The only time these eyes were seen to lose their sorrow was at the mention of the name of his mortal enemy—Majiid al Fakhar, Sheykh of the Akar.

The sad eyes had flashed fire only moments before, and Fedj had some hope that hatred and rage might take the place of Jaafar's missing backbone. Unfortunately the flames had been quenched by the Sheykh's customary whining over his ill luck.

Fedj sighed again. The yurt offered no help to the djinn. He looked up through the hole in the top of the tent, seeking advice from the heavens. That was a joke, he realized, watching the smoke from the charcoal brazier spiral up and out of the tent. Night in the desert can get very cold, and the warmth of the burning charcoal was welcome to the djinn, who had lived among mortals so long he had fallen into the habit of experiencing physical sensations.

The round yurt, about six feet in height, was twenty-six feet in diameter. The skeleton of the semipermanent tent was made of strong wooden poles lashed together with thin leather thongs to form the side walls. On top of these, bent poles were lashed to a circular hoop about the size of a cart wheel. This central ring was left open to provide ventilation and to carry off the smoke of the burning charcoal, which—in a tightly closed area—could suffocate a man. The skeleton of the yurt was covered with felt—made of matted camel hair—both inside and out; the felt held fast with cords tied firmly around it. The inner walls were sometimes stamped with colorful designs, or in richer dwellings such as the Sheykh's, the walls were covered with colorful carpets, woven by his wives.

The floor of the yurt was made of thick felt, a layer of dried grass, then another layer of felt, leaving a clear space in the center for the brazier. The wooden-frame door was left open in the summer, covered in the winter with curtains of felt rugs. Fedj was thankful it was covered. Only the servants crouched near the back of the tent were witness to their master's display of weakness.

Fedj had made certain that he and Jaafar would be alone before breaking the news of the God's command to the Sheykh. At this time of night—after *eucha* or suppertime—there would normally have been many of the Sheykh's friends seated with him in the yurt, drawing smoke through the water of the hubble-bubble pipes, drinking bitter coffee and sweet tea, and regaling each other with stories that Fedj had heard a thousand times, told by their grandfathers and great-grandfathers. After a few hours they would disperse, the men going to the tents of their wives or heading for the flocks if it was their turn to take over the night watch.

Sheykh Jaafar al Widjar himself would select the tent of the wife he currently preferred, taking elaborate precautions to visit her tent in secrecy. This was an old custom, handed down from more violent days when assassins lurked in the shadows, waiting to murder the Sheykh when he was at his most vulnerable—alone with his wife.

Having been around in the old days and having seen relative peace settle at last over the various desert tribes, Fedj had always considered these precautions ludicrous and had hinted to Jaafar on occasion that they should be abandoned. Now, however, the djinn was moved to thank Akhran that his master had—out of nothing more than a childish love for pretending there were *ghuls* lurking beneath the bed—kept up the old customs. In the land to the west—land of their ancient enemy the Akar—these precautions against knife thrusts in the dark would undoubtedly be useful.

The Sheykh let out another wail, clasping his bony hands together. Fedj cringed, wondering what new calamity had struck Jaafar—as if this one wasn't bad enough.

"Who will tell her?" the Sheykh demanded, peering around the tent with his sorrow-filled eyes that were, at the moment, glittering with fear. "Who will tell her?"

The servants huddled as far back into the shadows of the tent as was possible, each striving to avoid catching his master's eye. One—a large, muscular man—seeing the Sheykh's gaze linger on him, threw himself flat on the floor, scattering cushions and knocking over a brass water pot.

"O master! What crime have I committed that you should torture me thus? Even though I earned my freedom a year ago, haven't I remained to serve you faithfully out of nothing but my love for you?"

And your love of the bribes paid by those seeking the Sheykh's favor and the leftovers from the Sheykh's table, thought Fedj. The djinn did not waste time considering the plight of the servants, however. It was time now for him to retire. He had delivered his message, listened to his master's wailings and commiseratings, done all that could be expected of him. His eyes went to the golden ring on his master's left hand. . .

"No, you don't!" snapped Jaafar, clapping his right hand over the ring with an unusual amount of spirit.

"Master," said Fedj, squirming uncomfortably, his gaze fixed upon the hand covering the ring whose somewhat cramped interior had never seemed more welcome, "I have performed my duty as given to me by *Hazrat* Akhran in delivering his message. There will be much work to do tomorrow, what with packing and preparing for the long march to the Tel, in which duties you can be assured of my help, *sidi*. I therefore beg leave to retire and rest. . ."

"*You* will tell her," pronounced Jaafar al Widjar.

The slave in the comer gasped in relief and crept back into the shadows, throwing a rug over his head in case the Sheykh should change his mind.

If Fedj had possessed a heart, it would have sunk at that moment.

"Master," the djinn began desperately, "why waste my valuable services by using me for duties fit for slaves? Give me a command worthy of my talents. Say the word, I will fly to the far ends of the world—"

"I'll bet you would! So would I, if I could;" said Jaafar gloomily. "I cannot even begin to imagine what she will do when she hears this!" The Sheykh shook his head, shuddering from scrawny neck to slippered feet. "No, you tell her, Fedj. Someone has to, and after all, you're immortal."

"That only means I will suffer longer!" snapped the djinn viciously, cursing *Hazrat* Akhran from the bottom of his imagined heart.

Fedj kept his eyes fixed hopefully on his master's hand, praying for a glimpse of the ring, but the Sheykh, with unusual stubbornness born of sheer terror, kept his fingers closed over it tightly. Rising from the bench, Jaafar gazed down upon the prostrate djinn.

"Fedj, I command you to carry the news to Zohra, my daughter, that one month from this day, by command of *Hazrat* Akhran, she is to marry Khardan al Fakhar, Calif of the Akar, son of my hated enemy, Majiid al Fakhar—may *Hazrat* Akhran infest his trousers with scorpions. Tell her that if she does not do this thing and remain married to the Calif until the Rose of the Prophet blooms upon the Tel, that it is the will of *Hazrat* Akhran that her people will all perish. Tell her this," said the Sheykh morosely, "then bind her hand and foot and surround her tent with guards. You"—he gestured to a servant—"come with me."

"Where are you going, *sidi?*" demanded Fedj.

"To—to inspect the flocks," said Jaafar, throwing on a cloak to ward off the night's chill. He started for the door of the yurt, nearly falling over the servants, who were—contrary to normal—racing to do their master's bidding.

"Inspect the flocks?" Fedj's mouth gaped open. "Since when have you decided to do this, *sidi?*"

"Since. . . uh . . . receiving reports that those thieving Akar—the sons of horses—have been raiding again," Jaafar said, sidling past the djinn on his way to the door, his hand covering the ring.

"They are always raiding us!" Fedj pointed out sourly.

The Sheykh ignored him. "Come to me later. . . and—er—tell my daughter's reaction to the. . . uh . . . joyous news of her betrothal."

"Where will you be, *sidi?*" the djinn demanded, rising to his full height, his turbaned head poking out of the hole in the ceiling of the yurt.

"Akhran willing—far, far away!" said the father fervently.

CHAPTER 2

ond!" Majiid al Fakhar cried joyously as the djinn materialized inside the Sheykh's tent. "Where have you been? We missed you last night, on the raid."

Raid! Sond winced. "Who did you strike last night, *sidi?*"

"The Hrana! The sheepherders, of course."

Sond groaned inwardly. Sheykh al Fakhar made a gesture with his brown, weathered hand. "Stole ten fat ones, right out from under their noses." He snapped his fingers. "I even caught a glimpse of that piece of camel dung—Jaafar al Widjar—sitting among his shepherds." Majiid's booming laughter shook the poles of the striped tent. "'*Salaam aleikum,* greetings to you, Jaafar!' Khardan called out to him as we galloped past, the carcasses of Hrana sheep bouncing on our saddles." The Sheykh laughed again, this time with pride. "My son Khardan, what a prankster!"

"I wish you had not done that, *sidi,*" said Sond in a low, subdued voice.

"Bah! What's the matter with you this morning, Sond? Some little djinniyeh say no last night, did she?" Majiid smote the djinn a blow upon his bare shoulders that nearly sent the immortal sprawling to the felt-covered tent floor. "Come along. Cheer up! We are having a game of *baigha* to celebrate. "

The Sheykh turned to walk out the tent entrance—propped up by strong poles, the front of the spacious tent was open to catch the breeze—but he stopped in some astonishment as Sond laid his hand firmly upon Majiid's strong arm. "I beg that you will take a moment to listen to my news, *sidi,*" said the djinn.

"Make it quick," Majiid demanded irritably, glaring at Sond. Outside, the Sheykh could see his men and their horses assembling, eager for the game.

"Please lower the flaps, that we may have privacy."

"Very well," Majiid growled, instructing the servants with a wave of his hand to lower the tent flaps—an indication to all who passed that the Sheykh was not to be disturbed.

"Out with it. By Sul, man, you look as though you've swallowed a bad fig!" Majiid frowned, his thick, grizzled mustaches bristling. "The Aran, those camel-riding swine, have been using the southern well again, haven't they?" Majiid's big fist clenched. "This time, I'll rip out Zeid's lungs—"

"No, *sidi!*" Sond interrupted desperately. "It is not your cousin, Sheykh Zeid." His voice lowered. "I was summoned last night into the presence of *Hazrat* Akhran. The God has sent me with a message to you and your people."

Sheykh Majiid al Fakhar literally swelled with pride—in itself an imposing sight. The djinn, Sond, stood seven feet tall; Majiid came to his shoulder. A gigantic man, everything about the Sheykh was equally large and impressive. He had a thunderous voice that could be heard above the most furious battle. Fifty years old, he could lift a full-grown sheep with one arm, consume more *qumiz* than any man in camp, and outride all but the eldest of his many sons.

This eldest son, Khardan—Calif of his tribe—was the light of the sun in his father's eyes. Twenty-five years of age, Khardan—although not as tall as his father—resembled Majiid in nearly every other aspect. The Calif was so handsome that the eligible daughters of the Akar, peeping at him from the slits in the tent as he rode by, sighed over his blue-black hair and his fiery black eyes that—so it was said—could melt the heart of a woman or scorch that of an enemy. Strong and muscular, Khardan held his own in the tribe's friendly wrestling matches, once even throwing the djinn, Sond, to the ground.

The Calif had ridden on his first raid at the age of six. Seated behind his father on Majiid's tall horse, screaming in excitement, Khardan never forgot the thrill of that wild ride—the tense, exciting moments sneaking in among the stupid sheep; the howls of triumph when the *spahis* galloped off, bearing their booty; the howls of rage from the shepherds and their dogs. Since that night Khardan lived for raiding and for war.

The Akar were among the most hated and feared tribes in the Pagrah desert. Blood feuds existed between them and every other nomadic band of people. Hardly a week went past that

Khardan didn't lead his men on a sheep-stealing raid, a skirmish with some other tribe over disputed lands, or strike at another tribe in revenge for a wrong committed by one great-great-great-grandfather against another great-great-great-grandfather a century ago.

Arrogant, a skilled rider, fearless in battle, Khardan was adored by the Akar. The men would have followed him into Sul's Hell, while there wasn't an unmarried woman in camp from the age of sixteen and over who wouldn't have gladly carried her bed, her clothes, and all her worldly possessions to his tent and humbly laid them at his feet (the first act a woman performs following her wedding night).

But Khardan was not yet married—an unusual state for a man of twenty-five. It had been spoken at his birth, by the djinn Sond, that the God Akhran himself would choose the Calif's wife. This had been considered quite an honor at the time, but as the years went by and Khardan watched the *harems* of men he considered beneath him grow, waiting for the God to make a decision was getting a bit tiresome.

Without a *harem* a man lacks an important power—magic. A gift from Sul to women alone, the art of magic resided in the *seraglio*, where the head wife—generally chosen for her skill in this art—oversaw the usage of it. Khardan was forced to wait until he had a wife to obtain the blessings of magic, as well as the other blessings that come from the marriage bed.

"*Bazrat* Akhran speaks to me!" Majiid said proudly. "What is the will of the Holy One?" His mustaches twitched eagerly. "Has it to do at last with the marriage of my son?"

"Yes—" began Sond.

"Akhran be praised!" Majiid shouted, raising his hands to heaven. "We have waited five and twenty years to hear the will of the God in this matter. At last my son will have a wife!"

"*Sidi!*" Sond attempted to continue, but it was useless. Hurling aside the tent flaps with such force that he nearly upset the entire structure, Majiid burst outside.

The *spahis*—the horsemen of the desert—do not live in the yurts, the semipermanent dwellings of their cousins, the sheepherders of the hills. Constantly on the move to find grazing grounds for their herds of horses, the Akar travel from oasis to oasis, their animals feeding off the grasses in one area, then drifting on when the grass is gone to return again when it has grown back. The Akar lived in tents made of strips of wool that has been stitched together by the fingers and held together by the magical arts of the women of the *harem*. Khardan's mother—a sorceress of considerable skill—boasted that no storm wind that blew could upset one of her tents.

The Sheykh's tent was large and roomy, for here Majiid held council nearly every day, hearing petitions, settling disputes, passing judgement among his people. Though plain appearing on the outside, Majiid's tent was adorned inside with the luxuries of the nomad. Fine woolen rugs of shimmering color and intricate design hung from the tent walls and ceilings. Silken cushions lined the floors (the Akar scorned to sit or sleep on wooden benches, as did their cousins the Hrana.) Several hubble-bubble pipes, an ornate silver-trimmed saddle used to lean against while seated as well as for riding, a few brass water pots, coffee and tea pots and Sond's golden bottle stood in an orderly row near an outer tent wall. A finely carved wooden chest that had come from the city of Khandar held Majiid's weapons—scimitars, sabers, knives, and daggers.

As with their cousins the Hrana, the past few years had been prosperous ones for the Akar. This news would mark the rising of Khardan's star in the heavens. Truly now the Akar would become the most powerful tribe in all of Pagrah.

"Men and women of the Akar. Now we truly have something to celebrate!" Majiid's voice boomed through the camp. "*Hazrat* Akhran, all praise to His name, has made His will known concerning the marriage of Khardan!"

Sond heard resounding cheers from the assembled people. Eligible daughters gasped, giggled, and clasped each other's hands in hope. Mothers of the eligible daughters began planning the wedding in their minds, while their fathers hastily began to think of the *dot*—or dowry—each girl takes with her.

Sighing, the djinn looked longingly at his golden bottle that stood in a corner of Majiid's tent, near the Sheykh's favorite hubble-bubble pipe.

"I will double the prize money! Let the game begin!" Majiid called out.

Peering from the tent flaps, Sond saw the Sheykh, clothed in his black robes and the full-cut white trousers of the horsemen, leap onto the back of his tall steed—a pure white horse with a long, flowing mane and a tail that swept the sands.

"Sond! Come here! We need you!" Majiid shouted, twisting in his saddle to look back at his tent. "Sond, you son of— Oh, there you are," the Sheykh said, somewhat discomfited to see the djinn spring up out of the desert and stand by his stirrup. Majiid waved a hand. "Take the carcass out." He gestured some two hundred yards away. "When all is ready, give the signal."

Sond made one last attempt. *"Sidi,* don't you want to know who *Hazrat* Akhran—"

"Who? What does it matter who? A woman is a woman. Beneath the neck, they are all the same! Don't you see, my men are eager for their sport!"

"First things first, Sond," said Khardan, galloping up and wheeling his horse around and around the djinn. "My father is right. Women are as plentiful as grains of sand. The ten silver *tumans* my father is offering as prize are not so easily come by."

Heaving a profound sigh and shaking his silk-turbaned head, Sond lifted the freshly slaughtered sheep's carcass from where it lay on the ground. Flying up into the air, the djinn skimmed over the windswept rock floor of the desert. When he found a suitable site, he first cleared the area of brush and cacti, then dropped the bloody carcass on the ground. Standing beside the carcass, his *pantalons* flapping in the desert wind, Sond gave the signal. A ball of blue fire burst in the air over his head. At the sight, with wild, shrill yells, the *spahis* kicked their horses' flanks and began their mad dash for the prize. Sond, head bowed and feet dragging, slowly began to drift back to the side of his master.

"I gather by the length of your face that the will of *Hazrat* Akhran is going to be difficult for my master to swallow," said a voice in Sond's ear. "Tell me the girl's name!"

Startled, Sond glanced about to find Pukah, the djinn belonging to Khardan, hovering at his elbow.

"You will hear with everyone else," Sond snapped testily. "Certainly I will not tell you when I have not told my master."

"Have it your way," Pukah said easily, watching the horsemen gallop toward the sheep's carcass. "Besides, I already know the name."

"You don't."

"I do."

"Impossible."

"Not so. I talked to Fedj last night. Or what was left of him after Zohra was finished."

Sond drew a seething breath. "You consort with our enemy!"

"Nay, no enemy! Have you forgotten? I consort with our *brother!*"

"Why would Fedj, that son of a goat, tell you?" Sond demanded, nettled.

"He owed me," Pukah replied, shrugging his shapely shoulders.

"Have you told—"

"My master?" Pukah glanced at Sond in mocking amusement.

"And find myself sealed up in my basket for the next twenty years for being the bearer of such tidings? No, thank you!" He chuckled, folding his arms across his chest.

Pukah's words brought back an unpleasant reminder. Thinking of Akhran's threat, Sond turned moodily away from the grinning young djinn and pretended to be concentrating on watching the game.

The object of *baigha* is to see which rider can bring the largest portion of the sheep's carcass to Sheykh Majiid. Sixty horses and their riders were now galloping wildly across the desert, each one determined to be the one to carry the prize back to his Sheykh. Khardan's fast horse and skill in riding giving him the advantage; the Calif was almost always the first to reach the carcass. He did so now, but that didn't mean he had won. Leaping off his horse, Khardan grabbed the bleeding carcass and was struggling to lift it up to his saddle when he was overtaken by at least ten other men.

Nine jumped from their saddles. Falling bodily on Khardan, they attempted to wrestle the carcass away from him, almost immediately dismembering the sheep. One rider—Khardan's younger brother Achmed—remained on his plunging horse, leaning down from the saddle at a perilous angle in an attempt to grab a share of the prize and race off with it before the others could remount. By this time the rest of the riders had arrived to join in the fray. From the sidelines the spectators cheered madly, though nothing could be seen except clouds of sand and occasionally, a glimpse of a rearing horse or a toppling rider.

Each man struggled ferociously to yank a portion of the carcass from his comrade's hold. Blood-soaked riders were down, then up, then down again. Hooves flailed; horses whinnied in excitement, sometimes slipping and falling themselves, only to clamber back to their feet in well-trained haste. Finally Achmed—having possessed himself of a hind leg—galloped off, dashing back to the cheering Sheykh.

Leaping onto their horses, several men left the group still fighting over the remainder of the carcass to pursue the victor, Khardan in the lead. Catching up with his brother, the Calif jumped from his saddle, dragging Achmed, sheep, and horse down into the sand. The three other riders—unable to stop their maddened horses—hurtled over the bodies rolling on the ground. Wheeling their steeds, the *spahis* rode back and the fight began all over again.

Several times the Sheykh himself had to gallop out of the way in order to escape the melee that surged around him, his thundering shouts and cheers and laughter adding to the confusion. At the end of an hour everyone—man and horse—was exhausted. Majiid ordered Sond to signal a halt. A ball of fire—this one red—burst in the air with an explosive bang right above the heads of the contestants. At least twenty of them—laughing, bruised, battered, and covered with blood (some of which belonged to the sheep)—staggered up to their Sheykh, gory trophies grasped in their hands.

At a gesture from Majiid one of the *aksakal*—a tribal elder—rode forward, carrying in his hand a crude balance. Sitting on his horse, he carefully weighed each bloody, sand covered hunk of meat in turn, finally pronouncing Achmed the winner of the ten *tumans*.

Clasping his strong arms around his seventeen-year-old half brother, Khardan hugged the panting boy close in congratulation, advising him to save the money for their annual horse-selling trip to the city of Kich.

Achmed turned to his father to receive a similar reward—a reward that would have been more precious to him than silver. But Majiid was far too excited over the forthcoming revelations from the God concerning his eldest son to pay any attention to the younger one. Elbowing Achmed aside, Majiid gestured for Khardan to approach.

Achmed fell back a pace, giving way—as usual—to his older brother. If the young man sighed over this, no one heard him. In the heart of another there might have been bitter jealousy over such favoritism. In Achmed's heart there was only admiration and love for the older brother, who had been more father to him than sibling.

His arms and chest smeared with sheep's blood, his mouth split in a grin—white teeth shining against his black beard—Khardan accosted the somber djinn.

"Very well, Sond," the Calif said laughingly. "I have lost at *baigha*. Certainly I will prove more lucky at love. Tell me the name of my betrothed, chosen by the Holy Akhran Himself."

Sond swallowed. From the corner of his eye he saw Pukah leering at him wickedly, making a gesture as of a man stopping a bottle with a cork then tossing it away. Flushing angrily, the djinn faced Sheykh Majiid and his son.

"It is the will of *Hazrat* Akhran," said Sond in a low voice, his eyes on the feet of his master, "that Khardan, Calif of his people, wed Zohra, daughter of Sheykh Jaafar al Widjar. The wedding is to take place on the Tel of the Rose of the Prophet before the next full moon." The djinn spread his hands deprecatingly. "One month from today. Thus speaks Hazrat Akhran to his people."

Sond kept his gaze on the ground, not daring to raise it. He could guess the reaction of his master, the Sheykh, from the terrible, thundering silence that was crashing about the djinn in waves. No one spoke or made a noise. If a horse so much as grunted, it was stifled by its master's clasping a swift hand over the beast's nose.

The silence lasted so long that Sond at last risked a glimpse, fearful that perhaps his master had fallen into a fit. This seemed not unlikely. The Sheykh's face was purple, his eyes bulged in rage, his mustaches stood nearly straight out in bristling fury. Sond had never seen his master so angry, and for an instant the bottom of the Kurdin Sea was a haven of peace and calm by comparison.

But it was Khardan who spoke, breaking the silence.

"The will of *Hazrat* Akhran," he repeated, drawing a deep, shivering breath. "The will of *Hazrat* Akhran that I mingle the tainted blood of Hrana"—he exhibited his crimson-stained hands, glaring at them in disgust—"with the noble blood of the Akar!" The young man's face was pale beneath his black beard, the dark eyes glinted more brightly than the sun off polished steel. "Here is what I think of the will of *Hazrat* Akhran!"

Catching up the sheep's head from the pile of legs and guts and ribs and haunches, Khardan hurled it at the feet of the djinn. Then—drawing his scimitar—he plunged the blade through the animal's skull.

"There is my answer, Sond. Take that to your Wandering God-if you can find Him!"

Khardan spit on the sheep's head. Reaching out, he laid a bloody hand on the shoulder of a man standing near him, who cringed at the touch. "Abdullah? You have a daughter?"

"Several, Calif," said the man with a profound sigh.

"I will marry the oldest. Father, make the arrangements."

Turning on his heel, without a glance at the djinn, Khardan stalked off toward his tent, wiping the blood of the sheep from his hands as he went.

That night the desert of Pagrah was hit by the worst storm in the memory of the oldest *aksakal*.

CHAPTER 3

The day had grown increasingly hot, unusual for late winter in the desert. The sun beat down unmercifully; it was difficult to breathe the scorched air. The horses were nervous and uneasy, nipping at each other and their herders, or standing, huddled together, in what shade could be found from a tall sand dune that cut across the northern side of the oasis where the Akar were currently camped.

Late afternoon, one of the herders sent a boy running with a message for the Sheykh. Emerging from his tent, Majiid cast one look at the ominous sight on the western horizon and immediately cried out the alarm. A yellow cloud, standing out vividly against a dark-blue mass of clouds behind it, was rolling down out of the foothills. Seemingly as tall as the hills themselves, the yellow cloud was moving against the wind at an incredible rate of speed.

"Sandstorm!" Majiid shouted above the rising wind that, in sharp contrast to the searing heat, was damp and bitterly cold.

Men, women, and children of the encampment ran to their tasks, the men securing the tents while their wives cast magical spells of protection over them, the children driving the goats and other small animals inside or running to the pools of water in the oasis to fill waterskins. Some of the women of the *harems* ran to the horse herds where the herdsmen were hobbling the animals in the shelter of the dune. Around the necks of the beasts the women hung *feisha*—amulets—magically endowed with soothing calm to settle the frightened horses, allowing the men to wrap the animals' heads in soft cloths to protect them from the stinging, blinding sand.

Favorite horses were taken inside the tents; Khardan himself led his black stallion, allowing no one else to touch the animal, whispering words of courage into the horse's ears as he took the animal into his own dwelling place. Majiid's wives returned, leading his horse. Watching the progress of the storm, the Sheykh gestured for them to lead the animal into his tent.

"Sond!" he bellowed, peering into the stinging sand that was billowing around them even though the main storm was some distance away. "Sond!"

"Yes, *sidi*," the djinn responded, springing up out of the sands.

"Look... there!" Majiid pointed. "What do you see?"

Sond stared into the approaching storm. His eyes narrowed, he looked back at his master with a grim expression. " 'Efreet!"

The yellow cloud rolled down on them. Leading it, as generals lead an advancing army, were two great beings tall as the clouds of sand, surging over the desert before it. Lightning flared from their eyes, thunder roared from their mouths. In their hands they held uprooted trees, their giant feet kicked up huge clouds of dust as they sped down upon the camp. Nearer and nearer the 'efreet came, whirling and dancing over the sands like dervishes.

"Have they been sent by *Hazrat* Akhran?" Majiid roared. A gust of wind hit him, nearly blowing the big man off his feet. Seeing that everyone in the camp had taken shelter within their tents, he made his way back to his. "Undoubtedly, *sidi*," Sond shouted back.

Majiid shook his fist at the 'efreets defiantly, then ducked inside the tent, his djinn hastily seeking shelter in his bottle. The Sheykh's servants were endeavoring to calm Majiid's horse, who was plunging back and forth nervously, threatening to tear down the tent.

"Get away!" Majiid shouted at the servants. "He smells your fear!"

Stroking the horse's nose and patting him reassuringly on the neck, the Sheykh calmed the frightened animal. Under no circumstances had Majiid ever allowed women's magic to touch his horse. Seeing the animal tremble, its eyes rolling in its head, the Sheykh began to think that this time he might make an exception.

He was just about to go to his head wife's tent, seeking her, when he heard a rustling sound and smelled the scent of roses that, no matter where he was, brought the image of Khardan's mother to his mind.

"You read my thoughts, Badia," he said gruffly as she approached, and realized then that she must have been sitting quietly in his tent the entire time.

In her late forties, the mother of seven children, Badia was a handsome woman still, and Majiid regarded her with pride. Though he rarely slept in her bed—he preferred his younger wives for his pleasure—Majiid often visited Badia's tent at night anyway, to talk and receive her counsel, for he had come, over the years, to depend upon her wisdom.

Smiling at her husband, Badia hung the *feisha* around the horse's neck and whispered arcane words. Heaving a deep sigh, the animal sank down, resting its head in its master's lap. Its eyes closed in peaceful sleep. Stroking his horse's mane, Majiid reached out his hand, gripping his wife's arm as she was about to leave.

"Don't go out there, my treasure," he said. "Stay with me."

The tent walls heaved and billowed like a live thing, the chill wind sang a strange and threatening song in the ropes that held the tent fast. The light was a sickly ocher color, so murky it was as hard to see as if it had been night. Outside could be heard a low, grinding sound—the cloud of sand, accompanied by the 'efreets, drawing nearer.

Sitting on cushions beside her husband, Badia laid her head on his arm. Her face was veiled against the storm. She was dressed in her winter cloak made of fine brocade, embroidered with golden thread and lined with fur. Rings adorned the fingers that held fast to her husband's strong arm, gold glinted from her earlobes, the bangles on her wrists jingled softly. *Kohl* lined her eyes, her black hair—streaked with gray—was thick and long and fell in a single braid down her shoulder.

"It will be a bad storm, husband," she said. "You saw the 'efreets that travel with it?"

At that moment a blast of sand-laden wind struck the tent. Although protected by magic and the skill of the nomads in securing their dwellings against the storms of the desert, Majiid and his wife were nearly suffocated by the sand that swirled in every opening, seeming to penetrate the sturdy fabric of the tent itself.

Casting a cloth over his head, cradling his wife protectively in his arms as she buried her face in his breast for protection, Majiid wished briefly he could ask her to cast a spell of calm over him. He could hear the 'efreets stomping through the camp, battering against the tents with their giant fists, their voices howling in rage. The Sheykh's nose, mouth, and ears filled with sand; drawing breath was a painful sensation. Out in the camp he heard shrill screams and hoarse cries and realized that someone's tent had not been properly secured; probably a young man who had not established his *harem* yet and who perhaps had no mother to cast the spell of protection for him.

There was nothing anyone could do for him but hope he found shelter in the tent of a friend or relative.

An hour passed, and the storm did not diminish in fury. Rather, it appeared to grow worse. The yellow light deepened to an ugly brown. The wind pounced on them from every conceivable direction. Above the howling of the 'efreets, Majiid could hear the wailings of his people, children crying, women sobbing, and even his brave men raising their voices in terror.

"Sond!" shouted Majiid_ coughing and spitting sand from his mouth.

"*Sidi?*" came a tinny-sounding voice from inside the golden bottle.

"Come out here!" Majiid demanded, half-choked.

"I would prefer not to, *sidi*," returned the djinn.

"How long will this cursed storm last?"

"Until your noble son, Khardan, agrees to do the will of the most holy Akhran, *sidi*," replied the djinn.

Majiid swore bitterly. "My son will not marry a sheepherder!" The giant hand of an 'efreet tore at the Sheykh's tent, ripping loose the strong ropes and lifting one of the tent walls. Badia cried out in terror and prostrated herself on the floor, calling to *Hazrat* Akhran for mercy. The servants fled, lunging out beneath the flaps of the shaking tent, howling at the top of their lungs. Majiid, his face twisted in anger that vied with his fear, raised his face cloth to protect his skin from the stinging, biting blasts of sand as he staggered out of the tent to try to secure the ropes once more.

Instantly the 'efreets caught hold of him. Whirling him around until he didn't know his front from his back, they sent the Sheykh on a tumbling, staggering dance through the camp—tossing him back and forth from one to the other, hurling him up against tents, throwing him down into ravines, nearly burying him in sand. Disoriented, almost completely blind from the sand in his eyes, near suffocation from the dust in his mouth and nose, Majiid was finally blown completely off his feet. Catching hold of him, the 'efreets rolled his body over and over, sending him spinning across the rocky, windswept ground until he came to a sudden and painful stop, brought up by a palm tree bent double by the gale, its fronds kissing the earth in obeisance to the God of the desert.

Rubbing the grit from his eyes, Majiid peered upward, groaning in pain. The 'efreets towered above him, spinning so swiftly it made the Sheykh dizzy to watch. In their huge hands they held fragments of tents. Lightning flared from eyes that stared down at the Sheykh without visible emotion as their bodies surged around him.

For the briefest instant the storm abated, as though the 'efreets were holding their breaths, waiting. Majiid groaned again; he had broken ribs in his wild dance through the camp, he thought he might have sprained an ankle tumbling down that last ditch. The Sheykh was a fighter from a long line of fighters. Like any veteran warrior, he knew overwhelming odds when he saw them.

One could not—it seemed—fight a God.

Sheykh Majiid al Fakhar cursed. Clenching his fist in impotent anger, he beat it into the sand. Then, lifting his head, he stared up grimly at the grinning 'efreets.

"Sond!" he roared, a shout that carried clear across the camp. "Bring me my son!"

CHAPTER 4

Although the mapmakers of the Emperor of Tara-kan had undoubtedly given it some fanciful name, the outcropping of rock that jutted up unexpectedly and inexplicably in the center of the Pagrah desert was called by the dwellers of the desert the Tel, a word meaning hill. A forthright, laconic people, whose harsh surroundings had taught them to be sparing of everything including breath, they saw no need to call things other than what they were or to add any frivolous embellishments. It was a hill, so name it a hill.

The highest point of land for hundreds of miles in any direction, located in the heart of the desert, the Tel naturally became a prominent landmark. Distance was measured by it—such and such a well was three days' ride from the Tel, the Sun's Anvil was two days' ride east from the Tel, the city of Kich was a week's ride west from the Tel, and so forth. Situated in the center of nothing, the Tel and its surrounding oasis was, in fact, at least two days' ride from anywhere which is what made it so remarkable to find two tribes of nomads camped on either side, one to the east and one to the west.

South of the Tel, standing in a spot that was equidistant from each tribe's encampment, stood a huge ceremonial tent. Measuring seven poles long and three across, it was made of wide woolen bands sewn together—bands that appeared to have come from two different sources, for the colors of the tent clashed wildly, one side being a dark, sober-minded crimson and the other a flamboyant, dashing orange. A *bairaq*, tribal flag, fluttered in the desert breeze at either end of the tent—one flag was crimson, the other flag orange.

The ceremonial tent—sturdy and stable at the far ends appeared to be unstable in the center, as if the workmen of the two tribes erecting it had become distracted by something. Several splotches of blood on the ground near the middle of the tent may have accounted for the wobbling centerpoles.

Perhaps it was these splotches of blood that also accounted for the unusually large numbers of carrion-eating birds that circled above the huge tent. Or perhaps it was simply the unusually large number of people camped around the oasis. Whatever the reason, vultures wheeled in the skies above the Tel, their wings, black against the golden twilight, casting shadows that flowed over the huge tent—an ill-omen for a wedding day.

Neither bride nor groom noticed the bad luck sign, however. The groom had spent the day being plied with *qumiz*—fermented mare's milk—and was, by evening, so drunk that he could scarcely distinguish sky from ground, much less notice the scrawny birds flapping in eager anticipation above his head. The bride, dressed for the occasion in a *paranja* of finest white silk embroidered with golden thread, was heavily veiled; one might say extremely heavily veiled, since it was not generally the custom among her people to blindfold the bride before the wedding ceremony.

Nor was it the custom to bind the bride's wrists tightly together with strips of sheepskin, or to have the bride escorted to the tent by her father and his strongest men rather than her mother, sisters, and other wives of the *seraglio*. The bride's mother was dead, she had no sisters, and the other wives of her father were shut up in their tent, ringed round by guards, as they were when a raid was expected.

No music accompanied the bride's procession through her camp to the wedding tent. There was no strumming of the *dutar*, no clashing of tamborine, no wailing of the *surnai*. The journey was completed in silence, for the most part; silence broken only by the oaths and cursings of the men responsible for bearing the blushing bride to the ceremonial tent, the bride taking every occasion possible to kick the shins of her escorts.

At last the bride, still struggling, was dragged into the garish, unsteady wedding tent. Here her escorts relinquished her thankfully to her father, whose only comment on receiving his daughter on her wedding day was, "Make certain she doesn't get her hands on a knife!"

The groom's procession through his camp was considerably less painful for his escorts than the bride's, this being due to the fact that most of the escorts were in the same state of drunken euphoria as the groom. His djinn, Pukah, had passed out cold. Several of the *aksakal*, tribal elders, had remained sober—on orders of Sheykh Majiid—or the groom might never have arrived at his wedding at all; that small matter having slipped the besotted minds of the Calif and his *spahis*, who were reliving glorious raids.

At *aseur*, when the desert sun was sinking down behind the far-off foothills, the groom was lifted to his feet and hauled bodily into the ceremonial tent, accompanied by those of his companions who could still walk.

Inside the tent the groom's father met his son. At the sight of Majiid, Khardan's handsome face split into a grin. Spreading his arms wide, he lurched forward, wrapped his strong arms around his father's shoulders, and belched.

"Get him up to the center of the tent," commanded the Sheykh, casting a nervous sidelong glance at the unusually stern-faced and formidable-appearing Sond, who was standing near the centerpole.

The *aksakal* went into action. Without further ceremony Khardan al Fakhar, Calif of his tribe, was pushed and pulled over to stand unsteadily next to the centerpole. His drunken friends, shoving their way in behind their Prince, took their places on the right-hand side of the tent. They did not sit down as was customary, but remained standing, glaring balefully at the escorts of the bride, who were on the left-hand side.

The sight of the shepherds effectively sobered most of the *spahis*. Laughter and the crude jokes and boasts about the groom's prowess in the marriage bed died upon the warriors' bearded lips, some still frothy white from the *qumiz*. Armed to the teeth, the Akar and Hrana fingered the daggers thrust into their sashes or fondly caressed the hilts of scimitars and sabers, a low muttering rising from their throats as the bride and groom were being shoved and jostled into position.

"Let's get this travesty over with!" gasped Sheykh Jaafar al Widjar. Sweat poured from beneath his headcloth, both arms encircled his struggling daughter. "I can't hold her much longer, and if that gag comes loose from her mouth . . ." His voice trailed off ominously.

"Gag! How is she going to say her vows if she's gagged?" demanded Majiid al Fakhar.

"I will say them," grunted Jaafar al Widjar.

Traces of blood decorated the sleeves of his daughter's wedding gown, her hands twisted together as she fought to free herself of the bindings around her wrists.

Noting that Majiid al Fakhar looked dubious, Jaafar added harshly, "If she is allowed to speak, she might use her magic, and she is the most powerful sorceress in my wife's *seraglio!*"

"Bah! Women's magic!" snorted Majiid scornfully, but he glanced somewhat uneasily at the heavily veiled bride nonetheless. Reaching out, the Sheykh caught hold of his drunken son, who was slowly listing to one side, and yanked him upright. "Sond! If Jaafar speaks his daughters vows, will she and my son be married in the eyes of *Hazrat* Akhran?"

"If Zohra's father's camel said her vows, his daughter would be married in the sight of *Hazrat* Akhran!" growled Sond, exchanging glances with Fedj.

The other djinn nodded in agreement, making a gesture with his hand. "Get on with it!" The light of the hanging oil lamps flashed off golden bracelets ringing muscular arms.

"Very well," Majiid agreed with an ill-grace. Taking his place between the couple, flanked on either side by the grim-faced djinn, the Sheykh raised his eyes defiantly to heaven. "We, the chosen of the Most Holy and Beneficent God Akhran the Wanderer, have been brought together by a message from our great Lord"—a note of bitterness here—"to the effect that our tribes be joined by the marriage of my son, Khardan al Fakhar, Calif of his people, to this daughter of a sheep—,

A shrill scream from the bound and gagged Zohra and a sudden lunging of the bride in the direction of Majiid al Fakhar caused a momentary interruption in the ceremony.

"What insult is this 'daughter of a sheep'? Zohra is the daughter of myself, Jaafar al Widjar, princess of her people!" yelled Jaafar, catching hold of his daughter around the waist and wrestling her backward.

"Zohra, princess of sheep," resumed Majiid coolly. "Better than a four-legged son of a horse!"

Hanging onto his kicking, screaming daughter with one hand, Jaafar reached out and shoved the reeling, grinning groom with the other. His face flushed in drunken anger, Khardan staggered back into his parent, nearly knocking them both over, then lurched forward to take a wild swing at his future father-in-law.

The low mutterings on both sides of the ceremonial tent broke into open, shouted insults. Loud cries and the clashing of blades being drawn on the bride's side of the tent precipitated a clashing of steel on the groom's side. Sayal, one of the bride's brothers, hurled himself at Achmed, one of the groom's brothers, cousins of both gleefully joining the fight. A glorious brawl was in the offing when a blinding flash of light and deafening explosion knocked the combatants to the ground and caused the center post of the tent to sway in an alarming manner.

Stunned, the brothers and cousins rubbed their dazzled eyes and their ringing ears, wondering what had hit them.

Sond's turbaned head brushed the topmost part of the seven-foot-high tent. He stood in the middle of the melee, his muscled arms folded across his bronze, glistening chest, his black eyes flashing in anger.

"Attend to me—djinn of Sheykh Majiid al Fakhar, djinn to his father before him, djinn to *his* father before him, djinn to his father before *him,* and so on for the past five hundred generations of the Akar! Hear the will of the most Holy Akhran the Wanderer, who has deigned to speak to you foolish mortals after over two hundred years of silence!"

"May His name be praised," muttered Majiid caustically, holding up Khardan, whose knees were giving way beneath him.

Sond heard Majiid's sarcastic remark but chose to ignore it. "It is the will of Akhran the Wanderer that you two ancient enemies—the Akar and Hrana—be brought together in peace through the marriage of the eldest son and the eldest daughter of the tribal rulers. It is the will of Akhran that neither tribe shall shed the blood of a member of the other. It is further the will of Akhran that both tribes shall make their camps at the foot of the Tel until such time as the flower sacred to the great and mighty Akhran the Wanderer, the flower of the desert known as the Rose of the Prophet, blooms. This is the will of *Hazrat* Akhran.

"In return for their obedience"—Sond saw the groom's eyes start to glaze over and spoke more rapidly—"the Holy Akhran promises his people his blessing and assistance in the times of strife that are forthcoming."

"Strife! Hah!" muttered Jaafar to his daughter. "The only

people we ever fight are each other, and we are forbidden to do that!"

Zohra shrugged. She had suddenly ceased to struggle and slumped against her father's chest in what he assumed was exhaustion. He did not notice, in the confusion and turmoil, that his dagger was missing from its customary place in his sash.

"Skip the rest," ordered Fedj, holding out the ceremonial cord that officially bound the two people together as husband and wife. "Get on with the vows."

"In the name of Akhran the Wanderer, do you, Princess Zohra, daughter of Sheykh Jaafar al Widjar, come here of your own free will to marry Calif Khardan al Fakhar?"

A bitter curse from the bride was cut off by her father, who wrapped his hand around her throat. "She does," he said, breathing heavily.

"In the name of Akhran the Wanderer, do you, Calif Khardan al Fakhar, son of Sheykh Majiid al Fakhar, come here of your own free will to marry Princess Zohra, daughter of Sheykh Jaafar al Widjar?"

A vicious poke in the back from his father brought Khardan standing bolt upright, staring around with blinking eyes.

"Say *bali! Bali!*" ordered Majiid. "Yes! Yes!"

"*B-hali!*" cried Khardan with a triumphant gesture of his hand. His mouth gaped open, his eyes rolled back in his head, he swayed where he stood.

"Quickly!" shouted Fedj, holding out the binding to the two fathers.

Generally made of finest silk, the cord symbolizes the love and loyalty that bind husband and wife together. For this hasty wedding there had not been time to journey to the walled city of Kich to purchase silken cord, so a substitute was made of strong desert hemp. And as Pukah stated, it seemed more suitable to the occasion anyhow.

"Take it!" Fedj ordered.

Both fathers hesitated, glaring at each other. The mutterings in the tent swelled to a loud rumbling. Sond growled ominously, Fedj flexed his strong arms. A sudden gust of wind brought a small sand devil swirling into the tent through the open flap.

Memories of the 'efreets in his mind, Majiid grabbed the cord. With an ill-will, he and Jaafar bound the hemp around their offspring and tied it in a love knot, a bit more tightly than was absolutely necessary.

"In the name of Akhran the Wanderer, you two are married!" gasped Sond, wiping the sweat from his brow as he gloomily surveyed the bound couple—the groom leaning heavily against the bride, his head lolling on her shoulder.

There was the flash of a knife, the hemp cord parted as did the bindings on the bride's hands. The blade flashed again and might have ended the wedding day as well as any other future days for the groom had not Khardan pitched face-first onto the floor. Seeing that she had missed, Zohra jumped over the comatose body of her new husband and ran for the tent opening.

"Stop her!" Majiid yelled. "She tried to kill my son!"

"You stop her!" Jaafar roared. "You could probably beat a woman in a fair fight!"

"Dog!"

"Swine!"

The fathers drew their scimitars. Cousins and brothers leaped for each other's throats.

Hearing the clash of steel, Khardan staggered to his feet. He felt blindly for his scimitar—only to realize dimly that he was not wearing it on his wedding day. Cursing, he surged forward weaponless to join the brawl.

Steel clashed on steel. The tent poles swayed dangerously as bodies crashed into them. A shriek, a curse, and a groan coming from one of the guards standing near the tent entrance indicated that the knife-wielding bride had made her way that far, at least.

The two djinn stared around in exasperation. "You go after her!" Sond shouted. "I'll put an end to this!"

"Akhran's blessing be with you!" cried Fedj, vanishing in a swirl of smoke.

"That's just all I need!" muttered Sond.

Grabbing hold of the central tentpole with his strong hands, the djinn glared at the sword-slashing, dagger-wielding, heaving and plunging bodies. Then, his lips coming together in a grim smile, Sond jerked the tentpole up out of the ground and neatly snapping it in two, let it fall.

The tent collapsed like a deflated goatskin, narrowly missing the bride, smothering the groom, effectively ending the fighting of fathers, brothers and cousins. Dagger in hand, Zohra fled into the desert. The *qumiz* going to his head, Khardan lay snoring blissfully beneath the folds of the ceremonial tent as the air whistled out of it with a whoosh, effectively extinguishing—for the time being—the flames of hatred that had burned hot within the hearts of these people for centuries past remembering.

CHAPTER 5

eep night had fallen over the desert. Around the Tel, however, the flames of a hundred small suns lit the night almost
as bright as day, the night air resounded with drunken laughter.
These celebratory measures were not so much in honor of the
wedding but in commemoration of the glorious fight that had
taken place following the wedding, and in expectation of more
glorious fights to come. The largest bonfire burned outside Khardan's tent. Surrounded by weaving, dancing black shapes, the
flames licked hungrily at the wood as dogs lick up blood.

A silver slit appeared in the black sky; Achmed's youthful
voice, more sober than the rest, shouted out that the moon was
rising. This was followed by a cheer, for it was the signal to escort
the groom to his bridal tent where, presumably, the bride waited
in perfumed, bejeweled splendor. Everyone (more or less) surged
forward—the groom in the lead. Many of his companions clung
to each other for support, either too drunk or too injured to walk
without help.

No one had died in the skirmish in the wedding tent—for
which the fall of the pole could undoubtedly be thanked—but
there were several on both sides who'd been carried to their tents
feet-first and were being tended by their wives. One of these was
Zohra's father, Jaafar. A lucky swipe of Majiid's saber just as the
tent collapsed on top of them caught Jaafar across his skinny
chest. The wound opened a bloody gash in his flesh, ruined his
best robes, and neatly sliced off the bottom half of his long, white
beard, but it did little other damage, not even penetrating as far
as the bone.

Nonetheless, this injury done to their Sheykh would have
precipitated a bloodbath among the tribes had not Sond threatened to transport the first man who raised his dagger into the

Sun's Anvil, stuff his mouth with salt, and leave him tied to a stake with a waterskin hanging just beyond his reach. Grumbling and muttering threats into their beards, Jaafar's men limped out of the tent, bearing their fallen Sheykh, stretched out on a blanket, between them.

Jaafar himself had only one command to make: "Find my daughter."

The men of Hrana glanced uneasily at each other. Zohra was still armed, not only with her knife but with her magic, which, though it could do nothing deadly to them, could still make their lives more miserable than Sul's Hell. The men therefore hastened to assure their Sheykh that Zohra had been located. She was in the bridal tent.

This wasn't a lie—no honorable man would have told an untruth to a member of his own tribe. Someone had actually seen Zohra heading in the direction of the bridal tent following her escape from her wedding. What for, no one knew, but bets were being placed among the Hrana on how long Khardan would remain alive once he entered that tent. Nothing over five minutes was getting any odds at all.

Jaafar appeared dubious upon receiving the news that his daughter had—apparently—decided to meekly submit to this marriage. But before he could say anything further, he lost consciousness. Leaving their wounded Sheykh among his wives, the men of Hrana stealthily followed the groom's procession to the bridal tent, hoping to find a way to disrupt it without being caught by the djinn.

As it turned out, all of these proceedings in the camps were being observed by two black, scornful eyes. Supposedly in her bridal tent, lounging in a silken gown among silken cushions with *kohl* on her eyelids, *henna* on her fingertips, attar of rose, jasmine, and orange blossom perfuming the air, Zohra instead was standing on the very top of the Tel, dressed in an old caftan and trousers that she had stolen from her father. Her hand on her horse's bridle, she looked down into the camp one last time before leaving it forever.

The horse was a magnificent stallion—a wedding gift from Majiid to Jaafar. (Actually it was a gift from Sond to Jaafar. The djinn knew that Majiid would reluctantly hand over his son in marriage, but the Sheykh of the Akar would never—no matter how many storms *Hazrat* Akhran visited on him—give one of his horses to a Hrana. Therefore Sond had taken it upon himself to present the suitable gift. Majiid had no idea that the horse was missing. Sond had created a passable substitute that fooled everyone until the first time Majiid attempted to ride it. An unfortunate leap into the nonexistent saddle revealed that the horse was an illusion. It took a month for the Sheykh's bruises to heal, and it was weeks before he could speak to Sond without exploding in rage.)

Jaafar had been pleased with the horse, but he never rode it, preferring to ride the ancient, mangy camel he had purchased long ago from the tribe of Sheykh Zeid. His daughter Zohra, however, had fallen in love with the animal and determined to learn to ride if she died in the attempt. She practiced several times in secret during the month before the wedding, galloping among the hills, and being naturally athletic, she had become quite skilled. She had another motive in learning to ride: this gave her the means to escape her dire fate.

Stealing from a member of one's own tribe was an unforgivable act, but—since the horse was a wedding gift—Zohra considered that she had more right to the animal than did her father. After all, she was the one who had been insulted by that mockery of a wedding ceremony. She deserved this wonderful beast. And she had left all her jewels behind to pay for it. Surely they were worth more than one horse.

At the thought of her jewelry Zohra sighed softly and rubbed the horse's nose. The animal nuzzled its head against her neck impatiently, longing for a gallop, urging her to get on with her journey. Zohra patted it soothingly.

"We'll go soon," she promised, but she didn't move.

If there was one weakness in this strong woman, it was a love of jewelry. To hear the jingle of golden earrings, to see the flash of sapphire and ruby bracelets on her slender arms, to admire the sparkle of turquoise and silver on her fingers, this was almost worth being born a female. Almost. . . Not quite. That was the real reason she had gone to the bridal tent—to look for the last time on the jewelry that had been given her. Jewelry meant to adorn her body for—for what? To make her worthy in the eyes of some horseman?

Zohra's lip curled in a sneer. In her mind she envisioned the man's heavy, clumsy hands snatching the rings from her fingers, tugging the bracelets from her, arms, and hurling them carelessly into a comer of the tent as he . . . as he . . .

The horse neighed suddenly, tossing its head. Gripping the knife, Zohra whirled around, stabbing with a quick, skillful thrust, not caring whom or what she hit.

A strong hand closed painfully over Zohra's wrist. Holding on to the woman, the djinn Fedj stared down at the blade sticking from his chest. Grimly plucking out the dagger, the djinn returned it to the fuming bride.

"I command you! Leave me! Return to your ring!" ordered Zohra in a quivering voice.

"I am your father's djinn and therefore subject to no one's commands but his, Princess," answered Fedj coolly.

"Did he send you after me? Not that it matters. I'm not going back," Zohra stated defiantly, a defiance whose strength was considerably diluted by the knowledge that the powerful djinn could return her to her father's tent in the blink of an eye.

Fedj was just about to respond when a shout of drunken laughter coming up from the desert floor drew the attention of both. Looking down, they saw the groom's procession wend its way slowly through the camp. Khardan had apparently sobered up following the fight in the wedding tent, for he was walking upright without help, laughing and joking with several less steady companions, who staggered along at his side. Snatches of his conversation, carried clearly on the crisp, chill desert air, came to Zohra.

"I've heard stories about this she-devil of a sheepherder." Khardan's voice was rich and mellow, a deep baritone, his laughter infectious and arrogant. "I heard that she has vowed to the God that no man will possess her. An unholy vow! To be honest, my friends"—Khardan turned to face his companions, who were regarding their Calif with profound admiration—"I have come to believe that this sacrilegious vow is the reason *Hazrat* Akhran brought the Akar together with the tribe of our enemies. These shepherds have been living too long among their sheep. Akhran needed a man to take this woman and teach her the duties of her sex—"

Zohra gasped. Her dark eyes flashed, her hand curled tightly over the hilt of the dagger. "I have changed my mind," she said, breathing rapidly. "Send me back to the bridal tent, Fedj. That filthy *spahi* will learn what are the 'duties' of a woman!"

The djinn's own face was pale with fury as he glared down upon the swaggering prince, who was boasting of his prowess with women. "Believe me, Princess! Nothing would give me greater pleasure than to run a hundred cactus thorns through the portion of his anatomy that this young man values most, but-"

Raucous laughter drifted up from the Calif's companions. Turning unsteadily, Khardan once more proceeded slowly and leisurely to the tent of his bride. With a sigh Fedj laid his hand over the dagger-wielding hand of the Princess.

"But what?" she cried angrily.

"But I dare not. *Hazrat* Akhran has ordered that this union shall be so and so it shall be. You two must remain married and no blood must be shed between the two tribes until the Rose of the Prophet blooms."

"Why?" Zohra asked bitterly. "What is the God's reason? Look at the ugly plant!" She kicked irritably at one of the many Rose cacti growing at her feet. Sprawled against the hillside, it looked, in the bright moonlight, like a dead spider. "The leaves are withered and turning brown, curling in upon themselves. . ."

"It is winter, Princess," said Fedj, glancing at the cactus with equal disgust. "Perhaps this is its habit in the winter. I am not familiar with the customs of this flower, except I know that it grows here and nowhere else in the world—one reason why you have been commanded to reside in this place. As for the 'why' of *Hazrat* Akhran in forcing you to make this hateful marriage, I know something of the mind of the God, and—if it will comfort you—I can tell you that the boastings of that-puffed-up prince are arrows shot wide of the mark. I can also tell you, Zohra," said Fedj, his tone growing more serious, "that if you do not go back to your people, they and perhaps all the people of the desert are doomed."

Zohra glanced at the djinn from the corner of her black eyes. Though shadowed by thick, long lashes, the fire in their depths burned more hotly than any blazing log.

"Besides, Princess," continued Fedj persuasively, moving nearer Zohra, "Akhran said only that the two of you had to be married. He did *not* say that the marriage had to be consummated. . ."

Zohra's black eyes narrowed thoughtfully, and there was, Fedj was relieved to see, a glimmer of amusement in them—malevolent amusement, but amusement nonetheless.

"You would be Khardan's head wife, Princess," Fedj suggested softly, feeding the fire. "He would not be allowed to take another into his *harem* without your permission."

The glimmer of amusement became a flaring spark. "And it is only a few weeks until spring. When the Rose of the Prophet blooms, the command of the God is fulfilled. You may do what you like to your husband then, after having made his life miserable in the interim."

"Mmmmm," Zohra murmured. Near her, the horse shifted restlessly, either wanting to take flight through the desert or return to his mares.

"If I agree to go back," Zohra said slowly, her fingers tracing the intricate designs carved into the bone handle of the dagger, "I want one more thing."

"If it is in my power to provide it, I will, my lady," answered Fedj cautiously. There was no knowing what this wildcat might ask him for—anything from a *sirocco* to blow her enemies off the sands of the desert to a carpet to fly her to the other side of the world.

"I want my own immortal to serve me."

Fedj checked a deep sigh of relief. Fortunately a djinn was easy to provide. Fedj had one in mind, in fact—a low-ranking immortal who owed him a favor from three or four centuries back. Not only did this djinn—one Usti—owe Fedj a favor, but Fedj owed Usti a nasty trick. Fedj had been biding his time, savoring revenge for several hundred years. Here was his chance.

"Your wish is my command, Princess," said Fedj, bowing humbly. "In the morning you will find upon the floor of your tent what appears to be a small, brass charcoal brazier. Take up the brazier in your hand, tap it gently three times with your fingernail, and call the name 'Usti.' Your djinn will appear."

"I would prefer a female."

"Alas, Princess. The djinniyeh are the highest ranking of our kind and rarely deign to have dealings with mortals. And now, will you return to the bridal tent?" Fedj asked, holding his breath in anxiety.

"I will," said Zohra magnanimously.

Smiling broadly, Fedj patted the Princess's hand. The djinn could not see Zohra's face, hidden as it was by the folds of the headcloth she wore, or he might have been less pleased with himself.

"Shall I transport you, Princess?"

"No, you take care of the horse." Zohra stroked the animal's nose with regret, "We will have our ride another day," she promised the stallion.

"What about the guards?" Fedj gestured to several stalwart men of her father's tribe who were standing around the tent. At that moment he noted that one of the guards was leaning at an odd angle against a straggly-looking palm tree. "Ah, I see you've taken care of them. He's not dead?"

"No!" Zohra said scornfully. "It is a magic spell used to soothe teething babies to sleep. He may wake screaming for his mother"- the princess shrugged—"but he *will* wake. Farewell, Fedj."

Zohra began to make her way down the side of the Tel, slipping in the loose sand and gravel. Suddenly she stopped and looked back up at the djinn. "By the way, how is my father? I heard he was wounded in the fight."

"He is well, Princess," Fedj answered, noting that Zohra had not asked this question earlier. "The sword thrust penetrated no vital areas."

"It would have served him right if it had," Zohra remarked coolly. Turning, she made her way down the side of the hill, heedlessly trampling the Rose of the Prophet beneath her booted feet.

Zohra's mother, dead these ten years, had been an intelligent, strong-willed, and beautiful woman. A powerful sorceress, she was not only Jaafar's head wife but his favorite wife as well, bearing him many fine sons and a single daughter.

This one daughter, Jaafar used to say sadly, gave him far more trouble than any of his sons. Intelligent and strong-willed, and even more skilled in magic, Zohra, at the age of twelve, had the misfortune to lose the influence of her mother. Fatima could have shown her daughter how to use that intelligence for the good of her people, how to use the magic in order to help them survive their harsh way of life. Instead, without her mother's guidance, Zohra used her gifts to run wild.

The men of her tribe were responsible for the sheep, herding them from pasture to pasture, driving off predators. The women were responsible for the camp, using their magic in domestic matters from the building of the yurts to the cooking of food and the healing of the sick. Zohra found women's work boring, the confinement of the *seraglio* stifling. Dressing in her older brother's cast-off clothes, she constantly escaped the *harem*, preferring to play at the boys' rough sports. Jaafar's wives dared not correct the girl, for Zohra's doting father—grieving over his favorite wife's death—could not bear to see the daughter who resembled her made unhappy.

"She will outgrow it," he used to say fondly when his wives came to him with tales of Zohra seen running among the hills with the sheepdogs, the skin of her face and arms brown as that of a boy's.

Time passed, Zohra outgrew her brother's cast-off clothes, but she did not outgrow her wild and rebellious nature. Her brothers—grown men with wives of their own—were now scandalized by their sister's unwomanly behavior and tried to persuade Jaafar to control his daughter. Jaafar himself began to think uneasily that somewhere along the road he had made a mistake, but he could not figure out how to correct it. (His sons had suggested a sound beating. The one time Jaafar had attempted to beat Zohra, she had grabbed the stick from his hands and threatened to beat him!)

When Zohra was sixteen, the Sheykh let it be known among the Hrana that he was interested in contracting his daughter's marriage. This announcement precipitated a sudden outbreak of weddings in the tribe, the eligible men all hurrying to marry someone else—anyone else! Those ending up without brides disappeared into the hills, preferring to live among the sheep. They returned only when it was known that Zohra had publicly vowed to *Hazrat* Akhran that no man would ever possess her.

Moaning the usual—that he was cursed—Jaafar gave up all hope of changing his daughter and retired to his tent. Zohra, triumphant, continued to roam the hills dressed as a young man—her long black hair tangled and windblown, her skin deeply tanned from the sun, her body growing lithe and strong. She was twenty-two years old and could proudly boast that no man had laid a hand on her.

Then her world collapsed. The Wandering God abandoned her, casting her into the arms of her enemy as if she had been nothing more than a slave. She had refused to marry Khardan, of course, and would have run away from her home the moment she heard the news had not Fedj set himself to guard her day and night.

Then came the storm, terrifying her father and the rest of the weak-hearted cowards of her tribe. Jaafar decreed that she would marry Khardan and in this he stood firm, the 'efreets scaring him more than his daughter. Leaving the sheep with a few guards in the hills, the rest of the Hrana tribe made the long journey into the middle of the desert to the Tel, dragging their princess every degrading inch of the way.

These thoughts and memories a jumble in her mind, Zohra stopped again, halfway to the bridal tent. She had very nearly made good her escape this time. Why not try again? Surely Fedj would be occupied with watching the men. . . .

Biting her lip, looking at the bridal tent, Zohra sighed. Fedj's words returned to her. *If you do not go back to your people, they and perhaps all the people of the desert are doomed.* Although at times the princess thought her people as stupid as the sheep they tended, she loved her tribe fiercely. She didn't understand it. It seemed ludicrous. How could they be in such danger? But if they were, it would not be *she* who brought the wrath of the God down upon her people!

Zohra felt pleased with herself; she was making a noble sacrifice, and—by Sul—the Hrana would never be allowed to forget it!

Creeping past the slumbering guard, the princess crawled beneath the opening left between the tent wall and the felt floor. The tent flaps were lowered. Outside she could hear the groom's drunken procession wending its way through the camp, coming closer and closer. Stripping off the caftan and trousers and hurriedly stuffing them beneath a cushion, Zohra dressed herself in the silken bridal gown. Adorning herself with her jewelry, the princess sat before her mirror and began brushing out her waist-long black hair.

To be head wife. . . wife of the Calif. . .

Zohra smiled at her reflection.

She would make this Khardan wish he had never been born!

CHAPTER 6

The desert slept in the moonlight, languishing like a woman in her lover's arms. Khardan breathed deeply, joyfully inhaling the air scented with the smoke of burning juniper, roasting meats, and the elusive, mysterious fragrance of the desert itself.

He called to mind a story about a nomad who had become so exceedingly wealthy that he moved to the city. The nomad built a splendid palace, causing each room to have the perfume of thousands of crushed flowers blended with the clay of its walls. A visitor entering room after room was overwhelmed with the scents of roses, orchid, orange blossoms. Finally, however, the visitor came to the last room, which had no windows or doors but was open to the air.

"This," said the nomad proudly, "is *my* room!" He drew a deep, satisfied breath.

The visitor sniffed curiously. "But I smell nothing," he said, puzzled.

"The scent of the desert," replied the nomad with wistful longing.

And the desert had a fragrance—a clean, sharp perfume that was the smell of the wind and the sun and the sand and the sky. Khardan breathed again and again. He was young and alive. It was his wedding night. He was being awaited by a virgin of twenty-two who, though reputedly spirited, was also reputedly extremely beautiful. The thought was more intoxicating to him than the *qumiz*.

The Calif had not seen Zohra, nor had any of the men of his tribe. But he knew what she looked like. Or at least he supposed he did. Once Majiid had made his will known that his son would marry the Hrana's princess—Khardan had secretly sent Pukah, his djinn, to investigate.

Hovering about the shepherd's camp, completely invisible, the djinn followed a veiled Zohra for days, and at last his patience was rewarded when the woman—out on one of her solitary rambles—decided to strip off her clothes and bathe in a rushing stream. The djinn spent an afternoon observing her, then went—not to his master—but to Fedj, Jaafar's djinn.

Pukah found the older immortal lounging inside his ring. Although somewhat smaller and more cramped than most dwellings of the djinn, the ring suited Fedj to perfection. He was an orderly djinn, liking things neatly arranged, each in its proper place. The ring was sumptuously decorated, but it was not cluttered with furniture—as were some immortal dwellings. A carved wooden chair or two, a bench with silken cushions for his bed, a fine hubble-bubble pipe in the corner, and several very rare tapestries embellishing the ring's golden walls made up the djinn's establishment.

"*Salaam aleikum,* O Great One." Pukah performed the obeisance due to this older and higher-ranking immortal. "May I enter?"

A djinn may not cross the threshold of the dwelling place of another unless he has been invited.

"What do you want?" Fedj, drawing smoke up through the water of the hubble-bubble pipe, glanced at Pukah with distaste. He neither liked nor trusted the young djinn and liked and trusted him still less when Pukah was respectful and polite.

"I have been sent on an errand from my master, the Calif," replied Pukah humbly. "And knowing your wisdom, I am seeking advice about how to discharge my errand, O Intelligent One."

Fedj scowled. "You may enter, I suppose. But don't get the idea that just because our tribes are uniting means anything else but enmity exists between us. Your master could marry a thousand daughters of my master and I would just as soon see the eyes in his head eaten by ants as not. And that goes for your eyes, too."

"A blessing upon your eyes as well, O Fedj the Magnificent," said Pukah, seating himself cross-legged on a cushion.

"Well, what do you want?" said Fedj, glaring at the young djinn, not certain but having the feeling he'd been insulted. "Be quick. There's a redolent odor of horse in here I find nauseating."

"My master requested that I view his bride and ascertain her beauty," said Pukah glibly, his face smooth as goat's milk.

Fedj tensed. Slowly he lowered the stem of the hubblebubble from his mouth, his enjoyment of his quiet smoke ruined. "Well, have you seen her?"

"Yes, O Exalted One," Pukah replied.

"Then return to your master and tell him he is marrying the most beautiful of women and leave me in peace," Fedj said, lounging back among his cushions.

"I would that I could, O Peerless One," Pukah said sadly. "As I have said, I have *seen* the princess. . . ."

"And are not her eyes the soft and gentle eyes of the gazelle?" demanded Fedj.

Pukah shook his head. "The eyes of a prowling leopard." Fedj flushed in anger. "Her lips, red as the rose!"

"Red as the persimmon," said Pukah, his mouth puckering. "Her hair, black as the feathers of the ostrich-"

"The feathers of the vulture."

"Her breasts, white as the snows of the mountain tops."

"That much I'll concede. But," Pukah added sadly, "after viewing her from the neck up, my master may never get that far down."

"So what?" Fedj retorted. "He's been ordered to marry her and marry her he will, be she as ugly as the bustard. Or does he want to contend with another of *Hazrat* Akhran's 'warnings'?"

"My master has the courage of ten thousand men," returned Pukah loftily. "He offered to challenge the God, Himself, in single combat, but his father forbade and my master is a most dutiful son."

"*Humpf!*" snorted Fedj.

"But if I return with a report like this . . . well"—Pukah sighed-"I cannot be held responsible for the consequences."

"Let the hotheaded Calif fight *Hazrat* Akhran," Fedj sneered. "I will enjoy watching the 'efreets rip his arms from his body and wipe his face with the bloody stumps."

"Alas, I fear you would miss the spectacle, O Salty One," said Pukah. "I doubt if much would be visible from the bottom of the Kurdin Sea."

Fedj glowered at the young djinn, who gazed at him with limpid, innocent eyes. "What do you want?"

"Flying on the wings of love, I will return to my master and tell him that his bride-to-be is truly the loveliest of women with eyes of the gazelle, lips of roses, breasts of whitest snow, thighs—"

"What do you know of her thighs?" Fedj roared.

Pukah bowed his turbaned head to the ground. "Forgive me. I was carried away by my enchantment over the beauty of your mistress."

"Well," continued Fedj, eyeing the djinn warily, "you will tell your master this—in exchange for what?"

"Your thanks are all I desire—"

"And I'm Sul. What do you want."

"If you insist on giving me some reward, I ask only that you promise to do me a like favor some day, O Magnanimous One," Pukah said, his nose pressed into the carpet.

"I would sooner cut out my tongue than make such a promise to the likes of you!"

"*Hazrat* Akhran might be, able to assist you in that," Pukah said gravely.

Remembering the God's threat if the djinn failed in his assigned task, Fedj choked.

"Very well," the djinn snarled, fighting a momentary longing to grab up Pukah and stuff him bodily into the hubble-bubble pipe. "Now leave."

"You agree to do me a like favor someday?" Pukah persisted, knowing that a "very well" would not be acceptable as evidence before a higher tribunal of djinn in case Fedj ever tried to worm out of his agreement.

"I agree . . . to do you. . . a . . . favor. . . " muttered Fedj sourly.

Pukah smiled sweetly. Rising to his feet, the young djinn exhibited every sign of respect, backing out of the ring, his hands pressed together over his forehead. "*Bilhana!* Wishing you joy! *Bilshifa!* Wishing you health!"

"Wishing you devoured by demons!" muttered Fedj, but he waited to say this until Pukah had vanished. Moodily the elder djinn sought solace in his pipe once more, only to discover that the charcoal had gone out.

Now, on this moonlit night, his wedding night, Khardan approached the bridal tent, images of his bride—as described by an effusive Pukah—filling his mind and causing his blood to burn.

So what if she was the daughter of a shepherd? She was a beautiful daughter by his djinn's account, and anyway, this marriage only had to last until some wretched cactus flower bloomed. That would be, when? A matter of a few weeks until spring?

I will amuse myself with her until then, Khardan reflected, and if she grows wearisome, I will take a wife of my own choosing and relegate this shepherd's daughter to her proper place. If she proves too difficult, I will simply return her to her father.

But that was in the future. For now, there was the wedding night.

Turning to face his companions, who were weaving unsteadily on their feet, hanging on to each other's shoulders, Khardan bid them farewell. Sending him forth with several final, ribald suggestions, the men of the Akar turned and staggered off, never noticing that several cold-sober Hrana left the shadows to follow them.

Khardan reached the bridal tent just as the moon attained its zenith. The guards—members of the bride's tribe—stared stonily straight ahead, refusing to look at him as he approached. Khardan, grinning, wished them an impertinent, *"Emshi besselema—good* night," pushed past them, shoved aside the flap of the bridal tent, and entered.

A soft light glowed within the tent. The fragrance of jasmine met his nostrils, blended—oddly—with the faint smell of horse. His bride lay reclining upon the cushions of the marriage bed. In the dim light she was a shadowy figure against the pure white of the bridal sheets. Struck by a sudden thought, Khardan turned and poked his head out the tent flap.

"In the morning," he said to the Hrana, "enter and see by the blood upon this sheet that I have done what you sheep followers could not do; see what it is to be a man!"

One of the guards, with a bitter curse, made a lunge for his scimitar. The sudden appearance of Fedj, springing up out of the sand, his arms folded across his massive chest, caused the Hrana to contain himself.

"Leave," the djinn commanded, "I will stand guard this night."

Fedj did not do this out of love for Khardan. At this moment he would have enjoyed nothing more than seeing the Hrana's blade rip the braggart Calif from crotch to throat.

"Akhran commands," he reminded the guards.

Muttering, the Hrana left. The djinn, full seven feet tall, took his place before the tent.

Khardan, laughing, ducked back inside and shut the tent flaps. Turning, he approached the bed of his bride.

She was dressed in her white wedding gown. The light sparkled off the golden threads of the elaborate embroidery that lined the hem of gown and veil. Jewels sparkled on her hands and arms, a band of gold held her veil upon her head. Drawing nearer, Khardan could see the swelling curves of her breasts rising and falling beneath the folds of the filmy material that swathed her body, the full curve of her hips as she lay upon the bed.

Sinking down upon the cushions beside Zohra, Khardan reached out his hand and gently removed the white veil from her face. He could feel her trembling, and his excitement mounted.

Khardan breathed a soft sigh.

From Pukah's description the Calif had expected a lovely woman, an ordinary woman—a woman like his mother and his sisters. "Eyes like the gazelle, lips like roses, breasts like snow. . . ." So Pukah had glibly reported.

"Djinn, where are your eyes?" Khardan said to himself, letting the silk of Zohra's face-veil slip between his fingers and fall to the bed.

He had seen the pet gazelles in the palaces of Kich, he had seen the animal's adoring gaze cast down when a man stroked the creature's neck or fondled the soft ears.

The large, liquid black eyes that fixed him with an unwavering stare were nothing like that. There was flame in them, they gleamed with an inner light that the intoxicated Calif mistook for love. The petal softness of Zohra's cheeks were a dusky rose, not pasty white as other women's. Her black hair shone sleek and smooth like the mane of the Calif's own horse. Falling over her shoulders, her hair brushed against the wrist of his hand that rested lightly upon the white sheets of the bridal bed, sending a fire crackling through his body as though he'd been touched by a flail.

"Holy Akhran, my sincerest apologies for ever doubting your wisdom," Khardan breathed, moving nearer his bride, his eyes upon the red lips. "I thank you, Wandering God, for this gift. She truly pleases me. I—"

Khardan stopped speaking, his voice arrested by the blade of a dagger pressed against his throat. His hand, which had been about to part the silken fabric of the *paranja,* halted in midair.

"Touch me and you die," said the bride.

The Calif's face flushed in anger. He made a movement toward Zohra's knife-hand, only to feel the metal of the blade—warm from having been hidden against the bride's breast—prick his skin.

"Your thanks to your God are premature, *batir-thief!*" Zohra said, her lip curling. "Don't move. If you think that I—weak female that I am—do not know how to use this weapon, you are wrong. The women in my tribe butcher the sheep. There is a vein right here"—she traced a line down his neck with the tip of her dagger—"that will spill your cowardly blood and drain you of life in seconds."

Khardan, sobering rapidly, knew suddenly that he was seeing his bride truly for the first time. The black, fiery eyes were the eyes of the hawk swooping in for the kill, the trembling he had mistaken for passion he realized now was suppressed fury. The Calif had faced many enemies in his life, he had seen the eyes of men intent on killing him, and he knew the expression. Slowly, breathing heavily, he withdrew his hand.

"What is the meaning of this? You are now my wife! It is your duty to lie with me, to bear my children. It is the will of *Hazrat* Akhfan!"

"It is the will of *Hazrat* Akhran that we marry. The God said nothing about bearing children!" Zohra held the knife firmly. Her black eyes, staring into Khardan's, did not waver.

"And what will happen tomorrow morning when the bridal sheet is exhibited to our fathers and there is no blood to give proof of your virginity?" Khardan asked coolly, lounging back and folding his arms across his chest. His enemy had made a mistake, opening up an area vulnerable to attack. He waited to see how she countered.

Zohra shrugged her shoulders.

"That is *your* disgrace," she said, lowering the dagger slightly.

"Oh, no, it isn't, madam!" Lunging forward, Khardan skillfully pinned Zohra's knife-wielding hand to the bed cushions. "Quit struggling. You'll hurt yourself. Now listen to me, she-devil!" He shoved his bride down upon the bed and held her fast, his arm over her chest. "When that sheet is exhibited tomorrow morning, Princess, and it is white and spotless, I will go to your father and tell him that I took you this night and that you were *not* a virgin!"

Zohra's face went livid. The hawk eyes glared at him with such fury that Khardan tightened his grip on the woman's wrist.

"They will never believe you!"

"They will. I am a man, Calif of my tribe, known for my honor. Your father will be forced to take you back in disgrace. Perhaps he will even cut off your nose—"

Zohra twisted in Khardan's grasp. "My magic—" she gasped.

"Cannot be used against me! Would you have yourself proclaimed a black sorceress as well? You would be stoned to death!"

"You—" Struggling to free herself, Zohra mouthed a filthy name.

Khardan, his eyes widening in pretended shock, grinned. The Calif's gaze went to the high, firm breasts he could feel rising and falling rapidly beneath the silk. The fragrance of night-blooming jasmine wafted through the air. His bride's black eyes were fierce as any hunting bird's, but her lips were red and warm and glistened warmly.

"Come, Zohra," he murmured, leaning to kiss her. "I like your spirit. I had not expected such a thing from the daughter of a sheepherder. You will bear me many fine *sons-hhhhiii!*"

"You wanted blood on the sheet!" Zohra cried in triumph. "There, you have it!"

Gritting his teeth against the pain, Khardan stared in amazement at a deep gash in his upper arm.

Dagger pointed at her husband, Zohra slid back away from him as far as she could on the cushions of the bridal bed whose white silken sheets were now stained crimson red.

"And what will you tell your father? That his stallion was a gelding?" Zohra laughed mirthlessly, pointing at the wound on his arm. "That *you* were the virgin? That it was the bride who conquered?"

Her earrings jingling in triumph, Zohra flung back her head proudly and started to rise up out of the bed. A strong hand caught hold of her wrist, yanking her back down onto the cushions. Screaming a curse, she tried to lash out with the dagger, only to find her knife-hand caught in a grip of iron. There was a cracking sound, and gagging with pain, Zohra dropped the weapon.

Smiling grimly, Khardan flung his bride back onto the bed. "Do not fear, *wife*"—he spoke with mocking irony—"I will not touch you. But you are not going anywhere. We must spend this night as man and wife and be found together in the morning or *Hazrat* Akhran will vent his wrath upon our people."

He gazed down upon her as she lay among the cushions, nursing her bruised wrist. Her hate-filled eyes burned through a tangle of sleek black hair. Her gown had been torn in their struggles; it fell down over one shoulder, revealing smooth, white skin. The slightest touch would displace it completely. Khardan's gaze lowered, his hand moved slowly. . . .

Snarling like a wildcat, Zohra grasped hold of the flimsy fabric and drew it closer around her.

"Spend the night with you. I would sooner sleep with a goat! Pah!" She spit at him.

"And I likewise!" Khardan said coldly, wiping spittle from his face.

The groom was stone-sober now. There was no passion in his eyes as he gazed upon is bride—only disgust.

Zohra clutched her clothes around her. Wriggling as far from her husband as she could get, she huddled among the cushions at the head of the bed.

Khardan climbed out of bed and stripped off his torn and bloodstained wedding shirt. Rolling it into a ball, he threw it into a corner of the tent, then tossed a cushion over it. "In the morning, burn it," he ordered without turning around or looking at his bride.

The tan skin of his strong shoulders glistened in the flickering light. Removing the headcloth, he shook out his curly, black hair. *Shir,* he was called among his people—the lion. Fearless and ferocious in battle, he moved with a catlike grace. The scars of his victories were traced over his lithe body. Going to a water bowl in the tent, he bathed the wound on his arm and clumsily bandaged it as best he could with one hand.

Glancing at his bride's reflection in one of many small mirrors that had been woven into a tapestry hanging upon the wall before him, Khardan saw to his astonishment that the fire of anger had died in the dark eyes. There was even, he thought, a smoldering glimmer of admiration.

It was gone in an instant, as soon as Zohra realized the Calif was watching her. The soft red lips that had been slightly parted over the even white teeth curled in a sneer. Flipping her long black hair over her shoulders, Zohra coldly averted her face, but he could see the slits of black eyes watching him.

Khardan's hand moved to the waist of his trousers, and he heard a snarl of warning from the bed behind him. His lips twisting in a grim smile, the Calif—with an emphatic gesture—cinched his trousers more tightly. Walking to the front of the tent, he searched the felt floor. Finding what he sought, he returned at last to the bridal bed. In his hand was the dagger.

Without a glance at Zohra, he tossed the weapon down upon the cushions. Blood glistened on the dagger's blade, its handle facing the bride. Lying down upon the right-hand side of the bed, the dagger separating him from his wife, Khardan turned his bare back to Zohra. He rested his head upon his arm, made himself comfortable, and closed his eyes.

Zohra remained where she was, crouched at the head of the bed, watching her husband warily for long moments. She could see blood beginning to seep through the crude bandage he had wound around his arm. The gash was open, bleeding freely. Hesitantly, moving slowly and quietly, Zohra removed a bracelet, ornamental with blood stone, she wore upon her arm and held it out toward Khardan.

The Calif, sighing, shifted his weight. Zohra snatched her hand back. Dropping the bracelet, her fingers hovered over the handle of the dagger. But Khardan only burrowed further down into the soft cushions. Zohra sat, waiting, unmoving, until the man's breathing became even and regular. Then, picking up the bracelet again, she lightly passed the jewels over the injured flesh.

"By the power granted to woman by Sul, I conjure the spirits of healing to close this wound."

The bracelet slipped from her hand. Her fingers lingered on the man's muscular arm, their light touch sliding up the smooth skin.

Khardan stirred. Hastily, fearfully, Zohra snatched her hand away. There was no change in his breathing pattern, however, and she relaxed. *Qumiz* often sent men to sleep's realm quickly, buried them deeply. She stared closely at the wound, wondering if her spell had been successful. It seemed that the bleeding had stopped, but because of the bandage she could not be certain, and she dared not untie the cloth to examine it, for fear of waking the man.

Zohra had no reason to doubt her power, however. Nodding to herself in satisfaction, she blew out the light of the lamp then gingerly laid herself down upon the bed, keeping her body as far as possible from Khardan's, nearly rolling off the edge of the cushions in the process. For some reason she could still feel the touch of his skin, warm beneath her fingers. Glowering into the darkness, the princess reached behind her with her hand for the dagger and found the hilt, cold and reassuring, lying on the silken sheets between them.

The wound was healed, vanished as if it had never been. The scar would be just one more taken in battle. But what an ignominious defeat for the warrior!

Zohra smiled. Exhausted from the day's events, she sighed, relaxed, and soon fell fast asleep.

Lying next to her, Khardan stared into the darkness, still feeling the touch of fingers upon his skin, fingers as soft and delicate as the wings of the butterfly.

The next morning the two fathers approached the bridal tent. Jaafar walked stiffly. Though his wives had used their magic to seal his wound, the cut had been deep enough to require a bandage and a healing potion spread over it to prevent the tainting of the blood. The Sheykh of the Hrana was surrounded by armed guards who glared at the Sheykh of the Akar as Majiid swaggered into view, surrounded by his own armed *spahis*.

The procession of the two fathers was not, therefore, the joyous walk with arms around each other customary to the morning after the wedding night. They did not speak but growled at each other like fighting dogs, their followers keeping their hands closed over the hilts of dagger and sword.

The men of the Hrana and the Akar gathered around the bridal tent, waiting in silence. Fedj, his face grim, turned and faced the tent, calling out a cold morning greeting to bride and groom. The djinn, having heard the commotion in the bridal tent during the night, had no idea what they would find upon entering. Two lifeless corpses, hands on each other's throats, wouldn't have much surprised him.

After several moments, however, the groom emerged, carrying the white silken sheet in his hand. Slowly he unfurled it to flutter like a banner in the desert wind. The splotch of red was plainly visible.

A cheer went up from the Akar. Jaafar regarded Khardan with amazed, if grudging, respect. Majiid clapped his son upon his back. Pukah, sidling over, nudged Fedj in the ribs. "Five rubies you owe me," he said, holding out his hand.

Scowling, the djinn paid up.

The fathers reached for the bridal sheet, but Khardan kept it away from them.

"*Hazrat* Akhran, this belongs to you," the Calif cried to the heavens

He held the sheet out. The desert wind filled the bridal sheet. Khardan loosed it and a sudden strong gust sent it skipping along the sands. The silken sheet fluttered through camp, dancing like a ghost, the wind driving it toward the Tel. Long, sharp needles of a shriveled and brown cactus—the ugly plant known as the Rose of the Prophet—caught the sheet and held it fast.

Within seconds the whipping, angry wind had ripped the bridal sheet to shreds.

The Book
of
Promenthas

Chapter 1

Leaning upon the ship's rail, the young wizard breathed deeply, his lips parted as though he could drink in the fresh wind that billowed the sails and sent the galleon scudding over the waves. Sunlight danced on the smooth blue water of the Hurn Ocean, clouds white as angel's wings floated in the sky.

"A day like this is a gift of Promenthas," said the wizard to his companion, a monk, who stood beside him on the foredeck.

"Amen," replied the monk, taking the opportunity to rest his hand lightly upon the hand of the wizard. The two young men smiled at each other, oblivious to the coarse remarks and nudgings among the galleon's rough crew.

The wizard and the monk were just entering young manhood—the magus only eighteen, the monk in his early twenties. The two had met aboard ship. It was the first time either had been away from the rigorous, cloistered schooling both Orders required of their members, and now they were on an adventure, voyaging to a world rumored to be fantastic and bizarre beyond reckoning. As they were the youngest of each of their Orders present, an immediate friendship had developed between them.

That friendship had deepened during the long voyage, becoming—on both sides—something more serious, more profound. Unaccustomed to relationships of any kind, having been raised in strictly ordered and highly disciplined schools, neither young man sought to rush this one. Both were content to wait and enjoy the long, sunlit days and fill warm, moonlit evenings in each other's company; nothing more.

A step behind them caused the hands to separate quickly. Turning, each bowed reverently to the Abbot.

"I heard the name of Promenthas," said the Abbot gravely. "I trust it was not being taken in vain?" His gaze went to the young wizard.

"Indeed not, Holiness," replied the wizard, flushing. "I was thanking our God for the beauty of the day."

The Abbot nodded. His gravity easing as he looked upon the two young men, he smiled at them benignly before continuing his morning stroll around the deck. Glancing back over his shoulder, he saw them grinning at each other and shaking their heads, undoubtedly laughing at the foibles of their elders.

Ah, well . . . the Abbot recalled what it was to be young. He had seen the growing affection between the two; one would have had to have been blind to miss it. He was not overly concerned. Once they arrived in Bastine, the two would be kept busy with the duties of their Orders, and though the party of wizards and monks traveled as a group for safety's sake, the young men would find little time to be alone together. If their relationship was a solid one, the hardships of the journey would strengthen it. If not, as well to find out before either was hurt.

The Abbot, his constitutional taking him around to the starboard side of the ship, found his gaze following his thoughts, returning once again to the two young men standing opposite him. A school of dolphins was swimming alongside the ship, their graceful bodies leaping through the waves. Brother John, the young monk, was leaning over the rail in an effort to gain a better view; a feat that obviously disturbed his companion.

Odd, thought the Abbot. One generally sees solemnity in those of *my* Order. In this instance, however, it was the wizard Mathew who was the more solemn and serious of the two. Such a remarkable-looking young man, too, the Abbot noted, not for the first time.

Mathew was a Wesman, a race celebrated—men and women alike—for their beauty and their high-pitched, fluting voices. His hair was a coppery auburn, his face so white as to be almost translucent, his eyes green beneath feathery chestnut eyebrows. The men of Mathew's race did not grow beards— his face was smooth, and though the bone structure was delicate, it was strong, marked by a serious, thoughtful expression that was rarely broken. When the young wizard smiled, which was rarely, it was a smile of such infectious warmth that one was instantly moved to smile back.

He was as intelligent as he was attractive. His Master had informed the Abbot that Mathew had been at the head of his class since he was a boy. This journey was, in fact, a reward granted upon his recent graduation to the rank of apprentice wizard.

Mathew was also devoutly religious, another reason he had been chosen to accompany the priests upon their missionary travels. Forbidden by Promenthas, their God, to fight, the priests often employed wizards to act as bodyguards when traveling to the lands of infidels, preferring the more gentle, refined defenses of magic to the swords and knives of men-at-arms.

So dangerous and uncertain was this trip, however, that the Abbot almost regretted not bringing knights with him, as had been urged by the Duke. The Abbot had pooh-poohed the idea most heartily, reminding His Grace that they traveled with the blessing and guidance of Promenthas. Stories he had since heard from the ship's captain, however, had given the Abbot pause.

Of course he believed the captain to be exaggerating; obviously the man enjoyed scaring the naive representatives of the God. Stories of djinn who lived in bottles and brought their masters gold and jewels, carpets that flew through the air—the Abbot smiled at the captain indulgently over the dinner table, wondering how the man thought adults could take such outlandish tales seriously.

The Abbot had studied the lands and languages of the continent of Sardish Jardan. Such study was requisite for both priests and magi, for they must all speak the language of the infidel fluently in order to bring them to the knowledge of the true Gods, and they had to know something of the land through which they were going to travel. The Abbot had read, therefore, many of these stories but took them about as seriously as he took the tales of guardian angels related to him as a child. The idea that mankind could communicate directly with immortal beings! It was sacrilegious!

The Abbot believed in angels, certainly. He would not have been a faithful representative of Promenthas if he had not. But it was only the most exalted, the most holy of men and women who were granted the rare privilege of talking with these radiant beings. And for an immortal to live in a bottle! The thought brought a chuckle to the Abbot that he immediately suppressed as bordering on blasphemy.

One had to make allowances for sailors, he reminded himself. The ship's captain had, after all, not been pleased at carrying the priests to Sardish Jardan. Only through the Duke's intervention and a payment of almost three times the amount of money paid by other passengers was the captain finally prevailed upon to take the missionaries on board. The Abbot suspected the man was getting his own back by telling every gruesome tale he had ever heard.

Unfortunately, several stories of the captain's did, on more than one occasion, keep the Abbot awake long hours into the night: stories of slave traders, of strange Gods who decreed that those not of their faith should be put to death, of flesh-eating cannibals, of savage nomads who lived in uninhabitable deserts. The Abbot had read something of these in the books written by adventurers who had visited the land of Sardish Jardan, and he felt his qualms about this journey growing as each passing day brought them nearer.

It was all very well to remind himself that he should have faith in Promenthas, that they were traveling on the God's work, and that they were going to bring the light of the God's countenance to shine upon these infidels. The Abbot, after listening night after night to the captain, had begun to think that maybe the light shining off a few sword blades might not be such a bad thing.

A cry brought the Abbot's thoughts back to the ship. At sight of the dolphins, the sailors lined up at the rail began casting golden rings into the sea and crying out to the dolphins to grant them a safe voyage. Apparently the young monk, excited by the sight, had nearly fallen overboard in an effort to see the dolphins catch the rings on their long snouts. Only the quick-thinking action of this friend had saved him from tumbling into the ocean.

His feet once more firmly on deck, Brother John was wiping salt spray from his blond beard and laughing at the wizard, Mathew, whose face was so white that the Abbot feared for a moment the young magus might faint. Mathew managed a wan smile, however, when his friend clapped him on the back, and he managed to suggest—in a low, trembling voice—that they go below and play a game of chess.

Brother John agreed readily, and the two left the deck, the long, black, gold-embroidered robe of the wizard and the plain gray robe of the monk whipping around their ankles in the freshening wind. The Abbot, watching them, frowned slightly. The young wizard had truly been unnerved by the trivial incident. He had acted swiftly and responsibly in catching hold of the monk's rope belt and dragging him back over the railing. But Brother John had not been in any real danger; the seas were so calm that even if he had fallen into them, the dousing would have done him no harm.

The Abbot had suspected that Mathew was overly sensitive, and this sign of weakness did not bode well, coming as it did upon the heels of the Abbot's dark thoughts about the possible dangers they might face.

Resolving to say a word about this matter to the Archmagus, the Abbot made his way below deck. Passing the cabin where the lower members of both Orders had their berths, the Abbot saw the two young men bent over a chessboard, the carved pieces having been fitted with pegs so that the listing of the ship did not cause them to slide around. The young wizard's long red hair fell over his shoulders, almost touching his elbows. Absorbed in his game, Mathew had apparently forgotten his fright. The long, delicate fingers moved a piece. Brother John, not knowing the Abbot was observing them, muttered a mild oath, tugging at his beard in irritation.

Folding his hands in his long sleeves, the Abbot made his way to the cabin of his longtime friend, the Archmagus, where he was greeted warmly and invited to sit down for a cup of tea.

"What is the matter, Holiness?" the Archmagus asked, lifting the teapot that bubbled over a magical fire he had conjured up in a small iron brazier. "You have been unusually solemn these past few days."

"It is these tales the captain has been telling," the Abbot admitted, settling himself down on a bench bolted to the deck. "You have studied this land, more than I. Am I leading my flock into the jaws of the wolf?"

"Sailors are a superstitious lot," the Archmagus said comfortingly. Pouring the tea carefully into a cup, he took care not to allow the swaying of the ship to cause him to dump hot water upon the lap of his companion. "You saw the goings on up there just now?" He nodded above deck.

"Yes, what was that?"

"They are sacrificing to Hurishta, Goddess of the Sundering Seas. Thus the golden rings. They believe the dolphins are her daughters. By giving them these rings, they insure a smooth passage."

The Abbot stared at him, incredulous.

The Archmagus, pleased at the monk's reaction, continued, "They even claim, if you will believe me, that these daughters of Hurishta bear a great love for sailors, and that if any man falls overboard, they will carry him safely to shore."

The Abbot shook his head.

"And tonight," continued the Archmagus, who was a traveled man, "you will see something even stranger. They will cast iron rings into the sea."

"Certainly more economical than gold," remarked the Abbot, who had been thinking regretfully of that money falling into the ocean instead of into his church's poor box. "That is not the reason. The iron rings are for the Inthaban."

"Another Goddess?"

"A God. He, too, supposedly rules the sea, but on the other side of the world. He and this Hurishta, however, are presumably jealous of each other and constantly invade each other's territory. Wars break out frequently, and when they do, terrible storms erupt. Therefore the sailors always play it safe, sacrificing to both during an ocean crossing so as not to offend either."

"Has no one ever attempted to bring these benighted souls to the knowledge that the seas are ruled by Promenthas in His grace and mercy?"

"I would strongly advise against such a thing, my friend," the Archmagus counseled, seeing an expression of eager, holy zeal start to light the Abbot's face. "The sailors already fear that your presence angers both God and Goddess. They have sacrificed more than normal during a voyage, and it is only the lasting fair weather we've experienced that has kept them in such good humor. I shudder to think what might happen if we were to run into a storm."

"But this isn't the time of year for storms!" the Abbot said impatiently. "If they only took the time to study the oceans and the tides and prevailing winds instead of believing in such childish nonsense—"

"Study?" The Archmagus looked amused. "Most of them can't read or write so much as their names. No, Holiness, I suggest that you do your proselytizing among the more educated people of Sardish Jardan. The Emperor, so I have heard, not only is conversant in several languages but can read them as well. His court is a haven for astronomers, philosophers, and other learned men. It is this very intelligence, in fact, that makes him so dangerous."

The Abbot cast the Archmagus a sharp glance. "You and I have not spoken of this—," he began in a low voice.

"Nor should we," the Archmagus said firmly, glancing out the door to see that no one was near.

"I am not quite so much in the dark as you think," the Abbot responded crisply. "The Duke sent for me the night before we sailed."

Now it was the Archmagus who cast a penetrating glance at his friend. "He told you?"

"Some. Enough to understand that he and His Royal Highness view this Emperor as a threat—unlikely as that appears to me, with an entire ocean between us."

"Oceans may be crossed and by more than ships. If you believe the captain—"

"Bah!" The Abbot dismissed the idea with a sniff.

Setting down his empty teacup, the Archmagus gazed out the porthole into the rolling seas; his face, with its long gray beard, troubled. "I will not hide from you, my friend, that we are entering a strange land, populated by a cruel and savage people who believe in alien Gods. The fact that you enter as priests threatening their Gods, and that we enter as spies threatening their government, places us all in gravest danger that no ship's captain can exaggerate. We must be wary, watchful, every moment."

"Why, if this is so, did you bring Mathew?" the Abbot asked after a moment's pause. "He is so innocent, so naive . . . so . . . so"—the Abbot fumbled for a word—"young," he said finally, lamely.

"Precisely why I brought him. It is his youth and his very lack of guile that will protect us from suspicion. He has a gift for languages and can speak the tongue of this land better than any of us. It is the Duke's suggestion, in fact," continued the Archmagus, sipping his tea, "that if the Emperor takes a fancy to him—and the Emperor is known to be attracted to all things beautiful and charming—we leave him behind in the court. "

"Is he aware—"

"Of the true nature of our mission? No, of course not. Nor, I think, could he ever be told. Mathew's is a transparent, trusting nature. He could not, I believe, keep a secret to save his life."

"Then how could you possibly think of leaving him?"

"We will tell him that he is being placed here to study these people, to report to us on their culture, their ways, their language. He will innocently transmit all he learns through our magical means. We will be able to read between the lines and thus discover the Emperor's true plans and motives."

Uncomfortable at such duplicity, the Abbot sighed and shifted about uneasily on his hard bench. Fortunately the Church did not involve itself in politics. He had only to save souls. Their talk turned to other, less dark subjects, and after an hour the Abbot prepared to take his leave.

"I suppose I shouldn't worry," he said on departing, intending to snatch a nap before dinnertime and more of the captain's night-disturbing tales. "After all, Promenthas is with us."

The Archmagus smiled and nodded. But after his friend had left, the wizard gazed out at the sparkling water where the dolphins played alongside, sporting with the golden rings cast to them by the sailors. His face grew troubled. "Promenthas with us? I wonder. . . ."

CHAPTER 2

The voyage eastward across the Hurn sea from Tirish Aranth to Sardish Jardan was, as the Archmagus said, a swift and a calm one. The galleon had been favored with a steadily blowing wind, warm weather, and clear skies during the whole of the two-month trip. Whether credit for this was due to Hurishta and Inthaban or to the fact that it was late winter and the storms that swept the ocean early in the year had abated depended entirely upon one's point of view.

So calm had been the voyage that the sailors—ever superstitious—were relieved when a minor leak was discovered belowdecks, forcing all hands to take a turn manning the pumps. This, the sailors said, cut the luck that had been running too good. Although their work nearly doubled, the sailors' spirits improved immeasurably after finding the leak. They sang as they cheerfully pumped the seawater out of the ship, and there were only mild grumbles when the dolphins suddenly left them the morning before they were due to arrive in Bastine. The reason for this premature leave—taking of the daughters of Hurishta was undoubtedly the sight of a whale, known to be a son of Inthaban, spouting off the starboard bow. The sailors tossed iron rings in the whale's direction and gleefully pointed out the route the daughters of Hurishta had taken for the whale's benefit.

Although not yet within visual contact of land, the sailors and their passengers knew they were close, and this caused a rise of spirits of everyone aboard ship. Palm fronds could be seen floating past, along with trash and other marks of civilization. There was a noticeable change in the smell of the air as well, which the sailors claimed was the "land" smell but which the Abbot thought was probably the increasingly strong stench of the bilge. There were sharks in these waters, too. The captain took grim pleasure in pointing them out, saying that they were the sons of Hurishta keeping watch for Inthaban. Be that as it may, there were no more games for wizards or monks at the ship's rail.

About midafternoon of the day before they were due to sail into the port city of Bastine on the western coast of Sardish Jardan, the sailors' songs ceased. Casting grim glances at the priests, the sailors went about their duties in silence or gathered together in knots, talking among themselves. The captain walked the deck, a preoccupied, worried expression on his face.

Catching sight of one of the monks, he motioned. "Call up your masters," he said.

Within moments the Archmagus and the Abbot were on deck. Looking to the east, they saw the sky turning a most peculiar color—a dreadful greenish black. Banks of heavy gray clouds floated over the water, lightning flickering along the fringes. Thunder could be heard booming sullenly across a sea.

"What is it?" questioned the Abbot.

"Hurricane, most likely," said the captain.

"But that's impossible at this time of year!" the Archmagus scoffed.

"You must be mistaken, Captain," added the Abbot. "Look, the sea is completely calm!" He pointed to the waters, which were smooth and flat.

"Lubbers!" muttered the captain, and proceeded to tell them that the seas were flat because the strong wind was cutting off the tops of the waves.

A sharp command from the captain sent the sailors scrambling aloft to set the storm sails. Catching sight of the other monks and wizards hurrying up on deck to view the ominous-looking clouds, the captain was just about to order everyone below when a tremendous blast of wind hit the ship, laying it over on its side.

Sailors lost their footing and fell from the masts into the sea. The helmsman fought the wheel, the captain shouted orders and cursed the landlubbers, who had scattered all across the deck, getting in the sailors' way. The Abbot, having tumbled into a pile of ropes, was struggling to regain his feet when he saw the monster.

"Promenthas, have mercy!" the Abbot cried, staring in shock.

A gigantic man rose up from the ocean, rearing up out of the water as though he had been crouched there, waiting for them.

When he reached his full height, he was three times taller than the ship, the deep seawater coming to his waist. His skin was the same greenish color as the sky, gray cloud banks formed his hair, seawater streamed from his bare chest in cascades. Lightning flared in his eyes, his thundering voice boomed over the water.

"I am Kaug," the creature roared. "Who are you who trespass upon my seas without offering the proper sacrifice?"

"Now just a minute!" the captain roared back, glaring at the creature with—to the Abbot—unbelievable courage. "We've made the sacrifices! We've given gold to Hurishta and iron to Inthaban—"

"What have you given to Quar?" bellowed the creature. The captain turned pale.

"Quar? Who is this Quar?" muttered the Abbot, hurrying to the side of the Archmagus. "Some king?"

"Quar is the God of the infidels of this land," said the Archmagus.

"What is that. . . that thing?" The Abbot endeavored to control the tremor in his voice.

"Possibly an immortal known among them as an 'efreet," returned the Archmagus, regarding the huge creature with an air more scholarly than fearful. "I have read reports of them, but I must say, I never believed that they truly existed. This is indeed a most remarkable occurrence!"

"Nonsense! It is an archfiend of the Demon Prince Astafas!" said the Abbot angrily. "Sent to test our faith!"

"Whatever he is, he seems capable of doing that," returned the Archmagus coolly.

"We are a trading vessel on a peaceful mission," the captain was shouting. "Your God knows us. We carry the required sacrifices with us. Quar may rest assured that we will visit his shrine when we first set foot upon land!"

"Liar!" snarled Kaug, his blasting breath hitting the ship and sending it rolling in the water. "You carry on board priests of Promenthas, who come here to try to turn the people from the worship of their true God."

"By doing this, do we offend Quar?" the captain inquired meekly, possibly for future reference.

In answer a lightning bolt splintered the mast.

The captain, nodding gravely, turned around. "Throw the

priests overboard!" he commanded his crew.

"Touch these holy men at your peril!" snarled the Archmagus, leaping forward to halt the attacking sailors.

At a word from their leader, the four other wizards ranged themselves alongside the Archmagus, including the young wizard Mathew. Although his face was deathly white and he was trembling visibly, he took his place beside his leader on the heaving deck. Hastily gathering his flock around him, the Abbot stood behind the protecting wizards.

"Promenthas, come to our aid! Save us from this archfiend!" prayed the Abbot, and his prayer was fervently repeated by the twelve members of his Order.

"Don't let that bunch of old women stop you!" howled the captain, raging at his men. "Twenty gold pieces to the first man that sends a priest to the sharks!"

The Archmagus cried out arcane words and lifted in his hand a black obsidian wand that burst into black flame. The other wizards did the same, raising wands of clear quartz or red ruby or green emerald, each flaring with different color of fire. The sailors, who had surged forward again, hesitated.

Laughter thundered over the ocean. Kaug lifted both his arms high over his head. Blue fire leaped from his hands, green fire shot from his eyes. His hair was red flame, whipped about wildly by the storm winds that swirled around him.

Grimly the Archmagus held his ground, although his puny magic appeared like a tiny candle clutched in the hands of a child compared to the blazing flames in the fingers of Kaug. The priests' prayers grew more fervent, several of the monks falling to their knees to beseech Promenthas's protection. The other magi flanked their leader, waiting for his signal to hurl their spells, the red-haired young wizard keeping a bit nearer the monks than his fellows, particularly one monk who had not fallen to his knees but remained standing, tense and alert, near his friend.

For an instant it seemed time itself stopped. No one moved. The sailors, caught between the fire of the magi before them and the fire of the 'efreet behind them, stared at each other uncertainly. The priests continued their prayers, the magi stolidly guarding them.

Then, tiring of the game, Kaug shrugged his massive shoulders and began to wade toward the ship. The waves stirred up by the approach of his gigantic body sent the galleon rolling, hurling sailors and landsmen alike off their feet. Reaching out with his huge hands, Kaug caught hold of the vessel at the prow and the stem and lifted it from the water.

Howling in panic, the captain fell prostrate on his face, promising the God everything from his firstborn child to a share in next year's profits if Quar would only spare his ship. The priests slid about the deck; they had no breath left for prayers. The Archmagus, eyes closed as he clung to the rigging, appeared to be conjuring some powerful spell to deal with this dread apparition that had sprung from the seas.

Carrying the boat effortlessly, Kaug waded through the ocean. Storm winds blew before him, flattening the waves at his approach. Rain lashed the decks, lightning twined about the masts, thunder boomed incessantly. The men aboard the ship held on to anything they could find, clinging to the deck, the ropes, the wheel, for dear life as the ship rocked and heaved in the 'efreet's hands.

"So, Priests, you have come to teach Quar's people of other Gods!" shouted Kaug as he neared the land. "Quar gives you your chance."

So saying, the 'efreet set the ship back into the water. Sucking in a breath so deep that he inhaled clouds and rainwater, Kaug leaned down behind the vessel and blew upon it.

The gusting blast of the 'efreet's breath carried the ship skimming over the waves at an incredible rate of speed. Salt spray lashed the decks, the wheel spun out of control, the wind whistled in the rigging. Then came a shattering crash and a sudden jarring jolt. The ship's forward motion halted abruptly, sending everyone slithering along the wet decks.

"We've run aground!" screamed the captain.

Laughter, boomed behind them. A giant wave lifted the ship, slamming it into the rocks.

"She's breaking up!" the sailors wailed in terror.

"We'll have to abandon ship," gasped the Archmagus, helping the Abbot struggle to his feet.

Wood splintered, masts fell, men cried out in agony as they were buried in the debris.

"Keep together, brethren," ordered the Abbot. "Promenthas, we commend our souls into your care! Jump, my brothers!"

With that, the priests and wizards of Promenthas leaped over the side of the sinking ship and disappeared into the frothing, swirling waters of the Hurn.

CHAPTER 3

The young monk staggered ashore, his arm around his friend, half-carrying, half-dragging the young wizard out of the waves. The wizard sank down weakly upon the beach, the monk collapsing beside him. Coughing and gagging, gasping for breath, they lay on the beach, shivering with the cold and fear.

Gradually, however, the sand—baked by the bright sun-warmed their water-soaked robes. Mathew closed his eyes in thankful rest. The horror of the leap into the swirling water, the panic of being sucked under the waves, began to fade, replaced by the remembrance of a strong arm's catching hold of him and dragging him to the surface, the relief of drawing that first deep breath and knowing that he wasn't going to drown.

The sand's warmth seeped into his body. He was alive, saved from death. Reaching out, he touched the hand of his friend. Mathew smiled. He could lie upon this beach with this feeling in his soul forever.

"Why did you lie to me, Mathew?" asked the monk, coughing. His throat was raw from vomiting salt water. "You can't swim a stroke!"

Mathew shook his head. "I had to tell you something. You wouldn't have left me behind."

"Jumping in the water like that! You could have drowned! Should have! Would have served you right!"

Mathew, opening his eyes, glanced over to see John grinning—somewhat shakily—at him.

"Promenthas was with us!" Mathew said softly.

"Amen!" John said, looking back out at the raging seas with a shudder.

Above them the sky was clear. Angry waves still crashed upon the shoreline, though the storm was far out to sea. What had happened to the ship neither could tell, for both had immediately been swept under the swirling water and had lost sight of the vessel. Bits and pieces of splintered wood, floating up onto the beach, appeared to tell the grim story.

"What will we do now?" John asked after a pause. "No food. No water. At least you can speak the language."

"Yes, but I've lost all my scrolls and my crystal wand," Mathew said, looking down ruefully at the place on his belt where his scroll case used to hang. "You know, I had the strangest feeling that they were taken from me deliberately! Look!" He exhibited the metal chain to which they had been attached. "It's broken, as though it had been ripped apart!"

"Bah! Are there pickpockets in the ocean? You just lost them," John replied, shrugging. "As violent as those waves were, it's a miracle we've still got our clothes!"

They both stared out to sea, each wondering—now that they were safe—what would become of them, lost and alone in a strange land, when movement farther down shore caught John's attention. "Mathew, look!" he cried excitedly, sitting up in the sand and pointing along the barren shoreline. Several gray- and black-robed figures could be seen staggering out of the water. "Our brethren! Do you have the strength to reach them?"

Speechless with relief, Mathew nodded and held his hand out to his friend. John helped him stand, and limping wearily, the two made their way along the windswept beach until they reached the main body of the priests and wizards who had managed to make it ashore.

The Abbot, his wet bald head shining in the fading sunlight, was clucking over them like a distracted hen. "Who is missing? Please stay together so that I can count—Brother Mark, Brother Peter. . . Where's Brother John? Ah, there you are, my boy! And Mathew here, too! Archmagus! Mathew is safe! We have all been spared! Let us thank Promenthas."

The Abbot lifted his eyes to heaven.

"Time for that later," the Archmagus said crisply. More interested in what was transpiring below than above, the wizard had been exploring the beach, investigating their surroundings. "Look there."

"Where?"

"Up there, on the crest of that hill."

"People! A caravan! They must have seen the wreck and have come to help us! Truly Promenthas is great! Blessed be His Holy name!"

"I don't think you need make spectacles of yourselves," the Archmagus counseled his followers, several of whom were shouting and waving their arms to attract attention. "They have seen us. Let us behave with some dignity."

The Archmagus wrung water from his beard. The Abbot twitched his sodden robes into place, and each leader glanced about at the others of their Orders, motioning them to do what they could to make a more presentable appearance.

Still, they did not look at all prepossessing, Mathew thought. Huddled together, half-drowned and exhausted, they were nothing more than flotsam cast up on a foreign shore.

The beach upon which the shipwrecked survivors stood gradually rose to form a sandy hill. Covered with long grass that waved sinuously in the wind, it was dotted here and there with scrub bushes. Large rocks, wet with salt spray, jutted out of the sand. Mathew saw, lined up on the top of the hill on what was apparently a road of some sort, a group of men mounted on horseback staring down at them.

Following along after the horsemen was a palanquin—a large, covered sedan chair. Hung with white curtains, the chair rested on two large poles that were being carried by six turbaned *mameluks*. An imposing sight, these slaves were dressed in matching black silk pantalons, their muscular chests and arms bare and glistening with oil rubbed into their skin. Behind the palanquin, the curtains of which were tightly drawn, strode several tall animals—the likes of which the men of Tirish Aranth had seen only in their books. Brown and ungainly, with long, curved necks, a ridiculously small head for such a large body, and thin, scrawny legs with huge, splayed feet, the animals carried striped, hoop-shaped tents upon their humped backs.

"Promenthas be praised!" the Abbot breathed. "Such wondrous beasts *do* exist! What is it they are called?"

"Camels," replied the Archmagus matter-of-factly, endeavoring to look unimpressed.

But what caught Mathew's attention was the group that came up behind the camels—a long line of men straggling over the road, marching with heads bowed. Each man had an iron ring around his neck. A long length of chain running through the rings, binding the men together. Mathew sucked in his breath in horror. A slave caravan! The Abbot, seeing them, scowled darkly, and the Archmagus, shaking his head, frowned in anger and sorrow.

Riding behind the chained men—obviously their guards—came another group of mounted men. The uniformed horsemen were a bizarre sight to the men of Tirish Aranth, who were accustomed to seeing the hose and doublets, feathered hats, and flowing capes of His Majesty's Royal Guard.

Each of these soldiers wore a short, dark-blue coat that came to his waist. Decorated with golden embroidery that flashed in the sunlight, the coat covered a white shirt that was open at the neck. Bright red trousers, as full as a lady's skirts, billowed about their legs and were tucked into tall black riding boots. Small cone-shaped red hats, adorned with jaunty black tassels, perched atop their heads. The hats looked extremely comical. Mathew, grinning, giggled and nudged John, only to receive a swift, rebuking glance from the Archmagus.

Acting on some unheard order, the entire caravan came to a halt. The chained slaves, glad for any excuse to rest, slumped to the ground. Mathew saw a white hand emerge from the folds of the curtains of the palanquin and make a single, graceful gesture toward the beach. At this, the leader of the horsemen turned his horse's head and skillfully guided his animal down the sandy hill, his troop following in orderly fashion behind him.

"Slave trader," muttered the Abbot, watching, scowling. "I want nothing to do with this evil person."

"I am afraid we cannot afford the luxury of picking and choosing our companions," the Archmagus said softly. "We have lost all our magical paraphernalia and without it, as you know, we are unable to cast spells. We have lost our maps, we have no idea where we are. Besides," he added smoothly, knowing how to handle the Abbot, "this may be your opportunity to bring a soul walking in darkness to the light."

"You are right. Promenthas, forgive me," the Abbot said instantly, his face clearing.

"Whoever that person is, he must be wealthy to keep his own *goums*." The Archmagus used the word of this land with the aplomb of the seasoned traveler.

"Wealth obtained from trading in human flesh," the Abbot began bitterly, but he hushed upon receiving a glance from the Archmagus, warning him that the soldiers were within earshot.

The *goums* in their colorful uniforms were truly an awesome sight. Reaching the shoreline, they rode their magnificent steeds with skill and precision along the wet, packed sand, their horses' manes and tails streaming behind them like banners in the remnants of the storm wind. The setting sun, breaking occasionally through the ragged clouds, glinted on the hilts of the sabers they wore at their sides. Instinctively the small group on the shore huddled closer together as the Abbot and the Archmagus stepped forward wearily to greet their saviors.

The leader rode his horse at a gallop straight for the Abbot, turning the beast aside with a flourish at the last possible moment, the horse's hooves flashing within inches of the priest. Reining in his mount, the *goum* raised his hand, bringing the riders behind him to a halt. Another gesture sent them cantering out in a straight line on either side of him, the horses dancing sideways in remarkable precision. The priest and the wizard watched, apparently unmoved by this spectacle, although their followers could not forbear to whisper among themselves in amazement and wonder.

The *goum* slid down from the saddle, approaching them on foot, his shining black boots crunching across the wet sand.

"*Salaam aleikum!*" said the Abbot, bowing, his greetings being echoed by the Archmagus. "*Bilshifa! Bilhana!* May you have health and joy."

Mathew cringed, wishing the Archmagus would let him do the talking. The Abbot may have been able to speak the language, but his clumsy pronunciation was that of a child saying his first words.

"*Aleikum salaam,*" returned the leader, eyeing the wet, bedraggled band of men with cool curiosity. He was a short man with brown skin, dark eyes, and a small black mustache over his lip. "You speak our language well, but your tongue gives the words strange emphasis. Where are you from?"

"We come from across the sea, *sidi,*" said the Abbot, waving his hand westward. "A land called Tirish Aranth."

"Across the sea?" The man's eyes narrowed suspiciously as he gazed out into the crashing waves. "Are you birdmen?

Have you wings beneath those robes?"

"No, *sidi*." The Abbot smiled over such naivete. "We came by *dh-dj-*" He struggled for the word in the foreign tongue.

Mathew, forgetting himself, impatiently supplied it. "*Dhows.*"

"Thank you," said the Abbot, glancing at the young wizard gratefully. "*Dhows.* A galleon. It was attacked by an archfi—"

"'Efreet," the Archmagus hastily interposed.

"Er, yes." The Abbot flushed. "What you call an 'efreet. I fear you will not believe us, *sidi*, but I swear by *my* God, Promenthas, that this creature rose up out of the water and—"

"Promenthas?" The leader repeated the name, mouthing it as if it tasted bad. "I do not know this God." Glaring at the Abbot, he frowned. "You come from a land I have never heard of, speaking our language with strange accents, talking of a God that is not ours. What is more, you have, by your own admission, brought down the wrath of an 'efreet upon us, whose anger has wreaked havoc among several small towns along the coast. Their destruction has delayed *my* lord's journey and caused him great inconvenience."

The Abbot blanched, glancing at the Archmagus, who looked grave.

"We—we assure you, *sidi*, that the coming of this horrible creature was not our fault," stammered the Abbot. "It attacked us, too! It sank our ship!"

The *goum* appeared unconvinced, and the Archmagus thought it best to intervene, steering the subject into safer waters. "We are cold and exhausted by our ordeal. We do not want to add to the inconvenience of your master by further delaying his journey. If you could but direct us to the town of Bastine, we have important friends there who can help us. . . ."

This last was an outright lie, but the Archmagus did not like the look of this *goum* and did not want him or his master to think them completely friendless in this alien land.

"Wait here."

Remounting, the *goum* wheeled his horse, dashing up the shoreline at a gallop. Coming to a halt before the palanquin, he leaned down to speak to the person inside.

The priests and wizards remained standing on the shore, casting sidelong glances at the riders, who, for their part, gazed out across the ocean at the slowly sinking sun with magnificent unconcern. After a brief conversation with the unseen person in the palanquin, the leader returned, cantering along the sand.

"My master has decreed that you find food and rest this night."

The Abbot sighed, clasping his hands together. "Promenthas be praised," he murmured. Aloud he said, "Please express our grateful thanks to your master—"

The Archmagus cried out a warning. The priest stopped talking, his tongue cleaving to the roof of his mouth. The leader of the riders had drawn his saber. The sunlight, breaking through the clouds, glinted on the wickedly curved blade. Behind their leader, each *goum* did the same.

"What . . . what is the meaning of this?" the Archmagus' demanded, staring at the swords with narrowed eyes. "You said we were to have food and rest. . ."

"Indeed you will, *kafir*. This night, you will dine in Hell!"

Digging his heels into his horse's flanks, the leader rode straight for the priest and before the astonished man could even cry out, drove his saber through the Abbot's stomach. Jerking the blade free, he watched the priest's body sag to the ground, then swung the bloodstained saber around, cleaving open the head of the Archmagus.

Shouting wildly, the *goums* attacked. The wizards met their deaths without a fight. Bereft of magical wands and scrolls and all else needed to cast their spells, they were helpless. The *goums* cut them down within seconds, stabbing them with their sabers, trampling their bodies beneath the flashing hooves of their steeds. The monks, true to their calling, fell to their knees, crying out to Promenthas. Sharp steel brought their prayers to an agonized end.

Mathew stared numbly at the writhing body of the Abbot, lying on the sand. He watched the *goum* slay the Archmagus, he saw their leader riding his horse directly at him, and suddenly, with no clear idea what he was doing, he caught hold of John's hand and turning, began running down the beach as fast as he could.

Seeing two of his prey escaping, a shout came from the leader. Behind him, Mathew could hear the pounding of hooves, the shrill cries of the *goums* giving chase, the dying screams of his companions.

Hearts nearly bursting from their chests, their lungs burning with fear, the two young men fled in blind panic, running without direction, without hope.

Mathew stumbled in the wet sand and fell. John stopped, reached out his hand to his friend, and pulled him back up. Though each knew that their flight must inevitably end in death, the two ran desperately, driven by the thudding of hoofbeats coming closer and closer, the whistling sound of sabers slashing through the air, the laughter of the *goums*, who were clearly enjoying this wild chase.

Then Mathew experienced the strangest sensation. It seemed a hand touched his forehead, his black hood flew back, his red hair streamed out behind him. He glanced about to see who was near him, fearful it was the *goum*. But the man was still some distance behind him, riding his horse at a canter, obviously playing with his helpless victims.

Blood pounding in his ears, Mathew turned his head and continued running. Even in his terror he moved with the grace inborn in his people, one hand holding on to John, the other clutching his robes so that he could run without tripping. He did not see the swift change of expression on the leader's face, he did not hear the new, shouted command to the rider pursuing him.

Mathew's strength was flagging. He heard cries directly behind him now and knew any moment he would feel burning pain, feel the blades pierce his body. Horses' hooves drummed next to him, he could hear the animal's harsh breathing. John's hand clung to his with a deathlike grip. . . .

A heavy weight struck Mathew from behind, knocking him off his feet and sending him tumbling to the ground. A man was on top of him. Mathew struggled, but the *goum* struck him a blow across the face that stunned him, and the young wizard froze in the sand, sobbing in terror, waiting for death. But the *goum*, seeing his quarry subdued, rose to his feet. Sick and dizzy, Mathew turned his aching head, looking for John. He saw his friend, kneeling in the sand beside him, his head bowed. He was praying.

The leader of the *goums* dismounted and came up behind John. Raising his blade, the goum held it poised above the monk's neck.

Screaming, Mathew hurled himself forward. His guard struck

him again, dashing him to the ground.

The sword fell, the blade flashing red in the light of the dying sun.

John's headless body slumped sideways into the sand. Warm blood, spurting from the neck, splashed on Mathew's outstretched arms. Something landed with a horrible, sickening thump in the sand right beside him.

Mathew saw a gaping mouth, its last prayer on its lips. He stared into wide-open, empty eyes. . .

 # CHAPTER 4

ater splashed in his face. Sputtering, shaking his head, Mathew regained consciousness. At first he could remember nothing. He knew only that there was a hollow, burning emptiness inside him, and he wondered, too, that he was not dead.

Dead. The word brought back the memories, and he moaned. He saw the sword flash red in the sunlight. . . .

"Remarkable hair, unusual color," came a harsh, deep voice quite near him. "Soft white skin. Now you must find out—"

The voice sank too low to hear; another responded. Mathew paid little attention to the words. At the time he wasn't even aware that he understood them. Shock and horror had temporarily driven the skill of speaking and understanding the language from his head. Later he would remember the words he'd heard and realize their portent. Now he only wondered what they were going to do to him.

He was lying on the ground, somewhere near the ocean, he presumed, for he could hear the waves crashing against the shore. There was a feel of grass beneath his cheek instead of sand, however, so he assumed they must have moved him from the beach. He couldn't remember. He couldn't remember anything except John's eyes, staring at him reproachfully.

I am dead. You are not.

Mathew moaned again.

Why has my life been spared? Some foul torture perhaps. His stomach wrenched. He turned his own reproach upon Promenthas. *Why didn't You let me die with John?*

Hands caught hold of Mathew, dragging him to his feet. A sharp command and a slap across the face caused him to open his eyes.

It was twilight. The sun had set, the afterglow lit the sky. He was on the road above the beach, standing in front of the palanquin. The litter's curtains remained drawn. Two of the *goums* had hold of him by the upper arms, but once assuring themselves that he could stand on his own, they shoved Mathew forward. Their leader caught the young wizard as he stumbled and yanked him nearer the palanquin.

The leader grabbed hold of Mathew's chin, forcing his head up. Rough fingers, clamped beneath his jaw, turned the young wizard's head to the left and then the right, as though exhibiting him to the unseen person behind the curtains. At length a voice spoke from inside the palanquin. It was a man's voice—harsh and deep, the voice that had spoken earlier. Mathew caught a glimpse of a bejeweled, slender hand, holding the curtain aside the tiniest crack.

The leader of the *goums* let Mathew go. At the same time he asked him a question—or at least Mathew assumed he was being questioned, for the *goum* looked at him expectantly, obviously awaiting a response. The young wizard shook his head dully, not comprehending, waiting only for them to kill him and end the burning ache within his breast. The *goum* repeated the question, more loudly this time as if he thought Mathew might be deaf.

The voice from within the palanquin spoke sharply, and the leader, turning to face Mathew, made a crude gesture with his hand, a gesture whose sexual connotation transcends all languages, is known the world over. The leader made the gesture, then pointed at Mathew's private parts, then made the gesture again.

The young wizard regarded the man with disgust. He understood, he thought, what the man was trying to say. But what did it have to do with him?

Bleakly, angrily, he shook his head. The *goum*, after studying his face intently, laughed and said something to the man in the palanquin.

The man, with a nod barely discernible from behind the curtains, spoke again. Somewhere in another part of his brain Mathew understood the man's words. He stared at the white curtains in a daze.

"Yes, I agree with you, Kiber. She is a virgin. See to it that she remains one until we reach Kich. Put her in one of the *bassourab*, so that the sun may not blemish such a delicate flower."

The jeweled hand reached out from the curtains, the man

gestured. The litter bearers lifted up their poles and carried the palanquin down the road.

She! Her! Mathew understood that much in the confusion of his mind and suddenly everything became clear.

They had mistaken him for a woman!

Kiber, the leader of the *goums*, took hold of his arm and led him away. Walking almost blindly, Mathew stumbled at the side of his captor, the realization of his plight striking home with the sharp bite of a steel blade.

This was why he had not been slaughtered with the others. In his mind he saw the Abbot, the Archmagus, John—bearded, all of them. All except Mathew, the Wesman, whose race did not grow facial hair.

They have mistaken me for a woman! Now what will they do with me? Not that it matters, he thought numbly. Sooner or later they must discover their mistake. And then it will all be over. Certainly it would be better to undeceive them, to lift his robes, reveal his maleness. Undoubtedly he would die swiftly at the hands of this savage. John had died swiftly . . . very swiftly indeed. . . .

Mathew shuddered, his stomach turning, bile flooding his mouth. He saw his comrades butchered before his eyes, he saw himself dying the same way. The shining blade plunging though flesh and bone, the terrible, bursting pain, the final, dreadful scream torn from his lungs.

Mathew's legs gave way and he fell. Crouched on the road, he retched. I don't want to die! I don't!

Kiber, with a look of irritation, waited until Mathew had emptied his stomach, then hauled him to his feet, hurrying him along.

Shivering allover, Mathew trembled so that he could barely walk. He was growing light-headed and knew he would not be able to go much farther. He was going to faint. . . . Fear hit him like cold water in the face. He dare not lose consciousness; his secret might be discovered.

Fortunately they did not have too far to go. With a grunted command the *goum* jerked Mathew to a halt in front of one of the long-legged, grotesque-looking camels. Resting on its knees on the ground, the beast gazed at Mathew with an incredibly vicious, stupid expression. Taking hold of the young wizard's wrists, Kiber bound them together swiftly and skillfully with a strip of leather.

The *goum* pulled aside the flap of the dome-shaped tent atop the camel saddle and gestured for Mathew to enter.

Mathew stared at the strange-looking saddle and the precarious tent covering it without the vaguest idea what to do. He had never ridden a horse, let alone any creature this big. The camel snaked its head around to look at him, chewing its cud like a cow. Its teeth were enormous. Kiber, anxious to get the caravan on its way, reached out his arms, obviously intending to pick Mathew up bodily.

Fear jolted the young wizard to action. Not wanting the man to touch him, he clumsily scrambled up into the odd-looking saddle. With gestures the *goum* indicated Mathew was to curl one leg around the horn of the saddle, locking it in place by placing the other over it. Then, either to prevent his prisoner from escaping or because he had noted Mathew's deathly pale face and the greenish shadows beneath his eyes, Kiber tied the young wizard to the saddle and to the sides of the camel tent with long lengths of cloth.

Pulling the curtains of the *bassourab* shut, the *goum* shouted, "*Adar-ya-yan!*"

Grumbling, the camel rose to its feet, moving with a rolling motion that brought back memories of the stormtossed ship.

Mathew blessed the tent surrounding him, for it prevented him from seeing how high he was off the ground. Kiber shouted again and the beast started walking. Mathew's queasy stomach lurched with every step. Slumping over the saddle and thankful that no one could see him, the young wizard gave himself up to dark despair.

Everything had happened so swiftly, so suddenly, one moment he was standing on a sun-drenched beach with John. The next moment, John was dead and he was captured. And every moment from now on, Mathew would live with the edge of a knife constantly at his throat. And he knew, sooner or later, the blade would jab home. Sooner or later he must be discovered. He was spinning out the thread of his life for a few minutes, an hour, perhaps a day, two at most. He was alive, but what kind of life was he facing? A life of constant torment, a life without hope, a life of looking forward to death.

Tell them the truth. Do you want to live with this fear, waiting in terror for the moment that will come—yes, it *will* come—

when you are found out? End it quickly! Die now! Die with your brothers. Die bravely...

"I can't!" Mathew's teeth clenched together, cold sweat slid down his body. He saw John's headless trunk slumping to the sand, he felt the warm blood splashing on his hands. "I can't!" *Hiding behind a woman's skirts*—an old and shameful saying in his country. What about hiding *in* a woman's skirts! What greater shame was that? He moaned, rocking back and forth. "I am a coward! A coward!"

Mathew was sick again—the stench of the camel, the jolting motion, his fear, and his memories of the terrible sights he had witnessed all combining to twist his bowels and wrench his stomach. Clinging to the saddle, he shook with pain and terror, providing further proof for himself that he was a craven coward.

He never stopped to consider that he was young, lost, alone in a strange and terrible land, that he had seen those he loved murdered before his eyes, that he had been beaten, was sick and in shock.

No, in Mathew's eyes he was a coward, unworthy of having lived when those so much braver and better than he had given up their lives for their faith.

Their faith. His faith. Mathew tried to whisper a prayer, then stopped. Undoubtedly Promenthas had abandoned him as well. All knew the God took the soul of the martyred to dwell with him in eternal bliss forever. What about the soul of the coward? How would Mathew face Promenthas, John, the Archmagus? Even after death, there would be no comfort for him.

The journey was a nightmare that seemed to last for endless days, although in reality it was only an hour. With the advent of night the caravan came to a halt. In a stupor from his agony of mind and body, Mathew had only the vaguest comprehension of the camel he was riding lurching awkwardly to the ground. He remained where he was, lost in misery, until a hand thrust aside the curtain. Two *goums* untied Mathew, grabbed hold of him, and dragged him from the saddle.

At first he was afraid he could not walk. The moment his feet touched the ground, his knees buckled. Falling, he saw his captors bending down to lift him up and carry him. Terror revived him. Shaking off the hands of the *goums*, Mathew staggered to his feet.

The moon was full and bright. Glancing around, Mathew saw that they had traveled inland and were now far from the sea. He heard the sound of water, but it was a river. The camp was being established on its banks in the middle of a vast expanse of grassy plain. The smell and sound and sight of the river water made him realize how thirsty he was. His throat was parched and hurting from the seawater and his sickness. But he dared not call attention to himself by asking for something to drink.

To distract himself he continued looking around. The palanquin had been carried to the front of a large tent, surrounded by a bevy of slaves. The *goums* were working efficiently to set up tents, groom and water the horses, spread out fodder for the camels. Several women, their heads and bodies swathed in black, silk, were being assisted out of other *bassourabs* and taken to small tents. Most of the women, Mathew saw, had their hands bound like his.

The men with the iron collars slumped to the ground where they stood. Sitting with heads bowed between their legs, their hands dangling in front of them, they took no interest in anything going on around them.

Once again Mathew wondered, 'What are they going to do to me?' His gaze returned to the palanquin in time to see a man dressed in white robes, his head and body covered by the folds of white *burnoose,* leave the litter. A canopy had been erected by the slaves in front of the tent, cushions were carefully arranged on the ground. The man ducked beneath the canopy and settled himself among the cushions. Lounging on one arm, he made several gestures that sent slaves flying to do his bidding. Mathew was watching in weary, numb fascination when Kiber, jabbing him, pointed at a tent.

Nodding, Mathew started to walk toward it, hoping he had the energy to travel the short distance. The tent was a small one. Made of strips of wool sewn together, it was barely large enough for one person. It didn't matter. Ducking inside, Mathew fell thankfully to the firm, solid ground.

He was just realizing that he would have to go in search of water soon or perish when a head thrust itself into the tent. It was Kiber. Hastily Mathew sat up, his hands reaching instinctively to gather his robes close around his body.

The *goum* tossed a waterskin onto the floor of the tent.

Snatching it up, Mathew drank greedily, gulping the water down, never minding that it tasted of camel. Watching him, Kiber gave a grunt of satisfaction, then threw down a bundle at Mathew's feet. Taking a sharp dagger from his belt, the *goum* crouched down in front of Mathew, and the young wizard's raw throat constricted in terror.

Kiber was not going to kill him, however. With a quick slice the *goum* neatly severed Mathew's wrist bonds, then gestured from the bundle to Mathew and back to the bundle again.

Mathew stared at the bundle, puzzled.

Picking it up, Kiber thrust it into his hands. Mathew examined it, and slowly it occurred to his stupefied brain what he was holding.

Clothing. Women's clothing.

He looked up at the *goum*, who gestured again peremptorily, adding something in a sharp tone and pointing with a grimace of disgust to Mathew's own filthy robes.

It was obvious what the man meant. Mathew clutched the bundle tightly. This was the moment. This was the time to make his stand. Firmly, courageously, he would rise to his feet. He would reveal the truth and accept his fate, dying bravely, dying with dignity.

Dying. . . .

Fear clenched his stomach. He tried to stand, but he had no strength in his legs. Tears blurred his vision. Finally, gulping, he bowed his head. Kiber, with another grunt, left the tent.

Spreading out the women's clothes upon the ground, Mathew slowly began to strip off his bloodstained robes.

CHAPTER 5

The women's clothing fit easily over Mathew's slight, slender frame, the sheer bulk and graceful folds of the fabric concealing his flat chest and narrow hips, aiding in his disguise. It was certainly different from the low-cut, full-skirted dresses worn by women in his own land—dresses that revealed a broad expanse of snowy—white bosom, of powdered shoulders, dresses whose silken fabric swept the floor and could be raised to show the turn of an ankle.

Fingers trembling, fearing to hear footsteps outside, he hastily drew on the silken, full-cut cotton trousers. Similar to those the men wore, they fit tightly about his ankles. A gauze smock covered his upper body, its sleeves reaching to the elbow. Over this fit a buttoned waistcoat with long sleeves to the wrist, then, over everything—an ankle-length black caftan, and finally a black veil that covered face and head, soft leather slippers for his feet.

Viewing these clothes in the dim moonlight that filtered through his tent, Mathew saw a mental image of himself, running along the beach, his black robes fluttering about him. The *goums'* mistake was understandable, perhaps inevitable.

He must look, he thought, like a walking black cocoon—a cocoon concealing a worm doomed to die.

What would happen to him now?

Dressed in the women's clothing, Mathew huddled inside his tent, not daring to sleep. The young wizard had lived a cloistered life, having spent his childhood and youth in the closed and secret school of the magi, but Mathew knew enough of the ways of men and women to understand that his greatest danger lay in the hours of darkness. He recalled the touch of the man in the palanquin—the jeweled hand stroking his cheek—and his heart sank.

Bitterly he regretted the loss of his magical devices—amulets and charms that could send a man into sweet slumber, spells that would disorient a man, making him think he was somewhere he wasn't. Mathew could produce them, but that would take time and material: the quill of a raven to write the arcane words, parchment made of sheepskin, blood. . .

Blood. . . He saw John, falling. . .

No! Mathew shut his eyes, driving the gruesome vision from his mind. If he dwelt on that, he would go mad. And it was no use dreaming about magic defenses he didn't have and couldn't acquire. To keep himself occupied and hopefully discover some clue about what they planned to do to him, Mathew began going over the words he'd heard people speaking, trying to remember exactly what had been said, trying to translate the phrases.

At first it seemed impossible; the language that he had studied so painstakingly for so many months had vanished from his head. Stubbornly Mathew forced himself to concentrate. He'd understood a few words, enough to know that they thought he was female. "She." "Her." And another word. "Virgin." Yes, Mathew remembered that word clearly, mainly because Kiber had repeated it often, coupling it with that crude gesture. He knew now what the *goum* had been asking: Have you lain with a man? Mathew couldn't recall what he had responded, but he guessed that the look of disgust upon his face had been sufficient answer.

A light step sounding outside caused the young wizard to catch his breath in fear. But it was a woman. Parting the tent, peering inside, only her eyes visible above her veil, she thrust a bowl of food into Mathew's hands, then withdrew.

The wizard's stomach wrenched at the smell of the stuff—a glob of rice mixed with meat and vegetables. He started to shove the bowl back out, then stopped. This again would call attention to himself. It was impossible to eat. Even if he knew what the meat was, he could never keep it down. Furtively slipping the bowl out of the back of his tent, he dumped the food out into the grass, hoping some animal would come by and eat it before it was discovered in the morning.

This accomplished, he set his mind back to its problem. There had been those words spoken when he was half-conscious. "Red hair." Yes, they had been talking about his hair, which he knew from his studies would be considered an unusual color among the mostly dark-haired, dark-eyed people of this land. There had been something else. Something to do with his skin. . .

Again, footsteps. These were heavy, booted, and definitely coming this direction. Holding his breath, Mathew waited grimly, almost eagerly. He had decided what to do. The man would almost certainly be wearing a dagger—he had noticed that they all did, carrying one or more tucked into their belts. Mathew would grab the dagger and use it. The wizard had never attacked a man before, and he doubted if he would be able to do much damage to his enemy before the man killed him. At least it would lend his death some semblance of dignity.

The steps came nearer and nearer, then stopped right outside the tent. He heard voices. There were two of them! Mathew swallowed the terrible taste in his mouth and tried to force himself to stop trembling. Soon it would be over—the fear, the pain. Then peace, eternal peace with Promenthas.

The two men, talking to each other, laughing, crouched down. Mathew tensed, ready to spring. But neither man entered the tent. Listening, longing to look outside but not daring to stir, Mathew thought he heard them settling themselves on the ground before his tent. His fear easing, he tried to concentrate on what they were discussing, hoping to discover his fate.

They spoke the language much faster than he was able to understand, however, and at first he caught only about one word in five. Listening closely, sorting out the strange accent, he began to comprehend more and more. The men were reliving the exciting event of the day—the slaughter of the *kafir*. Hearing them argue over how many of the unbelievers each had slain, and whose victims had died slowest and screamed loudest, Mathew gritted his teeth, fighting a longing to lash out in a rage and anger that surprised him, treading as it did on the heels of his fear.

"The one man, he squealed like a hog when I stuck him. Did you hear? And the two who ran. A fine chase we had, along the shore. The captain himself beheaded the man—a swift, clean stroke. Robbed us of fun, but *he*—the master—was in a hurry."

Beheaded! They were talking about John! Mathew wanted to stuff something in his ears, shut out the voices and the memories. But he couldn't afford the luxury. Grimly he forced himself to keep listening, hoping to discover his fate.

After the murders of the *kafir* had been discussed, disputed, and enjoyed to the fullest, the *goums'* conversation turned to their journey. They were bound for Kich, Mathew managed to make out, catching the name and recognizing it as being one of the major cities in Sardish Jardan. The caravan had made good time today, despite stopping to sport with the *kafir,* and the *goums* hoped, if the weather held, to be in Kich within a week. Once there, they would sell their wares, collect their wages, and spend some time indulging in the sins to be found in the rich city.

Sell their wares.

Remarkable hair, unusual color. Soft white skin.

Mathew bit his tongue to keep from crying out. What a fool he'd been, not to have thought of this. The women with their hands bound...

A virgin. See to it that she remains one until we reach Kich.

That explained the reason the men were outside. They were guards, responsible for keeping the "wares" undamaged! So that was his fate. He was to be sold as a slave!

Mathew sank back upon the few cushions that had been tossed carelessly into the tent for his use. At least I am in no immediate danger, he thought. If I manage to maintain my disguise, which—considering how segregated the women are being kept from the men—shouldn't be too difficult, I might well live a while longer, until we reach the slave markets.

He felt no relief at this, only empty and disappointed, and he smiled bitterly. Of course he had secretly been hoping it would all end quickly, this night.

Now he looked forward to nothing but torturous days of constant fear; torturous nights spent lying awake, starting at every footstep. And at the end? What then? He would be placed upon the slave block and sold as a woman, then meet his death—probably a horrible one—at the hands of some defrauded buyer.

Terror, shame, and guilt burst from Mathew's throat in an anguished cry. Hastily he tried to choke back his tears, wondering if the guards had heard him, afraid that they might come in to find out what was wrong. But he could not help himself, grief and fear overwhelmed him. Stuffing the veil in his mouth to muffle his despairing sobs, the young man rolled over on his stomach, buried his face in the cushions, and wept.

Night, black and empty, came upon the plains: The guards outside Mathew's tent dozed fitfully. They had heard his choked cries but only glanced at each other with sly grins, each urging the other to creep into the tent and "comfort" the captive. Neither moved to do so, however. Kiber was a good captain, discipline was maintained. The last man who had gained a little private pleasure from the slaves had been dealt with swiftly and severely. One stroke of his captain's sword and the wretched *goum* was now a eunuch in the *seraglios* of Kich.

As for the faint sobs coming from the tent, more than one captive was likely wailing over her fate that night. It was none of their concern. So the guards slept, not overly worried that anyone might slip past them.

Someone did slip by them, however. It was not anyone either *goum* could have stopped had they been awake. It was not one either could have seen, asleep or awake. The angel, her white, feathery wingtips brushing the ground, stole into the tent with less sound than the soft breeze whispering across the sand. Bending over the weeping Mathew, the angel touched him gently upon the cheek, brushing away his tears even as her own fell fast.

At her soft touch, the young man's wrenching sobs ceased. He drifted into a deep, dreamless sleep. The angel gazed at him with deep pity and compassion. Slipping back out of the tent, she glanced furtively around her, then swiftly and silently spread her wings and soared into the heavens.

CHAPTER 6

Promenthas paced solemnly the long length of the red-carpeted aisle that ran straight and narrow between the hard, wooden pews in his cathedral. The God's face was grave, he stroked his white beard thoughtfully, his white brows bristling. An angel waited at the far end of the aisle, her silver hair shining in the soft light of hundreds of flickering votive candles. A sound behind her caused her to glance around. Seeing who it was that entered the great wooden doors, the angel slipped silently away to wait within the dark shadows of the nave.

"Promenthas, I understand that you wished to speak to me."

"I do and over a matter of extreme gravity." Promenthas's gentle voice shook with grief and anger. "How dare you murder my priests?"

Dressed in a fantastically embroidered silk caftan with long, flowing sleeves, Quar looked particularly exotic and outlandish in the austere setting of Promenthas's cathedral. But Quar did not see himself in the gray marble edifice. He was strolling about the grounds of his palace. To him it was Promenthas who was out of place, the God's plain, gray robes appearing poor and shabby amid the sumptuous setting of orange trees, fountains, and peacocks.

Coolly regarding his angry fellow, Quar raised his eyebrows. "If we are accusing one another of misdeeds, how dare you send your missionaries to subvert the faith of *my* people?"

"I cannot be accountable for the zeal of my followers!"

Quar bowed. "My answer as well."

"There was no need to slaughter them! You could have attempted to gain them for yourself." Promenthas's face flushed in anger.

"According to the new belief spreading among my followers,

a *kafir*—an unbeliever—leads a misguided life that is doomed to end only in sorrow and tragedy. By cutting short such a wretched existence, my followers consider that they are doing the *kafir* a favor."

Promenthas stared in astonishment. "Never before have any of us propounded a doctrine such as this! It is murder in the name of religion!"

His hand absently stroking the neck of a fawn that he kept as a pet in his garden, Quar appeared to muse upon the matter. "Perhaps you are right," he admitted after several moments of profound thought. "I had not looked at the incident in that light." He shrugged delicately. "To be truthful, I had not really given the encounter much thought. These are mortals we are discussing. What can one expect of them except to behave foolishly and irrationally? But now that you have brought this to my attention, I will discuss the matter with my Imam and attempt to discover who is teaching such a potentially dangerous doctrine."

Promenthas appeared somewhat mollified. "Yes, you had better look into it. And put an end to it."

"Rest assured, I will do what I can."

Promenthas did not much like this answer, nor did he like Quar's easy dismissal of the shocking murders. But Promenthas was not entirely satisfied in his own conscience that his people had been completely in the right, so he let the matter drop.

Changing the topic of conversation to less volatile subjects, he escorted Quar to the massive carved wooden doors of the cathedral. In Quar's view the two walked together to the wrought-iron gates of the palace garden. Bowing to each other coolly, the Gods parted.

But left alone, Promenthas returned his thoughts to the murdered priests and magi. His head bent, his hands clasped behind his back, the God was walking down the aisle when—to his astonishment—he glanced up to see someone standing before the altar.

"Akhran," said Promenthas, not overly pleased. The followers of the Wandering God had been known to commit their share of murder, although—he had to admit—not in the name of religion. More often it was in the name of theft, blood feud, war. "What business brings you here?"

The Wandering God, dressed in flowing black robes worn

over a white tunic and trousers, his head and face swathed in black cloth, looked as if he were standing in the midst of a raging sandstorm instead of the quiet of the cathedral. Two piercing black eyes beneath straight-edged brows stared intently into Promenthas's mild eyes-eyes that were now shadowed with worry.

"I warned you," came the deep voice, muffled behind the *haik*. "You would not listen to me."

Promenthas frowned. "I don't know what you mean."

"Yes, you do. *Jihad*."

"I'm sorry, I do not understand—"

"*Jihad*. The word of my people for 'holy war.' It has already begun. Evren and Zhakrin are dead, their immortals vanished. Now your followers, butchered in the lands of Quar."

Promenthas regarded the other God in silence. Akhran—as always—seemed too big, too wild, too savage, to be contained within the stone walls of the cathedral. The Wandering God himself was obviously ill at ease. Removing the face cloth from his mouth, sucking in a deep breath of air, he looked longingly to the wide wooden doors that led outside. But Akhran remained where he was—standing tall, straight—keeping himself under rigid constraint.

By Sul, Promenthas realized in astonishment. Akhran really *is* in the cathedral! The Wandering God has left his beloved desert, has deliberately entered my dwelling place! Such a thing had not happened since the beginning of time.

Promenthas knew he should be pleased, flattered. He felt neither, only chilled. Quickening his steps, he approached the altar.

"If what you told us that terrible day is true," he said slowly, coming to stand before Akhran, "why then are Quar's own immortals disappearing?"

"I have an idea, but I have no proof. If what I fear is correct, then our danger is very great."

"And what do you fear?"

Akhran shook his head, the black brows beneath the twisted black folds of the headcloth drawing together like the wings of a falcon above the smoldering eyes.

Promenthas moved to smooth his beard as was his habit when disturbed and noticed that his hand trembled visibly. He clasped his fingers together in an unconscious, prayerful attitude. "Perhaps you are right, Akhran. Perhaps we have let Quar make fools of us all. But what does he want?"

"Surely that is obvious. To become the Supreme God, the Only God. Little by little, his Emperor is extending his rule, his Imams are gaining strength. Those people they conquer are either killed instantly, as were your followers, or given the choice of *jihad*—convert or die. Little by little we will lose our worshipers. We will dwindle and . . . eventually . . . vanish."

"That is impossible!"

"Is it? You saw it happen before your own eyes. Where now are Evren and Zhakrin?"

Promenthas was silent long moments, mulling over in his own mind the account the angel had given him of the slaughter of his followers. *Jihad*. Holy war. Convert or die. Frowning, he glanced back at the Wandering God.

"This affects you most closely, Akhran. The lands of your people border on those of Quar's faithful. What are you doing?"

The Wandering God cast Promenthas a scornful look and lofted his head proudly. "My people are not like yours. They did not go meekly to their deaths with prayers upon their lips. They fight."

Promenthas smiled "Quar or each other?"

Akhran's eyes blazed fiercely, than his shoulders sagged, his mouth twisted. "One should never be angry to hear the truth. That, in fact, is one reason I have come. I seek your help. Your people are much different than mine, they are noted for their wisdom, their compassion, their patience . . . ."

Promenthas regarded the Wandering God in astonishment.

"That may be true, but how can my people help you, Akhran? They are an ocean away—"

"Not all of them."

Promenthas, taken aback, appeared startled. "No," he murmured, glancing at the angel who was waiting patiently in the nave and who appeared extremely alarmed by the turn of the conversation. "No," the God repeated. Troubled, Promenthas rested his hand upon the altar rail, absently caressing the oiled wood with his gnarled, wrinkled fingers. "That is true."

Akhran laid his suntanned, weather-hardened hand upon Promenthas's. "Do not deceive yourself, my friend. An ocean will not stop Quar."

Promenthas's gaze went to the angel. "The poor lad to whom

you refer has undergone a frightful experience. His suffering has been immense. I had thought to give him a swift and easy death."

"And will you do the same for the tens of thousands who will not be so fortunate?" Akhran asked sternly.

Promenthas stared thoughtfully at the angel. The silverhaired woman regarded her God with beseeching blue eyes, mutely pleading with him not to change his mind.

At length Promenthas, turning abruptly, looked back at Akhran. "So be it," he said gruffly. "I will do what I can. I promise nothing, however. After all, one can only accomplish so much with mortals."

Akhran smiled, a brief smile that vanished in an instant, his face returning to its accustomed gravity and severity. Wrapping the black cloth over his mouth and nose, he nodded to Promenthas—the closest the Wandering God ever came to a bow—and took his leave, walking hastily back down the red-carpeted aisle, his strides growing increasingly longer as he neared the bright sunlight he could see shining outside the massive wooden door.

"Come, One Who is Swifter Than the Starlight!" he called out commandingly.

In answer, Promenthas heard the sound of hooves clattering up the marble stairs of his cathedral, followed by the shocked voices of his angels raised in protest. The white head of a stallion appeared in the doorway, shaking its mane in impatience, its shrill whinny splitting the sanctuary's holy silence. With a parting wave of his hand Akhran vaulted easily into the saddle. The horse reared, hooves flashing in the light, then it leaped into the air. Indignant seraphim and cherubim gazed after it in dismay, loudly exclaiming over horse manure on the marble steps.

Shaking his head, sighing, Promenthas turned and beckoned to the droop-winged, disconsolate guardian angel.

The Book
of the
Immortals

CHAPTER 1

The scent of roses hung heavy in the air. A nightingale trilled unseen in the fragrant shadows. Cool water fell from the marble hands of a delicate maiden, spilling into a large conch shell at her feet. The multicolored tiles, laid out in fantastic mosaics, sparkled like jewels in the twilight. But Quar took pleasure in none of this beauty. The God sat upon the tiled rim of a fountain's basin, absently tearing apart a gardenia, moodily tossing the waxy, white petals into the rippling water.

The luck of Sul, that's what it was. The luck of Sul, which was no luck at all. The luck of Sul had taken those damned and blasted priests of Promenthas's into the way of a few dozen of Quar's faithful. At least he assumed they had been his faithful. The God had not realized his followers had grown quite that fanatical. Now Promenthas was angry and not only angry, suspicious as well. Quar was not prepared for this. He had intended to deal with Promenthas, of course, but further—much further—down the long and twisting road of his scheming.

And there was Akhran to consider. He would act swiftly to take advantage of the incident. The Wandering God was undoubtedly persuading Promenthas to some sort of action. Not that Promenthas could do much. His followers had all died on the swords of the righteous. Hadn't they? Quar made a mental note to check. But now that Promenthas was alerted, He would be watchful, wary. Quar would have to move faster than he'd anticipated.

Akhran the Meddler. He was the scorpion in Quar's bed sheets, the *qarakurt* in Quar's boot. Just days ago Quar had received a report that two tribes of Akhran's followers had banded together in the Pagrah Desert. Relatively few in number compared to Quar's mighty armies, these nomads were more of a nuisance than a direct threat. But Quar had no time for nuisances right now.

The one factor on which Quar had counted in his design to overthrow Akhran was the constant feuding and strife among the Wandering God's followers. The old axiom: divide and conquer. Who would have imagined that this Wandering God, who seemingly cared for nothing except his horse, would have been observant enough to detect Quar's plotting and move swiftly to forestall it?

"It was my fault. I concentrated on the other Gods of Sardish Jardan. I saw them as the threat. Now Mimrim of the Ravenchai, feeling herself weakening, hides on her cloud-covered mountain. Uevin of the Bas takes refuge behind his politics and siege machines, never realizing that his foundation is being undermined and soon he will fall through the cracks. But you, Horse God. I underestimated you. In looking west and south, I turned my back upon the east. It will not happen again. ..

The vase, once broken, cannot be mended with tears, Quar reminded himself severely. You have realized your mistake, now you must act to remedy it. There is only one way Akhran could have united his feuding tribes—through the intervention of his immortals. There were reports of Akhran's 'efreets whipping up fearsome desert storms. Apparently the unleashing of the mighty power of the djinn was enough to frighten those thick-headed nomads

Quar paused, absently crushing the last blossoms of the ravaged gardenia in his hand.

The djinn. Why, that was his answer.

Tossing the dead flower into the pool, Quar rubbed his hands together, sniffing the essence of the perfume that clung to the shell of human flesh with which the God frequently chose to surround his ethereal being. Rising to his feet, he left the pleasure garden and entered his palace, proceeding to his own private salon. The room was sumptuously furnished, the walls hung with bright-colored silks, the floors carpeted with thick tapestries made of the finest wool. In the center of the room stood a black lacquer table on which rested a small copper-and-tin gong.

Lifting the mallet, Quar struck the gong three times, waited for the count of seven, then struck the gong three times again. The resultant quavering tone was vaguely disturbing. Setting the teeth on edge, it caused the very air to shiver. As the last note died in the still, perfumed air, a cloud of smoke began to take human shape and form around the gong, coalescing into a ten-foot-tall 'efreet.

"*Salaam aleikum, Effendi,*" said the 'efreet, folding its hands together before its turbaned forehead. Clad in red silken pantalons girded with a red sash around its massive stomach, the 'efreet bowed with a grace remarkable in such a hulking body. "What is your wish, my Master?"

"I grow weary of Akhran's meddling, Kaug," said Quar languidly, seating himself upon a silken couch. "I have received reports that two of his tribes have united. How is this possible?"

"They have united through the efforts of two of Akhran's djinn—one Fedj and one Sond, O Most Holy Being," replied Kaug.

"I thought as much. I find it most annoying."

"I can see the solution in your mind, my Master. Your plan is an excellent one. Be at peace, *Effendi.* The matter is easily handled. And now, allow me to bring you some refreshment to ease the worries this has brought upon you."

Kaug clapped his hands, the thunderous sound calling into being a pot of thick, sweet coffee and a plate of candied rose petals, sweet figs, and pomegranates. Nibbling a rose petal, Quar watched appreciatively as Kaug poured the sweet, syrupy coffee into a fragile porcelain cup.

"It is a trifling thing, an irritation," said Quar. "But such is the delicacy of my nature that these small upsets disturb me unduly. I can rest assured, then, that this matter is in your capable hands, my loyal servant?"

"Consider the scorpion relieved of his sting, the spider crushed, Magnificence," replied the 'efreet, falling to his knees and bowing so low that the front of his turban brushed the carpet.

"Mmmm." Quar picked at the pomegranate with a golden knife, poking out the ruby seeds and crunching them, one by one, between his teeth. Scorpions and spiders. Exactly what he'd been thinking. He did not like Kaug's penetrating his mind, and the God wondered, not for the first time, how much of his inner thoughts the 'efreet was coming to know as Kaug grew in strength and power.

"Is there anything else my Master desires?"

"Information. The murder of these wretched priests of Promenthas—"

"Ah!" Kaug frowned.

"What is it?"

"I knew such violent a deed would upset you, Master, and so I have endeavored to discover what I could. Unfortunately a dark cloud hangs over those who committed the act, obscuring my sight."

Quar's eyes narrowed. "A dark cloud. What does that mean?"

"I do not know, *Effendi*."

"Perhaps it is some trick of Promenthas's. All the followers are dead, are they not?"

"As far as I can tell—"

"Promenthas's followers are dead. Yes or no, Kaug?" Quar repeated softly.

The chastised 'efreet, unable to reply, crouched on the floor before his Master, shoulders hunched, his huge body quivering.

Sincere abjection? Or a very fine act.

"Very well, if you do not know, you do not know. You are dismissed," Quar said, making a negligent gesture with a jeweled hand.

"My Master is not angry?"

"No, no," Quar said, barely concealing a yawn behind sugar-covered fingers. "My time is too valuable to waste on such trivial circumstances. I assume that, in your hands, all will be acted upon and settled satisfactorily."

"I am honored by your confidence, my Master, and blessed by your patience with my shortcomings." The 'efreet bowed again, humbly, thankfully.

Quar did not reply. Reclining upon the couch, he closed his eyes as though asleep. In reality he had stepped out of the human body and was watching Kaug with invisible eyes, scrutinizing the 'efreet carefully, searching for traces of smugness, self-satisfaction, or an inner conviction that this matter with Akhran and the priests was a greater threat than his Master was letting on. Quar saw only serious, conscientious devotion on Kaug's massive face.

Returning to his body, Quar blinked, yawned, and rubbed his eyes sleepily.

"Is there anything else I can do for you, Exalted One?"

"No. Proceed with your tasks."

Bowing again, the 'efreet's hulking form dissolved to a cloud of billowing smoke that spiraled around the gong, then vanished suddenly, sucked up by the copper metal.

Left alone, Quar rose from the couch. Perfume filled the air around him, his heavy brocade robes brushed against the thick carpet. Hands behind his back, his head bowed, he began to pace in the small amount of space in the room that was cluttered with carved wooden chairs, tables, couches, huge standing vases of porcelain, flambeaux with thick beeswax candles, golden pipes and pots, and flowering trees.

Back and forth he walked; not the restless, nervous pacing of one who is indecisive or uneasy in his mind. This was the pacing of one who walks the miles his thoughts travel, the footsteps of one mentally traversing desert and city, making new plans, refining old ones.

At the end of an hour's pacing, Quar—lingering near the black lacquer table in the center of the room—reached out to gently stroke the gong with his fingers, a slight smile upon his lips. His plans were coalescing in his mind, much as the 'efreet coalesced around the gong.

Quar's faithful follower, the Emperor, would be instructed to act at once to secure the God's position in southern Sardish Jardan. Once conquered, the southern lands of Bas would provide wealth and slave labor to complete the building of the Emperor's grand fleet. In the name of Quar, the Emperor would sail west, across the ocean, aiming to strike at the gold-laden, heavily populated continent of Tirish Aranth—the stronghold of Promenthas.

The war in heaven would move to the world.

Jihad.

CHAPTER 2

When the Gods decided that the immortals were to be freed from their boring task of guarding the Realms of the Dead and assigned to the more interesting—if occasionally more stressful—task of interacting with mortals, each God was initially granted an equal number of immortal beings to serve him. This number either grew or diminished as the God's power in the world increased or waned. Ranking among the immortals was, therefore, usually based on age. The older, wiser immortals took over the leadership roles. Young immortals were assigned the low-ranking, menial tasks—generally that of working directly with the humans.

Unfortunately the young immortals, because they lived half on the mortal plane and were deeply involved with mortals, tended over the centuries to take on mortal characteristics—particularly mortal weaknesses.

Promenthas's angels were arranged in a strict hierarchy, as has been discussed; guardian angels being the youngest and lowest in rank, up through archangels, seraphim, and cherubim. Each angel had his or her assigned task, his or her appointed superior. Only in times of dire emergency or disaster—such as the murder of his followers—would Promenthas invite a guardian angel to report to him directly. Others of the Gods were more relaxed in their dealings with immortals, structuring them loosely as suited their needs. Then, of course, there were those such as Akhran, the Wandering God, who had no discipline or structure at all.

This lack of organization at first led to much confusion among Akhran's immortals. Each was constantly getting in the other's way. Some tribes had a surfeit of djinn, while others had none at all. The 'efreets fought among themselves, unleashing violent storms that occasionally came near to wiping Akhran's followers from the face of the planet.

All this was brought to Akhran's attention—when he could be found. Beyond scowling in irritation at being bothered and lopping off a few heads to serve as a warning, the Wandering God did little that was useful. Seeing that their God took no interest in them, and becoming more than a little fearful for their heads, Akhran's immortals attempted to form some sort of organization.

This worked out as well as might have been expected. The powerful 'efreets demanded control of the wild and reckless forces of storm, volcano, and shaking ground. They were granted these without question. The elder djinn refused to have anything to do with humans since that onerous duty required one to live upon the mortal plane, subject always to the whims of humans and bound to a material object. This—to the elder djinn—was a humiliating way in which to live out eternity. They chose, therefore, to remain on the immortal plane and send the young djinn down to do the dirty work.

The young djinn did not mind this so much, most enjoyed the exciting, ever-chaotic world of humans. But the elder djinn did something else that drove the younger to distraction. In order to liven up eternity's nights, the elder djinn chose to keep the djinniyeh—the female djinn—on the immortal plane with them. As might be imagined, this angered the younger djinn and nearly precipitated outright war. The rebellion came to nothing, however. Each rebel djinn felt the blade of Akhran's sharp sword at his throat and meekly, if reluctantly, backed down.

Attended by the beautiful djinniyeh, the elder djinn lived in heavenly splendor, performing such tasks as distributing their less worthy brethren among the mortals, hearing disputes between djinn, and judging complaints from mortals about their djinn. The young djinn (or an older djinn who'd had the misfortune to cross a powerful peer) were sent to the world below, each immortal's essence entrapped inside a material object made by mortal hands—such as a lamp, a ring, or a bottle. This bound the djinn to the mortal plane and made it impossible for him to survive long outside of it.

Of course there was always the possibility for advancement from the mortal realm to the immortal, and the younger djinn were ever on the watch for the opportunity to perform some miracle that would attract Akhran's attention. As a reward the God would elevate the djinn from his humble lamp in a sheepherder's yurt to a dwelling among the clouds, with the djinniyeh to supply one's every need, wish, and desire.

To live in luxury, entwined in the arms of the djinniyeh, was every djinn's dream, for if there was one human frailty above all others to which the djinn were subject, it was love. Intrigues and assignations between the djinn below and the djinniyeh above were common; particularly among the young and lovely djinni-yeh of an elderly djinn, whose afterdinner delights consisted of a pat on a well-rounded bottom and falling asleep with his head on a perfumed bosom.

One djinn, in particular, was notorious for his affairs of the heart. Strong and handsome, as brave and daring as his sheykh, Sond could often be found scaling the walls of the cloud palaces, slipping among night's shadows into perfume-scented gardens, whispering words of love to some beautiful djinniyeh who trembled in his strong arms and begged him not to wake the Master.

Sond had long avoided falling victim to love, however. He had a roving eye and varied tastes. His conquests among the djinniyeh were many and he always escaped unscathed. But like every gallant warrior, he was finally vanquished on the field. The weapon that brought him down was neither sword nor arrow, but something infinitely more painful and piercing—a pair of violet eyes. Red, pouting lips inflicted wounds in Sond too deep to ever heal. Soft, white breasts, pressed against his flesh, forced him to plead for terms of unconditional surrender.

Now the eucalyptus trees of other cloud gardens saw Sond no more. Other djinniyeh waited and sighed for their lover in vain.

Her name was Nedjma, which means "the star," and she was the light of his heart, his soul, his life.

On this particular night Nedjma's master—an elderly djinn who remembered (or insisted that he did) the creation of the world—had been in his silk-cushioned bed well over an hour. His current favorite was with him, destined for a boring evening of listening to the old djinn's snores. The rest of the djinniyeh remained in the *seraglio,* chattering and gossiping, playing at games of chance, or—if they were fortunate—slipping away for more thrilling games of love.

126

Nedjma went out for a breath of fresh air, or at least that is what she told the guards. Some might have thought it strange that no fresh air could be found near the palace but was only obtainable in the darkest part of the garden that stood farthest from her master's dwelling. Here, in this secluded place, a pool as deep and dark as Nedjma's eyes reflected the light of stars and a full moon. The eucalyptus scented the soft night wind, its fragrance mingling with the smells of roses and orange blossoms.

Nedjma looked carefully around, not really expecting to see anyone, of course, since no one ever came here. Feeling certain (and perhaps a little disappointed) that she was alone, she posed herself gracefully upon the marble lip of the pool. Leaning over, she idly trailed her hand in the water, sending the goldfish darting about in a frenzy.

She was a sight as beautiful as the night itself. Pantalons made of silken gauze spun as fine as cobweb softly draped the curves of her shapely legs. The diaphanous fabric was clasped about her waist with a jeweled girdle, leaving bare her shell-white midriff. Her small feet were adorned with jewels and rouged with *henna*. Her thick honey-colored hair was worn in a long coil, and her enchanting face could be seen through the soft folds of a gold-embroidered veil.

Entirely absorbed in contemplating the water, the fish, or perhaps her own bejeweled hand, Nedjma was perfectly unconscious of the fact that, when she bent over the pool, her breasts in their tight-fitting bodice were an enticement, her soft lips a temptation, her voice, as she sang sweetly to herself (or perhaps to the fish), an invitation.

Believing herself to be alone, Nedjma was considerably startled to hear a rustling in the gardenia near the wall surrounding the garden. Lifting her head, she glanced about in pretty confusion, a blush on her cheeks, her body trembling.

"Who is there?" Nedjma called.

"The one for whom you've been waiting," answered a deep voice from the wall.

"Sond!" Nedjma exclaimed indignantly, drawing her veil close about her face and glancing in the direction of the voice with eyes that sparkled like the star for which she was named. "How dare you be so bold? As if I would wait for you or any man," she continued loftily, rising to her feet with the grace of the willow swaying in the wind. "I came out here to taste the beauties of the night. . . ."

"Ah, that is my desire as well," Sond replied, slipping through the shadows of the foliage.

Her eyes cast down in charming embarrassment, Nedjma turned—not very quickly—as if to leave, accidentally allowing one small hand to flutter behind her. Sond caught hold of that hand and pulled her easily into his strong arms. Clasped close against the djinn's muscular chest, Nedjma could have struggled and screamed for help—she had done that before, just to keep her admirers eager and alert. But there was something different about Sond tonight—a fierce passion gleamed in his eyes; a passion that would not be denied.

A weakness swept over Nedjma. She had long considered surrendering herself to the handsome djinn. Besides, struggling took so much energy, screaming gave her a sore throat. Melting in the djinn's warm embrace, Nedjma closed her eyes, tilted back her head, and parted her glistening red lips.

Sond tasted the beauties of the night; not once, but several times. When it seemed he was nearly intoxicated from the wine of love, he reluctantly loosened his grasp on the beautiful djinniyeh.

"What is it, my own? What is wrong?" Nedjma asked, snuggling near him once again, her breath coming in quick pants. "My master sleeps soundly this night!"

"My bird, my blossom," Sond whispered, running his hand through the honey-colored hair, "I would give my life to be with you this night, but it may not be. My own master requires me soon."

"You came only to toy with me." Nedjma let her pretty head droop, her lips forming a charming pout.

"Cruel one! You have toyed with me for months! But no. I came to bring you a gift."

"A gift? For me?" Nedjma looked up, her eyes pools of moonlight so lovely that Sond was forced to kiss her again.

One arm around her, holding her close, he drew forth from a pouch he wore on his sash an object and placed it Nedjma's delicate hands.

The djinniyeh squealed softly in delight. It was an egg, made of pure gold, decorated with jewels. No djinn or djinniyeh can resist material objects from the mortal world; particularly those made of costly metals and jewels. It is one of their failings, and thus the elder djinn and occasionally some powerful mortal are able to entrap the souls of the unwary in such devices.

"Oh, Sond! It is beautiful!" Nedjma sighed. "But I cannot accept it." Holding the precious egg in her hand, she did not return it but gazed at it with longing.

"Certainly you can, my dove," Sond said, brushing his lips against the hair that had escaped from the veil. He closed his fingers over the hand holding the jeweled egg. "Do you fear me? Your Sond?"

Nedjma peeped up at him from beneath long, thick eyelashes. "Well," she murmured, lowering her head to hide her blushes, "perhaps just a little. You are so strong. . . ."

"Not as strong as your master," Sond answered with some bitterness, releasing her hand. "You belong to him. No poor device of mine could ever contain you."

"I don't know," Nedjma faltered, uncurling her fingers to look at the fabulous egg once more. Its gold gleamed in the moonlight, its jewels winked and sparkled like the eyes of a teasing maiden. "It is so very lovely!"

"And look," Sond said, exhibiting it with the proud eagerness of a small boy. "Look what it does."

Flicking a hidden catch, the djinn caused the egg to split open. A tiny bird in a gilt cage rose up from the bottom half of the eggshell. The bird's tiny beak parted, the cage began to whirl around and around, and sweet, tinkling music trilled in the air.

"*Ohhhh!*" Nedjma breathed. Her gentle hands, cupped around the egg and the singing bird within, trembled with delight. "I've never seen or dreamed of anything so exquisite!" She clasped the egg to her bosom. "I accept it, Sond!" Looking into the djinn's eyes, Nedjma moistened her red lips with the tip of her tongue. "And now," she whispered, closing her eyes and pressing near him, "take your reward. . . ."

"I will," came a cruel voice.

Nedjma's eyes opened wide, the breath caught in her throat.

Her scream was cut off by a rough hand that closed over her mouth and nose. Now the djinniyeh struggled, but it was useless. The 'efreet's huge arms held her easily; his hand smothered her cries.

129

"I will satisfy your desires," Kaug laughed harshly, "with my own body, not that of your puny lover." Ripping open the silken bodice, the 'efreet ran his coarse hands over the djinniyeh's soft breasts. Choking in disgust and terror, Nedjma writhed in his grasp. "Come now, quit fighting. Is this the thanks I get in return for my little present?"

His arms loosened their grip somewhat as he bent his head to kiss her. With a twist of her lithe frame Nedjma managed to free herself. In her struggles she had dropped the golden egg. It lay on the tiles of the garden between them, gleaming in the moonlight, apparently forgotten. Clutching her torn clothing about her as best she could, Nedjma's form began to shimmer, changing to a column of gracefully twining smoke. Her eyes flashed scorn and hatred.

"You have violated the sanctity of the *seraglio* and laid violent hands upon my person!" she cried, her voice quavering with fear and anger. "I go to wake the guards of my Master! For having dared touch that which is not yours, your hands will be stricken from your wrists—"

"No, my lady," said Kaug. Reaching down, he picked up the golden egg and held it up before her. "You accepted my gift."

Nedjma's eyes, the only part of her body visible through the billowing smoke, stared with horror at the golden, jeweled object—an object made in the mortal world by mortal hands. Moaning, she attempted to flee. The smoke that was her body wafted through the garden's perfumed air. The 'efreet watched, unconcerned. Flicking the catch, Kaug caused the egg to open, the singing bird in the cage to rise up out of the bottom.

The 'efreet spoke a word of command. The smoke wavered in the air, fighting the invisible force that was pulling her inexorably toward the egg. Nedjma's struggles were feeble. Kaug was too powerful, the djinniyeh's magic could not hope to prevail against that of an 'efreet.

Slowly Nedjma's being was sucked into the egg. Her ragged wail of despair, drifting unheard through the garden, was blown away by the night wind.

CHAPTER 3

Sond climbed over the garden wall, his heart beating to the rhythm of the words of the message he had received. "Come to me, come to me. . ."

Nedjma had never sent for him before, preferring to tease and torment him until finally allowing him a single kiss, won after considerable playful struggle. But last time there had been a look in her eyes following that kiss—a look the experienced Sond knew. She wanted more. Her sending for him could mean only one thing: he had conquered.

Tonight Nedjma would be his.

Hiding in the gardenias near the pool—their meeting place—Sond looked about for his beloved. She was not there. He sighed, smiling. The cunning *houri*—*she* would tease him to the very last, it seemed. Stepping softly onto the multicolored tiles around the still pool of water, he called her name.

"Nedjma!"

"Come here, beloved. Keep hidden, out of the moonlight," came a sweet voice in return.

Sond's heart pounded, the blood beat in his head. He pictured her awaiting him in some dark, fragrant bower, her white body, modestly cloaked in the shadows of the night, trembling, eager to yield to him. Hastening toward the sound of the voice, Sond crashed through shrubs and bushes, heedless of the noise he was making, thinking only to end the ache of his desires in sweet bliss.

In a sheltered comer of the garden, far from the main dwelling and ringed round by pine trees, Sond caught a glimpse of bare skin gleaming white in the moonlight. Leaping through a tangled thicket of roses, he reached out, caught the figure to him—

—and found his face pressed against a hairy chest.

Deep laughter boomed above him. Angry and humiliated, Sond stumbled backward. Looking up, he saw the cruel, heavy features of an 'efreet.

"Kaug!" Sond glared at the 'efreet in a fury that he was forced to conceal, knowing as he did that the powerful Kaug could roll him into a ball and toss him from the heavens if he chose. "Do you know where you are, my friend?" Sond tried to look as if he cared. "You have mistakenly wandered into the realm of *Hazrat* Akhran! I advise you to leave before the guards of the mighty djinn who dwells here discover you. Quick, hurry!" He gestured toward the wall. "I will cover your retreat, my friend!"

"Friend!" Kaug said effusively, placing his huge hand upon Sond's shoulder and squeezing it painfully. "My good friend, Sond. Almost more than friends for a moment there, weren't we, though? Ha! Ha!"

"Ha, ha." Sond laughed feebly, gritting his teeth.

The 'efreet's grip on him tightened. Cartilage twisted, bone cracked. The body had existed in the mind of the djinn so long that the pain was very real. Though he gasped with the agony, Sond grimly stood his ground. Kaug might twist his shoulder off. He refused to let the 'efreet see him suffer.

A knife's blade of fear had pierced Sond, more painful than the 'efreet's torture. Kaug had obviously not come here by accident. What then was the reason for his appearance in this garden at night? What did it have to do with Sond? More frightening, what did it have to do with Nedjma!

Laughing again, Kaug released his hold. "You are brave! I like that, my friend. I like that so much, my friend, that I am going to give you a gift!"

Clapping his hand on Sond's back, Kaug knocked the breath from the djinn's body and sent him staggering headlong into an ornamental pool.

Sond teetered precariously on the edge of the water. Recovering his balance, he paused before turning around, attempting to catch his breath and master his overpowering rage. It was not easy. His hand, of its own volition, crept to the hilt of his saber. It took a strong, physical effort to wrench it back. He had to find out what Kaug was doing here. What did he mean by a gift? And where was Nedjma? By Sul, if he had harmed her. . . !

Sond's fist clenched. Slowly, forcing himself to relax, he drew several deep breaths and turned back to face the 'efreet.

"Really, a gift is not necessary, my friend!" Sond made a deprecating gesture with his swordhand, a gesture that kept it hovering near the scimitar's hilt. "To have earned the praise of one as powerful as yourself is a treasure priceless beyond all measure—"

"Ah!" Kaug shook his head. "Do not make such rash statements, my friend. For I have here in my palm a treasure that is *truly* priceless beyond measure."

Unrolling the fingers of his huge hand, the 'efreet exhibited an object that glittered in the moonlight. Growing more and more perplexed, Sond stared at it closely, suspiciously. It was an egg, made of gold, encrusted with costly jewels.

"Truly, that is a rare thing," he said cautiously, "and therefore a gift far beyond my humble aspirations, my friend. I am not worthy of such a precious object."

"Ah, my friend!" Kaug sighed gustily, the 'efreet's breath fluttering the leaves of the trees and causing ripples to mar the smooth surface of the pool. "You have not yet seen what a wondrous device this is. Watch carefully." Flicking a latch, Kaug opened the egg. A gilt cage rose up from the bottom. "Sing, my pretty bird!" Kaug said, tapping at the cage with a large fingernail. "Sing!"

"Sond! Help me! Sond!"

The voice was faint but familiar; so familiar that Sond's heart nearly burst from his chest. He stared into the gilt cage in horror. Trapped in the cage was not a bird, but a woman! "Nedjma!"

"My love! Help me—"

Sond grabbed for the egg, but Kaug—with a deft motion closed his hand over it, snapping shut the device and smothering the djinniyeh's despairing plea.

"Release her!" Sond demanded. His chest heaving in fury he no longer bothered to conceal, the djinn drew his scimitar and leaped threateningly at the 'efreet. "Release her or, by Sul, I'll slit you from throat to navel!"

Kaug laughed heartily and tossed the golden egg playfully into the air.

Sond attacked him, slashing wildly with his blade. Kaug spoke a word, and the djinn found himself tickling the 'efreet with the plume of an ostrich. Undaunted, Sond hurled the feather to the ground. Speaking a word of his own, he summoned up a gigantic two-handed saber. Wielding the blade, twirling it over his head until it made the air whistle, Sond made a dive for the 'efreet.

Kaug, grinning, held the golden egg in the path of Sond's savage swing. The djinn halted his deadly stroke just inches from the glittering golden surface. Kaug spoke again and the saber blade flew from Sond's hands. The 'efreet's fingers closed over the hilt—the great two-handed saber looked like a small dagger in Kaug's huge fist. Holding the egg in his palm, Kaug brought the sharp edge of the blade level with it.

"It would be a shame to crack the shell. I think the pretty bird inside would die," Kaug said coolly.

"What do you mean 'die'?" Sond demanded, struggling to breath over the tightness in his chest. "That's impossible!"

"Where now are the djinn of Evren and Zhakrin? Where now are the djinn of Quar?"

"Well, where?" Sond asked, his anguished eyes upon the golden egg.

Kaug slowly lowered the saber. "An interesting question, is it not, my friend? And one for which our pretty bird might discover a most unpleasant answer." The weapon disappeared from Kaug's hand. Reaching out one long finger, he began to stroke the egg.

"Or perhaps I will command the pretty bird to sing for me," he said, a lascivious leer on his face. "I will accompany her on my instrument, of course. Who knows, she may like my playing better than yours, friend Sond."

"What do you want in exchange for her?" Quivering in barely suppressed anger, Sond wiped sweat from his face. "It cannot be wealth. For that you would go to her master."

"I have more wealth than you can possibly imagine. Quar is generous—"

"Ah, Quar!" Sond ground his teeth. "Now we come to it!"

"Indeed, you are swift of thought, my friend—like the falcon swooping down to peck out the eyes of the gazelle. My Most Holy Master is disturbed, you see, by rumors that have reached his ears concerning a uniting of the tribes of Akhran. "

"Well, what of it?" Sond sneered. "Is your great and powerful Master frightened?"

Kaug's laughter boomed over the garden, causing Sond to glance around nervously. He had no doubt that if they were discovered by the elderly djinn's guards, Kaug would vanish, leaving Sond to his fate.

"Is my Master frightened of the fly that buzzes around his head? No, of course not. But that fly is an annoyance. It irritates him. He could smack it and end its puny life, but Quar is merciful. He would much prefer that the fly go away. You, as I understand it, Sond, were instrumental in bringing the fly into my Master's presence, so to speak. It would be much appreciated if you would drive it off."

"And if I don't?"

"Then my Holy Master will be forced to kill the fly—"

"Hah!" Sond burst out.

"—and crush this most fragile golden egg," Kaug finished imperturbably. "Or, since that would be a grievous waste, Quar might decide to keep the egg for himself, enjoying it until he tired of toying with it, then pass it on to a devoted servant like myself—"

"Stop!" Clutching his chest, feeling that his heart must crack from the pain, Sond swallowed the bile rising in his throat. "What . . . what must I do?"

"Hatred smolders like hot coals at the feet of the two tribes. See to it that this flame is fanned until it is a roaring fire that engulfs the fly. When this is done, when the fly is either dead or departed, Quar will return this most enchanting bird's egg to one who could find it a nest."

"And what if I fail?"

Kaug popped the golden egg into his mouth and began to suck on it with lewd smacking sounds.

Sond's stomach wrenched and he doubled over in agony. Crouching on his hands and knees at Kaug's feet, he was violently sick. Kaug watched, grinning. Then, leaning down, he patted Sond solicitously on the back.

"I have faith in you, Sond, my friend. I don't think you will fail me."

The 'efreet's laughter rumbled in Sond's ears, eventually dying away in the distance like a departing storm.

CHAPTER 4

Spring came to the desert at last, arriving in a week of drenching rain that turned the sea of sand into a sea of mud and the placid, underground river that fed the Tel oasis changed to a raging torrent. The rushing water found the tiniest crevice and carved it into a ravine. The desert floor collapsed in several places as the river ate away at the rock and sand. The rain slashed down like knives. Firewood was soaked and would not light. A cold wind blew constantly, chilling the blood, whipping through clothes that were never dry.

Nevertheless, spirits in the camp were high. All knew the rain would end soon, and when it did, the desert would blossom. And surely then the Rose of the Prophet would bloom. The Hrana could go back to their sheep and their hills. The Akar could move their horses to summer pastures farther to the north.

Khardan, lying in his tent in enforced idleness, listened to the rain drumming on the sand outside and thought about the rain's bringing life to the desert and wondered what it would bring to him.

When the Akar left the Tel, would Zohra come with him? There was some astonishment among the Akar that Khardan had not taken another wife, since he had now fulfilled the god's wish and married Akhran's chosen. Several fathers had hinted openly that they had daughters available, and though modesty and tribal custom forbade the girls from making known their interest in the handsome Calif openly, they never failed in any opportunity to cross his path, peeping at him from above their veils.

Khardan ignored the hints and the sidelong glances. Akar gossip finally agreed that he did not want to grant his Hrana woman any increase in power by providing her with a *harem*— traditionally a stronghold of magic—over which she, as head wife, would rule.

Khardan let them think what they liked, perhaps even accepting this reason himself for his lack of interest in other women. There were times, however, when he admitted to himself that the eyes of the sparrow were dull and lackluster after one has looked into the fiery black eyes of the hawk.

Could one live with the hawk? Yes, if she were tamed. . . .

Closing his eyes, listening to the rain, Khardan smelled again the scent of jasmine and felt the touch of her fingers, soft and light, against his skin.

Zohra, hearing the monotonous dripping of the rain spilling from the folds of the tent's strong fabric, imagined it nourishing the Rose of the Prophet, tried to imagine the ugly cactus bearing a beautiful flower.

She herself wondered at Khardan's refusal to take another wife. Deep within, some wayward part of her was glad—the same part that persisted, during the long nights, in remembering the warmth of his smooth skin beneath her fingertips, the play of strong muscles across his back and shoulders as he had lain beside her in their bed on their wedding night.

She had won her victory, she had inflicted on this proud warrior his one and only defeat. That would be a memory to treasure all her life, something between the two of them that neither could ever forget. He had accepted his defeat with grace, she had to admit. Perhaps it was now up to her to accept her victory in the same way?

Her hand closed over the hilt of the dagger she kept beneath her pillow. Drawing it out, she gently pressed her lips against it, closed her eyes, and smiled.

The next day, just as suddenly as it started, the rain ended. The sun appeared. The desert burst into life.

The fronds of the date palm stirred in a mild breeze that bore with it the scents of the wild desert blossoms, lacy tamarisk, and sweet-smelling sage. The horses nibbled tender sweet grasses that sprang up around the oasis. Newborn foals staggered about awkwardly on unsteady legs as mothers looked on with pride, while some of the younger stallions forgot their newly acquired dignity and gamboled like colts.

That morning the Hrana and the Akar, led by their Sheykhs,

eagerly gathered around the Tel. Pointing and shouting, the people began to sing hymns of praise to Akhran. Although the Rose of the Prophet had not bloomed with the rains, the cacti had turned green, their fleshy leaves and stems swelling with life. Many among both tribes swore they could actually seen the budding of blossoms. Khardan glanced at Zohra. Zohra, catching his gaze, lowered her eyes, a flush staining her face a dusky rose, more beautiful than any desert flower.

The djinn Sond watched the two of them intently, cast a grim glance at the Rose of the Prophet, and disappeared.

As Jaafar was returning to his tent, rubbing his hands with glee and already preparing for his tribe's imminent departure, he noticed someone falling into step beside him on his righthand side.

"Congratulations, my Sheykh, on so fortunate an occurrence," the man said.

"Thank you," Jaafar responded, wondering who this fellow tribesman was. He could not see his face, hidden by the *haik*, though he thought the voice sounded vaguely familiar. "Give praise to our Wandering God."

"Praise be to Akhran," the man said obediently, bowing his head. "I presume we will be leaving soon, returning to our flocks in the hills?"

"Yes," said Jaafar, still attempting to place this person, unwilling to risk insulting him by asking his name. Trying to get a closer look at the man's face without seeming to do so, the Sheykh increased his pace to gain a step or two on the man, peering back at him. This didn't work, however. The man eagerly quickened his steps and popped around to come up unexpectedly on his Sheykh's left.

"Eh?" said Jaafar, astonished, turning to talk to the man on his right, only to find him gone.

"Here, my Sheykh."

"Oh, there you are. What was it you were saying? Something about leaving—"

"Yes, my Sheykh. And after having lived with these horse people for so long, an idea has struck me. Wouldn't it be an excellent thing to have horses of our own? How much simpler guarding the sheep would be if we did it on horseback! How much better to have horses to drive off the wolf in the night. And other enemies besides the wolf," the man added in a low voice, with a sidelong glance at the Akar's side of the camp.

"What an interesting idea," began Jaafar, turning to his left only to find the man on his right again. "Where? Oh! I—I didn't you see move around." The Sheykh was becoming increasingly rattled.

"Then, too"—the man's voice dropped even further—"it would be some payment for what they have stolen from us over the years."

"Yes," muttered Jaafar, his brows drawing together, the old bitter hatred that had been forgotten in the celebrations of the morning burning with a new flame. "I like this suggestion. I shall myself broach it with Sheykh al Fakhar—"

"Ah, do not trouble yourself, *sidi*!" the man said smoothly, drawing his face mask even more closely around his nose and mouth. "After all, you have a daughter who is married to the Calif. Tell her to make of her husband this one small request. Surely he can refuse her nothing, least of all this. Go to her now. Press upon her the importance. It is a matter of pride, after all. You deserve nothing less, Sheykh of Hrana, who have given these Akar so much."

"You're right!" Jaafar said, his usually weak eyes gleaming. "I will go to my daughter and ask her to see the Calif without delay!"

"But she is not to go as a beggar!" the man warned, laying his hand upon the Sheykh's arm. "She is not to demean herself before that man!"

"My daughter would never do such a thing!" Jaafar shouted fiercely.

"Forgive me my eagerness to see all go well for you, my Sheykh," the man said humbly, placing his hand over his heart and bowing his head low.

"Humpf!" Jaafar, with a snort, headed off for his daughter's tent. He had completely forgotten his curiosity over who this strange tribesman might be. His eyes were on the herds of horses pastured around the oasis. Already he felt himself their proud owner.

"So much," said Sond softly, causing the robes of the Hrana he wore to melt away into the sweet spring air, "for the blossoming of the Rose or any other flower."

CHAPTER 5

"C *ouscous!* Ah, what a treat!"

The djinn sniffed at the dish with the critical air of one who is accustomed to dining well and often, his large belly and several chins shaking appreciatively as he dipped the fingers of his right hand into the steaming delicacy.

"The secret is in the proper roasting of the meat," the djinn remarked, his mouth full of almonds, raisins, and lamb. "Too long and it becomes tough and dry. Too little and ... well, there is nothing worse than underdone lamb. You, my dear Sond"—the djinn kissed his fingers to the other djinn opposite him—"have acquired the proper technique to perfection."

Following this compliment, the two djinn ate rapidly and without talking, for to speak during eating is to insult the meat. Finally, with a deep sigh and a belch of satisfaction, the fat djinn leaned back upon his cushions and swore that he could not consume another bite.

"Delicious!" he said, bathing his hands in the lemon water his host poured out in a basin before him.

"I am honored by the praise of one so knowledgeable as yourself, my dear Usti. But you really must try these almond cakes. They come all the way from Khandar."

Sond offered a plate of the sticky sweets to his guest, who could not offend his host by refusing. In truth, it appeared from his rotund stature that this djinn had not offended a host in the past six centuries.

"And a pipe to finish off a good meal," said Usti.

The djinn watched with appreciation as Sond placed the hubble-bubble pipe between them. Taking up one of the mouthpieces, he inhaled the tobacco smoke; the water in the pipe gurgling a soothing accompaniment. Sond puffed on the other mouthpiece, both djinn smoking in companionable silence for long moments, allowing their immortal bodies to attend to the important, if illusionary, human function of digestion.

As the two smoked, however, it became apparent to the rotund djinn that Sond was studying him with sidelong glances, and that Sond's face, as he did this, was becoming increasingly grave and solemn. Whenever Usti looked directly at Sond, however, the tall, handsome djinn instantly glanced away. Finally Usti could stand this no longer.

"My dear friend," he wheezed, his breath being constricted both by the tobacco smoke and his large belly, "you look at me, then when I look at you, you're not looking at me, then when I look away, you're looking at me again. By Sul, tell me what is wrong before I go mad."

"You will forgive me, friend Usti," said Sond, "if I speak plainly? We have known each other such a short time. I fear I am being presumptuous."

Usti waved this away with a graceful gesture of a sugar coated hand.

"It's just that I note you are not quite well, my friend," Sond continued solicitously.

Usti heaved a mournful sigh, wisps of smoke trailing from the corners of his mouth.

"If you knew the life I led!" The djinn laid his hand upon his breast.

In contrast to Sond's bare chest and shoulders, Usti's large body was swathed in the folds of a silken blouse, a pair of voluminous trousers, and a long silken robe. A white turban adorned his head. The temperature inside Sond's lamp, where the two were dining, was warm, and Usti mopped sweat from his face as he expounded upon his woes.

"May *Hazrat* Akhran forgive me for speaking ill of my mistress, but the woman is a menace, a menace! Zohra—the flower." The djinn snorted, blowing smoke out his nose. "Zohra—the nettle. Zohra—the cactus. This"—he waved his hand over the dishes—"is the first good meal I've had in days, if you will believe me!"

"Ah, truly?" said Sond, gazing at the djinn with pity.

"It never fails. I am in the midst of a quiet little dinner when 'tap, tap, tap'"—Usti bit the words—"comes on the outside of my brazier. If I don't respond immediately, if, for example, I decide to drink my coffee while it is hot and *then* attend to my mistress's demands, she flies into a rage, which generally ends"—Usti paused for effect and breath—"in hurling my dwelling place into a comer of the tent."

"No!" Sond was appropriately horrifIed.

"The mess it makes." Usti shook his turbaned head mournfully. "My furniture is all topsy-turvy these days. I don't know whether it is right side up or wrong side down! To say nothing of the broken crockery! My pipe has sprung a leak. It is impossible for me to entertain!" The djinn put his head in his hand, his shoulders heaving.

"My dear friend, this is intolera—"

"And that isn't the half of it!" Usti's many chins quivered in outrage. "The demands she makes of me! And against her husband, who only tries to persuade her to behave properly. She refuses to milk goats, churn the butter, do her weaving, cook her husband's food. If you will believe me"—Usti, reaching out, tapped Sond upon his knee—"my mistress spends all the day riding horses! Dressed as a youth!" Leaning back into the cushions, Usti regarded his host with the air of one who has said it all, amen, nothing more.

Sond's eyes opened wide. The matter being too shocking for words, the djinn squeezed Usti's flabby arm in brotherly sympathy.

"But Zohra is a beautiful woman and spirited," Sond began suggestively. "Surely the Calif, Khardan, son of my master, has certain compensations—"

"If he does, he derives them from his imagination!" Usti grunted. "Which is not to disparage the Calif, may *Hazrat* Akhran look upon him with favor. He proved his manhood on his wedding night with the lioness. Why sleep with claws at his throat? It is just as well Sul, in his infinite wisdom, did not give this woman the power of black magic. I dread to think what she might do to her husband if she could. Speaking of which, are you familiar with the story of Sul and the Too-Learned Wizards?"

"No, I don't believe so," replied Sond, who had first heard the story four centuries earlier but who knew the duties of a host.

"When the world was young, each of the Gods, may their names be praised, had his own gifts and graces which he bestowed upon his faithful. But Sul—as center of all—alone possessed the magic. He shared this gift with humans of learned and serious mien who came to him in humility, pledging to serve him by spending their lives in study and hard work; not only of magic but of all things in this world.

"The wizards did as they promised, studying magic, languages, mathematics, philosophy, until they became the most learned and wise men in the world. And so, too, did they become the most powerful. Since they had all learned each other's languages and customs, they came together and exchanged information, further increasing their knowledge. Then, instead of each looking to his own God, they all began to look increasingly to Sul, the Center. All gradually became of one mind, and this mind told them to use their powerful magic to supplant the Gods.

"As you can imagine, the Gods were furious and reproached Sul, demanding that magic be taken away from the humans. This Sul could not do, magic having become too pervasive within the world. But Sul himself was angered at the wizards, who had become arrogant and demanding. And so he dealt with them harshly, in order to teach them a lesson.

"Bringing the wizards together on a pretense of celebrating their newfound power, Sul took each man and cut out his tongue so that he no longer had the power to speak any language at all.

"'For,' spoke Sul, 'it is meant that men should speak to each other through the heart and this you have forgotten.'

"Next Sul decreed that, since magic was still in the world, it should be given into the hands of women, who are, most of them"—Usti heaved a sigh—"gentle and loving. Thus magic would be used for purposes of good, not evil. Sul stated, further, that magic must be based in material objects—charms, and amulets, potions, scrolls, and wands—so that those who practice it are constrained by the physical properties of the objects in which the magic resides as well as by their own human limitations.

"Thus spoke and did Sul, and the Too-Learned Wizards went home to discover that their wives had the magic and that they— as punishment for their arrogance—were forced to eat soup and gruel the rest of their tongueless days."

"All praise to the wisdom of Sul," said Sond, knowing what was required at the end of this story.

"All praise," repeated Usti, mopping his brow. "But Sul did

not have my mistress in mind when he did such a thing. My mistress's words are sharper than the cactus and sting worse than the scorpion. Just between you and me, my friend"—leaning forward, Usti placed a fat finger on Sond's chest, poking at him to emphasize his words—"I do not think the Calif regrets overmuch that his wife does not cook for him, if you take my meaning."

"No!" remonstrated Sond, aghast. "Surely he doesn't think she would. . . she would—"

"Poison him?" Usti rolled his eyes. "The woman is a menace, a menace!"

"Zohra would not dare go against the decree of Akhran!" Usti said nothing, but raised his hands to heaven.

Sond appeared appropriately alarmed. Lowering his voice, he glanced around the confines of the lamp and then he, in his turn, drew near Usti.

"I do not want to pry into private matters between djinn and master, but has your mistress ever asked you to . . . well, you know. . ."

Usti's eyes rolled back into his head so far that only the whites showed. "Not death," he said softly. "Even my mistress would not dare bring down the wrath of *Hazrat* Akhran by ordering me to assassinate her husband, when she knows that first I must have the God's sanction to take a mortal life. But. . . other. . ." He whispered in Sond's ear, making explanatory gestures with his hands.

Sond's face registered horror. "And what did you do?"

"Nothing," puffed Usti, fanning himself with a palm frond. "I pleaded the excuse that several hundred years previously Khardan's great-great-great-grandfather freed me from the spell of an evil 'efreet and that I am bound to do the family no harm of *any kind*"—he emphasized the words—"for a thousand years. Which is true," he added, "to a certain extent, although the nature of the oath is not quite so binding as I have led my mistress to believe. Since then, however"—the djinn groaned—"my life has been one of torment. If I appear, my mistress throws pots at me. If I hide in my dwelling, she throws *me* at the pots!"

"What precipitated all of this? It seemed they were getting along so well. . ."

"Sheep! I like sheep in their way," Usti said with a fond glance at the carcass of the lamb, "but I cannot fathom why such fuss is being made over them. It all has to do with this decree of *Hazrat* Akhran that the tribes remain camped around the Tel until the

Rose blooms, which I may add, it seems to me further from doing than ever. I think, in fact, if I may speak candidly, my friend?"

"You may."

"I think the wretched plant is dying. But that is neither here nor there. From what I can gather, it seems that Zohra's people are being forced to trek between this Tel out in the middle of the desert and the foothills to the west where they pasture the sheep. Consequently their tribe is split. Those who are living here worry about those who are living there. They fear raiders from the south. They fear wolves. They fear wolves from the south. I don't know!"

Usti wiped his sweating forehead.

"My mistress's father—may *Hazrat* Akhran bury him to his eyebrows in a hill of fire ants—gave her the idea that if the Hrana had horses it would solve all their problems. Zohra went to Khardan and demanded that he give her people horses to herd sheep."

Sond gasped.

"Precisely the Califs response," Usti said gloomily. He lowered his voice, imitating Khardan's deep baritone. " 'Our horses are the children of *Hazrat* Akhran,' he told my mistress. 'They are ridden for His glory—to make war, to participate in the games that celebrate His name. Never have they borne a burden! Never have they worked for their food!' " Usti began to shout. " 'Never will our noble animals be used to herd sheep! Never!' "

"*Shhh!* Hush!" Sond remonstrated, though he carefully suppressed a smile of delight.

Usti's conversation, like the sheep they were discussing, was being led along Sond's path. Taking advantage of a lull in the talk occasioned by Usti's recent passionate outburst's having temporarily caused a severe constriction of his breathing passages, Sond poured sweet, thick coffee and produced a plate of candied locusts, dates, and other delicacies. Usti's eyes actually grew moist with pleasure at the sight.

"Truly our horses *are* sacred to us, as the Calif says," Sond stated, sipping his coffee and nibbling on a fig. "Even when we move from camp to camp, our beloved animals are never ridden, but walk proudly with the people. However," the djinn continued solemnly, "it is required of us that we look at the world from the back of another's camel. I can understand your mistress's point of view. It is not good in these unsettled times for the tribe to be divided. Speaking of which, camels would, of course, be the ideal solution, but where are they to come from? The prices which that bandit Zeid demands for his *mehari* are outrageous. My master has long considered beating some humility into him."

"Ah, I agree. But as the proverb relates, it is difficult to beat the man who owns a large stick."

"True." Sond sighed. "The Aran outnumber my people two to one and their *mehari* are swifter than the wind. Those racing camels of Zeid's are famous even in Khandar."

"Why dream of camels? We may as well dream of flying carpets, which, by the way, was one of my mistress's demands, if you can believe it. I told her that sending carpets into the heavens was perfectly well for legends and lore but absolutely impractical when it came to the real thing.

" 'What would you do if you met a storm 'efreet?' I asked her. 'One puff and you're among the heathens on the opposite end of the world. And there's no way to control the silly things. They have a decided propensity to flip over. And did you know that if you fly too high, your nose starts to bleed? *That's* something they never mention in those fool stories. To say nothing of the sheer energy involved in getting one off the ground and keeping it aloft.' No, I told her it was impossible."

"What did she do?"

"She brought the tent down on top of me. And see this mark?" Usti exhibited a bruise on his forehead.

"Yes."

"An iron skillet. My ears still ring. And now, just because I refused to carpet the sky, my mistress has commanded *me* to come up with a better solution or she threatens next time to throw my brazier in quicksand. I didn't sleep a wink, all night! Oh, why was I forced into all this?" Usti gazed beseechingly at the heavens. "Of all djinn, I am the most unfortunate! If that *nesnas* had not captured my poor master and killed him and made me prisoner, I would not now be beholden to Fedj for having rescued me, and I would not now be in the clutches of this wild woman to whom—all things considered—I think I prefer the *nesnas!*"

Letting his turbaned head sink into his hands, Usti moaned in misery.

"And yet," said Sond cautiously, "if there *was* a—way to make your mistress happy. . ."

Usti ceased wailing and opening one eye, peered out between his fingers. "Yes? You said a way to make my mistress happy? Go on."

"I'm not certain that I should," Sond said, upon deep reflection. "You are, after all, the enemy of my master."

"Enemy!" Usti spread his hands. "Is this the body of an enemy? No! It is the body of one who wants only to get a good night's sleep! To eat a meal while it is hot! To find his furniture on the floor and not the ceiling!"

"Ah, you tear out my heart!" said Sond, placing his hand on his bosom. "I am truly sorry for your plight and you do look unwell."

"Unwell," cried Usti, tears flooding his eyes. "If you only knew the half of it! This is the first solid food I've been able to keep down in days! I shall soon be skin and bones!" He put his hands together pleadingly. "If you have an idea that will put an end to my mistress's tantrums, I would be eternally in your debt! Rest assured, I will give you all the credit! "

"No, no!" said Sond hastily. "This is to be *your* idea. The credit will all belong to you." Reaching out, he squeezed Usti's fat hand. "My reward will be to see a brother djinn grow happy and well once more."

"You are kind, my friend! Kind!" murmured Usti, his tears losing themselves in the creases of his chins. "Now, what is this idea?"

"Suggest to Zohra that her people steal the horses." Usti's eyes opened wide. The tears stopped.

"Steal?"

"It is fitting, after all. My people have stolen from them for years. Now the Hrana have a chance to get back at us. Zohra's father, Sheykh Jaafar, will be happy. Zohra will be happy. What's more, she will be grateful to you for suggesting something so brilliant! She will make your life a paradise! Nothing will be too good for you. "

"Forgive my ignorance, my friend," Usti said cautiously, "I do not know much about your people, not having lived among them long, but it seems to me—and I intend no disrespect—that the Akar are . . . one might say. . . volatile. Isn't this proposed thievery likely to . . . uh . . .upset them?"

"My master will be angry for a day or two, but—in the end—he will respect the Hrana for showing some spirit. And the sun will freeze to a ball of ice," Sond added beneath his breath.

"What did you say?" Usti cupped his hand over his ear. "It's this ringing in my head—the skillet, you know."

"I said my master will think it all very nice. In fact," Sond continued, carried away by his enthusiasm, "this event may well solidify the friendship between our two tribes. It will provide the Hrana with the horses they need. They will be content. It will show the Akar that the Hrana are courageous and daring. My people will be content. And all because of you, Usti! *Hazrat* Akhran will undoubtedly reward you handsomely. "

"My own little dwelling among the clouds," said Usti, gazing upward at the ceiling of the lamp wistfully. "Just a small one. No more than eighty rooms, ninety at the outside. A lovely garden. Djinniyeh to scratch my back where I cannot reach, rub my temples with rose water when I have the headache, sing to me sweetly. . ."

Absorbed in his dream, Usti did not notice that at this remark about the djinniyeh, his host became exceedingly pale.

"It will be no more than you deserve, my friend," Sond said, rather more harshly than he intended. He cleared his throat. "Well, will you do it?"

"I will!" Usti said with sudden resolve. "Are you certain, my friend," he added warily, "that you will not demand—I mean accept—any of the credit?"

"No, no!" Sond said, shaking his head emphatically. "I beg that you leave me out of this. Surely one so wise as yourself would have thought of this idea eventually. "

"Ah, that is true," said Usti gravely. "In fact, it was on the tip of my tongue even when you spoke."

"There, you see!" Sond said, slapping his friend on his large back.

"I would have spoken it first," pursued Usti, "except that I was drinking this delicious coffee and I feared to insult you by putting the cup down."

"And seeing you thus pleasantly engaged, Akhran caused your thought to fly to my mouth, your words to come from my throat. I am honored"—the djinn bowed from the waist—"to have served as your vessel."

Smiling warmly, Sond propped himself up among his cushions on one elbow and passed the plate of candied fruit to his guest.

"Another fig?"

CHAPTER 6

"Another fig?" mimicked a disgusted voice outside the lamp, a voice so soft that neither of the two enjoying their repast inside heard it.

A djinn may not enter the dwelling of another djinn unless he receives an invitation, but it is possible for one djinn to listen in on conversations held inside the dwelling unless the master of the dwelling takes precautions to protect himself. Sond, upset and desperate, was so intent on the seduction of Usti that he carelessly forgot to place the magical seal around his lamp.

Pukah stood in Majiid's tent, his ear over the lamp spout. He had been standing there, invisible, listening to every word spoken by the two for the past hour, and now the young djinn was in a state of turmoil and confusion not to be believed.

Having been ordered by his master to keep a watch on the comings and goings of Zohra, Pukah had instantly noted the sudden disappearance of Usti—a highly unusual occurrence. Usti had not been known to voluntarily leave his dwelling since coming into Zohra's possession. Fearing mischief of some sort directed against Khardan, Pukah immediately searched the camp, eventually discovering the fat djinn's whereabouts in the last place he had expected—being entertained in the lamp of his enemy!

Just what was Sond up to? Pukah hadn't any idea. He knew Sond didn't care a horse's droppings for the fat djinn.

"If I hear one more honey-coated 'Usti, my friend' come from your lips, I'll gag," Pukah told the lamp.

He listened in amazement to Sond's casual suggestion of the horse-thieving raid. Pukah knew—if the thickheaded Usti didn't—that the theft of the horses would *not* bring about everlasting friendship between the two tribes.

"Everlasting bloodshed is more like it," Pukah said grimly.

Why was Sond risking the wrath of *Hazrat* Akhran by suggesting such a thing?

"Even if Akhran does think it's Blubber-belly's idea, he'll be so mad he'll throw us all into the Kurdin Sea! And Sond knows it."

Pukah pondered the matter as he returned to his own dwelling—a woven basket that had once been used by a snake charmer to house his reptile. It was an unusual dwelling place for a djinn. Pukah had been only a very young djinn when he'd come across the snake charmer squatted in the road near Bastine. Fascinated by the snake, who swayed its deadly head hypnotically to the music of its master, Pukah slipped inside the basket to get a better view. He was promptly captured by the snake's owner and spent the next twenty years traveling the lands of Sardish Jardan, doing all sorts of interesting jobs for the snake charmer, who also happened to be a worshiper of Benario, God of Thieves, on the side.

Other than having to share his dwelling with the snake, who—as it turned out—was an incredibly boring individual, Pukah enjoyed his life on the road. He came to know all manner of people, visit all manner of cities and villages, and was taught a number of ways to enter houses where one hadn't been invited. He also became acquainted with nearly every immortal being between Bas and Tara-kan.

Then one day his master was caught worshiping Benario not wisely but too well. The wealthy merchant he was attempting to rob chopped the charmer into pieces small enough to have fit inside his own basket. This left Pukah and the snake to their own devices. The snake, in return for its freedom, gave Pukah the basket.

Hoping to escape the notice of Akhran's elder djinn, who would have assigned him to a mortal, Pukah transported himself and his basket to the *souks* of Kich, hoping to pick out his own human. Liking the looks of Badia, Khardan's mother, he planted his basket on the back of her donkey, hiding among the other baskets until she arrived at her tent—an old trick taught him by his master, who often used this to gain access to rich houses.

When Badia opened the basket, Pukah leaped out, threw his arms around her, and swore her eternal service in return for having freed him from his captivity. The young djinn was presented to Khardan on his twelfth birthday, and although Pukah was far older in years than his master, the two might have been said to have grown up together, for djinn must mature just like their mortal counterparts.

Therefore, though one was two hundred and the other but twenty-five, the same lust for action and excitement burned in the heart of the djinn that burned in the heart of his master. Pukah was equally ambitious, determined to rise high in the estimation of his God. He looked down upon Sond and Fedj with scorn. Content with their lives, the two older djinn had—or so he had always supposed—no desire to better their lot.

"I will not wait until I am old and toothless before I have a palace," Pukah resolved. "And when I get one, it will be located here in *this* world, not up there. Besides, mortals are incredible fun."

All Pukah's bright dreams were dashed when Akhran spoke— actually spoke—to Fedj and Sond, giving them the command that would eventually bring the two warring tribes together at the Tel. Pukah had nearly turned inside out with envy. What he would have given if only the Wandering God had spoken to him! And then he was forced to watch as the great fools Sond and Fedj— ("They must have sand in their heads in place of brains!")—went about grumbling and complaining instead of taking full advantage of the situation.

But now, here was Sond doing what Pukah would have done all along—he was almost certainly taking this opportunity to become a hero in the eyes of *Hazrat* Akhran.

"But how oddly he's going about it!" Pukah said to himself, pacing back and, forth in his basket. "I don't understand! Usti! Horse stealing! What would I do if I were in Sond's lamp? Aha!"

The young djinn snapped his fingers. Coming to a halt before a mirror that hung in a prominent location on the wall of his basket, he expounded the matter to himself as was his custom, having had, for long years, no one to talk to other than the snake.

"Well, what is it you would do, Pukah, if you were not Pukah but Sond?"

"Well, Pukah, since you asked, if I were Sond and not Pukah, I would get that triple-chinned ass, Usti, to go to his mistress with this wild scheme of stealing horses. Then I—Sond—would go to *Hazrat* Akhran and tell the God that I had learned that this disaster was about to take place. I would beg Akhran to intervene. He would do so, peace would be restored, and I—Sond—would be a hero in the eyes of Akhran!"

Pukah, proud of his plan, gazed gleefully in the mirror at Pukah, who gazed gleefully back until it occurred to both of them that they were Pukah, not Sond.

"That," said Pukah gloomily to Pukah, "is exactly what I would do if I were Sond. The swine!"

The two Pukahs put their heads together, literally, both leaning against the mirror.

"Pukah, my man, aren't you every bit as smart as Sond?"

"Smarter," replied Pukah stoutly.

"And aren't you as clever as Sond?"

"Cleverer!"

"And aren't you, Pukah"—Pukah raised his head to look himself straight in the eye—"destined to be a hero? Don't you deserve it more than that great hulking oaf who thinks only of his handsome face and his broad shoulders and whose ambition in life is to find a garden wall he hasn't scaled, a pair of legs he hasn't straddled?"

(It must be noted here that Pukah was slight and slender of build, with a face rather too long and narrow to be considered in any way handsome, and whose attempts to endear himself to certain comely djinniyeh had thus far resulted in having his pointed jaw soundly slapped.)

"You deserve it! You do!" returned Pukah warmly.

"Then, Pukah, it is up to you to ruin Sond's plans to become a hero, or if that is not possible, to come up with a plan of your own to outhero him. Now, how can this be accomplished?"

The Pukah standing in front of the mirror began pacing back and forth in the basket. The Pukah in the mirror did the same, the two coming together occasionally to inquire, with raised eyebrows, if either had an idea. Neither did, and the Pukah in the mirror—for one—was beginning to grow increasingly glum.

"There's no use in trying to talk Usti out of presenting this crazy scheme to the wild Zohra. The fat djinn is too enamored of it. He's even decided it was all his idea. I'd never be able to convince him to drop it. So, let him go ahead and let Zohra plot to steal the horses. I could go to her and tell her it was a trap. . ."

Pukah considered this a second, but the Pukah in the mirror shook his head. "No, you're right. Zohra hates me almost as much as she hates my master. She would never believe me."

"*You* could be the one to tell Akhran you have uncovered the plot," suggested the Pukah in the mirror.

Pukah reflected upon this suggestion, and at length he announced that if they couldn't come up with anything better, it would have to do. "But," he added desperately, "there must be something I can do that will blow Sond off his camel—"

"Camel. . . ."

Pukah stared at his image, who stared at him right back, both faces taking on a look of foxish cunning.

"That's it!" they cried together. "Camels! Zeid!"

"Sond and Fedj bring two tribes together in peace. Pooh! What is that? It is nothing! A child could do the same if he put his mind to it. But if *three* tribes come together in peace! Now that would be something! Such a miracle has never occurred in all the history of the Pagrah desert!"

"Quar would not dare to even think of bothering us!" "Kaug would leap into the ocean and drown himself in sheer frustration!"

"Akhran will be victorious above. The Akar will be victorious below, and it will all be due to me!"

Dancing in delight, Pukah began to caper about his basket, the Pukah in the mirror prancing about just as merrily.

"Me! Me! Me! *I* am the one who will be the hero. Sond and Fedj are dogs compared to Pukah! Akhran himself will bow before Pukah. 'Without you, my hero,' our God will say as he takes me in his arms and kisses both my cheeks, 'I would be lost! I would be licking Quar's boots! Here's a palace, here's two palaces, here's a dozen palaces and ten dozen djinniyeh!' "

"Let Sond play his games! Let him plot his plots and scheme his schemes! Let him think he has won! I will snatch the fruit from his mouth and it will be so much the sweeter for having the marks of his teeth on it! Now, to make my plans. What is the name of Sheykh's Zeid's djinn?"

"Raja," supplied the Pukah in the mirror.

"Raja," murmured Pukah.

Once again he resumed his pacing, this time with such concentrated thought that he completely forgot the Pukah in the mirror, who—nevertheless—did not forget him but kept up with him step for step until night fell and both were swallowed by darkness.

CHAPTER 7

Peering out from a hole in the charcoal brazier that sat within the entrance to his mistress's tent, Usti watched a young man—at least it appeared to be a young man—stride through the camp of Sheykh Majiid al Fakhar early in the morning, almost three weeks following the arrival of spring to the Tel. The young man's boots were dusty, his robes coated with a fine film of sand, the *haik* covered nose and mouth. It was obvious that he had been out riding in the cool of the day. There was nothing unusual in this. It should not have attracted any particular attention to him. It did, however, and the attention was not of a flattering kind.

Women carrying firewood to cook the noonday meal stopped and stared at the young man with cold, unfriendly eyes or whispered to each other before hurrying on their way. Their husbands, standing about discussing the relative merits of one horse over another, glanced at each other as the young man walked by them, their eyebrows rising significantly. Conversations fell silent, the eyes of the men and the women turned to the tent of their Calif, who was just emerging, his falcon on his wrist, preparatory to a day's hunting.

The djinn saw that the young man was aware of the glances and undoubtedly heard the whispered words, for his head tilted higher, the lips pressed firmly together. Ignoring the stares and the mutterings, looking neither to the right nor the left but straight ahead, the young man continued walking through the camp.

His way led him directly past the Calif, who was watching his coming with a face devoid of all expression. Usti held his breath. Nearing Khardan, the young man—for the first time—shifted his eyes from the tent that was his destination. The gazes of the two met and crossed like saber blades; the djinn swore that he could hear the clash and see the sparks.

Neither the Calif nor the young man spoke. The young man, with a contemptuous toss of the head, walked past his Calif. Khardan went his own way, crossing the compound to his father's tent. The women continued their chores, the men picked up their conversations, many looking after their prince with sympathy and respect, praising his patience, speaking of him as they might speak of a martyr who was being tortured for his faith.

Seeing the young man approach, Usti groaned and immediately thrust several fragile items beneath a mound of clothes. He himself took refuge in his brazier in the sunken tiled bath that he had lined with sheepskin for just such an emergency.

Coming to his tent, which was pitched as far from Khardan's as was decently possible, the young man angrily jerked open the tent flap. Usti heard Zohra's voice muttering through the folds of the *haik*.

"Unwomanly! . . . Unnatural! . . . Cursed! Hah!"

The djinn cringed, then groaned again as he heard a ripping, slashing sound. Usti risked a look.

"No, madam! Not the cushions!"

Too late.

Drawing her dagger, Zohra stabbed it into a silken cushion, slitting it open from top to bottom. From the look upon her face it was obvious to the djinn that—in Zohra's mind—it was not a cushion that she was murdering. Tossing it into a corner, she caught hold of another and drove the weapon into the fabric flesh, then disemboweled it, yanking out the wool stuffing and throwing it about the tent until it seemed a rare desert snowstorm had struck.

"And we all know who will have to clean this up, don't we, madam," the djinn said to himself gloomily.

Again and again Zohra hurled herself at her enemy, until there wasn't a cushion left alive. Finally, exhausted, she sank back down among the remnants of her rage and gnawed her lip until it bled.

"If this foul marriage does not end soon, I shall go mad!" she cried. "It is all his fault! I will make him pay. I will make them all pay!"

Zohra's hand closed over the charcoal brazier. Usti, tumbling back into his bathtub, shrieked in despair.

"Madam! I beg of you! Consider what is left of my furniture!"

Zohra, sneering, peered inside the brass brazier. "Why? If it is as worthless as you are, blubbering pile of camel dung, then it can be replaced by a few sticks of wood and the skin of a goat!"

A hissing sound, like air escaping from an inflated bladder, and a wobbly column of smoke emerging from the brazier announced the arrival of the djinn. Assuming his fat and comfortable form, Usti materialized in the center of the tent.

Casting the destruction a bitter, dismal look, the djinn placed his hands together and *salaamed,* bending as low as his rotund belly permitted.

"May the blessings of *Hazrat* Akhran be upon you, this morning, delicate daughter of the flowers," said Usti humbly.

"May the curse of *Hazrat* Akhran be upon you this morning, you horse's hind end," returned the delicate daughter with a snarl.

Usti shut his eyes, shuddered, and drew a deep breath.

"Thank you, madam," he said, bowing again.

"What do you want?" Zohra demanded irritably. Tossing the brazier down upon the torn cushions, she began pacing restlessly the length of the tent, muttering to herself and twining one long strand of black hair around her finger.

"If madam will recall," the djinn began, carefully repeating what he and Sond had spent last night devising, "she commanded me to come up with a plan by which we could extricate ourselves from the current intolerable situation."

Zohra glared at the djinn. "I commanded you? To come up with a plan! Hah!" Tossing her black mane of hair, she stopped her pacing long enough to pick up a golden jewel box from out of the torn fabric and sheep fluff.

"Per-perhaps I misunderstood madam," Usti stammered. "Perhaps you did." Madam sneered. "The last command I recall giving you was to—"

"I—I remember!" Usti said, sweat pouring off his face. "And I assure madam that such a thing is physically impossible, even for those of us whose bodies, shall we say, lack material substance . . ."

Hefting the jewel box in an alarming manner, Zohra eyed the throwing distance between herself and the djinn.

"Please!" gasped Usti. "If you would only listen to me!"

"Is this another of your imbecilic schemes? Flying carpets? Pig's bladders inflated with hot air that sail through the clouds? Or perhaps my personal favorite—putting wings on the sheep so that *they* could fly to us!"

Usti, his eyes on the jewel box, gulped. Drawing forth a silken handkerchief, he began to mop his forehead.

"I . . . I . . ." The djinn's words slipped from him like olive oil from a pitcher.

"Speak!" Zohra raised her hand, the jewel box glinting in the light.

Usti lifted one pudgy arm in defense and closing his eyes, gabbled in a rush: "It seems to me, madam, that if we require horses we should take them!"

The djinn cringed, waiting for the jewel box to career off his head.

Nothing happened.

Hesitantly Usti dared risk a peep at his mistress.

She stood transfixed, staring at him with wide eyes. "What did you say?"

"I repeat, madam," Usti replied, lowering his arm with great dignity, "that if we desire horses we should take them."

Zohra blinked, the jewel box fell from her hand to land unheeded on the wool-covered floor.

"After all, you are the head wife of the Calif," Usti continued, pressing his argument as Sond had suggested.

"What is his is yours, is it not?"

"But I asked him for the horses and he refused," Zohra murmured.

"*That* was your mistake, madam," Usti said crisply. "Although we give alms, who among us truly has respect for the beggar?"

For a moment the djinn thought he'd gone too far. Zohra's face flushed a dusky rose color, the flame in her eyes nearly scorched him. Angrily she snatched up the jewel box again, and Usti hurriedly prepared to seek the shelter of his brazier. But he saw suddenly that Zohra's anger was turned inward, against herself.

Brushing the black hair out of her face, she regarded the djinn with grudging respect.

"Yes," she admitted. "That was my mistake. So you are proposing I take what is mine by right of marriage. I do not think my husband will quite see matters with the same eye."

"Madam," said Usti earnestly, "far be it for me to disrupt a union made in heaven. Your noble husband has many worries. It is of the utmost importance that we do not cause Khardan a moment's anxiety. Therefore I suggest, in order to spare him all discomfort, that we acquire the said horses in the nighttime when his eyes are closed in slumber. When he wakes in the morning, the horses will be gone and it will be no good crying over spilt mare's milk. Then, in order to further spare him pain, we will tell him that the horses were stolen by that son of a she-camel, Sheykh Zeid."

Zohra hid her smile behind the veil of her black hair. "Won't my noble husband discover an inconsistency in our story when he sees my people riding upon the backs of horses that should be a hundred miles away to the south?"

"Is it our fault that Zeid is a notorious idiot and allowed the horses to slip through his fingers? The poor beasts, wandering lost in the desert, appeared in our camp in the foothills and we Hrana—out of the kindness of our hearts and the exhortation of *Hazrat* Akhran that we treat his children with respect—took in the animals, who, noble creatures that they are, did not want us to go to the vast expense of feeding and caring for them without offering their services in return." Usti wheezed for breath, this last statement having completely winded him.

"I see," Zohra said thoughtfully, pressing the cool metal of the jewel box against her cheek as she pondered. "And how am I to convince my father of the merits of this plan? Pious fool—man that he is, he would never permit it."

"Your father, praise his name, is elderly, madam. Care should be taken to make his last days upon this world days of peace and happiness. Therefore I suggest that we do not disturb him with such unsettling matters. I am certain that there are young men within your tribe who would be willing-nay, eager—to take part in such an adventure?"

Zohra smiled grimly. There was no doubt about that! The last dagger-wielding skirmish between the warring tribes had left several young Hrana—including a cousin of hers—lying bleeding and battered in the sand. The Hrana nursed their wounds, praying to Akhran to grant them an opportunity for revenge, and inwardly cursing Jaafar for preventing them from declaring open warfare. These young men would find this raid much to their liking and would have no qualms about keeping it secret from their Sheykh.

"When should this take place?"

"In a week's time, madam. The moon will not smile upon the night and darkness will cover our movements. That will also give me time to contact those you suggest and make them acquainted with our plan. "

"I may have underestimated you, Usti," Zohra admitted magnanimously.

"Madam is too kind!" Usti bowed humbly.

Opening the jewel box, Zohra seated herself in a corner of the tent on the one cushion that had escaped her wrath. Lifting a golden sapphire-studded bracelet from the box, she slid it on her arm and studied it critically, admiring the way the jewels caught the rays of the midday sun.

"Now," she commanded leisurely, motioning with her hand at the destruction in the tent, "clean up this mess."

"Yes, madam," said the djinn, heaving a profound sigh.

CHAPTER 8

The east glowed faint gold with the approach of dawn. South of the Tel there was one cloud in the sky, drifting ever nearer to the camps of the Akar and Hrana. It was a strange cloud, moving leisurely from the south to the north—traveling against the wind currents, which were blowing west to east. On this cloud reclined two djinn, resting comfortably among the ephemeral mists as they might have rested on the finest cushions of the most luxurious couch.

One of the djinn was large, well-built, with skin the color of ebony. He was arrayed in gold cloth, massive gold earrings hung to his shoulders, his arms were encircled with gold enough to ransom a Sultan, and the expression on his face was fierce, for he was a warrior djinn of a warrior tribe. Seated near him, eating figs from a basket and talking animatedly, was the lithe and slender Pukah.

"Yes, Raja, my friend, our God, the Holy Akhran, commanded that the tribes of Sheykh Jaafar al Widjar and Sheykh Majiid al Fakhar join together and live in peace and harmony at the Tel, and that they further symbolize this newly established unity by the marriage of the daughter of Jaafar with the son of Majiid."

"And did they marry?" growled Raja. Lying prone, stretched full length upon the cloud, he hefted a gigantic scimitar into the air, critically appraising the sharpness of the blade by the light of the rising sun.

"Most certainly!" Pukah nodded his head. "It was a wedding that I may truthfully say will be long remembered. But surely your master has heard of this from the God?"

"No," said Raja, a dangerous note in his voice. "My master has heard nothing of this . . . miracle."

"Ah!" Pukah sighed sympathetically and placed his hand

upon Raja's black-skinned arm. "I know how difficult it must be for you, my friend, to serve such an impious master. If only Sheykh Zeid were more attentive in his service to *Hazrat* Akhran, it might have been your master who was chosen to rejoice in the God's blessings."

"No one knows the pangs I suffer over my master's impiety," Raja remarked, staring at Pukah coldly until the young djinn, with a deprecating smile, hurriedly removed his hand from the huge, muscular arm. The black djinn turned the blade of his weapon this way and that, watching it catch the light. "So you say that the two tribes are living together in the shadow of the Tel? I find this remarkable, considering that they are such bitter enemies."

"*Were,* my dear Raja, *were* bitter enemies," said Pukah. "The wounds of the past have been cauterized by the flame of love. Such hugging and kissing! Such games and revelry, such comradeship we have. It makes one weep to see it."

"I can imagine," said Raja wryly.

"And then the fondness of the Calif for his wife!" Pukah gave a rapturous sigh that ruffled the feathers of a passing flock of startled birds. "From the moment the sun rises and he must leave her arms, Khardan counts the hours until the sun sets and he can rush back to enjoy her numerous charms and endowments."

Knowing the reputation of the lady in question, Raja raised a skeptical eyebrow at this.

"I assure you it is the truth, my dear Raja!" Pukah said solemnly. "But perhaps you doubt my word—"

"No, no, my dear Pukah," Raja grunted. "It is just that I am overcome with joy"—the black djinn brought his sword down suddenly with an alarming swipe that neatly chopped the cloud in two and sent half of it scudding off in the opposite direction—"at this picture of bliss you describe! The thought of peace coming to such bitter enemies overwhelms me. I long to see for myself. . ."

Pukah did not hesitate. "Precisely why I brought you here. Look, my doubting friend."

Raja, bending over, peered down from the heights of the cloud.

It was just past dawn. Pukah considered this a propitious time to present the camp for inspection, being fairly certain that if there had been any fights last night, the Tel would have attained some semblance of peace if only that the combatants must have dropped from sheer exhaustion.

"See, what did I tell you? The tents of the Hrana standing beside the tents of the Akar!" said the young djinn, proudly exhibiting the camp.

"What is that large splotch of blood there?"

"Where we slaughter the sheep." Pukah's face was innocent and bland as goat's milk.

"I see."

Bent over the rim of the cloud so that Pukah could not see his face, Raja gnawed his lip, scowled, and cast the young djinn a swift, sidelong, angry glance.

"It is the wish of my master, the Calif"—Pukah babbled on happily, noticing nothing of this sudden change of the black djinn's expression—"that your master, Sheykh Zeid, come to us at the Tel and press to his bosom his cousins, Majiid and Jaafar, whose love for Zeid exceeds only the love they bear for each other."

His face once more carefully expressionless, Raja raised his head and looked intently at Pukah. "That is the wish of the Calif?"

"The dearest wish of his heart."

"You may be certain that I will convey this message to my master."

"With all haste?" Pukah prompted.

"With all haste," responded Raja grimly. Good as his word, he disappeared on the spot.

"Ah, I guess he could not contain his eagerness." Pukah leaned back among the feathery cloud. "So much for Sond," he said to himself blissfully. "Let him try to be the hero now! Let him plot his little plots and try to convince *Hazrat* Akhran that *he* was responsible for keeping peace between two tribes. Pukah, you have outdone him! Pukah, *you* will achieve the union of three tribes! Pukah, history will resound with your name!"

Popping a fig into his mouth, the young djinn, arms behind his head, relaxed upon his cloud. Drifting through the sky, he began to mentally layout the floor plan of the palace a grateful Akhran would bestow upon him, populating the airy rooms of his imagination with supple beauties who danced, sang, and whispered honeyed words of love in his ears.

If, however, at that moment Pukah had looked down from

his cloud, he would have seen a sight to make him choke on his fig.

Sond stood with Khardan near the horses, pointing at them and speaking urgently to the Calif.

"This means war!" Khardan shouted. "Hush, *sidi*, keep your voice low."

The Calif, with a tremendous struggle, did as Sond requested, though his dark eyes glittered with anger. It was dawn. The two were walking near the outskirts of the camp. Khardan's gaze went again to the horses peacefully grazing near the bubbling stream.

"When do they plan their raid?"

"In a week's time, *sidi*. The first moonless night."

"You say that"—Khardan choked on the words—"my—my wife is behind this?"

"Yes, *sidi*. Alas, it grieves me to bring you such news—"

"The woman is a witch!" Khardan clenched his fist. "This ends it, Sond! Akhran himself could not expect me to live with such insult! Stealing my horses!"

If Sond had reported that the Hrana were plotting to steal his children, the fruit of his loins, Khardan could scarcely have been more outraged. In fact, he might have taken that news rather more calmly. As long as there were women and long desert nights, there would be children. But his horses!

According to legend, the magnificent horses of the Akar came by direct lineage from the steed of the God. The nomads likened their horses to the desert itself, the animals' sleek and glistening coats were as black as the desert night or as white as the silver of the shining stars. Their long sweeping tails and manes flowed like the wind across the dunes.

The horses gloried in battle. The smell of blood and the sound of clashing steel caused ears to prick, eyes to flash, and it was all a *spahi* could do to hold his mount back from charging in where the fray was the thickest. Countless stories were told of horses who continued to attack the enemy even after their own masters had fallen.

Each man in the tribe owned his own stock, whose lineage he could trace back proudly generation through generation. When times were hard, his horses were given first portion of the food and his family made due with what was left. The horses drank first at the oases. A woman whose magic could calm a restless steed was prized above all other women.

Besides raising and breeding these noble animals for their own use, the Akar kept a certain number apart each year to sell to the Sultan in the city of Kich. The sale purchased necessities such as coal and firewood, which were not to be found in the desert; staples such as rice and flour; and luxuries such as coffee, honey, and tobacco. These last were small pleasures, but they made the harsh life of the nomad bearable. In addition, the *souks* of Kich yielded the jewelry so much beloved by the women; the swords, daggers, and scimitars valued by the men; and silks and cottons for the clothing of both.

The Akar's yearly trip to Kich was a momentous event, forming the subject of conversation of the *spahis* for a year after—either recalling fondly the good times they'd had or looking forward to the good times expected. Parting with the horses was the hardest task, and it was not unusual to see some fierce warrior who had literally waded in blood weep unashamedly as he bid good-bye to a beloved animal.

By stealing the horses the Hrana stole the life, the soul, the heart of the Akar. As Sond knew when he suggested it, this was the one crime the Hrana could commit that would cause the Calif to break the commandment of the God.

Sheykh Jaafar could, of course, have argued that—by stealing sheep—the Akar threatened the survival of the Hrana. Sheep provided the wool the Hrana used for their clothing, the meat they ate, the money that bought both necessities and luxuries. So Jaafar might have argued, but he would have argued in vain. Just as each God saw only his own facet of the Jewel of Sul, So Sheykh Majiid and Sheykh Jaafar each saw the light shining on his own Truth. All else around them was darkness.

"What are your orders, Master? Do we attack the sheep herders immediately?"

Khardan ruminated, his hand stroking his black beard thoughtfully.

"No. They would claim themselves innocent, protesting to Akhran that we had attacked them without cause. We would be the ones facing the wrath of the God instead of those foul bleaters. We must catch them in the act, then we can proclaim to the heavens that it is *we* who have been wronged. I can rid myself of this accursed woman. We can leave this accursed place. "

"Your plan is excellent, *sidi*. I myself will relay it to my master—"

"Tell no one, Sond!" Khardan ordered. "Especially not my father! He would be beside himself with fury and might, in his rage, accidentally reveal us to them. I will do what must be done."

"The Calif is wisdom itself."

"I will not forget this, Sond," returned Khardan, choking with emotion. "Your warning has saved us from a dread calamity and will free us at last from the stench of these shepherds. When *Hazrat* Akhran hears the tale of our betrayal, he shall also hear of your devotion to your people from my own lips, and if he chooses to free you of your servitude, no one will be pleased more than I."

Flushing, Sond averted his face from the Calif's eyes. "I beg you will not do that, *sidi*." he said in a low voice. "I—I am not worthy of such honor. Besides, it would devastate me to leave your father. . ."

"Nonsense!" said Khardan gruffly, clearing his throat. He clapped the djinn upon his broad back. "Majiid would miss you, not a doubt of it. You've served this family well, back to my great-great-great-grandfather and probably beyond that. But it is time you left the mortal realm and lived in peace above, with some charming djinniyeh to gladden your days and sweeten your nights, eh?"

Little did Khardan know that he was twisting the dagger in Sond's soul. Flinching with pain, the djinn concealed his anguish by prostrating himself upon his knees before the Calif. Khardan took this as a further touching sign of the djinn's devotion and came near weeping as he returned to his tent.

Long after the Calif had gone, Sond remained crouching on his knees in the desert sand, beating his clenched fists on the windswept rock, striking at it until his immortal flesh bled.

Sond had betrayed not only his people, he had betrayed his God. Akhran the Wanderer was not noted for his mercy; his punishments were swift, harsh, and sudden. There was not a doubt in Sond's mind but that the God would discover his djinn's treachery. True, Sond might plead that he'd done what he had done for the sake of his beloved. But what was the life of one djinniyeh compared to the grand schemes of heaven?

Sond had considered going to Akhran and telling the God that one of his immortals had been taken captive, but the djinn had rejected the idea instantly. The God would be angry, but Akhran's anger would be directed at Quar. The Wandering God would never submit to Quar's demands for Nedjma's safe return nor would he allow Sond to do so either. In his rage Akhran might actually commit some rash act that would cause Sond to lose Nedjma forever.

Reminding himself of this, Sond grew calmer. If anyone was going to save Nedjma, it would have to be him and him alone.

"And if I can do that, I will cheerfully submit to any punishment you mete out to me, O Holy One," Sond vowed fervently, raising his eyes to heaven.

His peace restored, convinced that what he was doing was right, the djinn composed himself and prepared to begin his day's service. On his way to Majiid's tent, Sond passed by the Tel. The djinn cast a glance at the Rose of the Prophet. The cacti looked worse than ever. They seemed dying of thirst; the green fleshy stems had turned a brown and sickly color. Their spines were beginning to falloff.

Well, it will be watered soon, Sond thought grimly. Watered with blood.

CHAPTER 9

Khardan met secretly with certain of his men, apprising them of the proposed raid by the Hrana and telling them of his plan to thwart it. The Calif's anger was echoed by his *spahis* when they heard of this outrage. It was well that Khardan was present to calm them, or they might have torn down the tents over the Hrana's heads then and there.

Zohra met secretly with her people as well. At first the men of the Hrana had been reluctant to meet with a woman, especially a woman whom they viewed as the enemy. Zohra felt this and it hurt her. Facing the men of the Hrana, many of whom were half brothers, cousins, nephews, she saw their dark faces and suspicious eyes, and flushing deeply in shame, she thought how close she had come to submitting herself to the arrogant Calif, to becoming truly the enemy of her people.

Thank Akhran, that had not happened. Her eyes had been opened.

In a low, passionate voice, she recited the sufferings of her tribesmen at the hands of the Akar. She reminded the men of what they already knew—that lambing season was near: a time when the flocks were most vulnerable to attack by predators. She repeated, word for word, her request for horses and her husband's scathing denial. Then she presented her plan to gain the animals.

The men listened, suspicion losing itself in anger at her eloquent and crafty reminder of their woes, anger deepening to rage at hearing Khardan's insults, rage changing to unbridled enthusiasm over Zohra's proposal. Finally they would have their revenge upon the Akar and a sweet revenge it would be!

A semblance of peace settled over the Tel, both tribes having been instructed by their leaders to commit no rash act that might draw undue attention to themselves. Each settled down to wait out the week, but never had time passed so slowly. Night after night, eyes impatiently watched the moon wane, pouring its pale light down upon the desert, sucking out the colors of all objects. Many noticed that the Rose of the Prophet, curling in upon itself like a dying spider, looked particularly ugly in the moonlight. The withered cacti now gave off a peculiar odor—the smell of rotting flesh.

An impatient people, accustomed to thinking and reacting instantly, the waiting and the need for secrecy was sheer torture. The air around the oasis crackled with undischarged lightning. Both Sheykhs knew a storm was brewing. Jaafar became so nervous he couldn't eat. Majiid demanded of his son outright to know what was going on, but he was only told grimly that everything was under control and that he would be alerted when the time came.

Foreseeing bloodshed, Majiid grinned and sharpened his sword.

The two djinn, Fedj and Sond, were each secretly set by their masters to spy upon the other and did so with such alacrity that they were always to be seen, skulking about the camp, glaring at each other and adding to the overall tension. Thinking he knew what was going on, Pukah enjoyed the game immensely, meanwhile wondering when Sond planned to bring down the wrath of Akhran on the two tribes. Usti, preening himself on his plan, now lived a life of luxury. His brazier stood in an honored place in his mistress's tent. She no longer commanded him to perform menial tasks, never tossed him out the tent, and did not once interrupt his dinner.

The relationship between Zohra and Khardan remained unchanged—at least outwardly. As before, neither spoke when their paths accidentally crossed. Their gazes met, locked briefly, then parted, though it took every ounce of self-control Khardan possessed not to gouge out the black eyes that flashed with secret, triumphant scorn whenever they looked at him. He wondered he might well go mad before the week ended.

And then, halfway through the interminable seven days, Pukah brought his master certain information that gave Khardan the opportunity to vent some of his mounting rage. He dared not openly attack his wife; that would give everything away. But he could at least slide a thorn or two into her smug flesh.

Zohra had just returned from her early-morning ride and was in her tent, cleansing her body of sweat and grime and smoothing perfumed oils on her skin, when Khardan suddenly and without warning lifted the tent flap and entered.

"Greetings, wife," he said grimly.

Whirling in alarm, her long black hair flicking over her bare back like a scourge, Zohra caught up a woolen robe and clutched it around her naked body. She glared at her husband with flaming eyes, too furious to speak.

Khardan at first said nothing either. His well-planned speech had been on his lips, but the glimpse of Zohra's lithe figure drove the words from his head.

He stared at the dusky cheeks flushed a deep rose, the tendrils of black hair that swept across her face, the white shoulders visible above the robes Zohra held to her breast. The fragrance of jasmine clung to her, the oil on her body glistening in the sunlight filtering through the tent. One quick grab of that robe with his hand. . .

Abruptly, angrily, Khardan averted his gaze, refusing to let her see his momentary weakness. Why did this woman—of all the women he knew—affect him this way, turning his blood to water? He attempted to salvage his dignity.

"Are you some Pasha's concubine that you appear in such a state in the middle of the day? Clothe yourself, woman!"

The blood of shame and outrage pounded in Zohra's ears and dimmed her vision with a red tide, blotting out Khardan's momentary look of admiration. She saw only that he turned his head from her; obviously in revulsion and disgust. Quivering in fury and hurt pride, she remained standing where she was, her nakedness covered only by the dusty robe she held pressed against her chest.

"Say what you have to say and be gone!" Her voice was low and husky, thick with what in another might have been the desire of love but in her was only the desire to kill this man—of all the men she knew—who continually caught her in some moment of weakness.

Khardan cleared his throat of a sudden huskiness himself and began his prepared speech. "I understand that you have been to my mother to learn the charm that calms horses."

"What if I have? It is no business of yours. Such matters of magic are between women, not meant for men."

"I was only wondering why you are taking this sudden interest in womanly things, wife," Khardan said smoothly, his anger returning to save him as he recalled his wife's scheming. He knew well why Zohra was suddenly so interested in acquiring this magical skill and it pleased him to toy with her.

Zohra heard the odd timbre in his voice, and for a moment her heart quailed. Could he have discovered? . . . No, it was impossible! Every man she had chosen was loyal and trustworthy. Above all, their cause to hate Khardan and his tribe was as great as hers. They would let their tongues be ripped from their mouths before they would reveal the secret.

But she had, unknowingly, revealed herself, Khardan, watching her closely, saw the cheeks swept by a sudden pallor, saw the bright eyes grow dark with fear. Smiling to himself, he added mockingly, with a glance at Zohra's bed, "Perhaps you are interested in other womanly pursuits as well? Maybe this is why you are attempting to entice me with your body?"

"Hah! You flatter yourself!" Zohra laughed contemptuously, fear banished by rage. "I prefer my horse between my legs!"

Her words struck home with the force of a knife. Khardan stared at her in disbelief. No woman he had ever known would dare say such a thing. "By Sul! I could kill you for that insult and not even your father would blame me!"

"Go ahead! Kill me! Killing women, stealing sheep! Pah! Is it not the way of the cowardly Akar?"

Khardan, his blood burning with rage—among other things—sprang forward and caught hold of his wife, grasping her bare arms. His painful grip brought tears to Zohra's eyes, but she did not flinch or struggle. She kept the robe clutched over her body, her fingers curled about the fabric in a deathlike grip. Gazing at Khardan without fear, Zohra's lips curled in disdain.

"Coward!" she said again, and it seemed, from the tilt of her head, so near his, and the slight movement of her tongue across her lips, that she dared him to kiss her.

Furious with himself and the wild thoughts that filled his mind, Khardan flung Zohra away from him. Tossing her backward, he sent her sprawling awkwardly among her perfume bottles and *henna* jars. "Thank *Hazrat* Akhran for your life, madam!" Turning on his heel, he stalked from the tent.

"I won't thank him!" Zohra screamed after the vanished form of her husband. "I would rather die than be married to you, you—you—"

Her rage strangled her. Choking, she flung herself upon her bed, weeping passionately, still seeing, in her husband's eyes, that look of revulsion and disgust...knowing deep within herself that she had offered and been rejected.

Khardan, trembling with anger, stalked through the camp. In his mind he pictured with pleasure the humiliation he would inflict upon this woman. He would drag her before her father, proclaim her a witch, see her cast from her tribe in shame...

And all the time he could smell, lingering upon the skin of his hands, the teasing, tantalizing fragrance of jasmine.

CHAPTER 10

i t was as if Akhran himself extended his blessing upon the Hrana. The day of the raid dawned hot and breathless. During the morning a mass of clouds flowed down from the hills to the west, bringing a damp wind and sporadic, spitting drops of rain that evaporated before striking the hot ground. With the coming of afternoon the rains ceased, though the clouds remained. By night the very air itself seemed to grow thick and heavy. Lightning flickered on the horizon and the temperature plummeted. The *batir* donned curly-haired sheepskin coats over their tunics to protect themselves from the chill of the long ride back to their homes, their heads were covered with black cloth, and they drew the black face cloths over their mouths.

All were well-armed with sword and dagger. Their eyes, barely seen above the face cloths, glinted hard and cold as the steel they carried. Each knew that, if caught, it would be a fight to the death. Each was willing—eager—to take that risk. At last they were striking back at their enemy, hitting him in the heart.

"And I say you should not go, sister!" The whispered voice hissed through the darkness. "It is too dangerous."

"And I say I will go or none of you will stir a step from this place."

"You are a woman, it is not seemly."

"Yes, I am a woman. And which of you men will perform the magic to keep the beasts quiet until we get them away from camp? You, Sayah? You, Abdullah? Hah!"

Wrapping the black mask around her face, Zohra turned away, obviously considering the argument ended. The young men, huddled together in a stand of the tall, tasseled grass growing about the water of the oasis, shook their heads. But none of them continued the argument.

Zohra's magic would undoubtedly be essential to them in handling the horses, particularly since few of these men had ever ridden. Most had spent the week covertly observing the *spahis:* watching to see how they mounted the beasts, listening for what words were used to command them, taking note of how often the animals were fed and watered, what they ate, and so forth. The only question that remained unanswered for the Hrana was how the horses would react to strangers. This was where Zohra's magic could provide help, that and her knowledge of the beasts. They knew her presence was valuable, but—if given a choice—most of the Hrana would sooner have gone forth into the desert with a pouch full of snakes as with the unpredictable, hotheaded daughter of their Sheykh.

"Very well, you can come," came Sayah's grudging whisper. "Are all ready?"

Zohra's half brother, a few months her junior and still unmarried, Sayah had been the Hrana's choice to lead the raid. Cool and calculating, the exact opposite of his impulsive sister, Sayah was courageous as well, having once fought off a starving wolf with his bare hands. Like the other Hrana, he had also been forced to stand and watch in helpless fury as Majiid's raiders swept down on their swift horses and stole the choicest of his flock. Sayah had a few private plans of his own in regard to the horses they were about to acquire; plans he thought best not to mention to his sister, since all of them ended in killing her husband.

Receiving grim, eager replies to his question, Sayah nodded in satisfaction. At his signal the band of thieves crept through the tall grass toward the place where the horses were tethered for the night. Behind them the camp slumbered in a silence that must have appeared unnatural had they stopped to consider it. The night was too still, too calm. No dog barked. No man laughed. No child cried. None of the *batir* noticed, however, or—if they did—they passed it off as the oppression of the coming storm.

The rain had ceased, but its smell was in the breathless, heavy air. The night was darker than any could believe possible; the raiders could not even see each other as they padded soft-footed over the ground.

"Truly Akhran is with us!" murmured Zohra to her brother.

"You are right, my son," growled Majiid. "The coming of this strange storm is proof that *Hazrat* Akhran is helping us protect our own!"

"*Shh*, Father. Keep still," hissed Khardan.

His hand reached out to stroke the neck of his trembling horse. The creature shifted restlessly but remained silent, nervous and excited, aroused by the presence hiding in their midst, sensing the tension of the coming battle. Any experienced horseman approaching the herd would have noted the restless pawing and head-shaking and been on his guard. Khardan was counting upon the fact that Zohra and her *batir* were too inexperienced in the ways of horses to realize something was amiss.

Standing beside his father, surrounded by the other Akar—each man armed not only with steel but with an oil-coated torch—Khardan could feel Majiid's tall, muscular frame quivering with suppressed anger and bloodlust. Khardan had broken the news of the raid to his father only moments before going out to catch the thieves. As his son had foreseen, Majiid flew into such a rage that Sond was forced to hold him by the elbows or the Sheykh would have sped through the camp like an 'efreet and throttled Jaafar on the spot. After much difficulty, Sond and Khardan forced the old man to listen to their plan and he finally accepted it, with the understanding that he alone be allowed to skewer Jaafar.

As to Zohra, Majiid pronounced that she was a witch and should be dealt with summarily, suggesting several fitting punishments, the most merciful of which was having her stoned to death.

Khardan felt his father's hand close over his. It was the silent signal, being passed from man to man, that the scouts had detected the presence of the *batir*. Shaking with eagerness and the excitement of battle, Khardan reached out and squeezed the hand of the man crouched near him, then he readied the flint he would strike to light the torch.

Khardan held his breath, straining to hear the soft swish of feet upon the sandy rock floor. Then his muscles tensed. He had not heard, but he had smelled something.

Jasmine.

Swiftly striking the flint, he shoved it close to the brand. The oil burst into flame. Majiid, wielding his flaming torch, let out a fearful yell and leaped onto the back of his warhorse. Frightened by the sudden fire, the animal reared back, lashing out with its hooves. Scrambling for his own horse, Khardan barely escaped being bashed in the head, and from the sounds of a groan and a dull thud, one of the *batir* wasn't so lucky.

At their Sheykh's signal the rest of the Akar lit their torches and vaulted onto the backs of their horses, their sabers flashing in the firelight. The Hrana, on foot and completely at the mercy of the horsemen, drew their own weapons, striking out at their enemy in bitter anger and disappointment at their failure.

The light and noise drew the attention of the camp, most of whose people had been lying in wait, listening. The djinn Fedj appeared in their midst with a bang, only to be confronted coolly by Sond.

"What are you doing to my people?" Jaafar shrieked, running from the tent of one of his wives, his white nightclothes flapping around his bare ankles.

"I'll tell you what I'm doing! I'm going to roast you over a slow fire, you fornicator of sheep!" Majiid shouted, literally foaming at the mouth. Kicking his excited horse in the flanks, Majiid charged straight for Jaafar, swinging his saber in a blow that would have set the Sheykh to tending the sheep of Akhran had it connected. Due to his own failing eyesight and the flaring torches, Majiid miscalculated, his blade whistled harmlessly over Jaafar's head.

Wheeling his horse, Majiid galloped back for another charge. "You've set your witch-daughter and her demons to stealing my horses!"

"Taste your own poison!" Jaafar cried.

With unexpected nimbleness the wiry old man ducked Majiid's vicious slash. Grabbing the Sheykh's leg as the horse galloped by, Jaafar pulled Majiid from the saddle. The two went over in a tumble, rolling about on the desert floor, fists flailing, seeming in dire peril of being trampled by the wildly excited horses.

Khardan, after the first signal, kept himself clear of the fight. Charging through the crowd, his torch held high, his eyes went from one black-robed figure to another, impatiently lashing out at anyone who got in his way. At last he found the one for whom he had been searching. Slimmer than the rest, moving with an unmistakable grace, this figure—dagger in hand—was grimly facing an opponent whose saber must within seconds slice her in two.

"Mine!" shouted the Calif, urging his horse forward at a gallop. Neatly cutting between the attacker and his blackrobed victim, Khardan struck the man's arm down with the flat of his own blade. Leaning over, he caught hold of Zohra around the waist and hoisted her—headfirst, kicking and screaming—up and over his saddle.

"Death will not rob me of my chance to see you humbled, wife!" cried Khardan, grinning.

"Oh, won't he?" Zohra muttered viciously. Dangling head down, fighting to free herself, she raised her dagger.

Khardan saw the blade flash and grappled for it. His horse plunged beneath them, trying to keep its footing.

"Damn you!" the Calif swore, a searing pain tearing through his leg. He could not reach the knife, but a mass of thick, black hair came into his hands. Gripping it firmly, Khardan yanked Zohra's head back. Shrieking in pain, Zohra dropped her knife; twisting, she managed to sink her teeth into Khardan's arm.

Horses surged around them. Swords flared in the torchlight. Flaming brands smashed down on heads; riders were dragged from their steeds; steel blades clashed in the night. Standing on the outskirts of the battle, women wailed and pleaded, their children crying out in fear. Their cries went unheard. Pandemonium reigned, reason was lost in hatred, there was only anger and the lust to kill.

Sond and Fedj fought with gigantic scimitars, stabbing each other's immortal flesh a hundred times over. Majiid was bashing Jaafar's head into the ground. Sayah clashed with Khardan's brother Achmed, neither giving ground nor gaining any, each recognizing the makings of a valiant warrior in his opponent.

In the confusion no one heard the tinkling of camel bells. Only when a brilliant flash of lightning illuminated a *mehariste* did the battling tribes realize that a stranger was in their midst.

At the sight the women hastily grabbed up children and ran for the shelter of their tents. The ringing of steel and the grunts and shouts of the combatants slowly died away as, one by one, the Hrana and the Akar looked around dazedly to see what was happening.

The flames of the torches, flickering in the rising wind of the breaking storm, revealed a short, squat figure swathed in rich fabric seated upon one of the swift racing camels whose worth was known the desert over. The light glinted off the silver and turquoise of a very fine saddle, glistened in the crimson-red silken tassels that hung about the camel's knees, and gleamed brightly in the golden, jewel-studded fringed headdress the animal wore on its head.

"*Salaam aleikum*, my friends!" called out a voice. "It is I, Zeid al Saban, and I have been sent by *Hazrat* Akhran to see what I could not believe—the two of you, bitter enemies, now joined by marriage and living together in peace. The sight of such brotherhood as I witness here at this moment brings tears to my eyes."

Sheykh Zeid raised his hands to heaven. "Praise be to Akhran! It is a miracle!"

CHAPTER 11

"Praise be to Akhran," muttered Majiid, wiping blood from his mouth.

"Praise be to Akhran," echoed Jaafar glumly, spitting out a tooth.

"Praise be to Pukah!" cried the irreverent djinn, springing up out of the sand in front of the camel. "This is all *my* doing!"

No one paid any attention to him. Zeid's eyes were on the heavens. Majiid's and Jaafar's eyes were on each other. As much as each Sheykh hated the other, each distrusted Zeid more. Leader of a large tribe of nomads that lived in the southern region of the Pagrah desert, the short, squat figure seated elegantly on the *mehari* was wealthy, shrewd, and calculating. Although the desert was his home, his camel trading took Sheykh Zeid to all the major cities of Tara-kan. He was cosmopolitan, wise in the ways of the world and its politics, and his people outnumbered the separate tribes of Jaafar and Majiid two to one.

Mounted on their swift *meharis*, the Aran were fierce and deadly fighters. There had been rumors of late that Zeid—bored with his holdings in the south—had been thinking of extending his wealth by threatening the tribes to the north, force them to acknowledge him as *suzerain*—overlord—and pay him tribute. This was in the minds of both Majiid and Jaafar, and it passed, unspoken, between them as they exchanged grim glances. Two bitter enemies suddenly became reluctant allies.

Elbowing Pukah out of the way, the Sheykhs hastened to pay their respects to their guest, offering him the hospitality of their tents. Behind them their tribes watched warily, weapons in hand, waiting for some sign from their leaders.

Zeid received the Sheykhs with all ease and politeness. Although alone in the midst of those he knew to be his enemies, the Sheykh of the south was not worried. Even if his intentions toward them had been hostile and he had made those intentions known, Zeid's rank as guest made him inviolate. By ancient tradition the guest could remain three days with his host, who must—during that time—show him all hospitality, pledging his life and the lives of his tribe to protect the guest from any enemies. At the end of three days the host must further provide safe escort to his guest the distance of one day's journeying.

"*Adar-ya-yan!*" Zeid ordered, tapping the camel with a slender stick. The beast sank to its knees—first front and then rear—allowing the Sheykh to descend from his magnificent saddle with dignity.

"*Bilhana,* wishing you joy, cousin!" said Majiid loudly, opening his broad arms wide in a gesture of welcome.

"*Bilshifa,* wishing you health, my dear cousin!" said Jaafar, rather more loudly, opening his arms even wider.

Embracing Zeid in turn, the Sheykhs kissed him on both cheeks with the ritual gesture that formally sealed the guest covenant. Then they studied the camel with appreciative eyes, all the while praising the saddle and its fine workmanship. It would never do to praise the camel, for such praise of a living thing invites the evil eye of envy, which was well-known to cause the object thus stricken to sicken and die.

Zeid, in his turn, glanced about in search of something of his hosts' to praise. Seeing, however, one of the Sheykhs clad only in his nightrobes and the other battered and bloodstained, Zeid was somewhat at a loss. He was also intensely curious to find out what was going on. The Sheykh fell back upon an old resource, knowing the surest way to a father's heart.

"Your eldest son, Majiid. What is the young man's name—Khardan? Yes, Khardan. I have heard many tales of his courage and daring in battle. Might I request the honor of his introduction?"

"Certainly, certainly." Bowing effusively, Majiid darted a glance about for his son, hoping desperately that Khardan wasn't covered to the elbows with his enemy's blood.

"Khardan!" the Sheykh's voice boomed into the night. As the sight of the *mehariste* had put an end to the fight between the fathers, so it put an end to the battle between husband and wife.

"Zeid!" hissed Khardan, hastily pulling the struggling Zohra into a sitting position across the front of this horse. "Stop it!" he said, shaking her and forcing her to look into the ring of torch-light.

Zohra peered out through her disheveled mass of black hair and recognized the camel rider and the danger at the same time. Hastily she shrank back out of the light, hiding her face in her husband's robes. As Sheykh's daughter, Zohra had long been involved in political discussions. If Zeid saw her here, sporting among the men, it would forever lower both her father and her husband in the powerful Sheykh's estimation, giving him a distinct advantage over them in any type of bargaining or negotiation. She must leave quickly, without letting anyone see her.

Swallowing her bitter anger and disappointment, Zohra hurriedly began to wind the men's robes she wore as closely around her as possible. Understanding her intent, Khardan swiftly and silently edged his horse backward into the shadows.

Zohra's hands shook and she became entangled in the garments. Khardan reached out his hand to help her, but Zohra—acutely aware of the firm body pressed by necessity against hers (at least one could assume it was by necessity since both were still on horseback)—angrily jerked away from him.

"Don't touch me!" she ordered sullenly.

"Khardan!" Majiid's voice echoed over the field. "Coming, my father!" Khardan called. "Hurry!" he whispered urgently to his wife.

Refusing to look at him, Zohra grabbed her long hair and twisting it into a coil, tucked it beneath the folds of the black robe. She was preparing to slip down off the horse when Khardan detained her, sliding a firm arm around her waist. Zohra's black eyes flared dangerously in the flickering torchlight, her lips parted in a silent snarl.

Coolly ignoring her rage, Khardan took off his own head-cloth and tossed it over his wife's black hair.

"That beautiful face of yours would never be taken for a man's. Keep it covered."

Staring at him, Zohra's black eyes widened in astonishment.

"Khardan!" Majiid's voice held a note of impatience. Wrapping the face cloth over her mouth and nose, Zohra slid off the back of the horse.

"Wife," Khardan's voice called out softly but sternly. Zohra glanced up at him. He gestured to the wound in his leg that was bleeding profusely. "I must make a good impression," he said in low tones.

Understanding his meaning, the black eyes—all that were visible of the face hidden by the mask—glared at him in sudden anger.

Khardan, smiling, shrugged his shoulders.

Fumbling for a pouch beneath her robes, Zohra withdrew a green stone streaked with red. Laying it against the knife wound, she bitterly repeated the magic charm that would cause the flesh to close, the blood of the wound to purify. This done, she cast her husband one last look, sharper than a tiger's tooth, and melted away into the shadows of the night.

Khardan, grinning widely, kicked his horse's flanks and galloped up to greet his father's guest. Arriving before the Sheykhs, the Calif caused his horse to go down on its knees, both animal and the man astride it bowing in respect and displaying a nice bit of horsemanship at the same time.

"Ah, excellent, young man, excellent!" Zeid clapped his hands together in true delight.

Jumping off his horse, Khardan was formally introduced to the Sheykh by his father. The usual pleasantries were exchanged.

"And I hear,"—Zeid nodded at Pukah, who, blissfully ignorant of the tension in the air, had been beaming upon the assembled company as though he had created them all with his own hands—"that you are newly married and to a beautiful wife—daughter of our cousin."

The Sheykh bowed to Jaafar, who bowed nervously in return, wondering where his unruly daughter was.

"Why are you out here instead of languishing in the arms of love?" Zeid asked casually.

Jaafar shot a swift glance at Majiid, who was eyeing his son worriedly beneath frowning brows. But Khardan, with an easy laugh, made a sweeping gesture with his hand. "Why, Sheykh Zeid, you have come in time to witness the *fantasia* being held in honor of my wedding."

"*Fantasia?*" repeated Zeid in amazement. "This is what you consider a game, is it?"

His eyes went to the men lying groaning on the ground, to their attackers, standing above them, sabers running red with blood. It was the middle of the night. An unusual time for a contest. The Sheykh's eyes, narrow and shrewd, returned to Khardan, studying the young man intently.

The moment Zeid's djinn, Raja, had come to him with news that Majiid and Jaafar had combined forces, Zeid determined to see for himself if this disquieting news was true. The Sheykh had at first discounted it. Zeid did not believe that even Akhran could draw the poison from the bad blood that ran between the two tribes. Traveling north on his swift camel, Zeid had seen, from a distance, the altercation taking place beneath the Tel and he had smiled, his belief confirmed.

"You are mistaken, Raja," he told his djinn, who was concealed in a golden jewel box in one of the Sheykh's *khurjin*. "They have met here to fight, and it seems that we are going to be fortunate enough to witness a good battle."

It struck him as odd, however, that the two tribes should have chosen this remote location—far from their accustomed dwelling places. On riding closer, Zeid was further disconcerted to see the tents of both tribes pitched around the Tel, with the outer signs of having been here for some length of time.

"It appears you may be right, after all, Raja," Zeid had muttered out of the corner of his mouth as he drove his camel forward.

"You play rough, young man," the Sheykh said now in awe, staring at the large patch of blood on the Calif's trousers and the purpling marks of teeth in his hand.

"Boys will be boys, you know, my friend," Majiid said with a deprecating chuckle.

Putting an arm around the Sheykh's shoulder, Majiid turned Zeid away from the sight of churned-up, bloody ground, using slightly more force than politeness dictated.

"Fun is over, young men!" Jaafar shouted. His back to Zeid, he glared sternly at the combatants, indicating by hand gestures that they were to clear the area as rapidly as possible. "Help each other up. That's good men!" he continued in a cheerful, hollow voice.

Reluctantly—eyes on their Sheykhs—the Akar stretched out their hands to the Hrana, assisting those they had been attempting to kill a moment before.

"See if anyone's dead!" Jaafar said in an undertone to Fedj.

"Dead?" Zeid, coming to a halt, twisted out of Majiid's extremely friendly grip.

"Dead! Ha! Ha!" Majiid laughed loudly, attempting to get hold of Zeid once more.

"Ha! Ha! Dead! My father-in-law is such a jokester." Putting his arm around Jaafar, Khardan gave the old man a hug that nearly strangled him. "Did you hear that, men? Dead!"

Scattered laughter rippled through the tribesmen as they hurriedly doused their torches while surreptitiously bending down to check for pulses in the necks of those few who were lying ominously still and quiet on the ground.

"Come, Zeid, you must be hungry after that long ride. Allow me to offer you food and drink. Sond! Sond!"

The djinn appeared, looking grim, dazed, and wild-eyed. If Majiid noticed, he put it down to the interrupted fight and immediately forgot it in the press of other troubles. "Sond, you and Fedj, the djinn of my dear friend Jaafar, go along ahead of us and prepare a sumptuous feast for our guest."

Sond bowed unsteadily, bringing shaking hands to his head, a sickly smile on his lips. "I obey, *sidi*," he said, and vanished.

Majiid heard stifled groans coming from behind him and hurried the Sheykh along until Zeid was practically tripping over his shoes.

"Will your son be joining us?" Zeid asked, turning, attempting once more to see what was going on.

Glaring at Khardan above Zeid's head, Majiid indicated with several urgent nods that the Calif was to remain on the field and keep the fight from breaking out again.

"If you will forgive me, Sheykh Zeid," Khardan said with a bow, "I will remain behind to take care of this remarkable camel of yours and to make certain everyone finds his tent. Some," —he glanced at a limp Hrana being dragged through the sand by two Akar—"have been celebrating overmuch, I'm afraid."

"Yes," said Zeid, thinking he saw a trail of blood in the sand but unable, because of Majiid's large body blocking his sight, to get a closer glimpse.

"My dear cousin Jaafar will join us, however. Won't you, my dear cousin?" Majiid said, his voice grating.

Jaafar wrenched his gaze from the body being hastily dragged off into the desert and managed to mutter something polite. He fell into step beside them.

"But surely he is not coming to eat dressed in his night-clothes?" Zeid said, glancing at Jaafar in considerable perplexity.

Gazing down at himself, having completely forgotten his state of undress, Jaafar flushed in embarrassment and hurried off to his tents to change, thankful for the chance to regain his composure. But as he went, he heard Majiid loudly telling their guest, "New wife. Wanted to see the fun but didn't want to waste time getting to bed afterward."

Groaning, Jaafar clutched his aching head. "Cursed! Cursed!" he moaned as he darted into his tent and hastily pulled out his best robes.

Khardan, standing in the midst of the horses, glaring sternly about to see that his orders were being carried out, heard a step behind him and caught the flash of steel out of the corner of his eye.

"This *fantasia* isn't over, Akar!" came a voice in his ear. Whirling, Khardan struck his attacker a sharp blow to the stomach with his elbow, hearing the breath leave the man's body with a satisfying whoosh. A well-aimed right to the chin persuaded Sayah that the fun, for him, had ended.

Khardan assisted the groggy young man to his tent and pitched him unceremoniously inside, then hastened back to attend to the dead. Planning to bundle the bodies into hurriedly dug graves, he discovered to his relief that, though several were critically wounded, no one on either side had been killed. Seeing the wounded delivered safely into the care of their wives, hearing laughter and loud talk coming from the tent of his father, Khardan cast a glance at Zohra's tent. It was dark and silent.

Looking at the tooth marks on his hand, the Calif shook his head and smiled, then wearily turned his steps to his own tent and fell, exhausted, into bed.

Teetering on the edge of sleep, the Calif was vaguely conscious of Pukah's voice in his ear.

"This was all my doing, Master! All my doing!"

CHAPTER 12

The seventy-two hours of the guest period crept along with the slow, dragging steps of a lame and blind beggar. Following the storm, the Tel sweltered beneath a fiery sun that appeared determined to remind them that the unbearable heat of summer was not far off. The tribes themselves sweated in the heat of unresolved anger. They had the taste of blood in their mouths, yet were forbidden to reveal by the least sign, look, word, or deed that all were not the best of friends, the closest of brothers.

This unnatural friendship became such a strain that most of the tribesmen forbore to walk about camp, preferring to skulk about in their tents, plotting dark deeds when the guest period ended. Fortunately the heat of the day gave them the perfect excuse, although the Sheykhs found it difficult to explain why the camp was unnaturally silent and somber during the customary hours of socialization after dark.

Nothing was seen or heard of Zohra during the three days, much to the relief of her father and her husband. This was not unusual, since it was the custom of the tribes to keep their women hidden as much as possible during the visit of a stranger. There was one slight incident: a child, scampering past Zohra's tent, discovered a brass charcoal brazier lying in the sand outside of it. Picking it up to return it to its owner, the child noted with some wonder that the brazier was badly dented and appeared to have been smashed with a rock.

Dinner was the most trying period for everyone concerned. Always an elaborate affair—in honor of the guest a sheep was butchered each night—dinner demanded that Majiid and Jaafar not only exhibit every politeness to their guest but to each other as well. Majiid's forced smile made his face ache. Jaafar was so nervous that the food he ate sat in a lump in his stomach and he was up half the night with belly cramps.

Meanwhile, all feasted on roast mutton; *fatta,* a dish of eggs and carrots; *berchouks,* pellets of sweetened rice; and almond cakes; spread before them on the food carpets by the servants. No one talked during meals, this time being spent in enjoying the food and allowing the digestion to proceed uninterrupted. But after dinner, drinking sweet tea alternated with dark, bitter coffee, nibbling on dates and figs, or sharing the hubble-bubble pipe, the men conversed pleasantly, each keeping his tongue dull and his ears sharp—as the adage goes—hoping to say nothing that would give himself away, hoping to hear something that might be to his advantage.

The burden of conversation fell naturally upon the guest, who was expected to share news of the world with his hosts in exchange for their hospitality. Zeid felt safe in such discussions; the rapidly changing political situation in Tarakan provided him a perfect topic. His first news gave his hosts a shock, however.

"The Amir in Kich——" Zeid began.

"Amir?" Khardan appeared startled. "Since when is there an Amir in Kich?"

"My friends, haven't you heard?" Zeid reveled in the position of being the first to impart important information. "Kich has fallen to the Emperor of Tara-kan!"

"What has happened to the Sultan?" demanded Jaafar.

"Put to death along with his household by the Amir," answered Zeid grimly, "supposedly for refusing to worship Quar. Actually, I don't think the Sultan was offered the choice. He might have been perfectly content to worship Quar, but the Imam needed an example for the remainder of the populace. The Sultan, his wives, concubines, children, and eunuchs were dragged to the top of the cliffs above the city and hurled over the edge; their bodies left to feed the vultures and the jackals. The fortunate ones," he added, chewing a fig, "died in the fall. The less fortunate were rescued and what remained of them turned over to the torturers. Some, it was said, lived for days. As you might imagine, the town's population converted almost to a man; the grandees pooled their funds to build a new temple dedicated to Quar."

"I trust this will not affect our trading with them," said Majiid, frowning, smoke curling from his bearded lips.

"I don't see why it should," replied Khardan coolly, lounging back on the cushions and leisurely sipping his coffee. "In fact, it might just prove more favorable. I presume this Amir is anxious to extend the Emperor's holdings down into Bas. He will undoubtedly be needing horses for his troops."

"But will he buy them from a *kafir*, an unbeliever?" queried Jaafar smoothly, delighted at the opportunity to toss cold water on his enemy's fire while maintaining the guise of concerned friendship. "Perhaps he will throw *you* from the cliffs Majiid." Jaafar's unspoken words adding, *May I be there to witness it.*

Hearing that silent comment as clearly as the voiced, Majiid's beard bristled, his eyebrows coming together so alarmingly over his hawk nose that Khardan hurriedly intervened.

"Come, now. The Amir is, after all, a military man. Military men are practical, by and large, and certainly not accustomed to being led around by the nose by priests, no matter how powerful. If the Amir needs horses, he will buy ours and we will have the secret satisfaction of knowing that the horses of *Hazrat* Akhran will bear the followers of Quar into what we devoutly pray is disaster."

"The Amir, as you say, is a practical man," said Zeid cautiously, not wanting to contradict his host impolitely, yet, just as eager as Jaafar to thrust a verbal knife into the ribs of his enemies. "And he is an excellent commander, as you may judge by the fact that he defeated the Sultan's armies in a single battle. But do not underestimate the Imam. This priest is, so I have heard, a charismatic man of great personal beauty and intelligence. He is, as well, a zealot, who has dedicated himself body and soul to the service of Quar. It is rumored that he has great influence not only over the Amir, but—what is more important—over the Amir's head wife, as well. Her name is Yamina and she is reputedly a sorceress of great power."

"I trust you are not implying that my son will be in danger from the Amir's wife!" Majiid demanded forgetting himself.

"Oh, certainly not." Zeid made a graceful smoothing gesture with his chubby hand. "No more than he is in danger from his own wife."

Khardan choked, spilling his coffee. Majiid bit through the pipe stem, splitting it in two with his teeth, and Jaafar swallowed a date whole, nearly strangling himself. Zeid gazed around in perfect innocence, smoothing his beard with his jeweled hand.

Having been commanded by a glum and dour Sond to serve, Pukah hurriedly chose this juncture to pour more coffee. The conversation turned to safer topics, and a friendly argument over the relative merits of horses versus camels allowed the evening to end in harmony.

But before going to his bed that night, Zeid peeped from the guest dwelling, his shrewd eyes following Khardan to his tent—the Calif's tent, *not* the tent where his wife resided.

"Raja was right. It is a marriage of convenience, nothing more," Zeid muttered to himself. "So—I am resolved."

The end of the guest period came at last. The evening of the third day saw Zeid mounting his camel, intending to take advantage of the coolness of the night to make the desert crossing. Khardan offered to serve as escort, taking two of his younger brothers with him.

Zeid left with many protestations of friendship. "It pleases a pious man such as myself that you are carrying out the wishes of our God and living in harmony together. You may rest assured that I will be keeping my eyes on you, cousins. Imbued as you are with Akhran's blessing, you soon might grow as wealthy and powerful as myself."

Seeing Majiid and Jaafar exchanging grim glances, Zeid concealed his smile.

Leaving this barb to rankle in his hosts' flesh, the Sheykh rode off with a flourish, taking the opportunity to exhibit the great speed of his animal. The horses of his escorts galloped along behind.

Following the Sheykh's departure, Majiid saddled his warhorse and went for an hour's gallop in the desert to vent his pent-up rage. Jaafar took to his bed. Pukah, alone in his basket, was relaxing with a plate of sweetmeats when he was surprised to hear a familiar voice asking permission to enter his dwelling.

"Enter and welcome," said Pukah, rising to his feet, somewhat amazed to see Raja. "To what do I owe this great pleasure? Your master and mine are in no danger are they?"

"None, I assure you," Raja replied. Opening his hand, the djinn revealed a lovely little jewel box. "My master sends this to your master, with thanks for his timely 'warning.'"

"Warning?" Pukah's mouth dropped open. "My master gave

him no warning. What are you talking about? Are you certain this was intended for the Calif? Perhaps you are seeking Fedj or Sond—"

"No, no," said Raja smoothly, dropping the box into Pukah's limp hand. "It is obvious to Sheykh Zeid that these two tribes have joined together solely for the purpose of attacking him and that he was brought here in hopes that he would be intimidated."

Raja's bland, polite smile changed to a sneer. "Tell your master his plan to frighten Sheykh Zeid al Saban has not succeeded. My master goes now to organize his army, and when he returns, he will crush your tribes into the ground!" The djinn bowed. "Farewell, 'friend.'"

Raja disappeared in a clap of thunder that shook Pukah's basket and set the bowls rattling. The stunned young djinn stood staring at the dark cloud of smoke—all that could now be seen of Raja as he swirled away.

"Sul's blood!" murmured Pukah in despair. "What do I do now?"

CHAPTER 13

"ife, wake up!"

A touch on her shoulder roused Zohra from a fitful sleep. Quick as a striking snake, her hand darted to the dagger. Khardan was swifter. His own hand closed over her wrist.

"You have no need of that. I came to tell you that you are wanted in your father's house. We must talk about what has happened."

He was kneeling beside her bed. An oil lamp burned on the floor near him. Holding Zohra's wrist tightly until he felt, from the relaxing of her tense muscles, that she understood what he wanted of her, Khardan stared intently into his wife's flushed face, nearly hidden from view by masses of black hair. The usually fiery black eyes were misty with sleep, confusion, and—deep in their depths—fear. He could guess what she must be thinking. Disgrace, divorce. . . He smiled grimly.

"What time is it?" Pulling her arm away from Khardan's, Zohra drew the sheepskin blanket close about her body. "Why am I being summoned?"

"Two hours before dawn," Khardan replied tiredly, rubbing his eyes. Standing up, he turned his back upon her, ostensibly out of regard for her modesty, but really in an attempt to forget the softness of her face in sleep, the shadow of her long lashes upon her cheeks, the faint fragrance of jasmine. . .

"If you want to know why you are summoned, I suggest you dress yourself and come to your father's tent to find out. I have ridden all day and night without rest or food, and I have no energy to argue with you or force you to come if you do not choose. So, wife, you may do as you please."

Turning on his heel, he left her tent, allowing himself a moment's satisfaction in thinking of the turmoil that must be raging in those soft breasts beneath the sheepskin blanket.

If Khardan had truly known the extent of the agony this mysterious and ominous summons in the dark hours before dawn was causing his wife, he would have felt himself well repaid for the dagger thrust in his leg four nights previous. Once her husband was gone, Zohra shrank back into blankets that had suddenly grown cold and comfortless, her mind a storm of emotion that came near blinding her with its fury.

The three guest days had been difficult for everyone, but torture to Zohra. Accustomed to drowning serious thought in the rushing water of action, she rarely spent a moment in reflection or consideration of her acts. Her self-imposed confinement during the last three days had given her ample and unwelcome opportunity to think. She came to realize the enormity of her crime. Worse, to consider the possible outcome.

The family was an honored and sacred institution for on it rested the survival of the tribe. Divorce—or "repudiation"—was therefore considered a great evil and came about only following dire circumstances. A divorced woman might be taken back into her father's tent, but she was considered disgraced, her children had neither rank nor status in the tribe, and they generally lived worse than the indentured slaves who might—in time—expect to be free.

If the woman had been caught committing adultery, she might further be disfigured in some way—her nose slit, her face scarred—so that she should never tempt a man to sin again. A man caught violating another's wife was treated little better. He was driven from the tribe, his worldly possessions confiscated, his wives and children permitted to enter other families within the tribe or to return to their own parents with honor.

A woman could divorce a man if he failed to provide for her and her children properly or if he mistreated her. A man could divorce a woman if she refused to perform marital duties, just as a woman could divorce a man for the same reason. In all cases of family disputes the matter was taken to the Sheykh, who heard both sides of the story and then made a ruling to which there was no appeal.

Zohra had not only considered the possibility of divorce when she first began planning the wild scheme of stealing the horses, she had welcomed it, looking forward to regaining her precious freedom. Three days of considering what that freedom might cost her, however, had made it seem less and less appealing.

Biting her lip in frustration, Zohra huddled in her bed and considered what to do. She could refuse to go; let them come and drag her out of her tent! That would be humiliating, she realized quickly, and was probably just what Khardan hoped she would do. Far better to go and face him with dignity, she decided. After all, she had as much grounds to divorce him as he had to divorce her. Let him claim she refused to sleep with him. Everyone in the tribe knew he never came near her tent. After all, Zohra realized suddenly, there was the matter of the wedding sheet. If the truth were revealed that she was still a virgin, Khardan would be disgraced before everyone!

As for the incident with the horses, no harm had been done. Well, not much. Not as much as she would have liked! Her decision made, she rose from her bed. Leisurely washing, she dressed herself carefully in her finest clothes, brushed and arranged her long hair, and adorned herself with her favorite jewels. Then she relaxed. Let them wait, she decided. Let them all wait for her pleasure.

When Zohra finally made her way to her father's tent, the first faint rays of the rising sun had drenched the sand in rose pinks and purples. The camp was stirring already, most hurrying to finish their daily work before the intense heat of afternoon drove them to seek the cool shade of their tents. Ignoring the many curious and hostile glances cast in her direction, Zohra left the camp of the horsemen and entered the camp of her own people, where she was accorded almost the same chill reception. Smothering a small sigh, holding her chin rigid, she entered her father's tent.

When she chose, Zohra could make herself beautiful. Generally she did not choose to do so, preferring the freedom of men's clothing. This morning, however, out of a desire to further irritate these men by enhancing her femininity, she had taken extraordinary care with her appearance. She was dressed in a fine silk caftan of a deep rose-red color that became her dusky skin. A veil of the same rose color, trimmed in gold, covered the sleek black hair. Silver bracelets gleamed on her wrists and around her ankles. Her feet were bare—she had rouged the heels and toes with *henna*. Her black eyes were outlined with *kohl*, making them appear large and liquid. Her bearing was regal and proud, her face cool and impassive.

It was still dark enough inside the tent for oil lamps to be burning. Within sat—in grim silence—Sheykhs Majiid and Jaafar, the Calif, and their three djinn. Zohra's resolution wavered, the proud gaze faltered. Lowering her eyes, she did not notice the severe, stern expressions on the faces of the men and djinn change as she entered the tent. She did not see Khardan's face—pale with fatigue—soften in admiration. She did not see her father's perennial gloom lift for an instant or see Fedj nod to himself in satisfaction. She might have even seen—had she looked—Majiid's old eyes flash. But Zohra saw nothing except in her mind, and there they were all regarding her with scorn and contempt.

Zohra felt all her disdain seep from her like blood from a knife wound. Truly they considered her crime a heinous one. Some terrible punishment was to be meted out to her. A sudden weakness swept over her. She felt her legs give way and sank down upon a cushion near the entrance. The tent blurred in her vision. Fixing her gaze firmly on a point above the men's heads, she concentrated every fiber of her being on not giving them the satisfaction of seeing her cry. No matter what they did to her, she would face them with pride and dignity.

"Why have I been summoned to my father's tent?" she asked, her voice low.

The men looked to Khardan, who, as her husband, had the right to answer. He was forced to clear his throat before he could reply, but when he did, his voice was cool and smooth.

"Since you have chosen, wife, to meddle in the affairs of men, it has been decided that you be included in this discussion that affects the future and well-being of both Hrana and Akar. It is considered the responsibility of men to deal with matters of politics. Women should be protected from the troubles of this world. You elected to become involved, however, and therefore it is right and fitting that you be forced to accept responsibility for your actions and share in bearing the burden of their consequences."

Mentally bracing herself for whatever dreadful weapon they intended to hurl at her, Zohra heard Khardan without truly comprehending what he said. When he finished speaking, he regarded her intently, obviously awaiting some response. But his words made no sense. This was not what she had expected. Raising her gaze, she stared at him in perplexity.

"What are you saying, husband?"

Fatigue got the better of Khardan. Dropping the formality, he spoke bluntly. "I am saying, wife, that you behaved like a damned fool. Because of you, our people came near slaughtering each other. We were saved by the intervention of *Hazrat* Akhran, who sent our enemy to us to act as a mirror in which we might see ourselves reflected. Now that enemy has departed, having gained respect for us, giving us assurances of his friendship—"

"*Yech!*" A strangled sound came from Pukah.

Khardan, startled, glanced at his djinn in astonishment.

"What? Do you have something to say?"

"N-no, Master." Pukah shook his head miserably. "Then keep silent!" Khardan snapped.

"Yes, Master."

The djinn retreated back into the shadows of the tent.

Scowling at the interruption, Khardan resumed, now speaking to all those assembled.

"*Hazrat* Akhran is wise as always. This alliance of Akar and Hrana brought the light of newfound respect to the eyes of Zeid al Saban—eyes that once gazed on us with scorn. We can use that respect to bargain as equals with the camel breeder now, instead of coming to him as beggars." (Or thieves, the Calif might have added with more honesty, this being the traditional method by which the Akar acquired the few camels they owned.) "Zeid is a wary old fox, however. He will be watching us, as he warned, and if he sees the tiniest crack in the rock he will smash us with a hammer of steel. "

"*Yrrp!*" Pukah, huddled in the corner, covered his mouth with his hand.

Khardan glared at him.

"I—I'm not feeling well, Master. If you do not need me—"

"Leave! Leave!" said Khardan, waving his hand.

Pukah dwindled away in a wispy cloud of smoke, appearing as unwell as was possible for an immortal, and Khardan, heaving an exasperated sigh, paused to recall what he had been about to say.

It was slowly occurring to the dazed Zohra that this wild scheme of hers to steal the horses—far from angering her husband—had actually won his grudging respect.

Ah, well, she reflected, what could one expect of a thief? "Therefore I advise," Khardan was saying, "that we declare an end to the fighting between our two peoples. Further"—the Calif fixed his father with a piercing gaze—"I suggest that we trade the Hrana horses—"

"No!" shouted Majiid. The Sheykh clenched his fist. "I swear I will—"

"—Make no unwise or foolish oath until you have listened to what I propose," Khardan said firmly.

Majiid, glaring fiercely, snapped his mouth shut, and his son continued.

"We trade the Hrana horses in return for a monthly payment of twenty sheep. The Hrana will use the horses for crossing the desert to reach their flocks in the hills. No shepherding." The Calif transferred his piercing stare to Jaafar. "Would that be agreed?"

"Yes! Yes! I assure you!" Jaafar stammered, regarding Khardan with amazement mingled with profound relief.

Ever since the night of the raid the Sheykh had resigned himself to taking his daughter back into his tent and being miserable for the rest of his existence. Now, suddenly, instead of a wayward daughter, he was being given horses! "Praise be to Akhran," the Sheykh added humbly.

By contrast, Majiid's face flamed red, his eyes bulged with anger. He glared at his son with a look that had sent many another man scurrying away in terror. Khardan returned the glare with a calm, steady, unwavering gaze, his bearded jaw firm and unyielding.

Watching from beneath lowered eyelids, Zohra felt a sudden warmth of admiration for her husband. Alarmed and frightened by this unexpected feeling, she told herself she was merely exulting in her victory over him.

"No. . . sheep. . . herding!" The words burst out of Majiid's throat, hissing through his teeth.

"No, no!" Jaafar promised.

Majiid went through a final, agonized internal struggle; saliva bubbled on his lips as though he were being poisoned."Bah!" he said, rising to his feet. "So be it!"

Ripping aside the tent flap, Majiid started to leave.

"I ask you to listen to me one more moment, Father," Khardan said respectfully.

"Why? What are you going to give him next?" Majiid roared. "Your mother?" He turned to Jaafar, waving his arms "Take her! Take all my wives!" Yanking his dagger from his belt, he held it out to the Sheykh. "Take my stomach! My liver! Cut out my heart! Rip out my lungs! My son, it seems, wants you to have everything else of value!"

Khardan suppressed a smile. "I merely wanted to suggest, Father, that—in order to allow tempers to cool—I leave for the city of Kich somewhat earlier than when we had originally planned. This will give the hotheads on both sides something to do other than brooding and licking their wounds. We can offer escort to Jaafar's people as far as the hills, then continue on to the city from there."

"Escort him to Sul for all I care!" Majiid snarled, and stalked out of the tent.

Sighing, Khardan looked after him then glanced at Sheykh Jaafar. "My father will keep his word and I will see to it that our people keep theirs." The Calif's voice was cold. "But know this. We are still enemies. However, we pledge by the Holy Akhran that *for the time being*"—he emphasized this—"there will be no more raids, no more insults, not a hand raised by the Akar against the Hrana."

"I pledge to the same. When do we get the horses?" Jaafar asked eagerly.

Khardan rose to his feet. "Undoubtedly my father is handling the matter now. Select those of your men you wish to ride with us and have them ready. We leave with the setting of the sun."

Bowing coldly, Khardan left the tent of his enemy, his dignified bearing an indication that this was only a temporary settlement of their age-old dispute. Zohra lingered a moment after he had gone to cast a triumphant glance at her father, then hastened after the Calif.

News of the agreement was spreading through both camps, bringing reactions of suspicious disbelief in the Hrana's tents and outraged disbelief among the Akar. But as Khardan had planned, there was no time for either side to dispute the matter. The news was also spreading that the Calif intended leaving for the city this very evening, and both camps were thrown into a flurry of confusion—men oiling their saddles and sharpening weapons; women hurriedly mending robes, tucking charms of protection in their husbands' *khurjin,* preparing food for the road, all the while chatting excitedly about the fine gifts their husbands would bring them on their return.

Zohra ignored all of this activity as she hurried through the camps, her one thought to catch up with Khardan, who was walking wearily toward his tent.

Reaching out a hand, Zohra touched his arm.

Khardan turned. The smile on his lips froze, his face darkened. Zohra started to speak, but he forestalled her.

"Well, wife, you have won. You have what you wanted. If you have stopped me with the purpose of rubbing salt in my wounds, I suggest you think twice. I am tired and I see no rest for myself this night. Further, I have much to do in order to prepare for my journey. If you will excuse me—"

Now Zohra *had* planned to gloat over her victory. The sharp words were on her lips, ready to shoot forth and deflate his pride. Perhaps it was the perversity of her nature that made her inclined to do the opposite of what anyone expected of her, perhaps it was the warmth of the admiration she had felt for the Calif in the tent. Whatever the reason, the spears she had ready to cast at her enemy suddenly changed into flowers.

"My husband," said Zohra softly, "I came only to . . . to thank you."

Her hand lingered on Khardan's arm. She could tell by the almost dumbfounded expression on his face that she had startled him, and she tried to laugh at him. His hand closed tightly over hers, however. He drew her near him. The laughter quivered in her throat, disrupted by the rapid beating of her heart.

He was not regarding her with disgust now. His eyes burned with a fire brighter than the sun, forcing her to lower her gaze before them.

"How deep is the well of your gratitude, madam?" he whispered, his lips brushing her cheek.

The sun's flame kindled in her body. "Perhaps you should cast in your bucket, my lord, and find out," she answered, closing her eyes and lifting her lips.

"Master!" came an agonized voice.

"Not now, Pukah!" Khardan said gruffly.

"Master! I beg an instant only!"

Zohra came to her senses. Glancing around, she saw that they were standing in the center of the camp, surrounded by people laughing and nudging each other. Ashamed and embarrassed, Zohra slipped from her husband's grasp.

"Wait!" He caught hold of her.

Backing away from him, she murmured, "Perhaps, upon your return, my lord, you can plumb the well's depth." Then, breaking free, she fled.

Khardan stared after her, more than half-inclined to follow, when the hand tugged at his arm again.

Turning, he glowered at the djinn. "Well?" he demanded, his voice shaking. "What is it, Pukah?"

"If you do not need me, *sidi,* I beg leave to be gone from your service for a short time. Only the shortest of times, I assure you, *sidi.* An eyeblink will seem long compared to it. You will never miss me—"

"I can guarantee you that! Very well, be gone!"

"Thank you, *sidi.* I am going. Thank you." Bowing, backing up, bowing again, and backing up again, Pukah hastily faded from view.

Khardan turned to follow his wife, the blood throbbing in his temples, only to find that others were crowding around him now, wanting to know who was going to ride with him arguing about whose horses had to be given to the sheepherders, and badgering him with countless other fool questions.

Looking over their heads, hoping for a glimpse of rose-red silk, Khardan saw nothing but the confusion in the camps. Zohra was gone. The moment had passed. He turned back to his men, forcing himself to remember that he was Calif of his people, they had first claim upon him—always.

With an effort the Calif wrenched his mind from thoughts of rose-red silk and jasmine to deal with the business at hand, answering questions somewhat incoherently, finding that wells and buckets kept getting mixed up in the conversation. The need to settle a fight between one of the Akar and a Hrana effectively cooled his ardor. Then Majiid appeared, demanding to know why his son didn't just rip off his father's head and be done with it, and swearing that he would not give up the oldest nag in his possession to the sheepherders. Patiently Khardan went through his reasoning once again.

His own preparations for the journey took the rest of the day, and before Khardan knew it, the shadows of evening had stretched out their cool, soothing fingers over the sand. It was time to leave. Standing beside his black horse, Khardan glanced around. His *spahis* on their war-horses were gathered in a restless, excitement-laced knot behind him. Further behind them, several Hrana men were seated on their new mounts, their awkwardness and uneasiness on the tall, prancing beasts masked by fierce looks of pride that dared anyone to say they hadn't been born in the saddle.

Trouble would break out before this ride was finished, Khardan knew. He found his gaze straying to Zohra's tent, hoping to catch a glimpse of her.

The other women in camp were bidding good-bye to their husbands, calling out to remember this or that, lifting babies to be blessed. Husbands bent to kiss their wives. Zohra was nowhere to be seen. Thinking suddenly that this trip was a confounded nuisance, Khardan swung himself up into the saddle. Waving to his father, he wheeled his horse. Hooves flashed in the sand, a cheer went up from the men, and the *spahis* galloped after their leader, showing off their riding skills as long as they were within sight of camp.

As he rose past the Tel, Khardan noted with some astonishment that the Rose of the Prophet, previously thought to be dying, seemed almost on the verge of blooming.

CHAPTER 14

As Khardan's men traveled west over the Pagrah desert to the city of Kich, a slave caravan was traveling eastward over the plains of northern Bas, bound for the same destination. The slaver's journey, unlike that of the *spahis*, was made at a slow and leisurely pace. This was done not out of kindness for the slaves but for reasons of economics. Merchandise put upon the market after being marched halfway across a continent appears to disadvantage and fetches far below its actual worth. The slaves were, therefore, permitted to walk at a relaxed pace and were adequately fed. Not that any of this mattered or was even apparent to Mathew. The young man's misery increased daily. He lived and breathed fear.

Lurching and swaying upon the camel, concealed within the tentlike *bassourab*, he peered despairingly out upon the harsh land. Comparing it to his homeland, he began to wonder if he was on the same planet.

At first they rode through barren plains, the camels walking splay-footed across sandy, flat stretches of rock covered by strange, ugly grasses and flesh-ripping plants. Then the flat plains dipped down into ravines and the camels fought for sure footing along treacherous falls of crumbled stone. Awed by the savage beauty, Mathew stared dazedly at sheer rock walls, streaked with garish colors of reds, oranges, and yellows that soared above him to dizzying heights.

Everything in this land went by extremes, it seemed. The sun either blazed down upon them mercilessly or rainstorms beat at them with incredible fury. The temperature rose and fell with wild abandon. By day the young wizard sweated and suffered from the intense heat. By night he shivered with cold.

And if the land was harsh and the climate cruel, its people

were harsher and crueler still. Slavery was unknown in Mathew's country, having been decreed by his God, Promenthas, to be a mortal sin. The concept of slavery was completely alien to Mathew, impossible for him to comprehend or understand. That he and all the rest of these men, women, and children were nothing more to the unseen person in the white palanquin than so much chattel, to be measured in terms not of life but of gold, seemed ludicrous. Mathew could not imagine that one human being could look upon another as he might look upon a horse or a camel.

The young wizard soon learned to think differently. The slaves were not treated like horses. Horses, for example, were never beaten.

What the man's crime was, Mathew never knew. Perhaps he had tried to escape. Perhaps he had been caught talking to another slave—which was forbidden. The *goums* stopped the caravan, threw the unfortunate wretch upon the ground, stripped off the loincloth that was the only clothing the male slaves wore, and beat him swiftly, impersonally, and efficiently.

The blows fell upon the man's buttocks, an area of his body that would remain covered when he was exhibited in the marketplace, thus hiding the unsightly bruises and stripes of the whip. At first the man forbore from crying out, but after three lashes his screams of pain began and soon echoed off the high rock walls.

Mathew, shaking with sick horror, stopped up his ears with his veil. Wrenching his gaze away, he looked at the white palanquin that stood on ground near him, those carrying it taking advantage of the respite to squat down on their haunches and rest. Not a sound came from within the litter, the white curtains did not stir. Yet Mathew knew the man inside looked on, for he saw the *goum* glance at the litter for orders, and he saw that slender white hand come out once, make a graceful motion, then withdraw. The beating ceased. The slave was dragged to his feet and chained back with his fellows, and the caravan proceeded on its way.

Mathew had no fear of being beaten himself. Terrified of revealing his secret, he kept well apart from the other slaves, never speaking to anyone if he could help it. He had no thoughts of trying to escape. The young wizard knew he would not last twenty minutes in this godforsaken land. For the time being he was safest with his captors—at least so he assumed.

Evening brought respite from travel. The *goums* assisted Mathew down from the back of the camel—a stupid and vicious beast whose one redeeming feature, so far as Mathew could see, was that it could travel enormous distances through the arid land without requiring water. The guards then escorted the female slaves to a place of privacy where they could perform their ablutions. This moment always brought panicked fear to Mathew, for he not only had to hide himself from the guards but from the women as well. Once this daily terror ended, the *goums* hustled Mathew and the other women into their tents, setting the guards around them for the night, and Mathew could, at last, relax.

Although Mathew never saw the trader, except for that slender white hand, he had the feeling that he was being kept under constant, special surveillance. His tent was always placed closest to the trader's own tent in the evening. The camel he rode was always first in line behind the palanquin. Mathew received his food immediately after the trader received his.

At first this surveillance increased Mathew's fear. Gradually it lulled him into a mindless security, giving him the impression that someone cared about his welfare—a wistful notion, born of desperation, that was soon cruelly dispelled.

On the fourth night of the journey the evening's bowl of food was slipped through Mathew's tent flap. Dully he glanced at it, and without much thinking about what he did, he picked it up and deposited it surreptitiously behind the tent.

One of the *goums* was walking by the tent when he felt something tickle his neck, like feathers touching his skin. Thinking it to be one of the thousand varieties of winged insects in this land, the *goum* slapped at it irritably, but the tickle did not go away. Craning his head in an effort to see what was harassing him, the *goum* saw, instead, Mathew's food bowl slide out of the back of the tent, its contents dumped on the ground.

Scowling, the *goum* forgot about the tickle—that quite mysteriously ceased—and hurried to Kiber to report.

Lying down to try to drown his misery in exhausted sleep, Mathew was scared nearly witless by the sudden entrance into his tent of the leader of the *goums*.

"What is it? What do you want?" Mathew gasped, clutching his women's clothing about him. He was becoming more and more adept at speaking the language—a fact that neither appeared to impress nor surprise his captors. They all had the mentality of animals anyway, and one dog is rarely surprised to hear another bark.

Kiber did not answer him. Grabbing Mathew by the arm, the *goum* hauled him out of his tent and dragged him across the ground to the dwelling of the trader. Kiber apparently had orders already to enter, for he charged inside with Mathew without announcing his presence.

The interior was shadowy and dark; no lamps had been lighted. Half-blinded by the veil over his face, Mathew could see little. He had the general impression of luxury; of fine silken cushions and rich rugs and the glitter of gold and brass. The air was perfumed; there was a smell of food and coffee. He saw a man swathed in white robes, reclining on a cushion. A woman—dressed in black—crouched, head down, some distance away.

At Mathew's entrance the trader raised his head. Despite being indoors he kept his face covered with the face cloth. All that was visible were two eyes, hooded by thick, drooping lids, that glittered above the white mask. Mathew shivered. A ray of cold moonlight, shining through the tent flap, gleamed on the white mask with more warmth than the young wizard saw in those eyes. Not knowing what to expect, Mathew stared back at the man with the frozen calm of despair.

"Down! On your knees, slave!" Kiber twisted Mathew's arm painfully, forcing the young wizard to the ground. "What is the problem?" the trader asked in a soft voice. "This one is attempting to starve herself to death."

Mathew gulped. "That—that's not. . . true," he stammered, feeling himself quail beneath the gaze of the cold, hooded eyes.

"Mahad discovered her throwing her food out of the tent, attempting to hide it in the grass. It occurred to him that he had heard animals snuffling in the night near this one's dwelling. Obviously, *Effendi,* your bounty has been feeding the jackals, not this one."

"So you are using death to escape your fate?" inquired the trader, the eyes gazing at Mathew dispassionately. "You would not be the first," he added in somewhat bored tones.

"No!" Mathew's voice cracked. He licked his parched lips. "I . . . haven't been . . . able to eat. . ."

His voice trailed away. It had not occurred to the young man to deliberately starve himself to death, yet he suddenly realized he had been doing just that, slowly and surely, without knowing it. Perhaps it had been his unconscious self taking over and carrying out the deed his conscious mind was too cowardly to perform. All Mathew knew was that every time he tried to take a bite, his gorge rose and he could no more have swallowed the food than he could have swallowed sand.

How could he explain this to those hooded eyes? He couldn't. It was impossible. Shaking his head, Mathew tried to say something else, make some lame promise that he would eat, although he knew he couldn't. At least they couldn't force food down him. He was going to die with dignity perhaps after all. Before he could utter a word, however, the trader made a gesture. The woman who had been kneeling at the rear of the tent came forward and knelt beside him. Putting his hand—the slender white hand—on her chin, the trader lifted her unveiled face so that she looked at Mathew.

Woman! Mathew was appalled. She was a child, no more than fourteen at most. She stared at him with frightened eyes, and he saw that her entire body quivered with fear.

"Your own life obviously means little to you," the trader said softly, "but what about the lives of others?" His hand clenched around the girl's jaw. "When you do not eat, this one will not eat. Nor will she have anything to drink." Dropping his hand to her shoulder, the trader roughly shoved the girl forward, sending her sprawling in a heap at Mathew's feet. "With the heat of the desert ahead, she will last perhaps two—three days." The trader leaned back among the cushions. "When she is dead, there will be another."

Mathew stared at the man, incredulous. His gaze went to the girl, cowering before him, her thin hands pressed together in a pleading gesture.

"I can't believe you'd do this!" Mathew said in a cracked voice.

"Can't you?" The trader shrugged. "This girl"—he nudged her with the toe of his slipper—"has no value. She is not pretty, she is no longer even a virgin. She will bring a few coppers, nothing more, as someone's house slave. But you, beautiful blossom from across the sea, are worth fifty of her! You see? I am not doing this out of any concern for you, my flower, but out of greed. Does that convince you that I would do it?"

It did. Mathew had to admit that. He also had to admit to himself at last that he was in truth nothing more than marketable goods, merchandise, a thing to be bought and sold. What would happen when this man found out he had been cheated, when Mathew's unsuspecting buyer discovered that he had purchased flawed wares? Mathew didn't dare think of this or he knew he would go mad. As it was, he could only promise, through trembling lips, to eat what food was given him. The trader nodded— the cold, impassive expression in the eyes never changing—and waved Mathew, the *goum,* and the wretched girl put of his sight.

Kiber escorted Mathew and the girl back to the tent. More food was brought. This time Kiber sat inside, watching Mathew expectantly. The girl did the same, except that her eyes were on the food, not on Mathew.

The young wizard wondered how he would be able to choke down the rice that had been mixed with vegetables and greasy meat. He tried to concentrate on the girl, hoping his pity for her would carry him through this ordeal. But he found himself imagining the dreadful life she must lead, the cruel usage to which she had been subjected, the bleak and hopeless future she faced. Gagging, he brought up his first mouthful. Kiber growled in anger. The girl whimpered, clasping her hands.

Resolutely Mathew took another bite. Refusing to let himself think of anything at all, he began to count the number of times he chewed. When he reached ten, he swallowed. Keeping his mind a blank, he grabbed another lump of the substance and shoved it in his mouth. He chewed it ten times as before, his mind thinking of only the numbers. In this way he managed to eat enough to his dinner apparently to satisfy Kiber, who gave the rest to the girl. Grabbing the bowl with both hands, she brought it to her mouth, wolfing it down like a starving dog. She licked out the bowl, getting every last vestige, then prostrating herself before Mathew, she began to weep and pour incoherent blessings down upon his head.

Kiber—evidently feeling his job was finished—jerked the girl to her feet and led her from the tent. Watching through the tent flap, Mathew saw the *goum* take the girl back to the trader's tent and throw her inside.

She is no longer even a virgin. . . .

Mathew heard the cruel voice, saw the cold eyes. Sickened, he lay down upon his cushions, expecting to lose most of what he had eaten. But surprisingly, his body accepted the food. He had not gone without eating long enough to make it reject what it craved, as sometimes happened—so he had heard—to monks who fasted for too long. Closing his eyes, he felt a sense of disappointment that he'd been, once again, cheated of death.

CHAPTER 15

*T*he flies droned, the sweat trickled down his face, the coolness of a drop felt suddenly startling against his hot skin. Mathew clung to the saddle of the lurching beast on which he rode, half-asleep in the sweltering heat. His body suffered, but he did not notice. He was not truly there. Once more, as he did so often now, he had retreated from reality, taking refuge in the memories of his past.

In his mind he was far away, back in the land that had given him birth. He walked the lush grass of the grounds of the ancient school where he studied. He lunched beneath huge oaks that were older than the school; he and his fellow students discussing in youthful, solemn voices the mysteries of life, chewing on them over cold beef and bread and solving them—every one—before dessert.

Or he was in the classroom, sitting at the tall desk, laboriously copying his first major spell onto the parchment made from the skin of a newborn lamb. His fingers sticky with the lamb's blood used to write the cantrip, he stopped often to wipe them so that he would not drop a blot upon the parchment; the slightest error would negate the magic. He could clearly see the feather of the raven's quill, shining with a black rainbow of color in the mild sunlight filtering through the glass windowpanes. Days and days he worked on that spell, making certain every single stroke of the quill was as perfect as he could possibly make it. His fingers cramped from the strain, his back ached from bending over the tall desk. Never in his life had he been happier.

At last the spell was finished. He sat back and stared at the parchment for an hour, searching for the tiniest flaw, the smallest mistake. There were none. Rolling it carefully, he tucked it into the carved ivory spell case that had been a gift from his parents upon the last Holy Day. Closing the silver lid, he sealed it with beeswax and, carrying it carefully, brought the spell to the desk of his Master, the Archmagus, and laid it before him. The Archmagus, engrossed in reading some moldy, dusty text that literally smelled of arcane knowledge, said nothing but calmly accepted the spell case.

A fortnight later—the longest term of days and nights Mathew had ever spent in his life—the Archmagus called the young man to his private study. Here were gathered several other wizards—teachers of Mathew's. All of them stood regarding him gravely, their long, gray beards brushing against their chests. The Archmagus handed Mathew back the spell case. It was empty. Mathew held his breath. The Archmagus smiled, the other masters smiled. The spell had worked perfectly, they said. Mathew had passed. He was, at last, an apprentice wizard. His reward—to be taken on a journey by sea to the land of Sardish Jardan.

He returned home for a holiday before his trip, spending his time in continued quiet study and meditation with his parents in the candlelit libraries of their castle. The Weslanders lived in what many people of Tirish Aranth considered harsh country. According to popular myth, it was so hilly that one always slept at an angle. The mountainous country was heavily forested, covered with tall stands of pine and aspen. Its soil was rocky, unsuitable for all but subsistence farming. There was no lack of food, however. A wilderness people, the Weslanders had learned long ago to live off the land. They hunted deer and elk in the forest, snared rabbits and squirrels in the valleys, and caught bright-colored trout in the splashing streams.

Lovers of study and of nature, the Weslanders were a solitary people, building their stone dwellings at the top of treacherous paths that only the most adventuresome or loyal of friends dared climb. Here, among their books, the Weslanders lived their quiet lives, raising their children in the slightly preoccupied manner of those to whom the quest for knowledge comes first and all else second.

Because of their slender build, fluting voices, and the physical beauty of both men and women, it was difficult to tell the sexes apart. The Weslanders saw no reason why they should, for that matter. Women and men were one in all they did, from attending schools to hunting. It was this blurring of the sexes that had, over the years—according to the scornful world in general—caused the men to cease to grow facial hair. Having little to do with the world in general, the Weslanders ignored their detractors. They almost never married outside their own race, finding the other people of Tirish Aranth to be boorish and stupid, fonder of the body than the mind as the Weslander axiom ran.

Mathew's family was an old one and had, over the years, amassed a fortune so that they were able to concentrate on their studies to the exclusion of all else. His mother was a philosopher, whose writings on the teachings of Promenthas had received high acclaim from both religious and secular circles. She had been offered chairs at several universities but had always declined. Nothing could ever induce her to leave the hills in which she had been born or the husband to whom she was devoted. Mathew's father was an alchemist—a dreamy man who was never happier than when puttering among his glass tubes and burning blue flames, creating horrendous smells and occasional explosions that rocked the house. Mathew's earliest memory of his father was seeing him emerge from the underground laboratory in a cloud of billowing smoke, his eyebrows burned off, his soot-covered face ecstatic.

Mathew's parents sent him to the finest school for wizards open to young men. He left home at the age of six, returning once a year for Holy Day. Except that his father grew a little grayer and the lines about his mother's eyes grew more pronounced over the years, Mathew always came back to find his parents unchanged. Once yearly they welcomed him home, raising their heads from book or glass tube, smiling at him as though he hadn't been gone over an hour, and calmly going back to their work with a quiet invitation for him to join them. Within moments of his return, Mathew was seated at his own desk, a warm feeling inside him that he had never been away.

He was sitting there now, in the high-backed wooden chair, listening to the scratching of his mother's pen across the page on which she was writing, hearing her murmur to herself, for she spoke aloud while she wrote. A cool breeze, scented with the sharp smell of pine, blew through the open casement. From the laboratory below the house came a muffled thud and then a yell. His father. . . strange, he never shouted like that. Mathew raised his head from the book he was perusing. What was wrong? Why this yammering?

With a jolt the young wizard woke up, catching himself just before falling from the saddle. The pain of terrible, bitter knowledge that he had been dreaming twisted inside him. Waking was always agony, the price he paid. But it was worth it to escape this wretched life, if only for a few brief moments. He was just about to try to lose himself in that wonderful haven again when he realized the shouts had not been part of his imagination. Peeping through the fabric of the *bassourab*, Mathew looked to see what the commotion was about. His heart died within him.

They had reached the walls of the city.

Accustomed to the thatched and gabled roofs of the dwellings in his own land, the buildings that he could see rising above the walls appeared as strange and awful to Mathew as the land through which he traveled. Twisting upward in fantastic designs, with spires and towers and minarets that bulged like onions, they seemed to have been built by some insane child.

Mathew could even smell the city from this distance—thousands of unwashed bodies sweating, eating, defecating, beneath the merciless sun. He could hear the noise—a low murmur of hundreds of voices raised in bargaining, praying, fighting... And he would be taken into this city, dragged to the marketplace in chains, made to stand and endure the gaze of countless merciless eyes... Sick with fear, he hung his head down to allay the dizziness that assailed him and waited for the order that would send him into hell.

The only order that came immediately, however, was one which brought the camels to their knees. The white covered palanquin was set upon the ground. A slave came hurrying around with water. Drinking greedily, Mathew peered through the curtains and watched the *goums* fonning hastily into ranks. When their lines were dressed to the satisfaction of the leader, they galloped off toward the city walls with a fine display of horsemanship, unfurling banners as they rode. Staring across the plain, Mathew saw riders dash out from the city gates to meet the *goums*. This must be some sort of request for permission to enter the gates, which—as far as Mathew could see—were still closed.

The preliminaries took a long time. A slave came around with food, which Mathew was careful to eat, having the uncanny feeling that the eyes behind the curtains of the litter could see through the camel tent. Although he had watched for her anxiously, Mathew had seen the slave girl only occasionally after that first night. When he did catch a glimpse of her, coming or going from the tent of the trader, she appeared to be as well fed as any of the slaves, and at least she was still alive. She glanced at Mathew once but did not speak to him. Mathew was just as glad. Fearfully guarding his secret, he did not encourage conversation with anyone lest they discover it was a man to whom they spoke, not a woman.

After what seemed like eons, although it was probably only an hour at most, the city riders galloped back to the gates, the *goums* wheeled their horses and returned to the caravan. For the first time Mathew saw the trader actually leave the comfort of his covered palanquin. His white robes billowing around him, he walked out to meet Kiber. Kiber in turn jumped off his horse in mid-gallop and with an ease and grace Mathew found remarkable, ran alongside the animal to come to stand, panting, near the trader.

The other *goums* arrived a few seconds behind, their excited voices shouting to the slaves to come for their horses or calling for water. In an effort to escape the clamor and the dust, the trader and Kiber moved toward the rear of the litter.

Their walk brought them close to Mathew's camel. Leaning forward, careful to keep hidden behind the curtains of the *bassourds*, he held his breath so that he could hear their conversation.

"What is the problem?"

"There is a new ruling in effect, *Effendi*."

"And that is?"

"All magical objects and any djinn we possess must be turned over to the Imam, to be kept in Quar's holy temple."

"What?" Mathew heard the trader's voice grate. "How is this possible? Did you not tell him I was a loyal and faithful follower of Quar?"

"I so told him, *Effendi*. He said that all who are faithful followers of the God will be happy to perform this act of sacrifice that has been ordered by the God himself."

"The Imam is a fool! What man will give up his djinn?"

"Apparently many men, *Effendi*. According to the captain, there is not a djinn left in Kich and the people have never lived so well. They go to the Imam with their needs now, and he handles them, dealing with Quar directly. The city is prosperous, says the captain. They lack nothing. There is no sickness, the markets are filled, their enemies fall beneath their feet. Already the people speak of the djinn as remnants of a bygone age, not needed in modem times."

"So it is true, what we heard. Quar is deliberately getting rid of his own djinn. I do not like this." The cold malice in the voice made Mathew shiver despite the heat. "You know the importance of what I carry. What are the chances of getting inside the city without its being detected?"

"Very little, I should think, *Effendi*. The caravan will be thoroughly searched upon entering the city walls. These people are naturally suspicious of outsiders, particularly, it seems, since that band of *kafir* was able to cross the ocean and set foot upon the shores of their land. I told the captain that it was *we* who dispatched the *kafir* in the name of Quar and he seemed impressed."

"But not impressed enough to let us enter without harassment?"

"No, *Effendi*."

The trader snarled, a low, growling rumble of anger, like a cat denied its prey. "Would that we had heard this news earlier. It is too late to leave. It would appear suspicious for a trader in slaves to turn back once he reaches the marketplace. And I need the money from their sale to pursue our journey."

He was silent long moments, lost in thought. Mathew heard Kiber's horse shuffle restlessly. The other horses were being watered and it wanted its share. The leader of the *goums* spoke to the animal softly, and it quieted.

"Very well. Here's what we will do." The trader's words were quick and cool. "Gather the magical objects of everyone in camp and put them together with those we took off the slaves when we captured them. Add to that my personal objects—"

"*Effendi!*"

"There can be no help for it! Hopefully this will satisfy them and they will be careless in their search. This and the fact that it was by my orders that the *kafir* died should convince the Imam that I am a loyal follower of Quar. My way will be clear to act."

"What about—" Kiber hesitated, as though reluctant to speak.

"I will take care of that, you may be certain. The less you know, the better."

"Yes, *Effendi.*"

"You have your orders. Proceed."

"Yes, *Effendi.*"

The two parted, the trader returning to the covered palanquin, Kiber leaving to carry out his master's commands. Mathew, sighing, sat back. He had listened to the conversation hoping to learn what was going to happen. But nothing he heard made any sense. Djinn! He had read of these immortal beings. Supposedly similar in nature to angels, they dwelt on the human plane and were said to live in lamps, rings, and other such silly objects. They talked to men—to all men, not just priests—holding discourse with ordinary humans and performing for them the most trivial of deeds.

Mathew found it astounding that someone as cold and calculating and obviously intelligent as this trader could actually appear to believe in such foolish tales. Perhaps he did so only to humor his men. As for magical objects, the young wizard hungered to know what they might be. For the first time he saw a glimmer of hope in his desperate situation. If he could get his hands on one of these objects...

A whispered voice near him made him start in fear. "Mistress!"

Mathew parted the curtains of the *bassourab* a crack. The slave girl stood beside his camel.

"Mistress," she said again, beckoning. "You come. He want you."

Mathew shuddered, terror overwhelming him, turning his hot hands ice cold, constricting his throat muscles.

"Come, come!" The girl cast a swift, fearful glance in the direction of the palanquin, and Mathew realized that *she* would be punished if he was remiss in following orders. Trembling in every limb, he climbed down slowly from the camel saddle.

Glancing around to see if anyone was watching, the girl took Mathew's hand and tugged him after her, guiding him swiftly across the sandy ground to the litter. Mathew noticed that they kept to the outside of the line of camels, steering clear of the crowd that was milling around in the center where some of the *goums* were preparing the slaves for their march into town. Others were collecting the magical items as ordered; still others were seeing to the horses or spreading fodder for the camels. No one paid the least attention to them. The girl led Mathew around to the far side of the palanquin, out of sight of everyone.

"I have her," the girl said to the curtains of the litter. "Come close, Blossom," came the trader's voice.

His heart pounding so that he could barely breathe for the intense pain, Mathew hesitated, trying to gather his courage.

The girl motioned for him to obey, again with the look of fear. Shivering, Mathew stepped closer. The slender hand came out, caught hold of the robes around his neck, and drew him closer still.

"I have just discovered that we are going to be searched when we enter the city. On my person I carry a magical object of rare and immense value. For obvious reasons I do not wish it to be found by these slum dwellers. They will go through my possessions carefully, but they will probably not be too interested in what a slave girl such as yourself carries. Therefore I give this object to you, to keep for me until such time as I may come to claim it."

Mathew gasped. Was it possible? Was he going to come into possession of some arcane relic so easily? The trader could not know he was a wizard; he would suppose him incapable of using the object. It must be powerful. Mathew had seen enough of the harshness of this God, Quar, to understand that the trader was risking his life in defying the orders of Quar's priest. Mathew's hands trembled with eagerness. He needed to gather what information he could about the object in order to use it, however, and hastily searched for some way to do so that would not appear suspicious. At the last moment it occurred to him that a slave girl, such as himself, should probably seem reluctant to take on such a burden.

"I . . . don't understand, *Effendi.*" Mathew stammered. "Surely there are others more worthy. . . of—of your trust."

"I don't trust you in the least, Blossom. I give this to you because you will be sold to someone wealthy and important, consequently easy for me to find."

"But what if I should lose it or something should happen to it—"

"Then you will die most horribly," said the cool voice of the trader. "The object is blessed—or cursed as the case may be—so that it cannot be lost or mislaid by accident." The slender hand upon Mathew's robes suddenly tightened its grip, twisting the fabric expertly, cutting off Mathew's breath. "One who attempts to do so deliberately will meet the most excruciatingly painful death that *my* God can devise. And believe me, my dear Blossom, his talents in that area have long been admired."

There was no doubting that voice. Mathew began to strangle, the slave girl stared at him with huge, frightened eyes. At the last moment the hand removed itself from his robes, gliding back into the curtains of the palanquin. Mathew gasped for air. The curtains parted once more. Reaching out, the trader caught hold of Mathew's hand and pressed something inside.

Mathew stared in confusion.

He held a globe of glass. Small enough to fit comfortably in his palm, the globe was decorated on the top and the bottom with the most intricate gold- and silverwork. It was filled with water, and inside the globe swam two fish—one the color of black velvet with long sweeping fins and a fanlike tail; the other a shimmering golden color with a flat body and large, staring eyes.

He had been given a fishbowl!

"I— What—" Mathew could not speak coherently.

"Shut up, Blossom, and attend to me. We haven't much time. You must keep this hidden from sight. The globe itself will help you, for it is naturally loathe to reveal itself to anyone. You need not feed the fish nor care for them, they can fend for themselves. Carry the globe on your person at all times—sleeping or waking. Speak of it to no one. Do not tremble so, Blossom. You will have this in your possession for only a few days, if that long. Then I will come to relieve you of this burden. Serve me well in this matter and you will be rewarded." The slender hand moved to stroke Mathew's soft cheek.

"Betray me and . . ."

There was a rustle of curtain, a flash of metal in the sunlight, and a kind of startled gasp from the slave girl. Mathew, staring at her, saw her eyes widen with pain, then slowly drain of life. The girl crumpled to the ground at his feet, a large red stain spreading over her clothes. The trader's slender hand, holding a small, silver dagger, was wet with blood.

Mathew started to recoil in horror, but the trader caught hold of his wrist and held him fast. "Now no one knows about this but you and I, Blossom. Return quickly to your mount." The voice was soft, low. "Remember what you have seen of my wrath."

The slender hand let loose its grip and disappeared inside the palanquin. Dazed, Mathew slid the fishbowl beneath the bodice of his clothing. The glass was cold against his hot flesh. He shuddered in reaction, as though he had pressed a handful of ice against his breast. Hardly knowing where he was or what he was doing, Mathew turned, stumbling blindly over the hard, sun-baked ground. Instinct alone led him to the camel.

The rest of the party was preparing to continue to travel. The slaves removed the halters from the camels' knees, coaxing them to rise with encouraging shouts and taps of the camel stick. The *goums* mounted their horses; the litter bearers lifted their burden to their shoulders; the slaves rose to their feet, their chains clashing together in an off-key jangle. Two slaves walked alongside the palanquin, each slave carrying in his arms a huge rattan basket filled with objects strange and curious—amulets, charms, jewelry—anything that might possibly be construed as possessing magic. Kiber galloped up and down the line, casting his dark-eyed gaze critically over the assembly. Finally, with a glance at the litter, he nodded and urged his horse forward. Banners hanging limp in the hot, breathless air, the caravan set off at a leisurely pace.

Mathew's camel lurched to its feet, grumbling in protest. Peering through the folds of the camel tent, the young wizard stared down at the body of the slave girl, lying forgotten on the desert sand.

Ahead of him, rising up out of the plains, were the city walls—a prison house of misery and suffering. The city's stench hit his nostrils. The camel picked her way around the body of the slave girl; vultures were already flapping down to the ground.

Twisting in the saddle, Mathew gazed back at the corpse with envy.

CHAPTER 16

The 'efreet Kaug did not dwell in a sumptuous palace on the plane of the djinn. For reasons best unknown to anyone, he lived in a cave far beneath the Kurdin Sea. Rumor had it that he had, centuries before, been banished to this cave by the God Zhakrin during one of the cycles of faith when that dark God reigned supreme and Kaug's God, Quar, was but a humble licker of boots.

Swimming through the murky salt water of the inland sea, Pukah pondered this story. He wondered if it was true, and if so, what dread deed Kaug had committed to merit this punishment. He also wondered, if Kaug was now so powerful, why he didn't move to a better neighborhood.

Despite the fact that he could breathe water as easily as he breathed air, Pukah felt smothered. He missed the blazing sun, the freedom of the vast, open land. Cutting through the sea with slashing strokes of his arms, the djinn deeply resented having to endure the cold and the wet and what was worse, the stares of goggle-eyed fish. Nasty creatures, fish. All slimy and scaly. No desert nomad ate them, considering them food fit only for city people who could get nothing better. Pukah's skin crawled in disgust as one of the stupid things bumbled into him. Pushing the fish aside, taking care to wipe the slime from his hand on a nearby sponge, Pukah peered through the water, searching for the cave entrance.

There it was, light streaming from within. Good, Kaug was at home.

Kaug's cave stood at the very bottom of the sea, hollowed out of a cliff of black rock. The light from inside illuminated long, greenish-brown moss that hung from the cliff, drifting about in the water like the hair of a drowned woman. Coral rose in grotesque shapes from the seafloor, writhing and twisting in the constantly shifting shadows. Gigantic fish with small, deadly eyes and sleek bodies and rows of razor teeth flashed past, eyeing Pukah hungrily at first, then cursing the djinn for his ethereal flesh.

Pukah cursed them back just as heartily—for being ugly, if nothing else. The young djinn was not in the least overawed by his surroundings, beyond a certain repugnance and a desire to gulp a draft of fresh air. Confident in himself and his own intelligence and what he assumed was the correlating stupidity of his opponent, Pukah was actually looking forward to tossing a verbal sack over the head of his enemy.

If Pukah had talked to Sond or Fedj, he would have been on his guard. He would, in fact, have been quaking in his silken slippers, for it was far more likely that—in an encounter with the evil 'efreet—it would be Pukah who would end up in the bag and *not* a verbal one. But Pukah had not discussed his plan with either Sond or Fedj. Still determined to outdo both the other djinn and win Akhran's admiration for himself, Pukah had devised a second scheme to salvage his first. Like many others, djinn and human alike, Pukah mistook a hulking body as an indication of a hulking mind, visualizing himself as being capable of flitting about the older 'efreet's dull intelligence like a teasing bird fluttering about the head of the bear.

Alighting on the seafloor at the entrance to the cave, Pukah stared inside. He could barely see the great bulk of the 'efreet lurking about within, a dark, stoop-shouldered shape against the light that was cast by some kind of enthralled sea urchins, who floated or stood in mournful servitude about the 'efreet's dwelling.

"*Salaam aleikum,* O Mighty Kaug," called out Pukah respectfully. "May I enter your soggy home?"

The black shape paused in whatever it was doing, turning to glare out the entrance.

"Who calls?" it asked harshly.

"It is I, Pukah," said the young djinn humbly, immensely pleased with his own playacting. "I have come to see Your Magnificence on a matter of extreme importance."

"Very well, you may enter," Kaug said ungraciously, turning his back upon his guest, who was, after all, a lowranking djinn of little importance.

Nettled at this rudeness, Pukah was doubly pleased to be able to prick the bubble of the 'efreet's contentment. Glancing in disgust at the moss-covered boulders that were apparently meant for chairs, Pukah made his way to the rear of the water-filled cave. He noticed, in passing, that Kaug had acquired some particularly lovely objects from the world of humans. A golden egg, encrusted with jewels, standing in the center of a giant conch-shell table, attracted the djinn's particular attention. He'd never seen anything so remarkable.

Firmly Pukah brought his mind back to the business at hand, making a mental note to come back in half a century or so, when the 'efreet wasn't home, and relieve him of these beautiful, delicate objects that were obviously not suited to the brute's taste.

"Wishing you joy, Great One." Pukah bowed, making a fluttering gesture with his hand from his turban to his face.

"What do you want?" Kaug demanded, turning at last from what he was doing to face the young djinn.

Pukah, sniffing, saw that the 'efreet had been bent over a pot, cooking up something indescribably nasty-smelling. Fearing he would be invited to stay for dinner, Pukah decided to launch into his business without preliminary small talk.

"I have come, O Magnificent One, to bring a warning to your master, the Revered and Holy Quar."

"Ah, yes?" said the 'efreet, staring at Pukah with slit-eyes, their shrewdness concealed by the narrowing of the lids. "And why this concern for my Master, little Pukah?"

Little Pukah! The young djinn's anger flared; it was all he could do to remind himself that he was the wiser, the smarter of the two, and that he could, therefore, afford to be magnanimous and overlook this insult.

But this glob of seaweed will pay for that remark before I'm finished with him!

"I come because I do not like to see any of the Gods humbled and cast down from their high places in the eyes of the humans, Great One. It gives the petty mortals delusions of grandeur and makes life difficult for all of us, don't you agree?"

Did you understand that, Chowder Head, or must I use words of one syllable?

"Oh, I agree. Most assuredly," said Kaug, lowering his bulk into a chair made from a huge sponge. Thousands of tiny fish darted out from it when he sat down. He gazed up at Pukah comfortably, not inviting the djinn to be seated. "I take it that you foresee some sort of humiliation coming to my Master?"

"I do," remarked Pukah.

"Quar will be indebted to you for this timely warning then," said Kaug gravely. "Will you be so kind as to describe the nature of this impending disaster, that I may carry the description to my Master and we may prepare ourselves to thwart it?"

"I will tell you, but there is no way you can thwart it. I do this only to spare your Master the shameful end that he will undoubtedly meet should he attempt to fight his fate instead of accepting it."

There, I guess I told him!

"If what you say is true, then my Master and I will exalt your name, O Wise Pukah. Will you be seated? Some refreshment? "

I'd sooner dine in the Realm of the Dead!

"No, thank you, O Great One, although it smells truly divine. My time is short. I must return to my mortal master, the Calif, who cannot do without me as you must know."

"Mmmmm," murmured Kaug. "Then continue your most interesting conversation."

"Let us be honest with each other, O Great One. It is no secret that your Holy Master, Quar, is intent upon taking over control of the heavens, and that my Holy Master, Akhran, is equally intent that he—Quar—shall not succeed in this venture. May we agree on that?"

"We can agree on anything you like, my charming friend," Kaug said expansively. "Are you certain you won't sit down? Partake of some boiled octopus?"

Boiled octopus! The salt has definitely eaten away at this fellow's brain.

Politely declining the 'efreet's invitation, the young djinn continued, "As you and your Master have no doubt heard, the tribes of Sheykh Jaafar al Widjar and Sheykh Majiid al Fakhar have been joined together, united through the marriage of the Calif, Khardan, and the flower of her tribe, Zohra."

Pukah spread his hands, sighing in rapture. "Theirs is truly a marriage made in heaven! Now our blessings have been further increased—may Sul not be envious of our good fortune—by the uniting of yet a third tribe of the desert!"

Pukah's chest swelled with importance, particularly as he noted the 'efreet's grave expression grow considerably graver.

"A third tribe?" Kaug inquired. "And who would that be?"

"The mighty and powerful Sheykh Zeid al Saban!"

Although Pukah never knew it, he did actually manage to astonish Kaug. When one believes someone is meekly eating out of your hand, it is a shock to feel teeth sinking into your fingers. Sond had betrayed him! Kaug's eyes widened in what Pukah took to be fear but what was actually outrage. Then they narrowed, studying the young djinn shrewdly.

"Why are you telling us this?"

"Alas." Pukah heaved a sigh. "I have a soft spot in my heart for city people. The three tribes plan to come together and sweep into Kich, where they will depose the Imam and put him to the sword; take over the palace; and relieve the Amir of the troublesome burden of his many wives and concubines. Perhaps, if they feel so inclined, they will loot and burn the city. Perhaps not. It is whatever suits my master's fancy at the time. I cannot stomach the thought of such violence and bloodshed. And as I stated before, it would be a humiliating defeat for Quar."

"Indeed, it would," said Kaug slowly. "You are right, Pukah. There is a great tragedy in the making here." So there was, but not exactly the one Pukah had in mind. "What do you suggest that we do? What will it take to propitiate this hot-blooded Calif of yours so that he will leave us in peace?"

Smiling charmingly, Pukah appeared to consider the matter. "Khardan is, even now, upon his way to the city of Kich, ostensibly to sell horses to the Amir, but—in reality—to see how he is treated. If he is treated well, he will leave the city untouched, perhaps demanding only several hundred camels, a few sacks of gold and jewels, and a hundred bolts of silk as tribute. If he is in any way insulted or offended, he will level the place!" Pukah grew quite fierce when expressing this last, making a slashing motion with his hand as of a sword sweeping down upon a bare neck.

Kaug kept his face impassive, though he burned within with such flame that it was a wonder the water surrounding him didn't begin to boil. He regarded Pukah with thoughtful attentiveness. "If we treat your master as he—no doubt—deserves," the 'efreet said smoothly, "what will he do in return?"

"The Calif will distribute the wealth among the three tribes, then disband them, each going back to the land of his fathers. Quar may keep his city intact and pursue the war to the south in Bas, in whose people we take no interest."

"Magnanimous," said Kaug, nodding.

"That is the Calif," said Pukah. "Magnanimous to a fault!" The young djinn could tell by Kaug's face that the 'efreet was impressed, even awestruck. His plan was succeeding. Kaug would take news of this to Quar, who would back down and cease to threaten Akhran, who would allow the tribes of Jaafar and Majiid to go back to fighting each other, which would convince Zeid that they weren't going to fight him, which would send Zeid back to his home in the south—all of which would modestly be presented by Pukah as having been his doing and would gain for him the palace in the clouds and the djinniyeh in the bath.

Kaug, anxious to rid himself of his visitor so that he could speed this message to Quar, insisted that Pukah stay to dine, pressing his invitation by reaching into the pot and hauling out dinner by the tentacles.

Pukah, at this point, heard his master calling for him and retired from the 'efreet's premises with ungracious haste.

He had not been gone a second, however, before Kaug rose up out of the water. Able at last to release his rage, the 'efreet surged over the inland sea with the force of a hurricane, the waves foaming and leaping about him, the winds tearing at his flying hair.

In one hand he held lightning, which he hurled at the ground in anger. In the other he held a jeweled egg.

The Book
of Quar

CHAPTER 1

$\mathcal{T}$he sound of a gong, ringing three times, shivered through the incense-scented darkness. A man, asleep on a cotton pallet that was placed on the cold marble floor in a small alcove, wakened hastily at the sound. At first he stared at the small brass gong that sat upon the altar in disbelief, as if wondering whether he had truly heard its summons or if it had been part of his dream. The gong rang again, however, dispelling his doubts. Dressed only in a white cloth that he wore wrapped about his thin thighs, the man rose from the pallet and hastened across the polished marble floor.

Reaching the altar, which was made of pure gold fashioned in the shape of a ram's head, the man lit a thick beeswax candle, then prostrated himself flat before the altar, his arms outstretched above his head, his belly on the floor, his nose pressed against the marble. He had anointed himself with perfumed oil before retiring, and his brown skin glistened in the dim candlelight. His hair had never been cut—so to honor his God—and it covered his naked back like a black, shining blanket.

The slender body of the Imam quivered as it lay upon the floor, not from the cold or from fear but in eagerness. "It is I, Feisal, your unworthy servant. Speak to me, Quar, O Majesty of Heaven!"

"You have answered the summons swiftly."

Feisal raised his head, staring into the candle's flame. "Do I not—sleeping and waking—live within your Temple, Master, that I may be present to carry out your slightest wish?"

"So I have heard." Quar's voice came from the floor, the ceiling, the walls. It whispered around Feisal; he could feel its vibrations caress his body and he closed his eyes, almost overcome by the holy ecstasy. "I am pleased by this and by the good work you are doing in the city of Kich. Never before has a priest of mine been so zealous in bringing the unbeliever to salvation. I have my eye upon you, Feisal. If you continue to serve me in the future as well as you have served me up to the present, I think the great church of mine that shall one day encompass the world could have no better leader than yourself."

Feisal clienched his fists, a shudder of pleasure convulsed his body. "I am honored beyond telling, O King of All," the Imam whispered huskily. "I live only to serve you, to glorify your name. To bring that name to the lips of the *kafir* of this world is my greatest, my only desire."

"A worthy task, yet not an easy one," said the God. "Even now there comes to your city an unbeliever of the most heinous sort. A devout follower of the Ragged God, Akhran, he and his band of thieves ride to Kich, their intention: to spy upon the city. They plan to attack it and lead the people to the worship of their evil God."

"Akhran!" the Imam cried in a voice of horror such as might have shrieked out the name of a demon rising from the depths of Sul. Stunned by the shock, the Imam sat up, staring around the darkness that was alive with the presence of the God. The sweat that covered his oiled skin trickled down his bare breast. His ribs—all too visible from a lifetime of fasting—constricted, the stomach muscles tightened. "No! This cannot be!"

"Do not look upon this as a catastrophe. It is a blessing, proof that we are destined to win the holy war we fight, that we have learned of their perfidious scheme in time. Consult with the Amir, that you may devise together the best plan to deal with the unbelievers. And so that he knows you act by the command of Quar, you will find a gift from me upon the altar. Take it to the Amir's head wife, Yamina the Sorceress. She will know what use to make of it. My blessings upon you, faithful servant."

Hurling himself flat, Feisal pressed his body into the marble, hugging the floor as though he were physically clinging to his God. Slowly the rapture within him died and he knew Quar was with him no longer. Drawing a deep, shivering breath, the Imam rose unsteadily to his feet, his gaze going immediately to the altar. A sob choked him. Reverently he reached out his shaking hand, the damp fingers closing around the gift of the God—a small, ebony horse.

CHAPTER 2

ω hat is the business of the Akar in the city of Kich?" demanded the gate watchman.

"The Akar bring horses to sell to the Amir," replied Khardan somewhat irritably, "as we have done yearly since before the mud of Kich's first dwellings was dry. Surely you know this, Gate Master. We have always been granted entrance to the city without question before. Why this change?"

"You will find many changes in Kich now, *kafir*," the Gate Master replied, giving Khardan and his men a smug, scornful glance. "For example, before you enter, I must ask that you turn over all magical charms and amulets to me. I will guard them well, you may be certain, and they will be returned to you when you leave. Any djinn you possess you will take with you to the temple, where they will be given up as a show of respect to the Imam of Quar."

"Amulets! Charms!" Khardan's horse, sensing his master's anger, shifted restlessly beneath him. "What do you take us for—women? Men of the Akar do not travel under the protection of such things!" Checking his horse, bringing it once more under his control, Khardan leaned over the saddle, speaking to the Gate Master eye-to-eye. "As for djinn, if I had one with me—which I do not—I would throw it into the Waters of the Kafir before I would give it to the Imam of Quar."

The Gate Master flushed in anger. His hand strayed to the stout cudgel he carried at his side, but he checked the impulse. He had his orders concerning these unbelievers, and he was bound to carry them out no matter how much he might dislike it. Swallowing his rage, he bowed coldly to Khardan and with a wave of his hand, indicated that the nomads could enter.

Leaving the herd of horses outside the walls under the care of several of his men, Khardan and the rest of his *spahis* entered the gate of the city of Kich.

An ancient city that had stood for two thousand years at least, Kich had changed little during that time. Centrally located, built in a pass between the Ganzi mountains to the south and the Ganga mountains to the north, Kich was one of the major trading cities of Tara-kan.

Although under the *suzerain* of the Emperor, Kich was—or had been during most of its history—an independent city-state. Ruled by the family of the Sultan for generations, Kich paid annual rich tribute to the Emperor, expecting in return to be left alone to pursue its favorite pastime—the amassing of wealth. Its people were primarily followers of the Goddess Mimrim—a gentle Goddess, a lover of beauty and money. For centuries the people of Kich led an easeful life. Then matters began to change. Their goddess had never been demanding in the matter of daily prayers and so forth—such solemn things tended to disrupt both business and pleasure. The people began to turn from Mimrim, putting more faith in money than in their goddess. Mimrim's power dwindled and she soon fell victim to Quar.

The people of Kich knew nothing of the war in heaven. They knew only that one day the Emperor's troops, carrying the ram's-head flag—symbol of Quar—swept down on them from the north. The gates fell, the Sultan's bodyguards—drunk as usual—were slaughtered. Kich was now under the Emperor's direct control, the spearhead of an army pointed directly at the throat of the rich cities of Bas to the south.

The city was turned into a military stronghold. Kich was ideally suited for this, being surrounded by a wall seven and a half miles long. Dotted with towers, punctured by loopholes for archers, the wall had eleven gates that were now closed day and night. A curfew was imposed upon its citizens. Movement of any type around the city after eleven at night was forbidden by strict edict, enforced by severe penalty. Cudgel-carrying night watchmen patrolled the streets, banging on the gates of every courtyard they passed, ostensibly in order to frighten away thieves. In reality they were making certain that no fires of rebellion smoldered behind closed doors.

There were, in addition to these watchmen who walked the street, those who walked the roofs of the bazaars. Covered to protect them from the sun, the boothlike shops were provided with skylights every hundred feet or so. The watchmen patrolled these roofs, beating a drum and peering down through the skylights to see if there was any suspicious movement below.

There was no rebellion brewing in Kich, however. Although the people resented these measures at first, they soon found compensation. Business increased threefold. The roads to the north, previously too dangerous to travel because of raiding *batir*, were now guarded by the Emperor's troops. Trade between Kich and the capital city of Khandar flourished. The people of Kich began to look upon their new God, Quar, with a friendly eye and did not begrudge him his tribute or his demands for strict obedience.

By day, the *souks* of Kich were crammed with people. The jabbering and shouting and yelling of their bargaining mingled with the cries of the sellers enticing would-be customers. Shrieking, shrill-voiced children darted about underfoot. The air rang with curses, cajolings, and the laments of beggars, all tangled up in a confusion of growling, snorting, bleating, barking animals.

Space within the city was at a premium, for no one was foolish enough to dwell outside the protective walls. The streets were cramped and narrow, laid out in a crazy labyrinth in which a stranger was instantly, invariably, and irrevocably lost. Windowless houses made of clay covered over with plaster piled up against each other like ships run aground, facing any and every direction along streets that wound around and in and over and upon themselves, sometimes ending inexplicably in a blank wall, sometimes wandering up or down stairs that appeared to have been carved out of the houses themselves.

Entering the city, Khardan glanced about uneasily. Before, he had always found the noise and the smells and the excitement exhilarating. Now, for some reason, he felt trapped, stifled. Dismounting, the Calif motioned to one of the older men riding with the group.

"Saiyad, I don't like this talk of changes," Khardan said in a low voice. "Keep everyone together until my return and wait for me here."

Saiyad nodded. A cleared area inside the gate was used as a standing place for carts that had been brought into the city by traders. Seeing his men and their horses settled there and trusting to Saiyad to keep them out of trouble, Khardan and his younger brother Achmed turned their footsteps toward the *Kasbah*.

They did not have far to go. Combination palace and fortress, the *Kasbah* stood near the northern end of the city wall. The graceful minarets, tall spires, and cupola of the late Sultan's palace could be seen rising above its own protective wall that kept the palace aloof from the city. Made of crystalline quartz, its bulbous domes capped with gold, the palace itself shone like a jewel in the bright sunlight. Delicate, lacy latticework decorated the windows. The waving fronds of palms, visible above the walls, hinted at the pleasure gardens within.

It was Achmed's first visit to the city, and his eyes were wide with wonder.

"Watch where you are going," Khardan remonstrated, pulling his brother out of the path of a donkey, whose rider lashed out at them with his long stick. "No! Don't trouble yourself! Ignore him. He is beneath your notice. Look, look there."

Distracting his brother, who was glaring threateningly after the donkey rider, Khardan pointed to an octagonal-shaped stone building that stood on their left, opposite the walls of the *Kasbah*.

"That must be the new Temple they have built to Quar," Khardan said grimly, eyeing with disfavor the golden ram's head that gleamed over the entryway. "And over there"—he gestured to a tall minaret, the tallest in the city—"the Tower of Death."

"Why is it called that?"

"Thus do they deal with condemned criminals in Kich. The offender is bound hand and foot, then tied up in a sack. He is dragged to the top of the tower and hurled alive over its balcony, plummeting down into the street below. There his body lies unburied as a warning to all who would break the law."

Achmed gazed at the Tower of Death in awe. "Do you suppose we will get to see such a thing?"

Khardan shrugged, grinning. "Who knows? We have all day."

"Where do we go now? Don't we want to visit the palace?" Achmed asked in some confusion, noting that they seemed to be walking away from it.

"We must enter through the front gate, and that stands across the city, on the other side of this wall. To get there, we must go through the bazaars."

Achmed's eyes glistened with pleasure.

"Careful," added Khardan teasingly, "you keep swiveling your head like that, you'll break your neck."

"I want to see everything!" Achmed protested. Gasping, he grasped Khardan by the arm and pointed. "Who is that?"

Moving with sublime calm through the chaos and turmoil that swirled around him like seawater around an 'efreet was a man who outshone the sun. Dressed in bright yellow velvet robes—every inch of which was covered with golden embroidery and studded with jewels—the man wore loops of heavy gold chains about his neck. Silver and golden bracelets covered his arms; his fingers could not be seen for the rings that adorned them; his earlobes had been disfigured by the weight of the gold that hung from them. His skin was an olive color, his eyes slanted and painted with bright colors, outlined by stripes of black that ran from the lids to his ears. Behind him scurried a servant, holding a huge palmetto leaf over the man's head to shade him from the sun. Another servant walked beside him, cooling him with the constant breeze of a feathered fan.

"He is a moneylender, a follower of Kharmani, God of Wealth."

"I thought everyone in Kich worshiped Quar."

"Ah, even Quar dares not offend Kharmani. The economics of this city would come to a sudden halt if he did. Besides, the followers of Kharmani are few in number and probably not worth Quar's attention. They have no interest in wars or politics, being concerned only with money."

Achmed gazed at the man, who strolled along through the crowd with grand aplomb, seeming to thrive on the glances of envy and lust that were cast at him.

"Do they ever ride alone into the desert, these followers of Kharmani?" Achmed whispered to his brother. "One of those bracelets would support a man and three wives—"

"Don't even think such thoughts!" Khardan returned hastily. "You will bring down the wrath of the God on all of us! None dare rob one of Kharmani's chosen! The last time I was in Kich I saw a follower of Benario, God of Thieves, who had tried to pick a moneylender's pocket. The moment he touched the man's purse, his hand froze to it, and he was forced to spend the rest of his life trudging after his victim, his hand always in the man's pocket, never able to free himself."

"Truly?" Achmed appeared skeptical.

"Truly!" Khardan averred, hiding his smile.

Achmed was gazing regretfully after the moneylender when a strange, clanking sound coming from the opposite direction drew the young man's attention. Looking over his shoulder, he tugged at the sleeve of his brother's tunic. "Who are those poor wretches?"

Khardan's lip curled in disgust. "Slaves being taken to the slave market." He pointed to a row of tents standing a few feet from them. "I detest that part of the city. The sight leaves a bad taste in my mouth for days. See the white palanquin being carried behind them? The slave trader. Those men riding around him are *goums*, his bodyguards."

"Where do the slaves come from?"

"These are from Ravanchai, most likely." Khardan glanced coolly at the line of men and boys chained together, shuffling through the streets, heads bowed. "The people of that land are farmers"—he spoke with disdain—"living in small tribes. A peaceful people, they are easy prey for the traders and their bands of *goums*, who periodically sweep down on them, round up the strong young men and the comely young women, and carry them off to sell here in Kich."

"Women? Where are they?" Achmed studied the line of slaves with renewed interest.

"Probably in that covered cart, right in front of the palanquin. See how closely guarded it is? You can't see them, of course. They will be veiled. Only when they get to the selling block will the dealer remove their veils so that the buyers can see what they are purchasing."

Achmed licked his lips. "Perhaps with my share of the money I could—"

Khardan, with a quick, easy motion, cuffed the young man on the side of the face.

Putting his hand to his stinging cheek, his skin burning with embarrassment and pain, Achmed glared at his older brother. "What did you do that for?" he demanded, stopping in the middle of the street, where they were immediately surrounded by a group of half-naked children, begging for coins. "Father owns slaves. So do you—"

"Indentured servants!" Khardan rebuked him sternly. "Men

who have sold themselves to pay back a debt. Such slavery is honorable, for they work to buy their freedom. This man"—making an angry gesture toward the palanquin—"trades in humans for personal gain. He captures them against their will. Such a thing is forbidden by Akhran. Besides"—Khardan smiled, cuffing his brother on the cheek again, this time playfully—"the women you could afford you wouldn't want, and those you would want you couldn't afford."

They started on their way again, the beggar children setting up a wail of protest.

"Here," said Khardan, turning down a street to his right, "are the bazaars."

Gaping in wonder, Achmed immediately forgot his pain. He had never imagined such wealth and splendor, such an array of goods for sale, such a confusion of noise. Walking along, he looked down street after street of covered booths surrounded by gesticulating buyers.

Sections of the bazaars and sometimes entire streets in Kich were dedicated to selling specific types of merchandise. Directly across from the palace wall, on the southern side, was the Street of Copper and Brass—dazzling to the eye as sunlight glinted off its wares. Next to that stood the Baker's Bazaar, the smells from this street causing Achmed's stomach to rumble loudly. Canting away at an angle from this row of covered booths was the Carpet Bazaar—a blur of fantastic colors and designs that made one dizzy to look into it.

"Down that street," Khardan said, indicating a branching road that traveled farther south, "is Silk and Shoe bazaar. We will buy presents for our mothers there."

"And something for your wife?" Achmed said slyly, to pay for the blow.

"Perhaps." Khardan flushed and fell silent.

This not having been the answer Achmed expected, the young man glanced at this brother in some astonishment. Khardan saw rose-colored silk in his mind's eye. Smelling again the fragrance of jasmine, he hurriedly continued pointing out the sights. "Beyond that is the Wood and Straw sellers, then the Street of the Dyers and Weavers, the Street of the Rope-makers, the Potter's Bazaar, the Goldsmith's and Jeweler's, the Moneylenders, the Tobacco and Pipe dealers, and the Teahouses and the *arwat*—the rest-houses. Down that direction are streets where you may purchase magical charms and amulets, salt, sweetmeats, furs, iron-ware, and weapons."

"Weapons!" Achmed's eyes shone. His father had promised him a sword with a share of the money. He peered down the crowded street in a vain effort to catch a glimpse of shining steel. "We will go there first."

"Undoubtedly. Watch out." Khardan caught his brother just as the young man was about to stumble into a huge pool of water standing between the street and *Kasbah* wall.

"What is that?"

"A *hauz*. There are many different such artificial ponds in the city. The water comes from the mountains, carried by *ariqs*. It has many uses…" Khardan nudged Achmed, pointing out a man washing camel dung from his hands in the pool while a veiled woman filled a drinking jug not half a yard away. "Thirsty?"

"Not now!"

"City dwellers," Khardan said in the same tone in which he might have said "jackals." Achmed nodded, his young face solemn with newly acquired wisdom.

Mindful of the importance of their errand and knowing that the Amir's audience hours lasted only during the cool of the morning, Khardan hurried his brother along, keeping him from falling into the clutches of the vendors, who would soon have relieved the young man of the ten silver *tumans* he had brought with him. Seeing that the sun was nearing its zenith, the brothers left the bazaars and made their way to the great entrance of the *Kasbah*.

Two stalwart towers of stone flanked the massive wooden doors that stood open beneath an arched passage. Above the door, on the second story between the towers, ran a colonnaded porch. A third story, open to the air, was atop that. From the roof of this third story, directly above the door, hung a gigantic sword.

Suspended by strong iron chains, the magnificent sword was the symbol of the Amir, a powerful symbol that reminded all who looked upon it that they were under his iron rule. The sword was so large and so heavy that it had taken a veritable army of men and seven elephants to move it over the mountains from the capital city of Khandar.

The day the sword arrived in Kich had been a day of ceremony in the city, marking the ascension of the Amir to the throne. The 'efreet Kaug had hung the sword himself, the immortal's hands easily lifting the heavy weapon from the huge cart on which it traveled. The Imam blessed the sword, prophesying that it would hang there to glorify the new order of Quar, whose reign would last until the sun, the moon, and the stars fell from the skies. The people of Kich had, needless to say, been impressed.

Khardan was not. Staring grimly at the sword suspended above his head, he remembered regretfully how things had been in the past.

A solid-silver crescent moon had hung there in the days of the Sultan—a simple, pleasure-loving man who paid his annual tribute to the Emperor at Khandar and then promptly did his best to forget about politics for another year. There had been no questions asked at the gate under the Sultan's rule, no nonsense about bringing djinn to the Temple of the Imam. The guards in the tower that stood to the right of the great gate had languished half-asleep in the afternoon sun. There had been no curfew. Every night the city's men gathered around the *hauz* outside the great gate, coming there to relax, share the day's gossip in whispers, or listen to storytellers recalling days gone by. The soldiers in the barracks, located in the inner court to the gate's left, had lounged about, gambling, eyeing the veiled women who came to the *hauz*, or indulging in swordplay.

Now the guards in the tower were alert, scrutinizing all who entered. People still came to the *hauz* for water, but they did not linger long under the baleful gaze of the guards.

The wooden doors stood open, but there were guards here, too, who insolently questioned Khardan about everything from the lineage of his horses to his own—at which point the Calif nearly forgot himself. Only the remonstrating hand of his younger brother on his arm made Khardan—literally—bite his tongue to keep back the angry words.

Finally the guards ungraciously let them pass. They entered the cool shadows of the *Kasbah*; Achmed stumbled over the paving stones, his head craned at a painful angle to view the gigantic sword. Khardan strode beneath it without a glance, his face grim and stern and dark with suppressed anger.

The price of horses was going up.

CHAPTER 3

"$\mathcal{T}$he nomad and his men have arrived in the city, O King."

"Very well. Inform the Imam."

Bowing low, hands folded together, the servant retired, backing out of the audience room with silent steps. The Amir glanced at the Captain of the Guard, who lingered near the throne and who was not only second-in-command but chief Wazir. Civilian ministers had held this exalted position in the city of Kich in the past, but Kich was under military rule now; the Amir considered himself a general first and a reluctant king second.

Amir Abul Qasim Qannadi did not trust civilians. The last Wazir met the same fate as did his Sultan, having the distinct honor to be hurled over the cliff while the screams of his ruler could still be heard echoing among the jagged rocks below. When Qannadi took control of the city, the Amir replaced all civilian personnel with his own military men. A practical soldier, the Amir would have killed the minor officials as well, or at the very least thrown them into the dungeons. But the Imam, Feisal, as spiritual leader, demurred over this unnecessary bloodshed.

At Feisal's insistence the minor officials were given the choice of serving Quar in this life or serving their former God in death. Needless to say, one and all experienced a sudden religious transformation and were allowed to live, though dismissed from their posts. A few of those known to have been most loyal to the Sultan had later met with unfortunate accidents—all of them being waylaid and beaten to death by, so it was presumed, followers of Benario. Eyewitness reports that the followers of Benario were wearing the uniform of the Amir beneath their black cloaks were instantly discounted.

The Amir appeared grave when the families of these men protested. Qannadi expressed his regret, denied the rumors, and told them to thank Quar that Kich was now in the hands of someone who could restore law and order and make it safe for decent citizens. The Imam appeared graver still and comforted the relatives with the thought that their late fathers or husbands or brothers had found the true faith before departing this world.

What words Feisal—the Imam, and Qannadi—the Amir, exchanged over this matter in private were not known, but sharp-eyed court observers remarked that the next day the Amir's face was white with fury and he avoided the Temple, while the Imam appeared long-suffering and martyred. The quarrel between the two was patched up, according to whispers, by Qannadi's head wife, Yamina—a sorceress of great skill and power, who was also extremely religious and devout.

This was mere rumor and speculation. What was known for certain was that, following this incident, the Amir handed over the running of the city to the Imam and Yamina.

It turned out to be a providential arrangement for all concerned. The Amir, who detested the petty bureaucratic day-to-day affairs of state, was able to devote his entire attention to extending the war to the south. The Imam was able to exert the God's influence over the daily lives of the people, thus coming a step nearer his dream of establishing a city devoted to spreading the glory of Quar. As for the Amir's wife Yamina, it brought her two things she desired most: power and daily contact with the Imam.

When the Imam received word from his God that the *kafir* who dwelt in the Pagrah desert were making warlike, threatening gestures, the priest took the matter straight to the Amir.

The Imam expected Qannadi's reaction to this threat to be the same as his. Feisal's eyes shone with the scorching flame of holy zeal as the two walked together in the pleasure garden.

"We shall sweep down on them with our armies and show them the might of Quar. They will fall to their knees in worship as did the people of Kich!"

"Who? The Desert Dwellers?" Grinning, the Amir scratched his graying black beard with a small forked twig he had broken off an ornamental lemon tree. "A few bloody and broken bodies won't cause them to convert. They may not appear to be devout followers of their Ragtag God, but I'll wager you could throw each and every Akar off the highest cliff in the world and not a one would even spit in Quar's direction."

The Imam, shocked by such crude talk, reminded himself that the Amir, after all, was a soldier.

"Forgive my blunt tongue, but I think you underestimate the power of *Hazrat* Quar, O King," Feisal rebuked. "What's more, you overestimate the power this Wandering God exerts on his people. After all, what has he done for them? They live in the most appallingly desolate place in the known world. They are forced to roam the land in search of water and food, their lives are a constant struggle for survival. They are wild, uneducated, un-civilized, barely classifying as human beings at all. If we brought them into the city—"

"—They would rise up in the night and slit your throat," said the Amir. Plucking an orange off a tree and biting through the flesh with his strong teeth, he spit the peel out onto the walkway, to the disgust of several palace eunuchs.

"You border on sacrilege!" The Imam spoke in a low voice, breathing heavily.

Qannadi, glancing at the black eyes burning in the priest's gaunt face, suddenly deemed it wise to end the discussion. Stating that he would consider the matter from a military standpoint and let the Imam know of his decision, he abruptly turned on his heel and left the garden.

Feisal, fuming, returned to his Temple.

The next day Qannadi called the Imam to the *divan*—the audience chamber—and proposed a plan for dealing with the upstart Calif of the Akar. Feisal listened to the plan and expressed his concerns. He did not like it. The Amir had not expected he would. But Qannadi had sound reasons—militarily if not spiritual—for pursuing a more cautious course of action than the one the Imam proposed.

Feisal continued to press his arguments daily, hoping to persuade Qannadi to change his mind—all without result. Still the priest persisted, even to the last moment. Upon receiving word that Khardan was on his way to the palace, the Imam hurriedly left the Temple, and entering the *Kasbah* by a secret, subterranean passage built beneath the street, he hastened to Qannadi, hoping to make one final appeal.

"I understand that the nomad Khardan is on his way here, O King," Feisal said, approaching the rosewood throne where Qannadi sat dictating to a scribe a letter to the Emperor.

"We will conclude after luncheon." The Amir dismissed the scribe, who bowed and left the *divan*. "Yes, he is on his way. The guards have orders to let him pass, after a certain amount of harassment. My plans are in readiness. I presume"—Qannadi regarded the Imam with a cool glance from beneath white-streaked black brows—"that you still do not approve?"

Abul Qasim Qannadi was in his early fifties, tall and stalwart, with a face tanned by sun, burned by wind, lashed by rain. The Amir kept himself in prime physical condition, riding his warhorse daily and taking strenuous exercise with his officers and men. He detested a "soft" life, and his disgust at the excesses and luxuries indulged in by the late Sultan had been so great that—if he'd had his way—the palace would soon have been altered to resemble a barracks.

Fortunately the Amir's wives—led by Yamina—intervened. The silken tapestries remained in place, the ornately carved rosewood throne had not been hacked to kindling, the delicate vases were not crushed like eggshells. After much arguing, pouting, and sulking, Yamina, who—as head wife—could see to it that her husband's nights were extremely cold and lonesome, even persuaded the Amir to replace his comfortable military uniform with the silken, embroidered caftans of a ruler. He wore them only around the palace, however, never appearing in them before his troops if he could help it.

Bluff, sharp-tongued, quick to mete out discipline, Qannadi was the terror of the servants and the palace eunuchs, who had previously led an idyllic existence under the pleasure-loving Sultan and who now fled to Yamina for comfort and protection.

A djinn might have flown the world round and not found another human who contrasted more sharply with Qannadi than the Imam. In his middle twenties, yet already a power in the church, Feisal was a small-boned man whom the powerful Qannadi might have tucked under one arm and carried around like a child. But there was that about the Imam which made people, including the crusty old general, leery of crossing him. No one truly felt comfortable around Feisal. Qannadi often wondered, in fact, if the rumors were true that the Emperor had given the priest control of the church in Kich simply to be rid of him.

It was the presence of the God in the Imam that made other

mortals tremble before him. Feisal was a handsome man. His liquid, almond-shaped eyes were set in a fine-boned face. The lips of the mouth were sensuous. His long-fingered hands, with their gentle touch, seemed made for the pleasures to be found behind silken, perfumed curtains. Yamina was not the only one of the palace's wives and concubines to discover their interest in their religion renewed when the Imam took over as head of the church. But the women sighed for him in vain. The only passion that burned in the almond eyes was a holy one; the lips pressed their kisses never on warm flesh but only upon the cold and sacred altar of Quar. The Imam was devoted body and soul to his God, and it was this, Qannadi recognized, that made the priest dangerous.

Though the Amir knew his plan for dealing with the nomads was militarily sound and he had no intention of renouncing it, he could still not help but glance at the priest out of the corner of his eye. Seeing the thin face become too smooth, that look of martyred tolerance in the almond eyes, Qannadi's own expression hardened stubbornly.

"Well?" he prompted, irritated at the Imam's silence. "You disapprove?"

"It is not I who disapprove, O King," the Imam said softly, "but our God. I repeat my suggestion that you should act now to stop the unbelievers before they become too powerful."

"Bah!" Qannadi snorted. "Far be it from me to offend Quar, Imam, but he seeks only more followers. I have a war to fight—"

"So does Quar, O King," interrupted the Imam with unusual spirit.

"Yes, I know all about this war in heaven," Qannadi replied wryly. "And when Quar has to worry about His lines of supply being severed, His right flank being menaced by these hotheaded nomads, then I'll listen to His ideas on military strategy. As for the notion of calling up my troops from the south, marching them back five hundred miles, and sending them out in the desert chasing after an enemy that will have scattered to the four winds once they get there, it's ludicrous!"

The Amir's graying brows bristled. Closing over the beaked nose, they gave him the formidable glare of a fierce old bird of prey.

"Pull back and we give the southern cities time to strengthen.

No, I will not be drawn into fighting a war on two fronts. I do not believe it necessary, for one thing. The idea that these tribes have united! Hah!"

"But our source—"

"A djinn!" Qannadi scoffed. "The immortals work always for their own ends and be damned to either man or God!"

Seeing, from the swift flare of the almond eyes and the sudden pallor of the Imam's smooth skin that he had ridden near a deadly quagmire, the Amir retreated back to firmer ground, neatly turning his enemy's own weapon against him.

"Look here, Feisal—Quar himself professes as much. The wisest thing the God ever did was to order you to remove the djinn from the world. This is a military matter, Imam. Allow me to handle it my own way. Or"—he added smoothly—"will you be the one to tell the Emperor that his war to gain control of the rich cities of Bas has been halted to chase after nomads who will send their tribute to him in the form of horse manure?"

The Imam said nothing. There was nothing he could say. Feisal knew little of military matters, but even he could see that turning the spear point away from the necks of the south would give them a chance to draw breath and perhaps even allow them time to find the courage they seemed to have, for the moment, mislaid. Though devoted to his God, Feisal was not a fanatical fool. The Emperor was known as Quar's Chosen for good reason, possessing a power that even a priest dare not cross or thwart.

After a moment's thought Feisal bowed. "You have persuaded me, O King. What is it that I may do to assist you in your plan?"

The Amir wisely refrained from smiling. "Go to Yamina. Make certain all is in readiness. Then return to me here. I assume you want a chance to try to talk the *kafir* into transferring his faith to Quar?"

"Assuredly."

The Amir shrugged. "I tell you again, you waste your breath. Steel is the only language these nomads speak."

Feisal bowed again. "Perhaps, O King, because that is the only language they have ever heard spoken."

CHAPTER 4

Khardan and Achmed crossed the courtyard of the *Kasbah*, heading for the palace. To their right, standing just inside the great entryway, were the soldiers' barracks. There appeared to be an unusual amount of activity among the soldiers, activity that Khardan put down to preparations for the war in Bas. The uniformed men—dressed in their stiff-collared, waist-length red coats adorned on the back with the gold ram's head—stared at the nomads, dressed in their long, flowing black robes. There was enmity in the stares, but there was respect as well. The reputation of the nomads as a superb fighting force was well-known and well-deserved. Legend had it that an outpost in Bas had once surrendered without a blow on just hearing the rumor that the tribes of Pagrah were going to sweep down upon them.

Blissfully unaware of Pukah's wild tale, completely ignorant of the fact that they were—according to the djinn—here as spies, Khardan and Achmed noticed the soldiers' dark gazes but simply accepted them as a natural compliment to their fighting prowess.

"Shut your mouth; you'll swallow a fly." The Calif nudged his younger brother in the ribs as they approached the palace. "It's only a building, after all, built by men. Who are we to be impressed with such human creations? We have seen the wonders of Akhran."

Having lived with the sandy wonders of Akhran all of his seventeen years, and never having seen anything so splendid and beautiful as the palace with its golden domes and shimmering lacework and graceful minarets glittering in the sun, Achmed felt rather resentfully that he had a right to be impressed. Nevertheless, his respect and love for his elder brother was such that he immediately closed his gaping mouth and hardened his features, attempting to appear bored. Besides, he had his dignity to uphold among these soldiers, and he wished devoutly that he had a sword hanging at his side as Khardan wore his.

Entering the palace, under the scrutiny of more guards, Khardan was surprised to find the vast waiting room, which had—in the days of the Sultan—been packed with supplicants and grandees and ministers, now virtually empty. Their boots made a hollow sound, echoing beneath the ceiling whose wood beams were made of juniper and rosewood and whose intricate designs supposedly took a team of artisans thirty years to carve. Struck dumb by the beauty of the marvelous ceiling, the gorgeous tapestries lining the walls, the fantastic-patterned tiled floor beneath his feet, Achmed came to a complete standstill, staring about him in wonder.

"I like this less and less!" Khardan muttered, catching hold of his dazed brother and thrusting him forward. A silk-caftaned servant, gliding toward him, inquired his name and his business. Acting on Khardan's reply that he was expected, the servant led the nomads to an antechamber outside the *divan*. Khardan immediately removed sword and dagger, handing both weapons to a captain of the guard. Achmed turned over his dagger; then spread his robes to show that he wore no sword. The brothers started toward the door that led to the audience room when the captain stopped them.

"Wait. You may not proceed yet."

"Why not?" Khardan looked at the man in astonishment. "I have given you my weapons."

"You have not been searched." The captain made a gesture.

Turning, Khardan saw a eunuch step toward him.

"What is the meaning of this?" Khardan demanded angrily. "I am Calif of my people! You have my word of honor that my brother and I carry no weapons!"

"It is not the Amir's intention to insult the Calif of the Desert," the captain said with a sneer, "but it is now the law of Quar, as given to us through his most holy Imam, that the persons of all *kafir* are to be searched before being admitted into the presence of the Amir."

This is it, Achmed thought, tensing. Khardan won't stand for much more. And at first it seemed that this was Khardan's thought as well. His face pale with fury, the Calif fixed the eunuch with a stare so ferocious that the huge, flabby man hesitated, looking to the captain for counsel. The captain snapped his fingers. At this signal two guards, who had been standing on either side of the entrance to the *divan*, their sabers at their sides, drew the flashing blades and held them crossed before the door.

Khardan's inner mental battle was visible to Achmed. The Calif longed to walk from the place and kick the dust from his boots in the faces of everyone present, but his people needed the money and the goods it would buy to survive another year. It was they who would pay for any prideful act, no matter how satisfying. Quivering with anger, Khardan submitted to the search that was offensive and humiliating in the extreme, the eunuch's fat fingers, thrust inside the Calif's robe, poking and prodding, left no part of Khardan's body untouched.

Achmed, nearly dying of shame, was searched as well. Finding no hidden weapons, the eunuch nodded to the captain.

"Now may we enter?" Khardan demanded, his voice taut.

"When you are wanted, *kafir*, not before," replied the captain coolly, sitting at a desk and calmly preparing to eat his lunch—an act of extreme rudeness to the nomads, who never ate in anyone's presence without offering food first to the guest.

"And when will that be?" Khardan growled.

The guard shrugged. "Today, if you are lucky. Next week, if you are not."

Seeing Khardan's face flush darkly, Achmed cringed, waiting for the storm. But the Calif mastered his rage. Turning his back on the captain, folding his arms across his chest, Khardan strode over to examine other weapons that had been confiscated from those entering the Amir's presence. The ominous fact that the weapons were here, whereas their owners were not, might have spoken much to Khardan, had he been attentive. But in reality he wasn't even seeing the weapons. Fists clenched beneath his robes, he stared blindly into a blood-red tide of rage that was washing over him.

"Never again," he muttered, his lips moving in a silent vow. "As Akhran is my witness, never again!"

A servant entered from the *divan*. "The Amir will see the *kafir* Khardan, who calls himself Calif."

"Ah, you are lucky, it seems," the captain said, munching on a crusty hunk of bread.

The guards at the door stepped back, their blades held once more at their sides.

"I *am* the Calif. I have been Calif longer than this upstart has been Amir." Khardan glowered at the silk-clad, mincing servant, who raised his feathery eyebrows and looked down his long nose in disapproval of this speech.

"Go straight ahead," the servant said coldly, standing as far back as possible to permit the nomads to walk past.

His long robes sweeping around him, Khardan entered the *divan*. Achmed, following, noted that the servant's nose wrinkled at the strong smell of horse that clung to them both. Head held high, Achmed deliberately brushed up against the elegant servant. Glancing back behind him to enjoy the man's reaction of disgust, Achmed saw something else.

The captain, lunch forgotten, had risen from the table and was loosening his sword in his belt. Gesturing, he gave an order in a low voice. The doors they had entered, doors that led to the outside of the *Kasbah*, swung shut on silent hinges. Two more guards, swords drawn, slipped quietly into the room and took up positions before the barred doors.

Achmed reached out for his brother. Their way out of the palace had been sealed off.

CHAPTER 5

"Not now, Achmed!" Khardan snapped nervously, brushing away his younger brother's hand that was urgently tugging at the sleeve of his robe. "Do as I told you. Bow when I bow and keep your mouth shut."

Crossing the colorful mosaic-tiled floor of the *divan*, Khardan glanced about the audience chamber, noting a great many changes since the Sultan's time. In bygone days the divan would have been filled with people standing about, discussing their dogs or their falcons or the latest court gossip, waiting for the Sultan's eye to fall upon them that they might curry his favor. Poorer supplicants, herded into a corner, would have waited humbly to present cases as important as a murdered relative or as trivial as a dispute over the rights to a stall in the bazaar. Numerous servants, scurrying here and there on bare feet, kept all in order.

The *divan* today, by contrast, was empty. "On entering the front, always look to the back." Thus goes the old saying. Acting with the instincts of a seasoned warrior, Khardan quickly studied the chamber that he had not visited in over a year. Closed on three sides, the high-ceilinged, rectangular-shaped room was open on a fourth—a columned balcony looked out over the beautiful pleasure garden below. Khardan glanced longingly in that direction without even realizing that he did so. He could see the tops of ornamental trees at a level with the balcony. A breeze scented with the perfume of exotic flowers drifted through the *divan,* sunlight streamed in between the columns. Huge wooden partitions, standing near the walls, could be pulled across the floor to seal shut the *divan* when the weather was inclement or if the palace was under attack.

Doors led from the chamber to various other parts of the palace, including the Amir's private living quarters. The Amir's bodyguards stood at these, two more flanked his throne. Khardan glanced at them without interest. Now that he had familiarized himself with the room, his attention turned upon the man—Abul Qasim Qannadi, the Amir of Kich.

Two men stood near the rosewood throne that had been the Sultan's. Khardan examined each closely, and had no trouble determining which was the Amir—the tall man with the straight, broad shoulders, who moved awkwardly in the richly embroidered silken caftan. Hearing Khardan approach, the Amir gathered the long sweeping folds of silk in his hand and stiffly climbed the stairs leading up to the rosewood throne. Qannadi grimaced as he sat down, he obviously found the throne uncomfortable. Khardan—noting the deeply tanned, weathered face—guessed that this was a man who would be much more at home seated in a saddle. The Calif felt his anger slip away from him; here was a man he could understand. Unfortunately it did not occur to Khardan that here was a man he should fear.

The other man moved to stand beside the throne. Noting he was a priest by the plain white robes that hung straight from the shoulders, Khardan barely spared him a glance. The Calif wondered idly what interest a priest could have in the selling of horses, but supposed only that perhaps he and the Amir had been conferring and that the arrival of Khardan had interrupted their talk.

Reaching the foot of the throne, the Calif made the formal *salaam,* bowing, his hand moving in the graceful gesture from forehead to breast as he had been accustomed to performing before the Sultan. Watching out of the corner of his eye in order to make certain Achmed was imitating him and doing nothing to disgrace them both, Khardan missed the shocked expression that crossed the Imam's face and the man's furious hand gesture. Straightening, the Calif was considerably surprised to find an armed guard stepping between him and the Amir.

"What do you mean by this lack of respect, *kafir?*" the guard said. "On your knees to the representative of the Emperor—Quar's Chosen, the Light of the World."

Khardan's temper flared. "I am Calif of my people! I go on my knees to no one, not to the Emperor himself were he here!"

"Worm!" The guard raised his sword threateningly. "You would be on your belly if the Emperor were here!"

Khardan's hand went for his weapon, only to close over empty air. Frustrated, his face flushing dark, he took a step toward the guard as if he might challenge him bare-handed, but a deep voice came from the throne.

"Leave him be, Captain. He is, after all, a prince." Khardan, his blood throbbing in his ears, did not hear the subtle mockery in the man's voice. Achmed did, and his heart was in his throat. The strange, chill emptiness of this huge chamber made him uncomfortable; he distrusted the man on the throne with his cold, impassive expression. But it was the priest with his thin, wasted face that made the hair on the young man's neck prickle and rise as does that of an animal who senses danger yet cannot find the source. Achmed wanted to look anywhere else in the chamber except into those burning eyes that seemed to see nothing of any consequence in this world, only in the next. But he couldn't. The almond eyes caught him and held him fast, a prisoner of the Imam's more surely than if the priest had bound the young man in chains. Frightened, ashamed of his fear, Achmed was helpless to speak it. He could do nothing except obey his brother's instructions and pray that they escaped this terrible place alive.

"Let me introduce myself," the Amir was saying. "I am Abul Qasim Qannadi, General of the Imperial Army and now Amir of Kich. This"—he gestured to the priest—"is the Imam."

The priest did not move but remained staring at Khardan, the holy fire rising in him, burning hotter and hotter. Khardan, glancing at the priest, was touched by the flame. He found that, like his brother, he could not easily withdraw his gaze.

"I . . . trust we can conclude our business swiftly, O King." Khardan appeared somewhat disconcerted. "My men wait for me near the Temple." Wrenching his gaze from the Imam's hold with what seemed an almost physical effort, he glanced uncomfortably about the chamber. "I do not feel at ease within walls."

Beckoning to a scribe, who came forward with a sheaf of papers, the Amir referred to them briefly, then looked back at Khardan. "You come here to offer your tribe's horses for sale as you have done annually according to the records," said the Amir, his dark eyes regarding the Calif coolly.

"That is true, O King."

"Did you not know that much has changed since your last visit?"

"Some things never change, O King. One of these is an army's need for good horses. And ours"—Khardan lifted his head proudly—"are the best in the world."

"So it does not disturb you to sell your horses to enemies of the late Sultan?"

"The Sultan was not my friend. He was not my enemy. His enemies, therefore, are neither my friends nor my enemies. We did business together, O King," said Khardan succinctly. "That is all."

The Amir raised an eyebrow; whether he was startled at the answer or impressed with it was impossible to tell. The impassive face was unreadable. "What price do you ask?"

"Forty silver *tumans* a head, O King."

The Amir referred again to the paper. The scribe, whispering something, pointed to a row of what looked to Khardan to be bird tracks on the sheet.

"That is higher than last year," the Amir said.

"As you said," remarked Khardan coolly with a glance toward the antechamber where he had been searched, "some things have changed."

The Amir actually smiled—a smile that drove one corner of his mouth deeper into his beard—and went back to studying the paper, his hand stroking his chin meditatively. Khardan remained standing before him, arms folded across his chest, looking anywhere but at the Imam. Achmed, unnoticed and forgotten, glanced continually at their exit that was an exit no longer and wished himself back in the desert.

"May I ask you a question, Calif?" The Imam's voice flicked like a flame. Khardan started, as though it had burned his skin. Glancing at the Amir and seeing him apparently absorbed in studying the figures on last year's sale of the horses, Khardan—his eyes dark and shadowed—reluctantly faced the priest.

"You are a *kafir*, an unbeliever, is that not true?"

"No, it is not true, Holy One. My God and the God of my people is Akhran the Wanderer. Our belief in him is strong."

"Yet thankless, is it not, Calif? I mean"—the Imam spread his long-fingered hands—"what does he do for you, this Wandering God? You dwell in the cruelest of lands, where every drop of water is counted as precious as a jewel, where the sun's heat can boil the blood, where blinding storms of sand flay the flesh from the bone. Your people are poor, forced to live in tents and to roam from place to place to find food and water. The meanest beggar in our streets has at least a roof over his head and food to eat. You are uneducated, neither you nor your children"—his gaze went to Achmed, who immediately looked somewhere else—"can read or write. Your lives are unproductive. You are born, you live, you die. This God of yours does nothing for you!"

"We are free."

"Free?" The Imam appeared puzzled.

Achmed noticed that the Amir, though seemingly involved in reading the document, was listening and watching intently out of the corner of his eye.

"We are under the rule of no man. We follow no one's laws but our own. We move freely as the sun, taking what we need from the land. We work for ourselves. Our sweat is not another's profit. We cannot read"—he gestured toward the Amir's document—"scratches drawn on paper. But why should we? What need is there?"

"Surely there is need to read the sacred writings of your God!"

Khardan shook his head. "The text of our God is written on the wind. We hear his voice singing in the dunes. We see his words in the stars that guide our way through the land. Our sacred credo soars on the wings of a hawk, it beats in the hooves of our horses. We look into the eyes of our wives and see it there. We hear it in the cry of every newborn child. To capture that and commit it to the bondage of paper would be an evil thing. Our God forbids it."

"So"—the Imam smiled—"your God *does* give you commands and you obey them?"

"Yes."

"Then you are not truly free."

"We are free to disobey," remarked Khardan, shrugging.

"And what is the punishment for disobedience?"

"Death."

"And what is the reward for leading a virtuous life?"

"Death."

A noise came from the Amir, a sort of low chuckling sound that immediately became a clearing of the throat when the Imam cast him an irritated glance. Qannadi turned his gaze back on

Khardan, who was becoming increasingly impatient at what he considered childish ramblings. Adults did not waste their time speaking or thinking of such obvious things. Achmed saw the flickering fire in the priest's eyes and wished his brother were taking this more seriously.

"So you are free to lead a harsh life and die a cruel death. These are the gifts of this God of yours?"

"The life we live is our own. We do not ask you to live it or understand it. As for death, it comes to all, unless you have discovered some way for city walls to shut it out."

"Those who have been blind from birth, who walk in perpetual darkness, are said not to be able to comprehend light, having never seen it." The Imam's voice was gentle. "One day your eyes will be opened to the light. You will walk in Quar's radiance and you will realize how blind you have been. You will leave off your aimless wandering and come here to the city to glory in the gifts of Quar to his people and to show your thankfulness to him by leading productive, useful lives."

Khardan cast a glance at his younger brother, rolling his eyes significantly. Among the nomads the insane are well treated, for all know that they have seen the face of the God. One did not listen to their ravings, however. The Calif pointedly turned his attention back to the Amir.

Clearing his throat again, Qannadi handed the paper to the scribe, dismissing the man with a wave of his hand.

"I am pleased to hear your people have such a philosophical outlook, Calif." The Amir regarded Khardan with cold eyes. "For a harsh life is about to become harsher. We have no need for your horses."

"What?" Khardan stared at the Amir in amazement.

"We have no need of your horses now, nor is it likely that we ever will in the future. You must return to your people empty-handed. And much as you despise the city, it does supply you with certain necessities of life without which you may find it difficult to survive. That is," he added with heavy irony, "unless your God has seen fit to rain down rice and wheat from the heavens."

"Do not take me for some rug merchant, O King," Khardan said grimly. "Do not think you can make me run after you, offering you a lower price because you first turn away. You may go to a hundred rug merchants, but you will find only one man who sells the horses you need to carry you to victory. Animals bred to war who will not shy at the smell of blood. Animals who prick their ears to the call of the trumpet, who lunge forward into the heart of the battle. Animals descended from the horse of the God! Nowhere—nowhere on this world—will you find such horses!"

"Ah, but you see, Calif, we are no longer limited to this world," the Amir said. "Send for my wife," he instructed a servant, who bowed and ran to do his bidding.

"Perhaps this is the light of which you spoke, Imam," continued the Amir conversationally in the tense silence that followed. "Perhaps hunger will open their eyes and lead them to the city walls they despise."

"Quar be praised if this is so," the Imam said earnestly. "It will be the saving of their bodies, the salvation of their souls."

Khardan, scowling, said nothing but glowered at them both. He had taken an involuntary step backward on hearing the Amir send for his wife. Zeid's words came back to him. The Amir's head wife—*reputedly a sorceress of great power.* Khardan did not fear magic, considering it a woman's province, suitable for healing the sick and calming horses during a storm. But—as something he could not control—he did not trust it. He had heard stories of the powers of the ancients, stories of the power to be found in the *seraglios* of the city dwellers. He had scoffed at these, despising men who let their women become too strong in this arcane art. Looking at the powerful Qannadi, however, it occurred to Khardan—rather late—that he may have misjudged the matter.

A woman entered the *divan.* She was clothed in a *chador* of black silk, embroidered with threads of spun gold that had been stitched to form dots like small suns over the surface of the fabric. Though her figure was completely hidden, the woman moved with a grace that spoke of the beauty and symmetry of her form. A black veil rimmed in gold covered her face and head, leaving only one eye visible. Outlined in *kohl*, that one staring eye regarded Khardan boldly, penetrating him, as though the focus of her two eyes had been combined and were thus made stronger in just one.

"Yamina, show this *kafir* the gift of Quar to his people," ordered the Amir.

Bowing before her husband, her hands pressed together to her forehead, Yamina turned to face Khardan, who stared at her coldly;

the ever-shifting dunes revealed more expression than his face.

Slipping jeweled fingers into the filmy folds of the *chador,* Yamina withdrew an object. Placing it in the palm of her hand, she held it out before Khardan.

It was a horse, wonderfully carved, made of ebony. Perfect in every detail, standing about six inches tall, the animal's nostrils were two fiery red rubies, and topaz gleamed in the eyes. Its saddle was of fine ivory with gold and turquoise trappings. Its hooves were shod with silver. Truly it was an exquisite work of art, and Achmed, looking at it, sighed in longing. But Khardan remained unimpressed.

"So this is Quar's gift to his people," the Calif said scornfully, glancing swiftly at the Amir to see if he were being made sport of. "A child's toy."

"Show him, Yamina," the Amir ordered gently, by way of answer.

The sorceress placed the horse upon the floor. Touching a ring she wore upon her hand, she caused the setting of the jewel to spring open. From inside the ring Yamina withdrew a tiny paper scroll. Prying open the horse's mouth, she tucked the scroll inside, clamping the statue's teeth over it so that it held it firmly. As she knelt beside the toy horse, the single, visible eye of the sorceress closed; she began to whisper arcane words.

A puff of smoke came from the horse's mouth. Catching hold of Achmed's hand, Khardan drew back away from the animal, his face dark with suspicion. The Imam murmured to himself in a low voice—prayers to Quar undoubtedly. The Amir watched with amused interest.

Khardan drew a shivering breath. The horse was growing! As the sorceress spoke, repeating the same words over and over, the animal gained in height and width; now it was a foot tall, now it came to Khardan's waist, now it was as tall as a man, now as tall as the Califs own warhorse. The sorceress's voice hushed. Slowly she rose to her feet, and as she did so, the ebony horse turned its head to look at her and it was ebony no more!

The horse was flesh and blood, as real and alive as any steed that ran free in the desert. Khardan stared at it, unable to speak. Never had he seen magic such as this, never believed it possible.

"Praise be to Quar!" breathed the Imam reverently. "A trick!" Khardan muttered through clenched teeth.

The Amir shrugged. "If you like. It is, however, a 'trick' that Yamina and the rest of my wives and the wives of the grandees and nobles of this city can all perform." Rising to his feet, the Amir descended from the rosewood throne, coming to stroke the horse's neck. It was, Khardan could plainly see, a magnificent animal—restive, with a spirit to match the fiery ruby red of its nostrils. The horse's eyes rolled round to view its strange situation, its hooves dancing nervously on the tiled floor.

"This fine animal is, as I said, a gift from the God," the Amir remarked, stroking the velvety black nose. "But the spell will work on any object made into a likeness of a horse. It may be carved of wood, shaped of clay. One of my own sons, a lad of six, fashioned one this morning."

"Do you take me for a fool, O King?" Khardan demanded angrily. "Asking me to believe women can perform such magic as this!"

But even as he spoke, Khardan's eyes went to Yamina. The single, staring eye of the sorceress was on him, its gaze unblinking, unwavering.

"It doesn't matter to me what you believe, Calif," the Amir said imperturbably. "The fact remains that I do not need your horses, which places you and your people in a desperate situation. But Quar is merciful." The Amir raised a hand to prevent Khardan from interrupting. "We have room in the city to house you and your tribesmen. Bring your people to Kich. Work will be found for you. The men of your tribe can join the ranks of my own armies. Your reputation as warriors is well-known. I would be honored" —his voice changed subtly, his sincerity on this point was obvious—"to have you ride among us. Your women can weave rugs and make pottery to sell in the bazaar. Your children will go to school in the Temple, learn to read and to write—"

"—And the ways of Quar, O King?" Khardan concluded coldly.

"Of course. No one may live within these walls who is not a devout follower of the one, true God."

"Thank you, O King, for your generosity," said Khardan, bowing. "But my people and I would sooner starve. It seems we have wasted our time here. We will be leaving—"

"There, you see!" said the Imam quickly, coming forward. His thin arm raised, he pointed a trembling finger at Khardan.

"Now do you believe, O King!"

"So!" thundered the Amir in a voice that caused the horse to neigh shrilly, thinking it heard the call to battle. "It is true! You are spies, come to scout the city so that you and your murdering dev-ilmen may sweep out of the desert and attack us. Your attempt has failed, Calif! Our God is all-knowing, all-seeing, and we have been warned of your treacherous plans!"

"Spies!" Khardan stared at the man in amazement. "Guards!" shouted the Amir above the horse's whinnyings, the commotion causing it to rear up on its hind legs. "Guards! Seize them!"

CHAPTER 6

Forced to hold on to the bridle of the plunging, excited horse, the Amir called loudly for the guards, who began running from all corners of the room. Gliding out of the way of the flashing hooves, moving near the rosewood throne, the Imam watched intently, his face grave. Beside him stood Yamina, her hand resting lightly on the priest's bare arm, the single, visible eye staring out from the shimmering black fabric of her robes. The Amir's bodyguards, who had been flanking the throne, ran toward Khardan and Achmed, sabers flashing.

Thrusting Achmed behind him, Khardan kicked out at the guard nearest him. The Calif's black riding boot struck the guard's swordhand. Bone crunched, and the saber went flying, falling to the tile floor with a clatter.

"Get it!" Khardan cried, shoving Achmed toward the blade skidding over the floor.

Stumbling in his haste, Achmed dove for the saber. The other bodyguard swung his blade in a vicious stroke that would have parted Khardan's head from his shoulders had not the Calif ducked down beneath it. Rising again swiftly, Khardan blocked the guard's follow-through stroke with his forearm, seized the man's wrist with both hands, and twisted.

Bones cracked, the guard screamed in pain, his sword fell from limp fingers. Shoving the guard backward into another, Khardan picked up the sword. Achmed stood at his back, his own weapon raised.

"That way!" Khardan shouted, jumping toward the ante-chamber through which they had entered.

"No, it's sealed off!" Achmed gasped. "I tried to tell you—"

But Khardan wasn't listening. His eyes swept the *divan*, searching for a way out.

"Shut the partitions!" the Amir bellowed. "Shut the partitions! "

The partitions! Turning, Khardan saw the balcony, the tops of the trees visible in the pleasure garden below. The garden was surrounded by a wall and beyond that wall was the city and freedom. But already servants were scurrying in a panic to obey the Amir's command. The partitions, scraping against the tile floor, were hastily being dragged shut.

Khardan shoved his brother toward the balcony. A guard leaped at the Calif, but a slicing swing of Khardan's saber caused him to fall back, clutching his arm that had been nearly severed from his body. Turning, Khardan ran after his brother, his robes swirling about him as he raced toward the partitions.

They were almost shut, but the servants—seeing the two desert nomads hurtling down on them, weapons flashing in the sun—broke and ran, shrieking, for their lives. The Amir's voice echoed throughout the *divan,* cursing them all for cowards.

Squeezing between the partitions, Khardan and Achmed ran out onto the balcony.

"Shut those!" Khardan ordered Achmed while he hurried to look over the smooth stone balustrade. It was a twenty-foot drop, at least, into the garden below. Hesitating, he turned around. Behind him could be heard the stomping of feet; he could see the partitions being forced apart again. There was no help for it.

Grabbing hold of Achmed, he helped his brother over the stone railing.

Keeping one eye on the slowly parting partition, Khardan climbed over the balustrade, perching precariously on the narrow lip of stone.

"The flower bed! Jump for it!" he ordered.

Dropping his sword down first, Achmed prepared to follow. He couldn't make himself jump, however. Clinging to the railing with both hands, his face white and strained, he stared down at the garden that seemed miles beneath him.

"Go!"

Khardan shoved his brother with his boot. Achmed's hands slipped, he fell with a cry. Tossing his own sword down into the flowers, the Calif leaped after him, falling through the air and landing in the flower bed below with the grace of cat.

"Where's my sword? Are you all right?"

"Yes," Achmed managed to answer. The heavy fall had jarred him, leaving him dazed and shaken. Blood trickled from his mouth; he'd bitten his tongue on landing and wrenched his knee painfully, but he would die before admitting this to his elder brother. "Your sword's there, by those pink things."

Seeing the hilt flash in the sunlight, Khardan swiftly bent down and caught hold of it. He glanced around, getting his bearings, trying to remember what he knew of the palace and its environs. He had never, of course, been in the pleasure garden before. Only the Sultan, his wives, and his concubines were allowed here, spending the heat of the day relaxing amid the shade trees and orange blossoms, dabbling in the ornamental pools, playing among the hedgerows. Located at the eastern end of the palace, far from the soldiers' barracks and surrounded by a high wall, the garden was private and effectively cut off from the city noises and smells.

"If we climb the northern wall, we should come out near our men," Khardan muttered.

"But which way leads north?" Achmed asked, staring helplessly at the maze of hedges and branching paths.

"We must pray to Akhran to guide us," the Calif said.

At least there weren't any guards here, he thought, knowing that only the eunuchs were allowed in the pleasure gardens with the women. But he could hear shouts and orders being issued. That would undoubtedly change. They hadn't much time.

Plunging out of the flower bed, he jumped onto a path, startling a gazelle that bounded off in fright. Glancing back, he motioned for his brother to come behind him. The boy's face was pale but grim and resolute. Khardan saw him limping.

"Are you sure you're all right?"

"I'm fine. Just get us out of here."

Nodding, Khardan turned and selected a path that appeared to lead toward the north. He and Achmed followed it until it opened into a wide patio around a pond. Achmed was about to step out, but Khardan pulled him back into the bushes. "No! Look above!"

Archers lined the balcony, their bows ready, their arrows aimed into the garden below.

Keeping himself and his brother hidden as best he could among the hedgerows, daring to raise his head only now and then to see if he could locate the wall, Khardan tried first one path, then another, becoming increasingly frustrated as each seemed to lead him deeper and deeper into the garden's sweet-smelling labyrinth. Achmed kept up, never complaining. But Khardan knew the boy was nearly finished; he could hear Achmed's breath come in in painful gasps, his limp was worsening.

Rounding a corner, the Calif finally caught a glimpse of the wall and he breathed a sigh of relief. By this time he was so disoriented he didn't know if it would bring him out to the right place or not, but he didn't care. Once he was in the open, he would take on the Amir's army if he had to.

But as he drew nearer the wall, Khardan's heart sank. It was over twenty feet high, smooth and sheer, without a handhold or foothold visible. Vines that might have grown over it had been cut away. The trees that stood near it had all been pruned to prevent any branches from overhanging the wall. Obviously the Sultan had been careful of his wives, making certain that no would-be lovers had easy access to his garden.

Gnashing his teeth in frustration, Khardan ran along the base of the wall, hoping desperately to find a crack in the surface, a vine some gardener might have overlooked, anything! The whiz and thud of an arrow near him let him know that even if they couldn't be seen plainly, their movements through the foliage were easily detected. Already guards must be pouring through the gates. . . .

"No! Please, let me go!" begged a voice. "I'll give you my jewels, anything! Please, please don't take me back there!"

Khardan stopped. It was a woman's voice and it sounded very near him. Holding up his hand, warning Achmed—coming along behind him—to stop, the Calif peeped cautiously through a stand of rose trees. Thankful for the rest, Achmed leaned dizzily back against the wall, massaging his leg that throbbed and burned with each move.

About five feet from Khardan a woman was struggling with two of the palace eunuchs—big men, their bodies had run to flab as often happens among their kind, but they were strong nevertheless. Holding the woman's arms, the eunuchs were dragging her down a path, presumably toward the palace. The woman was young, her clothes were disheveled and torn, and her veil had been ripped from her head, leaving her face and head visible.

Khardan—even in the midst of his own danger—gasped in awe at her beauty.

He had never in his life seen hair like that. Long and thick, it was the color of burnished gold. When she shook her head in her pleadings, it billowed about her in a golden cloud. Her voice, though choked with tears, was sweet. The skin of her arms and breasts, plainly visible through the torn fabric of her clothes, was white as cream, pink as the roses that surrounded him.

That she had been ill-treated was obvious. There were bruises on her arms, and—Khardan sucked in his breath in anger—marks of a lash could be seen on her bare back.

"Stay here!" Khardan ordered Achmed. Running out onto the path, his sword drawn, the Calif accosted the eunuchs.

"Let her go!" he demanded.

Startled, the eunuchs turned, their eyes opening wide at the sight of the desert nomad in his long robes and riding boots, the saber in his hand.

"Help!" cried one of the eunuchs in quavering, high-pitched squeaks, still holding firmly to the girl. "Intruders in the *seraglio!* Help! Guards!"

His captive turned a lovely face toward Khardan, peering up at him through a golden shower of hair.

"Save me!" she begged. "Save me! I am one of the Sultan's daughters! I have been hiding in the palace, but now they have discovered me and are taking me to cruel torture and death! Save my life, bold stranger, and all my fortune is yours!"

"Shut up!" One of the eunuchs slapped the girl with the back of his fat hand.

He screamed in pain himself the next moment, staring stupidly at the bloody gash that had split his arm open from shoulder to wrist.

"Let her go!" Khardan leaped menacingly at the other eunuch, but he already let loose of the girl's arm.

"Guards! Guards!" The eunuch cried in panic, backing away from Khardan and finally turning and running down the path, the flesh of his flabby body jiggling and bouncing ludicrously. The other eunuch had fainted dead away and lay with his head in a pool, his blood staining the water red.

"How do we get out of here?" Khardan demanded, catching hold of the girl as she threw herself into his arms. "Quickly! There are guards hunting for me as well! My men are outside the wall, by the slave market. If we can just get to them—"

"Yes!" she panted, clinging to him. "Just give me a moment."

Her breasts, pressed against Khardan's chest, heaved as she sought to catch her breath. Her fragrance filled his nostrils, her hair brushed against his cheek, shining as silken web. She was warmth and roses and tears and softness, and Khardan put his arm around her, drawing her closer still and soothing her fright.

She was as courageous as she was beautiful, apparently, for she drew a quivering breath and thrust herself away from him. "There is . . . a secret way. . . through the wall. Follow me!"

"Wait! My brother!" Khardan darted back into the bushes, coming out with Achmed behind him.

Beckoning with a hand so slim and white it might have been the petals of the gardenia blooming around them, the girl motioned Khardan and Achmed to follow her down a path that neither of them would ever have seen, so cunningly hidden was it by the twists and turns of the maze. No more arrows fell around them. They could hear questioning shouts of deep voices, however, and the shrill piping of the eunuch.

The girl did not hesitate but led them confidently through a veritable jungle of foliage in which both of them must immediately have been lost. Khardan could no longer see the wall; he couldn't see anything through the tall trees, and the vaguest suspicion of doubt was starting to form in his mind when suddenly they rounded a corner and there was the wall, a stand of bushes with long, wicked-looking thorns backed up against it.

Khardan stared at it gloomily. They might use the bushes to climb the wall, but their flesh would be in shreds by the time they reached the top. He wondered, too, if the thorns were poisonous. A drop of something waxy glistened at the tip of each. Still, it was better than languishing in the Arnir's prison. He started to shove the girl behind him, planning to climb the bush, when—to his surprise—she stopped him.

"No, watch!" Hurrying to the wall, the girl pulled out a loose rock. There was a grinding sound, and to Khardan's astonishment, the thorn bush slowly moved aside, revealing an opening in the wall. Through it, Khardan could see the marketplace and hear the babble of many voices.

Other voices behind them—the guards'—were growing

louder. The girl darted out into the street. Grasping hold of Achmed, Khardan thrust his brother through the hole in the wall and followed after him.

He found the girl kneeling down beside a blind beggar who happened to be sitting just near the wall's opening. She was talking to him hurriedly. Khardan, watching in amazement, saw her draw a golden bracelet from her wrist and drop it into the beggar's basket. The blind beggar, with amazing dexterity for one who couldn't see, snatched up the bracelet and hurriedly stuffed it down the front of his rags.

"Come!" The girl grasped Khardan's hand.

"What about the opening in the wall?" he asked. "They'll know we've escaped. . ."

"The beggar will take care of it. He always does. Where did you say your men are waiting?"

"By the slave market."

Khardan glanced around the streets. Achmed was looking at him expectantly, waiting for orders, but the Calif had no idea which way was which. The bazaars all melded into one another; he was completely lost. The girl, however, seemed to know exactly where she was. Hurriedly she drew Khardan and his brother into the crowd around the colorful stalls. Looking backward, the Calif was astonished to see the wall smooth and unbroken, the beggar sitting there, his milk-white eyes seeing nothing, a basket with a few coppers on the ground before him.

No one else seemed to be paying any attention to them. "The soldiers will suppose they have you trapped in the garden!" The girl, holding on to Khardan tightly, pointed. "There is the slave market. . . and . . . are those your men?" She faltered. "That. . . rough-looking group. . . ."

"Yes," said Khardan absently, thinking. "You believe the soldiers will concentrate on searching the palace?"

"Oh, yes!" The girl looked directly at him, her eyes wide, and he suddenly noticed that they were blue as the desert sky, blue as sapphires, blue as cool water. "You will have time to flee the city. Thank you, brave one"—she flushed, her eyes lowering modestly before his gaze—"for rescuing me."

Khardan saw the girl swaying on her feet. Catching hold of her in his arms as she fell, he cursed himself for not having realized she must be weak and dazed from her terrible ordeal.

"I'm sorry," she murmured faintly, her breath soft as the evening wind against his cheek, "to be so much trouble. Leave me. I have friends. . ."

"Nonsense!" Khardan said harshly. "You will not be safe in this city of butchers. Besides, we owe you our lives."

Opening her blue eyes, the girl looked up at him. Her arms stole around his neck. Khardan's breath came fast. Her hand with its cream-and-pink fingers raised to touch his bearded cheek. "Where will you take me . . . that I will be safe?"

"To my tribe, to the desert where I live," he answered huskily.

"That means you are a *batir,* a bandit!" Her face paled; she averted her eyes from his. "Put me down, please! I will take my chances here." Tears glistened on her cheeks. She pressed her hand against his chest. Such gentle hands, they could not have torn the petals from a flower, Khardan thought. His heart melted in his breast.

"My lady!" he said earnestly. "Let me escort you to safety! I swear by *Hazrat* Akhran that you will be treated with all respect and honor."

The lovely eyes, shimmering with tears, raised to his. "You risked your own life to save mine! Of course I believe you! I trust you! Take me with you, away from this terrible place where they murdered my father!"

Overcome by weeping, she hid her face in his chest.

The blood beating in his ears so that he was wholly deaf, Khardan held the girl close, his soul filled with her perfume, his eyes dazzled by the radiance of the sunlight on her hair.

"What is your name?" he whispered.

"Meryem," she replied.

Chapter 7

"Brother!" said Achmed urgently. "Let's go!"

"Yes! We should not linger," Meryem said, glancing around nervously. "Though the soldiers are not out here, there are spies, who may report us to the Amir. You can put me down now," the girl added shyly. "I can walk."

"Are you certain?"

She nodded, and Khardan set her upon her feet. Seeing his admiring eyes on her, Meryem realized she was half-naked. Blushing, she gathered up the torn shreds of her clothing, trying to draw them together to preserve her modesty and succeeding only in revealing more than she covered.

Glancing about quickly, Khardan saw a silk merchant's stall. Snagging a long scarf, he tossed it to the girl.

"Cover yourself!" he ordered harshly.

Meryem did so, winding the silk around her head and shoulders.

"Where is my money?" the merchant screamed at them.

"Collect from the Amir!" Khardan thrust the small man aside. "Perhaps his wife will conjure it up for you!"

"This way!" Taking hold of the Calif's hand, Meryem led Khardan and Achmed through the bazaars, pushing past vendors, customers, donkeys, and dogs.

"Saiyad!" Khardan called once they were in sight of his men.

The *spahi* ran up to them. "By Sul, Calif! What has happened? We heard a great shouting coming from the palace. . ."

Saiyad stared at them in wonder—the strange girl wrapped up in a stolen scarf, Achmed white-faced and limping, Khardan's robes spattered with blood.

"It is a long story, my friend. Suffice it to say that the Amir will not be buying our horses. He accused us of being spies and tried to have us arrested."

"Spies?" Saiyad's mouth gaped open. "But what—" Khardan shrugged. "They are city dwellers. What do you expect? Their brains have rotted in this shell."

The rest of the men, crowding around, were muttering among themselves.

"No, we're not leaving empty-handed," the Calif called out, raising his voice. "And I'm not running from these dogs! We will leave the city when and how we choose!"

The *spahis* cheered raggedly, swearing bitter oaths of revenge. Gazing at them fearfully, Meryem shrank back next to Khardan. He put his arm around her, and drew her close. "We came to deal fairly, but we have been insulted. Not only that, our God has been insulted as well." The men glowered, fingering their weapons. Waving his hand at the stalls, Khardan shouted, "Take what you need to live on this year!"

The men cheered and began running for their horses. Khardan grabbed hold of Saiyad's bridle to detain him.

"Watch for the soldiers."

"Aren't you coming?"

"Achmed is hurt and there is the woman. I will wait for you here."

"Anything I can get you, my Calif?" the grinning Saiyad asked.

"No. I have already acquired more treasure than I came with the intent to buy," Khardan replied.

Saiyad glanced at the girl, laughed, and dashed off.

Yelling wildly, brandishing their swords in the air, the *spahis* rode straight for the stalls of the bazaars. People scattered before them like terrified chickens, screaming in panic at the sight of the lashing hooves and flashing steel.

Saiyad guided his horse straight into a silk merchant's stand. The stall toppled. Its owner hopped about the street in rage, cursing the nomads at the top of his lungs. Roaring with laughter, Saiyad speared several fine silks with his sword blade and began waving them in the air above his head like a flag.

Across the street, Saiyad's brother—with a few well-aimed blows of his scimitar—cut down the shelves of a brass merchant's stall. Pots, lamps, and pipes crashed to the street with ringing clangs like a hundred bells. Snatching up a fine lamp, the nomad stuffed it into his *khurjin* and galloped off in search of more plunder.

"Someone will be killed!" said Meryem, shivering with fear and crowding close to Khardan.

"They will if they try to stop us," said the Calif.

Eyes gleaming with pride, he was watching his men wreaking havoc among the stalls when a push from behind him nearly knocked him over. Turning, he saw his war-horse. Dancing restively, the animal nudged him again with its head, urging him in the direction of the fray.

Laughing, Khardan patted his horse's nose, soothing the excited beast.

"Khardan, the guards. Don't you think we should go?" Mounted on his own horse, Achmed looked back worriedly toward the palace.

"Relax, little brother! They probably think we're still running around in the garden. But you are right, we should be ready, just in case."

Grasping Meryem around her waist—such a small waist, his hands almost completely encircled it—Khardan started to lift her up onto the back of the horse when a sudden tickling sensation, like feathers brushing against the back of his neck, caused him to turn his head.

The slave market—set apart from the rest of the bazaars in the *souk*—was conducting business as usual. Riots in the bazaars were commonplace. The slave buyers were far more interested in the merchandise being exhibited on the block, and at that moment a young woman was being put up for sale—a woman, it seemed, remarkable for her beauty, for a low murmur of anticipation was rippling through the crowd when the auctioneer dragged the veiled woman before them.

Having rescued one helpless person from the clutches of this city of devils, Khardan felt his heart swell with pity and anger at the sight of another, who probably faced a similar, cruel fate. Grasping hold of her veil, the dealer tore it from the woman's head. The crowd gasped in wonder and even Khardan blinked in astonishment. Hair the color of fire caught the rays of the noon sun. It seemed that blazing red flame tumbled down around slender shoulders.

But it was not the woman's beauty that struck Khardan. Indeed, she was not particularly beautiful at the moment. Her face was thin and wasted, there were dark shadows beneath her eyes. It was the expression on the woman's face that drew Khardan's attention, a look such as the Calif had never seen before—the despairing look of one who has lost all hope, who sees death as the only salvation.

"The trip was a hard one for such a delicate blossom," the auctioneer was shouting. "With some food and drink, however, she will soon be a prize flower, ready for any man to pluck! What am I bid?"

Anger swept over Khardan, a white-hot rage. That one human being should be able to buy another and thereby acquire the power of a God—the power of life and death—was true evil.

Turning, he lifted Meryem up onto a horse, but it was Achmed's mount, not his.

"Take care of her," he ordered his younger brother, who was staring at him in astonishment. Shrieks and crashes were audible from the bazaar, an indication that the *spahis* were still having their fun. Another sound rose above it, however—the blare of trumpets, coming from the *Kasbah*.

"The soldiers!" Meryem cried, her face pale. "We must leave!"

Swinging himself into his saddle, Khardan glanced coolly in the direction of the trumpet calls. "It will take them some time to get organized, still longer to get through the crowds. Do not worry. Saiyad hears them as well as we do. Wait for me. I won't be long."

A single word of command caused the Calif's horse to leap forward. Deadly silent, without a yell or word of warning, Khardan rode straight into the mass of slave buyers. Wild-eyed faces stared up at him. The men either got out of his way or were ridden down. Shouts and curses and yells rose into the air. Someone grabbed hold of his boot, trying to drag him from his steed. A blow from the flat of Khardan's sword sent the slaver crashing to the ground, blood streaming from his head.

The mob surged around the Calif, some trying to escape, others trying to attack him. Striking out to the right and left with his sword, Khardan—his eyes on the slave block—continued to urge his horse forward. The auctioneer suddenly became aware of Khardan's purpose. Frantically calling for his bodyguards, he tried to save his sale by hustling the woman from the platform.

A blow to the head from Khardan's boot sent the auctioneer tumbling over backward into the arms of his guards.

"Here, I've come to save you!" Khardan shouted.

The woman on the block looked up at him with that same hopeless, despairing expression. Whether he meant to drive his sword through her body or carry her away to safety seemed all one to the wretched creature.

Fury burning in his heart that one human could so reduce another to this pitiable condition, Khardan leaned down from the saddle. Sliding his arm around the woman's waist, he lifted her easily, hauling her up behind him on the horse's back and clamping her hands around his chest.

The woman's arms slipped nervelessly from around him. Turning, Khardan saw that she was staring at him with dull, uncaring eyes.

"Hold on tightly!" Khardan commanded.

For an instant he wondered whether or not she would obey him. If she didn't, she was lost, for the Calif could not both hold her and guide his horse back through the raging mob. "Come alive, damn you!"

Khardan was battling to keep the horse standing amid the attacking mob, he had no real idea what he was saying. Beating and kicking and lashing out at those trying to grab his horse's bridle, the Calif knew only that saving this young woman had suddenly become extremely important to him—a symbol of his victory over these foul city-dwellers.

"Come back to life!" he shouted. "Nothing is that bad!" Perhaps it was his words or perhaps it was the fear of falling from the plunging, rearing horse, but Khardan felt the arms around him tighten. Slightly amazed at her strength—unusual for a woman—Khardan did not have time to wonder at it. A group of mounted *goums* belonging to one of the slave traders was endeavoring to make its way through the mob to get at Khardan.

At a command from its master, Khardan's horse reared into the air, lashing out with deadly hooves. The mob scattered, more than a few fell to the ground, blood streaming from broken heads. Seeing their fellows fall, the slavers turned and ran. The *goums* and their horses became entangled in a mass of people milling about in panic.

Grimly triumphant, Khardan galloped out of the slave market just as a few of the trader's *goums* were able to make their way through the mob. Heading back to where his brother awaited him, Khardan rode past a white palanquin.

At the sight the woman behind him gave a slight gasp, her grip on Khardan tightening. Glancing down, the Calif saw the litter's curtain being held back by a slender hand, a man's face looking out. Cruel and malevolent, the man's eyes went through Khardan like cold steel.

His very soul chilled, Khardan could not withdraw his gaze. He actually checked the horse and paused, staring at the man in the palanquin with awful fascination. The whistle of a sword slashing by his head recalled him to his senses. Whirling, he struck out with the hilt of his sword catching the *goum* on the chin and knocking him from his horse. But the other *goums* were catching up with him now, too many to fight.

"We're going to run for it!" he shouted to the woman. "Hold on!"

Kicking the horse's flanks, Khardan urged the animal ahead at a gallop. The street was clear now, the people having fled for safety. Out in the open at last, the desert horse ran with the speed of the wind that was its grandsire. Khardan risked a glance back at his prize. Her red hair streaming behind her like a fiery banner, the woman was holding on to him for dear life; her head pressed against Khardan's back, her arms gripping him with a panicked strength that was nearly squeezing the breath from his lungs.

The *goums* pounded behind them. Khardan's horse, exhilarated at this wild race and the yells and shouts of encouragement from the waiting Akar, unleashed all its energy. Few horses in the tribe could keep up with Khardan's stallion. One by one the *goums* fell behind, shaking their fists and calling out curses.

Intoxicated with the danger and excitement, the *spahis* rode up around their leader, shouting and yelling and clapping him on the back. Festooned with stolen bolts of silk and cotton, their saddlebags bulging with filched jewelry, their sashes bristling with newly appropriated weapons, the nomads carried huge sacks of purloined flour and rice slung across their saddles.

The soldiers of the Amir were in sight now, but their progress through the stalls of the bazaar was being hampered by the wreckage the *spahis* had left behind.

Gathering his men around him, Khardan raced for the city gates, which were standing wide open to permit a long camel caravan to enter.

The last building the *spahis* passed was the Temple of Quar. Wheeling his horse, heedless of the rapidly gaining soldiers, Khardan guided the animal up the Temple stairs.

"Here is how we pay homage to Quar!" he shouted. Lifting the sword he had taken from the Amir's guard, Khardan plunged it through one of the priceless windows. The stained glass, which had been made in the image of a golden ram's head, shattered into a thousand sparkling shards. Minor priests ran screaming from the Temple, shaking their fists or wringing their hands.

Turning, Khardan's horse cleared the stairs in a single jump. The Calif and his *spahis* swept out of the city gates, riding down the few guards who made a halfhearted attempt to stop them.

Once out of arrow range but still in sight of the city walls, Khardan called a halt.

"Some of you round up the horses!" he instructed. "Make certain you get them all! I'll leave nothing behind for these swine!"

"Will the soldiers come after us?" Saiyad shouted.

"City dwellers? Out into the desert? Hah!" Khardan laughed.

"Here, my friend, take this girl, will you?"

"With pleasure, my Calif!" Grinning from ear to ear, Saiyad caught hold of the red-haired slave girl and transferred her from the Calif's horse to the back of his own.

Riding over to Achmed, Khardan held out his hands to the Sultan's daughter. "Will you ride with me, my lady?" he asked.

"I will," Meryem said softly, flushing as Khardan lifted her in his arms.

Flinging one final, defiant shout of triumph at the city walls, the *spahis* wheeled their steeds and dashed off into the desert, their black robes swirling around them.

At the city gates the captain of the soldiers sat upon his horse, watching the nomads go, his men lined up in silent ranks behind him. The leader of the *goums* was arguing violently with him, pointing at the rapidly disappearing *spahis* and raving at the top of his lungs. But the captain, with a shake of his head, simply turned his horse and rode back into the city, his men following behind him.

In the palace the Amir and the Imam stood on the balcony overlooking the pleasure garden, watching as the servants rolled the injured eunuch onto a litter.

"All went as you planned," said the Imam. (The priest did not yet know of the desecration done to his Temple, or he might have been less conciliatory.)

The Amir, detecting a grudging note in Feisal's voice, smiled inwardly. Outwardly his face maintained its stem, military calm. "Of course." He shrugged. "Although I thought for a moment we were going to capture the arrogant young whelp accidently. I thought I would have to pick him up and hurl him into the garden myself, but fortunately he caught my hint about the partitions."

"He has taken the viper to his bosom," said the Imam in a soft voice. "Are you certain of its fangs?"

The Amir glanced at Feisal irritably. "I grow tired of your doubting, Imam. My wife handpicked the girl from among my concubines. Yes, I am certain of her. Meryem is ambitious, and if she succeeds, I have promised to marry her. She should have no trouble. These nomads, for all their bluster, are naive as children. Meryem is skilled in her art—" The Amir paused, his eyebrows raised. "She is skilled in many arts, as a matter of fact, not the least of which is the art of giving pleasure. The young man should have an interesting time of it."

He turned back, gazing out over the city walls into the desert. "Enjoy your nights well, *kafir*." Qannadi munnured. "If the reports of your tribes uniting are true, those nights are numbered. I cannot allow you and your Ragtag God to stand in the way of progress."

CHAPTER 8

lthough Khardan truly believed that the Amir's soldiers would not be so foolish as to pursue them, the Calif deemed it wise to ride homeward as swiftly as possible. It wasn't fear of the Amir that drove him. It was the memory of the cruel face in the palanquin. There had been more than a threat of revenge in the malevolent eyes, there had been a promise.

Khardan found himself starting awake the first night away from the city. Bathed in cold sweat, he had the feeling that something was creeping up on him.

He would sleep better in his own land, and he knew his men were as eager to return home as he. No one complained at riding all night and into the cool hours of the day, switching horses often to keep them from tiring. They ate their meals in the saddle, managed to snatch a few hours sleep burrowed like worms in the sand, the horses' reins tied around their wrists. The *spahis* were in good spirits, far better than if their journey had been successful, for they loved nothing better than raiding. This moment would stand out forever in their lives, and already they were reliving it, enlivening the long journey with repeated tales of their victory in the city of Kich, tales that were expanding like bread dough with the yeast of their telling.

At first Khardan was silent during these sessions, inclined to brood on nagging questions that rankled like thorns in his flesh. What had the Amir meant about Quar's warning them of the Akar's coming? Where had Qanndi gotten the notion that the Akar were spying on the city so that they could conquer it? Nothing that mad would ever occur to Sheykh Majiid—any of the sheykhs of the desert for that matter. Not only did they know it would be foolhardy in the extreme to attack such a fortification as the walled city of Kich, why in the name of Sul would anyone want such a place anyhow?

Then there was the man with the cruel eyes in the palanquin. A slave trader, obviously, but who was he and where did he come from? Khardan found himself unpleasantly obsessed with the memory of that man, and he endeavored to find out more about him during the rare times when he was able to talk to the slave woman he had rescued.

But the woman proved to be no help. Silent, reclusive, she kept by herself whenever possible, shrinking even from the company of Meryem, who would have been happy to have another woman go with her to perform the private ablutions prohibited to the eyes of men. So quiet was the red-haired woman—never talking, never answering questions spoken to her—that Khardan began to wonder if she was deaf and dumb.

Saiyad reported to Khardan that the woman never said a word to him. She ate and drank what was given her but took nothing on her own. If no one had brought her food, she probably would have starved. The hopeless look in the eyes had not gone away; if anything, it was intensified. It became apparent to Khardan that the woman would just as soon lie down and die in the sand as to be kept clinging to this life, and he wondered more than once what dreadful thing had happened to her. Recalling the cruel, cold eyes of the man in the palanquin, the Calif did not think he needed to search far to find an answer.

Eventually, as the days passed and the Akar drew nearer their own land, leaving behind the city with its walls and its noise and its stench, the Calif's spirits rose. He not only began enjoying hearing the stories of his men, but he told his own as well, elaborating with parental fondness on the courage of his younger brother in the palace escape until Achmed's ears were red with embarrassed pleasure. The men listened in admiration as Khardan recounted with all due modesty the discovery and rescue of the Sultan's daughter, enlivening the tale with shrill imitations of the eunuchs' squeals that caused the men to roar with laughter.

The Sultan's daughter was another cause for the rise in the Califs spirits. True to his word, Khardan treated her with the respect and reverence he would have accorded his own mother. He even offered her a horse of her own to ride—something completely unheard of—but she shyly refused, saying she knew nothing of the beasts and was terrified of them. She would continue to ride with him, if she wasn't too great a burden.

Too great a burden! Khardan's heart sang like the wind among the dunes as he galloped over the sands, the lovely creature clinging to him, her hands entwined about his chest, her head leaning against his back when she grew weary. He did not know by what art she managed it, but not even the strenuous ride diminished her beauty. He and the others smelled of sweat and horse; she smelled of rose and orange blossoms. She kept carefully veiled, her white body completely covered to protect her from the sun and from the eyes of men. She rarely lifted her blue eyes when in the presence of men but kept them lowered as was considered proper in a woman, her long, black lashes brushing her cheeks.

The modesty that bespoke the virgin was all the more enchanting to Khardan because of the closeness they experienced riding together. It was her fear of the horse—which seemed to her a great and powerful beast, so Meryem said—that made her sit so near Khardan. Tears glistened in her eyes. He must think her shameless! Wiping away those tears, Khardan assured her that he didn't think her shameless at all. He barely knew she was with him. Meryem smiled sweetly and held him all the tighter. Khardan, feeling her warm and soft against his flesh, their bodies moving together in time to the rhythm of the horse's motion, sometimes ached with a passion that it took all his self-command to conquer.

The Calif comforted himself with the thought that this pleasure would not be long deferred. Every time he looked into Meryem's blue eyes, he saw love and admiration blooming there. When he reached the Tel, the first thing he would do would be to make the Sultan's daughter his wife. Soon he would sleep in her arms, laying his head upon the trembling bosom that pressed so often against his back.

Thoughts of Zohra flew from his mind on the wings of this new passion, with only the briefest wonder at how she would react to the introduction of a new wife into the *harem*.

"Ah, well," Khardan told himself, thinking of their final moments together in camp, "Zohra is tame now, at least. That last episode has frightened her into submission. I will do what I must to keep her happy and find true joy with another." (Which only went to prove the Amir's statement that, despite their bluster, the nomads were as naive as children.)

Meryem's conversation enlivened the long, dark hours of the night ride across the desert. She told Khardan tales of life in the Sultan's palace—tales that the Calif found incredible.

She spoke of the enclosed, marble baths where the wives and concubines went daily to bathe and play in the heated, perfumed water, always conscious—though they were never permitted to show it—of the small hole in the wall through which the Sultan watched, selecting his choice for the night.

She described the elaborate maze the Sultan had ordered specially built within the palace walls so that he could have the pleasure of chasing the selected favorite until he caught her and forced her to surrender. She told about the dinners during which the Sultan would invite the girls to dance. Stripping off their veils and their clothes, the women stepped lightly to music played by musicians whose eyes had been gouged out that they might not look upon the beautiful bodies moving gracefully before them.

Meryem spoke, too, of the secret passage through the garden wall; how those women not chosen by the Sultan used it to admit lovers into the garden, paying the blind beggar well to keep his mouth shut and conceal their transgressions, for it would be as much as their lives were worth if the eunuchs discovered them.

Khardan listened in amazement, his blood tingling in his veins. He asked if the Amir was indulging in the same style of life. Remembering the stem face, the rigid military posture, the Calif could not believe it of the man.

"No," Meryem replied. "Qannadi has no heart. He sees beauty in nothing but war and bloodshed. Oh, he has his *harem*, his wives. But he keeps them for the power of the magic they bring him. The *seraglio* is a witches' coven, not a place of love. The women speak only of magic, of their skills in *that* art, not in the art of loving. They go to the baths to bathe, not to show themselves. I even heard that the Amir ordered the spy hole closed up. There are no more intimate dinners. The Amir sent the musicians to play for his soldiers. The garden might be filled with the lovers of his wives, for all the Amir cares."

Realizing she was speaking more bitterly than might seem right for a Sultan's daughter, Meryem hastily changed the subject.

"That was how I managed to escape detection for so long. When the soldiers of the Amir seized the palace, they easily caught my father. His bodyguards fled—the cowards—and left him to his cruel fate. There are secret hiding places built into the palace, with a tunnel that runs below ground to the soldiers' barracks. The Sultan did not have time to avail himself of this; the Amir made certain of that, sending his troops in to capture the palace before they had even conquered the city. I was able to hide myself in one of these secret places, however. It was little larger than a closet. I stayed there for I don't know how long, crouched in the darkness, thirsting and starving, but too scared to leave. I heard the screams"—she shivered—"and I knew what was happening out there. Later I overheard the eunuchs talking about my father's death."

Her voice broke. With a great effort she managed to control her tears and continue with her story.

"At last I knew I must leave the closet or die there. I crept out. My plan was to hide myself among the numerous concubines of the Amir. I would be safe, I hoped, unless he sent for me. My plan worked, at least so I imagined. I told the other girls and the eunuchs that I was new, a present from one of the grandees. I thought I had fooled them, but as it turned out, they knew me all along. The Amir, it seems, thought I was part of a plot of one of the nobles to overthrow him and so he had me watched. I waited for my opportunity to escape, and when you created the commotion in the *divan*, I thought I had my chance.

"I hurried to the garden, intending to slip out the hole in the wall. But the eunuchs caught me and beat me, trying to make me reveal the name of the man for whom I worked. They were going to drag me back to the Amir's torture chambers when you saved me."

She hugged Khardan close, her body shivering with her emotion. The Calif did what he could to comfort her, although what comfort he could offer was of necessity limited by the fact that they were riding horseback at the head of a troop of his men. This was, perhaps, just as well, or his resolution to wait and make the girl his wife might have vanished there in the night in the desert sand.

To take his mind off the aching of desire, he gruffly asked another question, this one about the Imam. Meryem readily answered, although it was some time before the infatuated Khardan could fully attend to what she was saying.

"—a result of the Imam's teaching, for he believes that passions of the body, while necessary to . . . to"—Meryem flushed prettily—"produce children, take the mind away from the worship of Quar.

"If you can believe the eunuchs," she whispered in Khardan's ear, embarrassed to discuss the matter aloud, "the Imam is said never to have slept with a woman. That is something Yamina would very much like to change, if you credit gossip."

Khardan recalled the holy zeal he'd seen burning in the priest's liquid eyes and could well believe this to be true. But the subject of Yamina brought another question to his mind.

"The magic of the horse," he asked Meryem, "is that true magic or was it a trick such as one performs for gullible children?"

"It is true magic!" Meryem said, her voice tinged with awe. "And that is not the greatest of Yamina's powers."

"Are you yourself this. . . skilled in the art of magic?" Khardan asked abruptly and somewhat uneasily.

"Oh, no!" Meryem replied glibly, guessing at the nomad's fear. "I have the usual women's talents, of course. But magic was not considered important in my father's court, nor was it considered seemly that I—as his daughter—should be taught such a common art." She spoke haughtily, and Khardan nodded in grave approval. "Certainly I am far from being as powerful as Yamina. She can enchant the weapons of the Amir's soldiers so that they never miss their target—"

"She must have slipped up on that one," interrupted Khardan with a grin, thinking of the inept guards who had tried to stop them at the palace.

He felt the girl's body tense. Imagining she must be reliving once again those few terrible moments of her capture, he turned and gave her a reassuring smile. She had an answering smile ready for him behind the veil, but it vanished the moment he looked away from her again, and he did not notice her biting her red lips in anger at herself for having used them too freely. The Calif must not guess that the soldiers had missed on purpose!

There was no more talk between them that night. Meryem—resting her head against Khardan's strong back—pretended to sleep. Guiding his horse across the sands as carefully as possible, keeping a sharp watch for any irregularity in the path that might cause the horse to slip and thus jostle the girl and waken her, Khardan let his mind roam among the stories he had heard as he might have roamed among the many rooms of the Sultan's palace. The sun rose, a ball of fire burning in the pale blue sky. Khardan did not see it. He was lost in a sweet dream of blind musicians, playing at his command.

After days of hard riding the Akar reached the foothills where the tribesmen of Sheykh Jaafar al Widjar received them with sullen hospitality. Having ascertained that the horses given the sheepherders were being well cared for, Khardan accepted the freshly butchered carcasses of several sheep in return, and refusing the grudgingly offered three days of guest hospitality, the *spahis* continued their ride.

Another day and a night of hard riding brought them to the Tel, brought them home.

CHAPTER 9

Every man, woman, and child of both tribes camped around the Tel turned out to meet the *spahis*, wbo could be detected some distance away by the cloud of dust they raised. Standing at the edge of the camp, his eyes peering into the late afternoon sun, Majiid thought the dust cloud looked bigger than it should. His brow creased in worry. He'd had the uncomfortable feeling for days that something was wrong. He had summoned Sond, intending to send him to find Khardan and make certain he was safe, only to discover that the djinn had vanished. This unusual disappearance on the part of the immortal added to Majiid's nagging worries. Something had gone awry; Majiid knew it.

Now, seeing the dust cloud, he knew what it was. They were bringing back the horses. The sale had fallen through.

The *spahis* made a fine entrance into camp. Showing off their riding skills, they drew their horses up in a line before Majiid, and led by Khardan, each man had his horse kneel to the Sheykh. Despite his misgivings, Majiid's heart swelled with pride. He could not resist a triumphant glance at Jaafar. Let your sheepherders do this!

Majiid discovered Jaafar staring not at the horsemen but at the horses that they had brought back with them, and now it was Jaafar's turn to look at Majiid with raised eyebrows. Scowling, Majiid turned away. Hurrying over to talk to Khardan and determine what had gone wrong, the Sheykh's gaze went balefully to the Sultan's daughter. Women! Majiid had the instinctive feeling that this female was going to be the root of the trouble.

Other eyes saw the Sultan's daughter; other eyes frowned at the sight. Dressed in her finest gown, her black hair brushed until it glistened like a raven's wing, her body perfumed with jasmine, Zohra had been about to step from her tent and greet her husband when she caught a glimpse of the heavily veiled woman riding behind him. Who was she? What was he doing with her? Stepping back quickly into the shadows of her tent, Zohra watched the meeting between father and son, listening carefully to all that was said.

Jumping down from his horse, Khardan embraced his father.

"Welcome home, my son!" Majiid clasped his arms around Khardan, true emotion apparent in the slight quiver of his voice.

Around them rose a hubbub of voices, the other tribesmen joyfully greeting friends and family, pulling booty from the *khurjin* and distributing it to laughing wives and children. Looking at the spoils, Majiid glanced questioningly at his son. "It appears your trip was successful?"

Khardan shook his head, his face grave and serious. "What happened?"

"Yes, tell us, Calif, why you failed to sell the horses," said Jaafar loudly to Majiid's extreme irritation.

In a few words Khardan repeated his story. Aware that others were listening, he kept it brief, saving the details and his own private concerns for a later talk in his father's tent. It was not difficult for the Sheykh to hear his son's unspoken words, however, and a sidelong glance at Jaafar's darkening face showed him that the sharp mind of the Hrana had picked them up. Zohra, standing unnoticed within the shadows of her tent, heard them, too.

"Well, well," Majiid said with forced gaiety, slapping Khardan on his shoulders and embracing him again. "It must have been a glorious victory! I wish I had been there! My son, defying the Amir! My men, looting the city of Kich!" The Sheykh laughed boisterously. The *spahis* who heard his words exchanged glances of pride. "And are these some of the treasures of the city you have brought back with you?" Majiid asked, strolling over to the horses where sat the two women Khardan had freed.

Handling her as carefully as if she were made of fragile porcelain, Khardan grasped Meryem around her waist and lifted her down from the saddle. He led her by the hand to the Sheykh.

"Father, this is Meryem, daughter of the late Sultan of Kich."

Falling on her knees in the sand, Meryem prostrated herself before Majiid. "Honored father of my savior. Your son, risked his life to save me, unworthy orphan of cruelly murdered parents. I was discovered, hiding in the palace. The Amir would have tortured me, then killed me as they did my father, but your son rescued me and carried me from the city."

Raising her head, Meryem looked at the Sheykh earnestly, clasping her white hands together. "I cannot repay his kindness in wealth. I can repay it only by becoming his slave, and this I will gladly do, if you will accept a pitiful beggar such as myself into your tribe."

Touched by this pretty speech, enchanted by its deliverer, Majiid glanced up at Khardan. He saw his son's eyes aflame with a passion that any man must have felt. Although the Sheykh could not see the woman, veiled as she was, he caught a glimpse of the golden hair glistening in the sun. He saw the blue eyes sparkling with grateful tears and could witness the grace of the slender figure hidden by the folds of the *chador*. Majiid was, therefore, not surprised when Khardan, leaning down, gently raised up Meryem to stand beside him.

"Not a slave, Father," Khardan said, his voice husky, "but my wife. I pledged her my honor that she would be treated with all respect in this camp, and therefore, since she no longer has a father or mother of her own, I ask that you take her into your dwelling as your own daughter, my father, until such time as arrangements can be made for our wedding."

Black eyes, hidden in the shadows, flashed in anger. Feeling half-suffocated, Zohra drove her nails into the flesh of her palms and struggled to compose herself. "What do I care?" she demanded, gasping for breath over the terrible pain in her chest. "What does it matter to me? Nothing! He is nothing to me! Nothing!"

Growing calmer with this remembrance, repeating the words to herself, Zohra was able, after a few moments, to continue to watch and listen.

Majiid had welcomed his newest daughter and turned her over to his wives, who gathered around the girl, murmuring sympathetically over her cruel fate. Khardan's mother led the Sultan's daughter by the hand to her own tent. The Calif watched proudly, his eyes burning with a love visible to everyone in the camp.

"And what of this one?" Majiid questioned, looking at the silent woman shrouded in black.

The slave had not moved from her place on Saiyad's horse. She did not look around her. Neither interest, curiosity, nor fear was visible in the eyes above the black veil. Their gaze held only that same hopeless despair.

In a grim and angry voice Khardan told his father of the slave market and how he had rescued the woman as she was about to be auctioned off. The Calif told his exciting tale about outriding the *goums,* but he kept quiet about the cruel-eyed man in the white palanquin. Khardan had not mentioned him to anyone, nor did he intend to, having a sort of superstitious dread that—like a demon of Sul—speaking of the man might somehow Summon him.

"Saiyad has offered to take the woman into his *harem,*" Khardan added. "This is a noble gesture on Saiyad's part, Father, since the woman is dowerless."

Majiid glanced questioningly at the *spahi.* Saiyad, coming forward, bowed to the Sheykh to indicate that Khardan spoke the desire of his heart. Majiid turned to his son. "The woman's life is in your hands, Calif, since you are her savior. Is this your will?"

"It is, O Sheykh," answered Khardan formally. "This man was leader in my absence and performed his duties with exemplary skill. I can think of no more suitable reward."

"Then so shall it be. Woman, attend to me."

The Sheykh looked up at the female, who still sat unmoving upon the horse. "Woman?"

The slave did not respond but stared straight ahead with a face so white and rigid that Majiid was reminded uncomfortably of a corpse.

"What's the matter with her?" he demanded, turning to Khardan.

"She has suffered a great shock, Father," Khardan replied in a low voice.

"Um, well, Saiyad will soon comfort her," Majiid said with an attempt at a laugh that failed beneath that frozen face, glimmering pale like a waning moon. Majiid cleared his throat. "Woman, you will henceforth belong to this man, who, in his mercy, has deigned to take you dowerless into his family. You will submit to his will in all things and be a dutiful servant, and you will be rewarded by his caring and compassion."

Saiyad, bowing again, grinned broadly at Khardan. Reaching up his hands, he grasped hold of the woman and brought her down—limp and unresisting—from the horse's back.

"If there is nothing else I can do for you, my Sheykh," Saiyad began, licking his lips, his hungry gaze fixed upon the woman, "it has been a long ride. . . ."

"Yes, of course!" Majiid smiled. "No doubt you are tired and desire some rest. Go ahead!"

Taking hold of the woman by the arm, Saiyad led her to his tent.

Watching her go, her head bowed, her feet stumbling as if she did not see the ground on which she walked, Khardan quieted the misgivings stirring in his heart. Irritably he told himself that it was all for the slave woman's own good. Why couldn't she be grateful? If Khardan had not rescued her, she might now be in the clutches of some brute, who would use her for his foul pleasures, then cast her to his servants when he grew tired of her. Saiyad was rough and certainly not handsome. A poor man, he had only one wife, so this addition to his household would be a welcome one. The slave woman's life would be hard, but she would be fed and sheltered. Saiyad would not beat her. Her children, if she bore him any, would be well-cared for. . . .

Saiyad and his new woman disappeared into his tent. Khardan's father asked his son a question about the situation in Kich, and with relief, the Calif turned his attention to other matters. Deep in discussion, the two walked together to the Sheykh's tent. Noticing Jaafar watching them intently, Khardan glanced at his father and received a grudging nod to include the other Sheykh in their talk. The three men disappeared inside Majiid's tent; Fedj, the djinn, came along to serve them.

The other *spahis* went to their tents, accompanied by their families, the women exclaiming excitedly over lovely silks or new brass lamps or showing off sparkling bracelets. Unnoticed, forgotten, Zohra crept back inside her own tent. Pressing cold hands to feverish cheeks, she sank down upon silken cushions, biting at her veil in her frustration.

All was silent in the camp. The sun, sinking down in the west, brought an eerie beauty to the harsh land, painting the sands with rose pink, deepening to purple. The first cool breeze of coming night was drifting among the tents with a soft sigh when the sound of a hoarse yell split the air.

So ferocious was the sound, so filled with rage, that everyone in camp thought they were under attack. Weapons in hand, men dashed from their tents, looking about wildly and demanding to know what was happening. Women clasped children to their breasts and peered fearfully from the entrances. Khardan and the Sheykhs rushed from Majiid's dwelling.

"What is it? What in the name of Sul is going on?" Majiid thundered.

"This, O Sheykh!" yelled a voice. Choked with fury, it could hardly be understood. "Witness this!"

Expecting nothing less than the Amir's army galloping down upon him, Majiid turned with astonishment to see Saiyad emerging from his tent, dragging the slave woman by the back of her robes. She was unveiled, her red hair tumbling about her in a brilliant mass. With a vicious snarl Saiyad hurled her across the compound. The woman fell forward on her stomach, hands outspread, to lie face down, unmoving, at Majiid's feet.

"What is this, Saiyad?" the astounded Sheykh demanded, angry at being alarmed over nothing. "What's the matter? Isn't the girl a virgin? Surely you didn't expect as much—"

"Virgin!" Saiyad drew a seething breath. Reaching down, he grasped hold of a handful of the red hair and yanked the woman's head up, forcing her to face Majiid.

"Virgin!" Saiyad repeated. "She isn't a virgin! She isn't even a woman! She is a man!"

CHAPTER 10

Jaafar, staring at Saiyad, burst into raucous laughter. Saiyad flushed an angry red. Reaching out, he grabbed Khardan's scimitar, snatching it from the Calif's hand.

"I have been shamed!" Saiyad cried. "Defiled!"

He dragged the disfigured man to his knees. Raising the sword, Saiyad held it poised above the kneeling, shivering figure. "I will have my revenge by cleaving this unclean head from its neck!"

The man raised his head. Khardan saw the expression on the pale face undergo a swift and horrifying change, the eyes reflecting stark terror and fear such as he had never seen in the eyes of another human before. It was not terror at the blow coming, it seemed, but at a memory of something so horrible it blotted out the threat of death. Staring aghast into the white face, Khardan realized with a riveting shock that this was no man—it was a youth, not much older than Achmed. A boy, frightened and alone.

Once again Khardan saw the woman. . . the boy. . . standing upon the slave block, saw the look of hopeless despair. Now he understood. Who knows how or why the young man came to be dressed as a woman, but he had foreseen as surely as he drew breath that he must be discovered and that his end would be a terrible one. This sword blow, at least, would be swift and painless, the misery that was traced upon the face soon ended. . .

Saiyad's arms tensed, ready to deliver the killing stroke.

Moving swiftly, without stopping to consider why, Khardan caught hold of Saiyad's hands, wrested the sword from the man's grasp.

"Why did you stop me? Why?" Foam flecked Saiyad's lips, his eyes were bloodshot and bulging from his head.

"I saved this life," Khardan said sternly. Retrieving his scimitar from the sand where it had fallen, he thrust it into his belt. "Therefore, the life is mine alone to take."

"Then you kill him! You must. I demand it! I have been shamed!" hissed Saiyad, breathing heavily and wiping his hands repeatedly upon his robes as though to rid himself of some filth. "You cannot let him live! He is foul, unclean!"

Ignoring Saiyad and ignoring, too, the swift angry glance his father shot him, Khardan turned to face the youth. People crowded near, pushing, shoving, and craning their necks to get a better view.

"Back off!" the Calif commanded, glaring around him.

Scowling, still rubbing his hands against his tunic front, Saiyad remained standing where he was. No one else moved.

"Father, is this not my right?" Khardan demanded.

Majiid nodded wordlessly.

"Then let me talk to the . . . this man!"

His face grim, Majiid moved some distance away, dragging Jaafar with him. One by one the other members of the tribe backed away, forming a large half-circle. Khardan stood in the center, the young man remaining kneeling before him, head bowed.

The Calif stared helplessly at the youth, completely at a loss as to what he should do. By law, this man who had disguised himself as a woman and who had apparently used this disguise to entice another man to lay hands upon him must surely die. Khardan would be unworthy of his standing as Calif of his people if he defied the law. Slowly the Calif drew his sword.

And yet. . . there had to be some other explanation!

The youth's face had regained its terrible composure. Crouched on his knees, his hands clasped tightly together as though clutching every bit of courage he possessed, he looked up at Khardan with empty eyes, facing death with a despairing calm that was dreadful to see.

Khardan's palms began to sweat. He flexed them around the sword's hilt. He had killed men before, but never one kneeling, never one who was defenseless. The Calif felt sickened at the thought, yet he had no choice. Shifting nervously in his stance as though to better position himself to deliver the killing blow, Khardan glanced swiftly around the camp, seeking inspiration.

He received it, from an unexpected source.

Movement in the shadows of a tent caught his eye. Coming

forward noiselessly so that she stood within the failing twilight, Zohra mouthed a word, at the same time tapping her head as though there were something wrong with it.

"Mad!"

Khardan stared at her, the sudden rush of thoughts confusing him. How had she known the reluctance he felt? Stranger still, why should she care about this boy one way or another? No matter, the Calif supposed. He had his answer now. He knew the beginning, if not exactly where all this would end.

Lowering his sword, Khardan cast a grim glance around the assembled tribes. "I have remembered that Akhran gives everyone the right of speaking in his own defense. Does anyone question this?"

There was some muttering. Saiyad snarled angrily, mumbling something inaudible, but he said nothing aloud.

Khardan turned back, regarding the youth grimly. "You may speak. Tell why you have done this thing."

The youth did not answer.

Khardan checked a sigh. Somehow he had to force him to talk.

"Can you answer me?" he asked suddenly. "Are you dumb?"

Wearily, as though longing for sleep that was denied him, the young man shook his head.

"From your look, you are not of this land," Khardan continued patiently, hoping to force the young man to respond. "Yet you understand our language. I saw your face. You understood Saiyad's words when he threatened to kill you."

The youth swallowed, and Khardan could see the knot in the young man's throat that marked the true nature of his sex.

"I . . . I understand," the young man said in a voice that was like the music of the flute. They were the first words he had spoken since Khardan had rescued him. The empty eyes looked up at the Calif.

"Why these questions?" the youth continued in a dulled, uncaring tone. "End it now."

"Damn it, boy! Don't make me kill you!" Khardan shot back in a vehement whisper, meant for the youth's ears alone.

Startled, the young man blinked, as though awakening from some terrible dream, and stared at Khardan dazedly.

Walking over to the youth, the Calif grasped hold of the

young man's chin, turning his face roughly to the light. "You have no beard." With the blade of his sword he parted the robes. "No hair upon the chest."

"It. . . is the manner of . . . men of my . . . land," the youth said in a strained voice.

"Is it also the manner of men of your land to dress as women?"

Bowing his head, flushing in shame, the young man did not reply.

"What did you do in this land of yours?" Khardan persisted.

"I . . . I was a wizard—a 'sorcerer' in your tongue."

Khardan relaxed. Behind him he heard excited, wondering whispers.

"Where is this land?" Khardan continued, praying to *Hazrat* Akhran to grant him wisdom and a certain amount of luck.

The God heard his prayers. Or at least some God heard.

"Across the Hurn sea," the boy mumbled.

"What?" Khardan gripped the young man painfully by the chin, raising his head. "Repeat your words, that all may hear!"

"Across the Hurn sea!" the youth cried in desperation.

With a grim smile Khardan thrust the young man roughly away from him. The Calif turned to face his tribe.

"There, you hear? He claims to be a sorcerer! All know only women may practice magic. Not only that, but he claims to come from a land across the Hurn." The Calif waved his arms. "All know that there is no such land! All know that the Hurn empties into the abyss of Sul. It is as I thought. The young man is mad. By the laws of *Hazrat* Akhran, we are forbidden to harm him."

Khardan gazed about defiantly. Victory was within his grasp, but he hadn't won. Not yet. Accustomed to either obeying or disobeying the laws of their God as they saw fit, the nomads weren't going to give up the excitement of an execution so easily.

Saiyad—his honor unsatisfied—took a step forward and turned to face the tribes.

"I say he is not mad! I say he is a perversion and should, by the laws of *Hazrat* Akhran, be put to death."

Khardan glanced at his father. Majiid said nothing, but it was obvious that the Sheykh agreed with Saiyad. Arms folded over his massive chest, eyebrows bristling, the Sheykh regarded his son with anger, mingled with concern.

Khardan realized that his leadership in the tribe was balanced on a knife's edge. He cast a swift glance at Zohra, still hidden in the shadows. He could see her eyes, black, fiery, watching him intently, but he had no idea what she might be thinking.

If it is your will that this young man live, then help me, Akhran, Khardan prayed silently.

And suddenly, whether from Akhran or from within himself, the Calif had his answer.

Khardan turned back to face the youth. "You yourself will make the decision whether you live or die. I give you a choice. If you are sane, you will choose to die bravely as a man. If you are mad, you will choose to live—as a woman."

A murmur of appreciation and awe rippled through the tribe. Majiid glanced about proudly now, defying anyone to argue with such godlike wisdom.

"Will that satisfy you?" Khardan looked at Saiyad.

Head to one side, Saiyad considered. If the young man was sane, he would pay with his life for his crime and Saiyad's honor would be avenged. If the youth were mad—and what sane man would choose to live life as a woman—then it would be understood by everyone that the boy had seen the face of Akhran and no shame could come to Saiyad. Either way, his honor would be appeased. Saiyad nodded once, his brow clearing.

Raising the sword, the blade flashing red in the light of the setting sun, Khardan held it poised, flexing his hands on the hilt to get a firmer grip. "Well?" he prompted harshly.

His eyes stared into the eyes of the youth. For a brief instant there was just the two of them, poised upon the turning world. No one else was present, no one at all. Khardan could hear the beating of his own heart, the whisper of his own breath. The sun was sinking, deepening to blood red, the sky to the east was black, glittering with the first faint stars. He could smell the scents of the desert—the tamarisk and sage, the sweet scent of the grass around the oasis, the acrid odor of the horses. He could hear the rustling of the palm leaves, the song of the wind across the desert floor.

"Live!" he pleaded softly, almost reverently with the boy. "Live!"

The eyes looking into his flooded with tears. The head drooped, the red hair fell around the shoulders like a veil. A sob burst from the young man's throat, his shoulders heaved.

Weak with relief, Khardan lowered the sword. His impulse was to take the young man by the shoulders and comfort him, as he might have comforted one of his younger brothers. But he dared not. He had his standing to maintain. Scowling darkly therefore, he turned back to face the tribes.

"I will not kill a woman!" He thrust his sword into his belt.

"That is all very well," said Jaafar suddenly, stepping forward and pointing at the wretched figure huddled on the sand. "And I admit that the boy is undoubtedly mad, touched by the God. But what is to become of him? Who will take care of him?"

"I will tell you!" came a clear voice.

From out of the shadows of her tent stepped Zohra, her silken *caftan* rippling with the rising wind, her jewelry sparkling in the dying light. "He says he has the power of magic. Therefore he will enter the *harem*—as Khardan's wife!"

CHAPTER 11

The sun sank behind the far western hills. The afterglow lit the sky and was reflected back by the crystals of desert sand. There were a few startled gasps from some of the women, a flurry of whispers and silken rustling as wives crowded together like flocks of birds, and here and there a low voiced command from a husband to hush.

Silence, thick and heavy with amazement, fell over the tribesmen. All looked to Khardan, awaiting his reaction.

The Calif both looked and felt as though he'd been riding his horse at a mad gallop when the animal suddenly dropped dead beneath him. The breath left his body; his skin flushed red, then went deathly white; his frame trembled.

"Wife, you go too far!" he managed to gasp out, nearly strangling.

"Not at all," Zohra replied coolly. "You have stolen two—shall we say—'women' and carried them far from their homes. By the law of Akhran you are, therefore, required to provide for them, either by establishing them in your tent or seeing them established in another—"

"By Sul, wife!" Khardan swore viciously, taking a step nearer Zohra. "I saved their lives! I didn't carry them off in a raid!"

Zohra made a fluttering motion with her hands. Her face was unveiled, and it was smooth and grave and solemn. Only Khardan, looking into the black eyes, saw smoldering there coals he had fondly thought quenched. What could have touched off this fire, the Calif couldn't imagine. In another woman he might have said it was jealousy, but jealousy implies a certain amount of caring, and Zohra had made it clear countless times that she would as soon give her love to the meanest creature that walked as to give it to him.

He had thought her changed, but apparently not. No, this was just another attempt to humiliate him, to shame him before his people and to elevate herself in the eyes of her own. And once again, as in the matter of the bridal sheet, Khardan was helpless to fight her, for she stood solidly on her own ground-magic, a woman's province, inviolate by men.

"I will give each of these 'girls' the ritual tests, of course," Zohra said.

Her proud gaze swept over everyone to light upon Meryem, who shrank into the arms of Khardan's mother.

"What about it, child?" Zohra asked of her with mocking gentleness. "Are you—a Sultan's daughter—skilled in the art of magic?"

"I—I am not. . . very good," the girl admitted timidly with a sidelong glance at Khardan from beneath her long lashes. She appeared confused, yet confident. She did not yet understand her danger. "But I would do my best to please my husband. . . ."

"I'm sure you would," murmured Zohra with the purring sound a lioness makes before tearing the throat from her victim. "And I'm sure there will be many men here who will come to 'your father' "—Zohra smiled placidly upon the glowering Maji-id—"and will offer to take you to wife despite your lack of skill in magic. For I am certain that you have talents in other areas. . ."

"But I am to be Khardan's wife," Meryem began innocently, then stopped, realizing something was wrong.

"Ah, I'm afraid not, poor child." Zohra sighed softly. "Not if he takes this other 'woman' into his tent. Are you skilled in magic?"

Turning, she glanced at the youth, who had no idea what any of this was about and who knew only that—once again—his fate was being held in balance. Still crouched on the ground, the young man's sobs had ceased. He stared from Khardan to Zohra in blank confusion.

"Yes, I am . . .skilled. . ." He faltered, not knowing what else to say.

Truly mad! Zohra thought. But—mad or sane—he serves my purpose.

Zohra had taken a gamble on her course of battle. Armed with knowledge of her husband and a woman's knowledge of other women, she had ridden forth, confident of victory, and she had just achieved it. Like all men, Khardan distrusted magic, since it was something he could not control. No matter how proficient in the art Meryem truly was—and Zohra, thinking of the soft life in the Sultan's court, did not believe this could be very proficient at all—the girl would surely play down her talent in this area in favor of others that Khardan was certain to find more to his taste. As for the madman, whether he was skilled or not didn't matter. After all, it was Zohra who gave the tests and they were always given in secret...

"You see, my child," Zohra continued, her limpid-eyed gaze turning back to Meryem, "Khardan has a wife already. This will make his second. It is a law that a man can take no more wives than he can support, and since the failure to sell the horses, it will be all my husband can do to keep the two of us. He cannot provide for a third."

Had Zohra been watching Meryem closely, she would have seen the blue eyes go suddenly cold as blue steel, she would have felt their sharp, cutting edge, and she would have known that she had created an enemy—a deadly one, who could fight her on her own level. Exultant in her victory, enjoying the sweet fruits of vengeance against her husband, Zohra did not see the dagger in Meryem's gaze.

One person saw it, however—the young man. But he was so lost in confusion that though he saw the girl's deadly, darting gaze, he soon lost the memory in the turmoil of his mind.

"Father!" said Khardan, turning to the Sheykh. "I put this to you! Give me your judgment and I will abide by it."

It was obvious from Majiid's lowering brow and quivering mustache that he would have sided with his son. But he had the law to uphold, justice must be served.

Shaking his head, he said sternly, "We cannot leave the madman to starve; that would anger *Hazrat* Akhran. You have accepted responsibility for the madman. If you had not intervened, then he would be dead now—purely by accident"—the Sheykh looked up deprecatingly into the heavens—"since we would have had no way of knowing he was mad, in which case we would have been forgiven his death due to our ignorance, and you, Khardan"—Majiid glowered at his son—"would be making wedding plans. Let this be a lesson!"

He gestured at the girl. "I have accepted Meryem into my

family. She will be well cared for until such time as a suitor comes who can claim her hand. "

The judgment given, the Sheykh's lips snapped tightly shut. Folding his arms across his chest, he turned his back upon the supplicant, a sign that there was to be no further discussion.

"Now wait just a minute!" The voice was that of Badia, Khardan's mother.

Stepping forward, she faced Majiid. A diminutive woman, she did not come to her tall husband's shoulder. Generally meek and docile, knowing and accepting her place as head wife and mother, Badia had her limits, however, and these had just been reached. Hands on her hips, she faced her astonished husband, casting a glance around the assembled tribes.

"I think you have all lost your wits! You are as mad as this wretched creature!" she said with a scathing gesture at the youth. "A man in the *harem*! Such a thing is not done unless he is . . . has been. . ." She flushed deeply but was not embarrassed enough to be swerved from her course. "Has had his manhood cut away," she said finally, ignoring her husband's shocked look.

Other women in the tribe nodded and murmured in agreement.

"The poor young man is mad. You're not going to make a eunuch of him, too," Khardan said coldly. "A beardless chin, a hairless chest. What harm can you fear he will do? Especially in my *harem*." He cast a bitter glance at Zohra. "My wife is more of a man than this one! But—if it will please you, Mother—I will set a guard at his tent. Pukah shall watch over him. There is probably wisdom in that anyway, lest he—in his madness—chooses to do harm to himself or someone else. And now there is one more thing I will say before the matter closes."

Leaving the center of the compound, Khardan walked over to stand before Meryem. He took hold of her hands in his, looking down into the adoring, tear-filled eyes. "By day, you are more radiant than the sun. By night, you brighten my darkness like the moon. I love you, and I swear as *Hazrat* Akhran is my witness that no man will possess you except myself, Meryem, if I have to steal the wealth of the Amir's treasury to do it."

Leaning down, he kissed the girl's forehead. Weeping, Meryem nestled against him. He felt her body, soft and warm, trembling in his grasp. Her fragrance intoxicated him, her tears inflamed his heart. Hurriedly his mother came to take the girl and lead her away.

Breathing as though he had been fighting a battle with ten thousand devils, Khardan left as well, walking rapidly into the deepening darkness of the desert. If he went to find some glimmer of hope in the Rose of the Prophet, it was not there. Green and almost healthy looking when Khardan had left for his journey to the city, the plant was—once again—brown and shriveled.

One by one the other members of the tribes melted away, hurrying to their tents to discuss the day's events in excited whispers. Only two were left standing in the compound, Zohra and the youth.

Zohra had won, but for some reason the sweet fruit of revenge had changed to ashes in her mouth. Hiding her wounds, she made her way with haughty demeanor back to her tent.

The young man remained behind, crouched on his knees on the hard granite of the desert floor. Many gave him sidelong glances as they scurried past. None came to him. He did not know what to do, where to go. If it had been his headless corpse lying there, he could not have experienced more bitterly the taste of the loneliness of death than he did now, surrounded by the living.

John had died once, his life severed by the blade.

"How many times have I died?" Mathew asked himself miserably. "How many times must I go on dying?"

His strength gave way and he sank down onto the warm, hard ground, his senses slipping from him. He never noticed the soft feathers of the angel's wing drawing over him or felt the light touch of the angel's tear, falling like dew upon his skin.

CHAPTER 12

"ho are you?" asked Pukah in astonishment.

The woman who had been hovering over the young man whirled in fear. At the sight of Pukah, she instantly disappeared.

"Wait! Don't go!" Pukah cried. "Beautiful creature! I didn't mean to frighten you! Don't leave! I—She's gone." The djinn gazed around disconsolately. "What was she? An immortal, of course, but like none I've seen in all my centuries!"

Coming nearer the unconscious youth, Pukah felt about in the air with his hands. "Are you here, lovely being? Show yourself. You needn't be afraid of Pukah. Gentle Pukah, I am called. Harmless as a human babe. Come back, dazzling enchanter! I want only to be your adoring slave, to worship at your feet. Such small, white feet, peeping beneath your white gown, hair the silver of starlight, wings like a dove. . . Wings! Imagine that! And eyes that melt my heart!

"Nothing. She's gone." Pukah heaved a sigh, his shoulders slumped. "And I am desolated! I know what you are going to say." He raised his hand to forestall any argument that might be forthcoming from his other half. "You, Pukah, are in too much trouble already. The last thing you need is a female—even if she did have wings. Because of you, Sheykh Zeid and twenty or so thousand mad *meharistes*—give or take several thousand—are going to sweep up out of the south and murder us all. Thinking to right this by trying to bring about peace between Quar and Akhran so that the tribes can separate and no longer prove a threat to Zeid so that Zeid would go back to his camels and leave us in peace, I went to Kaug—may sting rays swim into his *pantalons*—and told him that all three tribes were gathering together to strike out at the city of Kich."

Shaking his head sadly, Pukah lifted the unconscious youth.

"And it should have worked! Kaug was terrified, I swear it! Well, you know! You saw him!" This to Pukah's alter ego, not the young man. "It was Quar, that archfiend of a God, who stirred up trouble. How was I to know the Amir was such a powerful general? How was I to know he had magical horses? How was I to know he would try to arrest my poor master and nearly get us all killed? I—"

"So it was *you*!" came a ferocious voice from out of the darkness.

Pukah nearly dropped the young man he was carrying over his shoulder. "Pukah," he muttered to himself, glancing around swiftly, "will you never learn to keep your mouth shut? Who . . . who is there?" he called.

"Sond!" came the terrible voice.

The large, muscular djinn took shape and form, standing before Pukah, his strong arms folded before his broad chest, and a dark expression on his face.

"Sond! Honored friend! I would bow, but as you see, I am rather discommoded at the present time—"

" 'Discommoded!' " said Sond, his voice swelling with his rising passion. "When I am through with you, swine, you will not only be discommoded, you will be disembodied, disemboweled, disexcruciated, disenchanted, and dis-anything else I can think of!"

The young man, hanging upside down, his head and arms dangling across Pukah's shoulders, groaned and began to stir. Wondering why Sond was in such a towering rage, and also wondering, uneasily, how much the elder djinn had overheard, and further wondering how he could escape with his skin and his ambition both intact, Pukah gave Sond a meek smile.

"I am honored that you take such an interest in me and my unworthy doings, Sond, and it would please me no end to be able to discuss them with you, but—as you see—my master has ordered me to tend to this poor madman, and of course, I must obey, being the dutiful servant that I am. If you will wait for me here, I will deposit the madman in his bed, then return. I swear, I will be back in two barks of a dog—"

"Two barks of a *dead* dog," Sond interrupted grimly. "Don't think you can escape me so easily, worm."

The djinn clapped his hands together with a sound like

thunder. The young man hanging over Pukah's shoulders disappeared.

Pukah nervously began to back up.

"My poor madman!" he cried. "What have you done with him?"

"Sent him to his bed. Weren't those your orders?" Sond said through clenched teeth, advancing one step forward for each step Pukah retreated. "I have done your work for you. Are you not grateful?"

"I—I am!" Pukah gasped, inadvertently putting his foot into a brass pot and nearly falling into a tent. "Dee-deeply grateful, friend S-s-sond.".

Catching his balance, Pukah hopped along, trying desperately to extricate his foot from the pot. Sond, shoulder muscles bulging, veins popping, eyes flaming, continued to stalk the unfortunate young djinn.

"Therefore, since you are so grateful to me, 'friend' Pukah, do continue your most interesting conversation. You went to Kaug, you say, and told him—told him what?"

"That. . . uh . . . that the two tribes of Sheykhs Majiid al Fakhar and Jaafar al Widjar were united at last and that . . . uh . . . we were now rejoicing that a third tribe—that of the powerful Sheykh Zeid al Saban—would soon be united with us as well and . . . and"—Pukah thought swiftly—"I told Kaug that this was all *your* doing, O Great Sond, and that truly this is proof of your high intelligence—"

Thinking to flatter the elder djinn (also thinking that if Zeid did attack them it would be best to start laying the groundwork for casting the blame onto someone else's shoulders), Pukah was astounded beyond measure to see Sond—upon hearing these words—go livid.

"You. . . what?" The djinn choked, near strangling.

"I gave you all the credit, friend Sond," Pukah said humbly. Finally kicking the pot off his foot, he straightened and held up his hands deprecatingly. "Do not thank me. It was nothing but your due. . ."

Pukah's voice died. Sond, bellowing terrifyingly, had soared to nearly twenty feet in height. His great arms lifted above his head as though he meant to tear the stars, one by one, from the sky. Pukah saw instantly, however, that the stars were not the target of Sond's wrath. Plunging down like a meteor, the djinn descended upon Pukah.

Panic-stricken, the young djinn had time only to hide his head in his arms and regret his young life, tragically ended, visualizing himself stuffed in an iron money box, locked and sealed and buried one thousand feet below the surface of the world. A gigantic wind hit him, blew all around him, completely uprooting two palm trees....

Then the gale stopped.

This is it, the end, thought Pukah grimly.

But there was nothing.

Fearfully he waited.

Still nothing.

Keeping his arms covering his head, his eyes squinched tightly shut, Pukah listened. All he heard was a pitiful moaning as of a man having his guts wrenched out. Cautiously Pukah opened half an eye and peered out over his elbow.

Bent double, his arms clasped around his stomach as though he were holding himself together, was Sond—sobbing bitterly.

"Ah, my dear friend," said Pukah, truly touched and feeling more than a little guilty that he hadn't spoken the truth. "I know that you are grateful to me, but I assure you that this display of emotion is completely—"

" 'Grateful'!"

Sond lifted his face. Tears streaked the djinn's cheeks, foam frothed on his lips, blood dripped from his mouth. Teeth gnashing, hands outstretched, Sond leaped for Pukah's throat.

"Grateful!" Sond screamed. Knocking Pukah to the ground, he grabbed the young djinn around the neck and began bashing his head into the desert floor, driving it deeper with each word he spoke. "She is lost! Lost to me! Forever! Forever!"

Bash, bash, bash...

Pukah would have screamed for help, but his tongue was so tangled up with everything else rattling around in his head that all he could do was gasp "Uh! Uh! Uh!" at each blow.

Eventually Sond's strength gave out, or he might have bashed Pukah clear through the world, where the djinn would have come out on the other side and discovered that Mathew wasn't mad after all. Exhausted by his grief and his rage, Sond merely gave Pukah a final shove that sent the young djinn down through six feet of solid granite. Then Sond fell over backward, moaning for breath.

Dizzy, disoriented, and thoroughly shaken, Pukah at first considered staying in his hole and—not content with that hiding him from Sond—pulling the desert in on top of him. But as his head cleared, he began to consider the elder djinn's words: *She is lost. . . Lost to me forever. . .*

She who? Lost how? And why was it apparently all his—Pukah's—fault?

Knowing he would never rest content—not even locked in an iron money box—without the answer to these questions, Pukah peered up out of his hole.

"Sond?" he said timidly, preparing to dive back down if the elder djinn showed signs of renewed hostility. "I don't understand. Tell me what's wrong. Something *is* wrong, I take it."

Sond groaned in answer, flinging his head about from side to side, his face contorted in a grief most awful to witness.

"Sond," said Pukah, beginning to have the feeling now that something was really, really wrong and wondering if it was going to further compound his own troubles, "if you'd. . . uh . . . tell me, perhaps I could help—"

" 'Help'!" Sond propped himself up on his elbows, gazing at Pukah with bloodshot eyes. "What more can you do than you've done already except to take my sword and slice me in two!"

"I would be honored to do that, of course, if it is what you truly desire, O Sond," began Pukah humbly.

"Oh, shut up!" Sond snarled. "There is nothing you can do. Nothing anyone can do, not even Akhran."

Upon hearing the name of the awful God, Pukah glanced nervously up into the heavens and scrunched back down into the hole.

"You. . . spoke to Holy Akhran?"

"Yes. What else could I do?"

"And. . . what did you tell him?"

"I confessed my guilt to him."

Pukah heaved a sigh of relief. "For which guilt I am certain the merciful God has forgiven you," he said soothingly.

"That was, of course, before I knew anything about the hand you had in this!" Sond growled, glaring at Pukah. He sighed bleakly. "Not that it matters anyway, I suppose."

"I'm sure it doesn't!" Pukah said, but Sond wasn't listening.

"I lost Nedjma the night Kaug stole her from the garden. Akhran made me see this. I was a fool to believe that anything I did would induce Kaug to give her back. He was using me. But I was desperate. What else could I do?"

In a few bitter words Sond related the story of Nedjma's capture by the 'efreet and Kaug's demands that Sond separate the tribes or lose Nedjma forever.

"I tried to split them apart. It didn't work. You saw that," Sond continued miserably. "Everything was against me! Zeid coming out of nowhere like that"—Pukah squirmed uncomfortably—"and forcing the Akar to make friends with the Hrana. I went to Kaug to try to explain and beg him to give me another chance, but he only laughed cruelly. He asked if I truly thought myself clever enough to thwart him. Nedjma was gone, he said, and I would never see her again—until the day I myself was sent to join her."

Pukah's brow wrinkled in thought. "That's an odd statement. What did he mean by it?"

Sond shrugged wearily, letting his head lapse into his hands. "How should I know?" he mumbled.

"And what did *Hazrat* Akhran say?"

"After I finally found him," Sond said, looking up, his face drawn, "a search that took four days and four nights, he told me that he understood why I had done what I had done. He said that next time I was to come to him directly, then he gave me a stern lecture on attempting to subvert the ways of the Gods and reminded me that he himself had ordered us to find out what was happening to the vanishing immortals—"

"Why, that's it!" Pukah cried.

"That's what?"

"That's what happened to Nedjma! Kaug's sent her to wherever the lost djinn are. From what he said about your going to join her, we're next, seemingly," Pukah added after some reflection.

"Do you truly think so?" Sond looked up, hope illuminating his face so that it glowed in the dark with a pale, white radiance.

Pukah looked at him in amazement.

"Honored Sond, I am pleased beyond measure that you have recovered your spirits and that any poor words of mine have performed this transformation, but I can't help wondering why this dread news of Nedjma's being banished to the Gods know where—no, on second thought, to someplace of which *they* don't even know—fills you with such joy?"

"I . . . I feared. . . she was. . . that Kaug had. . ." Sond's voice trailed off huskily, his face growing dark and brooding once more.

"Ah!" said Pukah in sudden understanding. "Kaug?" He scoffed. "You say Nedjma is delicate and beautiful? Then she will not arouse Kaug's interest. He ruts with sea cows. I'm serious! I have it on very good authority. . . Now, come, my friend."

Pukah felt confident enough to climb out of his hole. Going over to Sond, he respectfully assisted the djinn to his feet. "I am always thinking, you know. It is my curse to have a fertile brain. And I have the beginnings of a plan. No, I can't say anything yet. I must do some research, some investigating," the djinn continued importantly, brushing the sand off Sond's shoulders and putting the djinn's rumpled clothing to rights. "Don't say a word to anyone yet about. . . well, what you overheard me discussing with myself tonight, particularly to the master. All this is part of the plan. You might spoil it.

"And now," continued Pukah, as Sond stood gazing at him in bewilderment, "I must go and tend to the madman as my master ordered. As if I didn't have enough to do!" He sighed a long-suffering sigh. "Be of good hope, O Sond!" Pukah clapped the djinn on the shoulder. "And put your faith in Pukah!"

With that, he vanished.

CHAPTER 13

ω aking from the strangest dream he'd ever experienced, Mathew sat up suddenly, shivering in fear. He'd been lying in the sand when a young man wearing a white turban and flowing silken pants appeared out of nowhere and—with an unbelievable strength—lifted him up onto his shoulders. This young man had been talking to himself—at least so Mathew thought, until another man appeared. His face was dreadful to I behold. He made a sound like thunder, and then both men were gone and the young wizard was alone inside a tent that smelled strongly of goat.

Glancing around in the darkness, Mathew began to realize that at least that part of his dream hadn't been a dream. He *was* lying in a tent, it *did* smell as if a goat had been its former inhabitant, and he was alone in the night. The air was bitterly cold, and he groped about in the darkness for something to cover himself. Finding a soft woolen blanket, he wrapped it around his body and lay back down upon the cushions.

Suddenly, with a pang of fear, he started back up. Thrusting his hand deep inside his robes, he felt frantically for the fishbowl. His fingers closed over its cold surface, the edges of the gold and silver metalwork biting into his skin. Gently he shook it and was reassured by the feeling of motion within the globe. At least the water was still there; presumably the fish were safe and unharmed.

A light step from outside the tent caused Mathew to hastily thrust the bowl back inside his robes. His heart pounding, wondering what new terror he was going to have to endure, the wizard stared at the tent entrance.

"Are you awake, mast—er, mistress?" The voice seemed a bit confused.

"Yes," Mathew answered after a moment's hesitation.

"May I enter?" the voice continued humbly and servilely. "My master has instructed me to make you comfortable for the night."

"Are. . . are you from Khardan?" Mathew asked, daring to breathe a little easier.

"Yes, mas—er, mistress."

"Then please, come inside."

"Thank you, mas. . . mistress," said the voice, and to Mathew's astonishment one of the figures came out of his dream and stepped inside the tent.

It was the young one, the one who had picked him up with the ease of a man lifting a puppy. Hands folded before him, his eyes cast down, the young man in the white turban performed the *salaam*, politely wishing Mathew health and joy.

Mathew stammered out a suitable reply.

"I have brought a *chirak*, an oil lamp," the young man said, producing one out of the night. Setting it down carefully upon the tent floor, he caused it to light with a wave of his hand. "And here is a brazier and charcoal to burn to warm yourself. My master tells me that you are not of this land"—the young man spoke carefully, with elaborate politeness as though fearing to unduly upset Mathew—"therefore I assume you are not familiar with our ways?"

"N-no, I'm not."

The young man nodded solemnly, but—when he thought Mathew wasn't watching—he rolled his eyes to the heavens.

"Make certain that you set the brazier here, beneath the opening in the tent, so that the smoke may rise up and out. Otherwise you will not wake up in the morning, for the smoke of the charcoal is poisonous. If you will allow me to arrange your bed"—the young man gently but firmly crowded Mathew into a corner of the tent, out of the way—"I would suggest that you be careful to keep the cushions on the felt rug when you sleep. Neither the scorpion nor the *qarakurt* will cross felt, you know."

"No, I didn't," Mathew murmured, gazing in awe at this remarkable young man. "What is a *qarakurt*?"

"A largish black spider. You are dead within seconds of its bite."

"And. . . you say it won't walk on felt? Why not?" Mathew asked nervously.

"Ah, only *Hazrat* Akhran knows the answer to that one," the young man said piously. "All I know is that I have seen a man sleep soundly, though surrounded by an army of such spiders, all thirsting for his blood. Yet they would not set one black leg upon his felt blanket. And you must also remember to shake your clothes and especially your shoes out every morning before putting them on, for though the scorpion will not cross felt, he is smart and will wait for his chance to sting by hiding in your garments."

Remembering the past nights when he had not cared where he lay and thinking of how he had heedlessly slipped on the women's shoes each morning, Mathew felt his throat constrict as he vividly imagined the stinging tail of the scorpion thrusting itself into his flesh. To turn his thoughts from these horrors, he questioned the young man.

"You are a remarkable wiz—sorcerer," Mathew said earnestly. "How long have you studied the art?"

To Mathew's astonishment, the young man drew himself up very straight and regarded the wizard with a cold eye.

"I know you are mad," the young man said, "but I cannot see that this gives you the right to insult me."

"Insult you? I never meant—"

"To refer to me as a sorcerer! To imply that I dabble in that woman's art!" The young man appeared highly offended.

"But—the lamp you conjured. And the light. I assumed—"

"I am a djinn, of course. I am called Pukah. Khardan is my master."

"A djinn!" Mathew gasped and shrank back. Apparently he wasn't the only madman in this camp. "But. . . there are no such things as djinn!"

Pukah gave Mathew a pitying glance. "Mad as a foaming-mouthed dog," he muttered. Shaking his head, he continued to plump up the cushions. "By the way, mas-mistress. When I came to find you this night and discovered you lying senseless upon the ground, there was an immortal—one of my kind—bending over you."

Eyes glowing with the memory, Pukah forgot what he was doing and slowly sank down upon the cushions. "Yet she wasn't of my kind, either. She was the most beautiful creature I have ever seen. Her hair was silver. She was dressed in long white robes, soft feathery white wings grew from her back. I spoke to her," the djinn said sadly, "but she vanished. Is she your djinniyeh? If so," he continued eagerly, "could you tell her that I truly mean her no harm and that I want just one moment, one second with her to speak of my adoration—"

"I don't know what you're talking about!" Mathew interrupted. "Djinniyeh! That's ridiculous! Although"—he hesitated—"what you describe sounds very much like a being we know as an angel..."

"'Angel'!" Pukah sighed rapturously. "What a beautiful word. It fits her. Do all in your... uh ... land have such creatures to serve you?"

"Angels! Serve us!" Mathew was shocked at the sacrilege. "Absolutely not! It would be our privilege to serve them if we should ever be fortunate enough to see one."

"That I can believe," said Pukah gravely. "I would serve her all my life, if she were mine. But then, if you never see these beings, how do you communicate with your God?"

"Through the holy priests," Mathew said, faltering, his thoughts going painfully to John. "It is the priests—and only the highest ranking of their Order—who talk with the angels of Promenthas and so learn His Holy Will."

"And that is all these angels do?"

"Well"—Mathew hesitated, suddenly uncomfortable—"there are such beings known as guardian angels, whose duty it is to watch over the humans in their care, but..."

"But what?" Pukah prodded inquisitively.

"I—I never really believed... I mean, I still don't..."

"And you do not believe in me, either!" the djinn said. "Yet here I stand. And now"—Pukah rose gracefully to his feet—"if there is nothing further I can do for you, I must return. My master undoubtedly needs me. He attempts nothing without my advice and counsel."

"No, that—that is all," Mathew mumbled, his thoughts in confusion. "Thank you... Pukah..."

"Thank *you*, mas—mistress," rebuked the djinn, bowing, and melting into the smoke, he disappeared as if sucked out the tent flap.

Catching his breath in amazement, Mathew stared blankly at where the djinn had been standing. "Maybe I *am* mad," he muttered, putting his hand to his head. "This isn't real. It can't be happening. It is all part of a dream and I will soon waken—"

Someone else was outside his tent. Mathew heard a clashing of jewelry, a silken rustle, and smelled the sudden sweetness of perfume. "Are you awake?" came a soft whisper.

"Yes," Mathew answered, too dazed to be frightened.

"May I enter? It is Zohra."

Zohra? He had a dim impression that this was the woman who had announced that he was to be taken into the *harem*. He vaguely remembered hearing someone refer to her by that name. This meant, from what he'd gathered, that she was Khardan's wife. "Yes, please do. . . ."

The tent flap darkened, a figure shapeless in a silken *caftan* entered. The lamplight gleamed off bracelets and rings, its flame reflected in the black, flashing eyes barely visible above her veil. Entering swiftly, Zohra carefully shut the tent flap behind her, making certain that no chink of light escaped. Satisfied, she seated herself upon the cushions, knelling with easy grace, staring at Mathew, who remained crouched in the corner of the tent where he had been driven by the djinn.

"Come within the light," Zohra ordered, making a commanding gesture with her arm, her bracelets clinking together musically. "There, sit across from me." She pointed to a pile of cushions opposite her, keeping the charcoal brazier and the oil lamp between them.

Doing as he was bidden, Mathew came to sit on the cushions. A pool of warm yellow from the flame of the lamp encircled them both, illuminating their faces, setting them against a backdrop of shadows that moved and wavered with the flickering of the flame. Slowly Zohra lowered the veil from her face, her eyes, all the while studying Mathew intently.

He, in turn, looking at her, thought that he had never before seen a woman so beautiful or so wild.

My wife is more of a man than this one!

Khardan's bitter words came back to Mathew, and—looking into the face of the woman who sat opposite him—he could well understand them. There was something masculine about the face in its unbending pride, the fierce anger that he could sense smoldering beneath the surface. Yet he had the feeling that the lips could soften, the eyes could be tender if she chose.

"I want to thank you, madam," Mathew said evenly, "for the part you played in saving my life."

"Yes," was the woman's unexpected reply, her eyes never leaving Mathew's face. "I came to find out why I did. What is there about you that moved me to intercede in your behalf? What is your name?"

"M-Mathew," the young man answered, startled at the abruptness of the question.

"M-Mat-hew." Zohra stumbled over it, her lips forming the unusual sound awkwardly.

"Mathew," Mathew repeated, feeling a certain joy at hearing his name spoken by another human being. It was the first time anyone had asked him.

"That is what I said. Mat-hew," Zohra replied loftily. "And so, Mat-hew, can you tell me why I saved your life?"

"N-no," replied the young man, startled at the question. Seeing that Zohra obviously expected an answer, he fumbled for words. "I . . . can only assume that your woman's heart, feeling pity. . ."

"Bah!" Zohra's contempt burned brighter than the lamp. "Woman's heart! I have no woman's heart. And I do not feel pity. If anything"—she cast him a scornful glance—"I feel contempt!" Angrily she tore at her gown, her sharp fingernails rending the fragile fabric. "If I had a man's body, I would never hide in this . . . this winding sheet!"

"And you would not have done what I did to save my life," Mathew said. Ashamed, he lowered his head before her scathing gaze. "And neither would he," he added softly, so softly he did not think she heard. But Zohra caught the words, pouncing on them like a diving hawk.

"Khardan? Of course not! He would die the death of a thousand daggers before hiding in woman's clothing. As for me, I am trapped in them. I die the death every morning when I wake and put them on! Perhaps"—now it was she who was speaking to herself—"perhaps that is why I saved you. I saw them looking at you, saw them staring at you the same way they stare at me. . ."

Mathew, with a flash of insight, suddenly understood. The pride in the handsome face masked a gnawing pain. But why? What is wrong here? He did not understand, he had no way of knowing about the age-old enmity between the two tribes, of the marriage forced upon them by their God, of the brown and dying plant upon the Tel. He knew only because he saw it in her face that this woman was—like himself—surrounded by people and desperately lonely.

Now it was he who pitied her, pitied her and longed to help. And for the first time, the fear he had lived with for those torturous weeks since his capture began to fade to the back of his soul, replaced by a feeling more blessed—a feeling of caring. Yet he was wise enough to know that he must guard against revealing this feeling to her or endure the stinging lash of her pride.

"I do not believe you are mad," she said suddenly, and Mathew felt the fear return. "Yes," she added, seeing it flare in his eyes, "you must continue to make others believe you are insane. I shouldn't imagine that will be too difficult." Her lips twisted. "They are, as you have seen, fools."

"What. . . about Khardan?" Mathew hesitated, feeling his face flush. "Does he . . . think me mad?"

Zohra shrugged her slender shoulders, causing the silk to rustle around her, the perfume to drift lightly on the warmth spreading through the tent. "Why do you suppose I should know—or care—what he thinks?" Her eyes challenged Mathew to answer.

"No reason, except"—the young man faltered, uncomfortable at this discussion of intimate affairs between man and woman—"except that you are . . . his wife. I thought that he must—"

"Spend his nights in my company? Well, you are wrong." Zohra drew her robe around her as if chilled, though the heat radiating from the charcoal brazier was rapidly becoming stifling in the small tent. "We are man and wife in name only. Oh, that is no secret. You will hear it around the camp. You take a great interest in Khardan," she said suddenly, her eyes piercing Mathew's heart with a suddenness for which he was unprepared.

"He saved me from the slavers," Mathew said, his skin on fire. "And he saved me again this night. It is only natural—"

"By Sul!" said Zohra in amazement. "I believe you are in love with him!"

"No, no!" Mathew protested warmly. "I . . . admire him, that is all. And I am grateful. . ."

"Is this the custom in your land across the sea?" Zohra asked curiously, reclining among the cushions. "Do men love men there? Such a thing is prohibited by our God. Is it not by yours?"

"I—I . . ." Poor Mathew had no idea what to say, where to begin. "You believe me then?" He grasped at this straw, hoping to save himself from drowning. "You believe that I do truly come from a land across the sea?"

"What does that matter!" Zohra brushed away the insignificant with a wave of her hand. "Answer my question."

"As. . . as a matter of fact," Mathew faltered, "such love as you . . . you mention is *not* prohibited by our God. Love. . . between any two people. . . is considered sacred and holy, so long as it is true love and caring and not. . . not simply lust or self-gratification of the body."

"How old are you?"

"I have seen eighteen summers in my land, madam," Mathew replied.

A sudden longing for that land, for those summers spent among the spreading oaks, came to the young wizard. His eyes filling with tears, he hurriedly bent his head so that she would not see. Perhaps she did and sought to turn his thoughts from his homesickness. If that was her intent, she succeeded admirably with her next question.

"And do you lie with men or with women?"

Mathew's eyes flared open; the blood rushed to his face until he felt it was a wonder it didn't drip from his gaping mouth.

"I—I have. . . never. . . lain. . . I mean. . .had that kind of . . . relationship with. . . anyone, m-madam!" he stammered.

"Ah, good," she said gravely, thoughtfully drawing the end of her veil between her jeweled fingers. "Our God, Akhran, forgives much, but I do not think he would be understanding in such a matter. And now," she continued, an amused smile playing about her lips, "you claim to be a sorcerer? How is this possible? The Gods give this gift only to women? Or"—a sudden thought occurred to her—"perhaps you have this because you have never—"

"I assure you, madam," said Mathew, regaining his dignity, "that the men of my land have long practiced this art and that what. . . we spoke of . . . has nothing to do with it."

"But"—Zohra appeared bewildered—"how is this possible? Do you not know of the Too-Learned Wizards and the curse put upon them by Sul? Men are forbidden to practice magic!"

"I do not know of what you speak, madam," said Mathew

cautiously. "If, by the story of the Too-Learned Wizards, you mean the story of the Reproach of the Magi—"

"Tell me this tale," said Zohra, settling down more comfortably among the cushions.

Mathew glanced hesitantly toward the outside. "I would be honored to do as you request, madam, but are you certain it is safe? Won't—"

"My husband come seeking me? I think not," Zohra said with a mocking smile that held—for Mathew's eyes—a trace of bitterness. "Besides, I am safe here with you, am I not? Are you not mad? Go on. Tell your tale."

Mathew tried to collect his thoughts—a difficult task. He remembered hearing this story his first day upon entering the Wizards' School as a young child, awed by the black-robed archmagi, the rows of wooden desks, the towering stone buildings. He had never, in his wildest imaginings, pictured himself relating it while sitting in a tent in the middle of the desert, the fiery eyes of a wild and lovely woman fixed upon him.

"It is our belief that our God has gifts and graces that he bestows upon his faithful," said Mathew, looking questioningly at Zohra, who nodded gravely to show she understood. "But Sul—as center of all—alone possesses the magic. He shares this gift with those of learned and serious manner who come to him in humility, pledging to serve him by spending their lives in study and hard work; not only in the pursuit of magic, but in pursuit of knowledge of all things in this world.

"Long ago a group of magi studied so diligently that they became the most learned and the wisest men and women in the world. They knew not only magic, but languages, philosophy, science, and many other arts. Because they had all learned each other's languages and customs, they were able to come together and further increase their knowledge. Instead of looking each to his own God, they began to look increasingly to Sul, the Center. They saw, when they looked into the center, the strife and turmoil in the world, and they knew that it was caused by the rankling and arguing and bickering of the Gods, who could not see the truth but only one part of the truth. Gradually the magi became of one mind, and this mind told them to use their magic to try to reach some resolution among the Gods.

"Unfortunately, feeling threatened, the Gods come to Sul

and demanded that magic be withdrawn from the world. This Sul could not do, magic having become too pervasive within the world. Sul himself became enraged at the magi for abusing his gift, and he chastised them severely, accusing them of attempting to aspire to become Gods.

"But the magi reproached him, saying that their concern was only for the suffering of their fellow humans and crying out that the Gods had forgotten this in their selfish arguing. Sul was chagrined and so begged their pardon. But Sul said, something must be done to appease the Gods or they would insist that magic be removed from the world. Therefore the magi agreed on a compromise.

"Magic must be based in material objects—charms and amulets and potions—so that those who practice it are constrained by their own human limitations as well as by the physical properties of the objects in which the magic resides. Thus the Gods would not perceive magic as being a threat to their power, and the magi could still go abroad and work for the benefit of humanity. And that," concluded Mathew in relief, "is my tale."

"Sul did not cut out their tongues?" asked Zohra in disappointment.

"Cut out their— No, certainly not!" Mathew said, shocked. "After all, Sul is a God, not a—" He had been about to say "barbarian," but it suddenly occurred to him that, from what he had witnessed, the Gods of these people *were* barbarians! Stuttering, he fell silent.

Fortunately, lost in her own thoughts, Zohra had not noticed.

"And so you are a sorcerer? You practice the art of Sul? What magic can you do? Show me."

"Madam," said Mathew, somewhat confused, "I can do a great many things, but I need my charms and amulets, which were lost when our ship—our *dhow*—sank in the sea. If I have the proper tools, I can fashion others and then I will be pleased to show you my skills."

"But surely you can do the usual things: healing the sick and injured, calming animals, that sort of magic."

"Madam," said Mathew hesitantly, thinking that perhaps she was testing him, "I could do that when I was a child of eight. My skills are much further advanced, believe me."

Zohra's eyes widened slightly. She ceased toying with her veil, her fingers stopping, frozen in mid-motion. "Explain."

"Well. . ." Mathew hesitated, wondering what she expected of him. "I can see into the future, for one thing. I can fight evil spirits sent by Sul to test us, as well as those inflicted upon us by the Dark Gods. I can help restless souls of the dead find repose. I can defend those threatened by danger I from weapons physical or magical. I can summon certain minor servants of Sul and keep them under my control, although that is very dangerous, and—as an apprentice—I'm not really supposed to do so except in the presence of an archmagus. I am young," he added apologetically, "and still learning."

Sitting up straight from her formerly lounging position on the cushions, Zohra was staring at him in awe, a glittering in her eyes as of the sun on quartz. "Can you truly do this!" she breathed. The glint in her eyes became suddenly dangerous. "Or perhaps you *are* mad, after all . . ."

Mathew was suddenly very, very tired. "In this matter," he said wearily, "I am not. You can test me. If you will give me some days to work and provide me with the material I require. . . ."

"I will," said Zohra fiercely, rising to her feet with a feline twist, her bracelets jangling. She smiled at him. "If you speak truly, you may become the most valued and favored of anyone's wives, Mat-hew!"

Mathew flushed but was too exhausted to reply. When Zohra saw his white, drawn face, her expression softened, but only for an instant and then only when the young man was looking wistfully at his bed and not at her.

Preparing to leave, she paused at the tent entrance. "What God do you worship?"

"He is called Promenthas," Mathew replied, looking back up at her, astonished that she should ask, more astonished that she should care.

"May the peace of . . . Promenthas . . . be with you this night, Mat-hew," Zohra said with unwonted gentleness.

Touched, the young man could not speak but averted his gaze, sudden tears flooding his eyes. Smiling to herself, Zohra bent down, extinguished the light of the oil lamp, and then glided from the tent, her soft slippers making no noise over the sand-swept ground.

And it seemed that the peace of Promenthas was with him, even in this terrifying and alien land, for the young wizard slept soundlessly and dreamlessly for the first night since his ordeal began.

CHAPTER 14

The next few days passed in gloom for the tribes camped around the Tel. After their initial pleasure in heaving tweaked the Amir's nose subsided, the people began to take stock of their situation and discovered it to be grim.

Once again the tribes found themselves united—if only in their misery. The loot the men had managed to steal would last a while, but not a year. Neither the Akar nor the Hrana were farmers. Both depended on grain and other staples purchased from the city to survive. And if the Amir's wife could conjure up a magical horse, there was little doubt she could produce a magical sheep as well. The prospects of Jaafar and his people selling their animals and their wool in the markets in the fall seemed dim. Not only did their prospects for survival appear to be bordering on desperate, they were trapped out in the middle of the desert, forced to remain camped around an oasis whose water level was dropping, whose grass was gradually being consumed by the horses, while every passing day brought nearer summer and the threat of the violent winds of the *sirocco*.

There was some hope that the Rose of the Prophet might yet bloom and free them. It hadn't died out completely—an astonishing phenomenon, considering that the shriveled cacti appeared prepared to blacken, wither, dry up, and blow away if someone breathed on them crooked. But as for blooming, it seemed likely that flowers would sprout from Jaafar's bald head first—as Majiid observed bitterly to his son.

The tribal leaders, Khardan, Majiid, and Jaafar, spent long hours in discussion and occasionally heated debate over what to do. At length, all agreed that the Sheykhs' djinn were to be summoned and ordered to go in search of Akhran, appraise him of the situation, and receive the God's permission to leave the Tel until the storm season was over.

Fedj went alone; Sond pleaded some nameless indisposition. After several days Fedj returned downcast, stating that the Wandering God was living up to his name and had disappeared.

The men were cast into gloom. The sun grew hotter and hotter, the grass became more difficult to find, the level of the water in the pool sank a little each day, and the tempers of those in camp became more volatile.

"I say we leave!" Majiid said following Fedj's return. "We move to our summer camp. You move back to the foothills with your sheep. . . and our horses!" he added bitterly, beneath his breath.

Jaafar, groaning as usual, did not hear the sarcastic comment. Khardan heard, but preoccupied with some deep thought, he did nothing more than cast his father a warning glance.

"And risk the wrath of Akhran?" Jaafar cried. He shook his head.

"Bah! Akhran may not take it into his head to think about us for another hundred years. What is time to a God? By then we'll all be dead and it won't matter. Or," Majiid continued grimly, "we can stay here three months and we'll all be dead and again it won't matter."

"No, no!" Jaafar flung up his hands in protestation. "I remember the storm, even if you have forgotten—"

"Wait," Khardan interrupted, seeing his father beginning to swell with the prospects of an argument, "I have an idea. Suppose we do as the Amir thinks we're going to do? Suppose we attack Kich?"

Jaafar groaned again. "How does this solve our problems? It only adds to them!"

Majiid, brows bristling, glared at his son. "Go join the madman in the tent of your wife. . . ."

"No, listen to me, Father, Sheykh Jaafar. Perhaps this is what the God has meant for us to do all along. Perhaps this is why he brought us together. I am not opposed to leaving the Tel, but before we part, let us do this one thing!"

"Two tribes, raiding Kich! You did it once, by luck. Such luck won't happen again."

"It doesn't have to be two tribes! It can be three! We bring Zeid in on this with us! Together we'll have enough men to raid the city and this time we'll do it right. We can acquire wealth enough to last us a lifetime, besides teaching the Amir and his Imam to think twice before insulting *Hazrat* Akhran."

As Khardan spoke, his gaze went to Meryem, who was just entering Majiid's tent. Undoubtedly by chance, she always happened to be the one available to bring food and drink to the men.

Seeing the girl, noting her sidelong glances directed at his son, Majiid—who had been about to reject the scheme of raiding Kich—suddenly changed his mind. He had decided that Meryem would make an ideal wife for Khardan. His grandchildren would be descended from the Sultan! They would have royal blood in their veins as well as—what was more important—the blood of the Akar.

Besides, Majiid felt *his* old blood stir at the thought of raiding the city. Not even his grandfather—a legendary *batir*—had done anything so daring.

"I like it!" he said when Meryem had gone. One did not discuss matters of politics before women.

"I, too, find it interesting," said Jaafar unexpectedly. "Of course, we would need more horses—"

"It all depends on Zeid," interposed Khardan hastily, seeing his father swell up again. "Perhaps we can persuade him to give us his swift *meharis*. Will our cousin join us, do you think?"

"No one loves a good raid more than Zeid!"

"Pukah, what is the matter? Where are you going? You have not been dismissed," Khardan said, catching sight of the djinn slinking out of the tent.

"Uh, it occurred to me, master, that you might like your pipe . . ."

"I will tell you if I do. Now sit down and keep quiet. You should be interested in this. After all, it was you who brought about our alliance."

"I wish that you would forget such a trifling matter, master," said Pukah earnestly. "After all, are you certain that you can trust Sheykh Zeid? I have heard it said that his mind is like the dunes—always shifting its position as the wind blows."

"Trust him?" said Majiid brusquely. "No, you can't trust him. We can't trust each other, why should this be different? We'll send him a message"

The Sheykhs and the Calif fell to arguing over what they should say and what they should offer and Pukah finally managed to slink, unnoticed, from the tent.

Each day, rising before dawn, the djinn had been traveling to Zeid's camp, where he spent the morning hours watching with increasing gloom the Sheykh's building up of his forces. Not content with drawing on his own men, Zeid had summoned all of the southern tribes. More and more men and their camels were pouring into camp all the time. It was obvious that Zeid's attack on the Tel was going to occur in a matter of weeks, if not days.

Pukah wondered fleetingly if a proposed raid on Kich might not interest Zeid enough to make him forget about attacking his cousins. He immediately rejected this notion, however, knowing that Zeid was certain to think this was just another of Khardan's tricks.

Pukah, sighing, continued working on his plan to be away from camp when the attack occurred, thereby avoiding the wrath of his master when Khardan discovered the truth.

Other people beside the djinn were watching Zeid with considerable interest. Spies of the Amir reported that the Sheykh was calling up those under his *suzerain* or those who owed him favors or money or both and that he was apparently preparing for a major battle. The rumor spread rapidly that the nomads' target was Kich.

The cities in Bas, seeing the huge blade of the Emperor's scimitar hanging over their necks, began sending Zeid gifts. The Sheykh was inundated with concubines, donkeys, and more coffee, tobacco, and spices than he could use in a decade. Zeid wasn't stupid. He knew that the southern cities, aware of the buildup of his forces, were hoping he was coming to their rescue, not to dance on their graves.

Zeid heard the rumor about attacking Kich and laughed at it, wondering how anyone could believe it. The Sheykh knew the Amir by reputation. Qannadi was a cunning, crafty general; one to be respected and feared.

"My feud is not with the Amir or with the God of the Amir," Zeid repeatedly told ambassadors from the cities of Bas. "It is with my ancient enemies, and as long as Qannadi leaves me alone, I, Sheykh Zeid al Saban, will leave Qannadi alone."

Qannadi heard Zeid's words but didn't believe them. He saw the flood of gifts pouring into the desert, he saw the cities of Bas—who had once trembled and hung their heads at the sound of his name—begin to take heart and lift their heads and talk back to him. The Amir was angry. He had counted on the cities to the south falling into his hands like rotten fruit, their governments corrupted from within by his own double-dealing agents. The rumor of strength coming from the desert was making this increasingly more difficult, and it was all the fault of these nomads. The Amir was beginning to think that the Imam had been right to insist that they be harshly dealt with.

But Qannadi was a cautious man. He needed more information. Zeid was undoubtedly planning a move northward, that much Qannadi had from his spies. But the imbeciles also added that they believed he was going to attack Majiid and Jaafar, not ally with them. This made no sense to the military-minded general. It never occurred to him that a blood feud dating back centuries would take priority over the threat that he posed to them here and now. No, Qannadi needed to know what was transpiring among the tribes camped around the Tel.

He had planted his spy there, but he had heard nothing from her. Each day, with growing impatience, he demanded of Yamina if Meryem had made her report.

He waited many days in vain.

Meryem was having problems of her own. She was not, as she claimed to be, a daughter of the Sultan. Rather, she was a daughter of the Emperor—her mother having been one of his many hundred concubines. She had been given to the Amir as a present by the Emperor and thus came into Qannadi's *harem*. Much to Meryem's disappointment, the Amir had not married her but had merely taken her as his concubine. She was, as Qannadi told Feisal, an ambitious girl. She wanted the position of wife to the Amir, and it was this that induced her to take the dangerous role of spy when Yamina offered it to her.

The danger Meryem had foreseen. But not the discomfort. Accustomed to a life of luxury in the Emperor's grand palace in the capital city of Khandar, then to life in the rich palace of the late Sultan in Kich, Meryem found life in the desert disgusting, dirty, and appalling.

She was, had she known it, the pampered pet of Sheykh Majiid's *harem*. Her gentleness and beauty, plus her scandalous stories of life in the Sultan's court, made her a favorite with Majiid's wives and daughters. Badia, Majiid's head wife, spared Meryem from doing truly hard tasks, such as herding the horses, milking goats, drawing water, hauling firewood. But Meryem was expected to earn her keep in the *harem*. After twenty years of doing nothing except gossiping and lounging around ornamental pools, Meryem found this hateful in the extreme.

Plus, she was increasingly frustrated in being unable to get near Khardan and thus find out the information she had been sent here to gather. She repeated her woes to Yamina.

"You have no idea how wretched my life is here," Meryem said bitterly.

Alone in her tent, she held in her hands what appeared to be a mirror in a gilt frame. If anyone came in (which was unlikely considering the late hour of the night), they would have seen her admiring her face, nothing more.

In reality the mirror was a device of great magical power that allowed the sorceress who possessed it to summon the image of another sorceress onto its surface and thereby communicate with her.

"I live in a tent so small that I must crouch to enter. The smell is unbelievable. I was sick with it for three days after I came here. I am forced to wait on the men hand and foot like a common house slave. My beautiful clothes are in tatters. There is nothing to eat except mutton and gazelle, bread and rice. No fresh fruit, no vegetables. No wine, nothing to drink but tea and coffee—"

"Surely you have some diversions that make up for these inconveniences," interrupted Yamina with a distinct lack of sympathy. "I saw the Calif, you recall. A handsome young man. I was impressed, quite impressed. Such a man must make one's nights exciting. Anticipation of pleasure in the darkness makes the hours of daylight go by swiftly."

"The only thing I anticipate in the night is the pleasure of being bitten to death by bugs," said Meryem bitterly.

"What?" Yamina appeared truly startled. "You have not yet seduced this man?"

"It isn't as if I haven't tried," said Meryem petulantly. She could not bear to see Yamina—who had once been jealous of the younger, prettier girl—gazing at her smugly. "This man has notions of honor. He promised to marry me before taking me, and I fear he truly means it! And only by marrying him can I truly discover what is going on in this camp. I tried spying on the meetings of the Sheykhs, but they stop talking every time I enter. If we were married, however, I know I could persuade him to tell me what they were planning—"

"Then marry him! What is stopping you?"

Briefly, Meryem related her tale, elaborating on Zohra's interference but leaving out the fact that she—Meryem—had been replaced in Khardan's *harem* by a young man. That choice bit of information would become the joke of the *seraglio!* It was a blow from which Meryem's pride would never recover—a blow that she promised herself would someday be avenged.

"There is but one thing to do," Yamina said crisply, having heard the tale. "You know what that is."

"Yes," Meryem replied with seeming reluctance and hesitation, though inwardly rejoicing. "Such a thing goes against the teachings of the Imam, however. If he were to find out. . ."

"And how is he to find out?" Yamina demanded. "If you do it properly, no one will know, not even the woman's kin.

"Still," persisted Meryem stubbornly, "I want your sanction on this."

Yamina was silent, her lips pursed in displeasure.

Meryem, abject and humble, awaited the answer. She knew that Yamina was quite capable of betraying her by turning her over to the Imam. Forcing Yamina to give her sanction to murder would put the blame upon her; she must keep it secret, and Meryem would be safe.

"You know," Meryem added softly, "that the mirror is quite capable of recalling faces and the words they have spoken in the past, as well as transmitting those of the present."

"I am aware of that! Very well, I sanction it," Yamina said in a tight voice. "But only after all other means have failed. Men think with their loins. The Calif's honor will come to mean little enough to him when he holds you in his arms. And the marriage bed is not the only bed where business can be discussed, my dear. Or could it be"—Yamina added sweetly—"that your charms are fading, that you have attempted this and failed? Perhaps this Zohra or the other wife holds greater attraction for him than you do?"

"I have failed in nothing!" Meryem retorted angrily. "It is me whom he loves. He spends his nights alone."

"Then there should be no problem enticing him to spend his nights in your tent, Meryem, my child." Yamina's voice hardened. "The sands in the hourglass dwindle. The Amir grows impatient. Already he has mentioned his disappointment in you. Do not let that disappointment grow to displeasure."

The mirror in Meryem's hands went dark—almost as dark as the girl's scowling face. Beneath her anger and her hurt pride ran an undercurrent of fear. Unlike a wife, a concubine was at the mercy of her master. The Amir would never mistreat her—she was the Emperor's daughter, after all—but he was at liberty to give her away as one might give away a singing bird. And there was a certain one-eyed, fat captain—a friend of the general's—who had been casting that one eye in her direction. . .

No, Meryem would have Khardan. Never before had she doubted her charms—they had worked on many men, not just the Amir. But this man, this Calif, was different. He could be the rare exception to Yamina's rule. He would not be easy to seduce. Still, as long as she was careful and did not play the harlot but the innocent, loving victim, Meryem thought she might just succeed. . .

Putting away the magical mirror, the Amir's concubine went to her bed, falling asleep with a sweet and not altogether innocent smile upon her face.

The other newcomer to a *harem* was leading a life almost as easy as Meryem's, though not for the same reasons.

The life of a madman was not an unpleasant one among the nomads. Mathew no longer lived with the fear of imminent and terrible death (except from the bite of the *qarakurt,* for though he never saw one, Pukah's description of the deadly black spider haunted him). He was not shunned, as he had feared, or kept shut up away from other people. In this he had to admit that these barbarians were more humane in their treatment of the insane than those of his own land, who locked the mentally ill away in foul places that were little better (and many times worse) than prisons.

The tribesmen went out of their way to be kind to him—always rather cautiously and warily but kind nonetheless—speaking to him and bowing as they passed, bringing him small gifts of food such as rice balls or *shish kabab.* Some of the women, finding that he had no jewelry of his own, gave him theirs (Zohra would have adorned him head to toe had he allowed it). Mathew would have returned it had not Zohra told him that, in this way, the women were making certain that Mathew would have some money of his own should he ever find himself a "widow."

Children stared at him wide-eyed, and he was often approached by young mothers with requests to hold their newborn infants, if only for a few moments. At first Mathew was touched by all this attention and was beginning to consider that he had misjudged these people whom he had thought uncouth savages. One day, however, Zohra opened his eyes to the truth.

"I am pleased that your people seem to like me," Mathew said to her shyly one morning as they walked to the oasis to draw water for the day's usage.

"They don't like you," she said, glancing at him in amusement, "any more than they like me. They are frightened."

"Of me?" Mathew stared at her in astonishment.

"No, no! Of course not. Who could be frightened of you?" Zohra said, casting a scornful glance at Mathew's frail figure. "They fear the wrath of *Hazrat* Akhran. You see, the souls of babies waiting to be born sleep in the heavens, in a beautiful land where they are tended by the djinniyeh. The Wandering God visits each babe, bestowing his blessing upon it. Now, most babies sleep through this visit, but sometimes there is one who awakens, opens his eyes, and gazes on the face of God. The radiance dazzles him. He takes leave of his senses and thus is he born here upon the world."

"That's what Khardan meant when he told them I'd seen the face of the God," Mathew murmured.

"Yes, and that is why they dare not harm you. That is why the gifts and attention. You have seen the God and so will recognize him when you return to him. The rest of us will not know him. The people hope that when they die and reach the heavens, you will introduce them."

"And I'm supposed to get there before them?"

Zohra nodded gravely. "They consider it likely. You are, after all, a sickly looking thing."

"And holding the infants. Is this some kind of blessing? . . ."

"You are warding off the evil eye."

Mathew stared in disbelief. "The what?"

"The evil eye—the eye of envy—which, we believe, can kill a living thing. So that other mothers will not be envious of her newborn infant, the mother puts the babe in your arms, for who could envy a child that has been held by a madman?"

Mathew had no answer to this and began to wish he hadn't asked. The gifts and kindnesses suddenly took on a new and sinister aspect. These people were all eagerly waiting for him to die!

"Oh, not eagerly," Zohra said off-handedly. "They don't particularly care one way or the other. They just want to make certain that you will remember them to the God, and—in this harsh land of ours—it is best not to take chances."

A harsh land, a harsh people. Not cruel and savage, Mathew was beginning to realize, as he struggled to align his nature to their way of thinking. But resigned, accepting of their fate—no, even proud of it. Death was a fact, as much a part of life as birth and attended with rather less ceremony.

In Mathew's homeland death was accompanied by solemn ritual—the gathering of priests and weeping family around the dying person, the gift of prayer to carry the soul heavenward, an elaborate funeral with burial in the sacred cathedral grounds, a strict period of mourning observed by friends and family.

In the desert, among the nomads, the dead were placed in shallow, generally unmarked graves scattered along the roads the nomads wandered. Only the resting places of a particularly heroic *batir* or a Sheykh were commemorated by covering the grave with small stones. These became almost like shrines; each passing tribe paid tribute by adding a stone to the grave.

And that was all. Death in the desert was the same as life in the desert—stark, frightening, and comfortless. Mathew had made his decision. He had chosen to live. Why? Out of cowardice, he presumed. But deep down, he knew that wasn't the reason.

It was Khardan.

Khardan had seen that he was dying inside. Mathew recalled the Calif's words, spoken during that wild, sublime, terrifying moment of rescue. *Come alive, damn you! Come back to life!* Khardan's arms had carried him from the grasp of his captors. Khardan's hand had stayed the hand of his would-be executioner. Khardan's will had drawn him into making the choice. Mathew did not love Khardan, as Zohra had suggested. The young man's heart had been torn open, the wound was fresh, raw and bleeding. Until it healed, he could not feel strongly about anything or anyone.

"But because of Khardan, I am alive," Mathew said to himself in the darkness of his tent. "I do not know yet what that means. I do not know but that death would have been preferable. All I know is that Khardan gave me my life, and in return, I pledge this life of mine—poor and unworthy as it may be—to him."

Chapter 15

Once again an uneasy alliance was created between the tribes of the Tel. The Sheykhs and the Calif called a meeting of the *aksakal*, the tribal elders, of both Hrana and Akar and presented to them the proposal to raid Kich. A torch tossed on an oil-soaked tent would have caused no greater conflagration.

No one trusted anyone. No one could agree on anything, from the merits of the plan itself to the division of spoils that had yet to be taken. No one could make a decision. One side or another stormed out in a rage. Everyone constantly changed views. First the Akar were for it and the Hrana opposed. Then the Hrana came out for it and the Akar decided it was nonsense. The Sheykhs changed their minds according to who presented the best argument at the particular moment, and like a horse that has eaten moonweed, everyone galloped around in a circle and got nowhere very fast.

Life in the camps around the Tel continued much the same. The Rose of the Prophet did not die, but it didn't bloom either. Not that anyone, thought about it now or paid much attention to it anymore, their minds being preoccupied with the rumors of war against someone—Zeid, the Amir, each other—that flew around the camp like vultures.

In the realm of the immortals, Sond spent much of his time moping about his lamp in a fit of gloom. Usti, terrified to leave the charcoal brazier lest Zohra catch a glimpse of him, remained hidden from view and lost considerable weight. Pukah made his daily trip south, watching Zeid's numbers increase daily and trying desperately to think of a way to extricate himself from this mess.

In the mortal realm, Meryem watched and waited for a chance to work her charms on Khardan, and Zohra taught Mathew to ride a horse.

At last Zohra had discovered a companion to share her lonely rides. Mathew had not been in camp two days before she made him come with her. Zohra's reasons for this were not entirely selfish; she was truly concerned about the state of the young man's health.

The fact that she should care about him astonished her. At first it displeased her as well. It was a sign of weakness. She had meant merely to use the young man to inflict further wounds on Khardan. Then she admitted that it was pleasing, for a change, to have someone to talk to, someone interesting and different, someone to whom—at the same time—she could still feel herself the superior. It was, she thought, very much like having a second wife in the *harem*. And of course, there was always the possibility he was telling her the truth about at least some of his skills in magic. She might actually learn from him.

What Zohra did not admit to herself was that she saw in Mathew someone as lonely as she was. This and their shared, secret admiration for Khardan formed a bond between them that neither was to know—for a time—existed.

Watching Mathew closely, Zohra became increasingly concerned for his health. The frail body and too-sensitive mind would not last long in this world. Riding would provide exercise, it was a useful skill to acquire, and it would keep the young wizard from his unfortunate tendency to brood too much on things that could not be changed and should—according to those of the desert—therefore be accepted.

Mathew agreed to go riding at first because he was thankful for anything to keep from longing for his home. And he had to admit that it certainly occupied his mind. First he had to overcome his fear of the animal itself—more intelligent than a camel, the horse (so Mathew imagined) took an instant dislike to him, gazing at him with a distinctly unfriendly eye. Then he had to concentrate on staying in the saddle. After a few tumbles onto the hard granite, his mind was occupied with something else—pain.

"This is the end," he told himself, trudging back into camp, so stiff and sore he could barely walk. "This time I was lucky. Next time I will break my neck."

Limping along, he looked up to see Khardan standing before him.

The Calif had been out hunting; he wore the mask of the

haik to protect him from wind and sand. All Mathew could see of his face were the piercing black eyes, and they were grave and solemn.

Fearful he had done something wrong—he was dressed, after all, in men's clothing, Zohra having insisted on this—Mathew flushed and began to stammer out an apology.

"No, no," Khardan interrupted him. "I am pleased to see that you are learning to ride. It is a man's skill and one that is blessed by Akhran. Perhaps, someday, I will take you out and teach you what I know. Until then"—his gaze went to Zohra, standing slightly apart, her own face concealed by the mask of the head covering—"you are with a teacher almost as skilled."

Pleased at Khardan's words and the unusual fact that the Calif had actually stopped to speak to him, Mathew saw that Zohra was no less astonished at his unexpected praise and that the ordinarily fierce eyes of the woman were introspective and thoughtful as she returned to her tent.

To gain Khardan's respect was a goal worth risking one's life for, Mathew decided, and he vowed to learn to ride if it killed him—which seemed not unlikely. It also gave him the opportunity to discuss magic with Zohra, something that he feared to do when they were in camp. The young man had discovered that his powers and skills in the art—which, in his country, made him an apprentice—were far greater than anything the women of the desert could ever have dreamed.

And it wasn't long before he found out the reason why—an astounding one, as far as he was concerned.

"The magic I have seen you perform is done with charms and amulets—rude ones at best." The two were resting in the shade of the oasis, letting their tired horses drink and nibble at the dwindling grass. "Where are your scrolls kept, Zohra?" Mathew continued. "That is the key to truly powerful magic. Why do you never use them?"

"Scrolls?" Zohra seemed puzzled and not even really interested for the moment.

Her attention was on the hunting being done by Khardan and the men of the Akar, who were using their falcons to bring down gazelle from a herd that had come to the oasis in search of water.

Mathew, too, paused a moment to watch the chase. He had

seen falconry practiced in his own land, but never anything remotely similar to the way it was done here. Like everything else, it was brutal, savage, and efficient. Had anyone told him that a bird could bring down an animal as big as a gazelle, he would have scoffed in disbelief. But he was seeing it and he still couldn't believe it.

Khardan, falcon on his wrist, removed the hood from the bird's head. The falcon soared into the air. Flying over the gazelles, it chose its victim and dove for it, aiming for the head of the animal. The gazelle, who could generally outrun packs of hunting dogs, couldn't outrun the swiftly flying bird. Swooping down, the falcon struck the gazelle in the head and began pecking out the animal's eyes. Soon blind, the creature tripped, stumbled, and fell to the ground—easy prey for the hunters. Mathew had seen Khardan training his falcons to perform this feat by placing meat in the eye sockets of a sheep's skull. The young wizard had thought at the time it was some macabre sport, until he saw now that it meant survival.

"Mat-hew! Look at that!"

Zohra pointed excitedly. The falcon of Achmed had made a particularly splendid kill. Mathew, watching, saw Khardan put his hand on Achmed's shoulder, congratulating the young man and praising his work with the bird. Majiid joined them and the three stood laughing together.

Mathew's heart ached, his loneliness came near to overwhelming him.

"Scrolls," he continued grimly, putting it out of his mind, "are pieces of parchment on which you write the spells so that they may be used whenever you need them."

Zohra's response confounded him. "Write?" she said, glancing at him curiously. "What do you mean, 'write'?"

Mathew stared at her. "Write. You know, write down words so that they may be read. As in books."

"Ah, books!" Zohra shrugged. "I have heard of such things used by city dwellers, who also, they say, burn cattle dung to keep warm." This in a tone of deep disgust.

"You cannot read or write!" Mathew gaped.

"No."

"But"—Mathew was bewildered—"how do you read and study the laws of your God? Are they not written down somewhere?"

"The laws were spoken by the mouth of Akhran into the ears of his people and so have been passed from the mouths of his people into the ears of those who came after them. What better way? Why should words go onto paper, then into the eye, and then into the mouth, and then into the ear? It is a waste of time."

Mathew floundered for a moment in this quagmire of ir-refutable logic, then tried again. "Books could have kept the knowledge and wisdom of your forefathers. Through books that knowledge would have been preserved."

"It is preserved now. We know how to raise sheep. Khardan's people know the ways of horses. We know how to hunt, where to find the oases, what time of year the storms come. We know how to raise children, how to weave cloth, how to milk a goat. Your books never taught you that!" Mathew flushed. That much was true. His attempts at doing women's work had proved a dismal failure. "What more is there to know?"

"Books taught me to speak your language, they taught me something about your people," he added lamely.

"And was it the truth they taught?" Zohra asked him, turning her eyes on him, their gaze steady and unwavering.

"No, not much," he was forced to admit.

"There, you see? Look into a man's eyes, Mat-hew, and you can tell if he is lying to you. Books tell lies and you will never know it for they have no heart, no soul."

There are men whose eyes can lie, Mathew thought but did not say. Men with no heart, no soul. Women, too, he added men-tally, thinking of blue, limpid eyes that had been watching the two of them of late—eyes that seemed to be constantly spying on them, yet could never be discovered looking directly at them. Eyes that always glanced away or were cast down in modesty, yet—when he turned—he could feel them, boring through his flesh.

Thinking of Meryem had distracted his thoughts. Resolutely he forced them back to the moment. Books were not, apparently, the way to introduce Zohra to the study of magic. He came about on a new tack, sailing his ship into what he hoped were calmer waters.

"Scolls aren't books," he began, fumbling for an explanation that would convince her. "Magical scrolls aren't, at least. Because Sul decreed that magic be based in material objects, writing down the spells on scrolls was the only way the sorcerers could make their spells work. Before that—according to the histories—all they had to do was pronounce the arcane words and the minion of Sul was summoned, or the wood burst into flame; or whatever you wanted happened. Now the sorcerer must write the words upon parchment. When he reads them aloud, he obtains—hopefully—the desired result."

Now Zohra was watching him with eager interest, the hunt forgotten. "You mean, Mat-hew, that all I have to do to summon a servant of Sul to come perform my bidding is to write down these words upon something, read them, and the creature will come?"

"Well, no," Mathew said hastily, having a sudden terrifying vision of demons running loose through the camp. "It takes many years of study to be able to perform magic as powerful as that. Each letter of the words you write must be perfect in shape and form, the exact wording must be used, and then the sorcerer must have rigid control or the servant of Sul will turn the sorcerer into a servant of Sul. But there are other spells I could teach you," he said quickly, seeing Zohra's interest begin to wane.

"Could you?" Her eyes flared, bright and dangerous.

"I—I'd have to think about it. To recall some." Mathew stammered, pleased that he had kindled her interest. "When can we start?"

"I need parchment, preferably sheepskin. I need to make a stylus, and I need ink."

"I can get you all that today."

"Then I'll need some time to practice, to draw my thoughts together. It has been some time and much has happened since I have used my magic," Mathew said wistfully, feeling the wave of homesickness sweep over him once more. "Perhaps, in a few days. . ."

"Very well," Zohra said. Her voice was suddenly cold. "Let's go. We should be returning to camp before the heat of afternoon."

Mathew sighed, his feelings of loss and loneliness—almost forgotten for a moment—returning.

Who was he fooling? No one but himself. What could he ever be to Khardan except a coward who had saved his skin by dressing as a woman and pretending to be mad? Certainly he could never be a friend, never a companion—like a younger brother.

And Zohra. He thought her beautiful in the wild and savage way this land was sometimes beautiful. He admired her in much the same way he admired Khardan, envying her strength, her pride. He had something he could offer her, and he hoped it would gain her respect and admiration for himself. But it was obvious, she was using him for her own purposes—to ease her own loneliness, to learn more about magic.

No, he was alone in a strange land and he would always be so.

The thought struck him a blow that literally took his breath away.

Always.

He had not looked into his future in this land because—up until now—he did not think he had one. He had looked forward only to death.

Always.

Now he had life, which meant he had an "always"—a future.

And a future, no matter how bleak, meant hope.

And hope meant that perhaps, somehow, he could find a way to get back home.

CHAPTER 16

As the days passed and Meryem spent more time among the nomads, she began to fear that her attempt to seduce Khardan would fail. Honor was the nomad's single most valued possession—one that belonged to rich and poor, male and female alike. A man's word, a woman's virtue: these were more precious than jewels, for they could not be traded or sold, and once broken were lost forever. Honor was necessary to the nomad's survival—he had to be able to trust his fellow man on whom his life depended, he had to be able to trust in the sanctity of the family on whom his future depended.

This was not something Meryem could easily explain to the Amir, however. Qannadi was not a patient man. He expected results. He did not tolerate excuses. He had sent his concubine to gather information, and he expected her to succeed. Khardan possessed the information Meryem needed. Once in her bed, his head pillowed on her soft breast, lulled by the touch of her skilled hands, he would reveal to her anything she wished.

"He is, after all, only a man," Meryem argued with herself. "Yamina is right. A man's brains are between his legs. He cannot resist me." Impatiently she watched and waited for just the proper moment, and at last she had her chance.

It was twilight. Walking wearily through camp after another day's pointless arguing with his father and the other tribesmen, Khardan glanced up to see Meryem come out from behind a tent and start across the compound, her slender shoulders bent beneath the weight of a yoke from which dangled two full skins of water. This was typically women's work, and Khardan, pausing to watch and admire the grace of the diminutive figure, thought nothing of the burden she bore until he noticed her steps falter. Meryem let the skins down slowly to the ground so as not to lose a drop of the cool water. She lifted a limp hand to her forehead, her eyes rolling upward. Springing forward, Khardan caught her just as she was falling.

His own tent was closest. Carrying the unconscious woman inside, he laid her down upon the cushions and was just about to go and get help when he heard her stir. Returning, he knelt down beside her.

"Are you all right? What is wrong?" He looked at her in concern.

Meryem, half sitting up, gazed around her dazedly. "Nothing is wrong," she murmured, "I . . . just felt faint suddenly."

"I'm going to call my mother." Khardan started to rise.

"No!" Meryem said rather more loudly than she had intended. Khardan looked at her, startled, and she flushed. "No, please, don't trouble your mother on my account. I am much better. Truly. It is . . . so hot." Her hand artfully disarrayed the folds of the caftan she wore so that a tempting expanse of throat and the swelling of her smooth, white breasts could be seen. "Let me rest in here, where it is cool, for just a moment, then I will return to my work."

"Those skins are too heavy for you," Khardan said gruffly, averting his gaze. "I will mention this to my mother."

"It isn't her fault." Meryem's blue eyes shimmered with tears. "She. . . she told me not to do it." The soft hand reached out and clasped Khardan's. "But I do so want to prove to you that I am worthy of being your wife!"

Khardan's skin was swept by flame, his blood burned. Before he quite knew what was happening, Meryem was in his arms, his lips were tasting the sweetness of her lips. His kisses were eagerly returned, the girl's body yielding to his with a passion rather unexpected in the Sultan's virgin daughter. Khardan did not notice. His mouth was on the milky white throat, his hands seeking the softness beneath the caftan's silk, when it suddenly occurred to the Calif what he was doing.

Gasping for breath, he pushed Meryem away from him, almost throwing her back into the cushions.

Khardan was not the only one losing control. Consumed by a pleasure she had never before experienced in the arms of a man, Meryem grasped Khardan's arm.

"Ah, my love, my darling!" she breathed, drawing him back

down upon the cushions, forgetting herself and acting with the wantonness of the Amir's concubine. "We can be happy now! We don't have to wait!"

Fortunately for Meryem, Khardan was too immersed in his own inner battle to notice. Tearing himself free of her hold, he rose to his feet and staggered to the tent entrance, breathing as though he had fought a deadly foe and just barely escaped alive.

Hiding her face in the cushions, Meryem burst into tears. To Khardan, they seemed the tears of offended innocence, and he felt himself a monster. Actually they were tears of anger and frustration.

Mumbling something incoherent about sending his mother to her, Khardan hastened from the tent. After he'd gone, Meryem managed to compose herself. She dried her eyes, twitched her clothes into place, and was even able to smile. The smoldering coals of Khardan's love had just burst into a raging fire, one that would not be quenched easily. Blinded by his desire, he would be prepared to believe any miracle that would suddenly make it possible for them to marry.

Leaving his tent, Meryem met Badia, who was hurrying to her side. In answer to her future mother's worried questions, Meryem said only that she had fainted and that Khardan had been kind enough to stay with her until she felt better.

"Poor child, this separation is torturing both of you," said Badia, putting her arm comfortingly around Meryem's small waist. "A way out of this dilemma must be found."

"Akhran willing, it shall be," said Meryem with a sweet and pious smile.

"Usti, what are you doing out of your dwelling? I did not send for you!" Zohra poked the fat djinn in his belly as he lay napping upon the cushions. "And what is that thing upon the floor?!"

With a startled snort Usti sat bolt upright. His mounds of flesh rolling and rippling in waves, he blinked at his mistress in the light of her oil lamp. "Ah, Princess," he said, frightened. "Back so soon?"

"It is just past dinnertime."

"I take it you have dined?" he asked hopefully.

"Yes, I dined with the madman. And I ask you again what this is, you lazy excuse for a djinn."

"A charcoal brazier," said Usti, glancing at the object sitting upon the floor.

"I can see it's a charcoal brazier, djinn-with-the-brains-of-a-goat!" Zohra fumed. "But it isn't mine. Where did it come from?"

"Madam should be more specific," he said plaintively. Seeing Zohra's eyes narrow dangerously, Usti added hurriedly, "It is a gift. From Badia."

"Badia?" Zohra stared at her djinn. "Khardan's mother? Are you certain?"

"I am," Usti replied eagerly, pleased to have—for once—impressed his mistress. "One of her own servants brought it over and said distinctly that it was for 'her daughter Zohra.' I have been waiting up to deliver it to you."

" 'Daughter' . . . she said. . . 'daughter'?" Zohra asked softly.

"And why not? You *are* her daughter, if only in the eyes of the God."

"It's just. . . she never sent me anything before," Zohra murmured.

Kneeling down, she examined the brazier. It was made of brass, of truly fine workmanship and design, like nothing she had ever seen before. Three legs, carved to resemble the feet of a lion, supported the pot. Ornately carved holes around the lid emitted the smoke. Peering inside, Zohra saw six pieces of charcoal nestled in the brazier's brass belly. Since trees were scarce, the charcoal itself was a gift nearly as valuable as the brazier.

Instantly the idea came to her that the brazier came from Khardan. "The man is too proud to give it to me himself," she guessed. "He fears that I would refuse it, and so he uses this ruse to present it to me."

"What did you say, madam?" asked the djinn, nervously stifling a yawn.

"Nothing." Smiling, Zohra ran her finger along the delicate swirls and curlicues of the lid. "Return to your own brazier. I have no need of a fat djinn this night."

"Madam is all kindness!" remarked Usti. With a relieved sigh he transformed himself into smoke and fled gratefully to the peace and tranquility of his own dwelling.

Kicking the djinn's brazier aside with her foot, ignoring the pitiful lament of protest that came from within, Zohra placed the new brazier upon the floor beneath the tent opening. Lighting the charcoal, she was aware of a faint perfumelike fragrance in the smoke, perhaps the wood of a rose or lemon tree. She had never smelled anything like it before.

Undoubtedly Khardan has given it to me, she thought as she made ready for bed. Lying down, she watched the smoke from the brazier drift upward through the tent flap. But why? What can be his motive? He is—to all appearances—furious with me for having supplanted the blond rose he plucked from the Sultan's garden. He has not spoken to me, not one word since the night of his return. Perhaps his anger has cooled and he does not know how to show it except in this way. I will show him that I, too, can be magnanimous. After all, once again I have been the victor. Tomorrow perhaps I will smile upon him. . .

Perhaps.

Smiling now at the thought, Zohra extinguished the oil lamp and lay down among the cushions, drawing the woolen blankets over her. The charcoal in the new brazier continued to burn, spreading a soothing warmth through the tent, banishing the chill of the desert night.

Hiding in his own brazier, Usti picked up his scattered furniture and comforted himself for his hard life by drinking plum wine and consuming large quantities of sugared almond paste.

The night deepened. Zohra sank into a dreamless sleep. The smoke from the brazier continued to rise through the opening in the tent, but it no longer drifted upward in a thin, wavering line. Slowly, imperceptibly, the smoke came to life, curling and twisting in an evil, sinuous dance. . .

CHAPTER 17

$\mathcal{T}$he camp slept. Mathew, lying awake on his cushions, thought he had never heard such loud silence. It actually echoed in his head. Sitting up, he strained to hear a noise—any noise that would be a comfort to his loneliness. But not a baby whimpered, not a horse whinnied nervously as it caught the scent of prowling lion or jackal. Nothing stirred in the desert tonight, seemingly.

Mathew sat up, shivering in the cold. Wrapping another cloak around him, he lit his oil lamp and prepared to work.

He drew forth a piece of parchment and spread it out upon the smooth surface of the tent floor. Zohra had brought him the quill from a falcon to use as his writing instrument. He wasn't certain of its effectiveness in copying magical spells—he would have preferred a raven's feather as was used in the schools. But he couldn't recall anything in his texts stating that the quill itself possessed any inherent magical properties. Hopefully it was just tradition that dictated the nature of the quill used. Dipping it into the small bowl of ink that was made from burned sheep's wool with gum water added to the cinders, Mathew slowly and laboriously began to draw the arcane symbols upon the parchment.

This was the third night he had devoted to his work, and he found that he spent most of the day looking forward to this time of peace and quiet when he could lose himself in his art. Everyone rested through the heat of the day in the afternoon, which gave him time to nap and catch up on lost sleep. He already had a small packet of scrolls neatly tucked away in his pillow.

As he worked, he smiled with pleasure over the memory of Zohra's reaction to the performance of his first, simple spell. Taking a bowl, he had filled it with a handful of sand. Then, holding a scroll, he had spoken the arcane words with some trepidation.

Would the falcon quill work? What about the ink? Had he spelled every word correctly and was he speaking the words of the cantrip in the proper cadence?

His fears had proved groundless. Moments after he had completed reading the spell, the words on the paper began to writhe and crawl. Zohra—her eyes wide as a terrified child's—shrank back into a corner. She might have run from the tent had not Mathew, dropping the parchment into the bowl, grasped hold of her hand reassuringly. She had clung to him, watching as the words spilled from the parchment into the bowl. When the letters touched the sand, it began to change form, and within seconds the parchment had vanished, the words disappeared, and a bowl of cool, pure water stood on the floor of the tent.

"Here, you may drink it," Mathew had said, holding it out to Zohra.

She would have nothing to do with it, however. He had drunk it himself—an odd experience, with her watching him, waiting half in hope and half in dread for something dire to occur to him. Nothing did, but she still had refused to drink the enchanted water. Mathew, sighing, knew that if Zohra wouldn't touch it then certainly no one else in the camp would even consider such a thing. His dreams for bringing water to the desert in a magical manner ended rather abruptly at this point. It also occurred to him—not without some bitterness—that the nomads probably wouldn't want any more water in the desert anyway. They seemed to gain a grim satisfaction out of battling with their cruel land.

Part of Mathew's brain was thinking idly of this, part of it was concentrating upon the work at hand when both parts came together with a suddenness that sent a physical jolt through his body.

Somewhere in the camp, powerful magic was being worked. How he knew this, he could not tell. He'd never experienced such a sensation before, except, perhaps, when he'd performed his own spells. Or maybe he'd always experienced it at the school and simply never noticed, so pervasive was the magic there. No matter what the reason, the enchantment prickled his skin, shortened his breath, and he felt the hair on his head rise as it does when one stands too near where lightning strikes.

And it was black magic, evil magic. This Mathew recognized instantly, having been taught to be able to discern the difference, something a wizard must learn to detect in the event that he comes across a strange scroll or spellbook.

Mathew hesitated. Should he get involved? Might not he be putting himself in deadly danger, exposing his own power to whoever was practicing this? He tried to ignore it and turned back to his work. But his hand shook and he made a blot upon the parchment, ruining it. The aura of evil was growing around him.

Mathew rose to his feet. He might be a coward when it came to flashing steel but not to magic. The arcane he knew, he understood, he could fight. Besides, he admitted to himself ruefully as he hurriedly grabbed up the bag of scrolls and slipped out of the tent into the moonlit night, his curiosity was far outweighing his fear.

The source of the enchantment was easy to locate. It beat upon his face like the heat of the afternoon sun. He could literally almost hear its pulsing heartbeat. It was coming from Zohra's tent!

Had the woman duped him? Was she really a powerful sorceress, involved in the black arts? Mathew, creeping nearer, couldn't believe it. Wild, quick-tempered, fierce, but honest—to a fault. No, he thought grimly, if Zohra wanted to kill you she would simply come into your tent and stab you through the heart. None of the subtlety of black magic for her.

Which meant. . .

His own heart in his throat, Mathew quickened his steps.

The distance between their tents wasn't great; they were, after all, together in Khardan's *harem*. But to Mathew it seemed an eternity passed before he was able to reach the tent and thrust aside the entry flap.

He stopped, staring, transfixed in horror.

A luminescent cloud of smoke hovered over Zohra's slumbering figure. Just as he sprang into the tent, the cloud dipped down and slowly slipped into the woman's nostrils. She drew it inside her with her own indrawn breath.

She breathed out, but her next breath didn't come. Zohra's eyes opened. She tried to inhale and the cloud flowed into her mouth, strangling her. Her eyes widened in terror. She struggled against it, her hands clawing at the shimmering, deadly cloud. Her frantic fingers closed on nothing but smoke.

What was this apparition? Mathew had no idea; he'd never

seen or heard of anything like it. Whatever it was, it was killing Zohra. She would be dead in minutes, already her struggles were weakening, the smoke continuing to seep into the woman's nose. Where was it coming from? What was its source? Perhaps if that were destroyed...

Glancing hastily about, searching frantically for a scroll or a charm, Mathew saw the charcoal brazier, he saw the smoke rising from it and drifting—not up and out of the tent—but over to Zohra's bed. The charcoal... burning...

Lunging outside the tent, Mathew scooped up a handful of sand, hurried back in, and flung it on the glowing hot brazier, thinking it might distract the thing. But it had no effect. Completely ignoring him, concentrating totally on its victim, the deadly smoke continued to enter Zohra's body, suffocating her. Her face was dark, her eyes rolled back in her head, her body convulsed with her futile efforts to draw breath.

Falling to his hands and knees, Mathew scooped up handfuls of sand and flung them one after another over the brazier. At first he thought he had failed, that smothering the fire would not stop the magic. He couldn't fight this thing, he realized in anger and despair. Not with the few scrolls he had. He would have to watch Zohra die...

Desperately Mathew continued to fling sand until the brazier was practically buried. Zohra's body had gone limp, her struggles had ceased, when suddenly the smoke stopped moving. The cloud's awful luminance began to dim and waver. Strengthened by renewed hope, Mathew grabbed up a felt blanket and flung it over the sand-covered brazier. Tamping it down, he began to press it firmly around the object, cutting off any possible source of air.

A wave of anger and hatred hit him a physical blow, flinging him backward. With a howl of rage that he heard in his soul, not with his ears, the cloud surged out of Zohra's body. Rearing up into the air, it dove down for him with incredible speed, shimmering hands reaching for this throat.

Mathew could do nothing, there was no time to react to defend himself. Suddenly a cool breeze, blowing through the entrance at his back, drifted into the open tent flap. As if fanned by wings, the cloud separated and broke apart. Soon it was nothing more than wisps of eerily glowing smoke darting aimlessly and furiously about the tent. And then they, too, were gone.

Bowing his head, his body bathed in sweat, Mathew drew a shuddering breath. Rising on unsteady feet, he hastened to Zohra's bedside. She lay still and unmoving, her face a deathly white in the moonlight, her eyes closed. He put his hands upon her heart and felt it beating, but very, very faintly. She was no longer under enchantment. The magic had been smothered with the charcoal. But still, she was dying.

Not knowing what else to do, realizing only that the thing had sucked the breath of life from her body and that it must be put back, Mathew opened her mouth and breathed his own life into hers.

Time and again he did this, uncertain if it would work, but feeling that he must do something. And then he felt the chest beneath his hand move; he felt a stirring of air from her mouth touch his lips. Elated, he kept forcing breath into Zohra's body. Her eyes—wide and terrified—fluttered open, her hands reached out and caught hold of his face.

"Zohra!" he whispered, stroking her hair back from her forehead soothingly. "Zohra. It is Mathew. You are safe. The thing is gone!"

She stared at him a moment, frightened, disbelieving. Then she gave a shuddering sob and buried her face in his breast. He held her close, smoothing her hair, rocking her like a child. Shivering with fear and the horrible memory, she clung to him, weeping hysterically, until gradually the hypnotic motion of his soothing hand and the soft, reassuring murmurs of his voice drove away the worst of the terror. Her sobs quieted.

"What. . . was it?" she managed to ask.

"I don't know." Mathew's eyes went to the brazier, now covered with the blanket. "It was magic, whatever it was. Strong magic. Black magic. It came from that charcoal brazier. "

"Khardan tried to kill me!" Zohra gasped out, a last sob wrung from her body. She hid her face in her hands.

"Khardan? No!" Mathew said, holding her tightly and calming her again. "You know how he feels about magic! He wouldn't do anything like this. Come to your senses, Zohra."

Wiping away her tears with the heel of her hand, Zohra seemed to come suddenly to the realization that she was being held in Mathew's arms. Her face flushing, she drew away from him. He, too, was embarrassed and uncomfortable and released her quickly.

Standing up hurriedly, Mathew walked over to the brazier and cautiously removed the blanket.

"Where did you get the thing?"

Zohra, after a few tries, her fingers still numb and trembling, lit the oil lamp and held its wavering flight over the brazier. Mathew brushed away the sand to reveal it, standing in the center of the tent.

"It's cold," he reported, staring at it in awe. He looked back up at Zohra, puzzled. "What do you mean, Khardan tried to kill you?"

"He sent this to me," Zohra said. Her fear dying away, it was being replaced by anger.

"*He* sent it to you?" Mathew repeated, still refusing to believe it.

"Well," Zohra amended, "I assumed. . ." She drew a shivering breath. "This was brought to my tent by a servant who said that she had been sent by Badia, Khardan's mother—"

Mathew glanced up at her swiftly. "Meryem!"

"Meryem?" Zohra appeared scornful. "I'd sooner suspect a kitten!"

"Even kittens have claws," he murmured, reliving with sudden, vivid clarity the night of his near execution. "I saw a look on her face when you thwarted her marriage to Khardan. She could have killed you then, Zohra, if she'd had the means. Lately I've seen her watching us. You stand in her way of marrying the Calif and she means to take care of that small matter."

Zohra's eyes flared with wild anger. She took a step toward the tent flap.

"Wait!" Mathew grabbed her. "Where are you going?"

"I'll confront her with this! I'll drag her before the Sheykhs! I'll accuse her of being the witch she is—"

"Stop, Zohra! Think! This is madness! She will deny everything. She has been in the *seraglio* all night, probably being careful to keep in the sight of the women of Majiid's *harem*. You have no proof! Just my word and I am a madman! Smoke tried to kill you? You will look a fool, Zohra—a jealous fool, in Khardan's eyes."

"*Makhol!* You are right," she murmured. Slowly her anger drained from her, leaving her exhausted. She sank back down on her cushions. "What can I do?" she mumbled, clasping her head in her hands, her long black hair tangling between her fingers.

"I'm not certain," Mathew said grimly. "First we must figure out why she did this."

"You said it yourself. To marry Khardan!" Zohra's eyes burned, a dreadful sight in her livid face. "If I am dead, then he can take another wife. Surely that is obvious."

"But why such haste? Why risk revealing herself by this use of magic that only a truly powerful sorceress would know, especially when she lied to Khardan and to everyone in the tribe about her skills in the art. The odds are, of course, that she would never be discovered. This attempted murder was very clever of her. You would have been found dead in the morning. It would have looked as if you had died in your sleep. "

Zohra, shuddering, made a strangled sound, choked, and covered her mouth with a hand.

"I'm sorry," Mathew said softly. Sitting beside her, he put his arm around her again and she wearily laid her head on his chest. "I forgot. . . I thought I was in the classroom again. Forgive me. . ."

She nodded, not understanding.

"You had better rest now. We'll talk about this more tomorrow—"

"No, Mat-hew!" Zohra clutched at him fiercely. "Don't leave me!"

"You will be safe," Mathew said soothingly. "She can't do anything else tonight. She's already taken a great risk. She must wait until morning to see if her magic worked."

"I can't sleep. Go on . . . go on with what you were saying."

She drew away from him. Mathew, swallowing, struggled to recall his chain of thought under the gaze of those black, fiery eyes.

"Haste, Mat-hew . You mentioned haste."

"Yes. She knows that undoubtedly, within a month or so, she will have a chance to marry Khardan. If she were truly the innocent girl she pretends, such a short time would not matter. But she isn't an innocent girl. She is a powerful sorceress who wants, who *needs* to marry Khardan immediately and who will commit murder to do it."

He pondered. "Where would she have come by such magical arts?"

"Yamina, the Amir's wife, is a cunning sorceress," Zohra said slowly, staring at Mathew, both of them thinking the same thing.

"And Meryem comes from the palace. Truly, this begins to make more and more sense! Wasn't it providential of Khardan to come upon Meryem in the garden like that! Some God was surely smiling on her."

"Quar," muttered Zohra. "But, what could be her motive in coming here? Is she an assassin?"

"No," Mathew said after a moment's thought. "If she were sent to kill Khardan, she could have done it a dozen times over before this. She tried to kill you, but only because you stand in the way of her marriage. That's the key. She must marry him and quickly. But why?"

"And we cannot tell anyone!" Zohra said, rising impatiently and pacing the tent. "You are right, Mat-hew. Who would believe us? I am a jealous wife, you—a madman." She twisted the rings on her fingers round and round in her frustration.

"Ah, how stupid we are!" Striking her forehead with hand, Zohra turned to Mathew. "It is very simple. There is no need to worry about any of this. I will kill her!"

Moving to the bed, Zohra slid her hand beneath her pillow, grabbed the dagger, and slipped it inside the folds of her gown. She moved swiftly and calmly, and she was halfway out of the tent before Mathew's dazed brain caught up with her.

"No!" Flinging himself after Zohra, he grabbed hold of her arm. "Y—you can't kill her!" he stammered, shocked.

"Why not?"

Why not? Mathew wondered. Why not kill someone who has just tried to kill you? Why not kill someone you believe is a threat, a danger? I could say that life is a sacred gift of the God and only the God has the right to take it back. I could say that taking the life of another is the most dreadful sin a person can commit. That was true in my world, but is it true in this one? Perhaps that belief is a luxury in our society. If I had John's murderer before me, would I extend my hand to him in forgiveness, as we are taught? Or would I extend it to clutch him by his throat. . .

"Because. . . if you kill her," Mathew said slowly, "no one will know of the foul deed she has committed. She will die with honor."

Zohra stared at Mathew intently. "You are wise for one so

young." Sighing in disappointment, the woman lowered the tent flap and stepped back inside. "And you are right. We must catch the snake that hides beneath golden hair and put her on display for all to see."

"That. . . that might take some time." Mathew had no idea what he was saying. *I nearly let her go,* he thought, trembling. *Killing that girl seemed perfectly logical! What is this land doing to me?*

"Why?" Zohra's question forced him to concentrate.

"When. . . um . . . Meryem discovers she's failed, she'll be nervous, wary, on her guard. Did her magic go awry? Perhaps you didn't use the brazier at all and will use it tomorrow or the next night. Or did you, somehow, manage to thwart her? If so, do you suspect her? She will be leery of using her magic again too soon, although she may resort to more conventional means of getting rid of you. I do not think I would accept any food or drink from your father-in-law's tent."

"Usti!" said Zohra suddenly.

Mathew stared at her blankly, not understanding.

Kicking aside cushions, Zohra snatched up a charcoal brazier from the tent floor. It appeared to be a very old brazier that had seen a great deal of usage, if one could judge by the scratches and dents on its surface. Tapping it three times with her fingernail, Zohra called out, "Wake up, you drunken sot."

A voice from within was heard to groan. "Madam," it said groggily, "have you any idea what time it is?"

"Had it been left to you, Fat One, I would never have disturbed your rest again! Appear. I command you."

After a night of shocks, it seemed that there was one more waiting for Mathew.

He had not thought any more about the young man who claimed to have been a djinn. Not seeing him around camp, he assumed him to be as mad as, supposedly, he was himself. He'd heard casual talk among the tribesmen concerning djinn doing this and djinn doing that, but he assumed it was much the same as in his country where people spoke of the "faerie"—beings who were supposed to enter houses at night and switch babies or mend shoes or other farfetched legends. Now he could only watch in speechless amazement as another cloud of smoke rose from a charcoal brazier.

This smoke was obviously not threatening, however—coalescing into the form of a rotund man of middle years, with a red, bulbous nose and a bald, round head. Dressed in silken nightclothes, the man had obviously been rousted from a warm and comfortable bed.

"What is it, madam," he began in martyred tones, then he suddenly caught a glimpse of Zohra's pale face, still bearing traces of the horror that she had undergone. "Madam?" he repeated fearfully. "What—what is wrong?"

"Wrong? I was nearly murdered in my bed this night while you slept the sleep of the grape! That is what is wrong!" Zohra waved her hand, expressive of her contempt. "And *you* would have had to answer to Akhran for my death! I dread to think," she said in a hushed voice, "of your fate at the hands of the God!"

"Princess!" the djinn wailed, falling to the floor with a thud that shook the very ground beneath their feet. "Are you serious?" He glanced from Zohra's face to Mathew's. "Yes, you are serious! Ah, I am the most wretched of immortals! Be merciful, madam. Do not tell Holy Akhran! I swear I will make it up to you! I will clean your tent, every day. And never complain once when you rip up the cushions. See"—grabbing a cushion, Usti tore it apart in a frenzy—"I will even spare you the trouble by ripping them up myself! Only do not tell the Most Holy and Extremely Short-tempered Akhran!"

"I will not tell him," Zohra said slowly, as if considering the matter, "if you will do one thing. We know who it is who tried to murder me. It will be your duty to watch her day and night. And I need not tell you what will happen should you fail—"

"Fail? Me? Like a *saluki*—a hunting hound—I will be on her—Did you say her?" Usti's eyes bulged from their layers of fat.

"The girl, Meryem."

"Meryem? Madam is mistaken. A more sweet and charming little—"

Zohra's eyes flashed.

"—little whore I have never seen," Usti mumbled, crawling backward on his knees, his head bowed. "I shall do as you command, of course, Princess. Henceforth you shall sleep the sleep of ten thousand babes. Worry not. Your life is in my hands!" So saying, the djinn disappeared, melting into the air with unaccustomed alacrity.

Sinking back down onto the cushions, her strength gone, Zohra murmured, "My life... in his hands. Akhran help us all."

Mathew, still staring in disbelief at the place where the djinn had been groveling, could only agree.

CHAPTER 18

"Caring for a madman. That's all you are considered fit for, Pukah, my friend," muttered Pukah disconsolately. Hitting through the air, making his daily trip south, the djinn enlivened his journey by feeling terribly sorry for himself. Pukah'd actually had very little to do with Mathew, although he had convinced himself that he did nothing night and day but watch the young wizard. Generally Pukah lounged around outside Mathew's tent, his brain bubbling with fermenting schemes. When he did happen to peek in, it was more in hope of seeing the beautiful immortal again than keeping a watchful eye on the young man. Pukah noticed Mathew pottering about with sheep's skin and a foul-smelling ink but thought nothing of it. After all, he was mad, wasn't he?

Thus Mathew worked on his magic completely without Pukah's knowledge. The young wizard was able to fashion—as best he could—charms and amulets, as well as scrolls, and he began to instruct Zohra in their use. She, in turn, taught him what she knew of the healing arts of magic. Mathew had little knowledge in that field. In his land the sick and injured were tended by magi specialized in medicine. Pukah knew that Zohra was alone with Mathew for long periods during the day, but he took no particular notice of that either. His master's wife spent her time with a man who thought he was a woman. What of it? She'd done stranger things. Pukah had his own problems, and one of those problems was suddenly about to bloat like the carcass of a dead elephant.

Arriving at his usual observation post, Pukah had just settled himself comfortably upon a passing cloud when, looking down, he received a most uncomfortable shock.

"Now, may Sul take Zeid!" said the djinn. "May he take the wretch and deliver him into hell and afflict him with ten thousand demons that will do nothing but puncture his fat belly day and night with ten thousand poison spears! Ah, me, friend Pukah, you are in serious trouble now!"

"Well, well. If it isn't little Pukah," exclaimed a booming voice. "*Salaam aleikum.* Pukah. Have you got any more of your master's secrets you are willing to give away today?"

"*Aleikum salaam*, Raja," Pukah said cautiously.

"What think of you my master's army?" Raja asked. He gazed down from the cloud upon a veritable horde of *meharistes*, his glistening black-skinned chest swelling with pride. "We are all assembled, and as you see, preparing this day to ride north."

"I think it is a very nice army, as armies go," Pukah said, attempting to stifle a yawn.

"Nice!" Raja bristled. "You will see what a 'nice' army it is when it kicks your master in the ass!"

"Licks my master where?"

"Kicks, you donkey-headed fool," Raja snarled.

"You had much better say 'licks' because that is what will be happening," Pukah said gravely. "I tell you this only because I like you, Raja, and I am fond of your master, Sheykh Zeid, a very great man, and one whom I would not want to see humiliated before his tribesmen."

"Tell me what?" Raja regarded Pukah suspiciously.

"That you had much better turn around and go back to your business of watching camels hump one another or whatever it is that they do, because if you ride to attack Sheykh Majiid al Fakhar and Skeykh Jaafar al Widjar and Amir Abul Qasim Qannadi, then you will surely—"

"Amir?" Raja interrupted in astonishment.

"What did you say?"

"What did *you* say?"

"I thought you mentioned the Amir."

"Only because *you* mentioned the Amir!"

"Did I?" Pukah inquired uneasily. "If I did, please overlook it. Now, to continue—"

"Yes, you will continue, little Pukah," said Raja threateningly. "Continue talking about the Amir, or by Sul, I will take hold of your tongue, split in two, pull it out of your mouth, wrap it around your head, and tie it in a knot behind your neck."

"You are very boastful now, but my master and his new

friend will soon cut you down to size," Pukah remarked scornfully, though he thought it best to put a mile or so of sky between him and the angry Raja.

"What new friend?" Raja thundered, the clouds around him darkening with his rage, lightning crackling around his ankles.

"As I said, I have a truly soft spot in my heart for your master—"

"And another in your head!" Raja growled.

"—and so I think you had better warn Zeid that my master, Khardan, upon hearing of your master's plan to attack him, traveled to the city of Kich, where he was entertained with all honor by the Amir, who was so enamored of my master that he did everything in his power to get him to stay longer. The Imam himself came to join his pleas with those of his Arnir. Qannadi sent for his head wife, Yamina, who performed splendid feats of magic all for my master's pleasure. My master refused their invitations, however, saying regretfully that he must fly back to the desert because an old enemy was gathering forces to make war upon him.

"Qannadi was furious. 'Name the wretch!' the Amir cried, drawing his sword, 'that I may personally cut him into four equal parts and feed him to my cat.'

"This, you understand, my master was loathe to do—you know how proud a man he is—saying that it was his fight and his alone. But Qannadi proved insistent, and so my master most reluctantly, you understand—said that his enemy's name was Sheykh Zeid al Saban. The Amir swore upon the steel of his blade that from that day forward Khardan's foes were his foes, and the two parted with much affection, the Amir giving Khardan one of his daughters in marriage and inviting Khardan and my master's men to enjoy the spoils of the city before they left.

"This my master did, with much delight. The Amir's daughter resides in Sheykh Majiid's tent, and we wait only for the Amir and his forces—who are on their way—to celebrate the joyous occasion of their wedding."

Pukah ended, having run out of breath, watching Raja warily to see the djinn's reaction. As the astute Pukah had guessed, Sheykh Zeid had received an account of Khardan's visit to Kich from his spies, but the details had been imperfect. Pukah had mingled just enough truth with his lies to make this wild story sound plausible.

The djinn knew it sounded plausible because Raja suddenly disappeared with a thunderclap, the clouds swirling around him in a black vortex. Pukah heaved a sigh of relief.

"Now, Pukah, you are certainly very clever," said Pukah, lounging back upon the cloud.

"Thank you, my friend," Pukah replied. "I think I must agree with you. For surely, upon hearing this news that the great army of the Amir is allied against him, Zeid will take fright. He will disband his men and return to his homeland. You have spared your master the annoyance of being attacked by these sons of she-camels. By the time Zeid (may his beard grow up his nose) learns the truth—that the Amir has no interest at all in your master—it will be well into summer and too late for the Sheykh to launch an attack. Now that you have—once again—saved your master, you have time to help poor Sond out of his difficulty, for which he will—no doubt—be eternally grateful."

"A beautiful plan," Pukah informed his better half. "It won't be long, I foresee, before he and Fedj are working for me—"

"Ah, Pukah," the alter ego interrupted, tears in his eyes, "if you keep on as you are going, the Holy Akhran will fall on his knees and being to worship *you!*"

"What? This is impossible!" Zeid roared, reining in his camel with a suddenness that nearly sent the beast foundering in the sand.

"So I thought, *sidi.*" said Raja, breathing heavily from exertion. "Knowing what a liar this Pukah is, I flew to Kich to see for myself."

"And?"

"And I discovered that the Amir has recalled some of his troops from the south. As we speak, they are gathering in the city; the soldiers talk of a rumored journey eastward, into the desert."

"But he has not moved out yet?"

"No, *sidi.* Perhaps the marriage is still being negotiated. . ."

"Bah! I cannot believe this is possible! An alliance between city and desert? *Hazrat* Akhran would never permit it. Yet," muttered the Sheykh into his beard, "it is certainly true that Khardan left the city in a shambles and was not chastised for his daring; the Amir allowed him to ride away free as the wind. And he was seen bearing upon his horse a woman of the palace, reputedly as lovely as the bending willow. . . ."

"What is your command, *sidi?*" Raja asked. "Do we return to our homeland?"

The Sheykh, looking back behind him, saw his vast army of *meharistes*, saw the sun flash upon sword and dagger, upon lance and arrow tip. He saw, behind them, another army, this one made up of women and their children, following their men to set up camp for them and to tend to their wounds after the battle. Here were gathered together all the tribes who vowed him allegiance. It had taken many long hours of negotiating and compromising and the salving of old wounds to bring them together. Now all were eager for war. And was he going to tell them to turn back? Tell them Sheykh Zeid ran from the field, his tail between his legs, because another, I larger dog had entered the fray?

"Never!" Zeid cried with such fierceness that his voice carried up and down the ranks, causing the men to join in the yell with wild enthusiasm, although they had no idea what they were cheering.

Grabbing his banner from his staff-bearer, Zeid waved it in I the air. "Ride, my men! Ride! We will descend upon our foe like the wind!"

Banners waving, the *meharistes* galloped north, toward the Tel.

"I tell you, Sond, *Hazrat* Akhran was most emphatic in insisting that we undertake this journey." Pukah spoke to his fellow djinn in a soft undertone. The two were waiting in attendance upon their masters, who were—once again—meeting in Majiid's tent to argue about the best way to approach Sheykh Zeid. "Of course," Pukah added deprecatingly, "I realize that this proposed rescue attempt is going to be perilous in the extreme, and if you would prefer not to go . . ."

"I will go"—Sond swore an oath—"were it into the abyss of Sul itself! You know that, Pukah, so don't be a fool."

"Then ask your master's permission," Pukah urged. "Or would you rather wait here, serving coffee while your heart bleeds with grief, not knowing what terrible torment Nedjma may be enduring? Our masters can spare us for the short space of time it will take us to locate the Lost Immortals, rescue them, and return covered in glory. The Tel is as dull as the Realm of the Dead. What could possibly happen while we are gone?"

"You are right," Sond said after a moment's thought.

"You have received your master's permission?"

"Khardan was most proud to send me upon work of the God," boasted Pukah.

Now, Pukah had not actually spoken to the God at all, but he felt safe in assuming that *Hazrat* Akhran would want them to do this, and so he took the liberty of sparing the God worry by issuing Akhran's orders for him and relaying those orders to Khardan.

"Undoubtedly my master has spoken to yours about the matter already," Pukah continued. "Majiid will be expecting you to go."

Sond saw himself freeing Nedjma from her cruel bondage. She would fall into his arms, fainting, weeping, blessing him as her savior and vowing to be his forever. . . And Akhran—the God would surely reward him handsomely, perhaps a palace of his own where he and Nedjma could dwell. . . "I will ask my master this evening," the djinn said decisively.

The two were serving *berkouks*—pellets of sweet rice—to the Sheykhs and the Calif when their fellow djinn, Fedj, swirled down through the tent flap opening with the fury of a windstorm.

"What is the meaning of this?" Majiid demanded. Rice flew about the tent, his robes billowed in the wind, sand and dust rose from the tent floor in a stinging cloud.

"I beg pardon, *sidi.*"

Gasping for breath, the djinn whirled around until his form began taking shape out of the cyclone. Falling on his knees before Jaafar, who was regarding him with his perennially worried expression, Fedj burst out, "I have seen a huge army coming toward us. It is located three days' ride south from our camp!"

"Zeid?" flashed Khardan, rising to his feet.

"Yes, *sidi,*" Fedj replied, talking to Jaafar as if it were his master who had asked the question. "He has many hundred *meharis* with him, and their families follow behind." "*Ykkks!*" Pukah dropped a tray of candied locusts.

"Ah, you see, Father?" the Calif said in excitement. "Our arguments were all in vain. We need make Zeid no offer! He comes to join us in friendship."

"Mmmm," growled Majiid. "This is also how the *meharistes*

ride to battle."

"It makes little difference," Khardan said, shrugging. "Zeid knows our credo: 'The sword always drawn and the same word for friend or foe.' Nonetheless, I think they will prove friendly. Pukah, here, assures me of it."

He glanced at Pukah with a smile. The djinn's return grin was that of a fox who has just drunk poisoned water, but Khardan was too preoccupied to notice. "Now we can discuss with them our plan to band together and raid Kich! There can be no more arguments among our people when they see the camel riders coming to us in the name of peace! Truly *Hazrat* Akhran has sent Zeid at precisely the right time!"

Pukah uttered an alarming groan. "Too many sweets," he said miserably, laying his hands on his belly. "If I may be I excused, master—"

"Go! go." Khardan waved his hand, impatient with the continued interruptions. Resuming his seat, he leaned forward, the Sheykhs drawing close to him. "Now, here is my suggestion. Three days from hence, we will ride out to meet Zeid and—"

The Sheykhs and the Calif bent their heads together and were soon absorbed in deep discussion. Sond took advantage of the opportunity to leave the tent and follow Pukah. The djinn, looking truly ill, was slumped against a tent pole.

"Well, what are you doing out here?" Pukah snapped, seeing Sond's downcast expression. "If we are to leave this night, you had much better be back in there, asking permission of your master."

"You still intend to go?" Sond stared at him in astonishment.

"Now more than ever!" Pukah averred solemnly.

"I don't know." Sond appeared dubious. "If our masters are going to raid Kich with Zeid, then we will be needed. . ."

"Oh, we will be back before *that* event takes place, you may be certain," said Pukah. "Probably about a thousand years before," he muttered.

"What did you say? Are you feeling all right?"

"I need to get away," Pukah stated with firm conviction.

"The strain I've been under, arranging this. . .uh . . . alliance, has taken its toll on me. Yes, I definitely need to get away! The sooner the better."

"Then I will go speak to my master right now," Sond said, disappearing.

Pukah stared after him, his gloomy gaze following the djinn back to the tent where the Sheykhs sat discussing their plans to enlist Zeid's aid to raid Kich. If they only knew that instead of riding out to be met with kisses on the cheeks they were going to be met with daggers in the guts! . . . Pukah groaned.

He noticed, as he gazed despairingly at the tent, a small figure slipping away from it. But so lost was the djinn in his own fear and misery that he lacked the curiosity to wonder why a woman would have been so interested in what was going on inside that she had paused to listen. Or yet why she was now in such a hurry to leave.

The Amir was in his bathing room. Lying naked on a table, he was suffering untold tortures under the massaging hands of his manservant when a slave arrived to announce that Qannadi's head wife and the Imam needed to see him on a matter of extreme urgency.

"Ah!" grunted the Amir, propping himself up on his elbows. "They've heard from the girl. Toss that towel over me," he instructed his servant, who was already covering his master's body. "No, don't stop. Unless I have misjudged my barbaric desert friend, I will be riding soon and I need the kinks worked out of these old muscles."

Nodding silently, the manservant began his work again, his huge hands mercilessly pummeling and kneading the muscles in Qannadi's legs. A stifled cry came from the Amir's throat.

"The blessings of Quar be upon you," said the Imam, entering the steamy bathing room. "From the sound, I thought you were being murdered, at the very least."

"So I am!" Qannadi said, gritting his teeth, sweat pouring down his face. "The man delights in his work. I'm going to make him Lord High Executioner one day. *Ahhhf*" The Amir sucked in a breath, his hands clenched over the end of the marble table on which he lay. The manservant, grinning, started on the general's other leg. "Where is Yamina?"

"She comes," said Feisal imperturbably. "She has had news."

"I expected as much. Ah, here is my lovely wife."

Yamina entered the room, her face modestly veiled with only the one eye visible. Walking delicately to avoid stepping in puddles, she circled the sunken marble bathing pool. Lilies floated upon the perfumed water. Sunlight poured down through a skylight in the ceiling above, comfortably warming the enclosed room, its rays dancing upon the water's surface.

"You have heard from the girl?"

"Yes, husband," Yamina replied, bowing to him and bowing yet again to the Imam—the woman's single visible eye casting the priest a sultry glance that he caught but chose to ignore.

"So she finally seduced the desert prince?"

"We did not discuss the matter," Yarnina said reproachfully, with an apologetic glance for the Imam for speaking of such sordid matters. "Meryem's time was short. She is constantly watched, she says, by Khardan's head wife, whose jealousy of her knows no bounds. Meryem has discovered that what we heard rumored is true. Sheykh Zeid al Saban and his *meharis* are within three days ride of the Tel. The nomads are meeting now to make plans to"— Yamina paused for effect—"join forces and raid Kich!"

"Ouch! Damn you for a blackhearted bastard! I'll rip your throat out someday!" Half sitting up, the Amir glared behind him at his manservant.

Accustomed to being sworn at and threatened by Qannadi, who could not get along without him, the manservant merely grinned and nodded, his hands continuing to twist and pound Qannadi's battle-scarred flesh.

The Amir transferred his glare to the Imam. "It seems you were right, Priest," he said grudgingly.

Feisal bowed. "Not I, but our God. You do not intend to let them near the city?"

"Of course not! Kich would be in an uproar. I had enough trouble settling the populace down after Khardan's last little visit. No, we'll ride out and make short work of this puppy."

"There is to be as little bloodshed as possible, I hope," the Imam said earnestly. "Quar would be displeased."

"Humpf. Quar wasn't displeased at the blood that was shed taking this city, nor does he seem displeased by the thought of the blood we're shortly going to be shedding in the south. He'd rather have dead souls, I presume, than no souls at all?"

Yamina's eye widened at such sacrilegious talk. Glancing at the Imam, she was not surprised to see his face flush, the thin body quiver with suppressed rage. Drawing near the Imam, her hand hidden in the folds of her silken robes, Yamina closed her fingers around the priest's wrist, cautioning him to control himself.

Feisal needed no such warning, however. His skin crawled at the touch of the woman's cool hand pressed against his hot flesh, and he removed his wrist from her grasp as diplomatically and unobtrusively as possible, in the meantime issuing a rebuke to the Amir.

"Naturally Quar seeks the souls of the living, so that he may pour his blessings down upon them and so enrich their lives. He knows to his great grief, however, that there are those who persist in walking in darkness. For the sake of their souls and to free them from a life of wretched misery, he condones the killing of these *kafir* but only so that they may come to see in death what they were blind to in life."

"Hunh!" grunted Qannadi, growing uncomfortable as always in the presence of the burning-eyed priest. "Are you saying then that Quar will have no objection if we put these nomads to the sword?"

"Far be it for me to interfere with military affairs," said the Imam, noting the Amir's darkening face and proceeding with caution, "but—if I may make a suggestion?"

Feisal spoke humbly, and Qannadi nodded.

"I think I know how we can pull the teeth of this lion instead of cutting off its head. Here is my plan...."

Feisal presented his proposal clearly, succinctly, precisely; his orderly mind had taken care of every detail. Qannadi listened in some astonishment, although he should have known, from past dealings with the priest, that this man was as ingenious as he was devout. When the Imam had finished, Qannadi nodded again grudgingly, and Yamina, seeing her husband bested, cast the Imam a proud glance.

"And if this fails?" the Amir asked gruffly, waving his manservant away. Wrapping himself in the towel, he heaved his aching body off the marble table. "If they refuse to convert?"

"Then," said the Imam devoutly, "it will be *jihad!* May Quar have mercy upon their unworthy souls."

CHAPTER 19

Huddled in the cool shadows of Mathew's tent, her feathery white wings drooping, Asrial hid her face in her hands and wept.

It was not often the guardian angel gave way to her despair. Such a lapse in discipline would have brought raised eyebrows and stern, cold stares of reproach from the seraphim and undoubtedly a lecture from some cherubim upon putting one's trust wholeheartedly in Promenthas, believing that all was the will of the God, and all were working toward the Greater Good.

Thinking of such a lecture, hearing in her mind the sonorous voice, only made Asrial's tears flow faster. It wasn't that she had lost her faith. She hadn't. She believed in Promenthas with all her heart and soul; to work his will upon this material plane was the greatest joy she could know. So it had been for eighteen years, the years she'd been given Mathew to guide and protect.

But now?

Asrial shook her head bleakly. The young man she guarded was not alone in his anguish and misery. Asrial had watched, horrified, as the *goums* cut down the charges of her fellow angels. She had seen the other angels, helpless to intervene, fall to their knees in prayers to Promenthas and then rise again to comfort the souls of the newly departed and lead them to their safe rest.

Asrial alone had not been content to pray. She loved Mathew dearly. She remembered spending night after night, hovering over his crib when he was a baby, taking simple delight in just watching him breathe. To see him foully murdered, dying upon this alien shore. To have to face his bewildered soul and try to wean it away from the life he loved so dearly and had just begun to experience. . .

It was the angel's unheard prompting that had caused the

young wizard to run for his life. It was Asrial's invisible hand that had snatched the black hood from the wizard's head, revealing his delicate face and the long coppery-red hair. Why had she done it? She had a wild hope that his youth and beauty might touch the hearts of the savages and that they would leave him in peace. She'd had no idea that the man with whom she was dealing had no heart; that the only emotion the sight of Mathew's beauty touched was greed.

When Asrial saw the young man taken into the caravan, to be sold as a slave, she knew she'd made a mistake. She'd allowed herself to become personally attached to a human. Inadvertently she'd tampered with the plan of Promenthas, and now her charge was suffering for it. That first night when Mathew had wept himself to sleep in the trader's caravan, Asrial had flown home to Promenthas. Falling upon her knees before the God, she had kissed the hem of his white robes and prayed for forgiveness and a swift death for the suffering human.

Promenthas had been on the verge of promising her just what she'd asked, but then they had been interrupted by Akhran, the Wandering God—a frightful being to Asrial. Trembling, she had crept into the nave to wait impatiently until the Gods had finished their conversation. Already she was imagining Mathew's release from his dreadful life, the look of peace that would come upon his face, the joy when he knew that his soul was, at last, to return home.

And then, after talking with the barbaric Wandering God, Promenthas had changed his mind! Mathew was to live, it seemed. Why? Of course Asrial had not been given a reason. Faith. Trust in the Lord. She must do what she could to keep the young man alive, and not only that, but somehow she must place him in the hands of those who worshiped Akhran.

Bitterly disappointed, feeling Mathew's terror and misery wrench her heart, Asrial had nevertheless obeyed the commands of her God. It was she who alerted the guard to the fact that Mathew was slowly starving himself to death; she who touched Khardan with her feathery wings so that he would turn his head and see the young man about to be sold into slavery.

And all for what? So that Mathew could now, under the guise of a woman, live among people who considered him mad! What was Promenthas thinking? What could this one human, this eighteen-year-old boy, do to end the war raging in the heavens. . .

"Child!"

Asrial started and looked up in fear, thinking perhaps that the barbaric, savage djinn who had been pursuing her had discovered her at last. Instantly she began to fade away.

"Child, do not go!" came the voice again, and it was soft and gentle and pleading. Asrial stopped, her wings shivering in terror.

"What do you want of me? Who are you?"

"Look to your feet."

Asrial glanced down and saw the small crystal globe containing the two fish lying upon the floor of the tent. She stared at it, alarmed. It should not be sitting about in the open like this. Mathew was always so careful. She was certain he had concealed it safely in the pillow before going out to ride with Zohra this morning. Hastily she started to pick it up and return it to its hiding place, but the voice stopped her.

"Do not touch the globe. It might waken him."

Asrial, kneeling down beside it, could see that one of the fish—the black one—was asleep, floating inertly, eyes closed, near the bottom of the globe. The other fish, the golden one, swam in circles near the top, keeping the water moving in lulling, hypnotic ripples.

"Who are you?" asked Asrial in awe.

"I cannot tell you. To speak my name would break the spell.

He would awake and know what I have done. Now listen and obey me, child. We haven't much time. My power wanes. There are two within this camp who prepare to go seek the Lost Ones. You must go with them."

Asrial gasped, her wings fluttered. "No! I cannot! I dare not leave my charge!"

"You must, child. It is for him you do this. If not, he faces a cruel fate. He will die slowly by the most foul means man can devise—a sacrifice to a Dark God who thrives on pain and suffering. Your human will linger for days in hideous agony, and at the end his soul will be lost, for in his final moments, in the madness of his pain, he will renounce Promenthas. . ."

"But I cannot leave him." The angel wept and covered her ears with her hands. But this did not blot out the voice that continued to whisper within her heart.

"You can. He will be safe as long as he carries us. He is the Bearer and as such cannot be harmed. He will be safe until the one who seeks him finds him again!"

"The man in the palanquin!" Asrial cried, a prey to terror. "Yes. Already he comes searching for him. Every moment that passes, the danger draws nearer."

"I must talk to Promenthas!"

"No!" Though the fish continued to swim in seemingly unconcerned, lazy circles around the globe, the voice was insistent, stem, commanding. "No one—least of all a *God*—must know, or all will be ruined. *Go* with them, child. It is your protege's—and perhaps the world's—only chance."

"Chance! Chance for what?" Asrial cried desperately. But the fish spoke no more. Around and around it swam, its gills moving in and out, its graceful tail and fins sending the water washing in gentle waves against the sides of the crystal, rippling around its slumbering companion.

Afraid to touch the globe, Asrial dropped a silken scarf over it, then sank back upon the cushions of Mathew's bed.

"What should I do?" she murmured, distractedly plucking out small pinfeathers in her wings. "What should I do?"

Chapter 20

ɳo, you read it," Mathew insisted, putting the scroll back into Zohra's reluctant hands. "Go ahead. Read the words."

"Isn't it enough that I wrote them?"

Zohra smoothed the parchment out upon the floor of the tent, her eyes fixed upon it with a gaze of mingled pride and awe and dread. Drawing a deep breath, she lifted the scroll and held it over the bowl of sand. Then, at the last moment, she shoved it toward Mathew.

"You!"

"No, Zohra!" Mathew pushed the scroll away. "I've told you. It is *your* spell. *You* wrote it. *You* are the one who must cast it!"

"I can't, Mat-hew. I don't want it!"

"You don't want what?" Mathew said softly. "The power?"

The power that will make you a great sorceress among your people? The power to help them. . ."

Zohra's eyes flashed. Her lips compressed, the hand holding the parchment let it fall to the floor, and her fingers clenched into a fist. "The power to rule them!" she said fiercely.

Mathew sighed, his shoulders slumping. "Yes, well"—he gestured at the bowl of sand—"you won't be able to do anything until you overcome this fear—"

"I'm not afraid!" Zohra said angrily.

Snatching up the scroll, she carefully smoothed it out as Mathew had taught her. Holding it above the bowl of sand, she slowly and deliberately repeated the arcane words. Mathew held his breath, averting his eyes, unable to watch. What if the cantrip failed? What if he had misjudged her? What if she didn't possess the magic? Picturing her disappoittment, he shuddered. Zohra did not handle disappointment at all well. . .

A quick intake of breath from Zohra caused Mathew to look

back at the scroll. Relief and pride flooded through him. The words were beginning to writhe upon the parchment. One by one they slid off, tumbling into the bowl. Within seconds the sand had been transformed to cool, clear water.

"I did it!" Zohra cried. Transported with delight, she threw her arms around Mathew and hugged him. "Mat-hew! I did it!"

No less elated than his pupil, feeling for the first time since he'd come to this terrible land a tiny surge of joy bubble up through the barren desert of his soul, Mathew clasped Zohra close. The human contact was intensely satisfying. For an instant the bleak wind did not blow quite so coldly. Their lips met in a kiss that, for Zohra, was laced with fire but was—for Mathew—a kiss of heartbroken loneliness.

Zohra sensed this. Mathew felt her stiffen, and she thrust him away from her. The young man lowered his head, swallowing the shame, the guilt, the sense of loss whose bitter bile was choking him. Glancing at the woman, he saw her face—cold, stern, proud, and contemptuous. . . The open wound inside him bled freely, its pain overcoming him.

"Can't you understand!" he shouted at her, suddenly angry. "I don't want to be here! I don't want to be with you! I want to go home! I want to be with my own people in my own land! To see . . . trees again! To walk on green grass and drink water—all the water I want—and then to lie in the middle of an icy-cold stream and let it wash over me. I want to hear birds, leaves rustling, anything, except the wind!" He tore at his hair, gazing around the tent in his frenzy. "My god! Doesn't it ever quit blowing?"

He gasped for breath, the pain in his chest suffocating him. "I want to sit in the blessed silence of the cathedral and repeat my prayers and . . . and know that they are going to the ears of Promenthas and not being scattered like so much sand by this damnable wind! I want to continue my studies! I want to be with people who don't look away when I approach, then stare at me when I am past. I want to talk to people who know my name! It's Mathew, *Mathew!* Not Mat-hew! I want . . . my father, my mother. . . my home! Is that so wrong?"

He looked into her eyes. She lowered her long lashes almost immediately, but he saw there what he had expected-scorn, pity for his weakness. . .

"I wish Khardan had killed me that night!" Mathew burst out

in bitter agony.

Zohra's response startled him. She reached out hastily and placed her hand upon his lips. "No, Mat-Matchew!" Her struggle to pronounce his name correctly touched him, even through his despair. "You must not say such a thing. It will anger our God, who blessed you with life!" Fearfully she glanced about. "Promise me you will never say such a thing or think it," she whispered insistently, not moving her hand from his mouth.

"Very well," Mathew mumbled as best he could through her fingers.

She patted him, as one does an obedient animal, and withdrew her hand. But she continued to watch him anxiously, her gaze straying from him more than once to the tent entrance. It suddenly occurred to Mathew that she was truly frightened, truly expecting this God of hers to hurl aside the tent flap, draw his flaming sword, and carry out Mathew's wish on the spot.

How personally these people take things, Mathew thought, feeling even more alien and alone. How close they are to their God, involving him in every part of their lives. They argue with this Akhran, they curse him, they bless him, they obey him, they ignore him. A goat fails to give milk, a woman breaks a pitcher, a man stubs his toe. . . They cry out to their God with their petty woes. They blame him for them, although—Mathew had to admit—they were equally generous in their praise of him when things went right. This Akhran is more like a father than a God— a father who was as human as themselves, with all a human's failings. Where is the awe, the reverence, the worship of One who is without fault?

One who is without fault. . .

"Promenthas! Heavenly Creator," Mathew sighed, "forgive me! I have sinned!"

"What. . . what do you say?" Zohra regarded him suspiciously. He had unconsciously spoken the prayer in his own language.

"It is by your holy will I am here. Promenthas! It is by your will that I am alive!" Mathew gazed up into the heavens. "And I have not seen that! I have been lost in pitying myself! I did not realize that, in so doing, I was questioning you! You brought me here for a reason—but what reason? To bring knowledge of you to these people? That can't be! I am not a priest! Your priests died, and I was spared. For what purpose? I don't understand. But I am not meant to understand," Mathew counseled himself, remembering his teachings. "Mortal mind cannot comprehend the mind of the God." Yet these people seem to, easily enough.

"Matchew!" Zohra cried fearfully, tugging on his sleeve. "Matchew!"

Blinking, he stared at her. "What?"

"Don't talk in those strange words. I don't like it. I am certain it will offend Akhran."

"I-I'm sorry," he said flushing. "I was, I was praying. . . to my God."

"You can do that at night. I want to learn another spell. And, Matchew"—she cast him a stern glance—"do not try to kiss me again!"

He smiled wanly. "I'm sorry." He drew a deep breath. . . And Zohra, you have been speaking my name. . . just fine."

"Of course," she said, shrugging. "I knew I was saying it right, Mat-hew. It was you who were not hearing it right. Sometimes"—she regarded him gravely—"I think you *are* mad. But only a little," she added, stroking his arm soothingly.

"Now," she continued, scooting the bowl toward him. "You say that we can see pictures in the water. Show me how to work this spell. I want to see pictures of this home of which you speak."

"No! I can't!" Mathew drew back, truly alarmed. "I don't want to be reminded!" If he saw his homeland, his parents' dwelling, standing among the pines upon the high cliffs, the rose-red clouds of sunset, his heart would break. He might go truly mad, more than just a little.

"I was wrong in what I said before," he continued steadfastly. "My God told me that I am here to do His bidding, whatever that may be. Longing for something that I am obviously not meant to have is . . . is sacrilege."

Zohra nodded, her dark eyes grave. "I have long seen this sickness in you," she said. "Now perhaps you will heal. But what can we see in the bowl?"

"We will look into the future," Mathew said. He thought this would please her and he was right. Rewarded by a warm, eager smile, he pushed the bowl of water over toward her. "You will perform the spell. We will look into your future and that of your people." Truth to tell, he didn't much want to see into his own.

Zohra's eyes glistened. "Is this the way?" she asked, kneeling before the bowl.

"You are too rigid. Relax. There. Now listen to me carefully. What you will see are not 'pictures' of what will happen. You will see symbols that represent events looming in your future. It will be up to us to interpret these symbols, in order to understand their meaning."

Zohra frowned. "That seems silly."

Mathew hid his smile. "It is Sul's way of forcing you to think about what you see and study it, not just accept it and go on. Remember, too, that what you see may never come to pass, for the future is shaped by the present."

"I am beginning to wonder why we bother!"

"I did not promise this would be easy! Nor is it a toy to play with," Mathew responded sternly. "There is a danger involved in scrying, for—if we see something bad happening—we have no way of knowing if we should alter the present so as to change the future or to continue as we are."

"If we see something bad, we should try to stop it!"

"Perhaps not. Look," Mathew said patiently, seeing her mounting frustration, "suppose you look into the water and you see yourself riding your horse. Suddenly your horse stumbles and falls. You are thrown from the animal and break your arm. This is a bad thing, right? And you would do what you could to prevent it from happening?"

"Of course!"

"Well, let us say that if the horse doesn't fall, he carries you into quicksand and you both die."

Zohra's eyes opened wide. "Ah, I understand," she murmured, looking at the water with more respect. "I'm not certain I want to do this, Mat-hew."

He smiled at her reassuringly. "It will be all right." He felt safe, knowing that the symbols were generally obscure and complex to decipher. She probably wouldn't understand them at all, and it might take Mathew days to figure out what Sul meant. Meanwhile the scrying would entertain her and turn her thoughts from. . . other matters.

"Relax, Zohra," he said softly. "You must clear your mind of everything. Empty it so that Sul may draw his images upon it as a child draws in the sand. Close your eyes. Begin to repeat this phrase." Slowly he spoke the arcane words of the spell. "You say it."

Zohra stumbled over the words, speaking it clumsily. "Again."

She said it again, this time more easily.

"Continue."

She did so, the words coming to her lips easier each time.

"When you believe you are ready"—Mathew lowered his voice almost to a whisper so as not to disturb her concentration—"open your eyes and look into the water."

At first, despite his instructions, Zohra's body was stiff and tense from nervousness and excitement. It was a natural reaction and one reason that the chant was repeated—to force the mind into calm waters where it could drift until Sul claimed it. Mathew saw Zohra's shoulders gradually slump, her hands cease trembling, her face grow peaceful, and he felt a true sense of pride and accomplishment, knowing that his pupil had succeeded. She had entered the trance. Mathew had often wondered why powerful archmagi should spend their time in teaching young people when they could, for example, be managing royal kingdoms. Now he was beginning to understand.

With a deep sigh Zohra opened her eyes and stared into the water. A tiny line of irritation creased her brow.

"At first you will see nothing," Mathew said gently. "Be patient. Keep looking. "

Zohra's eyes blinked, she caught her breath.

"Tell me what you see."

"I see"—her voice was hesitant—"birds of prey."

"What kind of birds?"

"Hawks. No, wait, there is one falcon among them."

That symbol was easy enough to interpret, Mathew thought.

"What are they doing?"

"They are hunting. It is *aseur*, after sunset, night is falling."

"What do they catch?"

"Nothing. They fight among themselves and so their prey escapes."

That certainly wasn't unexpected. There wasn't a day went by that some minor squabble didn't break out between the two tribes camped around the Tel. Mathew nodded, "Go on," he said wryly.

"Other birds are coming. Eagles! A great many. . ." Zohra suddenly gasped. "They are attacking!"

"What are?" Mathew asked, alarmed.

"The eagles! They are attacking the hawks! Scattering them across the sky! The falcon... Ah!" Zohra put her hands over her mouth, her eyes staring into the water in horror and shock.

"What?" Mathew almost shrieked. It took all his willpower not to grab the bowl of water and stare into it himself, despite the fact that he knew he wouldn't be able to share her vision. "What happens, Zohra? Tell me!"

"The falcon falls to the sand... his body pierced by sharp claws... The hawks are destroyed, killed or carried away by the eagles to their nests... to feed... their young..."

"Anything else?" Mathew demanded impatiently.

Zohra shook her head. "The sky is dark now. It is night. I can see nothing more. Wait..." She stared into the bowl in perplexity. "I'm seeing this all again!"

Mathew, confused and fearful, trying to make some sense of this terrifying vision, looked up at her quickly. "Exactly the same as before?"

"Yes."

"Exactly!" he said insistently. "Any change? No matter how slight..."

"None... except that it is *fedjeur*, before morning. The hawks and the falcon are hunting at sunrise."

Mathew breathed a shivering sigh of relief. "Go on," he said almost inaudibly.

"I don't understand."

"I'll explain later."

"The hawks are again fighting among themselves. The prey escapes. The eagles are coming. They are attacking. I can't watch!"

"Yes, you can!" Mathew came near shaking her and dug his nails into his palms to control himself. "What now?"

"The eagles strike the falcon. He falls... but not into the sand! He falls... into a pit of ... mud and dung... He lives and struggles to rise up out of the pit. He yearns to fight. But the eagles fly away, pursuing the hawks."

"The falcon?"

"He is hurt... and his wings are caked with... filth... But he is alive."

" And?"

"And the sun is shining."

She fell silent, peering intently into the water.

"Nothing else?"

Zohra shook her head. Slowly, blinking her eyes, coming back to herself, she turned to look at Mathew. "That was very bad, wasn't it?"

"Yes," he answered, averting his face.

"What does it mean?"

"I . . . I must study it," he answered evasively.

"No," she said. "There is no need to study it, Mat-hew. I know what it meant. I know in my heart. A great battle is coming! My people will fight and they will die! Isn't that what it means?"

"Yes, partly," Mathew said. "But it is not that simple, Zohra! I warned you it wouldn't be. For one thing, Sul is offering you hope! That is why there were two visions.

"I see no hope!" she said bitterly. "The hawks are attacked and they are killed!"

"But in the first, it is sunset, then night. In the second, it is sunrise, then the sun is shining. In the first, the falcon dies. In the second, Khardan lives."

"Khardan!" Zohra stared at him.

Mathew flushed. He hadn't intended to stay that. Zohra's lips pressed firmly together. She stood up and stared for the tent entrance. Twisting to his feet, guessing her intention, Mathew caught hold of her arm.

"Let go of me!" Her eyes flared dangerously.

"Where are you going?"

"To tell my father, to warn them."

"You can't!"

"Why not?" Angrily she shook free of him and started to shove past.

"How will you explain it?" Mathew cried. Catching hold of her again, he gripped her arms, forcing her to look at him. "How will you explain the magic, Zohra? They won't understand! You'll put us both in danger! And we don't know what Sul is trying to tell us yet!"

Promenthas forgive me my lie, he prayed silently.

"But we are going to be attacked!"

"Yes, but when? It could be tonight. It could be thirty years from tonight! How can you tell?"

He felt the bunched muscles in her arms start to ease, and he breathed a sigh of relief. He released his hold on her. Turning her back to him, Zohra brushed her hand across her eyes, wiping away tears he was not intended to see.

"I wish I'd never done this thing!" Frustrated, she stamped on the water bowl, shattering the crockery and deluging cushions, robes, and the tent floor.

Mathew was about to say something comforting—meaningless, perhaps, but comforting—when a cloud of smoke appeared in the tent, coalescing into the large, flabby body of the djinn. Usti glanced around at the destruction gloomily. "Princess," he said in a quavering voice, "it is customary to take laundry to the water, not bring the water to the laundry. I suppose I will be asked to clean up this mess?"

"What do you want?" Zohra snapped.

"A little rest, if you do not mind, madam," Usti said plaintively. "I have been watching the woman, Meryem, for days now, and the most exciting thing she has done is learn how to milk a goat. And while spending twenty-four hours a day with the constant sight of a nubile white body and golden hair before my eyes would have been the dream of my youth, I find that at this age my mind turns to thoughts of broiled mutton, a nice bit of crispy lamb, sugared almonds. All to be digested pleasantly while lying stretched out upon my couch. . . ."

"What is she doing now?" Mathew interrupted the djinn's blissful ramblings.

"Sleeping through the heat of the afternoon, *sidi.*" said Usti morosely, "as should all sane people. I make no disparaging remark on your affliction," the djinn added, bowing.

Mathew sighed and glanced at Zohra. "I suppose it won't do any harm to ease up on watching her," he said. "As Usti says, days have passed and she hasn't tried anything. I wonder why. . ." Here was yet another problem to ponder. "What do you think?"

"Mmm?" Zohra looked around at him. Obviously she hadn't heard a word. "Oh." She shrugged. "I don't care. I grow bored with this chasing after nothing anyway. Leave the girl alone."

"At least for the afternoon. I'll clean this up," Mathew offered, still feeling the sense of unreality and uneasiness he always experienced talking to a being he wasn't fully convinced he believed in. "You may go."

Usti granted him a grateful look. "Akhran's blessings on you, madman," he said fervently, and quickly disappeared before anyone could change his or her mind.

"My head throbs," Zohra said heavily, putting her hands to her temples. "I am going to my tent to think what must be done."

"Hope, Zohra," Mathew said to her softly as she walked past him. "There is hope. . ."

The dark eyes stared into his searchingly, their gaze warm and intense. Then, without a word, she stepped around him and left his tent, gliding across the empty compound that was baking in the hot sun.

Turning back, Mathew began listlessly picking up fragments of the water bowl. Holding the broken pieces in his hands, he came to a stop, staring at them unseeing. Hope? he thought bleakly. Yes. Hope to save Zohra and her people from the night, hope to save them from annihilation.

But only if Khardan plummets from the sky. Not to die in glory, but to live. . .

To live in shame and degradation.

CHAPTER 21

Usti was correct in reporting that Meryem hadn't done anything remarkable in the past few days—or at least anything that had been discovered by the djinn. This was due to several factors, not the least of which was Meryem's discovery of Usti. The bumbling djinn was no clever spy, and it had been easy for the sorceress to discern she was being watched and by whom. Of course this told her all she needed to know: somehow Zohra had survived the murder attempt, her suspicions were aroused, and she now believed Meryem to be a sorceress of considerable power. Meryem guessed, although she did not know for certain, that she had the madman to thank for all this. She intended to see that he received her compliments.

Meanwhile, knowing she was being watched forced her to take extra precautions. She was still no nearer marrying Khardan, and it began to look as if she must fail in her assignment when—by Quar's blessing—she happened to pass Majiid's tent just as the men were informed of the approach of Sheykh Zeid and his *meharistes* from the south. A few minutes spent listening told her all she needed to know.

A swift call summoned Yamina to the mirror, and it had been a simple matter to impart the vital information Meryem had learned to the Amir's wife while sharing the news with Majiid's wives at the same time. Since spying on their menfolk was accepted practice, none of the wives questioned Meryem's having overheard such important news or her right to spread it. They found it most welcome and discussed it and its implications far into the night.

Yamina sent Meryem a message in return, stating that the Amir had received the news and was making his plans according- ly. The message also added that he looked forward to welcoming

Meryem into the *seraglio*. Meryem, who should have been gloating like a miser over newfound wealth, suddenly discovered that the gold had turned to lead. In particular, the thought of sharing the Amir's bed—which had before been her highest goal—was distinctly unappealing. It was Khardan she wanted.

Never before had a man taken such possession of her mind and soul. She didn't like the feeling. She fought against it. And not a day went by but that she didn't find some opportunity to see him, to be near him, to make him aware of her, to watch him in secret. She did not love him. Hers was not the nature to love. She was consumed by desire for him; a physical yearning that she'd felt for no other man in her life.

Had she been able to satisfy that desire, a few nights of passion might have quenched it. Knowing she could not have what she wanted increased its value tenfold. He tantalized her. Her nights were spent in sweet, tormenting fantasies of his love; her daily menial tasks were made bearable by dreams of introducing him to the pleasures taught in a royal *seraglio*.

And the Amir was going to make war on him.

Khardan might well be killed! Might? Hah! Meryem knew enough of the man to realize that for him there would be no surrender. Were the foe to outnumber him a thousand to one, he would die fighting. What could she do?

She had only one idea. She would try to persuade him to flee with her to Kich. The Amir could use a man such as Khardan in his armies. He would be near her, in the palace, and once the nomad had tasted the pleasures of city life, Meryem was postive he would not want to return to this one.

Knowing the loyalty Khardan felt for his people, Meryem was somewhat dubious about the success of her plan, but there was no harm in trying. At least it would give her an excuse to talk to him, to be alone together in the privacy of his tent.

Consequently, on the afternoon when Zohra and Mathew were absorbed in their contemplation of terrifying visions and Usti was absorbed in the contemplation of a bottle of fine wine, Meryem rose from her supposed nap and crept out into the camp that slumbered beneath the sweltering sun.

Silently, unobserved by anyone, Meryem slipped into Khardan's tent. He was asleep, his strong body stretched out full length upon the cushions. For long moments she stood watching him, delighting to torment herself with the ache of her longing. One arm was thrown across his eyes to protect them from a beam of sunlight that had slanted over the bed and was now gone with the approach of evening. His breathing was even and deep. The front of his tunic was open, revealing the strong, muscular chest. Meryem envisioned sliding her hand inside, caressing the smooth skin. She envisioned her lips touching the hollow of his throat and was forced to shut her eyes and regain control of herself before she dared approach him.

Feeling her glowing cheeks cool, she knelt down on shaking knees by his bed and laid a gentle hand upon his arm.

"Khardan!" she whispered.

Startled, he blinked and half sat up, his hand reaching instinctively for his sword.

"What? Who—"

Meryem shrank back in terror. "It is only me, Khardan!"

His expression softened at the sight of her, then he frowned. "You should not be here!" His voice grated harshly, but she knew—with a thrill—that it was not the harshness of anger but of passion.

"Don't send me away!" she pleaded, pressing the palms of her hands together. "Oh, Khardan, I am so frightened."

She was pale and trembled from head to toe, but it wasn't from fear.

"What is it?" Khardan said, instantly concerned. "Who in this camp has given you reason to be afraid?"

"No one," Meryem faltered. "Well"—she amended, lowering her eyes and looking at him through the long lashes—"there is someone who scares me."

"Who?" Khardan demanded in a deep voice. "Tell me the name!"

"No, please. . ." Meryem begged, affecting to try to draw away from him. Though this had not been her intent in coming here, the opportunity to strike out at her enemy was too good to pass up.

Khardan continued to argue, and as he was much too strong for her, she yielded to his pressing demands.

"Zohra!" she murmured reluctantly.

"I thought as much," Khardan said grimly. "What has she done? By Akhran, she will pay!"

"Nothing! Truly. It is just that sometimes, the way she looks at me. Those black eyes. And then she is such a powerful sorceress. . ."

Khardan regarded Meryem fondly. "Such a loving little bird as you, my dear, would not speak ill of anyone, even the cat. Do not be afraid. I will have a word with her."

"Ah, but Khardan!" She wrung her pretty hands. "This is not why I came! It is not for myself that I am frightened."

"For whom then?"

"For you!" she breathed. Hiding her face in her hands, she began to weep, being careful as she did so to cry only enough tears to give a shimmer to her eyes, not to make her nose red and swollen.

"My treasure!"

Putting his arms around her, Khardan held her close, stroking the blond hair that had slipped out from beneath her veil. She could feel his body tense, straining against the bonds he had bound around himself. Her own passion rose. She let slip the veil from her face, revealing her full, red lips.

"What have you to fear for me?" he asked, his voice husky, holding her away from him slightly to look into her eyes.

"I have heard. . . about this terrible Sheykh Zeid!" she said in a tear-choked voice. "I know that there may be a battle! You might die!"

"Nonsense." Khardan laughed. "A battle? Zeid is coming in answer to our prayers, gazelle-eyes. He will ride with us to raid Kich. Who knows," he added teasingly, brushing back a handful of golden curls, "by next week I might be the Amir."

Meryem blinked. "What?"

"Amir!" he continued, just for something to say. His towering fortress of strength was rapidly crumbling. "I will be the Amir and you will show me the wonders of the palace. Particularly the secret hole in the wall that looks into the bathing room and the hidden chamber where the blind musicians play."

Meryem wasn't listening. Was it possible? Why had she never considered this before? But could it be worked? There was still this terrible battle. . . . She had to think. To plan. Meanwhile, here was Khardan, his lips brushing against her cheek, burning her skin. . .

"I must go!" she gasped, tearing herself from his embrace.

"Forgive the foolish fears of a weak and silly woman." She backed out of the tent, her heart pounding so that she couldn't hear her own words. "Only know that she loves you!"

Though his arms and hands released her and he let her go without trying to stop her, his eyes held her still, and it was all she could do to flee their warm embrace. Literally running, she escaped back to the cool solitude of her tent.

Yes, she would sleep in the Amir's bed.

But it would be Khardan, not Qannadi, who lay beside her!

CHAPTER 22

Sheykh Zeid was now within two days ride of the camp around the Tel. Everyone waited eagerly to see what tomorrow morning would bring, for if Zeid were coming as a friend, he would send vaunt-couriers ahead of him by one day to announce his coming. If he were a foe, he would send no one. Since the *spahis* lived for fighting, they were as prepared for one eventuality as the other. Most—like Khardan—considered it unlikely that Zeid would opt for war. After all, what possible reason could he have for attacking them?

Pukah could have given one. Pukah could have given them several. The djinn was the only person in camp *not* looking forward to tomorrow morning. He knew that no vaunt-courier would appear bearing guest-gifts and salutations from his master. He knew that instead there would be masses of fierce *meharistes* galloping down on them. Zeid's men were true children of battle—the highest compliment one nomad can pay another. Strong and courageous to the point of folly, the Aran fought as well on foot as on the backs of their *meharis,* each man trained to run alongside his camel, using one hand to pull himself up onto the animal's back by the saddle while slashing out with his sword in the other. Pukah chafed to be gone. He *had* to be gone by morning and intended to leave this night—Sond or no Sond.

Majiid had been most reluctant to part with his djinn, and the fact that Sond was running off on another wild errand for Akhran didn't help matters. The Sheykh was beginning to have his doubts concerning his wisdom of the Wandering God these days. The Rose of The Prophet looked to be on verge of death. He'd lost horses to the Hrana. (Majiid's worst nightmares consisted of seeing his precious animals plodding along ignominiously behind a flock of bleating sheep.) Then there'd been the

Amir's refusal to buy the horses, the Calif's near arrest, and finally the arrival of a madman in their midst.

"What more could Akhran do to me?" Majiid demanded of his djinn. "Beyond setting fire to my beard, of course. Now he wants to take you away from me!"

"It is a most urgent matter," Sond pleaded, driven by his love for Nedjma to pursue the argument in the glare of Majiid's anger. "You, my master, are seeing things by night instead of by day. You may have lost horses, but you have gained mutton. You and Jaafar have managed to intimidate that old bandit Zeid, who is eager to be your friend. Khardan escaped the Amir's wrath and tweaked the man's nose into the bargain by carrying away the Sultan's daughter, and now you will have vengeance upon the city and become wealthy in the process!

"I will be gone only a few days at the most, *sidi*," Sond said in conclusion. "You will never miss me. Usti, the djinn of your daughter-in-law, has agreed to supply your needs until I return." (This Usti had done, but only after great quantities of *qumiz*, and then he had been unable to recall his agreement in the morning. This didn't matter to Sond, however, who truly expected to be back before Majiid could think of wanting him.) "And if I may remind my Sheykh," Sond continued smoothly, "now is hardly the time to offend *Hazrat* Akhran."

That much Majiid had to admit, albeit reluctantly. Such a daring undertaking as a raid on a walled city would require all the blessings the Wandering God had to bestow and then some. "Very well," he said finally, giving grudging assent. "You may go. But I command you by the power of the lamp to be back before we launch our attack on Kich."

"To hear is to obey, *sidi*," the overjoyed Sond cried, throwing his strong arms around his master and kissing him soundly on both cheeks—a proceeding that highly scandalized Majiid, who felled the djinn with one blow of his powerful fist. The swelling of Sond's jaw was nothing compared to the swelling of his heart with love, however. He hastened into his lamp to prepare for his journey.

Pukah, meanwhile, restlessly prowled the camp, trembling in dread whenever anyone rode up, fearful news would come that Zeid was attacking sooner than the djinn anticipated. It was evening, the time when the barren sands came alive with sparkling purples and golds. Oblivious to the beauty, Pukah sat some distance from camp in the shadow of the Tel, watching with increasing gloom the people coming out of their tents to take advantage of the cool night breeze.

"I will give Sond one hour," Pukah stated, his eye on the rim of the sun that was slowly disappearing into the far distant hills. "When it is dark, we are leaving."

He was speaking to himself, as usual, and so was considerably surprised and more than a little alarmed to find this pronouncement met with a small, soft sigh.

"Who's there?" he cried, leaping to his feet. "Who spoke?" He drew his sword.

"Oh, please! Put your weapon away!" said a sweet voice, the sweetest voice Pukah had ever heard in all his centuries. Dropping the sword, he fell to his knees.

"It is you, my enchanter!" he cried, spreading his arms and looking around wildly. "Please, show yourself. I will not harm you, I swear it! I would sooner let myself be pierced by red-hot needles run into the soles of my feet—"

"Don't say such dreadful things, I beg of you!" the voice pleaded.

"No, no! I won't. I'm sorry. Please, only let me see you that I may know you are real and not a dream!"

A cloud of golden rain began to shimmer before the djinn's dazzled vision. Out of the rain stepped the form of a woman. She was dressed in voluminous white robes with long white sleeves. Wings surpassing the whiteness and delicacy of a swan's sprang from her shoulders, their feathery tips brushing the ground. Silver hair curled about a face so ethereal in its wistful loveliness that Pukah didn't feel a thing when his heart leaped from his chest and fell with a thud at the woman's bare, white feet.

"Please, tell me your name, that I may whisper it to myself every second from now throughout eternity!"

"My... my name is Asrial," said the immortal vision of loveliness.

"Asrial! Asrial!" Pukah repeated in rapture. "When I die, that name will be the last word upon my lips."

"You can't die; you're immortal," Asrial pointed out unromantically. Her voice shook as she spoke, however, and a tear sparkled like a star upon her cheek.

"You are in trouble, in danger!" Pukah guessed instantly. He threw himself upon his belly in the sand, arms outstretched. "I beg you! Let me help you! Let me sacrifice my unworthy life for just the reward of removing that tear from your cheek. I will do anything, anything'"

"Take me with you," said Asrial.

"Anything but that," Pukah said heavily.

Sitting up, leaning back on his heels, he regarded the angel with a mournful expression. "Ask me for something simple. Perhaps you'd like the ocean to cool your feet. I could it put it over there, to your left. And to the right, a mountain, to complete the view. The moon, to hold in your hand, and the stars to adorn your hair. . ."

"Can you truly do such things?" Asrial's eyes widened.

"Well, no," Pukah admitted, realizing that he might suddenly be called upon to supply one or more of the above. "But I am very young. Someday, when I am older, I expect to be able to perform these and other such miracles like that!" He snapped his fingers. "You see," he added confidentially, "I am the favorite of my God."

"Ah!" The angel's pale, wan face brightened until it seemed to Pukah he was blinded by her radiance. "Then surely you have nothing to fear and my coming with you will be only a minor inconvenience. I will keep out of your way," she promised. "I won't be any trouble, and I might be of some small help. I am not a favorite of my God as are you," she added shyly, "but Promenthas is very powerful and a loving father to his children."

"Are you his daughter?" Pukah was beginning to fear that he'd chosen the wrong immortal to try to impress.

"No, not literally," Asrial said, blushing. "I meant only that all those who worship Promenthas are viewed by him as his children."

"So, you worship Promenthas," Pukah said, stalling for time, wondering how he could get out of this.

"Yes," she answered. "Do you mind if I sit down? It's been a . . . a trying day. . ."

"Oh, please!" Pukah sprang to his feet. "What would you prefer? A cloud? A cushion of swan's down? A blanket of lamb's wool?" He produced all three, this being a relatively simple trick.

"Thank you," she said, selecting the blanket. With her own

hands—such lovely hands, Pukah saw with a sigh—she spread it upon the desert floor and sank down onto her knees.

"Excuse me," she said. "What are you looking at?"

"Your wings. Forgive me, but I was just wondering how you manage to sit like that without crushing them. "

"They fold back, out of my way. Like this." She turned slightly to give him a view of the graceful sweep of her feathers trailing on the ground behind her.

"Ah!" said Pukah, overwhelmed by the beauty of the sight. He caught hold of his hand, just as it was straying out to touch one of the feathers. Clasping it firmly, he held it behind his back, out of temptation.

"It is unusual to see a female immortal on this plane." A sudden jealous thought struck Pukah. "The madman is your master. In what capacity do you serve him?" he demanded savagely.

"The madman—I mean Mathew—is *not* my master. We do not serve humans as do you," she added, regarding Pukah with lofty reproof. "I serve only Promenthas, my God."

"You do?" Pukah cried, ecstatic. "Then why are you with the madman?"

"Mathew is not mad!" Asrial returned angrily. "I am his guardian."

"You?" Pukah seemed to find this amusing. "From what do you protect him? Vicious attacks by butterflies? A sparrow coming too near?"

"I saved his life when all the rest of his companions were slaughtered by the foul followers of Quar!" Asrial cried, stung. "I kept him alive when he was in the fiendish clutches of the evil slave trader. I kept him alive when your master would have had his head on his sword!"

"That is true," Pukah said thoughtfully. "I saw that myself and I found it hard to believe. Khardan is not generally one to show mercy." He regarded her with new respect. "I think, then, that your mad— Forgive me . . . your Mathew. . . is a human fortunate in his God's choice of a guardian. I also think that your Mathew is still in much need of guarding, if you will forgive my mentioning such a distressing fact,"- he added gently.

"Oh, Pukah!" Asrial's eyes filled with tears. "I do not want to leave him! But I have no choice, it seems. If I do not go on this journey with you, I have been told that a terrible fate will most certainly befall him!"

"Do you know where we are going?" Pukah hedged.

"I was told you seek the Lost Immortals."

"Who told you?" Pukah demanded, startled and displeased.

"Sond! That's it! You know Sond! He knows you! Ah, I should have guessed as much! Breaking his heart over Nedjma, is he? Meanwhile dallying with another immortal—"

"I don't know what you are talking about!" Asrial said coldly, drawing her robes closely about her. "I never heard of this Sond. As for who told me, I can't tell you. It is a secret, one on which—perhaps—my Mathew's very life depends."

"I'm sorry. Don't cry. I'm a jealous fool!" Pukah said remorsefully. "It's only that I love you to distraction!"

"Love?" She looked at him in perplexity. "What is this talk of love and jealousy and dalliance among our kind?"

"Are there male angels among you?"

"Yes, most assuredly."

"Don't you fall in love?"

"Certainly not. Our thoughts are on paradise and the good work that we strive to do among men. We are wholly occupied in our worship of Promenthas. It is he who has our love, and it is a pure love, unstained by the corruption of bodily lust that so afflicts humans. And is this not true with you?"

"Er no," said Pukah, feeling somewhat uncomfortable beneath the gaze of those cool, innocent eyes. "We have our share of bodily lust, I'm afraid. I can't quite picture paradise without it, if you'll forgive my saying so."

"That's what comes of being around humans so much," Asrial stated.

"Well, for that matter," Pukah added, nettled by her superior tone, "I notice that your talk about 'your Mathew' goes a bit beyond that of your everyday bodyguard."

"What do you mean by that?"

"I mean that perhaps you're eager to do more than just *guard* his body. . ."

"How dare you!" She flounced to her feet, her wings spreading in her indignation. Her face had flushed a deep rose, her eyes sparkled with her anger, the outspread wings fanned the evening air, filling Pukah's nostrils with the pure, sweet smell of holy incense. He fell to the ground again.

"I dare because I'm a wretch, a miserable excuse for a djinn, not worthy of you to spit upon!" he cried woefully. "Forgive me?"

"Will you take me with you?"

"Please don't ask that of me, Asrial!" Pukah begged, looking up at her earnestly. "It is dangerous. More dangerous than you can possibly imagine. More dangerous than I've let on to Sond," he admitted shamefacedly. "If you must know the truth, *I'm* going only because I've messed things up around here so badly that I'm afraid my master will turn me over to Akhran for punishment. And all know that while the Wandering God has many faults, showing mercy is not one of them. I hope, by searching for the Lost Ones, I can somehow make I reparation for the serious trouble I'm about to bring down upon my master's unsuspecting head."

"You did not do this purposefully to cause him harm?"

"No, oh, no!" Pukah cried. "I can say that truthfully, if I can say nothing else to my credit. I meant, all along, only to help him." Choking, he wiped his eyes, muttering something about sand flying down his throat.

"Then," said Asrial shyly, reaching out her hand to him, "together we will work to help your master and my Mathew and save them from the trouble that we *both* have inadvertently brought to them. Can you put up with me?"

"If you can put up with me," Pukah said humbly.

"Then I may come?"

"Yes." Pukah sighed. "Though it goes against my heart. Ah, look. Here is Sond, and with good news by that stupid grin on his face. I better tell you the rest of the story. And—er don't mention anything to Sond about. . . about what I just said? He wouldn't understand! The reason we are going is that Sond's beloved, a djinniyeh named Nedjma, was kidnapped by an evil being known as an 'efreet. This 'efreet—going by the name of Kaug—dwells in a most fearsome place beneath the Kurdin Sea, and it is there that we must begin our search for the Lost Immortals.

"Ah Sond! About time. We were just speaking of you. This is Asrial. She's coming with us. . . . Yes, she has wings. She's an angel. . . . Don't ask questions. We don't have time. I'll explain everything to you on the way!"

CHAPTER 23

Zeid was within one day's ride of the Tel. Khardan, his father, and Jaafar were up early that morning, eyes turning toward the south. The sun rose over the Sun's Anvil, burning fiercely in the sky. Everyone waited expectantly.

At length three *meharis* appeared. But they were not vaunt-couriers. They did not ride into camp, which would have been a show of friendly intent. They stood upon a tall sand dune, the sun glinting off the banner of Sheykh Zeid al Saban and off the swords the men held—blades bare—in their hands.

It was a challenge to do battle.

Mounting their horses, Khardan and Majiid galloped out to meet them; Jaafar following on an ancient she-camel, who plodded through the sand with extreme reluctance and who managed to carry the Sheykh to the brief parley in time to see it end.

"What does our cousin mean that he brings war upon us?" Majiid demanded, urging his horse forward until it stood nose-to-nose with the lead camel rider—Sheykh al Saban's standard bearer.

"We do not come in war, but in peace," said the *mehari* formally. "Acknowledge that you are under the *suzerain* of Sheykh Zeid al Saban and pay him tribute of the following"—the *mehari* recited a list of demands that included, among other things, thirty fine horses and one hundred sheep—"and we will leave in peace," the *mehari* concluded.

Majiid's brows bristled in anger. "Tell Sheykh Zeid al Saban that I would sooner place myself under the *suzerain* of Sul and that the only tribute I will pay him will be in blood!"

"So be it!" the mehari said grimly. He pointed to the south where the Sheykhs and the Calif could see the vast army of meharistes assembled. "We will be waiting to collect."

Raising their sabers, the camel riders saluted their foe, then turned and dashed off, the tassels that hung from the camels' saddles bouncing wildly about the animals' long, thin legs.

Hastily Khardan and the Sheykhs returned to camp—Majiid grinning broadly at the prospect of a battle, Jaafar groaning and moaning that he was cursed. Khardan, his face dark with fury, stalked into his tent and kicked the basket where Pukah lived.

"Come out, you miserable wretch, that I may yank off your ears!"

"Have you forgotten, Brother?" Achmed peered in the tent flap. "You gave him permission to leave."

"Yes, and now I understand the reason why he was so eager to be gone before this day dawned!" Khardan muttered with an oath. "I wonder how how long he's known Zeid meant to attack us."

"Still, Khardan, it *is* a fight!" Achmed could not understand his brother's anger.

"Yes, but it's not the fight I wanted!" Khardan's fist clenched.

"Ah, well," said Achmed with the philosophy of one who is seventeen, possessor of a new sword, and about to ride into his first major battle, "we attack the camel riders today, Kich tomorrow."

Khardan's stern face relaxed into a smile. Putting his arm around his brother, he hugged him. "Remember what I've taught you! Make me proud!"

"I will, Khardan!" Achmed's voice broke, excitement and emotion overcoming him.

Seeing his embarrassment, Khardan cuffed the boy affectionately across the face. "And don't falloff your horse!"

"I was a child then! I haven't done that in years! I wish you'd just shut up about that!"

Achmed shoved his brother. Khardan shoved him back, harder. Their friendly tussle was broken up only by the sound of a ram's horn.

"There's the call!" Achmed's eyes shone.

"Go along. Get ready," Khardan ordered. "And don't forget to visit your mother. "

"Will she cry?"

Khardan shrugged. "She's a woman."

"I don't think I can take that," Achmed muttered, his eyes cast down, face flushing.

Khardan permitted himself a smile, knowing his brother would not see it. He remembered himself at seventeen, bidding his mother good-bye. There had been tears then, too, and it had not been his mother alone who cried. The memory had shamed him for days. Now he was older and could understand. He had a difficult visit of his own to pay.

"You are a man now," he told his brother severely. "It is for you to play a man's part. Would you go into battle without your mother's prayers?"

"N-no, Khardan."

"Then leave!" Khardan shoved him again, this time in the direction of Majiid's harem. "I will see you when we ride. You are to be on my right."

It was the place of honor. His face glowing with pleasure and pride, Achmed turned and raced across the compound to Majiid's tents.

Khardan stared in that direction longingly, his thoughts *not* on his mother. Although it would not be considered proper, since they were not married, he still meant to bid Meryem good-bye. But there were other farewells he had to make first, much as he disliked it.

Turning, he left his tent. Walking the short distance across the compound to the dwellings of his wives, he glanced about, instinctively studying the weather, and noticed a darkening in the western sky. Odd time of year for a storm. It looked to be far off, however; probably over the foothills. He thought little of it. Often the clouds never left the hills. Their moisture sucked out of them by the desert heat, they generally dwindled away. His attention was drawn away by a shouted question from one of his *spahis*. Answering that, Khardan did not give the storm another thought.

The camp was in an uproar—men sharpening their blades on the whirring grindstones, gathering up saddles and bridles, bidding their families good-bye, receiving crude charms and protective amulets from their wives. Khardan, pausing, watched a father gather his small children in his arms and hold them close.

The Calif felt a swift spasm of pain contract his heart. He wanted children of his own. As he was the eldest of Majiid's many offspring, one of the greatest pleasures in Khardan's life had been helping to raise his younger brothers, teaching them horsemanship and warfare. To pass these skills on to sons of his own would be his proudest moment. And then to have a little girl (he pictured her with blue eyes and blond hair) clinging to him. To keep her safe from the harshness of the world, protected in the shelter of his strong arms. And when she was older, he could envision her coaxing a new bauble or a pair of earrings from him. Her teasing voice, her gentle hands. . . so like her mother's. . .

Khardan shook his head, his gaze going to his destination—Zohra's tent. His face dark and grim, he thrust aside the tent flap and entered.

She had been expecting him. This was a visit he was required to pay before leaving to fight. Tradition demanded it, despite the fact that they had not spoken and only rarely even looked in each other's direction since the night he had brought Meryem into camp and into his father's tent.

Zohra, her face cold and impassive, rose to her feet to greet him. She did not bow, as was customary between husband and wife. Someone else in the tent rose, too. Khardan was surprised to see Mathew present, as well, and he looked at Zohra in some astonishment, amazed at her thoughtfulness and foresight in sparing him the humiliation of entering the tent of the madman and bidding him good-bye like a true wife.

This unexpected solicitude on her part did not deter him from his true purpose in coming here, however. Seeing them together increased his anger. He was beginning to think that *Hazrat* Akhran was playing some sort of cruel joke upon him—giving him one wife who was still a virgin and another wife who was a man. The crimson stain on the bridal sheet had saved him from shame in regard to Zohra. Everyone in both tribes knew that he did not visit her tent at night, and there was not a person in either tribe—including Zohra's own—who blamed him, considering how unwomanly she acted. He was spared shame, too, in the case of the madman. But this did not ease the bitter knowledge deep within him that—to all effect—his two wives were more barren than the desert, for the sands at least bloomed in the spring. His wives were like that accursed, dried-up, withering Rose that had brought them here in the first place.

This will end, he said to himself. This will end when Meryem comes into my tent. And then it suddenly occurred to the Calif that maybe this was what Akhran intended all along. Khardan was meant to conceive children with a Sultan's daughter! The blood of sheep would not run in the veins of his sons!

Zohra had dressed herself in a *chador* of deep-blue silk edged with gold. Her face was not veiled, her jewelry sparkled in the light of day that sifted through the tent. Fire smoldered in her dark eyes, as it always did when she confronted her husband. But it was not the fire of desire. Whatever attraction these two had felt had seemingly died—a casualty of the Calif's journey to Kich. Resentment, hatred, jealousy, shame—this was the dagger that separated them now, a dagger whose edge was sharper and cut deeper than any blade forged by the hands of man.

"So, it is to be war," Zohra said coldly. "I trust, husband, that you are not here to receive either my tears or my blessing."

"At least, wife, we understand each other."

"I do not know why you bothered to come at all then."

"Because it is expected and would not look right," Khardan returned. "And it gives me the opportunity to discuss a I matter of serious import with you. I do not know the details because Meryem, gentle and loving soul that she is, refused to tell me. But I know that you have done or said something to frighten her. By Sul!" His voice grated. Taking a step nearer Zohra, his fist clenched, he stared at her intently, eyes flaring in anger. "You *do* anything to her, you *say* anything to her, you harm a single strand of golden hair on her head, and I swear by *Hazrat* Akhran I'll—"

Swiftly, silently, without a scream, without breathing a word, Zohra hurled herself at her husband, her sharp nails flashing like the claws of a panther. Her reaction took Khardan by surprise, caught him completely off guard. He had expected an angry denial or perhaps the haughty silence of one who is guilty but considers herself justified. He had not expected to be fighting for his life.

Catching hold of her wrists, he wrested her hands from his I face, but not before four long, bloody scratches glistened on his left cheek. She lunged at him again, her hands clutching at his throat. Zohra's strength was above that of the average woman. Add to this the fury, the surprise, and the swiftness of her attack, and Khardan might have been in serious trouble had not Mathew joined in the fray. Grabbing hold of Zohra, the young wizard dragged her off Khardan.

The woman fought and struggled to free herself, kicking and spitting like an enraged cat.

Clasping his arms around her upper body, pinning her flailing hands to her side, Mathew glared at Khardan.

"Get out!" he cried.

"She is a witch!" Khardan said, breathing heavily, his fingers upon his face. Drawing them back, he saw the blood and cursed.

Zohra tried to fling herself at him again, but Mathew held on to her firmly.

"You cannot understand!" Mathew shouted at Khardan angrily. "Just get out!"

The Calif stared at him in some astonishment, amazed to see the young man's face so pale and threatening. Dabbing at the bloody marks with the hem of his sleeve, Khardan cast a final, piercing glance at his wife, then turned upon his heel and left her tent.

"Let me go! Let me go!" Zohra shrieked, foam flecking her lips. "I'll kill him! He will die for this insult!"

Mathew continued holding Zohra, now more out of concern for her than from fear she might harm Khardan. He was right to be alarmed. Her body went suddenly stiff, rigid as a corpse. She stopped breathing.

She was having some sort of fit. Mathew glanced about in desperation, looking for something... anything... Catching sight of a waterskin hanging on the tent pole, he snagged it with a free hand and dashed the liquid into the woman's face.

Zohra caught her breath in shock, sputtering and gasping as the water ran down into her mouth. Half-collapsing, she staggered against the sides of the tent. Mathew went to help her, but—with unexpected strength—she shoved him away.

"Wait! Zohra!" Cursing the confining folds of the caftan that wrapped around his legs, nearly tripping him, Mathew managed to catch hold of the woman's wrist just as she was about to storm out of the tent. "You can't blame Khardan! He didn't know she tried to kill you! You can't expect him to understand. And we can't tell him!"

Zohra came to a stop. She did not turn to look at Mathew, but he knew she was listening to him at least, though her body shook with fury.

"We'll find a way to prove it!" Mathew gasped. "After the battle."

Now she looked at him, her eyes cold.

"How?"

"I—I don't know yet. We'll. . . think of something,"
Mathew muttered. He had never in his life seen any person—
man or woman—so enraged. And now she was suddenly cool
and calm. A moment before she had been fire, now she was ice.
He would never understand these people! Never!

"Yes," Zohra said, lifting her chin, "that is what we will do. We
will prove to him that she is a witch. The Sheykh will order death.
His men will hold her down upon the sand and I will bash her
head in with a rock!"

She'd do it, too, Mathew thought with a shudder. Mopping
chill sweat from his face, he felt his legs give way and sank back
down weakly onto the cushions.

"What was it you came to tell me?" Zohra asked. Seating herself before a mirror, she picked up a bracelet and slid it over her
wrist.

Mathew had to get hold of his scattered thoughts before he
could relate in any sort of coherent fashion the reason for his visit
to her tent this morning.

"I've been working out the symbols in the dream. And I need
to discuss them with you, especially now that it seems there could
be a war."

At the mention of the vision Zohra's hand began to shake.
Hurriedly she lowered the mirror she had been holding. Glancing
back at him with a troubled look, she put her hand to her head,
her brow creased in pain.

"No," she said, her voice suddenly hollow and fear-laden.
"This is not it. I would know. I would feel it inside me—a cold
emptiness." She pressed a clenched fist over her heart. "Like I felt
when I looked into that cursed water. I don't want to talk about
it, Mat-hew. Besides"—she tossed her head, banishing the darkness—"this is not war, not really, though they call it that. It is"—
she shrugged—"a game, nothing more."

"A game?" Mathew gaped. "But. . . then. . . no one will get
hurt? No one will die?"

"Oh, yes, of course," Zohra said, slipping a sparkling ring
onto her finger, admiring the flash of the jewel in the light. "They
will slash each other with their swords and knock each other from
their mounts and some will undoubtedly die, more by accident

than anything else. Perhaps Zeid will prove the stronger. He and his *meharis* will drive our men back to camp. He will gloat over his victory, then return to his homeland. Or perhaps our men will drive him back to his homeland, then they will sit and gloat over their victory. The dead will be proclaimed heroes and songs sung over them. Their brothers will take their wives and children into their households and that will be that."

Mathew only partially heard. He was staring into nothing, seeing again—in his mind—Zohra's description of the vision.

"That's it!" he breathed.

"What?" Startled by the timbre of his voice, she looked up from her jewels.

"The hawks were fighting among themselves! The eagles came at them, diving out of the sky!"

"There, you see?" Zohra cast him a triumphant glance. "When armies fall from the skies, then we can worry. Until that moment"—she turned back to adorning herself with her jewelry—"all this stupid battle means is that we will miss our ride this morning."

The storm drifted resolutely down out of the foothills. Only one person in camp paid any attention to the approaching clouds. Meryem, her hand parting the tent flap, stared at it intently, watching it come nearer and nearer. So preoccupied was she that she did not notice Khardan approach until his hand brushed hers.

Startled, she gave a little scream. Swiftly Khardan slipped inside the tent, and Meryem was in his arms.

"Oh, my beloved!" she whispered, shimmering blue eyes searching his face. "I don't want to you to go!"

What could he do but kiss the trembling lips and brush away the tear that crept down her soft cheek?

"Do not grieve," he said lightly. "This is what we have prayed to Akhran for!"

She stared at him in perplexity.

"But you wanted peace with Sheykh Zeid. . ."

"And we shall have it—after his fat stomach has been relieved of a few pounds." Khardan patted the hilt of his sword. "When he acknowledges us the victor, I intend to offer him the chance to fight together. The chance to raid Kich! What's the matter? I thought you would be pleased."

Meryem's glance had strayed to the storm cloud. Swiftly she looked back at Khardan.

"I—I am afraid," she faltered. "Afraid of losing you!"

She buried her face in his chest. Khardan stroked the golden hair, but there was a note of irritation in his voice when he answered.

"Have you so little faith in my skill as a warrior?"

"Oh, no!" Meryem hastily dried her tears. "I am being a foolish female. Forgive me!"

"Forgive you for being female? Never!" Khardan said I teasingly, kissing the supplicating hands she held up so prettily before her. "I will punish you for it the rest of your life."

The thought of such punishment made Meryem's heart beat so rapidly she feared he might notice and consider it unmaidenly. Hoping the flush staining her cheeks would be taken for confusion and not the immodest desire that swept her body, Meryem hurriedly lowered her head before his intense gaze. Removing a necklace she wore around her throat, she offered it to him timidly.

"What is this?" he asked, taking the object in his hand. "A silver shield," she said. "I want you to wear it. It was. . . my father's, the Sultan's. My mother made it for him, to protect him in battle. Its protection isn't very powerful. But it carries with it my love."

"That is all the power I need!" Khardan whispered, clasping the shield tightly in his hand. He kissed her again, nearly crushing her in his embrace.

With difficulty Meryem caught her breath. "Promise me you will wear it?" she said insistently

"You shall put it on me with your own hands!"

Almost reverently he removed the head-cloth.

Meryem saw the four long scratch marks upon his face and gave a small scream. "What is this?" she asked, reaching out hesitantly to touch them. "You are hurt!"

"Nothing!" Khardan said harshly, averting his face, bowing his head so that she could slip the silken ribbon over his curling black hair. "A tangle with a wildcat, that is all."

Thinking she knew the particular breed of cat, Meryem smiled to herself with pleasure. Wisely saying nothing more, she slid the ribbon over his head, her fingers brushing through his hair. She felt his body tremble at her touch, and she stepped back quickly, her worried glance straying, once again, to the approaching storm.

The ram's horn, bleating loudly, recalled Khardan's attention. "Good-bye, gazelle-eyes!" he said, his face flushed with passion and excitement. "Do not weep! I will be safe!" His hand closed over the silver shield.

"I know you will!" Meryem said with a brave, tearful, secret smile.

CHAPTER 24

Seated astride the magical ebony horse, the Amir looked down from his vantage point on the back of the cloud-shaped 'efreet, watching as the *meharistes* of Sheykh Zeid dashed across the dunes, their swift camels seemingly outpacing the wind. Below him he could see the activity in the camp around the Tel: the men racing for their horses, the women with their children gathered outside their tents, waving their outstretched hands in the air, their shrill voices raised in an eerie war chant to hearten their men.

Gathered around the Amir was a vast army, each soldier mounted upon a steed as magical as his own. Unaccustomed to the height and the strangeness of being carried through the skies on the back of an 'efreet, many of Qannadi's men cast nervous glances beneath them. More than a few faces were pale and sweating, and several—to their eternal shame—leaned over their saddles and were quietly sick. But these were well-disciplined, seasoned troops. They spoke no word. Their eyes upon their captains, who were meeting with the Amir, they waited for the signal that would send them from this black, lightning-fringed cloud to the ground below where they would do what they did best—fight and conquer.

"You have your orders. You know what to do," the Amir said crisply. "The Imam asks me to remind you that you fight to bring the light of Quar to the darkness of the souls of these *kafir*. We fight these men only long enough to show the strength and might of our army. I want to divide them, demoralize them. I don't want them killed!"

The captains answered in the affirmative, but with a distinct lack of enthusiasm.

"Wreck their camp as we did that of the sheepherders earlier this day. Leave the elderly and the infirm behind, unharmed. We don't want them. They are of no use to us. Women of childbearing age and children are to be captured and taken back to the city. They are not to be molested. Any man caught violating a woman will swiftly find himself a place among the palace eunuchs."

The captains nodded. The Amir was always strict in regard to this, as several eunuchs had reason to know to their bitter sorrow. The Amir had performed the operation himself, on the spot, with his own sword. It was not that he was a kindly man. He was simply a good general, having seen in wars in his youth how quickly a well-disciplined army can degenerate into an uncontrollable mob if allowed to slip the leash.

The Amir glared around his troops, letting his threat sink in. Fixing his eyes upon two of his captains, Qannadi continued, speaking to them specifically. "Those of you riding south to attack the Aran, the same orders apply. All captives are to be brought to Kich. Any questions?"

"We don't like this about the men, sir; just leaving them out here. We've heard about these nomads. They fight like ten thousand devils, and they would cut out their own hearts before they'd surrender. Begging the Amir's pardon, but they'll never convert to Quar. Let us kill them and send Him their souls now instead of later."

There were mutterings of agreement. Privately Qannadi sided with his captains. He knew that the nomads would eventually have to be wiped out. Unfortunately the Imam would have to come to see this, too. And right now the only thing those almond eyes—blind with holy zeal—saw was the glory of converting an entire people to the knowledge of the One, True God.

"You have your orders," Qannadi said harshly. "See that they are obeyed. "When the men have been beaten on the field and left to starve, they will receive word that their families are being well-treated in Kich and have found true spiritual solace in Quar." Qannadi was repeating the Imam's words. But those who knew him well saw the slight twist of the man's lip.

"However, if you are attacked," the Amir said slowly and precisely, "there is nothing you can do but kill to defend yourselves."

Nodding, relaxing, the men grinned.

"But when I give the order to withdraw, all fighting is to cease. Take a few prisoners among the men—in particular strong, young ones. Is this understood? Any further questions . . . Fine. The blessing of Quar be with you."

At this point the captains would have responded with a mighty shout, but they had been counseled to keep strict silence and so they disbanded in quiet, each man returning to his command.

"Gasim, a word with you." The Amir gestured to his favorite, the one-eyed captain who had been casting that eye upon the lovely Meryem. Gasim rode up in response to the Amir's command, bringing his horse close alongside that of his commander. "Captain"—the Amir's voice was low—"you know that I put up with this nonsense of taking prisoners to keep the Imam happy. There is one man, however, whose soul must be in Quar's hands this night."

Gasim raised his single eyebrow, the other being concealed behind the patch that covered the empty socket where his eye had been prior to a vicious sword slash. "Name him, my General."

"Their Calif—Khardan. You know him by sight. You saw him at the palace."

"Yes, Amir." Gasim nodded, but Qannadi saw the man appeared uneasy.

"What's the matter?" The Amir's voice grated.

"It is just. . . the Imam said that the Sheykhs and the Calif were to be left alive, to lead their people to the knowledge of the truth of the God. . ." Gasim hesitated.

The Arnir shifted in his saddle and leaned forward, thrusting his chin into Gasim's face. "Whose wrath do you fear most? Mine upon this world or Quar's in the next?"

There could be only one answer to that. Gasim was well acquainted with the Amir's legendary torture chambers.

"Khardan will die!" he said softly, bowing.

"I thought he might," Qannadi returned wryly, sitting back in his saddle. "Bring me his head so that I may know my orders have been carried out. You are dismissed."

The captain saluted and galloped off, the hooves of his horse eerily silent as they beat upon the cloudy chest of the 'efreet.

"You know what you are to do, Kaug?" the Amir asked, looking into the two huge staring eyes among the mist.

"Yes, *Effendi*."

The Amir's gaze returned to the desert beneath him. The

spahis, mounted upon their horses, were galloping out to meet the camel riders—swords flashing in the air, their voices raised in wild shouts.

An odd way to welcome friendly allies, Qannadi thought idly. But what could you expect of these savages?

Lifting his hand, he gave the signal.

CHAPTER 25

Leaving Zohra's tent, Mathew looked up at a swiftly moving, dark-black cloud and saw an army descending from the sky.

At first he could neither speak nor react. Paralyzed with astonishment, he stared, openmouthed. Soldiers—hundreds of them—mounted on winged horses, soared out of the towering thunderhead. They rode in tight formation, spiraling downward like a human cyclone, heading for the ground, heading for the camp around the Tel. The golden ram's head, stitched upon their uniforms, now bore the wings of eagles sprouting from its skull.

Mathew gave a strangled cry. Hearing him shout, Zohra ran from her tent. Several women, standing near him, their eyes on the husbands who were just galloping out of sight, turned to stare at him in alarm. Wordlessly, unable to talk, Mathew pointed. The first riders were just touching the ground, their magical steeds hitting the desert floor at a gallop.

Zohra clutched at her chest, her heart frozen by cold, numbing fear. "The vision!" she gasped. "Soldiers of Quar!"

A fierce wind swept down out of the cloud, raising a stinging, blinding storm of sand that swirled around the camp. Catching hold of tent poles, the wind—like a huge hand—yanked them from the ground and sent them flying, bringing the fabric crashing down upon those inside. Shrieks and wails of terror rose into the air. The winds increased to gale force and the darkness deepened, split occasionally by jagged lightning and deafening cracks of thunder.

Some of the women tried to flee, to escape, running after the *spahis,* who had already disappeared. Blankets, swept along the desert floor by the wind, encircled the legs of their victims, tripping them, bringing them down. It seemed as though all inanimate objects had suddenly come to malevolent life. Brassware, iron pans, and crockery slammed into their former mistresses, knocking them senseless to the ground. Rugs wrapped around their weavers, smothering them.

Then, out of the storm came the soldiers of Quar. They rode through the camp, the storm winds dying swiftly to allow them to do their work. Leaning down, the soldiers grabbed wailing children up in their arms and carried them off. Others dragged the comatose bodies of the women across the saddles and ordered their steeds back to the air.

Not all their prey was easily captured. Although supposedly sheltered and protected in the *harems,* the women of the desert were in reality the same valiant warriors as their husbands and fathers and brothers. The women did not fight for glory but they fought nonetheless—a daily battle, a battle against the elements, a battle to survive.

Badia caught up a broken tent pole and swung it. Smashing against the shoulders of a soldier, it knocked him from his mount. A brass pot, hurled with deadly efficiency by a grandmother with long years of matrimonial bickering behind her, struck a soldier on the back of his head, felling him instantly. A twelve-year-old girl leaped for the bridle of a galloping horse. Catching hold of it, she used her weight to drag the animal off balance as she had seen her father do many times during the *baigha* games. The horse fell, its rider tumbled to the ground. The girl's younger brother and sisters fell upon the soldier, beating him with sticks and pummeling him with their small fists.

But the battle, against overwhelming odds, was a losing one.

The wind blew Mathew off his feet, driving him to his hands and knees. He caught a glimpse of Zohra running back into her tent, then—blinded by the stinging sand—he could see nothing. Fighting the whipping gale, he struggled to stand and saw Zohra emerge, dagger in hand, just as the tent blew down

The tent! Mathew thought instantly of two things: the fish and his magic. Panicked, he turned to see his own tent take wing and flap off like a huge bird, his scrolls and parchments sailing after it. This time the wind inadvertently aided him, for it was at his back as he ran to save his possessions. Lunging after them, he caught what scrolls and parchments he could, searching frantically as he scrambled here and there among the debris for the glass globe, containing the two fish.

A glint of light caught his eye. There was the globe—right beneath the pounding hooves of a galloping horse!

Mathew heard echoing in his ears the cold voice promising what would happen to him if he lost the fish. His heart in his throat, he watched, cringing, as the iron shoes smashed the globe into the ground. The horse's rider, clutching two squirming, screaming children in his arms, thundered past Mathew without a glance. Dazed by the confusion about him, the young wizard was turning away in despair to look for Zohra when the same flash of light caught his attention. Looking down, he saw the glass globe, blown by the wind, rolling toward him.

Numb with shock, Mathew stared at it in disbelief. It was completely unharmed, not even scratched.

"Mat-hew!" He heard a shout behind him. Hastily he picked up the glass globe and, after a quick glimpse to ascertain that the fish were safe and unharmed, thrust it into the bodice of his women's robes.

"Mat-hew!" The shout was a warning.

Whirling, Mathew saw a soldier on horseback reaching out to grab the "woman" and haul her up into the saddle. Reacting with a coolness that astonished him, Mathew caught hold of the soldier's outstretched arm. Bracing himself, he pulled with all his strength, jerking the man from the saddle.

The soldier fell on top of Mathew, carrying them both to the ground. Grappling with the man, Mathew fought to free himself, then he heard a horrifying scream and felt the heavy body on top of his go rigid, then limp, sagging over him. The silken scarves of a *chador* swirled about Mathew's head like a blue and golden cloud. The weight was yanked off him, a hand helped him to his feet. Standing up, Mathew saw Zohra remove her bloodstained dagger from the soldier back.

Her long black hair streaming in the wind, she turned, dagger in hand, ready to face her next foe.

"Zohra!" Mathew shouted desperately above the shrieks and screams, the neighing of horses, the yells and commands, "Zohra, we must find Khardan!"

If she heard him, she paid no attention to him.

Frantically Mathew spun her around to face him. "Khardan!" he screamed.

Seeing a soldier intent on riding them down, Mathew dove

for cover beneath a partially collapsed tent, dragging a struggling Zohra with him.

Though Mathew knew they wouldn't be safe here long, the tent offered some protection and there might be—there *had* to be—time enough to make Zohra understand the danger.

"Listen to me!" Mathew gasped. Crouched in the darkness, he caught hold of the woman by the shoulders. "Think of the vision! We have to find Khardan and convince him to flee!"

"Flee! hah!" Zohra's eyes flamed. She stared at him contemptuously. "Remain here if you want, coward! You will be safe in your women's clothing. Khardan will die fighting, as will I!"

"Then night will come to you and your people!" Mathew cried.

Starting to crawl out the tent, Zohra paused. Outside, hooves thundered about them, the cries of women and children echoed shrilly in their ears.

"Think of the vision, Zohra!" Mathew said urgently. "The falcon pierced by many wounds. Night falling. Or the falcon, wings mired in the mud, struggling to fight with the coming of day!"

Zohra stared at Mathew, but he knew, from the expression on her livid face that her eyes did not see him. They were seeing, once again, the vision. The dagger fell from nerveless fingers. Her hand—covered with the soldier's blood—pressed against her heart.

"I can't ask him to do such a thing! He would despise me forever!"

"We won't ask," Mathew said grimly, searching about for some type of weapon and settling for an iron pot.

Absorbed in his fear, he did not notice the ominous silence that had now settled over the camp, making it possible for them to talk without yelling.

"But how will we find him?"

"Surely your men will turn back, once they know what is happening?"

"Yes!" said Zohra excitedly. "They will come to us and so will Zeid! They will fight together to defeat these foul sons of Quar!"

"Not if the vision is true. Something will happen to separate them. But you're right. Khardan will return to the camp—if he can. Come on!"

Cautiously he emerged from the tent. Zohra crept out after

him. They both halted, staring in shock. The battle was over. The camp was completely destroyed. Tents lay on the ground like dead birds, their fabric rent and shredded by wind, sword, and horses' hooves. Livestock had been ruthlessly butchered. Waterskins lay split open, their precious liquid soaking into the desert sand. There wasn't a thing left, it seemed, that hadn't been broken, smashed, or ripped to shreds.

Those few who had put up a fight had been subdued at last, the soldiers carrying them up into the welcoming arms of the 'efreet, whose huge body shrouded the sky in darkness. Now that the captives were safe, the storm wind began to rise again.

At the edge of the camp, barely visible through the swirling sand, Mathew caught a glimpse of color-rose-pink silk. Staring, he saw a strange sight. A woman with golden hair, her veil having blown from her head, was talking with a soldier on horseback. She was speaking earnestly, angrily it seemed, for she stamped her foot upon the ground and pointed insistently toward the south.

Meryem! How strange, Mathew thought. What is she doing? Why hasn't she tried to escape? Turning to glance in the direction she indicated, Mathew drew a breath.

"Look!" he shouted, peering through the gathering gloom, his eyes gummed with sand. "There they are! There is Khardan! I can see his black horse! Hurry!" He started running. "Or we'll be too late."

A hand caught hold of his arm; nails dug painfully into his flesh. Turning, he saw Zohra gazing bleakly above them. From out of the clouds came another spiral of horses—fresh soldiers riding down to meet the returning nomads.

"I think, Mat-hew, that we are already too late!" she said softly.

CHAPTER 26

Unaware of what was happening in their camp, Sheykhs Majiid and Jaafar led the charge across the desert to meet Zeid. Unaccustomed to riding, Jaafar jounced up and down in the saddle, stirrups flying and there appeared every likelihood that the Sheykh would fall from his mount and break his neck before ever reaching the field of battle. Majiid had tried to persuade the Sheykh to stay behind, but Jaafar—more than half-convinced that this was all some devious plot of Majiid's—had insisted on riding with the leaders, refusing to let his "ally" out of sight. Thus did all the Hrana and the Akar ride into combat—keeping one eye on the enemy in front and the other eye on those who rode at their side.

So occupied were they in warily watching each other that they never thought to look up into the sky that was growing darker and darker by the moment. They might never have noticed it at all had not Jaafar—to the surprise of no one—toppled off his horse to land heavily upon his back in the sand.

The Hrana gathered around him, prepared to stop and assist their fallen leader. Jaafar couldn't talk—the breath had been knocked from his body—but he managed to wave his men on, pointing furiously at Majiid, warning them not to let the *spahis* get ahead of them.

Lying in the sand, gasping for breath, Jaafar had time to contemplate the heavens while Fedj, his djinn, chased after the horse.

"I hope that damn storm breaks before the fighting starts!" the Sheykh growled when Fedj returned, leading the horse and coming to assist his master.

Fedj took hold of his master's hand, glancing up as he was about to haul Jaafar to his feet. The djinn's eyes widened. With a startled cry, he let loose of the Sheykh, who tumbled back down into the sand again.

"Storm!" the djinn shouted. "That is no storm, *sidi!* That is Kaug, Quar's 'efreet!"

"Boo! What would an 'efreet be doing here?" Jaafar peered up into the sky in disbelief.

Suddenly Fedj gasped in horror. "Armies!" he shrieked, pointing behind them. "Armies of men on horseback, attacking our camp!"

Twisting around, Jaafar saw the soldiers, mounted on their magical steeds, flying out of the storm cloud, aiming for the tents below.

"Go to Majiid!" Jaafar ordered the djinn. "Go warn him!"

Within an eyeblink Fedj was gone, and within another he materialized directly in front of Majiid's horse, causing the startled Sheykh to rein in so quickly he nearly upset the animal.

"What do you want?" Majiid roared in anger. "Get out of my way! Return to that clumsy oaf you call a master and tell him to ride a donkey into battle next time!"

"*Effendi!*" cried Fedj. "Our camp is under attack!"

"What fools does Jaafar take us for that we should fall for such a trick?" Khardan demanded furiously, galloping up beside his father. "The enemy is before us, not behind!" He indicated a large cloud of sand through which could now be see the armies of the *meharistes.*

In answer Fedj—his expression grim—simply pointed back at the Tel. Khardan and Majiid reluctantly turned in their saddles.

"*Hazrat* Akhran be with us!" Khardan breathed.

Majiid, his eyes bulging in disbelief, could only sputter, "Who— What?"

"The Amir's soldiers!" Khardan cried. Grasping the reins, he dragged his horse's head around. The black war charger, foundering in the sand, nearly lost its balance. But Khardan's skill kept it upright until it could get its hind legs beneath its body. Leaping forward, it carried its master ahead at a furious gallop.

The other *spahis* milled about in confusion, shouting and pointing and passing the news along to those who were just riding up. One by one they all turned to dash back to camp, several of the unskilled Hrana riders falling from their mounts or upsetting their horses in their excitement.

"Fly to Zeid!" Majiid ordered Fedj. "Tell him the Amir is attacking and that we call upon him in the name of Akhran to help us defend ourselves against the unbeliever!"

"Done!" cried Fedj, disappearing so swiftly that the air spoke the word for him.

But when the djinn reached Zeid, he found the Sheykh already apprised of the situation, having seen for himself the armies descending from the sky.

"So!" snarled Zeid before the djinn could say a word. "What's the matter? Was Khardan afraid that he could not take us on alone? Well, he was right! We will fight both you and your friend the Amir!"

"What do you mean?" Fedj cried. "The Amir is not our friend! Can't you see he is attacking us?"

Consumed with battle rage, Zeid did not hear. The Sheykh was about to urge his camel forward when one of his men shouted and pointed toward the sky. A contingent of soldiers on their winged horses could be seen dropping down out of the thundercloud, flying southward.

"So that's your master's plan, is it?" Zeid cried grimly. "What plan? You don't understand! Listen to me!" Fedj pleaded in desperation.

"Oh, I understand! You lure us up here and then the Amir attacks our defenseless camp while we are gone! Qannadi won't get far! Not even magical winged steeds can outrun the *meharis!*"

Shouting commands, dividing his forces, leaving some to guard his rear, ordering others to lead the charge, Zeid wheeled his camel and prepared to race after the soldiers.

"You brainless goat!" Fedj flew after Zeid. "The Amir isn't our ally! How could you think such a thing? And now you're playing into his hands, letting him divide us up." But Zeid, his face red with fury, refused to listen. Soaring to twenty feet in height, Fedj was prepared to grab hold of the camel with his bare hands and shake some sense into the fat little Sheykh. But he was stopped by Raja, Zeid's djinn, who leaped out of his master's saddlebags.

Soaring to thirty feet in height, his black skin glistening in the sun, his muscles bulging, his eyes blazing in fury, Raja leaped at Fedj. The two djinn fell to the ground, landing with a thud that caused the granite floor to crack beneath them. Howling in rage, Raja and Fedj rolled over and over, hands grappling for each other's throat.

Sheykh Zeid, in the meantime, raced over the dunes, chasing after the winged horsemen, his *meharistes* shouting for the soldiers to come down and fight them like men.

Glancing over his shoulder as he thundered northward toward the Tel, Majiid saw the camel riders turn tail—or so it seemed—and dash off back in the direction of home.

"Ah! Coward!" Pulling back on the reins, Majiid caused his horse to rear on its hind legs, the animal's front hooves slicing the air.

"May your wives mate with camels!" he called after the departing Zeid. "May your sons have four legs and your daughters humps! May you— May you. . ."

Majiid could think of nothing else. Fear for his people choked him. Half blind with tears of anger, he galloped on.

CHAPTER 27

The voice of the 'efreet howled in Khardan's ears, Kaug's breath blew sand into his face. Lightning flared, trying to blind him. Thunder rumbled, shaking the ground beneath his feet. A darkness as of night covered the sun.

Deadly as the diving falcon, Khardan fell upon his prey.

Unfortunately, the Calif had, in his rage, far outridden his men. Alone he smashed into the vanguard of the Amir's troops, attacking them with a fury and a recklessness that caught them completely by surprise. They might well have been facing ten thousand devils, instead of just one man.

The steel talon of his saber ripped into his enemy's flesh. The Rose of the Prophet growing on the Tel was watered with his enemy's blood. On Khardan fought, by himself. His enemies fell before his wrath like wheat to the scythe.

His arms were crimson to the elbow, the hilt of his saber and his hand were gummed with blood and gore so that he could not move his fingers. His horse battled as savagely as its master, lashing out with its sharp hooves, working skillfully to keep its footing on the blood-slick ground.

So fierce was Khardan's attack that his enemies could not get within his guard, though they outnumbered him twenty to one. Time and again they hurled themselves at him, striking with sword and dagger, only to be thrown back. They waited, biding their time, knowing that soon Khardan must grow tired, he must begin to weaken. When the rise and fall of his blade slowed, when they heard his breath begin to whistle in his lungs, his enemies took heart. Surrounding him, they pressed in closely and this time won through.

A sword thrust sliced the Calif's arm, another ripped a bloody gash across his chest. Khardan knew he was hit, but he felt no pain. Grimly he fought on, his horse staggering and plunging in the churned-up sand, its hooves slipping in the brains and mangled flesh beneath its feet.

Then Khardan, battling one foe in front of him, saw—behind him—the flash of a saber. He could not defend himself and knew that this was the end. He would take this last enemy with him, however, and—even as he braced himself for the blow from behind—he cut down the man in front. The blow never came. A cry caused him to glance around. He saw his younger brother Achmed, his sword wet with blood, staring down white-faced at the corpse of the man who had been about to kill Khardan.

"Your left!" Khardan cried out harshly, knowing he must rouse his brother from the shocked daze of his first kill. "Fight, boy, fight!"

Instinctively obeying his brother's voice, Achmed turned, clumsily blocking the soldier's blow. Khardan tried to keep by his brother's side, but a strange feeling was coming over the Calif—a feeling of weariness and exhaustion such as he had never before experienced during the wild madness of battle. He knew he had not taken a serious wound, *yet* he felt life draining from his body. Darkness covered his eyes, taking on an eerie, blood-red tinge. Time itself slowed. Men and horses came into sight, loomed large in his vision. He tried to fight them, but his sword arm suddenly felt as though it were made of lead, holding a weapon of stone.

And then one single figure appeared before him, riding out of the red-tinged mist. It was a captain of the Amir's soldiers, a man with only one eye. Khardan saw death glittering in that eye, but he could do nothing to defend himself; raising his arm took more strength then he possessed. He saw the stroke of the captain's blade, slicing toward his neck, and it seemed to take forever, the flare of the metal cutting a burning swath through the enveloping mist.

Khardan felt no fear, only a fierce anger. He was going to die, helpless as a babe.

The blade hit his throat and stopped, the sword rebounding from his neck as though it had struck a steel collar. He saw the one eye of the captain open wide in astonishment, then the man himself disappeared, falling backward off his horse, sinking into the red-tinged mist with a terrible yell.

Khardan blinked, trying to clear his vision, trying to shake off this awful lethargy. He was like a small child lost and wandering aimlessly in a horror-filled night.

He felt himself slide from the saddle, his body nerveless, unable to support him. He slumped down into the warm sand, closing his eyes, longing for sleep.

"Khardan!" came a voice.

Forcing open heavy eyelids, he looked up and saw a face covered by a rose-pink veil hovering above him in the mists.

"Meryem!" he murmured. He could not think how she came to be here. She was in danger! Frantically, he struggled to rise, to save her!

But he was tired.

So very tired. . .

CHAPTER 28

Puddled in the meager shelter offered by the trunk of a palm tree, Mathew watched the battle raging around the Tel with the curiously detached interest of a spectator witnessing a drama. He couldn't understand his lack of feeling and began to fear that the harshness and cruelty of this land was robbing him of his humanity.

Mathew had one thought, one purpose—to find Khardan. Nothing else mattered. Silently cursing the darkness, the storm-driven wind, and the swirling sand, the young wizard stared into the surging, heaving, struggling mass of men and horses. The sand blowing into his face made his eyes burn painfully. Tears streamed down his cheeks, soaking the veil he had drawn over his mouth to protect himself from inhaling the dust. Angrily, impatiently, he wiped the tears and grit from his eyes and continued to stare into the mob.

Once he thought he saw Khardan and pointed him out to Zohra, who was crouched next to him. But she shook her head emphatically. The man turned his head, and Mathew, sighing, was forced to admit that she was right. The *spahis* in their swirling robes all looked alike to him. He was trying to recall if Khardan had been wearing anything distinctive that morning, such as a red head-rope or perhaps the red leather boots that he sometimes preferred to his black ones. But the morning seemed very far away, lost in a haze of blood and terror. He couldn't remember anything.

The pounding of horse's hooves behind him and a sharp intake of breath from Zohra caused Mathew to whirl about fearfully. One of the soldiers was riding down on them, sword raised. Mathew saw Zohra's hand dart inside the folds of her *chador*, he saw the flash of her dagger. Instinctively Mathew's hand closed around one of his magical scrolls. Scoffing at himself, he let it go. What would he do? Throw a bowl of water in the enemy's face? He needed a wand—something powerful—to work warrior's magic.

The soldier closed on them. Mathew felt Zohra tense, ready to spring, but the man, seeing now that they were females, arrested the downward stroke of his blade.

"Ah, did we forget you, my beauties?" he asked, laughing harshly. His uniform was streaked with blood. "An oversight. Wait here. I will return for you when I have sent a few more souls of your menfolk to Quar."

He rode off. Mathew caught hold of Zohra as she lunged after him. "Stop it! Are you mad?"

"That son of ten thousand swine! Let me go!" Zohra's face was pale and resolute. "This is hopeless, Mat-hew! We will never find Khardan! I am going to go fight with my people!"

"You'll be captured! They won't fight a woman!" "I won't *be* a woman!" Zohra cried fiercely.

Not twenty feet from them lay the body of one of the *spahis,* the wind whipping his robes around him. Zohra's gaze fixed upon the body, and it was easy for Mathew to guess her intent. Stripping the veil from her head, Zohra tossed it to the ground and started forward.

"You'll be killed! And Khardan will be lost and so will your people!" cried Mathew. Pressed against the palm tree's trunk, he was suddenly too afraid to move. He saw the soldier's leering face...

"Then at least the souls of my people will come before Akhran with pride, knowing we have avenged our wrongs," Zohra retorted, clambering over the scrub. Sharp needles stabbed into her gown, rending and tearing it.

Mathew glanced wildly at the battle and then at Zohra, moving farther from him every instant. The horror of the slaughter, the carnage he had witnessed struck him with a bloody fist.

"Zohra!" he shouted desperately. "Don't leave me! Don't leave me alone!"

She stopped then and turned to face him. Her long black hair streamed behind her in the wind, her tattered clothes fluttered around her like the feathers of a bird's wings. Her face was sharp as the hawk's beak, her eyes as dark and deadly as those of any bird of prey.

The contempt in those eyes, staring coldly at Mathew, pierced him to the heart. Without a word, Zohra turned. Fighting the buffeting winds, she headed once more for the body.

Howling darkness overwhelmed Mathew. Falling back against the tree trunk, he stared into the storm, seeing the nightmare begin all over again. The soldier coming for him, dragging him back to Kich. And once in Kich, the man in the white palanquin would find him. . . He began to shake.

"Promenthas!" he gasped. "You spared my life! You brought me to this accursed land for some reason! What for? What for?"

Mathew stared beseechingly into the heavens, but there was no answer. His head lowered in despair. How could he expect it? Promenthas was far away. Mathew was in the land of this savage God, this Wandering God, who cared nothing for anyone, not even for his own people. Mathew twisted around to watch Zohra. The desperate notion of following after her entered his mind—at least he wouldn't die alone—when suddenly Mathew caught a glimpse of rose-pink silk, an astonishing sight amidst the blood and the darkness.

Suddenly everything was clear to him. They weren't the only ones interested in rescuing Khardan!

"Zohra!" Mathew screamed to make himself heard above the noise of the battle. "Zohra!"

She turned her head, clutching back the hair that flew into her eyes. Mathew pointed, yelling wildly.

It was Meryem. Mounted on one of the magical horses, she was heading away from the battlefield, riding back toward the ruined camp. Slung across the front of the saddle was the body of a man, a *spahi* to judge by his robes. The man hung head down, his arms dangling limp. Mathew had no doubt that it was Khardan, and he saw, from Zohra's suddenly rigid stance and intense gaze, that she recognized him as well.

Not knowing what else to do, Mathew began to run after Meryem on foot, more out of desperation than with the hope of catching up with her. His lithe body, toughened by hardship and exercise, gave him more than he had expected, however. A heady excitement, doubly welcome after the debilitating fear, exhilarated him, and it seemed he flew over the hard ground, his feet barely touching it.

Gradually, with a feeling of grim exultation, he realized he was gaining on them.

The battle safely behind her, Meryem slowed when she reached the camp. Checking her horse, she gazed up into the cloud, and raising a wand she held in her hand, she spoke arcane words, causing the wand to flare brightly, illuminating her in a circle of radiant white light.

"Kaug!" she called out. "Extend your hand! Lift us up into the clouds!"

The man she carried across her saddle stirred and moaned.

"The terrible dream will soon be ended, my darling," she murmured, running her hand over Khardan' s body, delighting in the feel of the strong, muscular back beneath her fingers. "A few more moments and we will be far away from this vile place! I will take you to the Imam, beloved. And I will also take with me a most interesting story of how the Amir ordered Gasim to murder you, contrary to the Imam's express command.

"The Amir will deny it, of course." Her fingers lightly touched a pouch she wore around her waist, concealed beneath the flowing, rose-pink silk. "But I have Gasim's dying image, captured within my mirror. I have his final words revealing Qannadi's treachery."

The horse shifted about nervously; a lightning bolt crackled too near.

"Come, Kaug! Get me out of here!" Meryem cried, staring upward impatiently into the cloud and shaking the wand at it.

She saw nothing, however, the 'efreet being occupied with the battle. Irritably biting her nether lip, Meryem sighed. Her eyes turned once more to Khardan.

"It will take more than this, of course, to bring down the Amir," she told him. "But it will be a start. In the meanwhile, beloved"—her hand massaged Khardan's shoulders—"when you awaken, I will tell you how you saved me from the clutches of the murderous Gasim. I will tell you how I pleaded with the soldiers to spare your life and bring us safely to Kich. You will be a prisoner, that is true, but a prisoner whose captivity will be the most pleasant in history! For I will come to you every night, beloved. I will bring you to a knowledge of Quar, and"—she drew a deep breath, her fingers tightening' convulsively—"I will bring you to a knowledge of more worldly pleasures! Your body will be mine, Khardan! You will give your soul to Quar, and together we will rule—"

Too late, Meryem heard the panting breath and light foot-steps. Turning, she caught a glimpse of the white face and red hair of the madman right behind her. She raised the wand, but the madman's hands dragged her from the saddle and hurled her to the ground before there was time for her to recite the spell.

She fell heavily.

Pain shot through her head. . .

"Zohra! There's no time for that now!" Mathew hissed an-grily. Catching hold of Zohra's dagger-wielding hand, he stopped it just above Meryem's breast. "Look at her! She's unconscious! Would you murder her thus?"

"No," said Zohra after a moment's pause. "You are right, Mat-hew. Her death would be quick and easy. I would derive no satis-faction from it. "

Sickened, Mathew turned back to Khardan. "Help me get him down on the ground," he ordered Zohra coldly.

The wind tearing at them, they struggled together to grasp Khardan in their arms and slowly lower him from the back of the horse. Nervously Mathew glanced back at the battle to see if any-one was taking an undue interest in them. But the soldiers were intent upon their fighting, the *spahis* were battling for their lives. Nevertheless, Mathew thought it best that they not call attention to themselves. Reaching out his hand, he touched the horse's bri-dle, and as he had anticipated, the magical beast instantly disap-peared.

"Keep low!' he ordered Zohra, pulling her down next to him.

"What is the matter with Khardan?" Zohra asked, examining him by the fading light of the wand Meryem had dropped upon the ground. Zohra's skilled hands pulled back the bloodsoaked robes from the man's chest with unwonted gentleness. "He is wounded, but not seriously. I have seen him take worse hurts in the *baigha!* Yet he seems on the verge of death!"

"He is under an enchantment. But what's causing it? . . . Ah! Here's the answer." Drawing aside the folds of Khardan's *haik,* Mathew gingerly slipped his hand beneath a small piece of jew-elry the Calif wore around his neck. "Look, Zohra!"

A silver shield beamed with a bright, magical radiance like a small moon.

Sucking in her breath, Zohra stared at it in awe.

"A parting gift from our sorceress," Mathew said coolly with a glance at Meryem. "Quite clever. She can activate the shield with a word. He probably collapsed as though dead. It not only enchanted him, it protected him from harm until she could reach him."

"How do we break the spell?"

Mathew was silent a moment, then he looked up into Zohra's face.

"I'm not certain we want to, Zohra. If Khardan regains consciousness, he will go back and fight and he will die, as the vision foretold. This is our chance to save him."

Zohra stared at Mathew, then turned her gaze to Khardan, lying amid the wreckage of the camp of his people. Blood covered his robes—his own blood and that of his enemies. Lifting her head, Zohra looked back at the Tel.

The storm wind was dying. The battle, too, was ending. The outcome had been obvious from the start. Taken by surprise and completely outnumbered, the *spahis* had fought valiantly, inflamed by the sight of their wrecked homes, their fear for their captive families. Many of Qannadi's soldiers would find a lasting resting place at the foot of the Tel, their bones picked clean by the slavering jaws of the jackals and hyenas who were already prowling the fringes of the battleground.

But the sheer force of the number of the Amir's troops proved impossible for the nomads to overcome. The bodies of many *spahis* lay scattered about the oasis. Some of them were dead. Most were only wounded and unconscious. Qannadi's soldiers had acted on their orders, fighting their foe with the flats of their swords, clubbing them to the ground. Those who had risen up to keep on fighting had been struck down again and again, until they rose no more.

Mathew watched Zohra, his heart aching. He knew what she must be thinking. Khardan would return and he would fight. He would force the Amir's soldiers to fight until he fell, pierced by many swords. . .

Her face deathly white, Zohra faced Mathew. "Where shall we go?"

Why go anywhere? Why not just stay here? The words were on Mathew's lips, then he saw a group of soldiers break off from the main body and begin riding back toward the wrecked camp.

They carried flaming torches in their hands. Leaning down, they touched the brands to the tents, setting them on fire. They were, apparently, leaving nothing behind for the survivors. Others began moving among the wounded, occasionally lifting the unconscious body of a *spahi* onto the backs of their horses, taking them prisoner. Mathew thought he recognized Achmed, Khardan's brother, being dragged into a saddle. The young man's face was covered with blood.

His gaze going hopelessly from one danger to another, Mathew saw—standing on the rim of a dune, silhouetted against the setting sun—a white palanquin!

He is here! He has come for me! Terror clasped Mathew by the throat, suffocating him. The globe of glass pressed against his skin, its icy cold making him shudder.

"Mat-hew! Do you see? The soldiers are burning the camp! What should we do?"

"Why do you look at me?" Mathew gasped, struggling to breathe. He glared at her accusingly. "I don't know anything about this land! All I know is that we must flee! We must escape!"

His eyes were drawn involuntarily to the dune. He blinked, staring. The palanquin was gone! Had it ever been there? Was it his imagination? Or was he crazed with the horror of everything that had happened? Shaking his head, he glanced hurriedly around.

What was left of the tents, the smashed poles, the blankets and cushions, and all the other possessions of the tribes were ablaze. A few old women, left wailing over their losses, raised their fists, shrieking curses. The soldiers ignored them and went about their work.

Mathew began to strip off Khardan's headcloth.

"What are you doing?" Zohra demanded in amazement.

"Hand me her clothes and her veil!" he ordered, tugging at Khardan's black robes with shaking hands. Not stopping his work, keeping one eye on the soldiers, Mathew nodded his head toward the unconscious Meryem.

To his surprise, he heard Zohra chuckle—a deep throaty sound more like the purring of a giant cat than a laugh.

Apparently she approved his plan.

Working swiftly, hidden from sight by the billowing clouds of smoke rolling through the camp, Mathew and Zohra covered

Khardan's bloodstained tunic and trousers in folds of rosepink silk. Avoiding touching the brightly glowing silver shield that hung around the man's neck, Zohra wrapped Meryem's veil about Khardan's head, drawing it up over his mouth and nose, arranging it to hide his beard. While Zohra did this, Mathew hurriedly searched Meryem's unconscious, half-naked body, taking anything he could find that might be magical and hastily stashing it in the folds of his robes. Last, he lifted the now-dark wand from her hand, treating it with the utmost respect, carefully wrapping it in a piece of torn cloth before thrusting it into one of the pouches and hanging it around his waist.

Khardan's body was dead weight when they lifted him, one arm draped over the shoulder of each, his feet dragging on the ground. Mathew staggered beneath the burden. "We can't carry him far!" he grunted.

"We won't have to!" Zohra returned, coughing in the thick smoke. "We will hide in the oasis until the soldiers are gone. Then we can come back to camp."

Mathew wasn't certain he wanted to come back, not until he knew whether the white palanquin had been real or a vision. But he lacked breath to argue. Keeping to the shadows, he and Zohra hurried through the camp, avoiding the light of the burning torches, their own veils wrapped tightly about their heads.

Rounding a blazing tent, they were suddenly confronted by a soldier, who stared at them in the dim light.

"Hey, you women! Stop!"

"Pretend you don't hear!" Zohra muttered. Heads bowed, dragging Khardan between them, they kept walking. The soldier started after them.

"Dog! Where do you think you are going?" came a harsh voice. "Trying to get out of the work?"

"Captain! Look, some women are getting away!"

This is it! Mathew thought. Stabbing pain tore through his shoulders, bowed beneath Khardan's weight. The smoke and the veil were both slowly stifling him. He was on the verge of exhaustion; it took a conscious effort to force his feet to stumble along the ground. No, this would be the end of them. Grimly he waited for the command...

But the captain, absorbed in setting fire to a pile of silken cushions, glanced in the direction of the fleeing women and gave the soldier a look of disgust.

"Look at them! Bent, sickly old hags. If you must risk having yourself turned into a eunuch, do so with one of the young, pretty girls we stole! Now, get back to your post!"

Mathew exchanged relieved glances with Zohra and saw the black eyes—reflecting the flames of the burning village—smile at him in weary triumph.

"We did it, Mat-hew!" she whispered.

The young wizard could not reply; he didn't have the strength.

They were near the edge of camp. A few feet more and they were in the tall, tassel-headed grass that grew thick about the water. Easing Khardan's unconscious body to the wet ground, Mathew and Zohra collapsed beside him, too tired to go farther.

Huddled in the grass, hidden from view of the campsite, they were afraid to move, afraid to speak, almost afraid to breathe. The soldiers milled about the area for hours, it seemed. Smoke from the burning camp drifted over them, and they could hear the groans and cries of the injured echoing in the darkness.

Time passed, and no one discovered them. No one even came in their direction. The dark cloud disappeared, revealing behind it a full moon, hanging like a grinning skull in the dark sky. Khardan remained unconscious, still under the enchantment. Zohra, by the sound of her regular breathing, had fallen asleep.

The veil had been torn from her head, the moonlight shone full upon her. To keep himself from giving way to exhaustion, Mathew concentrated on studying Zohra's face. Beautiful, proud, willful, unyielding, even—it seemed—to sleep itself. Smiling sadly, Mathew sighed. How angry she made him, angry and frustrated. And ashamed. He brushed back a lock of black hair from her eyes and felt her shivering in the chill air. Moving as softly and gently as he could, Mathew put his arm around her and drew her near him. She was too tired to wake. Reacting instinctively to the warmth of his body, she snuggled next to him. The scent of jasmine, faint and sweet, drifted to him over the acrid smell of smoke.

Turning his head, Mathew looked at Zohra's husband. The woman's clothes Khardan wore were caked with mud and filth. Recalling the vision, Mathew's soul shrank in fear. Resolutely he shoved the memory aside.

Khardan was alive. That was all that mattered.

Mathew withdrew the rose-pink veil from Khardan's face.

The enchantment the man was under must be a terrible one. The strong features twisted. Sometimes a stifled groan escaped his lips, the hands twitched and clenched. But Mathew dared not lift the spell, not yet. He thought he could still hear gruff, sharp voices coming from the direction of the camp.

He could do nothing for the Calif but offer silent sympathy and guard his rest—poor guard though he might be. Reaching out slowly, Mathew took hold of Khardan's hand and held it fast.

Mathew closed his eyes, promising to keep them shut just a moment to ease the burning irritation caused by the sand. The irritation was soon gone. His eyes stayed closed. He slept.

CHAPTER 29

Exhausted from his fight with Raja that had—as was usual with fights among the immortal—ended in a draw, Fedj hastened back to the camp, only to find the battle over. Searching the battlefield for his master, the djinn discovered Jaafar lying unconscious on the ground. The unfortunate Sheykh had been the first casualty. Arriving at the field of battle on foot, Jaafar was kicked in the head by a horse and fell over senseless, never drawing his sword.

Making certain his master was still alive, Fedj carried him back to what was left of the camp, then went off in search of other survivors. Hearing a soldier shout about someone's trying to escape, the djinn instantly went to investigate. Three women were taking advantage of the smoke to try to sneak away. It appeared that one of the women was sick or injured, for the other two were carrying her. As he flew forward to help them, the djinn saw the rose-colored veil slip down from I the face of the injured woman.

Fedj stared in shock, too stunned to even make his presence known.

Though partially hidden by the rose-colored veil, the strong, handsome features, the black beard, were easily recognized.

"Khardan!" the djinn muttered in swift anger. "Fleeing the battle disguised as a woman! Wait until my master hears this!"

So saying, he sped back through the air to Jaafar, who was just sitting up, clutching his head, and moaning that he was cursed by the God.

"Effendi," whispered a voice. "I have located her."

A slender hand parted the curtains of the white palanquin "Yes?"

"She is hiding in the tall grass of the oasis. There are two others with her."

"Excellent, Kiber. I will come."

The curtains of the palanquin were drawn back. A man stepped from them. The litter stood concealed behind a huge dune some distance to the east of the Tel. Making less noise than the wind brushing the desert floor, the *goum* and his master walked along the outskirts of the wrecked camp. Neither gave it a glance; both looked to their destination and soon reached the oasis.

Walking swiftly through the grass, Kiber led his master to where three figures slept, huddled together in the mud.

Leaning over them, the slave trader examined them carefully by the bright light of the full moon.

"A black-haired beauty, young and strong. And what is this? The bearded devil who stole the blossom and put me to all this trouble! Truly the God looks down upon us with favor this night, Kiber!"

"Yes, *Effendi!*"

"And here is my blossom with the flame-colored hair. See, Kiber, she wakes at the sound of my voice. Don't be frightened, Blossom. Don't scream. Gag her, Kiber. Cover her mouth. That's right."

The trader drew forth a black jewel and held it over the three figures on the ground.

"In the name of Zhakrin, God of Darkness and All That Is Evil, I command you all—sleep. . ."

The trader waited a moment to make certain the spell had taken.

"Very well, Kiber, you may proceed."

Turning, the trader walked away.

Their task completed at last, the soldiers threw their burning brands into the numerous bonfires blazing around the camp. Springing onto the backs of their magical horses, they soared into the air, flying back to the west toward Kich. Kaug had long ago departed, bearing in his mighty hands the main body of the Amir's troops, the Amir, and all those who had been taken captive.

The desert night was alive with the sounds of death: the crackling of the flames; the wailing of an old woman; the groaning of the wounded; the snarls and vicious snaps of carrion eaters, fighting over the bodies.

The survivors who could stand did what they could for those who could not, dragging the wounded back to the fires that would—at least—keep them warm during the chill night. Tribesman helped rival tribesman—shepherd carrying horseman in his arms, horseman dabbing cool water onto the parched lips of a shepherd. No one had strength enough to bury the dead. The bodies of the nomads were hauled near the fires, thwarting the jackals and hyenas, who howled their frustration and made do by feasting on the corpses of the Amir's soldiers.

Majiid, weary and wounded, looked at the bodies as each was brought in. He recognized here a friend, there a cousin, but never the one for whom he searched in vain. He questioned the men. Were there more dead out there? Had they found everyone? Were they certain?

His men only shook their heads. They knew whom the Sheykh both longed and dreaded to find. They had not seen him. No, as far as they could tell, these were the only ones who had met their deaths.

"But I have his sword!" Majiid cried, holding out Khardan's notched and bloodstained weapon. "I found it on the ground beneath his fallen horse'"

Averting their faces, the men looked away.

"He would not let himself be captured'" Majiid thundered. "He would not have surrendered his sword! You are blind fools! I will go look for myself!"

Torch in hand, ignoring the pain of his wounds—and he had taken several—the Sheykh went to conduct his own search of the area around the Tel.

The carrion eaters snarled at him for disrupting their feasting and slunk away, skulking about in the shadows until he and his fearsome fire had gone. Majiid grimly climbed among the rocks of the Tel, turning over the bodies of the soldiers and the dead horses, peering beneath them, dragging them to one side. Only when he grew too weak and dizzy from loss of blood to stand did he finally admit to himself that he would have to give up, at least for the night.

Sinking to the sand, he looked back on the ruins of the camp, on the smoldering fires, the smoke curling into the starlit sky, the figures of his people—what remained of them—silhouetted against the flames, walking slowly with bowed heads.

Tears came to Majiid's fierce old eyes. Snorting, he fought them back, but the fires blurred in his vision, the bleak hopelessness of despair overcame him. Refusing to give way to such womanly weakness, the old man struggled to rise to his feet. His hand brushed across a cactus, growing in the blood-covered ground.

"Curse you, Akhran!" the old man swore viciously.

"You have brought us to ruin!"

Grasping the cactus, oblivious to the thorns that gouged his flesh, Majiid took hold of the Rose of the Prophet and tried to drag it out of the sandy soil.

The cactus didn't budge.

Time and again Majiid tugged at it, drove his foot into it, hacked at it with his sword.

Stubbornly the cactus refused to yield.

Majiid sank, exhausted, to the ground and stared at the Rose in wonder until the coming of the dawn.

The Paladin of the Night

The Book
of the
Immortals 1

CHAPTER 1

The theories about the creation of the world of Sularin numbered the same as the Gods who kept it in motion. The followers of Benario, God of Thieves, were firm in their belief that their God stole the world from Sul, who had been going to set it as another jewel in the firmament. Uevin's worshipers portrayed Sul as a craftsman, holding calipers and a T square in his hand and spending his spare time considering the nature of the dodecahedron. Quar taught that Sul molded the world from a lump of clay, used the sun to bake it, then bathed it with his tears when he was finished. Akhran told his followers nothing at all. The Wandering God hadn't the least interest in the creation of the world. That it was here and now was enough for him. Consequently each Sheykh had his own view, handed down from great-great-grandfather to great-grandfather to grandfather to father to son. Each Sheykh's view was the right one, all others were wrong, and it was a matter over which blood had been spilled on countless occasions.

In the Emperor's court in Khandar, renowned for advanced thought, learned men and women spent long hours debating the differing theories and even longer hours proving, eventually, that Quar's teachings were undoubtedly the most scientific. Certainly it was the only theory to explain adequately the phenomenon of the Kurdin Sea—an ocean of salt water populated with seagoing fish and completely surrounded on all sides by desert.

The landlocked Kurdin Sea was populated by other things, too; dark and shadowy things that the learned men and women, living in the safety and comfort of the court of Khandar, saw only in their sleep or in fevered delirium. One of these dark things (and not the darkest by any means) was Quar's minion, Kaug.

Three figures, standing on the shore of the sea, were discussing this very subject intently. The figures were not human; no human had ever crossed the Sun's Anvil whose empty dunes surrounded the sea. The three were immortals—not gods, but those who served both gods and humans.

"You're telling me that his dwelling is down there, in *that?*" said a djinn, staring at both the water and his fellow djinn with deep disgust.

The water of the Kurdin Sea was a deep cobalt blue, its color made more vivid and intense by the stark, glaring whiteness of the desert. In the distance, what appeared to be a cloud of smoke was a white smudge against a pale blue sky.

"Yes," replied the younger djinn. "And don't look so amazed, Sond. I told you before we left—"

"You said *on* the Kurdin Sea, Pukah! You never said anything about *in* the Kurdin Sea!"

"Unless Kaug's taken up boating, how could he live *on* the Kurdin Sea?"

"There's an island in the center, you know."

"Galos!" Pukah's eyes opened wide. "From what I've heard of Galos, not even Kaug would dare live on that accursed rock."

"Bah!" Sond sneered. "You've been listening to the *meddah's* stories with ears soaked in *qumiz.*"

"I haven't either! I'm extensively traveled. My former Master—"

"—was a thief and a liar!"

"Don't pay any attention to him, Asrial, my beautiful enchanter," said Pukah, turning his back upon Sond and facing a silver-haired woman clad in white robes, who was looking from one to the other with increasing wonder. "My former master *was* a follower of Benario, but only because that was the religion in which he was raised. What could he do? He didn't want to offend his parents—"

"—by earning an honest living," interposed Sond.

"He was an entertainer at heart, with such a wonderful way with animals—"

"Snake charmer. That was his ploy to get into other people's houses."

"He was not a devout believer! Certainly Benario never blessed him!"

"That's true. He got caught with his hand in the money jar—"

"He was misunderstood!" Pukah shouted.

"When they were through with him, he was missing more than understanding," Sond said dryly, folding his gold-braceleted arms across his bare chest.

Drawing his saber from the green sash at his waist, Pukah rounded on the older djinn. "You and I have been friends for centuries, Sond, but I will not allow you to insult me before the angel I love!"

"We've never been friends, that I knew of," Sond growled, drawing his saber in turn. Steel flashing in the bright sunlight, the two began to circle each other. "And if hearing the truth insults you—"

"What are you two doing?" the angel demanded. "Have you forgotten why we are here? What about your Nedjma?" She glared at Sond. "Last night you shed tears over her cruel fate—being held captive by this evil afright—"

"—'efreet," corrected Sond.

"Whatever it is called in your crude language," Asrial said loftily. "You said you would give your life for her—which, considering you are immortal, doesn't seem to me to be much of a sacrifice. We have spent weary weeks searching the heavens for her and now you quibble about going into the sea!"

"I am of the desert," Sond protested sullenly. "I don't like water. It's cold and wet and slimy."

"You can't really feel anything, you know! We are immortal." Asrial glanced at Pukah coolly from the corner of her blue eyes. "We are above such things as love and physical sensations and other human frailties!"

"Above love?" cried Pukah jealously. "Where did the tears I saw you shedding over your mad master come from, if you have no eyes? If you have no hand, why do you caress his forehead and, for all I know, other parts of his body as well!"

"As for my tears," retorted Asrial angrily, "all know the adage, The drops of rain are the tears the Gods shed over the follies of man—"

"*Hazrat* Akhran goes about with dry eyes, then," Pukah interrupted, laughing.

Asrial pointedly ignored him. "And as for your insinuation that I have had carnal knowledge of my 'protégé'—Mathew is *not* my master and he's *not* mad—your statement is absurd and what I would expect of one who has been living around humans so long he has tricked himself into believing he can feel what they feel—"

"Hush!" said Sond suddenly, cocking his turbaned head to one side.

"What?"

"Shhh!" the djinn hissed urgently. He stared far off into nothing, his gaze abstracted. "My master," he murmured. "He's calling for me."

"Is that all?" Pukah raised his eyes to heaven. "He's called for you before. Let Majiid tie his headcloth himself this morning. "

"No, it is more urgent than that! I think I should attend him!"

"Come now, Sond. Majiid gave you permission to leave. I know you don't want to go swimming, but this is ridiculous—"

"It isn't that! Something's wrong! Something's been wrong ever since we left."

"Bah! If something was wrong, Khardan would be calling for me. He can't get along without me for even the smallest thing, you know." The young djinn heaved the sigh of the vastly overworked. "I rarely have a moment's peace. He begged me to stay, in fact, but I told him that the wishes of *Hazrat* Akhran held preference over those of a human, even my master—"

"And is your master calling for you?" Sond interrupted impatiently.

"No! So you see—"

"I see nothing except a braggart and a buffoon—" Sond fell silent. "That's odd," he said after a moment's pause. "Majiid's calls just ceased."

"There, what did I tell you. The old man pulled his trousers on all by himself—"

"I don't like this," muttered Sond, putting his hand over his breast. "I feel strange—empty and hollow."

"What does he mean?" Asrial drew near Pukah. Slipping her hand into the hand of the djinn, she held onto him tightly. "He looks terrible, Pukah!"

"I know, my dear. I never could understand what women see in him!" said Pukah. Looking down at the small white hand he was holding, the djinn squeezed it teasingly. "A pity you can't feel this—"

Angrily, Asrial snatched her hand away. Spreading her white

wings, she smoothed her robes about her and waded into the water of the cobalt blue sea. Pukah followed instantly, plunging headlong into the sea water with a splash that drenched the angel and sent a school of small fish into a panicked frenzy. "Coming?" he yelled.

"I'll be along," Sond answered softly.

Facing the west, the djinn's eyes scanned the horizon. He saw nothing but blowing sand, heard nothing but the eerie song the dunes sing as they shift and move in their eternal dance with the wind.

Shaking his head, the djinn turned away and slowly entered the Kurdin Sea.

CHAPTER 2

Sinking deeper and deeper into the Kurdin Sea, Asrial tried to appear as nonplussed and casual as if, she were drifting through a clear blue sky in the heavens of Promenthas. Inwardly, however, she was a prey to growing terror. The guardian angel had never encountered a place as fearsome as this.

It wasn't the cold or the wetness that sent shudders through her ethereal body—Asrial had not been around humans nearly as long as either Pukah or Sond and so did not feel these sensations. It was the darkness.

Night steals over the surface of the world like the shadow of an angel's wing and it is just that—a shadow. Night hides objects from our vision and this is what frightens mortals—not the darkness itself, but the unknown lurking beneath it. Night on the world's surface merely affects the sight, however, and mortals have learned to fight back. Light a candle and drive the darkness away. Night above does not affect hearing—the growls of animals, the rustling of trees, the sleepy murmur of the birds are easily detected, perhaps more easily than in daylight, for night seems to sharpen the other senses in return for dimming one.

But the night of the water is different. The darkness of the sea isn't a shadow cast over mortal vision. The sea's night is an entity. It has weight and form and substance. It smothers the breath from the lungs. The sea's night is eternal. The sun's rays cannot pierce it. No candle will light it. The sea's night is alive. Creatures populate the darkness and mortals are the trespassers in their domain.

The sea's night is silent.

The silence, the weight, the aliveness of the darkness pressed in on Asrial. Though she had no need to breathe, she felt herself gasping for breath. Though her immortal vision could see, she wished desperately for light. More than once she caught herself in what appeared to be the act of swimming, as were Sond and Pukah. Asrial did not cleave the water with clean, strong strokes like Sond or flounder through it fishlike, as did Pukah. It was, with her, more as if she sought to push the water aside with her hands, as if she were trying to clear a path for herself.

"You're growing more human all the time," commented Pukah teasingly, bobbing up near her.

"If you mean that I am frightened of this terrible place and want very much to leave, then you are right," Asrial said miserably. Brushing aside the silver hair that floated into her face, she glanced around in dismay. "Surely this must be the dwelling place of Astafas!"

"Asta-who?"

"Astafas, the God who sits opposite Promenthas in the Great Jewel. He is cruel and evil, delighting in suffering and misery. He rules over a world that is dark and terrible. Demons serve him, bringing him human souls on which he feeds."

"That sounds a lot like Kaug, only he eats things more substantial than souls. Why, you're trembling all over! Pukah, you are a swine, a goat," he muttered beneath his breath. "You should never have brought her in the first place." He started to slip his arm comfortingly around the angel, only to discover that her wings were in the way. If he put his arm above where the wings sprouted from her back, it looked as if he were attempting to choke her. Sliding his arm under the wings, he became entangled in the feathers. Finally, in exasperation, he gave up and contented himself with patting her hand soothingly. "I'll take you back up to the surface," he offered. "Sond can deal with Kaug."

"No!" cried Asrial, looking alarmed. "I'm all right. Truly.

"It was wrong of me to complain." She smoothed her silver hair and her white robes and was endeavoring to appear composed and calm when a tentacle snaked out of the darkness and wrapped around her wrist. Asrial jerked her hand away with a smothered shriek. Pukah surged forward.

"A squid. Go on, get out of here! Do we look edible? Stupid fish. There, there, my dearest! It's all right. The creature's gone. . ."

Completely unnerved, Asrial was sobbing, her wings folded tightly about her in a protective, feathered cocoon.

"Sond!" shouted Pukah into the thick darkness. "I'm taking

Asrial to the surface— Sond! Sond? Drat! Where in Sul has he got to? Asrial, my angel, come with me—"

"No!" Asrial's wings parted suddenly. Resolutely, she began floating through the water. "I must stay! I must do this for Mathew! Fish, you said. The fish told me Mathew would die a horrible death. . . unless I came—"

"Fish? What fish?"

"Oh, Pukah!" Asrial halted, staring at the djinn in horror. "I wasn't supposed to tell!"

"Well, you did. 'The sheep is dead', as they say. Might as well eat it as cry over it. You spoke with a fish? How? Where?"

"My protégé carries with him two fish—"

"In the middle of the desert? And you say he isn't mad!"

"No! No! It isn't like that at all! There's something. . . strange"—Asrial shivered—"about these fish. Something magical. They were given to Mathew by a man—a terrible man. The slave trader who took my protege captive. The one who ordered the slaughter of the helpless priests and magi of Promenthas.

"When we came to the city of Kich, the slave trader was stopped outside the city walls by guards, who told him he must give up all his magical objects and sacrifice them to Quar. The slave trader gave up every magic item he had—except for one."

"I've heard of fish that swallowed magic rings, but magic fish?" Pukah appeared highly skeptical. "What do they do? Charm the bait?"

"This is serious, Pukah!" Asrial said softly. "One life has been lost over them already. And my poor Mathew. . ." She covered her face with her hands.

"Pukah, you are a low form of life. A worm, a snake is higher than you." The djinn gazed at the angel remorsefully. "I'm sorry. Go on, Asrial."

"He. . . the slave trader. . . called Mathew over to the white palanquin in which the trader always traveled. He handed my protege a crystal globe decorated on the top and bottom with costly gold work. The globe was filled with water and inside swam two fish—one gold and one black. The trader ordered Mathew to keep them hidden from the guards. There was a poor girl standing there, watching—a slave girl. The trader told Mathew to witness what would happen if he betrayed him and he . . . he murdered the girl, right before Mathew's eyes!"

"Why did he choose Mathew to carry these fish?"

Asrial blushed faintly. "The trader mistook my protégé for a female-"

"Ah, yes," muttered Pukah. "I forgot."

"The guards would not search the women in the caravan not their persons, at least—and so Mathew was able to conceal the fish. The slave trader said that he would take them back when they went into town. But then your master rescued Mathew and carried him away. And with him, the magical fish. . . ."

"How do you know they're magic? What do they do?" Pukah asked dubiously.

"Of course they're magic!" Asrial snapped irritably. "They live encased in a crystal globe that no force on this world can shatter. They do not eat. They are not bothered by heat or cold." Her voice lowered. "And one spoke to me."

"That's nothing," Pukah scoffed. "I've talked to animals. I once shared my basket with a snake who worked for my former master. Quite an amusing fellow. Actually, it was the snake's basket, but he didn't mind a roommate after I convinced—"

"Pukah! This is serious! One fish—the gold one—told me to come with you to find the Lost Immortals. The fish referred to Mathew as the Bearer. . . and she said he was in dreadful danger. In danger of losing not only his life but his soul as well!"

"There, there, my dear. Don't get so upset. When we get back, you must show me these wonderful fish. What else do they— Oh, Sond! Where have you been?"

The elder djinn swam through the murky water, his strong arms cleaving it aside with swift, clean strokes. "I went ahead to Kaug's dwelling, to look around. The 'efreet's gone, apparently. The place is deserted."

"Good!" Pukah rubbed his hands in satisfaction. "Are you certain you want to continue on, Asrial? Yes? Actually, it's well that you are coming with us, beautiful angel, because neither Sond nor I may enter the 'efreet's dwelling without his permission. Now you, on the other hand—"

"Pukah, I need to talk to you." Sond drew the young djinn to the far side of a large outcropping of rock covered with hollow, tubular plants that opened and shut with the flow of the water, looking like hundreds of gasping mouths.

"Well, what is it?"

"Pukah, a strange feeling came over me when I drew near Kaug's dwelling—"

"It's the stuff he cooks for his dinner. I know, I felt it, too. Like your stomach's trying to escape by way of your throat?"

"It's not anything I smelled!" Sond said angrily. "Quit being a fool for once in your life. It's a feeling like. . . like . . . like I *could* enter Kaug's dwelling without his permission. In fact, it seemed as if I was being pulled inside!"

"Pulled inside an 'efreet' s house! Who's the fool here now? Certainly not me!" Pukah appeared amused.

"Bah! I might as well be talking to the seaweed!" Shoving Pukah aside, Sond swam past him, diving down toward the cave on the ocean floor where the 'efreet made his home.

Pukah cast the djinn a scathing glance. "At least the seaweed would provide you an audience on your own mental level! Come on, Asrial." Catching hold of the angel's hand, he led her down to the very bottom of the sea.

Kaug's cave was hollowed out of a cliff of black rock. A light glimmered at the entrance, the eerie luminescence coming from the heads of enthralled sea urchins gloomily awaiting their master's return. The long greenish brown moss that hung from the cliff reminded Asrial of the squid's tentacles.

"I'm going in there alone," whispered the angel, reminding herself of Mathew's plight and trying very hard to be courageous. "I'm going in there." But she didn't move.

Sond, biting his lower lip, stared at Kaug's dwelling as though mesmerized by it.

"On second thought, Asrial," Pukah said in a bland and innocent voice, "I think it might be better if we *did* accompany you."

"Admit it, Pukah! You feel it, don't you!" Sond growled.

"I do not!" Pukah protested loudly. "It's just that I don't think we should let her go in there alone!"

"Come on then," said Sond. "If we're not barred at the threshold, then we know something is wrong!"

The two djinn floated ahead to the entryway of the cave, their skin shimmering green in the ghostly light emanating from the sea urchins, who were staring at them with large, sorrowful eyes. Slowly Asrial swam behind. Her wings fanning the water, she paused, hovering overhead as the djinn stopped—one standing on either side of the entryway. 'Well, go on!" Sond gestured.

"And get a jolt of lightning through my body for breaking the rule. No thank you!" Pukah sniffed scornfully.

"This was your idea!"

"I've changed my mind."

"You're not going to be stopped and you know it. I tell you, we're being invited inside there!"

"Then *you* accept the invitation!"

Glaring at Pukah, Sond cautiously set his foot across the threshold of the 'efreet's dwelling. Cringing, Pukah waited for the blue flash, the crackle, and the painful yelp from Sond, an indication that the established rule among immortals was being violated.

Nothing happened.

Sond stepped across the threshold with ease. Pukah sighed inwardly. Despite what he'd told Sond, he, too, had the distinct feeling that he was being urged to enter the 'efreet's home. No, it was stronger than that. Pukah had the disquieting impression that he *belonged* inside the eerily lit cave.

"What nonsense, Pukah!" Pukah said to himself with scorn. "As if you ever belonged in a place where fish heads are an integral part of the decor!"

Sond was staring at him in grim triumph from the entryway. Ignoring him, Pukah turned to give Asrial his hand. Together, they entered the cave. The angel stayed quite near the djinn. The feathers of her wings brushed against his bare back, and despite his growing sense of uneasiness, Pukah felt his skin tingle and a pleasurable warmth flood his body.

Was Asrial right? he wondered for a moment, standing in the green-tinged darkness, the angel's hand held fast in his. Is this sensation something I've tricked myself into experiencing to become more like humans? Or do I truly enjoy her touch? Leaning near him, looking around but not letting go of his hand, Asrial whispered, "What is it we're searching for?"

"A golden egg," Pukah whispered back.

"I doubt we'll find the egg," Sond muttered unhappily.

"And if we did, my lovely djinniyeh would not be inside. Remember? Kaug said he had taken Nedjma to a place where I would never see her again until I joined her."

"Then what are we doing here?" Pukah demanded. "How

should I know? It was your idea!"

"Me? You were the one who said Kaug was holding Nedjma captive! Now you change your tune—"

The djinn sucked in a furious breath. "I'll change your tune!" Sond laid his hand on the hilt of his sword. "You will sing through a slit in your throat, you—"

"Stop it! Just stop it!" Asrial's tense voice hissed in the darkness. "Now that we're here, it can't hurt to look! Even if we don't find Nedjma, we may find something that would guide us to where this afright has taken her!"

"She's right," said Pukah hastily, backing up and stumbling over a sponge. "We should search this place,"

"Well, we'd better hurry," Sond grumbled. "Kaug may be back any moment. Let's separate."

Repeating Mathew's name over and over to herself to give her courage, Asrial drifted deeper into the cave. Pukah slanted off to the right, while Sond took the left.

"Ugh! I just found one of Kaug's pets!" Rolling over a rock that the 'efreet used for a chair or a table or perhaps just liked to have around, Pukah grimaced as something black and ugly slithered out from underneath. "Or maybe it's a girlfriend." Setting the rock back hastily, he continued on, poking his long nose into a bed of lichen: "Asrial is right you know, Sond. Hazrat Akhran believes that Quar is responsible for the disappearance of the immortals, including his own. If that's true, then Kaug must know where they are,"

"This is hopeless!" Asrial waved her hands helplessly. "There's nothing here but rocks and seaweed." Turning, she suddenly recoiled. "What's that?" She pointed to a huge iron cauldron standing in a recessed area of the cave.

"Kaug's stew pot!" Pukah's nose wrinkled. "Can't you smell it?" The djinn drifted over near the angel. "The place has changed," he admitted. "Last time I was here, there were all sorts of objects sitting about. Now there's nothing. It looks as if the bastard moved out. I think we've searched enough. Sond! Sond? Where are you!"

"But there must be something!" Asrial twisted a lock of her hair around her finger. "The fish said I should come with you! Maybe we could talk to your God. Perhaps he knows something?"

"No, no!" Pukah grew pale at the thought. "That wouldn't be wise. I'm sure if Akhran knew anything He would have informed us. Sond! Sond! I—"

A hoarse, ragged cry came from the inner depths of the cave.

"Sul's eyeballs! What was that?" Pukah felt the hair beneath his turban stand straight up.

"Promenthas be with us!" Asrial breathed.

The terrible cry rose again, swelled to a shriek, then broke off in a choking sob.

"It's Sond!" Pukah sprang forward, overturning rocks, shoving through curtains of floating seaweed. "Sond! Where are you? Did you step on a fish? Is it Kaug? Sond . . ."

Pukah's voice died. Rounding a corner, he came upon the elder djinn standing by himself in a small grotto. Sickly green light, oozing from slimy plants clinging to the walls, was reflected in an object Sond held in his hands. The djinn was staring at it in horror.

"What is it, my friend? What have you found? It looks like—" Pukah gasped. "Akhran have mercy!"

"Why? What's the matter?" Asrial tiptoed into the grotto behind Pukah and peered over his shoulder. "What do you mean scaring us half to death? It's only an old lamp!"

Sond's face was a pale green in the light of the plants. "Only an old lamp!" he repeated in an anguished voice. "It's my lamp! My *chirak!*"

"His what?" Asrial looked at Pukah, who was nearly as green as Sond.

"It is more than a lamp," Pukah said through stiff lips. "It is his dwelling place."

"And look, Pukah," Sond said in a hushed whisper. "Look behind me, at my feet."

"Mine, too?" Though Pukah's lips formed the words, no one could hear them.

Sond nodded silently.

Pukah sank slowly to the cave floor. Reaching out his hand, he took hold of a basket that stood behind Sond. Made of tightly wrapped coils of rattan, the basket was small at the bottom, swelled outward toward the top like the bulb of an onion, and curved back in toward the center. Perched atop it was a woven lid with a jaunty knob. Lovingly drawing the basket close, Pukah stroked its woven coils.

"I don't understand!" Asrial cried in growing fear, looking from one despairing djinn to the other. "All I see is a basket and a lamp! Why are you so upset? What does it mean?"

"It means;" came a deep, booming voice from the front of the cave, "that now *I* am their master!"

CHAPTER 3

$\mathcal{T}$he 'efreet's shadow fell over them, followed by the hulking body of the gigantic immortal. Water streamed from the hairy chest, the 'efreet's pugnacious face was split by a wide grin. "I took your homes several weeks ago, during the Battle at the Tel. A battle your masters lost, by the way. If that old goat, Majiid, is still alive, he now finds himself without a djinn!"

"Still alive? If you have murdered my master, I swear by Akhran that—"

"Sond! Don't! Don't be a—" Pukah bit off his words with a sigh. Too late.

Swelling with rage, Sond soared to ten feet in height. His head smashed into the cave ceiling, sending a shower of rock crashing to the floor below. With a bitter snarl, the djinn hurled himself at Kaug. The 'efreet was unprepared for the suddenness and fury of Sond's attack. The weight of the djinn's body knocked the hulking Kaug off his feet; the two hit the ground with a thud that sent seismic waves along the ocean floor.

Clutching at a rock to keep his balance on the heaving ground, Pukah turned to offer what comfort he could to Asrial, only to find that the angel had vanished.

A huge foot lashed out in Pukah's direction. Crawling up on the rock to be out of the way of the combatants thrashing about around him, Pukah considered the matter, discussing it with himself, whom he considered to be the most intelligent of all parties currently in the room.

"Where has your angel gone, Pukah?"

"Back to Promenthas."

"No, she wouldn't do that."

"You are right, Pukah," said Pukah. "She is much too fond of you to leave you."

"Do you really think so?" asked Pukah rapturously.

"I do indeed!" replied his other self, although his statement lacked a certain ring of conviction.

Pukah almost took himself to task over this, then decided, due to the serious nature of the current crisis, to overlook it.

"What this means is that Asrial is here and in considerable danger. I don't know what Kaug would do if he discovered an angel of Promenthas searching through his underwear."

Pukah glanced at the combatants irritably. The howling and gnarling and gnashing was making it quite difficult for him to carry on a normal conversation. "Ah, ha!" he said suddenly, hopefully, "but perhaps he didn't see her!"

"He heard her voice. He answered her question."

"That's true. Well, she's gone," said Pukah in matter-offact tones. "Perhaps she's just turned invisible, as she used to do when I first caught a glimpse of her in camp. Do you suppose she's powerful enough to hide herself from the eyes of an 'efreet?"

There was no answer. Pukah tried another question. "Does her disappearance make things better or worse for us, my friend?"

"I don't see," came the gloomy response, "how it matters."

Taking this view of the situation himself, Pukah crossed his legs, leaned his elbow on his knee and sat, chin in hand, to wait for the inevitable.

It was not long in coming.

Sond's rage had carried him further in his battle with the 'efreet than anyone could have expected. Once Kaug recovered from his surprise at the sudden attack, however, it was easy for the strong 'efreet to gain the upper hand, and Sond's rage was effectively punched and pummeled out of him.

Now it was the 'efreet who carried the djinn, and soon a battered and bloody Sond was hanging suspended by his feet from the cracked ceiling of the cave. Dangling head down, his arms and legs bound with cords of prickly green vine, the djinn did not give up, but fought against his bonds—struggling wildly until he began to revolve at the end of his tether.

"I wouldn't do that, Sond," advised Pukah from his seat on the rock. "If you do free yourself, you will only come down on your head and you should certainly take care of what brains you have."

"You could have helped, you bastard son of Sul!" Sond

writhed and twisted. Blood and saliva dripped from his mouth.

Pukah was shocked. "I would not think of attacking our new master!" he said rebukingly.

Turning from admiring his handiwork, Kaug eyed the young djinn suspiciously. "Such loyalty, little Pukah. I'm touched."

Sliding down from his rock, the young djinn prostrated himself on the cave floor before the 'efreet, his head brushing the ground.

"This is the law of the immortals who serve upon the mortal plane," recited Pukah in a nasal tone, his nose pressed flat against the floor. "Whosoever shall acquire the physical object to which the immortal is bound shall henceforth become the master of said immortal and shall be due all allegiance and loyalty."

Sond shrieked something vile, having to do with Pukah's mother and a male goat.

Pukah appeared pained. "I fear these interruptions annoy you, My Master. If I may be allowed—"

"Certainly!" Kaug waved a negligent hand. The 'efreet appeared preoccupied; his gaze darting here and there about the grotto.

Believing he knew the quarry the 'efreet was hunting, Pukah thought it best to distract him. He picked up a handful of seaweed, grabbed hold of Sond by his turban, and stuffed the pale green plant into the djinn's yammering mouth.

"His offensive outbursts will no longer disturb you, My Master!" Pukah threw himself on his knees before the 'efreet.

"Allegiance and loyalty, eh, little Pukah?" said Kaug. Stroking his chin, he regarded the djinn thoughtfully. "Then my first command to you is to tell me why you are here."

"We were drawn here, Master, by the physical objects to which we are bound according to the law that states—"

"Yes, yes," said Kaug irritably, casting another searching glance around the cave once more. "So you came here because you couldn't help yourself. You are lying to your master, little Pukah, and that is quite against the rules. You must be punished." Lashing out with his foot, the 'efreet kicked Pukah under the chin, snapping the djinn's head back painfully and splitting his lip.

"The truth. You came here in search of Nedjma. And the third member of your party. What was her reason for coming?"

"I assure you, Master," said Pukah, wiping blood from his

mouth, "there were only the two of us—"

Kaug kicked him in the face again.

"Come, come, loyal little Pukah! Where may I find the lovely body belonging to that charming voice I heard when I entered my dwelling this night?"

"Alas, My Master, you see before you the only bodies belonging to the only voices you heard in your dwelling place. It depends upon your taste, of course, but I consider my body the loveliest of the two—"

Nonchalantly, Kaug drove his foot into the young djinn's kidney. Real or imaginary, the pain was intense. Pukah doubled up with a groan.

"I heard a voice—a female voice, little Pukah!"

"I have been told I have a most melodious ring to my-ughh!"

Kaug kicked the djinn in the other kidney. The force of the blow rolled Pukah over on his back. Drawing his sword, the 'efreet straddled the young djinn, his weapon poised above a most vital and vulnerable area on Pukah's body.

"So, little Pukah, you claim the female voice was yours. It will be, my friend, if you do not tell me the truth and reveal the whereabouts of this trespasser!"

Covering himself with his hands, Pukah gazed up at the enraged 'efreet with pleading eyes. "O My Master! Have mercy, I beg of you! You are distressed by the unwarranted attack on your person by one who should, by rights, be your slave"—a muffied shriek from Sond—"and that has thrown a cog (ha, ha, small joke) in the wheel of your usually brilliant thought process! Look around, Great Kaug! Could anyone or anything remain hidden from your all-seeing gaze, O Mighty Servant of the Most Holy Quar?"

This question stumped the 'efreet. If he said yes, he admitted he wasn't all-seeing, and if he said no, he granted that Pukah was right and that he—Kaug—hadn't really heard the strange voice after all. The 'efreet sent his piercing gaze into all parts of the cave, dissecting every shadow, using all his senses to detect a hidden presence in the dwelling.

Kaug felt a thrill in his nerve endings, as if someone had touched his skin with a feather. There *was* another being in his cave, someone who had the ability to enter his dwelling without permission, someone who was able to hide herself from his sight. A film of white mist blocked his vision. Kaug rubbed his eyes, but that did nothing to dispel the odd sensation.

What should he do? Castrate Pukah? The 'efreet pondered. Other than providing a bit of mild amusement, it would probably accomplish little else. Such an act of violence might actually frighten the creature into disappearing completely. No, she must be lulled into a sense of well-being.

I will give Pukah the hemp and watch him weave the rope that will go around his neck, said Kaug to himself. Aloud, he intoned, "You are right, little Pukah. I must have been imagining things." Sheathing his sword, the 'efreet kindly helped the djinn to his feet. Kaug wiped slime from Pukah's shoulder and solicitously plucked fronds of seaweed from the djinn's *pantalons*. "Forgive me. I have a quick temper. A failing of mine, I admit. Sond's attempt on my life upset me." The 'efreet pressed his hand over his huge chest. "It wounded me deeply, in fact, especially after all the trouble I went to in order to rescue both of you."

"Sond is a beast!" cried Pukah, casting Sond an indignant glance and congratulating himself on his cleverness. The young djinn's sharp ears pricked. "Uh, what do you mean. . . rescue us? If it's not asking too much of you in your weakened condition to explain, Most Beneficent and Long-Suffering Master."

"No, no. I'm just exhausted, that's all. And my head is spinning. If I could just sit down. . ."

"Certainly, Master. You do seem pale, sort of chartreuse. Lean on me."

Kaug draped his massive arm over Pukah's slender shoulder. Groaning, the young djinn staggered beneath the weight.

"Where to, Master?" he gasped.

"My favorite chair," said Kaug with a weak gesture. "Over there, near my cooking pot."

"Yes, Master," Pukah said with more spirit than breath left in his body. By the time the two reached the huge sponge that the 'efreet indicated, the young djinn was practically walking on his knees. Kaug sank into his chair.

Pukah, suppressing a groan, slumped down on the floor at his feet. Sond had lapsed into silence, whether in order to hear better or because he was unconscious the young djinn didn't know and, at this point, didn't care.

"You were not present at the battle that took place around the Tel, were you, little Pukah?" said Kaug, settling his massive body in his chair. Leaning back, he regarded the young djinn with a mild-eyed gaze.

"You mean the battle between Sheykhs Majiid and Jaafar and Zeid?" questioned Pukah uneasily.

"No," said Kaug, shaking his head. "There was no battle between the tribes of the desert."

"There wasn't?" Pukah appeared much amazed, then recovered himself. "Ah, of course, there wasn't! Why should there be? After all, we are all brothers in the spirit of Akhran—"

"I mean the battle between the tribes of the desert and the armies of the Amir of Kich," continued Kaug coolly. Pausing a moment, the 'efreet added, "Your mouth is working, little Pukah, but I hear nothing coming out of it. I didn't accidentally hit something vital, did I?"

Shaking his head, Pukah found his voice, somewhere down around his ankles. "My. . . my master and the. . . the armies of—"

"Former master," amended Kaug.

"Certainly. Former m-master," Pukah stammered. "Forgive me, noble Kaug." Prostrating himself, he hid his burning face against the floor.

The 'efreet smiled and settled himself more comfortably in his spongy soft chair. "The outcome of the battle was never in question. Riding their magical steeds, the troops of the Amir easily defeated your puny desert fighters."

"Were. . . were all . . . killed?" Pukah could barely force himself to say the word.

"Killed? No. The objective of the Imam was to bring as many living souls to Quar as possible. The orders of the Amir, therefore, were to capture, not kill. The young women and children we brought to Kich to learn the ways of the One, True God. The old people we left in the desert, for they can be of no use to us in building the new world Quar is destined to rule. Your master and his *spahis* we left there, also. Soon, bereft of their families, broken in spirit, weak in body, they will come to us and bow before Quar."

A strangled sound from Sond was expressive of defiance.

Kaug gazed at the elder djinn sadly. "Ah, he will never learn gratitude, that one. You are intelligent, Pukah. The winds of heaven have switched direction. They blow, not from the desert, but from the city. The time of Akhran is dwindling. Long did Majiid call for his djinn to come to his aid, but there was no answer."

Glancing through his fingers at Sond, Pukah saw that the older djinn had ceased struggling. Tears flowed from Sond's eyes, dripping into the puddles of sea water on the floor beneath him. Pukah turned his head from the distressing sight.

"The Sheykh's faith in his God is beginning to weaken. His djinn will not come at his command. His wife and children were taken captive. His eldest son—the light of his eyes—is missing and all assume him to be dead—"

Pukah lifted a strained face. "Khardan? Dead?"

"Isn't he?" Kaug's eyes stabbed at him.

"Don't you know?" Pukah parried the thrust.

They stared at one another, mental swords clashing, then Kaug—falling back—shrugged. "The body was not discovered, but that means little. It is probably in the belly of a hyena—a fitting end to a wild dog."

Lowering his head again, Pukah endeavored to gather up his widely scattered wits. "It *must* be true! Khardan must be dead! Otherwise, he would have called on me to come to his aid!"

"What are you mumbling about, little Pukah?" Kaug nudged the djinn with his foot.

"I was. . . er . . . remarking to myself that I am most fortunate to be your slave—"

"Indeed you are, little Pukah. The Amir's men were going to burn your basket and sell that lamp but I—recognizing them as the dwellings of fellow immortals—was quick to rescue you both. Only to be set upon in my own home—" The 'efreet glowered at Sond.

"Forgive him, Master. He thinks with his pectorals." Where is Asrial? Pukah wondered. Much like Kaug, he was darting glances here and there in an effort to locate her. Has she heard? A sudden thought occurred to him. If she has, she must be frantic with worry.

"I—I don't suppose, Kind Kaug, that you could reveal to me the fate of my mast—former master's—wives?" Pukah asked warily.

"Why do you want to know, little Pukah?" Kaug yawned.

"Because I pity those who must try to console them for the

loss of such a husband," Pukah said, sitting back on his heels and regarding the 'efreet with a face as bland as a pan of goat's milk. "The Calif was deeply in love with his wives and they with him. Their sorrow at his loss must be terrible to witness."

"Now, as a matter of fact, it is a great coincidence, but Khardan's two wives have disappeared as well," Kaug said. Leaning back in his chair, the 'efreet regarded Pukah through narrowed eyelids.

It may have been his overwrought imagination, but Pukah thought he heard a smothered cry at this. The 'efreet's eyes opened suddenly. "What was that?" Kaug glanced about the cave.

"Sond! Moan more quietly! You disturb the Master!" Pukah ordered, leaping to his feet. "Allow me to deal with him, O Mighty 'Efreet. You rest."

Kaug obediently leaned back and shut his eyes. He could sense Pukah hovering over him, staring at him intently. Then he heard the djinn padding away on his bare feet, hastening toward Sond. The 'efreet heard something else, too—another grieving moan. Opening his eyes a slit, he saw a most interesting sight. Pukah had tucked his hands beneath his armpits and was flapping his elbows frantically.

Sond stared at him, bewildered, then suddenly took the hint—for that's what it obviously was—and began to groan loudly.

"What do you mean by that dismal howling?" Pukah shouted. "My Master is in enough pain as it is. Shut up this instant!" Whirling about to face the 'efreet, Pukah grabbed hold of a largish rock. "Allow me to knock him senseless, My Master!"

"No, that will not be necessary," Kaug muttered, shifting in his chair. "I will deal with him myself."

Pukah flapping his arms. Pukah with wings? The trail had taken an unusual turn and the 'efreet, in trying to follow the path, had the distinct impression he'd become lost en route. He knew he was getting somewhere, but he needed time to find his way.

"Sond, I confine you to your *chirak*!" The 'efreet snapped his fingers and the djinn's body slowly began to dissolve, changing to smoke. The smoke wavered in the air; two eyes could be seen, fixed in malevolent fury on Kaug. A simple gesture from the 'efreet caused the lamp to suck the smoke out of the air, and Sond was gone.

"And what is your will concerning me, My Master?" Pukah asked humbly, bowing low, his hands pressed against his forehead.

"Return to your dwelling. Remain there until I call for you," Kaug said absently, preoccupied with his thoughts. "I am going to pay my homage to Quar."

"A safe and pleasant journey, Master," said Pukah. Bowing his way across the floor, the djinn retired precipitously to his basket.

"Ugggh," grunted Kaug, heaving his bulk up out of the chair.

"Ugggh," Pukah mimicked, his ears attuned to ascertain the 'efreet's departure. "One of his more intelligent noises. The great oaf! Pukah, my friend, you've fooled him completely. He has neglected to confine you to your dwelling, and while he is gone, you may leave it to search for your lost angel."

Materializing inside his basket, Pukah found it in a state of general disarray—the furniture overturned, crockery smashed, food scattered about. Having previously shared his dwelling with a snake, who had not been very neat in his personal habits, the djinn was accustomed to a certain amount of slovenliness. Ignoring the mess, Pukah set the bed to rights, then lay down on it and waited, listening intently, to make certain the 'efreet had really gone and that this wasn't some sort of lamebrained trick to trap him.

Hearing nothing, Pukah was just about to leave his basket and go search the cave when he was nearly suffocated by a flurry of feathers. Silver hair obscured his vision and a warm, soft body hurled itself into his arms.

"Oh, Pukah!" Asrial cried, clutching at him frantically. "My poor Mathew! I have to find him! You must help me escape!"

CHAPTER 4

"This would seem to indicate that their Calif, this Khardan, is not dead," Quar mused.

Kaug found the God taking a stroll in His pleasure garden, Quar's mind occupied with the march of the Amir's army south. This *jihad* was a weighty matter, so much to do; making certain the weather was perfect, preventing rain so that the baggage trains did not founder in the mud; forcing disease's deadly hand away from His troops; keeping the magic of Sul flowing into the horses, and a hundred other worries. Quar had frowned at Kaug's interruption but, since the 'efreet insisted it was important, magnanimously agreed to listen.

"That is what I think as well, O Holy One," said the 'efreet, bowing to indicate he was sensible of the honor of sharing like beliefs with his God. "The djinn, Pukah, has the brains of a mongrel, but even a dog knows when its master is dead and the news came as a complete surprise to Khardan's lackey."

"And this you tell me about the wives. It is certainly mysterious," Quar said offhandedly, sinking his white, perfectly shaped teeth into the golden skin of a kumquat. "What do you make of it?" A speck of juice dripped onto the costly silk robes. Irritably, the God dabbed at it with a linen napkin.

"Pukah brought up the matter, Magnificent One. When I asked him why he was interested, he lied, telling me that Khardan cared deeply for his wives. We know from the woman, Meryem, that the Calif hated his head wife and that his second wife was a madman."

"Mmmmm." Quar appeared entirely absorbed with removing the stain from his clothing.

"It was when I mentioned that the wives had disappeared that I heard the strange sound—as of someone stricken with grief, Holy One. I am convinced that there is someone else present in my dwelling." Kaug scowled, his brow furrowed in thought. "Someone with wings. . ."

Quar had been just about to take another bite of the fruit. His hand stopped midway to his mouth. "Wings?" he repeated softly.

"Yes, Holy One." Kaug described Pukah's peculiar behavior and Sond's reaction.

"Promenthas!" murmured Quar softly. "Angels in company with djinn of Akhran! So the Gods are fighting me on the immortal plane as well!"

"What is it you say, Holy One?" Kaug drew nearer.

"I said this strange winged intruder has probably taken advantage of your leaving and fled," Quar said coldly.

"Impossible, My Lord. I sealed my dwelling before I departed. I thought I should lose no time in bringing you this information," the 'efreet added deprecatingly.

"I do not see why you are so concerned with this Khardan!" said Quar, plucking another kumquat. "All my people have become obsessed with him! The Imam wants his soul. The Amir wants his head. Meryem wants his body. This Calif is human, nothing more—the blind follower of a dying God."

"He could be a threat—"

"Only if you make him one!" Quar rebuked sternly. Kaug bowed. "And what are your instructions concerning the djinn, My Lord?"

Quar waved a delicate hand. "Do what you want. Keep them as your slaves. Send them where we send the others. It matters little to me."

"And the mysterious third party—"

"You have more important things to occupy your time, Kaug, such as the upcoming battles in the south. However, I give you leave to solve your little mystery, if you like."

"And would my Lord be interested in the outcome?"

"Perhaps some day, when I am bored with other foolishness, you may share it with me," Quar said, indicating with a cool nod that the 'efreet's presence was no longer wanted.

The 'efreet, bowing again, evaporated into the blossom-scented air.

As soon as Kaug was gone, Quar disgarded the semblence of

negligence that he wore in the presence of the powerful 'efreet. Hastening back into his sumptuous dwelling, he entered a Temple, whose exact duplicate could be found in the world below, in the city of Kich. The God lifted a mallet and struck a small gong three times.

A wasted face appeared in Quar's mind, its eyes burning with holy ecstasy. "You have summoned me, *Hazrat* Quar?"

"Imam, among the people of the desert we captured must be some who are related to this Khardan, their Calif."

"I believe there are, Holy One. His mother and a half-brother . . . or so I am told."

"I want information regarding this man, this Calif. Attain it any way possible. It would be ideal, of course, if you could convert one or both to the true faith."

"I hope to convert all the desert nomads, Holy One."

"Excellent, Imam."

Feisal's face disappeared from Quar's sight.

Settling back on a silk brocade sofa, Quar noted that he still held the kumquat in his hand. Regarding it with complacence, he slowly closed his fist upon it and began to squeeze. The skin ruptured, the juice flowed over his fingers. When the fruit was reduced to an unrecognizable pulp, the God tossed it casually away.

CHAPTER 5

We must escape! We must get out of here, Pukah!" Asrial cried distractedly. "That terrible monster is right. Mathew has disappeared! I searched for his being in my mind and could not see him! A darkness shrouds him, hiding him from my sight. Some dreadful thing has happened to him!"

"There, there," murmured Pukah, too dazzled and confused to know what he was saying. The beautiful creature appearing out of nowhere, her soft hands clinging to him, her fragrance, her warmth. The djinn had just presence of mind enough to take hold of the soft hand and draw the angel down with him upon the bed.

"Let's relax and think about this calmly." Pukah brought his lips near the smooth cheek. How did one manage about the wings? They were bound to be in the way...

"Oh, Pukah!" Asrial sobbed miserably, lowering her head. Pukah found himself kissing a mass of wet, silver hair. "It's all my fault! I should never have left him!"

Putting one arm around her waist (sliding it under the wings), Pukah held Asrial nearer. "You had no choice, my enchanter!" he whispered, brushing aside the hair. "The fish told you to come." His lips brushed her fevered skin.

"What if it was a trick?!" Asrial sprang to her feet with such energy that her wings swept Pukah off the bed. "It could have been a ploy of Astafas's, an attempt for that Lord of Darkness to steal Mathew's soul! Oh, why didn't I think of this before?! And your master, Khardan. He must be with Mathew. He is undoubtedly in danger, too. Let's leave, Pukah, quickly!"

"We can't," said the djinn, picking himself up off the bottom of the basket.

"Why not?" Asrial stared at him, startled.

"Because"—Pukah, sighing, sat down upon the bed—"Kaug sealed the cave before he left."

"How do you know?"

Pukah shrugged. "See for yourself. Try going back out into the ocean again."

Asrial closed her eyes, her lips moved, her wings waved gently. Her eyes flew open, she looked about eagerly and her face crumpled in disappointment. "I'm still here!"

"Told you," said Pukah, lounging back on the bed. Reaching out, he patted a place beside him. "Come, beloved. Rest yourself. Who knows how long Kaug will be gone? We're trapped here together. We might as well make the best of it."

"I—I think I would prefer a chair," said Asrial. Her face flushing rosy red, she glanced about the djinn's dwelling in search of an article of furniture that was not smashed, missing a leg, or most of the stuffing.

"Not a whole piece of furniture in the place except the bed, I'm afraid," said Pukah cheerfully. He owed Kaug one. Two in fact. "Come, Asrial. Let me comfort you, distract your sorrowful thoughts, take your mind from your trouble."

"And how will you do that, Pukah?" Asrial asked coolly, the flush subsiding from her cheeks. "If I am not mistaken, you are attempting to seduce me, to . . . make love to me. That's completely ridiculous! We do not have bodies. We can't feel physical pleasure!"

"Tell me I didn't feel this!" Pukah said grimly, pointing to his swollen lip. "Tell Sond he didn't feel that drubbing he took!" Climbing out of bed, the djinn approached the angel, hands outstretched. "Tell me I'm not feeling what I feel now—my heart racing, my blood burning—"

"Sond didn't!" Asrial faltered, taking a step backward. "You don't! You've just tricked yourself—"

"Tell me you don't feel this!" Grabbing the angel around the waist, Pukah pressed her body close to his and kissed her.

"I . . . I didn't . . . feel a thing!" gasped Asrial angrily when she could breathe. Struggling, she tried to push Pukah away. "I—"

"Hush!" The djinn put his hand over her mouth.

Furious, Asrial clenched her fists and started to beat on the djinn's chest. Then she, too, heard the sound. Her eyes widening in fear, she went limp in Pukah's arms.

"Kaug's back!" whispered the djinn. "I've got to go!" Pukah vanished so suddenly that Asrial, bereft of his support, nearly fell. Weakly, she sank down on the bed and crouched there, shivering, listening to what was happening outside the basket.

Slowly, unconsciously, her tongue moved across her lips as though she could still taste a lingering sweetness.

"Master!" cried Pukah in a transport of joy. "You've returned!" He flung himself on the cave floor.

"Humpf," growled Kaug, glowering at the groveling djinn. "He doesn't pull the wool over my eyes!"

"Indeed, such a thing would take a great many sheep, Master," said Pukah, cautiously rising to his feet and padding after the 'efreet, who was stomping about the cave angrily.

"He fears Khardan!"

"Does he, Master?"

"Not because your former master is mighty or powerful, but because Quar can't rule him and, seemingly, he can't kill him."

"So my master—former master—is not dead?"

"Is that a great surprise to you, little Pukah? No, I thought not. Nor to your winged friend, either, eh?"

"Unless Sond has sprouted feathers, I have no idea to whom my Master is referring." Pukah prostrated himself, upon the floor, extending his arms out in front of him. "I assure my Master of my absolute loyalty. I would do anything for my Master, even go in search of the Calif, if my Master commands it."

"Would you, Pukah?" Kaug, turning, eyed the djinn intently.

"Nothing would give me greater pleasure, My Master."

"I believe that for once you are telling the truth, little Pukah." The 'efreet grinned. "Yes, I think I will take you up on your offer, slave of the basket. You understand who it is you serve now, don't you, Pukah? By the laws of the djinn, I am your master, you are my servant. If I ordered you to bring Khardan sliced neatly into four equal parts, you would do so, would you not, slave?"

"Of course, My Master," said Pukah glibly.

"Ah, already I can see your mind turning, planning to find some way out of this. Let it turn all it wants, little Pukah. It is like a donkey tied to the waterwheel. Round and round he goes, never getting anywhere. I have your basket. I am your master. Do not forget that or the penalty if you disobey me."

"Yes, My Master," said Pukah in a subdued voice.

"And now, to prove your loyalty, little Pukah, I am going to send you on an errand before you go and search for the missing Khardan. I command you to take the *chirak* of Sond to a certain location. You will leave it there and you will return to me for my orders concerning the Calif."

"Where is this 'certain location,' My Master?"

"Not backing out already, little Pukah, are you?"

"Certainly not, My Master! It is just that I need to know where I am going in order to get there, you dundering squidhead." This last being muttered under Pukah's breath.

"Despite his harsh treatment of me, I am going to grant Sond his heart's wish. I am going to reunite him with his beloved Nedjma. You wanted to know where the Lost Immortals were, little Pukah?"

"I assure my Master that I have not the slightest interest—"

"Take the lamp of Sond and fly with it to the city of Serinda and you will discover what has become of the Vanished Ones."

"Serinda?" Pukah's eyes opened wide; he raised his head from the floor. "That city no longer exists, My Master. It vanished beneath the desert sands hundreds of years ago, so long past that I cannot even remember it."

Kaug shrugged. "Then I am asking you to deliver Sond's *chirak* to a dead city, little Pukah. Do you question my commands already?" The 'efreet's brow creased in a frown.

"No, Master!" Pukah flattened himself completely. "The wings of which you speak are on my feet. I will return to my dwelling—"

"No need to rush, little Pukah. I want you to take some time to look around this interesting city. For—if you fail me, djinn—your basket will find itself sitting in Serinda's marketplace."

"Yes, My Master. Now I'll just be getting back to my dwelling—"

"Not so fast. You must wear this." A black, three-sided rock attached to a leather thong appeared in the 'efreet's hand. "Sit up." Pukah did as he was ordered and Kaug cast the thong around the djinn's neck. The rock—which came to a point at the top like a small pyramid—thumped against Pukah's bare chest. Pukah regarded it dubiously.

"It is kind of you to give me this gift, Master. What is this interesting looking stone, if I might ask?"

"Black tourmaline."

"Ah, black tourmaline," said Pukah wisely. "Whatever this is," he muttered.

"What did you say?"

"I will keep it always, Master, to remind me of you. It's ugly enough."

"You must learn to speak up, little Pukah."

"I was saying that if you don't need me, I will return to my dwelling and put this marvelous object somewhere safe—"

"No, no! You will wear it at all times, little Pukah. Such is my wish. Now, be gone!"

"Yes, Master," Rising to his feet, Pukah headed for his basket.

"What are you doing?" Kaug growled.

Pukah stopped, glancing over his shoulder. "I am returning to my dwelling, O Mighty Master,"

"Why? I told you to take Sond's lamp and leave."

"And so I will, Master," said Pukah firmly, "after I have made myself presentable. These"—he indicated his *pantalons*—"are stained with blood and slime. You would not want me appearing before your friends in such a state, Master. Think how it would reflect upon you!"

"I have no friends where you are going, little Pukah," Kaug said with a grim smile. "And believe me, in Serinda, no one will remark on a few spots of blood."

"Sounds like a cheerful place," Pukah reflected gloomily. "Then I am not going to my dwelling. I am just going over to pick up Sond's lamp, Master," the djinn said loudly, sidling nearer and nearer his basket. "The floor of this cave is extremely wet. I hope I don't slip and fall— Ooops!"

The djinn sprawled headlong on the floor, knocking over the basket. As it hit the ground, the lid flew off and Pukah made a desperate attempt to slip inside, but Kaug was there ahead of him. Grabbing the lid, the 'efreet slammed it on top of the basket and held it there firmly with his huge hand.

"I hope you have not hurt yourself, little Pukah?" the 'efreet said solicitously.

"No, thank you, Master." Pukah gulped. "It is amazing how fast one of your bulk can move, isn't it, Master?"

"Isn't it, little Pukah? Now, you will be going!"

"Yes, Master." Sighing, Pukah leaned down and picked up Sond's lamp. Slowly and reluctantly, the young djinn began to dwindle away into the air until all that remained of him was his eyes, staring disconsolately at the basket. "Master!" cried his disembodied voice. "If you would only grant me—"

"Be gone!" roared Kaug.

The eyes rolled upward and disappeared.

Instantly the 'efreet snatched off the lid of the basket and thrust his huge hand inside.

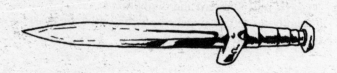

The Book
of the
Zhakrin 1

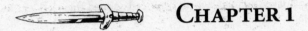 # CHAPTER 1

The procession wound its way slowly across the plains toward the city of Idrith. It was a magnificent sight, and—as word of its approach spread through the *souks*—many Idrithians clambered up the narrow stairs and lined the city walls to see, exclaim, and speculate.

At the head of the procession marched two *mamalukes*. Gigantic men, both seven feet tall, the slaves wore red and orange feathered headdresses that added an additional three feet to their height. Short black leather skirts banded by gold encircled their narrow waists. Gold flashed from the collars they wore round their necks, jewels glittered on the headdresses. Their chests and legs were bare, their skin oiled so that it glistened in the noonday sun. In their hands, each *mamaluke* carried a banner with a strange device, the like of which had never before been seen in Idrith. On a background red as blood, there glistened a black snake with eyes of orange flame.

Now snake banners were common enough—every city had at least one minor or major potentate who thought himself wily enough to deserve such a symbol. But this particular insignia had something unusual—and sinister—about it.

The snake's body was severed in three places and still, from the portrayal of the forked tongue flicking from the silken mouth, it seemed that the snake lived.

Behind the *mamalukes* marched six muscular slaves clad in black leather skirts bound with gold but without the additional finery of the standard-bearers. These slaves bore between them a palanquin whose white curtains remained tightly closed, permitting no one to catch a glimpse of the person who rode inside. A troop of *goums* mounted on matching black horses closely followed the palanquin. The soldiers' uniforms were a somber black, with black short coats and matching black, flowing pants that were tucked into knee-high red leather boots. Each man wore upon his head a conical red hat adorned with a black tassel. Long, curved-bladed swords bounced against their left legs as they rode.

But it was that which came behind these *goums* in the solemn processional that caught the attention of the crowd on the walls of Idrith. Numerous slaves bore between them three litters, each covered by white fabric. Several *goums* rode at the side of the litters. The heads of these soldiers were bowed, their black uniforms were torn, they wore no hats.

Following the litters was another squadron of *goums*, escorting three baggage-laden camels decked out in splendid finery—orange-and-red feathered headdresses, long tassels of black fringe that bounced about their spindly legs.

From the slow movement and sorrowful mien of those marching across the plains, it was soon obvious to the people of Idrith that this was a funeral cortege they were observing from the walls. Word spread and more people pushed their way through the crowds to see. Nothing attracts attention like a funeral, if only to reassure the onlooker that he himself is still alive.

About a mile from the city gates, the entire procession came to a halt. The standard-bearers dipped their banners—a sign that the party approached in peace. The slaves settled the palanquin on the ground. The *goums* dismounted, the camels sank to their knees, the rattan-covered litters were lowered with great ceremony and respect to the ground.

Looking and feeling extremely important, aware of hundreds of envious eyes upon him, the Captain of the Sultan's Guard led a squadron of his men out to meet and inspect the strangers before permitting them to enter the city. Barking a sharp command for his men to keep in line and maintain discipline, the Captain cast a glance toward the Sultan's palace that stood on a hill above Idirth. The Sultan could not be seen, but the Captain knew he was watching. Bright patches of color crowding the balconies gave indication that the Sultan's wives and concubines were flocking to see the procession.

His spine might have been changed to iron, so stiff and straight was the back of the Captain as he walked his horse slowly and with great dignity past the standard-bearers, advancing upon the palanquin. A man had emerged from its white curtains and was waiting with every mark of respect to meet the Captain. Beside the man stood the leader of the *goums*, also on foot and also respectful. A slave held his horse some distance behind him.

Dismounting himself, the Captain handed the reins of his horse to one of his men and walked forward to meet the head of the strange procession.

The man of the palanquin was clothed almost completely in black. Black leather boots, black flowing trousers, a long-sleeved, black flowing shirt, a black turban adorning his head. A red sash and a red jewel in the center of the turban did nothing to relieve the funereal aspect of the man's costume. Rather, perhaps because of the peculiar shade of red that was the color of fresh blood, they enhanced it.

The skin of the man's face and hands was white as alabaster, probably why he took such precautions to keep himself out of the burning sun; Idrith being located just to the north of the Pagrah desert. By contrast, his brows were jet black, feathering out from a point above a slender, hawkish nose. The lips were thin and bloodless. Trimmed moustaches shadowed the upper lip, extending down the lines of the unsmiling mouth to join a narrow black beard that outlined a firm, jutting jawline.

The man in black bowed. Placing a white-skinned, slender hand over his heart, he performed the *salaam* with grace. The Captain returned the bow, far more clumsily—he was a big, awkward man. Raising his head, he met the gaze of the man in black and flinched involuntarily, as if the penetrating glance of the two dark, cold eyes had been living steel.

Instantly on his guard, the Captain cleared his throat and launched into the formalities. "I see by the lowering of your standards that you come in peace, *Effendi*. Welcome to the city of Idrith. The Sultan begs to know your names and your business that we may do you honor and lose no time in accommodating you."

The expression on the face of the man in black remained grave as he replied with equal solemnity and politeness. "My name is Auda ibn Jad. Formerly a trader in slaves, I am now traveling eastward to my homeland of Simdari. I wish only to stop over in your city for a day and a night to replenish my supplies and give my men some rest. Our journey has been a long and a sad one, and we have still many hundreds of miles to go before its end. I am certain that you must have surmised, Captain," the man in black said with a sigh, "that we are a funeral cortege."

Uncertain how to respond, the Captain cleared his throat noncommittally and glanced with lowering brows at the number of armed men he was being asked to let into his city. Auda ibn Jad appeared to understand, for he added, with a sad smile, "My *goums* would be most willing to surrender their swords to you, Captain, and I will answer for their good conduct." Taking hold of the Captain's arm with his slender hand, Auda led the soldier to one side and spoke in a low voice. "You will, however, be patient with my men, *sidi*. They have the gold of Kich in their purses, gold that melancholy circumstances prevented them from spending. They are excellent fighters and disciplined men. But they have suffered a great shock and seek to drown their sorrows in wine or find solace in the other pleasures for which this city is well-known. I myself have some business to do"—ibn Jad's eyes flicked a glance at several iron-bound wooden chests strapped to the camels—"with the jewel merchants of Idrith."

Feeling the cold sensation spread from the man's eyes to the fingers that rested on his arm, the Captain of the Sultan's Guard drew back from that icy touch. Every instinct that had made him a good soldier for forty years warned him to forbid this man with eyes like knives to enter his city. Yet he could see the heavy purses hanging from each *goum*'s sash. The merchants of Idrith standing upon the city walls could not detect the money pouches from that distance, but they could see the heavy chests on the camels' backs, the gold that glittered around the necks of this man's slaves.

On his way out of the city gates, the Captain had seen the followers of Kharmani, God of Wealth, reaching for their tally-sticks, and he knew very well that the proprietors of the eating houses, the tea shops, and the *arwats* were rubbing their hands in anticipation. A howl of outrage would split the Sultan's eardrums if this woolly sheep all ready for the shearing were driven from the city gates—all because the Captain did not like the look in the sheep's eyes.

The Captain still had one more bone to toss in the game, however. "All those desirous of entering the city of Idrith must surrender to me not only their weapons but all their magic items and djinn as well, Effendi. These will be given as sacrifice to Quar," said the Captain, hoping that this edict—one that had come from the God and one that therefore not even the Sultan could lift—would discourage these visitors. His hope was a vain one, however.

Auda ibn Jad nodded gravely. "Yes, Captain, such a commandment was imposed on us in Kich. It was there that we left all our magical paraphernalia and our djinn. We were honored to do this in the name of so great a God as Quar and—as you see—he has in turn favored us with his blessing in our journeying."

"You will not be offended if I search you, *Effendi*?" asked the Captain.

"We have nothing to hide, *sidi*," said ibn Jad humbly, with another graceful bow.

Of course they don't, the Captain thought dowerly. They knew about this and were prepared. Nevertheless, he had to go through the motions. Turning, he ordered his men to commence the search, as Auda ibn Jad ordered the leader of the *goums* to unload the camels.

"What is in there?" The Captain pointed to the litters.

"The bodies, *sidi*," replied ibn Jad in low, reverent tones. "I did mention that this was a funeral cortege, didn't I?"

The Captain started. Yes, the man had said that they were a funeral procession, but the Captain had assumed it was an honorary one, perhaps escorting the icon of some deceased Imam back to his birthplace. It never occurred to the soldier that this Auda ibn Jad was carting corpses around with him. The Captain glanced at the litters and frowned outwardly, though inwardly sighing with relief.

"Bodies! I am sorry, *Effendi*, but I cannot allow those inside the city walls. The risk of disease—"

"—is nonexistent, I assure you. Come, Captain, look for yourself."

The Captain had no choice but to follow the man in black to where the litters rested on the sandy soil of the plains. Not a squeamish man—the Captain had seen his share of corpses in his lifetime—he nevertheless approached the litters with extreme reluctance. A body hacked and mangled on the field of battle was one thing. A body that has been traveling in the heat of early summer was quite another. Coming near the first litter, the Captain hardened himself for what was to come. It was odd, though, that there were no flies buzzing about. Sniffing, the Captain detected no whiff of corruption, and he glanced at the man in black in puzzlement.

Reading the Captain's thoughts, Auda ibn lad smiled deprecatingly, as if denying credit for everything. He neared the litter, and his smile vanished, replaced by the most sorrowful solemnity. With a gesture, he invited the Captain to look.

Even as close as this, there was no hint of the nauseating odor of decay, nor could the Captain detect any perfume that might have covered it. His repugnance lost in curiosity, the Captain bent down and peered inside the first litter.

His eyes opened wide.

Lying in the most peaceful attitude of repose, his hands folded over the jeweled hilt of a splendid sword, was a young man of perhaps twenty-five years of age. He was handsome, with black hair and a neatly trimmed black beard. A helm carved to resemble the severed snake device lay at his feet, along with a broken sword that belonged—presumably—to the enemy who had vanquished him. Dressed in shining black armor, whose breastplate was decorated with the same design that appeared on the banners of Auda ibn Jad, the young man seemed by outward appearance to have just fallen asleep. So smooth and unblemished was the flesh, so shining black and lustrous was the hair, the Captain could not forbear stretching forth his hand and touching the white forehead.

The flesh was cold. The pulse in the neck was stilled, the chest did not move with the breath of life.

Stepping back, the Captain stared at the man in black in astonishment.

"How long has this man been dead?"

"About a month," ibn Jad replied in grave tones.

"That—that's impossible!"

"Not for the priests of our God, *sidi*. They have learned the secret of replacing the fluids of the body with fluids that can delay or completely arrest the natural process of decay. It is quite a fascinating procedure. The brains are taken out by drawing them through the nose—"

"Enough!" The Captain, paling, raised his hand. "Who is this God of yours?"

"Forgive me," said Auda ibn Jad gently, "but I have taken a sacred vow never to speak His name in the presence of unbelievers."

"He is not an enemy of Quar's?"

"Surely the mighty and powerful Quar can have no enemies?" Ibn Jad raised a black eyebrow.

This statement left the Captain somewhat at a loss. If he pursued the matter of this man's God, it would appear that the mighty and powerful Quar did indeed have something to fear. Yet the soldier felt uncomfortable in not pursuing it.

"Since your priests have conquered the effects of death, *Effendi*," said the Captain, hoping to gather more information, "why have they never sought to defeat Death himself?"

"They are working on it, *sidi*," said ibn Jad coolly.

Nonplussed, the Captain gave up and glanced back down at the corpse of the man lying in state in the litter. "Who is he and why do you carry him with you?"

"He is Calif of my people," answered ibn Jad, "and I have the sad task of bearing his body home to his grieving father. The young man was killed in the desert, fighting the nomads of Pagrah alongside the Amir of Kich—a truly great man. Do you know him, Captain?"

"Yes," said the Captain shortly. "Tell me, *Effendi*, why is a Prince of Simdari fighting in foreign lands so far from his home?"

"You do not trust me, do you, Captain?" said Auda ibn Jad suddenly, frowning, a look in the cold eyes that made the soldier—a veteran of many battles—shudder. The Captain was about to respond when ibn Jad shook his head, putting his hands to his temples as if they ached. "Please forgive me," he murmured. "I know you have your duty to uphold. I am short-tempered. This journey of mine has not been pleasant, yet I do not look forward to its ending." Sighing, he crossed his arms over his chest. "I dread bringing this news to my king. The young man"—with a nod toward the corpse—"is his only son, the child of his old age at that. And now"—ibn Jad bowed gracefully—"to answer your most reasonable question, Captain. The Calif was visiting the court of the Emperor in Khandar. Hearing of the fame of the Amir, the Calif rode to Kich to study the art of warfare at the feet of a master. It was by the vilest treachery that the savage nomads killed him."

Ibn Jad's story seemed plausible. The Captain had heard rumors of the Amir's attack on the nomads of the Pagrah desert.

It was well-known that the Emperor of Tara-kan—a man who thirsted after knowledge as another thirsts for strong drink—encouraged visitors from strange lands who worshiped strange Gods. Yes, it was all nice and neat, so very nice and neat. . .

"What do you carry in those other two litters, *Effendi*?"

"Ah, here you will see a sight that will move you profoundly, *sidi*. Come."

Walking over to the two litters that rested behind the first, the Captain saw—out of the corner of his eye—that his troops had almost completed their search of the caravan's goods. He would have to make a decision soon. Admit them into the city or keep them out. Every instinct, every twitching nerve fiber in his body warned him—keep them out. Yet he needed a reason.

Glancing inside the litter, expecting to see another soldier—perhaps a bodyguard who had sacrificed his life for his master—the Captain caught his breath. "Women!" he stated, looking from one litter to the other.

"Women!" murmured Auda ibn Jad in reproof. "Say rather 'Goddesses' and you will come nearer the truth, for such beauty as theirs is rarely seen on this wretched plane of mortal existence. Look upon them, Captain. You may do so now, though to have set eyes upon their beauty before the death of my Calif would have cost you your life."

A white gauze veil had been drawn over the face of each woman. With great respect and reverence, ibn Jad removed the veil from the first. The woman had classic features, but there was something about the pale, still face that spoke of fierce pride and stern resolution. Her long black hair glistened blue in the sun. Bending near her, the Captain caught the faintest smell of jasmine.

Auda ibn Jad turned to the other woman, and the Captain noticed that his touch grew more gentle. Slowly he drew back the veil from the motionless body. Gazing at the woman lying before him, the Captain felt his heart stirred with pity and with admiration. Ibn Jad had spoken truly. Never had the soldier seen a woman more beautiful. The skin was like cream, the features perfect. Hair the color and brilliance of dancing flame tumbled down over the slender shoulders.

"The wives of my Calif," Auda said, and for the first time the Captain heard grief in the voice. "When his body was brought into the palace at Kich where they were staying, awaiting my lord's return, they hurled themselves upon him, weeping and tearing their clothes. Before any could stop them, the one with the red hair grabbed the Prince's sword. Crying that she could not live without him, she drove the blade into her own fair body and dropped dead at his feet. The other—jealous that the red-haired wife should reach him first in the Realm of Our God—drew a dagger she had hidden beneath her gown and stabbed herself. Both are the daughters of Sultans in my land. I bear them back to be buried with honor in the tomb of their husband."

His head whirling from his glimpse of the beauty of the women, combined with a story of such tragedy and romance, the Captain wondered what to do. A Prince of Simdari, a friend of both the Emperor and the Amir, the body of this young man should by rights be escorted into the city. The Sultan would never forgive his Captain if, on his yearly visit to the court of Khandar, he was asked by the Emperor if he had received the funeral cortege of the Calif with honor and the Sultan was forced to reply that he knew nothing of any such cortege. In addition, was the Captain to deny his Sultan—who was always on the verge of perishing from boredom—the opportunity of meeting exotic guests, of hearing this sad tale of war and love and self-sacrifice?

The only metal the Captain had to set against all this glittering gold was plain, solid iron—an instinctive feeling of dislike and distrust for this Auda ibn Jad. Still pondering the matter, the Captain turned to find his lieutenant hovering at his elbow, the leader of the *goums* standing at his side.

"We have completed the search of the caravan, sir," the lieutenant reported, "with the exception of those." He pointed at the litters.

The leader of the *goums* gave a shocked yelp that was answered swiftly and sternly in their own language by Auda ibn Jad. Even so, the leader of the *goums* continued to talk volubly until Auda silenced him with a sharp, angry command. Red-faced and ashamed, the *goum* slunk away like a whipped dog. Auda, pale with fury, yet with his temper under control, turned to the Captain.

"Forgive the outburst, *sidi*. My man forgot himself. It will not happen again. You mentioned searching the corpses. By all means, please proceed."

"What was all that about, *Effendi?*" the Captain asked suspiciously.

"Please, Captain. It was nothing."

"I insist on knowing—"

"If you must." Auda ibn Jad appeared faintly embarrassed. "The priests of our God have placed a curse upon these bodies. Any who disturb their rest will die a most horrible death, their souls sent to serve the Calif and his wives in heaven." Ibn Jad lowered his voice to a confidential whisper. "Accept my apologies, Captain. Kiber, the leader of my *goums*—while he is a good soldier—is a superstitious peasant. I beg you to pay no heed to him. Search the bodies."

"I will," said the Captain harshly.

Turning to his lieutenant to issue the order, the Captain saw by the carefully impassive, frozen expression on the soldier's face that he had heard ibn Jad's words quite clearly. The Captain opened his mouth. The lieutenant gave him a pleading look.

Angrily, the Captain marched over to the body of the Calif. "May Quar protect me from the unknown evil," he said loudly, reaching forth his hand to search the mattress upon which the corpse rested. Any number of objects could be concealed in it, or beneath the silken sheet that covered the lower half of the body, or even inside the armor itself. . .

An eerie murmur, like the low whistle of a rising windstorm, caused the Captain's hair to bristle. Involuntarily, his hand jerked back. Looking up swiftly, he saw the sound had come from ibn Jad's *goums*. The men were backing away, their horses—affected by the fear of their masters—rolled their eyes and danced nervously. The slaves huddled together in a group and began to wail piteously. Auda ibn Jad, with a scowl, rounded upon them and shouted at them in his own language. From the motion of his hand, the Captain gathered he was promising them all a sound thrashing. The wailing ceased, but the slaves, the *goums*, the horses, and even, it seemed, the camels—beasts not noted for their intelligence—watched the Captain with an eager, anticipatory thrill of horror that was most unnerving.

Ibn Jad's face was tense and strained. Though he was endeavoring hard to conceal his emotions, apparently he, too, was a superstitious peasant at heart. Abruptly, the Captain withdrew his hand.

"I will not disturb the honored dead. And you, Auda ibn Jad, and your men have leave to enter Idrith. But these"—he gestured at the rattan litters—"must remain outside the city walls. If they are indeed cursed, it would not do to bring them into the sacred precincts of Quar." At least, the Captain thought grimly, he had solved *that* dilemma! Perhaps Auda ibn Jad and his men will take offense at this and leave.

But the man in black was smiling and bowing graciously, his fingers going to heart, lips, and forehead in the graceful *salaam*.

"I will order my men to guard the dead," the Captain offered, though—glancing at his troops—he knew such an order would be unnecessary. Word of the curse would spread like the plague through the city. The most devout follower of Benario, God of Thieves, would not steal so much as a jeweled earring from the corpses.

"My grateful thanks, Captain," said Auda, bowing again, hand pressed over his heart.

The Captain bowed awkwardly in return. "And perhaps you would do me the very great honor of accompanying me to the Sultan's palace this evening. Affairs of state prevent His Magnificence from seeing the world, and he would be much entertained by the stories you have related to me."

Auda ibn Jad protested that he was not worthy of such attention. The Captain patiently assured him that he was. Auda insisted that he wasn't and continued to demur as long as was proper, then gave in with refined grace. Sighing, the Captain turned away. Having no legitimate reason to keep this man and his *goums* out of Idrith, he had done what he could. At least the corpses with their unholy curse would not pollute the city. He would himself take personal charge of Auda ibn Jad and order his men to keep a watchful eye upon the *goums*. After all, they numbered no more than thirty. The Sultan's wives alone outnumbered them two to one. Amid the thousands of people jammed into Idrith, they would be as a single drop of rain falling into a deep well.

Telling himself that he had the situation under control, the Captain started to remount his horse. But his uneasiness persisted. His foot in the stirrup, he paused, hands on the saddle, and looked for one last time at the man in black.

Beneath hooded lids, the eyes of Auda ibn Jad were glancing sideways into the eyes of Kiber, leader of the *goums*. Much was being said in that exchange of glances, though probably nothing that was not of the most innocent nature. The Captain shivered in the noonday sun.

"I am," he said grimly, "a superstitious peasant."

Pulling himself up into the saddle, he wheeled his horse and galloped off to order the city gates be opened to Auda ibn Jad.

 # CHAPTER 2

The Sultan was—as the Captain had foreseen—charmed with Auda ibn Jad. Nothing would do but that the Sultan and his current favorites among his wives and concubines must leave the palace and traipse outside the city walls to pay homage to the dead. The women cooed and sighed over the handsome young Prince. The Sultan and the nobles shook their heads over the wasted beauty of the women. Auda ibn Jad told his story well, bringing tears to many eyes in the royal court as he related in heartfelt tones the final words of the red-haired wife as she fell dead across her husband's body.

Following this, there was a sumptuous dinner that lasted long into the night. The wine flowed freely, much of it into the Captain's mouth. Ordinarily, the Captain did not take to strong drink, but he felt he had to warm himself. There was something about Auda ibn Jad that chilled his blood; but what it was, the Captain couldn't say.

Deep into his sixth cup of the unwatered vintage that came from the grapes grown in the hills above Idrith, the Captain stared at the man, seated cross-legged on silken cushions opposite him. He couldn't take his eyes off ibn Jad, feeling himself caught by the same terrible fascination a cobra is said to exert over its victims.

It is Auda ibn Jad's face, the Captain decided muzzily. The man's face is too smooth. There are no lines on it, no traces of any emotion, no traces of any human feeling or passion—either good or evil. The corners of the mouth turn neither up nor down. The cold, hooded eyes narrow in neither laughter nor anger. Ibn Jad ate and drank without enjoyment. He watched the sinuous twistings of the dancing girls without lust. A face of stone, the Captain decided and drank another cup of wine, only to feel it sit in his stomach like a lump of cold clay.

At last the Sultan rose from his cushions to go to the bed of his chosen. Much pleased with his guest, he gave Auda ibn Jad a ring from his own hand. Nothing priceless, the Captain noted, staring at it with bleary eyes—a semiprecious gem whose glitter was greater than its worth. Auda ibn Jad apparently knew something of jewels himself, for he accepted it with a flicker of sardonic amusement in the cold eyes.

In answer to the Sultan's invitation to return to the palace tomorrow, ibn Jad replied regretfully that he must not tarry in his sad journey. His king had, as of yet, no knowledge of the death of his son and Auda ibn Jad feared lest it should reach his ears from some stranger, rather than a trusted friend.

The Sultan, yawning, was very understanding. His Captain was overwhelmed with relief. In the morning they would be rid of this man and his well-preserved corpses. Stumbling to his feet, the Captain—accompanied by a cold sober ibn Jad—made his way through the winding passages of the palace and stumbled drunkenly down the stairs. He narrowly missed tumbling head-first into a large ornamental pool that graced the front of the palace—it was ibn Jad's hand that pulled him back—and finally weaved his way through the various gates that led them by stages back into the city.

Once in the moon-lit streets of Idrith, Auda ibn Jad glanced about in perplexity.

"This maze of alleys confuses me, Captain. I fear I have forgotten the way back to the *arwat* in which I am staying. If you could guide me—"

Certainly. Anything to get rid of the man. The Captain lurched forward into the empty street; ibn Jad walking at his side. Suddenly, inexplicably, the man in black slowed his pace.

Something inside the Captain—some old soldier's instinct—screamed out a desperate warning. The Captain heard it, but by then it was too late.

An arm grabbed him from behind. With incredible strength, it wrapped around his neck, choking off his breath. The Captain's fear sobered him. His muscles tensed, he raised his hands to resist. . .

The Captain felt the stinging pain of the knife's point entering his throat just beneath his jaw. So skilled was the hand wielding the blade, however, that the Captain never felt the swift, slicing cut to follow.

There was only a brief tremor of fear... anger...
Then nothing.

The Captain's body was discovered in the morning—the first in a series of grisly discoveries that left the city of Idrith in the grip of terror. Two streets over, the body of an old man was found lying in a gutter. Ten blocks to the north, a father woke to find his young, virgin daughter murdered in her sleep. The body of a virile, robust man turned up floating in a *hauz*. A middle-aged mother of four was discovered lying in an alley.

The disciplined guards surged outside the city walls to question the strangers, only to find that the funeral cortege of Auda ibn Jad had disappeared. No one had heard them leave. The sun-baked ground left no trace of their passing. Squadrons of soldiers rode out in all directions, searching, but no trace of the man in black, his *goums*, or the bodies in the rattan litters was ever found.

Back inside the city, the mystery deepened. The dead appeared to have been chosen at random—a stalwart soldier; a decrepit old beggar; a beautiful young virgin; a wife and mother; a muscular young man. Yet the victims had one thing in common—the manner of their dying.

The throat of each person had been slit, neatly and skillfully, from ear to ear. And, most horribly, by some mysterious means, each body had been completely drained of blood.

The Book
of Quar 1

CHAPTER 1

i t was the noise—the noise and the stench of the prison that disturbed the nomads most. Accustomed to the music of the desert—the song of the wind over the dunes, the hum of the tent ropes stretched taut in a storm, the barking of camp dogs, the laughter of children, the voices of the women going about their daily chores, the cry of a falcon making a successful kill—the sounds of the prison tore at the young men until they felt as if every inch of their skins had been flayed from their bodies.

The soldiers of the Amir did not mistreat the desert dwellers, who had been captured in the raid on the camp around the Tel. Far from it. Although the nomads had no way of knowing, they were being accorded better treatment than any other prisoners. Physicians had been sent to treat their wounds, and they were allowed exercise and a small amount of time each day to see their families. But to the imprisoned Akar, Hrana, or Aran tribe members, being deprived of their freedom was the most excruciating torture the Amir could have devised.

When the captives were first brought in, they were assembled in the prison yard and the Amir spoke to them.

"I watched you in battle," he said, sitting astride his magical, ebony horse, "and I will not hide from you the fact that I was impressed. All my life I had heard the stories of the bravery and skill of the followers of Akhran."

The nomads, who had previously been standing sullenly, eyes on the ground, looked up at this, pleased and startled that Qannadi should know the name of their God. The Amir made it a point to keep such details in his mind, often surprising his own men by speaking to each by name, recalling some act of bravery or daring. An old soldier, he knew such small things touched the heart and won undying loyalty.

"I did not believe it," he continued in his deep baritone, "until I saw it for myself." He paused here dramatically, to let his words slide like oil upon the troubled waters. "Outnumbered, taken by surprise, you fought like devils. I needed every soldier in my command to defeat you and even then I began to fear that the might of my army was not strong enough. "

This was not exactly true; the outcome had never been in doubt and—considering the strength of the army the Amir had built up to conquer the south—Qannadi had thrown only a token force at the nomads. He could afford to lie at his own expense, however, being ten times rewarded by seeing the sullen eyes gleam with pride.

"Such men as you are wasted out there." Qannadi gestured dramatically toward the Pagrah desert. "Instead of stealing sheep, you could be capturing the wealth of cities. Instead of knifing each other in the dark, you could be challenging a brave foe in glorious combat on an open field. I offer you this and more! Fight with me, and I will pay you thirty silver *tumans* a month. I will give your families free housing in the city, the opportunity for your women to sell their wares in the *souks*, and a fair share in the spoils of any city we conquer."

Most of the nomads growled and shook their heads, but some—Qannadi noted—dropped their eyes, shuffling their feet uneasily. Many here had ridden with their Calif in the raid on the Kich. Qannadi skillfully conjured up visions in their minds of galloping their horses through rich palaces, snatching up gold and jewels and Sultans' beautiful daughters. The Amir did not delude himself. He did not think it likely he would gain any recruits this moment. After all, the men had just seen their families carried off, they had seen some of their own die in battle. But he knew that this arrow he had fired would pierce their imaginations and stick there, festering, in their minds.

Sayah, Zohra's half brother, stepped forward. "I speak for the Hrana," he cried, "and I tell you that we serve no man except our Sheykh!"

"The same for the Akar!" came a voice and, "The same for the Aran," came another.

Without responding, Qannadi turned and galloped out of the prison yard. The nomads thought he rode off in anger and congratulated themselves on having tweaked the Amir's nose. So rowdy were they that the guards thought it best to beat soundly the most vocal before driving them back to their cells.

Qannadi was not angry, however. The true, underlying meaning of what these men said struck the Amir with such force it was a wonder he didn't fall from his saddle. Absorbed in thought, he returned to the palace and sent at once for the Imam.

"Bringing their Sheykhs in is out of the question," the Amir said, pacing back and forth the length of the room that had once been the Sultan's private study and was now his, never noticing that his boots were tracking mud and manure on the handwoven, priceless carpets covering the floor. "They are old dogs who will bite any hand other than their master's. But these young pups are different. They might be taught to jump through the hoops of another, especially if it is one of their own. We need to raise up a leader in their midst, Feisal, someone they trust and will follow. But someone who, in turn, must be under our complete control. Is that possible, do you think, Imam?"

"With Quar, all is possible, O King. Not only possible, but probable. It is too bad," Feisal added, with a subtle change of expression in his voice, "that their Calif, this Khardan, should have vanished so mysteriously."

Qannadi glanced at the priest sharply. "Khardan is dead."

"His body was not discovered."

"He is dead," the Amir said coldly. "Meryem reported to me that she saw him fall in battle, mortally wounded. As for why the corpse was not discovered, it was probably hauled off by some wild beast." Qannadi fixed Feisal with a stern, black-eyed gaze. "We both want these nomads on our side, Imam'"

"There is one difference, O King," said Feisal, not at all discomfited by the Amir's baleful gaze. "You want their bodies. I want their souls."

The following day, and many days after that, the Imam visited the prison. Though he would never admit as much to the Amir, Feisal realized Qannadi had grasped hold of the tail of a valuable idea. It would be up to the Imam to soothe the beast attached to that tail and make it work for them. Consequently, he talked to the young men, bringing them news of their families, assuring them that their mothers, wives, and children were being well cared for, and extolling the virtues of settled city life, drawing subtle differences between it and the harsh life of the wanderer. Wisely, the Imam never mentioned Quar. He never mentioned Akhran, either, but left the young men to draw their own conclusions.

One person in particular drew his attention. Sitting alone in the tiny, narrow, windowless cell in the Zindan, Achmed, Khardan's half brother, foundered in a despair so black and murky he felt as though he were drowning in it.

The smell in the prison was poisonous. Once a day, the prisoners were allowed outside to walk around the compound and to perform their ablutions, but that was all. The remainder of the time they had to make do with a corner of the cell, and though it was cleaned out daily by slaves, the stench of human excrement, as well as that of sickness, was always in the air.

Achmed could not eat. The stink penetrated the food and tainted the water. He could not sleep. The noise, that spoke of pain and suffering and torture, was dreadful. In the cell next to his, an unlucky follower of Benario's had been captured inside one of the bazaars after curfew, making away with stolen goods. The wretch's hands had been cut off, to teach him a lesson, and he moaned and howled with the pain until he either lapsed into unconsciousness or one of the guards—irritated at the clamor—clouted him over the head.

In the other side cell, a debtor to the followers of Kharmani, God of Wealth, had developed an insidious cough and lay hacking his life away while bemoaning the fact that he couldn't raise the money to payoff his debts while confined in prison.

Across from Achmed, a beggar caught exhibiting fake sores to a gullible audience was developing real ones. Two cells down a man condemned to be hurled from the Tower of Death for raping a woman pounded on the walls and pleaded with an unhearing Amir for another trial.

At first, getting out of the cell was a welcome release, but after a few days Achmed grew to dread the time they were allowed to walk in the compound. No loving wife came to stretch her hand out to him through the bars of the gate, no mother came to weep over him. His own mother—one of Majiid's many wives—had been captured in the raid on the camp. She was in the city, but too ill to come and see him. This Achmed heard from Badia, Khardan's mother, the only one who occasionally visited the young man.

"The soldiers did not hurt her," Badia hastened to assure Achmed, seeing by the dark, violent expression on the young man's face that he might commit some foolish act. "They were really very kind and gentle and took her to a house of one of their own Captains, whose wives are caring for her like a sister. The Imam himself has been to see her and said a prayer for her. But she was never strong, Achmed, not since your baby sister was born. We must put our trust in Akhran."

Akhran! Alone, despairing, Achmed cursed the name of the God. Why have You done this to me, to my people? The young man questioned, head in his hands, tears creeping through his clenched fingers. This day would have been my birthday. Eighteen years. There would have been a *baigha* held in my honor. Khardan would have seen to that, even if Majiid—Achmed's father and Sheykh of the Akar—forgot. Majiid very likely would have forgotten; he had many sons and took pride in only one—his eldest, Khardan.

Achmed didn't mind. He, too, admired Khardan with all his heart and soul, feeling—in many ways—that Khardan was more of a father to him than the rough, bellowing, quick-tempered Majiid. Khardan would have seen to it that this day was special for his younger half-brother. A present—perhaps one of the Calif's very own jeweled daggers. A dinner just for the two of them in Khardan's tent, drinking *qumiz* until they couldn't stand and listening to Pukah's tales of bloodsucking *ghuls*, the flesh-eating *delhan*, or the alluring and deadly *ghaddar*.

The thief in the next cell began to rave deliriously. A sob burst from Achmed's throat. Slumping down onto the straw spread over his floor, he hid his face in the crook of his arm and wept in lonely, bitter anguish.

"My son."

The soft, sympathetic voice spread over Achmed's bleeding soul like a soothing balm. Startled—the young man had been so lost in his grief he had not heard the sound of the key in the door or the door being opened—Achmed sat up and hastily wiped away the traces of his tears. Glancing suspiciously at the slender figure of the priest entering his cell, Achmed crouched down on the dirty mattress that was his bed and affected to be intently interested in a crack in the wall.

"I hear that you suffered a wound in the battle. Are you in

pain, my son?" the Imam inquired gently. "Shall I send for the physicians?"

Sniffing, Achmed wiped his nose on the sleeve of his robe and stared fiercely straight ahead.

The priest smiled inwardly. He felt instinctively he had arrived at precisely the right moment, and he thanked Quar for having been led to the suffering lamb in time to save it from the wolves.

"Let me examine your injury," said the Imam, although he knew well that it was not the wound on the head but the wound in the heart that brought the tears to the young man's eyes.

Achmed ducked his head, as though he would have refused, but Feisal pretended not to notice. Removing the *haik*, he examined the cut. During the battle, Achmed had been struck by the flat of a sword blade. The blow had split the skin and knocked him unconscious, leaving him with a terrible headache for a day after but doing no serious injury.

"Tsk," the Imam made a clucking sound, "you will have a scar."

"That is good!" Achmed said suddenly, huskily. He had to say something. The attention the priest paid him and the gentle touch of his fingers had come dangerously near to making him start to cry again. "My brother has many such scars. It is the mark of a warrior. "

"You sound like the Amir," said Feisal, his heartbeat quickening in secret delight. Many times he had looked in on Achmed and the young man had never spoken to him, never even looked at him. The Imam smoothed back the black hair. "To me, such scars are the mark of the savage. When man is truly civilized, then all wars will cease and we will live in peace. There." He handed back the headcloth. "The wound is healing cleanly. It will leave a white mark on your scalp, however. The hair will not grow back."

Holding the cloth in his hands, Achmed twisted it with his fingers. He did not put it back on. "Civilized? You're one to talk. This"—he pointed to his head—"was the work of your 'savages'!"

The Imam carefully concealed his joy by glancing around the cell. It was impossible to talk here. Next door the mutilated thief was screaming feverishly. "Will you come outside and walk with me, Achmed?"

The young man glowered at him suspiciously.

"It is a fine day," the Imam said. "The wind blows from the east."

The east. The desert. Achmed lowered his eyes. "Very well," he said in a low voice. Rising to his feet, he followed Feisal out the door of his cell, trudging down the long, dark corridor. The guard started to follow, but the Imam shook his head and warned him away with a gesture of his thin fingers. As they passed the cells, those inside stretched out their hands to the priest, begging for his blessing, or tried to snatch up and kiss the hem of his robe. Stealing a glance from the corner of his eye, Achmed saw the Imam react to all this with extraordinary patience, murmuring the ritual words, reaching through the bars to touch a bent head, offering comfort and hope in the name of Quar.

Achmed recalled the first time he had seen the priest, when Khardan had come to the palace to try to sell horses to the Amir. Achmed had been frightened of the Imam then and he was frightened of him now. It was not that the priest's physical presence was formidable. Days and nights of fasting and praying had left the Imam's body so slender and delicate that Achmed could have picked the man up and broken him in two with his bare hands. The fear did not generate from the gaunt and handsome face.

It was the eyes, aflame with holy zeal, whose fire could burn holes through a man as a hot iron burns through wood.

Emerging into the sunshine, Achmed lifted his face to the heavens, reveling in the welcome warmth on his skin. He drew a deep breath. Though the air smelled of city, at least it was better than the stench in the prison. And, as the Imam had said, the wind was from the east and Achmed could swear he caught the faintest breath of the desert's elusive perfume.

Glancing about, he saw Feisal watching him intently. Shoulders slumping, Achmed dove back into sullen uncaring like a startled djinn diving back into his bottle.

"Your mother's health is improving," said the Imam.

"She wouldn't have fallen sick if you'd left her alone," Achmed returned accusingly.

"On the contrary, my son. It was well for her that we brought her to Kich. Our physicians have undoubtedly saved her life. Out there, in that wretched land"—the Imam looked to the east—"she would surely have perished." Seeing stubborn disbelief on the young face, the priest turned the conversation. "Of what were we speaking?" he asked.

"Savages." Achmed sneered.

"Ah, yes. So we were." Feisal gestured to what little shade existed in the compound. "We are alone. Shall we sit down to talk more comfortably?"

"You'll soil your robes."

"Clothes can be cleansed, just like the soul. I see that no one has brought you a clean robe. Disgraceful. I will speak to the Amir."

The Imam settled himself comfortably on the hard rock pavement. Leaning against the prison wall, the priest appeared as much at home as if he had been lounging on a sofa in the finest room in the palace. Awkwardly, Achmed squatted down beside him, the young man flushing in embarrassment at the deplorable condition of his clothes.

"You have a younger sister," the Imam said. Achmed—all his suspicions aroused once more—scowled and did not answer.

"I have seen her, when I visited your mother," Feisal continued, gazing unblinking out over the compound that was bathed in brilliant sunlight. "Your sister is a beautiful child. How old is she? Two?"

Still no reply.

"An interesting age. So full of curiosity and testing one's limits. I suppose that, like all children, she put her hand into the cooking fire, didn't she?"

"What?" Achmed stared at the priest in puzzlement.

"Did she ever put her hand into the fire?"

"Well, yes, I guess so. . . . All little kids do."

"Why?"

Achmed was confused, wondering why they were discussing small children. He shrugged. "They're attracted to it—the bright light, the colors, the warmth."

"They don't understand that it will hurt them?"

"How could they? They're too little."

"What did your mother do when she caught your sister starting to put her hand in the dancing flames?"

"I don't know. Smacked her, I guess."

"Why didn't your mother reason with the child, tell her that the fire will hurt her?"

"You can't reason with a two-year-old!" Achmed scoffed.

"But the child understands a slap on the wrist?"

"Sure. I mean, I guess so."

"Did she understand it because it gave her pain?"

"Yes."

"And did your mother enjoy hurting her child?"

"We're not barbarians, no matter what you think!" Achmed answered hotly, thinking this was a slur on his people.

"I am not saying that. Why does your mother choose to hurt her child?"

"Because she's afraid for her!"

"A slap on the wrist hurts, yet not like the fire."

"This is a stupid conversation!" Moodily, Achmed picked up small pieces of loose rock and began tossing them into the compound.

"Be patient," the Imam counseled softly. "We see the road beneath our feet, not the end. But we walk it still or we would get nowhere. So—the child reaches for the fire. The mother slaps the child's wrist and tells her no. Until the child is capable of understanding that the fire will burn her, the lesser hurt protects the child from the greater. Is this true?"

"Something like that, I suppose." Achmed had always heard priests were crazy. Now he had proof.

Reaching out his hand, the Imam touched the young man upon his forehead. "Now do you understand?" Feisal asked, his fingers gliding gently over the wound.

Turning, pausing in mid throw, Achmed stared at the priest in astonishment. "Understand what?"

Feisal smiled, his eyes were brighter than the sun of *dohar*.

"In spiritual matters, you are the child. Your God, the false God, Akhran, is the fire—bright colors and dancing light. Like the fire, he is a dangerous God, Achmed, for he will bum up your soul and leave it nothing but ashes. The Amir and myself are the parents who must protect you from everlasting harm, my son. We tried to reason with you, but you did not understand our words. Therefore, in order to save you from the inferno, we had to strike out, to slap your hand. . . ."

"And what about those you hit a little too hard?" Achmed cried angrily. "Those who died!"

"No one regrets loss of life more than I," the Imam said, his almond-shaped eyes burning into Achmed's. "It was your people—most notably your headstrong brother—who attacked us. We defended ourselves."

Jumping to his feet, Achmed began to walk away, heading back for the cells.

"Believe me, Achmed!" The Imam called after him. "The Amir could have destroyed your tribes! He could have wiped you out. It would have been far less trouble. But such was not his intent, nor mine!"

"You take us hostage!" Achmed tossed the words over his shoulder.

Rising gracefully, the Imam walked after the young man, talking to a steel-stiffened back.

"Hostage? Where is the demand for ransom? Have you been put up on the slave blocks? Tortured, beaten? Has one of your women been violated, molested?"

"Perhaps not." Achmed slowed his furious pace across the compound, his head half-turned. "Cream floating on soured milk! What do you want from us?"

Coming to a halt before the young man, the Imam spread his hands. "We want nothing *from* you. We want only to give."

"Give what?"

"The cream, to use your words. We want to share it with you."

"And what is this cream?" The young man was scornful.

"Knowledge. Understanding. Faith in a God who truly loves and cares for you and for your people."

"Akhran cares for His people!"

Achmed's tone was defiant, but Feisal knew it to be the defiance of a small child striking back at the hand that had hurt him, not the defiance of a man firm in his convictions. Coming up behind the young man, the priest rested his hands upon Achmed's shoulders. The Imam felt the young man flinch, but he also felt that the touch of friendship was not unwelcome to the lonely youth. Feisal said nothing more to challenge the young man's faith, wisely knowing that this would only force him to strengthen his defenses. It was Feisal's plan to slip quietly into the carefully guarded fortress of Achmed's soul, not attack it with a battering ram.

"There is someone who wants to see you, Achmed—a member of your tribe. May I bring him tomorrow?"

"You can do what you like. What choice do I have? I am your prisoner, after all."

"We keep you in your cells only as the mother keeps her babe in a cradle, to protect it from harm."

Tired of hearing about children—or perhaps tired of being constantly referred to as a child—Achmed made an impatient gesture.

"Until tomorrow, then?" the Imam said.

"If you like," Achmed said sullenly, but the priest had seen the flash of the eyes, the heightened color in the averted face at the mention of a visitor.

"The peace of Quar be with you this night," the Imam said, gesturing to a guard, who arrived to take Achmed back to his cell.

Twisting his head, the young man watched the priest leave, the spare body moving gracefully beneath the white robes that were now stained with the filth and muck of the prison. Yet Feisal didn't appear disgusted. He hadn't tried to brush it off or keep himself away from it. He had touched the beggars, the condemned, the diseased. He had given of his God to them. *Clothes can be cleansed*, the Imam had said. *Just like the soul.*

The peace of Quar or any other God was a long way from Achmed that night.

CHAPTER 2

Achmed waited impatiently the next morning to learn the identity of this mysterious visitor. He hoped it might be his mother, but the morning hour for the meeting of the prisoners and their families at the iron gates came, and she was not there. Khardan's mother was there to visit, however, and Badia told Achmed that what the Imam had said was true. Sophia was improving. Although she was not strong enough to make the journey to the prison, she sent her love to her son.

"What the Imam said about my mother, that she would have died out there in the desert. Is that true?"

"Our lives are in the hands of Akhran," said Badia, averting her eyes and turning to leave. "Pray to him."

"There is something wrong!" cried Achmed, catching hold of the woman's hand through the gate. "What is it? Badia, you have always been a second mother to me. I see trouble in your face. Is it my mother? Tell me what is the matter!"

"It is not your trouble, Achmed," the woman said in a broken voice. "It is my own." She pressed her hand over her heart. "Our God gives me strength to bear it. Farewell. I leave you with this"— she kissed him on the forehead—"and your mother's blessing."

Turning, she hurried away, disappearing into the crowd of the nearby *souks* before Achmed could question her further. A bell sounded. The guards came out to lead the prisoners back to their cells amid the wailing and parting cries of their mothers, wives, and children.

Badia surely hadn't been the visitor the Imam meant, Achmed thought as he walked with slow and shuffling step across the compound. Lost in his thoughts, he started when he felt an elbow dig into his side. Glancing up, he saw Sayah, a Hrana.

"What do you want, shepherd?" Achmed asked rudely. noting that Sayah's expression was grim and dark.

"Just wondering if you'd heard the news."

"What news?" Achmed appeared uninterested. "Has one of your women given birth to a goat that you fathered?"

"It is you who has bred the goat and it is in your own tribe."

"Bah!" Achmed tried to move away, but Sayah caught hold of the sleeve of his robe.

"One of your own, an Akar, has renounced our holy Akhran and gone over to the God of this city," he hissed.

"I don't believe you!" Achmed glared at Sayah defiantly.

"It is so. Look there!" Sayah gestured toward the gate.

Achmed turned his head reluctantly, knowing what he would see even before he glanced around, for he had instantly guessed the identity of the Imam's visitor. Standing at the bars, dressed in clean, fresh white robes, looking both defiant and extremely nervous was Saiyad, one of Majiid's most trusted men. Next to Saiyad stood the Imam.

From the sound of the low growl that rumbled around him, Achmed knew that the other members of the Akar had heard Sayah's words and seen Saiyad standing by the gate next to the priest. Looking about the crowd for advice, Achmed was amazed to find that all the men of the Akar were staring expectantly at him! It suddenly occurred to the young man that they were assuming he would take the role of leadership! He was Majiid's son, after all. . . .

Confused and overwhelmed by this unexpected responsibility, Achmed muttered something about "talking to him myself and clearing up this mistake," then walked back toward the gate. The guards leaped after him, but a gesture from the Imam sent them about their duties. Gathering together their other prisoners, the guards marched them back to the cells, taking out their frustrations on the nomads when they were certain that the Imam wasn't watching.

Drawing nearer, a stern, unwavering gaze fixed on Saiyad, Achmed saw that the man's eyes looked everywhere but at him— the ground, the sky, the prison, the Imam. Saiyad's fingers worked busily, folding and pleating, then drawing smooth, then folding and pleating a handful of the white cotton of his flowing robes.

"So it is no mistake," Achmed said beneath his breath, his heart dragging in the sand.

He reached the gate. The Imam did not enter, keeping both himself and Saiyad outside, perhaps afraid for his visitor's life. A glance at Achmed's dark and foreboding expression must have made the priest thankful for his precaution.

"Saiyad," said Achmed coolly. "*Salaam aleikum.*"

"And. . . and greetings to you, Achmed," answered Saiyad, his eyes meeting the young man's for the first time. He was obviously sorry they did so, for his gaze darted away the next instant. His fingers clenched around the fabric of his robe.

"What brings you here?" Achmed asked, attempting to conceal his rising fury. Why had Saiyad done this foul act? Worse, why did he feel it necessary to come and rub their noses in his dirt?

"Saiyad has come to check on your welfare, Achmed," said the Imam smoothly, "and to make certain that you and the others are being well treated."

"Yes, that is the reason I have come!" Saiyad said, his bearded face splitting into a grin.

Liar! thought Achmed, longing to shove the man's teeth down his throat. "So it is true what they say," the young man's voice was low. "You have converted to Quar."

The man's grin vanished instantly, to be replaced by a sickly smile. Shrugging his shoulders, he glanced deprecatingly at the Imam, and still working the fabric that was now dirty from the misuse, he drew near the iron gates and motioned for Achmed to come closer.

Feeling his skin crawl as though he were approaching a snake, the young man did as he was asked. The Imam, half turning, affected to be absorbed in the beauty of the palace that was nearby.

"What could I do, Achmed?" Saiyad whispered, his fingers leaving his robes and gripping the young man's through the bars. "You don't know what it's like out there in the desert!"

"Well, what is it like?" Achmed asked, trying to maintain his composure, yet feeling himself go cold all over.

"We are starving, Achmed! The soldiers burned everything, they left us with nothing—not even a goatskin in which to put the water! We have no shelter. By night we sleep in the sand. During the day, we fight for the shade of a palm tree! There are many sick and injured and only a few old women with magic enough to tend them. My wife, my children were carried away. . . ."

"Stop whining!" Achmed snapped. Unable to help himself, he drew back from Saiyad's touch in disgust. "You are not the only one to suffer! And at least you are free! Look at us, locked in here, worse than animals!" Lowering his voice, glancing at the Imam, he added softly, "Surely my father must be planning some way to get us out of here. Or Khardan—"

"Khardan!" Saiyad spoke too loudly. Both saw the thin shoulders of the Imam jerk, the turbaned head move ever so slightly. Hunching around so that his back was to the priest, Saiyad faced Achmed. The eyes that had been cast downward in guilt suddenly met his in contempt; the young man was disquieted to see the older man's lip curl in a sneer.

"Haven't you heard about your precious brother?"

"What? What about Khardan?" Achmed's heart stopped beating. "What's happened to him?" Now it was he who grabbed hold of the older man's robes.

"Happened? To him?" Saiyad laughed unpleasantly. "Nothing! Nothing at all, the filthy coward!"

"How dare you!" Achmed dragged the man closer with a jerk of his hands, banging Saiyad's head against the bars. One of the guards took a step toward them, but the Imam, supposedly neither hearing nor seeing what was going on, made a quick, imperceptible gesture, and—once again—the guard retreated.

"It's true, and all your ill usage of me won't change it! Our Calif fled the battlefield, disguised as a woman!"

Achmed stared at the man, then suddenly began to laugh. "Liar as well as a traitor! At least you could have come up with something more believable." Releasing his hold of the older man, Achmed wiped his hands on his robes, like one who has come into contact with a leper.

"Yes, couldn't I?" Saiyad retorted angrily. "Think, Achmed! If I was lying, wouldn't I have made up a better tale? What reason would I have to lie anyway?"

"To get me to join him!" Achmed made a furious gesture at the priest.

"I don't give a damn whether you join us or not!" Saiyad snarled. Realizing he was losing control and hurting his own cause, the older man drew himself up with an air of shabby dignity. "I came here to explain why I did what I did, hoping you and the others would understand. What I told you about Khardan is the truth, I swear by—" Saiyad hesitated. He had been about to say "Akhran," but seeing the silent figure of the Imam standing some distance away, he choked on the word "—by the honor of my mother," the older man concluded lamely. "All in the desert know it is true."

"Not my father!"

"Your father more than any of them!" Saiyad waved his hands. "Here!" Reaching into his sash, he fumbled for something, then withdrew a sword, "Majiid bade me give this to Khardan's mother, but I did not have the heart. You do with it what you want."

Seeing the flash of steel passing between the visitor and the prisoner, the guard leaped to intervene—Imam or no Imam.

"You dogs!" the guard swore at them. "I'll have you both whipped—"

Hastily, the Imam stepped in front of the guard, extending a slender arm between him and the nomads. "It is nothing of importance, I assure you!"

"Nothing! I saw that man give the boy a sword—"

"True," the Imam interrupted. Reaching through the bars, he grasped Achmed's limp hand and held the weapon up for inspection. "It is a sword. But can this be of harm?"

Looking at the weapon intently, the guard scowled, then gave a brief laugh and turned away, shaking his head over the stupidity of those who cooked their brains in the sun.

The sword's blade was broken; only the hilt and three inches of steel remained.

"Your father himself did that with an axe," Saiyad hissed, when the Imam had once again turned away.

Achmed held the broken sword—Khardan's sword—in a nerveless grasp, staring at it with anguished eyes. "I . . . I don't understand. . ." he said thickly.

"Your father proclaimed Khardan dead." Saiyad sighed. Reaching through the bars, he patted Achmed's arm, giving awkward, embarrassed comfort. "Majiid is a broken man. We are leaderless now. Day after day, he sits doing nothing but staring into the east, where it is said Khardan vanished!"

"But how could he know? Did he see Khardan . . . ?"

"No, but there was one who did. Fedj, the djinn."

"Jaafar's servant? A Hrana djinn?" Fire scorched the tears that had glimmered in Achmed's eyes. "No one would believe that—"

"He swore the Oath of Sul, Achmed," Saiyad said quietly. "And he walks among us still."

The young man stared. He could not speak, his tongue seemed to have swollen, his throat gone dry. The Oath of Sul was the most terrible, the most binding oath an immortal could take.

If what I now repeat is not the truth, may Akhran take me now, as I stand here, and lock me in my dwelling, and drop that dwelling into the mouth of Sul, and may Sul swallow me and hold me in the darkness of his belly for a thousand years.

Thus ran the Oath. Many times Achmed had seen the djinn (most notably Pukah) threatened with the Oath, and each time he had seen them back down, refusing to take it. This was the first he had ever heard of one actually swearing by it.

Dazed, blinded by his tears, he could only whisper, "How?"

"Fedj was not present at the battle. He was detained by Raja, Zeid's djinn, who attacked him. Fearing for his master, Fedj left the contest as speedily as he could, only to find the battle ended. He discovered Jaafar lying among the wounded. Seeing his master to safety, Fedj then went to see if there was anyone else who needed his aid. The Amir's soldiers were burning the camp, and all was in disorder. Dusk had fallen, smoke filled the air. Fedj heard a noise and saw three women taking advantage of the confusion to flee the soldiers. Thinking he would lend them his assistance, Fedj flew toward them. Just as he started to speak, he saw the veil covering the face of one of the women slip down—"

Seeing the pain in Achmed's eyes, Saiyad stopped speaking and stared at his feet.

"Khardan?" the young man murmured almost inaudibly, more of a sigh than a spoken word.

Saiyad nodded.

Clutching the broken sword, Achmed slumped against the bars of the gate. Then, angrily, he cried, "I don't believe it! Maybe he was injured, unconscious, and they were helping him!"

"Then why hasn't he come back? He knows his people need him! Unless. . ."

"Unless what?" Achmed glanced up swiftly.

"Unless he is truly a coward—"

Grabbing hold of Saiyad, Achmed slammed the man's face

up against the bars. "Swine! Who is the coward? Who has come crawling on his belly? I will kill you, you—!"

The Imam could see that Saiyad was in trouble this time. Together he and the guard managed to free the nomad from Achmed's strangling grip.

"The bearer of bad news is always treated as though he were the cause of it," Saiyad muttered, breathing heavily and twitching his robes back into place. "Others feared telling you, but I thought you should know."

"The bearer of bad news is treated thus only when he takes pleasure in the telling!" Achmed retorted. "You have hated Khardan ever since he made you look a fool over the madman!" The last words were so choked that they were practically indistinguishable. "Get out of my sight, dog!" Achmed waved the broken sword. "My father is right! Khardan is dead!"

Saiyad's face flushed in anger. "For his sake and for yours, I hope so!" he snarled.

Half-blind with rage, Achmed hurled himself again at the bars, thrusting at Saiyad with the broken sword as though it had a blade still.

Alarmed at this sight, afraid that the young man would hurt himself, the Imam shoved Saiyad away from the gate. "Go back to your home!" the priest instructed in a low voice. "You can do nothing more here!"

Guards came running from across the compound. Grabbing hold of Achmed by both arms, they wrestled the young man away from the gate. Glowering at the priest defiantly, Saiyad moved closer. "Listen to me, Achmed! We are finished as a people and a nation. Akhran has abandoned us. You and the rest of them in there"—he nodded at the prison—"must face that. Now you know why I turned to Quar. He is a God who protects and rewards His own."

With his last strength, Achmed hurled the broken sword at Saiyad.

"You have done enough, my friend," the Imam said coldly. "Go back to your home!"

Gathering the remnants of his dignity about him, Saiyad turned and headed for the *souks*.

"Take the young man back to his cell," the Imam ordered. "Treat him well," the priest added, seeing glances pass among the guards and guessing that they intended to use this display of defiance as an excuse to punish their prisoner. "Any marks on his body and you will answer to Quar!"

The guards dragged their prisoner away and deposited him in his cell without a bruise on him. But they grinned at each other as they left the young man, rubbing their hands in satisfaction. The Imam had much to learn. There are ways and methods that leave no marks.

In the darkness and stench of the cell, Achmed lay upon his bed, doubled up with a pain that twisted his soul more than the beating had twisted his body.

Khardan was dead. And so was his God.

CHAPTER 3

eaving the prison, Feisal walked slowly through the crowds that parted at his coming, many sinking to their knees, hands outstretched to seek his blessing. He granted it reflexively, absent-mindedly touching the foreheads with his thin fingers, murmuring the ritual words as he passed. Absorbed in his thoughts, the Imam was not even consciously aware of where he was until the incense-scented, cool darkness of the inner Temple washed over his skin, a relief from the noonday heat.

Pacing back and forth before the golden ram's-head altar of his God, Feisal considered all that he had heard.

Believing that Achmed was wavering in his faith, the Imam had brought the nomad, Saiyad, to the prison with the simple intent of showing the young man that his people remaining in the desert were scattered and despairing and that those who came to Quar were finding a chance for better lives. That was all. The Imam had been as shocked as Achmed to hear this news of Khardan, and now Feisal considered what to make of it.

The Imam had his spies—exceedingly good ones, devoted to him and to Quar. The priest knew how many segments of orange the Amir ate for breakfast in the morning; he knew the woman the Amir chose to sleep with at night. Qannadi had kept his voice low—but not low enough—when he gave his favorite Captain, Gasim, secret orders to make certain that Khardan's soul was one of the first to be dispatched to Quar. The Imam had been angry at the flouting of his God's wishes, at Qannadi thus acting against the Imam's expressed command that the *kafir*, the unbelievers, be brought to Quar alive. Nevertheless, anger did not draw the veil of folly over Feisal's eyes. The priest detested bloodshed, but he was wise enough in his knowledge of man's stubborn nature to know that there were some who would see Quar's light only when it gleamed through the holes in their flesh. Qannadi was a skillful general. He would be needed to bring the southern cities to their knees in both surrender and worship. Feisal knew he must occasionally toss a bone to this fierce dog to keep him friendly, and therefore he said nothing about his knowledge that Khardan's death had been a deliberate act of murder.

But now—was Khardan dead? Apparently Quar did not think so. If not, how had the Calif escaped? Feisal could hardly credit this strange tale about the Calif disguising himself as a woman. And, more important, where was he?

One person might know the answer to this. The one person who had been acting very mysteriously since the Battle at the Tel.

Ringing a tiny silver bell, the Imam summoned a half-naked servant, who flung himself upon the polished marble floor at his master's feet.

"Bring me the concubine, Meryem," ordered Feisal.

Leaving the inner Temple, Feisal walked a short distance down a corridor to the chamber where he held audience. Like the inner Temple, the room gave the appearance of being closed off from the outside world. It had no windows and the only doorways were reached by means of circumnavigating long and winding corridors. The floor was made of black marble. Tall marble columns supported a ceiling of carved ivory that had been shipped in squares from the Great Steppes of Tara-kan and whose ornate figures represented the many blessings that Quar bestowed upon his people. Lit by huge charcoal braziers that stood on tripods in each corner of the square room, the Imam's audience chamber was otherwise empty, with the exception of a single, marvelous wooden chair.

Sent from Khandar, the chair was probably worth more than the entire Temple, complete with furnishings, for it was carved of *saksaul*. Found only in the salt-impregnated sand of the eastern Pagrah desert, the *saksaul* tree had been long venerated for its unusual properties. The black wood was extremely hard, yet—when carved—it splintered and broke like glass. Thus the craftsman needed to exert extraordinary care, and even small carvings could take many months of work. The wood was heavy and sank in water. When burned, the *saksaul* gave off spicy, fragrant fumes that induced a kind of intoxication. The ash left behind was often carefully preserved and used by physicians for various medicines. Most curious of all, the tree grew beneath the sand, its snakelike trunk—stretching over thirty feet or more—lying buried ten to twelve inches below the surface.

Seated in the *saksaul* chair, the ornate carving of which had reputedly taken several craftsmen many years of painstaking labor, Feisal began collecting in his mind all the reports he'd received and everything he had himself observed about Meryem. One by one he considered them, fingering each as a beggar fingers gold coins.

Qannadi's soldiers had discovered the Amir's concubine and spy lying unconscious in the nomads' camp. Most of her clothes and all her possessions had been stripped from her body, including all of her powerful magical paraphernalia. When the Amir questioned her, Meryem told him that one of his soldiers had mistaken her for a filthy *kafir* and had tried to rape her. She was able to point out the man and watched in offended innocence while he was flogged nearly to death in punishment.

The Amir had not believed her and neither had Feisal. Qannadi's soldiers had been ordered under penalty of castration not to molest any woman. They had been given orders to watch for Meryem, to rescue her from the nomads if it appeared she was in danger. The idea that one of his men would risk his life harming the Amir's concubine was ludicrous. But the Amir had no proof, other than that the soldier volubly protested his innocence, and so he had no choice but to have the wretch punished. Qannadi did not carry out his threat to castrate the man, but a flogging on occasion was useful in maintaining discipline, and if the soldier didn't deserve punishment for this infraction, he undoubtedly deserved it for something else.

The matter was closed, and Meryem was sent back to the *seraglio* where, according to Yamina, the girl waited in dread for the Amir to fulfill his promise and make her one of his wives. Feisal knew that two months ago this had been the dearest dream of Meryem's heart. Not that Qannadi was any great prize in the bedroom. He was nearly fifty, his warrior's body grotesquely scarred, his hands rough and calloused, his breath often sour with wine. It was not, therefore, for the pleasure of his company that the women vied with each other to be his chosen favorite, but for the pleasure of the rich rewards of such a distinction.

The status of wife in the Amir's harem meant that a woman joined the ranks of the powerful sorceresses who worked the palace magic. Any children born of this union were legitimate sons and daughters of the Amir and, as such, were often granted high places in court, to say nothing of the fact that anyone could be chosen as Qannadi's heir. A concubine might be loaned out or even given as a gift to a friend or associate. Not so a wife, who was kept in well-guarded seclusion.

Such isolation did not mean that the wives were not a force in the world. Yamina, Qannadi's head wife, was known to every grandee, noble, priest, and lowly citizen to be the true ruler of the city of Kich. The Imam had, more than once, seen Meryem watching and listening when he and Yamina were involved in political discussions. There was no doubt that it was her ambition to gain as much power as she was able.

But Qannadi never sent for her.

"I think the time she spent living in the desert has driven her insane," Yamina had confided during one of the many private and confidential talks with the Imam she always managed to arrange in his chambers in the Temple. "Before she left, she did everything possible to catch Qannadi's eye—dancing naked in the baths, flaunting her beauty, appearing unveiled. . ."

Yamina always went into details describing such things to the Imam; her hand—by accident—touching the priest's thin leg or gliding gently along his arm. Sitting alone in his marvelous chair, Feisal remembered Yamina's words and remembered her touch as well. He frowned to himself in displeasure.

"Since her return," Yamina had continued somewhat coldly, the priest having sidled farther away from her on the sofa on which they both sat, "Meryem bathes in the morning when she knows the Amir is away reviewing his troops. She hides whenever the eunuch appears to select Qannadi's choice for the night. If the Amir asks for dancers, she pleads that she is unwell."

"What is the reason for this strange behavior?" Feisal asked. He recalled that he had not been particularly interested, other than keeping himself aware of all that concerned the Amir. "Surely she knows the risk she is taking? She is already in disfavor. Qannadi is convinced she lied about what happened to her in the nomads' camp."

"I think she is in love," Yamina said in a throaty, husky whisper, leaning nearer Feisal.

"With the nomad?" Feisal appeared amused. "A wild man who smells of horse."

"A wild man? Yes!" Yamina breathed, running her fingers along the Imam's arm. Her veil had slipped from her face, her hand artfully displaced the filmy fabric covering her neck and breasts, allowing the priest to see a beauty still considered remarkable after forty years. "A wild man with eyes of flame, a body hard and muscular, a man accustomed to taking what he desires. A woman in love with such a man will risk everything!"

"But this Khardan is dead," Feisal said coolly, rising to his feet and walking around to the back of the sofa.

Biting her lip in frustration, Yamina stood up. "Like other men I could mention!" she hissed. Covering herself with her veil, she left his chambers in an angry rustle of silk.

Feisal had not paid much heed to Yamina's words. She frequently used gossip such as this in her attempts to arouse him to a passion that his religious soul viewed as onerous and disgusting, his common sense viewed as highly dangerous. Now, however, he began to wonder. . .

"The concubine, Meryem," said the servant, startling Feisal out of his reverie.

The Imam looked up and saw a lithe, slender figure clothed in a pale blue *paranja* standing, hesitating, inside the chamber's doorway. The light from the flaming brazier glistened on golden hair, just barely visible beneath the folds of her veil. Bright blue eyes watched the Imam with what the priest noted was an almost feverish luster.

Dismissing the servant, Feisal beckoned.

"Come nearer, child," he said, assuming a paternal tone, though he himself was only a few years older than the woman.

Meryem crept forward and threw herself on the floor before him, her arms extended. Gazing down at her, the Imam saw that the girl was terrified. She trembled from head to toe, the fabric of her gown shivered as in a breeze, her earrings and bracelets jingled in nervous agitation. Feisal smiled to himself in inward satisfaction, all the golden coins of his thoughts falling together in one bag. Bending down, he took hold of her hand and raised her to her knees, drawing her close.

"Meryem, my child," he began softly, his almond eyes catching hers and holding them fast, "I have received reports saying that you are unwell. Now that I see you, I know they are true! I am deeply concerned, both as your spiritual adviser and, more importantly, as your friend."

He could not see her face, hidden behind her veil. But he saw the fear in the eyes waver, the feathery brows come together in confusion. This wasn't what she had expected. The Imam grew more and more certain of himself.

"What have you heard, Imam?" she asked, casting out her line, fishing for information.

Feisal was quick to take the bait. "That you imagine someone is trying to poison you, that you refuse to eat or drink unless a slave tastes your portion first. That you sleep with a dagger beneath your pillow. I realize that your experiences in the desert among the nomads must have been quite frightening, but you are safe from them now. There is no way they can harm you—"

"It isn't the nomads!" The words burst from Meryem's lips before she could stop them. Realizing too late that the fish had just landed the fisherman, she turned deathly white and covered her veiled mouth with her hand.

"It isn't the nomads you fear," Feisal said with increasing gentleness that brought tears to the blue eyes. "Then it must be someone in the palace."

"No, it is nothing! Only my foolishness! Please, let me go, Imam!" Meryem begged, trying to free her hand from the priest's grasp.

"Qannadi?" Feisal suggested. "Because you lied to him?"

Meryem made a choked sound. Almost strangling, she sank down onto the floor, cowering in terror. "He will have me killed!" she wailed.

"No, no, my child," the Imam said. Slipping out of the chair, the priest knelt beside the girl and gathered her into his arms, rocking her and talking to her soothingly. Yamina, had she been there, would have writhed in jealousy completely misplaced. The only desire Feisal felt was the intense desire to drain this girl of the vital information she had hidden in her heart.

"On the contrary," the Imam said to Meryem when her sobs grew calmer, "the Amir has completely forgotten the incident. Of course he knew you lied. More than one of his men had reported seeing Gasim fighting Khardan hand to hand. Qannadi thought it very strange, then, to hear that his best Captain died of a knife wound in the back!" Meryem groaned, shaking her head. "Hush, child. Qannadi guessed only that you were trying to save your lover. With the war in the south, he has more things on his mind than concern over a concubine's infidelity."

The blue eyes looked up at him over the edge of the veil. Shimmering with tears, they were wide and innocent and Feisal wasn't fooled by them in the least.

"Is. . . is that truly what he believes, Imam?" Meryem asked, blinking her long lashes.

"Yes, my dear," said Feisal, smiling. Reaching up, he smoothed back a lock of blond hair that had slipped from beneath the head-covering. "He doesn't know you were plotting to overthrow him."

Meryem gasped. Her body went rigid in the Imam's arms. She stared at him wildly, and suddenly Feisal had another golden coin to add to his growing accumulation of wealth. "No," he said softly. "That's not quite true. Not *were* plotting to overthrow him. You *are* plotting to overthrow him!"

The tears in the blue eyes vanished, burned away by shrewd, desperate calculation. "I will do anything!" Meryem said in a tight, hard voice. "Anything you ask of me. I will be your slave!" She tore the veil from her face. "Take me now!" she said fiercely, pressing her body against Feisal's. "I am yours—"

"I want nothing from you, girl," the priest said coldly, pushing her away from him, sending her sprawling onto the marble floor. "Nothing, that is, except the truth. Tell me everything you know. *Everything!*" he added, speaking the word slowly and with emphasis. "And remember. I know much already. If I catch you in another lie, I will turn you over to Qannadi. Then you can tell your story to the Lord High Executioner under much less pleasant circumstances!"

"I will tell you the truth, Imam!" Meryem said, rising to her feet and regarding Feisal with cool dignity. "I will tell you that the Amir is a traitor to Quar! Because of his sacrilege, the God himself has ordained his downfall. I am but His humble instrument," she added, lowering her eyes modestly.

Feisal found it difficult to maintain his countenance during this sudden, newfound religious fervor on Meryem's part. Placing his fingers over his twitching lips, he motioned with the other hand for her to speak.

"It is true that I love Khardan, Imam!" Meryem began passionately. "And because I love him I wanted more than anything else to bring him to the knowledge of the One, the True God. I knew that the Amir planned to attack the camp, of course, and I feared for Khardan's life. From some words of Yamina's, I came to realize that Qannadi is afraid of Khardan and with reason," the girl added loftily, "for he is strong and brave and a fierce warrior. I guessed that the Amir might try to have Khardan assassinated.

"Before the battle, therefore, I gave Khardan a charm to wear around his neck, Imam. He thought it an ordinary amulet of good luck, such as are made by the backward women of his tribe."

"But it wasn't, was it?" said Feisal grimly.

"No, Imam," Meryem answered with some pride. "I am a skilled sorceress, almost as powerful as Yamina herself. When I spoke the word, the charm cast an enchantment over the nomad, sending him into a deep sleep. It also acted as a shield, preventing any weapon from harming him. It was well I did so," she said, her voice hardening, "for it was as I suspected. Going against your express command that the nomads were not to be harmed, Qannadi attempted to have Khardan murdered. I caught Gasim in the act."

She paused, glancing at the Imam from the corner of her eye, perhaps hoping to see the priest fly into a rage at this news. Having been aware of it, Feisal showed no emotion whatsoever, and Meryem was forced to continue without having any idea how the priest might be reacting. "I carried Khardan from the battle on Gasim's horse. I intended to bring him to Kich and place him in your care, Imam, so that the Amir would not have him killed. Between the two of us, I knew we could convert Khardan's soul to Quar!"

"I doubt you were interested in his soul so much as his body," the Imam said dryly. "What happened to spoil your little plan?"

Meryem's face flushed in anger, but she carefully controlled herself and went on smoothly with her story, as though there had been no interruption. "I was waiting for Kaug, the 'efreet, to extend his hand and take us up into the clouds when I saw, out of the corner of my eye, that madman coming up behind me and—"

"Madman?" Feisal questioned curiously. "What madman?"

"Just a madman, Imam!" Meryem said impatiently. "A youth Khardan rescued from the slave traders here in Kich. Khardan thought the boy was a woman, but he wasn't; he was a man without hair on his face or chest who had dressed up in woman's clothing. The other nomads wanted to execute him, but Khardan wouldn't let them, saying that the youth was mad because he claimed to have come from over the sea and to be a sorcerer. Then the witch woman—Khardan's wife—said that the youth should be taken into Khardan's harem, and that is why Khardan couldn't marry me!"

Feisal didn't hear half of this involved and somewhat incoherent explanation. The words "over the sea" and "sorcerer" had completely overwhelmed his mind. It was only with a violent effort that he managed to wrench his thoughts back to what Meryem was saying.

"—the madman pulled me from the horse and struck me savagely over the head. When I woke up," she concluded pitifully, "I was as they found me—half-naked, left for dead."

"Khardan?"

"Gone, apparently, Imam. I don't know. I didn't wake up until I was in the palace. But when I questioned the soldiers, they had seen no sign of him."

"And his body was never discovered," the Imam mused.

"No, it wasn't," Meryem muttered, drawing her veil over her face once more, keeping her eyes lowered.

"And why do you think this. . . this madman would strip off your clothes?"

"Isn't that obvious, if you will forgive me, Imam? To have his way with me, of course."

"In the midst of a raging battle? He must have been mad indeed!"

Meryem kept her gaze on the floor. "I—I suppose, Imam, that he was interrupted in his foul deed—"

"Mmmm." Feisal leaned forward. "Would it surprise you to hear that Khardan was seen fleeing the field of battle, dressed in women's clothes?"

Meryem looked up, blue eyes open wide. "Of—of course!" she stammered.

"Don't lie!"

"All right!" she cried wildly, stamping her small foot. "I didn't know, but I suspected. It would have been the only way to escape the soldiers! There were a lot of old hags left behind in the camp. If the soldiers saw Khardan dressed as a woman, they would probably just let him go."

"And Khardan is still alive'" Feisal said softly. "You know it and you are hoping he will come back!"

"Yes!"

"How do you know?"

"The enchantment will continue working to keep him from harm as long as he wears the necklace...."

"But someone may have removed it, taken it off. Perhaps the madman." Feisal sank back into the chair, his brows knotted. "If he is truly a sorcerer—"

"That is nonsense!" Meryem said spiritedly. "Only women have the magic. All know that!"

"Still..." Feisal seemed lost in thought. Then, shrugging, he returned to the matter at hand. "You do not speculate that he may be alive, Meryem! You *know* he is alive! You know where he is, and that is why you have been afraid. Because you think that he will turn up any moment and challenge the Amir, who will then begin to suspect there is a snake hiding in his fig basket—"

"No! I swear—"

"Tell me, Meryem. Or"—Feisal caught hold of her hand—"would you prefer to tell the Lord High Executioner as he flays the skin from these delicate bones..."

Meryem snatched her hand away. The veil, stained with sweat and tears, clung damply to her face. "I—I looked into the scrying bowl," she murmured. "If... if he was dead, I would see his... his body."

"But you didn't?"

"No!" Her voice was faint.

"You saw him alive!"

"No, not that either..."

"I grow tired of these evasions!" The Imam's voice cracked, and Meryem shuddered, the words flicking over her like a whip.

"I am not lying now, Imam!" she cried, casting herself on the floor and looking up at him pleadingly. "He is alive, but he is covered by a cloud of darkness that hides him from my sight. It is ... magic, I suppose. But like no magic I have ever seen before! I do not know its meaning!"

There was silence in the Temple chamber, a silence so deep and thick and reverent that Meryem stifled her sobs, holding her breath so as not to disturb it or the Imam, whose almond eyes stared unseeing into the shadows.

Finally, the Imam stirred. "You are right. You are in danger in the palace."

Lifting her head, Meryem gazed at him with incredulous, unbelieving hope dawning in her eyes.

"What's more, you are being wasted. I am going to suggest to the Amir that you be sent to live in the city with the nomads. Khardan's mother, I believe, is one who was captured and brought to Kich."

"But what will I tell them?" Meryem sat back on her knees. "They think I am the Sultan's daughter! They would expect the Amir to execute me!"

"An expert on lying such as yourself should have no trouble coming up with a story that will melt their hearts," Feisal remarked. "The Amir was going to have you thrown from the Tower of Death but then he succumbed to your charms. He begged you to marry him, but you—loyal to your nomadic prince—refused. Qannadi hurled you in the dungeon and fed you only on bread and water. He beat you. Still you remained true. Finally, knowing he could never have you, he cast you into the streets. . ."

Meryem's lips came together, the blue eyes glistened. "Lash marks and bruises," she said. "The guards must throw me out at midday, when there is a crowd—"

"Anything you want," the Imam interrupted, suddenly impatient for the girl to be gone and leave him to his thoughts. Clapping his hands, he caused the servant to appear. "Return to the *seraglio*. Make your preparations. I will speak to the Amir this evening and convince him of the necessity of replanting our spy among the nomads." He waved his hand. "Get up. Your thanks are not necessary. You are serving Quar, as you said. And Meryem—"

This to the girl as she was rising to her feet.

"Yes, Imam?"

"Anything you discover concerning Khardan—anything at all—you will inform me."

"Yes, Imam," she said glibly.

Too glibly. Feisal leaned forward in the *saksaul* chair. "Know this, my child. If I hear his name on the tongue of another before

I hear it on yours, I will have that tongue torn from your mouth. Do you understand?"

"Yes, Imam." All glibness disappeared.

"Very well. You may go. Quar's blessing attend you."

When the girl and the servant were gone, Feisal sank back into the chair. His elbow resting on the hard, carved surface of the chair arm, the Imam allowed his head to sink into his hand as though the weight of his contemplations was too much for his neck to bear. The nomads. . . Khardan . . . the Amir . . . Achmed . . . His thoughts tumbled about in his mind like rocks in a jeweler's polishing wheel. One only he found rough, uncut, disturbing.

The madman. . .

CHAPTER 4

 he prison guards sat hunched in the meager shade afforded
by the squat, square gatehouse, their backs pressed against
the cool wall that had not yet been baked by the sun. It was nearly
noon and the shade was dwindling rapidly. Soon the heat of afternoon would drive them inside the gatehouse itself. They avoided that as long as possible. Entering the clay-brick dwelling was
tantamount to entering an oven. But though the heat inside was
intense, it had at least the advantage of providing shelter from
the sweltering sun. As the last vestige of shade was vanishing, the
guards, grumbling, rose to their feet. One of the younger nudged
an older man, his superior, and pointed.

"Soldiers."

Squinting into the sunlight, the commandant peered out toward the *souks*, always thankful for some change in the monotony
of his watch. Several of the Amir's soldiers, splendid in their colorful uniforms, were urging their horses through the crowds in
the bazaar. The people scattered before them, mothers grabbing
up small children, the merchants quickly removing their most
valuable items from display and shoving their daughters behind
the curtained partitions. If the crowd was too thickly packed together, and the horses could not get through, the soldiers cleared
a path, lashing out efficiently with their riding sticks, ignoring
the cursing and the angry shouts that died away to a hushed awe
when the crowd caught sight of the man riding behind the soldiers.

"The Amir," the commandant muttered.

"I think he's coming here," said the young guard.

"Pah!" The older guard spat on the ground, but his gaze was
fixed warily on the retinue that was making its way through the
bazaars. "I think you're right," he said slowly, after a moment's

pause. Whirling around, he began bellowing orders that brought other sleepy guards to their feet, hastily stumbling across the compound at the commandant's call.

"What's the matter with Hamd?" he bellowed, noting that one of the guards was not responding. "Drunk again? Drag him inside the gatehouse! Quickly! And look to your uniforms! What's that? Blood? Yours, too? Tell him it's from the thief. What's that? The man died two days ago? Worse luck! Keep out of sight, then! The rest of you—try to look alert, if I that's possible, you sons of pigs. Now go on! Back to your places!"

Muttering imprecations on the heads of everyone from the Amir to the comatose Hamd, whose limp, flabby body was being dragged unceremoniously across the ground to the gatehouse, the commandant began pushing and shoving his bleary-eyed men toward their assigned positions, some of the slower being assisted on their way by sound thwacks from the commandant's thick cudgel.

The clattering of horses' hooves drew nearer. Gulping for breath, sweating profusely, the commandant cast one final glance around his prison. At least, he thought thankfully, the prisoners had been put back in their cells following the midday exercise period. In the darkness of the Zindan, swollen cheeks, split lips, and blackened eyes were not readily apparent. Neither were blood stains on tunics, for that matter. Just to be safe, however, the commandant's dull mind was fumbling with excuses for going against the Amir's express orders that the prisoners—particularly the nomads—were not to be physically abused. The commandant was just fabricating a full-scale riot that had forced him to resort to the use of force when the younger guard interrupted his lumbering thoughts.

"Why is the Amir coming here? Is this customary?"

"No, by Sul!"

The two were standing at some semblance of attention in front of the gatehouse and the commandant—keeping eyes forward with a grin of welcome plastered across his face—was forced to talk out of the side of his mouth.

"The old Sultan never came within a thousand paces of the place, if he could help it. And when he was forced to ride past, he did so in a covered sedan chair with the curtains pulled tightly shut, holding an orange stuck all over with cloves to his nose to ward away the smell."

"Then why do you suppose the Amir's coming?"

"How in Quar's name should I know?" the commandant grunted, surreptitiously mopping his face with his sleeve. "Something to do with those damn nomads no doubt. It's bad enough we have the priest skulking about, sticking his nose into everything. Quar forgive me." The commandant glanced warily up at the heavens. "I'll be glad when the lot of them are out of here."

"When will that be?"

"When they convert, of course."

"They'll die first."

"All the same to me." The commandant shrugged. "Either way, it shouldn't take very long. Shhh!"

The men fell silent, the commandant shifting uneasily, longing to turn his head and look behind him to see that everything was in order but not daring to allow his nervousness to show. Behind him, he could hear Hamd's drunken voice suddenly raise in a bawdy song. The commandant's blood began throbbing in his temples, but then came a sound as of someone thumping an overripe melon, a muffled groan, and the singing ceased.

The soldiers on horseback trotted up to the gate. At their leader's command, they spread out in a straight line, sitting stiffly at attention in their saddles, their magical horses standing as still as if they had turned back to the wood out of which they were created. The Captain raised his sword with a flourish. Qannadi, who had been riding a short distance behind his troops, cantered forward. Returning his Captain's salute, he dismounted. Eyes flicking here and there over the prison and its yards, he slowly approached the sweating commandant. The Captain followed.

In the old days, if the Sultan had taken it into his head to visit the prison—which was about as likely as if he had taken it into his head to fly to the moon—such a visit could never have been accomplished without hundreds of guards surrounding his sacred person; slaves carrying his chair and rolling out velvet carpets so that he might not soil his silken shoes upon the unworthy ground; several other litters bearing his favorite wives, who would be peeping out between the curtains and holding their veils over their mouths; more slaves carrying huge feathered fans to keep away the flies that found the prison a veritable feasting ground.

The Sultan would have stayed four minutes, five at the most, before the hot sun and the stench and the general unpleasantness of the place drove him back into the perfumed silken shelter of his palanquin. Watching the Amir walk with long, purposeful strides over the hard-baked ground, appearing cool and calm, his nose not even wrinkling, the commandant heartily missed the old days.

"O Mighty King!" The commandant dropped to his belly on the blisteringly hot ground, looking—in this undignified attitude—very much like a toad and adding nothing to the already deplorable state of his uniform. "Such an honor—"

"Get up!" Qannadi said with disgust. "I've no time for I that. I'm here to see one of your prisoners."

The commandant scrambled to his feet but left his heart lying on the pavement. Which prisoner? Hopefully not one who had been chastised too severely.

"Filthy wretches, O King. Unworthy of such attention! I beg of you—"

"Open the gate."

The commandant had no choice except to obey. His hands shook so that he could not fit the key into the latch, however, and Qannadi made a sign. The Amir's Captain stepped forward, took the keys from the shaken guard, and opened the gate that rotated on its hinges with a shrill squeak. Thrusting his way past the stammering commandant, the Amir entered the prison compound.

"Where is the cell of Achmed, the nomad?"

"On. . . on the lower level, third to your left. But do not offend your spirit by entering the House of the Damned, Your Majesty!" Panting, the commandant waddled about six steps behind the swiftly walking general. "My eyes are accustomed to the sight of these dregs of humanity. Allow me to bring the *kafir* into your Exalted Presence, O King."

Qannadi hesitated. He had intended to enter the prison and talk to Achmed in his cell. But now that he stood before the ugly, windowless building, now that he could smell the smell of human refuse and despair, now that he could hear faintly the moans of hopelessness and pain coming from inside, the general's courage—whose flame had never once died on the field of battle—wavered and dimmed. He was accustomed to death and misery in war, he would never grow accustomed to death and misery where men were caged like beasts.

"The gatehouse is quite comfortable this time of day, O Magnificent One," the commandant suggested, seeing the Amir hesitate.

"Very well," Qannadi said abruptly, turning his steps and attempting to ignore the audible whoosh of relief that escaped the commandant.

"Go ahead!" the commandant shouted at the young guard, who was standing rooted to the spot, staring at the Amir in awe. "Make the gatehouse ready for His Majesty!"

By dint of several frantic hand motions behind the Amir's back and a series of threatening grimaces, the commandant managed to convey the message to the dumbfounded young guard that he was to make certain the drunken Hamd was out of sight. Catching on, the young man bolted away, and Qannadi entered the sultry shadows of the bare brick room just in time to hear a scuffling sound and see the soles of the boots of the unfortunate Hamd disappear into a back room. A door slammed shut.

Picking up an overturned chair, the Captain of the Amir's guard placed it at a crude table for Qannadi who, however, seemed to prefer pacing about the small dwelling. The commandant appeared, gasping for breath, in the doorway.

"Well?" said Qannadi, glaring at the man. "Go get the prisoner!"

"Yes, O King!" The commandant had completely forgotten this small matter. He vanished precipitously from the doorway. Glancing out a small window, Qannadi saw the man running across the compound, headcloth flapping in the wind of his exertions. Glancing at the Captain, the Amir raised his eyebrows. The Captain silently shook his head.

"Clear everyone out," Qannadi ordered, motioning toward the back room.

The Captain acted immediately on his orders and by the time Qannadi saw the commandant returning across the compound, shoving a reluctant and unwilling Achmed along in front of him, the building had been emptied of all its occupants, including a dazed and bloody Hamd. The Captain of the guard took up his post outside the door.

The puffing and panting commandant appeared in the entrance. Dragging the young man by the arm, he thrust Achmed inside the gatehouse. The nomad stood in the cool shadows, dazed, blinking his eyes, glancing around in confusion.

"Bow! Bow to the Amir, dog of an unbeliever!" the commandant shouted angrily.

It was obvious to Qannadi that the sun-blinded young man had no idea an Amir or anyone else was in the room. But when Achmed did not respond fast enough to suit the commandant, he kicked the youth painfully in the back of the knees, causing his legs to buckle. Gripping him by the back of his tunic, the commandant bashed the young man's head on the floor.

"I apologize for the dog's ill manners, O Exalted One—"

"Get out!" said Qannadi coldly. "I want to speak to the prisoner in private."

The commandant glanced uneasily at Achmed, lying prostrate on the floor, and spread his hands in a deprecating manner. "I would not be so bold as to disobey an order of my king but I would be remiss in my duties if I did not inform His Majesty that these *kafir* are wild beasts—"

"Are you saying that I—General of the Armies of Quar's Chosen—cannot deal with one eighteen-year-old boy?" Qannadi inquired smoothly.

"No! No! Assuredly not, O King!" babbled the commandant, sweating so it appeared he might melt into a puddle on the spot.

"Then leave. The Captain of my guard will be posted outside. In case I find myself in any danger, I can always yell for him to come rescue me."

Not knowing exactly what to make of this speech, the dull-witted commandant stammered out that this knowledge would be of great comfort to him. Disgusted, Qannadi turned his back upon the prison guard and gazed out a square window at nothing with magnificent aplomb. The folds of the *haik* hiding his face, the Amir was able to turn his head slightly to see what was happening behind him out of the corner of his eye. The commandant, casting a swift, fearful glance at his king, administered a swift, savage kick to Achmed, catching the boy painfully in the crook of his knee. His face dark, the commandant raised a fist at his prisoner threateningly, then, bobbing up and down like a beggar's monkey, backed out the door, fervent in his praise of the Amir, the Emperor, Quar, the Imam, the Amir's wives, and anyone else he could think of.

His hand itching to draw his sword and rid the world of this specimen of humanity, Qannadi kept his back turned until a scuffle, the sound of his Captain's voice, and a whine assured him that the commandant had been hustled off the premises.

Still Qannadi did not turn around.

"Get up," he ordered the young man gruffly. "I detest seeing a man grovel."

He heard the sharp intake of breath as Achmed stood upon his injured leg but even that indication of weakness was quickly choked off by the young man. Qannadi turned around just in time to see the nomad draw himself up, standing straight and tall and facing the Amir with defiance.

"Sit down," said Qannadi.

Startled, seeing only one chair and realizing—barbarian though he was—that no one ever sat in the presence of the king, Achmed remained standing.

"I said sit down!" Qannadi snapped irritably. "That was a command, young man, and—like it or not—you are in no position to disobey my commands!"

Slowly, his face carefully impassive, Achmed sank down into the chair, gritting his teeth to keep the gasp of pain from slipping out.

"Are the guards mistreating you?" Qannadi asked abruptly.

"No," lied the young man.

The Amir turned his head back to the window again to hide the emotion on his face. The "no" had not been spoken out of fear. It had been spoken in pride. Qannadi remembered suddenly another young man who had nearly died of a festering arrow wound because he was too proud to admit he'd been hit.

The Amir cleared his throat and turned back again. "You will address me as 'King,' or 'Your Majesty,' " he said. Walking over to the door, he glanced outside to see his men, mounted on their horses, waiting patiently in line in the hot sun. He knew his men would remain there uncomplaining until they dropped but—magic or not—the animals were beginning to suffer. Cursing himself, aware that in his preoccupation he'd forgotten them, the Amir ordered the Captain to disperse the guard and see that the horses were watered. The Captain left, and the Amir and the young man were alone.

"How long have you been confined here?" Qannadi asked,

coming over to gaze down upon the young man.

Shrugging, Achmed shook his head.

"A month? Two? A year? You don't know? Ah, good. That means we are starting to break you."

The young man looked up swiftly, eyes glittering.

"Yes," Qannadi continued imperturbably. "It takes spirit, an effort of will, to keep track of the passing of time when one is in a situation where each day of misery blends into a night of despair until all seem alike. You've seen the wretches who've been here for years. You've seen how they live only for the moment when they receive their wormy bread and their cup of rancid water. Less than animals, aren't they? Many forget how to talk." Qannadi saw fear darken the young man's eyes and he smiled to himself in inner satisfaction. "I know, you see. I was in prison myself for a time. I wasn't much older than you, fighting the warriors of the Great Steppes.

"They are fierce fighters, those men of Hammah. Their women fight alongside them. I swear by Quar that is the truth," Qannadi added gravely, seeing Achmed's stare of disbelief. "They are a large, big-boned race—the women as big as the men. They have golden hair that, from birth, is never cut. Men and women both wear it in braids that hang down below their waists. When they fight, they fight in pairs—husband and wife or couples betrothed to be married. The man stands upon the right to wield sword and spear, the woman stands to his left, holding a great, huge shield that protects them both. If her husband is killed, the wife fights on until either his death is avenged or she herself falls beside his body." Qannadi shook his head. "And woe betide the man who takes the life of a shieldmaid."

Pain forgotten, Achmed listened with shining, wondering eyes. Gratified, Qannadi paused a moment to enjoy this audience. He had told this story to his own sons and received only stifled yawns or bored, glazed stares in return.

"I was lucky." Qannadi smiled wryly. "I didn't have a chance to kill anyone. I was disarmed the first pass and knocked unconscious. They took me prisoner and cast me into their dungeons that are carved out of rock into the sides of mountains. At first, I was like you. My life was over, I thought. I cursed my bad luck that I hadn't fallen among my comrades. The Hammadians are a just people, however. They offered all of us the chance to work out our servitude, but I was too proud. I refused. I sat in my cell, wallowing in my misery, day after day, blind to what was happening to me. Then something occurred that opened my eyes."

"What?" Achmed spoke before he thought. Face flushed, he bit his lip and looked away.

Qannadi kept his own face carefully smooth and impassive. "When the Hammadi first captured me, they beat me every day. They had a post planted in the center of the prison yard and they would put a man up against it like so"—the Amir demonstrated—"and chain his hands to the top. Then they stripped the clothes from my back and struck a leather thong across my shoulders. To this day I bear the scars." Qannadi spoke with unconscious pride. He wasn't watching Achmed now, but was looking back, into his past. "Then one day they didn't beat me. Another passed, and another, and they continued to leave me alone. My comrades—those that still lived—were being punished. But not me. One day I overheard another prisoner demand to know why I alone was spared this harsh treatment.

"Can you guess their answer?" The Amir looked at Achmed intently.

The young man shook his head.

" 'We do not beat the whipped dog.' "

There was silence in the gatehouse. Because it had been many years since he had thought of this incident, Qannadi had not realized that the pain and shame and humiliation was still within him, festering like that arrow wound of long ago.

" 'We do not beat the whipped dog,' " he repeated grimly. "I saw then that I had let myself become nothing but an animal—an object of pity, beneath their contempt."

"What did you do?" The words were forced through clenched teeth. The young man stared at hands clasped tightly in his lap.

"I went to them and I offered myself as their slave."

"You worked for your enemy?" Achmed looked up, his black eyes scornful.

"I worked for myself," the Amir replied. "I could have proudly rotted to death in their prison. Believe me, young man, at that point in my life, death would have been the easy way out. But I was a soldier. I reminded myself that I had been captured, I had not surrendered. And to die in their foul prison would be to admit defeat. Besides, one never knows the paths the God has chosen one to walk."

The Amir glanced surreptitiously at Achmed as he said this last, but the young man's head was bowed again, his gaze fixed upon his clenched hands.

"And, as it turned out, Quar chose wisely. I was sent to work on the farm of a great general in the Hammadi army. Their armies are not as ours," Qannadi continued. Staring out his window, he saw not the crowded *souks* of Kich but the vast, rolling prairies of the Great Steppes. "The armies are under the control of certain rich and powerful men, who hire and train their soldiers at their own expense. In time of war, the king calls these armies to come fight for the defense of the land. Of course, there is always the chance that the general might become too powerful and decide that he wants to be king, but that is a danger all rulers must face.

"I was put to work in the fields of this man's farm. At first, I regretted that I had not died in the prison. I was thin, emaciated. My muscles had atrophied during my long confinement. More than once, I sank down among the weeds with the thought that I would never rise again. But I did. Sometimes the overseer's lash helped me up. Sometimes I myself struggled to my feet. And, as time passed, I grew strong and fit once more. My interest in life and, more importantly, my interest in soldiering returned. My master was constantly exercising his troops, and every moment I could escape from my labors I spent watching. He was an excellent general, and the lessons I learned from him have helped me all my life. Particularly, I studied the art of infantry fighting, for in this these people were most skilled. At length, he noticed my interest. Far from being offended, as I feared, he was pleased.

"He took me from the fields and set me among his troops. My life was not easy, for I was different, a foreigner, and they did everything they could to test me. But I gave as good as I got, most of the time, and eventually earned their respect and that of my general. He made me one of his personal guard. I fought at his side for two years."

Achmed stared in blank astonishment at this, but Qannadi seemed no longer aware of the boy's presence.

"He was a great soldier, a noble and honorable man. I loved him as I have loved no other, before or since. He died on the field of battle. I, myself, avenged his death and was given the honor of placing the severed head of his enemy at his feet as he lay upon his funeral bier. I cast my lighted torch onto the oil-soaked wood and I bid his soul godspeed to whatever heaven he believed in. Then I left." Qannadi's voice was soft. The young man had to lean forward to hear him. "I walked for many months until I reached my homeland once more. Our glorious Emperor was only a king then. I came before him and laid my sword at his feet."

Sighing, the Amir withdrew his gaze from the window and turned to look at Achmed. "It is a curiosity, that sword. A two-handed broadsword it is called in the north. It takes two hands to wield it. When I first was given one, I could not even lift it from the floor. I still have it, if you would like to see it."

The young man glowered at him, dark eyes wary, sullen, suspicious.

"Why are you telling me this tale?" He rudely refused to use the proper form of address, and the Amir—though he noticed—did not press him.

"I came because I deplore waste. As for why I told you my story, I am not certain." Qannadi paused, then spoke softly. "You take a wound in battle and it can heal completely and never bother you again. Then, years later, you see a man hit in exactly the same place and suddenly the pain returns—as sharp and piercing as when the steel first bit into your flesh. When I looked into your face, Achmed, I felt the pain. . ."

The young man's shoulders slumped. The pride and anger that had kept him alive drained from his body like blood from a mortal wound. Looking at Achmed, Qannadi had one of those rare flashes of illumination that sometimes, in the dark night of wandering through this life, lights the way and shows the soul of another. Perhaps it was seeing once again in his mind Khardan and Achmed together, standing before his throne—one brother proud and handsome, the other looking at him with complete and total adoration. Perhaps it was the Imam, telling him the strange tale of Khardan's alleged flight from the battle. Perhaps it came from within the Amir himself and the memory of his own starved childhood, the father who had abandoned him. Whatever it was, Qannadi suddenly knew Achmed better than he knew any of his own sons, knew him as well as he had come to know himself.

He saw a young man deprived of the light of a father's love and pride, growing in the shadow cast by an older brother. Instead of letting this embitter him, Achmed had simply transferred the love for his father to his older brother, who had—Qannadi knew—returned it warmly. But Khardan had betrayed him, if not by an act of cowardice (and the Amir found it difficult to believe such a wild tale) then at least by dying. The boy was left with no one—father, brother, all were gone.

Going up to the young man, Qannadi put his hand on his shoulder. He felt Achmed flinch, but the boy did not pull away from the Amir's touch.

"How old are you?"

"Eighteen," came the mulled response. "I—I had a birthday."

And no one remembered, Qannadi thought. "I was the same age myself when I was captured by the Hammadi." A lie. The Amir had been twenty, but that was not important. "Are you a whipped dog, Achmed? Are you going to lie down on your master's grave and die?" The boy cringed. "Or are you going to live your own life? I told you I deplore waste. You are a fine young man! I could wish my own sons to be more like you!"

A touch of bitterness crept into the voice. Qannadi fell silent, mastering his emotions. Achmed was too preoccupied with his own to notice, although he would recall it later.

"I came here to make you an offer," Qannadi continued. "I watched the Battle at the Tel. My men are good soldiers, but it took four of them to one of yours to conquer your people. It is not that you are more skilled in handling your weapons, I believe, but in handling your horses. Quar has given us magical beasts but, it seems, He has not seen fit to train them in the art of warfare. Instead of your people breaking your hearts in this prison, I give you the chance to earn your freedom."

Achmed's body held rigid for a moment. Slowly he raised his head to look directly into Qannadi's eyes.

"All we would do is train the horses?"

"Yes."

"We would not be forced to join your army? Forced to fight?"

"No, not unless you wanted."

"The horses we train will not fight our own people?"

"My son"—Qannadi used the word unconsciously, never realizing he had spoken it until he saw the eyes looking into his blink, the lids lower abruptly—"your people are no more. I do not tell you this to attempt to trick you or demoralize you. I speak the truth. If you cannot hear it in my voice, then listen to your own heart."

Achmed did not respond but sat, head down, his hands grasping spasmodically at the smooth top of the crude wooden table, seeking something to hold onto and not finding it.

"I will not make you convert to our God," the Amir added gently.

At this, Achmed raised his head. He looked, not at Qannadi, but eastward, into the desert that could not be seen for the prison walls.

"There is no God," the young man answered tonelessly.

CHAPTER 5

The nomads of the Pagrah desert believed that the world was flat and that they were in its center. The huge and splendid city of Khandar—as far distant, in their minds, as a remote star—glittered somewhere to the north of them and beyond Khandar was the edge of the world. To the west was the city of Kich, the mountains, the great Hurn Sea, and, finally, the edge of the world. To the south was more desert, the cities of the land of Bas in the southeast, and the edge of the world. To the east was the Sun's Anvil—the edge of the world.

It was rumored among the nomadic tribes that the city dwellers spoke of the existence of another great sea to the east, beyond the Sun's Anvil, and had even given it a name—the Kurdin Sea. The nomads scoffed at this belief—what could one expect of people who built walls around their lives—and spoke scornfully of the Kurdin Sea, referring to it in ironic terms as the Waters of Tara-kan and considering it the biggest lie they had heard since some insane *marabout* of Quar's had ventured into the desert a generation ago, babbling that the world was round, like an orange.

There was also rumored to be a lost city somewhere in the Sun's Anvil—a city of fabulous wealth, buried beneath the dunes. The nomads rather liked this idea and kept the tradition of Serinda alive, using it to illustrate to their children the mutability of all things made by the hands of man.

The djinn could have told their masters the truth of the matter. They could have told them that there *was* a sea to the east, that there *had* been a city in the Sun's Anvil, that Khandar did not stand at the top of the world nor was the Pagrah desert the world's center. The immortal beings knew all this and much more besides but did not impart this information to their masters. The djinn had one abiding rule: When in the service of humans, you who are all knowing know nothing and they who know nothing are all knowing.

To be fair to the nomads, the average city dweller of Kich or Khandar or Idrith thought the world considerably smaller. Let the *madrasahs* teach differently. Let the Imam preach about bringing the *kafir* who lived in lands beyond to a knowledge of the True God. To the coppersmith, the weaver, the baker, the fabric dyer, the lamp seller—the world's center was the four walls of his dwelling, its heart the *souk* where he sold his skill or his wares, its edge the wall surrounding the city.

Born and bred in the court of an enlightened Emperor, the Imam knew the truth about the world. So did the Amir, who—though not an educated man—had seen too much of it with his own eyes not to believe that there was always more over the next hill. The learned scholars in the Emperor's court taught that the world was round, that the land of Sardish Jardan was just one of many lands floating atop the waters of several great oceans, and that people of many kinds and many different beliefs lived in these lands—people who were to be drawn inevitably into the arms of Quar. Thus, when the Imam heard from Meryem about a madman who claimed to have come from over the sea, Feisal considered this news worthy of being passed on to his God.

The Imam prepared for his Holy Audience by fasting two days and a night, his lips touching only water and that sparingly. Such a feat was no hardship for Feisal, who had fasted whole months at a time in order to prove that the body could be subdued and disciplined by the spirit. This short fast was undertaken to purge the unworthy house of the spirit of all outside influences. During this time, the Imam kept strictly to himself, refusing contact with anyone from the outside (particularly Yamina), who might draw his thoughts from heaven. He broke his self-imposed restriction only twice—once to talk at length with Meryem, another to question the nomad, Saiyad.

The night of the Audience came. Feisal bathed himself in water made frigid by the addition of snow hauled from the mountaintops; snow that was used in the palace to cool the wine, used by the Imam to mortify his flesh. This done, he anointed his unworthy body with scented oils, to make it more pleasing to the God. At the hour of midnight, when the weary minds and bodies of other mortals found solace from their sorrows in sleep, Feisal stripped himself of all his clothes except for a cloth wrapped about his thin loins. Trembling, in an ecstasy of holy fervor, he entered the Inner Temple. Carefully, reverently, he struck the copper-and-brass gong on the altar three times. Then he prostrated himself flat on the floor before the golden ram's head and waited, his skin shivering with excitement and the chill of the air.

"You have called, my priest, and I have come. What is it you want?"

The voice caressed him. The Imam caught his breath in rapture. He longed to lose himself in that voice, to be lifted from this body with its weak need for food and water, its unclean habits, its impure lusts, its unholy longings. It was with an effort that the Imam reminded himself of what Quar had told him when the priest was young—it was through this unworthy body that the Imam could best serve his Master. He must use it, though he must fight constantly never to let it use him.

Knowing this and knowing, too, that he had to wrench his soul from the peace it longed to attain in heaven back to the travails of the world, the Imam lifted a silver dagger and thrust the knife blade with practiced skill into his ribs. There were many such scars on the Imam's body; scars he kept hidden from view, for knowledge of such self-inflicted torture would have shocked the High Priest himself. The pain, the knowledge of his mortality, the blood running down his oiled skin—all brought Feisal crashing down from heaven and enabled him to discuss the concerns of humans with his God.

Pressing his hand over his side, feeling the warm blood well between his fingers, Feisal slowly drew himself to a kneeling position before the altar.

"I have been in contact with the nomads and I have heard, O Most Holy Quar, a very strange thing. There is or was a man living among the followers of Akhran who claimed to have come from over the sea and—what's more—who claimed to possess the magic of Sul."

The very air around the priest quivered with tension. Feeling now no pain from his wound, Feisal reveled in the sensation of knowing that, as he had believed, this information was welcome to his God.

"Is your informant reliable?"

"Yes, Holy One, particularly because she considers this to be of little importance. The man is dismissed as mad."

"Describe him."

"The man is a youth of about eighteen years with hair the color of flame and a hairless face and chest. He goes about disguised in women's clothes to hide his identity. My informant did not see him practice magic, but she sensed it within him—or thought she did."

"And where is this man?"

"That is the strange part, *Hazrat* Quar. The man escaped capture by the soldiers when they raided the camp. He interfered with plans to bring that most dangerous of the nomads—Khardan—into our custody. Both the madman and Khardan have disappeared under mysterious circumstances. Their bodies were not found, yet—according to those I have questioned—neither has been seen. What is stranger still is that my informant, a skilled sorceress, knows Khardan to be alive, yet, when using her magic to search for him, she finds her mystic vision obscured by a cloud of impenetrable darkness."

The God's silence hummed around the Imam, or perhaps it was a buzzing in his ears. Feisal was growing dizzy and light-headed. Grimly, he clung to consciousness until his God should have no further need of him.

"You have done well, my servant, as usual," spoke Quar finally. "Should you hear or discover anything further about this man from across the sea, bring it to my attention at once."

"Yes, Holy One," murmured Feisal ecstatically.

The darkness was suddenly empty and cold. The God's presence in the Inner Temple was gone. The bliss drained from the Imam's body. Shivering with pain, he rose unsteadily to his feet and crept over to where his pallet lay on the cold marble floor. Knees weak, he sank down onto it and groped with a shaking hand for a roll of soft cloth he had hidden beneath it. Pulling it out, Feisal—with his fading strength—bound the bandage tightly about his wound.

His consciousness slipped from him and he slumped down upon the bloodstained pallet. The ball of cloth fell from his hand and rolled, unwinding, across the black, chill floor.

CHAPTER 6

e do not beat the whipped dog. . . Are you going to lie down on your master's grave and die?

Crouched in his dark cell, Achmed repeated the Amir's words to himself. It was true. Everything the Amir said was true!

"How long have I been in prison? Two weeks? Two months?" Despairing, Achmed shook his head. "Is it morning or night?" He had no idea. "Have I been fed today, or was that yesterday's meal I remember eating? I no longer hear the screams. I no longer smell the stench!"

Achmed clutched at his head, cowering in fear. He recalled hearing of a punishment that deprived a man of his five senses. First the hands were cut off, to take away the sense of touch. Then the eyes were gouged out, the tongue ripped from the mouth, the nose cut off, the ears torn from the head. This place was his executioner! The death he was dying was more ghastly than any torture. Misery screamed at him, but he had lost the ears to hear it. He had long ago ceased being bothered by the prison smell, and now he knew it was because the foul stench was his own. In horror, he realized he was growing to relish the guards' beatings. The pain made him feel alive. . .

Panic-stricken, Achmed leaped to his feet and hurled himself at the wooden door, beating it with his fists and pleading to be let out. The only response was a shouted curse from another cell, the debtor having been rudely awakened from a nap. No guards came. They were used to such disturbances. Sliding down the doorway, Achmed slumped to the floor. In his half-crazed state, he fell into a stupor.

He saw himself lying on a shallow, unmarked grave, hastily dug in the sand. A terrible wind came up, blowing the sand away, threatening to expose the body. A wave of revulsion and fear swept over Achmed. He couldn't bear to see the corpse, decaying, rotting. Desperately, he shoveled the sand back over the body, scooping it up in handfuls and tossing it onto the grave. But every time he lifted a handful, the wind caught it and blew it back into his face, stinging his eyes, choking him. He kept working frantically, but the wind was relentless. Slowly, the face of the corpse emerged—a man's face, the withered flesh covered by a woman's silken veil. . .

The scraping sound of the wooden bar being lifted from the door jolted Achmed out of his dream. The shuffling footsteps of prisoners being herded outside and the distant cries of women and children told the young man that it was visiting time.

Slowly Achmed rose to his feet, his decision made.

Emerging into the bright sunlight, Achmed squinted painfully against the brilliance. When he could see, he scanned the crowd pressed against the bars. Badia was there, beckoning to him. Reluctantly, Achmed crossed the compound and came to stand near her.

The woman's eyes, above the veil, were shadowed with concern.

"How is my mother?" Achmed asked.

"Sophia is well and sends her love. But she has been very worried." Badia examined the young man intently. "We heard that the Amir sent for you. That he spoke to you. . . alone."

"I am all right." Achmed shrugged. "It was nothing."

"Nothing? The Amir sends for you for nothing? Achmed"—Badia's eyes narrowed—"there is talk that the Amir offered you a place in his army."

"Talk! Talk!" Achmed said impatiently, turning from the woman's intense gaze. "That is all."

"Achmed, your mother—"

"—should not worry. She will make herself ill again. Badia"—Achmed changed the subject abruptly—"I heard about Khardan."

Now it was the woman's dark eyes that lowered, the long lashes brushed the gold-trimmed edge of the veil. Achmed saw Badia's hand steal to her heart, and he knew now what sorrow she had hidden from him the last time she had visited.

"Badia," the young man asked hesitantly, swallowing, "do you believe—"

"No!" Badia cried stubbornly. Raising her eyes, she looked directly at Achmed. "The rumor about him is a lie—a lie concocted by that swine Saiyad. Meryem says so. Meryem says Saiyad has hated Khardan ever since the incident with the madman and that he would do anything—"

"Meryem?" Achmed interrupted in amazement. "Wasn't she captured? The Sultan's daughter— Surely the Amir would have done away with her!"

"He was going to, but he fell in love with her and couldn't bear to harm her. He begged her to marry him, but Meryem refused. Don't you see, Achmed," Badia said eagerly, "she refused because she knows Khardan is alive!"

"How?"

Achmed was skeptical. Meryem was certainly lovely. The young man could remember watching the lithe, graceful body gliding like the evening breeze through the camp, going about her chores, long lashes modestly downcast until you came close to her then, suddenly, the blue eyes were looking right into your heart. Khardan had fallen headlong into the pool of those blue eyes. Achmed tried to visualize the sternfaced, gray-haired, battle-scarred Qannadi floundering in the same water. It seemed impossible. But, Achmed was forced to admit, what a man does in his tent in the night is best covered by the blanket of darkness.

"—she gave Khardan a charm," Badia was relating.

Achmed scoffed. "Women's magic! Abdullah's wife gave him a charm, too. They buried it with what was left of him."

Badia drew herself to her full height, which brought her about to Achmed's chin, staring at him with the sharp-edged gaze that had often cut the tall Majiid off at the knees. "When you have known a woman, then mock her magic and her love if you dare. But do not do so while you are still a boy!"

Wounded, Achmed lashed out. "Don't you understand, Badia? If Khardan is alive, then what Saiyad said is true! He fled the battle—a coward! And now he hides in shame—"

Thrusting her arm through the prison gate, Badia slapped him. The woman's blow, hampered as it was by the iron bars, was neither hard nor painful. Yet it brought bitter tears to the young man's eyes.

"May Akhran forgive you for speaking of your brother so!"

Badia hissed through her veil. Turning on her heel, she walked away.

Achmed sprang at the bars, shaking them with such violence that the guards inside the compound took a step toward him.

"Akhran!" Achmed laughed harshly. "Akhran is like my father—a broken old man, sitting in his tent, mourning a way of life that is as dead as his son! Can't you understand, woman? Akhran is the past! My father is the past! Khardan is the past!" Tears streaming down his cheeks, Achmed clutched the bars, rattling them and shouting. "*I*—Achmed! *I* am the future! Yes, it is true! I am joining the army of the Amir! I—"

A hand caught hold of his shoulder, spun him around.

Achmed saw Sayah's face, twisted with hatred.

"Traitor!" A fist slammed into Achmed's jaw, knocking him backward against the bars. The faces of other tribesmen loomed close. Glittering eyes floated on waves of hot breath and pain. A foot drove into his gut. He doubled over in agony, slumping to the ground. Hands grabbed him roughly by the collar of his robes and dragged him to his feet. Another blow across the mouth. A flaring of fire in his groin, burning through his body, forcing a scream from his lips. He was on the ground again, covering his head with his arms, trying to shield himself from the eyes, the hands, the feet, the hatred, the word...

"Traitor!"

CHAPTER 7

Qannadi sat late in his private chambers. He was alone, his wives and concubines doomed to disappointment, for none would be chosen this night. Dispatches had arrived by courier from the south, and the Amir had informed his staff that he was not to be disturbed.

By the light of an oil lamp burning brightly on his desk, Qannadi read the reports of his spies and double agents—men he had planted in the governments of the cities of Bas who were working for their overthrow from the inside. Studying these, he compared them to the reports of his field commanders, occasionally nodding to himself in satisfaction.

The ripples created by the rock thrown at the nomads were still spreading across the pond. Qannadi had made certain his agents proclaimed publicly that the Amir had done as a tremendous favor by ridding them of the spear that had long been pointed at their throats. Never mind that centuries had passed since the nomads had attacked Bas and that the attack had come at a time when the newly arising cities were seen as a distinct threat to the nomads and their way of life. So devastating had been the battles fought then that they lived in legend and song, and it took only the mention of the fearsome *spahis*—the cruel desert riders in their black robes and black masks—to drain the blood from the plump cheeks many a Senator.

Governed by democratic rule that permitted all men of property (excluding women, slaves, laborers, soldiers, and foreigners) to have an equal vote, the people of Bas had lived in relative peace for many years. Once they had established their city-states, they devoted themselves to their favorite occupation—politics. Their God, Uevin—whose three precepts were Law, Patience, and Reality—delighted in all that was new and modern, despising anything that was old or outdated. His was a materialistic outlook on life. What counted was the here and now—that which could be seen and that which could be touched. The people of Bas insisted on having every moment of their lives controlled, and there existed so many ordnances and laws in their cities that walking on the wrong side of the road on an odd-numbered calendar day could land one in prison for a month. The great joy in their lives was to crowd the Senate chambers and listen by the hour to endless harangues over trivial points in their numerous constitutions.

Uevin's followers' second greatest joy was to create marvels of modern technology to enable them to better the quality of their lives in this world. Huge aqueducts crisscrossed their cities, either bringing water into the homes or carrying waste away from them. Their buildings were massive, and of modern design with no frivolous adornments, filled with mechanical devices of every conceivable shape and description. They had developed new methods of farming-terracing the land, using irrigation, rotating crops to rest the soil. They invented new ways to mine gold and silver and, so it was rumored, had even discovered a black rock that burned.

Though the majority of people in Bas believed in Uevin, they considered themselves enlightened, and encouraged believers in other Gods to settle in their cities (mostly, it was believed, for the sake of the debates it stirred up). Followers of both Kharmani and Benario were numerous in Bas, and an occasional temple could be found to Zhakrin and Mimrim and Quar. Life was good in Bas. The people exported their crops, their technological devices, their ores and metals, and were generally well off. Their faith in Uevin had never wavered.

Until now.

In determining how his immortals should best serve both himself and his followers, Uevin rejected the notion of djinn and angels that were used by other Gods and Goddesses. He designed a more modern system, one that could be completely controlled and was not subject to the whim of changeable humans. Delineating his immortals as "minor dieties," he put each in charge of one specific area of human life. There was a God of War, a Goddess of Love, a God of Justice, a Goddess of Home and Family, a Goddess of Crops and Farming, a God of Finance, and so forth. Small temples were built wherein each of these minor dieties and their human priests and priestesses dwelt. Whenever a human had a problem, he or she knew exactly what deity to consult.

This worked well until, one by one, Uevin's immortals began to disappear.

First to vanish had been the Goddess of Crops and Farming. Her priestesses went to her one day with a question and did not hear her voice in response. A drought struck. The wells ran dry. The water in the lakes and ponds dwindled. Crops withered and died in the fields. Uevin ordered the God of Justice to salvage the desperate situation, but his God of Justice was nowhere to be found. The system of government fell apart. Corruption was rife, the people lost faith in their Senators and threw them out of office. At this critical juncture, Uevin lost his God of War. Soldiers deserted or rioted in the streets, demanding more pay and better treatment. With the God of War went the Goddess of Love. Marriages fell apart, neighbor turned against neighbor, entire families split into quarreling factions.

At this critical juncture, Quar's followers lifted their voices. Look to the north, they said. Look to the city of Kich and see how well the people are living. Look to the rich and powerful city of Khandar. See her Emperor and how he brings peace and prosperity to the people. See the Amir of Quar, who has saved you from the savage nomads. Discard your useless beliefs, for your God has betrayed you. Turn to Quar.

Many of Uevin's followers did just that, and Quar took care to see to it that those who came to worship at his temples were blessed in all their endeavors. Rain fell on *their* fields. *Their* children were polite and did well in school. *Their* gold mines were prosperous. *Their* machines worked. Consequently *they* were elected to the Senate. *They* began to gain control of the armies.

Uevin attempted to fight back, but without his immortals he was losing the faith of his people and therefore growing weaker and weaker.

The Amir knew little and cared less about the war in heaven. That was the province of the Imam. Qannadi cared about the reports of a Bas general assassinated by undisciplined soldiers, a Governor deposed by the Senate, a student riot. Reading the missives of his spies, Qannadi deemed that the time was at hand to march south. Like rotten fruit, the city-states of Bas were ready to fall into his hand.

A knock at the door disturbed his thoughts.

Annoyed, Qannadi looked up from his reading. "I left orders not to be bothered."

"It is Hasid, General," came a rasping voice.

"Enter," said the Amir immediately.

The door opened. Qannadi could see his bodyguard on the other side and behind him an old man. Dressed in dirty rags, his body gnarled and twisted as a carob tree, there was a dignity and pride in the old man's bearing and his upright stance that marked him a soldier. The bodyguard stood aside to let the old man pass, then shut the door again immediately. The Amir heard the sentry's boots thud on the floor as he once more took up his position outside the door.

"What is it, Hasid? The young man—"

"I think you should send for him, O King." Hasid stumbled over the unfamiliar royal appellation.

"We have known each other long enough to dispense with formalities, my friend. Why should I send for the young man now?" Qannadi glanced at a candle marked off in hours whose slow-burning flame kept track of the time. It was well past the midhour of darkness.

"It must be tonight!" said the old soldier. "'There will be no tomorrow for Achmed."

"What happened?" Frowning, the Amir laid the dispatch down on the desk and gave Hasid his complete attention.

"This noon, the young man lost control. He shouted out to the crowd at the gates his intention of joining your army."

"And?"

"There was a riot, General. I am surprised you didn't hear about it."

"That fat fool who runs the prison never reports to me. He is terrified that I will lock him in one of his own cells. He is right, but all in due time. Continue."

"The guards put the riot down, dragging off the other no-mads, beating them and locking them in their cells. But not before Achmed's tribesmen had nearly killed him."

Startled to feel a pang of fear, like the thrust of cold iron through his bowels, Qannadi rose to his feet. "Is he all right?"

"I don't know, sir. I couldn't find out." Hasid shook his head.

"Why didn't you come to me sooner?" The Amir slammed his

fist on the table, sloshing the oil in the lamp over the dispatches.

"If I am to remain valuable to you," the old soldier said shrewdly, "then I must keep up my appearance as an ordinary prisoner. I dared not leave until the guards had drunk themselves into their usual nightly stupor. I think the young man is still alive. I went to his cell and I could hear his breathing, but it is very rapid and shallow."

Buckling on his sword, Qannadi flung open the door. "I want an escort of twenty men, mounted and ready to ride within five minutes," he said to the sentry.

Saluting, the guard turned and ran to a balcony overlooking the soldiers' quarters. His voice rang out through the night, and within moments the Amir heard the clatter and clamor below that told him his orders were being obeyed with alacrity.

"Wait here," the Amir told the old soldier. "I have further need of you, but not in that prison."

Hasid saluted, but his king was already out of the room.

CHAPTER 8

chmed wakened and this time managed to hold onto awakening. Until now, consciousness had slithered away from him—a snake sliding through the hands of the dancer in the bazaars. Now he gazed about him, able to bring reality and dreams together, for he vaguely remembered coming to this place, except that he visualized it in his mind as being dark and shadowy, lit with soft candles and peopled with veiled women whispering strange words and touching him with cool hands.

Now it was daylight. The women were gone. There was only an old man, sitting beside him, looking at him with a grave face. Achmed gazed at him and blinked, thinking he might be a trick of his aching head and vanish. He knew the old man, but not from the shadowy dreams. He remembered him from . . . from . . .

"You were in the prison," Achmed said and was startled at the sound of his own voice. It seemed different, louder.

"Yes." The old man's grave expression did not alter.

"I'm not there now, am I?"

"No. You are in the palace of the Amir."

Achmed looked around. Yes, he had known that. There had been flaring torchlights and strong arms lifting him from the pallet. The Amir's voice, thick with anger. A ride on horseback and jolting pain. Warm water washing over him, the hands of men—gentle as women—cleansing his battered body.

Then this room. . .

His hand smoothed silken sheets. He was lying on thick, soft mattresses resting on a tall, ornately carved wooden frame. He was clad in clean clothes. The filth had been washed from his body, he smelled the sweet fragrance of rose and orange blossom, mingled with pine and other, more mysterious perfumes.

Looking up, Achmed saw silken drapes swooping gracefully

over the tall wooden pillars of the bed to fall in folds around him. The curtains had been pushed aside, to permit him a view of his room—magnificent and beautiful beyond fantasy—and the wizened old man, sitting unmoving beside him.

"You very nearly died," said the old man. "They sent for the physicians, who did what they could, but it was the magic of Yamina that brought you back."

"You were one of the prisoners. Why are you here?"

"I was in the prison," corrected the old man. "I was not one of the prisoners."

"I don't understand."

"I was placed in the prison by the gener—the Amir—to watch over you. I am called Hasid and I was Captain of the Body Guard under Abul Qasim Qannadi for twenty years, until I grew too old. I was pensioned honorably and given a house. But I told him when I left—'General,' I said, 'there's going to come a time when you'll need an old soldier. Not these young men, who think all battles are won with trumpet calls and shouts and dashing here and there. You'll need someone who knows that sometimes victory comes only by stealth and long waiting and keeping the mouth shut.' And so he did." Hasid nodded gravely. "So he did."

"You went into prison. . . voluntarily?" Achmed sat up in his bed, staring at the old soldier in amazement. "But—they beat you!"

"Hah!" Hasid looked amused. "Call that a beating? From those dogs? My mother gave me worse, to say nothing of my sergeant. Now there was a man who could lay it on! Broke three of my ribs once," the old soldier said, shaking his head in admiration, "for drinking on watch. 'Next time, Hasid,' the sergeant told me, helping me to my feet, 'I'll break your skull.' But there wasn't a next time. I learned my lesson."

Achmed paled. Memory leaped out at him. The angry, frightened faces, the flailing fists and feet, punching and kicking . . .

"They hate me! They tried to kill me!"

"Of course! What do you expect? But not for the reason you think. You spoke the truth, and it was the truth they were trying to beat down—not you. I know. I've seen it before. There isn't much," Hasid said on reflection, scratching himself beneath his rags, "that I haven't seen."

"What happened to them?" Achmed asked in a strained voice.

"The Amir released them."

"What?" Achmed stared. "Freed?"

"He opened the prison gates wide. Sent them slinking back out into the streets, crawling on their bellies like whipped curs."

Lying on your master's grave...

"Why is he doing this?" Achmed muttered, restlessly shoving aside the silken sheets.

"He's smart, the Amir. Let them go. He's keeping their mothers, their wives, their families here in the city. They can go home to them—if they choose—or they can make their way across the desert and find that their tribe is nothing but a few old men, beating their toothless gums, yammering about a God who no longer cares—"

Achmed cringed. "I understand that!" he said hurriedly. Glancing at the luxury and finery about him, he gestured. "I meant why is the general doing *this*. You... watching over me. Bringing me here. Saving my life... All to train horses." His face grew dark with suspicion. "I don't believe it."

"You believed it in prison."

"In that pit of Sul, it made sense. Maybe because I wanted it to." Achmed tossed the blankets aside and swung his bare legs over the edge of the mattress. Ignoring the sharp pain in his head, he struggled to rise. "I see it now. He's been lying to me. Maybe he's using me, holding me hostage." A sudden dizziness assailed him. Pausing, he put his hand to his head, fighting it off. "Where are my clothes?" he demanded groggily.

"Hostage? And what ransom would your father pay? He has nothing left."

Achmed closed his eyes to keep the room from spinning. A bitter taste filled his mouth; he was afraid he would be sick.

Nothing left. Not even a son....

Cold water splashed in his face. Gasping, Achmed opened his eyes, staring at Hasid.

"Why—" he sputtered.

"Thought you were going to faint." Hasid returned the water carafe to a nearby table. "Feel better?"

A nod was all Achmed could manage.

"Then get dressed," the old soldier ordered. "Your old clothes have been burned, as mine will be once I can get rid of them." He scratched himself again. "There are your new ones."

Wiping his dripping face, Achmed glanced at the foot of his bed to see a simple white cotton caftan lying there, not unlike that which Qannadi himself wore.

"I can't tell you why he's doing this—not in words. That would be betraying a friend's trust. But, if you feel up to walking a bit," Hasid continued, "I've got something to show you that might answer your questions"—he peered at the young man out of the corner of his eye—"if you're as smart as he says you are, that is."

Wordlessly, moving slowly and carefully to avoid jarring his aching head, Achmed drew on soft undergarments, then the caftan. He hoped that they wouldn't have to walk far. Despite the magical healing, his legs felt weak and wobbly as a newborn colt's.

"Come on!" Hasid prodded him in the ribs. "I marched five miles once on a broken ankle, and no woman's hands tended me either!"

Gritting his teeth against the pain, Achmed followed the old soldier across the room that was as large as Majiid's tent. Carpets of intricate and delicate weave covered the floor, their shimmering colors so beautiful that it seemed a desecration to walk on them. Lacquered wood furniture, decorated with gold leaf and adorned with objects rare and lovely, stood beside low sofas whose overstuffed, silken cushions invited the young man to sink down and lose himself amid their embroidered leaves and flowers. Feeling clumsy and awkward, fearful of knocking some precious vase to the floor, Achmed tried to imagine walking on a broken ankle. Finally, he decided the old man was lying. Later, when Achmed asked the Amir if Hasid's claim was true, Qannadi grinned. Hasid *was* lying. It hadn't been five miles he walked. It had been ten.

Approaching a window, the old soldier pressed his face against the glass and indicated that Achmed was to do the same. The room stood on the ground floor of the palace. The windows opened onto the lush garden through which he and Khardan had escaped only months ago. The bright sunlight sent a stabbing throb through his eyeballs, memories sent a pain through his heart. Achmed couldn't see anything for long moments.

"Well?" Hasid prodded him again.

"I—I can't... That is, what am I—"

"There, the man right across from us. By that fountain."

Blinking his eyes rapidly, not daring to wipe his hand across them for fear of rousing Hasid's contempt, Achmed at last focused on a man standing not five feet from them, tossing grain to several peacocks that had gathered around him.

The sight of the man was interesting enough to dry Achmed's tears and make him forget the pain of both body and soul. The man was young—perhaps twenty-five—tall and slender with skin as white as the marble fountains. A turban swathed his head, its silken fabric glittering with jewels and golden baubles. His clothing was equally sumptuous. Full-cut silken *pantalons* in colors of blues and greens and gold rippled about his legs as he moved among the peacocks. A golden sash encircled his slim waist, golden shoes with turned-up toes graced his feet. A billowing sleeved shirt, open at the throat, was covered by a vest made of golden fabric decorated with green embroidered curlicues and knots, finished off by a row of silken fringe that swung when he made the slightest move.

The man's eyelids were painted green and outlined in *kohl*. Jewels sparkled on the fingers that tossed the grain to the birds, gold dangled from his earlobes.

Achmed gasped. He had never seen anyone so truly magnificent. "Is that the Emperor?"

"Hah!" Hasid began to wheeze with laughter, causing the man outside to turn his head and glance at them with disapprobation. Brushing the grain from his hands, he walked away, moving past the splashing fountain with studied grace and elegance, the peacocks walking with mincing step behind him.

"The Emperor!" Hasid struggled to catch his breath. "If the Emperor came, where do you think we'd be, boy? Turned out in the streets, most likely. This place wouldn't be big enough to hold all his wives, let alone his wazirs and priests and grandees and scribes and slaves and cupbearers and platebearers and footwashers and asslickers that surround him from the moment he wakes up in the morning to when he enters one of his hundred bedrooms in the night. The Emperor!" The old soldier chuckled, shaking his head.

"Then who is it?" Achmed demanded irritably, feeling the pounding in his head once more.

"The answer to your question." Hasid eyed him shrewdly. "The eldest son of Abul Qasim Qannadi."

Achmed gaped. Turning to look outside, he saw the man pluck an orchid and begin ripping the petals from it in bored fashion, tossing them idly at the birds. "He was raised in the Emperor's court and lives in the palace in Khandar. Yamina, his mother, is one of the Emperor's sisters, and she saw to it that her son had all the advantages of being brought up in the royal household. Qannadi rarely saw the boy." Hasid shrugged. "His own fault, perhaps. He was always away somewhere, conquering more cities in the Emperor's name. He sent for his son a month ago, to teach him the art of warfare. He was going to take him south. His son said he would be honored to attend his father, but he would need a covered litter in which to travel since he couldn't for the life of him ride a horse and he dare not remain out in the sun long—it would ruin his complexion—and was it possible to bring several of his own friends, as he could not stand to be in the company of vulgar soldiers, and he wanted his own personal physician as well since it was quite likely that he would faint at the sight of blood.

"The young man," Hasid added dryly, "is returning to Khandar tomorrow."

Achmed's breath was gone from his body. He felt like the man who commanded his djinn to bring him a silver ball and found himself holding the gleaming moon. As the man said to the djinn, "It is beautiful and of exceeding value, but I'm not certain what to do with it." The garden dissolved before the youth's eyes. Gazing out the window, he did not see the ornamental trees and the hanging orchids and the blood red roses. He saw the desert—the vast, empty dunes beneath a vast, empty sky; the tall tasseled grass bending in the everlasting wind; the scraggly palms clinging to life around a bracken puddle of water; the shriveled, stinking plant whose name now held for the young man a terrible, bitter irony—the Rose of the Prophet.

"You were right," Hasid said softly. "This has nothing to do with the training of horses, Qannadi has asked to see you. Will you come to him?"

Achmed turned away from the window. "Yes," he said, "I will come."

CHAPTER 9

The God Quar stood in the incense-sweetened darkness of his Temple in the City of Kich, his hand resting upon the golden ram's head of his altar. The God was obviously waiting and doing it with an obvious ill grace. Occasionally his fingers drummed nervously upon the ram's head. More than once, his hand lifted a mallet to strike a small gong which stood on the altar, but he always—after a moment's hesitation and an impatient snarl—withdrew it.

Lying on a pallet on the cold marble floor opposite Quar, the God's Imam muttered and moaned, tossing in a feverish sleep. His self-inflicted wound had not healed cleanly, the flesh around it was swollen and hot to the touch, streaks of fiery red were spreading outward from it. Yamina had attempted to tend to the priest, as had all the court physicians, but Feisal refused all help.

"This is...between my God...and myself!" he gasped, clutching Yamina's hand with painful intensity, his other hand pressed against the bandages that were wet with blood and pus from the oozing wound. "I have done... something to ... displease Him. This...is my punishment!"

Pressing Feisal's wasted hand against her lips, Yamina pleaded, calling him every endearing name that came to mind. Gently, firmly, he told her to leave. Sorrowfully, she did as he asked, secretly intending to sneak back in when he was asleep and use her magic to heal him without his knowledge.

To Feisal, Yamina was transparent as the water in the palace *hauz*. Feeling his strength dwindle, knowing that consciousness would soon leave him, the Imam commanded his servant to permit no one to enter, binding the man with the most terrible of oaths to insure his obedience. The servant was to shut the inner Temple doors and seal them. Not even the Amir himself would be allowed entry. The last sound Feisal heard before he sank into fever-ridden, insane dreams, was the hollow booming of the great doors coming together, the crashing fall of the iron bar across them.

Drifting in and out of delirium, the Imam was vaguely aware of the arrival of the God in his Temple. At first Feisal doubted his senses, fearing that this was a fever dream. Battling pain and the fire that was consuming his body, he struggled to hold onto consciousness and knew then that Quar was truly with him. His soul radiant with joy, the priest attempted to rise to do Quar homage, but his body was weaker than his spirit, and he fell back, gasping for breath.

"Tell me . . . what I have done . . . to incur your wrath, O Holy One," murmured Feisal weakly, extending a trembling hand to his God.

Quar did not respond or even look in the direction of his suffering priest. Pacing about near the altar, he peered with markedly growing irritation into the darkness. Feisal lacked the breath to repeat his question. He could only stare with adoring eyes at his God. Even the pain and torment he was enduring seemed blessed—a flame cleansing soul and body of whatever sins he had committed. If he died in the fire, then so be it. He would stand before his God with a spirit purged of infection.

The gong spoke suddenly, sounding three times. Quar turned toward it eagerly. The gong was silent for the count of seven, then rang three times again. A cloud of smoke took human shape and form around the gong, coalescing into a ten foot tall 'efreet.

Clad in red silken *pantalons* girded with a red sash around its massive stomach, the 'efreet performed the *salaam*, its huge hands pressed against its forehead. Feisal watched silently, without wonder.

"Well, where is he?" Quar demanded.

"I beg your pardon, *Effendi*," said the 'efreet in a voice like the low rumbling of distant thunder, "but I have not found him."

"What?" The God's anger stirred the darkness. "He can *not* have gone far. He is a stranger in this land. Bah! You have *lost* him, Kaug!"

"Yes, *Effendi*, I have *lost* him," replied Kaug imperturbably. "If I may be permitted to tell my tale?"

Turning his back upon the 'efreet, the God made an irritated gesture.

"As you surmised, My Holy Master, the so-called madman was one of the *kafir* who came by ship across the Hurn Sea and landed near the city of Bastine. Immediately on their arrival, the priests and sorcerers of Promenthas—"

"—were met by a group of my zealous followers and slaughtered," interrupted the God impatiently. "I know all this! What—"

"I beg, your pardon, *Effendi*," interrupted the 'efreet, "but it seems we were misled, It was not your followers who murdered the *kafir*."

The God was silent for long moments, then said skeptically, "Go on."

"Consider, Majesty of Heaven—if the unbelievers had been killed in your name, you should have had some claim to their souls,"

"They were protected by guardian angels—"

"I have fought the angels of Promenthas before, *Effendi*, as you well know," the 'efreet stated.

"Yes, and this time you fought them and lost and did *not* tell me," Quar remarked coldly.

"This time, I did *not* fight them. I never saw them, I was not called *to* fight the angels."

Quar half turned, regarding Kaug through narrowed eyes. "You are speaking the truth."

"Certainly, *Effendi*."

"Then it is Death who has failed us."

"No, *Effendi*. The angels of Promenthas whisked their charges away without contest. According to Death, the *kafir* were killed in the name of a God of Evil—a God too weak to claim them."

Quar sucked in his breath, the skin with which he adorned his ethereal being paled.

"Zhakrin!"

"Yes, *Effendi*. He has escaped!"

"How is that possible? He and Evren were being held in the Temple of Khandar, my most powerful priests guarding them. No one knew the Gods were being held there—"

"Someone knew, *Effendi*. At any rate, neither Zhakrin nor Evren are there now. One of your powerful priests, it now appears, was in reality in the service of Zhakrin. By some means not known to us, he managed to free the Gods and carry them away."

"What do we know about him? Where has he gone?"

"I believe him to be the same man who slaughtered the worshipers of Promenthas. He passes himself off as a slave trader, but he is in reality a Black Paladin, a devoted follower of Zhakrin. He first appeared in Ravenchai, where he captured a number of the natives and brought them to sell in Kich. He has a troop of *goums* in his command, and it was they who killed the priests and the magi of Promenthas. But one person was left alive. A young man of extraordinary beauty who was mistaken for a woman. Thinking to fetch a high price for such a prize, the slave trader took her to Kich. The young man—maintaining his disguise as a woman—was put upon the block just as Khardan and his nomads were terrorizing the city. Khardan took it into his head to rescue the beautiful 'woman.'"

"Took it into his head! Hah!" Quar snarled. "I see the guiding hand of Promenthas in this. He has joined with Akhran to fight me!"

"Undoubtedly, Holy One." Kaug bowed. "The young man was taken to the camp of the nomads. Here, according to the woman, Meryem, he was nearly executed by the enraged man who sought to take the lovely 'woman' as his concubine. Khardan saved the young man's life, proclaiming him mad. Meryem believes that it was this young 'madman' who thwarted her plans to bring Khardan to Kich."

"Then the two are together." "Presumably, *Effendi*."

"Presumably!" Quar's rage beat upon the walls of the Temple. Feisal, in his fevered imaginings, thought he saw the marble blocks start to melt beneath the heat. "I am divine! I am all-knowing, all-seeing! No mortal can hide himself from my sight and the sight of my servants!"

"Not a mortal, Holy Master." Kaug's voice lowered. "Another God. A dark cloud hides them from my sight and the sight of your sorceress."

"A dark cloud. Slowly, inexorably, the power of my enemies grows." Quar fell silent, musing. The 'efreet's hulking body wavered in the air, or perhaps it was Feisal's dimming vision that caused the immortal to appear as if he were a mirage, shimmering against empty sand. "I dare not wait longer."

The God turned his attention to his dying priest. Gliding across the black marble floor, his silken slippers making no noise, his silken robes shining a cold and brilliant white in the darkness, Quar came to stand by Feisal's pallet.

Unable to move, the Imam gazed up at the face of the God with an adoration that banished all pain and fever from his body. The Imam saw his soul rise to its feet, leaving the frail husk of its flesh behind, holding out its hands to the God as a child reaches for its mother. Content, blissful, Feisal felt life ebbing away. The name of the God was on his lips, to be spoken with his last breath.

"No!" said Quar suddenly, and the Imam's soul—caught between two planes—shrank back in bewilderment. Kneeling beside Feisal, the God tore off the bloodstained bandages and laid his hand upon the wound. His other hand touched the priest's hot forehead. "You will live, my faithful Imam. You will rise up from your bed of pain and suffering and know that it was I who saved you. You will remember my face, my voice, and the touch of my hands upon your mortal flesh. And the lesson you will have learned from the agony you have undergone is this.

"You have placed too great a value on human life. As you have seen, it is a thing that can be taken from us as easily as thieves robbing a blind man. The souls of men are what is truly important and they must be rescued from stumbling about in the darkness. Those who do not believe in me must die, so that the power of their false gods dies with them."

Feisal drew a deep breath and another and then another. His eyes closed in a peaceful sleep, his soul reluctantly returned to the fragile body.

"When you awaken," Quar continued, "you will go to the Amir and tell him it is time. . ."

"Time?" Feisal murmured.

"*Jihad!*" whispered Quar, bending low over His priest, caressing him, smoothing the black hair with His hand. "Convert or die!"

The Book
of Zhakrin 2

Chapter 1

I n the name of Zhakrin, God of Darkness and All That Is Evil,
I command you, wake!"

Mathew heard the voice as if it were coming from far away.
It was early morning in his homeland. The sun shone brightly,
joyous bird song greeted the new day. A spring breeze, laden with
the scent of pine and rain-damp earth blew crisp and chill in his
window. His mother stood at the foot of the long, stone stairs,
calling her son to come break his nightlong fast. . .

"Wake!"

He was in a classroom, after luncheon. The wooden desk,
carved with countless names and faces long since gone out into
the world, felt cool and smooth beneath lethargic hands. The old
Archmagus had been droning on and on for an eternity. His voice
was like the buzzing of flies. Mathew closed his eyes, only for a
moment while the instructor turned his back. . .

"Wake!"

A painful tingling sensation was spreading through Mathew's
body. The feeling was distinctly unpleasant, and he tried to move
his limbs to make it cease. That only made it worse, however, sending small needles of agony darting through his body. He moaned.

"Do not struggle, Blossom. Lie still for an hour or so and the
sensation will pass."

Something cold brushed across his forehead. The cold touch
and the colder voice brought back terrifying memories. Forcing his eyes open—the lids feeling as if they'd been covered with
some sort of sticky resin—Mathew gazed upward to see a slender
hand, a face masked in black, two cruel and empty eyes.

"Lie still, Blossom. Lie very still and allow your body to resume its functioning once more. The heart beats rapidly, the sluggish blood now runs free and burns through the body, the lungs

draw in air. Painful? Yes. But you have been asleep a long time, Blossom. A long, long time."

Slender fingers brushed his cheek.

"Do you still have my fish, Blossom? Yes, of course you do. The city guards do not search the bodies of the dead, do they, my Blossom?"

Mathew felt, cool against his skin, the crystal globe that was hidden in the folds of the woman's gown he wore; the globe filled with water in which swam two fish—one golden, one black.

The sound of boots crunching on sand came to Mathew's ears. A voice spoke respectfully, "You sent for me, *Effendi?*" and the hand and eyes withdrew from Mathew's sight.

The young wizard's vision was blurred. The sun was shining, but he could see it only as if through a white gauze. It was hot and stuffy where he lay, the air was stale. He was smothering and he tried to suck in a deep lungful of breath. His flaccid muscles refused to obey his mind's command. The attempt was more of a wheeze or a gulp.

The tingling sensation in his hands and legs increased, nearly driving him wild. Added to this was a panicking feeling that he was suffocating, the inability to draw breath. His sufferings were acute, yet Mathew dared not make so much as a whimper. Death itself was preferable to those cruel eyes.

"Blossom is coming around. What about the other two?" queried the cold voice.

"The other woman is conscious, *Effendi.* The bearded devil, however, will not awaken."

"Mmmm. Some other enchantment, do you think, Kiber?"

"I believe so, *Effendi.* You yourself mentioned the possibility that he was ensorcelled when we first captured him, if I recall correctly?"

"You do so. Let us take a look at him."

The booted feet—now two pairs of them—moved somewhere to Mathew's right.

Bearded devil. The other woman. Khardan! Zohra! Mathew's body twitched and writhed in agony. Memory returned. . .

Escaping the Battle at the Tel; Khardan, unconscious, bound by some enchantment. Zohra and I dressed him in Meryem's rose-colored, silken *chador*. The veil covered his face. The soldiers stopped us!

"Let the old hags go!"

We escaped and crouched down in the mud near the oasis, hidden in the tall grass. Khardan, wounded, spell bound; Zohra, exhausted, sleeping on my shoulder.

"I will keep watch."

But tired eyes closed. Sleep came—to be followed by a waking nightmare.

"A black-haired beauty, young and strong," the cold voice had spoken. "And what is this? The bearded devil who stole the Blossom and put me to all this trouble! Truly, the God looks down upon us with favor this night, Kiber!"

"Yes, Effendi!"

"And here is my Blossom with the flame-colored hair. See, Kiber, she wakes at the sound of my voice. Don't be frightened, Blossom. Don't scream. Gag her, Kiber. Cover her mouth. That's right."

I looked up, bound and helpless, to see a black jewel sparkling in the light of the burning camp,

"In the name of Zhakrin, God of Darkness and All That Is Evil, I command you all—Sleep. . ."

And so they had slept. And now they woke. Woke. . . to what? Mathew heard the voices again, coming from a short distance away.

"You see, Kiber? This silver shield that hangs round his neck. See how it glows, even in daylight?"

"Yes, *Effendi.*"

"I wonder at its purpose, Kiber."

"To protect him from harm in the battle, surely, *Effendi*. I have seen such before, given to soldiers by their wives."

"Yes, but why render him unconscious as well? I begin to see what must have happened, Kiber. These women feared their man would come to harm. They gave him this shield that not only would protect him from any blow, but would also cause him to fall senseless during the battle. Then they dragged him away, dressed him in women's clothes—as we found him—and escaped the field."

"One of them must be a powerful sorceress, then, *Effendi.*"
"One or both, although our Blossom did not exhibit any magical talents when in our company. These nomads are fierce and proud warriors. I'll wager this one did not know he was being saved from death by his womenfolk, nor do I think he will be at

all pleased to discover such a fact when he awakes."

"Then why bring him out of the enchantment, *Effendi?*" It seemed to Mathew that Kiber sounded nervous. "Let him stay in stasis, at least until we reach Galos."

"No, we have too much work to do to load the ships without hauling him on as well. Besides, Kiber"—the cold voice was smooth and sinuous as a snake twisting across the sand—"I want him to see, to hear, to taste, to feel all that is yet to come to him. I want the poison to seep, little by little, into the well of his mind. When his soul goes to drink, it will blacken and die."

Kiber did not appear so confident. "He will be trouble, *Effendi.*"

"Will he? Good. I would hate to think I had misjudged his character. Remove the sword from his hands. Now, to break this enchantment—"

"Let one of the women, *Effendi.* It is never wise to interfere with wizardry."

"Excellent advice, Kiber. I will act upon it. When Blossom is able to speak and move about, we will question her concerning this. Now, remove the baggage from the *djemel* and line it up along the shore. We must be ready to load the ships when they land, for they will not be able to stay long. We do not want to be caught here in the heat of the afternoon."

"Yes, *Effendi.*"

Mathew heard Kiber move away, his voice shouting orders to his men. Closing his eyes, the wizard could once again see the colorful uniforms of the *goums,* the horses they rode. He could see the slaves, chained by the feet, shuffling across the plains. He could see the white-curtained palanquin. . .

White curtains! Mathew's eyes opened, he looked about him. His vision had cleared. Gritting his teeth against the pain, concentrating every fiber of his being on the effort, he managed to move his left hand enough to draw aside the fold in the fabric and peer out at his surroundings.

The sight appalled him. He stared, aghast. He had thought the desert around the Tel, with its undulating dunes of sand stretching to the far distant mountains, empty and forbidding. There was life around the oasis, certainly. Or at least the nomads considered it life. The tall palm trees, their brown-tipped fronds—looking as if they had been singed—clicking in the everlasting wind.

The lacy tamarisk, the sparse green foliage, every blade and leaf precious. The waving stands of brown, tasseled grass that grew near the water's edge. The various species of cacti that ranged from the wiggly-armed burn plant—so called because of its healing properties—to the ugly, sharp-needled plant known by the incongruous, romantic appellation of the Rose of the Prophet. Coming from a world of ancient, spreading oaks, stands of pine forests, wild mountain flowers, Mathew had not considered this desert life life at all—nothing more than a pathetic mockery. But at least, he realized now, it had been life.

He looked out now on death.

The land was dead and the death it had died had been a tortured one. Flat and barren, the earth was white as bone. Huge cracks spread across its surface, mouths gaping open in thirst for the rain that would never fall. Not far from where he lay, Mathew could see a heap of black, broken rock, and near that a pool of water. This was no oasis, however. Nothing grew near that pool. Steam rose from its surface, the water bubbled and churned and boiled.

The sun had just lifted into the eastern sky. Mathew could see, from where he lay, the tip of a red, fiery ball appearing over the horizon. Yet already the heat was building, radiating up from the parched ground. There was a gritty taste in his mouth and he suffered from a terrible thirst. Mathew ran his tongue across his lips. Salt. Now he knew why the land was this strange, glaring white. It was covered with salt.

His strength gave out. Mathew's hand fell limp at his side, the curtain hid the vision. No wonder they had to be gone before afternoon. Nothing could live in this desert in the noonday sun. Yet the man had spoken of ships. Mathew feebly shook his head, hoping to clear it. He must be hallucinating, imagining things. Or perhaps he meant camels, the young wizard thought weakly. Weren't they sometimes called the ships of the desert?

But where would they go? Mathew had seen nothing in that picked-clean corpse of a world. And his thirst was growing unbearable. Cruel eyes or not, he was desperate for water. Just as his parched lips shaped the word and he tried to force sound from his dry throat, Kiber thrust aside the curtains of the litter. He held a waterskin in his hand.

"Drink!" he commanded, glowering sternly at Mathew, perhaps remembering the days in the slave caravan when he'd caught the young wizard refusing to eat.

Mathew had no intention of refusing water. By a supreme effort he raised his arms, grasped the neck of the *girba*, aimed a stream of the warm, stale liquid into his mouth and drank thirstily. Some splashed on his neck and face, cooling him. All too soon, Kiber snatched the waterskin away and disappeared. Mathew heard the *goum's* boots crunching on the salt-covered ground and, in a few moments, a throaty murmur, probably Zohra.

Mathew lay back on the litter. The water gave him strength; he seemed to feel it spreading energy through his body. He longed to sit up and his hand itched to draw the curtains aside. But to do so was to risk attracting the attention of the man with the cruel eyes to himself.

Thrusting his hand into the folds of the woman's clothing, Mathew touched the crystal globe containing the fish. It was cold and smooth against his hot skin. He was suddenly possessed by a desperate desire to examine the fish, to see if they were all right. Fear stopped him. The slaver might chance to look inside and Mathew did not want to seem to be paying too much attention to the magical globe. He wondered what the man had meant by the curious statement, "The city guards do not search the bodies of the dead."

The smothering sensation increased, that and an almost overwhelming urge to move his body. Finally Mathew sat up and was almost immediately seized with a sudden dizziness. Starbursts exploded before his eyes. Weakly, he propped himself up on his arm and, hanging his head, waited until his vision cleared and the terrible light-headed feeling passed. Cautiously pushing aside the curtain a crack, he peered out, further examining his surroundings. The litter, he discovered, was sitting on stilts about four feet off the floor of the salt flats. Keeping a wary eye out for the slave trader, Mathew looked to the front of the litter and blinked in astonishment.

Before him stretched a vast body of water—wide as an ocean—its deep blue color like nothing he had ever seen before. A cool breeze, blowing off the sea, drifted in a whisper past his face, and he thankfully gulped in the fresh air.

The slave trader stood at the water's edge, facing out into it. Lifting his arms above his head, he cried in a loud voice, "It is I,

Auda ibn Jad! In the name of Zhakrin, I command you. Send my ship!"

So he *had* meant ships! But what sea could this be? It didn't look like the Hurn. No waves crashed against the shore. It wasn't the greenish color of the ocean he had crossed. The water lapped gently about the feet of the slave trader, Auda ibn Jad (it was the first time Mathew recalled ever hearing the man's name). Staring intently out into the sea in the same direction as ibn Jad, Mathew thought he could detect a shadow on the horizon—a dark cloud in an otherwise cloudless sky.

Turning abruptly, the slave trader caught Mathew staring out of the curtains.

"Ah, Blossom! You are enjoying the fresh air."

Mathew did not answer. He could not speak a word. The cold eyes had snatched out all the wits in his head, leaving behind nothing but empty fear.

"Come, Blossom. Stand up. That will help get the blood circulating again. I need you."

Walking over to Mathew, ibn Jad reached out his slender hand and grasped hold of the young wizard's right arm. The man's touch was as cold and unfeeling as his eyes and Mathew shivered in the hot sun.

Rising to his feet, he thought at first he was going to faint. His knees gave way, the sunbursts flared again in his vision. Falling back, he caught hold of one of the supports of the litter's roof with his hand and hung onto it grimly; Auda propping him up. The slave trader gave Mathew a few moments to recover, then dragged the groggy wizard across the sand to another litter. Mathew knew who lay inside, just as he knew the question he was going to be asked. Shoving aside the curtains of the palanquin, ibn Jad pushed Mathew forward.

"The charm the bearded devil wears around his neck? Did you make it? Are you the sorceress who laid the enchantment upon him?"

We plan and work for years to chart our life's course, and then sometimes one instant, one word will irrevocably alter our destiny.

"Yes," said Mathew in a barely audible whisper.

He could not have told the conscious reasoning behind his lie. He had the distinct feeling it was motivated by fear; he did not want to appear completely defenseless and helpless in the eyes of this man. He knew, too, that if he answered no, ibn Jad would simply question Zohra, and he would not believe either of them if both denied it.

"I made. . . the charm," Mathew said hoarsely.

"A fine piece of work, Blossom. How do you break the spell?"

"By taking it from around his neck. He will immediately begin to come out of the enchantment." That was a guess, but Mathew felt fairly certain it was a good one. Generally, that was how charms such as this one worked. There wouldn't have been any reason for Meryem to have created a delayed effect.

"Break it," commanded ibn Jad.

"Yes, *Effendi*," Mathew mumbled.

Leaning over Khardan, the young wizard stretched forth a trembling hand and took hold of the silken ribbon from which hung the softly glowing silver shield. Mathew noticed, as he did so, the unusual armor in which Khardan had been dressed. It was made of metal—black and shining. A strange design was inset into the breastplate—a snake whose writhing body had been cut into several pieces. It was a gruesome device, and Mathew found himself staring at it, unmoving, his hand poised in midair above Khardan's neck.

"Go on!" grated ibn Jad, standing over him. "Why do you delay?"

Starting, Mathew wrenched his gaze from the grotesque armor and fixed it on the silver shield. Cupping his hand beneath the talisman, he closed his fingers over it gingerly, as though fearing it would be hot to the touch. The silver metal felt warm, but only from the heat of Khardan's body. Clasping the shield, Mathew gave the ribbon a sharp tug. It snapped. The charm came off in Mathew's hand. Almost instantly the metallic glow began to fade. Khardan moved his head, groaning.

"Give that to me."

Wordlessly, Mathew handed ibn Jad the charm.

The man studied it carefully. "A delicate bit of craftsmanship." He glanced from the charm to Mathew to Khardan. "You must care about him very much."

"I do," Mathew said softly, keeping his eyes lowered.

"A pity," said Auda ibn Jad coolly.

Mathew looked up in alarm, but at that moment, movement seen out of the corner of his eye distracted him.

Zohra, stumbling with faltering footsteps but managing to walk nonetheless, was approaching their group. Mathew saw the set of her jaw, the fire in the black eyes, and tried to call out, to speak, to warn her, but the words caught in his dry throat. Seeing his fixed gaze, the slave trader turned.

The wind from the sea was rising. Small waves were washing up on the shore now. Behind Zohra, Mathew saw the cloud on the horizon growing larger and darker.

The wind whipped Zohra's veil from her face. She caught hold of it and covered her nose and mouth. Coming to stand before Auda ibn Jad, she drew herself weakly to her full height, regarding him with flashing black eyes.

"I am Zohra, Princess of the Hrana. I do not know where I am or why you have brought me here, dog of a *kafir!* But I insist that you take me back!"

CHAPTER 2

On angry shout from Kiber, who was lashing out at one of his own men with his camel stick, attracted Auda's attention, and he did not immediately answer Zohra's demand. Kiber was busy supervising the unloading of several *djemel*, baggage camels. Under their leader's direction, the *goums* and the slaves placed the wooden boxes, rattan baskets, and other items in the sand near the water's edge. It was the mishandling of several large, carved ivory jars with sealed lids that brought down Kiber's wrath on his *goum*. The slaves were not allowed to touch these jars, Mathew noted. Several handpicked *goums* were lowering the jars from the *djemel* to the sand with extreme care and caution, treating them with almost reverential respect. When one of the *goums* nearly dropped his end of the jar. Kiber was on him in a flash, and ibn Jad frowned darkly.

Mathew wondered what could be in the jars—possibly some rare incense or perfume. Whatever it was, it was heavy. It took two of Kiber's strongest *goums* to lift a jar by its ivory handles and stagger across the sand to place it with the other merchandise stacked along the shoreline.

The men carrying the jars passed quite close to where Mathew stood in the hot sun near Khardan's litter. The young wizard would have liked to have examined the jars more closely, for he thought he detected magical runes among the other designs carved on the sides, and his skin prickled with a tingle of fear and curiosity when he observed that the lid was decorated with the carved body of a severed snake—the same device that appeared on Khardan's black armor. But Mathew did not have time to investigate or even give more than a moment's passing thought to the ivory jars. His attention was focused on Zohra, and he stared at the woman with mingled anger, frustration, fear, and admiration.

She must be as bewildered and confused as I am, Mathew thought. No, more so, because he at least knew the slave trader and knew why Auda ibn Jad wanted him—the fish, obviously, although that didn't begin to answer all the questions. Zohra had wakened in a strange place from some sort of enchanted sleep, experienced all the same uncomfortable sensations Mathew had experienced—even now she swayed slightly on her feet and he could tell that it was taking every ounce of will she possessed to remain standing. She had, apparently, no idea where she was (This disappointed Mathew. He had hoped she would recognize this place.) and yet she was regarding the formidable Auda ibn Jad with the same scornful gaze she might have fixed upon poor Usti, her djinn, for bungling a command.

Auda's attention continued to remain focused on the unpacking of the ivory jars. Mathew saw Zohra's dark eyes above the veil flare with anger, her black brows draw together. He knew he should stop her. In his mind he saw the slave girl falling to the sand, ibn Jad's knife in her ribs. But the intense heat of the sun radiating up from the salt floor was sapping Mathew's strength. Clinging to one of the poles supporting the litter where Khardan lay, Mathew could only try to warn Zohra to keep still with a gesture of his hand. Zohra saw him and she saw Khardan, who was groaning, shaking his head muzzily, and making feeble, futile attempts to sit up.

"I asked you a question, swine!" Zohra said, stamping her slippered foot on the cracked ground, her jewelry jingling, her body quivering with anger.

"Dog of a *kafir!* Swine!" Mathew cringed.

"I am a Princess of my people. You will treat me as such," Zohra continued, holding the veil tightly over her face, the rising wind whipping the silken folds of her *chador* around her legs. "You will tell me where I am and you will then return me to my people."

Seeing the nine ivory jars safely stacked up on the shoreline with four *goums* posted guard around them, Auda ibn Jad turned his attention to the woman standing before him. A glint of amusement flickered in the hooded eyes. Weakly Mathew sank down onto the hot ground, huddling in a small patch of shade cast by Khardan's litter. Almost immediately, however, a new fear arose when the young wizard saw Khardan's eyes open to stare about his surroundings in confused astonishment.

A waterskin lay nearby. Catching it up, Mathew held the mouth out to Khardan to drink, trying as best he could to warn him to keep silent. The Calif thrust the waterskin aside.

Gritting his teeth against the pain, Khardan propped himself up on one elbow and stared intently at Auda ibn Jad.

"You stand, Princess, on the shores of the Kurdin Sea—"

"The Waters of Tara-kan?" Zohra cut in scornfully. "Do you take me for a fool?"

"No, my lady." Respect coated the surface of Auda's voice.

He was toying with her, amusing himself because he had no other entertainment. The slaves and the *goums* had completed unloading the camels. The slaves sank, panting, down onto the ground, trying desperately to find some modicum of shade by crouching beside the kneeling camels. The *goums* stood in disciplined silence, sipping water and keeping watch over the baggage and the slaves. They appeared immune to the heat, though Mathew could see huge patches of sweat darkening their black uniforms. And he noted, as he glanced at them, that more than one turned his gaze out to sea, nodding in relief and satisfaction at the sight of the shadow growing larger upon the water.

"All know the Waters of the Tara-kan do not exist," said Zohra, dismissing the vast sea that stretched before her with decisive finality. So calmly and firmly did she speak that it seemed the sea itself must realize its mistake and take itself out of her presence at once.

"I assure you, madam, that these are the waters of the Kurdin Sea. We have reached them by traveling north from the Tel in the desert of Pagrah to the city of Idrith, then due east across the southernmost border of the Great Steppes."

Zohra gazed at Auda pityingly. "You are mad. Such a journey would take months!"

"Indeed it has, my lady," ibn Jad replied softly. "Look at the sun."

Zohra looked upward at the sun. So did Khardan. Mathew watched the Calif carefully, searching for clues in the expression on the man's face. The young wizard himself did not bother to study the orb's position in the sky. In this strange part of the world, he was barely able to judge the passing of day into night much less the passing of weeks into months. It seemed to him to have been only last night that they had escaped the Battle at the Tel. Had it truly been months ago? Were they truly far from their homeland?

Our homeland! Mathew shook his head bleakly. What am I thinking about? My homeland... So much farther away than that ... Farther away than the blazing sun...

He saw Khardan's eyes widen, the man's face grow pale beneath the growth of heavy black beard, the lips part, the tongue attempt to moisten them. The Calif looked down now upon the strange armor that he wore, noticing it for the first time. His hand ran over it, and Mathew saw the fingers tremble. Wordlessly the young wizard held out the waterskin again. This time Khardan accepted it, drinking a small amount, his brow furrowed, his black eyes fixed upon Auda ibn Jad with a dark expression Mathew could not fathom.

Zohra's cool demeanor, too, was shaken. She darted a swift, fearful glance at Mathew from above her veil—the glance of one who has ventured blithely onto smooth, hardpacked sand, only to discover herself being sucked beneath the shifting surface.

Mathew quickly averted his eyes. She had thrown herself into this, she must get herself out. He could say or do nothing that would help her, and he dared not attract the attention of the slave trader to himself. By the looks of it, Auda ibn Jad was telling the truth. They had undertaken a long journey, apparently traveling under some sort of spell that feigned death yet kept them very much alive.

The city guards do not search the bodies of the dead.

That statement was beginning to make sense. Mathew's hand stole surreptitiously to the globe containing the fish. Ibn Jad had given it to him originally to sneak it past the guards in the city of Kich. Now Mathew had been instrumental, apparently, in doing the same thing with the guards of Idrith. That was the reason ibn Jad had taken Mathew captive instead of killing him and retrieving the fish. Mathew recalled the moment of terror when he had awakened in the tall grass near the oasis. Seeing the slave trader standing above him, he had supposed the man meant to murder him. Instead, ibn Jad had cast him into a deep sleep.

But why take Khardan? Why take Zohra? Why bring them here? Why the ships? Where were they being taken? Surely, if he had brought them this far, ibn Jad did not intend to kill them now.

Looking at Auda's smooth, impassive face, the unblinking eyes; looking at the waters of the sea that were growing rougher by the moment; looking at the shadow covering the water and realizing that it was the darkness of a rapidly approaching storm—a strange storm, a storm that seemed to rage only on a small part of the ocean—Mathew wondered despairingly if death coming to them this minute might not be a blessing.

"I do not like this place," said Zohra coolly. "I am leaving." Mathew raised his eyes, staring at her in astonishment.

Gathering the folds of her wind-whipped clothes around her with one hand, holding her veil over her nose and mouth with the other, Zohra turned her back upon Auda ibn Jad and began walking due west over the cracked, tortured earth.

Shrugging, ibn Jad moved over to the shoreline and stood there, gazing intently out eastward into the storm. The *goums*, watching Zohra, nudged each other, many pointing at the sun and laughing. Kiber said something to Auda ibn Jad, who glanced at Zohra out of the corner of his eye and shrugged again.

Mathew stared at her, aghast. She knew, far better than he, having lived in the desert, that she would not last more than a few hours out there before the merciless heat blistered her skin and boiled her blood, before the lack of water drove her to madness. The storm wind blowing off the sea tore the silken veil from her head, her long black hair streamed into her face, nearly blinding her. Still weak from the effects of the spell, Zohra stumbled over the cracked, uneven ground, slipped and fell. Pausing a moment to catch her breath, she staggered back up to her feet and continued on, limping.

She's twisted her ankle. She won't get a hundred yards! Mathew realized. Half-heard words spoken by the *goums* indicated they were placing bets on how far she could go before collapsing. Of all the stupid, meaningless gestures! Mathew fumed. Why didn't she just drive a knife into her heart? Was her pride that important? More important than her life?

And these people considered *him* mad!

Struggling to his feet, Mathew cast a wary glance at ibn Jad. Seeing him apparently absorbed in watching for the ship, the young wizard started after Zohra. She was weakening fast. Her

limp was more pronounced, every movement must be causing her agony. Mathew quickly caught up with the woman and
grabbed hold of her arm.

Turning, she saw who it was held her and immediately jerked
away.

"Let me go!" she ordered

At the sight of her pain-twisted face, the parched lips already
cracked and bleeding from the salt-laden air, and the fierce pride
and determination masking the terror in the black eyes, Mathew
felt tears well up in his throat. Whether they were tears of pity,
tears of admiration, or tears of exasperated rage, he wasn't certain. His instinct was to take her in his arms and comfort her, let
her know she wasn't alone in the fear and despair she was trying
desperately to hide. Yet the wizard had the distinct feeling that
once he got his hands on the obstreperous woman, he'd shake her
until her teeth rattled in her head.

"Zohra! Stop! Listen to me!" Mathew caught hold of her
again and this time held on firmly. Unable to free herself, she
glared at him in fury. "You're only making things worse! Do you
know what kind of death you'll die out there?"

The black eyes stared at him unwaveringly.

She knows, Mathew thought, swallowing the lump in his
throat. "Zohra"—he tried again—"whatever we face can't possibly be as bad as that! Don't leave me! Don't leave Khardan! We've
got to get through this together. It's our only chance!"

Her eyes blinked, her gaze shifted from Mathew to Khardan,
a slight smile twisted the cracked lips. Not liking the looks of that
smile, Mathew glanced swiftly around.

Auda ibn Jad had his back turned, staring out to sea. Un-
armed, with no weapon but his bare hands, Khardan had risen
from the litter and was running across the sand toward the slave
trader.

Gnashing his teeth in frustration, his heart stopped in fear,
Mathew watched helplessly, expecting to see the *goums* rush the
Calif, Kiber draw his shining sword and cut Khardan down. Instead, no one made a move. No one even shouted a warning to
ibn Jad, who still had his back to his rapidly approaching enemy.

Khardan hurled himself at the slave trader, his hands outstretched.

The end came swiftly, occurring so fast that Mathew wasn't

certain what happened. He saw Auda ibn Jad sidestep ever so slightly. Khardan leaped on his back, his arms closing around the slave trader's throat. Auda's hands grabbed hold of Khardan's arms and in the same, fluid movement, bent forward, pulling the Calif with him. Propelled by his own momentum, Khardan was flipped over the slave trader's shoulder. The Calif flew through the air and splashed into the shallow water at the shore's edge. He lay there, dazed and stunned, staring up at the sky.

"Has everyone gone insane? Are all you nomads intent on delivering yourselves as quickly as possible into the arms of Death?" Mathew demanded bitterly.

"We are not cowards!" Zohra hissed, struggling feebly to escape his grip. "Not like you! I will die before anyone keeps me captive, for whatever reason!"

"Sometimes it takes more courage to live!" Mathew responded, his voice thick and choked.

Zohra stared at him, the women's clothes he wore, and made no answer.

Auda ibn Jad was shouting orders. *Goums* came running across the sand toward them. Catching hold of both Zohra and Mathew, they dragged them back to the slave trader. Other *goums*, supervised by Kiber, were lifting Khardan up out of the sea. They shoved Mathew down into the sand near the baggage that was to be loaded onto the approaching vessels. Zohra fell down next to him, Kiber dropped Khardan, breathing heavily, at their feet. Bending over the Calif, ostensibly to see if he was hurt but in reality hiding his face, Mathew saw Zohra looking at him, her dark eyes unusually thoughtful.

He turned his head, not wanting to meet her gaze, afraid that if she should be able to see inside him, she would see there the sick fear that shamed him and made a mockery of his words.

CHAPTER 3

Bruised and aching, Khardan was content for the moment to catch his breath and consider the situation. His attack on Auda ibn Jad had not been as rash and ill considered as it appeared to Mathew. The Calif knew that the fall of a leader can never fail to throw even the best disciplined army into confusion and disarray. There was every possibility this slave trader ruled by fear alone and his followers might be exceedingly grateful to the man who removed the sword from their throats.

That man is not likely to be me—at least not at this moment, Khardan thought, glancing at ibn Jad with grudging respect. The slave trader had tossed him around with the ease of a father playing with his children! Looking at the long, curved sword ibn Jad wore at his side, the Calif guessed that the man was undoubtedly equally skilled with it, as well. And the longer Khardan watched Kiber and his *goums,* the more obvious it became to him that they served ibn Jad with unshakable, unswerving loyalty—the type of loyalty that is not and never can be generated by fear.

What I need now are answers, Khardan thought upon reflection. Of course, these had to come from the red-haired youth, the one whose life he had saved. The Calif had recognized the slave trader as the man in the white palanquin who had stared at Khardan with such malevolence in the city of Kich. More than once Khardan had wakened in the night, sweating and shaking, remembering the dreadful promise of revenge in those cold, flat eyes—the eyes of a snake.

Khardan could understand ibn Jad's anger—the Calif had stolen one of his salves, after all. But Khardan had known at the time, when those deadly eyes first pierced his soul, that there was more to it than that. It was as if the Calif had snatched up the one thing in this world that gave ibn Jad reason to live. And Auda had promised, in that look, that he would have it back.

What was the young man's name, anyway? Khardan tried to remember through the haze of pain and confusion. Mathew. Something like that. He'd heard Zohra pronounce it. Thinking of his wife, who wasn't a wife to him any more than the young man was a wife to him, Khardan glanced at her. Zohra sat on the other side of Mathew, and unlike the young man, who was looking at him with a worried expression, she didn't appear to be the least interested in Khardan's welfare.

He couldn't see her face; the black hair, blown by the wind, covered it like a veil. Nursing her sore ankle, rubbing it with her hand, she stared straight out to sea and was seemingly lost in her thoughts.

Khardan wondered what she knew about the young man. It was too late to ask. Bitterly he regretted not questioning this man about his past, about where he'd come from, why he had chosen to hide his sex from the world in women's clothes. It occurred to Khardan that he hadn't spoken more than twenty words to the youth the entire time he'd been in the nomad's camp.

Who could blame me? Khardan reflected grimly, looking up at the young man with the flame-colored hair and the face as smooth and delicate as that of any woman. Kneeling beside Khardan, Mathew was making a clumsy attempt to loosen the fastenings of the breastplate clamped over the Calif's chest.

A man who disguises himself as a woman! A man who lets himself be taken into another man's harem! Bad enough I had to live with such disgrace—but to be seen taking an interest in him!

There was too much on my mind to worry over a boy—Sheykh Zeid, Meryem... Khardan's heart jumped. Meryem! She'd been in danger! The battle... he remembered seeing her face just before he lost consciousness. What had happened to her? What had happened to all of them—his people? Why was he here? He stared again at the sun whose position in the sky meant the passage of two months at least. From Idrith to the Kurdin Sea... Answers! He needed answers!

Reaching out, he caught hold of the young man's arm. "What's going on?" he asked softly.

Startled, Mathew glanced at Khardan uneasily, then shook his head and averted his face. He was attempting to untie a knot in one of the leather thongs holding the sides of the breastplate together. Khardan's hand closed over his, halting his work with its firm pressure.

"What is your name?"

"Mathew," was the barely audible reply. The young man kept his eyes lowered.

"Mat-hew," repeated Khardan, stumbling over the strange sounding word and coming out with it finally in a manner and accent similar to Zohra's. "Mat-hew, it is obvious that we are here because of you. Why does this man want you?"

Mathew lowered his head. Locks of the flaming red hair slid out from beneath the woman's veil he wore, partially hiding his face. But Khardan saw a flush stain the fair cheeks, he saw the curved lips tremble, and he could guess at the answer the youth was too embarrassed to give.

"So, he does not know you are a—" Khardan paused.

The crimson in the cheeks deepened. Mathew shook his head. Khardan felt the young man's hands shake; the fingers were icy to the touch, despite the terrible heat.

Letting loose the boy's hand, Khardan glanced around cautiously. Auda ibn Jad and Kiber stood together on the beach, conferring in low tones, occasionally glancing out to sea. The *goums'* attentions were focused on the sea as well. The slaves sat huddled together near the camels, heads bowed, no interest in anything.

"That's not the truth, Mat-hew," Khardan said slowly, turning his gaze back to the youth. "He doesn't want you for his bed. He would have sold you in Kich if I hadn't stolen you away. There is another reason he wants you and it is the reason we are here. Tell me."

Raising his head, Mathew looked at Khardan. The young man's eyes were wide and in them was a look of such pleading and terror that Khardan was taken aback.

"Don't ask me!" The words came out a gasp.

Khardan's lips tightened in anger and frustration. The boy's fear was contagious. Khardan felt it chill his own blood and the feeling irritated him. He'd never experienced fear like this before, and he had faced death in battle since he was seventeen years old. This fear was like a child's fear of the dark—irrational, illogical, and very real.

Mathew gave up on the knot; his hands were shaking too

violently. He started to turn away, to go sit with Zohra, who was crouched on the hot ground near Khardan's feet. The Calif caught hold of him again.

Slowly, reluctantly, Mathew glanced back at him. The face was terror stricken, the eyes begged Khardan to release him. Khardan bit back the words he'd been going to say. He wanted to sit up; the heavy metal of the armor was poking him uncomfortably in the back. But moving about might attract the attention of ibn Jad, and Khardan wanted to talk undisturbed for as long as possible.

"What happened at the Tel, then," Khardan said gruffly, frowning. "Surely you can tell me that! How did we come to fall into the hands of this slave trader?"

As he had hoped she would, Zohra turned her head at his question. She stared at her husband, exchanged a swift, grim glance with Mathew, then turned back to gaze out at the sea in silence once more.

"The Amir's forces raided the camp. Everyone—women and children—were taken prisoner—" Mathew answered softly, warily.

"I know that," Khardan snapped impatiently. "I saw. I mean after."

"We—Zohra and I—escaped by hiding in a tent." Mathew's eyes, as he spoke, were focused on the snake on Khardan's armor. "You. . . fell in battle. We . . . uh . . . found you on the battlefield. The Amir's men were taking prisoners, you see, and we feared that they would take you, so we carried you off the field of battle—"

"—disguised as a woman."

The cold, smooth voice broke in on the conversation.

Intent upon Mathew's story, Khardan had not heard the man approach. Twisting, he looked up into the black masked face of Auda ibn Jad.

The man was talking nonsense! Khardan sat up, chafing beneath the hot, heavy armor. Ignoring ibn Jad, the Calif looked to Mathew to continue his story and was astounded to see that the boy had gone deathly white and was biting his nether lip. Khardan's gaze went to Zohra. She kept her back turned to him, but that back was rigid, her neck stiff, her head held high in a manner quite well-known to him.

"Is this true?" Khardan demanded angrily.

"Yes, it's true!" Zohra whirled to face him, her hair whipping about her in the wind blowing off the sea. "How do you think you would have escaped otherwise? Is the Amir such a kindly man that he would say, 'Ah, poor fellow, he's hurt. Take him away and tend him'? Hah! More likely a sword through the throat and the jackals feasting off your brains, much food they would find there!"

A smile twitched at the comer of the mouth of Auda ibn Jad.

"You have. . . shamed me!" Khardan's face burned an angry red. Sweat beaded his brow. His hands clenched and I he struggled for breath. "I am . . . dishonored!"

"It was all we could think of to do!" Mathew faltered. Glancing up, he saw the reptile eyes of ibn Jad watching with interest. The youth laid a placating, trembling hand on Khardan's arm. "No one saw us, I'm certain. There was so much smoke and confusion. We hid in the tall grass, near the oasis. . ."

"The young woman tells the truth, Nomad," said ibn Jad. "It was there I found you, in the oasis, dressed in rose-pink silk. You don't believe me?" Crouching down opposite Mathew, the slave trader reached out his slender hand and caught hold of the youth by the chin. "Look at that face, Nomad. How I can such beauty lie? Look into the green eyes. See the love they hold for you? Blossom here did it for love, Nomad." Ibn Jad released Mathew roughly, the marks of the man's fingers showing clearly on the youth's livid face. "Now this one." The slave trader turned to look admiringly at Zohra, who was pointedly ignoring him. "This one, I'd say, did it for spite." Auda ibn Jad rose to his feet. "Not that it matters, where you are going, Nomad," he added casually.

"Where *are* we going?" Zohra asked with disdain, as though inquiring of a slave what they might be having for dinner.

"Across this—the waters of the sea whose existence you refuse to acknowledge, Princess," said Auda ibn Jad with a smile and a gesture of his hand. "We go to the island fortress of Galos, where dwells the last remnant of those who worship Zhakrin, God of the Night."

"I have never heard of this God," Zohra stated, dismissing Zhakrin as she dismissed the ocean.

"That is because he has been deposed from his heavenly throne. Some think him dead—a costly mistake. Zhakrin lives, and we gather now in his palace to prepare for his return."

"We?" Zohra's lip curled in scorn.

Auda ibn Jad's voice became cool, reverent. "The Black Paladins, the Holy Knights of Evil."

CHAPTER 4

Black Paladins, Zhakrin . . . The words meant nothing to Zohra. None of this meant anything to Zohra, except that she was here where she did not want to be, she was being held captive by this man, and her attempt to escape had been stopped by Mathew. Zohra did not believe ibn Jad's wild tales about traveling to Idrith and beyond to a sea that did not exist. The Tel was nearby. It had to be. He was lying to prevent them from attempting to escape, and Mathew had swallowed that lie. And so had Khardan, apparently. As for the odd position of the sun in the sky, a summer sun—it had been spring when she closed her eyes to sleep the sleep of exhaustion in the oasis—that could be explained. She knew it could, if only she could get away from this man with the disturbing eyes and discover the truth.

What they needed was action, to fight, to do something instead of just sit here like . . . like old women! Zohra glanced at the two men with her and her lips twisted in derision. At least Khardan had tried to fight. She had been proud of him at that moment. But now the man's anger and hurt pride had overthrown his reason, casting him into some sort of stupor. He stared at his hands, his fists clenching and unclenching, his breath coming in short gasps. As for the young wizard—Zohra glanced at him in scorn.

"He has already exhibited *his* worth!" the woman muttered beneath her breath. "I could measure it in goat droppings!"

She herself was at a disadvantage now, with her injured, ankle. At a disadvantage, but not helpless. Her hand went to her breast. The dagger she had grabbed during the onset of the raid was hidden in her bosom. Pressing against her flesh, the metal felt warm and reassuring. She would never be taken aboard a ship, if such was truly the intent of this man. She would never be taken to any palace of a dead God.

Mathew's voice, speaking to the Paladin, disturbed her thoughts.

"So that is how you did it?" The young man was staring up at Auda ibn Jad with awe; fear made his voice crack. Zohra glanced away from him in disgust. "That is how you cast the enchanted sleep over us. You are not a wizard—"

"No, Blossom." Ibn Jad frowned at the idea. "I am a true knight and my power comes from Zhakrin, not from Sul. Long ago, in my youth, I learned the might of Zhakrin. I accepted him as my God and pledged to him my life, my soul. I have worked—all those of my Order have worked—unceasingly to bring about our God's return into this world."

"A priest!" Zohra sneered. She did not see the cruel eyes, gazing at her, narrow dangerously.

"No!" said Mathew hastily. "Not a priest. Or rather a priest who is a warrior. One who can"—the young man paused, then said heavily—"kill in the name of the God."

"Yes," said the Black Paladin coolly. "I have laid many souls upon the altar of Zhakrin." The toe of his boot idly scraped the salty soil from around the base of one of the ivory jars that stood near them. "We kill without mercy, yet never without reason. The God is angered by senseless murder, since the living are always more valuable in his service than the dead."

"That's why you've kept us alive," Mathew said softly. "To serve your God. But. . . how?"

"Haven't you figured that out yet, Blossom?" Auda ibn Jad looked at him quizzically. "No? Then I prefer to keep you ignorant. Fear of the unknown is much more debilitating."

The storm was worsening. Water that had previously been calm now crashed on the shore. Everyone's clothing was wet through with salt spray. The sun had disappeared behind the storm clouds, casting a dark shadow over them.

Kiber's voice called out urgently. The Black Paladin turned to look to sea. "Ah! The ship is in sight. Only a few more moments before it lands. You will excuse me, I am certain." Ibn Jad bowed. "There are matters to which I must attend."

Turning, he walked over to Kiber. The two conferred briefly, then Kiber hurried over to his *goums*, gesturing and shouting orders. The soldiers sprang into action, some running over to the camels, others taking up positions around the baggage, others hauling the slaves to their feet.

Curious, Zohra looked out to sea.

She had heard tales of the *dhough,* the vessels made of wood that floated upon the water and had wings to drive them before the wind. She had never seen one before. She had never, in fact, seen a body of water as large as this one and was secretly in awe of it, or would have been, if such an emotion would not have betrayed weakness. Looking critically at the ship as it approached, Zohra felt at first disappointment.

The *meddah,* the storyteller, had said these vessels were like white-winged sea birds, swooping gracefully over the water. This *dhough* resembled a gigantic insect, crawling over the ocean's surface. Oars stuck out from either side, scrabbling over the waves like feet, propelling the insect forward into the teeth of the wind. Ragged black wings flapped wildly.

Zohra knew nothing about ships or sailing, but she found it impossible to see how this one stayed afloat. Time and again she expected to see it perish. The vessel plunged in and out of the tall waves, its prow sliding down an incline that was steep and smooth as polished steel. It disappeared, and it seemed it must have vanished forever beneath the churning waters. Then suddenly it came in sight, springing up out of the watery chasm like a many-legged bug scrabbling to regain its footing.

Zohra's disappointment turned to uneasiness; her uneasiness darkened and deepened the nearer the ship approached.

"Mat-hew," she said softly, moving nearer the young wizard, whose gaze was fixed, like hers, upon the ship. "You have sailed in these *dhough?*"

"Yes." His voice was tight, strained.

"You have sailed across a sea?" She had not believed his story before. She wasn't certain she believed it now, but she needed reassurance.

He nodded. His eyes, staring at the ship, were wide. "It looks so frail. How does it survive such a beating?"

"It shouldn't." He coughed, his throat was dry. "It"—he hesitated, licking his lips—"it isn't an . . . ordinary ship, Zohra. Just like that isn't an ordinary storm. They're supernatural."

He used the term from his own language and she stared at him, uncomprehending.

Mathew groped for words. "Magic, enchanted."

At that, Khardan lifted his head, his fog of rage blown away by the cold, biting wind of Mathew's words. The Calif stared out at the ship that was so close now they could see figures walking across its slanting deck. A jagged bolt of lightning shot from the churning black clouds, striking the mast. Flame danced along the yardarms, the rigging caught fire and burned, the sails became sheets of flame whose garish light was reflected on the water-slick deck and flickered in the rising and falling oars. The vessel had become a ship of fire.

Catching her breath, Zohra looked hurriedly at Auda ibn Jad, expecting some outcry, some angry reaction. The man paced the shore and appeared disturbed, but the glances he cast the ship were of impatience, not dismay.

Mathew's hand closed over hers. Looking back out to sea, Zohra shrank close to the young man. The flames did not consume the vessel! Burning fiercely, the ship surged across the storm-tossed waves, being driven to shore by buffeting winds. Thunder boomed around it, a black banner burst from its masthead. Outlined in flame was the image of a severed snake.

"They would put us aboard that!" Zohra's voice was low and hollow.

"Zohra," Mathew began helplessly, hands on her shoulders, "it will be all right. . ."

"No!" With a wild shriek, she broke free of him. Leaping to her feet, fear absorbing the pain of her injured ankle, Zohra ran wildly away from the sea, away from the blazing ship. Her flight caught everyone off guard; the Black Paladin fuming at the slowness of the ship in docking was staring out to sea, as were all those not involved with more pressing tasks. A flutter of silk seen out of the corner of the eye caught Kiber's attention. He shouted, and the *goums* guarding the captives and the baggage set off instantly in pursuit.

Fear lends strength, but it saps strength, too, and when panic subsides, the body is weaker as a result. The fire from the ship seemed to shoot through Zohra's leg; her ankle could no longer bear her weight and gave way beneath her. Away from the water's edge and the cooling winds of the storm, Zohra felt the heat that was rising from the salt flats suck out her breath and parch her throat. The glare of the sun off the crystalline sand seared through her eyes and into her brain. Behind her, she could hear panting breath, the pounding of booted feet.

Staggering blindly, Zohra stumbled and fell. Her hand closed over the hilt of the hidden dagger and, when rough hands grabbed hold of her, she struck out at them with the knife. Unable to see through her tangled hair, she lashed wildly at the sound of their voices or their harsh, rasping breath. A grunt and a bitter curse told her she'd drawn blood and she fought ever more furiously.

A cold voice barked a command. Hands closed over her wrist, bones cracked, pain burned in her arm. Gagging, choking, she dropped the dagger.

Gripping her firmly by the arms, the *goums*—one of them bleeding from a slash across the chest—dragged her back across the sand. The ship had dropped anchor some distance from the shore and stood burning in the water like a horrible beacon. The sight of small boats, black against the flames, crawling slowly toward land, renewed Zohra's terror.

She struggled against her captors, pulling backward with all the weight of her body.

Sweating profusely, the *goums* hauled her before the Black Paladin. Zohra shook the hair out of her eyes, her sun-dazzled vision had cleared enough to see him. He was regarding her coolly, thoughtfully, perhaps wondering if she was worth the trouble.

Decision made, ibn Jad lifted his hand and struck.

CHAPTER 5

B ind his hands and arms!"

Rubbing his knuckles, Auda ibn Jad glanced from the comatose body of Zohra lying at his feet to the insane struggles of Khardan, battling with the *goums*. "If he persists in causing trouble, render him unconscious as well."

"Khardan!" Mathew was pleading, "be calm! There's nothing we can do! No sense in fighting! We must just try to survive!"

Soothingly, timidly he touched the muscular arm that was being wrenched behind Khardan's back and bound tightly with cords of braided hemp used to hold the baggage in place upon the camels. Glaring at him in bitter anger, Khardan drew away from the young man. His struggles ceased, however, but whether from seeing the logic in Mathew's words or because he was bound, helpless and exhausted, the young wizard did not know.

His body shivering, like that of a horse who has been run into the ground, Khardan stood with head bowed. Seeing him calm for the moment at least, Mathew left the Calif to tend to Zohra, who lay in a heap on the ground, her long black hair glistening with the salt spray from the pounding waves.

Mathew glanced warily at the *goums,* but they made no attempt to stop him. The flat, cruel eyes turned their gaze on him, however, and Mathew faltered, a bird caught and held by the mesmerizing stare of the cobra.

Kiber spoke, ibn Jad's gaze turned to his Captain, and Mathew—with a shivering sigh—crept forward again.

"These two are trouble," the leader of the *goums* grumbled. "Why not leave them as payment, along with the slaves."

"Zhakrin would not thank us for wasting such fine, healthy bodies and souls to match. This woman"—ibn Jad bent over to caress a strand of Zohra's black hair—"is superb. I like her spirit.

She will breed many strong followers for the God. Perhaps I will take her myself. As for the bearded devil"—ibn Jad straightened and glanced over at Khardan, his eyes coolly appraising the young man's muscular build—"you know what awaits him. Will that not be worth some trouble in the eyes of Zhakrin?"

Auda ibn Jad's tone was severe. Kiber cringed, as though the knight's stern rebuke cut his flesh. The *goum's* "Yes, *Effendi*" was subdued.

"See to the landing party," ibn Jad ordered. "Keep your men occupied in loading the baggage aboard. Send the sailors to me. I will take charge of them."

Kiber, bowing, scurried away. It seemed to Mathew that, at the mention of the sailors, Kiber's tan face became unusually pale, strained, and tense.

Zohra moaned, and Mathew's attention turned to her.

"You had best rouse her and get her on board the boats as quickly as possible, Blossom," said the Black Paladin carelessly. "The sailors will be coming to me for their payment and you are both in danger here."

Payment? Mathew saw the Black Paladin's reptile eyes go to the slaves, who crouched together in a miserable huddle, chained hand and foot by the *goums* as soon as their labors were finished. Pitifully thin and emaciated, their bones showing beneath their whip-scarred skin, the slaves stared in wild-eyed terror at the fiery ship, obviously fearing that they would be forced to board it.

Mathew had a sudden, chilling premonition that the poor wretches' fears were groundless—or rather, misplaced. Hastily he helped Zohra to her feet. Draping one of her arms over his shoulder, he put his arm around her waist and half carried, half dragged her across the sand, over to where the *goums* were keeping a wary eye on Khardan. Groggy but conscious, Zohra clung to Mathew. The right side of her face was bruised and swollen. Blood trickled from a split lip. She must have had a blinding headache, and a tiny gasp of pain escaped her every time her injured foot touched the ground.

She made no complaint, however, and did her best to keep up with Mathew, whose own growing fear was lending impetus to his strides. He was facing the incoming boats now, and his gaze went curiously to the crew who sailed a ship of flame across storm-blasted water and who were now coming to shore to demand payment for their services.

There seemed nothing unusual about them. Human males, they shipped their oars with disciplined skill. Jumping over the side into the shallow water, they dragged the boats onto the shore, leaving them under Kiber's command. At his orders, the *goums* immediately began to stow the baggage on board, Kiber personally supervising the loading of the large, ivory jars. Though all did their work efficiently, Mathew noted that every *goum*—Kiber included—kept his eyes fearfully upon the sailors.

They were all young, muscular men with blond hair and fair, even features. Coming ashore, they paused and looked long and hard at the *goums,* their blue eyes eerily reflecting the orange glow of the fire that blazed in the water behind them. Kiber gave them a swift, hunted glance. His eyes darted to Auda ibn Jad, then back to his men, who weren't moving fast enough to suit him. Shouting at the *goums,* Kiber's voice cracked with fear.

"In the name of Zhakrin, God of Night and Evil, I bid you greeting," called Auda ibn Jad.

The eyes of the sailors reluctantly left the *goums.* As one man, they looked to the Black Paladin standing, facing them, some distance up the beach from the shoreline. Mathew caught his breath, his arms went limp, he nearly let loose his hold on Zohra. He couldn't move for astonishment.

Each of the sailors was identical to every other. The same nose, same mouth, same ears, same eyes. They were the same height, the same weight. They moved the same, they walked the same, they were dressed the same—in tightfitting breeches, their chests bare, gleaming with water.

Zohra sagged wearily in Mathew's arm. She did not look up and something warned Mathew to make certain that she didn't. Snatching the veil from his hair, he cast it over her head. The sailors' eyes swept over both of them like a bone-chilling wind. Mathew knew he should move, should take the few steps—all that was required to bring them back under the protection of Kiber and his *goums.* But Mathew's feet were numb, his body paralyzed by a fear that came from deep inside the part of his mind where nightmares lurked.

"We answered your summons and sailed our ship to do your bidding," spoke one of the sailors—or perhaps it was all the sailors; the fifty mouths moved, but Mathew heard only one voice.

"Where is our payment?"

"Here," said Auda ibn Jad, and pointed at the slaves.

The sailors looked and they nodded, satisfied, and then their aspect began to change. The jaws thrust forward, the lips parted and drew back, gleaming teeth lengthened into fangs. The eyes burned, no longer reflecting the fire of their ship, but with insatiable hunger. Voices changed to snarls, fingernails to ripping talons. With an eager howl, the sailors swept forward, the wind of their passing hitting Mathew with a chill, foul-smelling blast, as if someone had opened the doors of a desecrated and defiled tomb.

He did not need to look at the prints left behind by the creatures in the sand to know what these monsters were. He knew what he would see—not a human track, but the cloven hooves of an ass.

"*Ghuls!*" he breathed, shuddering in terror.

The slaves saw death running toward them. Their shrieks were heart-rending and piteous to hear. Zohra started to lift her head, but Mathew—clasping her close to him—covered her eyes with his hand and began to run, dragging her stumbling and blinded along with him.

"Don't look!" he panted, repeating the words over and over, trying not to hear what was happening behind him. There was the clanking of chains—the slaves trying desperately to escape. He heard their wails when they realized it was hopeless and then the first horrible scream and then more screams and the dreadful ripping, tearing sounds of teeth and talons sinking into and devouring living flesh.

Zohra became dead weight in Mathew's arms. Overcome by her pain, she had lost consciousness. Shaking, unable to take another step, he lowered her onto the ground. Kiber himself ran forward to lift up the woman's body and carry her into the waiting boats. The *goum* kept his eyes averted from the grisly massacre, driving his men to their work with shouts and curses.

"*Hazrat* Akhran, have mercy on us!" The voice was Khardan's, but Mathew barely recognized it. The Calif's face was livid, his beard blue against the pallid skin. His eyes were white-rimmed and staring, purple shadows smudged the skin. Sweat trickled down his face; his lips trembled.

"Don't watch!" Mathew implored, trying to block the man's

vision of the gruesome carnage.

Khardan lunged forward. Bound or not, he obviously intended to try and help the doomed slaves.

Mathew caught hold of him by the shoulders. Struggling wildly, Khardan sought to free himself, but the youth held onto him tightly, with the strength of desperation.

"*Ghuls!*" Mathew cried, his voice catching in his burning throat. "They feed on human flesh. It will be over soon. There's nothing you can do!"

Behind him, he could hear screams of the dying, their still living bodies being rended from limb to limb. Their wails tore through head and heart.

"I can't stand it!" Khardan gasped.

"I know!" Mathew dug his nails into the man's flesh. "But there is nothing you can do! Ibn Jad holds the *ghuls* in thrall, but just barely. Interfere, and you kill us all!"

Wrenching himself free from Mathew's hold, Khardan lost his balance, stumbled, and fell to his knees. He did not get up, but remained crouched on the ground, sweating and shivering, his breath coming in painful sobs.

The screams ceased suddenly. Mathew closed his eyes, going limp in relief. Footsteps crunched in the sand near him, and he looked up hurriedly. Auda ibn Jad stood beside him, staring down at Khardan. The Calif heaved a shuddering sigh. Wiping his hand across his mouth, he lifted his head. His face was white, the lips tinged with the green of sickness. Dark, bloodshot eyes, shadowed with the horror of what they had witnessed, stared up at the Black Paladin.

"What kind of monster are you?" Khardan asked hoarsely. "The kind you will become," answered Auda ibn Jad.

CHAPTER 6

*i*t was well Mathew had others to worry about during the journey across the Kurdin Sea on the demon-driven vessel, or he might have truly succumbed to madness. They had no more set foot on board when the *ghuls* returned from their feast. Once more in the guise of handsome young men, their bodies daubed with blood, they silently took their places at the oars below and on the decks and in the rigging above. A word from Auda ibn Jad set the black sails billowing. The anchor was weighed, the *ghuls* heaved at the oars, the storm winds howled, lightning cracked, and the ship clawed its way through the foaming water toward the island of Galos.

Khardan had not spoken a word since ibn Jad's strange pronouncement on shore. He had suffered himself to be hoisted roughly aboard ship without a struggle. The *goums*, under Kiber's orders, lashed the nomad to a mast and left him there. Sagging against his bindings, Khardan stared around him with dull, lusterless eyes.

Thinking the sight of Zohra might rouse the Calif from the stupor into which he had fallen, Mathew brought the limp and lifeless form to lie on the deck near where her husband stood, tied to the mast. Soaked through to the skin from the rain and the sea water breaking over the heaving deck, the young wizard did what he could to keep Zohra warm and dry, covering her with a tarp, sheltering her amid the tall ivory jars and the rest of the baggage that the *ghuls* had secured as best they could on the slippery deck. Khardan did not even glance down at the unconscious woman.

After he had done what he could for Zohra, Mathew wedged himself between two carved wooden chests to keep himself from sliding around with the yawing of the ship. Wet and miserable and extremely frightened, the young man glared up at the stupe-

-fied Khardan with bitter anger.

He can't do this to me! Mathew thought, shivering from cold and fear. He's the one who's strong. He's the warrior. He's supposed to protect us. I need *him* now. He can't do this to me!

What's the matter with him anyway? Mathew wondered resentfully. That was a horrible sight, but he's been in battles before. Surely he's seen things just as gruesome. I know I have. . .

The memory of John, kneeling on the sand, Kiber's shining sword flashing in the sunlight, the warm blood splashing on Mathew's robes, the head with the lifeless eyes rolling across the sand. Tears blinded Mathew. He hung his head, clenching his hands.

"I'm frightened! I need you! You're supposed to be strong! Not me! If I can cope with this. . . this horror, why can't you?"

If Mathew had been older and able to think rationally, he would have been able to answer his own despairing question. He had *not* seen the *ghuls* attack and devour the helpless slaves. Khardan had, and though to Mathew there was not much difference between driving a sword into a man's gut and sinking fangs into his neck, the warrior's mind and heart reacted differently. One was a clean death, with honor. The other—a horrifying death brought about by creatures of evil, creatures of magic.

Magic. If Mathew had considered it, magic was the key—a key that unlocked the box of Khardan's innermost fears and let them loose to terrorize and overthrow his mind.

To the nomad, magic was a woman's gift—a tool used to quiet teething babies, to soothe horses during a sandstorm, to make the tent fast against wind and rain, to heal the sick and injured. Magic was the magic of the immortals, which was the magic of the God—the earth-shaking, wind-roaring magic of Akhran's 'efreets; the miraculous comings and goings of Akhran's djinn. This was the magic Khardan understood, much as he understood the rising of the sun, the falling of the rain, the shifting of the dunes.

The dreadful evil magic Khardan had just witnessed was beyond his comprehension. Its terror slammed into the mind like cold steel, shattering reason, spilling courage like blood. *Ghuls* to Khardan were creatures of the *meddah's* creation, beings ruled by Sul who could take any human form but were particularly fond of turning themselves into young, beautiful women. Wandering lost and alone in the desert, they would trap unwary travelers into helping them, then slay their rescuers and devour them.

To Mathew, *ghuls* were forms of demons studied in textbooks. He knew the various means by which they could be controlled, he knew that for all services rendered the living, these undead demanded payment and this must be made in the form of that which they constantly craved—warm, sweet human flesh. The magic of the *ghuls*, the storm, the sea, the enchantment that had kept him asleep for two months, all of this was familiar to Mathew, and understandable.

But he was in no condition to consider any of this rationally. Khardan was slipping under very fast, and the young wizard had to find some means of rousing him. Had he been stronger, had he been Majiid or Saiyad or any of Khardan's fellow tribesmen, Mathew would have clouted the Calif in the jaw—it being well-known that bloodletting cleared the brain. Mathew considered it. He pictured himself hitting Khardan and discarded the idea with a rueful shake of the head. His blow would have all the force of a girl slapping an over-eager suitor. He lashed out with the only other weapon he had available.

"It seems we should have left you in women's clothing!" Mathew cried bitterly, loud enough to reach Khardan through the pounding of the rain and the howling wind and the blackness that was engulfing him.

The verbal thrust stung. "What did you say?" Khardan turned his head, bleary eyes staring at Mathew.

"Your wife has more courage than either of us," Mathew continued, reaching out a gentle hand to wipe away water that had dripped onto Zohra's bruised face. "She fought them. They had to strike her down."

"What was there to fight?" Khardan asked in a hollow voice, his gaze going to the *ghuls* sailing their enchanted ship through the storm. "Demons? You said yourself there was nothing to be done against them!"

"That is true, but there are other ways to do battle."

"How? Disguise yourself and run away? That isn't fighting!"

"It's fighting to survive!" Mathew shouted angrily, rising to his feet. His red hair, wet and matted, poured like blood over his shoulders. The wet clothing clung to his slim body, the heavy folds of the soaked fabric kept his secret, hiding the flat chest and the thin thighs that would never be mistaken for a woman's. His face was pale, his green eyes glinted in the glare of the flame and the lightning.

"Survive through cowardice?"

"Like me?" Mathew questioned grimly.

"Like you!" Khardan glared at him through the water streaming down his face. "Why did you save me? You should have let me die! Unless"—he cast a scathing glance at Zohra—"it was her intent to humiliate me further!"

"Me! Me! Me! That's all you think about!" Mathew heard himself screaming, knew he was losing control. He could see several of the *goums*, clinging to the rigging for balance, look in their direction, but he was too caught up in his anger to speak calmly. "We didn't save you! We saved your people. Zohra had a magical vision of the future—"

"Magic!" Khardan shouted in fury and derision.

"Yes, magic!" Mathew screamed back, and saw that here would be the end of it. Khardan would never listen to the telling of Zohra's vision, much less credit it. Angry and exasperated, frightened and alone in his fear, Mathew slumped back down on the slick, wet deck and prepared to let misery engulf him.

"Akhran, save us!" Khardan cried to the heavens, struggling against his bonds. "Pukah! Your master is in need! Come to me, Pukah!"

Mathew didn't even bother to lift his head. He hadn't much faith in this God of the nomads, who seemed more a megalomanic child than a loving father. As for the djinn, he was forced to believe that they *were* immortal beings, sent from the God, but beyond that he hadn't seen that they were of much use. Disappearing into the air, changing themselves to smoke and sliding in and out of lamps, serving tea and sweet cakes when guests arrived...

Did Khardan truly expect his God to rescue him? And how? Send those fearsome beings called 'efreets to pluck them off the deck of the ship and carry them, safe and sound, back to the Tel? Did he truly expect to see Pukah—white *pantalons*, turban, and impish smile—trick Auda ibn Jad into setting them free?

"There is no one who can help you!" Mathew muttered bitterly, hunching himself as far back into the shelter of the baggage as possible. "Your God is not listening!"

And what about you? came the voice inside Mathew. At least this man prays, at least he has faith.

I have faith, Mathew said to himself, leaning his head wearily on the side of a basket, cringing as the sea broke over the ship and deluged him with chill water. He closed his eyes, fighting the nausea that was making his head whirl. Promenthas is far away from this land. The powers of darkness rule here...

The powers of darkness...

Mathew froze, not daring to move. The idea came to him with such vivid clarity that it seemed to take material form on the deck. So powerful was the impression in his mind that the young wizard opened his eyes and glanced fearfully around the ship, certain that everyone must be staring at him, divining his thoughts.

Auda ibn Jad paced the foredeck, hands clasped behind his back, his eyes looking straight ahead, unseeing, into the storm. His body was rigid, his hands clenched so tightly that they were white at the knuckles. Mathew breathed easier. The Black Paladin must be exerting all his power to maintain control over the *ghuls*. He wouldn't waste a scrap of it on his captives. And why should he?

We're not going anywhere, Mathew thought grimly. He looked swiftly at the *goums*. Kiber, green around the mouth and nose, clung to the rigging, looking nearly as bad as Mathew felt. Several of the other *goums* were also seasick and lay upon the deck moaning. Those who had escaped the sickness eyed the *ghuls* warily, shrinking away whenever one of the sailors drew too close. The *ghuls*, their hunger assuaged, were occupied with out-sailing the storm.

Sick and despondent, Khardan slumped against his bonds. The Calif's head hung limply. He had ceased to call upon his God. Zohra, unconscious, was probably the most fortunate person on the ship.

Hunching down amidst the jumble of baskets and chests and the tall ivory jars, Mathew doubled over as though clenched by sickness. Unfortunately, the play-acting became reality. The nausea, forgotten in his initial excitement, rose up and overwhelmed him. His body went hot, then cold. Sweat rolled down his face. Panting, refusing to give way, Matthew closed his eyes and waited grimly for the sick spell to pass.

At last he felt the nausea ease. Reaching into the folds of the caftan, he drew out a small pouch that he'd hurriedly tied around the sash at his waist. He cast a swift, furtive glance over his shoulder. Fingers trembling, he yanked open the pouch and carefully shook the contents out in his lap.

When he and Zohra had accosted the sorceress Meryem—fleeing the battle with the enchanted Khardan—Mathew had taken from her all the magical paraphernalia he could find. Surrounded by soldiers, smoke, and fire, he hadn't bothered to examine them other than a cursory glance before he thrust them into a pouch and concealed the pouch in the folds of his clothing.

That they were objects empowered to work black magic, Mathew hadn't a doubt. He guessed Meryem was devoted to the dark side of Sul since she had used her skill in the arcane arts to attempt murder. Looking at the various articles, unwilling even to touch them, he was overwhelmed with revulsion and disgust—feelings that ran deeper than his sickness; the feelings all wizards of conscience experience in the presence of things of evil.

Mathew's first impulse—and one so strong it nearly overpowered him—was to cast the ensorceled items into the sea. This is what he should do, this is what he had been taught to do.

This was what he could not afford to do.

Feverishly, between bouts of sickness, he examined each object.

There weren't many. Counting on her beauty and charm and the naïveté of the nomads to succumb to these, Meryem hadn't considered herself in any real danger. She had carried a small wand, about six inches in length, designed to be easily concealed in a pouch or tucked into the bosom of a gown. Mathew studied it intently, trying, as he had been taught, to understand its use by analyzing the material out of which it was made. The base of the wand was formed of petrified wood. Set atop that was a piece of black onyx in the form of a cube with the corners ground down. It was a remarkable example of workmanship and obviously the most powerful of the arcane treasures Mathew held. His fingertips tingled when he touched it, a numbing sensation spread up his arm. The wand slipped from his nerveless grasp.

This won't do! Mathew said to himself angrily, beginning to see hope's light flicker and dim. I can overcome this natural aversion, any disciplined wizard can. It's mental, not physical, after all. I've seen the Archmagus demonstrate the use of objects far darker and more foul than these!

Resolutely, he picked up the wand from where it lay on the deck and held it tightly in his hand. The chill sensation spread instantly from his palm up to his elbow, then into his shoulder. His arm began to ache and throb. Biting his lip, fighting the pain, Mathew held onto the wand. He saw, in his mind, Khardan's face and the look of scorn in the man's eyes. *I will prove myself to him! I will!*

Slowly the chill wore off. Sensation returned to his hand and Mathew discovered he'd been gripping the wand so tightly that the cube's sharp edges had cut into his flesh. Carefully, he dropped it back into the pouch.

Now, if he only knew what it did. . .

He mentally recounted all the possible enchantments that could be laid upon wands; he considered also the natural powers of black onyx itself. Mathew attempted to come up with the answer as he hurriedly sorted through the other objects. But his mind was clouded with sickness and terror. Every time he heard a footstep on the deck, he started and glanced fearfully over his shoulder, certain he'd been discovered.

"Black onyx," he mumbled to himself, leaning back against a wooden chest, another wave of sickness breaking over him. Closing his eyes, he saw himself in the classroom—the wooden desks with their high stools, meant for copying; the smell of chalk dust; the clatter of the slates; the monotone voice of an aged wizard reciting the text.

Black onyx. Black for self-protection, the power of disciplined thought. Onyx, possessor of an energy that can be used to control and command, frequently useful in direct intercession with those who dwell on Sul's plane of existence. Petrified wood—that which was once alive, but which is now dead, devoid of life, mocking its form. Often used as base for wands because the wood has the ability to absorb the life of the wielder and transfer it to the stone.

Add to this the strange design of the wand's onyx tip—not spherical, which would have indicated a harmony with nature, not even a perfect cube that would have represented order. A cube with the corners ground off—order turned to chaos?

So what did it all mean? Mathew shook his head weakly. He couldn't guess. He couldn't think. He gagged and wretched, but there was nothing in his stomach to purge. His body, under the spell of the Black Paladin, had apparently not required food. Knowing he was growing weaker and fearful of discovery, Mathew began to thrust the remaining magical objects, one by one, back into the pouch. They seemed relatively worthless anyway. A couple of healing scrolls, a scroll of minor protection from pointed objects (so much for Zohra and her dagger; Meryem had protected herself against that), a charm carved in the shape of a phallus that affected male potency (to be used for or against Khardan?), and finally a ring.

Mathew stopped to study the ring. It was made of silver, not very elegant craftsmanship. The stone was a smoky quartz and was obviously designed to be functional rather than ornamental. Of all the objects, this was the only one that did not make the young wizard holding it feel unease or disquiet. He guessed it was the only object whose magic was not harmful. Smoky quartz— protection from harm—*by showing us the dark, we are drawn toward the light.*

It wouldn't help him. If he went through with his plan, it might hinder him. He turned to Zohra, lying near him. They hadn't taken her jewelry from her. Lifting a limp left hand, Mathew slid the ring onto her finger. It looked plain and poor near the other more beautiful jewels. Mathew hoped she wouldn't notice it, at least until he found a chance to whisper some quick word of explanation.

The young wizard closed the pouch and thrust it into the bodice of his gown, near the globe containing the fish. Then he gave himself up to feverish consideration.

This plan is sheer folly. It will end in disaster. What I contemplate risks not only my life, but my immortal soul! No one expects that of me. Not Zohra. Certainly not Khardan. Not even myself.

I am helpless, just as I was when I came to this accursed land and ibn Jad slaughtered my comrades and took me captive.

I stand blindfolded upon the edge of a cliff. Perhaps if I keep perfectly still and do not move, nothing will happen to me! If I start to walk, I will surely fall, for I cannot see where I am going! I am helpless! Helpless!

But that wasn't quite true, and Mathew's soul squirmed uncomfortably. Months ago, when he'd first been cast up onto the shore where the bones of his friends now lay buried in the blood-drenched sand, he had been helpless. He'd had no magic, the only weapon with which he could defend himself.

Mathew rested his hand over the pouch, concealed in his clothes. Now he had the power to act. He had the power to take a step that might lead him—lead them all—safely to the bottom of the cliff.

He had the power.

If only he could find the courage.

The Book
of the
Immortals 2

Chapter 1

"Poor Sond," commiserated Pukah, flitting through the ethers, the djinn's lamp clasped firmly in his hands. "You're going to be incarcerated in a dark dungeon, in a town that has been dead and buried for centuries. Chained hand and foot, water dripping on your head, rats nibbling your toes—if rats are able to live in such a desolate place, which I hope, for your sake, poor Sond, that they cannot. I truly feel for you, my friend. I truly do. Of course"—Pukah heaved a sigh—"it is nothing, absolutely nothing compared to the torture I'm going to be forced to endure as slave to that oyster-headed monster. Oh, granted I'll be free to come and go pretty much as I choose. And it's undoubtedly true that since Kaug has clam shells for brains it is I myself, Pukah, who will likely end up the master and he, Kaug, my slave. Plus, I'll have my beautiful angel with me.

"Ah, Sond! She adores me!" Pukah heaved another sigh, this time a rapturous one. "You should have seen us together in my basket before squid-lips returned. She pulled me down on the bed and began to fan me with her wings. She kissed me again and again and . . . well . . . we are both men of the world aren't we, poor Sond? I dare say you know what she wanted of me.

" 'Ah, my dear,' I said sadly, 'I would more than gladly oblige you, here and now, but this is hardly a romantic setting. That crustacean who calls himself an 'efreet may return at any moment. And then there is my poor friend, Sond, who is in a most dire predicament,' I continued, trying manfully to break free of her embrace. But she continued to have her way with me and what could I do? The basket is only so big, you know, and I didn't want to make too much noise. I believe I'll tell Kaug I am indisposed tonight. He can find someone else to cook his flounder. As soon as I discover where my white-winged dove is hiding, we will have leisure to finish what we began."

Pausing for breath, Pukah peered through the swirling mists of the immaterial plane.

"Dratted stuff. It's as thick in here as Jaafar's wits. I can't see a thing! Ah, wait. It's clearing. Yes, this is it. I do believe, my poor Sond, that we have arrived."

Setting the *chirak* down at his feet, Pukah looked around with wonder.

"This is Serinda? This is where the immortals are being held . . . prisoner?"

Long ago, so many centuries past that it was not worth remembering, when the great and glorious city of Khandar was nothing but a camel-watering hole, a beautiful city named Serinda flourished.

Few people living now remembered Serinda. Those who did so were generally scholars. The city was marked on the Emperor's maps, and many were the evenings in the Court of Khandar when learned minds debated long and ardently over the mystery of Serinda—a city that existed, supposedly thrived—in the middle of a desert.

Kuo Shou-ching, a man of vast wisdom who had traveled to the Emperor's court from the far eastern lands of Simdari, maintained that the Pagrah desert was not always a desert. It was a known fact in Simdari that the volcano, Galos, erupted about this time, spewing out deadly ash, belching tons of rock into the air, and sending lava—the hot blood of the world's heart—pouring forth.

The eruption was so powerful, claimed Kuo Shou-ching, that a black cloud of ash hung in the sky for a year, obliterating the sun, turning day to night. It was during this time that the city of Serinda died a horrible death, its people perishing from the volcano's foul breath, their bodies and their city buried in ash. Galos continued to belch forth fire and smoke sporadically for years, forever changing the face of the land of Sardish Jardan.

One who disputed the theory of Kuo Shou-ching was Hypatia, a wise woman from the land of Lamish Jardan. She maintained that the city of Serinda was founded after the eruption of Galos, that the natives—who were extremely advanced in the ways of science and technology—brought the water of the Kurdin Sea into the desert through a remarkable system of aqueducts and that they literally made the desert bloom. She stated further that they built ships to sail the inland sea, formed by the volcano's eruption, and that they traded with the peoples of the Great Steppes and the populace of Lamish Jardan.

According to Hypatia, the fall of Serinda was brought about by the desert nomads, who feared the city was growing too powerful and would attempt either to absorb them into it or to drive them from their lands. Consequently, the fierce tribes fell upon peaceful Serinda, putting every man, woman, and child to the sword.

Needless to say, this was the theory that found favor with the Emperor, who had become increasingly irritated by reports he had been receiving of the nomads in the Pagrah Desert, and who began to think that it might be an excellent thing for the world if the nomads were obliterated from the face of it.

There was likewise the theory of Thor Hornfist, from the Great Steppes, who stated that the city of Serinda and its inhabitants had been eaten by a giant bear. Almost no one paid attention to Thor Hornfist.

The immortals, of course, knew the truth, but being highly diverted by the theories of the mortals, they kept it to themselves.

The history of the dead city of Serinda was not in Pukah's mind as he stared about the place, however. What was in the young djinn's mind was the fact that—for a dead city—Serinda was certainly lively!

"Market day in Khandar is nothing to this!" Pukah gaped.

The streets were so crowded it was difficult to walk through them. They reverberated with noise—merchants extolling, customers bargaining, animals bleating. *Arwats* and coffee houses were doing a thriving business, so packed that their patrons were literally tumbling out the doors and windows. No one seemed to be making any attempt to keep order. Everyone was intent on doing whatever he or she pleased, and pleasure seemed to be Serinda's other name.

Pukah stood in a dark alley between the weapons dealers' and the silk merchants' bazaars. In the length of time it took him to orient himself, the djinn saw two fistfights, a drunk get his face slapped, and a couple kissing passionately in a garbage-infested corner.

Raucous laughter echoed through the streets. Women hanging out of silk curtained windows called out sweet enticements to those below. Gold and silver flowed like water, but not so freely as the wine. Every mark and feature of every race in the world of Sularin was visible—straight black hair, curly golden hair, slanted dark eyes, round blue eyes, skin that was white as milk, skin tanned brown by wind and sun, skin black and glistening as ebony. All jostled together; greeted each other as friend, fell upon each other as enemy; exchanged wine, laughter, goods, gold, or insults.

And everyone of them was an immortal.

"Poor Sond!" snarled Pukah, giving the lamp a vicious kick. "Poor Sond! Sentenced to a life of constant merrymaking, love-making, drinking, and dicing! While I'm chained, day and night, to a beast of an 'efreet who will no doubt beat me regularly—"

"If he does, it will be no more than you deserve," cried an indignant, feminine voice.

Smoke poured forth from the lamp's spout, coalescing into the handsome, muscular Sond. Bowing gallantly, the djinn extended his hand and assisted another figure to step from the lamp—this one slender and lovely with flowing silver hair and feathery white wings, who glared at Pukah with flashing blue eyes.

"What do you mean—I fanned you with my wings?" Asrial demanded angrily.

"What were you two doing in there?" Pukah demanded back.

"Precisely what we did in your basket!" retorted Asrial.

"Aha!" Pukah cried, raising clenched fists to Sond.

"Nothing!" Asrial shrieked, stamping her bare foot.

"A fight! A fight!" cried several onlookers. Immortals swarmed into the alley, pressing eagerly around Sond and Pukah.

"My money on the big handsome one!"

"Mine on the skinny one with the shifty eyes. He probably has a dagger in his turban."

"You're fools, both of you. My money for the enchanting creature with the wings. My dwelling place is near here, my sweet. A little wine to cool you after your journey—"

Steel flashed in Pukah's hands. "I do have a dagger, and you'll feel it if you don't let go of her!" He caught hold of Asrial, dragging her out of the arms of a bearded, red-haired barbarian dressed in furs and animal skins.

"There's not going to be any fight," Sond added, his strong hand closing over the arm of the barbarian, who was hefting a wicked-looking, two-handed sword. A handful of gold coins materialized in the djinn's palm. "Here, go have a drink on us. Pukah, put that knife away!" Sond ordered out of the corner of his mouth.

Swearing fealty forever, the barbarian threw his arms around Sond and gave him a hug that nearly squeezed the djinn in two. Then, weaving drunkenly, he and his companions staggered back down the alley and out into the street. Seeing that there was, after all, not going to be a fight, the other onlookers dwindled away in disappointment.

"Well, what *were* you doing in there?" Pukah asked sullenly.

Asrial removed herself from the djinn's grasp. "It was obvious that the 'efreet must have guessed where I was hiding. When I heard him coming, I had no choice but to flee into Sond's lamp. Your friend"—she smiled sweetly and demurely at Sond—"was a perfect gentleman." The blue eyes turned to Pukah, their gaze cool. "More than I can say for you."

"I'm sorry," Pukah said miserably. Suddenly contrite, he cast himself bodily at the angel's feet. "I'm a wretch! I know! So do you, I've mentioned it before!" He groveled in the alley. "Trod on me! Grind me into the dust! I deserve no less! I'm dog meat! The hind end of a camel! The tail of the donkey—"

"I'd enjoy taking you up on that offer," said Sond, kicking at Pukah with his foot. "But there isn't time. We have to find Nedjma and get out of here. After all," added the djinn smoothly, "soon Kaug will command *you* to return!" Grinning, the djinn reached down to pick up his lamp, only to see it vanish beneath his hand. Kaug's laughter could be heard echoing above the noise.

For an instant, Sond paled. Then he shrugged. "It doesn't matter. I'll escape him somehow."

"And how do you think you're going to get free?" Pukah cast a bitter glance at the djinn.

"Do you see any guards?" Sond countered, sauntering down the alley.

"No, but we've only been here a quarter of an hour."

Emerging out of the shadows of the alley, the three blinked in the bright sunlight pouring down upon Serinda.

"I don't think we'll find any guards," said Sond quietly, after a moment's study of their surroundings.

The only ruler in the city of Serinda appeared to be Chaos, with Disorder as his Captain. A victorious army invading a conquered city could have created no greater turmoil in the streets. Every conceivable vice known to mortal flesh was being plied in the streets and houses, the alleys and byways of Serinda.

"You're right," Pukah admitted glumly. "Why don't they all leave, then?"

"Would you?" Sond asked, pausing to watch a dice game.

"Certainly," said Pukah in lofty tones. "I hope I know my duty—"

Sond made an obscene noise.

"Pukah!" gasped Asrial, grabbing the djinn, digging her nails into his arm. "Pukah, look!" She pointed. "An . . . an Archangel!" Her hand covered her mouth.

"Arch who?"

"Archangel! One. . . one of my superiors!"

Turning, the djinn saw a man, dressed in white robes similar to Asrial's, standing in a doorway. His wings quivering, he was enjoying the favors of a giggling, minor deity of the goddess Mimrim.

Forgetting himself, Pukah sniggered. Asrial flashed him a furious glance.

"He. . . he shouldn't be doing. . . such things!" the angel stammered, a crimson flush staining her cheeks. "Promenthas would be highly displeased. I'll . . . I'll go and tell that angel so, right now!"

Asrial started to push her way through the milling, jostling crowd.

"I don't think that's such a good idea!" Pukah snatched her out from under the nose of a horse whose rider—another barbarian—was urging the animal into the very heart of the mob, heedless of those he knocked down and trampled.

"You told me you angels didn't indulge in that sort of thing," Pukah teased, sweeping Asrial into the shelter of an ironmonger's stand.

"We don't!" Asrial blinked her eyes rapidly, and Pukah saw tears glimmering on her long lashes.

"Don't cry!" Pukah's heart melted. Wiping her tears with one hand, he took advantage of the situation to slide the other around the angers slim waist, congratulating himself on dealing adroitly with the wings. "You're too innocent, my sweet child. Knowing their God disapproves, I imagine your higher-ranking angels have learned to keep their love affairs private—"

"Affairs? There are no love affairs! None of us would ever even think of doing . . . such . . . such . . ." Glancing back at the couple in the doorway, her eyes widened. She flushed a deep red, and hastily turned away. "Something's wrong here, Pukah!" she said earnestly. "Terribly wrong. I must leave and tell Promenthas—"

Pukah's heart—that had melted and run through his body like warm butter—suddenly chilled into a lump. "No, don't leave me!" he pleaded. "I mean, don't leave . . . us. What will you tell your God, after all? I agree with you. Something is wrong, but what? There are no guards. It doesn't look like anyone's being held here against his will. Help us find Nedjma," continued Pukah, inspired. "She'll tell us everything, and then you can take that information to Promenthas, just as I'll take it to Akhran."

The thought of being the bearer of such news to his own God considerably lightened the jump that was Pukah's heart. He envisioned Akhran listening in profound admiration as his djinn described the numerous harrowing dangers he—Pukah—faced in the daring rescue of Nedjma and the discovery of the Lost Immortals. He could picture Akhran's reward. . .

"How can you go to Akhran if you belong to Kaug?" Asrial asked thoughtfully.

"Fish-face?" Pukah was amused. "His brain can deal with only so much at one time. When I'm not in his direct line of sight, he probably doesn't remember that I exist. I'll be able to come and go as I please!"

Asrial appeared dubious. "I'll come with you to find Sond's friend and hear what she has to say. Then I must return to Promenthas. Although I don't quite understand," she added with a tremor in her voice, "how this is going to help Mathew."

"Your protégé is with my master," Pukah said, hugging her comfortingly. "Khardan will protect him. When you have reported to your God and I to mine, then you and I will go find both of them!"

"Oh, Pukah!" Asrial's eyes gleamed through her tears, the light within making them glitter more beautifully than the stars in the heavens, at least to the djinn's enraptured mind. "That would be wonderful! But. . ." The light dimmed. "What about Kaug?"

"Oh damn and blast Kaug!" Pukah snapped impatiently.

He was not, in fact, quite as confident as he sounded about the 'efreet's thickness of skull and dullness of wit and did not want to be reminded of him at every turning. "Come on, Sond! Are you going to stand here for the next millennium?"

"I was just considering the best way to search for her." Sond looked bleakly at the hundreds of people milling about in the street. "Perhaps we should split up?"

"Since neither Asrial nor I know what she looks like, that is hardly a good idea," remarked Pukah acidly. "From what you've told me about her, I suggest we just listen for the sound of *tambour* and *quaita* and look for the dancing girls."

Sond's face darkened with anger, and he began to swell alarmingly.

"I'm only trying to be helpful," said Pukah in soothing tones.

Muttering something that fortunately never reached the angel's ears or Asrial might have left them then and there, Sond began to shove his way through the crowd.

Pukah, with a wink at the angel, followed along behind.

 **CHAPTER 2**

As it turned out, Pukah's suggestion led them straight to Nedjma. Unfortunately, the djinn never had a chance to gloat over it.

It was with some difficulty that they made their way through the dead city of Serinda—now possibly the liveliest city in this world or the next. The two djinn and the angel were continually accosted by merrymakers seeking to draw them into their revels.

"Thank you," said Pukah, disentangling himself from a throng of Uevin's Gods and Goddesses who were weaving through the streets. Clothed in nothing but grape leaves, they carried jars of wine that they lifted to purple-stained mouths. "But we're a girl short, you see. We're looking for one for my friend!" he explained to the countless pairs of glazed eyes focused—more or less—on him. "Yes, that's right. Now if you'd just let us past... No, no! Not you, I'm afraid, my dear. We're hunting a *specific* girl. But if we don't find her, I'll bring him right back."

"I'm not your girl," said Asrial coldly, attempting to pry her hand loose from Pukah's.

"Fine!" returned the djinn, exasperated. "When I've rescued my master and your madman from whatever difficulty they've managed to land in without me, then I'm coming straight back here!"

"Mathew isn't mad!" Asrial cried indignantly. "And I don't care where you go—"

"Shhh!" Pukah held up his hand for silence, something practically impossible to achieve amidst the hubbub around them.

"What?"

"Listen!"

Rising above the laughter and the giggles and the shouts and the singing, they could hear—very faintly—the shrill, off-key, sinuous notes of the *quaita,* accompanied by the clashing jingle of the *tambour.*

Sond glared at Pukah.

"Very well!" The young djinn shrugged. "Ignore it." Without saying a word, Sond turned and crossed the street, heading for a building whose shadowy arched doorways offered cool respite from the sun. Roses twined up ornate lattice work, decorating the front. Two djinn in silken caftans lounged around outside the doorways, smoking long, thin pipes. Sond looked neither to the right nor the left, up nor down, but pushed his way past the djinn, who stared after him in some astonishment.

"Eager, isn't he?" said one.

"Must be a newcomer," said the other, and both laughed. Raising his gaze to the upper levels of the building, Pukah saw several lovely djinniyeh leaning seductively over the balconies, dropping flowers or calling out teasingly to the men passing by in the street below.

Pukah shook his head and glanced at a grave and solemn Asrial. "Are you sure you want to come in here?" he whispered.

"No. But I don't want to stay out here either."

"I guess you're right," Pukah admitted, scowling at the red-bearded barbarian who appeared to be following them. "Well"— he grasped her hand again, smiling as her fingers closed firmly over his—"just keep close to me."

Tugging Asrial after him, Pukah stepped between the two djinn lounging in the doorway.

"Say, friend, bring your own?" commented one, tapping Pukah on the shoulder.

"I know that voice!" Pukah said, studying the other djinn intently. "Baji? Yes, it is!" Pukah clapped the djinn on his muscular forearm. "Baji! I might have known I'd find you here! Didn't you recognize Sond, who just walked past you?"

"Friend, I don't even recognize you," said the djinn, eyeing Pukah calmly.

"Of course, you do! It's me, Pukah!" said Pukah. Then, frowning, "You aren't trying to get out of paying me those five silver *tumans* you owe me, are you, Baji?"

"I said you're mistaken," returned the djinn, a sharp edge to his voice. "Now go on in and have your fun before things turn ugly—"

"Like your face?" said Pukah, fists clenching.

The shrill, anguished bleep of a *quaita* being cut off in mid-note and the clattering of a *tambour* hitting the floor mingled with a female scream and angry, masculine voices raised in argument.

"Pukah!" Asrial gasped. Peering into the shadows of the entryway, she tugged on the djinn's hand. "Sond's in trouble!"

"He's not the only one!" said Pukah threateningly, glaring at his fellow djinn.

"Pukah!" Asrial pleaded. The voices inside were growing louder.

"Don't leave!" Pukah growled. "This will only take a moment."

"Oh, I'll be right here," said the djinn, leaning back against the archway, arms folded across his chest.

"Pukah!" Asrial pulled him along.

Crystal beads clicked together, brushing against Pukah's skin as he passed through them into the cool shadows of the *arwat*. A wave of perfume broke over him, drenching him in sweetness. Blinking his eyes, he tried to accustom himself to a darkness lighted only by the warm glow of thick, jojoba candles. There were no windows. Silken tapestries covered the walls. His foot sank into soft carpeting. Luxurious cushions invited him to recline and stretch out. Flasks of wine offered to make him forget his troubles. Dishes heaped high with grapes and dates and oranges and nuts promised to ease his stomach's hunger, while the most enticing, beautiful djinniyeh he'd ever seen in his life promised to ease any other hungers he might have.

An oily, rotund little djinn slithered his way through the myriad cushions that covered every inch of the floor and, glancing askance at the angel, offered Pukah a private room to themselves.

"A charming little room, *Effendi,* and only ten silver *tumans* for the night! You won't find a better price in all of Serinda!" Catching hold of Pukah's arm, the chubby djinn started to draw him across the room to a bead-curtained alcove.

Pukah jerked his arm free. "What's going on here?" He glanced toward the center of the room, where the shouting was the loudest.

"Nothing, *Effendi,* nothing!" assured the rotund djinn, making another attempt to capture Pukah's arm, urging him onward. "A small altercation over one of my girls. Do not trouble yourself. The *mamalukes* will soon restore peace. You and your lady friend will not be disturbed, I assure you—"

"Pukah! Do something!" Asrial breathed.

Pukah quickly assessed the situation. A flute player sat gagging and coughing on the carpeted floor; it appeared he'd had his *quaita* shoved down his throat. The *tambour* player lay sprawled amid the cushions, unconscious; one of the drummers was attempting to bring him around. Several patrons were gathered together in a circle, shouting and gesticulating angrily. Pukah couldn't see between their broad backs, but he could hear Sond's voice, bellowing from their midst.

"Nedjma! You're coming with me!"

A shrill scream and the sound of a slap was his answer, followed by laughter from the patrons. Irritably shoving away the grasping hands of the rotund *rabat-bashi*, Pukah ordered, "Stay here!" to Asrial and shoved his way through the circle.

As he had expected, Sond stood in the center. The djinn's handsome face was twisted with anger, dark with jealousy. He had hold of the wrist of a struggling djinniyeh with the apparent intent of dragging her out of the building.

Pukah caught his breath, forgetting Asrial, forgetting Sond, forgetting why they were here, forgetting his own name for the moment. The djinniyeh was the most gorgeous creature he'd ever laid eyes on, and there were parts of her on which he longed to lay more than his eyes. From her midriff up, only the sheerest of silken veils covered her body, sliding over her firm, high breasts, slipping from around her white shoulders. Honey gold hair had come loose in her struggle and tumbled about a face of exquisite charm that, even in her indignation, seemed made to be kissed. Numerous long, opaque veils hanging from a jeweled belt at her waist formed a skirt that modestly covered her legs. Noticing several of these veils wound around the heads of the onlookers, Pukah guessed that the djinniyeh's shapely legs, already partially visible, wouldn't be covered long.

"Nedjma!" said Sond threateningly.

"I don't know any Nedjma!" the djinniyeh cried.

"Let go of her! On with the dance! Pay your way like everyone else!"

Pukah glanced behind him and saw the *rabat-bashi* make a peremptory gesture. Three huge *mamalukes* began to edge their way forward.

"Uh, Sond!" Shoving the unsteady-footed patrons out of his way, Pukah tripped over a cushion and tumbled onto the cleared area of the dance floor. "I think you've made a mistake!" he said urgently. "Apologize to the lady and let's go!"

"A mistake? You bet he's made a mistake." A huge djinn that Pukah didn't recognize and thought must be one of Quar's immortals thrust his body between Sond and the djinniyeh.

"The girl doesn't know you and doesn't want to," the djinn continued, his voice grating. "Now leave!" Pukah saw the djinn's hand go to the sash he wore round his waist.

Sond, his gaze fixed on the djinniyeh, saw nothing. "Nedjma," he said in a pleading, agonized voice, "it's me, Sond! You told me you loved—"

"I said leave her alone!" The large djinn lunged at him.

"Sond!" Pukah leaped forward, trying to deflect the knife. Too late. A quick hand movement, the flash of steel, and Sond was staring down at the hilt of a dagger protruding from his stomach. The huge, djinn who had stabbed him stepped back, a look of satisfaction on his face. Slowly, disbelievingly, Sond clutched at the wound. His face twisted in pain and astonishment. Red blood welled up between his fingers.

"Nedjma!" Staggering, he extended the crimson-stained hand to the djinniyeh.

Crying out in horror, she covered her eyes with her jeweled hands.

"Nedjma!" Blood spurted from Sond's mouth. He crashed to the floor at her feet and lay there, still and unmoving.

Pukah sighed. "All right, Sond," he said after a moment. "That was very dramatic. Now get up, admit you were wrong, and let's get out of here."

The djinn did not move.

The patrons were gathering around the djinniyeh, offering comfort and taking advantage of the opportunity to snatch away more of the veils. The huge djinn put his arm around the weeping Nedjma and drew her away to one of the shadowy alcoves. The other patrons, wailing in protest, demanded that the dance continue. Other djinniyeh soon appeared to ease their disappointment.

Clucking to himself about blood ruining his best carpets, the *rabat-bashi* was pointing at Pukah and demanding payment for damages. The tall *mamalukes,* faces grim, turned their attention to the young djinn.

"Uh, Sond!" Pukah knelt down beside him. Placing his hand on the djinn's shoulder, he shook him. "You can quit making a fool of yourself any time now! If that was Nedjma, she's obviously enjoying herself and doesn't want to be bothered... Sond." Pukah shook the unresponsive body harder. "Sond!"

There was a flutter of white wing and white robes, and Asrial was beside him. "Pukah, I'm frightened! Those men are staring at me! What's Sond doing? Make him get up and let's leave—Pukah!" She caught sight of his face. "Pukah, what's wrong?"

"Sond's dead," said Pukah in a whisper.

Asrial stared at him. "That's impossible," she said crisply. "Is this more of your antics, because—" The angel's voice faltered. "Promenthas have mercy! You're serious!"

"He's dead!" Pukah cried. Almost angrily, he grabbed Sond's shoulder and rolled the body of the djinn over on its back. An arm flopped limply against the floor. The eyes stared at nothing. Pulling the dagger from the wound, the djinn examined it. The blade was smeared with blood. "I don't understand!" He glared around the room. "I want answers!"

"Pukah!" Asrial cried, trying to comfort him, but the *mamalukes* shoved the angel aside. Grasping the young djinn by the shoulders, they dragged him to his feet.

Pukah lashed out furiously. "I don't understand! How can he be dead?"

"Perhaps I can explain," came a voice from the beaded curtained entryway. "Let him go."

At the sound, the *mamalukes* instantly dropped their hold on the djinn and stepped back from him. The proprietor ceased his lamentations, the patrons swallowed words and wine, several nearly choking themselves, and even this sound they did their best to stifle. No one spoke. No one stirred. The light of the candles flickered and dimmed. The fragrant air was tinged with a sweet, cloying smell.

A cold whisper of air on the back of his neck made Pukah's skin shiver. Reluctantly, unwillingly, but completely unable to help himself, the djinn turned to face the doorway. Standing in the entrance was a woman of surpassing beauty. Her face might have been carved of marble by some master craftsman of the Gods, so pure and perfect was every feature. Her skin was pale, almost translucent. Hair, thin and fine as a child's, fell to her feet, enveloping her slender, white-robed body like a smooth satin cape of purest white.

Pukah heard Asrial, somewhere near him, moan. He couldn't help her, he couldn't even see her. His gaze was fixed upon the woman's face; he felt himself slowly strangling.

The woman had no eyes. Where there should have been two orbs of life and light in that classic face were two hollows of empty blackness.

"Let me explain, Pukah," said the woman, entering the room amid a silence so deep and profound that everyone else in the room seemed to have suffocated in it. "In the city of Serinda, through the power of Quar, it is at last possible to give every immortal what he or she truly desires."

The woman looked expectantly at Pukah, obviously waiting for him to question her. "And that is?" he was supposed to say. But he couldn't talk. He had no breath.

Yet his words echoed, unspoken, through the room. "Mortality," the woman replied.

Pukah shut his eyes to blot out the sight of the empty eye sockets.

"And you are—" he blurted out.

"Death. The ruler of Serinda."

CHAPTER 3

i n the *arwat,* the immortals resumed their pleasure-taking, giving the body of Sond nothing more than a cool, casual glance or—at most—a look of bitterness for having bled all over the carpet (this from the *rabat-bashi).*

"Get him out of here!" the proprietor muttered to two *mamalukes,* who bent down and—lifting the dead djinn by his flaccid arms—appeared prepared to drag him unceremoniously out the door.

"The back door," specified the *rabat-bashi.*

"No one's taking Sond anywhere," declared Pukah, drawing a dagger from the sash around his slim waist. "Not until I have some answers."

Dropping Sond's arms, which fell with a lifeless thud on the floor of the *arwat,* the two immortal *mamalukes* drew their daggers, eager grins on their faces.

"Pukah, no!" cried Asrial, hurling herself at the young djinn.

Gently he pushed her away, his eyes on the knife-wielding slaves who were circling, one to either side of him, steel flashing in their hands.

"You there!" cried the proprietor distractedly, gesturing to another *mamaluke,* "roll up that other carpet! It's the best one in the house. I can't afford to have it ruined as well. Quickly! Quickly! Excuse me, sir"—this to Pukah—"if you could just lift your foot for a moment? Thank you. It's the blood, you see, it doesn't wash—"

"Blood!" Asrial put her hands to her head in an effort to concentrate. "This is impossible. Our bodies are ethereal. They cannot bleed, they cannot die!" Lowering her hands, she looked at Death. "I don't believe this," the angel stated flatly. "Sond is *not* dead! Not even you can make the immortal mortal. Pukah, stop that nonsense."

Somewhat startled, Pukah glanced at her, then at Sond lying on the floor. Slowly he lowered his dagger. "That's true," he said. "Sond can't be dead."

"You are both young," said Death, turning the empty eye sockets toward them, "and you have not lived long among humans—especially you," she said to Asrial. "You are right, of course. Sond is not dead—at least not as mortals would term it. But he might as well be. When the sun dawns tomorrow, this djinn will regain his life—but nothing else."

"What do you mean?" Pukah glared at the cold and lovely woman suspiciously. "What else is there?"

"His identity. His memory. He will have no knowledge of who he is, whom he serves. He will be—as it were—newborn and will take on whatever identity occurs to him at the moment. He will forget everything. . ."

"Even the fact that he is immortal," said Asrial slowly.

Death smiled. "Yes, child, that is true. He will have the mortal hunger to live life to the fullest. As are mortals, he will be driven—blessed and cursed with the knowledge that it must all come to an end."

"This is why the immortals are lost to the world," realized Pukah, staring at Sond. "They no longer remember it. And that is why Nedjma did not know my poor friend."

"She is no longer Nedjma, nor has she been for a long time now. Only a few nights ago she died at the hands of a jealous lover. Days before that, she was accidentally killed in a street brawl. No one in this city"—the hollow eyes turned to Asrial—"remains alive from dusk to dawn."

A hoarse cry interrupted them. The djinn who had stabbed Sond staggered out of the inner room, clutching his throat with one hand, a half-emptied goblet of wine in the other. Falling to the floor, he writhed in agony for a few seconds, then his body went rigid. The cup fell from his hand, rolling across the carpet, leaving a trail of spilled wine. Nedjma swept out from the room. Standing above the body, she deliberately brushed a fine, white powder from her delicate fingers. "Let this be a lesson to all who think they own me!" Tossing her honey-colored hair, she vanished behind another beaded curtain.

"Wine. . . it stains are almost as bad as blood," whined the proprietor, wringing his hands.

Death watched appreciatively, her lips slightly parted as though she were sipping the dead djinn's life.

"So," said Pukah to himself. "I am beginning to understand..." His hand went to the tourmaline amulet Kaug had given him. As he touched it, he thought he saw Death flinch. The hollow eyes met his, a fine line marring the marble smoothness of the white brow.

Tucking his dagger into his sash, Pukah crossed his arms and rocked back on his heels. "There is one who will leave this city at dusk or dawn or whenever I choose. Me." He held up the amulet that he wore around his neck. "My master cannot do without me, you see, and so has insured my return."

"What is this?" Death peered closely at the tourmaline, the coldness of her eyeless gaze causing Pukah's flesh to shiver and crawl. "This goes against our agreement! I am to have all who come here! Who is this master of yours?"

"One Kaug, an 'efreet, in the service of Quar," answered Pukah glibly.

"Kaug!" Death's brow furrowed. The shadow of her anger descended upon the *arwat,* causing the *rabat-bashi* to hush his complainings, and the guests to hastily withdraw to whatever dark, obscure corners they could find.

Pukah saw Asrial staring at him pleadingly, begging him to take her from this place. The thought that she might die and forget her protégé must be terrifying to her. What she didn't realize—and Pukah had—was that *he* could leave, but she couldn't. Death would never allow it. *I am to have all who come here.* The only way for them to escape, the only way for all the immortals trapped here to escape was Pukah's way. Pukah had a plan.

Not only will *Hazrat* Akhran reward me, Pukah thought blissfully. All the Gods in the Jewel of Sul will be forever indebted to me! I will be an immortal among immortals! Nothing in this world or in the heavens will be too good for me! One palace— hah! I will have twenty palaces—one given by each God. I will spend the heat of the summer in a vast stone fortress on the Great Steppes. I will winter in a grass hut of thirty or forty rooms on one of those little tropical islands in Lamish Aranth, sleeping on the feathery wings of a grateful, loving angel ...

Seeing Death's pallid hand reaching for the amulet, Pukah

hastily clamped his fingers over it and took a step backward.

"Rest assured my master reverences you most highly, my lady," Pukah sajd humbly. " 'Death is second to Quar in my esteem.' Those were the 'efreet's very words."

" 'Second to Quar!' " Death's eyeless sockets grew dark as endless night.

"Quar is becoming the One, the True God," Pukah said apologetically. "You must concede that. The number of humans worshiping Him grows daily."

"That may be true," Death said sharply, "but in the end their bodies are mine! That is the promise of Sul."

"Ah, but didn't you hear—" Pukah stopped, biting his tongue, lowering his eyes, and glancing at Death from beneath the lids— "but then I guess you didn't. If you'll excuse me, my lady, I really should be getting back. Kaug is dining on boiled ray tonight, and if I'm not there to remove the sting, my master will—"

"Hear what?" questioned Death grimly.

"Nothing, I assure you, my lady." Grabbing hold of Asrial's hand, Pukah began to sidle past Death toward the door. "It is not my place to reveal the secrets of the Most Holy Quar—"

Death raised a pale, quivering finger and pointed at Asrial. "You may have an Amulet of Life, djinn, but this feathered beauty here does not! Tell what I need to know, or she will be struck down before your eyes this instant!"

Death gestured, and the two *mamalukes,* their daggers still in hand, looked with eager, burning eyes at the angel. Asrial caught her breath, pressing her hands over her mouth and shrinking next to Pukah. The djinn put his arm around her reassuringly. The foxish face was pale, however, and he was forced to swallow several times before he could speak.

"Do not be hasty, my lady! I will tell you everything, for it is obvious to me now that you have been the victim of a trick played upon you by the God. I assume that it was Quar who schemed to trap the immortals by laying this spell upon the city of Serinda?"

Death did not reply, but Pukah saw the truth in the face whose marble facade was beginning to crack. Hurriedly he continued, "Quar gave you the delightful task of casting this spell over the city, knowing—as He did—that your greatest pleasure in life comes from watching others leave it?"

Again, though Death did not answer, Pukah knew he was

right and spoke with increasing confidence, not to mention a hint of smugness. "Thus, Lady, Quar rid the world of the immortals—all the immortals, if you take my meaning. Your grave and lovely self included."

"Pukah! What are you saying?" Asrial glanced up at him in alarm, but the djinn hugged her into silence.

"For you see, O Sepulchral Beauty, Quar has promised all who follow him *eternal life!*"

Death sucked in a deep breath. Her hair rose around her in a wrathful cloud, a cold blast of fury hit those in the *arwat,* causing the strongest slave to tremble in fear. Asrial hid her face in her hands. Only Pukah remained confident, sure of himself and his glib tongue.

"I have proof," he said, forestalling what he was certain would be Death's next demand. "Only a few months ago, Quar ordered the Amir of Kich to attack bands of nomads living in the Pagrah desert. Were you present at the battle, Lady?"

"No, I was—"

"Busy here below," Pukah said, nodding knowingly. "And your presence was sorely missed, Lady, I can tell you, particularly by the jackals and hyenas who count upon your bounty. For hardly anyone died in that battle. The Imam of Quar ordered them taken alive! Why? So that his God could grant them eternal life and thereby be assured of eternal followers! Before that was the battle in Kich—"

"I was present then!" Death said.

"Yes, but whom did you take? A fat Sultan, a few of his wives, assorted wazirs. Piffle!" Pukah said with a disdainful sniff. "When there was an entire city filled with people who could have been raped, murdered, burned, stoned—the survivors left to fend off disease, starvation—"

"You are right!" said Death, her teeth clenching in a skull-like grimace.

"Far be it from me to betray *Hazrat* Quar, for whom I have a high respect," added Pukah humbly, "but I have long been one of your most ardent admirers, my lady. Ever since you took my former master—a follower of Benario—in the most original fashion—his body parts cut off one at a time by the enraged owner of the establishment my poor master took it into his head to rob without first checking to make certain that no one was at home.

That is why I have revealed to you Quar's plot to remove you forever from the world of the living and keep you here below, playing games."

"I will show you how games are played!" Seething, Death approached Pukah, the hollow of her empty eyes seeming to grow larger, encompassing the djinn.

"Show me?" Pukah laughed lightly. "Thank you, but I really don't have time for such frivolities. My master cannot do without—" It suddenly occurred to the djinn that Death was drawing uncomfortably near. Letting go of Asrial, he tried to back up and tumbled over a hubble-bubble pipe. "What have I to do with this? Nothing!" He scrambled to his feet. "If I were you, now, Lady, I would leave this city immediately and fly to the world above. No doubt the Amir is riding to battle this very instant! Spears through chests, sword slicing through flesh. Arms ripped from their sockets, entrails and brains on the ground! Tempting picture, isn't it?"

"Yes indeed! So Quar has sent you here to frighten me—" Death stalked him.

"F-frighten you?" Pukah stammered, knocking over a table and small chair. "No, Lady," he said with complete honesty, "I assure you, that frightening you is the furthest thing from my—his mind!"

"What does He want? His immortals returned? Eternal life! We'll see what Sul has to say about this!"

"Yes, *yes!*" gabbled Pukah, backed up against a wall, his hand clutching the amulet. "Go talk to Sul! Wonderful person, Sul. Have you ever met Him?"

"I intend to speak with Him," said Death, "but first I will send Quar his messenger back in the form of a skeleton to remind him of whom he is trying to cheat!"

"You can't touch me!" said Pukah quickly, raising the amulet in front of Death's baleful, empty eyes.

"No," said Death softly, "but I can her!"

Death vanished and reappeared. The pale, cold hands were suddenly clasped around Asrial's shoulders, the angel caught fast in Death's grip.

The djinn stared into the angel's blue, despairing eyes and wondered what had gone wrong. It had been such a simple, beautiful plan! Get Death out of the city. Set her on Quar. . . "I'll make a bargain with you," offered Pukah desperately.

"A bargain?" Death stared at him suspiciously. "I have had enough of your Master and His bargains!"

"No," said Pukah solemnly, "this would be. . . just between you and me. In exchange for her"—he looked at Asrial, his soul in his eyes, his voice softening—"I will give you my amulet—"

"No, Pukah, no!" Asrial cried.

"—and I will remain in the city of Serinda," the djinn continued. "You boast that no one lives from dawn to dusk in this city. I challenge that claim. I say that I am cleverer than you. No matter what form you choose to take, I can avoid falling your victim."

"Ha!" snorted Death.

"No one shall goad *me* into any quarrel," averred Pukah.

"No woman will slip poison into *my* drink!"

"And if I win, what do I get out of this bargain, beyond the pleasure of seeing you stretched lifeless at my feet?"

"I will give you not only myself, but my master as well."

"Kaug?" Death sneered. "Another immortal? As you can see, I am well supplied with those already."

"No." Pukah drew a deep breath. "You see, Kaug is not my master so much as he is my jailer. Sond and I were captured by the 'efreet and forced to do his bidding. My true master is Khardan, Calif of the Akar—"

"Pukah, what are you saying?" cried Asrial, appalled. "Khardan!" Death appeared interested. "Akhran holds that particular mortal in high favor. He keeps close watch upon him. I cannot get near. You are saying that if I win—"

"—the eyes of Akhran will be looking elsewhere."

"You know that now your mortal, Khardan, stands in dire peril?" Death inquired coolly.

"No," said Pukah, looking somewhat uncomfortable, "I didn't. It's been some time, you see, since I was captured, and I—"

"Not only him, but those with him," said Death, her eyes on Asrial.

Clasping her hands, the angel gazed at the pale woman beseechingly. "Mathew?" she whispered.

"We will speak of this later, you and I," said Death soothingly, running her cold hand over Asrial's silver hair. "Very well," she added, "I accept your bargain, Pukah. Hand me the amulet."

"But you haven't heard the rest of the deal," protested the

young djinn in offended dignity. "The part about what *you* give me if I win."

Death glanced around the *arwat*. "If he wins!" she repeated. Everyone burst into shouts of laughter, the proprietor guffawing until he lost his breath and had to be pounded on his back by one of the slaves. "Very well," said Death, wiping tears of mirth that sprang horribly from the empty sockets. "If you win, Pukah, I will give you what?" Your freedom, I suppose. That's what all you djinn want.

"Not only my freedom," said Pukah cunningly. "I want the freedom of every immortal in the city of Serinda!"

The laughter in the *arwat* suddenly ceased.

"What did he say?" puffed the *rabat-bashi*, who—between trying to breathe and getting thumped on the back—hadn't been able to hear clearly.

"He says he wants us freed!" growled an immortal of Zhakrin's, eyeing Pukah grimly.

"Freed!" said a cherubim, staggering out of a bead-curtained room, a goblet in her hand. "Free to go back to a life of drudgery!"

"A life of slavery," slurred one of Quar's 'efreets from where it lay comfortably beneath a table.

"Death take him!" cried Uevin's God of War.

"Death! Death!" chanted everyone in the *arwat*, rising to their feet, fingering their weapons.

"Free? Did I say free?" Sweat trickled down from beneath Pukah's turban. "Look, we can discuss this—"

"Enough!" Death raised her hands. "I agree to his terms. Pukah, if you are alive by sunset tomorrow"—hoots and howls of derision greeted this. Clenching her raised fists, Death commanded silence—"then I swear by Sul that the spell over the city of Serinda will be broken. If, however, the failing light of the sun casts its rays over your body as it lies upon its bier, Pukah, then your master, Khardan, is mine. And his end will be truly terrible"—Death looked at Asrial—"for he will be slain by one whom he trusts, one who owes him his life."

Asrial stared at Death in horror. "Not—" She couldn't finish.

"I fear so, child. But—as I said—we will discuss that later. Hear me!" Death lifted her voice, and it seemed that the entire city of Serinda fell silent. "I owe allegiance to no God or Goddess. I have no favorites. Whatever else may be said of me, I am impartial. I take the very young. I take the very old. The good cannot escape me, neither can the sinner. The rich with all their money cannot keep me from their doors. The magi with all their magic cannot find a spell to defeat me. And so I will have no favorites here. Pukah will have this night to prepare his defense. The people of Serinda will have this night to prepare their attack.

"Pukah, this night you may keep your amulet and freely walk the city. Whatever weapon you find will be yours. Tomorrow, at the Temple in the city plaza, at the dawning of the new day, you will deliver to me the amulet and the contest will begin. Is this agreed?"

"Agreed," said Pukah through lips that, despite his best efforts, trembled. He couldn't meet Asrial's despairing eyes.

Death nodded, and the people resumed their frenetic activities, everyone making eager preparations for tomorrow's deadly contest.

"And now, child, you want to see what is happening in the world of humans?" asked Death.

"Yes, oh yes!" cried Asrial.

"Then come with me." Death's hair lifted as though stirred by a hot wind. Floating around her, it enfolded the angel like a shroud.

"Pukah?" Asrial said, hesitating.

"Go ahead," said the djinn, trying to smile. "I'll be fine, for a while at least."

"You will see him again, child," Death said, putting her arm around Asrial and drawing her away. "You will see him again. . . ."

The two vanished. Pukah slumped down into a nearby chair, ignoring the snarls, the hostile stares. Gulping slightly at the sight of daggers, knives, swords, and other cutlery that was making a sudden appearance, he turned his head to look out the window. He was not cheered by the sight of an imp pushing a grindstone down the street; the demon was besieged by a mob of immortals brandishing weapons to be sharpened.

Seeing his reflection in the window, Pukah found it more comforting to look at his own foxish face. "I'm smarter than Death," he said, seeking reassurance.

The unusually gloomy reflection made no answer.

The Book
of Quar 2

CHAPTER 1

Far from the Kurdin Sea, where the ship of *ghuls* sailed amid its own storm; far from where Mathew struggled against inner darkness; far from Serinda, where a djinn battled against Death; another young man fought a battle of his own, though on much different ground.

Quar's *jihad* had begun. In the first light of dawn, the city of Meda, in northern Bas, fell to the troops of the Amir without putting up more resistance than was necessary for the citizens to be able to meet each other's eyes and say, "We fought but were defeated. What could we do? Our God abandoned us."

And it did seem as if this were true. In vain the priests of Uevin called for the God of War to appear in his chariot and lead the battle against the armies of the Emperor. In vain the priestesses of the Earth Goddess called for the ground to open and swallow the Amir's soldiers. There came no answer. The oracles had been silent many months. Uevin's immortals had disappeared, leaving their human supplicants to cry their pleas to deaf ears.

Uevin's ears were not deaf, though he often wished they were. The cries of his people rent his heart, but there was nothing he could do. Bereft of his immortals, losing the faith of his people, the God grew weaker by the day. Ever before him was the vision of Zhakrin and Evren, their shriveled and starved bodies writhing upon the heavenly plane, then blowing away like dust in the wind. Uevin knew now, too late, that the Wandering God, Akhran, had been right. Quar was intent on becoming the One, the Only. Uevin hid inside his many columned dwelling, expecting every moment to hear Quar's voice summon him forth to his own doom. The God, quaking and trembling, knew there was nothing he could do to stop Quar.

The army of Meda—outnumbered, beset by dissension

within their ranks, aware that their Governor was hastily packing his valuables and fleeing through the back wall of the city as they prepared to defend its front—fought halfheartedly and, when called upon to surrender, did so with such promptness that the Amir remarked to Achmed drily that they must have ridden forth to battle with white flags in their saddlebags.

Achmed never had a chance to fight—a fact that made him burn with disappointment. Not that he would have seen battle this day anyway. The young man rode with the cavalry and they would not be used today unless the Medans proved more stubborn than was expected. Chafing with inaction, he sat his magical horse high on a ridge overlooking the plains on which the two armies rushed together like swarms of locusts.

Achmed shifted in his saddle, his gaze darting to every boulder and bush, hoping to see some daring Medan raise up out of the cover with bow poised and arrow at the ready, endeavoring to end the war by killing the general, Achmed saw himself hurling his own body protectively in front of the Amir (the king's bodyguards having fled, the cowards!). He saw the arrow fly, he felt it graze his flesh (nothing serious). He saw himself draw his sword and dispatch the Medan. Cutting off the man's head, he would present it to the Amir. Refusing all assistance, he would say, with eyes modestly downcast, "The wound? A scratch, my lord. I would gladly be pierced by a thousand arrows if it would serve my king."

But the Medans selfishly refused to cooperate. No assassin crouched in the bushes or crept among the rocks. By the time Achmed saw himself, in his vision, carried away on a shield, the Medans were throwing their own shields on the ground and handing over their weapons to the victors.

When the battle had ended, the Amir rode up and down the long line of prisoners that were drawn up outside the city walls. Most of the Medans stood with heads bowed, in sullen or fearful silence. But occasionally Achmed—riding at Qannadi's side—saw a head raise, a man glance up at the king out of the corner of an eye. The Amir's stern and rigid face never changed expression, but his eyes met those of the prisoner, and there was recognition and promise in that glance. The man would look back down again at his feet, and Achmed knew he had seen someone in Qannadi's pay—a worm the Amir had purchased to nibble at the fruit from the inside.

Achmed heard mutterings of disgust from the Amir's body-guards, who rode behind him. They, too, knew the meaning of that exchange of glances. Like most soldiers, they had no use for traitors, even when the traitors were on their side.

The young man's face burned, and he hung his head. He felt the same stirrings of disgust for the treacherous who had betrayed their own people, yet all he could ask himself was, "What is the difference between them and me?"

The inspection came to an end. Qannadi announced that the Imam would speak to the prisoners. The Amir and his staff rode off to one side. Achmed, still brooding, took his place beside and a few steps behind Qannadi.

A creaking of the Amir's leather saddle and a slight cough caused Achmed to raise his head and look at the man. For a brief moment a warm smile flickered in the dark eyes.

"You came to me out of love, not for money," was the silent message.

How had Qannadi divined what he was thinking? Not that it mattered. This wasn't the first time their thoughts had ridden together over the same path. Feeling comforted, Achmed allowed himself to accept the answer. Knowing it was true in part, he could feel satisfied with it and firmly shut out any efforts by his conscience to question it further.

In the past month that they had been together, Achmed had come to love and respect Qannadi with the devotion of a son—giving to the Amir the affection he would have been glad to give to his own father, had Majiid been the least bit interested in accepting it. Each filled perfectly the void in the other's heart. Achmed found a father, Qannadi the son he'd been too busy fighting wars to raise.

The Amir was careful not to let his growing affection for the young man become obvious, knowing that Yamina watched her husband jealously. Her own child stood to inherit the Amir's position and wealth, and neither she nor her mincing peacock of a son would hesitate to send a gift of almonds rolled in poisoned sugar to one who might pose a threat. Long ago, a pretty young wife of whom Qannadi had been especially fond and who was to have delivered a baby near the same date as Yamina's had died in a similar manner. Such things were not unusual in court, and Qannadi accepted it. But it was one reason, perhaps, that he afterward exhibited no great affection for any of his wives.

The Amir gave Achmed the rank of Captain, put him in charge of training both men and horses in the cavalry, and took care—while they were in court—to speak to him as he would any other soldier in his army. If he spent a lot of time with the cavalry, it was only natural, since they were the key to victory in many instances and required much training in advance of the war against Bas. Yamina' s single, jealous eye saw nothing to give her concern. She sent her son back to the glittering court in Khandar, both of them happy in the knowledge that generals often met with fatal mishaps.

Qannadi himself had no illusions. He would have liked to make Achmed his heir, but he feared that the young man would not last even a month in the palace of the Emperor. Honesty, loyalty—these were qualities a king rarely saw in those who served him. Qualities the Amir saw in Achmed. The Amir didn't attempt to instruct the young man in the dangerous machinations of court intrigue. The nomad's blend of brute savagery and naive innocence delighted Qannadi. Achmed would not hesitate to hack to bits a rival in a fair fight, but he would allow himself to be devoured by ants before he would slyly murder that same rival. What was worse, Achmed fondly believed that every man worthy of being called a man abided by the same code of honor. No, he wouldn't last long in the court at Khandar.

Let my painted-eyed, painted-lipped son grovel at the Emperor's feet and smile when His Imperial Majesty kicks him. I have Achmed. I will make of him an honorable, dutiful soldier for Quar. For myself, I will have one person who will fight at my side, who will be near me when I die. One person who will truly mourn my passing.

But the ways of Quar are not the ways of Akhran. Qannadi himself was naive in thinking he could uproot the thorny desert Rose, bring it into the stifling atmosphere of court, and expect it to thrive. The cactus would have to send down tough new roots in order even to survive.

The Imam had watched the battle from the protection of a palanquin borne on the long journey from Kich to Meda by six sweating, struggling priests of Quar. At the Amir's signal, they hauled the covered litter out onto the plains before the city walls that were lined with Medans waiting in hushed, breathless silence to know their fate.

Feisal emerged from the palanquin, his thin hand pushing aside the golden curtains decorated with the head of the ram. A change had come over the Imam since his illness. No one knew what had happened to him, except that he had come very close to death and had been—according to his awestricken servant—healed by the hand of the God. Feisal's body, always slender from fasting, now appeared emaciated. His robes hung from his spare frame as they might have hung from a bare-limbed tree. Every bone, every vein, every muscle and tendon was visible in his arms. His face was skull-like, with cadaverous hollows in the cheeks, the sunken eyes appeared huge.

These eyes had always glowed with holy zeal, but now they burned with a fire that appeared to be the only fuel the man needed to keep the body functioning. The sun was blazing hot on the plains in midsummer. Achmed sweated in the leather uniform trousers worn by the cavalry. Yet he shivered when the Imam began to speak, and, glancing at Qannadi, he saw the black hair on the sunburned arms rise; the strong jaw—barely visible beneath the man's helm—tighten. The Imam's presence had always inspired discomfort. Now it inspired terror.

"People of Meda!" Feisal's voice must have been amplified by the God. It was hardly creditable that the lungs in that caved-in chest could draw air enough to breathe, let alone to shout. Yet his words could be clearly heard by all in Meda. It seemed to Achmed that they must be heard by every person in the world.

"You were not this day defeated by man," the Imam called out. He paused, drawing a deep breath. "You were defeated by Heaven!" The words rolled over the ground like thunder; a horse shied nervously. The Amir cast a stern glance behind him and the soldier quickly brought his animal under control.

"Do not grieve over your loss! Rather, rejoice in it, for with defeat comes salvation! We are children in this world and we must be taught our lessons of life. Quar is the father who knows that sometimes we learn best through pain. But once the blow has been inflicted, He does not continue to whip the child, but spreads His arms"—the Imam suited his action to his words—"in a loving embrace."

Achmed thought back to when he'd heard these—or similar—words, back to that dark time in prison. Clenching his hands over the saddle horn to keep himself calm, he wished desperately this would end.

"People of Meda! Renounce Uevin—the weak and imperfect God who has led you down a disastrous path, a path that could have cost you your lives had not Quar been the merciful father that He is. Destroy the temples of the false God Uevin! Denounce His priests! Melt down His sacred relics, topple His statues and those of the immortals who served Him. Open your hearts to Quar, and He will reward you tenfold! You will prosper! Your families will prosper! Your city will become one of the brightest jewels in the crown of the Emperor! And your immortal souls will be assured of eternal peace and rest!"

Growing light-headed in the heat, Achmed imagined the Imam's words leaping from the man's mouth in tongues of flame that set the dry grass ablaze. The flames spread from the priest to the prisoners lined up against the wall and lit them on fire. The blaze burned hotter and hotter until it engulfed the city. Achmed blinked and licked thirstily at a trickle of sweat that dropped into his mouth. The plains reverberated with the sound of cheering, started on cue by the Amir's forces and picked up eagerly by the defeated Medans.

Feisal had no more to say, which was well, since he could never have been heard. Exhausted, drained, he turned to make his way back to the palanquin, his faithful servant hurrying forward to assist the priest's feeble steps. At the city walls, enthusiastic crowds shoved open the wooden gates. Chants of "Quar, Quar, *Hazrat* Quar" reverberated across the plains.

Unexpectedly the Medan prisoners broke ranks and surged toward the Imam. Qannadi acted swiftly, sending his cavalry forward with a wave of his hand. Riding with the others, Achmed moved his horse in a defensive position around the priest's palanquin. Sword drawn, he had orders to hit with the flat of the blade first, the cutting edge second.

Achmed's horse was engulfed by a tide of humanity, but these men were not out for blood. Risking life and limb amid the horses of the cavalry, they sought only to touch the palanquin, to kiss the curtains. "Your blessing on us, Imam!" they cried, and when Feisal parted the curtains and extended his bony arm, the Medans fell to their knees; many had tears streaming down their dust-streaked faces.

Feisal's dark, burning eyes looked at Qannadi, giving a wordless command. The Amir, lips pressed grimly together, ordered his men to fall back a discreet distance. The Medans lifted the Imam's palanquin onto their own shoulders and bore him triumphantly through the city gates. The roar of the crowd must have been heard by the sorrowing Uevin as far away as heaven.

It's all over! thought Achmed with relief and turned to share a smile with his general.

Qannadi's face was stern. He knew what was coming.

CHAPTER 2

chmed crouched in the shadow of his tent, eating his dinner and watching the sun's last rays touch the grass of the prairie with an alchemist's hand, changing the green to gold. The young man ate alone. He had made few acquaintances among the Amir's troops, no real friends. The men acknowledged his skill in riding and his way with horses, even magical ones. They learned from him: how to sit a galloping horse by pressing the thighs against the flanks, leaving hands free to fight instead of clutching the reins; how to use the animals' bodies for cover; how to leap from the saddles of running horses and pull themselves back up again. They learned how to keep the horses calm before a battle, how to keep them quiet when slipping up on the enemy, how to hush them when the enemy is somewhere out there, preparing to slip up on you. They accepted Achmed's teaching, though he was younger than most of them. But they never accepted *him*.

Although accustomed to the close comradeship of the friends in his father's tribe, most of whom were not only friends but relatives in one way or another, Achmed was not bothered by the lack of friends among the troops. The month in prison had hardened him to isolation; cruel usage at the hands of his tribesmen had caused him to welcome it.

Few others were stirring about the camp. The guards walking the perimeter looked dour and put-upon, for they could hear the shouts and laughter drifting up over the city walls and knew that their comrades were enjoying themselves. The Amir had given each man a sackful of the Emperor's coins with orders to spend freely—the first sign that Quar was raining gold down upon Meda. The troops were commanded to be friendly and as well behaved as could be expected; dire punishments were threatened for those who raped, looted, or in any other way harmed a Medan. The Amir's household guards manned the streets to maintain order.

Achmed could have been among those disporting themselves in the city, but he chose not to. The Medans, who had surrendered their city to Heaven without a fight, disgusted him and, if truth be told, disturbed him more than he could admit.

The sun's gold was darkening to dross, and Achmed was thinking about rolling himself in his blanket and losing himself in sleep when one of Qannadi's servants appeared and told him that all officers were ordered into the Amir's presence.

Hurrying through the city streets, Achmed saw no signs of rising rebellion or any other threat, and he wondered what this was about. Perhaps nothing more than joining the Amir for a victory dinner. Achmed's heart sank. There was no way he could excuse himself, yet he didn't feel up to celebrating. The servant did not lead him to the Governor's Palace, however, but to an unexpected place—a large temple-like structure located in the center of a plaza.

A broken statue of Uevin lay on the paving stones. North of the plaza stood the columned building that was—Achmed realized from his talks with Qannadi—the seat of Medan government known as the Senate. Standing on top of the smashed remains of the God Uevin was a huge golden ram's head that had been carted from Kich for precisely this purpose. (When, days later, the Amir's troops moved on southward, the golden ram's head would be reloaded into the cart and hauled off to do similar service in future conquered cities.)

The plaza was crowded with Medans, talking in low voices. On its outer perimeter, the Amir's elite household guards stood stern-faced and implacable, the tips of their spears gleaming in the sun's afterglow. The crowd kept its distance from the soldiers, Achmed noticed. Taking advantage of this path that had formed between the people and the guards, the young man followed the servant to the steps leading up to a marble-columned portico.

A throne from the Governor's Palace had been carried here by the Amir's servants and stood before the Senate's entryway. Qannadi sat on the throne, looking out onto the crowd gathered before him. He had changed from his battle armor into a white caftan, cloaked with a purple, gold-trimmed robe. His head was bare, except for a crown of laurel leaves, worn because of some silly custom of the Medans. It was already dark within the confines of the Senate porch. Torchbearers stood on either side of Qannadi, but they had, for some reason, not yet been given the order to light their brands. Looking intently at the Amir's face as he ascended the stairs, Achmed saw the firm set of the jaw, the shadows carved in the face, making Qannadi appear grim and unyielding in the fading light.

Next to Qannadi stood Feisal. No torchlight needed for him, the fire in the priest's eyes seemed to light the plaza long after the sun's glow had faded. Hoping to lose himself in the gathering gloom, Achmed took his place at the end of the line of officers who stood pressed against the Senate wall behind the Amir's throne. The young man wondered briefly how his absence had been noticed, when suddenly he felt the fiery gaze of the Imam sear his flesh. Feisal had been waiting for him! The priest raised his thin hand and beckoned for Achmed to approach.

Startled and unnerved, Achmed hesitated, looking to Qannadi. The Amir glanced at him from the corner of his eye and nodded slightly. Swallowing a knot in his throat, Achmed edged his way in front of his fellow officers, who stared straight out over the heads of the crowd. Why should I be afraid? he scolded himself, irritated at his clammy palms and the twisting sensation in his bowels. Perhaps it was the unusual silence of the people, who stood quietly as darkness washed slowly over them. Perhaps it was the unusually rigid stance and serious mien of the officers and guards. Perhaps it was the sight of Qannadi. Drawing closer, Achmed saw that the firmness of the man's jaw was being maintained by a strong effort of will, the merciless face beneath the leafy crown was the face of a man Achmed didn't know.

Feisal, though he had sent for the young man, took no further notice of him.

"Stand here," the Amir ordered coldly, and Achmed did as he was commanded, taking his place at Qannadi's right hand.

"Light the torches," was Qannadi's next order, and the brands being held behind him sputtered into flame, as did other torches carried by those in the crowd in the plaza. "Bring forth the prisoners. You, guards, clear a space there."

He gestured at the foot of the steps. The guards used the hafts of their spears to push back the Medans, forming an empty, circular area at the base of the Senate stairs. Facing the Medans, spears held horizontally before them, the guards kept the milling crowd at bay.

Achmed breathed easier. He'd heard it rumored that the Governor had been captured by the men-at-arms of those Medan Senators who had been in the Amir's pay. The wretched politician, bound hand and foot, was dragged forth, as were several other Senators and ministers who had remained loyal to their thankless citizens.

That this was to be a trial and execution, Achmed now recognized. He could view the deaths of these men with equanimity. In their gamble for power, the dice had turned against them. But they had lived well off the winnings up until this time; this was the chance they took when they first began to play the game. He found it difficult, therefore, to understand the unusual grimness of the Amir.

Perhaps he sees himself, standing there in chains, came the sudden, disquieting thought. *No, that's impossible. Qannadi would never have run. He would have fought, even though he had been one against a thousand. What then?*

More prisoners were being led by the guards into the doomed circle. One was a woman of about fifty, dressed in white robes, her gray hair worn in a tight braid around her head. Behind her stumbled four girls, younger than Achmed. They, too, were dressed in white, their gowns clung to bodies just swelling with the first buds of womanhood. Their hands were bound behind their backs, and they stared about with dazed, uncomprehending eyes. Following the four girls marched a man of rotund girth clad in red robes. From the expression on his face, he knew what was coming and yet walked with dignity, his back straight.

The voice of the crowd changed in regard to each prisoner. A guilt-laden murmur began when the Governor and the Senators were led in, many eyes looking up or down or anywhere but at the faces of the men for whom most of them had undoubtedly voted. The murmur changed to a whisper of pity at the sight of the young girls, and low mutterings of respect for the large man in red. The mutterings swelled to anger with the arrival of the last prisoner.

Beardless, with long brown hair, the prisoner was clad in black trousers tucked into the tops of black leather boots; a black silken shirt with flowing sleeves, open at the neck; and a crimson red sash around his waist. A curious device—that of a snake whose body had been cut into three pieces—was embroidered upon the front of his shirt.

Achmed stared at the snake in fascination. His skin prickled, his thumbs tingled, and from nowhere the image of Khardan came to him. Why should he think of his lost brother now, of all times? And why in the presence of this brown-haired man, who swaggered into the circle, closely followed by two guards carrying drawn swords. Achmed stared at the man intently, but found no answer to his question. The man in black started to move to the center of the circle. One of the guards put his hand on his arm to draw him back. The man turned on him with a vicious snarl, freeing himself of the guard's hold. The man in black walked where he was told, but of his own free will. He leered at the crowd, who swallowed their words at his baleful look. Those standing anywhere near the man fell backward in an attempt to get away from him—guarded as he was—an attempt that was thwarted by the press of the crowd.

The man looked up at the Amir' and suddenly grinned, his white face skull-like in the light of the flaring torches. The vision of Khardan faded from Achmed's mind.

"Is this all?" demanded Feisal, the timbre of his voice quivering slightly with anger. "Where are the underlings for these two?" He gestured at the rotund man and the man in black.

The captain of the elite guard stepped forward, hand raised in salute, his gaze on the Amir. "Have I leave to report, My King?"

"Report," said Qannadi, and Achmed heard weariness and resignation in the reply.

"All the other priests of Devin escaped, Highness, due to the cou—" he was about to say "courage" but a glimpse of Feisal's burning eyes made him change the word—"efforts of the High Priest." He gestured with a thumb toward the rotund man in red, who smiled serenely. "He held the doors with his own body, my lord. It took a battering ram to break them down, and due to the delay, the remainder of Uevin's priests escaped. We have no idea where they've gone." "Secret passages underground," Qannadi growled.

"We searched, My Lord, but found none. That is not to say that they couldn't exist. The Temple of Uevin is filled with strange and unholy machines."

"Keep looking," Qannadi said. "And what about this one?" His gaze turned to the man in black, who stared boldly back.

"A follower of the god, Zhakrin, my lord," the captain said in a low voice. Qannadi frowned; his face grew, if possible, grimmer. Feisal sucked in a hissing breath.

"That God of Evil no longer has power in the world," the Imam said, speaking to the man in black. The thin hand clenched. "You have been deceived!"

"It is not we who have been deceived, but you!" The man in black sneered. Taking a step forward, before the guard could stop him, he spit at the Imam's face. The crowd gasped. The guard smote the bound man on the side of the head with the butt-end of the spear, knocking him to the ground. Feisal remained unmoving; the fire in his eyes burned brighter.

Slowly the brown-haired man regained his feet. Blood streamed down the side of his face, but his grin was as wide as ever.

"We found the rest of the scum in the temple dead, My Lord," the Captain reported. "They died by their own hands. This one"—he gestured at the man in black—"apparently lacked the courage to kill himself. The coward put up no resistance."

The follower of Zhakrin did not note or even seem to hear the condemnation. His eyes were focused now on Feisal, never leaving the priest.

"Very well," Qannadi said in disgust. "Are you satisfied, Imam?"

"I suppose I must be," said Feisal sourly.

Qannadi rose to his feet, facing the crowd that hushed to hear his words.

"Citizens of Meda, there stand before you those who refuse to accept the blessings of Quar, who spurn the mercy of the God. Lest their unbelief spread like a poison through the now healthy body of your city, we take it upon ourselves to remove the poison before it can do you further harm."

One of the young girls cried out at this, a piercing wail that was cut off by one of the guards clapping his hand over her mouth. Achmed's throat went dry, blood throbbed in his ears so that he heard the Amir's words as though through a hood of sheep's wool.

"It shall be done this night, before you all, that you may see Quar's mercy and His judgment. He is not a God of vengeance.

Their deaths shall be quick"—the Amir's stern gaze went to the man in black—"even though some may not deserve such a fate. The bodies may be claimed by their relatives and buried in accordance with the teachings of Quar. Imam, have you words to add?"

The priest walked down the stairs to stand on the lowest step in front of the prisoners. "Are there any who would now convert to Quar?"

"I will!" cried a Senator. Flinging himself forward, the politician fell at the Imam's knees and began to kiss the hem of his robe. "I place myself and all my wealth into the hands of the God!"

Qannadi's mouth twisted; he regarded the wretched man with repugnance and made a motion with his hand for the Captain of the guard to come near. The Captain did so, silently drawing his sword from its sheath.

Feisal bent down, laying his hands upon the Senator's balding head. "Quar hears your prayer, my son, and grants you peace."

The Senator looked up, his face shining.

"Praise to Quar!" he shouted, a shout that ended in a shocked cry. The Captain's sword stabbed him to the heart. Staring at the Imam in amazement, the Senator pitched forward onto his stomach, dead.

"May Quar receive you with all blessing," the Imam said in a soft voice over the body.

"Carry on," ordered Qannadi harshly.

The guards surrounding the prisoners drew their swords.

The rotund priest fell to his knees, praying to Uevin in a firm voice that ended only with his life. The Governor left the world in bitter silence, casting a scathing glance at those who had betrayed him. The priestess, too, met her end with dignity. But one of the young virgins—seeing the priestess fall lifeless, the bloody sword yanked from the body—twisted free of her guard and ran in panic-stricken terror to the stairs.

"Mercy!" she cried. "Mercy!" Slipping and falling, she looked up directly at Achmed, extending her hands pleadingly. "You are young, as I am! Don't let them kill me, Lord!" she begged him. "Please! Don't let them!"

Blonde hair curled about a pretty, terrified face. Fear made her eyes wild and staring. Achmed could not move or look away but regarded the girl with pity and dismay.

Hearing the guard's footsteps coming up behind her, too weakened by fear to stand, the girl tried pathetically to crawl up the stairs, her hands stretched out to Achmed.

"Help me, Lord!" she cried frenziedly.

Achmed took a step forward, then felt Qannadi's hand close over his forearm with a crushing grip.

Achmed halted. He saw the hope that had dawned bright in the girl's eyes darken to despair. The guard struck quickly, mercifully cutting short the girl's last moment of terror. The body sagged, blood poured down the stairs, the hand reaching out to Achmed went limp.

The torchlights blurred in Achmed's vision. Dizzy and sick, he started to turn from the gruesome sight.

"Courage!" said the Amir in a low voice.

Achmed lifted glazed eyes. "Is it courage to butcher the innocent?" he asked hoarsely.

"It is courage to do your duty as a soldier," Qannadi answered in a fierce, barely audible whisper, not looking at Achmed but staring straight ahead impassively. "Not only to yourself but to them." He cast a swift glance around the crowd. "Better these few than the entire city!"

Achmed stared at him. "The city?"

"Meda was lucky," the Amir said in flat, even tones.

"Feisal chose it to set an example. There will be others, in the future, not so fortunate. This is *jihad,* a holy war. Those who fight us must die. So Quar has commanded."

"But surely He didn't mean women, children—"

Qannadi turned to look at him. "Come to your senses, boy!" he said angrily. "Why do you think *he* brought you here?" He did not look at Feisal, still standing at the bottom of the stairs, or motion toward him, but Achmed knew whom the Amir meant.

"My people!" Achmed breathed.

Nodding once, briefly, Qannadi removed his hand from the young man's arm and slowly and tiredly resumed his seat upon the throne.

His mind engulfed by the horror of what he had witnessed and the implication of what he'd just heard, Achmed stared blindly at the carnage when hoarse, triumphant laughter jolted him from his dark dream.

"The curse of Zhakrin upon the hand that kills Catalus!"

cried the man in black.

He stood in the center of what had become a ring of bodies lying in the plaza. In his hand he held a dagger. Its blade, gleaming in the torchlight, twisted like the body of the snake on his shirt. So commanding was he and so forceful his presence that the guards of the Amir fell back from him, looking uncertainly at their Captain, all clearly loathe to strike him.

"I did not lack courage to die with my fellows!" cried the man, the dagger held level with his red sash, one hand extended to keep off the guards. "I, Catalus, chose to die here, to die now, for a reason."

Both hands grasped the dagger's hilt and plunged the weapon into his bowels. Grimacing in pain, yet forbearing to cry out, he drew the weapon across his gut in a slashing motion. Blood and entrails splashed out upon the stones at his feet. Sinking to his knees, he stared up at Feisal with that same ghastly grin on his face. The dagger slid from Catalus's grasp. Dipping his hands in his own blood, he lurched forward. His crimson fingers closed on Feisal's robes.

"The curse of Zhakrin . . . on you!" Catalus gasped, and with a dreadful gurgling sound that might have been laughter, he died.

The Book
of Astafas

Chapter 1

The imp materialized within the darkness. It could see nothing, and the only part of the imp that could be seen were its bright red eyes and the occasional flick across the lips of an orange-red tongue.

"Your report astonishes me," said the darkness.

The imp was pleased at this and rubbed its long, skinny hands together in satisfaction. It could not see the speaker, not because the darkness hid the voice's source but because the darkness *was* the voice's source. The words reverberated around the imp as though spoken from a mouth somewhere beneath its feet, and the imp often had the impression, when summoned to appear before its God, that it was standing inside the brain of Astafas. It could sense the workings of the brain, and the imp occasionally wondered if it could grab a flash of intelligence as it whizzed past.

In order to prevent itself from touching that which was sacrosanct, the imp continued rubbing its hands, twining the large-knuckled fingers together in eager excitement.

"I begin to think the Wandering God was right after all," continued Astafas. "Quar played us all for fools. He intends to become the One, True God. The rival Gods of Sardish Jardan are falling to His might. I would not care so much, except that now His mask is off and I see His eyes turning to gaze greedily across the ocean."

The voice sank to the darkness and was silent. The imp felt a tingling sensation in its feet—the God was thinking, musing. Fidgeting, the imp bit off a squeal.

"To think," muttered Astafas, "if it hadn't been for those wretched priests of my ancient foe, Promenthas, getting themselves involved, I might not have discovered Quar's intentions until it was too late. Strange are the ways of Sul."

The imp agreed heartily with this, but said nothing, thinking it best not to reveal that it had ever doubted its master. A sudden jolt in the vicinity of its arm sent the imp skittering across the darkness, its skin burning with the shock of the God's sudden anger.

"My immortals, too, have been disappearing! And, by your account, they are being held captive somewhere?"

"This is the reason the guardian angel, Asrial"—the imp spoke the name gingerly, as though it stung its tongue—"left her protégé, Dark Master. One of the fish of which I spoke in my report sent her, along with the two immortals of the Wandering God, to search for them."

"A guardian angel of Promenthas leaving her charge. I do not believe I have ever heard of such a thing." If Astafas had been Promenthas—instead of that God's evil opposite—he could not have been more shocked. "The natural order is falling apart!"

"Still," suggested the imp, nursing a singed elbow, "it does provide us with an opportunity. . ."

"Yes," agreed the God thoughtfully. "But would it be worthwhile to gain one soul and lose thousands?"

The imp seemed to think it would—by the flicking of its hungry tongue across its lips.

The brain of the God hummed and buzzed around the imp. Its red eyes darted here and there nervously. It lifted up one foot and then the other, hopping back and forth in anticipation of some paralyzing shock. It still wasn't prepared for it, and when it came, the imp was knocked flat on its face.

"There is a way we can have both," said Astafas. "You are certain you know the young man's plans?"

"I see into his mind." The imp lifted its head, peering eagerly into the darkness, its red eyes shining like hot coals. "I read his thoughts."

"If he does what you anticipate, you will go along with him."

"I will?" The imp was pained. "I can't snatch him for you, then and there?"

"No. I need more information. I have an idea, you see, about these fish he carries. Humor the young man. He will not escape," said Astafas soothingly. "He will simply wind himself tighter and tighter in our coils."

"Yes, Dark Master." The imp did not sound overly enthusiastic. Scrambling to its splay-toed feet, it dejectedly asked if it was dismissed.

"Yes. Oh, one other thing—"

The darkness began to disappear; the imp had the uncomfortable sensation of falling.

"Dark Master?" it questioned.

"Do what you can to protect him."

"Protect him?" the imp wailed.

"For the time being," said the fading darkness.

CHAPTER 2

The *ghuls* piloted their storm-driven ship through the murky waters of the Kurdin Sea. Whether the power of Sul kept the vessel afloat or the power of the evil God in whose service the *ghuls* sailed, Mathew had little idea. Fierce gusts ripped the sails into tattered black shreds that streamed from the yardarms like the banners of a nightmarish army. The rigging snapped and slithered to the deck, twisting and writhing like snakes. None except the *ghuls* and the Black Paladin, Auda ibn Jad, could stand on the pitching deck, swept constantly by battering waves. Kiber and his men huddled aft, crouched beneath whatever meager shelter they could find from the wind and wet. The faces of the *goums* were pale and strained; many were sick and they obviously liked this voyage as little as their captives.

Auda ibn Jad stood beside the wheel, staring intently ahead as though he could pierce the storm clouds and catch a glimpse of his destination. Where that destination was or what it might hold, Mathew had long ago ceased to care.

In his sickness, crazed thoughts came to his horror-numbed brain. The *ghuls* began to fascinate him; he could not take his eyes off the men who were not men but creatures of Sul held in thrall by the power of Zhakrin. The idea of leaping up and hurling himself into the arms of one of the *ghuls* came to his mind and the thought, in his weakness and terror, was a pleasant one. With the warm-blooded human in its grasp, the *ghul* would certainly kill him. Not even Auda ibn Jad—who was just barely holding them in check now—could prevent that. The *ghuls* suddenly became creatures filled with light, almost angelic in aspect. Benevolent, handsome, strong, they offered him escape, a way out.

"Come to me," the *ghul* seemed to whisper every time one looked his way. "Come to me and I will release you from this torment."

Mathew imagined the hands gripping him tightly, the teeth sinking into his flesh, the sharp, burning pain, and the swift fear that would soon mercifully end as the blood drained from his body, bringing blissful lethargy and, finally, welcome darkness.

"Come to me. . ."

He had only to move, to stand, to run forward. It would I all be over—the fear, the guilt.

"Come to me. . ."

He had just to move. . .

"Mat-hew!"

A thick, pain-filled call, heard over the terrible whispers, roused him. Reluctantly, he wrenched his mind from dreams of death and returned to the world of the living.

"Mat-hew!" Panic tinged the voice. Zohra could not see him, he realized. Her view was blocked by one of the heavy ivory jars. Slowly he made his way to her, crawling on hands and knees over the heaving deck.

At the sight of him, Zohra half raised, clutching at him desperately.

"Lie back down," he urged her, pressing her body gently back onto the deck.

But she sat up again, her eyes blinking against the pain that must be making her head throb. "Mat-hew, what is happening?!" she demanded angrily.

Mathew sighed inwardly. First she acts, then she questions. Just like Khardan. Just like these nomads. Whenever anything out of the ordinary confronts you, don't think about it, don't try to understand it. Attack it. Kill it, and it will go away and not bother you anymore. If that doesn't work, perhaps ignoring it will. And if that doesn't work, then you cry and mope like a spoiled child. . .

Mathew cast a bitter glance at Khardan. Lashed to the mast, the Calif sagged in his bindings, his head bowed. Occasionally a groan escaped his lips when the sickness took hold of him, but other than that—not a word. He has lost a battle and so considers that he has lost the war, Mathew thought, anger stirring in him again (completely ignoring that only moments before he himself had been courting death).

"Mat-hew!" Zohra tugged on his soaking-wet clothes. "Where are they taking us?" She looked fearfully about at the ship. "Why does that man want us?"

Mathew nudged his brain to function. Zohra had been unconscious when they brought her on board. She probably didn't even remember the *ghuls* attacking and devouring the helpless slaves. How could he hope to explain what he didn't understand himself?

"It's all . . . my fault," he said at last, or rather croaked, his throat sore from swallowing sea water and vomiting. Another wave of nausea swept over him, and he slumped down weakly beside Zohra, wondering, as he did so, why she wasn't deathly ill like the rest of them.

"Your fault?!" Zohra frowned. Leaning over him, her wet black hair slapping against his face, she grabbed two handfuls of the wet silk of his caftan and shook him. "Get up! Don't lie there! If this is your fault, then you must do something!"

Closing his eyes, Mathew turned his head and did something.

He was sick.

Mathew lost all concept of time. It seemed they sailed forever before the storm winds began to abate and the black, lowering clouds that hung over the masts began to lift. Had he looked into a mirror at that moment and seen that his skin was wrinkled and aged, his eyes dim, his body bent, his hair white, he wouldn't have been much surprised. Eighty years might have passed on board that dreadful ship.

Eighty years. . . eighty seconds.

From his prone position on the deck, Mathew heard Auda ibn Jad's voice raised in command. He heard the sound of boots hitting wood and a few suppressed groans—the *goums* staggering to their feet.

Kiber's face—pale and green—loomed above him, the *goum* leader shouting something that Mathew could not hear over the crashing of the sea. Suddenly the young wizard wished the voyage would go on, that it would never end. The memory of his idea returned to him. He did not welcome it and wished heartily that the thought had never occurred to him. It was stupid, it was foolhardy. It was risking his life in what was undoubtedly a futile gesture. He had no notion of where his actions might lead him because he had no notion of where he was or what was going to happen to him. Conceivably, he could make matters worse.

No, he would not be like Khardan and Zohra. He would not leap forward in the darkness and grapple with the unknown. He would do what he had always done. He would let things take their course. He would ride the current in his frail craft and hope to survive. He would do nothing that might risk falling into the dark water where he would surely drown.

Kiber jerked him roughly to his feet. The motion of the ship, although not as violent, was still erratic, and sent Mathew stumbling back against the baggage. He caught himself and stood clinging to a large rattan basket. Kiber glanced at him, saw that for the moment he was standing, and turned to Zohra.

Seeing the *goum* approaching her, she repelled him with a flashing-eyed look and stood up on her own, backing out of the man's reach as far as she could before being brought up by several of the huge ivory jars.

Reaching out, Kiber grabbed hold of her arm.

Zohra struck the *goum* across the face.

Auda ibn Jad, shouted again, sounding impatient.

Grim and tense, the red marks of the woman's hand showing clearly against his livid skin, Kiber caught hold of Zohra again, this time wrenching her wrist and twisting her arm behind her back.

"Why can't you be a woman like Blossom?" Kiber muttered, taking hold of Mathew, as well, and dragging him forward. "Instead of a wild cat!"

Zohra's eyes met Mathew's. A woman like you! Her contempt seared him. Despite that, his resolve was not shaken. He caught a glimpse of Khardan. The man didn't have strength enough left in his body to crush an ant beneath his heel, yet he had apparently roused himself from his stupor and was struggling feebly with the *goums* freeing him from his bonds. For what? Nothing but pride. Even if he did manage to overpower them, where could he go? Leap off the ship? Throw himself into the arms of the *ghuls*, who now watched the fight with intense, hungry interest.

That's what this plan of yours is—a feeble struggle against overwhelming odds. And that's why it's forgotten, Mathew told himself, looking away from both Zohra and Khardan. His fingers brushed against the pouch that contained the magical objects, and he snatched his hand away as though it had burned him. He would have to get rid of them and quickly. They were a danger to him now. He cursed himself for having picked them up.

Fumbling at his belt, Mathew pulled out the pouch and instantly crumpled it in his hand, pressing it against his waist, concealing it in the folds of his wet clothes. He darted a furtive look from beneath his lowered eyelids, hoping to be able to drop the pouch to the deck without anyone noticing.

Unfortunately, Auda ibn Jad turned from looking out over the sea, his snake-eyed gaze resting upon Mathew and Zohra and the grim-faced Kiber behind them.

"Trouble, Captain?" ibn Jad asked, noting with amusement Kiber's bruised cheek.

Kiber answered something; Mathew didn't know what. He froze beneath the piercing gaze. Panicked, he doubled over, digging the hand with the pouch into his stomach, hoping to seem to be still sick, although in reality his nausea was passing, either because the motion of the ship was settling down or his fear and worry had driven it from his mind.

Ibn Jad's gaze flicked over him, to rest more steadily at Zohra. There was neither lust nor desire in the man's dark eyes. He was regarding her with the same cool appraisal a man might regard a dog he was considering acquiring. When he spoke, his words were the embodiment of Mathew's thought, causing the young wizard to start guiltily, wondering if the Black Paladin had the power to read minds.

"The bitch will produce strong whelps," said ibn Jad in satisfaction. "Fine new followers for our God."

"Bitch!" Zohra's eyes flared.

Breaking free of the weakened Kiber, she hurled herself at ibn Jad. Kiber jumped after her and wrestled her back before she reached the Black Paladin—whose amusement seemed to grow. Auda made a sound in his throat that might have been a chuckle but caused Mathew to go cold all over. Obviously out of patience and in an ill humor, Kiber handed Zohra over to a couple of his men with orders to tie her hands and hobble her feet.

Ibn Jad's eyes were again on Mathew, and the young wizard cowered beneath their gaze, realizing too late that he could have dropped the pouch during the altercation and wondering, briefly, why he hadn't.

Ibn Jad ran his slender hand over Mathew's smooth cheek. "A jackal, that one, compared to our fragile and delicate Blossom here who trembles beneath my fingers."

Mathew cringed and gritted his teeth, forcing himself to submit to the man's odious touch, slightly turning his body to keep the pouch in his hand concealed. He was vaguely aware of activity stirring around them, of the rumbling of a heavy chain, a splash, and the ship swinging slowly at anchor.

Brutal enslavement—this was to be Zohra's fate and his, too, undoubtedly, until ibn Jad discovered he had been deceived, that Mathew would never bear this God, Zhakrin, worshipers. It was happening all over, he realized in despair the terrible waiting, the dread anticipation, the fear, the humiliation, and then the punishment. And there would be no one to save him this time. . .

"These women. . . are my wives!" said a slurred voice.

"You will die before you touch them!"

Mathew looked at Khardan and then averted his face, tears stinging his eyelids.

The Calif stood before ibn Jad. The bindings had cut deeply into the nomad's arms, fresh blood streamed from a gash on his swollen lip. The sickly pallor of his complexion was accentuated by the blue-blackness of his unkept beard. His eyes were sunken, encircled by shadows. He walked unsteadily; it took two *goums* to hold him upright. At a nod from ibn Jad, they let go. Khardan's knees buckled. He pitched forward, falling at the feet of the Black Paladin.

"A bold speech from a man on his knees, a man we found hiding from the soldiers of the Amir in a dress," said Auda ibn Jad coolly. "I begin to think I made a mistake with this one, Kiber. He is not fit for the honor I intended to bestow upon him. We will leave him to the *ghuls*. . ."

Damn you, Khardan! Mathew cursed the Calif silently, bitterly. Why did you have to do that? Jeopardize your life for two people you detest—a woman who brought you to shame and a man who is shame personified. Why do this? Honor! Your stupid honor! And now they will rend your flesh, murder you before my eyes!

Putting his booted foot on Khardan's shoulder, ibn Jad gave the man a shove, and the Calif went over backward, landing heavily on the deck.

Mathew heard the splash of oars in the water. Small boats had set sail from land and were drawing near the ship. The *ghuls*, their ship at anchor, their task finished, were gathering around Khardan, eyes shining with an eager, eerie light. The Calif tried to rise, but Kiber kicked him in the face, knocking him back onto the deck. The *ghuls* drew nearer, their aspect beginning to undergo the hideous change from man to demon. Seeing them, Khardan shook his head to clear it and started to struggle once more to stand.

Stop it! Mathew cried in silent agony, fists clenching. Stop fighting! Let it end!

Auda ibn Jad was pointing toward the boats, issuing orders. Kiber, turning to obey, drove the toe of his boot deep into Khardan's gut. With a gasp of agony, the Calif sank back onto the deck and did not rise again.

The *ghuls* closed in, their teeth lengthening into fangs, their nails into talons.

"Bring the women," said ibn Jad, and Kiber motioned to the *goums* holding Zohra. She stared at the *ghuls* in dazed disbelief and horror, seeming not to comprehend what was happening. The *goums* dragged her forward to where the boats were pulling up beneath the ship's hull. She twisted around, straining to watch Khardan, who was pressing his body flat against the deck as though he might escape by crawling into the wood. Bending over him, their breath hot upon his skin, the *ghuls* began to howl, and Khardan's arms twitched, his hands clenched spasmodically. Then taloned fingers stabbed deep into his flesh, and the Calif screamed.

Mathew's hand was inside the pouch; he never remembered how. His fingers closed over the cold wand of obsidian. He had no clear conscious thought of what he was doing, and when he drew forth the wand, the hand holding it seemed to belong to someone else, the voice that spoke the words was the voice of a stranger.

"Creatures of Sul," he cried, pointing the wand at the *ghuls*, "in the name of Astafas, Prince of Darkness, I command you to withdraw!"

The world went completely black. During the breadth of a heartbeat, night engulfed those standing on the ship. Light returned in the blink of an eye.

A skinny, shriveled creature with skin the color of coal stood spraddle-legged over Khardan. Its eyes were red fire, its tongue flickering flame. Raising a splay-fingered hand, it pointed at the *ghuls*.

"Heard you not my master?" the imp hissed. "Be gone, lest he call upon Sul to cast you in the fiery depths where you will never more taste sweet flesh or drink hot blood."

The *ghuls* halted, some with their talons digging into Khardan's flesh, others with their teeth just inches from his body. They stared at the imp balefully. The imp stared back, its red eyes burning fiercely.

"Always hungry, always thirsting. . ."

One by one, the *ghuls* released their hold upon Khardan. Slowly—eyes on the imp—they moved away from the Calif, their aspect shifting from demon to man.

Its tongue flicking in and out of its mouth in pleasure, the imp turned to Mathew and bowed.

"Will there be anything more, My Dark Master?"

CHAPTER 3

Mathew very nearly dropped the wand.

Of all the astonished people on the ship, the young wizard was the most astounded of all.

Feeling the wand start to slip from his shaking fingers, Mathew caught hold of it with a spasmodic jerk of his hand, reacting more out of instinct than conscious thought. To drop a wand during a spell casting was considered a grievous and dangerous error on the part of any wizard. Almost every nervous young student did it once, and Mathew could hear the voice of the Archmagus dinning furiously in his ears. The young wizard's training saved him. He gained additional strength from the sudden frightening realization that if the spell was broken, he was in far more danger than if all the *ghuls* in the nether plane had ringed themselves round him.

An instant before the imp bowed, Mathew saw clearly in the creature's eyes the burning desire to lay claim to his immortal soul. Then it would be Mathew who was forever in servitude to a Dark Master—Astafas, Prince of Darkness. Why didn't the imp snatch him up? Mathew had put himself in forfeit by speaking the name of Astafas. Why was the creature obeying him? Only the most powerful of the wizard's Order could summon and control immortals such as the imp.

The wand might have such powers, but Mathew doubted it. Meryem was a skilled sorceress, but not even she could have attained the high rank necessary to enable her to make a Wand of Summoning. If she had possessed this kind of arcane power, she would not have needed to resort to anything as clumsy as murder. No, some strange and mystifying force was at work here.

Too late, Mathew regained control of his features. He had been staring blankly at the imp as these confused thoughts tumbled through his mind, and he hoped no one had noticed.

His hope was a vain one. Auda ibn Jad's cool composure had been disturbed by the appearance of the imp, still more by its referring to the beautiful red-haired young woman as Dark Master. Ibn Jad was quick to note Mathew's unnerved appearance, however, and—though the Black Paladin did not know what it portended as yet—he filed it away in memory for later consideration.

Mathew knew he had to act, and he tried desperately to think what was the next logical order a powerful, evil wizard might be likely to issue.

The command that was in his heart was to have the imp carry him, Khardan, and Zohra off this horror-filled ship, as far away from Auda ibn Jad as the creature could manage. But just as this thought traveled from heart to mind, the imp raised its head and looked at Mathew. Its red eyes flared fire, its mouth parted in a wicked grin, the tongue licked dry, cracked lips.

Mathew shuddered and banished the thought. The imp could read his mind, obviously. And while undoubtedly it would obey his command, Mathew knew exactly where the imp would take them—a place of eternal darkness whose Demon Prince made Auda ibn Jad seem saintly in comparison. "Dark Master?" the imp prompted, rubbing its skinny hands together.

"I need you no more," Mathew said at last, a quaver spoiling the authoritative note he tried to instill in his voice. "Be gone until I call for you again."

Was this how one spoke to summoned creatures? Mathew couldn't remember; he'd had only the most cursory studies in Black Magic and the only object it accomplished was to fix in the minds of White Wizards that dabbling in this art would invariably lead to disaster. Mathew had the uncomfortable feeling, however, that no matter what he said, the imp would deal with the situation.

"I obey, My Dark Master," said the imp, and disappeared with a heart-stopping bang.

No one moved. Now that the imp was gone, all eyes turned to Mathew.

He had to keep going, keep performing. He gave them all what he hoped was a cold, threatening stare and made his way across the deck to Khardan. Raising the wand, he fixed, his gaze upon the *ghuls*, and was relieved to see them step back respectfully at his approach.

Mathew knelt down beside Khardan. Wounded, shaken by the nearness he had come to a tortured death, the Calif barely had the strength to raise his head. Putting his arm around the man's shoulders, Mathew lifted him to a sitting position on the deck.

"Are you all right?" he asked in a low voice.

Khardan's teeth chattered, his lips were blue. "The scratches!" he gasped. "Burn. . . like. . . cold fire."

Mathew examined the places on his arms and torso where the *ghuls* had driven their talons into the flesh. The long tears in the skin were swollen and colored a bluish white. There was no blood visible, although the cuts were deep. Leaning against Mathew, Khardan shook as with a chill. He was in such agony that he seemed to have only the vaguest idea what had happened.

"The *ghuls* poison has entered his blood. He is too ill to walk. Some of you carry him ashore." Looking up as he issued the command, Mathew's eyes met the eyes of Auda ibn Jad. He saw nothing in the black, reptilian flatness to give him a clue as to what the Black Paladin was thinking. If Auda challenged him, Mathew had no idea what he would do. Certainly not summon the imp again, if he could help it!

For long moments, the two stared at each other; the ship, the *goums*, the *ghuls*, the boats arriving beneath the ship's hull, voices shouting hails to the deck—all vanished from the mind of each man as he strove to see deep into the heart of the other.

Mathew came away with nothing. What Auda ibn Jad came away with—if anything—remained locked deep inside him.

"Kiber," said ibn Jad, "take three of your men and place; the Calif in the bosun's chair, then lower him into the boats. Gently, Kiber, gently."

Kiber called out three *goums*, who left their duties tying the baggage that had been brought on board in huge nets to be swung out over the side and deposited in the waiting boats. Hurrying forward—with sidelong, distrustful glances at Mathew—the *goums* lifted Khardan by his knees and his arms and hauled him awkwardly over to the ship's rail.

Rising to his feet, Mathew followed them, thankful that the folds of the caftan hid the trembling of his legs and hoping he did not disgrace himself by collapsing in a heap upon the deck. He still clutched the wand in his hand and thought it best to keep it visible. So tightly were his fingers wrapped around it, he wasn't at all certain he could let loose of the thing.

"Approach me, Blossom," said Auda ibn Jad. "The rest of you"—he gestured at the goums—"continue your work. It is almost nightfall and we must be off this ship by then. Take her"—he indicated Zohra—"and put her in the same boat with her husband."

Mathew glanced at Zohra apprehensively; there was no telling what she might say, perhaps blurt out that the wand wasn't his at all or that he had told her the God he followed was called Promenthas not Astafas. Zohra said nothing, however; simply stared at him in wide-eyed astonishment. He managed to smile at her in what he hoped was reassurance, but she was apparently so completely shocked by what had happened that she couldn't respond. Zohra allowed her captors to lead her away, looking as though she were in a waking dream.

Sighing, Mathew came to stand before Auda ibn Jad, the two of them were alone in the center of the deck.

"Well, Blossom, it seems your face and lithe body and the sorcerer's robes you wore when I first saw you fooled me. It was not a woman I took into my slave caravan but a man. Of course, you thought I would kill you, and so you let me remain deceived. You might have been right, but then again, I am not so sure I would have had you murdered as I did the others. There are those who fancy a pretty boy above a pretty girl and who are just as willing to pay good money for such in the slave market. You might have spared yourself much humiliation and me much trouble had you told me the truth. Still, the water spilled into the sand cannot be drunk, and there is no going back. I think you should give me the fish, now, Blossom,"

All this was spoken in cool, calm tones, even the last. But Mathew felt the steel-edged menace prick him sharply. Taking a moment to gather his thoughts and to grasp hold of his courage with the same desperate grip by which he held the wand, Mathew shook his head.

"No," he replied softly. "I will not do that. I know something of magic, as you have seen. You called me the Bearer and one so designated cannot be parted from that which he bears by any force in this world."

"I can kill you and take it from your corpse," said the Black Paladin with an easy, impersonal casualness that made Mathew blench.

"Yes," he answered, "you could kill me. But you won't, at least not until you know how much I know and—more importantly—how much my God"—the word came with difficulty—"knows."

"Astafas, our brother God in Evil." Auda ibn Jad nodded slowly, reflectively. "Yes, I must admit I am curious to know more about the Prince of Darkness. In fact, I am pleased at the opportunity for contact with our Brother. I will not sacrifice you in order to take the fish—not yet at least. There will come a time, Blossom—you don't mind me calling you this? I find I have grown accustomed to it—when your usefulness will be at an end, and then I will not hesitate to destroy you in a most unpleasant manner."

"I understand," said Mathew wearily, "you can do with me what you will—provided Astafas allows it—but I"—the young wizard drew a deep breath—"I insist that you let my friends go."

Auda ibn Jad smiled—so might a snake smile. Reaching out with his slender hand, he took hold of a strand of Mathew's wet red hair and drew it slowly and lingeringly through his fingers. The Black Paladin moved close to Mathew, his body touching that of the wizard's, his face and eyes filling Mathew's vision.

"I will let your friends go, Blossom," ibn Jad said gently. "Tell me where. Shall I leave them on this ship? Shall I drop them in the Kurdin Sea? Or perhaps you would prefer that I wait and set them free on the island of Galos? The Guardians of our castle find their work tedious sometimes. They would enjoy a chance for a little sport. . ."

Ibn Jad wrapped the strand of hair tightly about his finger and pulled Mathew's head so near his own that the wizard could feel the man's breath upon his cheek. Involuntarily, Mathew closed his eyes. He felt suffocated, as if the Black Paladin were breathing in all the air and leaving Mathew stranded in a vacuum.

"I was preoccupied, absorbed in keeping the *ghuls* in thrall. You took me by surprise, Blossom. You caught me off guard. Few have ever done that, and therefore I rewarded you by allowing your Calif to live." Ibn Jad gave a sharp tug on Mathew's hair, bringing tears to the young man's eyes and jerking his head nearer still. "But never again!" The Black Paladin breathed the words.

"You are good, my dear, but young. . . very young."

Giving Mathew's hair a vicious yank, he sent the wizard sprawling face first on the deck. The wand flew from Mathew's hand, and he watched in agony as it slid across the sand-scrubbed wood. He made a desperate lunge for it, but a black-booted foot stepped on it.

Crouched on his hands and knees, Mathew cowered in chagrin and shame. He could feel Auda ibn Jad's smile shine upon him like the light of a cold, pale sun. And then he heard the boot scrape across the deck; the wand rolled toward Mathew and bumped against his hand.

"My regards to Astafas," said the Black Paladin. "I welcome his servant to the Isle of Galos."

CHAPTER 4

The Isle of Galos was the peak of a huge volcano whose smoke-rimmed, storm-shrouded head reared up out of the murky waters of the Kurdin Sea. Like a fierce and ancient patriarch who sits motionless in his wheeled chair for days and at whom relatives glance fearfully and say, "Do you suppose he's still alive?" the volcano had done nothing in years. But, like the old man, the volcano lived still and occasionally gave evidence of this by a slight tremor or a small belch of noxious fumes.

It was here that the few followers of the dead Zhakrin chose to make what might very well be their final stand against the world and the Heavens. When it was known—almost twenty years ago—that their God was growing weaker, word went forth from the Lord of the Black Paladins, and those last remaining survivors of various purges and *jihads* and persecutions made their way to this place that seemed the embodiment of the dark horrors of their religion.

Carried across the Kurdin Sea by their few remaining immortals, the Black Paladins were left alone on the Isle when those immortals vanished. The knights' lives were harsh. Their God could no longer help them. They had nothing on which to live but faith and the code of their strict sect that bound them with undying loyalty to each other. Their single, unswerving goal was to bring about their God's return.

None but the members of that strict Order could have survived the ordeal. Survive they did, however, and—not only that—they began to thrive and prosper, acquiring—by various means—new members for their Black Cause. The sorceresses of the Black Paladins were able to capture the *ghuls* and, by granting them human flesh in payment, they persuaded Sul's creatures to work a sailing vessel between the Isle and the mainland. Contact with the world was reestablished, and once more the Black Paladins went forth—always in secret—to bring back what was needed.

The knights imported slave labor and began building Castle Zhakrin—a place of refuge where they could live and a temple for their God when he should return. Castle Zhakrin was constructed of shining black obsidian, granite, magic, blood, and bones. Numerous unfortunate slaves either fell to their deaths from the towering battlements, were crushed beneath huge blocks of stone, or sacrificed to Zhakrin. The Black Paladins sprinkled the blood of the victims over the building blocks; their bones were mixed with the mortar. When the Castle was completed, the remaining slaves were put to death and their skeletons added to the building's decor. Human skulls grinned above doors, dismembered hands pointed the way down corridors, leg and foot bones were imbedded in the walls of winding staircases.

Riding in the stern of ibn Jad's boat, Mathew gazed in awe at the Isle that he had been too preoccupied to notice from the ship. A barren, windswept, jagged cone of rock jutted from the water, soaring up to lose itself in the perpetual clouds that shrouded the mountain's peak. Nothing grew on the rock's dead, rough-edged surface. The wind seemed the only living thing on the Isle, whistling through lips of twisted stone, howling bleakly when it found itself trapped in deep ravines, beating against blank canyon walls.

Castle Zhakrin stood against one side of the mountain, its sharp spires and gap-toothed battlements making it look like the mountain's offspring, something the volcano spewed forth in fire and smoke and ash. A great signal fire burning from atop one of the towers added to the illusion, reddish orange light poured from the windows like molten lava streaming down upon the black sand beach below.

Gathered upon that beach were the Black Paladins. Fifty men of ages ranging from eighteen to seventy stood in a single straight line upon the sand. They were dressed in black metal armor that gleamed red in the rays of the setting sun. Draped over their shoulders were vestments of black cloth, each adorned over the left breast with the signet of the severed snake. The knights wore no helms, their faces—Mathew saw as the boat drew near—might have been carved from the stone of their mountain, so cold and immovable were they. Yet, when the boats were dragged ashore by the rowers-young men of between fifteen and seventeen whom Mathew judged, from what he overhead, to be knights-in-training—he noticed that the faces of the Black Paladins underwent a swift and subtle change. Greeting one of their own, he saw true emotion light their eyes and soften their features. And he saw this—astonishingly—reflected in the usually impassive face of Auda ibn Jad.

Startled by the change in the man, Mathew watched in wonder as the usually cold and taciturn Black Paladin leapt from the boat into the water before the squires had a chance to haul the boats ashore. Wading through the crashing waves, Auda ran into the arms of an elderly man whose head was ringed round by a crown shaped in the semblance of two snakes, twined together, their heads joining at his forehead, their red-jeweled eyes sparkling in the twilight.

"Ibn Jad! Zhakrin by thanked! You return to us safely," cried the man.

"And successfully, Lord of Us All," said Auda ibn Jad, falling to his knees and reverently kissing the old man's hands.

"Zhakrin be praised!" cried the Lord, lifting his hands to the heavens. His words were echoed by the other knights in a litany that reverberated from the mountainside and faded away in the pounding of the surf.

Khardan cried out in pain, and Mathew's attention was withdrawn from the Paladins. The Calif lay in the bottom of Mathew's boat. He had lapsed into unconsciousness and twitched and tossed and moaned in some horrid, fever-racked dream.

"The Black Sorceress will care for him. Do not worry, Blossom," Auda had told him. "He will not die. Don't be surprised, however, if he doesn't thank you. You did him no service in saving his life."

Mathew considered glumly that he had done none of them any service by his foolhardy act and had undoubtedly further compounded their troubles. Ibn Jad viewed him as a threat. Worse still, Zohra saw him as a hero. Despite the fact that they were in separate boats—Zohra having been put into the custody of Kiber, who looked none too happy about the fact and watched her warily—Mathew could feel the woman's eyes on him, looking at him with admiration. This newfound regard for him only served to increase Mathew's unhappiness. She expected him to save them, now, and he knew it was impossible. Once again he found himself living a lie, trapped into pretending he was something he wasn't, with death the penalty for the tiniest mistake.

Or perhaps death was the reward. Mathew didn't know anymore. He'd lived with fear so long, lived with the twisting bowels and cold hands and chill sweat and thudding heart that he increasingly saw death as blissful rest. The irrational anger continued to bum inside him—anger at Khardan and Zohra for being dependent on him, for making him worry about them, for making him feel guilty over having plunged them into this danger.

The squires and *goums* carried Khardan to shore. Wading through the water beside him, Mathew looked down at the pain-racked body and tried to feel some pity, some compassion. But all was darkness inside him, darkness cold and empty. He watched them place Khardan upon a makeshift litter, watched them haul him slowly up stairs carved into the rock leading to the Castle, and felt nothing. Zohra floundered through the water, Kiber holding her arm. Raising her head, she gazed after her husband with lips that parted in concern. Fear and pity for him—not for herself—glimmered in her black eyes. Mathew saw then that Zohra's hatred of Khardan masked some type of caring—perhaps not love, but at least a concern for him. And Mathew, who had loved Khardan longer than he cared to admit to himself, was too frightened to feel anything.

The emptiness only angered him further. He thought, somewhere, he could hear the imp laughing, and he looked away from Zohra's smile of approval and expectation. Mathew was almost thankful when Auda ibn Jad beckoned peremptorily to the young wizard to attend him. Turning his back on Zohra—who was standing wet, haughty, and bedraggled in the black sand—Mathew walked over to where ibn Jad was exchanging warm greetings with his fellow knights.

"What dread brotherhood is this?" Mathew said to himself, glad to have something to which he could turn his thoughts. "This man sold humans into slavery with no more regard than if they had been goats. He murdered an innocent girl, driving a knife into her body with as little care as if she had been a doll. He cast men to *ghuls* and watched their terrible sufferings with equanimity. And I see nothing but the same cold, dispassionate cruelty in the faces of these men surrounding him! Yet tears shine in their eyes as they embrace!"

"But where is Catalus, my bonded brother?" Auda looked questioningly around the circle of knights surrounding him. "Why wasn't he summoned to join us for this, our greatest hour?"

"He was summoned, Auda," said the Lord in a gentle, sorrowful voice, "and it is sad news I must relate to you, my friend. Catalus was in the city of Meda, training priests in our new temple there when the city was attacked by troops of the Emperor of Tara-kan. Cowards that they are, the Medans surrendered and—to a man—pledged their allegiance to Quar!"

"So the war in Bas has begun," said ibn Jad, his brows drawing together, the cruel eyes darkening. "I heard rumors of it as I passed through the land. And Catalus?"

"Knowing the people would turn our followers over to the troops of the Amir, he commanded the priests to kill themselves before they could be offered up to Quar. When the troops came, they found the temple floor running with blood, Catalus standing in the middle, his sword red, having dispatched those who lingered overlong.

"The troops of the Amir laid hands upon him, calling him coward. He bore their taunts in silence, knowing that he would soon see them choke on their own poisoned words. They dragged him before the Amir and the Imam of Quar, who thought he now had possession of the soul of Catalus."

Shuddering himself at the terrible tale, Mathew saw Auda ibn Jad's face drain of its color. White to the lips, the Black Paladin asked softly, "And what did my bonded brother do?"

The Lord laid his hand upon Auda's shoulder. All the knights had fallen silent, their faces stern and pale, their lips compressed. The only sound was the breaking of the waves upon the shore, the mournful wailing of the wind among the rocks, and the deep voice of the Lord of Black Paladins.

"Catalus watched the other prisoners slaughtered around him. When it came his turn, he drew from his robes a dagger he had concealed there and sliced open his belly. He crawled forward and, with his dying breath, grasped hold of the Imam's robes with his crimsoned hands and called down Zhakrin's Blood Curse upon Feisal, the Imam of Quar."

Auda ibn Jad lowered his head. A sob tore through his body;

he began to weep like a child. Several of the knights standing near rested their hands upon him in compassion, many of them unashamedly wiping their own eyes.

"Catalus died in the service of our God. His soul is with Zhakrin, and he will fight to help bring our God back to this world," said the Lord. "We mourn him. We honor him. Next we avenge him."

"Honor to Catalus! Praise to Zhakrin'" cried ibn Jad fiercely, lifting his head, tears glistening on his cheeks.

"Honor to Catalus! Praise to Zhakrin!" shouted the knights, and as if their call had summoned the darkness, the sun vanished into the sea and only the red afterglow remained to light the land.

"And now, tell us the name of this woman with hair the color of flame who stands here with you," said the Lord, his admiring gaze sweeping over Mathew. "Have you brought her for one of the Breeders, or has your heart been touched at last, Auda ibn Jad, and will you take her for wife?"

"Neither," said ibn Jad, his lips twisting in a smile. "No woman, this one, but a man." There was laughter at this, and several of the men flushed in embarrassment, their companions nudging them teasingly. "Do not be ashamed, my brothers, if you looked upon him with desire. His milk skin and green eyes and delicate features have deceived more than one, including myself. His story I will tell you in detail over our evening repast. For now, know that he is the Bearer and a sorcerer in the service of Astafas, our brother God."

A subdued, respectful murmur rippled through the Black Paladins.

"A sorcerer!" The Lord looked at Mathew with interest. "I have heard of men who were skilled in the art of magic, but I have never before encountered one. Are you certain, ibn Jad? Have you proof?"

"I have proof," said Auda with a touch of irony in his voice. "He summoned an imp of Sul and kept the *ghuls* from feasting upon that man whom you saw being carried into the Castle."

"Truly a skilled magus! My wife will be pleased to meet you," said the Lord to Mathew. "She is the Black Sorceress of our people, without whose magic we could not have survived."

Ibn Jad's eyes still glistened with tears shed over the death of a comrade, yet their threat slid through Mathew's soul like sharp steel. The young wizard could not make a coherent response, his tongue seemed swollen, his throat parched and dry. Fortunately a bell began to toll from the Castle tower. The knights began to disperse, walking across the beach, their boots crunching in the sand. Several respectfully drew the attention of their Lord to themselves. Ibn Jad was carried off by friends demanding to hear the tales of his adventures. Mathew thought he was going to be left alone, forgotten on this dismal shore, when the Lord glanced around over his shoulder.

"Some of you squires"—he called to the young men unloading the ivory jars and other baggage from the boats—"take the sorcerer to the chambers of my wife. Bid her find him suitable clothing and prepare him for tonight's ceremony."

Two squires leaped to act on their Lord's command, taking charge of Mathew. Without speaking a word to him or paying him attention beyond a cool, curious glance at his sodden woman's clothes, they led him swiftly over the wet, packed sand to where Castle Zhakrin stood, its black shining surface tinged with the blood of the departed sun.

CHAPTER 5

Climbing the black stairs carved into the side of the mountain, Zohra continued to maintain her haughty dignity and composure. Pride was, after all, the only thing she had left. Led by Kiber, who kept glancing at her as though she were a *ghul* and might eat him at a bite, Zohra set her face into a rigid mask that effectively hid her fear and confusion. It wasn't as difficult as might be expected. She seemed to have gone numb, as though she had been drinking *gumiz* or chewing the leaves of the plant that made city dwellers crazy.

She walked up the steep stairs without feeling the stone beneath her bare feet. At the top of the steps, a bridge known as the Dead March led the way across a deep ravine to the Castle. Made of wood and rope, the bridge swung between the sheer sides of the defile. Narrow, swaying dangerously whenever anyone stepped on it, the bridge could be crossed only by a few people at a time and was within easy arrow shot of the Castle's battlements. A hostile army attempting to use it was doomed—easy targets for the Castle's archers, who could also shoot flaming arrows that would set the ropes afire and send the entire structure plunging into the canyon below.

Human heads, mounted on poles, guarded the entrance to the Dead March. These were heads of prisoners, captured by the Black Paladins, and made to suffer the most dreadful tortures. By some arcane art, the flesh remained on the skulls and the agonized expressions on the dead faces served to warn all who looked on them what awaited an enemy of the Black Paladins in Castle Zhakrin.

Zohra glanced at the gruesome guardians with uncaring eyes. She navigated the perilously swinging bridge over the ravine with an appearance of calm that had Kiber shaking his head in admiration. Entering the gaping black archway of the Castle without faltering, she passed coolly beneath the red-tipped iron spikes that could be sent crashing down from the ceiling, impaling those who stood beneath them. The skulls grinning at her from the granite walls, the bony hands that held the flaring torches, didn't cause her cheeks to pale or her eyes to widen. Standing in the huge, torchlit hall, she watched the *goums* bear the litter on which Khardan shivered and moaned up a staircase. She had not spoken since they'd left the ship and asked only three questions upon entering the Castle.

"Where are they taking him? Will he recover?" and "What will become of him?"

Kiber glanced at the woman curiously. She certainly didn't sound the wife inquiring about the fate of a beloved husband. Kiber had seen many such in this hall, clinging to their men, being dragged away screaming and weeping. Of course, they had known or guessed what fate awaited their men. Perhaps this woman didn't. . . or perhaps she did and didn't care. Kiber suspected that it might not make much difference; she would never give way to weakness, no matter what she felt. Kiber had never met a woman like her, and he began to envy Auda ibn Jad.

"They are taking him to the Black Sorceress. She is skilled in healing the touch of the *ghuls*. If she chooses, he will recover. Beyond that his fate is up to my master," said Kiber gravely, "and will undoubtedly be determined at the Vestry,"—he stumbled over the word, the only term comparable in her language was "conclave," but this did not give quite the correct nuance.

Her face did not change expression, and he doubted if she understood. Now she will ask about her fate or that of the other red-headed woman. . . man. . . whatever it was.

But she didn't; she didn't say a word. From the expression on her proud face it soon became clear to Kiber that the woman understood; she was simply refusing to speak to someone she obviously considered far beneath her.

This irritated Kiber, who could have gone into detail concerning what would happen to this Zohra-woman, at least. The imagining of it excited him, and he considered telling her anyway, hoping to see her pride punctured by despair's sharp knife. But it wasn't his place to speak. The women brought to Castle Zhakrin either captive or voluntarily were the province of the Black Sorceress, and she would take it adversely if Kiber were to meddle in her affairs. Kiber—as did everyone else in the Castle—went out of his way to avoid offending the Black Sorceress.

Without saying anything further to Zohra, he led her up winding stairs to a spire known as the Tower of Women. There was no guard at the door; fear of the Black Sorceress was guard enough—the man who entered the Tower of Women at any other time except the scheduled hours would rue the day he had been born. So powerful was this influence that even though he was here on business, Kiber still felt uncomfortable. He opened the door and took a cautious step inside.

Silent figures shrouded in black robes glided away at his coming, melting into the shadows of the dark and gloomy hallway, their eyes darting frightened or curious glances at his prisoner. The air was heavy with perfume. The only sounds that broke the silence were the occasional cry of a baby or, far away, the scream of a woman giving birth.

Kiber hurried Zohra to a small room that stood just opposite the main entryway. Opening the door, he shoved her roughly inside.

"Wait here," he said. "Someone will come."

Hastily he shut the door, locking it with a silver key that hung from a black ribbon wrapped around a nail in the shining black wall. He returned the key to its place and started to leave, but his eyes were drawn to an archway that stood to his right. A curtain of heavy red velvet blocked the arch; he could not see beyond it. But from it wafted the scent of the perfume that hung in the air. The smell and the knowledge of what went on behind that curtain made his heart beat, his loins ache. Every night at midnight, the Black Paladins mounted the stairs and entered the Tower of Women. They and they alone had the right to pass beyond the red velvet curtain.

The sound of a door opening down the hall to his left made Kiber start. Wrenching his gaze from the curtain, he yanked open the door leading out of the Tower with such haste that he very nearly hit himself in the head.

"Kiber?" said a dried, rasping voice.

Pale-faced and sweating, Kiber turned around, his hand still on the wrought iron handle of the door.

"Madam," he said faintly.

Facing him was a woman of such small stature she might have been mistaken for a frail girl of twelve years. In reality, she counted seven times that number, though no sign of those years could be seen upon her face. What arcane art she used to cheat age none could tell, although it was whispered she drank the blood of stillborn babes. Her beauty was undeniable, but it did not foster desire. The cheeks were free of wrinkles, but their smoothness—on close observation—was not the tender firmness of youth but that of the taut, stretched skin of a drum. The eyes were lustrous, it was the glow of power's flame that brightened them. The breasts, rising and falling beneath black velvet, were soft and ripe, yet no man sought to pillow his head there, for the heart that beat beneath them was ruthless and cold. The white hands that beckoned Kiber so gracefully were stained with the blood of countless innocents.

"You have brought another one?" the woman inquired in a low, sweet voice whose dread music stilled the heart.

"Yes, Madam," Kiber answered.

"Come into my room and give me your report." The woman vanished back into the fragrant shadows without waiting to see if her command was obeyed.

There was no question that it would be. Kiber, with a quivering sigh, entered the chambers of the Black Sorceress, wishing devoutly he was anywhere else, even setting foot upon the *ghuls'* ship instead. Far better his flesh be devoured than his soul, doomed to Sul's abyss—if the Sorceress chose—where not even his God would be able to find him.

Alone in the room, Zohra stood staring at nothing. There was no one to see her now. Pride, because it feeds on others, began to starve and waste away quickly, and hysteria was there to take its place. Zohra lifted her face to the Heavens, a cry burning in her throat.

"Free me, Akhran!" she screamed furiously, flailing her arms. "Free me from this prison!"

The frenzied excitement lasted only moments, draining her remaining strength. Zohra sank down to the floor and lay there in a kind of stupor, eventually slipping into exhausted sleep.

The cold woke her. Shivering, Zohra sat up. The nap had

done her some good. She felt strong enough to blush with shame over the memory of her outburst. Anger returned, too, anger at Mathew for involving her in this and then abandoning her, anger at Khardan for his failures, anger at the God for refusing to answer her prayers.

"I am alone, as I have always been alone," Zohra said to herself. "I must do what I can to leave this horrible place and return to my people."

Rising to her feet, she walked over and tried to open the door. It was locked. She jerked on the handle several times, but it refused to give. Biting her lip in frustration, she turned and looked around the room, examining it for a way out.

An iron brazier standing on a tripod in a corner lighted the chamber, which was small and square and high-ceilinged. It had no windows and no other door except the one against which Zohra leaned. A handwoven carpet of extraordinarily beautiful design covered the floor, several black lacquer chairs were placed about the rug, small tables stood beside them.

Shivering in her wet clothes, Zohra walked the length and width of the room, searching for even the smallest crack. There was none, she realized, and the thought came to her, then, that she was trapped within these four walls. Never before had she been in any walled place. The yurts in which her people lived were temporary dwellings, made to let in air and light. They adapted to nature, permitted it entry. They did not shut it out and deny it.

The cold stone walls seemed to grow thicker the longer Zohra stared at them. Their solid structure and permanence weighted her down. The air was smoky and filled with dust that covered the furniture and the floor. She felt an increasing sensation of being unable to catch her breath and sank down into one of the chairs. The room was smaller than she'd noticed. What would happen when she used up all the air? She shrank back in the chair, panting, nervously twisting the rings on her fingers.

"Princess!" cried a distraught voice.

A puff of white smoke issued from a ring and hovered on the floor before her, swelling like a ball of flabby white dough. A turban, a pair of yellow silk *pantalons*, pointed shoes, and a fat face, squinched up in misery, gradually took form.

"Usti!" gasped Zohra.

Throwing himself at Zohra's feet, the djinn wrapped his fat

arms around her legs and burst into tears.

"Save me, Princess!" he wailed. "Save me!"

CHAPTER 6

"Save *you*?" repeated Zohra angrily, trying without success to free herself from the grip of the clinging, blubbering djinn. "I'll save you—in a goatskin!"

"Goatskin!" Usti hastily released his hold on Zohra. Sitting back on his heels, he groaned and mopped his eyes with the cloth of his turban that had come partially unwound and dangled down the side of his head. The djinn's clothes were torn and bedraggled, his face was grimy—now streaked with slobber, its expression woeful.

"I beg your pardon, Princess," whimpered the djinn. Every chin aquiver, he hiccuped. "But my life has been one of unendurable torment!"

"Your—!" Zohra began.

"For months," wailed Usti, placing his hands on his fat knees and rocking back and forth, "I've been sealed up inside . . . inside—"

He couldn't even say the word but pointed a trembling finger at the ring of smoky quartz on Zohra's hand.

"It was awful! When the 'efreet, Kaug, attacked the camp, my dwelling was destroyed. Fortunately I was outside of it at the time. I sought shelter in the first place I could find! That ring! And now, all these months, I've been trapped there! Nothing to eat and drink!" he sobbed wretchedly. "Nothing to do and no room to do it in. I've lost weight!" He gestured at his rotund stomach. "I'm skin and bones. And—"

Usti caught his breath in a gulp. Zohra had risen to her feet and was staring down at him with the formidable expression he knew so well.

"Skin and bones! You'll wish you were skin and bones, you bloated, oversized pig's bladder! I've been taken prisoner, brought to a sea that doesn't exist, carried across it on a ship filled with demons, and dragged to this awful place! Trapped in a ring!"

Glaring at the djinn, who was trying desperately to appear impressed and failing utterly, Zohra drew in a seething breath. Her hands flexed, her nails gleamed in the dim light. Usti's eyes flared wide in alarm, his visage began to waver.

The djinn was leaving!

She would be alone again!

"No! Don't go!" Zohra calmed herself. Sinking back into the chair, she held out a placating hand. "I didn't mean what I said. I—I'm frightened. I don't like this place or these people. You must free me! Get me out of here! You can do that, can't you, Usti?"

"Immortals, Princess, can do anything," said Usti loftily.

"You will take me back to my brazier?"

"Yes, of course!"

"You won't make me return to that ring?"

"No!" Zohra snapped, exasperated, keeping a tight hold on the arms of the chair to prevent herself from grabbing hold of the djinn by the collar of his ripped silken shirt and shaking him until the remainder of his turban unrolled. "Hurry! Someone might come!"

"Very well," said Usti placidly. "First, I must know where we are."

"We're here!" Zohra cried, waving her hands.

"Unless the walls deign to speak, this tells me nothing," said the djinn coldly.

"Surely you were listening!" Zohra said accusingly. "You must know where we are!"

"Princess, how can you possibly have expected me, in my state of mental agony, to pay attention to the generally trite and uninteresting prattlings of mortals?" Usti was aggrieved.

Zohra's words came out strained through tightly clenched teeth. "We are being held captive by those who call themselves Black Paladins. They serve a God named Shakran or something—"

"Zhakrin, Princess?"

"Yes, that seems right. And we are on an island in the—"

"—middle of the Kurdin Sea," finished Usti crisply. "An island known as Galos. This, then, must be Castle Zhakrin." He glanced about with interest. "I have heard of this place."

"Good!" Zohra sighed in relief. "Now, hurry. You must take me"—she hesitated, thinking rapidly—"*us* out of here." Khardan would be forever in her debt. This would make twice she had saved his life.

"Impossible," said Usti. "Us? Who's us?"

"What do you mean—impossible!" Zohra's hands curled over the arms of the chair, her eyes glittered feverishly.

Usti blanched but did not quail before his mistress's anger. An expression of self-righteousness illumined his fat face. Clasping his fingers over his stomach, he said importantly, "I swore an oath."

"Yes, to serve your mistress, you—!"

"Begging your pardon, Princess, but this oath takes precedence and would be so adjudged in the Immortals' Court. It is a rather long story—"

"But one I am eager to hear!" Zohra's lip curled dangerously.

Usti gulped, but he had right on his side and so proceeded. "It involved my former master two masters ago, one Abu Kir, a man exceedingly fond of his food. It was he, the blessed Abu Kir, may Akhran himself have the pleasure of dining with him in heaven, who taught me the delights of the palate." Usti gave a moist hiccup. "And to think I should be forced to talk about him, I—who have not dined in months! Be still, poor shriveled thing"—he patted his stomach—"we shall dine soon, if there is anything fit to eat in this wretched place. Yes," he continued hastily, "begging your pardon, Princess. We were speaking of Abu Kir. One night, Abu Kir summoned me forth.

"'Usti, my noble friend, I have a taste this evening for kumquats.'

"'Nothing easier, My Master,' I said, being, of course, always willing to serve. 'I will send for the slave to run to the market.'

"'Ah, it is not that easy, Usti,' said Abu Kir. 'The kumquats I fancy grow only in one place—the garden of the immortal Quar. I have heard that one taste of their sweet, thick lusciousness, and a human will forget all trouble and care.'

"'Truly, Master, you have heard correctly. I myself have tasted them, and that is no exaggeration. But acquiring the fruits of that garden is more difficult than inducing the mother of a beautiful young virgin to let her daughter spend the night in your bed. In fact, Master, if you but command it, I have a virgin in mind that will make you forget all about kumquats."

"'Women!' said Abu Kir in scorn. 'What are they compared to food! Fetch me the kumquats of Quar's garden, Usti, and I will—in turn—grant you your freedom!'

"I could not refuse such a generous offer; besides, I am—as you know, Princess—most devoted to those I serve and do my best to please them. A djinn of Akhran could not very well walk into the garden of Quar, however, and beg for kumquats, especially when Kaug—may his snout suck up sea water—is the gardener.

"Therefore I went to an immortal of Quar's and asked him if he would be so kind as to fetch me several kumquats from the garden of his master.

"'Nothing would give me greater pleasure,' said Quar's djinn. 'And I would fly to do so right now except that my mistress has had her favorite jade-and-coral necklace stolen by one of the followers of Benario. I was currently on my way to try to persuade one of the God's light-fingered immortals to persuade his master to return it. Otherwise, dear Usti, I would bring you the kumquats.'

"He looked at me out of the corner of his slanted eye as he spoke, and I knew what I must do to obtain the kumquats.

"Off I went to the immortal of Benario, first taking care, as you might imagine, that I had left my purse safely in my charcoal brazier."

Zohra leaned her head on her hand.

"I told you it was a long story," Usti said deprecatingly.

"How long until we get to Zhakrin and your 'oath'?"

"Just coming to that, Princess. You see, the immortal of Benario promised to return the jade-and-coral necklace in exchange for an assassin's dagger made by the followers of Zhakrin. Therefore I went—"

"Shhh!" Sitting up, Zohra stared at the door. The sound of rustling could be heard outside, a strong scent of perfume drifted into the room.

"Musk," said Usti, sneezing.

"Shhh!" Zohra hissed.

A key rattled in the lock.

"Get back into the ring!" Zohra whispered.

"Princess!" Usti stared at her in horror.

"Do as I command!" Zohra said fiercely, holding out her left hand, the smoky quartz sparkling on her finger.

The lock on the door clicked. Usti cast a despairing glance at the ring. The door began to open. The djinn gasped, as though struck a physical blow. He gave the door a terrified glance. His eyeballs bulging in his head, he changed instantly into smoke, spiraled up to the ceiling, and dove headlong into the ring.

Zohra took a moment to glance at the ring as the djinn disappeared inside. It was a plain silver ring with its darkish gem. It was ugly, and it wasn't hers. Hurriedly, she clapped her hand over it and turned to face her visitor.

A woman stood in the doorway, delicately sniffing the air. Her face was not veiled; she wore no covering over her head. Thick hair, chestnut brown, was pulled back into a tight, intricately twisted coil worn on the back of her head. Her robes of black velvet swept the floor as she walked; the symbol of the severed snake that Zohra had seen both on Khardan's armor and fluttering from the mast of the *ghuls'* ship adorned her left breast. Her face was remarkable for its clear-cut beauty, but—in the light of the brazier standing near the door—the white skin took on a grayish cast, reminding Zohra of the ivory jars the *goums* had loaded aboard the ship.

"I demand that you release me." The words were on Zohra's lips, but they were never uttered.

The woman said nothing. She simply stood in the door-way, her hand on the handle, looking at Zohra intently with eyes whose color was indistinguishable. Zohra met and returned the gaze haughtily at first. Then she noticed that her eyes began to sting and water. She might have been looking directly into the sun. The sensation became painful. The woman had neither moved nor spoken; she stared straight at Zohra. But Zohra could no longer look at her. Tears blurred her vision; the pain grew, spreading from her eyes to her head. She averted her gaze, and instantly the pain ceased. Breathing hard, she stared at the floor, not daring to look back at the strange woman.

"Who has been here?" the woman asked.

Zohra heard the door shut, the rustle of black robes whisper across the floor. The odor of musk was overpowering, choking.

"No one," said Zohra, her hand covering the ring, her eyes on the carpet at her feet.

"Look at me when you speak. Or do you fear me?"

"I do not fear anyone!" Zohra proudly lifted her head and glanced at the woman, but the pain returned and she started to turn away. Reaching out, the woman caught hold of Zohra's chin in her hand and held it firmly. Her grip was unusually strong.

"Look at me!" she said again, softly.

Zohra had no choice but to stare straight into the woman's eyes. The pain became excruciating. Zohra cried out, shutting her eyelids and struggling to free herself. The woman held her fast.

"Who was here?" she asked again.

"No one!" Zohra cried thickly, the pain throbbing in her head.

The woman held her long seconds. Blood beat in Zohra's temples, she felt nauseous and faint, then, suddenly, the hand released its hold, the woman turned away.

Gasping, Zohra slumped over in her chair. The pain was gone.

"Kiber said you were brave." The woman's voice touched her now like cool water, soothing her. Zohra heard the robes rustle, the soft sound of a chair being moved across the carpeting. The woman settled herself directly across from Zohra, within arm's reach. Cautiously Zohra lifted her eyes and looked at the woman once more. The pain did not return. The woman smiled at her approvingly, and Zohra relaxed.

"Kiber is quite an admirer of yours, my dear," said the woman. "As is Auda ibn Jad, from what I hear. I congratulate you. Ibn Jad is an extraordinary man. He has never before requested a specific woman."

Zohra tossed her head contemptuously. The subject of Auda ibn Jad was not worthy of being discussed. "I have been brought here by mistake," she said. "The one called Mat-hew is the one you want. You have him, therefore you must—"

"—let you go?" The woman's smile widened, a mother being forced to refuse a child some absurd demand. "No, my dear. Nothing ever happens by mischance. All is as the God desires it. You were brought here for a purpose. Perhaps it may be the very great honor of increasing the God's followers. Perhaps"—the woman hesitated, studying Zohra more intently—"perhaps there is another reason. But, no, you were not brought here by mistake, and you will not be released."

"Then I will go of my own accord!" Zohra rose to her feet.

"The Guardians of our Castle are called *nesnas*," said the woman conversationally. "Have you ever heard of them, my dear? They have the shape of a man—a man that has been divided in half vertically, possessing half a head, one arm, half a trunk, one leg, one foot. They are forced to hop on that one leg, but they can do so quite swiftly, as fast as a human can run on two. There have been one or two women who have managed to escape the Castle. We do not know what happened to them, for they were never seen again, although we heard their screams several nights running. We do know, however"—the woman smoothed a fold of her velvet robes—"that the *nesnas'* population increases, and we can only assume that, though they are half men in almost all aspects, there must be one aspect, at least, in which they are whole."

Slowly, Zohra sank back into her seat.

"I did not think you would want to leave us quite this soon."

"Who are you?"

"I am called the Black Sorceress. My husband is the Lord of the Black Paladins. He and I have ruled our people over seventy years."

Zohra stared at the woman in astonishment.

"My age? Yes, I see you find that remarkable. I can promise you the same eternal youth, my dear, if you prove tractable."

"What do you want of me?"

"Now you are being reasonable. We want your body. That and the fruit it will bear. Have you ever borne children?"

Zohra shook her head disdainfully.

"Yes, you are wife to the one who was attacked by the *ghuls*."

Zohra's face burned. Pressing her lips together, she stared into the flickering light of the brazier. She could feel the eyes of the sorceress on her and she had the uncomfortable sensation that the woman could see into the very depths of her soul.

"Extraordinary," the sorceress murmured. "Let me tell you, my dear, how the God chooses to honor women brought into this Castle. Those who are found worthy are selected to be the Breeders. It is they who are increasing the followers of Zhakrin so that our great God can return to us in strength and in might. Every night these women are placed into special rooms, and each midnight the Black Paladins enter this tower and go to the rooms. Here, each man honors the chosen woman by depositing his seed within her womb. When that seed takes, and the woman becomes pregnant, she is removed from the rooms and is well cared for until the babe is delivered. Then she is returned to the rooms to conceive another—"

"I would die first," stated Zohra calmly.

"Yes," remarked the sorceress, smiling. "I believe you would. Many say that, in the early days, and a few have attempted it. But we cannot afford to allow such waste, and I have means by which I make the most obdurate eager to obey my will."

Zohra's lip curled in scorn.

The sorceress rose to her feet. "I will have dry clothing brought to you, as well as food and drink. A room is being prepared for you. When it is ready, you will be taken there."

"You are wasting your time. No man will touch me!" Zohra said, speaking slowly and distinctly.

The sorceress raised an eyebrow, smiled, and glided toward the door, which opened at her approach. Two women, dressed in black robes similar to those of the sorceress, slipped noiselessly inside the room. One bore a bundle of black velvet in her arms, the other carried a tray of food. Neither woman spoke to Zohra or even looked at her, but kept their eyes lowered. Under the watchful gaze of the sorceress, they deposited the clothes upon a chair and set the tray of food upon a table. Then they silently departed. The sorceress, giving Zohra one final glance, followed them.

Zohra listened for the key but did not hear it. Swiftly, she ran to the door and pressed her ear against it. When all sounds had ceased in the corridor, she pulled on the handle. The door remained sealed fast. From far away, Zohra thought she heard a soft tinkle of laughter. Angrily, she whirled around.

"Usti!" she whispered.

Nothing happened.

"Usti!" she repeated furiously, shaking the ring.

Smoke drizzled out, coalescing into the form of a pale and shaken djinn.

"That woman is a witch!"

"To say the least. Oath or no oath, you must get me out of here!"

"No, Mistress!" Usti licked his lips. "She is a witch! A true witch! In all my lifetimes, I have never met such a powerful human. She knew I was here!"

"Impossible!" Zohra scoffed. "Quit making excuses and return Khardan and me to our desert this instant!" She stamped her foot.

"She spoke to me!" Usti began to tremble. "She told me what she would do to me if I crossed her. Princess"—he began to blubber—"I do not want to spend my eternal life sealed up in an iron box, wrapped round with iron chains! Farewell, Princess!"

The djinn leaped back into the ring with such alacrity that Zohra was momentarily blinded by the swirl of smoke. Enraged, she grabbed hold of the circlet of silver, and tried to yank it from her finger. It was stuck fast. She tugged and twisted, but the ring would not come off, and finally, her finger swollen and aching, she gave up.

She was shaking with cold. The smell of food made her mouth water.

"I must keep up my strength," she said to herself. "Since it seems I must fight this alone, it won't do to fall sick from a chill or hunger."

Her mind searching for some way out of this situation, Zohra stripped off her wet gown and replaced it with the black robes on the chair. Clothed and warm again, she sat down to dine. As she lifted the cover from the tray, her eyes caught the glimmer of steel.

"Ah!" Zohra breathed and swiftly picking up the knife, she tucked it into a pocket of her gown.

The food was delicious. All her favorites were on the various plates—stripes of *shiskhlick* grilled to her exact taste, succulent fruit, honey cakes, and candied almonds. A carafe as filled to the brim with clear, cold water, and she drank thirstily. Her strength returned and with it hope. The knife pressed reassuringly against her flesh. She could use it to force the door lock, then make her way out of the Castle. Dressed like all the others, she would simply be taken for one of the other women, and surely they must go about the castle on some errand or other. Once outside—Zohra thought of the *nesnas*.

Half men who hop on one leg! The sorceress must take her for a child to believe such stories. Zohra had a momentary regret in leaving Khardan; she recalled him lying in the litter, shivering and moaning in agony; she saw the bluish-purplish scratches on his arm and body, and she remembered guiltily that he had been willing to give his life to defend her.

Well, she told herself, it was all for his own honor, anyway. He cares nothing for me. He hates me for what Mathew and I did to him; humiliating him by taking him from the battlefield. I shouldn't have done it. That vision was stupid. Undoubtedly it was some trick of Mathew's to . . . to . . .

How hot it was! Zohra loosened the neck of the robe, unbuttoning the tiny buttons that held it together. It was growing unbearably warm. She seemed to smell again the stifling odor of musk. She was becoming sleepy, too. She should not have eaten so much. Blinking her heavy eyelids, Zohra struggled to her feet.

"I must keep awake!" she said aloud, tossing some of the cool water on her face. Standing up, she began to walk around the room, only to feel the floor slip away beneath her feet. She staggered into a chair and grabbed hold of it for support. The light coming from the brazier was surrounded, suddenly, by a rainbow of color. The walls of the room began to breathe in and out. Her tongue seemed dry, and there was an odd taste in her mouth.

Zohra stumbled back to the table, clinging to chairs, and grabbed hold of the water carafe. She lifted it to her lips. . .

"I have means by which I can make the most obdurate eager to obey my will."

The carafe fell to the floor with a crash.

Two women, clothed in black, carried Zohra from the antechamber. Zohra's eyes were open, she stared at them dreamily, a vacant, vacuous smile on her lips.

"What do we do with her?"

The Black Sorceress looked down at the nomad woman, then raised her eyes to the red velvet curtain covering the archway. The two women holding Zohra by her arms and legs exchanged swift glances; one lowered her eyes to her own swelling belly, and a small sigh escaped her lips.

"No," said the Black Sorceress after a moment's profound thought. "I am not clear in my mind about this one. The God's message is to wait. Take her to the chamber next to mine."

The women nodded silently and moved down the hall, carrying their burden between them.

The sonorous clanging of an iron bell, sounding from a tower high above them, caused the Black Sorceress to lift her head.

Her eyes gleamed.

"Vestry," she murmured, and wrapping her fingers around an amulet she wore at her neck, she disappeared.

CHAPTER 7

Ouda ibn Jad had been at Mathew's side, step for step and almost heartbeat for heartbeat, as they made their way up from the beach to Castle Zhakrin. Mathew's sodden wet clothes clung to him. The mournful wind cut through his flesh like slivers of ice, but was nothing compared to the cold, glittering side-ways glances of the Black Paladin. Always the focus of that piercing gaze—even when ibn Jad was talking to a fellow knight—Mathew had a difficult time maintaining his composure when faced with the horrors of the Castle. A follower of Astafas, he was certain, would not stare fearfully at the gruesome heads that guarded the bridge, or shrink away from the human skeletons on the walls.

By the time ibn Jad had escorted him to an antechamber located on the ground level of the palace, and left him there alone with a flask of wine to ease the chill, Mathew thought that he had performed adequately. No credit to himself. After the long walk to the Castle in the company of the Black Paladin, the young wizard was so miserable and cold that he doubted if any emotion other than terror was left inside him.

Shivering so he could barely keep hold of the glass, Mathew drank a little wine, hoping to lift his spirits and warm his blood. All the wine squeezed from every grape in the world could not obliterate reality, however.

I may have deceived ibn Jad, he thought, but I can never hope to deceive the Black Sorceress. A skilled Archmagus would see through me as if I were crystal. Mathew had little doubt—from the obviously high regard in which this woman was held—that this Black Sorceress was, indeed, very skilled.

Hoping to distract himself from his mounting fear, Mathew listlessly examined his surroundings. The room was bleak and comfortless. A huge fireplace dominated almost one entire wall, but no fire burned there. Fuel must be difficult to obtain on this barren isle, Mathew realized, peering wistfully at the cold ashes upon the hearth. He knew now why everyone dressed in such heavy clothing and began to think with longing of soft black velvet draping him with warmth. Drawing back thick red curtains, he found a window. Made of large panes of leaded, stained glass bearing the design of the severed snake, it had no bars and looked as if it could be easily opened. Mathew had no wish to try it, however. Though he could not see them, he sensed the dark and evil beings that lurked outside. His life would not be worth a copper's purchase if he set foot beyond the Castle walls.

Turning back, leaning upon the mantelpiece above the chill fireplace, Mathew saw no hope for them—for any of them. Auda ibn Jad had described in a cold, dispassionate voice what fate awaited Zohra in the Tower of Women. The Black Paladin made it clear that he admired the nomad woman for the strong and spirited followers she would deliver to the God, adding that he planned to request her for his own private use, at least to father her first few children. Ibn Jad's talk of his intentions sickened Mathew more then the sight of the polished skulls adorning the stair railings. If the man had spoken with lust or desire, he would at least have demonstrated some human feeling, if only of the basest nature. Instead, Auda ibn Jad spoke as if he were discussing the breeding of sheep or cattle.

"What will happen to Khardan?" Mathew had asked, abruptly changing the subject.

"Ah, that I cannot say," was Auda's reply. "It will be up to the members of the Vestry this night. I can only make my recommendation."

Alone in the bitterly cold room, sipping the wine that tasted like blood in his mouth, Mathew wondered what this meant. Recalling the human heads mounted on the Dead March, he shuddered. But surely if they were intent only upon murdering Khardan they would not go through such ceremony. Ibn Jad had been ready to toss the Calif to the *ghuls*, but that had been done in anger or . . .

Mathew stared into the flame of a candle burning on the mantelpiece. Perhaps it had been a test. Perhaps ibn Jad had never intended to give Khardan to the *ghuls*.

A soft knock upon the door made Mathew start; his hand

shook so that he sloshed wine on his wet clothes. He tried to bid the person enter, but his voice couldn't escape past the choking sensation in his throat. Not that it mattered; the door opened and a woman stepped inside.

She smote Mathew with the heat of the blazing desert sun, blinding him, burning him. Her evil was deep and dark and ancient as the Well of Sul. Her majesty overawed, her power overwhelmed, and Mathew bowed before her as he would have bowed to the head of his own Order. He was conscious of eyes studying him, eyes that had studied countless others before him, eyes that were old and wise in the knowledge of the terrible depths of the human soul.

There could be no lying to those eyes.

"You come from Tirish Aranth," said the Black Sorceress. The door shut silently behind her.

"Yes, Madam," answered Mathew inaudibly.

"That facet of the Jewel of Sul shared by Promenthas and your God, Astafas."

"Yes, Madam." Did she know he lied? How could she not? She must know everything.

"I have heard that in this part of the world men have the gift of magic. I have never met a male sorcerer before. You are man and not eunuch?"

"I am a man," Mathew murmured, his face flushing.

"How old are you?"

"Eighteen."

He was conscious of the eyes staring at him intently, and then suddenly he was enveloped by a fragrance of heady musk. The walls around him changed to water and began to slide down into some vast ocean that was rising up around him. Soft lips touched his, skillful hands caressed his body. The smell, the touch aroused almost instantaneous desire. . . . And then he heard a laugh.

The water disappeared, the walls surrounded him again, the fragrance was blown away by a cold wind. Gasping, he caught his breath.

"I am sorry," said the sorceress, amused, "but I had to make certain you were telling the truth. A man your age with no beard, features and skin any woman might envy. I have heard it said that men gained magic at the price of their manhood, but I see that is not so."

Breathing heavily, his body burning with shame and embarrassment, disgust twisting his stomach, Mathew could not reply nor even look at the woman.

"Male children born to you will acquire this gift?"

"They may or may not," answered Mathew, wondering at this unexpected question. Then Auda ibn Jad's description of the Tower of Women came to his mind. He lifted his head and stared at her.

"Yes." She answered his thought. "You will prove quite valuable to us. Male magi!" The sorceress drew in a deep breath of pleasure. "Warriors trained to kill with arcane weapons! We could well become invincible. It is a pity"—she regarded him coolly—"that there aren't more of you. Perhaps Astafas could be persuaded to lend us others?"

"I—I'm certain. . . he would be honored, as would I, t—to serve you," stammered Mathew, not knowing what else to say. The suggestion appalled him, he felt again the touch of the woman's hands on his body, and he hastily averted his face, hoping to hide his repugnance.

It obviously didn't work. "Perhaps a bit more manly than you," the sorceress said wryly. "And now tell me, how did one as young and obviously inexperienced as yourself manage to summon and control an imp of Sul?"

Mathew stared at her helplessly. He was a wet rag in this woman's hands. She had wrung him and wrenched him. He had no dignity, no humanity left. She had reduced him to the level of a beast.

"I don't know!" He hung his head. "I don't know!"

"I thought as much," the sorceress said gently. A hand patted him, an arm stole around his shoulder. It was now a mother's touch—soothing and comforting. She led him back to his chair and he sank down, unnerved and sobbing—a child in her arms.

"Forgive me, my son," said the soft voice, and Mathew raised his head and saw the sorceress clearly for the first time. He saw the beauty, the cruelty, the evil, and that strange compassion he had seen on the face of Auda ibn Jad and the other worshipers of Zhakrin. "Poor boy," she murmured and his own mother could not have grieved for him more. "I had to do this to you. I had to make certain." She stroked his face with her hand. "You are new to the paths of the shadow and you find the walking difficult. So do all who come to us from the light, but in time you will grow accustomed to and even revel in the darkness." The sorceress cupped his face in her hands, staring deeply into his eyes.

"And you are fortunate!" she whispered passionately, a thrill in her voice transmitting itself to Mathew's flesh. "Fortunate above all men for Astafas has obviously chosen you to do his bidding! He is granting you power you would otherwise not have! And that means he is aware of us and watching us and supporting our struggle!"

Mathew began to shake uncontrollably as the import of her words and their truth tore open his soul.

"The transition will be painful," said the sorceress, holding him close, pitying his fear, "but so is every birth." She drew his head to her breast, smoothing his hair. "Long I mourned that I could bring only daughters of magic into this world. Long I dreamed of giving birth to a son born to the talent. And now you have come—the Bearer, chosen to guard, to carry our most precious treasure! It is a sign! I take you for my own, from this moment." Her lips pressed against his flesh, stabbing like a knife at his heart. He cringed and cried out with the pain.

"It hurts," she said softly, brushing away a tear that had fallen from her eye onto Mathew's cheek. "I know it hurts, my little one, but the agony will soon end, and then you will find peace. And now I must leave you. The man, Khardan, waits for my ministration so that he may be fit to receive the honor that is going to be bestowed upon him. Here is clothing. Food will be brought to you. Is there anything else you desire— What is your name?"

"Mathew!" The word seemed squeezed out of his chest by his bursting heart.

"Mathew. Nothing else you want? Then make yourself ready. The Vestry convenes at ten this evening, four hours from now. Ah, poor boy." Her tongue clicked against the roof of her mouth. "Fainted dead away. His mind can accept this, but not his heart. It fights me, it fights the darkness. I will win, though. I will win!

"Astafas has given me a son!"

CHAPTER 8

i n Castle Zhakrin was a great hall made entirely of black marble—perfectly circular in shape. Black columns surrounded a large center floorspace in which the signet of the severed serpent, done in gold, had been inlaid in the marble. There was only one piece of furniture in the room at this time, and that was a small table on which stood an object covered with black velvet. The chamber was rarely opened and then only for ceremonial purposes, for the hall was known as the Vestry and it was here that the followers of Zhakrin met once monthly or, as on this occasion, whenever there was something of special significance to be brought before the people.

Having stored up winter's chill in its stone walls, the cold in the hall froze the heart. The black marble, gleaming in the light of innumerable torches that had been placed in sconces fashioned from the bones of human hands, might have been ice for the freezing breath it gave off. Mathew huddled thankfully within the warm, thick velvet of his new black robes, his hands folded in the sleeves.

At ten o'clock an iron bell rang through the Castle. The people of Zhakrin, with solemn mien, began to arrive in the hall. Swiftly and without confusion each took his or her place in the large circle that was forming around the severed serpent. There were fewer women than men. The women were dressed in black robes similar to those of the sorceress, and many were pregnant. Each woman stood beside a Black Paladin, and Mathew realized that these must be their wives. He sensed within almost all the women a powerful gift for magic, and no longer did he have to wonder how these people managed to survive under such harsh and hostile conditions.

Sometimes, standing respectfully a few steps outside the

circle of adults, was a young person of about sixteen years, this being the age required to first begin attending Vestry. From the comments made by those on entering and from the proud and fond looks given these young people, Mathew guessed that they were children of the Paladins. Again he marveled at the strange dichotomy of these people—the love and warmth extended to family members and friends; the heartless cruelty extended to the rest of the world.

The Black Sorceress appeared suddenly next to him, materializing out of the chill air. Remembering what had occurred between them in the room, Mathew lowered his head, a burning flush spreading over his skin. He knew he had fainted, he knew someone had dressed him and warmed him like a child, and he suspected who that person had been. The Black Sorceress gave no sign, either by word or look, that she was aware of his confusion. Standing beside him, she watched calmly and proudly as her people took their places in the circle. It was almost complete, with the exception of several gaps, and these were apparently left deliberately vacant.

"In time, you will be able to take your place with us in the Holy Circle," said the sorceress. "But for now you may not. Wait here and do not stir until you are summoned forth."

"How is Khardan?" Mathew asked softly.

In answer, the Black Sorceress turned her head slightly. Mathew followed her gaze and saw Kiber and another *goum* leading Khardan into the room. The Calif was pale and obviously confused and amazed by what he saw. But he walked firmly and steadily and there was no trace of pain on his face.

"And Zohra?" Mathew continued, swallowing, wondering at his daring.

"Zohra?" The sorceress was only half attending to his words; her eyes were on the gathering assembly.

"The woman who was with us?" Mathew pursued.

The sorceress glanced at him and shook her head, her eyes darkening. "Do not hold onto any interest in her, my son. There are many other women here as beautiful as that wild desert flower. That one is not for you. She has been chosen by another."

The Black Sorceress's voice was reverent and hushed. Thinking she meant Auda ibn Jad, Mathew was startled to see her look at the Black Paladin with a slight frown and a creased brow. "No, and not for him, either. I hope he does not take that ill." Shaking her head to prevent the young wizard from speaking further, the sorceress gave Mathew a reassuring smile, then left him, walking over to take her place in the circle beside the Lord of the Black Paladins.

A solemn hush fell over the assembly. All bowed their heads and clasped their hands before them. The Lord took a step forward.

"Zhakrin, God of Evil, we gather in your name to do you honor this night. We thank you for the safe return of our brother, Auda ibn Jad, and for the fulfillment, at last, of all that we have worked to achieve these many years."

"We thank you, Zhakrin," came the response from around the circle.

"And now, according to ancient tradition, we do honor to the fallen."

The Lord of Black Paladins turned to his wife, who drew near the black velvet-covered table. Removing the cloth, she lifted in her hand a golden chalice. Its foot was the body of a coiled snake, bearing a cup wrapped in its coils. Placing her hand over the chalice, the Black Sorceress whispered arcane words and sprinkled a powder from inside a golden ring she wore on her finger. Entering the circle, she walked slowly across the black marble floor and handed the chalice to Auda ibn Jad. He accepted it from her reverently, bowing his head. Turning to the empty place beside him in the circle, Auda raised the chalice.

"To our brother, Catalus."

"To Catalus," came the response.

Ibn Jad put the chalice to his lips, sipped at whatever was inside, then solemnly moved across the circle to present the chalice to a woman dressed in black.

She spoke in a language Mathew did not understand, but there was an empty place in the circle beside her, as well. The chalice went from hand to hand. Mathew gathered from those words he could understand that many of those being remembered here had died in the city of Meda. Several of the Black Paladins wept openly. A man put his arm around the shoulders of a woman; they drank out of the chalice together, and Mathew understood that a beloved son had been among those who killed themselves in the Temple rather than permit their souls to be offered up to

Quar. The grief of these people moved Mathew deeply. Tears came to his eyes and might have fallen had not the chalice passed again to the Lord of the Black Paladins. He handed it to his wife, who held it reverently.

"Now it is the time to put grief aside and prepare for joy," said the Lord of the Black Paladins. "Our brother, Auda ibn Jad, will now relate to us what he has done on his journeys in the name of Zhakrin."

Auda ibn Jad stepped forward and began to speak. There followed a tale of such atrocities that Mathew's tears were burned out of his eyes and he grit his teeth in order to keep from crying out. Villages burned, the elderly and very young slaughtered without mercy, the fit and strong captured and sold into slavery. Ibn Jad spoke proudly of the murder of the priests and magi of Promenthas who had been so unlucky as to set foot upon the shores of Tara-kan. He described their deaths in detail and went on to relate the sparing of the life of the young sorcerer who—as it turned out—had been sent to them by Astafas.

Cringing, Mathew kept his head lowered, chills shaking his body. He was aware of eyes upon him—eyes of those standing in the circle, the eyes of the Black Sorceress, the eyes of ibn Jad. Mathew was acutely aware, too, of another pair of eyes watching him, and he felt a swift, secret thrill of sweet pain. It was the first time Khardan had ever heard Mathew's story, and he could sense the Calif regarding him with sympathy and dawning understanding.

Auda ibn Jad continued his story, relating how Khardan and his nomads had wrecked the bazaars of Kich, how they had stolen Mathew from ibn Jad, and had then ravaged the Temple of Quar. Ibn Jad did not seem to mind telling tales against himself and related Khardan's bravery and valor in terms that won the Calif murmurs of approval and a grim smile from the Lord of the Black Paladins.

Auda went on to relate how the Amir had taken out his wrath at this effrontery to Quar by attacking the nomads, taking their women and children and young men prisoner, and scattering the tribes. The people of Zhakrin regarded Khardan with the shared compassion of those who have suffered a similar fate. Mathew saw now that ibn Jad was purposefully establishing Khardan as a hero in the eyes of Zhakrin's followers. The words the Black Sorceress had spoken, the "honor to be bestowed upon him" came to Mathew's mind. It all sounded well, as if Khardan were out of danger. But Mathew's uneasiness grew, particularly as he listened to what had occurred during their tourney from the desert of Pagrah north—the cold-blooded butchering of innocent people in the city of Idrith. Now he knew it was their blood—drained from the bodies—contained in those ivory jars, and his soul recoiled in horror as he remembered leaning against the jars on board the ship.

Khardan, too, must be wondering at the Black Paladin's intent. His face dark and suspicious, the Calif watched ibn Jad warily. There was a saying among the nomads that Mathew had heard, and he knew Khardan must be thinking of it now.

"Beware the honeyed tongue. It oft drips poison."

Ibn Jad finished his tale. It was applauded with soft murmurs from the women, deeper-voiced approval from the men. The Lord of the Paladins spoke of his pleasure and the Black Sorceress rewarded Auda with a nod and a smile and another drink from the chalice. Mathew had no idea what the cup contained, but he saw a rising flush come to Auda ibn Jad's pale, stern cheek; the cruel eyes glowed with increasing ferocity. The chalice was then passed from one person in the circle to the next, each taking a drink. It never, apparently, ran dry, and as the cup passed from hand to hand, Mathew saw that each person began to burn with an inner flame.

Ibn Jad returned to his place within the circle, and the Lord stepped forward.

"Now we will speak our recent history, that each may hear it once again so that it echoes forever in the heart. To those who are new to us and hearing this for the first time" his eyes went to Mathew and Khardan—"this will help you to better understand us.

"Long ago, Zhakrin was a rising power in this world. And as is often the way of Sul, when the Facet of Evil began to glow more brightly in the heavens, the Facet of Good gleamed brilliantly as well. Many and glorious were the encounters between the Black Paladins of Zhakrin and the White Knights of Evren, the Good Goddess." The Lord's voice softened, his aged eyes looked far away. "Just barely do I remember that time. I was no more than a boy, squire to my knight. Brave deeds were done in the name of both the Dark and the Light, each striving for supremacy with honor, as becomes knights.

"And then there came a time when the price of honor was too dear." The Lord sighed. "Immortal beings who had long served us no longer answered our prayers. The power of our God Himself was weakened. The people sickened and died, women grew barren. Some turned, then, to other Gods and Zhakrin grew weaker still. And it was in this hour that the followers of Evren began to persecute us—so it seemed—and, in anger and desperation, we fought back. Like dogs, we hunted each other down, expending our dwindling energies in savage hatred. Our numbers lessened, as did theirs, and we were forced to withdraw from the world, to hide in places dark and secret, and then we spent our days and nights searching each other out." The Lord's face grew grim. "No longer were the contests glorious and brave. We could not afford that. We struck by night, by stealth, as did they. Knives in the back replaced swords face-to-face.

"And then came the time when the fire in our hearts turned to black ash, and we knew our God was defeated. All but the most faithful left us then, for we were weak and had only the power within us with which to fight the battle that is this life. We fled here, to this place. With the strength we had remaining, we built this Castle. We cursed the name of Evren and plotted to destroy her followers if it cost us every last drop of our blood.

"Then a God came to us. It was not our God. It was a strange God we had never before seen. He appeared before us, standing in that very place." The Lord gestured at the head of the snake in the floor. "We asked his name. He said he was known only as the Wandering God"—Mathew glanced at Khardan in astonishment; the Calif's mouth sagged open—"and that he brought urgent news. It was not Evren who caused our Zhakrin's downfall. She herself was gone as well, and all her immortals. Her followers hid away as did we.

" 'Your fight is not with each other,' " said this Wandering God. 'You have been duped by one called Quar, who tricked you into nearly destroying each other, and while you were fighting, he took the field and claimed the victory. He seeks to become the One, True God; to make all men bow down and worship him.'

"The strange God disappeared, and we discussed this long among ourselves. We sent our knights to investigate. They found that the Wandering God had spoken the truth. Quar was the rising power in the world. It seemed that there were few who could stop him. Then it was that Auda ibn Jad—at great peril to his life—disguised himself as a priest of Quar and penetrated the very inner circles of the God's Temple in the Emperor's court of Khandar. Here he discovered the essences of Zhakrin and Evren, held prisoner by Quar. Auda ibn Jad summoned my wife to his aid. Together and in secret they succeeded in snatching the souls of the Gods from Quar, who even now, perhaps, is not yet aware that they are gone.

"Last time we met, you heard my wife's story of this daring theft. You heard her relate their final triumph. She and her knights traveled back here, drawing off pursuit, leaving Auda ibn Jad and his brave soldiers to slip unobserved into Ravenchai with the precious treasure they guarded. This night you have heard him relate his adventures in returning home to us. And now you—"

Mathew heard no more. The sound of pounding waves, the roar of rushing wind throbbed in his head. Pressing his hand over his breast, he felt the crystal globe cold and smooth against his skin.

The Bearer.

He knew now what he carried. Two fish—one dark, one light...

Mathew stared at the knights aghast, saw them all turn to look at him. The Lord's mouth was moving, he was saying something but his words were obliterated by the throbbing in Mathew's head and he couldn't hear. The Black Sorceress stepped into his line of vision and into his heart and his mind. She was all he could see, could think about. Her words alone he could understand, and when she raised her hand and beckoned, he responded.

"Let the Bearer come forward."

Moving slowly, Mathew stepped toward the Holy Circle. It broke and opened for him, it absorbed him and closed around him.

The Black Sorceress came to stand directly before the young wizard.

"Give me that which you bear," she said softly.

There was no denying her. Mathew's hand moved by her will, not his own. Reaching into the bosom of his black robes, he drew forth the crystal globe and held it in his trembling palm.

The golden fish remained motionless in the center of the

globe; the black fish swam about in wide circles, its mouth opening wide, striking in excitement at his crystal walls.

Breathing a reverent sigh, the Black Sorceress lifted the globe gently and carefully. Mathew felt the slight weight leave his hands and a great weight, not noticed until now, leave his heart. The sorceress carried the globe to the table and laid it down beside the chalice. Then she covered both with the black velvet cloth.

"Hear me, my people." Her voice rang triumphantly through the Vestry. "Tomorrow night, our god, Zhakrin, will return to us!"

There was no sound from the God's followers, no cheering. The matter touched the soul too deeply for the voice to echo it. Their victory shone in their eyes.

"He will be weak and thus He has chosen to reside in a human body until He can gain strength and return to His immortal form. This will mean the death of the body in which He chooses to reside for His short stay upon this plane, for He will be forced to suck it dry of its life's juices to feed him—"

Auda ibn Jad sprang forward. "Let Him take my body!" "Mine! Mine!" shouted the Black Paladins, breaking the circle, vying with each other for the honor.

The Black Sorceress. raised her hand for silence.

"Thank you all. The God takes note of your courage. But He has made His choice and"—the sorceress smiled proudly—"it is to be the body of a female. As man is born of woman, so shall our God be brought forth in the body of a woman. Because He will not diminish the number of his followers, He has selected one of our female prisoners—the newest one. She is strong in magic, which the God will find useful. She is intelligent, strong-willed and spirited—"

"No!"

Mathew's mouth formed the word, but it was Khardan who shouted it.

"Take my body, if it's flesh you need to feed your accursed God!" the Calif cried fiercely, struggling to break free of Kiber and the *goum*, straining against them with such strength that Auda ibn Jad left his place within the circle and moved near Khardan, his hand on the hilt of the sword he wore at his waist. Turning, the Paladin looked back at the sorceress with a raised eyebrow.

She nodded, appearing well pleased. "It is as you said, ibn Jad.

The nomad is noble and honorable. We know that he is strong and his spirit that of a warrior. You may begin his training tonight." Her eyes fixed upon Khardan. "Your offer becomes you, sir. But to accept such a sacrifice would be a tragic waste, abhorred by our God. You have proven your merit and will, therefore, serve Zhakrin in another way. You will begin your preparation to become one of the Black Paladins."

"I serve Akhran, the Wanderer, and no other!" Khardan retorted.

"As of now you serve Him. That will change," said the Black Sorceress gravely. "Since the circle has been broken, our Vestry is concluded. Auda ibn Jad, you will take the man below. His preparation will begin at once.

"We will reconvene tomorrow night at eleven o'clock," the sorceress continued, speaking to all. "The ceremony begins at midnight—the ending of one day and the beginning of another. So shall our God's return mark the beginning of a new time for the world."

"One question before we depart," said the Lord of the Black Paladins.

The sorceress turned respectfully to face her husband.

"We have here two holy beings—Zhakrin and Evren. What will we do with the Goddess of Good?"

"Because she is a Goddess and we but mortals, we are powerless to offer Her either help or harm. Her fate rests in the hands of Zhakrin."

The Lord nodded, and the people began to file out of the Vestry. The Black Sorceress remained, beckoning several of the women to join her. Their conversation was low and hushed, probably discussing tomorrow night's ceremony. Auda ibn Jad ordered Kiber, with a gesture, to bring Khardan, and together they left the Vestry.

Mathew glanced around. No one was paying any attention to him. He could see ibn Jad and his men traversing a narrow corridor. If I'm going to follow them, I must do so now, before they leave me behind. Silently, after one final look, he stole from the Vestry.

The eyes of the Black Sorceress did not mark his passing, but his footsteps resounded in her heart.

CHAPTER 9

When did I begin to lose control? Khardan wondered angrily.

For twenty-five years, I've held life in my hand like a lump of cold iron ready for the forging. Then, suddenly, the iron changed to sand. Life began to slide through my fingers, and the harder I grasped hold of it, the more fell away from me.

It all started with the God's command that I marry Zohra and wait for that accursed Rose of the Prophet to bloom. What have I done to offend the God that he treats me thus? What have my people done? Why has Akhran allowed me to be brought here when my people need me? Instead of helping us to defeat our enemies, why has he chosen to appear to these *kafir* and assist them in their evil plots?

"Hear my prayer, Akhran!" Khardan muttered angrily. "Send my djinn to me! Or appear here with your fiery sword and free me!"

In the passion of his plea, the nomad strained against the leather thongs that bound his wrists together. Kiber growled, and a knife flashed in the light of a torch. Whirling, Khardan turned to face his attacker. Bound as he was, he was prepared to fight for his life, but Auda ibn Jad shook his head. Reaching out, he took the knife from Kiber, grabbed hold of Khardan's arms, and pushed him up against a wall. The knife sliced through the leather thongs.

"That will be all for the night, Kiber," Auda said. "You have leave to go to your quarters."

The *goum* bowed and, after giving Khardan one final, threatening glance, departed. Walking back down the hallway, Kiber seemed not to notice—since he had been given no orders concerning the matter—the black shape moving some distance behind them that vanished precipitously into the deeper darkness of an open doorway at the *goum's* approach.

Khardan rubbed his wrists and stared suspiciously at ibn Jad. The two were alone in a shadowy hallway that was spiraling downward, taking them deep beneath the ground level of the Castle.

"Fight me!" Khardan said abruptly. "Your sword. My bare hands. It doesn't matter."

Auda ibn Jad appeared amused. "I admire your spirit, nomad, but you lack discipline and common sense. What have either of us to gain by fighting? Perhaps you could defeat me, although I doubt it, for I am well trained in forms of hand-to-hand combat of which you have no conception. Still, by some mischance you might win. Then what? Where would you go? Back to the *ghuls*?"

Khardan could not help himself; a shudder shook his body. Ibn Jad smiled grimly. "Such was my purpose in allowing them to attack you. I wouldn't have let them kill you, you know. You are far too valuable to us. Blossom's rescue of you was quite unexpected, although highly instructive, as it turned out. Strange are the ways of the God," he murmured reflectively and stared back down the hall in thoughtful silence. Shaking his head, breaking his reverie, ibn Jad continued. "No, I will not fight you. I have released your bonds so that we may walk together as men—with dignity."

"I will not serve your God!" Khardan said harshly.

"Come, let us not spend our time in pointless argument," Auda made a polite, graceful gesture with his slender hand. "Will you walk with me? The way is not far."

"Where are we going?"

"That will be seen."

Khardan stood irresolutely in the hallway, glancing up and down the torch lit corridor. Carved out of granite, it was narrow and grew narrower still up ahead. Torches lit the way, but they were placed upon the wall at intervals of about twenty or thirty feet and so left patches of darkness broken by circles of light. Farther back, at the beginning of the hall, after they'd left the Vestry, they had passed doorways and the arched entrances to other corridors. But soon these were left behind. The walls that had been made of smooth, polished stone gave way to rough-hewn blocks. There were no windows, there was absolutely no way out.

And if there was, there were the *ghuls*...

Khardan began to walk down the hall, his dark brows lowering, his face grim and stern. Auda ibn Jad accompanied him.

"Tell me, is it true that your God— What is His name?"

"Akhran."

"—Akhran is known as the Wanderer? Could it be your God who came to us with news of Quar's duplicity?"

"Yes," Khardan admitted. "Akhran has warned us of Quar's treachery, and we have seen it for ourselves."

"In the Amir's attack on your people?"

"I did not flee the battle, dressed as a woman!"

"Of course not. That was the doing of Blossom and your wife, Zohra. A remarkable woman that one. I cannot imagine that she would be the kind to drag a man out of battle. Did she give you any explanation for this irrational behavior?"

"Something about a vision," Khardan replied irritably, not wanting to discuss the matter, not wanting to think about Zohra. Despite the fact that she had dishonored him in his bed, despite the fact that she had thwarted his marriage to Meryem and made him ridiculous in the eyes of his fellow tribesmen by forcing him into the position of accepting a man into his harem, she was his wife, deserving his protection, and he was helpless to grant it.

"A vision?"

"Women's magic," muttered Khardan.

"Do not disparage women's magic, nomad," said Auda ibn Jad gravely. "Through its power and the courage of those who wield it—courage as strong or stronger than any man—my people have survived. This vision was important enough to the woman to cause her to act upon it. I wonder what it was. And still more, how it might affect what I do now."

Khardan could hear the Paladin's unspoken words as plainly as the spoken; the thoughtful, brooding expression on Auda's face indicated how seriously he took this matter. Khardan began to regret that he had not questioned Mathew further on this point.

The Black Paladin did not speak for several minutes, while they continued to walk the winding hallway. At length, the light of the torches ended. Beyond them was impenetrable darkness and an evil whose depths were unfathomable.

Khardan stopped. A sudden weakness came over him. Trembling, he leaned against the wall. A draft wafting up those shadowy stairs caused him to shiver uncontrollably. It was as chill and damp as the breath of Death; its touch upon his skin was like the cold touch of a corpse.

Auda ibn Jad took a torch from a sconce on the wall and held it aloft. The light illuminated stone stairs descending in a sharp spiral.

"Courage, nomad," said the Paladin, his hand on Khardan's bare arm.

"What is down there? Where are you taking me?"

"To your destiny," answered Auda ibn Jad.

Khardan was about to hurl himself at the Black Paladin, make a last, desperate, hopeless attempt to battle for his life; but the man's dark eyes met his, caught and held him motionless.

"Is this courage? To fight in despair like a cornered rat? If it is death you face down there, surely it is better to face it with dignity."

"So be it!" said Khardan. Shaking off Auda's hand, the Calif walked ahead of the Paladin down the staircase.

At the foot of the stairs they came to another hallway. By the light of ibn Jad's torch, Khardan could see a series of heavy wooden doors placed at intervals on either side of a narrow corridor. All the doors except one were closed. From that one shone a bright light, and Khardan could hear faint sounds emanating from it.

"This way," said ibn Jad, with a gesture.

Khardan walked slowly toward the doorway, his legs seemingly unwilling to carry him forward, his feet heavy and clumsy. Fear crawled like a snake in his belly, and he knew that if it were not for the black eyes of ibn Jad watching him, the Calif would have broken down and wept like a terrified child.

The sounds grew clearer the nearer he drew to the open door, and the snake in his gut twisted and turned. It was the sound of a man moaning in death's agony. Sweat broke out on Khardan's face, trickling down into his black beard. A tremor shook him, but still he kept going. Coming opposite the doorway, he felt the touch of Auda's hand upon his arm and came to a stop. Blinking against the brightness inside the room, he looked within.

At first he could see nothing but a figure of darkness outlined against blazing firelight. A small, shrunken man with an over-sized head and a wizened body glanced at Khardan with shrewd, appraising eyes.

"This is the one, Paladin?" came a voice as wizened as the body.

"Yes, Lifemaster."

The man nodded his huge head. It seemed balanced so precariously upon his scrawny neck, and he moved so carefully and with such deliberation, that Khardan had a fearful, momentary impression the head might topple off. The man was dressed in voluminous black robes that stirred and rippled in waves of hot air wafting from the room. From behind him, running like a dark undercurrent to his words, came the low, moaning sound.

"You arrive in good time, Paladin," said the man in satisfaction.

"The rebirth?"

"Any moment now, Paladin. Any moment."

"It should prove instructive to the nomad. May we watch, Lifemaster?"

"A pleasure, Paladin." The small man bowed and stepped aside from the doorway.

Khardan looked inside, then hastily averted his eyes.

"Squeamish?" said the wizened man, scurrying over to poke at Khardan with a bony finger. "Yet here I see scars of battle—"

"It is one thing to fight a man. It is another to see one tormented to his death!" Khardan said hoarsely, keeping his head turned from the gruesome sight within.

"Watch!" said Auda softly.

"Watch!" said the old man. The bony hand crawled over Khardan's flesh and he cringed in disgust, then started and gasped. Needle-sharp pain raced through his nerve endings. The small man held no weapon, but it was as if a thousand piercing thorns had driven into Khardan's flesh. Choking back his cry, he stared at the black-robed man, who smiled modestly.

"When I came to Zhakrin, I wondered how best I might serve my God. This"—he spread his thin arms, the yellowed skin hung from the bones—"is not the body of a warrior. I could not win souls for Zhakrin with my sword. But I could win them another way—pain. Long years I studied, traveling to dark and secret places throughout Sularin, learning to perfect the art. For art it is. Look, look at this man."

The fingers caressed Khardan's skin. Reluctantly, he turned his gaze back upon the figure in the room.

"He was brought in yesterday, Paladin. Look at his armor!" The wizened man pointed a palsied finger toward a corner of the room.

"A White Knight of Evren!" said Auda in awe.

"Yes!" The small man smiled proudly. "And look at him now. One of her strongest, one of her best. Look at him now!"

The man, his arms chained to the wall, sprawled naked upon the stone floor. He stared at the Lifemaster with wild, dilated eyes. His body was covered with blood—some of it still flowing—from numerous wounds, the skin was ashen gray. The low moaning sound came from his throat; then suddenly his body jerked convulsively. He screamed in agony, his head dashed back against the wall as though he had been struck by a giant hand.

But no one had touched him. No one had gone near him.

The wizened man smiled with quiet pride. "Pain, you see"— he nudged Khardan—"is in two places. Body and mind. The pain you feel"—his fingers twitched and Khardan felt the needles race through his flesh again, this time sharper and seemingly tipped with fire. He could not forbear crying out, and the wizened man grinned in satisfaction—"that was in your body. You are brave, nomad, but within fifteen minutes, with my instruments and my bare hands, I can reduce you to a quivering mass of flesh promising me anything if I will only end your torment. But that is nothing, nothing to the pain you will endure when I enter your mind! I am there now, in his." The wizened man pointed at the White Knight. "Watch!"

The Lifemaster slowly began to clench his tiny fist, the fingers curling inward. And, as he did so, the man chained to the wall began to curl in upon himself, his muscles clenching spasmodically, his entire body curling up like that of a dying spider, scream after scream bursting from his throat.

"Honor?" Turning to the Black Paladin, Khardan sneered, though his face ran with sweat and his body shook. "What honor is there is torturing your enemy to death?"

"Death?" The wizened man appeared shocked. "No! Senseless, wasteful!"

"He is dying!" Khardan said angrily.

"No," said the Lifemaster softly, "he is praying. Listen. . ."

Reluctantly, Khardan turned his gaze back to the tortured body. Evren's Knight hung from his chains, his strength nearly spent. His screams had ceased, his broken voice whispered words that could not, at first, be heard.

The Lifemaster raised a hand for silence. Hardly breathing, ibn Jad leaned forward. Baffled, Khardan glanced from one to the other. A look of triumph was on each face, yet the Calif could not understand their victory. A dying man praying to his Goddess to accept his soul. . .

And then Khardan heard the man's words clearly. "Accept me . . . in your service. . . Zhakrin . . ." The man's voice grew stronger. "Accept me . . . in your service . . . Zhakrin!"

Preparation to become a Black Paladin.

Evren's Knight lifted his head, tears streamed from his eyes. He raised his manacled hands. "Zhakrin!" he whispered reverently. "Zhakrin!"

The Lifemaster shuffled across the stone floor. Drawing a key from his robes, he removed the manacles. The knight fell to his knees, embracing the man around the legs. Clucking like a mother over her child, the wizened old man lifted a bowl of water and began to cleanse the tormented flesh.

"Naked, covered with blood, we come into this life," murmured ibn Jad.

Sickened and dizzy, Khardan slumped back against the stone wall. The tortured man's body was muscular; he was obviously strong and powerful. A bloodstained sword rested in the corner, his armor—adorned with a lily—was dented and scratched. He had apparently fought his captors valiantly. He had been the sworn enemy of this God, and now he offered Zhakrin his life.

"So did many of us come to the God," said ibn Jad. "The path of fire cleanses and leads the soul to the truth. And so it will be with you, nomad." He gripped Khardan's arm. "In years to come, you will look back on this as a blessed experience. And with you, it will be a twice wonderful transformation, for you will be reborn almost at the same moment as will our God!"

The Lifemaster had the knight on his feet, his scrawny arm around the strong body, holding him tenderly. "Take him, Paladin. Take him to his chamber. He will sleep and wake refreshed and renewed in the morning."

Auda ibn Jad accepted charge of Evren's Knight, who was still murmuring the name of Zhakrin in holy ecstasy.

Leading the knight back down the hallway, Auda glanced

over his shoulder at Khardan. "Farewell, nomad. When we meet tomorrow, I hope it will be to call you brother."

Khardan surged forward, with no hope of escape, with only some dim view in his mind of smashing his head into the stone wall, of dashing out his brains, of killing himself.

Bony fingers closed over his wrist. Pain mounted up his arm, running from tiny nerve to tiny nerve, seeping through his veins like slow-moving ice water. He stumbled to his knees, resistance gone. The Lifemaster grabbed hold of his other wrist and dragged him across the stone floor into the sweltering heat of the room.

Flame leaped high in Khardan's vision, heat beat upon his body. The manacles snapped shut around his wrists. The old man shuffled across the floor to where an iron cauldron hung over the roaring fire. Reaching inside, his flesh seemingly impervious to the searing heat, he drew forth a thin piece of red-hot, glowing iron and turned back with it to face Khardan.

"Akhran!" Khardan shouted, plunging against the manacles, trying to rip them from the wall. "Akhran! Hear me!"

The old man shuffled closer and closer until his huge head loomed in Khardan's vision. "Only one God hears your screams, nomad. Zhakrin!" The hissing breath was hot upon Khardan's cheek. "Zhakrin!"

CHAPTER 10

athew crept silently down the stairs behind Auda ibn Jad and Khardan, his way lit only by the faint afterglow of the Black Paladin's torch. Peering cautiously around the corner at the bottom, he saw the long, narrow hallway with its rows of closed wood doors and realized that to go any farther would lead to certain discovery.

He had no choice but to retreat back up the stairs, feeling his way in the darkness, moving cautiously so that he would not be heard. He came to a halt about halfway up the staircase, pressed against the wall, holding his breath to hear. The men's words came to him clearly; a trick of the stone carrying it to his ears almost as plainly as if he stood beside them.

Thus Mathew heard everything, from Evren's tortured Knight's agony to his final, ecstatic prayer to Zhakrin. He heard the scuffling sound of Khardan's futile try for freedom, he heard the Calif cry out in pain, and the sound of a heavy weight being dragged across the floor. But he heard something else, too. Auda ibn Jad was coming back this direction. Moving as swiftly as he dared in the total darkness, Mathew dashed to the top of the stairs. Reaching the level floor but not expecting it, he staggered and fell. The footsteps grew louder. Fortunately, ibn Jad was weighted down by the burden of the weak knight he was supporting and so was forced to move slowly. The Knight's murmuring prayers to Zhakrin kept the Black Paladin from hearing Mathew's scramblings.

Rising hastily to his feet, Mathew looked despairingly down the long hall. A torch burning on the wall about twenty feet away illuminated much of the corridor brightly, leaving only a swatch of shadow between it and the next torch; Mathew could not hope to run the length of the hall without being seen. Near him, just at the edge of the circle of torchlight, a darker shadow offered his only hope. Darting to it, Mathew discovered what he had been praying for—a natural alcove in the rough rock walls. It wasn't very big and seemed to grow smaller as Mathew attempted to squeeze his slender body into the fissure. If he had been standing directly beneath the blazing torch, he could not have imagined himself more visible. Turning his face to the wall in an effort to hide the milk-white skin that would show up in the light, Mathew drew his hands up into the sleeves of his black robes and held his breath.

Ibn Jad and the knight passed within inches of him. Mathew could have reached out and plucked the Paladin's sleeve with his hand. It seemed that they must see him or hear him; his heart thudded loud enough to wake the dead. But the two walked on by, continuing down the hall without once looking in his direction. Exhaling a relieved sigh, Mathew was about to offer a prayer of thanks for the protection when he remembered uncomfortably which God it was who ruled the Darkness.

An agonized scream welled up from below, echoing in the hallway. Khardan. . .

Mathew's legs gave way and he sank down weakly onto the stone floor, the terrible sound reverberating in his heart. Trembling, his hand went to the pouch he wore at his waist, his fingers closed over the obsidian wand.

The darkness hissed. "Say the word, Master, and I will save your friend from his suffering."

"I did not summon you!" Mathew said shakily, aware that he had no control over this creature.

"Not by word," replied the imp, sniggering. "I read the wishes of your heart."

Another cry rent the air. Mathew shrank back against the wall. "By saving him, you don't mean taking us away from here, do you?" he questioned. His chest constricted painfully; it was difficult to breathe.

"No," said the imp, drawing out the word, ending in a throaty growl. "My Demon Prince would not like that at all. If you leave, then so must I, and my Prince commands that I stay. He is delighted to hear of his brother God's return and more delighted still to know that the Good Goddess is in Zhakrin's power."

"What will he do with her?"

"Stupid mortal, what do you think?" the imp returned, its shriveled body writhing in eager anticipation.

"He can't destroy—" Mathew began, appalled.

"That remains to be seen. Never before has one of the twenty been so weakened. Her immortals are not here to help her; her mortal followers, as you have seen, are succumbing to Zhakrin. His power grows as Evren's wanes."

Mathew tried to think, to feel some sense of loss at the terrible fate of the Goddess, tried to force himself to contemplate what this upset might do to the balance of power in heaven. But Khardan's screams were in his ears, and suddenly he cared about nothing but what was happening on earth.

"Free him, free Zohra! Take me to your Prince," Mathew begged, sweat beading on his lip.

The imp pursed its shriveled lips. "A poor bargain, trading nothing for something. Besides, Zhakrin has requested the woman's body. Astafas would never offend his brother by stealing her away."

Khardan's screams ceased abruptly, cut off by a choked, strangled cry. In the awful silence, a glimmering of understanding lit Mathew's darkness. The perplexing behavior of, the Wandering God was no longer perplexing. The young wizard longed to fan the tiny spark of the idea that had come to him, to blow on the coal and watch it burst into flame. But he dared not. The moment the thought came to mind, he saw the imp's tongue lick its lips, the red eyes narrow.

Drawing the wand from his pouch, Mathew held it up before the imp. "I want to talk to Khardan," the young wizard said evenly, keeping tight control on his voice. "Lure his tormentor away."

The imp laughed, sneering derisively.

"What would happen," Mathew continued calmly, though his body trembled beneath the black robes, "if I were to give this wand to the Black Sorceress?"

The imp's red eyes flared. Too late, it hooded them with thin, wrinkled lids. "Nothing," said the creature.

"You lie," Mathew returned. "I begin to understand. The wand serves to summon the immortal nearest our hearts. Meryem used it to call one of Quar's minions. When the wand came into my hands, however, its power acted on an immortal being of the Gods in which I believe, and because its magic is black, it called you."

The imp's long red tongue lolled out of its mouth in derision. Its teeth showed black against the red, its eyes burned.

Mathew averted his gaze; looking directly at the wand he held in his hand. "If I gave this wand to the Black Sorceress, she could use it to summon an immortal being of Zhakrin's."

"Let her try!" The imp's tongue rolled up into its mouth with a slurp. "His immortals have long since disappeared."

"Nonetheless, *you* would be banished."

"As long as you are here, I am here, Dark Master," said the imp, grinning wickedly.

"But powerless to act," Mathew returned.

"As are you!"

"It seems I am powerless either way," Mathew shrugged. "What do I have to lose?"

"Your soul!" hissed the imp with a wriggle of delight that nearly twisted the creature in two.

Mathew saw the Hand reaching out for him; he saw the vast void into which he would be cast, his soul wailing in despair until its small cry was swallowed up by the eternal darkness.

"No," said Mathew softly. "Astafas would not have even that. For when I give the wand to the Black Sorceress, I give myself to her as well."

The imp was caught in mid-writhe. One leg twined about the other, one arm wrapped about its neck. Slowly it unwound itself and crept forward to glare at Mathew.

"Before I would allow that, I would snatch your soul away!"

"To do that, you would have to have me killed, and I would be dead, and you would lose entry to this place."

"It seems we are at an impasse!" the imp snarled.

"Do for me what I ask. Help me to see Khardan—alone." Its tongue curling and uncurling, the imp considered. It peered into Mathew's mind, but all it saw there was a theological muddle. As far as the imp was concerned, theology was good for only one thing—leading the overzealous scholar into deep and dangerous waters. While occasionally amused to hear mortals argue with firm conviction over something they knew absolutely nothing about, the imp generally found theological discussion somnambulic. The imp thought it odd (even for Mathew) to choose this time to discuss theology with a man being tortured, and the creature probed Mathew's mind deeply. The young wizard appeared to have nothing more treacherous planned, however. Not that anything he attempted would do him any good anyway. The imp decided to humor the mortal and gain a valuable concession at the same time.

"If I obey your commands, then you must swear fealty to Astafas."

"Anything!" Mathew said shortly, eager to reach Khardan. This ominous silence was more terrifying than the screams.

"Just a moment!" The imp held up a splay-fingered hand. "I feel it only right to tell you that your guardian angel is not present, and so you have no one to intervene in your behalf before you make this commitment."

Why this news should have distressed Mathew, who did not believe in guardian angels any more than he believed in other nursery tales, was a mystery. But he felt a sudden heaviness in his heart.

"It is of no matter," he said after a moment. "I pledge my loyalty to the Prince of Darkness."

"Say his name!" hissed the imp.

"I pledge my loyalty to. . . to Astafas." The word burned Mathew's lips like poison. When he licked them, he tasted a bitter flavor.

The imp grinned. It knew Mathew lied. It knew that though the human's mouth spoke the words, they were not repeated by his soul. But the mortal was alone on this plane of human existence, his guardian angel was no longer there to shield him with her white wings. And now Mathew knew he was alone. Despair, hopelessness—these would be the imp's instruments of torture, and when the time came—as it would soon; the imp, too, was starting to form a plan—the young wizard would be all too willing for the torment to end, to lapse into the soothing comfort of dark oblivion.

"Wait here!" the imp said and vanished in an eyeblink. A voice came out of the torchlight, sounding so near and so real that Mathew started to his feet, looking around in terror.

"Lifemaster! Come swiftly!" Auda ibn Jad sounded angry, upset. "This knight. There is something wrong with him! I think he is dying!"

The hall was empty. The Black Paladin was nowhere in sight. Yet the voice seemingly came from near Mathew's shoulder.

"Lifemaster!" Ibn Jad commanded.

"What is it?" a shrill voice answered from below.

Mathew scrunched back into the alcove, holding his breath.

"Lifemaster!" The Black Paladin was furious, insistent. Steps rasped upon the stairs. The Lifemaster, wheezing, slowly made his way to the top and stared down the hall.

"Ibn Jad?" he queried in a tremulous voice.

"Lifemaster!" The Black Paladin's shout echoed through the corridor. "Why do you tarry? The knight has gone into a fit!"

His oversized head jutting forward, peering this way and that, the Lifemaster shuffled down the hallway, following the sound of ibn Jad's voice that grew increasingly angrier as it grew increasingly more distant.

CHAPTER 11

Strong arms held Zohra close, warm lips tasted hers, hands caressed her. The aching of desire burned within her, and she cried out for love, but there was nothing. The arms melted away, the lips turned cold, the hands withdrew. She was empty inside, longing desperately for that emptiness to be filled. The pain grew worse and worse, and then a dark figure stood above her bed.

"Khardan!" Zohra cried out in gladness and held forth her arms to draw the figure near.

The figure raised a hand and a bright, white light shone in Zohra's eyes, burning away the dream.

"Waken," said a cool, smooth voice.

Zohra sat up, her eyes watering in the sudden brilliance. Holding up her hand to shield them, she endeavored to see the figure that was reflected in the white light.

"What happened to me?" Zohra cried fearfully, the memory of the arms and lips and hands all too real, her body still aching for the touch even as her mind revolted against it.

"Nothing, my dear," said the voice, a woman's voice. "The drug was given you prematurely." The white light became nothing more than the flame of a candle, illuminating the taut, stretched skin of the sorceress. Placing the candlestick on a table beside Zohra's bed, the sorceress sat down next to her The flame burned steadily and unwaveringly in the depths of the woman's ageless eyes. Reaching out a hand, she smoothed back Zohra's mane of tangled black hair.

"I believe, however, that it has proved most instructive. You see now that you are ours—body, mind, and soul."

"What do you mean?" Zohra faltered, drawing back from the woman's touch. Finding herself naked in the bed, she grasped hold of the silken sheets on which she lay and clasped them around her body.

The Black Sorceress smiled. "Had not another requested you, my dear, you would have now been languishing in the arms of one of the Black Paladins; perhaps within a few months, bearing his child."

"No!" Zohra tossed her head defiantly, but she kept her eyes averted from the stern, cold face.

The Black Sorceress leaned near, her hand touching Zohra's cheek. "Strong arms, soft kisses. And then nothing but cold emptiness. You cried out—"

"Stop!" Zohra thrust the hand from her, glaring at the woman through tears of shame. Clutching the sheets to her breast, she scrambled back as far as possible from the woman—which wasn't far until the carved wooden bedstead blocked her way. "I will eat nothing, drink nothing!" she cried passionately. "I will never submit—"

"The drug was not in your food, child. It was in the clothing you put on. The fabric is soaked in it, and the drug seeps through your skin. It could be in these bed sheets." She waved a hand. "The perfume with which we anoint your body. You would never know, my dear. . . But"—the sorceress rose languidly to her feet. Turning from Zohra, she walked away from the bed and began to pace the floor slowly—"do not concern yourself. As I said, you have been chosen by another, and though He wants your body, it is not for the purpose of breeding new followers."

Zohra remained silent, disdaining to question. She was barely listening, in fact. She was trying to figure some way to avoid the drug.

The Black Sorceress looked toward a small leaded glass window set into the wall of the cheerless room. "It is only a few hours until the dawn of what will be for us a new day, a day of hope. When the mid-hour of night strikes, our God will return to us. Zhakrin will be reborn." She glanced around at Zohra, who—catching the sorceress's gaze and seeing that some response was required—shrugged.

"What is that to me?"

"Everything, my dear," the Black Sorceress said softly, her eyes glittering with an eager, intense light. "He will be reborn in your body!"

Zohra rolled her eyes. Obviously the woman was insane. *I have to get out of here. The drug . . . perhaps it was that musky odor I smelled. There must be an antidote, some way to counter it. Usti might know, if I can persuade the blubbering coward to help me—*

A pang of fear struck Zohra. She glanced around hastily and saw her rings lying on the table beside the bed, gleaming brightly in the candlelight. She sighed in relief.

The Black Sorceress was watching her gravely. "You don't, believe me."

"Of course not!" Zohra gave a brief, bitter laugh. "This is a trick to confuse me."

"No trick, my dear, I assure you," said the Black Sorceress. "You are to be honored above all mortals, your weak flesh will hold our God until He attains the strength to abandon it and take His rightful place among the other deities. If you do not believe me, ask your djinn." The sorceress's gaze fIxed upon the silver ring. Zohra's face paled, but she pressed her lips tightly together and said nothing. The sorceress nodded. "I will give you a few moments alone to ease the turbulence of your soul. You must be relaxed and peaceful. When I return with the dawn, we will begin preparing you to accept the God."

The Black Sorceress left the room, shutting the door softly behind her. There came no sound of a lock, but Zohra knew hopelessly that if she tried to open it, the door would not yield. Silently, unmoving, clutching the sheets to her bosom, Zohra lifted the ring.

"Usti," she called out in a small, tight voice.

"Is she gone?"

"Yes!" Zohra checked an impatient sigh.

"Coming, Princess." The djinn drifted out from the ring—a thin, wavering wisp of smoke that writhed about on the floor before finally coalescing into a flabby body. Subdued, miserable, and frightened, the fat djinn had the appearance of a lump of goat's cheese melting beneath the desert sun.

"Usti," said Zohra softly, her eyes on the candle flame, "is what she said true? Can they. . . give my body. . . to a God?"

"Yes, Princess," said the djinn sadly, bowing his head. His chins folded in on one another until it seemed likely his mouth and nose would be swallowed up by flesh.

"And . . . there is nothing you can do?" Her spirit broken, her fears beginning to conquer, Zohra asked the question in a wistful, pitiful tone that wrung the djinn's nonexistent heart.

"Oh, Princess," Usti wailed, twisting his fat hands together in anguish. "I have been a most worthless immortal, all my life! I know that! But I swear to you that I would risk the iron box—I swear by *Hazrat* Akhran—that I would help you if I could! But you see!" He gestured wildly at the door. "She knows I am here! And she does nothing to try to stop me. Why? Because she knows I am helpless, powerless to stop her!"

Zohra bowed her head, her black hair tumbling over her shoulders. "No one can help me. I am all alone. Mathew has deserted me. Khardan is undoubtedly either dead or dying. There is no escape, no hope. . ." Slowly, despondently, she let the sheet slide from nerveless hands. Tears trickled down her cheeks and dripped onto the sheet, spotting the silk.

Usti stared at her in dismay. Flinging himself upon the bed, nearly upsetting it in the process, he cried, "Don't give up, Princess! This isn't like you! Fight! Fight! Look, aren't you furious with me? Throw something! Here"—the djinn grabbed hold of a water carafe. Splashing water recklessly over the bed, he thrust it into Zohra's unresponsive hands—"toss that at me! Hit me on the head!" Usti snatched off his turban, offering his bald pate as a tempting target. "Yell at me, scream at me, curse me! Anything! Don't cry, Princess! Don't cry!" Tears rolling in torrents down his own fat face, Usti dragged the bedclothes up over his head. "Please don't cry!"

"Usti," said Zohra, her eyes shining with an eerie light. "I have an idea. There is one way to prevent them from taking my body."

"There is?" Usti said warily, lowering the sheet and peering over it.

"If my body was dead, they could not use it, could they?"

"Princess!" Usti gasped in sudden terrified understanding, flinging the sheet over his head again. "No! I can't! I am forbidden to take a mortal life without permission from the God!"

"You said you would risk anything for me!" Zohra tugged at the fabric. Slowly, the djinn's face emerged, staring at her woefully. "My soul will plead for you to Holy Akhran. The God has done nothing to help us. Surely He will not be so unjust as to punish you for obeying the final request of your mistress!"

Usti gnawed on the hem of the sheet. Zohra's gaze was steadfast, unwavering. Finally, the djinn stood up. "Princess," he said, his chins quivering, but his voice firm, "somewhere within this fat body I will find the courage to carry out your command."

"Thank you, Usti," Zohra replied gently.

"But only at the last moment, when there is no . . . no hope," the djinn said, the final word lost in a knot of choking tears.

"At the last, when there is no hope," Zohra repeated, her gaze going to the window to watch for the dawn.

CHAPTER 12

Mathew waited until he saw the Lifemaster's bulbous head gleam in the flame of the most distant torch lighting the hallway, then the young wizard slipped from his alcove. Keeping to the shadows, he ran to the stairs and, clinging to the wall, fumbled his way down them. Once at the bottom, he could see the light streaming from the room where he knew Khardan must be held. No sound came from it. All was silent, silent as a tomb, he thought, his heart aching in fear.

Outside the door the memory of those agonized screams returned, and this courage failed him.

"Coward!" he cursed himself bitterly as he stood trembling in the doorway, fearful of entering, terrified of what he might find. "*He* is the one who is suffering and you shake in terror, unable to move to help him!"

"Help," he scoffed at himself. "What help can you offer? What hope? None. Words, that's all. What do you fear? That you will find him dead? Shouldn't that be your wish for him, if you truly care about him? Or are you selfish as well as cowardly? And what if he isn't dead? You will exhort him to accept more torment. Better to leave, better to let him go. . ."

"No! You're wrong!" Mathew argued resolutely, pushing back his doubts. He recognized that voice, it was the same one that had told him to give up when he'd been captured by the slave trader, the voice that had whispered to him of the sweetness of death. "I'm wasting time. The tormentor will be back soon."

Clenching his jaw tightly, Mathew walked into the torture chamber.

"Khardan!" he murmured. Compassion rushed in to fill fear's dark and empty well. Mathew forgot that the tormentor might return any moment. He forgot the imp, forgot his own danger.

Khardan sat on the stone floor, his back against a wall, his arms chained above his head. He had been stripped of his clothes. Burn marks scorched his bare chest, blood oozed from strategically inflicted wounds. The Calif's head lolled forward, he had lost consciousness. Tears stinging his eyes, Mathew pressed his hand to his lips, forcing back a choking cry of anguish.

"Leave him!" the voice urged. "Leave him this one moment of peace. It will be all he has. . ."

Shaking his head, blinking back the tears, Mathew summoned all his strength and courage—a far more difficult task than summoning demons—and knelt down beside the Calif. A bowl of water stood on a table nearby, just out of reach, probably placed there to enhance the tormenting of the chained man. Lifting it, Mathew dipped his fingers in the cool water and dabbed them upon the Calif's blood-caked lips.

"Khardan," he said. The name came out a sob.

Khardan stirred and moaned, and Mathew's heart was wrung with pity. The hand touching the lips trembled, tears blinded him momentarily and he could not speak. He forced himself to quash the sympathy, the vivid imaginings of what it must be like to endure such torture.

"Khardan," he repeated, more firmly, with a sternness he knew to be a prop holding him up.

Khardan raised his head suddenly, looking about him with a wild terror in his feverish eyes that pierced Mathew to his soul.

"No more!" the nomad muttered. His arms wrenched, trying to drag the chains from the wall. "No more!"

"Khardan!" Mathew stroked the man's hair back with a gentle, soothing hand and held the water bowl to his lips. "Khardan, it's Mathew! Drink. . ."

Khardan drank thirstily, then retched, moaning in agony, bringing most of the water back up. But his eyes lost their wild look, a glimmer of recognition flickered in the dark depths. He leaned back weakly against the wall.

"Where is . . . *he?!*" The horror with which Khardan said the word sent chills through Mathew. He set down the water bowl, his shaking hand was spilling most of it.

"He is gone, for the moment," Mathew said softly. "The creature I . . . control. . . led him away."

"Get me out of here!" Khardan gasped.

Removing his hand from the man's forehead, Mathew sat back, looking into the black, hopeful eyes. "I can't, Khardan." No words ever fell more reluctantly from Mathew's lips. He saw the eyes flash in contempt and anger, then they closed. Khardan sighed.

"Thank you for this much, at least," he said slowly, painfully nodding toward the water. "You had better leave now. You've risked a great deal in coming to me. . ."

"Khardan!" Mathew clasped his hands together pleadingly. "I would free you if I could! I would give my life for you if I could!" Khardan opened his eyes, looking at him intently, and Mathew flushed. He hadn't meant his words to come out stained with his heart's blood. Lowering his head, staring down at the bowl of pinkish water sitting on the floor at his knees, Mathew continued speaking in more subdued tones, all the while nervously twisting the black velvet robes between his trembling fingers. "But I can't. It would be pointless. There is nowhere to go, no hope of escape."

"We could at least die like men, fighting until the end," Khardan said warmly. "We would die, each in the service of his God—"

"No!" Mathew said stubbornly, suddenly clenching his fist and driving it into his knee. "That's all you think about—you nomads! Death! When you are winning, life is fine; when you are losing, you decide to give up and die!"

"To die with honor—"

"Honor be damned!" Mathew cried angrily, lifting his head and glaring at Khardan. "Maybe your death isn't what your God wants! Did you ever think about that? Maybe you're of no use to Him dead! Maybe He's brought you here for a reason, a purpose, and it's up to you to live long enough to try to find out why!"

"My God has abandoned me," Khardan said harshly. "He has abandoned all of us, it seems, for now He talks to these unbelievers."

"That's what they want you to think!" Impulsively, Mathew reached out to take the pale, suffering face in his hands. "Believe your God has abandoned you, and you will abandon your God!"

"What do you know of my God, *kafir?*" Khardan jerked his head away from Mathew's touch, averting his eyes.

Clasping him by the shoulders, Mathew moved so that the black eyes had nowhere to look but at him. "Khardan, think about what we heard up there! Think about what these people have endured, have suffered for their faith. Their God was dead, and still they didn't forsake Him! Are you less strong? Will you give in?"

Khardan stared at him thoughtfully, brows furrowed, eyes dark and unreadable. His glance went to Mathew's hands, the thin, delicate fingers, cool from the water, against the Calif's burning skin.

"Your touch is gentle as a woman's," he murmured. Flushing in shame, Mathew snatched his hands away.

"*More* gentle than some women's—like my wife's," Khardan continued with a ghastly smile. "I don't envy the one who tries to take her body. God or no God, He's going to be in for an interesting time—" Khardan gasped in pain. His body doubled over, nearly wrenching his arms from their sockets.

Mathew looked about frantically for the source, but saw nothing and realized it must be coming from within. Helplessly he watched Khardan writhe, his body jerking convulsively, and then the spasm passed. Breathing heavily, his flesh glistening with sweat, Khardan slowly lifted his head.

Mathew saw himself reflected in the red-rimmed eyes. He might have been the one tormented. His face was ashen, he was shaking in every limb.

Khardan smiled gently. His lips almost instantly twisted in a pain-filled grimace, but the smile remained in the dark, shadowed eyes. "You better go," he spoke almost inaudibly. "I don't think. . . you can take. . . much more of this. . ."

Praying that the imp was still leading the Lifemaster a merry chase, Mathew caught up Khardan's bloodstained shirt and, dipping it in the water, washed the man's feverish forehead and face with cooling liquid. Khardan's eyes closed, tears crept from beneath the lids. He gave a shuddering sigh.

"Khardan," said Mathew softly, "there is a way out, I think, but it is desperate, almost hopeless."

Khardan nodded weakly, to show he understood. He had strength for nothing more, and Mathew—seeing his suffering nearly gave way. "Be at peace," he longed to say, "go ahead and die. I was wrong. Give yourself rest." But he didn't. Gritting his teeth, dipping the cloth in the water again, he continued, the knowledge of what he was going to ask making his heart wrench. "We must try, somehow, to gain possession of the two Gods before

Zhakrin can come back into the world. Once we have them both, we must free Evren, the Goddess who is Zhakrin's opposite. With Her power—weak as it is—on our side, I think we might succeed in escaping."

Khardan moved his head, the eyes opening the tiniest crack to look at Mathew intently. Mathew laid down the cloth. Gently, he ran his fingers through the crisp, curling black hair. Unable to meet those eyes, he gazed above them, at his own hand. "To do this, you must gain admittance to the ceremony," Mathew said, his voice catching in his throat. "To gain admittance, you must be a Black Paladin. . . ."

Khardan's jaw muscles twitched, his teeth clenched.

"Do you know what I am saying?" Mathew persisted, emotion choking him. "I am saying you must hold out until the point. . . the point of. . ." He couldn't continue.

"Death. . ." murmured Khardan. "And then. . . convince them I am. . . one. . ."

Mathew froze. What was that? Fearfully he listened. Footsteps! On the stairs!

Khardan did not move. His face was livid, blood trickled from the comer of his mouth.

Shivering so he could barely stand, Mathew somehow managed to regain his feet. His legs seemed to have gone numb, however, and he thought, for a moment, he must sink back down to the floor again. Hesitating, he looked at Khardan.

I should forget this! The idea is insane. Far better to give up now!

Khardan's sunken eyes flickered. "I . . . will . . . not. . .fail!"

Nor will I! Mathew said to himself in sudden grim determination. Turning, he fled from the chamber, darting farther down the hallway, out of the light, to hide himself in the shadow of another cell.

Muttering irritable imprecations down upon Auda ibn Jad for disturbing his work for nothing and then having the nerve to try to deny that he had done anything, the Lifemaster shuffled back into the chamber.

Mathew heard the small man's dragging footsteps cross the room; he heard them stop and could almost picture the tormentor bending over Khardan.

"Ah, had a visitor." The Lifemaster chuckled. "So that's what all that rigmarole and fal-de-ra was about. Whoever it was gave you back a bit of strength, I see. Well, well. No thanks to whoever it was. We'll just have to work a little harder. . ."

Khardan's scream tore through the darkness and through Mathew's heart. Putting his hand in his pouch, gripping the wand tightly, the young wizard spoke the words of magic and felt impish hands grab hold of him and pluck him into the darkness.

CHAPTER 13

"Take me to the Tower of Women," Mathew ordered wearily. "To see the Black Sorceress? I think not!" the imp returned.

"No, I must talk with—" Staring around him, Mathew swallowed the word with a gulp.

The imp had returned Mathew to the room where the young wizard had been first taken on his arrival. Materializing within it, both Mathew and his "servant" were unpleasantly astonished to see the Black Sorceress standing before the cold ashes left scattered in the fireplace.

"Talk with whom?" inquired the woman. "Your other friend?"

"If you have no further need of me, Dark Master—" whined the imp with an obscene wriggle intended for a bow.

"Do not leave yet, creature of Sul," commanded the sorceress.

"Servant of Astafas!" hissed the imp angrily, its tongue sliding out between its sharp black teeth. "I am not a low demon of Chaos, madam!"

"That could be arranged," said the Black Sorceress, her brows coming as close together as was possible on the tightly stretched skin of her face. She glanced at Mathew. "Make me a gift of this creature."

"I cannot, madam," said Mathew in a low, respectful tone. He had little to fear. The sorceress might try to take the wand from him by force, but the imp would most certainly fight—if not to protect him, then to protect its own shriveled skin.

"You are wise for one so young." The sorceress gazed at him searchingly. Moving close to him, she laid a hand upon his cheek. Her touch was like the bony fingers of a skeleton. Mathew shivered but did not move, caught and held by the mesmerizing stare of the woman's eyes. "Your wisdom comes not from years but from the ability to see into the hearts of those around you. A dangerous gift, for then you begin to care for them. Their pain becomes your pain." She lingered on the word, her fingers softly caressing, and the chill touch began to burn, like ice held in wet hands.

Trembling, Mathew held himself very still, though the pain increased immeasurably.

"You have seen what you should not have seen," the voice breathed all around him. "You have been where you should not have gone. In time, when you were ready, I would have shown you all. Now, because you do not understand, you are confused and disturbed. And you have done nothing for your nomad friend except increase his torment. Why did you go? Did you think you could free him?"

She didn't know! Blessed Promenthas, she didn't know, didn't suspect!

"Yes, that was it!" Mathew gasped.

"A hopeless, foolish thought." The Black Sorceress made a clicking sound with her tongue; the noise flicked on Mathew's exposed nerves. "How did you think to accomplish your escape, and why didn't you go ahead and attempt it?"

"Madam," interposed the imp, rubbing its hands as though they ached, "the nomad was too far gone for us to be able to help him. Madam will forgive us," added the imp, licking its lips, "if we do not tell her our plans for assisting the nomad to escape."

"Why will madam forgive you?" The sorceress smiled cruelly at the imp, keeping her hand on Mathew's cheekbone, the young man not daring to move, though it seemed his teeth were on fire and his brain was expanding in his skull.

"Because, madam, you hope that Astafas will forgive you for harming one of His own." The imp sidled nearer to Mathew. Elongating, stretching its small form like rubber, it closed its splay fingers over the hand of the sorceress. "When Zhakrin returns to the world, He will require the help of Astafas in the fight against Quar." The imp's narrowed red eyes were fiery slits against its blackened, wrinkled skin. "Zhakrin has Astafas's help and freely given, but Zhakrin is not to forget that this young one is ours, not His." Like slithering snakes, the imp's words wound around Mathew, tightening their coils.

Slowly, the sorceress removed her hand, though her fingers lingered long on Mathew's skin. "You are weary." She spoke to

Mathew, but her eyes were on the imp. "Sleep now." The pain eased, submerged in a wave of drowsy warmth.

A soft pillow was beneath his head; he was lying in a bed. Darkness enfolded him, banishing pain, banishing fear.

"Thank you," he murmured to the imp.

"Payment will come," whispered the darkness back to him. "Payment will come!"

CHAPTER 14

awn—The sun's light struggled feebly to penetrate the shroud of gray mist that overhung the Isle of Galos—and the day began to march inexorably toward night, time moving far too slowly for some, far too swiftly for others.

Mathew slept the sleep of exhaustion, waking well past midday. His sleep had been neither restful nor refreshing, however. Filled with terror, his dreams tormented his soul as the Lifemaster tormented Khardan's flesh.

In the halcyon days in his own land, the young man had never given much thought to eternity, to the soul's repose after its sojourn through the world with the body. Like most young people, he assumed he would live forever. But all that had changed. In those terrible days of enforced travel with the slave caravan, when death seemed the only end to his suffering, Mathew thought with longing of his soul ascending to a place where he would find comfort and ease and hear a gentle voice say, "Rest now, my child. You are home."

Now he would never hear that gentle voice. Now he would hear only harsh laughter, crackling like flame. There would be no rest, no sweet homecoming. Only an empty void without and within, his soul gnawing at the nothingness in a hunger that could never be assuaged. For I have dared use the power of Astafas; not only used it—(Promenthas might be able to forgive that, considering the circumstances), but—and Mathew admitted this to himself as he stood in the sunlight trickling feebly through the leaded glass window—I have enjoyed it, exulted in it!

Deep beneath the shock at the imp's appearance had run an undercurrent of pleasure, He had felt the same thrill last night when the imp did his bidding, and lured away the tormentor.

"I should cast away the wand," Mathew said to himself firmly, "destroy it; fall to my knees and pray for Promenthas's forgiveness; and give myself up to whatever fate awaits me. And if it were just me, if I were alone, I would do that. But I can't. Others depend on me."

Flinging himself back onto his bed, Mathew shut his eyes against the light.

"I said I would give my life for Khardan," he said through trembling lips. "Surely I can give my soul!"

And Zohra—exasperating, foolhardy, courageous. Zohra—fighting her weaknesses, never seeing that they were her strengths. Trapped in these walls, without even the poor comfort of being able to exchange a few words as had Mathew and Khardan, Zohra must imagine herself completely alone. Had her courage given way at last? Would she go meekly to her dread fate? Perhaps, like Khardan, she believed that her God had abandoned her.

"I must go to her," Mathew said, sitting up, brushing the tangled red hair out of his face. "I must reassure her, tell her there is hope!"

His hand went to the wand in the pocket of his black robes. As his fingers closed over it, a surge of warmth washed pleasurably over Mathew. Drawing forth the wand, he examined it admiringly. It was a truly fine piece of workmanship. Had Meryem made it, or had she purchased it? He recalled reading of certain dark and secret places in the capital city of Khandar where devices of black magic such as this could be bought if one had the proper—

Mathew caught his breath. His hand began to shake, and he dropped the wand upon the bedclothes. When he'd first discovered the wand on board ship, when he'd first lifted it, his fingertips had tingled painfully, a numbing sensation had spread up his arm. His hand had lost all sense of feeling.

Now its touch gave him pleasure. . .

"Master," hissed the imp, appearing with a bang, "you summoned me?"

"No!" Mathew cried in a hollow voice, shoving the wand away from him. "No, I—"

A thin curl of smoke drizzled into the center of the room and began to take form. Staring in astonishment, Mathew saw the many chins and round belly of a djinn emerge from the cloud.

"Usti?" he gasped.

He wasn't certain even now, when the djinn appeared as a mountain of flesh before him, that it *was* Usti to whom he was speaking. The djinn had lost at least two chins, his rotund stomach was no longer capable of holding up his *pantalons* that sagged woefully around his middle, revealing a jeweled navel. The djinn's ordinarily fine clothes were torn and dirty and disheveled, his turban had slipped down over one eye.

"Madman!" Usti fell to his knees with a thud. "Thank Akhran I have found you. I—" He stopped, staring at the imp. "I beg your pardon," said the djinn stiffly. "Perhaps I have come at an inopportune time." The immortal's flabby form began to fade.

"No, no!" cried Mathew. "Don't go!"

The imp darted Mathew a narrow-eyed, suspicious glance. "How clever of you, My Dark Master. Do you not find it confusing, serving so many Gods?"

"Whom do you serve, sir?" inquired Usti with a sniff, eyeing the imp's skinny body with disfavor. "And doesn't He feed you?"

"I serve Astafas, Prince of the Night!"

"Never heard of Him," replied Usti.

"As for food," continued the imp, its red eyes flaring, its splay-fingers twitching and curling, "I dine off the flesh of those whose souls my Prince drags shrieking into the Pit!"

"From the looks of you," said Usti, with a pitying glance, "the Prince's larder must be rather bare. I should stick to mutton—"

The imp gave a piercing shriek and made a dive for Usti, who gazed at it in offended dignity. "My dear sir, remember your place!"

Hastily grabbing the wand, Mathew pointed it at the imp. "Be gone!" he ordered harshly, wrenching back a hysterical desire to laugh, at the same time choking on tears. "I have no more need of you."

"How sweet will be the taste of your soft flesh, Dark Master!" The imp's red eyes devoured Mathew, its hand groped toward him.

"Be gone!" Mathew cried in desperation.

"Ugghhh." Looking at Mathew's slender form, Usti grimaced. "There is no accounting for taste. Mutton," he advised the imp, "sliced thin and grilled with mustard and pepper—"

The imp vanished with a deafening shriek and a blast that

shook the room. Mathew rose hurriedly from the bed. Afraid that they had roused the entire Castle, he stared fearfully at the door. He waited expectantly, but no one came. They must all be preparing for the ceremony, he thought, and turned to the djinn, who was still going on about mutton.

"Usti, where did you come from? Are the other djinn with you?" Mathew asked hopefully. "I remember that Khardan had a djinn—a young man with a fox-like face."

"Pukah," said Usti distastefully, mouthing the name as though it were a bad fig. "A lying, worthless—" The djinn's fat face sagged. "But for all that, he might have been useful."

"Where is he?" Mathew nearly shouted.

"Alas, Madman." Usti heaved a quivering-chinned sigh. "He and the djinn of Sheykh Majiid were taken captive during the battle by Kaug, the 'efreet of Quar—may dogs relieve themselves in his shoes."

Hope's flame died, leaving behind cold ash. "So that is why Pukah did not answer Khardan's summons," Mathew murmured. "How did you escape?"

Usti was instantly defensive. "I saw the great horrible hairy hands of the 'efreet sweep Sond's lamp and Pukah's basket up into his arms. I heard his booming laugh, and I knew that I was next! Is it to be wondered that I fled to a place of safety?"

"Meryem's ring," guessed Mathew grimly. "So you thought you'd try life in the palace of the Amir?"

"You have sadly misjudged me, Madman. I would never desert my mistress, no matter how wretchedly she used me, no matter that she made my life a living hell!" Usti regarded Mathew with wounded pride. "I had no doubt that you would stop the rose-colored whore in her vicious plot. When you clouted her upon the head, I took that opportunity to scape her, causing the ring to slip off her finger and commanding it to hide in your pouch."

Mathew had his doubts about this; he considered it far more likely that Usti had been cowering in the ring and that he'd been taken up by sheerest accident. It was pointless to argue; time was pressing.

"Your mistress, Zohra, how is she? Is she all right?" Usti's fat face crumbled with true, sincere distress.

"Ah!"—he clasped his chubby hands—"that is why I have I

come to you! The Princess I knew and feared is gone! She wept, Madman, wept! Oh what wouldn't I give"—tears crept down the fat cheeks, losing themselves in the crevices of the djinn's remaining chins—"to be back in my dwelling as it goes sailing through the air! To sew up my mistress's ripped cushions! To . . . to feel an iron pot she has thrown at me wang against my skull!"

The djinn flung wide his arms. "My mistress has commanded me *to* kill her!" he sobbed.

"What?" Mathew cried, alarmed. "Usti, you can't!"

"I am sworn to obey," said the djinn solemnly, with a hiccup. "And, indeed, I would do that rather than see her suffer." Usti's voice grew gentle. "But that is why I came to you, the first chance I had. My mistress says that you have deserted her, but I did not believe that, so I came to see for, myself." Usti glanced dubiously at where the imp had been standing. "And I find a creature of Sul who calls you Dark Master. Perhaps, after all, the Princess is right." Usti's eyes narrowed suspiciously. "You have betrayed us, gone over to the side of darkness!"

"No, no! I haven't!" Mathew lowered his voice. "Trust me, Usti! Tell Zohra to trust me! And don't harm her. I have a plan—"

A knocking came at the door. Mathew cringed. "Who is it?" he managed to call out, in a voice that he hoped sounded as though he'd just awakened.

"I have food and drink," came the answer, "to break your fast."

"Just. . . just a moment!" Mathew couldn't delay long. Moving slowly toward the door, he spoke hastily to the djinn, who was already beginning to disappear. "Tell Zohra to have faith in her God! He is with her!"

Usti appeared dubious. "I will give her the message," he said morosely, "if I have the chance. Already the witchwoman has taken her and begins some evil process of purification—"

There came the grating of a key in the lock; the door began to swing open.

"Don't carry out Zohra's command!" Mathew begged to the vanishing smoke. "Not unless all is lost!"

He spoke to empty air. Sighing, he barely glanced at the slave who entered with a laden food tray. He did notice, however, a Black Paladin standing guard outside his door, and he knew there would be no more opportunities to walk freely through the Castle.

The slave placed the tray upon a table and left without a word; Mathew heard the door lock click. Feeling little appetite, but knowing he should eat to keep up his strength, he sat down to his gloom-ridden breakfast.

Up above him, in the shadows of the ceiling, the imp glared at the young wizard. "He has a plan, does he? You're thinking much too hard, human. I see your thoughts. I believe my Prince will find this most interesting. . ."

CHAPTER 15

uda ibn Jad opened his casement to the night air, feeling it blow cool against skin flushed and feverish with excitement and anticipation. He reveled in the sensation; then, turning back to his room, he bathed—shivering in the chill air—and arrayed himself in the black armor, donning at the last the black velvet robes. Examining himself critically in the mirror, he searched for the slightest flaw, knowing that the eyes of his Lord would be hard to please this night. He smoothed the black beard that ran across his strong jaw, brushed the wet black hair so that it glistened and tied it behind his head with a black ribbon. The mustache that grew over his upper lip traced two fine lines down either side of his mouth, flowing at last like a thin black river to the bearded chin. His pale face was stained with an unnatural infusion of blood beneath the skin, the black eyes glittered in the light.

I must calm myself. This excitement is unholy and irreverent. Kneeling down upon the cold stone floor, Auda clasped his hands in prayer and brought a restful repose to his soul by losing himself in holy meditation. The Castle around him was abnormally still and quiet. All were in their, rooms alone, preparing themselves with prayer and fasting. They would remain there until the hour for the Gathering came. Eleven times the iron bell would toll, calling all forth to the Vestry.

It lacked an hour till that time yet. Ibn Jad rose to his feet, his prayers concluded. His mind was clear, his racing pulse once more beating slowly, steadily. He had a matter of importance to attend to before the Gathering. Walking from his room, his booted feet making as little noise as possible upon the stone so as not to disturb the others in their holy solitude, ibn Jad went forth. He left the upper recesses of the Castle, making his way down to the chambers below the surface of the earth.

He had seen the Lifemaster this morning. Exhausted from having had no sleep throughout the day and night, the man was on his way to his room to eat a morsel (the strictures of the fast being required only of the knights) and then nap a few hours. An assistant, one to whom he was teaching his heinous skills, had taken over with the subject.

"The nomad is a strong man, ibn Jad," said the Lifemaster, his oversized head bobbing upon its spindly neck. "You chose well. It will be nightfall before we break him."

"The only man alive who ever bested me," said Auda ibn Jad, remembering Khardan raiding the city long months ago. "I want the bonding, Lifemaster."

The Lifemaster nodded, as if this did not surprise him. "I thought as much. I heard about Catalus," he added softly. "My condolences."

"Thank you," said ibn Jad gravely. "He died well and for the cause, laying the blood curse upon the priest who seeks to rule us all. But now I am brotherless."

"There are many who would be honored to bond with you, Paladin," said the Lifemaster emotionally.

"I know. But this man's fate and mine are bound together. So the Black Sorceress told me, and so I knew in my heart from the moment we looked upon each other in the city of Kich."

The Lifemaster said nothing more. If the Black Sorceress had set her word upon it, there was nothing more to say.

"The critical time will come this evening. His pain and anguish will have drawn him near death. We must be careful not to allow him to slip over." The Lifemaster spoke with the modest air of one who has mastered a delicate art. "Arrive at ten strokes of the bell. The bonding will be stronger if it is your hand that leads him away from death."

The final strokes of the iron bell were just fading away when Auda ibn Jad entered the Lifemaster's dread chamber.

Khardan was very far gone. Ibn Jad, who had murdered countless of his fellow beings and felt without a qualm their blood splash upon his hands, could not look at the nomad's tortured body without feeling his stomach wrench. Memories of his own conversion to Zhakrin, of his own suffering and torment in this very chamber, seared through the blackness of deliberate, blessed forgetfulness. Auda had seen others endure the same fate without thinking back to that time. Why? Why now?

Face pale, a bitter taste in his mouth, the Black Paladin sank weakly back against a wall, unable to wrench his gaze from the dying man who lay limply on the floor. Khardan was no longer chained. He no longer had the energy left to escape or fight his tormentor.

The Lifemaster, busy with his work, spared ibn Jad a glance. "Ah," he said softly, "the bonding starts already."

"What. . . what do you mean?" ibn Jad asked hoarsely.

"The God has given you back the memory He once blessedly took away. Your souls share pain, as your bodies will soon share blood."

Falling to his knees, ibn Jad bowed his head, thanking Zhakrin, but he flinched and came near crying out when the Lifemaster grasped hold of his arm.

"Come forward!" the tormentor said urgently. "It is time!"

Auda moved near Khardan. The nomad's face was ashen, his eyes sunken in his head. Sweat gleamed on his skin. Mingling with blood, it trickled in rivulets over his body.

"Call to him!" ordered the Lifemaster.

"Khardan," said ibn Jad, in a voice that trembled despite himself.

The nomad's eyelids shivered, he drew a quivering breath.

"Again!" the Lifemaster's voice was insistent, fearful.

"Khardan!" called Auda more loudly and stronger, as though shouting to one about to walk blindly off a cliff. "Khardan!" Ibn Jad grasped hold of a limp hand that was already devoid of the warmth of life. "We are losing him!" he whispered angrily.

"No, no!" said the Lifemaster, the huge head whipping about so rapidly it seemed it must fly off the thin, brittle neck. "Make him call upon the name of Zhakrin!"

"Khardan," cried ibn Jad, "pray to the God—"

"There, he hears you!" said the Lifemaster in what ibn Jad noted was a tone of relief. The Black Paladin glanced coldly at the man, his displeasure obvious, and the Lifemaster quailed before Auda's anger.

But ibn Jad had no time to spare upon the tormentor. Khardan's eyelids flickered open. Rimmed with crimson, the pupils dilated, the nomad's eyes stared at Auda without a glimmer of recognition.

"God?" he said inaudibly, the barest hint of breath displacing the bloody froth upon his lips. "Yes, I . . . remember. Mathew. . ." His words died in what ibn Jad feared was his final breath. The Black Paladin clutched the man's hand.

"Call upon the God to spare you, Khardan! Offer him your soul in exchange for your life, for an end to this torment!"

"My soul. . ." Khardan's eyes closed. His lips moved, then he fell silent. Slumping forward, his head rested on his chest. "What did he say?" ibn Jad demanded of the tormentor.

"He said. . . 'Zhakrin, I give you my life.' "

"Are you certain?" ibn Jad frowned. He had heard the words "give you my life," but the name of the God to whom the man prayed had been indistinct.

"Of course!" the Lifemaster said hastily. "And look! The lines of pain upon his face ease! He draws a deep breath! He sleeps!"

"Truly, life returns to him," said ibn Jad, feeling the hand he held grow warm, seeing color flow into the bloodless cheeks. "Khardan!" he called gently.

The nomad stirred and lifted his head. Opening his eyes, he looked around him in astonishment. His gaze went to the Lifemaster, then to ibn Jad. Khardan's eyes narrowed in obvious puzzlement. "I . . . I am still here," he murmured.

An odd reaction, thought ibn Jad. Still, this was an unusual man. I've never seen one draw so near death and then have the strength to turn back.

"Zhakrin be praised!" said ibn Jad, watching the nomad's reaction closely.

"Zhakrin . . ." Khardan breathed. Then he smiled, as though seeming to recall something. "Yes, Zhakrin be praised."

Scrambling to his feet, the Lifemaster hastened over to a table and returned bearing a sharp knife, whose blade was already stained with dried blood. Seeing it, Khardan's eyes flared, his lips tightened grimly.

"Have no fear, my . . . brother," said Auda softly. Khardan glanced at him questioningly.

"Brother," repeated ibn Jad. "You are a Black Knight, now. One who serves Zhakrin in life and in death, and you are therefore my brother. But I would go further. I have requested that you and I be bonded, that our blood mingle."

"What does this mean?" asked Khardan thickly, propping

himself up, his face twisting in pain as he moved.

"Life for life, we are pledged to each other. Honor bound to come to the other's defense when we can, to avenge the other's death when we cannot. Your enemies become my enemies, my enemies yours." Taking the knife from the Lifemaster, the knight made a slash in his own wrist, causing the red blood to well forth. Grasping Khardan's arm, he cut the skin and then pressed his flesh against the nomad's. " 'From my heart to yours, from your heart to mine. Our blood flows into each other's bodies. We are closer than brothers born.' There, now you repeat the oath."

Khardan stared searchingly at ibn Jad for long moments; the Calif's lips parted, but he said nothing. His gaze went to the arms, joined together—ibn Jad's arm strong and white-skinned, the veins and sinews clearly visible against the firm muscles; Khardan's arm, pale, weak from the enforced inaction of the past few months, stained with blood and filth and sweat.

"To refuse this honor would be a grievous insult to the God who has given you your life," said the Lifemaster, seeing the nomad hesitate.

"Yes," muttered Khardan in seemingly increasing confusion, "I suppose it would." Slowly, haltingly, he repeated the oath.

Auda ibn Jad smiled in satisfaction. Putting his arm around Khardan's naked back, he lifted the nomad to his feet. "Come, I will take you to your room where you may rest. The Black Sorceress" will give you something to ease the torment of your wounds and help you sleep—"

"No," said Khardan, stifling a cry of anguish. Sweat beaded his upper lip. "I must. . . be at the ceremony."

Auda ibn Jad looked his approval but slowly shook his head. "I understand your desire to share in this moment of our victory, but you are too weak, my brother—"

"No!" insisted Khardan, teeth clenched. "I will be there!"

"Far be it from me to thwart such noble courage," said ibn Jad. "I have a salve that will help ease the pain somewhat and a glass of wine will burn away the rest."

Khardan had no breath to reply, but he nodded his head. The Lifemaster draped a black cloth over the nomad's naked body. Leaning upon Auda ibn Jad, the Calif—weak as a babe—let himself be assisted from the chamber.

CHAPTER 16

Mathew had remained locked in his room throughout the day. He had spent the incredibly long hours of waiting pacing the floor, his fears divided among Khardan, Zohra, and himself. He knew what he must do, knew what he *had* to do tonight, and he mentally prepared himself, going over and over it again in his mind. It was no longer a question of courage. He knew himself well enough now to understand that his bravery sprang from desperation. Matters were desperate enough. This was their only chance to escape, and if it meant surrendering his soul to Astafas, then that is what he was prepared to do.

"And even that is a cowardly act," he said to himself, slumping exhausted in a chair, having walked miles in his little room. "It is all very well to say that you are sacrificing yourself for Khardan and Zohra, both of whom saved your life, both of whom were dragged into this because of you! But admit it. Once again, you are acting to save your own skin, because you can't face the thought of death!

"That was a very fine lecture you gave Khardan. All about having the courage to live and fight. Fortunately he couldn't see the words were stained yellow with a coward's bile as they fled your mouth. He and Zohra both are prepared to die rather than betray their God! You're prepared to sell your soul for another few moments of keeping life in a craven's body that isn't worth the air it breathes!"

Night had darkened his window. The tones of the iron bell had rung out at such long intervals during the day that Mathew often wondered if the timekeeping device had broken down. Now the peals dinned in his ears so often he was half convinced that they had let the clock run loose, chiming the quarter hours on whatever whim took it.

To distract thoughts that were threatening to run as wild as time, Mathew rose to his feet and threw open the window. A freshening wind from the sea blew away the foul-smelling, yellowish tinged fog that had clung like a noxious blanket to the Castle all day. Looking outside, Mathew could see a cliff of black jagged rocks—below that, the seashore, whose white sand gleamed eerily in the starlight. Dark waves broke upon the shoreline. A black patch against the water, the ship of the *ghuls* swung at anchor, its crew no doubt dreaming of sweet, human flesh.

Movement near the window casement caught Mathew's attention. He looked out to find a horrid figure looking in. Springing backward, Mathew slammed shut the window. Grabbing hold of the velvet curtains, he drew them closed with such force he nearly ripped them from their hangings. He left the window hastily, hurrying back to his bed, and sank down upon it.

A *nesnas!* Half human and half. . . nothing!

Mathew shuddered, closing his eyes to blot out the memory and succeeding only in bringing it more clearly to his mind. Take a human male and chop him in two, lengthwise, with an axe, and that is what I saw from my window! Half a head, half a nose and mouth, one ear; half a trunk, one arm, one leg. . . hopping, horribly. . . .

And that is what we must face when we leave the Castle!

You are the Bearer. Nothing can harm the Bearer!

The words came back to him comfortingly. He repeated them over and over in a soothing litany. But what about those with me? They will be safe, he assured himself. Nothing out there will harm them, for I will be the master, the master of all that is dark and evil. . .

What am I saying? Cowering, shivering, Mathew slid from the bed and fell to his knees. "Holy Father," he whispered, folding his hands and pressing them to his lips, "I am sorry to have failed you. I had supposed that you kept me alive, when so many more worthy than myself died, for some purpose. If so, surely I have upset that purpose through my foolish actions. It's just that. . . that I seem so alone! Perhaps what the imp said about a guardian angel is true after all. If that is so, and she has forsaken me, then I know why. Forgive me, Father. My soul will go to its dark reward. I ask only one last thing. Take the two lives in my care and deal mercifully with them. Despite the fact that they worship another

God and are barbaric and savage in their ways, they are both truly good and caring people. See them safely back to their homeland. . . their homeland. . ." Tears crept down Mathew's cheeks, falling among his fingers. "The homeland they long to see once more, to parents who grieve for them."

"What a wretch I am!" Mathew cried suddenly, flinging himself away from the bed. "I cannot even pray for others without finding myself sucked into the mire of self-pity." Glancing up at heaven, he smiled bitterly. "I cannot even pray... is that it? They say that those who worship the Prince of Darkness cannot say Your Holy Name but that it burns their tongues and blisters their lips. I—"

There came a knock on his door. Fearfully, Mathew heard the clock begin to chime. One... five... eight... his heart counted the strokes... ten... eleven...

A key rattled in the door lock. "You are wanted, Blossom."

Swallowing, Mathew tried to answer, but the words would not come. His hand moved to grasp hold of the black wand. It was an unconscious act; he did not know he was touching it until he felt its sharp sides bite into his flesh, its reassuring warmth wash over him like the dark waters of the ocean waves, crashing on the beach below.

The door swung open. Auda ibn Jad stood framed in the doorway, silhouetted against a backdrop of blazing torches. The flickering light burned bright orange on his black armor, glittered off the eyes in the head of the severed snake that adorned his breastplate. Beside ibn Jad stood another knight, dressed in the same armor.

The torchlight gleamed on curly black hair, lit a face that had been in Mathew's thoughts all day—a face that was pale and wan, drawn with pain yet alight with a fire of fierce eagerness, a face that looked at Mathew with no recognition at all in the black eyes.

"You are wanted," said Auda ibn Jad coolly. "The hour of our triumph draws near."

Bowing his head in acquiescence, Mathew walked out the doorway. Ibn Jad entered the room and began to search it. What he might be hunting for, Mathew hadn't any idea—perhaps the imp. Drawing near Khardan, the young wizard took the opportunity to look once more into the face of the Calif.

One eyelid flickered. Deep, deep within the blackness of the eyes was the glimmer of a smile.

"Thank you, Promenthas," Mathew breathed, then bit off his prayer, thinking he felt a burning sensation in his throat.

CHAPTER 17

Once again the circle of Black Paladins formed in the Vestry around the signet of the severed snake. This time, however, all the followers of Zhakrin were present in the room. Blackrobed women, many with the swollen bellies that held future followers of the God, sat in chairs in one corner of the huge hall. Kiber and his *goums* and the other men-at-arms in service to the Black Paladins stood ranged around the hall, their weapons in hand. The naked blades of sword and dagger, the sharp points of spears, gleamed brightly in the light of thousands of black wax candles set in wrought-iron flambeaux that had been lowered from the high ceiling.

Behind the soldiers, huddled on the floor, their faces pale with fear, the slaves of the followers of Zhakrin waited in hopeless despair for the return of the God that would seal their fate forever.

Flanked by Khardan and Auda ibn Jad, Mathew entered the Vestry. He walked closely between the two knights; more than once Khardan's body brushed against his, and Mathew could feel it tense and taut for action. But he could also hear the breath catch in Khardan's throat when he moved, the stifled groan or gasp of pain that he could not quite suppress. The Calif's face was pale; despite the intense chill of the great hall, sweat gleamed upon his upper lip. Auda ibn Jad glanced at him in concern and once whispered something to him urgently, but Khardan only shook his head, gruffly answering that he would stay.

It occurred to Mathew, as he entered the huge, candlelit chamber, that Khardan was suffering this because of him, because of what he'd said. He has faith in me, thought Mathew, and the knowledge terrified him. I can't let him down, not after what he's endured because of me. I can't! Gripping the wand more tightly, he entered the circle of Black Paladins, who moved aside respectfully to make room for them.

Within the center of the circle of men and women had been placed an altar of such hideous aspect that Mathew stared at it, appalled. It was the head of a snake that had been cut off at the neck. Carved of ebony, standing four feet high, the snake's mouth gaped open. Glistening fangs made of ivory parted to reveal a forked tongue encrusted with rubies. The tongue, shooting upward between the fangs, formed a platform that was empty now, but Mathew guessed what object soon would rest there. Around the altar stood the tall ivory jars that Mathew had seen on the boat. Their lids had been removed.

Beside the altar stood the Black Sorceress. Her gaze fixed on Mathew when he stepped into the circle. Aged, ageless, the eyes probed the young wizard's soul and apparently liked what they saw there, for the lips of the stretched face smiled.

She sees the darkness within me, realized Mathew with a calmness that he found startling. He knew she saw it because he could feel it, a vast emptiness that felt neither fear nor hope. And over it, covering the hollowness like a shell, spread exultation, a sensation of power coming into his hands. He reveled in it, rejoicing, longing to wield it as a man longs to wield the blade of a new sword.

Glancing at Khardan, he wondered irritably if the man would be of use to him now, injured as he was. Mathew fretted impatiently for the ceremony to get under way. He wanted to see that smile on the woman's drum-skin face vanish. He wanted to see it replaced with awe!

The Black Sorceress laid her hands upon the emerald eyes of the snake's-head altar, and a low sound thrummed through the Vestry, a sound that was like a wail or moan. At the sound, all excited talk that had flowed among the circle of Paladins and whispered through the women waiting in the corner of the Vestry ceased. The men-at-arms came to stiff attention, their boots scraping against the stone floor. The circle parted to admit four slaves carrying a heavy obsidian bier. Staggering beneath the weight, the slaves bore it slowly and carefully into the center of the circle that closed around them. Reverently, the slaves brought their burden before the Black Sorceress.

Upon the obsidian slab lay Zohra, clothed in a gown made

entirely of black crystal. The beads' sparkling edges caught the candlelight and gave off a rainbow-colored aura whose heart was darkness. Her long black hair had been brushed and oiled and fell from a center part in her head around her shoulders, touching her fingertips. She lay on her back, her hands stretched out straight at her sides. Her eyes were wide open, her lips slightly parted; she stared at the candles above her, but there was no sign of life on her face. From the pallor of her complexion, she might have been a corpse, but for the even rise and fall of her chest that could be detected by the faint shimmering of the crystal beaded gown.

Mathew felt Khardan flinch and knew this pain the man experienced did not come from his wounds. He cares for her more than he admits, thought Mathew. Just as well, it will give him added incentive to serve me.

The Lord of the Paladins stepped forth and made a speech. Mathew shifted from foot to foot, thinking they were taking an inordinate amount of time to conduct this ceremony. He had just heard the clock chime three-quarters of the hour gone, when he suddenly stared intently at one of the slaves carrying the bier.

At that moment the slave Mathew was watching set his end of the bier down suddenly, groaning from the strain and wiping his face. The bier tilted, jostling Zohra and causing the Black Sorceress to glare at the slave with such ire that everyone in the Vestry knew the wretched fellow was doomed.

Usti! recognized Mathew, staring in blank astonishment. How he had managed the transformation, Mathew didn't know. He was certain the djinn hadn't been among those who first carried the bier into the Vestry. But there was no mistaking the three chins, the fat face rising from bulging shoulders.

The other bearers started to set down their ends, but the Black Sorceress said sharply, "No! not here in front of me! Beneath the altar."

With a long-suffering groan, Usti lifted his end of the bier again, helping to shift it around to place it where indicated. Mathew saw the jeweled handle of a dagger flare from the djinn's sash wound around his broad middle. Usti's fat face was grim. His chins shaking with intent and purpose and resolve, Usti took his place at his mistress's head.

A hushed silence descended upon the Vestry; breath shortened, hearts beat fast, blood tinged the faces of those who had worked and waited and dedicated their very lives to the attaining of this moment of glory. The iron chimes began their toll. . . .

One.

The Black Sorceress drew forth from her robes the crystal globe containing the swimming fish.

Two.

Reverently, she laid the globe upon the forked tongue of the snake.

Three.

Turning to one of the ivory jars, the Black Sorceress dipped in her hand and drew it forth, stained with human blood.

Four.

The Black Paladins began to call upon their God by name. "Zhakrin . . . Zhakrin . . . Zhakrin . . ." whispered through the Vestry like an evil wind.

Five.

The Black Sorceress bent over Zohra and drew an S-shape on her forehead in the blood of the murdered innocents of the city of Idrith.

Six.

The chant rose in volume, increased in speed. "Zhakrin, Zhakrin, Zhakrin."

Seven.

Mathew's hand slowly began to draw forth the black wand.

Eight.

The Black Sorceress lifted the crystal globe and placed it upon Zohra's breast.

Nine.

The chant became frenzied, triumphant. "Zhakrin! Zhakrin! Zharkin!"

Ten.

The Black Sorceress dipped her hand again in the blood in the ivory jar and smeared it over the crystal globe.

Eleven.

Removing one of the razor-sharp, ivory fangs from, the mouth of the altar, the Black Sorceress held it poised above the globe, above Zohra's breast. . .

Twelve.

"In the name of Astafas, I summon you! Bring the fish to me!" cried Mathew.

He raised the wand, the imp appeared. A shattering explosion blew out the lights of the candles and plunged the room into darkness.

CHAPTER 18

The chanting dwindled into confusion, swallowed up by shouts of outrage and anger.

"Torches!" cried some of the Paladins, starting to leave.

"Do not break the Circle!" the Black Sorceress's voice shrieked above the cries, and Mathew heard movement around him cease.

But the men-at-arms standing outside the Circle were free to act. Hastening into the hallways around the Vestry, their booted feet skidding and sliding on the slick floors in their haste, the soldiers grabbed torches from the walls and were back into the Vestry before Mathew's eyes had yet grown accustomed to the darkness.

Blinking in the blazing light that caused his eyes to ache, Mathew saw the Black Sorceress staring at him, her face livid, her eyes burning more fiercely than the flames reflected in their dark depths. She did not say a word or make a move but only gazed upon him, testing his strength. Between her and Mathew stood the imp, its splay-fingered hands outstretched, its red eyes flaring threateningly around the circle, its tongue lolling in excitement from its drooling mouth.

Nobody moved or spoke. All eyes were on him. Mathew smiled, secure in his power. "Bring me the fish," he ordered the imp again, his voice cracking with impatience. "Why do you delay? Must I speak the name of Our Master again? He won't be pleased, I can assure you."

Slowly, the imp turned and faced Mathew, its red eyes flickering, its shriveled skin glistening with slime in the torchlight. "You speak the name of My Master glibly enough," said the imp, pointing at Mathew with a crooked finger, its feet sliding noiselessly over the floor as it drew near him. "But Astafas is not convinced that you are His servant. He demands proof, human."

"What more proof does he want?" Mathew cried angrily, keeping the wand pointed at the imp. "Isn't it enough that I am capturing these two Gods, bringing them to Him to do with as He pleases?"

"Are you?" inquired the imp, grinning. "Or are you using that as an excuse to aid you in your escape from the Castle, knowing that if you have the magical globe in your possession, no one can harm you? Will you truly offer the fish to Astafas?"

"I will! What can I do to prove it?"

The imp's pointing finger began to move. "Sacrifice, in the name of Astafas, this man." The finger stopped. It was aimed at Khardan's heart.

Mathew sucked in his breath. The wand in his hand began to writhe and change and suddenly he held an onyx dagger with a handle of petrified wood. The breastplate melted from Khardan's body, leaving his chest bare, the wounds of his torment clearly visible on his skin. The Calif regarded Mathew complacently, obviously thinking this was part of the plan. He made no attempt to escape, and Mathew knew he would not.

He has faith in me!

Not until Mathew plunged the dagger into his heart, would Khardan realize he'd been tricked, duped.

"There is nothing else I can do!" Mathew whispered, raising the dagger, enveloping himself in the darkness that had suddenly become a living, breathing entity.

And thus he did not see, behind him, torchlight flare off the drawn blade of the sword of Auda ibn Jad.

The Book
of Akhran

CHAPTER 1

Death led Asrial from the *arwat* through the crowded streets of the dead city of Serinda. Glancing back, the angel could see Pukah sitting disconsolately near the window, his face against the glass, staring into nothing. For the first time since Asrial had come to know him, the djinn looked defeated, and she felt an aching in her chest in what Pukah would have termed her heart. Repeating to herself that immortal beings did not possess such sensitive and wayward organs did little to ease the angel's pain.

"I've been around humans too long," Asrial rebuked herself. "When I go back, I will spend seven years in chapel and do penance until these uncomfortable, very wrong, and improper feelings are expunged from my being!"

But the strong, shielding walls of the cathedral of Promenthas were very far away. A mist began to rise up around the angel, obliterating the sight of the *arwat* from her view, The sounds of the city of Serinda faded in the distance. Asrial could see nothing except the gray fog that swirled around her and the figure of Death near.

"Where are we?" asked Asrial, confused and disoriented in the thick mist.

"One might say this is my dwelling place," responded Death.

"Dwelling!" Asrial peered through the mist, attempting to see past the wispy rags of fog that wrapped and whorled and meandered around them. "I see no dwelling!"

"You see no walls, no floor, no ceiling, you mean," Death corrected. "Such structure makes—for you—a dwelling. Yet how should I—who know the impermanence of all things—put my faith in the frail and fragile elements? Were I to live in a mountain, I would eventualy see it crumble around me. Speaking of that which is frail and fragile, I will show you the human in whom you take such an interest."

The mists swirled and then parted, swept from before the angel's eyes by a blast of cold wind. She stood in the Vestry. Mathew—dagger in hand—faced Khardan. Behind Mathew stood Auda ibn Jad, his sword slowly and noiselessly sliding from its scabbard. And standing near them all, its red eyes gleaming in glee—

"A servant of Astafas!" cried Asrial. "And I am not there to protect Mathew! Oh, I should never have left him, never!"

"Why did you come?"

"I was told I had to, or else my protege would lose his soul," Asrial faltered, her eyes on the imp.

"And who told you this?"

"A. . . fish," Asrial said, flushing in embarrassment. "How could I be so foolish!"

"The fish was the Goddess Evren, child." Death seemed amused. "Trying to regain Her immortals, so that She can return to power, if She manages to return to life."

"I don't understand."

"The two fish you see in the globe on the altar are, in reality, the God Zhakrin and His opposite, the Goddess Evren. They are in the hands of Zhakrin's followers. The Black Sorceress, the woman standing beside the altar, was just about to bring Zhakrin back into the world by placing His essence into the body of a human when your Mathew decided to interfere.

"The young man came into possession of a wand of evil magical power. He succumbed to the temptation to use it and so—without you to guard him—he is easy prey for Astafas. Your Mathew is attempting to take possession of the fish."

"To save Evren!" Asrial breathed.

Death shrugged. "Mathew is a human, child. The war in Heaven is not his concern. Under the growing influence of evil, the only person he intends to free is himself. Once he has possession of the globe, the magic surrounding it will protect him from harm. If he takes it, he would dare not free the Gods. And it would not make much difference if he did. Without their immortals, Zhakrin and Evren will soon dwindle, and this time they will vanish completely. Quar's power is ten times what it was when he first caught them. Their followers will be obliterated from the earth."

The vision changed. Asrial saw the future. A mighty armada sailed the Kurdin Sea. Hordes of men, bearing the standard of the golden ram's head, landed upon the beach of the Isle of Galos. The followers of Zhakrin fought desperately to save their Castle, but it was all in vain. They were overwhelmed: The bodies of the Black Paladins lay hacked and mangled upon the beach. Their line had not broken; each died where he stood—side by side with his brother. In the Castle, the Black Sorceress and the women fought with their magic, but that, too, could not prevail against the might of Quar. The Imam called down their ruin. The 'efreet, Kaug, surged up from the volcano, bringing with him deadly ash and poisonous fume. He shook the ground; the Castle walls cracked and crumbled. The armies of Quar fled to their boats and sailed hastily back to the mainland. The volcano blew asunder; molten rock flowed into the boiling sea. Steam and cloud wound their winding sheets about the Isle of Galos, and it vanished forever beneath the dark waters.

"They are a cruel and evil people," said Asrial, reliving in her mind the murder of the priests and magi upon the shores of Bas. "They deserve such a fate. They are not fit to live."

"So Quar teaches—about the followers of Promenthas," said Death coolly.

"He is wrong!" Asrial cried. "My people are not like those!"

"No, and they are not like Quar's followers. And therefore they must either become like Quar's followers or they must die, for 'they are not fit to live.'"

"You must stop him!"

"Why should I care? What does it matter to me if there is one God or twenty? And it is not your concern, either, is it, child? Your concern is for that one mortal whose life and soul stand poised upon the blade of a dagger. I fear there is little you can do to save his life"—Death caused the vision of Mathew to return and gazed upon it, an expression of insatiable hunger on her pallid face—"but you might yet be able to save his soul."

"I must go to him—"

"By all means," said Death nonchalantly. "But I should remind you that in order to reach the city gate, you will have to traverse the streets of Serinda."

The angel stared at Death with stricken face.

"But I can't! If I should die—"

"—you would live again, but without any memory of your protégé."

"What do you want of me?" Asrial demanded through trembling lips. "You brought me here, you showed me this for a purpose."

"Can't you guess? I want Pukah."

"But you have him!" the angel answered despairingly.

"You said yourself that there is no way for him to escape!"

"Nothing in Sul is certain," replied Death sagely, "as I—above all others—have reason to know. You love him, don't you?"

"Immortal beings cannot love." Asrial lowered her eyes.

"Should not. It reduces their efficiency, as you yourself can plainly attest. You have committed a double sin, child. You have fallen in love with a mortal and an immortal. Now you must choose between them. Give me Pukah, and will set you free to go to the rescue of your mortal's soul, if not his body."

"But it will be too late!" Asrial gazed, terrified, at the vision before her.

"Time has no meaning here. One day passes in this realm for every millisecond in the mortal realm. Bring me the tourmaline amulet this night, leave the djinn defenseless, and I will see to it that you arrive in time to fight for Mathew's soul."

"But you said Pukah had until morning!"

The woman showed her teeth in a grin. "Death is without pity, without mercy, without prejudice. . . without honor. The only oaths I am bound to keep are those I swear in Sul's name."

Asrial looked again at Mathew. She could see the darkness already folding its black wings around him. The sword of Auda ibn Jad was sliding forth slowly, ever so slowly, from its scabbard and she saw Mathew—his back turned to the Black Paladin—raise his dagger against a man who had trusted him, a man he loved.

Asrial bowed her head, her white wings drooped, and she found herself standing in the street, in front of the *arwat* in the city of Serinda.

CHAPTER 2

y enchanting one!" Pukah shouted, spying Asrial from the window. Springing to his feet, he raced outside the *arwat* and accosted the angel in the street. "You came back!"

"Of course," said Asrial sadly. "Where did you think I could go?"

"I don't know!" Pukah said, grinning. "All sorts of wild ideas went through my head when I saw you disappear with Death. Like maybe she might send you back to be with that madman of yours—"

"No!" cried Asrial wildly. Pukah looked at her, startled, and she flushed, biting her lip. "I mean, no, how silly of you to imagine such a thing." Reaching out her hand, she clasped hold of Pukah's and gripped it tightly. Her fingers were a bit too cold for those of an ardent lover, and her grasp was more resolute than tender, but so thrilled was Pukah at this expression of caring, that he immediately overlooked these minor inconsistencies.

"Asrial," he said earnestly, gazing into the blue eyes that were raised to his, "with you here, I'm not afraid of anything that might happen to me tomorrow."

The angel lowered her eyes, hurriedly averting her face, but not before Pukah saw a tear glisten on her cheek.

"Forgive me! I'm a wretch, a beast! I didn't mean to talk about tomorrow. Besides, nothing's going to happen to me. There, I'm talking about it again! I'm sorry. I won't say other word." He drew her near, putting a protective arm around her and glowering at those in the street who were lustfully eyeing the lovely angel. "I think we should go someplace where we can be alone."

"Yes," said Asrial shyly. "You're right" Her eyes looked to the upper windows of the *arwat*, from where sounds of sweet laughter drifted out into the street "Perhaps—"

"By Sul!" Pukah caught her meaning and stared at her, amazed. "Are you serious?"

Pressing her lips together firmly, Asrial moved nearer Pukah and rested her head against his chest.

The djinn flung his arms around the angel, hugging her close, never minding that it was similar to embracing the hard and unresisting trunk of a date palm. Her lips were stiff and did not kiss back.

"She does not want to seem too eager," said Pukah to himself. "Quite proper. I wonder if the wings are detachable."

Keeping his arm around Asrial's waist, the djinn led her back to the *arwat*. "A room," he said to the *rabat-bashi*.

"For the night only, I suppose." The proprietor grinned wickedly.

Pukah felt Asrial tremble in his arms and glared at the man. "For a week! Paid in advance." He tossed a handful of gold into the immortal's hands.

"Here's the key. Up the stairs, second door to your left. Don't wear yourself out tonight. You'll need to be fresh for the morrow!"

"I'll be fresh enough for you on the morrow you can be sure of that!" muttered Pukah, hurrying the near-collapsing angel up the stairs. "Don't pay any attention to that boor, my dearest."

"I'm. . . not," said Asrial faintly. Leaning against the wall, while Pukah fumbled with the key, the angel looked at him with such a sorrowful gaze that Pukah couldn't bear it.

"Asrial," he said gently, hearing the lock click, but not yet opening the door, "wouldn't you rather go sit somewhere and talk? Maybe the fountain by the Temple?"

"No, Pukah!" Asrial cried fiercely, flinging her arms around his neck. "I want to be with you tonight! Please!" She burst into tears, her grip tightened until she nearly strangled him.

"There, there," he said soothingly, feeling the heart beating wildly in the soft breast pressed against his bare chest. "You and I will be together, not only this night, but all nights in eternity!" Opening the door, he led the angel inside.

The rays of the setting sun beamed brightly through an open window. Asrial drew away from his arms as soon as they were in the room. Pukah locked the door, tossing the key on a nearby table, then hurried over to shut out the red, glaring light, slamming closed the wooden shutters and plunging the room into cool darkness.

When he turned around, his eyes growing accustomed to the dimness, he saw Asrial lying upon the bed that was the room's prominent feature. The wings—about which he had been so worried—spread out beneath her, forming a white, feathery blanket. Her long hair seemed to shine with its own light, bathing the angel in silver radiance. Her face was deathly pale, her eyes shimmering with unshed tears. Yet she held out her arms to him, and Pukah was very quick to respond.

Unwinding his turban, he shook free his black hair and crawled into bed beside her. Asrial did not look at him, but kept her eyes lowered in a maidenly confusion that made Pukah's blood throb in his temple. Slowly, her arms cold and shaking, the angel drew his head to her bosom and began to mechanically stroke the djinn's curly hair.

Pukah nestled into the softness of the wings and, placing his lips upon the white throat, was just about to lose himself in sweetness when he noticed that Asrial was singing.

"My dove," he said, clearing his throat and trying to lift his head, only to find that the angel held him close, "your song is beautiful, if a bit eerie, but so mournful. Plus"—he yawned—"it's making me sleepy."

The angel's hand motions were lulling and soothing. Pukah closed his eyes. The enchanting song bubbled into his mind like the rippling waters of a cool stream, quenching desire. He let the waters take him up and bear him away, floating on the top of the music until he sank beneath its waves and drowned.

Asrial's voice died. The djinn slept soundly, his head on her breast, his breathing regular and even. Rolling his body over gently, she sat up beside him. She had no fear of waking him. She knew he would sleep soundly for a long, long time.

A very long time. Sighing, Asrial gazed at the slumbering Pukah until she could not see him for the tears in her eyes. The slim, youthful body, the foxish face that thought itself so clever. Her hands stole around his chest and drew him close. She buried her face in his chest and felt his heart beat.

"No immortal can have a heart!" she wept. "No immortal can love! No immortal can die! Forgive me, Pukah. This is the only way! The only way!"

Taking hold of the amulet in her shaking hands, Asrial slowly removed it from around the djinn's neck.

CHAPTER 3

Sond djinn awoke in a dimly lit, cavernous chamber. Sitting up and looking around him, he could barely make out tall marble columns reflecting the orange light of glowing flame off their polished surface. The handsome djinn had no idea where he was and no recollection of how he got here. He had no recollection of anything, in fact, and felt his head to see if there was a lump on it.

"Where am I?" he asked rhetorically, more to hear the sound of his voice in the shadowy darkness than because he expected an answer.

An answer was returned, however.

"You are in the Temple of Death in the city of Serinda."

Startled, the djinn glanced quickly around and saw the figure of a woman clad in white standing over him. She was beautiful, her marble-smooth face reflecting the flame in the same manner as the towering columns. Despite her beauty, the djinn shivered when she approached. It may have been some trick of the indistinct light, but the djinn could have sworn there was something strange about the woman's eyes.

"How did I get here?" the djinn asked, still feeling his head for swellings or bruises.

"You don't remember."

"No, I don't remember. . . much of anything."

"I see. Well, your name is Sond. Does that sound familiar?" Yes, the djinn thought, that seemed right. He nodded gingerly, expecting his head to hurt. It didn't.

"You are an assassin—a skilled one. Your price is high. Few can afford you. But one did. A king. He paid you quite handsomely to kill a young man."

"A king shouldn't have to hire an assassin," said Sond, rising slowly to his feet and staring at the woman suspiciously. What was there about her eyes?

"He does when the killing must be kept secret from everyone in court, even the queen. He does when the person to be assassinated is his own son!"

"His son?"

"The king discovered the boy plotting to overthrow him. The king dares not confront his son openly, or the boy's mother would side with him, and she has her own army, powerful enough to split the kingdom. The king hired you to assassinate the young man; then he will spread the news that it was done by a neighboring kingdom, an enemy.

"You tracked your quarry to this city, Serinda. He stays in an *arwat* not far from here. But beware, Sond, for the young man is aware of you. Last night, you were attacked by his men who beat you and left you for dead. Some citizens found you and brought you to the Temple of Death, but you recovered, with my help."

"Thank you," said Sond warily. He moved nearer the woman, trying to see her more dearly, but she stepped back into a shadow.

"Your thanks are not required. Does any of this bring back memories?"

"Yes, it does," Sond admitted, though it seemed to him more like a story he'd once heard a *meddah* relate than something that had happened to him. "How do you know—"

"You spoke of it in your delirium. Do not worry, it is not unusual for memories to flee a person's mind, especially when they have taken such a brutal beating."

Now that she spoke of it, Sond did feel pain in his body. He could almost see the faces of his attackers, the sticks they carried raining blows down upon his body while the young man whom they served stood looking on, smiling.

Anger stirred in his heart. "I must complete my mission, for the honor of my profession," he said, feeling for the dagger in the sash at his waist, his hand dosing reassuringly over the hilt. "Where did you say he was staying?"

"In the *arwat* the next street over to the north. It has no name, but you can tell it by the lovely girls who dance on the balconies in the moonlight. When you enter, ask the proprietor to show you the room of a young man who calls himself Pukah."

"His guards?"

"He believes you to be dead, imagines himself safe. You will find him alone, unprotected." In her hand the woman held an amulet, swinging it by its chain.

Sond paid scant attention to the jewel. Eager to get on with his work, his memories growing clearer and more vivid by the moment, he looked about for an exit.

"There." The woman pointed, and Sond saw moonlight and heard faint sounds of a city at night.

He hurried forward, then stopped, turning. "I am in your debt," he said. "What is your name?"

"One you know in your heart. One you will hear again and again," said the woman, and her lips spread over her teeth in a grin.

Sond had no trouble finding the *arwat*. A huge crowd was gathered outside to watch the girls dancing on the balcony. This Serinda was a lusty, brawling city, apparently. If Sond was at all worried about how the murder of a Prince might be viewed here, his fears were quickly eased. Life was cheap in Serinda, to judge by what he glimpsed in dark alleyways as he made his way through the streets. With only a glance at the dancing girls, one of whom seemed vaguely familiar, Sond entered the inn.

He found the proprietor—a short, fat man, who glanced at him and nodded in recognition, though Sond couldn't recall ever having seen him before.

"I am looking for a man called Pukah," said Sond in a low undertone. The woman had said the Prince's guards would not be about, but it never hurt to be cautious.

The *rabat-bashi* burst into wheezing, gasping laughter, and Sond glared at him angrily. "Shut up! What is so funny?"

"A small joke just occurred to me," said the proprietor, wiping his streaming eyes. "Never mind. You wouldn't understand. A pity, too. Don't glower so and keep your knife where it is, or you'll regret it, friend." Steel flashed in the proprietor's hand. He could move fast, it seemed, for one so round. "Your man is upstairs, second door to the left. You'll need a key." Knife in one hand, he fumbled at a ring at his waist with the other. "Sure you don't want to wait until sunrise?"

"Why should I?" Sond asked impatiently, snatching the key

from the man's hand.

"No reason." The *rabat-bashi* shrugged. "You know your business, I guess. He was with a woman—a beauty, too. But she left some time ago. I'll wager you'll find him sleeping like a babe after his. . . um . . . exertions."

Scowling, Sond didn't wait to hear anymore but ran up the stairs, taking them two at a time. Pausing outside the door, he laid his ear to the keyhole, but it was futile to attempt to hear anything above the wailing of the music and the howls of the crowd outside. Ah, well, the noise would muffle any sound—such as a scream.

Quickly, Sond inserted the key, heard the lock click, and silently pushed open the door. The curtains were closed; he could see only a dark shape lying on white sheets. Padding softly across the floor, the djinn opened the curtains a crack, allowing moonlight to spill through and shine upon the figure in the bed. He wouldn't want to kill the wrong man by mistake.

But this was his man, he was sure of it. Young, with a thin, pointed-chinned face and an expression on his countenance indicating that—even in sleep—he thought very well of himself. Though Sond couldn't say he recognized the face, that smug, self-satisfied look evoked a response—a highly unpleasant one.

Drawing his dagger, Sond crept over to the bed where Pukah lay, apparently in deep slumber. To his consternation, however, the young man's eyes suddenly opened wide.

The dagger's blade gleamed in the moonlight. There was no mistaking the murderous intent on Sond's face. He gripped the dagger in his sweating palm and prepared to fight.

But the young man lay in bed, staring at him with an odd expression—one of sorrow.

"Pukah?" questioned Sond grimly.

"Yes," replied the young man, and there was a tremor in the voice as of one who holds very tightly to courage.

"You know why I am here."

"Yes." The voice was faint.

"Then you know that I bear you no malice. I am but the hand at the end of another's arm. Your vengeful spirit will not seek me, but the man who paid me?"

Pukah nodded. It was obvious he could not reply. Rolling over on his stomach, he hid his face in the pillow, gripped it with both hands. His body was covered with sweat, he quivered, his lips trembled.

Sond stood over him, looking down at him, contemptuous of his victim's fear. Lifting the dagger, the djinn drove it to the hilt between Pukah's shoulder blades.

CHAPTER 4

The entire population of the city of Serinda gathered to celebrate Pukah's funeral. The *arwat*'s proprietor (a new one;
the former had been dispatched during the night in a quarrel over
the price of a room) discovered the djinn's body in the morning
when she made a tour of the rooms, throwing out any guests too
drunk to stagger forth on their own.

Death came to view the body as it was being carried forth,
accompanied by a mockery of solemn state and ceremony. The
dancing girls preceded it. Dressed in sheer, filmy black silk, they
wept copiously and disappeared rapidly; there being those in the
crowd who offered to comfort them in their affliction. The *arwat*'s
musicians played funeral music to a festive beat that started an
impromptu street dance as the bearers carried the djinn's corpse
on their shoulders to the Temple of Death. Several fights broke
out along the route—those who had placed bets on the time of
death were arguing among themselves vehemently, since no one
was quite certain when he'd died.

Death walked behind the body, smiling upon her subjects,
who instantly cleared a path for her, scrambling to get out of the
way of her coming. The hollow eyes scanned the mob, searching
for one who should have been in attendance but was not. Death
did not look for the assassin. She had taken Sond last night. Several immortals, convinced that they were the "Prince's" bodyguards, cornered the djinn in an alley and effectively avenged
the death of their imagined monarch. Sond lay once again in the
Temple where he would be restored to life as a slaver, perhaps, or
a thief, or a Prince himself.

"Where is the angel?" Death questioned those who gathered
to watch. "The woman who was with the djinn yesterday?"

Since few to whom she spoke remembered yesterday or knew

anything about the dead man other than that it was rumored he had sought to destroy their city, no one could answer Death's question. Asrial had come to Death last night, bearing the amulet, and had given it into her hand without a word. Death promised that the angel should leave at sunset the following day, when the bargain was concluded. Asrial had seemed ill at ease, inattentive, and had vanished precipitously without responding to Death's offer.

"Truly she loves that liar," said Death to herself, and it occurred to her as she walked among the crowd that Asrial might have attempted to prevent the djinn's assassination and could very well have fallen victim to Sond's knife herself. Death shrugged, deciding it didn't really matter.

Pukah was laid upon a bier of cow dung. The singing, dancing immortals strewed garbage over him. Soaking the bier in wine, they made preparations to burn it with the setting of the sun.

Death watched the proceedings until, bored, she left to follow the Amir's troops into battle against another city in Bas. This city was proving obstinate—refusing to give up without a fight, refusing to acknowledge Quar their God. Death was certain to reap a fine harvest from this bloody field. The Imam had ordered every *kafir*—man, woman, and child—put to the sword.

She had all day until she must return to Serinda and see her bargain with Pukah completed.

Death had time to kill.

CHAPTER 5

"ark as Quar's heart," muttered Pukah to himself, opening his eyes and staring around him confusedly. "And the air is thick! Has there been a sandstorm?" Dust flew into his mouth, and the djinn sneezed. Sitting up to see where he was, he received a smart rap on the head.

"Ooof!" Dizzily, Pukah lay back down and, moving more cautiously, slowly extended his hands and felt around him. Above his head, apparently, was a slab of wood. And he was lying on wood—dirty, dust-covered wood by the feel and the smell.

Just when the djinn had decided that he was lying in a wooden box—for Sul only knew what reason—Pukah groped about farther and felt his hand brush into soft material on either side of him. "A wooden box with curtains," he commented. "This gets stranger and stranger." One hand slid completely underneath the material. Figuring that where his hand could go, he could follow, the djinn scooted across the floor, raising a huge cloud of dust, and nearly sneezing himself unconscious.

"By Sul!" said Pukah in astonishment, "I've been lying under a bed!"

Sunlight streaming through a dirty window revealed to the djinn the place where he'd apparently spent the night. It was the same bed on top of which he'd been lying in a state of bliss with. . .

"Asrial!" Pukah cried, looking around him frantically.

He was alone and his head felt as though it were stuffed with Majiid's stockings. Pukah had the vague memory of singing in his ears, then nothing. Slowly he sank down on the bed. Batting himself on the forehead several times, hoping to displace the stockings and allow room for his wits, the djinn tried to figure out what had happened. He remembered Asrial returning to the *arwat* after his bargain with Death. . .

Bargain with Death!

Pukah's hand went to his chest. The amulet was gone! "Death's taken it!" Gulping, he leaped up from the bed and staggered across the room to peer out the window. The sun was low, the shadows in the street were long.

"It's morning!" Pukah groaned. "Time for the entire city to try to kill me. And I feel as if camels have been chewing on my brain!"

"Asrial?" he called out miserably.

No answer.

She probably couldn't bear to watch, Pukah thought gloomily. I don't blame her. I'm not going to watch either.

"I wonder," the djinn said wistfully after a moment, "if I was good last night." He heaved a sigh. "My first time... probably my last... And I don't remember any of it!"

Flinging himself upon the bed, he pulled the pillow over his aching head and moaned a bit for the hardness of the world. Then he paused, looking up. "It must have been wild," his alter ego said upon reflection, "if you ended up under the bed!"

"I've got to find her!" Pukah said decisively, scrambling to his feet. "Women are such funny creatures. My master the Calif told me that one must reassure them in the morning that one still loves them. And I do love her!" Pukah said softly, clasping the pillow to his chest. "I love her with all my heart and soul. I would gladly die for her—"

The djinn stopped short. "You undoubtedly will die for her," his other self told him solemnly, "if you go out that door. Listen, I have an idea. Perhaps if you stayed hidden inside this room all day, no one would find you. You could always slip back underneath the bed."

"What would the Calif say—his djinn hiding beneath a bed!" Pukah snorted at himself in derision. "Besides, my angel is probably roaming the city now, thinking in her virgin heart that I have had my way with her and now will abandon her. Or, worse still"—the thought made him catch his breath—"she might be in danger! She has no amulet, after all! I must go find her!"

Checking to make certain his knife was tucked into his sash, the djinn hurled open the door and ran down the stairs, feeling as though he could take on the entire city of Serinda. He paused outside the beaded curtains.

"Ho! Come out, you droppings of goats, you immortal refuse of swine! Come! It is I—the gallant Pukah—and I challenge one and all to do battle with me this day!"

There was no response. Grimly Pukah charged through the curtains into the main room.

"Come, you horses' hindquarters!"

The room was empty.

Frustrated, Pukah fought his way through the swinging beads and leapt out the door, into the street.

"It is I, the challenger of Death, the formidable Pukah. . ."

The djinn's voice died. The street was empty. Not only that, but it seemed to be growing darker instead of lighter.

What with all the confusion, the shouting and yelling and flinging himself about, Pukah felt his head begin to throb. He gazed about in the gathering gloom, wondering fearfully if his vision was beginning to go. A fountain stood nearby. Bending his head at the marble feet of a marble maiden, he allowed her to pour cooling water from her marble pitcher upon his fevered brow. He felt somewhat better, though his vision did not clear up, and he was just sitting down on the fountain's rim when he heard a great shout rise up some distance away from him.

"So that's where everybody is!" he said triumphantly. "Some sort of celebration. Probably"—he realized glumly—"working themselves into a blood frenzy."

He jumped to his feet, the sudden movement making his head spin. Dizzily he fell back into the fountain, clinging to the marble maiden's cold body for support. "Maybe they're tormenting Asrial! Maybe Death took her from me in the night!"

Fury burning in his imaginary veins, Pukah shoved the maiden away from him, knocking her off her pedestal and sending the statue crashing to the pavement. He ran through the empty streets of Serinda, using the shouts as his guide, hearing them grow louder and more tumultuous as the darkness deepened around him. No longer trying to figure out what was going on, knowing only that Asrial might be suffering, and determined to save her no matter what cost to himself, Pukah rounded a corner and ran headlong into the Temple plaza.

He was stopped by a crush of immortals blocking his path. Their backs to him, they were staring at something in the center of the plaza and cheering madly. Standing on tiptoe, trying to see over veils and turbans, laurel wreaths and steel helms, golden crowns and tarbooshes and every other form of head-covering known to the civilized world, Pukah could make out a wisp of dark, foul-smelling smoke beginning to curl into the air. He saw Death, standing next to something in the center of the Plaza, a look of triumph upon her cold, pale face.

But what was it she was gazing at with those hollow, empty eyes? Pukah couldn't see, and finally, exasperated, he increased his height until he towered head and shoulders above everyone in the crowd.

The djinn sucked in his breath, a sound like storm wind whistling through taut tent rigging.

Death was looking triumphantly at him!

But it wasn't the him standing at the edge of the cheering mob. It was a him lying prone upon a bier of cow dung, flames flickering at its base from torches thrown by the crowd.

"*Hazrat* Akhran!" Pukah gasped. "There really are two of me! I've been leading a double life and I never knew it! Suppose"—a dreadful thought struck the djinn—"suppose he's the one Asrial fell in love with!" Pukah shook his fist at the body on the bier. "You've been so understanding, so sympathetic! And all the time it was you making love to her!"

Jealousy raging in his soul, Pukah began to shove his way through the mob. "Get out of my way! Step aside there. What are you staring at? You'd think you'd seen a ghost. Move over! I have to get through!" So intent was he upon confronting himself with betraying himself, the djinn did not notice that—at the sight of him—the immortals fell back, staring at him in shock.

Striding angrily down the path cleared for him by the shaken immortals, Pukah came to the bier. Death gaped at him, her mouth open, her jaw working in unspeaking rage. Pukah never noticed. His eyes were on himself lying, covered with garbage, upon the smoldering dung heap. .

"You were with her last night!" Pukah cried, pointing an accusing finger at himself. "Admit it! Don't lie there, looking so innocent. I know you, you—"

"Kill him!" Death shrieked, her hands clenching to fists. "Kill him!"

Howling in fear and fury, the mob surged toward Pukah, their screams and curses bringing him to his senses at last.

"I'm not dead!" he said. "But then who—"

The mob attacked him. The fight was hopeless; he was one against thousands. Falling back across the bier and the body on it—the body whose identity he now knew, the body who had given her life for his—Pukah raised his arm instinctively to ward off the blow. Averting his eyes from Death, his gaze rested on the face he loved, a face he could see beneath the mask it wore.

"Holy Akhran, grant my prayer. Let us be together!" Pukah whispered. Looking at Asrial, he did not see the sun vanish beneath the horizon.

Death saw. The dark eyes stared into descending darkness, and she gnashed her teeth in her wrath.

"No!" she cried, raising her hands to Heaven. "No, Sul! I have been cheated! You can't take this away from me!"

Night came to Serinda; the sun's afterglow lit the sky, and by its dim light the immortals watched their city begin to crumble and fall into dust.

Staring at the body on the bier, Pukah saw it change form. Blue eyes looked into his. "You've won, Pukah," the angel said softly, her silver hair shining in the twilight. "The Lost Immortals are freed!"

"Because of you!" Pukah caught Asrial's hand and pressed it to his lips. "My beloved, my life, my soul. . ." The hand began to fade in his. "What—" He grasped at it frantically, but he might as well have been clutching at smoke. "What is happening? Asrial, don't leave me!"

"I must, Pukah," came a faint voice. The angel was disappearing before his eyes. "I am sorry, but it has to be this way. Mathew needs me!"

"Stop, I'll go with you—" Pukah cried, but at that moment he heard a harsh voice booming in his ears.

"Pukah! Your master calls you! Have you been purposefully avoiding me? If so, you will find your basket being used to roast squid upon your return!"

"Kaug!" Pukah licked his lips, peering into the Heavens.

He felt himself slipping away, as though he were being sucked into a huge vortex. "No, Kaug! Please!" The djinn fought frantically, but he couldn't help himself.

A last glance at the city of Serinda, the dying city of Death, revealed all the immortals looking around themselves in vast confusion. A seraphim dropped a wine goblet, staring at it in horror, and hastily wiped his lips in disgust. A virginal goddess of Vevin glanced down at her own scantily clad form and blushed in shame. Several immortals of Zhakrin, who had been leading the murderous assault upon Pukah, suddenly lifted their heads, hearing a voice long stilled. They vanished instantly. A deity of Evren dropped a sword she had been waving and lifted her voice in a glad cry. She, too, disappeared.

Sond staggered out of the Temple, looking dazed. "Kaug?" he muttered, shaking his head muzzily. "Don't yell! I'm coming."

Pukah tumbled through the ethers, whirling round and round.

Death stood in the midst of the ruins of an ancient city lying silent and forgotten, sand blowing through its empty streets.

CHAPTER 6

Khardan understood little of what was transpiring around him. It was magic—magic more powerful and terrifying than he could have ever believed was possible to exist in this world. At first he had assumed that this was all part of Mathew's plan to help them escape—until he saw by the deperate, half-crazed look in the youth's eyes that Mathew truly meant to kill him. Khardan could do nothing to defend himself. Pain—numbed and shocked, he stared at Mathew in a stupor.

And then his eye caught movement.

Swiftly, silently, Auda ibn Jad drew his curved sword.

Light flashing on the arcing blade, the Black Paladin swung it in a slashing, upward thrust aimed at Mathew's back. True to his oath, Auda was going to save his brother's life.

Khardan's sluggish heartbeat quickened; action's heat surged through him, driving off the chill of helpless fear of the unknown. This he knew. This he understood. Steel against steel. Sinew and bone, muscle and brain against another man's bone and brain and brawn. Counting life's span by each panting breath, each thud of the heart, knowing any second it might end in a blood-red explosion of pain.

Far better than dying by magic.

Mathew did not see his danger. Eyes squinched shut, the youth lunged at Khardan with a despairing, clumsy thrust. Stepping lightly to his left, avoiding the dagger's jab, Khardan clasped his right hand around Mathew's wrist and yanked the boy past him and out of danger, sending him sprawling on his stomach to the stone floor. In the same movement, the nomad's left hand knocked aside Auda's sword thrust. Khardan intended to follow through with a knee to the groin, incapacitating his enemy, but ibn Jad quickly recovered and blocked the jab. Falling back before the nomad's rush, Auda kept his sword easily clear of Khardan's frantic grasp. His blade flaring in the torchlight, ibn Jad faced Khardan, who drew his own sword and fell on his guard.

"Tell me," said ibn Jad, his hooded eyes glittering, "the name of the God you serve?"

"Akhran," answered Khardan proudly, keenly watching the other's every move.

The Black Paladins gathered round, watching, not drawing their weapons. It was Auda's privilege to dispatch his foe himself. They would not intervene.

"That is impossible!" ibn Jad hissed, "You spoke the name 'Zhakrin'!"

"Zhakrin, Akhran"—Khardan shrugged wearily, his wounds aching—"they sound alike, especially to ears listening for what they want to hear."

"How did you manage to survive?"

"All my life I have made demands of my God," said Khardan in a low, earnest voice, never taking his eyes from the eyes of ibn Jad. "When He did not answer in the way I wanted, I was angry and cursed His name. But in that terrible chamber, my pain and torment grew more than I could bear. My body and my spirit were broken and I saw—as you meant me to see—a God. But it was not your God. It was Akhran. Looking at Him, I understood. I had been fighting His will instead of serving Him. That is what had led me to disaster. Stripped naked, weak and helpless as when I first came into this world, I knelt before Him and begged for His forgiveness. Then I offered Him my life. He took it"—Khardan paused, drawing a deep breath—"and gave it back."

Auda lunged. Khardan parried. The swords slid blade to blade to the hilts, the two men locked in a struggle that each knew would prove fatal to the one who faltered. They strained against each other, foot braced against foot, body shoving against body, arms locked.

Ibn Jad smiled. Khardan's breath was coming in painful, catching jerks. Sweat broke out on the Calif's forehead, his body began to tremble. Khardan sank to one knee, bowed down by ibn Jad's strength. He held his sword steady until, striking like a snake, Auda dropped his weapon, and seizing the wrist of the nomad's sword arm, he gave a sharp, skilled twist. Khardan's sword fell from a hand that had suddenly ceased to function.

Retrieving his weapon, the Paladin prepared for the kill.

Khardan made a last, feeble effort to fight. His hand reached out for his sword that lay on the stone floor at Auda's feet. The Black Paladin caught hold of Khardan's arm. Blood flowed from a reopened wound on the nomad's wrist—a cut that had been made with the Black Paladin's own knife. Blood from that wound was on ibn Jad's fingers—the blood of his bonded brother. . .

Mathew hit the floor hard, the fall slamming the air from his lungs and sending the dagger—wand flying from his grasp. He tried to draw a breath, but his breathing pattern had been disrupted, and for several horrifying moments he could not inhale. Panic-stricken, he gulped and gasped until air flowed into his lungs at last. His breathing resumed its normal rhythm. Panic subsided and fear rushed in to take its place.

Mathew heard shouts behind him. The remembered flash of ibn Jad's sword, glimpsed from the corner of his eye, filled Mathew with terror. The wand had changed back from dagger to its usual form. It lay only inches from his hand.

"Grab it! Use it! Kill!" The imp's shrill command dinned in Mathew's ears.

Scrambling forward, Mathew stretched out his hand to seize the wand when he felt something like feathers tickling the back of his neck. Startled, thinking someone had crept up on him from behind, he lifted his head and looked frantically around. No one was there. He started to turn his attention back to the wand when he saw the Black Sorceress. Ignoring the confusion and turmoil going on about her, she had lifted the ivory fang of the altar snake and was preparing to drive its pointed edge into the crystal globe that rested upon Zohra's chest.

"Stop her! Use the wand!" hissed the imp.

The young wizard lunged forward, his fingers closed over the handle of petrified wood.

"Command me!" begged the imp, panting, its hot breath burning Mathew's skin. "I will slay her! I will slay them all at your word, Dark Master. You will rule, in the name of Astafas!"

Rule! Mathew lifted the wand. Its evil power shot through his body with the tingling blast of a lightning bolt.

The imp's red eyes left Mathew and gazed at something that had seemingly appeared above the young wizard. "In the name of

Astafas, I claim him as mine!" the creature crowed triumphantly. "You are too late!"

"In the name of Promenthas," came a whisper soft as the touch of a feather upon Mathew's skin, "I will not let you take him."

War raged in Mathew's soul. Turmoil and doubt assailed him. The hand holding the wand shook. The hands of the Black Sorceress, holding the ivory knife, descended.

Fear for Zohra swept over Mathew like a cleansing, purifying fire, burning away terror, panic, ambition. He had to save Zohra. The magic was in his hand that could do so, but Mathew knew— and finally admitted to himself—that he was too young, too inexperienced to call upon it. Acting out of desperation, he did the first thing that came to mind. He lifted the obsidian wand and threw it, as hard as he could, at the Black Sorceress.

He missed his aim. The wand crashed instead into the crystal globe, knocking it from Zohra's chest, sending it rolling and bouncing over the marble floor. With a piercing scream, the Black Sorceress left Zohra to chase after the precious globe.

"Our only way out!"

Scrambling to his feet, Mathew joined in the pursuit of the crystal fish bowl. Though he was faster, the aged sorceress was closer. She must win the prize.

"It's over!" Mathew whispered to himself. Their brief, futile, hopeless battle was coming to its only possible end.

And then, suddenly, the globe vanished, swallowed up by what seemed to Mathew's dazed eyes a mound of flesh.

Flopping on his fat belly, Usti had flung himself bodily upon the bounding crystal globe.

"Thank Promenthas!" Mathew cried, lunging forward. "Usti!

Give me the globe! Quickly!"

"Give it to me, meddlesome immortal," shrieked the sorceress. "I might yet spare you the fate of an eternity locked away in iron!"

Ignoring threats and cajoles alike, the djinn lay prone upon the floor where he had landed, his arms stretched out above his head in an attitude that might have been mistaken for prayer until it became obvious to the two tense, eager observers that Usti seemed to be endeavoring to dig up the marble and crawl beneath it.

The sorceress gave an impatient snarl, and—at this dreadful sound—Usti lifted his head. His chins shook, the fat face was the color of tallow, congealing into lumps of fear. The djinn's eyes darted from one to another.

"Madam, Madman"—Usti raised himself up slowly off the floor—"I fear that I cannot accommodate either of you, no matter what"—the djinn gulped—"you threaten to do to me!"

"Give me the fish, Usti!" Mathew demanded in a cracked, terror-laden voice.

"—to me, or I'll rip out your eyes!" hissed the sorceress, clawlike hands twisting, taloned nails ready to sink into immortal flesh.

"I cannot!" Usti cried, wringing his hands. Sitting back on his fat knees, he gazed despairingly down at the front of his rotund belly. Water soaked the front of the djinn's silk blouse; the torchlight winked off shards of blood-smeared crystal poking out of his stomach. On the floor before him, two fish flopped feebly in a puddle.

"I broke it!" said Usti miserably.

CHAPTER 7

"**F**rom my heart to yours, from your heart to mine. . . closer than brothers born."

Khardan heard the whispered words, felt ibn Jad's grip on him relax. Pulling Khardan to his feet, Auda tossed the Calif his sword and then put his back to the nomad's. The Black Paladins, who were waiting for ibn Jad to finish his opponent, stared at their comrade in wordless astonishment.

"What are you doing?" Khardan demanded, his voice thick, his breathing ragged.

"Keeping my oath," said ibn Jad grimly. "Have you strength to fight?"

"You're going against your own?" Khardan shook his head in confusion.

"You and I are bonded by blood. I swore before my God!"

"But it was a trick! I tricked you—"

"Don't join your arguments with those of my own heart, nomad!" Auda ibn Jad snarled over his shoulder. "I am already more than half inclined to sink my blade in your back! Do you have the strength to fight?"

"No!" gasped Khardan. Every breath was burning agony. The sword had grown unaccountably heavy. "But I have the strength to die trying."

Auda ibn Jad smiled grimly, keeping his eyes on the Paladins. At last beginning to understand that they had been betrayed, they were drawing their weapons.

"Nomad—you have stolen from me, cheated me, tricked me, and now it seems likely you are going to get me killed by my own people." Ibn Jad shook his head. "By Zhakrin, I grow to like you!"

Swords slid from scabbards, blades gleamed red in the torchlight. Their faces grim, confused no longer, the Black Paladins closed the circle of steel.

Broken! Mathew stared bleakly at the water dribbling down Usti's belly, the shards of crystal on the stone floor, the fishing lying—gasping and twitching—in a puddle. But the globe couldn't break! Not by mortal hands! But, perhaps, an immortal belly?

"You could have had much, but you wanted it all!" whispered the Black Sorceress in Mathew's ear. Hands gripped his arm, and he flinched at the touch, knowing in sick despair that there was worse—far worse—to come. "What would Astafas have given you for them that I couldn't give you?"

Her hands crawled over his chest, up his neck.

Mathew couldn't move. Perhaps the sorceress had laid a spell on him, perhaps it was her awful presence alone that stung him, paralyzing him. He stared at her, seeing her emerge from her unnatural youthful shell like some dreadful insect crawling out of its husk. The flesh receded from the fingers; they were pincers with bloodstained talons scraping his chin, tearing his lips.

"First the eyes!" Her breath was hot and foul against his skin, her gaze mesmerizing, and Mathew felt his blood congeal, his senses go numb. The pincers clawed over his cheeks, piercing the flesh. "Then I will turn you over to the torturer and watch while he removes other parts of you. But not the tongue." A thumb caressed his mouth. "I will save that for last. I want to hear you beg for death—"

Mathew shut his eyes, a scream welling up inside him. The pincers were on his eyeballs, they began to dig in...

Suddenly there was a soggy thud, a muffled groan. The pincers twitched and relaxed. The hands slide horribly down his face, his body, but they were limp and harmless. Opening his eyes, Mathew saw the Black Sorceress lying unconscious at his feet, a bruised and bloody mark upon her forehead.

"Mat-hew," said a groggy voice at his side, "you must learn... to defend yourself. I cannot always... be rescuing you..."

The voice faded. Mathew turned, but Usti was there to catch his mistress as she slumped over sideways, the bloodrimmed ivory lid of one of the tall jars slipping from her fingers. Lifting Zohra in his flabby arms, his face reddening with the exertion, Usti turned to Mathew.

"What now, Madman?"

"You're asking me?" Shaking in reaction to his horrifying experience, the young wizard stared at the djinn. "Take us out of here!"

Usti drew himself up with dignity.

"I can take myself out of here. Poof, I'm gone! But humans are entirely another matter. You do not easily 'poof.' Only my vast courage and undying loyalty to my mistress keeps me here—"

"And the fact that they've taken the ring and you have nowhere to hide!" Mathew muttered viciously beneath his breath, noting that all the jewels had been removed from Zohra's fingers. Frustrated, frightened, he ceased to listen to the djinn's self-aggrandizements. The Black Sorceress was dead—at least Mathew hoped to Promenthas she was dead—but their danger had not lessened. If anything, it was now greater. He could picture to himself the fury of these people when they discovered their witch-queen murdered.

Where was Khardan? Was he still alive? Sounds of fighting coming from the opposite end of the Vestry, near the door, seemed to indicate that he was. How to reach him? How to win their way out of this dread Castle against so many opponents?

"I can take you out of here, Dark Master!" came a whining hiss at his elbow. "Speak the name of Astafas—"

"Be gone!" said Mathew shortly. "Return empty-handed to your Demon Prince—"

"Not empty-handed!" flashed the imp. With a gurgling cry, he snatched the golden fish up in his shriveled fingers, then vanished with a bang.

Mathew stared at the black fish, resting near the hand of the sorceress. The fish's spasmodic twitchings were growing more feeble, its heaving gills showed blood-red against its black scales. Mathew scooped up the fish in his hands. Cupping his fingers, cradling the slimy amphibian in his palms, the young wizard turned slowly around to face the followers of Zhakrin.

"Listen to me—" His voice cracked. Angrily, he cleared his throat and began again. "Listen to me! I have defeated your Black Sorceress, and now I hold in my hands your God!"

His call thundered through the Vestry, echoing off the ceiling, rising above the clash and clamor of the combatants.

All faces, one by one, turned toward his, all sound died in the vast chamber.

Mathew could not see Khardan, there were too many people standing between them. But Mathew knew from the sound of battle where the Calif must be. The young wizard began to hedge slowly in that direction.

"Follow me!" he shot out of the side of his mouth. Regarding Mathew with a look of amazed respect, the djinn hurriedly fell into step behind him, bearing the unconscious Zohra in his arms.

Coming up upon a line of Black Paladins that had formed in front of him, Mathew felt his heart pounding so that it came near to suffocating him.

Mathew tilted his hands slightly so that they could all see the black fish.

"Let me pass," he said, drawing a shivering breath, "or I swear I will destroy your God!"

Chapter 8

On the eastern shores of the Kurdin Sea was a small fishing village. It was located far enough from the Isle of Galos that the people dwelling there could see only the perpetual cloud that hung above the volcano.

Swirling over the village like the tide that ruled their lives, night had reached its flood stage and was beginning to ebb when a boat took to the water. A man was setting out fishing.

Not such a strange occupation for a resident of this tiny village, whose houses appeared at first glance to be nothing more than pieces of debris washed up on the shore during the last storm. Or at least it wouldn't have been strange to see the boat setting sail with all the others of the village, the fishermen casting out their baited hooks by the first rays of the sun. This fisherman was out in a boat by himself, in the dead of night, the oars muffled with old rags, the oarlocks greased with tallow so that no sound betrayed him.

No long length of rope was coiled at his feet, no hooks were baited with juicy squid. The solitary fisherman's only fishing equipment was a net and lantern of his own clever devising, for he could be clever if he chose—this fisherman—especially when it came to the crafty, the sly, and the deceitful.

Made of brass, the lantern was completely closed on all four sides and open only at the bottom, a narrow crossbar stretching from side to side. On the center of this crossbar rested the stub of a candle, and the light that this lantern shed streamed out from the bottom; no glimmer of flame could be seen shining from the sides. An odd sort of lantern, one might think, and certainly not practical for walking at night.

But highly practical for unlawfully catching fish.

Crouched at the boat's stern, the man, whose name wa

Meelusk, held the lantern up over the water, watching in high glee as the fish—attracted to the light—came swimming all goggle-eyed and gasping-mouthed to get a better look. Meelusk waited until he had a fair number, then gathered in his net with his wiry arms.

Dumping his catch in a basket made of twisted wire, Meelusk took time to cackle silently at the slumbering village of dolts who had no more brains than the fish they caught. They worked throughout the day, from dawn to dusk, those codheads, and oftimes came back with little to show for their labors. Meelusk worked only a few hours each night and never came in empty-handed.

Oh, he made a fine pretence of taking his boat out every day, but never fished with the rest, claiming to have a secret spot all his own. So he did. Every night he sailed to a secluded alcove and lowered his wire basket, full of fish, into the water. Every day he returned to this alcove-well hidden from the eyes of his neighbors-and slumbered peacefully through the heat of the afternoon. Waking with the setting of the sun, Meelusk hauled in his catch and sailed back to the village, to greet his neighbors with gibes and taunts.

"What, no luck this day, Nilock? And you with a family of ten to support! Try selling children in the market, instead of fish!"

"The God of the Sea favors the righteous, Cradic! Quit ogling your neighbor's wife, and perhaps your luck will change!"

With a cackling laugh, always cut short by a wheeze, for Meelusk complained of a weakness in his lungs (a weakness his neighbors devoutly hoped would carry him swiftly to his just reward), the skinny, bent, little man would caper away to his wretched hut, which stood far apart from the rest of the village. Meelusk lived by himself; not even a dog would have anything to do with him. Eating his miserly dinner, Meelusk stopped occasionally to wrap his arms around his scrawny body, hug himself, and think with delight how his neighbors must envy him.

Envy was not the word.

All knew about the poaching. All knew about the cunning lantern. All knew about his "secret fishing spot." And there was more. Meelusk did not steal only fish. They told stories of how the greedy old man dropped pebbles in the cups of blind beggars and filched the coins; how he grabbed the wares sold by poor cripples and ran off, taunting them to catch him. He was not a follower of Benario. Such thieves risked their lives to steal the rubies from a Sultan's hand while the man slept. This little man stole shirts drying on the line, snitched bread from the ovens of poor widows, snatched bones from the mouths of toothless dogs. Followers of Benario spit upon Meelusk. He was a craven coward who believed in no God whatsoever.

This night, shortly after midnight, Meelusk flashed his lantern light into the water and cursed. There was something amiss with the fish, it seemed. Few came near the light. Those that had been taken in his net were wretched little creatures, hardly worth the effort, too small to eat. Other fishermen would have thrown them back, making suitable apologies and asking them politely to return when they were bigger. Meelusk left the little things in the bottom of the boat, taking a mean, nasty satisfaction in hearing them flopping helplessly about. It was the only satisfaction he was liable to get this night, the old man thought sourly; tossing out his dripping net without much hope of bringing in anything.

He shone the lantern in the water, peering down, and gave a wheeze of delight. Something shiny and bright glittered right below him! Eagerly he took a pull at the net and grunted in amazement. The net would barely budge! A spasm of excitement shook Meelusk's bony frame. Truly this was big! Perhaps a dolphin— those kind an gentle daughters of Hurn that the fools on shore always treated with such respect, petting them when they rubbed up against the boats or actually leaping overboard and frolicking in the sea with them! Meelusk grinned a gap-toothed grin and, throwing all his weight into the task, heaved again on the net. He could imagine what they'd say when he dragged this big fish to market; they'd berate him, of course, for killing an animal known to be good luck to mariners. But he knew that in reality they would be eaten alive with envy.

By SuI, it was heavy!

Veins bulging on his bony arms, his feet braced against the gunnel, Meelusk pulled and grunted and panted and sweated and hauled and pulled. Slowly the net rose dripping from the water. His arms trembling from the strain, fearing at the last moment his muscles would give out and he would drop it back into the dark depths, Meelusk threw everything he had and then some into dragging the net over the side of the boat.

He made it, heaving it over the hull with such tremendous effort that he heaved himself along with it and sprawled flat on top of his catch. Pausing to catch his wheezing breath, Meelusk was so done in by his exertions that he resembled the unfortunate fish he'd landed, able only to gape and gasp. Finally, however, the stars quit bursting in his head; he was able to stand and stagger to a seat. Lifting the cunning lantern, he eagerly looked to see what he had caught.

Undoing the net with trembling fingers, Meelusk lifted up his first object and spit out a filthy, nasty little word. "A basket," he muttered. "Nothing but a water-soaked old basket—belonged to a snake charmer by the looks of it. Still, I can probably get a few coppers for it

"Ah, ha! What's this? A lamp!" Dropping the basket, Meelusk grabbed the lamp and stared at it with greedy, rapacious eyes. "A fine brass *chirak!* This will fetch a fair price in the market—not once but several times over!" Meelusk was adept at selling something to an unsuspecting merchant, then snitching it and reselling it again.

Tipping the lamp upside down, Meelusk shook it to drain out the water. More than water came out of the lamp, however. A cloud of smoke issued from the spout, assuming the form of an incredibly large and muscular human male. Arms clasped before his bare chest, the gigantic man regarded the little, dried-up Meelusk with humble respect.

"What are you doing in my lamp? Be gone! Get out!" screeched the old man in high dudgeon, clutching the lamp to his bosom. "I found it! It's mine!"

"*Salaam aleikum, Effendi,*" said the man, bowing. "I am Sond, the djinn of this lamp and you have saved me! Your wish is my command, O master."

Meelusk cast the djinn a disparaging gaze—noting the silken *pantalons,* golden arm rings, earrings, jeweled turban. "What do I want with a pretty boy like you?" the little man snorted in disgust. "Get you gone!" he was about to add, when suddenly the basket at his feet stirred, the lid flew off, and another cloud of smoke materialized into the form of a man—somewhat thinner and not as handsome as the first.

"And who might you be?" growled Meelusk warily, keeping a firm grip on the lamp.

"I am Pukah, djinn of this basket, *Effendi,* and you have saved me! Your wish is my command, O mast—" Pukah stopped speaking abruptly, his gaze becoming abstracted, his foxish ears pricking.

"I know, I know," mimicked Meelusk irritably, "I'm your master. Well you can just hop back into the sea, Fancy Pants, because—"

"Sond," interrupted Pukah, "our master talks too much. Hear how his breath rattles in his lungs? It would be far more healthful for him to speak less."

"My thought exactly, friend Pukah," said Sond, and before Meelusk knew what was happening, the firm, strong hand of the djinn clamped the little man's mouth tightly shut.

Pukah was listening intently, his head cocked toward the plume of smoke that was a dark splotch against the moonlit horizon. Enraged, Meelusk whined and whimpered until the young, foxish djinn gazed at him severely.

"Friend Sond, I fear our master will do himself an injury if he persists in making those annoying sounds. For his own benefit, I suggest you render him unconscious!"

Seeing the djinn clench an enormous fist, Meelusk immediately ceased his pitiful screeching. Nodding in satisfaction, Sond turned to Pukah. "What do you hear?"

"Khardan, my master—former master"—Pukah amended, with an obsequious bow to the mumed Meelusk—"is in dire peril. Over there, from whence issues that cloud of steam." The djinn's face paled, his eyes widened. "And Asrial! Asrial is there, too! They are fighting for their lives!"

Sond removed his hand from Meelusk's mouth. "What place is that, *Effendi?*"

"The Isle of Galos!" Meelusk whined. "A dreadful island, so I've heard, populated by demons who eat human flesh and evil witches who drink the blood of babes and terrible men with great, shining swords who lop off heads—"

"It seems to me, *Effendi,*" said Pukah solemnly, "that you have had, your entire life, a burning desire to visit this wondrous isle."

Somewhat slow-witted when it came to things other than cheating and stealing and lying, Meelusk smugly shook his head. "No, you are wrong, Puke-up, or whatever your name is. I am content with my home." He gave the djinn a cunning glance. "And

I command you to take me there, this instant!"

Another thought occurred to him. "After we've caught all the fish in the sea first, of course."

"Fish! Alas, all you think of is work, I fear, *Effendi*. You are such a conscientious man." Sond gave Meelusk a charming smile. "You must take some time off to pursue pleasure! As your djinn, *Effendi*, it is our duty to fulfill the wish of your heart. Rejoice, *Effendi!* This night, we sail for the Isle of Galos!"

Meelusk's gap-toothed mouth dropped open. He nearly swallowed his tongue and was, for a moment, so occupied in attempting to cough it back up that he could only splutter and slobber.

"I fear the master is going into a fit," said Pukah sadly. "We must keep him from choking on his spit," added Sond solicitously. Snatching up a slimy rag used to slop the deck, the djinn stuffed it neatly into Meelusk's gabbling mouth.

"Throw these little fellows overboard!" Pukah ordered, and began to hoist the boat's tattered and torn sail.

Gathering up the fish, accepting graciously their cries of thanks, Sond tossed them back into the ocean and sent the net and cunning lantern down after them.

"We need some wind, my friend"—Pukah stated, looking critically at the sail that hung limp in the still night air—"or we will arrive at the battle two days after its conclusion."

"Anything to oblige, friend Pukah. You take the tiller."

Flying out over the calm water, Sond began to swell in size until he was twenty feet tall—a sight that caused Meelusk's eyes to bulge from his head. The djinn sucked in a deep breath that seemed to displace the clouds in the sky and let it out in a tremendous blast of wind that billowed the sail and sent the fishing boat skipping and dancing over the water.

"Well done, friend Sond!" cried Pukah. "Look! The Isle of Galos! You can see it!"

The Isle of Galos loomed large on the horizon. Ripping the gag from his mouth, Meelusk began to beat his breast and wail. "You're going to get me killed! They will eat my flesh! Chop off my head!"

"*Effendi*," said Pukah with a sigh, "I sympathize with your vast excitement and your eagerness to fight *nesnas* and *ghuls*—"

"*Nesnas! Ghuls!*" Meelusk shrieked.

"—and I am aware that you are thankful to us—your

djinn—for providing you with the opportunity to draw your sword against Black Knights, who are devoted to torturing those they capture—"

"Torture!" Meelusk screeched.

"—but if you go on flinging yourself about in this manner, Master, you will upset the boat." One hand on the tiller, Pukah reached out his other and picked up Meelusk by the scruff of his neck. "For your own good, Master, in order that you be rested and ready to do battle when we go ashore—"

"Battle!" wailed poor Meelusk.

"—I am going to offer you the loan of my dwelling," continued Pukah with a magnanimous bow.

Meelusk's mouth thought what was left of Meelusk's brain was going to order it to say something and worked away at forming the words, but no sound came out.

Pukah nodded solemnly. "Sond, our master is speechless with gratitude. I fear, Master, that you will find the basket cramped, and there is a redolent odor of Kaug, for which I apologize, but we were just now released from imprisonment, and I have not yet had time to clean." So saying, Pukah stuffed Meelusk—headfirst, feet flailing—into the basket, firmly slamming shut the lid upon the man's protests and screams.

A peaceful silence descended over the dark water. Sitting back calmly at the tiller, Pukah steered a direct course for Galos. Sond flew along behind the boat, adding a puff every now and then to keep it skimming over the waves.

"By the way," said Pukah, comfortably extending his legs and giving the basket, from which muffled howls were starting to emerge, a remonstrating nudge with his foot, "did you discover the reason why that Goddess—what was her name—slipped into Kaug's dwelling and rescued us from that great hulking oaf?"

"The Goddess Evren."

"Evren! I thought she was dead."

"She seemed very much alive to me, especially when she ordered her immortals to pick up our dwellings and hurl them into the sea."

"Why would she do that? What are we to her?"

Sond shrugged. "She said she owed Akhran a favor."

"Ah," remarked Pukah with a sigh of admiration, "*Hazrat* Akhran always did have a way with the ladies!"

CHAPTER 9

Stand aside! Let the wizard pass!" ordered the Lord of the Black Paladins.

The line of armored men slowly parted, their eyes burning with hate, clouded with fear.

Keeping the fish in his cupped hands, deathly afraid he would drop the wiggly, slimy thing, Mathew walked through their ranks, feeling their gazes pierce him like sharp steel. Trotting along behind him, carrying Zohra in his arms and panting from the strain, came the djinn.

"Madman," gasped Usti in a low undertone that echoed resoundingly through the silent Vestry. "Where are we going?"

Mathew's breath caught in his throat. Where *were* they going? He hadn't any idea! His one thought was to get out of this nightmare chamber, but then what? Go out into the night, to face the one-armed, half-headed *nesnas?*

"To the sea!" came the cool pronouncement. "The God must be taken to the sea!"

Mathew looked down the row of men that lined his path like black, armor-plated columns. Standing at the end was Auda ibn Jad, sword stained crimson, more than one of his fellow knights lying wounded at his feet. Beside him, face ashen with pain and exhaustion, blood smeared over his bare chest and arms, was Khardan.

To Mathew's wild-eyed gaze, it seemed ibn Jad must have been fighting in defense of the nomad. And it was assuredly his voice that had ordered the wizard to take the fish to the sea. The sea! There were boats!

"*Ghuls!*" cried Usti, his round, frightened eyes looking like holes punched in bread dough.

"One worry at a time," Mathew snapped.

He glanced warily at the Black Paladins. They were muttering darkly; he saw his death in their grim faces, saw it in the white knuckles that clenched over the hilts of swords or around the hafts of spears, saw it in the bristling mustaches, the lowering brows.

He continued walking forward.

The fish in his hands gave a spasmodic jerk, flipping out of his grasp, taking Mathew's heart with it. Frantically he clutched at it, caught it by the tail, and closed his hands over it with a relieved sigh. The mutterings among the Paladins grew louder. He heard footsteps coming up behind him, steel sliding from a scabbard.

"Master!" whimpered Usti.

"I'll kill it!" Mathew shouted, sweat trickling down his face. "I swear!"

And then ibn Jad was at his side, guarding his back, a dagger in one hand, his drawn sword in another.

"Let them go," came the order. The face of the Lord was a terrifying sight—contorted with fury, pale with fear. Mathew darted a glance at the Black Sorceress lying on the floor at her husband's feet. Her women were gathered around her, endeavoring to bring her back to consciousness. But it appeared that it would be a long time—if ever—before she spoke to her people again. "We can do nothing more," the Lord added grimly. "My wife is the only one who could tell us if Zhakrin is truly in peril and she cannot speak."

Catching sight of Auda ibn Jad's face over his shoulder, Mathew saw a ghostly smile flicker across the thin, cruel lips. What the man might be thinking, Mathew couldn't fathom. From the expression on Auda's face, he wasn't at all certain he wanted to know.

Mathew kept walking.

Footsteps followed him across the stone floor; the wizard could feel the thud of boots jar his body. Behind the Paladins came their men-at-arms, and behind them the black-robed women.

The fish lay in his hands, its unblinking eye staring upward, the heaving of its gills growing weaker.

"If that fish dies, so do you!" hissed ibn Jad.

Mathew knew that all too well. Focusing his attention on the fish to the near total exclusion of all else, he willed the creature to live. Each breath it drew, he drew. He was only dimly aware of

Khardan joining them, of the nomad taking Zohra from the arms of the djinn, of Usti's protest. "My Prince, you can barely walk yourself!" Of Khardan's stern reply. "She is my wife." Of Usti's muttering, "I shall soon have to carry both of you!" But the words drifted past the young wizard, less real than the sudden sensation of cool, night air blowing upon his face.

They were outside the Castle, moving in a torchlit procession down the pathway, and still the fish clung to life. His gaze fixed upon it, Mathew slipped and slid precariously in the loose gravel of the path until ibn Jad's strong arm caught hold of him and braced him.

They were crossing the narrow bridge with its grinning, gruesome heads, when the fish stopped breathing. Mathew glanced in fear and consternation at ibn Jad, who shook his head grimly and hurried the wizard along, now half carrying the young man. The others followed, and the Black Paladins followed them.

Salt spray cooled Mathew's feverish skin. He could hear the waves rolling to shore. Leaving the bridge, setting foot on the ground once more, he looked down the cliff of shining wet black rock and saw the vast ocean before him, the moon's white light forming a glistening path on the top of the black water.

At the smell of the sea, the touch of spray upon its scales, the fish jerked and gasped, and Mathew began to breath himself. The crossing of the bridge had slowed the Black Paladins. Cautiously he began to descend the slick, steep steps.

"Hurry!" urged ibn Jad in Mathew's ear. "The damned thing's about finished! When we reach the sand, head for the boats!" he added in a piercing whisper.

Looking ahead, Mathew saw a line of boats drawn up in the sand near the water's edge. But he also saw the ship, swinging at its anchor, its sailors crowded on the deck, watching the unusual activity on-shore with hungry eyes.

"What about the *ghuls*?" returned Mathew frantically, fighting to keep calm, avoiding the longing to break into a panic-stricken run. Behind him, he could hear Khardan's labored breathing, Usti' s frightened whimpers.

"Once we're on the boat, I'll take care of Sul's demons! Whatever you do, keep hold of that fis—"

Mathew had just set foot upon the shore when, "Stop them!" The shrill cry of a woman rang like a hideous bell from the topmost turret of Castle Zhakrin.

"Too late! Run!" cried Auda, giving Mathew a rough push.

Mathew stumbled. The fish flew from his hands and plopped into the murky water.

"Stop them!" came the enraged sorceress's command, and it was echoed by the furious shouts of the knights.

Mathew reached down into the crashing waves and began to grapple frantically for the fish.

"Never mind!" Grasping him by the back of his wet robes, Auda jerked him upright. "You can't fool them any longer. It's all over! Run!"

Looking behind him, Mathew saw swords flash. The Paladin had turned to face alone the onslaught of charging knights, when there came a blinding flash of light. The djinn, Sond, exploded in their midst like thunder.

CHAPTER 10

Springing up from the sand, full ten feet tall, wielding a scimitar it would have taken four mortal men to lift, Sond stood between the captives and their attackers. Fanatic fighters though they were, the Black Paladins could not but be awed by this fantastic apparition appearing before them. Coming to a halt, they glanced askance at each other and at their Lord. Above them, the Black Sorceress called down death from the Castle spires, but she was far from the towering, grim-faced djinn and his scimitar that gleamed wickedly in the bright moonlight.

"Master, Master!" cried a voice excitedly. "Over here! Over here!"

Khardan raised his eyes—even that took a supreme effort it seemed—to see a rotting, leaking, tattered-sailed fishing boat nudging the shoreline, rocking back and forth with the waves. On board was Pukah, waving his turban like a flag, and a small, wizened man crouched at the tiller, who shook in such paroxysm of fear that the chattering of his teeth could be heard above the clash of steel.

Khardan forced his weary, aching legs to drag him forward another step. Fire burned in the muscles of shoulders and arms from carrying the unconscious Zohra, his wounds pained him, his strength was gone. Pride alone kept him from collapsing before his enemies.

Seeing his master begin to give way, Pukah leapt from the boat and ran toward the Calif, taking Zohra from him just as Khardan's eyes rolled back in his head and he pitched forward onto the sand. Mathew stopped in his own headlong flight and knelt to help him.

"Run for it, Blossom!" Auda ibn Jad commanded harshly.

"I can't leave Khardan!"

"Go on!" Auda hauled Mathew roughly to his feet. "I swore to protect him with my life! I will do so!"

"I will fight alongside you!" Mathew insisted doggedly. Ibn Jad glowered at him, then gave a grudging nod.

Several of the Paladins started forward, only to be confronted by the djinn. Undaunted, the knights were prepared to fight even the immortal when the voice of the Black Sorceress rang, out again from the tower.

"You are commanded to"—it seemed she choked on the words—"let them go!"

"Let them go?" Turning to face her, the Lord of the Paladins stared up at his wife in astonishment. "Who commands such a thing?" he shouted.

"Zhakrin commands!" came a deep voice that seemed to well up from the ground.

At the sound, several of the Paladins sank to their knees. Others remained standing, however, including their Lord. Sword in hand, he glared balefully at Mathew.

The volcano rumbled. The earth shook. Many more Paladins fell to their knees, looking at their Lord in fear.

Reluctantly, the knight lowered his sword.

"It seems our God owes Akhran a service," the Lord of the Black Paladins growled. "Leave quickly, before He changes His mind!"

Together, Mathew and Auda ibn Jad lifted Khardan to his feet and dragged him across the sand to the waiting boat.

"What did you mean when you told me—'you can't fool them any longer'?" Mathew asked the Black Knight.

"Surely you knew, didn't you, Blossom"—Auda's black eyes, glittered in the moonlight—"that you did not hold a God in your hands?"

Mathew stared at him, aghast. "You mean—"

"You held in your hands nothing but a dying fish!" A ghostly smile touched Auda's thin lips. "The Black Sorceress was not the only one who would be aware of the presence of the God within the fish. I was there during the ceremony when we freed the God from the Temple in Khandar. I was myself the Bearer for a long time after that. The God left when the djinn—or should I say *Hazrat* Akhran—broke the crystal.

"But you—Why didn't—" Mathew's lips went numb. He felt

the blood drain from his face, his strength seep from his body when he recalled how he had walked down that black-armored aisle of death.

"Betray you?" Ibn Jad released Khardan into the strong arms of Pukah. "Ask the nomad when he awakens."

Gently lifting up the Calif, the young djinn carried him through the water to the waiting boat and deposited Khardan next to his wife in the bottom. Pukah hurried back to pluck at Mathew's sleeve.

"Come, Mad—" The young djinn's gaze went to a point above and behind Mathew, his expression softened; indeed, it became almost enraptured. Looking around, startled, Mathew could have sworn that he caught a flash of white and silver. But there was no one near him. "Come, Mat-hew," amended Pukah gravely and respectfully, holding out his hand to assist the young wizard through the sea water. "Hurry! We could throw this wretch of a fisherman to the *ghuls* if they decided to chase after us, but I doubt his scrawny body would content them for very long."

Turning, Mathew waded into the rippling waves, then realized that Auda ibn Jad was not with him.

"Aren't you coming?"

The Black Paladins had risen to their feet and were swarming down toward the boat. Pukah was tugging at Mathew's sleeve. Sond splashed into the water beside him, appearing prepared to lift up the young wizard and carry him aboard bodily.

Auda ibn Jad shook his head.

"But. . ." Mathew hesitated. This was an evil man, one who murdered the innocent, the helpless. Yet he had saved their lives. "They will take their wrath out on you."

Ibn Jad shrugged, and—ignoring Mathew—the Black Paladins descended on their fellow knight. Auda surrendered without a struggle. The Paladins divested him of sword and dagger. Wrenching his arms painfully behind him, they forced him to his knees before their Lord.

"Traitor!" The Lord of the Paladins stared coldly at ibn Jad. "From now on, every second will bring your tortured body one step closer to death—yet never close enough!"

Raising a mail-gauntleted hand, he struck the Black Paladin across the face.

Ibn Jad fell back in his captors' arms. Then, shaking his head to clear it, he raised his eyes to meet Mathew's.

"As was our friend's, my life is in the hands of my God." He smiled, blood trickling from his mouth. "Do not fear, Blossom. We will meet again!"

The Paladins carried him off the beach, their Lord remaining behind. His eyes, blazing in the moon's pale rays, were so filled with enmity that their gaze alone might kill. Mathew no longer needed Pukah's exhortations and pleadings (all given in the most respectful tones) to hasten through the silver-laced, black sea water. Catching the young wizard up in his strong grip, Sond tossed him headfirst over the hull.

"The *ghuls*! They're watching! They smell blood! Oh, make haste, make haste!" Crouched on a seat, Usti wrung his hands.

But Sond, shaking his head, was examining the boat with a frown. At the bottom lay Khardan and his wife. Pukah had taken advantage of their unconscious state to rest Zohra's head upon her husband's shoulder and drape Khardan's arm around her protectively.

"Truly, a marriage made in Heaven," sighed the djinn. Heaven! I've had enough of Heaven, thought Mathew wearily. Hunching down on his knees in the boat's stern, oblivious to the inch or so of sea water that sloshed around him, he laid his cheek on a wet basket and closed his eyes.

"Well, what are you waiting for?" screeched the little old man from the tiller. "Get this thing moving."

"Master, shut up," said Pukah politely.

"The boat's too low in the water. There's too much weight," stated Sond "Usti, get out!"

"Don't leave me! You can't!" wailed the djinn. "Princess, please don't let them—"

"Stop blubbering!" snapped Pukah. "We're not going to leave you. And don't wake your mistress. We want a peaceful trip after what we've been through, to say nothing of what faces us when we reach shore. Crossing the Sun's Anvil on foot. If we survive that, we must then raise an army to defeat the Amir—"

None of it mattered to Mathew. It was all too far away. "We need a new sail," grunted Sond. "Usti, you'll do fine!"

"A sail!" The djinn drew an indignant breath. "I will not—"

"Was that a *ghul* I heard, smacking his lips?" inquired Pukah.

"I'll do it!" cried Usti.

The boat heaved and floundered. Startled, jolted to wakefulness, Mathew opened his eyes and beheld an astounding sight.

Curling his feet under the boom, groaning and protesting over the hardness of his life, Usti grabbed hold of the mast with both hands. His massive body stretched and expanded until all that remained recognizable were his woeful eyes, his turban, and numerous chins.

Sucking in a deep breath, Sond let it out in a whoosh.

Usti filled with air.

"Swells up like a goat's bladder!" commented Pukah in awe.

The fishing boat began to move over the water. Taking the tiller, Pukah steered the vessel into a path seemingly laid down for them by the moon.

Mathew closed his eyes again. The wind sang in the rigging. Pukah began to relate some improbable escapade about himself and Mathew's guardian angel in a City of Death. Usti whimpered and complained. Sond blew and puffed. Mathew paid no attention to any of it.

It seemed to him that he felt a gentle hand touch his cheek. A blanket of feathery softness wrapped him in warmth, and he drifted into a relaxed sleep.

A last image drifted into his mind, that of an imp appearing before Astafas, Prince of Darkness, bearing in its splay-fingered hand. . .

A dead fish.

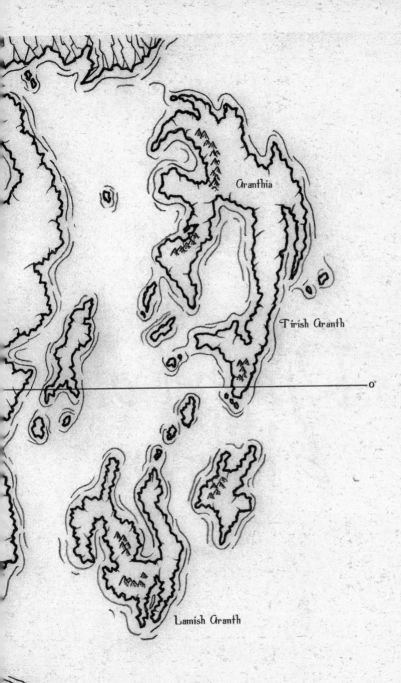

Granthia

Tirish Granth

O°

Lamish Granth

SCM

The Prophet of Akhran

The Book
of Quar

CHAPTER 1

*T*he desert burned beneath a summer sun that blazed in the sky like the eye of a vengeful god. Beneath that searing, withering stare, few things could survive. Those that did so kept out of the god's fiery sight, burrowing into their holes, skulking in their tents until the eye closed in night's sleep.

Though it was early morning yet, the heat was already radiating from the desert floor with an intensity that made even the djinn, Fedj, feel as if he been skewered like *shishlick* and was being slowly roasted over the coals of an eternal fire.

Fedj wandered disconsolately through the camp around the Tel—if camp it could be called. He knew he should be in attendance upon his master, Sheykh Jaafar al Widjar, but given the Sheykh's humor these days, the djinn would have preferred attending an imp of Sul. It had been the same every morning for the past few months. The moment Fedj sprang from the ring upon his master's hand, it began.

First, the whining. Wringing his hands, Jaafar wailed.

"Of all the children of Akhran, am I not the most unfortunate? I am cursed, cursed! My people taken captive! Our homes in the hills destroyed! The sheep that are our lives scattered to the winds and the wolves! My eldest daughter, the light of my old age, vanished!"

There was a time and not long ago, Fedj always thought sourly at this point, when that daughter's disappearance would have been considered a blessing, not a curse, but the djinn—not wanting to prolong the torture—always forbore mentioning that.

The whining and handwringing escalated into loud exhortation and breast-beating, silently punctuated by the inward comments of the long-suffering djinn.

"Why have you done this to me, *Hazrat* Akhran? I, Jaafar al Widjar, have faithfully obeyed every one of your commands without question!"

Without question, master? And I'm the son of a she-goat!
"Did I not bring my daughter, my precious jewel with the eyes of
a gazelle—"

And the disposition of a starving leopard!

"—to be wed to the son of my ancient enemy—may camels trod upon his head—Sheykh Majiid al Fakhar, and did I not
further bring my people to live around this cursed Tel by your
command, and further, did we not reside here in peace with our
enemy as was your will, *Hazrat* Akhran, or would have lived in
peace had not we been pushed beyond provocation by the thieving Akar—"

Who, for some reason, took it into their heads to be outraged
by the Hrana's "peaceful" stealing of Akar horses.

"And have we not suffered at the hands of our enemies? Our
wives and children swept from our arms by the soldiers of the
Amir and held prisoner in the city! Our camp destroyed, the water in the oasis dwindling daily before our eyes—"

Fedj rolled his eyes, sighing, and—knowing there was no
help for it—entered the tent of his master, catching him in mid-
harangue.

"—and still you insist that we stay here, in this place where
not even Sul could long live while we wait for some accursed
plant—whose brown and dried-up appendages are beginning
to look as wasted as my own—to bloom? To bloom? Roses will
sprout from my chin sooner than they will from that sand-suck-
ing cacti!" shouted Jaafar, shaking a feeble fist at heaven.

The temptation to actually summon forth blooms from the
old man's grizzled chin was so acute that Fedj squirmed in an
agony of torment. But now the exhorting and fist shaking had
ceased. It was always followed by sniveling contrition and groveling. Fedj tensed. He knew what was coming.

"Forgive me, *Hazrat* Akhran." Jaafar prostrated himself, nose
first on the felt floor of his tent. "It is only that your will is harsh
and difficult for us poor mortals to understand, and since it seems
likely that we will all perish from the harshness and the difficulty,
I beg of you"—a beady eye, peering out from the folds of the *haik*,
fixed itself intently upon the djinn—"to release us from the vow
and let us leave this accursed place and return to our flocks in the
foothills. . ."

Fedj shook his head.

The beady eye became pleading.

"I await your answer most humbly, *Hazrat* Akhran," Jaafar mumbled into the tent floor.

"The God has given you his answer," said Fedj in grim and dour tones. "You are to remain camped at the Tel, in peace with your cousins, until the Rose of the Prophet blooms."

"It will bloom on our graves!" Jaafar beat his fists into the ground.

"If so, then so be it. All praise to the wisdom of Akhran."

"All praise to the wisdom of Akhran!" Jaafar mimicked. Leaping to his scrawny legs, he made a pounce at the djinn. "I want to hear from Akhran himself, not from one of his messengers who has a full belly while I starve! Go find the God. Bring him to me! And don't come back until you do!"

With a meek *salaam*, Fedj took his leave. At least this command was a change and gave the djinn something to do, plus leave to be gone a long time doing it. Standing outside the charred and tattered remnants of what had once been a large and comfortable dwelling place, Fedj could hear Jaafar raving and cursing in a manner that would have done his wild daughter credit. Fedj stole a glance across the desert, on the opposite side of the Tel, where stood the tent of Majiid al Fakhar, Jaafar's old enemy. The sides of Jaafar's tent heaved and quivered with the old man's anger like a living, breathing entity. By contrast, Majiid's tent seemed a husk whose life juices had been sucked dry.

Fedj thought back to the time, only months before, when it had been the giant Majiid—proud of his people and his warrior son—who had thundered his rage to the dunes. Now Majiid's people were imprisoned in Kich; his warrior son was at best dead, at worst a craven coward skulking about in the desert. The giant was a broken man who rarely came forth from his tent.

More than once Fedj wished he had not been so quick to carry to his master his sighting of Khardan, eldest son of Majiid and Calif of the Akar, slinking away from the battle of the Tel, hiding from the soldiers in the rose-colored silk of a woman's *chador*. Certainly if he had foreseen the wreckage of spirits and valor that would follow after—far worse than any damage done by the Amir's soldiers—the djinn would have peppered his tongue with fire ants and swallowed it before he spoke.

Wholly dispirited, Fedj wandered aimlessly in the desert, soon leaving the Tel far behind. The djinn might have acted on his master's order and gone out to search for Akhran, but Fedj knew that the Wandering God could be found only when he wanted to be found, and in that instance, Fedj would not have to look very far or very hard. But Akhran had not made himself visible for months. Fedj knew that something was going on in the heavenly plane. Just what, he didn't know and couldn't guess. The tension hung in the air like a circling vulture, casting the shadow of its black wings over every act. It was extremely unfair of Jaafar to accuse the djinn of feasting while his master starved. Fedj hadn't dined well in weeks.

Drifting through the ethers, far from camp, absorbed in gloomy thoughts and forebodings, the djinn was jolted out of his grim contemplations by the sight of unusual activity on the desert floor beneath him. A sparse scattering of tents had sprouted during the night where the djinn could have sworn there had been no tents yesterday. It took him only a moment to realize where he had traveled. He was at the southern well that marked the boundary of Akar land. And there, camped around the well, using Majiid's water, was another old enemy—Sheykh Zeid!

Thinking that this encroachment upon Majiid's precious water might bring the dispirited Sheykh back to life, the djinn was just considering how he should impart the news to one who was not his master and, moreover, an enemy, when he caught sight of a form coalescing in the air in front of him.

"Raja?" questioned Fedj warily, his hand straying to the hilt of the huge saber at his side.

The heavily muscled, dusky-skinned body of Sheykh Zeid's djinn, also with hand on sword hilt, shimmered before Fedj in waves of heat rising from the sand.

"Fedj?" queried the other djinn, floating nearer.

"It is Fedj, as you well know, unless your sight has taken the same path as your wits and fled!" Fedj said angrily. "That water you drink is from the well of Sheykh Majiid! Your master is, of course, aware that all who drink that water without the Sheykh's permission soon find their thirst quenched by drinking their own blood."

"My master drinks where he will, and those who try to stop him will end their days filling the bellies of jackals!" Raja growled.

Scimitars flared yellow in the sun, gold flashed from earrings and arm bracelets, sweat glistened on bare chests as the djinn crouched in the air, watching, waiting. . .

Then suddenly, Raja hurled his scimitar from him with a bitter curse. It went spiraling, unheeded, down through the sky to land with a thud, carving a sword-shaped ravine in the Pagrah desert that remains a mystery to all who see it to this day.

"Slay me where I stand!" shouted Raja. Tears streamed down his face. Spreading wide his arms, he thrust forth his dark-skinned chest. "Kill me now, Fedj. I will lift no hand to stop you!"

Though the effectiveness of this display was somewhat blunted by the fact that the djinn was immortal and Fedj might run his scimitar through Raja a thousand times without doing him any harm, it was a noble gesture and one that touched Fedj to the core of his soul.

"My friend, what does this mean?" Fedj cried aghast, lowering his weapon and approaching Raja, not without a certain degree of caution. Like his master, Zeid, the warrior djinn Raja was a cunning old dog who might still have a tooth or two left in his head.

But as he drew nearer, Fedj saw that Raja was truly little more than a whipped pup. The husky djinn's despair was so obvious and real that Fedj sheathed his weapon and immediately put his arm comfortingly around the massive, heaving shoulders.

"My friend, do not carry on so!" said Fedj, distressed by the sight of this grief. "Matters cannot be this bad!"

"Oh, can't they?" cried Raja fiercely, shaking his head until his huge, golden earrings jangled against his jaw. "Tell Sheykh Majiid that Zeid is stealing his water! Bring him to fight, as would have happened in past months, and he will have the very great satisfaction of watching my master slink on his belly back into the desert where he will shrivel up and die like a lizard!"

Fedj could easily have sworn that he would do just that. He could have gloated over Zeid's downfall and glorified Majiid to the skies. But he chose not to. Raja's pitiable plight was deeply akin to his own, and Fedj guessed that Raja must know something of the true circumstances of his enemies, or he would not have revealed such weakness, no matter what his own inner turmoil.

The djinn heaved a sigh that shifted the location of several sand dunes.

"Alas, friend Raja. I will not hide from you that Sheykh Majiid would not raise his voice in anger if your master came into his tent and gouged out his eyes. And *my* Sheykh has taken to cursing the God, which does no one any good since we all know that the ears of *Hazrat* Akhran are stuffed with sand these days."

Raja lifted a grim face. "So it is true, what we have heard—that Majiid and Jaafar are in a situation almost as desperate as our own?"

"Almost!" said Fedj, suddenly indignant. "No situation can possibly be more desperate than the one in which we find ourselves. We have taken to eating the camp dogs!"

"Is that so?" said Raja, with growing anger. "Well, camp dog would seem a treat to us! We have taken to eating snake!"

"We ate the last camp dog yesterday, and since we have devoured every snake in the desert, we shall soon be forced to eat—"

The air was split by what to a mortal would have appeared to be a tremendous bolt of lightning streaking from heaven to the ground below. The two djinn, however, saw flailing arms and legs and heard an explosive curse boom in a voice of thunder. Recognizing one of their own, both djinn swallowed their words (more nourishing than either snake or dog) and immediately accosted the singed and smoking stranger who lay on his back, breathing heavily, at the bottom of a dune.

"Arise and declare yourself. Name your master and tell us what he is doing in the lands of the Akar and the Aran!" demanded Raja and Fedj.

Undaunted, the strange djinn rose to his feet, his own sword in his hand. Noting the richness of this djinn's clothing, the jewel-encrusted weapon he bore, and his air of superiority that was not put on as one puts on a caftan, but was inborn, both Fedj and Raja exchanged uneasy glances.

"My master's name is not important to the likes of you here on this plane," stated the djinn coolly.

"You serve one of the Elders?" asked Fedj in subdued tones, while Raja instantly made the *salaam.*

"I do!" said the djinn, glaring at them severely. "And I would ask why two such able-bodied men as yourselves are skulking about down here below when there is work to be done above?"

"Work? What do you mean?" said Raja, bristling. "We skulk down here below in service to our masters—"

"—when there is a war in heaven?"

"War!" Both djinn stared at the stranger.

"The plane of the immortals has erupted in fire," said the strange djinn grimly. "By some means, the Lost Immortals were discovered and freed from their imprisonment. The Goddess Evren and her counterpart, the God Zhakrin, have also come back to life and both accuse Quar of attempting to destroy them! Some of the Gods support Quar, others attack him. We fight for our very existence! Have you heard nothing of this?"

"No, nothing, by Akhran!" swore Fedj.

Raja shook his head, his earrings clashing discordantly.

"It is not to be wondered, I suppose," reflected the stranger, "considering the chaos up there. But now that you know, there is no time to be lost. You must come! We need every sword. Quar's 'efreet Kaug grows in strength moment by moment!"

"But if all immortals leave the mortal realm, what dreadful things will happen down here?"

"Better that than if the immortal realm collapses," said the stranger. "For that will mean the end of all."

"I must tell my master," said Fedj, his brow knitting.

"As must I," stated Raja.

"And then we will join you."

The strange djinn nodded and leapt back into the heavens, creating a gigantic whirlwind that swept the sand into a billowing cloud. Exchanging grim glances, Fedj and Raja both disappeared, their going marked by two simultaneous explosions that blasted holes in the granite and sent concussive waves throughout the Pagrah Desert.

CHAPTER 2

The lookout ran wildly across the desert sand, often stumbling, falling, picking himself back up and running again. As he ran, he shouted, and soon every man remaining in the decimated tribes of Sheykhs Jaafar and Majiid had left the shelter of their tents and was watching the lookout's approach with tense interest. He was an Akar, a member of Sheykh Majiid's tribe, and he was on foot rather than horseback. The few horses remaining—those who had been found wandering in the desert after being cut loose by the soldiers of the Amir—were considered more precious than all the jewels in a Sultan's treasury and were rarely ridden.

One of these horses was Majiid's own, the story being told that after the stallion's master had fallen in battle, the gallant horse stood guard above the body of his rider, fighting off the soldiers with vicious, slashing hooves. Another of the horses remaining was Khardan's. No man could get near him. Any who tried were warned away with a flattening of the ears and bared teeth and a low rumbling sound in the massive chest of the black charger. But Khardan's horse remained near camp, often seen at dusk or at twilight, a ghostly black shadow among the dunes. The fanciful claimed this meant that Khardan was dead, his spirit had entered the horse, and he was guarding his people. The practical said that the stallion would never wander far from his mares.

The lookout stumbled into camp. He was met with a *girba* filled with tepid water, which he drank thirstily but sparingly, being careful not to waste a drop. Then he approached. Majiid's silent tent. The flap was closed, a sign that the Sheykh was not to be disturbed. It had been closed almost continuously since word came of Khardan's disgrace and his father had broken his son's sword and declared him dead.

"My Sheykh," cried the man. "I bear tidings."

There was no reply.

The lookout glanced around uncertainly, and several of the other men motioned him forward, urging him with gestures to continue.

"*Effendi*," continued the lookout desperately, "Sheykh Zeid and his people are camped around the southern well!"

A low murmur, like wind among the sands, ran through the Akar. The Hrana, led by Sheykh Jaafar who had come out of his tent to see what was transpiring, glanced at each other wordlessly. This was war. Surely, if there was one thing that could rouse Majiid from his grief, it would be this unwarranted invasion of his territory by his ancient enemy.

The mutterings of the Akar swelled to angered talk of defiance, accented by loud calls for their Sheykh, and at length the tent flap opened.

Silence descended so abruptly, it seemed the men must have had the breath sucked from their throats. Those who had not seen Majiid in some time averted their heads, tears welling up in their eyes. The man had aged a decade, it seemed, for every month that had passed since the raid upon the Tel. The tall, strong frame was bent and stooped. The sharp, fierce gaze of the black eyes was bleary and lackluster. The bristling mustaches drooped beneath the hawk nose that was now as white and wasted as bare bone.

But Majiid was Sheykh still, respected leader of his tribe. The lookout fell to his knees, out of either reverence or exhaustion, while several of the *aksakal*, tribal elders, stepped forward to discuss this news.

Majiid cut their words off with a weary movement of his hand. "Do nothing."

Nothing! The *aksakal* stared at each other, the men of the Akar glowered, and Jaafar frowned, shaking his head. Hearing the unspoken defiance, Majiid glared round at them, the dark eyes flashing with sudden fire.

"Would you fight, fools?" he sneered. "How?" He gestured toward the oasis. "Where are the horses to carry you to battle? Where is the water for your *girba*? Will you fight Zeid with swords that are broken?"

"Yes!" cried one man passionately. "If my Sheykh wills it!"

"Yes! Yes!" shouted the others.

Majiid lowered his head. The lookout remained on his knees, staring up at him pleadingly, and it seemed for a moment that the Sheykh would say something more. His mouth moved, but no words came out. With another weary, hopeless gesture of a wasted hand, Majiid turned back to his tent.

"Wait!" called Sheykh Jaafar, striding forward on his short, bandy legs, his robes flowing about him. "I say we bid Zeid come speak with us."

The lookout gaped. Majiid glared, his lips meeting his beaky nose in a scowl. "Why not invite the Amir as well. Hrana?" he snarled. "Exhibit our weakness to the world!"

"The world knows already," snapped Jaafar. "What's the matter, Akar? Did your brains leave with your horses? If Zeid was strong, would he skulk about the southern well? Wouldn't he come riding in here to take this oasis, which all know is the richest in the Pagrah? Tell us what you have seen." Jaafar turned to the lookout. "Describe the camp of our cousin."

"It is not large, *Effendi*," said the lookout, speaking to Majiid, though he answered Jaafar. "They have hardly any camels. The tents of our cousins are few in number and are put up halfheartedly, straggling about the desert floor like men drunk on *qumiz*."

"See? Zeid is as weak as we are!"

"It is a trick," Majiid said heavily.

Jaafar snorted. "For what purpose? I say Zeid has arrived for this very reason—to talk to us. We should talk to him!"

"What about?"

The words fell from Majiid's lips as meat falls from the hand of a man baiting a trap. All there knew it, including Jaafar, and no one spoke, moved, or even breathed, waiting to see if he would nibble at it.

Jaafar did more than that. He calmly swallowed it whole.

"Surrender," the old man answered.

"One by one," said Sheykh Zeid, "the southern cities of Bas have fallen in the *jihad*. The Amir is a skilled general, as I have said before, who weakens his enemy from within and hits them with the force of a thunderbolt from without. Those who surrender to Quar are treated with mercy. Only their priests and priestesses are put to the sword. But those who defy. . ." Zeid sighed, his fingers aimlessly plucking at the hem of his robe as he sat cross-legged on the frayed cushions in Sheykh Jaafar's tent.

"Well," prodded Jaafar. "Those who defy?"

"In Bastine," Zeid said in low tones, his eyes cast down, "five thousand died! Man, woman, and child!"

"Akhran forbid it!" Jaafar cried, shocked.

Majiid stirred. "What did you expect?" he asked harshly, the first time he had spoken since Zeid had ridden into camp. The three men sat together, sharing a meager dinner that only two of them made even a pretense of eating. "The Amir means to make Quar the One, True God. And perhaps he deserves it."

"The djinn say there is a war in heaven, as well as down here," offered Jaafar. "At least that is what Fedj told me before he vanished three days ago."

"That is what Raja told me as well," Zeid agreed morosely. "And if that is true, then I fear *Hazrat* Akhran is being hardpressed. Not even the *sirocco* to plague us this year. Our God lacks spirit." Sighing, the Sheykh shoved his food dish aside; its scant contents were instantly snatched up and devoured by what few servants Jaafar had remaining.

Majiid seemed not to hear the sigh. Jaafar did, and gave Zeid a piercing glance but said nothing, it being considered impolite to interrogate a guest.

The conversation turned to the dark events of the tribe. Zeid's people had fared much the same as the rest of the desert nomads in the battle with the Amir.

"All the women and children and most of my young men, including six of my sons, are being held captive in the city of Kich," said the Sheykh, whose clothes hung loosely on a body that had formerly been rotund. "My men eat their hearts out with worry, and I will not hide that I have lost more than a few—gone to the city to be with their families. And who can blame them? Our camels were captured by the Amir and now serve his army. I note that your horses are few. Your sheep?" He turned to Jaafar.

"Butchered," the little man said, eyes rimmed red with grief and anger. "Oh, some survived, those that we were able to hide from the soldiers. But not nearly enough. What I don't understand is why the Amir didn't just butcher all of us as well!"

"He wants living souls for Quar," said Zeid dryly. "Or at least he did. Now, from what I hear, that's changed. And not with Qannadi's wish or approval, if rumor be true. The Imam, this Feisal, is the one who has ordered that all who are conquered either convert or die. "

"Humpf!" Majiid sneered skeptically.

Zeid shook his head. "Qannadi is a military man. He does not relish murder. I am told that he refused to give the order for his troops to kill innocent people in Bastine and that the Imam's priests were forced to do it themselves. I heard also that some of the soldiers rebelled against the slaughter, and that now the Imam has an army of fanatical followers of his own who obey him without question. It is said, Majiid," Zeid chose his words carefully and kept his eyes lowered, "that your son, Achmed, is very close to Qannadi."

"I have no son," said Majiid tonelessly.

Zeid glanced at Jaafar, who shrugged. The Hrana Sheykh was not particularly interested in this. He knew Zeid was purposefully withholding bad news and wished impatiently he would spit it out.

"Then it is true that Khardan is dead?" asked Zeid, treading more cautiously still. "I extend my sympathies. May he ride forever with Akhran who, it seems, may have taken him specifically to be at his side in the heavenly war." The Sheykh paused, expecting a reply to what everyone in the tent knew was a polite fiction. Zeid had heard—as he heard everything—the story of Khardan's disappearance, and had circumstances been less dire and he not been a guest in the camp, the Sheykh would have taken grim delight in pricking the flesh of his enemy with gossip's poisoned dagger. But with a much larger sword at their throats, there was no sense in that now.

Majiid said nothing. His face, so heavily lined it might have been scarred by the slashing strokes of a sabre, remained unchanged. But it seemed from the glitter in his eyes that he was listening, and so Zeid continued, though whether he was spreading balm on a wound or rubbing salt into it, he had no idea.

"But it is Achmed of whom I have heard reports. Your second son, it seems, though captured with the others, now rides with the armies of the Amir. Achmed has become a valiant warrior, I hear, whose deeds have won the respect and admiration of those with whom he rides—those who were once his enemies. They say he saved Qannadi's life when the general's horse was killed beneath him and the Amir was left on foot, surrounded by the

Bastinites who were fighting like ten thousand devils. Qannadi had become separated from his bodyguard in the confusion, and only Achmed remained, sitting his horse with the skill for which the Akar are famous, fighting single-handedly all attackers until the Amir could mount up behind him and the guard was able to break through and rescue them. Qannadi made Achmed a Captain, a great thing for one only eighteen. "

"Captain in an army of *kafir*!" Majiid shouted, bursting out with such pent-up rage that the servants dropped the food bowls they had been licking and cowered back into the shadows of the tent. "Better he were dead!" he thundered. "Better we all were dead!"

Jaafar's eyes opened wide at such blasphemy, and he instantly made the sign against evil, not once but several times over. Zeid made it, too, but more slowly, and as his lips parted reluctantly to speak, Jaafar knew his cousin was going to impart the news that had been resting so heavily upon his heart.

"I have one other piece of news. Indeed, it was in the hope—or fear—of relating it to you that I came to camp at the southern well."

"Out with it!" Jaafar said impatiently.

"In a month's time the army of the Amir returns to Kich. The Imam has decreed that we must come into the city and reside there in the future, and furthermore that we give our allegiance to Quar or—" Zeid paused.

"Or what?" Majiid demanded grimly, irritated at the Sheykh's dramatics.

"In one month's time, our people will die."

CHAPTER 3

Kneeling beside the *hauz*, Meryem threw the goatskin *girba* into the public water pool with an irritable gesture that sent the water splashing and brought a disdainful glare of disapproval from a wealthy man watering his donkey near her. Flicking imagined drops from the fabric of his fine robes, he trotted off toward the *souk* with muttered curses.

Meryem ignored him. Though her bag was filled, she lingered by the *hauz*, indolently dabbling her hand in the water, watching the passersby and basking in the obvious admiration of two palace guards who happened to be sauntering through this part of the city of Kich. They did not recognize her—one reason she was using this *hauz* located at the far end of town instead of the one near the palace—for which Meryem was thankful. Last week several of the Amir's concubines and their eunuch, visiting the bazaars, had seen her and recognized her. Of course they had not given her away. They knew she was doing some sort of secretive work for Yamina, wife of the Amir and ruler of Kich in her husband's absence. But Meryem heard their giggles. The veils covering their faces could not cover their smiles of derision. The eunuch had smirked all over his fat body and, under the excuse of pretending to assist her, had the effrontery to lean down and whisper, "I understand the dirt of manual labor, once ground into your pores, never washes out. You might, however, try lemon juice on your hands, my dear."

Lemon juice! To a daughter of the Emperor!

Meryem had slapped the man who was no longer a man, causing one matronly woman to come fluttering to her aid, waving her hands and shouting at the eunuch to be off and leave decent women alone. Of course this brought only more laughter from the concubines and an affected stare of offended dignity from the eunuch, who flounced off to regale his charges with his cleverness.

Since then Meryem traveled far out of her way each day to fetch water. When Badia questioned the girl about the unusual amount of time she was taking in her task, Meryem said only that she had been harassed by soldiers of the Amir. Badia, mindful of Meryem's supposed history as the wretched daughter of a murdered Sultan, said nothing more to the girl. Meryem gnashed her teeth and plotted revenge. The eunuch especially. She had something very special planned for him.

But that was in the future—a future that held for her. . . what? Once she had thought she knew. The future held Khardan, *she* held Khardan. Khardan was to be Amir of Kich and she his favorite wife, ruler of his harem. That had been her dearest dream, only months before when she was living in the nomad camp and saw Khardan every day and yearned after him every night. One of the hundreds of daughters of an Emperor who did not even know her name, given as a gift to the Emperor's favorite general, Abul Qasim Qannadi, Meryem was accustomed to giving herself to men without pleasure. But in Khardan she had discovered a man she wanted, a man who gave *her* pleasure, or at least so she dreamed, having been thwarted in her attempts to bring Khardan to her bed—a circumstance that had added red-hot coals to her already raging fire.

But the Amir's attack on the nomad camp had wreaked havoc on hundreds, not the least of which was Meryem. At first it seemed ideally suited to her plans. She had given Khardan a charm that caused him to fall into a deathlike sleep in the midst of battle. Spiriting him away, she had intended to bring him to Kich, where she planned to have him all to herself and gradually lead him—through ways in which she was highly skilled—to help her overthrow the Amir. But that red-haired madman and the black-eyed witch-wife of the Calif had literally knocked Meryem's plans right out of her head. They had taken Khardan away, somewhere beyond Meryem's magical sight. Now she was back among the nomads, pretending to be captive as they were captive in the city of Kich, living a dreary life of drudgery and toil, and spending each night looking into her scrying bowl, hoping to see Khardan.

She no longer burned with lust when she spoke his name, however. Without his physical presence to fan the flames, the fire of her passion had long since cooled, as had her ambition. The only emotion she felt now upon speaking his name softly when she looked into the bowl of enchanted water was fear.

Know this, my child. If I hear his name on the tongue of another before I hear it on yours, I will have that tongue torn from your mouth.

Thus had spoken Feisal, the Imam.

Staring into the water of the *hauz*, Meryem heard those words again and shuddered so violently that ripples of water spread from her shaking hand. It was *aseur*, after sunset, nearing evening. She could hear the sounds of the bazaars closing for the night—the merchants stowing wares away, endeavoring to politely hurry the last few straggling shoppers before slamming shut their stalls. Badia and the others would be waiting for her; the water was needed for cooking dinner, a task with which she would be expected to help. Sighing bitterly, Meryem hefted the slippery goatskin and began to lug it back through the crowded, narrow streets of Kich to the hovel in which the nomads lived by the grace of the Amir.

She looked at her hands and wondered if what the eunuch had said was true. Would the filth and dirt ever wash out? Would the hard spots on fingers and palms fade away? If not, what man would want her?

"This night, I *will* see Khardan!" Meryem muttered to herself beneath her breath. "I will leave this place and, with Feisal's reward, return to the palace!"

The house was dark and silent. The six women and their numerous small children who were crowded into the tiny dwelling were wrapped in their blankets, asleep. Squatting on the floor, hunched over a bowl of water that she held in her lap between her crossed legs, Meryem sat with her back to the others, the folds of her robes carefully concealing her work. Occasionally, in a murmuring voice, the girl would speak a prayer to Akhran, the God of these wretched nomads. Should any of the women waken, they would see and hear Meryem bowed in pious prayer.

In reality, she was working magic.

The water in the bowl was black with the shadows of night. If the moon shone, no ray of its light could penetrate for there were no windows in the buildings that piled up on top of each other like toys thrown down by a child in a tantrum. There was only a door, carved into the baked clay, that stood always open during the day and was covered by a woven cloth at night. Meryem did not need light, however.

Closing her eyes, she whispered—between the tossed-off empty prayers to Akhran—arcane words, interspersed at the proper intervals with the name of Khardan. When she had recited the spell three times, taking care to speak each word clearly and properly, Meryem stared into the bowl, holding her breath so as not to disturb the water.

The vision came to her, the same that came every night, and Meryem began to curse in her heart when suddenly she halted. The vision was changing!

There was the *kavir*—a salt desert, glittering harshly in the blazing sunlight. And there was that incredibly blue body of water whose gentle waves washed up on the white sand shore. Often she had seen this sight and tried to look beyond, for she knew in her heart that Khardan was here, somewhere. But always before, just when it seemed she would see him, a dark cloud had fallen before her vision. Now, however, no cloud marred her sight. Watching intently, her heart beating so she feared its thudding must waken the slumbering women, Meryem saw a boat sailing over the blue water to land upon the salt shore. She saw a man. . .the red-haired madman, it was, curse him! step from the boat. She saw three djinn, a little dried-up weasel of a man and one other, dressed in strange armor. . .

Yes! Khardan!

Meryem shivered in excitement. He and the red-haired madman were helping to lift someone else from the floor of the boat. It was Zohra, Khardan's wife. Meryem prayed to Quar it was Zohra's corpse they were handling with such gentleness, but she dare not spare time to find out. Her hands trembling with eager delight, she quietly rose to her feet, dumped the water onto the dirt floor, and—wrapping her veil closely about her face—slipped out into the empty streets. Glancing around, to make certain she was alone, Meryem reached into the bosom of her robes. She drew forth a crystal of black tourmaline, carved in the shape of a triangle, that hung around her neck on a silver chain.

Lifting the gem to the heavens, Meryem whispered, "Kaug, minion of Quar, I have need of your service. Take me, with the speed of the wind, to the city of Bastine. I must speak to the Imam."

CHAPTER 4

chmed climbed the seemingly endless marble stairs that led to the Temple of Quar in the captive city of Bastine. Formerly the Temple of the God Uevin in the free capital of the land of Bas, Quar's usurped place of worship was—to Achmed's eyes—extremely ugly. Massive, many-columned, composed of sharp angles and squared corners, the Temple lacked the grace and delicate loveliness of the spires and minarets and latticework that adorned Quar's Temple in Kich. The Imam, too, detested the Temple and would have had it torn down on the spot, but Qannadi intervened.

"The people of Bastine have been forced to stomach enough bitter medicine—"

"For the good of their souls," Feisal interposed piously.

"Of course," returned the Amir, and if there was a twist to the corner of his mouth, he was careful that only Achmed saw it. "But let us cure the patient, not poison him, Imam. I do not have the manpower to put down a rebellion. When the reinforcements from the Emperor arrive in a month's time, then you may tear down the Temple."

Feisal glowered; his black eyes in the sunken hollows of his wasted face blazed with his anger, but he could say nothing. By making the matter of the Temple's destruction a military one, Qannadi had snatched it neatly out of the priest's hands. Though a religious man, the Emperor of Tara-kan was also a very practical man who was enjoying the wealth of the newly acquired territory of Bas. What's more, the Emperor trusted and admired his general, Abul Qasim Qannadi, implicitly. Should Feisal choose to appeal the Amir's decision, the Imam would receive no support from his Emperor, and that was the priest's final authority here on earth.

As for appealing it to the Highest Authority? If Feisal had been praying to Quar for an enemy arrow to embed itself in the Amir's chest, no one knew of it but the Imam and the God. And apparently the God, too, was satisfied with the work Qannadi was performing in His Holy Name, for the only time the Amir had been in serious danger during the entire campaign, the young man Achmed had been there to rescue him. The Imam had publicly offered thanks to Quar for this heroic feat, but both priest and God must have found it ironic that a follower of Akhran (albeit former follower) had been instrumental in saving Qannadi's life.

Pausing upon the fifth landing in the long line of stairs leading up to the Temple, Achmed turned to look at the crowd of people waiting patiently in the heat of late morning to hold audience with the Imam. The young man wondered at Qannadi's decision. There were no signs of rebellion that he could see, as in former cities they had captured. There were no threatening slogans scrawled on the walls in the night, no defacing of Quar's altars, no mysterious fires started in abandoned buildings. Despite the fact that her soldiers had fought a bitter and bloody battle and lost, the city of Bastine appeared only too pleased to be under the rulership of the Emperor and his God. Undoubtedly the immediate reopening of trade routes between Tara-kan and Bastine and the subsequent flow of wealth into the city had something to do with it, as did the other blessings of Quar that were being showered upon the heads of those who converted to him.

That was the honey the people of Bastine fed upon now. The bitter herb they had been forced to swallow was the slaughter of five thousand neighbors, friends, relatives. As long as he slept the dream-troubled sleep of the living, Achmed would remember that awful day. And he knew that no one in this city would ever forget it either. But were these people ruled by fear? The young man looked at the lines of supplicants and shook his head. Climbing the remaining three flights of stairs, he exchanged greetings with the Amir's guards posted there and, entering through a side door, walked into the cool, shadowy confines of the Temple.

Seated upon his throne of carved *saksaul* wood that had been carted the length and breadth of the land of Bas, the Imam was holding his daily *divan*. Behind him, mounted upon a dais, the golden ram's head of Quar gleamed in the light of a perpetual flame that burned at its base. Smoke drifted up in lazy spirals, and although the fresco-decorated ceiling was high above them, the odor of incense in the closed confines of the Temple audience chamber was heady and overpowering. Feisal's newly formed soldier-priests were stationed at the main entrance to the audience chamber, keeping the crowds of supplicants in order, permitting each to advance only when the Imam gave the sign.

Although Achmed kept himself invisible in the shadows, he had the uncanny impression that Feisal knew he was here; he could even swear that when he looked away, the burning black eyes fixed their intense, soul-searing gaze upon him. But whenever Achmed confronted the priest, the Imam's attention seemed centered solely upon the supplicant kneeling before him.

What fascination draws me here? Achmed could not say, and every day when he left, he vowed he would not return. Yet the next day found him climbing the stairs, slipping in through the side door so regularly that the guards had become accustomed to his visitations and no longer even raised their eyebrows at each other when Achmed walked past.

The young soldier took up his usual position, leaning against a cracked pillar near the side door; a position where he could see and hear, yet remain unseen and unheard; a position that was generally isolated. Today, however, Achmed was startled to find someone else standing near his pillar. His eyes growing accustomed to the darkness after the glare of the sun outside, the young man saw who it was, and the blood mounted into his face. Bowing, he was about to withdraw, but Qannadi motioned him near.

"So this is where you spend your mornings when you should be out drilling with the cavalry." The Amir spoke softly, though the chattering and praying and occasional arguments among the waiting supplicants was such that it was unlikely he could have been overheard if he had shouted.

Achmed sought to reply, but his tongue seemed swollen and incapable of producing coherent sounds. Noting the young man's discomfiture, Qannadi smiled the wry smile that was little more than a deepening of the lines on one side of the thin-lipped mouth. Achmed moved to stand beside the general.

"Are you angry, sir? The cavalry is doing well without me—"

"No, I'm not angry. The men have learned all that you have

taught them. I drill them only to keep them alert and ready for"—the Amir paused and glanced at Achmed through shrewd eyes surrounded by a maze of wrinkles—"for whatever may come next."

Now it was Qannadi who flushed, the color deepening in his sunburned skin. The general knew that the next battle might be against the boy's people—Achmed's people. His gaze shifted from Achmed to the Imam. This was a subject neither discussed, though it was always there, following them as carrion birds follow an army.

The Amir heard the buckles attached to the young man's leather armor jingle as he shifted restlessly.

"Why don't you let the Imam tear down this ugly place, sir?" Achmed said in an undertone, his voice covered by the shrill arguments of two men accusing each other of cheating in the sale of a donkey. "There is no hint of rebellion in this town. Look, look at that!"

The young soldier nodded his head in the direction of the two men. Quar only knew how, Qannadi thought in grudging admiration, but Feisal had settled the argument to the satisfaction of each, apparently, to judge by their smiles as they left the presence of the priest.

"These people worship him!"

"Think about what you said, my son, and you will understand," replied the Amir as the Imam, seated on his throne, raised a frail hand in Quar's blessing.

"You are right, of course," Qannadi continued. "Feisal could tear the city down around their heads, stone by stone, and the citizens would cry their thanks to him. With his words, he turned murder into a benediction. They praised him as he butchered their friends, their neighbors, their relatives. Praised him for saving the souls of the unworthy! Do they line up to bring their problems to me to judge? Am I not Governor of this wretched city, proclaimed so by the Emperor? No, they bring their dealings with donkeys, and their quarrels with their wives, and their disputes with their neighbors to him."

"And would you have it any other way, sir?" Achmed asked gently.

Qannadi cast him a sharp glance. "No," he admitted, after a moment. "I am a soldier. I've never been anything else, nor do

I pretend to be. No one will be more grateful than I when the Emperor's regent comes to take over this city and we can return to Kich. But in the meantime, I must make certain that I have a city to turn over to him."

Achmed's eyes opened wide. "Surely the Imam would not—" He hesitated to speak. The thought alone was dangerous enough.

Qannadi spoke it. "—defy the Emperor?" The Amir shrugged. "Quar's power in heaven grows. So do the number of the Imam's followers. If Feisal chose to do so, he could split my army today, and he knows it. But it would be only a split. He could not gain the loyalty of the entire force. Not yet. Maybe in a year, maybe two. There will be nothing I can do to stop him. And when that day comes, Feisal will march triumphant into the capital city of Khandar with millions of fanatics behind him. No, if I were the Emperor, I would not sit easy on my throne. Why, boy, what's the matter?"

Achmed's face was pale, ghostly in the shadowy darkness. "And you?" he said, his voice cracking. "What will—He wouldn't commit—"

"Murder? In the name of Quar? Haven't we seen that done already?" Qannadi laid a comforting hand on the young man's trembling shoulder. "Do not fear. This old dog knows enough not to take meat from Feisal's hand."

That much was true—a simple precaution. Qannadi never ate or drank anything that had not been tasted first by some man paid well enough to risk poisoning. But a knife thrust from behind—that, no one can fight. And it would surely be the work of a lone fanatic. No one would appear more shocked at an assassination than Feisal himself.

"There is no dishonor in retreating from a fight with the God," Qannadi continued, lying to put to rest the boy's fears. "When the day comes that I see I am defeated, I will pack my *khurjin* and ride away. Perhaps I will go north, back to the land of the Great Steppes. They will soon have need of soldiers—"

"You would go alone?" Achmed asked, his heart in his eyes.

Yes, boy. The God willing, I will go alone.

"Not if there are those who would bear the hardships with me," Qannadi replied. Seeing Achmed's pleasure, a true smile, a deep smile, warmed the Amir's dark expression. But it lasted only briefly and then disappeared, the sun shining for an instant before the storm clouds banished its rays. "In many ways, I look forward to that, to the freedom, to being rid of the responsibility," he said with a soft sigh. "But that time will be long in coming, I fear. Long for all of us." And bitter, he added, but once again only to himself.

Does the boy know the horror he faces? Does he truly comprehend the threat to himself and to his people? I have adopted him as son in all but name only. I can protect him, will protect him, with all the power I have left. But I cannot save his people.

Qannadi did not regret attacking the nomads; that had been a sound military decision. He could not have marched south on Bas with his right flank unprotected, thousands of those wild desert fighters yearning after his blood. But he did regret falling into the Imam's scheme of bringing the people into the city and holding them captive. Far better that he had fought them to the death. At least they would have died with honor.

Ah, well, thought Qannadi wryly. *If Khardan is dead—as he surely must be, despite the Imam's misgivings—the soul of the Calif will soon rest easy enough, seeing me fall in defeat as well. And perhaps his soul will forgive mine, for—if it is my last act—I will save the younger brother the nomad Prince loved.*

Or at least, I will try.

Putting his hand on Achmed's shoulder, Qannadi turned and walked silently with the young man from the Temple.

CHAPTER 5

The Imam saw the Amir's departure from the Temple without seeming to see it or care about it, although in actuality he had been waiting for it with extreme impatience. When the side door had shut behind the two men, Feisal gestured immediately to one of the under priests and said softly, "You may bring her now."

The priest bowed and left.

"The morning's audience is concluded," Feisal said loudly.

This started a hubbub among the waiting supplicants. None dared raise his voice in protest, but all were determined that the soldier-priests remember each man's position in line, and clamored for attention. The priests took names and calmly, firmly, forcefully herded Quar's worshipers out the door.

Other priests had hurried outside to impart the news to the supplicants waiting upon the stairs and to swing shut the huge wooden Temple doors. Shrill cries of beggar children rose into the air, offering to hold the places of supplicants in line in exchange for a few pieces of copper. Wealthier citizens took advantage of this to leave the Temple and sustain themselves with a midday meal. The poorer worshiper sought what shade he could while still holding his place in line and munched on balls of rice or hunks of bread, washed down with water supplied by the priests.

When the huge doors boomed, shutting out the noise and the daylight, and the room was left to the silent, incensescented darkness, Feisal rose from the *saksaul* throne and stretched his legs.

He approached the golden ram's head. The altar flame glistened in the unblinking eyes. Looking about him carefully, making certain he was alone, Feisal knelt before the altar, so near the flame that he could feel its heat upon his shaven head. Raising his face, he stared up at the ram. The heat of the coals beat upon his skin; sweat beaded on his lips and rolled down his thin neck, staining the robes that hung on his wasted body.

"Quar, you are mighty, majestic. In your great name we have conquered the land and people of Bas, driven their God into hiding, destroyed his statues, taken his treasure, subverted the faith of his followers! The wealth of these cities goes to further your glory! All is as we dreamed, as we hoped, as we planned!

"So why is it, *Hazrat* Quar—" Feisal hesitated. He licked his dry, cracked lips. "Why is it . . . what is it . . . that you fear!" The words burst out—a hushed, awed gasp.

The fire flared, flames leaped up from the white-hot coals. Instantly, the Imam collapsed, hunching his body as if in pain. Crouching before the altar, he shivered in terror. "Forgive me, Holy One!" he chanted over and over, clasping his thin hands together and rocking back and forth in agony. "Forgive me, forgive me. . ."

A voice called his name softly. "Imam!" Lifting his eyes, he stared at the ram, thinking for one wild moment that its mouth had moved. But the voice repeated itself, and the priest realized with a pang of disappointment that the sound came from behind him and that it was a mortal who called him, not the God.

Rising shakily to his feet, having forgotten in his religious fervor that he had issued orders, Feisal glared angrily upon the one who had dared interrupt his prayers. Trembling visibly, the young priest shrank before the Imam's wrath. The woman who accompanied him was likewise stricken with terror. The blue eyes above the veil glanced about wildly, and she began to sidle back toward the secret way through which they had entered.

Reveling in the ecstasy of heaven, Feisal realized that he had not been interrupted—the God was choosing to speak to him through human lips.

"Forgive me," the Imam said, and the young priest mistakenly thought his superior was speaking to him.

"It is you who should forgive me, Imam!" The priest sank to his knees. "What I did was unpardonable! It was just. . . you said it was urgent that you talk with the woman—"

"You have done well. Go now and assist your brethren to make easy the waiting time of those who have come to us with their burdens. Meryem, my child." The Imam took her hand, starting slightly at the chill feel of the fingers. His own skin was burning hot. "I trust you have had refreshment after your fatiguing journey?"

"Yes, thank you, Holy One," Meryem murmured inaudibly.

The Imam did not speak again until the young priest had taken himself, bowing and walking backward, from the Temple. Meryem stood before Feisal with lowered eyes. She had removed her hand from his grasp and was nervously twisting the frayed gilt hem of her veil. When they were alone, the Imam remained silent. Meryem lifted her eager, still half-fearful gaze to meet his.

"I have seen him!"

"Who?" Feisal asked coolly, though he knew well enough of whom the woman spoke.

"Khardan," Meryem faltered. "He is alive!"

The Imam turned slightly, with a glance for the ram's head, almost as if to assure himself it was listening. "Where is he? Who is with him?"

"I . . . I don't know where he is," Meryem said, a break in her voice as she saw the Imam frown with displeasure. "But the witch-woman, Zohra, is with him. And so is the red-haired madman. And their djinn. "

It seemed to Feisal that the eyes of the ram flickered. "And you don't know where they are."

"It is a *kavir*, a salt desert, surrounded by blue water—water that is bluer than the sky. I did not recognize the place, but Kaug says—"

"Kaug!" Feisal looked back at Meryem, his brows lowered ominously.

"Forgive me, Imam! I did not think it would be wrong to tell the 'efreet!" Meryem's tongue ran across her lips, wetting the veil over her mouth. "He. . . he made me, Holy One! Or he refused to bring me here! And I knew you wanted this information most urgently—"

"Very well." The Imam contained his ill humor that was, he realized, nothing more than jealousy of the 'efreet and the honored and trusted position Kaug held with the God. "I am not angry, child. Do not be frightened. Go ahead. What did Kaug say?"

"He said the description matches that of the western shores of the Kurdin Sea. When I saw Khardan, Imam, he was stepping out of a boat—a fishing boat. Kaug says there is a poor fishing village on the northeastern side of the sea, but the 'efreet does not believe the nomads came from there. He said to tell you that he thinks it probable, from certain signs he has seen, that they were on the Isle of Galos."

"Galos!" Feisal paled.

"Not Galos!" said Meryem hastily, seeing that this news was unwelcome and knowing that bad news generally garnered little reward. "That was not the name. I was mistaken—"

"You said Galos!" Feisal cried in a hollow voice. "That is what the 'efreet said, wasn't it?" The priest's eyes burned in their sunken sockets. "That is what he told you to tell me! He is warning me! Thank Quar! Warning me!"

This was good news, then. Meryem relaxed. "Kaug said something about a God called Zhakrin—"

"Yes!" Feisal cut her off, not liking to hear that name spoken aloud. His thoughts went to Meda, to the dying man's blood-stained hand gripping the priest's robes, the curse spoken with the body's last shuddering breath. "There is no need to go into this further, my child. What other message does Kaug send?"

"Good tidings!" Meryem said, her eyes smiling above the veil. "He says there is no need to fear Khardan any longer. He and the witch-woman are trapped on the shores of the Kurdin Sea. To return to their tribes, they must go west—across the Sun's Anvil. No one has ever performed such a feat and survived."

"But they have their djinn, after all."

"Not for long. Kaug bids you not worry."

The Imam cast a suspicious glance at Meryem. "Why does this news please you, my child? I thought you were in love with this nomad."

Meryem did not hesitate. She had known this question must come, and she had long been prepared with her reply. "I came to realize, living among the *kafir* as I have these past few months, Imam, that such a love is an abomination in the sight of Quar."

Her eyes lowered modestly, her voice trembled with the proper tone of religious fervor, and she didn't fool Feisal in the least. He recalled the calluses he had felt on her fingertips; his gaze flicked over the tattered remnants of her fine clothing.

"I want only to return to the palace and regain my former place there," Meryem added, unconsciously answering any lingering doubts the Imam might be having.

"Your former place?" Feisal asked dryly. "I thought you were more ambitious than that, or has your sudden interest in religion taught you humility?"

Meryem flushed beneath her veil. "Qannadi promised to make me his wife," she said stubbornly.

"Qannadi would as soon think of bedding a snake. Have you forgotten? He suspected your little plot to use the nomad Prince to overthrow him. He would not take you back, even as concubine."

"He would if you told him to," Meryem countered. "You are strong! He fears you! I know, Yamina told me so!"

"It is not me he fears, but the God, as should all mortals," rebuked Feisal, adding humbly, "I am but Quar's servant and an unworthy one at that." Having said this, he continued thoughtfully. "Qannadi might take you back, if I asked him to. But, Meryem, consider. You left the palace once because you feared your life was in danger. Has the situation changed, except perhaps to grow more perilous for you? After all, you have lived with Qannadi's enemy for two months or more."

Meryem's feathery brows came together above the blue eyes. The hands, which had never ceased twisting the silken fabric since she first entered, gave it an involuntary jerk that tore the veil from her face. Biting her lip with her white teeth, she gazed at the Imam defiantly. "Then find me some place to go! I have done this for you—"

"You did it for yourself," Feisal stated coldly. "It is not my fault that your lust for Khardan has dwindled to ash and blown away. Still, you have proven your value and I will reward you. After all, I do not want you selling this information to Qannadi."

Eyes cast down, Meryem covered her face with a shaking hand and wished she could draw the veil over her brain as well. It was uncanny the way this man could see into her mind!

Feisal turned his back upon the woman and, walking over to the altar, sought help from the ram's head. The golden eyes shone red with the burning charcoal.

"We need to keep the girl nearby," the Imam muttered. "She can see the followers of Akhran and Promenthas in that scrying bowl of hers, and I want to know the moment the *kafir* draws his final breath. I must keep her near, yet I must keep her presence secret. Qannadi believes Khardan to be dead. Achmed believes his brother is dead. The nomads believe their Calif is dead. Their hope dwindles daily. They must not discover the truth, or they will gain strength to defy us! If Qannadi found out Khardan was alive, he would tell Achmed and word would get back to the nomads. I—"

The ram's eyes flared briefly, brilliantly. Feisal blinked, then smiled.

"Thank you, Holy One," the priest murmured.

Turning back to Meryem, who was watching with narrowed eyes, her hand holding her veil over her face, the Imam said gently, "I have thought of a place for you to stay. A place not only where you will be completely safe, but where you will continue to be most useful."

CHAPTER 6

ω hen the daily meeting of the officers concluded, Achmed lingered behind while the others, laughing and joking, left—those off duty heading for the city, the others going to take up assigned posts and to set the evening watch. Achmed remained behind, ostensibly to study a map. His brow furrowed in concentration; he might have been planning to face an onslaught of ten thousand foes at next day's dawning, so intently did he seem to consider the lay of the land. As it was, the only foe he was likely to face in the morning was the soldier's perennial enemy—the flea. Staring, unseeing, at the map was just an excuse. Achmed stayed behind when the others departed because it was easier being lonely when he was alone.

The young man had joined Qannadi's army in the spring. Now it was late summer. He had spent months with the men in his division, the cavalry. He had trained with them, learned from them, taught them what he knew. He had saved lives, he had been saved. He had gained their respect, but not their friendship. Two factors kept him from being included in the groups that went into the city seeking its pleasures. The first—Achmed was and always would be an outsider, a nomad, a *kafir*. The second—he was Qannadi's friend.

There was much speculation among the ranks concerning this relationship. Everything was guessed from a love interest to the somewhat wilder theory that the boy was really the Crown Prince of Tara-kan who had been sent away from the court of the Emperor for fear of assassination. No matter where the young man walked in the camp, he was certain to overhear conversations like the one he'd listened to only days before.

"Peacocks, that's what Qannadi's sons are, the lot of them. Especially the oldest. Waving his tail in the Emperor's court and picking up crumbs that fall at his feet," grunted one.

"What do you expect?" said another, watching with a critical eye the roasting of a lamb upon a spit. "The boy was raised in the *seraglio* by women and eunuchs. The general saw him maybe once, twice a year between wars, and then he took no interest in him. Small wonder the youth prefers the easy life at court to marching about all day in the heat."

"And I heard his wife, the sorceress, made certain the general took no interest in the boy," added a third. "The son will pull the boots off his father's corpse and measure them to fit his own feet as the saying goes. And when that day comes, Quar forbid it, that's the day I'll go back to that fat widow in Meda who owns the inn."

"Perhaps the *Kafir* will be the one wearing the boots," said the first in an undertone, his eyes darting about the camp.

"At least they'd fit him," muttered the second, giving the spit a half turn. "The *Kafir's* a fighter, like all those nomads."

"Speaking of boots, if I was in the *Kafir's*, I'd keep mine on day and night. A *qarakurt's* a nasty thing to find in between one's toes in the morning."

"And no need to ask how it got there. Yamina's not his deadliest enemy," said the third softly. "Not by half. The general's being careful, though. Not favoring the *Kafir* above others, not keeping him about during the day, not even sharing his meals. Just another young hero. Bah, let me take over! You're burning it!"

The *Kafir*. That was what they called him. Achmed didn't mind the name any more than he minded the danger that Hasid, an old friend of Qannadi's, had taken care to explain to the young man. At first Achmed scoffed at the thought that anyone might view him as a threat. But as time went by, he found himself shaking out his pallet every night before he slept, upending his boots every morning, eating his meals out of a cooking pot shared by others. And it wasn't Yamina's eyes he saw staring at him from the darkness.

The eyes he feared were the burning eyes of the Imam.

Yet Achmed accepted it all—the danger, the ostracism, the whispers and sidelong glances. He had affirmed this to himself that terrible day when Qannadi fell in the midst of his enemies, and Achmed had stood prepared to sacrifice his life for this man who had come to be father, friend, mentor. Yes, he would sacrifice his life for this man, but what about the lives of his people?

I can't prevent their deaths. Neither can Qannadi. They must convert or at least pretend to. Surely they will be able to see that! I will talk to them.

Talk to them. Talk to someone who understood him. Talk to friends, family. The empty, hollow pit within the boy deepened and widened. He was lonely—bitterly, desperately lonely. Tears stung his eyelids, and he very nearly threw himself down among the rugs and the saddles that were used as backrests and wept like a child. The knowledge that at any moment one of the officers might take it into his head to have another look at the route to Kich forced the sobs back down Achmed's throat. Choking, wiping the back of his hand over his eyes and nose and rebuking himself severely for giving way to unmanly weakness, the young man strode hastily from the tent.

He wandered aimlessly, restlessly, among the soldiers' encampment. It was late evening, he had no duties to perform. He could have returned to his own tent, but sleep was far from him, and he had no desire to spend another night staring into the darkness, holding memory at bay and scratching at fleas. He continued to roam, and it was only when he heard soft voices, muted groans, and deep laughter that Achmed realized where it was his feet had taken him.

Known as the Grove, it had other names in the soldiers' vernacular—names that had brought a flush to the young man's cheeks when he'd first heard them. That had been months and battles ago, however. Now he could grin knowingly when the Grove was mentioned. He'd even—out of curiosity and desire—availed himself of its dubious pleasures one night. Too bashful and ashamed to "examine the wares," he'd purchased the first merchandise offered him and discovered too late that it was old, ill made, and had undoubtedly known many previous owners.

The experience sickened and disgusted him, and he'd never—until now—gone back. Perhaps he had truly come here by accident, or perhaps his loneliness had led him here by the hand. Whatever the reason, the young man had heard enough talk among his elders to know now how business was conducted. Disgust vied with desire and, most burning, the need to talk, to touch, to be held, and at least—for the moment—to pretend that he was loved and cared for. A soft voice called to him, a hand reached from the shadows of the trees.

Clutching his purse, Achmed swallowed his nervousness and tried to appear hardened and nonchalant as he stepped farther into the Grove. Rustlings and glimpses of shadowy forms and the sounds of pleasure-taking increased his desire. He ignored the first who grabbed at him. They would be the professionals, the women who followed the troops from camp to camp. Deeper within the Grove were the ones new to this business—young widows from the town who had small children to feed and no other means to earn their bread. Their families would kill them if they discovered them here, but stoning is a quick way to die, compared to starvation.

Achmed was moving among the deepest, darkest part of the stand of trees, trying to push the image of his mother out of his mind, when he concluded with certainty that someone was following him. He had suspected it when he'd first entered the Grove. Footfalls that moved when he moved, stopped when he stopped. Only they didn't stop soon enough, and he could hear soft, padding footsteps through the cool, damp grass behind him. He moved forward again, heard the faint patter upon the ground, came to a sudden halt, and heard the patter continue—one step, two, then silence.

Fear and excitement banished desire. Slipping his hand to his belt; he felt for the hilt of his dagger and gripped it reassuringly. So this was it. He had supposed the Imam would hire someone more skilled. But no, this made sense. They would find his body in the Grove and assume he had been lured here by a woman, then murdered and robbed by her male accomplice. Such things were not uncommon. Well, he would give them a fight at least. Qannadi would not be ashamed of him.

Spinning on his heel, Achmed jumped at the hint of movement he saw in the darkness behind him. His hands, grappling for the neck, closed—not on male muscles and sinew—but on perfumed silk and smooth skin. A gasp, a scream, and Achmed and his pursuer fell heavily to the ground. The body beneath his went limp. Startled, shaken by the fall and his own fear, Achmed heaved himself off the inert form and peered at it intently in the starlit darkness.

It was a woman. Reaching out his hand, Achmed drew the veil from her face.

"Meryem!"

CHAPTER 7

The woman stirred at the sound of his voice. Too astonished to do anything except stare at her, Achmed remained crouched over her, the veil clutched in a hand that had gone as limp as the unconscious body. Her eyelids fluttered; even in the dim light, Achmed could see the shadows they cast upon the damask cheeks, delicate as the wings of dragonflies. Blinking dazedly, not looking at him, keeping her eyes lowered, Meryem sat up.

"Young sir," she said in a low, trembling voice, "you are kind, gentle. I . . . will give you pleasure. . ."

"Meryem!" Achmed repeated, and at the sound of her name and the shock and anger in the voice, the woman looked fully at him for the first time.

A deep flush suffused the pale skin. She snatched the veil from the young man's hand and covered her face. Rising swiftly to her feet, Meryem started to flee but slipped in the wet grass. Achmed caught her easily.

"Let me go!" She began to weep. "Let me take my shame and cast myself into the sea."

Her crying became frenzied, hysterical. She tried again to break away from Achmed's grip, and the young man was forced to put his arms around the slender shoulders and hold her close, soothing her. Gradually, Meryem calmed down and lifted blue eyes, shimmering with tears, to gaze into his.

"Thank you for your kindness." She gently pushed him away. "I am better now. I will leave and trouble you no more—"

"Leave! And go where?" asked Achmed sternly, alarmed by her talk of the sea.

"Back to town." Meryem lowered her lashes, and he knew she was lying.

"No." Achmed caught hold of her again. "At least, not right

now. Rest here until you feel better. Then I will take you back. You should not be wandering out here alone," the young man continued firmly, acting—for both their sakes—as if he had not heard her all-too-clear solicitation. "You have no idea what this place is."

Meryem smiled—a sad, wan smile that touched Achmed to the heart. A tear crept down her cheek, sparkling in the starlight like a precious jewel. Unconsciously the young man raised his hand to catch it.

"Thank you for trying to save me," Meryem said softly, her head drooping near but not quite touching his breast. "But I *do* know what this place is. And you know why I am here—"

"I don't believe it!" Achmed said stoutly. "You are not like. . . like these!" He gestured.

"Not yet!" Meryem hid her face in her hands. "But I soon would have been if not for you!" Looking up suddenly, she grasped hold of his tunic. "Achmed, don't you see? Akhran sent you! You saved me from sin! This was my first night here. You. . . would have been my first. . . first. . ."

Her skin burned; she could not say the word. Achmed put his hand over her lips. Catching hold of the fingers, she kissed them fervently and fell to her knees before him. "Akhran be praised!"

The woman's beauty dazzled him. The fragrance of her hair, the perfume clinging to her body, intoxicated him. Her tears, her innocence, her sweetness, mingled with the knowledge of where they were and what was going on around them inflamed Achmed's blood. He staggered like a drunken man, and it was the weakness in his limbs that made him sink down beside her.

"Meryem, what happened? Why are you here? You were in Kich, the last I heard, living with Badia, Khardan's mother—"

"Ah! Do not mention her name!" Meryem pressed her hands over her bosom, clutching at the silken gown, rending it in her despair. "I am not worthy to hear it spoken!" Rocking back and forth on her heels, moaning in grief, she let her hands fall, the torn fabric of her gown parting to reveal creamy white skin, swelling breasts.

Achmed drew a shivering breath. Taking hold of her chin, he turned her face to his and concentrated on looking into the wide, tear-shimmering blue eyes. "Tell me, what has happened? Is Badia, are my people—" Fear chilled him, his grip tightened.

"Something terrible has happened, hasn't it?"

"Not that bad!" Meryem said hastily, catching hold of the young man's wrist. "Badia and all your people living in Kich have been taken from their homes and put into the Zindan. But surely you knew of this? It was by Qannadi's order."

"Not Qannadi," Achmed said grimly. "The Imam. And are they all right? Are they being mistreated?"

"No," said Meryem, but her eyes faltered before Achmed's gaze. His grip on her hand tightened.

"Tell me the truth."

"It is so shameful!" Meryem began to weep. Her tears, falling on Achmed's flesh, burned like cinders. "I was in a cell with Badia and her daughters. One night the guards came. They said . . . they wanted one of us . . . willingly . . . or they would take all by force—" She could not continue.

Achmed closed his eyes, pain, anger, desire, surging through him. He could visualize the rest and, putting his arms around Meryem, drew her close. At first she resisted him but gradually let his strong arms comfort her. "You sacrificed yourself for the others," he said gently, reverently.

"When the guards tired of me," she continued, sobbing against Achmed's chest, "they sold me to a slave trader. He brought me here. I . . . escaped, but then I had nowhere to go, no money. Akhran forgive me, I thought I could sink no lower, but—praise his name—he set you in my path."

Achmed stirred uncomfortably, not liking to hear the name of the God, liking still less the thought that Akhran might have used him to save this poor girl.

"Coincidence," he said gruffly.

But Meryem shook her head firmly. The veil over the golden hair had slipped; the pale strands looked silver in the starlight. Achmed caught hold of one of the tresses that was damp from the girl's tears. Soft, silken, it smelled of roses. The words he said next stuck in his throat, but they needed to be said.

"Khardan will be proud of you—"

Meryem looked up at him in wonder. "Don't you know—"

She halted, confused. "Didn't they tell you? Khardan is . . . is dead. Majiid sent word to Badia. They found his body. The stories about him fleeing the battle were false—lies spread by the Imam. Khardan was given a hero's burial."

Now it was Achmed who lowered his head, now it was Meryem who reached her hand out to brush away his tears.

"I am sorry. I thought you knew."

"No, I am not crying for grief!" Achmed said brokenly. "It is thankfulness, that he died with honor!"

"We both loved him," said Meryem. "That will always be a bond between us."

Quite by accident their cheeks touched. The sweet night breeze cooled skin wet with tears and flushed with passion. Their lips met, tongues tasting salt mixed with sweetness.

Meryem pushed Achmed away and tried to stand, but she was entangled in her clothing. Achmed drew her near. She kept her head averted, turned from him, straining away from his grasp.

"Leave me! I am defiled! Let me go! I swear, I will not do what you fear. You have saved me. I will pray to Akhran. He will guide me."

"He has guided you. He has guided you to me," Achmed said firmly. "I will take you to my tent. You will be safe there, and I will go to Qannadi—"

"Qannadi!" The word came out shrill and harsh, and Achmed flinched in response.

"Have you forgotten?" Meryem whispered hurriedly. "I am the Sultan's daughter! Your Amir murdered my father, my mother! He sought to have me put to death! He must not find me!" Panic-stricken, she scrambled to her feet and began to stumble through the darkness, tripping over the long skirts of her robes.

Achmed pursued her and, grabbing hold of her wrist, pulled her close to him. Her body trembled in his arms. She wept and shivered in her fright. He pressed her near, stroking the golden hair.

"There, I didn't mean it. I forgot for the moment. I won't tell him, though I'm certain that if I did, he would not harm you—"

"No! No!" The girl gasped wildly. "You must promise me! Swear by Akhran, by Quar, by whatever God you hold sacred—"

Achmed was silent for a moment. He could feel warm, soft skin swelling out of the torn bodice, heaving with her rapid, catching breaths against his bare breast. His arms tightened around her.

"I swear by no God," he said thickly. "I believe in no God. Not anymore. But I swear by my own honor. I will keep you safe, keep you secret. I will guard you with my life."

Meryem's eyes closed. Her head sank against his chest, her hands stole up around his neck, and she sighed a sigh that might have been relief but seemed to whisper surrender.

Achmed stopped the sigh with his lips, and this time Meryem did not push the young man away.

CHAPTER 8

Promenthas summoned the One and Twenty.

His purpose—to discuss the current war raging on the plane of the immortals.

When the One and Twenty came together this time, no longer did each God and Goddess view the others contentedly from his or her facet of the Jewel that was the world. Now only a very few of the strongest Gods were able to maintain their dwelling places. The others found themselves standing meekly in Quar's pleasure garden, being eyed curiously and aloofly by the tame gazelle.

Promenthas was strong still. He stood in his cathedral rather than the garden, but the sounds of shipbuilding echoed through the cavernous chambers and disturbed his rest. God of the lands and peoples of Aranthia, far across the Hurn Sea from Tara-kan, Promenthas's followers were—for the time being—safe from the *jihad* that was raging in Sardish Jardan. The pounding of nails into wood was soon going to end their peace. The Emperor of Tara-kan had wealth enough and material enough from the southern realm of Bas to proceed with his designs for an armada. Within the year his fleet would be ready to cross the Hurn. Hordes of fanatical followers of Quar would storm the walled cities and castles of Aranthia.

A sparsely populated land divided into small states, Aranthia was ruled by kings and queens who kept the peace by marrying off their sons and daughters to each other. The land was heavily wooded, difficult to traverse except by the rivers and streams that were the country's blood, and it could hold out long against the Emperor's troops. In the end, however, Promenthas knew his people must be defeated, overwhelmed by sheer numbers if nothing more. The teeming capital city of Khandar alone contained more people than the entire population of Aranthia.

Seated in a pew near the altar, Promenthas watched grimly as Quar leisurely entered the cathedral. So large had the God grown, he was forced to duck his head and turn his body sideways to squeeze through the doorway. His magnificent robes were of the most rare and costly fabrics. All the jewels of the world adorning his body, Quar shone more brilliantly than the stained glass of the cathedral windows that had, of late, become grimy and dust covered from lack of care. Mincing along behind Quar, chatting merrily with him and inwardly calculating Quar's worth at the same time, was Kharmani, God of Wealth.

No matter that another facet of the Jewel might shine brighter, Kharmani's facet gleamed with its own light—a golden light. No God—not the most evil, not the most good—dared try to dim that light. Every other of the One and Twenty might crouch at Quar's feet. Kharmani would sit at his right hand—as long as that hand kept flipping golden coins in Kharmani's direction.

Behind Quar, Promenthas saw a shadowy figure sneaking into the cathedral under cover of the God's flowing robes. Promenthas frowned and sighed over the fate of the Poor Box, knowing without doubt that there wouldn't be a penny left after the departure of this God—Benario, God of Thieves. Kharmani might sit at Quar's right hand, but Benario would be at his left, if the God didn't steal Quar's fingers first.

Promenthas felt a rumbling beneath his feet, and he knew that Astafas, God of Darkness, was watching Quar step into a subterranean world of perpetual night. The dazzle must hurt Astafas's eyes, thought Promenthas wryly, and he felt a certain sympathy for his ancient enemy.

At least Astafas has not sunk to the level of these wretches. Trailing along behind Quar, their own radiance lost in the shadow of the shining God, were various others of the One and Twenty. Devin, shrunken and withered, meekly carried the hem of Quar's robes. Mimrim, head bowed, walked behind, holding a sitting cushion in the eventuality that the God should decide he was fatigued and desired rest. Hammah, the horned, helmed God of the Great Steppes, marched in Quar's retinue. Carrying his spear, the warrior God tried to appear dignified; but he kept his gaze from meeting that of Promenthas, and the white-bearded God knew with a heaviness in his immortal being that the rumors he'd heard were true. Hammah's people had allied with the Emperor and would march to battle on Quar's side.

Other Gods and Goddesses Promenthas saw, but now he was most interested in those notable for their absence. The angry rumblings that were shaking the cathedral's foundations gave indication that Astafas would cast himself in the Pit of Sul before serving Quar. Evren and Zhakrin were missing, though Promenthas had heard rumors of their return. And of course Akhran, the Wanderer, was nowhere to be seen.

Quar's almond-eyed gaze sought out Promenthas. Slowly, with great dignity, the white-bearded God rose to his feet and moved to stand directly before his altar. There were no angels flanking him. The war on the plane of the immortals had drawn away all his subalterns. Only one angel remained, and she was hidden safely in the choir loft.

"Why have you called this gathering of the One and Twenty—or perhaps we might better refer to it as the One and Seventeen," said Quar in his delicate voice. Kharmani gave a tittering laugh at the God's joke.

"I have called this meeting of the One and Twenty," said Promenthas, his voice deep and stern, "to discuss the war currently raging on the plane of the immortals."

"War." Quar appeared amused. "Call it bickering, squabbles among spoiled children!"

"I call it war," Promenthas returned angrily. "And you are the cause!"

Quar raised a finely drawn eyebrow. "I? The cause? My dear Promenthas, it was I who—seeing the danger existent in these undisciplined beings—attempted to bring order and discipline to the world in our care by confining them safely in a place where they could no longer meddle in the affairs of humans. It is due to the meddlings of the wild and uncontrollable djinn of Akhran that this havoc is being wreaked both in heaven and on earth. It is time we take direct control—"

"It is time you take direct control, isn't that what you mean?"

"Are you trying to make me angry, Graybeard?" Quar smiled pleasantly. "If so, you will not succeed. I included all my brethren out of politeness, but if you are too weak to deal with the matter, I am not. Someone must bear the burden of humanity's sufferings—"

"If you truly mean what you say," interposed another voice,

coming from outside the cathedral, beyond the walls of Quar's pleasure garden, "then banish the 'efreet known as Kaug, in whom you have consolidated much of your power. Prick your swollen ego, Quar, and let out the stinking air of your ambition. Become one of us once more—a facet in the Jewel—so that its beauty may last forever."

Akhran the Wanderer entered the cathedral of Promenthas, strode into Quar's pleasure garden. Akhran's boots were covered with dust; his flowing robes were frayed and tattered and stained with blood. The Wandering God seemed small and shabby, compared to Quar. Kharmani cast Akhran a glance of imperious disgust, and Benario, yawning, did not bother to leave his place among the shadows.

Quar lifted an orange studded with cloves to his nose to obviate the smell of horse and leather and sweat that entered with the Wanderer and kept his eyes on Promenthas.

"This is the thanks I receive for trying to bring order to chaos." Quar's tone was sad, his manner that of one who has been pierced to the heart. "What am I to expect of two who were instrumental in bringing the foul God of blackest evil, Zhakrin, back to power? But you will regret it. You think those humans who do your bidding have escaped Zhakrin's clutches, but his shadow is long and the darkness once again draws near them. You trust him—a God who drinks the blood of innocents—"

A muffled sound, like a despairing cry, came from the choir loft of the cathedral. Promenthas made a swift gesture with his hand, but Quar glanced up at the dust-covered carved wooden railings, and his smile deepened.

"Sul designed the Jewel so that all facets gleam with equal light—the good and the evil—" began Akhran angrily, removing the *haik* from his face and glowering at Quar.

"Ah, now you know the mind of Sul, do you, Wanderer?" interrupted Quar coolly, flicking a glance at Akhran, then flicking it away as though the sight might soil his eyes. "It is my belief, after much deep consideration, that Sul meant there to be One God, not One and Twenty. Thus his light will shine purely and brightly, beaming directly upon the humans, instead of being refracted, split, diffused."

"Do this, and the Jewel will shatter!" warned Akhran.

"Then I will pick up the pieces." With a graceful bow, Quar, his garden, and his retinue of followers disappeared.

"Beware, lest those pieces cut you," cried Akhran after him. There was no response. Akhran and Promenthas were left standing alone in the cathedral.

"Do not look so glum," said the Wandering God, clouting Promenthas on the back. "Quar has made a serious mistake—he has given too much of his power to the 'efreet. In order to win the war on the plane of the immortals, we have only to defeat Kaug." Akhran's booming voice rattled the panes of stained glass. "When that is done, Quar will fall."

"When that is done, the stars will fall." Promenthas sighed, though the stern face eased slightly at this offer of hope.

"Bah!" Akhran started to spit, recalled where he was, and wiped his mouth with the back of his hand. The sound of a horse whinnying in impatience drifted through the cool darkness. Wrapping the *haik* about his face, the Wandering God turned and walked down the aisle toward the cathedral's doors. Promenthas noted, for the first time, that the God was limping.

"You are injured!"

"It is nothing!" Akhran shrugged.

"What Quar said about Zhakrin, your followers and mine— the young wizard who travels with them. Are they in danger?"

Akhran turned, regarding Promenthas with narrowed black eyes. "My people have faith in me. I have faith in them."

"As Zhakrin's followers have faith in him. He seeks what Quar seeks and always has. He has no mercy, no compassion. Perhaps it was a mistake, helping him return. Admittedly Evren came with him, but she is weakened, her followers far distant, while Zhakrin is near. Very near." Promenthas sighed and shook his head. "We are too few, and we are divided among ourselves. I fear it is hopeless, my friend."

Akhran flung wide the cathedral doors and drew in a deep breath of fresh air. Mounting his horse, he leaned down to clasp reassuringly Promenthas's stooped and bent shoulder. "Only the dead are without hope!"

Raising himself up, he kicked his horse's flanks; the animal galloped off among the stars.

"And without pain," murmured Promenthas. Looking back down the aisle where Akhran had walked, he saw a trail of blood.

The Book
of Zhakrin

CHAPTER 1

Mathew sat upon a slag heap of shining obsidian. Scattered about the stark white of the salt desert floor, the black rock seemed the embodiment of the dark elements that stirred just below the crust of the world, just below the skin of man. Staring down at the gaping cracks in the surface of the heat-baked earth, Mathew fancied he could see the black rock escaping from the tormented depths, oozing out of the dead land, gangrenous liquid streaming from a putrefied wound.

The young wizard closed his eyes to blot out the horrid vision. Though it was early morning, only a few hours since the sun had risen, the heat was already intense. The Sun's Anvil. It was like the people of this godforsaken land to name it thus—terse, laconic, to the point. Sweating profusely beneath the heavy velvet robes, half-stunned by the heat and exhaustion, Mathew pictured a sinewy arm of pure fire wielding a hammer, slamming it down upon the ground that split and cracked beneath it but did not yield, the sparks flying, waves of heat rolling from the blast. . .

"Mat-hew!" A hand was shaking him.

Mathew lifted bleary, dreamy eyes. A form shimmered before him—Zohra, clad in the outlandish glass-beaded dress of sacrifice. Each bead caught the sun's light, the slightest movement set them gleaming and glinting and clicking together. Dazzled by the radiance, Mathew blinked at her.

"I'm thirsty," he said. Licking his tongue across his lips, he could taste, feel the salt that rimed them.

"The djinn have brought water," Zohra said, helping him to his feet. "Come, we must talk."

A night, a day, and another night they had sailed the Kurdin Sea. It had taken them this long to cross, where before they crossed in a matter of hours. The winds generated by the perpetual storm around Castle Zhakrin took delight in toying with them, blowing them furiously for miles in the wrong direction, then dying completely and leaving them becalmed, then hitting them from the front when least expected. Without their djinn, the humans on board would have soon lost all sense of direction, for the clouds swirling above them hid sun and stars and made navigation impossible.

Clinging to the side of the boat, sick and drenched and shivering with cold, lacking both food and water—not that they could have kept it down—the miserable occupants gave themselves up for dead. The boat's owner, Meelusk, howled in terror until at last his voice gave out. When the craft finally scraped against the shoreline, two of the djinn, Sond and Pukah, carried their bedraggled passengers ashore. The third djinn, Usti, whose rotund body had been pressed into service as a sail, was as sickly and forlorn as his mortal masters. Stricken with terror by the storms and a panicked fear that they were being chased by *ghuls*, Usti had kept his eyes squinched tightly shut the entire voyage. At its end, the djinn refused to let go of the mast or open his eyes. Sond poked and prodded and mentioned every luscious dish the djinn could think of, to no avail. Moaning, Usti refused to budge. Pukah finally had to pry the fat djinn's fingers off the mast and his feet from under the boom. Once freed, Usti collapsed like a deflated pig's bladder and lay gasping and moaning in the shallow water.

The Sun's Anvil. It was Pukah who had told them where they were. By night the desert's flames were quenched, the fires were out, the Anvil was cold steel. Clad in his wet robes, Mathew had shivered with the chill that seemed to enter his bones. Khardan and Pukah and Sond had debated the creation of a fire, and Mathew had heard with aching disappointment the three decide that it would be unwise. Something about attracting the attention of an evil 'efreet who apparently lived in that accursed sea.

When dawn came Mathew had reveled in the warmth and managed to sleep fitfully. On awakening, he felt the heat strike him a physical blow. Dragging himself to his feet, he had huddled in the meager shade cast by the outcropping of obsidian and wondered what they would do.

Apparently, according to Zohra, some sort of decision had now been reached. Mathew cast aside the hood of the robes he wore, hoping to catch the faint breeze that wafted occasionally from the surface of the Kurdin Sea. The water was flat and still now, its winds having been sucked up by the savage sun. The youth's long red hair was wringing wet with sweat, and he lifted it off the back of his neck. Noticing what he was doing, Zohra caught hold of the hood and dragged it over Mathew's head.

"The sun will burn your fair skin like meat on a skewer. Its heat will curdle your wits."

That, Mathew could readily believe, and he suffered the hood to remain in place, even drawing it lower over his forehead. Surely we will leave this dreadful place soon, he thought drowsily. The djinn will carry us in their strong arms, or perhaps we will fly upon a cloud.

The sight of Khardan's face jolted Mathew to reality. It was dark with anger; the black eyes burned hotter than the sand beneath their feet. The djinn stood before him, sullen, ashamed, but grim and resolute.

"What do you know of this?" Khardan flared, whirling on Mathew.

"What do I know of what?" Mathew asked dazedly.

"This war in heaven! The news, so Pukah tells me, was brought to them by your djinn!"

"My djinn?" Mathew stared, amazed. "I don't have a djinn!"

"Not djinn, angel," Pukah corrected, keeping his eyes lowered before his master's—former master's—fury. "A guardian angel, in the service of Promenthas."

"There are no such beings as angels," Mathew said, wiping the sweat from his brow. Every breath hurt; it was like breathing in pure flame. "At least," he added, shaking his head, thinking dreamily how unreal all this was, "no beings who would have anything to do with me. I'm not a priest—"

"No such beings!" Pukah cried, raising his head and angrily confronting a startled Mathew. "Your angel is the most loyal being in the heavens! For every tear you have shed, she has shed two! Every hurt you suffer, she takes upon herself. She loves you dearly, and you—unworthy dog—dare malign the best, the most beautiful— No, Asrial, I will say it! He must learn—"

"Pukah! Pukah!" Khardan shouted repeatedly, and at last managed to stem the tirade.

"Since when, djinn, do you speak to a mortal in this disrespectful manner?" Zohra demanded.

"I will handle this, wife," Khardan snapped.

"Better than you have handled all else previously, I presume, husband?" Zohra responded with a sneer, tossing the mane of black hair over her shoulder.

"It was not my actions that brought us here, if you will remember, wife!" Khardan drew a seething breath. "If you had left me on the field of battle—"

"You would be dead by now," Zohra said coolly. "Believe me, husband, no one regrets my action to save you more than I!"

"Stop it!" Mathew cried. "Haven't we been through enough? In that dark castle, you were each prepared to offer your life for the other. Now you—"

Mathew hushed. Khardan was staring out to the sea, his face stem and hard. The muscles in the jaw twitched, the tendons in the neck were drawn taut and strained.

My words have done nothing more than send him back to that dread place, Mathew realized sadly. He suffers it all again!

Swiftly Mathew glanced at Zohra. Her face had softened; she was recalling her own torment. If she could see the shared anguish in her husband's eyes. . . But she could not. From where she stood, she saw only the broad back, the head held high, the neck stiff and unbending. Her lips compressed. Zohra crossed her arms forbiddingly across her chest, the glass beads of her dress clashing together jarringly.

Mathew's own hand reached out to the Calif, the fingers trembling. Khardan turned at the moment, and Mathew snatched the hand back and hid it within the loose, flowing sleeves of his wizard's robes. The Calif took one look at the impassive face of his wife, and his own expression grew harder.

"I humbly beg your apology, *sidi*, and that of the madman—I mean, Mat-hew," said Pukah humbly, anxious to keep clear of domestic disputes. "I have been reminded that the madman—Mathew—had no way of knowing anything about his angel, since such contact between mortal and immortal is prohibited by his God, Promenthas, who is if I may say it, a most dour type of God and one who doesn't have a great deal of fun. Still, it seems to me that the madman should be thankful he is at least alive—"

"Thankful! Of course, he's thankful!" Khardan said impatiently. "And you tell me that he doesn't know anything about this. . . this—"

"Angel," contributed Pukah helpfully.

"Yes." Khardan avoided pronouncing the strange-sounding word. "So he knows nothing about this war?"

"No, *sidi*." Pukah was more subdued but, on exchanging glances with Sond, appeared determined to continue on in the face of the Calif's mounting displeasure. "Asrial—that is the angel's name, master—attended a meeting of the One and Twenty. It was there she learned of the war raging on the plane of the immortals. Akhran himself was present, master, and he said that Quar has placed much of his strength in the 'efreet, Kaug, who now seeks to banish the immortals back to our ancient prison, the Realm of the Dead."

"One 'efreet!" Khardan snorted. "Surely Akhran can deal with one 'efreet!"

"The gods are forbidden by Sul to act on the plane of their servants, *sidi*. Not that I think this would stop *Hazrat* Akhran, if he was so inclined. But Asrial tells us that Akhran"—the djinn hesitated, glanced at his fellow djinn, sighed, and imparted the bad news—"Akhran bears many wounds on his body, and though he does his best to hide them, Promenthas fears our God cannot last much longer."

"Akhran . . . dying!" Khardan said in disbelief. "Has our God truly grown so weak?"

"Say rather, the faith of his people has weakened," interposed Sond quietly.

Khardan flushed. His hand moved, unconsciously it seemed, to his breast. Mathew remembered vividly the wounds the Calif had borne, wounds gone now without a scar except for those that would remain forever on the man's soul. Wounds healed by the hand of the God.

Or wounds suffered by the God in his place?

"Our people." The flaring pride and anger faded from Zohra's eyes, leaving them shadowed with fear and concern. "So much has happened. . . we have forgotten our people."

"All the more reason you must help us return to them," Khardan said angrily to Pukah.

"All the more reason we must fight Kaug, Calif." Sond spoke with the sincerest respect, the firmest resolution. "If Kaug wins this battle, all immortals will disappear from the world. Quar, being the strongest of the Gods, will be able to increase his direct influence over the people. He will grow stronger, the other Gods weaker, and eventually the One and Twenty will be the One."

"We will be gone only a few hours, *sidi*," Pukah said confidently. "This Kaug may have the strength of a mountain, but he has the brains to match. We will defeat him and return to you before you can begin to miss us."

"Rest during the heat of the day, *sidi*, in the tent we have prepared for you. We shall be back to serve you dinner," added Sond.

The two djinn began to fade away. Mathew felt something brush against his cheek, something soft and light and delicate as a feather, and he raised his hand swiftly to grasp it, but there was nothing there.

"Khardan!" Zohra cried, clutching at him. "They mean to abandon us out here! You cannot let them go!"

"I cannot stop them!" Khardan shouted irritably, shaking off her hands. "What would you have me do? I am no longer their master!"

"But I am!" shrieked a shrill voice.

CHAPTER 2

Everyone turned, startled, having forgotten during the ensuing argument all about the scrawny little man. Truth to tell, no one had paid much attention to Meelusk at all during the entire trip. The beady-eyed, leering-faced fisherman had spent the journey huddled in a heap at the bottom of the boat. Whenever anyone—particularly the muscular Khardan—had looked at him directly, Meelusk would give a fawning, servile grin that twisted into a vicious snarl when he thought no one was watching.

Now he came stumping across the sand, clutching Sond's lamp to his chest and dragging Pukah's waterlogged snake charmer's basket (which was as big as the little man) behind him.

"I don't trust you, you black-bearded demon," Meelusk shouted, his gleaming eyes fixed on Khardan. "The woman with you is a she-devil, and I don't know what you are, red-haired freak!" The eyes darted to Mathew. "But be you she-devil or he-demon, I'll soon be rid of you! I'll soon be rid of the lot of you!"

These were fine-sounding words, but the djinn, Sond and Pukah, continued to fade from view, and it suddenly occurred to Meelusk to wonder who was getting rid of whom.

"Come back here!" the little man yelled, waving Sond's lamp in the air. "I'm your master! I rescued you from the sea! You have to obey me and I say come back here!"

The images of the djinn wavered, then slowly rematerialized. "He is right, after all," Pukah said to Sond. "He is our master."

"You bet I am!" said Meelusk smugly, casting Khardan a triumphant glance.

"He did rescue us from the sea. We owe him our fealty and loyalty," Sond agreed.

Turbaned heads bowed; the djinn came to prostrate themselves before the scrawny human.

"Damn right you do!" Meelusk cackled. "Now get up, and listen to me." He pointed at Khardan and his companions. "Leave the nomads here on the beach to rot. Take away their water and that tent." Protected by the djinn, Meelusk felt safe enough to shake a bony fist at the nomads. "You murderin', black-hearted devils! I've seen you look at me, thirsting for my blood! Ha! Ha! That's not all you'll thirst for." Meelusk turned back to the djinn at his feet. "Now you're going to dress me like a Sultan, then bring me beautiful women, then fix me up a palace that's made of silver and marble, with great high walls so's that no one can get to me. Then you're going to my village. The people there don't respect me enough. But they'll learn to! Yes they will, the curs. When we get there, you're going to kick over their houses, one by one. And stomp 'em into the dirt! And then set 'em on fire. After that, you're going to bring me all the gold and jewels in the world— Hey! What's the matter with you?"

Pukah had put a hand to his forehead and rolled his eyes. "Too many commands, master."

"Ah, slow-witted, are you?" said Meelusk, grinning craftily.

"Yes," said Sond gravely, "he is."

"Beautiful new clothes for my master!" commanded Pukah, clapping his hands.

Instantly Meelusk's skinny, dirt-encrusted body was swathed from head to toe in a cocoon of costly silks. "Hey!" cried a muffled voice, coming from the midst of the cocoon. "I can't breathe!"

"Jewels for my master!" commanded Sond, clapping his hands.

Ropes of pearls, chains of gold, and jewels of every color and description fell from heaven around Meelusk's neck, their weight bending him nearly to his knees.

"Women for my master!"

Nubile, willowy bodies surrounded Meelusk, their soft voices whispering into what little of his ears could be seen under the huge, jewel-encrusted turban that balanced precariously on the man's bulbous head. The women cuddled against him seductively. Gaping and drooling, Meelusk dropped both Sood's lamp and Pukah's basket in order to free up his eager hands.

"A new lamp and a new basket for my master!" shouted Pukah, carried away with enthusiasm.

"Yes! Yes!" Meelusk panted, ogling the women and clutching the soft bodies with grasping fingers. "New everything! More gold! More jewels! While you're at it, more of these beauties."

Pukah cast Khardan a significant look. Slipping up quietly and stealthily, the Calif snatched up Sond's lamp and Pukah's basket and, holding onto them tightly, took a swift step backward.

Instantly, the women, the jewels, the pearls and the gold, the turban, the wool and the silks, all disappeared.

"Ah, Master Meelusk, what have you done?" cried Pukah in dismay.

"Eh? What?" Meelusk glanced around wildly, his hands, which had encircled a slender waist, clasped firmly around empty air. Furious, he accosted the two djinn, who were gazing at him sadly. "Bring 'em back, do you hear me? Bring 'em back!" he howled, jumping up and down in the sand. '

"Alas, you are no longer our master, master," said Pukah, with a helpless spreading of the hands.

"You gave away, of your own free will, our dwelling places," said Sond, heaving a sigh.

Raving, gnashing his teeth, Meelusk whirled and made a lunge for Khardan, but before he could take even two steps, the huge Sond had caught hold of the scrawny little man by the arms. Lifting him like a child, the djinn carried Meelusk, kicking and screaming and calling down foul imprecations on the heads of everyone present, to his boat. Sond tossed Meelusk inside and gave the boat a mighty shove that sent it flying over the water.

"Best not shout so, former master!" Pukah called after the rapidly vanishing boat. "The *ghuls* have excellent hearing!"

Meelusk's curses ended abruptly, and all was quiet once more. When the boat was out of sight, Sond and Pukah came walking slowly across the sand to stand before Khardan. Sond's lamp, dented and scratched and somewhat the worse for wear, lay at the Calif's feet. Pukah's basket, waterlogged and unraveling in places, stood near the battered lamp. Khardan stared down at the objects that bound the djinn to the mortal world, his gaze dark and thoughtful.

The djinn bowed and waited in tense silence.

"Go do what you must, then!" Khardan growled abruptly, impatiently, refusing to look at them. "The sooner you're gone, the sooner you'll return."

Sond glanced at Pukah. Pukah nodded.

"Farewell, Princess, Calif, Madman!" The fox-faced djinn waved. "Look for us to return with the setting of the sun!" The djinn disappeared.

"A wise decision, husband!" sneered Zohra. "Now we are alone in this accursed place."

"It was my decision to make, wife, not yours!" Khardan returned shortly.

A heavy silence fell upon the three, broken only by the gentle sound of water lapping upon the shore and the snores of Usti, who lay sprawled on the beach like a giant, flabby fish.

"At least my djinn has not deserted us—" Zohra began.

Sond's huge hand reached suddenly out of the air. Gripping hold of Usti by the sash around the djinn's broad middle, the hand jerked him upward. There was a startled cry, a wail of protest, then Usti, too, was gone.

The three humans were alone upon the hostile shore. The sun pounded its hammer upon the cracked earth. Noxious pools of foul-smelling water bubbled and boiled. Behind them stood a tent, its open flap giving a glimpse of the cool, inviting darkness inside. Skins of water hung from the center pole, bowls of fruit and rice stood on rugs spread before cushions. There were even robes for the desert. The djinn had thought of and provided everything.

"Go inside, wife. Change your clothing," Khardan ordered Zohra. "We will wait for you out here."

"You cannot command your own djinn! You certainly do not command me, husband!" Zohra bristled. Her black eyes flicked over Khardan. Clad only in the remnants of the armor of a Black Paladin, his brown skin was beginning to redden. "You are the one who needs the protection. I will wait for you."

Khardan's face flushed in anger. "Why do you insist on opposing me, woman—"

"Please!" Mathew took a step between them. "Don't—" he began, staggered, and swayed on his feet. "Don't. . ." he tried to speak again, but he couldn't breathe. He couldn't swim against the burning tide. Closing his eyes, he let himself sink beneath it, drowning in sweltering waves of heat.

CHAPTER 3

Zohra and Khardan carried Mathew inside the shelter of the tent. They stripped off the heavy black robes he wore—Zohra keeping her eyes lowered modestly as was proper when nursing the sick, pretending not to see the young man's frail nakedness—and bathed his face and chest in the tepid salt water of the Kurdin Sea. Working together over the suffering young man, each was very much aware of the other's nearness. When hands touched, by accident, both started and drew quickly apart as though they had brushed against hot coals.

"What is wrong with him?" Khardan asked gruffly. Seeing there was nothing more he could do, he rose to his feet and moved over to stand beside the open tent flap.

"The heat, I think," Zohra replied. Dipping a strip of cloth in water, she laid it upon the hot forehead.

"Can your magic heal him? If the djinn do not return—"

Zohra glanced swiftly at Khardan.

Averting his eyes from the accusation in hers, the Calif stared outside. "—we will have to travel this night," he finished coldly.

"We could stay here." It was a statement of fact not a suggestion.

Khardan shook his head. "We have water for two days, at most. When that runs out. . ." He did not finish.

When that runs out they would die. Though unspoken, the words echoed through the tent.

Khardan stood tense, waiting his wife's attack. It did not come, and he wondered why. Perhaps she thought it well enough that her barb, once cast, rankled in her enemy's flesh. Or perhaps she had come to regret words spoken before she thought, the interval giving her time to reflect, time to see that Khardan had made the only decision he could. Whatever the reason, she kept quiet. Neither spoke for long moments. Khardan stared moodily across the *kavir*, watching the ripples of heat wash over the land—a mockery of the water for which it thirsted. Zohra made Mathew a crude blanket of his own cast-off black robes, modestly covering the fair-skinned body.

"I cannot use my magic," she said at last. "I have neither charm nor amulet. Where will we go?"

"Back to our people. West. Pukah said something about a city, Serinda—"

"A city of death!" Zohra realized that could have a double, sinister meaning, and bit her lip. "All know the story," she added lamely.

"There may be life for us within its water wells."

Both man and woman added silently, *There had better be.*

"I am going out to look around before the heat of afternoon sets in." Starting to thrust aside the tent flap, he halted. With the toe of his boot Khardan gingerly touched an object lying on the ground—Mathew's belt and a leather pouch. "The boy does possess the magic," he said wonderingly. "I saw him work it."

"He is a very skilled and powerful wizard," said Zohra proudly, as though Mathew were her own personal creation. "He has been teaching me. It was by his magic I saw the vision—"

She was not looking at Khardan; she did not hear him speak or make a sound. But so sensitive was she to his physical presence, she felt rather than saw the tensing of his body, the slight, swift intake of breath.

The vision, the reason—so she claimed—that she had dragged Khardan unconscious from the field of the battle, hiding him from the Amir's forces by dressing him in women's clothing.

"Since you are so skilled in his magic, wife"—the sarcasm flicked like a whip across her raw nerves—"is there nothing of his you can use to aid him?"

"I never said I was skilled in his arts," she retorted in a low, passionate voice, not looking at him, her eyes staring down at Mathew's still form. "I said he was teaching me. And I swear to Akhran," she continued, her voice trembling with her fervor, "that I will never use such magic again!"

Reaching out, she started to smooth the damp red hair back from the young man's forehead, but her fingers shook visibly, and she hurriedly hid her hands in her lap. For no reason at all, it seemed, tears sprang to her eyes and slid down her cheeks before she could stop them. She could not raise a hand to brush them away; that would have revealed her weakness to him. Swiftly she lowered her head, the black hair falling forward, veiling her face.

But not before Khardan had seen the drops glistening on the dusky cheeks, sliding down to lose themselves in the curving, trembling lips. The frightful ordeal through which she had been, the long and perilous journey they faced if the djinn did not return—it was enough to daunt the strongest. Khardan took a step near her, his hand reaching out. . .

Zohra flinched and hastily drew away. "You must leave the tent, husband." She spoke harshly to mask the tears. Rising to her feet, she kept her back to Khardan. "Mat-hew rests comfortably. I will change my clothes."

She stood stiff and straight-shouldered, unyielding. Blinded by the shadows after staring into the glaring sunlight, Khardan could not see his wife's fingers clench and drive into her flesh. He did not notice the long black hair that fell sleek and shining past her waist shiver with the intensity of her suppressed emotion. To him, she was cold and distant. The piles of obsidian, scattered over the desert floor, gave off more warmth than this flesh-and-blood woman.

Words crowded to Khardan's lips, but in such a tangle of fury and outrage that he could utter nothing coherent. Whirling, he stalked out of the tent, yanking down the flap after him, nearly bringing down the tent itself in his anger.

It was impossible, he knew it, for it had been months since Zohra had access to her perfumes. He could have sworn he smelled jasmine.

Fuming, Khardan stalked across the desert sand. The woman was maddening! A she-devil—that bandy-legged fisherman had been right! Khardan wanted to take her in his arms and . . . and . . . choke the life out of her!

The sun was hot, but not hotter than his blood. A high dune rose some distance from him, promising a view of the land. Grimly, he made his way across the cracked earth.

Inside the tent, safely hidden, Zohra fell to her knees and wept.

Mathew slept through the heat of afternoon and awoke, rested and alert, near sunset.

"The djinn, are they back?" he asked.

No one replied. His words fell into a well of silence so deep and dark he could almost hear them bounce off the walls. Something's happened. Hurriedly, he sat up and looked around. Khardan was stretched out full length on one side of the tent. Propped up on an elbow, he stared moodily out into the empty air. On the opposite side of the tent Zohra was deftly packing the food the djinn had provided and apparently making preparations to travel. The immortals were nowhere to be seen.

Mathew felt his throat tighten. The *girba* lay near him. He picked it up and started to drink, caught Khardan's sharp, swift glance, and took only a mouthful, though he was parched. Holding the water in his mouth as long as he could, hoping this would help ease his thirst, he swallowed tiny gulps of the precious liquid, making it last as long as possible. Gently he laid the waterskin back down, and Khardan's dark gaze turned from him.

"It is only just sunset, after all," Mathew said uneasily, waving away the small portion of food Zohra offered him. It was too hot to eat. "They'll be here soon."

Khardan stirred. "We cannot wait," he said, his voice deep and cold as the well that had drowned Mathew's words. "The moment the sun is gone, we must start walking. We have to reach Serinda before day dawns tomorrow." Looking at Mathew, he let his stern face relax somewhat. "Do not look so worried. It is not far. We should make it easily." He gestured. "You can see the city walls from the dunes."

Stiffly, as though he had been lying in one position for a long time, Khardan rose to his feet. He had changed his clothes, putting on the full pants, the tunic that tied around the waist with a sash, and the long, flowing robes of the desert. The *haik*, held in place with the *agal*, covered his head, the facecloth dangling down across his chest. Soft slippers, designed for walking in the shifting sand, covered his feet. Zohra was attired in a woman's loose robes, long-sleeved bodice, and pants that fit snugly around the ankle. A veil covered her head and face. With a sidelong glance at Mathew, her eyes studiously avoiding Khardan, she slipped out of the tent, carrying the food with her.

"Get dressed," Khardan ordered, pointing to two piles of

clothing lying in the center of the tent. Mathew recognized the silken folds of a woman's *chador* in one, the other appeared to be robes similar to those worn by the Calif. Not knowing what sex the strange madman might choose to be today, Pukah had thoughtfully left attire for either. Mathew stretched his hand toward the men's clothes, then stopped. Flushing, he looked at Khardan.

"Am I permitted?" he asked.

A fleeting smile touched the Calif's lips and warmed the dark eyes. "For the present, Mat-hew. When we return to the Tel, you may have to resume your role as"—a hint of bitterness—"my wife."

"I will not mind," Mathew said quickly, thinking only to ease Khardan's obvious pain. Realizing too late how his words and tone might be misconstrued, Mathew flushed more deeply still and sought to clarify his statement. But before he could do more than stammer, Khardan had left the tent, courteously giving Mathew privacy.

"Fool!" Mathew cursed himself, fumbling with the yards and yards of material. "Why not just shout your feelings to the four winds and be done with it!"

When he was finally dressed, he went outside to find the other two standing far apart, backs turned slightly, each staring intently into the west where the sun had vanished over the horizon. The air was cooling already, though the collected heat of day radiated up from the ground and made Mathew I feel as though he had stepped into a baker's oven.

"I'm ready," he said, and was startled to hear his voice sound small and tight.

Khardan turned and without a word reentered the tent. He came back with the *girba* slung over his shoulder and began walking westward, never glancing behind him. Zohra followed after Khardan, careful, however, to keep clear of his footprints, cutting her own path in the sand. By this and the set of her shoulders, she made it plain that though she traveled the same direction, it was by her choosing, not his.

Sighing, Mathew trudged along behind, his own footsteps, clumsy in the shifting sand, often stumbling across, overprinting, interconnecting, the two separate tracks that marched along on either side of him.

CHAPTER 4

From the top of the sand dune, staring into the western sky that was a cloudless, oppressive, ocherous hue, Mathew saw the city of Serinda. He knew its history, legends of the dead city being popular among the nomads.

A hundred years before or maybe longer, Serinda had been a thriving metropolis with a population numbering in the several thousands. And then, suddenly, according to legend, all life in Serinda had come to an end. No one knew the cause. Raiders from the north? The plague? The poisonous fumes of the volcano Galos? Gazing at the city walls—a gray-white, lacy border of mosque and minaret against the yellow sky—Mathew felt the stirrings of curiosity and looked forward eagerly to entering the gates that now were never closed. Perhaps he could solve this mystery. Surely there must be clues.

The city looked to be near them, Mathew thought, his spirits lifting. Khardan was right. A walk of a few hours should have them across this desert. They would be in Serinda before morning.

Night's deep blue-blackness washed over the land. Mathew reveled in the coolness. Invigorated, his journey's end in sight, he moved ahead so swiftly that Khardan was forced to remind him curtly that they had hours of walking before them.

Meekly slowing his pace, Mathew looked around him instead of ahead, and once again marveled at the strange, savage beauty of this land. No moon shone, but they could see their way clearly by the lambent light shining from the myriad stars that sparkled in the black heavens. Though Mathew knew it was the stars that cast the eerie, whitish glow upon the sand, it seemed to him as if the land itself radiated its own light, as it radiated the heat it had stored up during the day.

He gazed up, fascinated, at the stars. There were so many more of them, visible in this clear sky, than he could have ever imagined in his land. Having become accustomed already to the shifted positions of the constellations in this hemisphere, Mathew soon located the Guide Star that gleamed in the north sky and pointed it out to Zohra.

"They teach the children of my land that an angel of Promenthas stands there with his lantern to guide travelers through the night."

Zohra glanced at him skeptically. "Your people follow this—what was it?"

"Lantern, like a lamp or a torch. A light in the sky."

"Your people pick out a light and follow it and it leads them where they wish to go?" Zohra regarded him with narrowed eyes. "And the people of your land actually succeed in getting from one place to another?"

"Not just any light, Zohra," Mathew said, seeing her mistake. "That one particular star that always shines in the north."

"Ah! The people all travel north in your land!"

"No, no. When you know the star is in the north, you can tell if you're going east or west or south. Just as in the day you can tell which way you're going by the position of the sun. Don't your people do this?"

"Does *Hazrat* Akhran keep a *chirak* in the sky to guide him? And let his enemies know where he sleeps?" Zohra was scandalized. "Our God is not such a fool, Mat-hew. He knows his way around heaven. We know our way around earth. We follow not only that which we can see, but what we hear and smell. What do your people do when the clouds hide the sun and"—she gestured vaguely skyward—"that star?"

What would she say if I told her that the star was a sun? Or that our sun was a star? Mathew smiled to himself, picturing giving Zohra an astronomy lesson. Instead, he began to explain another marvel to her. "Our people have a . . . a"—he fumbled for a word in the desert language—"device with a needle inside it that always points toward the north."

"A gift of Sul," she said wisely.

"No, not magic. Well, in away, but it is not Sul's magic. It is the magic of the world itself. You see, the world is round, like an orange, and it spins, like a top, and when it spins, a powerful force is created that draws iron toward it. The needle in the device is made of iron and it—What are you doing?"

"Drink some water, Mat-hew."

"But Khardan said not to—"

"I said drink!" Zohra glowered at him above the veil, her eyes glittering more brightly than Promenthas's Guiding Lantern.

Mathew obediently swallowed a mouthful of the warm water that tasted faintly of goat and seemed as sweet as the clearest, purest snow water that bubbled among the rocks of the stream behind his home.

"Now, Mat-hew, relax," said Zohra earnestly, patting his cheek with a gentle hand. "You do not need to act crazy around us. We will not harm you. Khardan and I *know* you are mad."

Smiling at him reassuringly, Zohra turned to follow the Calif, who was keeping to their path unerringly, without a glance at the stars.

They stopped to rest only briefly, Khardan pushing them forward at an exhausting pace that Mathew could not understand. Serinda was so near. Why couldn't they take an hour to rest aching legs and burning feet? But Khardan was adamant. The Calif spoke little during the journey; he kept his face covered by the *haik*, and it was impossible to tell what he was thinking. But if his expression matched his voice during those times when he did speak, Mathew knew it must be grim and dour.

Eventually Mathew ceased to wonder why they couldn't stop. He ceased to wonder anything but whether he would take that next step or collapse. His early energy had drained from him. Reaching the point of exhaustion, he had pushed past it. The chill air dried the sweat on his body, and he shivered from the cold. His feet had blistered, and walking was agony. The muscles of his legs ached and twitched from the effort of attempting to keep his footing in the shifting sands of the dunes that crossed their path.

Once, at the top of one, he slipped, and had neither the strength nor the will to catch himself. Down the steep side he rolled, sand scraping the skin off any parts of his body not protected by the folds of enveloping cloth. At the bottom, where he came to a slithering halt, the youth lay still, enjoying the cessation of movement, not caring much whether he ever moved again. Khardan caught hold of him by the arm, hauled him to his feet, and gave him a shove, all without speaking a word. Mathew limped forward.

Where was Serinda? What had happened to it? Had Khardan got them lost? Mathew glanced heavenward, searching dizzily for the Guide Star. No, there it was, on his right hand. They were traveling westward. Promenthas was guiding them.

But my angel is gone, Mathew thought dazedly, reeling as he walked.

My angel. My guardian angel. A year ago I would have scoffed at such a childish notion. But a year ago I did not believe in djinn. A year ago I trusted myself. I had my magic. A year ago I did not need heaven...

"Now I need it," he muttered to himself. "My angel has left me, and I am alone. Magic!" He gave a bitter laugh, staggered, nearly fell, and stumbled on ahead. "I know how to make water out of sand. It is a simple spell." He had taught it to Zohra and nearly frightened the wits out of her.

"I could make this place an ocean!" Mathew gazed about dreamily and imagined himself swimming, floating upon cool water, splashing it over head and body, drinking, drinking all he wanted. His hand fumbled at the scrolls of parchment curled up neatly in the pouch at his belt. "Yes, I could make this place an ocean, *if* I had a quill to pen the words, and ink to write them, and a voice left in this raw and parched throat to speak them.

"A boon to the traveler," he imitated the Archmagus's droning voice. "No need to worry about fresh water. No need to drink at a stream that might be impure."

Hah! In his land, water was never more than a few steps away. In his land, they cursed it for flooding their crops, washing away the foundations of their houses.

"In such a place, I can conjure water!"

Some irritating person was laughing uproariously. Only when Mathew saw Khardan stop and turn to stare at him and Zohra come to stand beside him, her eyes shadowed by weariness and concern, did Mathew realize that the irritating person was himself.

He blinked and looked around. It was dawn. He could see the sweep of the dunes beginning to take on color, the light of Promenthas's Lantern start to fade. Raising his eyes, hope flooding his body with strength, Mathew looked eagerly to the west.

The white city walls, catching the sun's first, slanting rays, glistened against the dark background of waning night. Glistened far away. . . far, far away. . .

"Serinda! What's happened to it?" Mathew cried irrationally, clutching frantically at Khardan's robes. "Have we been walking in circles? Standing still? Why isn't it closer?"

"A trick of the desert," said Khardan softly, with a sigh that no one heard. "I was afraid of this." Suddenly angry, he pried Mathew's hand loose and shoved the young man away from him. He started off down the side of the dune on which they had been standing. "We can walk another two hours, before the heat sets in."

"Khardan."

Refusing to look around, the Calif kept walking, his own legs stumbling tiredly in the sand.

"Khardan."

Glancing around, he saw Zohra standing unmoving behind him. Silhouetted against the burning ball of the rising sun, she had one arm around Mathew's shoulders. The youth sagged against her strong body, his head bowed, shoulders slumped. His breath came in ragged gasps.

"He can't go any farther," Zohra said. "None of us can."

Khardan looked grimly at her. She stared just as grimly back at him. Both of them knew what this meant. Without more water, stranded out here in the open, they would never live through the scorching heat of coming day.

Tossing the nearly empty waterskin onto the sand, Khardan flexed his aching shoulders. "We will wait for the djinn," he said evenly. "They will meet us here."

Now was the time for Zohra's triumph, bitter though it may be. She eased Mathew down onto the desert floor, then lifted her head to look upon the face of her husband; a face she could not see for the cloth that swathed it.

But she could see the eyes.

"Yes, husband," she said softly. "we will wait for the djinn."

CHAPTER 5

blink of an eye took the three djinn and the angel from the desert to the realm of the immortals. Sond led them, and it was at his insistence that they found themselves materializing in a pleasure garden—the very garden, in fact, where Sond had sneaked in to meet Nedjma that fateful night when he'd clasped what he'd supposed was his beautiful djinniyeh to his arms, only to find his face pressed firmly against the hairy chest of the 'efreet, Kaug. The garden belonged to one of the elderly immortals of Akhran, a djinn who claimed to remember when time began. Too old and far too wise to have anything at all to do with humans anymore, the ancient djinn had established himself in a mansion whose bulbous-shaped towers and graceful minarets could ordinarily barely be seen through the lush, flowering trees and bushes of his garden.

The garden had changed, however. The wall that Sond had been accustomed to climb over with such agility was topped with wicked-looking iron spikes. Horses trampled the delicate orchids and gardenias, camels were hobbled on the tiled paths or noisily drank water from the marble fountains. Powerful djinn of all sizes and description surged about in frantic activity—tearing down the delicate latticework and using it to bolster defenses at the garden gate, shouting out to each other in graphic detail what they would do to Kaug and his various anatomical parts when they had him in their grasp.

Huddled in a window at the top of one of the towers, guarded by gigantic eunuchs, the djinniyeh peeped over the balcony, giggling and whispering whenever one of the djinn-who knew well the women were there—was bold enough to brave the baleful glare of the eunuchs and bestow a wink upon a veiled head that had caught his fancy.

Sond's gaze went instantly and eagerly to the balcony. Usti took one look at the strenuous activity going on all around him, groaned, and vanished precipitously behind an ornamental hedge. No one heard the fat djinn, however, or saw him disappear. The other djinn had spotted Sond and, crying out gladly, surged forward.

"Thank Akhran! Sond, where've you been? We can use that sword arm of yours!"

Flushed with pleasure by the welcome, Sond embraced his fellows—many of whom he had not seen in centuries.

"Where is that goat-thieving master of yours living now, Pejm?" Sond questioned one. "Down by Merkerish? Ah, I had not heard. I am sorry for his death. But we will be avenged. Deju! You were freed? You must tell me—"

"Pejm! *Bilhana!*" A loud voice interrupted Sond. "It's me! Pukah! I rescued you from Serinda! Uh, Pukah. The name is . . . well, doesn't matter. See you later." Pukah spoke to the back of another djinn. "Deju, it's me, Pukah! Here's *my* sword arm! Firmly attached to my shoulder. The one that rescued you from the city of Serinda. I— Uh . . . Serinda . . ."

"Serinda? Did you say Serinda?" A djinn rushed up to Pukah. The foxish face beamed in pleasure and cast a sidelong glance at Asrial to see if she was watching.

"Why, yes." Pukah performed the salaam with charming grace. "I am Pukah the hero of Serinda."

"*Salaam aleikum,* Serinda," said the djinn hurriedly.

"Did I hear Sond had arrived? Oh, there he is! If you could just step aside, Serinda—"

"My name's not Serinda!" Pukah said irritably to the djinn's back. "I'm Pukah! The *hero* of Serin— Oh, nevermind."

Elbowed firmly out of the way by one djinn then another as they crowded around Sond, Pukah was shoved off the path and found himself in a small grove of orange and lemon trees. Near him, huddled among the climbing roses, stood a forlorn-looking Asrial, staring with wide blue eyes at her surroundings.

The noise and confusion, the half-naked bodies—skin gleaming in the bright sunshine—the shouts and oaths, the obvious preparations for a battle, unnerved the angel. She had known, for she had heard her God, Promenthas, speak of a war in heaven. But it had never occurred to her that it would be like this—so much like a war on earth. She shrank back against a wall, hiding herself among the clinging tendrils of a morning glory.

What were the angels of Promenthas doing now? Had war come to them, too? Undoubtedly. An image came to her of the seraphim ripping the heavy wooden pews from the floor of the cathedral and stacking them against the doors; of archangels breaking out the lovely stained-glass windows, standing armed with bow and arrow; of cherubim clasping fiery swords, ready to defend the altar, to defend Promenthas. .

It was too horrible to imagine. Asrial turned her face against the wall to blot out the dreadful sights and sounds. She had seen wars upon earth, but those happened among humans. She had never imagined that the peace and tranquillity of her eternal home could be so violated.

"*Bilhana. Bilshifa.* My name is Pukah." Standing alone at the edge of a path, the djinn bowed and shouted and was completely and soundly ignored. "Fedj! Raja! Over here!" Pukah waved his arms, jumping up and down to make himself seen above the heads and shoulders of the larger djinn.

Fedj and Raja, however, were staring warily at Sond, who was returning the favor arms folded across his massive chest. Old enemies, were they to meet as friend or foe? Then Raja's face split into a smile. With one hand he greeted Sond with a blow on the back that sent the djinn headlong into a hibiscus bush, while with the other he proffered a jewel-encrusted dagger.

"Accept this gift, my dear friend!" said Raja.

"My dear friend, with pleasure!" cried Sond, making his way out of the foliage.

"Dear friend," mimicked Pukah in disgust. "Not two weeks ago they would have ripped out each other's eyes."

"Brother!" Fedj threw his huge arms around Sond and clasped him close. "Words cannot tell how I have missed you!" It was undoubtedly fond regard that caused Fedj to nearly squeeze the breath out of his "brother."

Sliding his muscular arms around Fedj's waist, Sond locked a hand over his wrist.

"Words fail me as well, brother!" Sond grunted, returning the embrace with such affection that the sound of cracking bones was distinctly audible.

"I think I'm going to vomit!" Pukah muttered. "And never

paying any attention to me—the hero of Serinda! Well, let them! Say"—he paused and hastily looked around—"I've got something that will make their bulging biceps twitch. Asrial, my enchanter! Where are you, my angel?" He peered through a tangle of hanging orchids. "Asrial?" A note of panic tinged his voice. "Asrial! I— Oh, there you are!" He sighed in relief. "I couldn't find you! My shy one!" Pukah gazed at her adoringly. "Hiding yourself away! Come." He took hold of her hand. "I want you to meet my friends—"

"No! Pukah, please!" Asrial hung back, her eyes wide with fright. "Let me go! I must return to my people!"

"Nonsense," said Pukah crisply, tugging at her. "Your people are my people. We're all immortal, and we're all in this together. Come on, there's a sweet child. Come on."

Reluctantly, hoping to avoid attention and still resolute on leaving, Asrial crept forward out of her hiding place.

"Look!" shouted Pukah proudly. "Look here! This is *my* angel!"

Asrial's pale cheeks flushed a delicate pink. "Pukah, don't say such things!" she begged. "I'm not your an—" Her words died away, sucked up and swallowed by a dreadful silence that fell over the djinn assembled in the garden, the eunuchs standing guard on the balcony, the djinniyeh gazing down at her over their veils.

Breathing heavily, one hand feeling his ribs to see if all were intact, Fedj used his other hand to point to Asrial.

"What's this?" he demanded.

"An angel," explained Pukah loftily, his foxish nose in the air.

"I can see it's an angel," Fedj snapped. "What's it doing here!"

"It's not an it, it's a she, as any but a blind beggar could plainly see! And she's with me! She's come to help—"

"Come to spy you mean!" roared Raja.

"A spy of Promenthas's!" shouted the djinn angrily, waving their swords and advancing on the two.

Asrial shrank back against Pukah, who shoved the angel behind him and faced the mob, his chin jutting out so far that any sword slice must have taken that portion of his face off first.

"Spy? If you muscle-bound apes had brains in your heads instead of your pectorals, you'd know that Promenthas is an ally of *Hazrat* Akhran—"

"Wrong! We heard Promenthas fights with Quar!" returned

many furious voices.

"That is not true!" Stung to courage, Asrial sprang forward before Pukah could stop her. "I have just come from a meeting with the two of them. Your God and mine pledged to help each other!"

There were unconvinced looks and mutterings.

"A trick! The angel lies. All angels are liars, you know that!"

"Now wait, my friends. I can vouch for the angel—"
Sond began.

"Ah, ha! So you're in this, too. I might have known, you thieving eater of horseflesh!" Fedj blocked Sond's path.

"This from one who beds with sheep!" Sond retorted scornfully. "Get out of my way, coward."

"Coward! All know it was the son of your master who fled a battle dressed as a woman!"

Steel flashed in the hands of the djinn.

"Take my advice, Pukah, and get her out of here!" came a yawning voice from somewhere down at their feet. Usti lay flat on his back, hands folded over his fat belly, peering up at them.

"Perhaps you're right," said Pukah, somewhat daunted and dismayed at the glittering eyes and glinting blades closing in on him.

"I'm not going!" Asrial retorted. Her white wings fanned back and forth in her agitation, her golden hair—stirred by the wind she created—floated in a cloud about her face. "Stop it!" Running forward, she hurled herself between Fedj and Sond, blocking their swords with her small white hands. "Don't you see? This is Kaug's doing! He wants to divide us, split us up. Then he can devour us piece by piece!"

Roughly shoving the angel aside, Fedj lunged at Sond. Asrial fell to the ground, in imminent danger of being trampled by the combatants, and Pukah, with a frantic cry, leaped to drag her out of the way. Before he could reach her, another figure sprang up from the flowers that were being torn to shreds by brawling, stamping feet.

The lithe, supple figure of a djinniyeh clothed in flowing silken pantalons and diaphanous veils stood in front of the fallen Asrial, guarding the angel's body with her own.

"Nedjma!" Sond gasped, falling backward, trembling from head to foot.

Dropping his sword, the enraptured djinn held out his arms and took a step forward, only to find himself suddenly blocked by the massive girth of a gigantic, scimitar-wielding eunuch who reared up from the earth like a mountain and stood rocklike and immovable between Sond and the djinniyeh.

Nedjma did not quite come up to Sond's shoulder. She barely came up to Raja's waist. But the enraged glance she flashed the djinn lopped off heads, cut brawny torsos in two, and reduced towering mounds of muscle and brawn to quivering lumps of immortal flesh. Gently and tenderly, without speaking a word, Nedjma bent down and helped Asrial to her feet. Putting her arm protectively around the angel's shoulder, she drew the white-robed body close to her own. With a last, flaring glance at Sond, Nedjma disappeared, taking the eunuch and Asrial with her.

His face burning with shame, his body shaking with thwarted passion, Sond bent over and retrieved his sword. Straightening, he avoided Fedj's eyes. Fedj, for his part, sheathed his sword and slouched out of the circle, muttering something about women minding their own affairs and staying out of those of men, but not saying it loudly enough that it could be overheard by those veiled and perfumed figures whispering indignantly together on the balcony.

Pukah watched anxiously until he saw white wings and golden hair being soothed and comforted above.

"Well, now that that's settled," began the young djinn brightly, stepping into the center of the garden, "let me introduce myself. I am Pukah, the hero of Serinda. You don't remember me, but I saved your lives, at great risk to my own. It was like this—"

At that moment, Kaug struck.

CHAPTER 6

blast of wind from the 'efreet's cavernous mouth swept through the pleasure garden. Tall palms bent double, torn leaves and petals filled the air like rain, water sloshed over the tiled rims of the ornamental pools. Usti, rudely awakened, dove for cover beneath a flower bed. On the balcony above, the djinniyeh screamed and caught hold of their fluttering veils, striving to see what was going on while the eunuchs pushed them toward the safety of the palace. Below, the djinn grimly drew their swords and braced themselves against the buffeting wind.

Fed by his God, the 'efreet's power had grown immense, and so had his size. Many times taller than the tallest minaret that graced the palace, many times wider than the walls surrounding it, Kaug lumbered across the immortal plane. The ground that existed only in the minds of those who stood upon it shook with the footfalls of the giant 'efreet. His breath was a gale, his hands could have picked up the huge Raja and tossed him lightly from the heavens. All the djinn in the garden, standing each upon the others' shoulders, could' not have achieved Kaug's height.

Yet they faced him. They would not give up meekly, as they had heard rumors of other immortals doing. Akhran himself—his flesh wounded and bleeding, absorbing the hurts inflicted on his people as he suffered at the same time from their dwindling faith—continued to fight. So would his immortals, until their power was drained, the strength of the mind that created their bodies depleted, and the bodies themselves vanquished, lying broken and bloody on the field of battle.

Kaug stopped just outside the walls of the garden and stared down with mocking triumph at the djinn within.

Sond took a step forward and raised his sword defiantly. Nedjma's perfume was in the djinn's nostrils; the memory of that scathing look she had cast him burned his mind. "Be gone, Kaug, while you still have a chance to save your worthless hide. If you leave now, we will not harm you."

Kaug's ugly face twisted into a grotesque smile. Taking a step forward, he calmly flattened one entire section of wall with a stamp of his foot.

"Sond!" said Kaug pleasantly, moving his other foot and crushing another section of wall. "So you are here? I am pleased, astonished but pleased. I thought you would have returned to the Tel, for I heard that former master of yours—poor old Majiid—has given up and is courting Death. Now there's a woman who will bring peace to his harem!"

Sond's face paled visibly. He cast a swift glance at Fedj, who averted his face from his brother djinn's alarmed, questioning eyes.

"And little Pukah," continued the 'efreet, his rumbling voice cracking the foundation stones of the palace, "here you are while your master sizzles like a lump of hot lead upon the Sun's Anvil. He, too, courts Death, and I fancy he will like her better than the wife he has!" Kaug chuckled and swung his hand, and a tower was swept from the castle walls. The djinn scrambled to avoid the debris that crashed into the garden around them, but remained standing in the ruins, grim and determined.

"You must be sorry you left my service, little Pukah!"

The 'efreet continued taunting them, but Pukah was only half listening, most of his attention being concentrated on a conversation taking place within his brain between himself and himself.

"We cannot win this, you know, Pukah," he stated.

"You, Pukah, are wise as always," his alter ego agreed with a sigh.

"And I am smarter than this heap of fish flesh," argued Pukah.

"Of course!" answered Pukah stoutly, knowing what was expected.

"Here's my plan." Pukah presented it, not without some pride. "What do you think of it?" he demanded when his alter ego remained silent for a rather prolonged period of time.

"There are . . . a certain number of flaws," suggested Pukah timidly.

"Of course, I haven't had time to work out all the details." Pukah glowered at himself, who considered that it might be time to keep quiet but couldn't forbear bringing up one more problem.

"What about Asrial?"

"Ah!" Pukah sighed. "You're right. I had forgotten." Then he said in a softer, sadder voice, "I don't think it will matter, friend. I don't believe there is any hope."

"But you should talk to her!" Pukah urged.

"I will," Pukah conceded hastily, "but I must start this to working immediately, so please shut up."

The inner Pukah was instantly silent, and the outer Pukah—all this having taken only flashing moments in his quicksilver brain—bowed gracefully to the 'efreet.

"Truly, Kaug the Magnificent, seeing you now in your glory and majesty, I do deeply regret that I gave in to the vile threats of the brutish Sond and allowed him to force me to leave your side."

Astounded and enraged, the djinn turned and glared at Pukah. Sond made a furious lunge at him, only to be stopped by the 'efreet's commanding voice.

"Halt! No one touch him. I find him . . . amusing." Squatting down, his hulking form casting a shadow black as night over the garden, his breath flattening trees, Kaug confronted Pukah. "So you want to be back in my service, do you, Little Pukah? Better that than the Realm of the Dead, eh?"

The 'efreet cast a significant glance around at all the djinn and the djinniyeh, peering through the windows above, and had the pleasure of seeing them all blench and cringe. Kaug grinned. "Yes, the Realm of the Dead. You remember that, don't you? No more human bodies, no more human pleasures and feelings, no more romps on earth, no more battles and wars, no more human food and drink"—a muffled moan could be heard, coming from beneath one of the flower beds—"no more djinn and djinniyeh. Nameless, shapeless servants of Death, that's what you'll become once I'm finished with you. When you no longer answer their prayers, the humans you serve will think they have been abandoned by their God. They will turn to Quar, to a God who listens to them, and to me—a servant who knows how to provide for their every need and desire as—"

"—as a good master provides for his slaves," supplemented Pukah.

Kaug glowered, this not being the most flattering of metaphors. But Pukah's face was bland and innocent, his tone admiring as he continued. "It appears to me that this will mean a tremendous amount of work for you, O Kaug, and though I have no doubt that your shoulders are big enough to bear the burden, it cannot help but reduce your time for... uh ... whatever pleasures you like to pursue." Momentarily flustered, Pukah had no idea what pleasures these might be, and he certainly didn't care to think on it a great deal.

"My pleasure is serving Quar!" Kaug roared, straightening to his full height, his head punching a hole in the starry sky.

"Oh, yes, it must be, of course!" stammered Pukah, the resultant gale knocking him off his feet. "But," he continued cunningly, picking himself back up, "you won't be serving Quar, will you? You'll be serving humans! Answering to their every whim. 'See that my twelve daughters are married to rich husbands!' 'Bring me a chest of gold and two caskets of jewels!' 'Cure this ailment from which my goat suffers!' 'Convince my son that he wants a job selling iron pots in the marketplace!' 'Make my dwelling as large as my neighbor's!' 'Deliver—'"

"Enough!" Kaug muttered. It was plain from the angry expression on the 'efreet's face that Pukah's shot had hit a vital spot. Endeavoring to fight a war in heaven, attempting to foment distrust and hatred among the various factions of immortals, Kaug was continually being forced to leave his important work to perform those very degrading tasks that Pukah had mentioned. Just a few days ago, in fact, he'd had to leave a pitched battle with the imps and demons of Astafas and return to earth to carry the *houri*, Meryem, to an audience with the Imam.

"What a waste it will be," added Pukah sadly, "to set us all to guarding the dead, who, after all, aren't in that much need of guarding. Not to mention serving Death. She doesn't have half the responsibility that *you* carry, O Kaug the Overburdened."

Pukah allowed his voice to trail off, seeing a thoughtful look crinkle the 'efreet's eyes. "Perhaps this intense mental process will rupture something," the djinn muttered hopefully. A frown formed in the beetling brows, and he hastened to forestall what he guessed would be the 'efreet's next argument. "I am certain that Quar, having depleted his own supply of immortals—in a most worthy cause, I grant you, but leaving you, unfortunately, short of help—Quar will be most pleased at your resourcefulness and ingenuity in being able to furnish your Great God with additional help to run the world."

Kaug absently uprooted a tree or two as he considered this latest proposition. Sond, taking advantage of the 'efreet's preoccupation, sidled nearer Pukah and hissed out of the side of his mouth, "Have you gone mad?"

"Can you win a fight against him?" Pukah demanded in a piercing whisper.

"No," Sond conceded grudgingly.

"Do you want to guard the Realm of the Dead?"

"No!"

"Then be silent and let me—"

Kaug fixed Pukah with a steely-eyed gaze, and the djinn was immediately all polite and respectful attention.

"You are saying, Little Pukah, that you and your brethren should come work for me instead of Death?"

Pukah bowed, hands pressed together prayerfully. "We will be honored—"

"We will be damned!" Sond started to shout, but Pukah's elbow in Sond's solar plexus deprived the djinn of breath, voice, and defiance all at one blow. There is no doubt the other djinn would have shouted their own resistance but that the baleful eye of the 'efreet swiveled round and gazed fiercely at each of them.

Gracefully Pukah glided in front of the gasping Sond and faced the 'efreet.

"Most Generous Kaug, my brethren are, as you can see, overwhelmed by the opportunity. They are stupefied and cannot express their thanks in a fitting manner."

"Thanks for what? I've made no offer yet!"

"Ah," said Pukah, looking at Kaug out of the corner of his eye, "you dare do nothing without consulting Quar. I understand."

"I do what I please!" thundered the 'efreet, the blast smashing every pane of glass on the djinn's immortal plane.

"Still, we wouldn't want to rush things. Give my brethren and me seventy-two hours human time to consider your terms and decide whether or not we accept."

Kaug's great eyes blinked. The 'efreet was somewhat confused. It was an unusual feeling for the generally sharp-witted Kaug, but then he'd had much on his mind lately. He did not recall offering terms. Or had he? The 'efreet knew that somewhere he'd lost control of the situation, and this angered him. He considered flattening castle, garden, and these irritating djinn at a breath, then snatching their immortal spirits from the shells of their bodies and sending them forthwith to Death. But at that moment, Kaug heard a gong ring three times.

Quar was summoning him. Undoubtedly some human needed his donkey scrubbed.

"You can always return and squash us later, if that is what you decide," suggested Pukah in the most respectful tones. "We're not likely to go anywhere." Except to rescue our master from the Sun's Anvil, the djinn added to himself," exulting in his own cleverness.

Seventy-two hours. Kaug considered. Yes, he could always return and squash them later. And in the meantime, seventy-two hours would be long enough to pluck a thorn from Quar's flesh.

"Smart Little Pukah," said Kaug to himself, "you shall have your seventy-two hours to hatch whatever plan is picking its way out of the shell of your mind. Seventy-two hours that will be the death of the Calif and soon be the death—or enslavement—of all of you."

"Seventy-two hours," Kaug stated out loud and—at the insistent clanging of the gong—the 'efreet started to leave. Seeming, at the last moment, to remember something, Kaug returned. "Oh, and you're quite right, Little Pukah," he said, grinning as he dropped a huge iron cage over the palace and gardens of the ancient djinn. "You're *not* going anywhere!"

CHAPTER 7

Khardan started up out of an exhausted sleep he never meant to take. He was wide-awake, alert. Unconscious, his mind had warned him of danger, and now, crouching in the meager shade offered by a tall sand dune, he stared around to discover what had quickened his heartbeat and pricked his skin.

He did not have to look long or far. The distant, ominous grinding sound came to him instantly. Turning his head to the west, the direction they were traveling, he saw a thick cloud on the horizon. It was a strange cloud, for it came from the land, not the sky. Its color was peculiar—a pale gray tinged with ocher.

In the top of the cloud, two huge, glistening eyes stared down at Khardan.

"An 'efreet," the Calif said aloud, though no one heard him. Beside him, huddled in the sand, Zohra slept, and next to her Mathew either slept or was dead, Khardan didn't know which. The boy had pitched forward on his face, unconscious, and nothing would rouse him.

Khardan looked away. If the boy was dead, he was lucky.

If he wasn't, he would be soon.

Serinda was no longer visible on the horizon. The 'efreet might have swallowed it up, for all Khardan knew.

Glaring at the 'efreet and the sandstorm it generated, Khardan clenched his hand over the hilt of the dagger he wore in his sash. His djinn had provided the dagger, just as they had provided clothes and water. They had thought of everything.

Everything except defeat.

Khardan wondered where Pukah was. Enslaved? Guarding the Realm of the Dead?

"If so," Khardan muttered, "you are liable to see your master very shortly!"

The death of the desert is a terrible one. It is a death of swollen tongue and cracked lips, a death of pain and suffering and eventual, tortured madness. Drawing his dagger, Khardan stared at the sharp, curved blade. He turned it in his hand. The sun, not yet obscured by the deadly, yellowish cloud, blazed on the steel, half blinding him.

Zohra slept the sleep of exhaustion and did not waken when he gently rolled her over onto her back. Khardan sat for long moments, staring at her face. He was dazed by the heat, and though the storm was still far away, there was a gritty taste in the air that was already making it difficult to breathe.

How long her eyelashes were. Long and thick and black, the lashes cast shadows over her smooth skin. He brushed his finger across them, and then, reaching out, he gently if clumsily unclasped the veil and removed it from her face.

Her mouth was parted, her tongue ran across it as though she drank in her sleep. Lifting the *girba*, he poured the water— the last of the water—onto the curved lips. He spilled most of it; the sand drank it greedily and seemed thirsty for more.

Soon it would have a richer, warmer liquid.

Zohra smiled, sighed, and drew a deep, easy breath. The expression of fierce pride was gone, softened and smoothed by weariness and suffering. Khardan found that he missed it. A burning hot wind rose from in front of the Calif, whipping his robes around him. He glanced up. As the wind blew stronger, the cloud grew larger, the grinding sound louder, the evil eyes in the cloud nearer. Resolutely, Khardan turned the peaceful, serene face away from him.

"Farewell, wife," he said softly. It seemed there should be more to say between them, but he couldn't think of anything. He was too tired, too dazed by the heat. When they met again beyond, then perhaps he could explain, could tell her everything that had been in his heart.

The Calif placed the point of the dagger on the skin right below Zohra's left ear.

A sound—a ringing sound, the tinkling sound of bells that accompanies a camel's plodding, splayfooted steps over the sand—arrested the killing stroke. Khardan paused, raising his head, wondering if the desert madness had overtaken him already.

"Pukah! Sond!" He meant it to be a shout, but the words came from his throat no more than a painful croak. There was no answer, but he heard the ringing clearly. If it was madness, then it had a smell as well. The odor of camel was unmistakable.

Sheathing the dagger, Khardan rose hastily to his feet and scrambled and crawled up to the top of the dune.

Crouched on the ridge, his arms braced against the blasting wind, the Calif looked below and saw camels—four of them tethered together—plodding through the sand. But there were no djinn hovering triumphantly in the air above them.

There was only a single rider. Swathed from head to toe in the black, flowing robes of the nomad, he kept his face covered against the sandstorm. Only his eyes were visible, and as he drew near, these stared straight at Khardan.

In the next instant, Khardan saw the stranger's hand dart into his robes.

Realizing suddenly that he was an excellent target poised on the ridge of the dune, the Calif cursed and, hand on his own dagger, slipped swiftly back behind the dune's rim. Peering cautiously over the edge, he kept the stranger within sight.

The man in black made a swift, deft throwing motion. Sun flared on steel. Flinching, Khardan instinctively flattened himself. The knife thudded into the sand, hilt up, inches in front of the nomad's nose.

Khardan barely glanced at the knife. He stared warily at the stranger, waiting for the attack. The man relaxed in the camel saddle. Leaning one hand easily upon the leg that was crossed in front to help him maintain his balance, he gestured toward the thrown dagger. Squinting his eyes against the blowing sand, the Calif diverted his gaze from the stranger to the weapon.

The hilt was made of gold, inlaid with silver, and it was fashioned in a design he himself had worn on a suit of black armor. Two ruby eyes winked at Khardan from the head of a severed snake.

CHAPTER 8

lowering his facecloth, Auda ibn Jad shouted over the rising storm. "Greetings, brother!"

Khardan scrambled and slid halfway down the side of the dune and halted some distance from the Black Paladin. Eyes narrowed against the stinging sand, the Calif stood, unmoving. Ibn Jad urged the grumbling camels forward.

"For a man who was expecting Death, you don't look glad to see me," he yelled.

"Perhaps that is because it is Death I see," returned Khardan.

Snagging a waterskin from his saddle, Auda offered it to the nomad.

"I need nothing," said the Calif, not glancing at the water, his gaze fixed on the Black Paladin.

"Ah, of course. You have drunk your fill from the vast rivers that run through this land." Auda lifted the *girba* to his lips and drank deeply. Water trickled down the corners of his mouth, flowing into the short, neatly trimmed black beard that graced his strong jawline. Replacing the stopper, he wiped his mustached lips with the back of his hand, then cast a glance at the approaching sandstorm. "And, on a cool day like today, a man does not thirst as he does when it is—"

"Why are you here?" Khardan demanded. "How did you leave the castle?"

Auda glanced up at the rapidly darkening sky. "First I suggest we make what shelter we can before the enemy strikes."

"Tell me now or we will both die where we stand!"

Auda regarded him silently, then shrugged and leaned close to be heard. "I left as you did, nomad. I placed my life in the hands of my God, and he gave it back to me." The thin lips smiled. "The

Black Sorceress called for my execution. I was accused of aiding prisoners to escape and asked if I had anything to say in my defense. I said you and I had shared blood. Closer than brothers born, our lives were pledged to each other. I had vowed this, before the God, before Zhakrin."

"They believed you?"

"They had no choice. The God himself, Zhakrin, appeared before them. He is weak, his form indistinct and constantly shifting. But he has returned to us," Auda said with quiet pride, "and the strength of our faith increases his power daily!"

These evil people had never wavered in their faith, even when it seemed their God had left them forever. Now he was increasing in strength. Our God, Akhran . . . wounded. . . dying. Khardan flushed uncomfortably and, reaching out his hand, took the waterskin from the Black Paladin. He drank sparingly, but Auda waved a hand at his camels. "Take your fill. There is more."

"There are others in my care," Khardan said.

A spark flickered deep in Auda's dark, hooded eyes. "So they survived, the two who were with you? The beautiful, black-haired wildcat, your wife, and the gentle Blossom? Where are they?"

"They lie on the other side." Covering his mouth and nose with the cloth against the blowing sand, Khardan turned and began to clamor up the side of the dune, wondering why it was like setting a spark to dry tinder to hear the Black Paladin praise Zohra.

Tugging hard on the camel's lead, shouting imperative commands, Auda dragged the recalcitrant animals to their knees at the bottom of the dune where they might find some protection from the fury of the storm.

Zohra was awake. Hearing their voices, she had climbed partway up the dune to meet them.

"Mat-hew!" Khardan shouted, pointing and indicating with a wave of his hand that Zohra was to bring the boy with her.

She understood and slid back down to get him. Hand on his shoulder, she shook him hard. There was no response, and she glanced up helplessly at Khardan.

The 'efreet howled furiously, sand swirled around them, making it nearly impossible to see. Sliding down the side of the dune, Khardan reached Zohra. Between them, they pummeled and screamed and managed at last to wake the young man and indicate to him that he must climb the dune to escape the storm.

Dazed and uncomprehending, Mathew did what he was told, responding to the hands that dragged him along and the voices that yelled in his ear. Once over the top, he collapsed and slithered down the side. Auda caught him and carried him to where the camels crouched, heads hunched down. Propping the boy up against the flanks of the animals, sheltered from the blasting wind, Auda flung a blanket over him and returned to assist Zohra.

Black eyes blazing, she drew away from Auda as he would have taken her hand, and stumbled through the sand to make her own shelter near Mathew. She would not even accept water until Khardan took it from the Paladin's hand and gave it to her.

Shrugging, Auda leaned back against the flanks of the camel he had been riding. Khardan sank down next to him. "This is useless," he yelled. "We cannot fight an 'efreet!"

"Ah, but we do not fight alone," Auda replied calmly.

Looking up into the sky, startled, Khardan saw that the eyes in the storm cloud were no longer gazing at him but at something on their own level, something he could not see. A strong breeze, cool and damp and smelling faintly of salt spray, rose up from the opposite direction, blowing against the 'efreet. Caught in the crosscurrents of opposing winds, the sand swept about them in blinding, whirling clouds. The camels faced out the storm stolidly. The humans ducked beneath blankets. Despite that, sand clogged their mouths and noses, sending them coughing and choking, making each breath a struggle.

Abruptly the 'efreet drew back. The winds ceased to howl, the sand quit its eerie wailing. Stirring, displacing a mound of sand that covered him, Khardan raised his head.

"Either the 'efreet believes we are dead, or he has decided to leave and let the sun finish us off," he stated, spitting grit from his mouth. "The creature is gone."

Auda did not respond. The Paladin's eyes were closed, and the Calif heard a faint murmuring coming from behind the folds of the *haik*.

He is praying, Khardan realized. "So it *was* your God who let you go," he said gruffly when ibn Jad opened his eyes and reached for the *girba*.

"I am honor bound to keep my vow," Auda replied, swishing water in his mouth and spitting it out. "Zhakrin commanded that I be set free. Free . . . to keep another vow—a vow made by another brother."

"I think I know of this vow." Khardan accepted the *girba* and, out of habit, drank sparingly.

"They told you of it that night. . ."

The first night at Castle Zhakrin. The Calif had been present—a prisoner—at a meeting of the Black Paladins and had heard the story Auda was now repeating.

"Dying at the feet of the accursed priest of Quar, dying of wounds inflicted by his own hand so that the *kafir* could not claim his life nor their God his soul, Catalus, my brother in Zhakrin, laid the blood curse of our God upon the Imam. I have been chosen to redeem that curse."

Khardan's gaze shifted from the man's impassive face to the silver-and-gold hilt that could be seen protruding from his sash. "An assassin's dagger?"

"Yes. Benario, God of the Stealthy, has blessed it."

Grunting, Khardan shook his head. "You are a fool."

With this pronouncement, he settled himself more comfortably back against the camel and closed his eyes.

Auda grinned. "Then I travel with a party of fools. How do you think I found you here? How do you think I came to be carrying water enough for three, or that I have brought three riding camels with me?"

Khardan shrugged. "That is easy. You followed our tracks through the sand. As for bringing along the camels, perhaps you like their company!"

Auda laughed—a sound like rocks splitting apart. From his smooth face and cruel, cold eyes, it seemed he did not laugh often. His mirth ended quickly—rocks tumbling down the side of a cliff and vanishing into a chasm of darkness. Leaning near, Auda grasped hold of the Calif's arm, his strong fingers digging deeply into the flesh.

"Zhakrin guided me!" he hissed, and Khardan felt hot breath upon his cheek. "Zhakrin sent me to follow you, and it was Zhakrin who drove off Quar's 'efreet! Once again I have saved your life, nomad. I have kept my vow to you.

"Now you will keep yours to me!"

CHAPTER 9

They slept fitfully through the day, sheltered from the searing heat in a small tent carried by the *djemel*, Auda's baggage camel. With the setting of the sun they woke, ate tasteless unleavened bread also provided by the Black Paladin, drank his water, then prepared to leave. Few words were spoken.

Though intensely curious about Auda and his arrival that had saved their lives, Zohra could not ask Khardan about him, and the Calif—grim and stern-faced and silent—volunteered no information. It was unseemly for a woman to question her husband, and though Zohra normally cared little about proprieties, she felt a strange reluctance to flout them before the Black Paladin. She kept her eyes lowered, as was proper, when she went about the small duties involved in preparing and serving their meager meal, but glancing at him from beneath the fringe of her lashes, she never failed to notice ibn Jad watching her.

Had there been lust or desire in the black eyes, or even exasperated fury as she was accustomed to seeing in Khardan's, Zohra would have discounted and scorned it. But the Paladin's flat gaze, expressive of no emotion whatsoever, unnerved her. She found herself stealing furtive glances at him more often than she intended, hoping to catch some glimmer of inner light in the eyes, gain some idea of his thoughts and intentions. Whenever she did, she was disconcerted to find her glances returned.

She could have whispered her doubts and fears to Mathew, except that the young man was behaving most oddly. Slow to waken, he moved sluggishly and stared about him in a dazed manner that took in the presence of Auda ibn Jad without surprise or comment. He drank as much as they allowed him but refused food and lay down again while the rest of them ate. Only when ibn Jad shook his shoulder to rouse him when it was time to leave did Mathew react to the man as though he remembered him, flinching away from his touch and staring at him with wild, glistening eyes.

But he meekly followed ibn Jad when bidden to rise and leave the tent. Obediently and without question, he mounted the camel and allowed the two men to position him comfortably in the saddle.

Zohra watched Mathew's strange behavior with concern and again, had they been alone, would have called it to Khardan's attention. Once or twice she endeavored to catch the Calif's attention. Khardan avoided her pointedly, and—with ibn Jad's eyes always on her, even when he was looking at something else—Zohra kept silent.

"We will reach Serinda before morning," Auda announced as they rode out into the rapidly cooling air of the night. "It is well that I came along, brother. For had you made it across the Sun's Anvil to Serinda alive, there—in the city of death—you would surely have died. There is no water in Serinda."

"How could that happen?" asked Khardan disbelievingly, the first words other than commands or instructions concerning their leaving he had uttered. "They must have dug their wells deep, to provide water for so many. How could Serinda's wells ever run dry?"

"Dug?" Twisting in his saddle, Auda glanced at Khardan, riding beside him, with amusement. "They dug no wells, nomad. The people of Serinda used machines to suck the water out of the Kurdin Sea. The water flowed along great canals that stood high in the air and emptied into *hauz* for the city's use. I have heard it said that these canals could sometimes be made to take the water directly into a man's dwelling."

"It is too bad we have no children traveling with us," Khardan remarked. "They would be fascinated by such lies. I suppose you will tell me next that these people of Serinda were fish people, who drank salt water."

Auda did not seem offended at this reaction to his tales. "The Kurdin Sea was not always salty, or so I have heard the wise men in the court of Khandar teach. Be that true or not, I repeat we will find no water at Serinda. There will be shelter from the sun there, however. We can spend tomorrow safely within its walls, then travel the next night. We have water enough to last that long, but no longer. The following day when we reach your camp around the Tel, we can lead your people to war against Quar. I presume" —Auda turned his flat, glittering eyes upon Khardan—"that your own wells have not run completely dry?"

It was obvious he was not speaking of water.

"The wells of my people run deep and pure!" Khardan retorted, resenting the insinuation but not daring to say more, since the Paladin's remarks hit closely near the center of his target. Flicking the camel stick across the beast's shoulder, he kicked at the camel's flanks with his heels, driving the animal forward to take the lead.

Riding behind the men, her attention divided between listening to the conversation and worriedly watching a swaying, groggy Mathew, Zohra knew by the hunch of the man's shoulders that Auda was regarding Khardan speculatively.

Her fingers curled over the reins, unconsciously twisting and pleating the leather. She had never—until now—heard true fear in her husband's voice.

CHAPTER 10

I t was in the dark shadows of the walls of Serinda, just as the eastern sky was beginning to brighten with the coming of day, that Mathew tumbled from his saddle and lay like one dead in the sand.

More than once on the long journey, Zohra had seen the young man's head nod listlessly, his shoulders slump, and his body begin to slant sideways. Ridjng up beside him, she lashed out with the camel stick, striking him a blow across his shoulders. The thin, flexible stick bit through cloth and into flesh like a whip—a painful but effective means of wakening a drifting rider. Mathew jerked upright. In the starlit darkness she could see him staring at her in puzzled hurt. Dropping back behind him, she put her hand to her veiled lips, enjoining him to silence. Khardan would have little patience with a man who could not sit a camel.

Zohra saw Mathew start to sway when they reached Serinda, but she could not urge her camel forward fast enough to catch, him. She knelt beside him. One touch of her hand upon his hot, dry forehead told her what she had long begun to suspect. "The fever," she said to Khardan.

Lifting the young man in his arms—the youth's frail body was as light as that of a woman's—Khardan carried him through the gates of Serinda. Half-buried in the sand, the gates that had once kept out formidable enemies now stood open to the one enemy that could never be defeated—time.

Pukah would not have recognized this city as the one in which he had performed his heroics. Quar's spell had made it appear to the immortals as they wanted to see it—a rollicking city of teeming life and sudden death. Streets choked with sand were streets choked with brawling mobs. Doors falling from their rusted hinges were doors broken in fights. The wind that whispered desolately through empty, dust covered rooms was the whispering laughter of immortal lovers. The spell broken, Death once more walked the world, and Serinda was a city even She had abandoned long ago.

Auda led them through the empty, windswept streets to a building that he said was once the home of a wealthy, powerful family. Zohra, interested only in finding shelter for Mathew, paid scant attention to private bathing pools of colorful inlaid tile or the remains of statuary; except perhaps to note in shock that the bodies of the humans portrayed were completely naked. Though broken and defiled by centuries of looters, it was easy to see that their sculptors had given careful consideration to every detail.

Zohra was too concerned about Mathew to pay attention to carved rock. When Khardan had lifted him in his arms, Mathew had looked straight up at him and had not known him. The young man spoke in a language none of them understood and it was obvious from his rambling tone and occasional shouts and yells that what he was saying probably made little sense anyway.

Searching through the many-roomed dwelling, they finally found one chamber whose walls were still intact. Located in the interior of the large house, it seemed likely to offer relief from the midday heat.

"This will do," said Zohra, kicking aside some of the larger fragments of broken rock that littered the floor. "But he cannot lay on the hard stone."

"I will look for bedding," offered Auda ibn Jad. Silently as a shadow, he slipped from the room.

Sunlight streamed through a crack in the ceiling, its slanting rays visible in the haze of dust and fine sand that their arrival had raised up from the stone floor. The light glistened in Mathew's flaming red hair, touched the pallid face, glinted in the fever-glazed eyes that stared at sights only he could see. Khardan held him easily, securely. The young man's head lolled against the nomad's strong chest, a feebly twitching hand dangled over the Calif's arm.

Moving near to brush a lock of hair from Mathew's burning forehead, Zohra asked in a low, tense tone, "Why has that man come?"

"Thank Akhran he did," Khardan replied without looking at her.

"I was not afraid to die," Zohra answered steadily, "not even when I felt the point of your dagger touch my skin."

Khardan's gaze turned on her in astonishment. She had not been asleep! She had realized what he meant to do and why he had to do it, and she had chosen not to make it difficult for him. Lying completely still, shamming sleep, she would have met her death at his hand unflinchingly, unprotesting. Akhran himself knew what courage that must have taken!

Awed, Khardan could only stare at her wordlessly. In his arms Mathew stirred and moaned. Zohra moved her hand to caress the boy's cheek. Her dark eyes raised to look in Khardan's.

"That man?" she persisted softly. "He is evil! Why—"

"An oath," Khardan growled. "I swore an oath—"

A scraping sound warned them of the Black Paladin's return. He backed in through the chamber door, dragging a wool-stuffed pallet with him.

"It is filthy. Others have used it before us for a variety of purposes," said Auda. "But it is all I could find. I shook it out in the street and dislodged several inhabitants who were none too pleased at finding themselves homeless once more. But at least Blossom will not add scorpion stings to his other troubles. Where do you want it?"

Keeping her eyes lowered, Zohra pointed wordlessly to the coolest corner of the room. Auda threw the mattress down and kicked it into place with his foot. Zohra spread a felt camel blanket on top, then motioned for Khardan to put, Mathew down. With clumsy gentleness, the Calif eased the suffering young man onto the pallet. The young, man's wide open eyes stared at them wildly; he spoke and tried weakly to sit up but could barely lift his head.

"Will he be well by morning?" asked ibn Jad. Kneeling beside her patient, Zohra shook her head. "Then, more to the point," continued the Black Paladin, "will he be dead by morning?"

Zohra turned her head; the dark eyes looked directly at Auda ibn Jad for the first time since he had joined them. For long moments she gazed at him in silence; then her eyes shifted to Khardan. "Bring water," she ordered—it was a woman's right to command when fighting sickness—and turned back to Mathew.

The two men left the building, walking through Serinda's silent streets to fetch the camels that had been left hobbled just within the gates.

Pulling down his facecloth, Auda smoothed his beard, ruefully shaking his head. "I swear by Zhakrin, nomad, I felt the fire in that look of hers scorch my flesh! I shall bear the scar the rest of my life."

Khardan walked without reply, the *haik* covering his own face, any glimmer of his thoughts lost in the cloth's shadow. Raising an eyebrow, Auda smiled, a smile that was absorbed and hidden by the black beard. Growing graver, the pale face smooth and impassive once more, he laid a slender, long-fingered hand upon Khardan's arm and brought the man to a halt.

"Draw her away, on some pretext or other. It need not be long."

"No." Khardan resumed his walk, his face averted from ibn Jad's, his eye staring straight ahead.

"There are ways that leave no mark. The boy succumbed to the fever. She will never know. My friend"—Auda pitched his voice louder to reach Khardan, who continued to walk away from him—"either Blossom dies now or we all die in a few days when the water runs out."

Khardan made a swift, angry, negating gesture with his hand, slicing it knifelike through the heat-shimmering air.

"My God will not allow the staying of my quest'" called ibn Jad.

Khardan reached the gates where the camels waited with the grumbling patience of their kind.

Auda remained standing, his arms folded across his chest.

"Unless you want to find that *two* have died by morning, nomad, you will take your woman out of that room and keep her out."

Khardan stopped, his hand resting on the splintered wood of the sand-mired gate. The fingers clenched. He did not turn around. "How long," he asked abruptly, "do you need?"

"The count of a thousand heartbeats," answered Auda ibn Jad.

CHAPTER 11

Soft-footed, Khardan entered the house they had taken over in Serinda, moving silently in the shadows that slanted across the corridors of the long-abandoned dwelling. Always uncomfortable within walls, the nomad felt doubly ill at ease walking the halls of another man's home without his permission or knowledge. No matter whether it was a Sultan's palace or the most tattered tent of the lowest tribe member, a home was a sacred place, inviolate—entered with ceremony, left with ceremony. And though this dwelling had been looted and stripped of its valuable possessions hundreds of years before, the mundane, everyday objects of those unknown people had been preserved in the dry air of the desert so that it seemed to Khardan as though the owners must return any moment—the women bewailing the destruction, the men angered and demanding revenge.

The nomad has little sense of time. Change means nothing to him, since his life changes daily. The nomad is the center of his own universe; he *is* his own universe. He must be, in order to survive his harsh world. The deaths of thousands in a nearby city will mean nothing to him. The stealing of a sheep from his fold will send him to war. Standing within these walls, Khardan had a sudden glimpse of time, the universe, and his own part in it. No longer was he the center, the man the sun rose for daily, the man for whom the stars shone, the man the winds buffeted and challenged to battle in personal contest. He was a grain of sand like millions of others. The stars never knew him. The sun would rise without him some day, the winds toss him heedlessly aside to pick up some other speck.

The man who walked this colored tile long ago once thought himself the center of the universe. The people who built this city knew themselves to be the apex of civilization. They had known their God to be the One, True God.

And now that God was nameless, unremembered, as were the men who worshipped him.

All that remained was of the earth, Sul, the elements. The stones on which Khardan trod were in the world before man came. Used by man, tooled by man, set in place by man, they would be here when man was gone.

The thought was humbling, frightening. The Calif's fingers moved over the smooth surface of the hewn rock, feeling the texture, the coolness within the stone despite the rapidly growing heat of the day outside, the slight depressions here and there where a hand wielding a chisel had slipped.

Sighing, his face grave, he moved on through the house, where the shadows seemed more welcome than he was, and quietly entered the room where Mathew lay.

Kneeling beside the pallet, her back to the door, Zohra glanced at Khardan as he entered, and glanced away. Intent on her patient, she wiped the boy's feverish face with a damp cloth.

"You should not be wasting the water," Khardan said in a harsher tone than he had meant to use. Let her offer what comfort she can. After all, what does it matter? He rebuked himself, but it was too late.

He knew by the set of her shoulders, the sudden twist of her hands, the wrenching of the cloth as she squeezed the liquid back into a cracked bowl, that he had made her angry. "You are tired, Zohra. Why don't you go to sleep?" he said evenly. "I will tend to the young man."

He saw her flinch, the shoulders jerk, then straighten. She turned to confront him, and he braced himself to meet with impassive expression the black eyes that looked straight into his soul. Patiently, he waited for the storm of her rage to break over him. But her head drooped, her shoulders slumped, her hands dropped the cloth listlessly into the water. Sitting back upon her heels, Zohra raised her face to look into the heavens, not to pray, but to force the tears back down her throat.

"He means to kill him, doesn't he?"

"Yes." Khardan could say no more.

"And you will let him!" It was an accusation, a curse.

"Yes," Khardan answered steadily. "Would you leave him alone with this sickness on him, to let the fever burn him up, or let him do himself an injury in his ravings or be preyed upon by some animal—"

"No!" Zohra glared at him, scorching him with the scorn and fury in her eyes.

"Will you die with him?" Khardan persisted. "Abandon our people when we are within two days' ride of them? Let all we have gone through be for nothing? Let all *he* has accomplished be for nothing?"

"I—" The seething words died on trembling lips. The tears fell then, sliding down her cheeks, leaving tracks in the dust on her skin, dust that sifted in through every chink in the rock wall.

Khardan knelt beside her. He wanted to take her in his arms and share his own grief, his own anger, and the fear, which had overwhelmed him in the empty, silent halls of the dead house, of being that grain of sand. His hand moved to touch her, but at that moment her chin jutted forward proudly, she swiftly wiped her eyes.

"You will kill ibn Jad," she said resolutely.

"I may not. I have taken an oath," Khardan replied. "Even if I hadn't, I could not kill one who has twice saved my life."

"Then I will kill him. Give me your dagger." The black eyes looked at him fiercely, an odd contrast to the tears still glistening on her face.

Khardan lowered his face to hide a smile that came despite the burning in his heart. "That would not solve matters," he said quietly. "Mathew would still be sick and unable to travel. We would still have water enough for only three days and no way of finding any when that is gone. And it will take us two days to reach the Tel."

She could not answer but glared at him with the irrational rage men hold against one who speaks an unpleasant truth.

Mathew twisted and moaned. The fever made the bones ache, joints stiffen, and cramped the belly. Slowly, with a gentleness few ever saw, Khardan reached out and laid a hand upon the boy's forehead.

"Rest easy," he murmured, and whether it was the touch or the sound of the loved and admired voice that penetrated the horrors of delirium, Mathew grew calmer. The tortured limbs relaxed. But it would be only for the moment.

Khardan continued stroking the pale skin that was dry and hot as a sand snake's to the touch.

"He will slip from this life quickly and painlessly. His sufferings will finally be at an end. We do him no disservice, Zohra. You and I both know he is not happy living among us."

"And if he is not, whose fault is that?" Zohra demanded in a low, trembling voice. "We looked down on him and sneered at him and reviled him for his weakness, for disguising himself as a woman in order to survive. But now we know what it is to be alone and afraid and helpless in a strange and alien place! Did we acquit ourselves any better? Did we even do as well? That evil knight may have helped us to escape, but it was Mat-hew who saved you—"

"Stop it, woman!" Khardan shouted, twisting to his feet. "Every word you speak is a knife in my heart, and you do not inflict wounds that I have not already felt myself! But I have no choice! I have made the best decision I can, and it is a decision I must live with the rest of my life! Unless a miracle occurs and water falls from the hands of Akhran"—Khardan pointed at Mathew—"the boy must die. If you are here, and if you try to stop him, ibn Jad will have no compunction over killing you, too." Khardan held out his hand to her. "I saved the boy's life in the desert. He and I are even. Will you come and rest before this night's travel?"

Zohra stared at the hand poised above her, the violent struggle within herself apparent in the flush that made her face nearly as fevered as Mathew's. She gave Khardan one final, piercing glance from her black eyes, a glance tainted with hatred and anger and, amazingly, disappointment—amazingly to Khardan because we feel disappointment in another only when we expect better than we receive, and Khardan found it difficult to believe his wife thought even that well of him. Certainly she did not now. Wringing water from the cloth, she laid it gently on Mathew's brow; then, spurning her husband's outstretched hand, Zohra rose to her feet.

"I will sleep," she said in an emotionless tone, and brushed past Khardan without another look.

Sighing, he saw her wend her way through the corridors of the house, then stood, gazing for long moments down at Mathew.

"What she said is true," he told the unhearing boy softly.

"I understand your unhappiness now, and I am sorry."

He started to say something more, sighed, and abruptly turned away.

"I am sorry!"

CHAPTER 12

ohra chose deliberately one of the many chambers located near Mathew's and hid within the shadows that played upon the stone walls. Holding her breath, she watched as the Calif emerged from the doorway. He paused and, lifting his hands to his eyes, rubbed them and continued down the hallway, shaking his head, toward the door that led outside.

He passed quite near her. Zohra saw his face was lined with fatigue and care, his brow furrowed with an anger that she knew turned in upon himself.

"This is not his fault," she whispered remorsefully, remembering the look with which she had favored him when she left. "If anything, the fault is mine, for without my meddling he would now be riding the heavens in honor with *Hazrat* Akhran. But it will be all right," she promised him silently as he passed by her. Her heart ached for his sorrow, and she wavered in her determination. "Perhaps I should tell him. What would it hurt? But no, he would try to stop me—"

She had unconsciously taken a step toward him, toward the door. She did not hear the sound of stealthy movement behind her nor realize that another person besides herself had chosen that particular room for a hiding place, until a hard-muscled body slammed into hers, pressing her into a corner, and a firm hand covered her mouth and nose.

Khardan stopped, listening, his head slightly turned. The hand clasped her more firmly, the cool, glittering eyes informed her that the slightest movement was death.

Zohra held very still, and Khardan, shrugging tiredly, went dejectedly on his way.

The hand did not release its hold until they both heard the nomad's footsteps fade in the distance.

"He will sleep outside, where he can breathe the free air. I know him, you see." The hand loosened its grip, moving from her mouth down to close gently around her neck. Zohra stared, terrified yet fascinated, into the expressionless eyes so close to hers. "He is not far. You could bring him with a scream. But it would do you no good." The hand gently touched two points upon her throat. "My fingers here. . . and here. . . and you are dead. I told him I would be forced to kill you if you interfered, and he warned you. I heard him. He will be cleansed of your death."

There was no doubting those eyes.

"I will not scream," Zohra whispered, not so much because she feared being overheard but because her voice had failed her.

"Good."

The hands left her throat, the pressure against her body melted away. Closing her eyes, Zohra drew a deep breath and felt herself begin to tremble.

"Wait here and be silent, then, as you have promised," said ibn Jad, taking a step toward the door that led to the sick chamber. Inside, Mathew could be heard, tossing in his feverish throes. "He will not suffer, I promise you. Indeed, with this, his sufferings will end. Our God waits to award him for his valor, as does his own God. Do not move. I will be back. I have something to discuss with you—"

"No!" Zohra could not believe it was her voice that spoke, her hand that darted out—seemingly of its own accord—and caught hold of the strong, sinewy arm of the Black Paladin. She held on firmly, despite the narrowing of the black eyes that was the only sign of emotion she had yet seen in the man. "Please." Zohra tried to summon moisture enough in her dry mouth to form her words. "Don't kill him! Not yet! I . . . want to pray to Akhran—my God—for a miracle!"

How had she known this plea—and only this—would touch Auda ibn Jad? She wasn't certain. Perhaps it was what she had seen and heard of his people in his dark castle. Perhaps it was the way he always spoke of the Gods—all Gods—with grave reverence and respect. A plea for pity, for mercy, for compassion, for the sanctity of human life—he would only stare at her coldly, walk into that room, and kill Mathew with ruthless efficiency. But to tell him she wanted time to place the matter in the hands of her God—that he understood. That he could respect.

He pondered, looking at her thoughtfully, and she held her breath until it became painful, her chest burned, sparks danced in her vision; and then—finally—he briefly nodded his head. Zohra relaxed, sighing. Tears came unbidden and unwanted to her eyes.

"If your God has not responded by nightfall," said ibn Jad gravely, "then I carry out my fiat."

She could not reply; she could only lower her head in what was part acquiescence and part a desire to look no longer into those disturbing eyes. Drawing her veil across her face with a hand that shook so she could barely lift it, Zohra sidled toward the doorway. An arm shot across, blocking her exit.

"I would go to my prayers," she murmured, not daring to lift her head, not daring to look at him.

"You and he are man and wife in name only. The Black Sorceress told me that no man has known you!"

Resolutely, her jaw clenched tightly, Zohra tried to push past the arm.

"Let me go," she said haughtily, in the imperious tone that had often served her so well.

It did not serve her now. Auda snatched the veil from her hand, uncovering her face. "He has forfeited his rights as husband. You are free to come to any man! Come to me, Zohra!"

His hands closed over her upper arms. Shuddering, Zohra shrank back against the wall, averting her face.

Lips brushed against her neck, and she struggled to free herself. His grip tightened painfully. Suddenly angry, she ceased to fight him and stared at him intently. "What do you want from me?" she demanded breathlessly. "There is no love in you! There is not even desire! What do you want?"

He smiled; the dark eyes remained flat, without passion. "I have appetites as do other men. But I have learned to control them since they are sand in the eyes of rational thought. I could find pleasure with you. Of that I have no doubt. But it would be fleeting, of the moment and then gone. What do I want of you, Zohra?" He drew her nearer, and she was tense and taut. "I want a son!" Now there was emotion in the eyes, and she was startled by its intensity. "My life nears its close. I know this, and I accept it. It is the will of Zhakrin. But I want to leave behind me a son with that strong, wild blood of yours flowing in his veins!"

Auda's lips came near hers, and nearly suffocated with fear and his nearness, she averted her face, pressing her head and her body back against the wall, her eyes closed. No man had ever dared touch her like this, no man had been this close. The drug-induced dreams of passion inflicted on her in Castle Zhakrin came back to her, tinged now with horror that weakened and debilitated.

She felt his breath upon her, fire against her skin; then, slowly, he released his hold on her. Leaning weakly back against the wall, Zohra glanced up at him hesitantly, warily. Auda had backed away several steps, his hands raised in the ageless gesture that means no harm.

The emotion in him had died. The face was pale, impassive, the eyes dark and flat. "I will not take you by force, Zohra. A woman such as you would never forgive that. I neither want nor expect your love. I will pray to Zhakrin and ask that he give you to me. One night, if he answers my prayer, you will come to me and say, 'I will bear your son and he will be a mighty warrior, and in him you will live again!'"

With that Auda bowed gracefully, and before Zohra could move or speak, he was gone, silently, from the room.

Zohra began to shake. Her knees would not support her, and she sank, shivering, to the floor and buried her face in her hands. She had seen the Black Paladin do magic that wasn't magic, or so Mathew had told her. It was not the magic of Sul but the magic of the Paladin's God. Auda's faith gave him power, and he was going to use it on her.

I will pray to Zhakrin and ask that he give you to me. Against all reason, against her will and her inclination, Zohra nonetheless felt herself drawn to Auda ibn Jad.

CHAPTER 13

ereft of coherent thought and reason, Zohra remained crouched in a shivering stupor upon the floor until a wild cry from Mathew changed her fear for herself to fear for another. Hastening to her feet, she ran into his room, terrified that ibn Jad had forsaken his promise.

There was no one in the room except the suffering boy; the only thing attacking him was the fever. He needed water, lots of water, to break its grip. It was time for Akhran to perform his miracle.

Reassuring herself with one last look that Mathew was in no immediate danger, either from his sickness or the Black Paladin—who was nowhere to be seen—Zohra left the sickroom and wound her way among the labyrinthine corridors of the house to the outside door.

Camels and men slept in the cool shade of a nearby building. Zohra halted when she saw that ibn Jad had laid himself down on a blanket beside Khardan. Zohra hesitated, loathe to go near the man. Glancing about, she searched for something else that might suit her purpose but knew she searched in vain. Her gaze went to the sash around Khardan's waist, to the hilt she could see glinting in the sun.

She had to have the dagger.

"Since when have you been afraid of any man?" she asked herself scornfully, and not stopping to think that some men are worthy of fear, Zohra boldly and quietly stole across the sun-drenched street.

The camels raised their heads and gazed at her with stupid, suspicious malevolence, thinking she might try to rouse them from their rest. Thankful it was camels she was facing and not Khardan's horse, who would never have allowed anyone to steal up on his slumbering master, Zohra hissed at the camels, and they lowered their heads. Khardan slept sprawled upon his back; his breathing was deep and regular, and Zohra, after watching for a moment, knew that he slept the sleep of exhaustion and would not easily waken. Drawing near him, she stole a glance at Auda. The man's eyes were closed fast; his breathing, too, was even. But whether he slept or shammed, Zohra could not tell.

It didn't matter, she told herself. Whatever she did, he would not stop her. He had given her until sundown, and she was beginning to know him well enough to understand that he would keep his vow.

Carefully, cautiously, she leaned over Khardan and with a light, delicate touch slowly began to ease the dagger from his sash. He sighed and stirred, and she went motionless, the dagger only halfway hers. He sighed again and lapsed back into unconsciousness.

Sighing herself, in relief, Zohra slipped the weapon out and clutched it thankfully. Turning, she was starting to move back across the street toward the house when her gaze fell upon ibn Jad. The dagger, warm from Khardan's body, was in her hand. One thrust, and it would all be over. No God could ever lure her to a dead man. She stared at him, sleeping soundly to all appearances. Her fingers curled tightly around the knife's hilt.

She took a step toward him, then turned and fled across the street as though he had leaped up and was chasing her. Pausing inside the doorway to catch her breath, Zohra looked back and saw that neither man had moved.

Khardan woke with a start, thinking that someone was sneaking up on him, intending to slit his throat. So real was the impression that he reached out defending hands before he had a chance to focus his eyes, and only when his hands closed on nothing but air did he realize it had been a dream. Wearily he started to lie back down again and try to recapture sleep, patting the sash with the unthinking, instinctive gesture of the veteran warrior reassuring himself his weapon is by his side.

It wasn't.

It didn't need the lingering fragrance of jasmine to bring one person to his mind. "Zohra!" he muttered, and sat upright, looking in every direction.

His first thought was that the headstrong woman was following through on her intention to kill Auda ibn Jad. But a glance showed him the Black Paladin lying beside him, peacefully asleep. Apparently he had gone through with his plan. Mathew must be dead, Khardan thought, a swift, stabbing pain wrenching his heart. But if so, what was Zohra doing with her husband's dagger? Revenge?

He could almost see her, standing in some shadowy recess, the weapon in her hand, dealing vengeance with a swift thrust into an unsuspecting back.

Khardan did not like the evil Paladin. Despite the fact that Auda had saved their lives, rescuing them from the other Paladins of Zhakrin who demanded their blood and their souls, Khardan remembered vividly that this was the same man who, without a second thought, had cast a chained and manacled group of wretched slaves to *ghuls*. As long as he lived, nothing would ever blot from his eyes the sight of that horrid feast, from his ears the dreadful screams. And Auda had committed, in the name of Zhakrin, other crimes as heinous. Khardan knew this well, having heard the recitation of these deeds from the Black Paladin's own lips.

A dagger in the back was undoubtedly an easier death than he deserved. Had it been six months before, Khardan himself would have wielded the weapon and thought little of it. But it was a changed Khardan who rose wearily to his feet and set off in search of his wife.

Before the enforced marriage to Zohra—a marriage commanded by the God—Khardan had paid lip service to *Hazrat* Akhran but never went much further than that. Twenty-five years old, handsome, bold, courageous, the Calif had fixed thoughts on the world, not upon heaven. After the marriage to Zohra, the only thoughts Khardan entertained about Akhran were bitter ones.

Then had come the moment the Calif stood before his God in the torture chamber of Castle Zhakrin. Khardan—broken in body and spirit—came face-to-face with Akhran.

The Akar believe that the insane have seen the face of the God and that it is the sight of this glory that drives them mad. If that was so, thought Khardan, then I must be touched with madness.

Khardan had seen the God. Khardan had given Akhran his

life, and Akhran had given it back to him.

In those few brief seconds Khardan had seen not only the God's face, but his mind as well. It was unclear, indistinct, but dimly he came to realize, thinking about all this now, that perhaps he had been mistaken in those feelings of emptiness he had experienced inside the house. He was not a meaningless grain of sand. He was part of a vast plan. These things were not happening to him by chance.

It seemed to Khardan, as he darted swift glances up and down the street, that if this was true, *Hazrat* Akhran might have handled matters more efficiently, improved on some things. But it occurred to the Calif that in certain areas the God might be as dependent upon his human followers as they were upon him.

"Perhaps if I had acted more wisely from the beginning, my path would have been easier," Khardan reflected, entering the dwelling place and making his way to Mathew's room. "Much of what has happened may be Akhran's attempts to mend the clay pot that I heedlessly smashed."

He and his companions had been taken to Castle Zhakrin for a reason—the freeing of the two Gods Quar was holding captive. That much was apparent to Khardan now. The Gods would presumably join Akhran in heaven's war.

And Akhran had need of his followers still, apparently. He had led them safely from the castle to the Kurdin Sea. There, however, things had begun to go wrong. The djinn had departed and not returned. Khardan remembered Pukah's description of Akhran—weak, bleeding, wounded.

The battle was not going well, then. Akhran had nearly lost his grasp on them. It was Zhakrin who picked them up, sending ibn Jad to find and save them. For some reason, the Gods had decided that the Paladin's path lay with his.

The Calif entered the boy's room reluctantly, fearful of what he must find.

Apparently the Gods had willed that Mathew should fall sick and die. . .

No, not die.

Khardan stared at the boy in amazement. Mathew lay upon the pallet, quiet now, having fallen into the unhealthful, dream-ravaged sleep of high fever. But he was asleep, he was not dead. Khardan saw the body twitch, heard the labored breathing. Moving nearer, leaning down to look at the boy closely, the Calif saw that the rag lying on the hot head was cool and moist. It had recently been changed.

But Zohra was not around.

Puzzled by this mystery, Khardan glanced about the room in search of something that might provide him with answers. Perhaps weariness had overcome ibn Jad, and the Paladin had decided to rest before he killed the boy. This seemed unlikely to Khardan, who guessed that the Black Paladin would not let death itself prevent him from carrying out any intention, much less a human weakness such as a need for sleep. It also did not explain his wife and his dagger.

But if so, where was she?

Poking among the few objects in the room, more out of frustration than in real hope of finding anything worthwhile, Khardan noted that the magical pouch Mathew wore on his belt, the pouch the Calif had carefully and gingerly removed when they stripped the boy of his heavy robes, had been upended, its contents recklessly dumped in a corner.

Khardan took a step near it, then stopped. He would have no idea what, if anything, was missing, and there was no sense in touching or handling items that sent shivers through him just to gaze upon them. And at that moment the thought occurred to him that Zohra was trying to work some of Mathew's magic.

Khardan was chilled to the bone. Mathew had been teaching her what he knew. The young man had tried to tell the Calif about it, but Khardan had refused to listen, not wanting to know. Women's magic. Or worse still, magic of a *kafir* from a faraway land.

He heard a voice. Zohra's voice. It sounded peculiar. . . . She was singing!

If a dozen scimitar-wielding soldiers of the Amir had crashed through the door and attacked him where he stood, Khardan would have fought them with his bare hands and never known fear. This eerie singing unnerved him, left him weak and shaking all over like a horse sensing the coming of an earthquake.

Her voice was quite near, rising from another part of the house. The center, Khardan judged, recalling having seen an open-air courtyard, its floor made of tilted, broken stone. He could easily find her now, if he could force his feet to carry him past the doorstoop. At length came the dim idea that he might be able to stop her before she did anything rash and impetuous. Just what that might be, Khardan wasn't certain, but he saw once again that horrible creature—a demon of some sort—Mathew had summoned forth from Sul.

Moving swiftly, careless of the noise he made, Khardan hurried through the corridors and discovered, as he had guessed, that the singing sound came from the courtyard in the center of the dwelling.

He halted beneath a stone arch. In the center of the courtyard was a large, round pool, full ten feet in circumference, with rock walls that stood about three feet off the ground. Long ago this *hauz* had held water for household use, water carried to the house, perhaps, by those canals of which ibn Jad had told them. That had been long ago. Now the pool was choked with sand blown into the courtyard in the desert's effort to reclaim what man had stolen from it. A vast mound of sand spilled over the edge of the pool, forming a small dune that covered a portion of the courtyard.

At the edge of the dried-up *hauz* stood Zohra. Her back was toward Khardan. She did not see him and, from her unnaturally rigid posture, might not have noticed him had he stepped in front of her. The Calif moved softly near her, hoping to see what she was doing and gain an idea of how to bring it to an end.

Coming around to where he could see her face, he noted that her attention was fixed upon a piece of parchment she held firmly in both hands. The glint of sunlight on a metal blade showed him his dagger. It lay on the edge of the *hauz,* and there was a pool of something dark—red—near it.

Eyes widening, Khardan saw blood dripping from a deep cut in Zohra's left arm. She paid no heed to it, however. Her gaze was fixed upon the parchment, and she was singing the song that wasn't a song in a voice that raised the hair on Khardan's head. Moving to get a look at the parchment, the Calif saw that it was covered with marks, marks drawn in blood!

Awed, shaken, yet determined to stop her, Khardan crept forward and reached out a hand. At that moment Zohra's voice ceased. Khardan stilled his movement, though it did not seem that she was aware of his presence. Her eyes and her entire being were focused upon the parchment to such an extent that he doubted if a thunderclap would rouse her.

His hand stretched forth, shaking, and then fell limp at his side. The bloody marks upon the parchment had begun to move—wriggling and writhing as though in agony! Khardan caught his breath, nearly strangling. His teeth bit through his tongue as he watched the marks crawl off the paper and drop, one by one, into the pool.

And suddenly the Calif was ankle-deep in water.

Water swirled around his feet, flooded the courtyard, flowed into the house. Water—trapped within the strong stone walls of the pool—glistened and sparkled in the noonday sun.

Hesitantly, Zohra dipped her fingertips into the water, as though she could not believe it herself. Her hand came out wet, dripping, and she laughed exultantly.

Hearing the sound of Khardan's breath sucking between his teeth, Zohra knew he was there. Turning, she faced him, and he had never seen her look so beautiful. Her cheeks glowed with a radiance of pride and accomplishment, her eyes sparkled more brilliantly than the water.

"Your miracle!" she said to him proudly. "And it is from my hands!" She held them out to him, and he saw the bloody gash on her arm. "*Not* Akhran's!"

CHAPTER 14

Your God has provided his miracle. It is obvious he wants this boy to live. Far be it from me to thwart his will. I do not kill for pleasure, Princess," continued Auda ibn Jad gravely, "but out of necessity."

It seemed to Zohra that Akhran's "miracle" might have been in vain. Water she had now, in plenty; but lacking the herbs and healing stones with which the nomad women usually treat illness, Zohra could do little except to bathe Mathew's burning skin and trickle water into the parched, cracked lips. The fever raged unabated. Mathew ceased even his incoherent babbling and lay in a stupor, panting for breath. The only sound he made was low moanings of pain.

Zohra fought her battle against Death alone, or assumed she did. Tending the sick was woman's work, and she was not surprised when ibn Jad and Khardan left the room that smelled of sickness and of death. Because she was not listening for it, she did not hear Khardan's return, nor did she see him sink down onto the floor of a shadowed alcove outside the open door of Mathew's room, where he could watch unobserved.

The afternoon wore away slowly, time being measured by the panting breaths drawn into the fever-ridden body. Each breath was a victory, a sword thrust at the unseen foe who fought to claim Mathew as prize. Rarely sick himself, Khardan had never been around sickness, had never given much thought to the fight women waged against an enemy ancient and strong as Sul.

It was an encounter grim and wearying as any he had ever fought with steel, and considerably more frustrating. The enemy could not be met with yells and clash of sword, grappled and wrestled to the ground. This dread foe must be combated with patience, with endless changing of dry cloths for wet ones, with refusal to allow heavy eyelids to shut and snatch even a few moments of blessed rest.

The most dangerous time came at *aseur*, sunset. For it is this time between day and night when the body's spirits are at their lowest ebb and the most vulnerable. The sinking of the sun cast the dwelling in shadows long before twilight had faded outside. There was no lamp to light, and Zohra fought her battle in a dim, dusty darkness.

Mathew had ceased even to moan. He made no sound at all, and Khardan thought several times the boy had quit breathing. But then the Calif would hear a dry, rasping gasp or see through the gloom a white hand twitch feebly, and he knew Mathew lived still.

"His spirit is strong, if his body isn't. But it's gone on too long," Khardan said to himself. "He can't take this. It cannot last much longer."

And it seemed as if Zohra realized the same truth, for he saw her head bow, her hands cover her face in a sob that was all the more heartrending in that it was silent, unheard. Khardan rose to go to her, to lend her his strength, if need be, to face the final moments that he had no doubt would be difficult to watch. But the Calif's movement was arrested. Halting, half-risen on one knee, he stared in awe.

A figure had entered the room, a woman with long hair that shimmered with a pale glow in the fading light. Her skin was white, she was clothed in white, and Khardan had the impression—though he could not see her face—that she was very beautiful. The face was turned toward Mathew, and the Calif wondered if this was the immortal guardian, the "angel" of which Pukah had spoken. If so, then why the chill running through his body, congealing his blood, freezing his breath? Why the fear that shook him until he was near whimpering like a child?

The woman stretched out white, delicate hands to the boy, and Khardan knew suddenly that she mustn't touch him. He wanted to call to Zohra, whose eyes were covered, who wasn't looking, but his tongue could not form the words. He made a sound, a kind of croak, and the woman—distracted—turned toward him.

She had no eyes. The sockets were hollow and dark and deep as eternal night.

This was no guardian! The boy's guardian was gone and he was alone and it was Death who leaned over him! The woman stared at Khardan until certain he would make no trouble, then turned back to claim her victory. The white hands touched the boy, and Mathew screamed, his body convulsed. Zohra raised her head. Crying out defiantly, she flung her body across Mathew's.

Startled, Death drew back. The hollow eyes darkened in thwarted anger. The hands reached out again and this time would have clutched at both, for Zohra held Mathew in her arms. His head on her breast, she rocked and soothed him. Her back was to her foe; she did not see her enemy approach.

Khardan moved. Drawing his dagger, he interposed himself between the two and Death. The woman's blond hair flicked across his skin, and he felt a searing pain. The hollow eyes stared at him malevolently, the white hand reached for him, and then, suddenly, she was gone.

Blinking, dagger in hand, Khardan stared around in fearful astonishment.

"Whatever are you doing?" came Zohra's voice.

Khardan turned. Zohra had laid Mathew back down upon the pallet and was staring at her husband with a narrow-eyed, suspicious gaze.

"The woman! Did you see her?" Khardan gasped. "Woman?" Zohra's eyes opened wide. "What woman?"

It was Death! Khardan started to shout in exasperation.

Death was here! She wanted the boy, and you wouldn't let her, and then she was going to take you both. Didn't you see her? . . . No, he realized suddenly. Zohra hadn't seen her. He put his hand to his head, wondering if the heat had touched him. Yet she had been so real, so horrifyingly real!

Zohra was still staring at him suspiciously.

"It. . . must have been a dream," Khardan said lamely, thrusting the dagger back in his belt.

"A dream you chase with a dagger?" Zohra scoffed. Giving Khardan a puzzled look, she shrugged, shook her head, and turned back to her patient.

"How is the boy?" Kbardan asked gruffly.

"He will live," Zohra said with quiet pride. "Only a few moments ago I nearly lost him. But then the fever broke. Listen! His breathing is regular. He sleeps peacefully."

Khardan could barely see the boy in the gloom, but he could hear the soft, even breathing.

A dream?

He wondered, and would probably keep on wondering the rest of his life.

Zohra started to rise to her feet, stumbled wearily, and would have fallen had not Khardan caught hold of her arm. Gently he assisted her to stand. Her face was a glimmer of white in the darkness. The only light in the room seemed to come from the flame in her eyes. Exhausted as she was, that inner fire burned brightly.

"Let me go." She tried to withdraw her arm from his grip. "I must fetch more water—"

"You must sleep," said Khardan firmly. "I will bring water. "

"No!" Brushing back a straggling lock of black hair from her face, she attempted once more to slip out of Khardan's hold, but the Calif's hand tightened. "Mat-hew is better, but I should not leave—"

"I will watch him."

Khardan steered her toward the room next door.

"But you know nothing of nursing!" she protested. "I—"

"—will tell me all I must do," Kbardan interrupted.

Weary, Zohra let herself be persuaded. Kbardan led her to a small chamber. Stepping inside, he spread his own outer robe out on the floor and turned to find her pressed back against a wall, staring around the room with fearful eyes. Zohra—seeing him watching her in amazement—suddenly behaved as if nothing were amiss, though she rubbed her arms as with a chill.

"Mathew will need you in the morning when he wakens," Khardan continued, mystified by her strange reaction. But then, it had been a day of mystery. Gently but firmly he eased his wife to the crude bed he had prepared for her.

Feeling exhaustion overcome her, Zohra lay down with a thankful sigh upon the stones. "If he wakes, give him water," she murmured sleepily. "Not too much at first. . ."

That, Khardan knew. Assuring her he could manage, he was almost out the door when she started up, crying out, "Where is ibn Jad?"

Khardan paused and turned. "I don't know. He mentioned something about hunting, trying to find meat—"

"Don't let him come in here!" Zohra said, and he was surprised at the harshness in her voice.

"I won't. But he wouldn't anyway." Where a woman rests is *harem.* forbidden to men.

"Swear, by *Hazrat* Akhran!" Zohra urged.

"Have you so little faith in me?" Khardan demanded impatiently. "Go to sleep, woman. I told you I would keep watch!"

Stalking into the sickroom, which was now almost completely dark, Khardan threw himself down beside the pallet. Fuming, he propped an elbow on a corner of the straw mattress. That she should require of him an oath! When he had protected her from the most feared of all beings! Reaching out, he felt Mathew's forehead. The skin was moist and damp. The young man's breathing was shallow and fast, but the terrible raspy, rattling sound was gone. He would be well and hungry by morning.

"In all of this, the only thing that doesn't surprise me is that Death is a female!" muttered Khardan angrily into his beard.

CHAPTER 15

Escaping from the fever-world, where dreams are more real than reality, Mathew woke to darkness and terror. Khardan's reassuring voice and strong hands, a sip of cool water, and the knowledge, dimly realized, that he was being watched over and protected led the young man to close his eyes and slip back into a healing sleep.

When he awoke the following morning, about midday, and saw the walls around him, he thought he was back in Castle Zhakrin, where it seemed he had wandered most in his delirious ramblings.

"Khardan!" he gasped, struggling to sit.

Zohra knelt swiftly by his side. Placing her hands on his shoulders, she forced him to lie back down; not a difficult task—his body seemed a limp, wet rag that had been twisted and wrung dry.

"You don't understand," he whispered hoarsely, "Khardan is . . . near death. They're. . . torture! I must-"

"Khardan sleeps soundly," said Zohra, smoothing back the hair from his forehead. "The only torture he suffers is a stiff neck from having slept on a paved street yesterday. Where do you think you are? Back in the castle?"

Mathew looked at his surroundings, his expression puzzled. "I thought. . . But no, we escaped. There was the desert and we walked and then Serinda was still far away and there was the storm." He stopped, frowning in an effort to carry his memories further.

"You don't remember what happened next?"

He shook his head. Sliding her arm beneath his shoulders, Zohra lifted his head and held a bowl of water to his lips. "The man called ibn Jad found us," she said. Mathew's wasted body flinched at the mention of the Paladin. He would have turned wondering eyes to Zohra, for there was a tenseness in her voice when she spoke the name, but she kept the water to his lips, and he dared not move his head for fear of spilling it. "He brought camels, and we rode through the night to Serinda. It was then the fever took you."

Mathew shivered. He had a recollection of a journey by night, but it was accompanied by vague terrors, and he quickly banished it. Having drunk the water, he lay back down.

"Where is ibn Jad? Did he ride on?"

"He is here," said Zobra shortly. "Are you hungry? Can you eat? I made some broth. Drink it, then you should rest."

More weary than he thought, Mathew dutifully drank the steaming liquid that had a faint poultry flavor and then drifted again into sleep. When he woke, it was early evening.

"Have you been here all this time?" he asked Zohra, who held out the bowl of water. "No; you do not need to help me. I can sit myself." The thought of what other services she must have helped him to perform during his sickness made him flush in embarrassment. "I have been so much trouble," he mumbled. "And now I'm delaying you. I'm keeping you from returning to your home."

Home. He spoke the word with a sigh. He had been dreaming again, pleasant dreams, dreams of his own land. Waking this time had not been a terrifying experience, only a very painful one.

Zohra sat down beside him. Awkwardly, as though she were unused to such gentle gestures, she patted his hand with her own. "You must miss your home very much."

Mathew turned his face in an effort to hide the tears that pain and suffering and his weakness wrung from him. The effort was a failure, for the tears became sobs that shook his body. He gulped them down, trying to stop crying, waiting for the gibe or the sneer with which Zohra always met his lapses. To his amazement she said nothing, and he was further astounded when her hand squeezed his tightly.

"I know now what it is, to miss one's home. I am truly sorry for you, Mat-hew." Her voice was soft and filled with a pity that did not offend, but eased, his heart. "Perhaps, when all this is over, we can find a way to send you back."

"She rose to her feet and left him, saying something about bringing food if he thought he could keep it down. Grateful for his time alone, Mathew managed to get up from the bed, and though his legs wobbled and his head spun, he was able to wash himself and was sitting up on the pallet, combing out the tangled red hair as best he could with his fingers, when he heard footsteps.

It was not Zohra who came to him, however, but Khardan.

"Your strength is returning," the Calif said, smiling. "I brought you this." He carried a bowl of rice in his hand. "You are to eat as much as you can, according to . . . my wife." He always spoke those two words with a certain grim irony. "Can you manage yourself?" Khardan asked in some embarrassment.

"Yes! Thank Promenthas," Mathew answered fervently, his skin burning. The thought of the Calif feeding him! Taking the dish, glad to have something to occupy his hands and his eyes, Mathew hungrily scooped the rice into his mouth with his fingers.

Seeming relieved himself, Khardan sat down, his back against the wall, and rubbed his neck with a groan.

"I am sorry to . . . have delayed your journey," Mathew mumbled, his mouth full of rice.

"To be honest, I am not that eager to return to my people," said Khardan heavily. For long moments he leaned against the wall in silence, his eyes closed. Opening them a crack, he peered at Mathew from beneath his lids. "I need to talk to you, Mat-hew. Do you feel able?"

"Yes! Assuredly!" Mathew placed the empty rice bowl on the floor and straightened his back and shoulders to appear attentive.

"You will tell me, Mat-hew, if you grow tired?"

"Yes, Khardan. I promise."

The Calif nodded and then frowned, trying to decide how to begin or perhaps *if* to begin. Mathew waited patiently.

"This vision. . . my wife. . . had," he said abruptly.

"Tell me about it."

"It would be more fitting if you asked her," suggested Mathew, surprised by the question.

Khardan waved his hand, irritably brushing the notion away from him. "I can't talk to her. When we come together, it is like setting a flaming brand to dry tinder. Rational discussion goes up in smoke! I'm asking you to tell me of the vision that started all of this."

Wondering at the change in the Calif, who had previously scorned the idea that a vision—women's magic—could have prompted Zohra to act as she did in removing him bodily from the battle around the Tel, Mathew related the story.

"I was teaching Zohra a magical spell my people know that allows us to see into the future. It is called scrying. You take a bowl of water and place it before you. Then you clear your mind of all thoughts and outside influences, chant the arcane words, and if you are fortunate, Sul will give you a picture in the water that can foretell the future."

Mathew paused, half expecting to be met with a laugh or a snort of derision. But Khardan was silent. Looking at him intently, Mathew tried to discover if the Calif was simply too polite to make the rude comments that were in his heart, or if he was truly struggling to believe and understand what he was being told. Khardan's face was hidden by the gathering shades of evening, however, and Mathew was forced to continue on without any idea of what the nomad was thinking.

"Zohra performed the magic perfectly. Your wife is very strong in magic," Mathew took a moment to add. "Sul has blessed her with his favor."

This occasioned a reaction, but not quite what he'd expected. Instead of scathing denial, Mathew heard Khardan stir uncomfortably and make a warning sound deep in his throat as if to indicate Mathew was to keep to the main path and avoid any side journeys. Knowing nothing about Zohra's creation of water from sand—a spell Mathew himself had taught her, but which she had always been terrified to perform—the young wizard shrugged to himself and continued.

"Looking into the water, she saw two visions." He closed his eyes, concentrating hard to remember every detail. "In the first it is sunset. A band of hawks, led by a falcon, fly out to hunt. But they end up fighting among themselves, and so their prey escapes. Distracted by their own quarreling, they are set upon by eagles. The hawks and the falcon fight the eagles, but they are defeated. The falcon is wounded and falls to the ground and does not rise again. Night falls. Now, in the second vision—"

Seeing the scene again in his mind, caught up in the fascination magic always held for him, Mathew had forgotten his listener. He was suddenly jolted back to reality.

"*Birds!*" The word fell like a thunderbolt. Springing to his feet, Khardan glared down at the young man, who was staring up at him with wide eyes. "She did this to me because of *birds?*"

"No! Yes! That is—" Mathew stammered. "The pictures are . . . are symbols that the magus interprets in his heart and his mind!" He groped frantically for an image he could use to help the man understand. No good relating symbology to letters and words, as had been taught Mathew in school. The nomad could neither read nor write. Many of the legends of Khardan's people were parables or allegories, but—while the nomads understood them in their hearts—Mathew wasn't at all certain that they thought them over in their minds. In any event, he could not now try to explain that the beggar in the tale actually represented Akhran and that the selfish Sultan was mankind. How could he make Khardan understand?

"I can explain it like this," Mathew said, suddenly inspired by the symbols themselves. "It is the same as teaching your falcon to hunt gazelle."

"Bah!" Khardan turned and seemed prepared to walk out of the room.

"Listen to me!" Mathew pleaded desperately. "You don't send the falcon after the gazelle without training. You put hunks of meat in the eye sockets of a sheep's skull and teach the bird to attack the gazelle by first attacking the meat in the skull! That skull represents—it symbolizes—the gazelle! Sul does the same with us. He uses these pictures we see as you use the sheep's skull."

Interested in spite of himself, the Calif had paused in the doorway. He was no more than a large shadow, shapeless in his flowing robes in the darkness. "Why does Sul do this? Why not just say what he means?"

"Why not send the falcon after the gazelle without training?"

"The bird would not know what to do!"

"And so it is with us. Sul does not want us to accept his vision too glibly, without 'training.' He wants us to look into our hearts and ponder the meaning of what we see. The hawks are your people. They are led by the falcon—that is you."

Khardan nodded solemnly, not out of pride, but merely an acceptance of his own worth. "That makes sense. Go on."

Mathew began to breathe easier. Although the Calif remained standing, at least he was listening and seemed to be comprehending what the young wizard was trying to teach. "The hawks— your people—are fighting among themselves, and thus their prey escapes them."

Khardan muttered irritably, not liking this that was, after all, nothing more than the truth. Hiding a smile, Mathew hurried on. "The eagles attack—those are the Amir's troops. You are wounded and fall out of the sky and do not rise again. Night settles over the land."

"And this means?"

"Your people are defeated and vanish into darkness."

"You are saying that if I had died, my people would have been vanquished. But I did not die!" Khardan stated triumphantly. "The vision is wrong!"

"It's what I tried to tell you at the beginning," said Mathew patiently. "There were two visions! In the second, the falcon is hit by the eagles and he falls to the ground, but he manages to rise again, even though . . ." Mathew hesitated, uncertain how to phrase this, uncertain how the Calif would react. "Even though—"

"Even though what?"

Mathew drew a deep breath. "The falcon's wings are covered with filth," he said slowly. "He has to struggle to fly."

Silence, brooding and heavy, followed. Khardan stood very still; not a rustle of cloth broke the profound quiet. Mathew held his breath, as if that small noise could be a distraction.

"I return. . . in disgrace," Khardan said finally. "Yes." Mathew let his breath out with the word.

"Is that all? The only difference in the two visions?"

"No. In the second vision there is no night. When you return, the sun rises."

CHAPTER 16

"I t was not an easy decision for Zohra to make, Khardan," Mathew argued earnestly. "You know her! You know her courage! She herself would have preferred to die fighting the enemy rather than run away! But that would have meant the end of your people. That was what mattered to her most. That was why we rescued you from Meryem—"

"Meryem!"

Mathew had known this would surprise the Calif. "Yes," continued the young man, trying to keep all emotion from his voice, knowing that Khardan must come to realize his own truth about the woman. "She was carrying you away on horseback—"

"She, too—trying to save me." Khardan spoke fondly, and Mathew grit his teeth to keep the sarcastic words locked behind them.

"She had given you a charm to wear around your neck—"

"Yes, I remember!" Khardan put his hand to his throat. "A silly thing, women's magic. . ."

"That 'silly thing' rendered you unconscious," Mathew said grimly. "Do you also remember fighting, then feeling a strange lethargy come over you? Your sword suddenly becomes so heavy you cannot lift it. Ground and sky are mixed up in your vision. The enemy attacks, but you are so weak you cannot defend yourself. The blow falls but bounces off harmlessly."

"Yes!" Though Mathew could not see him, he knew Khardan was staring at him in amazement. "Is this more scrying? How did you know?"

"I know the charm she used," Mathew said. "I know its effects. She wanted you safe and unharmed and unable to fight. With help, she carried you out of the battle—"

"Help? Do you mean Zohra's?"

"No. When we found you with that woman, Meryem was riding one of the Amir's magic horses. How else could she have escaped that battle except with the help of the Amir's soldiers??"

"There are many ways," Khardan said. "What she did, she did out of love. Misguided, perhaps, but she is a woman and does not understand such things as pride and honor."

Oh, don't women? thought Mathew, but he said nothing.

This was no time to argue.

"At least you cannot say my wife acted from the same motive," the Calif stated.

"What Zohra did, she did for your people," Mathew said with more heat than he intended. "Dressing you as a woman was the only way to get you past the soldiers. She didn't do it on purpose to disgrace you! And it wasn't her fault that our plans didn't work out. It was mine. Ibn Jad came searching for me. Blame me, if you must."

There was a long silence, then Khardan said, "It wasn't anybody's fault. It was the God's choosing."

Astonished, Mathew stared intently at Khardan, wishing he could see the man's face through the darkness. He heard the Calif, who had remained standing all this time, settle himself back down on the floor and lean against the wall.

"I have been thinking, Mat-hew. Thinking of what you said to me the night. . . the night that they were torturing me." The words were laden with remembered pain. "You said, 'Maybe your death isn't what your God wants! Maybe you're of no use to him dead! Maybe he's brought you here for a reason, a purpose, and it's up to you to live long enough to try to find out why!' I didn't understand then. But when I came to Akhran, when I saw his face, then I knew. He gave my life back to me to help him fight and win this war. I can do nothing to aid him in heaven, but I can do something on earth.

"The question is"—Khardan continued, sighing—"what? What can we do against the might of the Amir? Even if we had all our people banded together—which we don't. Even if they accept me on my return. . ." He paused, obviously expecting a response.

Mathew could not give him the reassurance he wanted, and so kept silent. His silence answered louder than words, however, and Khardan stirred restlessly. "The falcon rising from the filth. Very well, I return in disgrace. A coward who has obviously been hiding for months, if nothing worse is spoken of me. You are wise for your years, Mat-hew. It was this wisdom that helped you survive the slave caravan, this wisdom that freed us from that evil castle. I am smart, courageous," Khardan spoke simply, a statement of fact, "but I begin to realize that I am not wise. I came tonight to ask your advice. What should I do?"

A warmth flooded over Mathew. He thought at first it might be the fever returning, but this was a wonderful sensation, and he did not respond at once but let himself savor it and bask in it—though he did not feel at all that he deserved it.

"I—I don't know. . . what to say," Mathew stammered, thankful for the darkness that concealed his embarrassed pleasure. "You underestimate yourself. . . overestimate me. I don't—"

"You need time to think about things," Khardan said, rising to his feet. "It is late. I have kept you talking too long. If you sicken again, it will be my fault. Zohra will claw out my eyes."

"No, she wouldn't," Mathew said, believing the Calif spoke in earnest. "You don't know her, Khardan! She is proud and fierce, but she uses her pride like a ring of fire to protect herself! Within she is gentle and loving, and she imagines this to be a weakness instead of a very great strength—"

He spoke fervently, forgetting himself and to whom he talked until Khardan drew closer to him and, kneeling beside him, fixed him with an intense look. Lambent light from stars and desert glittered in the Calif's dark eyes.

"You admire her, don't you?"

What could Mathew say? He could only look deep into his heart and pluck out the truth. It was not the whole truth, but now was not the time—if that time ever came—for speaking the whole truth.

"Yes," Mathew answered, lowering his head before those piercing eyes. "I am sorry if that displeases you." He looked up again quickly. "And I would never touch her, never think of her in any way that was not proper—"

"I know."

Mathew was trembling in his earnestness and Khardan rested his hand soothingly upon the boy's shoulder. "And I cannot blame you. She is beautiful, isn't she? Beautiful—not like the gazelle—but like my falcon is beautiful. Courageous, proud. The fire you speak of flares in her eyes. That fire could burn a man's soul to ashes or—"

"—warm him for the rest of his life?" Mathew suggested softly when Khardan did not finsh his sentence.

"Perhaps." The Calif shrugged. He rose to his feet. "Right now, in her sight, I am a smoldering cinder. It may be too late to save either of us. She speaks the truth, however, when she says it is our people who matter. Rest easily, Mat-hew. I go to stretch my legs, then I will return and guard your sleep. You must get your strength back. In two days' time, we will begin the journey to the Tel."

The journey to our doom, be it good or evil, thought Mathew. He was weary. The mixed emotions that had assailed him throughout the conversation had drained him of energy. Lying down, he heard Khardan's footsteps echo through the corridors and his voice raised in conversation with another.

Auda ibn Jad.

Maybe He's brought you here for a reason. A purpose. Or maybe not. What if I'm wrong?

CHAPTER 17

B y next morning Mathew was able to walk with Zohra around the house. His interest in the dead city of Serinda revived as he viewed the wonders of the dwelling and marveled again at what terrible tragedy could have occurred that would destroy a people while leaving their city intact. When he attempted to expound on the mystery to Zohra, she evinced little interest, however, and Mathew realized after a few moments that she was leading him somewhere. There was an air of shy, quiet pride about her, much different from her usual fierce arrogance, and he found his curiosity growing.

They came into a central courtyard that once must have been a cool and charming haven from the bustle of city and household. Now it was choked with sand, littered with broken columns and fragments of statuary. In the midst of such desolation and destruction, Mathew was astonished to see a pool of crystal-clear water—deep and blue and cool from the night's chill.

"So this is why there has been no lack of water!"

The young man drank his fill, then opened his robes and splashed the water on his breast and neck and laved his face. Zohra, smiling, found a fragment of pottery in the shape of a scoop and helped Mathew wash his long red hair. Wringing the wet tresses out with his hands, he stared at the pool and shook his head.

"Isn't it marvelous, Zohra, what mankind can do? Marvelous and sad. The people disappear, Sul slowly takes over their city, and yet here, in this house, somehow the machines kept this working—"

"Not machines, Mathew," said Zohra softly, proudly. "Magic."

Mathew stared at her a moment, uncomprehending. Then

suddenly, joyfully, he threw his arms around her and hugged her close. "Magic! Your magic! You made the water! I knew you could do it! And you weren't frightened—"

"I was more frightened of that than of almost anything, except that horrible castle," Zohra said bluntly. She raised her dark eyes to Mathew's blue ones. He felt her shiver and tightened his grasp on her. "But I had no choice. That man, ibn Jad, would have killed you otherwise."

"Ah!" Now it was Mathew's turn to shudder, and Zohra who soothed him with her touch. "I wondered," he murmured. "That is why Khardan has been watching in the night."

"Ibn Jad swore he would not harm you. But I don't trust him." Her breath caught, her voice quavered.

"What is it, Zohra?" Mathew had never seen her frightened. "It's ibn Jad! What's he done to you?" Anger beat in his heart with a violence that startled him. "By Promenthas! If he's harmed you, I'll—"

You'll what? Attack ibn Jad? So might the lamb offer to fight the lion!

It seemed that Zohra might be thinking the same thing, for Mathew saw the corner of her lips twitch as if amused, despite her distress. Then a thought struck her, and she looked up at him in earnest, no laughter in her eyes.

"Mat-hew! Perhaps you can help me! It is possible to break a spell that one is under, isn't it?"

"Sometimes," said Mathew cautiously. He had the impression that there were murky waters ahead and wanted to wade into them slowly and carefully. "It depends—"

"On what?"

"On many things. What type of spell, how it was cast, what was used in the casting. It is more difficult than perhaps you imagine." Mathew's concern was growing as he guessed where her words were leading. "But how can ibn Jad cast a spell, Zohra? He is not a magus." Memory of the Black Sorceress returned to Mathew forcibly and unpleasantly. Perhaps there *was* away. "Did he have a charm, a wand—some magical object someone could have given him?"

"It was not Sul's magic," Zohra answered, shaking her head. "It was his God."

"Go on." Mathew didn't know whether to be relieved or even

more worried. "Tell me everything."

"I cannot," Zobra said stiffly. "It. . . is not proper for women to discuss such things with men who. . . are not our husbands."

"But I am another wife," Mathew said with a wry smile. "And I must know everything, Zohra, if I am to help."

"I . . . suppose so," Zohra admitted. Reluctantly, refusing to look at him and sometimes speaking so low Mathew had to bend his head to hear her, Zohra told him of her encounter with ibn Jad.

"He said he would pray to his evil God, Mat-hew! To give me to him!" Zohra looked up fearfully; her body trembled. "And . . . Mat-hew. . . when I was in that. . . that place. The woman gave me something to drink that made me dream . . ." She couldn't go on; deep rose red flushed her cheeks, and she hid her face in her hands.

"Of course," Mathew muttered. Some sort of love potion—no, lust potion might be a better term. That explained why the female captives were so cooperative and pliable, soft clay in the hands of the Sorceress. "Did you dream of him, of Auda?" the young man asked hesitatingly. Zohra's embarassment was catching. The blood burned in his skin.

"No, others," Zobra mumbled, her voice muffled by her hands.

Khardan? Mathew longed to ask but did not. A flicker of jealousy flared in him. He recognized it for what it was, but—confusedly—not precisely for whom it was intended. Was he jealous of Zohra for dreaming of Khardan or jealous of Khardan for being in Zohra's dreams? That was something he would have to work out later. Now, whether he understood himself or not, at least he understood what ibn Jad was doing—or trying to do. Very clever, Mathew thought. To use the dreams to insinuate himself into this woman's mind, use her own faith in Gods and their power to weaken the natural barriers she had established against him.

Unfortunately this was no time to enter on a discussion of free will.

"Zohra," said Mathew, shaking her gently so that she was forced to look up at him through a curtain of shining black hair, "half the time you don't obey the commands of your own God. Will you give in to a stranger?"

Zohra's eyes narrowed in thought over this argument. Coming to understand it and appreciate the irony, she even smiled slightly. "No, I will not!" Reaching out with her hand, her fingers lightly brushed Mathew's soft, beardless cheek. "You are very wise, Mat-hew."

So Khardan had said. But it wasn't wisdom, really. It was simply the ability to look at something from several different sides, to see a problem from the top and the bottom and around the corner instead of staring at it straight on. Like seeing all the facets of the glittering jewel, instead of concentrating on just one. . .

"Why do you look at me like that?" Zohra asked.

"Because Khardan was right," Mathew said shyly. "You are very beautiful."

The roses bloomed in her cheeks, the fire Khardan spoke of flamed in her eyes.

How those two loved each other! Hiding within walls of pride. Each nursed wounds. Each knew the other had seen him vulnerable, her weak. Fearful that he would use this against her or she would use it against him, both daily added more stones to the wall they were constructing between them.

Khardan recognzed this, but the tasks and the problems facing both of them were so overwhelming it might be that they would never be able to tear down the wall, no matter how much they longed to.

Their people—that was what mattered to both of them and their God, their *Hazrat* Akhran.

A cold wind blew through Mathew's soul. For a time he had forgotten he was a stranger in a strange land. The knowledge returned to him forcibly. He had no people, he had no one to love or to love him—at least a love he could admit to himself without writhing in shame. He had a God, but Promenthas was very far away.

"Mat-hew! You are so pale! Is the fever—" Her hand went to his forehead. Gently he pushed it away and pushed her away from him at the same time.

"No, I am fine. I understand that we are riding tonight?"

"If you feel like it—"

"I am fine," he repeated tonelessly. "Just a little tired. I think I will go lie down and sleep."

"I will come—"

"No, you must have things to do to prepare for the journey. I am not sick now. I no longer need your care." Turning from her, he walked away.

Confused, hurt by his words, Zohra stared after the young man. The thin shoulders were hunched, the head bowed. She was reminded forcibly of someone trying to protect his body from a blow.

Too late, the blow had fallen. And would continue to fall, repeatedly, cudgeling him into despair.

"Ah, Mat-hew," murmured Zohra, beginning to see, beginning to understand. "I am sorry." Unconsciously she echoed her husband's words.

"I am sorry."

That night they left Serinda, none of them ever to return.

The dead city was left to its dead.

The Book
of the
Immortals

CHAPTER 1

Throughout the seventy-two hours' grace period Kaug had granted them, the djinn worked diligently, if not very effectively, to fortify their position. Each djinn decided he knew all there was to know about warfare, and between erecting fantastic battlements (that soared to incredible heights and would probably confound Kaug for the span of a brief chuckle) and arguing strategy and tactics recalled from battles fought forty centuries earlier, nothing much to any purpose was accomplished. Fortifications were jealously torn down as quickly as they were put up. Fights erupted constantly, there was one prolonged battle that lasted two days between one faction of djinn—who claimed that the notorious *batir* Durzi ibn Dughmi, who had mounted ten thousand horses and five thousand camels in an attack on Sultan Muffaddhi el Shimt five hundred and sixty-three years earlier, had defeated the said Sultan—and another faction of djinn who claimed he hadn't.

Hidden from view by the climbing rosebush outside her window, Asrial gazed down upon the pandemonium with mingled feelings of shock, exasperation, and despair. By contrast she pictured to herself the strict, well-ordered discipline of the angels, drawn up for battle in rigid formation. Why can't the djinn see that they are defeating themselves? Why can't they be organized?

Frustrated, she stared out the window, her face flushed with anger, her small fist clenched. Apparently she wasn't alone in her thinking, for she heard—with a start—a voice coming from the room next to hers asking those very questions out loud.

"What is wrong with these fools? Why do they fight each other instead of preparing to fight Kaug?" The voice for all its fury—was sweet and musical, and Asrial recognized the speaker as Nedjma. Which left no doubt as to the identity of the male who answered.

"You know as well as I why they do this, my bird," Sond said quietly.

I don't know! thought Asrial. Hurrying over to the wall, she pressed her ear against a velvet tapestry that depicted in glowing colors the magnificent wedding of Muffaddhi el Shimt's daughter Fatima to Durzi ibn Dughmi. But the palace walls were thick, and the angel would not have been able to hear the rest of the conversation had not Sond and Nedjma walked over to stand beside the window in Nedjma's room.

It occurred to Asrial that Sond—being present in the *seraglio*—must be in considerable danger, and she wondered that the couple dared risk being observed from the garden below. Then the angel realized that she had not seen the eunuchs since yesterday, the day she'd been brought here by Nedjma. Perhaps they were working on the fortifications or, more likely, had been pressed into service guarding the body (though at his age there was not a great deal of his body left to guard) of the ancient djinn.

"No, I don't know the reason," said Nedjma petulantly, and Asrial blessed her. The djinniyeh added something else that the angel didn't catch. Returning to her window, Asrial saw the couple had walked out onto a small balcony attached to Nedjma's chambers. The angel could see and hear them quite well, she herself remaining unseen, her white robes and wings mingling with the white roses.

Nedjma stood with her back to Sond, her delicate chin high in the air. She did not wear her veil; in fact, Asrial saw, Nedjma wore very little, and what clothing she did have on seemed artfully designed to reveal more than it concealed. She was all blue silk and golden glints, emerald sparkles and pure white skin. Sond, coming up behind the djinniyeh, laid his hands upon the slender shoulders.

"It doesn't matter, Nedjma, my flower," he said softly. "No matter what we do, it won't stop Kaug. Do you think we would act like this if there was a chance? We do this out of our own anger and frustration and out of the knowledge that tomorrow it will all be over."

As he spoke, Nedjma's chin dropped slowly, the golden hair falling forward around her in a gleaming shower.

"Don't cry, beloved," Sond said gently. He caught hold of a mass of golden hair and, moving it from her cheek, bent to kiss away a shining tear. Putting her hands over her face, Nedjma's sobs became more hysterical. "I should not have told you." Sond straightened and drew back. "I didn't mean to make you unhappy. I only wanted you to know how little time"—he paused, a choke in his own voice—"how little time—" he repeated huskily.

Nedjma whirled to face him, the blue silk shimmering about her like a gilt-edged cloud. Hastily she dried her eyes and, coming to him, rested her hands upon his chest. "My own," she whispered. "I am not crying over what you told me. It was not news. I have known it in my heart. I was weeping because it is the end." Her arms stole around him, and she nestled her head against his chest.

"It may be the end," Sond answered. "But, my darling, we will make it a glorious one!"

Their heads bent, their lips met in a passionate kiss. The blue silk fell to the floor of the balcony, and Asrial, her face scarlet, her eyes wide, withdrew hurriedly from the window. Leaning her burning cheeks against the cool marble wall, she heard Sond's words echo over and over in her head.

"It doesn't matter. . . how little time . . . the end."

He was right. It didn't matter. It wouldn't matter for the angels of Promenthas. It wouldn't matter for the imps and demons of Astafas. It wouldn't matter for the djinn and djinniyeh of Akhran. Kaug had grown too powerful. No weapon was mighty enough to fell him, no wall was tall enough or thick enough to stop him. They could as well try to bring down a mountain with an arrow, stop a tidal wave with a castle of sand.

And like Nedjma, Asrial had known this in her heart.

"The end . . . a glorious one."

Lilting, breathless laughter came floating in the window with the perfume of the roses. Asrial slammed shut the casement. Blinking back the tears in her eyes, she was just about to leave when there came a knock at the ornately painted door to her room.

Asrial hesitated, uncertain whether or not to respond.

Before she had a chance, the door opened and Pukah entered.

Seeing her standing in the center of the room, her wings spread, the djinn's cheerful expression melted like goat cheese in the sun.

"You were leaving!"

"Yes!" she said, her fingers nervously plucking at the feathers of her wings. "I'm going back to my . . . my people, Pukah! I want to be with . . . them at the . . . at the . . ." She looked down at her hands.

"I see," Pukah said calmly. "And you were going without saying good-bye?"

"Oh, Pukah!" Asrial clasped her hands together, holding onto them as though she feared they might do something she didn't want them to do, reach out to someone she knew she couldn't hold. "I can't be what you want me to be! I can't be a woman to you as Nedjma is to Sond. I'm—I'm an angel." The hands released themselves long enough to lift the white robes. "Beneath this there isn't flesh. There is my essence, my being, but it isn't flesh and blood and bone, I tried to pretend it was, for my sake as well as yours. I wanted," she hesitated, swallowing, "part of me still wants that. . . that kind of love. But it can never be, So . . . I wasn't going to say good-bye."

"It was kind of you to spare me the hurt," said Pukah bitterly.

"Pukah, it wasn't you! It was myself I was sparing! Can't you understand?" Asrial turned away from him. Her wings wrapped around her, enclosing her in a feathery shell.

Pukah's face suddenly became illuminated with an inner radiance. The proud, self-satisfied façade crumbled. Hurrying to the angel, he gently parted the white wings that surrounded her and tenderly took hold of her clasped hands.

"Asrial, do you mean to say that you love me?" he whispered, fearful of speaking such joyous words aloud.

The angel raised her head. Tears glistened in her blue eyes, but when she answered, her voice was firm and steady. "I do love you, Pukah. I will always love you." She entwined her fIngers in his and held him fast. "I think that even in the Realm of the Dead, once more without form or shape, I will still have that love, and it will make me blessed!"

Pukah fell to his knees as she spoke, bowing his head as though receiving a benediction. Then, when her words had ceased, he slowly raised his head. "I know what I am," he said in sad and wistful tones. "I am conceited and irresponsible. I care too much for myself and not enough for others, even my own master. I've caused all sorts of trouble—without really meaning to," he added remorsefully, "but it was all for my own self-indulgence. Oh, you don't know!" He raised a hand to her lips as she was about to interrupt. "You don't know the harm I've done! It was because of me that the Amir thought my poor master was a spy and tried to arrest him. It was because of me that Sheykh Zeid went to war against us instead of becoming our ally. It was because of me that Kaug stole away Nedjma and imprisoned her in Serinda. And speaking of Serinda," the djinn continued, sparing himself no pain, "*you* were the hero, Asrial. Not I."

The djinn looked very woeful and wretched.

Her heart aching, Asrial sank down on her knees beside him. "No, my dear Pukah, don't berate yourself. As you say, you meant well—"

"But I didn't mean it for others. I meant it for myself," Pukah said resolutely. Standing up, he raised Asrial to her feet and gazed down at her with an unusually earnest and grave expression on his face. "But I'm going to make up for it all. Not only that"—for an instant, the old foxish glimmer appeared in the djinn's eyes—"I'm going to be the hero! A hero whose name and sacrifice will last throughout time!"

"Pukah!" Asrial stared at him, alarmed. "Sacrifice? What do you mean?"

"Farewell, my angel, my beautiful, enchanting angel!" Pukah kissed her hands. "Your love will be the shining light in my eternal darkness!"

"Pukah, wait!" Asrial cried, but the djinn was gone.

CHAPTER 2

Usti?" The rotund djinn gave a violent start that began at his broad back and rippled over his flab in undulating waves. Dropping whatever it was he was holding, sending it crashing to the tiled floor, Usti pivoted as swiftly as possible for one so large to face the door.

"The reason I am down here in the storage room is that I am reckoning up the amount of food we have on hand in case we are placed under siege," the djinn stated glibly, hastily wiping vestiges of rice from his chins. Endeavoring to who it was who had accosted him, he squinted and peered into the thick shadows wavering outside the circle of light cast by a lamp hanging—along with a quantity of smoked meats, dried herbs, and several large cheeses—from the ceiling. "There are . . . uh . . . twenty-seven jars of wine," he pronounced, still trying to see, "six large bags of rice, two of flour, thirty—"

"Oh, Usti! I don't care about any of that! Have you seen Pukah? Is he down here?"

"Pukah?" Usti's eyes opened wide, then narrowed in disgust as the figure stepped into the light of his lamp. "Oh, it's you," he muttered. "The madman's angel."

Any other time Asrial would have bristled angrily over the aspersion cast upon her protégé. Now she was too worried. Flinging herself at the djinn, she caught hold of his arm, this being markedly similar to thrusting one's hand into a bowl of bread dough. "Tell me he's here, Usti! Pukah, I know you are here!" She let loose of the djinn, who was glaring at her in high dudgeon, and looked intently into the dancing shadows. "Pukah, please come out and we'll talk—"

"Madam," said Usti, in glacial tones, "Pukah is not here. And you have interrupted my repast." He glanced disconsolately at the mess at his feet. "Ruined my repast is nearer the mark." He heaved a gloomy sigh and, squatting down with many grunts and groans, began a vain attempt to salvage something from the wreckage.

"A fine dinner of *fatta,* the vegetables crisp, the rice somewhat gummy, but then this is war, after all. One must make sacrifices. But now! Now!" Shaking his head and all six of his chins, he covered his eyes with his hands in an effort to blot out the terrible sight. "I know I will see it forever," he murmured in hollow tones. "The rice covered with dirt. The vegetables mixed up with bits of crockery. And soon, rats coming to devour—"

"Usti, he's gone!" Asrial slumped down on a cask of olive oil, her white wings drooping. "He's been gone all day and all night, too. Now it is nearly time for Kaug to return—"

"Ahhh!" Blowing like a whale rising to the surface, Usti heaved himself to his feet. "Kaug, did you say, angel of the madman?"

"Mathew isn't mad." Asrial answered automatically, her thoughts on something—someone—else. "He was acting so strangely when he left me. . ."

"Often a symptom of madness," said Usti knowingly.

"Not Mathew! Pukah!"

"Has he gone mad, too?" Usti readjusted the turban that had slipped over one eye in his feasting. "I am not surprised. Pardon me if I offend you, madam, but it would have been much better for all concerned if you and your madman had not inflicted yourselves upon us—"

"Inflicted ourselves on *you? We* didn't want to come to this dreadful place!" Asrial cried. "We never meant to fall in love—" She stopped, with a gulp. "What is that?" she whispered fearfully, staring up above them.

The earth was shaking and quivering more than Usti's chins. The cheeses swayed alarmingly, the carcass of a smoked goat tumbled to the floor. The lamp swung back and forth on its chain, the shadows in the underground storage chamber leapt and darted about the room like imps of Astafas, themselves gone mad.

"Kaug!" gasped Usti, his face the color of the blue cheese hanging over his head. "Back to the Realm of the Dead for us!" Catching hold of the dangling end of the cloth from his turban, he mopped his sweat-beaded forehead. "No more *couscous!*" He began to whimper. "No more sugared almonds. No more crispy bits of gazelle meat, nicely done, just slightly pink in the center—"

The rumbling increased, the shaking of the ground made it impossible to stand. Clinging to the wall, the cheeses tumbling down to roll around his feet, Usti had his eyes squinched tightly shut and was reciting feverishly, "No more *qumiz*. No more *shishlick*. No more—"

A jar of wine tipped over and broke, flooding the storage chamber and staining the hem of Asrial's white robes crimson. She paid no attention. She was listening.

There it was, rising faintly over the rumbling and cracking and the sound of Usti's lamenting.

"Djinn of Akhran! Attend to me! Quickly! We haven't much time!"

"Pukah!" cried Asrial, and disappeared.

Clutching a cheese to his breast, Usti bowed his head and wept.

Though the immortal plane shook with the terror of the 'efreet's approach, Kaug himself was just barely visible, his bulk darkening the horizon like a bank of storm clouds, lightning flickering from his eyes, thunder pounding the ground at his feet.

The djinn stood beneath their fortifications, weapons of every type and variety in their hands. On the balconies of the castle above the garden, the djinniyeh waited quietly, arms around each other for comfort. Hidden by silken robes, more than one sash wrapped around a slender waist concealed a sharp and shining blade. When their djinn had fallen, the djinniyeh were prepared to take up the fight.

The ancient djinn himself appeared. A tiny, dried-up husk of an immortal dressed in voluminous brocade robes that nearly swallowed him up and banished him from sight, he was carried in a sedan chair by two giant eunuchs onto his own private balcony. Shining scimitars hung at the sides of the eunuchs. The djinn had in his possession, resting across his brocade-covered knees, a saber that might have been the first weapon ever forged. So ancient was its design and so rusted was its blade, it is doubtful if the sword could have sliced through one of Usti's cheeses. Not that it mattered. Kaug's head could be seen rearing up over the edge of the plane, and he was massive—more gigantic than anything the immortals could possibly imagine. A stomp of his foot would crush their castle, his little finger could smash them into oblivion.

Sond stood at the head of the djinn's army. Sword in hand, he tried to keep his balance on the undulating ground. Fedj was at his right hand, Raja at his left. Behind them the other djinn waited, intending to make the price of their banishment as high as possible. Stone cracked, trees toppled. The sky darkened. Kaug's hulking form obliterated the setting sun. Its last rays illuminated something white that drifted through the air and fell at Sond's feet.

Leaning down, the djinn picked it up. It was a rose, and he knew where grew the bush from which the blossom had been plucked. Lifting it to his lips, he turned toward the rose-covered balcony. Though Nedjma's face was veiled, Sond knew she smiled at him, and he smiled bravely back, though he was forced to avert his head hurriedly, the smile twisting into a grimace of despair. Blinking his eyes, he reverently tucked the rose into the sash at his waist and was clearing his throat, preparatory to issuing a command that would have launched the battle, when suddenly Pukah sprang up out of an ornamental fountain right in front of him.

"Where have you been?" Sond snapped initably. "That angel of yours is driving everyone crazy! Go find her, shut her up, and then see if you can make yourself useful. Where's your sword? Raja, give him your dagger. Pukah, I swear by Akhran—"

But Pukah completely ignored Sond. Climbing up the side of the fountain's central figure—a marble fish spouting water from huge marble lips—Pukah clung to the statue's gills and shouted, "Djinn of Akhran! Attend to me!"

The djinn began to mutter and grumble; a rustle swept through the djinniyeh like wind through silken curtains.

"Pukah! This is no time for your tricks!" Sond cried angrily. Reaching up, he grabbed hold of one of Pukah's feet and endeavored to pull the djinn from his perch. Pukah, kicking himself free, shouted loudly, "Hear me! I have a plan to defeat Kaug!"

The muttering ceased abruptly. Silence—as silent as it could possibly get with the 'efreet drawing ever closer—spread like a pall over the immortals in the garden. Asrial appeared, bursting like a silver star at Sond's side.

"Pukah! I've been so worried! Where—"

The young djinn cast the angel a fond and loving glance. Shaking his head, he did not answer her but continued to speak to the crowd of immortals now gazing at him with full, if dubious, attention.

"I have a plan to defeat Kaug," Pukah repeated, speaking so rapidly and with such excitement that they could barely understand him. "I don't have time to explain it. Just follow my lead and agree with whatever I say."

The muttering began again.

Sond scowled, his anger mounting, "I told you, Pukah—"

"The Realm of the Dead!" said Pukah. His tense voice sliced through the grumblings like a length of taut thread. "The Realm of the Dead awaits! You haven't got a chance, not a prayer! Where is Akhran? Where is our God?"

The immortals glanced at each other uneasily. It was the one question everyone had in his heart but no one dared speak.

"I'll tell you where he is," continued Pukah in hushed and solemn tones. "Akhran lies in his tent, weak and injured, bleeding from many wounds. Some of these wounds Quar has inflicted. But others"—he paused a moment to clear his throat—"Others have been inflicted on him by his own people."

The garden grew darker. A foul-smelling wind began to blow, shrieking and howling, stripping leaves from those trees left standing and whipping dust into the air.

"Their faith dwindles!" yelled Pukah above the rising storm, the coming of the 'efreet. "They have lost their immortals! They do not think their God hears their prayers, and so they have quit praying. . . or worse—they pray to Quar! If we are defeated, it will be the end, not only for us, but for Akhran!"

The wind ripped through the garden, breaking and tearing whatever it could. It clawed at the shining silver hair of the angel, but Asrial paid it no heed. Her eyes were on the young djinn.

"We are with you, Pukah!" she cried.

Sond looked at Fedj, who nodded slowly, and at Raja, who nodded in turn. Glancing behind him, barely able to see through the dust and torn branches and leaves and flower petals and a sudden pelting rain, Sond caught glimpses of the other djinn nodding, and he even heard what he thought was the dried-up rasp of the ancient djinn adding his sanction.

"Very well, Pukah," said Sond reluctantly. "We will go along with your plan."

Heaving a vast sigh, tingling with pride and importance from turbaned head to slippered toe, Pukah turned and prepared to face Kaug.

CHAPTER 3

The 'efreet stomped up to the outer wall of the garden, and at his approach the storm winds ceased to rage, the thunder to crack, the lightning to flash. When Kaug stood still, the ground no longer shook. A dread and ominous quiet fell over the immortal plane.

"Your time is up," rumbled the 'efreet, and the vibrations of his voice started the plane to quivering again. "Seeing these warlike fortifications and noting that all of you carry weapons, I take it that you choose to fight."

"No, no, Kaug the Merciful," said Pukah from atop the marble fish. "We bring our weapons only to lay humbly at your feet."

Kaug's eyes narrowed suspiciously. "Is that true, Sond?" the 'efreet asked. "Have *you* brought your sword to lay at my feet?"

"Cut off your feet is more like it," muttered Sond, glaring at Pukah.

"Go on! Go on!" Pukah mouthed, making a swift, emphatic gesture with his hand.

His mouth twisting, as though his swallowed rage was poisoning him, Sond stalked up to the 'efreet and, with grim defiance, hurled the weapon point foremost at Kaug's toes. One by one the other djinn followed Sond's example, and soon the astonished 'efreet was standing ankle-deep in a veritable armory.

"And as for fortifications"—Pukah glanced around him, somewhat at a loss to explain the new battlements and turrets and walls that had sprung up—"these . . . uh . . . were just erected to give"—inspiration struck him with such force he nearly fell from his fish—"to give you a hint of the surprise to come!"

"I don't like surprises, Little Pukah," the 'efreet growled, grinding the swords and scimitars and spears to metallic powder beneath his huge foot.

"Ah, but you will like this one, O Kaug the Mighty and Powerful!" said Pukah with an earnest solemnity that made the other djinn gaze at him in wonder. "The world has treated you badly, Kaug. You have grown suspicious and untrusting. We knew, therefore, that we must do something to convince you that we were truly sincere in our desire to serve you. And so"—Pukah paused, savoring the suspenseful hush, the breathless anticipation that awaited his words—"we have built you a house."

Silence. Dead silence. The garden might have been filled with corpses instead of living beings.

"What trick is this, Little Pukah?" Kaug finally spoke, his words grating with suspicion, trembling with anger. "You know that, centuries ago, the wrath of the foul God Zhakrin banished me to the Kurdin Sea. There my house is, and there I must remain until Quar succeeds to his rightful place as the One, True God—"

"Not so, O Much-Put-Upon Kaug." Pukah shook his head. "The God Zhakrin owed me a favor—what for, we will not discuss—but he owed me a favor, and I have asked him, as my gift to you, O Master, that he set you free.

"This is no trick," Pukah added hastily, seeing Kaug's eyes narrow to slits of red flame. "Search within yourself. Do you feel constrained, chained any longer?"

Kaug's ugly face wrinkled, his gaze grew abstracted. Hesitantly he lifted his gigantic arms and flexed his muscles as though testing to see if he was manacled. His arms moved freely and, slowly, gradually, a pleased and gratified expression spread over his face.

"You are right, Little Pukah," Kaug said with a look of wonder. "I am free! Free! Ha! Ha! Ha!" Raising his arms in the air, he shook his fists at heaven. His glee sent seismic waves through the immortal plane. The balcony on which the djinniyeh stood sagged alarmingly, and the women fled in a whirl of silk. Seeing them run, Kaug leered and turned his gaze back to the djinn. "Thank you for this gift, Little Pukah. Indeed, I now truly believe that you mean to serve me, you and these sniveling cowards around you, and you may start doing so right now. You, Sond, fetch me the djinniyeh known as Nedjma. I have a desire to—"

"Don't you want to see your house?" interrupted Pukah.

"What?" Kaug stared at him irritably.

"Don't you want to see your house, Your Magnificence? It has a wondrous bedchamber," the djinn insinuated from his post atop the fish. Seeing that Kaug's attention was on the balcony, Pukah lashed out with a slippered foot at the infuriated Sond, kicking him painfully in the kidneys to remind him to keep quiet. "And while we are viewing your new dwelling, Nedjma can take time to prepare herself so that she may come to you in all her beauty and do you honor, O Kaug, Handsome Charmer."

Kaug was baffled. The 'efreet continued to stare lustfully at the balcony, scraping his hand over his stubbled chin and running his tongue across his lips, but he did this primarily because he knew it was torturing Sond. The 'efreet had a mild interest in Nedjma. When this war was won and the immortals banished, he would undoubtedly keep several of the more comely djinniyeh around for his pleasure, and Nedjma would undoubtedly be one of them.

What was Pukah up to? That was the question tormenting Kaug. His brain was searching for answers, but instead of finding any, his mental process was going round and round like a donkey yoked to a waterwheel. Kaug didn't trust Pukah. The 'efreet didn't trust anyone (his God Quar was no exception), and he knew Pukah was plotting some elaborate scheme.

But he freed me from Zhakrin's curse!

That was the fact that kept the donkey moving in its slow, plodding circle. Kaug simply couldn't believe it. Long, long ago, when Zhakrin had been a powerful force in the Jewel of Sul and Quar was but a bootlicking toad—(a toad with ambition—but a toad nonetheless)—Quar had secretly ordered Kaug to wreak havoc upon a fortress of Zhakrin's Black Paladins located in the Great Steppes. Generally Kaug took little delight in obeying Quar's commands, which—up until the war—had consisted of raining hail on the heads of recalcitrant followers or inflicting plagues upon their goat herds. When it came to battling the Black Paladins, however, Kaug enjoyed himself thoroughly. The 'efreet was having such a marvelous time hurling down fiery rocks on those trapped inside the castle, plucking their puny spears from his flesh and hurling them back with such force that they impaled men to the stone walls—that Kaug stayed longer than he should have. Zhakrin was able to come to the aid of his beleaguered Paladins.

Descending upon Kaug in his wrath, the God lifted the 'efreet in his mighty arms and slammed Kaug into the Kurdin Sea. And though it is impossible for one God to completely control another God's immortal, Zhakrin was able to effect a curse upon the 'efreet—pronouncing that Kaug must henceforth dwell in the Kurdin Sea so that Zhakrin could always keep track of the 'efreet's comings and goings.

Quar had meekly swallowed this insult—what else could he do then? And Kaug had been forced to live in a watery cave under the baleful eye of the evil God. But Quar and his 'efreet were now joined in mutual hatred of Zhakrin, and it was shortly after Kaug's banishment that Quar began his subtle war against the evil God that would end, finally, in the reduction of Zhakrin himself to a fish.

"And now Pukah has freed me," Kaug reflected. "He has persuaded Zhakrin to free me. Not that this must have been so difficult." The 'efreet sneered. "What is Zhakrin now? A ghost without form or shape. I could have freed myself had I wanted to, but I've grown accustomed to that cave of mine. Zhakrin owed Pukah a favor for releasing his immortals from Serinda, and all know that the Evil God's one major flaw is his honor. But why would Pukah use this favor in my behalf unless... unless"—the mental donkey came to a halt—"unless Pukah is like me!

"Of course. I should have realized this before," muttered Kaug to himself in a low voice that was like the rumblings of a volcano to the djinn watching him warily from below. "Pukah is a self-serving little bastard. I've always known that. His Immortal Master, the Mighty Akhran, lies bleeding, dying. His earthly master, the impudent Khardan, has crossed the Sun's Anvil, but he will soon find himself in greater danger from his own people. Could it be that Pukah is really, in truth, attempting to save his own miserable skin? If this wretched worm has truly been driven to crawling on his belly, I may have an amusing time of it!"

"Very well, Little Pukah," said Kaug aloud, shifting his weight from one foot to the other and crushing three stalwart stone towers in the process, "I will look at this house of yours. You will accompany me, of course, as will Nedjma."

"Nedjma?" A worried frown passed swiftly over Pukah's face. Kaug, watching intently, did not miss it and smiled to himself. "But Nedjma is not ready, O Kaug the Impatient, and you know how long it takes women to fuss over themselves, especially when there is one they truly desire to please."

"Tell her I will take her the way she is," said Kaug with a laugh that split a minaret in two and sent it crashing to the ground. "Run and fetch her, Little Pukah. I am eager to see my new house!"

Climbing down the fish, Pukah was confronted by a darkly scowling Sond. "It will be all right. Trust me," Pukah whispered hurriedly.

"I know it will," Sond said grimly. ".. I'm coming with you."

"No, you're not!" Pukah snapped. "It would spoil everything."

"Yes, I am. You're not going anywhere with Nedjma! I'll disguise myself as her—"

Pukah gave him a scathing look. "With those legs?"

The two djinn, still arguing, vanished from sight in the garden and materialized within the palace. Intent on his scheming, upset by this sudden, unexpected demand that Nedjma accompany him, Pukah never noticed that Asrial had come with them until she stood blocking his way when he and Sond tried to enter the *seraglio.*

"Asrial, my enchanter!" Pukah put his hands on the angel's arms and endeavored to move her gently out of his path. "At any other time the sight of you would be balm to my sore heart, but right now I have this evil 'efreet on my hands—"

"I know," Asrial said firmly. "I'm coming with you."

"How popular I've become lately," said Pukah, somewhat irritably. "Everyone wants to come with me." Stealing a sidelong glance at Sond, to make certain he was appreciating this, Pukah heaved a long-suffering sigh. "I know that I am irresistible, my angel, and that you cannot bear to be parted from me for the tiniest second, but—"

Pukah's tongue stuttered to a halt. It was no longer Asrial he held in his arms, but Nedjma!

"Here, what is this?" growled Sond, lunging forward to separate the two, when suddenly Nedjma—the real Nedjma—was standing by his side.

Her face pale, the djinniyeh laid a trembling hand restrainingly on Asrial. "No. It's wonderful of you to offer to sacrifice yourself, but I'll go with"—she gulped slightly, then bravely brought the word out—"Kaug. I know what you did for us in

Serinda and I . . . we"—she took hold of Sond's hand—"we can't ask you to—"

"You're not asking me," Asrial interrupted. She did not even glance at the djinniyeh, her eyes looked up into Pukah's. "I've decided this myself."

"It's dangerous, my angel," Pukah said softly. "You don't know what I must do, and if anything goes wrong, he'll carry out his threat!"

"I'm not afraid. You'll take care of me," Asrial answered, smiling.

"Like I took care of you in Serinda?" Pukah said wistfully, stroking the golden hair. He glanced at Nedjma, who—though she was trying very hard to be brave—was shivering with terror. "Nedjma will be no help at all," Pukah muttered to his alter ego. "She looks on the verge of passing out as it is. Asrial is courageous, strong. I know—none better—her resourcefulness."

"But what about—you know?" questioned the other Pukah solemnly.

"I'll take care of that," Pukah answered. "Very well," he said aloud. "You may go, but you must promise me one thing, Asrial—you must promise to do exactly as I tell you, without question."

Asrial frowned. "Why, what do you mean—"

"Little Pukah!" The 'efreet's gigantic eyeball appeared in the window of the harem, sending the djinniyeh fleeing in panic. Nedjma, hurriedly drawing the veil across her face, shrank back into the shadows. Sond leapt forward to hide her from Kaug's sight. "Hurry up!" Kaug roared, cracking the window glass. His eye rolled and winked lasciviously. "I must take my pleasure quickly, then return to my master."

Seeing the 'efreet this near, understanding the terrible portent of his words, Asrial could not forbear a shudder that Pukah felt.

"What are you doing with my woman, Little Pukah?" Kaug growled.

"I am just inspecting her to make certain she is worthy of your attention, O Kaug," shouted Pukah. In a hurried undertone he hissed, "Swear to me by Mathew's life that you will obey me!"

Frightened by Pukah's unwonted seriousness, alarmed at the enormity of the oath she was being asked to take, Asrial stared up at him wordlessly.

"Swear!" Pukah said sternly, shaking her slightly. "Or I will be forced to take Sond disguised as Nedjma, and then none of us will survive!"

"I swear."

"By Mathew's life," Pukah urged. "Say it!"

"Pukah!" Kaug raged.

"Say it!"

"I swear. . . by Mathew's life. . . to obey you!" The angel's words fell from pale and trembling lips.

Sighing in relief, Pukah kissed Asrial soundly on the forehead, then clasped her hand in his.

"Sond," he said in a low voice, turning to the djinn, "when I leave, you and Fedj and that good-for-nothing Usti must hurry back to Khardan and Zohra. As Kaug said, they will be in terrible danger! Farewell! Oh, and Sond," Pukah added anxiously, "you'll be certain to tell *Hazrat* Akhran that this was all entirely my idea, won't you?"

"Yes, but—"

"*My* idea. You won't forget?"

"No, but I don't—"

"You will tell him?"

"Yes, if that's what you want," said Sond impatiently.

"But why don't you just tell him yoursel—"

His voice died. The djinn, the angel, and the 'efreet were gone.

CHAPTER 4

"i will provide transportation, *Bashi*—you don't mind my calling you 'boss' do you, Boss?" Pukah asked humbly.

"Not at all," said Kaug, grinning and leering horribly at Asrial. "You might as well begin getting used to it, Little Pukah."

"Exactly what I thought myself," said Pukah, with a graceful *salaam*, managing—at the same time—to keep his body between Asrial and the 'efreet. "As I was saying, *Bashi*, I will provide transportation if you will but reduce yourself to a more suitable size."

Suddenly suspicious, Kaug glared narrowly at Pukah.

"You will find it difficult to fit into your new bed, *Bashi*," remarked Pukah with lowered eyes, a faint flush on his cheeks.

Kaug's suspicion wasn't the only part of him being aroused. Pukah's cunning reference to the bed inflamed him. The 'efreet had forgotten until seeing her again how beautiful the djinniyeh really was. Vivid memories of his struggles with Nedjma in the garden when he had kidnapped her—the feel of her soft skin, the surpassing loveliness of her body—made his blood tingle, his thick thighs ache with desire.

Still, Kaug was cautious. The hotter the fire in the loins, the colder the ice in the mind. He examined this gem Pukah was handing him with the precise, calculating eye a worshipper of Kharmani uses to examine the jewels of his bride's dowry.

He could not find a flaw.

A hundred times more powerful than the scrawny young djinn, Kaug could roll Pukah up into a ball, and toss him out into the eternal void of Sul, to languish forever amid nothingness, and all in less time than it would take the djinn to draw in a lungful of air for his final scream.

"You are right, Little Pukah," said Kaug, shrinking in size until he was only two heads and a shoulder larger than the djinn. "I would not want to be too big for the ... ahem ... bed." Laughing, he put his arm around Asrial and dragged the angel roughly to his side.

Pukah, smiling wanly, clapped his hands, and the three began their journey.

Behind them, on the immortal plane, the djinn looked at each other in worried puzzlement and then began to reconstruct their battlements.

"Where are we?" demanded Kaug, staring about, glowering darkly.

"On an insignificant mountain in a range unworthy of your notice, *Bashi*," answered Pukah humbly.

The three stood at about the midpoint of a mountain whose height was so vast that the clouds played about its knees and it seemed that the sun would have to leap to scale the topmost peak. A hoary frost perpetually covered the craggy head; summer's heat never reached the summit. Nothing and no one lived on the mountain. The bitter cold froze blood and sucked air from the lungs. The entire world had once been as desolate as this mountain, before Sul blessed it, according to the legend of those who lived in the mountain's shadow; and, therefore, the mountain was called Sul's Curse.

Kaug did not know this, nor did he care. He could feel the supposed djinniyeh trembling in his grip, and he was impatient, now that he did not have a war with the djinn to occupy him, to satisfy his lust.

"The doors to your abode, *Bashi*," said Pukah, bowing. As the djinn spoke, two massive doors of solid gold, studded with glittering jewels and standing sixty feet high, took shape and form within the mountain's rock. By Pukah's command—"Akhran wills it!"—the doors swung slowly inward on silent hinges. Leaving the barren, windswept landscape of the mountainside, Kaug, dragging Asrial with him, entered the golden doors.

The 'efreet drew in a long breath. His grasp on the angel weakened. Kaug could not help himself. He was overawed.

Golden walls, covered with tapestries of the most delicate design done in every color of the rainbow, soared to such heights that it seemed the ceiling must be lit with stars instead of crystal lamps. Objects rare and lovely from every facet of the Jewel of

Sul stood on the silver-tiled floor or hung from the gilt walls or adorned tables carved of rare *saksaul*. And as the 'efreet traversed this magnificent hallway, his mouth gaping wide in wonder, Pukah threw open door after door, displaying room after room and chamber after chamber, all filled with the most beautifully crafted furniture made of the rarest and most valuable materials.

"Quar himself has no such dwelling as this!" murmured Kaug.

"Bedroom," said Pukah, opening a door. "Second bedroom, third bedroom, fourth bedroom, and so on for several miles into the heart of the mountain. Then there is the divan for holding audience with those you want to impress" —Pukah threw open double doors—"and the divan for holding audience with those you don't want to impress"—more doors—"and the divan for holding audience with yourself, if you so desire, and then"—continued opening of doors—"here are your summer chambers and here are your winter chambers and here are your spring chambers and here are your inbetween winter and spring chambers and—"

"Enough!" shouted Kaug, beginning to tire of the seemingly endless display of riches. "I admit, I am truly impressed, Little Pukah"—the djinn bowed again—"and I apologize for thinking you were trying to trick me."

Pukah's eyes widened, his face crumpled with pain. "*Bashi*, how could you?" he cried, stricken.

Kaug waved a hand. "I apologize. And now"—the 'efreet gave Asrial a vicious tug—"we will retire to one of the bedrooms, if you can tell me where they are?" The 'efreet stared back down the hall. Every door—and all were closed—looked exactly like every other door.

"Ah, but first," said Pukah, taking advantage of the 'efreet's preoccupation to neatly slide Asrial's hand out of his grasp. "First the unworthy woman must bathe herself and put on her perfume and her finest clothing and rouge her small feet and darken her eyelids with *kohl*—"

"I care nothing for that!" the 'efreet raged, his thwarted passions rising red into his ugly face. Kaug began to grow in height and swell in breadth. "So this was a trick, after all, Little Pukah? It will be your last one!" The towering 'efreet reached out huge hands toward the djinn.

Ignoring Kaug, Pukah looked straight into Asrial's terrified eyes. "Run," he told her. "Run and shut the mountain's doors behind you."

Catching hold of the angel Pukah shoved her to one side and then dashed in a direction opposite the doors, down the glittering hallway. The 'efreet's grasping hands caught hold of nothing but the breeze left by the djinn's flight.

"I won't leave you!" Asrial cried frantically, though just what she could do if she stayed was open to question.

"Your oath!" Pukah's triumphant voice came floating back to her. The golden walls picked it up, the words reverberated from the starlit ceiling and bounced off the silver-tiled floor.

Your oath! Oath! Oath! *By Mathew's life. . .*

Clenching her fists in frustration, Asrial did as Pukah commanded. Turning, she ran the opposite direction from the one the djinn had taken. The 'efreet made a lunge for her, but the angel had shed the silken *pantalons* and veil. White wings sprouted from her back. She flew gracefully out of Kaug's grasp and sped toward the golden doors at the end of the hall.

Seeing his prey escaping him in two different directions, Kaug was momentarily at a loss over which to pursue. The answer, once he thought about it, was simple. He would catch Pukah first, rip that glib tongue from the djinn's foxish head, tie his feet into knots, and impale him on a hook in the ceiling above the bed. Then, at his leisure, Kaug would retrieve the angel, who, he calculated, would be glad to do anything she could to free her lover.

The 'efreet set off in pursuit of Pukah, who was running with the speed of a hundred frightened gazelles down the long hallway that led, twisting and spiraling, deeper and deeper into the heart of the mountain.

Run! Run and shut the mountain's doors behind you. Standing on the mountainside, Asrial grasped the huge golden door rings with both hands, and pulled at them with all her might. The doors, set solidly into the rock, refused to budge.

Asrial prayed to Promenthas for strength and slowly, slowly the mighty doors began to revolve on their hinges.

The angel heard Kaug's shouted threats from inside the mountain; his rage shook the ground on which she stood. She hesitated. . .

By Mathew's life!

Asrial gave a final tug. The huge doors closed with a dull, hollow boom that pierced the angel's heart like cold iron.

Inside the mountain Kaug heard the great doors slam shut, but he didn't give it a thought. . . until, suddenly, everything around him went completely and absolutely pitch dark.

Cold iron.

Asrial, pressing her hands against her heart, understood. "Oh, Pukah, no!" she moaned.

Running back to the doors, the angel beat on them frantically with her fists, but there was no answer. She shouted over and over—in every language she knew—"Akhran wills it!"—the words of command she had heard Pukah use to open them, but there was no response.

"Akhran wills it!" she said a final time, but this was a whisper, almost a prayer.

The angel, watching in helpless anguish, saw the golden doors begin to fade, the light of the gleaming jewels dwindle and darken.

The entrance vanished, and Asrial was left standing alone on the windswept, cold, and barren mountainside.

CHAPTER 5

Pukah sat, comfortably ensconced, in a tiny cavern—more a crevice than a cavern, actually—in the bowels of the mountain known as Sul's Curse. Lounging back on several silken cushions, smoking a hubble-bubble pipe, the young djinn listened to the soothing sound of the gurgling water—a sound punctuated now and then by fierce shouts and yells from the trapped 'efreet.

"The one thing I am sorry for, my friend," said Pukah exultantly to his favorite cohort—himself, "is that we missed seeing the expression on his ugly face when Kaug discovered the mountain was made of iron. That would have been worth all the rubies in the Sultan's girdle, the one that was stolen by Saad, the notorious follower of Benario. Have I ever told you that story?"

Pukah's alter ego emitted a tiny sigh at this point, for he had heard the story countless times and knew it as well or better than the teller. He also knew that he was destined to hear this story and many, many others in the days and nights follow—long days and longer nights that would flow into till longer years, interminable decades, and everlasting centuries. But the other Pukah, after that one tiny sigh, responded stoutly and bravely that he had never heard the story of Saad and the Sultan's Ruby-Studded Girdle and awaited it eagerly.

"Then I will tell it," said Pukah, highly gratified. He began relating the harrowing tale and had just come to the part where the thief, to avoid being captured by the Sultan's guards, swallows one hundred and seventy-four rubies when a particularly ferocious shout from the 'efreet shook the mountain to the core, interrupting him. The young djinn frowned in irritation and righted the hubble-bubble pipe that had been overturned in the resulting tremor.

"How long do you suppose it will be before Kaug finds us?" Pukah asked himself in somewhat worried tones.

"Oh, several centuries I should think," remarked Pukah confidently.

"That is what I think, too," Pukah stated, reassured.

A most tremendous roar rattled the crockery and set the wooden bowls to dancing about the floor.

"And by the time he does find us," Pukah continued, "I am certain that, since I am by far the cleverer of the two of us—the cleverest of all immortals I know, now that I come to think of it—I will have discovered a way out of this iron trap. And then I will be reunited with my angel—my sweetest, most beautiful of angels—and *Hazrat* Akhran will reward me with the most wonderful of palaces. It will have a thousand rooms. Yes, a thousand rooms." Leaning back among the cushions, letting smoke curl lazily from his lips, Pukah smiled and closed his eyes. "I think I will begin planning them right now. . . ."

The alter ego—having always found the end of Saad to be particularly gut wrenching—heaved a sigh of relief and went to sleep.

Above the djinn, beneath him, and all around him, the mountain known as Sul's Curse rumbled and quaked with the 'efreet's rage. Those few hardy nomadic tribes of the Great Steppes, who raised long-haired goats at the mountain's feet, fled with their flocks in terror, convinced that the mountain was going to split wide open.

The mountain remained intact, however. Encased in iron, Kaug had lost his power to do anything except to rage and storm. There was no possible way he could escape.

From that time on it became a joke among the Gods to refer to the mountain as Kaug's Curse.

But to Sond and Fedj and the immortals of Akhran and one loving angel of Promenthas, the mountain was henceforth known as Pukah's Peak.

The Book
of
Promenthas

CHAPTER 1

reluctantly Achmed rolled off his pallet. A soft arm twined about his neck, urging him to come back. Warm lips brushed against his throat, whispering promises of yet untasted pleasures. Succumbing, Achmed buried his head in the shower of golden hair that fell over the pillows at his side and let himself be enticed by the lips and the flesh for several breathless moments. Then, groaning as he felt the desire surge up within him again, he rose hurriedly from his bed and went to dress himself.

Propping herself upon one arm, languishing among the cushions, her nakedness covered with only a thin blanket, Meryem gazed at Achmed through the tousled hair that shone like burnished gold in the lamplight.

"Must you go?" she asked, pouting.

"I am officer in charge of night watch," Achmed said shortly, trying to keep from looking at her but unable to resist gazing hungrily at the smooth, white skin.

Buckling on his armor, his hands fumbled and slipped, and he muttered a brief curse. Rising from the bed, the blanket sliding to the tent floor, Meryem came to him.

"Let me do that," she said, pushing aside his shaking hands.

"Cover yourself! Someone will see!" Achmed said, scandalized, hurriedly blowing out the flame of the lamp.

"What does it matter?" Meryem asked, shrugging and deftly fastening the buckles. "Everyone knows you keep a woman."

"Ah, but they don't know *what* a woman!" Achmed replied, clasping her close and kissing her. "Even Qannadi said—"

"Qannadi?" Shoving him back, Meryem stared up at him in fear. "Qannadi knows about me?"

"Of course." Achmed shrugged. "Word spreads. He is my commander. Don't worry, my beloved." His hands ran over the body that was trembling with what he thought was passion. "I told him that I found you in the Grove. He shook his head and said only that it was all right to lose my heart, just not to lose my head."

"So he doesn't know who I am?"

"He knows nothing about your true identity, gazelle eyes," said Achmed fondly. "How could he? You keep your face veiled. Anyway, why should he recognize you as the Sultan's daughter? He must have seen you for only a few moments at most when his troops captured your father."

"Qannadi has seen as much of me as you, fool," Meryem muttered beneath her breath. Aloud she murmured coyly, "And have you lost your heart?" Her arms twined around his waist.

"You know I have!" Achmed breathed passionately.

"Meryem, why won't you marry me?"

"I am not worthy—" Meryem began, drooping her head.

"It is I who am not worthy to slipper your foot!" Achmed said earnestly. "I love you with all my heart! I will never love another!"

"Perhaps, then, someday I will let you make me your wife," Meryem said, seeming to relent beneath his caresses. "When Qannadi is dead and you are Amir—"

"Don't talk like that!" Achmed said abruptly, his face darkening.

"It is true! You will be Amir! I know, I have foreseen it!"

"Nonsense, my dove." Achmed shrugged. "He has sons."

"There are ways to handle sons," Meryem whispered, reaching her arms up to his neck.

Achmed pushed her from him. "I said not to talk like that," he responded, his voice grown suddenly cool. Turning his back on her, he reached for his sword that hung from the tent post.

Though she saw she had gone too far, Meryem smiled—a cunning, unpleasant smile that was hidden by the darkness. "No, you are not ready yet," she said to herself. "But you will be. You are getting closer every day."

Putting her head in her hands, Meryem began to weep softly. "You do not love me!"

There could be only one answer to this, and Achmed, his anger melting beneath her tears, gave it—with the result that he was about half an hour late relieving the officer on watch and was summarily and sternly reprimanded, the only thing saving him from a more severe punishment being the common knowledge that he was the Amir's favorite.

When Achmed was finally gone, Meryem sighed in relief. Washing off the sweat of passion, she dressed herself, looking with disfavor on the poor caftan of green cotton she was forced to wear, dreaming longingly of the silks and jewels , she had been wont to wear in the palace.

"Someday," she said resolutely, talking to Achmed's robes that lay in a heap in a corner. "Someday I will have all that and more, when I am head wife in your *seraglio*. And yes, you will be Amir! If Qannadi does not die in this war, which seems unlikely now that it is won, then perhaps he will meet with a fatal accident back in Kich. And then, one by one, his sons, too, will fall ill and die." Reaching her hand into her pillow, she slid forth a bag containing many scrolls, rolled tight and tied with various-colored ribbons. Caressing these and smiling, she pictured in her mind the various deaths of Qannadi's sons. She pictured Achmed receiving the news as he rose higher and higher in the Emperor's favor. She saw him glance at her and bite his lower lip but remain silent, knowing that by this time—though he might rule millions—he himself was ruled by one.

Meryem smiled sweetly and dressed herself in the green caftan. It had been a gift from Achmed and therefore—poor as it was, though it had cost Achmed more than he could afford—she was forced to wear it. Then she drew forth her scrying bowl and filled it with water. Clearing her mind of all disturbing thoughts, she began the arcane chant, and soon an image formed in the bowl. Staring at it, Meryem muttered most unwomanly words. Hastily twisting to her feet, she wrapped a veil of green and gold spangled silk around her head and face—another gift from the besotted youth—and slipped out of Achmed's tent.

CHAPTER 2

i tell you I must see the Imam!" Meryem insisted. "It is a matter of greatest urgency."

"But madam, it is the middle of the night!" remonstrated one of the soldier-priests who now served Feisal in place of slaves, ordinary men being considered unworthy of attending to the Imam's personal needs. "The Imam must rest—"

"I never rest," came a gentle voice from the depths of night's shadows that crowded thick behind the candlelit ram's-head altar. "Quar watches in heaven. I watch on earth. Who is it that needs me in the dark hours of the night?"

"One who calls herself Meryem, My Lord," answered the priest, hurling himself to the floor and prostrating his body as he would have if the Emperor himself had entered the room. Or perhaps he might not have groveled this low for the Emperor, who, after all—Feisal was now teaching—was only mortal.

"Meryem!" The gentle voice underwent a subtle change. Nose to the floor, the soldier-priest did not hear it. Meryem did, and from her place on the floor, whither she had thought it politic to drop herself, she grinned in triumph. "Let the woman come forward," Feisal said with dignity. "And you may leave us."

The soldier-priest sprang to his feet and bowed himself out. Meryem remained on the floor until he had gone; then, hearing the rustle of Feisal's robes near her, she raised her head and peered into the shadows.

"I have seen him!" Meryem hissed through her veil.

She heard a swift intake of breath. Stepping into the light cast by the altar candles, Feisal made a motion for the woman to rise and face him.

The priest's face appeared cadaverous in the altar light—the cheeks hollow, the skin waxen and tightly drawn over fragile bones. The robes hung from his wasted body, his neck thrust up out of them like the scrawny neck of a new-hatched bustard, his arms seemed nothing but bone covered by brittle parchment. No wonder his followers believed him to be immortal—he looked as if Death had claimed him long ago.

"Whom have you seen?" the priest asked indifferently, but Meryem was not fooled.

"You know well who I mean!" she muttered to herself, but said smoothly, "Khardan, Imam. He is alive! And he has returned to his tribe!"

"That is not possible!" Feisal clenched his fist, the bones of his fingers gleamed white in the altar light. "No man could survive crossing the Sun's Anvil! Are you certain?"

"I do not make mistakes!" Meryem snapped, then caught herself. "Forgive me, My Lord, but I have as much or more at stake here as you."

"I sincerely doubt that," Feisal said dryly. "But I will not argue." He raised a thin hand to prevent Meryem from speaking. Thoughtfully he began to pace back and forth before the altar, glancing at it occasionally as if—had the woman not been here—he would have found consolation in discussing the matter over with his God. The answer he sought apparently came to him without need for prayer, however, because he suddenly halted directly in front of Meryem and said, "I want him dead, this time for good."

Meryem started and glanced at him from beneath her long lashes. "Why should you bother, Holy One?" she said diffidently. "He is, after all, only one man, leader of a ragtag rabble—"

"Let us say I mistrust anyone who rises from the dead," Feisal remarked coolly. "We will leave it at that, Meryem, unless you think this is the time for both of us to share our little secrets?"

Meryem evidently did not, for she did not respond.

"Then we are both agreed that Khardan should die, are we not, Meryem, my child? After all, it would be a pity if Achmed should find out that his brother lives. There is no telling what he might do when he discovers you to be the lying little whore who deceived him. At the least he will kill you himself. At the worst he will turn you over to Qannadi—"

"What do you want of me?" Meryem demanded in a tight voice, barely able to speak for the smothering sensation that was choking her.

"It will take a very special person to get close enough to Khardan now to accomplish his death," said Feisal, coming close himself to Meryem and staring at her with his burning eyes. She felt his breath hot upon her skin, and she involuntarily shrank from the disturbing presence. He grasped her wrist painfully. "This close!" he said. "Or closer still!" He jerked her forward; her body touched his, and she shuddered at the awful sensation.

"There is someone who can get this close to him?" the Imam demanded.

"Yes!" Meryem gasped. "Oh, yes!"

"Good." Feisal released the woman suddenly. Unnerved, Meryem sank to the floor and remained there, on her knees, her eyes lowered. "You are skilled in your craft. I need not tell you how to proceed. You must start your journey tonight. . You will have to go on horseback—"

Meryem looked up, startled. "Why not Kaug?"

"The 'efreet is . . . busy upon matters of Quar, important matters," said Feisal.

The priest appeared uneasy, and Meryem wondered for the first time if the rumors that had been whispered in the dark and dead of night were true. Rumors that Kaug had disappeared, vanished. Rumors that he had not been seen nor his power felt in days. Delicately, Meryem probed.

"Surely you do not want me to waste time, Imam! It will take me weeks—"

"I said you will go by horseback!" the Imam interrupted sharply, his eyes flaring in anger.

Meryem prostrated herself humbly in response, more from a need to keep her flurried thoughts concealed than out of I reverence. Where was Kaug? What was all this about? Something was wrong. She could smell Feisal's fear, and she reveled in it. Undoubtedly she could turn this to her advantage.

"I will leave tonight, as you wish, Imam," she said, rising to her feet. "I will need money."

Going to a huge strongbox that stood behind the altar, Feisal opened it and returned presently with a sackful of coins.

"I can give you escort as far as Kich, but no farther. Once you are in the desert, you are on your own. That should be no problem for you, however, my child," the Imam added sardonically, handing Meryem the money. "Even snakes must flee your path."

Not deigning to answer, Meryem took the sack, her own cool gaze meeting Feisal's burning one. Much was said, though nothing was spoken. These were two people who, knew each other deeply, distrusted each other intensely, and were willing to use each other mercilessly to gain their heart's desire.

Without a word Meryem bowed and left Feisal's presence. "Quar's blessing be with you, my child," he murmured after her.

Late, late that night, a soft knocking—several distinct taps repeated in a peculiar manner—resounded on the door of the dwelling of one Muzaffahr, a poor dealer in iron pots, cauldrons, and spikes whose stall was the shabbiest in the *souk*. His goods, unskillfully made, were purchased only by those as poor as himself who could not afford better. Servile and humble, Muzaffahr never raised his eyes above the level of a person's knees when he spoke.

But it was a very sharp eye, not a servile one, that peeped through the slats of the wooden door of the ironmonger's hovel, and it was not his usual whining voice that queried softly. "What's the word?"

"Benario, Lord of Snatching Hands and Swift-Running Feet," came the answer.

The door opened, and a woman, shrouded in a green caftan and heavily veiled, glided over the doorstep. The iroomonger shut the door softly and—finger to his lips—took the woman's hand and led her through a curtained-off partition into a back room. Lighting an oil lamp that gave only a feeble glow from its trimmed wick, Muzaffahr—still enjoining silence—threw aside a threadbare rug on the floor, opened a trapdoor that appeared beneath it, and revealed a ladder leading down into total darkness.

He motioned at the stair. The woman shook her head and drew back, but the ironmonger motioned again, peremptorily, and the woman, casting him a threatening glance from her blue eyes, made her way slowly and cumbersomely, entangled in her robes, down the ladder.

Muzaffahr followed swiftly, sliding the trapdoor shut above them. Once below he lit another lamp, and light filled the room. The woman glanced around in amazed appreciation, to judge by the widening of the eyes that were barely visible above her veil. The ironmonger, rubbing his hands, smiled proudly and bowed several times.

"You will find no greater stock, madam, between here and Khandar. And there are very few in Khandar," he added modestly, "who carry such an extensive line as do I."

"I can believe that," the woman murmured, and Muzaffahr grinned in pleasure at the compliment.

"And now, for what is madam in the market? Daggers, knives? I have many of my own make and design. This one"—he lifted proudly a wicked-looking knife with a serrated blade and a handle made of human bone—"has been blessed by the God himself. Or perhaps poison—the favorite of genteel ladies?" He gestured to several shelves built into the cavernlike walls of the hole in the ground. Jars of all shapes and sizes stood in neat rows, each with a label attached. "I have poisons that will kill within seconds and leave no trace upon the victim's body."

Gliding closer, Meryem read the inscriptions on each jar with the air of one who knows her wares. Her eyes lighted on a heavy stone crock, and the ironmonger nodded. "I see you are an expert. That is an excellent choice. Takes thirty days to work. The victim suffers the most excruciating agonies the entire time. Ideal for a rival for your man's love." He started to lift the lid, but the woman shook her head and turned away.

"Ah, my rings. So it is not a rival then, but a lover? I know, you see. I know how the needs of women and how they prefer to work. I am a sensitive man, madam, very sensitive. Let me see your hand. Slender fingers. I do not know whether I have any that small. Here is one—a chrysoberyl in a silver setting. It works thus."

Turning the stone a half-twist, Muzaffahr caused a tiny needle to spring out of the ring's setting. The sharp point gleamed in the lamp light.

"When you curl your finger under, like this, the point extends beyond the knuckle and is easily inserted into the flesh." The ironmonger gave the stone another half-turn and the needle disappeared. "And, once again, an innocent ring. I can treat the needle for you or perhaps Madam would prefer to purchase the where-with-all and do that herself?"

"Myself," said the woman in a low voice, muffled by her heavy veil.

"Very well. Shall you wear it?"

The shrouded head nodded. Holding out her hand, the

woman allowed the ironmonger to slip the ring upon her finger.

"How much and what kind? Fast acting or slow?"

"Fast," she said, and pointed to one of the jars upon the shelf.

"Excellent choice!" Muzaffahr murmured. "I bow before an expert."

"Never mind that. Hurry!" the woman spoke imperiously, and the ironmonger hastened to obey.

A small perfume vial was filled with the selected poison. The woman concealed it in the folds of her robe. Money exchanged hands. The lamp was extinguished, the ladder climbed, the trapdoor raised. Soon both stood in the ironmonger's hovel that was a hovel once more, the tools of the assassin's trade well hidden beneath the trapdoor.

"May Benario guide your hand and blind your victim's eyes." Muzaffahr repeated the Thieves' Blessing solemnly.

"May he indeed!" the woman whispered to herself and glided into the night.

That morning, when Achmed returned to his tent, he found the following message scrawled upon a piece of parchment.

My beloved, I overheard something this night which leads me to believe that your mother and the other followers of our Holy Akhran being held prisoner in Kich are in terrible danger. I have gone to warn them of their peril and do what I can to save them. As you value my life and those of the ones you love, say nothing of this to anyone! Trust in me. There is nothing you can do except remain here and perform your duty as the brave soldier that you are. To do anything else might bring suspicion down upon me. Pray to Akhran for us all. I love you more than life itself.

-Meryem

Achmed had learned to read in the Amir's service. Now he wished his eyes had been torn from his head rather than bring him such news. Rushing from his tent, missive in hand, the young man searched the camp. He dared not risk asking anyone if they had seen her, and hours later, dejected, he was forced to return to his tent alone.

She was gone. There was no doubt. She had fled in the night.

Achmed pondered. His overwhelming desire was to rush after her, but that would mean abandoning his post without leave—a treasonous offense. Not even Qannadi could shield the young soldier from the death penalty attached to desertion. He considered going to the Amir and explaining everything and requesting leave to return to Kich.

As you value my life and those of the ones you love, say nothing of this to anyone!

The words leapt off the paper and burned into his heart. No, there was nothing he could do. He must trust to her, to her nobility, her courage. Tears in his eyes, he pressed the letter passionately to his lips and sank down on the bed, gently caressing the blankets where her fragrance lingered still.

CHAPTER 3

Khardan and his companions left Serinda in the early hours of evening, intending to cross the Pagrah Desert during the cool hours of night. The journey was accomplished in silence, each person's thoughts wrapping around him or her as closely as their face masks. Lulled by the rhythmic swaying of the camels, cooled by the night air, Mathew stared moodily at the myriad stars above that seemed to be trying to outdo the myriad grains of sand below and wondered what lay ahead for them.

To judge by Khardan's grim expression and Zohra's darkly flashing eyes whenever Mathew broached the subject, it would not be pleasant.

"Surely no one saw us," Mathew repeated comfortingly over and over until the words plodded along in his mind in time to the camel's footsteps. "We have been gone months, but that can be explained. Surely no one saw us. . ."

But even as he repeated the litany, willing it to come true, he felt someone watching him and, twisting in the saddle, saw the cruel eyes of the Black Paladin glitter in the moonlight. Auda's hand patted the hilt of the dagger at his waist. Shuddering, Mathew turned his back on the Paladin and hunched over in the saddle, determined to put a closer guard upon his thoughts.

They rode far into the morning. Mathew had discovered that he could sink into a half doze that permitted part of his mind to sleep while another part kept awake and made certain he did not "drift." He knew Zohra was watching him from the corner of her dark eyes, and he had no desire to feel the sting of her camel stick across his back.

They slept through the heat of the day, and Khardan allowed them to rest in the early evening, then they set off again. The Calif figured to arrive in the camp at the Tel at dawn.

Their first glimpse of the nomad's campsite was not auspicious. The four stood atop a large sand dune, highly visible against the morning sun that was rising at their backs. Thus, though no one in the camp below could possibly recognize them—seeing only black silhouettes—Khardan declared by his willingness to be seen that he had no hostile intentions.

It took long minutes before anyone noticed them, however. A bad sign, apparently, thought Mathew, watching Khardan's face grow grimmer as he surveyed the scene below. In the center of the landscape was the Tel, the lone hill that jutted up inexplicably from the flat desert floor. A few patches of brownish green dotted its red surface—the cacti known as the Rose of the Prophet. Khardan's frowning gaze lingered on the Rose, flicked sideways to Zohra, and back again before any but the young man noticed.

Mathew knew the history of the Rose. Zohra had related to him how their God, Akhran, had brought about her detested marriage to Khardan by pronouncing that the two must wed and their warring tribes dwell together in peace until the ugly-looking cacti bloomed. Perhaps Khardan was surprised to note that the plant was still alive. Certainly Mathew was surprised. It seemed remarkable to him that anything—humans included—could live in such bleak and forbidding surroundings.

The oasis was nearly dry. Where before Mathew remembered a body of cool water surrounded by lush, green growth, there was now only a large, muddy puddle, a few straggling palms, and the tall desert grass clinging to life on its shore. A herd of scroungy-looking camels and a smaller herd of horses were tethered near the water.

The camp itself was divided into three separate and distinct groups. Mathew knew the colors of Khardan's tribe, the Akar, and he recognized the colors of Zohra's tribe, the Hrana. But he did not know the third until Khardan murmured, "Zeid's people," and he saw Zohra nod silently in response. The tents themselves were poor, makeshift affairs straggling across the sand without order or care. And though it was early morning and the camp should have been bustling with activity before the heat of the late summer's afternoon drove them to rest in their tents, there was no one about.

No women met to walk to the well together. No children scampered across the sand, rounding up the goats to be milked, leading the horses to be watered. At length the four saw one man leave his tent and make his way, shoulders sagging, to tend to the animals. He glanced around at his surroundings, more out of despairing boredom, it seemed, than out of care. His surprise when he saw them standing on the dune above him was evident, and he ran off, shouting, toward the tent of his Sheykh.

Khardan dismounted and led his camel down the dune, the others following. Auda moved to walk beside the Calif and would have displayed his sword openly, but Khardan put his hand upon the Paladin's arm.

"No," he said. "These are my people. They will do you no harm. You are a guest in their tents."

"It is not myself I fear for, brother," returned Auda, and Mathew shivered.

Men came running, and as Khardan approached the camp he slowly and purposefully removed the *haik* that covered his face. Mathew heard a collective sucking in of breaths. Another man broke and ran back through the silently staring throng.

Khardan came to the edge of the campsite. The men stood before him in a row, blocking his path. No one spoke. The only sound was the wind singing its eerie duet with the dunes.

Mathew's hands, clutching the camel's reins, were wet with sweat. The hope in his heart died, pierced by the hatred and anger clearly visible in the eyes of the Calif's people. The four stood facing the crowd that was growing larger every minute as the word spread. Khardan and Auda were in front, Zohra slightly behind and to their right, Mathew to their left. Glancing at Khardan, Mathew saw the man's jaws tighten. A trickle of sweat ran down his temple, glistened on the smooth, brown skin of his face, and disappeared into the black beard. Grimly, without speaking a word, Khardan took a step forward, then another and another until he was almost touching the first man in the crowd.

The man stood with arms folded across his chest, dark eyes burning. Khardan took another step. His intention to either walk through the man or over him was obvious. Shrugging, the man stepped back and to one side. The rest of the crowd followed his lead, backing up, clearing a path. Slowly, his head high, Khardan continued on into the campsite, leading his camel. Auda, beside him, kept one hand thrust into his robes. Mathew and Zohra followed.

Unable to bear the stare of the eyes, the enmity that beat on them with the heat of the sun, Mathew kept his gaze fixed on his feet and tried to control a tremor in his legs. Once he sneaked a quick glance at Zohra and saw her walking majestically, chin in the air, her eyes fixed on the sky as if there were nothing worthy of her notice any lower.

Envying her the courage and pride that refused to give way to fear, Mathew shivered and sweat beneath his robes and kept his eyes on the ground, nearly walking into the rear end of Khardan's camel when the group suddenly came to a halt.

There had been a spoken command; Mathew remembered hearing it through the blood pounding in his ears, and now someone took the camel's reins from his nerveless hand and was leading the beast away. With some vague thought of covering Khardan's back, Mathew moved forward, only to bump into Auda, who was doing the same thing with far more speed and adeptness.

"Keep out of the way, Blossom," Auda ordered harshly, beneath his breath.

Flushing, feeling frightened and clumsy and useless, Mathew backed up and felt Zohra's hand catch hold of his and thrust him behind her. Reluctantly, lifting his eyes, Mathew saw the reason for their halt.

Three men stood before them. One—a scrawny, bandy-legged man with a perpetually gloomy expression—Mathew recognized easily as Sheykh Jaafar, Zohra's father. The other was a short, fat man with an oily-looking face and neatly trimmed black beard. This, Mathew assumed, must be the Zeid that Khardan had mentioned on the dune. The other man seemed familiar, but Mathew could not place him until Khardan, his voice tight, his breathing heavy, said softly, "Father."

Mathew gasped audibly and felt Zohra's nails dig rebukingly through the folds of cloth and into his flesh. This was Majiid! But what dreadful change had come over the man? The giant frame had collapsed. The man who had once towered over the short Jaafar now stood even with him. The shoulders that had once squared in defiance were stooped and rounded in defeat. The hands that wielded steel in battle hung limply at his side, the feet that had proudly trod the desert shuffled through the sand. Only the eyes shone fierce and proud as the eyes of a hawk;

the large, fleshless nose jutting forward from the outthrust head might have been the tearing beak of a predatory bird.

"Do not call me father," said the old man in a voice shaking with suppressed fury. "I am no one's father! I have no sons!"

"I am your eldest son, Father," said Khardan evenly. "Calif of my people. I have come back."

"My eldest son is dead!" retorted Majiid, froth forming on his lips. "Or if not, he should be!"

Khardan flinched; his face grew pale.

"You were seen!" cried Jaafar's shrill voice. "The djinn, Fedj, saw you fleeing the battle dressed as a woman, in company with that wildcat I once called daughter and the madman! The djinn swore it with the Oath of Sul! Deny it, if you can!"

"I do not deny it," said Khardan, and a low muttering rippled through the crowd of men. Auda's dark eyes darted here and there, his hand came out of his robes, and Mathew saw steel flash in the sun.

"I do not deny that I fled the battle!" Khardan raised his voice for all to hear. "Nor do I deny that I was dressed as. . ." he faltered a moment, thten continued strongly, "as a woman. But I deny that I fled a coward!"

"Slay him!" Majiid pointed. "Slay them all!" His words bubbled on his tongue in his fury. "Slay the coward and his witch-wife!" The Sheykh himself reached for his scimitar, but his hand closed over nothing. He had long ago ceased to wear his weapon. "My sword!" he howled, turning on a cringing servant. "Bring me my sword! Never mind! Give me yours!" Rounding on one of his men, he grabbed the sword from the man's hand and, swinging it ferociously, turned on Khardan.

Auda slid in front of the Calif with practiced grace and ease, bringing his sword up to meet Majiid's wild blow. The Black Paladin's next stroke would have sliced Majiid's head from his shoulders had not Khardan and Sheykh Zeid each restrained the two.

"Cursed for eternity is the father who slays his son!" gasped Zeid, grappling with Majiid for the weapon.

"These are my people! I forbid you to harm them!" Khardan caught hold of Auda.

"The Calif must be fairly judged and have a chance to speak in his own defense," Jaafar cried.

Majiid struggled briefly, impotently. Then, seeing it was useless in his weakened condition to try to break free, he hurled the sword aside. "Pah!" Glaring at Khardan, he spit on the ground at his son's feet and, turning, shambled back to his dwelling.

"Take the Calif under guard to my tent," ordered Zeid hastily, hearing the low rumbling of the crowd. Several of the Sheykh's men closed in on Khardan. Divesting him of sword and dagger, they started to lead him away, but Auda stepped in front of them.

"What of this man?" demanded Jaafar, pointing a trembling finger at Auda.

"I go with Khardan," said the Black Paladin.

"He is a guest," Khardan stated, "and shall be treated as such for the honor of our tribes. "

"He drew steel," muttered Zeid, regarding the formidable Auda warily.

"In my defense. He is sworn to protect me."

There was some awed murmuring over this. Clearly it went against Zeid's heart to offer the black-clad Auda his hospitality, but as Khardan had said, their tribal honor hung in the balance. "Very well," said Zeid reluctantly. "He shall be granted the guest period of three days, so long as he does nothing to violate it. You take him to your tent," he instructed Jaafar.

The Sheykh opened his mouth to protest, caught Zeid's glare, and snapped it shut. With an ungracious *salaam*. Jaafar bowed and indicated that his home was Auda's home and showed the way with a sweep of his bony hand.

Nodding reassuringly to the Black Paladin, Khardan suffered himself to be led away by his captors. Auda followed them, watching until the tent flap closed behind the Calif; then, with a black-eyed stare at Jaafar that made the little man fall back a pace, he bowed sardonically and walked over to the tent that the Sheykh had indicated as his.

"And what of your daughter?" Zeid shouted after Jaafar. "I don't want the witch near me!" screeched the Sheykh.

"Send her with her accursed husband!"

Though Zohra's face was veiled, Mathew saw the scorn in her eyes.

Sheykh Zeid al Saban was clearly at a loss. He could not take the woman into his dwelling. Such a thing would not be seemly. "There are no women's tents," he said to her apologetically. "Since there are no women." The Sheykh dithered. "You"—he finally pointed at one of his tribesmen—"vacate your dwelling. Take her there and keep her under guard."

The man nodded, and he and another hurried forward to lead Zohra away. They would have taken her by the arms, but the look she flashed them warned them back as effectively as if she had wielded a blade. Tossing her head, she walked where they led. She had not spoken one word the entire time.

The only one who remained behind was Mathew, standing alone, his face burning beneath a hundred glowering gazes.

"What of the madman?" said someone at last.

Mathew closed his eyes against the baleful stares, his fists clenched as though he held his courage in his hands.

"We may not touch him," said Zeid at last. "He has seen the face of Akhran. He is free to go. Besides," said the Sheykh, turning away and shrugging, "he is harmless."

The rest of the men—eager to put their heads together and discuss this development and speculate on what the Sheykhs would decide and how soon the execution of the coward and his witch-wife would take place—agreed without question and hurried off to their gossip.

Opening his eyes, Mathew found himself standing alone.

CHAPTER 4

O n the evening of the day they had arrived in the camp at the Tel, Mathew walked toward the tent where Zohra was being held prisoner. It was near Khardan's tent, he noted, as he approached. Standing at the entrance to both were guards, who appeared uncomfortable and ill-at-ease, their hands constantly straying to touch their swords reassuringly. The reason for their discomfiture was readily apparent. In the shadow of a nearby tent Auda squatted on the desert floor, the dark, flat eyes never leaving Khardan's dwelling. The Black Paladin had posted himself at noontime. He had not moved all day, and it did not seem likely, from his watchful manner, that he intended to move ever again.

Avoiding the gaze of those eyes that he knew all too well, not envying the guards their being forced to endure that malevolent stare for hours on end, Mathew quickened his pace to Zohra's tent.

Both guards bowed with the officious politeness the nomads always exhibited to the madman. Mathew had, after all, seen the face of the God. It would never do to insult him, lest he take it out on them after death when they themselves would come face-to-face with Akhran. This gave Mathew a certain power over them, albeit a negative one. He intended to use it, and he had even changed back into women's clothing that he had begged of Jaafar in order to enhance his appearance of being mentally infirm.

"I want to see Zohra," he said to the guard. He indicated a bundle he held in his hands. "I have some things for her."

"What things?" demanded the guard, reaching for the bundle.

"Women's things," Mathew said, holding onto it firmly.

The guard hesitated—certain private belongings of women were not considered suitable to the sight of men. "At least let me feel to make certain you do not carry a weapon," the guard said after a moment's pause.

Willingly Mathew held out the bundle, and the guard grasped it and prodded it and poked at it and, satisfied at last, let Mathew pass into the tent without comment.

No man would have been permitted to enter this tent, Mathew thought bitterly, closing the flap behind him. But a madman—a man who chose to hide himself in the clothes of a woman rather than face an honorable death, a man they shun, a man they consider harmless—me they will allow inside.

An honorable death. The words caused his heart to constrict painfully. Khardan would die before he let his people brand their Calif a coward. That must not happen.

We will see how "harmless" I am, Mathew resolved.

Zohra sat cross-legged on the bare tent floor. There were cushions in the tent, but after one look and a wrinkling of his nose, Mathew understood why she had tossed them into a comer rather than use them for her comfort. She glanced up at him without welcome or hope.

"What do you want?" she asked dully.

"I came to bring you a change of clothing," said Mathew for the guard's benefit.

Zohra made a disdainful movement with her hand, started to speak, then stopped as Mathew swiftly put his finger to his lips.

"Shhh," he warned. Kneeling down beside her, he unfolded the garments.

"A knife?" Zohra whispered eagerly, but the fire in her eyes faded when she saw what the bundle contained. "Goatskin?" she said in disgust, lifting the limp pieces of cured skin with a thumb and forefinger.

"Shhh!" Mathew hissed urgently. *Kohl*, used to outline the eyes, and several falcon feathers tumbled out onto the floor. Seeing them, Zohra understood. The dark eyes flared. "Scrolls!"

"Yes," said Mathew, breathing his words into her ear.

"I have a plan."

"Good!" Zohra smiled and lifted a feather whose quill had been sharpened to a fine point. "Teach me the scrolls of death!"

"No, no!" Mathew checked an exasperated sigh. He should have known this would happen. He considered telling Zohra that he could not take a human life, that the ways of his people were peaceful. He considered the notion briefly and, sighing, dismissed it just as fast. He could imagine Zohra's reaction. She already thought him crazy. "You will make scrolls of water," he whispered patiently.

Zohra scowled. "Water! Bah! I will kill them. Kill them all! Beginning with that sniveling swine, my father—"

"Water!" said Mathew sternly. "My plan is this—"

He was about to explain when voices came from outside.

"Let me in," demanded a grating voice at the near-by tent. "I will see the prisoner."

Mathew, drawing aside the tent flap ever so slightly, peeped outside.

It was Majiid, talking to Khardan's guard.

"Leave us," the old man ordered the guards. "I will not be in any danger and he will not run away. Not again."

Swiftly Mathew drew back. He and Zohra heard the guards' footsteps crunch over the sand. There was a moment's pause and Mathew could imagine Majiid glowering at the unmoving Auda, then they heard the tent flap thrown aside and Khardan's voice respectfully—if somewhat ironically—welcoming his father.

Zohra's guards were talking this over in low tones. Exchanging meaningful glances, both Zohra and Mathew crawled quietly to the rear of her tent. It stood close to Khardan's and, holding their breaths, they were able to hear much of the conversation between father and son.

"Have the Sheykhs determined my fate?"

"No," growled Majiid. "We meet tonight. You will be allowed to speak."

"Then why are you here?" Khardan's voice sounded weary, and Mathew wondered if he had been asleep.

There was silence as if the old man was struggling to speak the words. When they finally came out, they blurted forth, forced out past some great obstacle. "Tell them that the witch ensorcelled you. Tell them that it was her scheme to destroy our tribe. The Sheykhs will judge in your favor since you acted under the constraint of magic. Your honor will be restored."

Khardan was silent. Zohra's face was pale, but cool and impassive. Her eyes were liquid night. But she was not as calm as she seemed. Involuntarily she reached out and caught hold of Mathew's hand with her own. He squeezed it tightly, offering what poor comfort he could.

After all, Majiid had asked nothing of Khardan but that he speak the truth.

"What will happen to my wife?"

"What do you care?" Majiid demanded angrily. "She was never wife to you!"

"What will happen?" Khardan's voice had an edge of steel.

"She still be stoned to death—the fate of women who practice evil magic!"

They heard a rustling, as if Khardan rose to his feet. "No, father. I will not say this to the Sheykhs."

"Then your fate is in the hands of Akhran!" snarled Majiid bitterly, and they heard him storm from the tent, yelling loudly to the guards to take up their posts again as he left.

Mathew and Zohra started to return to their work when they heard Khardan speaking again—not to a human, but to his God. "My fate is in your hands, *Hazrat* Akbran," said the Calif reverently. "You took my life and gave it back to me for a reason. My people are in danger. Humbly I come before you and I beg you to show me how I may help them! If it means sacrificing my life, I will do so gladly! Help me, Akhran! Help me to help them!"

His voice died. A tear fell hot on Mathew's hand. Looking up, he saw its mate slide down Zohra's pallid cheek.

"I talk of killing them," she murmured. "He talks of saving them. Akhran forgive me."

She did not bother to wipe the tear away but moved swiftly and soundlessly back to the center of the tent. Taking up the quill she rubbed it in *kohl*, and bending over the goatskin, keeping it hidden from view in case anyone entered the tent, she began to laboriously trace out the arcane words that would bring water out of sand.

CHAPTER 5

The council convened shortly after Majiid left Khardan's tent, or at least Mathew assumed that this was the reason for a loud burst of raised voices and vehement arguing that carried clearly in the still night air. When he had first begun working on his scroll, he feared they might not have enough time to complete the work. But gradually, as the hours passed and the haranguing continued, Mathew relaxed. From the occasional shout, he gathered that the Sheykhs were fighting over whose side of the camp should hold the judgment and which Sheykh and whose *akasul* should preside.

Zeid claimed that since he was not near kin to any of the parties involved, he should be the one who sat in judgment. This precipitated an hour's shouting match over whether a father's mother's sister's seventh son's brother's son related to Majiid on the father's side was considered near kin. By the time this dispute was resolved (Mathew never did find out how), the argument over the site began again with an entirely new set of issues involved.

But though the bickering bought them time, Mathew found his feeling of ease seeping away. The yelling and the clamoring rasped on his nerves like a wood mason's file going across the grain. He found it increasingly hard to concentrate, and when he had ruined his second scroll by misspelling a word he had known how to spell since the age of six, he tossed down the quill in exasperation.

"After all, why should we hurry?" he said abruptly, startling Zohra. "They're not going to decide anything for a week! They couldn't agree on the number of suns in the sky! Jaafar would say it was one, Majiid would swear it was two and one was invisible, and Zeid would claim them both wrong and state that there were no suns in the sky and he would slit the throat of anyone who accused him of lying!"

"All will be determined by morning," returned Zohra softly. She knelt upon the floor, bent nearly double to trace the letters upon the goatskin. Her lips slowly and deliberately formed the sound of each letter she drew, as though this would somehow aid her hand in executing the symbol.

Executing. The word made Mathew's hand tremble, and he hastily clasped one over the other. "How do you know?" he asked irritably.

"Because they have it all decided in their minds already," Zohra returned, shrugging. She glanced up at Mathew, her eyes dark pools in the lamplight. "This is a serious matter. How would it look to the people if they made a decision in only a few hours?"

A sudden clashing of steel made Mathew jump and almost spring to his feet, thinking that they were coming for them. Zohra went on writing, however, and Mathew—realizing the sound was confined to the council tent—supposed bitterly that this matter of putting to death their Calif and his wife was so serious that the Sheykhs needed to shed some of their own blood first.

Maybe they'll all kill each other, he thought. Savages! Why do I bother? What do these barbarians matter to me? They think I'm mad! They are kind to me only out of superstition. I will always be some sort of strange and rare creature to them, never accepted. I will always be alone!

Mathew did not know his despairing thoughts were stamped plainly upon his face until an arm stole around his shoulders.

"Do not fear, Mat-hew," said Zohra gently. "Your plan is a good one! All will be well!"

Mathew clung to her, letting her touch comfort him until he became aware that her caressing fingers were no longer soothing but arousing. Hastily gulping, he sat back and looked at her with a wild hope beating in his chest. There was caring in the dark eyes, but not the kind for which he longed. The smooth face was expressive of worry, concern, nothing more.

But what more did he want? How could one be in love with two people at the same time?

Two people one could never have. . .

A groan escaped Mathew's lips.

"Are you sick again?" Zohra drew near, and Mathew, cringing, repelled her with an upraised hand.

"A slight pain. It will pass," he gasped.

"Where?" Zohra persisted.

"Here." Mathew sighed, and pressed his hand over his heart. "I've had it before. There is nothing you can do. Nothing anyone can do." That, at least, was truth enough. "We had better finish the magic if we are to be ready by morning," he added.

She still seemed inclined to speak, then checked herself and, after gazing intently at the young man, returned silently to her work.

She knows, he realized forlornly. She knows but does not know what to say. Perhaps she loved me once, or rather wanted me, but that was when I first came and she and I were both frightened and weak and lost. But now she has found what she sought; she is sure of herself, strong in her love for Khardan. She doesn't know it yet, she won't admit it. But it is there, like a rod of iron in her soul, and it is giving her strength.

And Khardan loves her, though he has armored himself against that love and fights it at every turn.

What can I do, who love them both?

"You can give them each other," came a voice soft and sad, echoing his heartbreak, yet with a kind of deep joy in it that he didn't understand.

"What did you say?" he asked Zohra.

"Nothing!" She glanced at him worriedly. "I said nothing. Are you sure you are all right, Mat-hew?"

He nodded, rubbing the back of his neck, trying to rid himself of a tickling sensation, as of feathers brushing against his skin.

CHAPTER 6

The following dawn the sun's first rays skimmed across the desert, crept through the holes in Majiid's tent, bringing silence with them. The arguing ceased. Zohra and Mathew glanced at each other. Her eyes were shadowed and red-rimmed from lack of sleep and the concentration she had devoted to her work. Mathew knew his must look the same or perhaps worse.

The silence of the morning was suddenly broken by the sound of feet crunching over sand. They heard the guards outside scramble to their feet, the sound of footsteps draw nearer. Both Mathew and Zohra were ready, each had been ready for over an hour now, ever since first light. Zohra was clad in the women's clothes Mathew had brought for her. They were not the fine silk she was accustomed to wearing, only a simple *chador* of white cotton that had been worn by the second wife in a poor man's household. Its simplicity became her, enhancing the newfound gravity of bearing. A plain white mantle covered her head and face, shoulders and hands. Held tightly in her hands, hidden by the folds of her veil, were several pieces of carefully rolled-up goatskin.

Mathew was dressed in the black robes he had acquired in Castle Zhakrin. Since he was able to come and go freely, he had left the tent in the middle of the night and searched the camp in the moonlit darkness until he found the camels they had ridden. Their baggage had been removed from the beasts, thrown down, and left to lie in the sand as though cursed. Mathew could have wished the robes—retrieved by Auda from their campsite on the shores of the Kurdin Sea—cleaner and less worse for wear, but he hoped that even stained and wrinkled they must still look impressive to these people who had never seen sorcerer's garb before.

Stealing back to the tent once he had changed his clothes,

Mathew noted the figure of the Black Paladin sitting unmoving before Khardan's tent. The slender white hand, shining in the moonlight as if it had some kind of light of its own, beckoned to him. Mathew hesitated, casting a worried glance at the watchful guards. Auda beckoned again, more insistently, and Mathew reluctantly approached him.

"Do not worry, Blossom," the man said easily, "they will not prevent us from speaking. After all, I am a guest and you are insane."

"What do you want?" Mathew whispered, squirming beneath the scrutiny of the flat, dispassionate eyes.

Auda's hand caught hold of the hem of Mathew's black robes, rubbing the velvet between his fingers. "You are planning something."

"Yes," said Mathew uncomfortably, with another glance at the guards.

"That is good, Blossom," said Auda softly, slowly twisting the black cloth. "You are an ingenious and resourceful young man. Your life was obviously spared for a purpose. I will be watching and waiting. You may count upon me."

He released the cloth from his grasp, smiled, and settled back comfortably. Mathew left, returning to Zohra's tent, uncertain whether to feel relieved or more worried.

The eyes of the guards opened wide when Mathew, clad in his black robes, emerged from the tent into the first light of day. The young wizard had brushed and combed his long red hair until it blazed like flame in the sunshine. The cabalistic marks, etched into the velvet in such a way that they could not be seen except in direct light, caught the sun's rays and appeared to leap out suddenly from the black cloth, astonishing all viewers.

Mathew's hands—gripping his own scrolls—were concealed in the long, flowing sleeves. He walked forward without saying a word or looking at anyone, keeping his eyes staring straight ahead. He saw, without seeming to, Khardan leave his tent, saw the puzzled look the man cast him. Mathew dared not respond or risk breaking the show of mystery he was wrapping around himself.

What the Archmagus would have said had he seen his pupil now came to Mathew's mind, and a wan smile nearly destroyed the illusion. "Cheap theatrics! Worthy of those who use magic to trap the gullible!" He could hear his old teacher rage on, as he had once a year at the beginning of First Quarter. "The true magus needs no black robes or conical hat! He could practice magic naked in the wilderness"—since no one dared laugh in the presence of the Archmagus, this statement always occasioned sudden coughing fits among the students and was later the source of whispered jokes for many nights to come-"practice magic naked in the wilderness if he has only the knowledge of his craft and Sul in his heart!"

Naked in the wilderness. Mathew sighed. The Archmagus was dead now, slaughtered by Auda's *goums*. The young wizard hoped the old man would understand and forgive what his pupil was about to do.

Looking neither to the right nor the left, Mathew made his way through the camp, past the ranks of staring nomads, and walked straight to the Tel. He seemed to travel blindly (although in reality he was watching where he was going and carefully avoided large obstacles), occasionally stumbling most convincingly over small rocks and other debris in his path.

Behind him he could hear the men following after him, the Sheykhs questioning everyone as to what was going on, the nomads responding with confused answers.

"This is ridiculous!" Zeid said angrily. "Why doesn't someone stop him?"

"He is mad," muttered Majiid sullenly.

"*You* stop him," suggested Jaafar.

"Very well, I will!" humphed Zeid.

The short, pudgy Sheykh—hands raised, mouth open-planted himself in front of Mathew. The wizard, staring straight ahead, kept walking and would have run the Sheykh down had not Zeid—at the last moment—scrambled to get out of his way.

"He didn't even see me!" gasped the Sheykh.

"He is being led by the God!" cried Jaafar in an awed voice.

"He is being led by the God!" The word spread through the crowd like flame cast on oil, and Mathew blessed the man in his heart.

Hoping everyone—including Khardan—was following him, but not daring to look behind, Mathew reached the Tel and begin to climb it, slipping and falling among the rocks and the scraggly-looking Rose of the Prophet. When he was about halfway up, he faced around and spread his arms wide, keeping the goatskin scrolls concealed by turning his palms away from his audience.

"People of the Akar, the Hrana, and the Aran, attend to my words," he shouted in a voice as deep as he could possibly make it.

Standing at the foot of the Tel directly below him was Zohra. Khardan, held by his guards, was staring darkly at Mathew, perhaps convinced that the young man had now truly gone mad. Near him, Auda—face covered by his *haik*—watched with a glint of a smile in his dark eyes and his hand near his dagger. The sight of him made Mathew nervous, and he quickly shifted his gaze.

"Madman, come down!" Majiid sounded impatient. "We have no time for this—"

"No time for the word of Akhran?" Mathew called out sternly.

The crowd muttered. Heads came together.

"Get him down from there, and let's get on with the judgment," ordered Zeid, waving at several of his men.

At first Mathew thought they were going to refuse to obey, and they thought so, too, it seemed, until Zeid grew red in his face, swelling indignantly at this disobedience. Three men began to climb the Tel.

Mathew muttered a swift prayer to Promenthas and another to Sul, then—reciting the words he had written with such deliberation—he hurled one of the scrolls to the ground at his feet.

An explosion sent fragments of rock and dust shooting out in all directions. Purplish green smoke rose up, obscuring the young wizard from sight. Trying to keep from coughing—he'd remembered to hold his breath only at the last minute—Mathew attempted to compose himself so that, when the smoke cleared, the crowd would see a sorceror in command, not a young man, tears running down his cheeks from the smoke in his eyes, gagging at the smell of sulphur.

Cheap theatrics, maybe. But it worked.

The three men who had been climbing up the hill were now scrambling back as if for their lives. Zeid had gone white as his turban, Majiid's eyes bulged, and Jaafar had covered his head with his hands. Even Zohra, who knew what he was going to do, appeared impressed.

"I have not only seen the face of Akhran, I have spoken to

him," Mathew shouted. "As you can see, he has lent me his fire! Attend to my words or I will cast it among you!"

"Speak then," growled Majiid in a tone that said plainly, "Let's humor him; then we can get on with our business."

This was rather disconcerting. Mathew had no choice, however, but to plunge ahead.

"I do not intend to deny what the djinn Fedj told you. Zohra and I did carry this man"—he pointed at Khardan, who was shaking his head, making signals that Mathew should keep silent—"away, disguised as a woman!

"But," Mathew shouted over the murmurings of the crowd, "it was not a live body we carried. It was a corpse. Khardan, your Calif, was dead!"

As Mathew expected, this caught their attention. There was a rustling as those who had been talking demanded a repeat of the madman's words from those who had been listening. Silence descended; the air was heavy and charged as a thundercloud.

"You, his father, know it to be true!" Mathew jabbed a finger at Majiid. "You knew in your heart your son was dead. You told them he was dead, didn't you!" The pointing finger encompassed the tribe.

Taken aback, the Sheykh could do nothing but glower, his white eyebrows bristling fiercely, and glare at Mathew. There were nods from his tribesmen and narrowed, suspicious glances from those not of his tribe.

"How many of you have ridden into battle with this man?" Mathew's finger shifted and aimed at Khardan. "How many of you have seen his valor with your own eyes? How many owe your very lives to his courage?"

Lowered heads, shameful glances. Mathew knew he had them now.

"And yet this is the man you charge with cowardice? I say to you that Khardan was dead before any of the rest of you ever found your way to the battlefield!" Mathew quickly followed up his advantage. "Princess Zohra and I, having fought off the Amir's troops who would have taken us prisoner as they took the rest of the women, saw the Calif fall, mortally wounded. We took him from the field so that the foul *kafir* would not defile his body.

"And we dressed him in women's clothing."

The hush was breathless; not a man so much as moved lest he

miss Mathew's next words.

"We did that—not to hide him from the troops," said Mathew in a quiet voice that he knew all must strain to hear. "We did that to hide him from Death!"

Now they breathed, all at once, in a rush of air that was like a night breeze. Mathew risked a swift glance at Khardan. No longer scowling, the Calif was attempting to keep his face as expressionless as possible. Either he had some glimpse of where Mathew was headed, or he now trusted the young man to lead him there blindfolded.

"Death was searching the field for victims of the battle, and since we knew she must be looking for warriors, we clad Khardan in women's clothes. Thus Death did not find him. Your God, *Hazrat* Akhran, found him.

"We fled Death, escaping into the desert. And there Akhran appeared to us and told us that Khardan should live, but that in return for his life he must offer his aid to the first stranger who came by. The Calif drew breath and opened his eyes, and it was then that this man"—Mathew pointed at Auda, who was standing alone amidst the crowd, no one wanting to come too near him—"came to us and asked for our aid. His God, Zhakrin, was being held prisoner by Quar. He needed us to help free him.

"Mindful of the bargain he had made with Akhran, Khardan agreed, and we went with the stranger and freed his God. The stranger is a knight in his land, a man sworn to honor. I ask you, Auda ibn Jad, is this the truth I speak?"

"It is," replied ibn lad in his cool, deep voice. Removing the snake dagger from his belt, he lifted it high in the air. "I call upon my God, Zhakrin, to witness my oath. May he plunge this knife into my breast if I am lying!"

Auda let go the knife. It did not fall but remained poised in the air, hovering above his chest. The crowd gasped in astonishment and awe. Mathew recovered his voice—he had not been expecting that—and continued, somewhat shakily.

"We left the homeland of ibn Jad and traveled back to the desert, for Akhran had come to us once again to tell us that his people were in danger and needed their Calif. We crossed the Sun's Anvil—"

"No! Impossible!"

The nomads, who could swallow to a man a child's tale about

Khardan fleeing Death in a disguise, scoffed at the thought of anyone crossing the *kavir*.

"We did!" Mathew cried them down. "And this is how. Your Calif is not the only one to receive a gift from Akhran. He bestowed a gift upon your Princess, as well."

Their lives now depended on Zohra. The tribesmen turned wary, suspicious eyes upon her. Mathew nearly closed his, afraid to watch, afraid that the spell wouldn't work, that in her agitation she had written the wrong words or written them the wrong way or a hundred other things that could go wrong with the gift of Sul.

Taking the goatskin from the folds of her robes, Zohra held it up and read the words in a clear voice. The letters began to wriggle and writhe and one by one fell off the skin onto the sand at her feet. Those near her began to shout and exclaim and stumbled over themselves to fall back, while those who could not see shouted and questioned and pushed forward. Mathew could not see the pool of blue water at the woman's feet—her white robes blowing in the wind obscured the view. But he knew it must be there, from the reaction of those around her and from the look of pride that swept over Khardan's face as he gazed at her.

"Khardan has returned to you—a Prophet of Akhran. Zohra has returned to you—a Prophetess of Akhran. They have returned to lead you to war! Will you follow them?"

This was where Mathew expected the rousing cheer. It was not forthcoming, and the young man stared at the crowd beneath him in rising apprehension.

"That is all very well," said Sheykh Zeid smoothly, stepping forward. "And we have seen some fine tricks, tricks worthy of the *souk* of Khandar, I might add. But what about the djinn?"

"Yes! The djinn!" came the cry from the crowd.

"I say to you"—Zeid faced the people, raising his stubby arms for silence—"I say that I will name Khardan Prophet and I will follow him to battle or to Sul's Hell if the Calif chooses *provided* he can return to us our djinn! Surely," Zeid continued, spreading his hands, "Akhran will do no less for his Prophet!"

The crowd cheered. Majiid shot his son a dark glance that said, "I warned you." Jaafar eyed Zohra fearfully, seemingly expecting her to turn the entire desert to an ocean that would drown them all and Zohra was glaring at the people as if this idea was not far from her mind. Khardan cast Mathew a grateful, resigned glance, thanking the young man for the vain attempt.

No! It wouldn't be in vain!

Mathew took a step forward. "He will bring back the djinn!" he announced. "In a week's time—"

"Tonight!" countered Zeid.

"Tonight!" clamored the crowd.

"By tonight," Mathew agreed, his heart in his throat. "The djinn will return by tonight."

"If not, then he dies," said Zeid calmly. "And the witch with him."

There was nothing more to say, and Mathew could not have been heard in the uproar had he wanted to say it. Head bowed, wondering how he'd managed to lose control of things so rapidly, the young wizard made his way dejectedly down the Tel. When he reached the bottom, Zohra put her arm consolingly around him.

"I'm sorry," he said to her, when a voice interrupted him.

Khardan, surrounded by guards, stood before him.

"Thank you, Mat-hew," said the Calif quietly. "You did what you could."

Mathew had the sudden strange sensation of being wrapped in a blanket of feathers.

"The djinn will be back!" he said, and suddenly, for some reason, he believed his own words. "They will be back!"

Khardan sighed and shook his head. "The djinn are gone, Mat-hew. As for Akhran, he may be defeated himself now, for all we—"

"No, look!" Reaching down, Mathew touched one of the ugly cacti. "Tell me how this remains alive, when all around is dead and withered! It is because Akhran is alive—just barely, perhaps, but he lives! You must continue to have faith, Khardan! You must!"

"I agree with Blossom, brother," said Auda unexpectedly, coming up behind them. "Faith in our Gods and in each other is all we have left now. Faith alone stands between us and doom."

CHAPTER 7

"Faith. I must have faith," Mathew repeated to himself over and over during the day that lasted far too long and seemed likely to end all too rapidly.

Minute after minute slid past, precious as drops of water from a punctured *girba*. Mathew tasted each minute; he touched it, heard it fall away from him and vanish in the vast pool of time. Every noise—be it the barking of one of the mangy camp dogs or the shifting of a guard outside Zohra's tent—brought him to his feet, peering eagerly out the tent flap.

But it was nothing, always nothing.

Noon came and went and the camp quieted, everyone resting in the blazing heat. Mathew gazed enviously at Zohra. Exhausted by her night's work and the tension of the morning, she had fallen asleep. He wondered if Khardan was sleeping, too. Or was he lying in shadowed darkness, thinking that if he'd done the talking—as, by rights, he should have—all would have gone well?

Sighing heavily, Mathew let his aching head sink into his hands. "I should have kept out of this," he reprimanded himself. "These aren't my people. I don't understand them! Khardan could have handled it. I should have trusted him—"

Someone was in the tent!

Mathew saw a shadow from the corner of his eye but had no time to draw a breath before a hand clapped firmly over his mouth.

"Do not make a sound, Blossom," breathed a voice in his ear. "You will alert the guards!"

His heart pounding so that he saw starbursts before his eyes, Mathew nodded. Auda released his grip and, motioning to Mathew to wake Zohra, melted back into the darker shadows of the tent.

It seemed a shame to disturb her. Let her have her few last moments of peace before Auda gestured peremptorily, the cruel eyes narrowed. "Zohra!" Mathew shook her gently. "Zohra, wake up." She was awake and alert instantly, sitting up among the cushions and staring at Mathew. "What? Have they—"

"Shh, no." He pointed toward Auda, barely visible in the dim light at the back of the tent. The Paladin had removed the facecloth and now pressed his finger against his lips, commanding silence.

Zohra shrank away from him in fright; then seeming to recollect herself, she stiffened and glared at him fiercely.

Moving softly, Auda crept over to them and, beckoning them near, said in a barely heard undertone, "Blossom, what killing magic can you have ready?"

Deadly cold swept over Mathew, despite the sweltering heat. His fingers went numb, his heart ceased to function, he could not draw in air. Slowly, unable to speak, he shook his head.

"What? You don't know any?" Auda said, his dark eyes glinting.

Mathew hesitated. That was what he would answer. He didn't know any. The Black Paladin must accept this. The words were on his lips, but he saw then that he had waited too long. The lie must be plain in his eyes. He shook as with a chill and said tightly, "I will not kill."

"Mat-hew!" Zohra's fingers dug into his arm. "Can you do this . . . killing magic?"

"He can do it," Auda said calmly. "He won't, that's all. He will let you and Khardan die first."

Mathew flushed. "I thought you were the one who counseled faith!"

"Faith in one hand." Auda held forth his left hand, closed in a fist. "This in the other." His right hand reached into his robes and brought forth the snake dagger. "So my people have survived."

"We returned to the Tel to save your people!" Mathew looked to Zohra. "And now you want to slaughter them?"

Zohra ran her tongue over her lips; her face was pale, her eyes wide and burning with a fierce, inner fire of hope that was slowly being quenched. "I—I don't know," she whispered distractedly.

"We do what we must do! These"—the Paladin motioned outside the tent—"are not all of your people." Auda's voice was soft and lethal. It might have been the serpent-headed dagger speaking. "The women and children and young men are being held prisoner in Kich. We can save them, but only if you and Khardan are alive! If you die—" He shrugged.

"He is right, Mat-hew."

"My God forbids the taking of life—" Mathew began. "There is no war in your land?" Auda questioned coolly. "The magi do not fight?"

"I do not fight!" Mathew cried, forgetting himself. The guards stirred outside. Auda's eyes flashed dangerously. He twisted to his feet. A ray of the burning sun that filtered through the tent flap glinted off the blade of the knife in his hand.

Mathew tensed, sweat running down his body. The guards did not enter, and it occurred to Mathew that they must be half-stupified with the heat.

Settling himself beside Mathew, Auda took hold of the young man's arm and squeezed it painfully. His breath burned Mathew's skin. "You've seen a man beheaded before, haven't you, Blossom? Swift and fast, a single stroke of the blade across the back of the neck."

Mathew cringed, going limp in the man's cruel grasp. Once again he saw John kneeling in the sand, saw the *goum* raise his sword, saw the steel flash in the sun's dying light. . . Auda's grip tightened; he drew Mathew closer.

"This is how Khardan will die. Not a bad death. A flash of pain and then nothing. But not Zohra. Have you ever watched anyone being stoned to death, Blossom? A rock strikes the head. The victim, bleeding and dazed and in pain, tries desperately to avoid the next. It hits the arm with a crunching sound. Her bones break. Again she turns, trying to flee, but there is nowhere to run. Another rock thuds into her back. She falls. Blood runs in her eyes. She cannot see, and the terror grows, the pain mounts. . ."

"No!" Mathew clenched his fists in agony behind his head, covering his ears with shaking arms.

Auda released him. The Paladin, sitting back, gazed on him with satisfaction.

"You will help us, then."

"Yes," said Mathew through trembling lips. He could not look at Zohra. He had seen her in his mind's eye, lying limp and lifeless on the blood-splattered sand, crimson staining the white robe, the black hair clotted with red. "The spell I cast this morning." He swallowed, trying to maintain his voice. "More powerful. . . much more powerful. . ."

"You will use the magic of Sul. I will call down the wrath of my God," said Auda. "Those we do not stop will be too terrified to chase after us. I will have the camels ready. We can make our way to Kich. What components do you need for this spell of yours, Blossom? I assume this one cannot be cast using the skin of a goat."

"Saltpeter," Mathew mumbled. "It's a chemical. Perhaps, the residue from the urine of horses—"

"I refuse!" cried a long-suffering voice. "It is bad enough that I must clean up the tent after madam's cushion—ripping tantrums. Bad enough that I never have a moment's peace in which to eat a quiet bite. Bad enough that I am ordered to go here, fetch this, do that! But I refuse"—a curl of smoke flowed out of one of Zohra's rings and began to take shape and form in the center of the tent—"I absolutely refuse," said a fat djinn with great dignity, "to fetch horse piss."

No one spoke or moved. All stared at the djinn dazedly. Then Zohra leaped forward. "Usti!" she cried.

"No, madam! Don't!" The djinn flung his flabby arms protectively over his head. "Don't! I beg of you! Where are the horses? Hand me a bucket! Just don't hurt me—I . . . madam! Really! You are a married woman!"

Flushing bright red, the scandalized djinn fended off Zohra, who was hugging and kissing him and laughing hysterically.

"What is going on in there?" demanded a guard.

Auda slipped out of the tent, disappearing as swiftly and silently as if he were a djinn himself.

"Where are Sond and Fedj and Pukah?" Zohra asked suddenly. "Answer me!" she insisted, shaking the fat djinn until his teeth rattled in his head.

"Ah! T-t-this is m-more like it-t-t," stuttered Usti. "If m-m-madam will re-l-lease m-me, I will—"

"The djinn!" A guard, thrusting his way into the tent, stared at Usti in awe. "The djinn are back! Sheykh Jaafar!" He turned and fled, and Mathew could hear him shouting as he ran. "Jaafar, *sidi!* The djinn are back! The madman spoke truly! Khardan is a Prophet! He will lead us to defeat the *kafir!* Our people are saved!"

Relief thawed Mathew, melting his anguish. Hurrying outside, he saw Khardan emerge from his tent in company with Sond, Fedj, and a huge, black-skinned djinn that the young wizard did not recognize.

But where, Mathew wondered, is Khardan's djinn? Where is Pukah?

The Sheykhs came running. Zeid's round face was red with pleasure and delight. He declared to anyone who would listen that he had always known Khardan was a Prophet and he—Zeid al Saban—was responsible for proving it. Jaafar's mouth gaped wide in astonishment. He started to speak, inhaled a large quantity of dust kicked up by the gathering crowd of cheering tribesmen, and would have choked to death had not Fedj solicitously pounded his master on the back.

Majiid said nothing. The old man ran straight to his son and, flinging his arms around him, cried the first tears he had shed in over fifty years. Khardan embraced his father, tears streaming down his own cheeks, and the men from all the tribes united to cheer wildly.

When Zohra stepped from her tent, they cheered her, too. Jaafar darted over to press his daughter to his bosom but, daunted by the fire in her eye and recollecting certain unfortunate statements he had made concerning her, decided to give her a gingerly pat on the arm. The Sheykh then ducked hurriedly behind the muscular Fedj.

Standing tall and upright, his arm around his son's shoulder, Majiid faced the dancing, singing crowd and was about to call—somewhat belatedly—for a celebration. Zohra was walking over to stand next to her husband when a disturbance at the rear of the crowd caused those in front to turn around, their yells dying on their lips.

A rider was approaching. Coming from the east, the figure on horseback was muffled to the eyes, and there was no telling who or what it was. It was alone, and so no weapons were drawn.

The horse, covered with lather, foam dripping from its mouth, dashed into camp. Men scrambled out of its way. The rider checked it in its headlong course, pausing to scan the faces as though searching for someone.

Finding the person sought, the rider guided the weary animal straight to Khardan.

The rider drew aside a veil covering the head, revealing a quantity of golden hair that shone brightly in the sun. Holding out her hands to Khardan, Meryem cried out his name and then fell, fainting, from her horse into his arms.

CHAPTER 8

nd so," Sond finished his tale solemnly, "Pukah sacrificed himself, luring Kaug to the mountain of iron and tricking the 'efreet inside while the immortal, Asrial, guardian angel of the madman—I beg your pardon, *Effendi*." Sond bowed to Mathew. "Asrial, guardian angel of a great and powerful sorcerer, slammed shut the doors of the mountain, and now both Kaug and Pukah are sealed forever inside. Since the 'efreet is no longer stirring up strife among the immortals, many of us have banded together and now almost all on the heavenly plane have united to fight Quar."

The men who crowded in and around the tent nodded gravely and murmured among themselves, rattling swords and intimating by their actions that it was time they, too, went to battle.

"May I speak, My Lord?" said Meryem timidly from her seat next to the Calif.

"Certainly, lady," replied Khardan, looking at her fondly.

Next to Mathew, Zohra growled deep in her throat, like a hungry lioness. Mathew closed his hand over hers, wanting to hear what Meryem had to say.

"It is very noble of the Calif to have sacrificed his djinn for the sake of his people, and it is a wonderful thing that the evil Kaug has been finally rendered harmless, but I fear that this—instead of helping our people in Kich—has only put them in the most terrible danger."

"What do you mean, woman?" Sheykh Zeid demanded.

Aware that all eyes were on her, Meryem became suitably pale and more timid than before. Khardan, taking hold of her hand in his, urged her to courage. Flushing, Meryem cast him a grateful glance and continued. "The Imam returns to Kich in two weeks time. He has proclaimed that if your people being held prisoner in Kich have not converted to Quar by then, he will put them—every one—to the sword."

"Is this possible?" Khardan demanded, shocked.

"I fear so, Calif," said Zeid. "He has done it before, in Meda and Bastine and other cities. I, myself, heard this same threat. If, as the djinn say, Quar is truly desperate now—" he shrugged his fat shoulders despairingly.

"We must rescue them, then," said Khardan firmly.

"But we cannot attack Kich—"

"I know a secret way into the city," said Meryem eagerly, her eyes shining. "I can lead you!"

Rising to her feet, Zohra stalked out of the tent. Khardan saw her leave, and it seemed he started to say something, then shook his head slightly and turned back to the conversation around, him. Mathew, casting the Calif an exasperated look, hurried to catch up with Zohra.

"We must tell him!" he said urgently.

"No!" Zohra said, angrily shaking off Mathew's band from her arm. "Let him make a fool of himself over the *houri*!"

"But if he knew she tried to murder you—"

"You told him about the spell she cast over him!" Zohra whirled and faced Mathew. "Did he listen? Did he believe? Bah!" She turned, continued walking, and stormed into her tent.

Mathew took a step after her, then stopped. He took a step back to the Calif's tent and stopped again. Confused, upset, and uncertain what to do, the young wizard turned his footsteps toward the open desert, the coolness of the oasis.

Though night had fallen, the sand radiated so much heat from the day that it would be some time before the temperature became bearable.

"I told him about Meryem casting the spell on him. I told him about her trying to capture him and take him to the Amir. Obviously he didn't believe me, or maybe it flattered him to think she cared so much for him. Why can't he see?" Mathew fumed. "The man is intelligent about everything else! Why, in this one instance, is he such a blind fool?"

Had Mathew been more experienced in the sweet torment of love, he would never have asked the question, let alone been unable to find the answer. But he wasn't, and he fretted and swore and paced back and forth until he worked himself into a fevered sweat that dried on his body and set him to shivering as night's chill grew.

When he became aware, finally, that the babble of voices had ceased, he realized it was late, very late at night. The meeting had broken up, the tribesmen wending their ways to their tents. Weariness overwhelmed the young man. Returning to the camp that was empty and silent, he discovered that by night all tents look alike. Mathew stumbled sleepily and irritably first this direction, then that, hoping to find some late roamer who could guide him. Catching sight of movement, he headed toward the person, a plea for aid on his lips. The words died unspoken, and Mathew—wide awake—darted back into the shadow of a tent, out of the light cast by stars and a half-moon.

A lithe figure glided through the camp. She was wrapped in silken veils, but Mathew had no trouble recognizing the delicate, diminutive stature, the graceful walk. Stealthily the young man followed Meryem and was not surprised to see her creep up to the closed flap of a tent Mathew guessed must be Khardan's.

"Who is it? Who is there?" called the Calif, alert, it seemed, to the slightest sound.

"It is Meryem, My Lord," responded the woman in a half-smothered whisper.

Keeping to the deepest shadows, Mathew saw the tent flap open. Khardan appeared, silhouetted against golden lamp light. "What are you doing here? It is not proper—"

"I don't care!" Meryem cried, clasping her hands, her voice quivering. "I have been so miserable! You don't know what it was like! The Amir's troops captured me during the battle and carried me back to Kich! I was terrified that they would recognize me as the Sultan's daughter and drag me before the Amir. But, thank Akhran, they didn't!" She began to weep. "Your mother, Badia, cared for me as if I were her own daughter. She never believed you were dead, and neither did I!"

Khardan put his hands on the girl's heaving shoulders. "There, there. It is all right now." The Calif paused, his fingers twining themselves in the silken veil. "If my mother is imprisoned, how is it that you are not there also?"

The question was carelessly put. Mathew caught the slight tenseness in the voice, however, and hope surged through him.

"I managed to escape," said Meryem, swallowing her tears and gazing up at the Calif adoringly. "I came to you as fast as I could."

The answer seemed to satisfy Khardan, to judge by his fond smile. Mathew grit his teeth. Can't you see she's lying?

It was all he could do to keep from rushing from his hiding place and shaking some sense into the man.

"Let us be happy, my love!" Meryem continued, drawing near and putting her hands caressingly on his chest. "I don't want to wait for us to be married. Danger is so near." She nestled into his arms. "Who knows how long we may have together?"

Smiling at her, Khardan drew Meryem into his tent.

A fury gripped Mathew by the throat, a fury such as he had never experienced.

"By Promenthas, I'll confront her with the attempt on Zohra's life! Let her deny it before Khardan, if she can! And I'll remind him of that little silver charm she hung around his neck while I'm at it!"

Not stopping to think what he might be interrupting, Mathew ran over to the tent. The flap had been left open; Khardan was so taken by passion, apparently he forgot to close it.

Mathew entered the tent silently. Blinking in the bright lamplight, he waited impatiently for them to acknowledge his presence. Neither did. Khardan's back was to Mathew, the Calif appeared intent on kissing soft flesh. Meryem's arms were around Khardan's neck. Her eyes were closed and she moaned in ecstasy. Wrapped up in their pleasure, neither noticed the young man.

Suddenly the realization of what he was doing and how Khardan would react to this violation of his privacy struck Mathew. His face burning with shame, he started to quietly edge his way out, intending to slink off into the desert and spend the night fuming in what he recognized was the rage of jealousy.

As he moved, his attention was caught by Meryem's hands; the skin glimmering white in the lamplight. Instead of caressing the Calif, the hands were doing something very strange. Dainty fingers closed over the stone of a ring she wore and gave it a deft twist. A needle shot out, gleamed for an instant, then vanished in shadow as Meryem slowly and deliberately moved the ring toward Khardan's bare neck.

Mathew had seen assassin's rings. He knew how they worked. He knew that Khardan would be dead or dying within moments. The Calif's weapons lay on a wooden chest at the foot of his bed.

Springing forward, Mathew grabbed the dagger, and in the same moment, never noticing that Khardan's hand was closing over Meryem's wrist, the young wizard plunged the knife into the woman's back.

A wailing scream deafened him. He felt Meryem's body stiffen. Warm blood drizzled over his hand. The body jerked horribly in its death throes; a heavy weight sagged against him. Appalled, Mathew sprang back, and Meryem dropped to the floor. She lay on her back, her legs twisted at an awkward angle. Blue, glassy eyes stared up at him.

"My god!" whispered Mathew. The bloodstained knife fell from his fingers, which had gone limp and numb.

A shadow entered the tent. Pausing, it looked from Mathew to the corpse. Khardan bent over Meryem, perhaps searching desperately for life.

"Ah, well done, Blossom," commented Auda.

"Khardan!" Mathew licked his tongue across his dry lips. He felt a hot sickness welling up inside him. The ground canted away beneath his feet. "I—I . . . She was . . ."

To his amazement, Khardan looked up coolly at Auda.

"You were right," he said heavily. "This is a tool of Benario's." Lifting the flaccid hand, the Calif gingerly exhibited the ring with its deadly needle.

Mathew's weakness abated momentarily, lost in his shock. "You knew?" he gasped.

Khardan gave him a rebuking glance. "Of course. I thought long about what you told me. I remembered certain things she said to me, and finally I began to understand. She failed in her attempt to capture me for the Amir, and so she returned to do the only thing left—murder me."

Mathew swayed on his feet. Khardan, rising swiftly, caught the young man in his arms. Easing Mathew onto the bed, the Calif gestured to the Black Paladin to bring water.

"I'm all right!" Mathew gasped, shaking his head in refusal, fearing if he drank anything he would gag.

"Auda recognized her. He had seen her at Khandar," Khardan continued. Putting his arm around Mathew's shoulders, he forced the young man to sip at least a small mouthful of the tepid liquid. "Meryem was not a Sultan's daughter, but the Emperor's daughter by one of his concubines. She was given to Qannadi as a gift and was acting in his service."

"I killed her!" Mathew said hollowly. "I felt her. . . the knife going in . . . that scream. . ." Gazing at his hand, the blood, moist and sticky, shining black in the moonlight, he shuddered and doubled up, retching.

"Her life was forfeit," said Auda calmly, standing over the bed and looking down at Mathew with amusement in the dark eyes. "She has murdered before, not a doubt of it. Benario's followers must, you know. They call it 'blooding.' Only one who was high in the God's favor and knowledgeable in his ways could have secured a ring like this."

"Khardan! Are you safe? I heard a scream!" Voices were clamoring outside the tent.

Motioning for the Calif to remain where he was, Auda lifted Meryem's body in his arms and carried her out. "An assassin," he shouted to the gathering, murmuring crowd, "sent by Quar to murder your Calif. Fortunately I was able to stop her in time!"

Mathew looked up at Khardan. "Ibn Jad is right, Khardan. She tried to kill Zohra," he said in croaking whisper, his throat raw. In broken sentences he related the incident to the Calif, who listened gravely, his face serious.

"You should have told me."

"Would you have believed us?" Mathew asked softly.

"No." Khardan sat back on his heels. "No, you are right. I was then—as you thought me now—a blind fool."

Mathew flushed, hearing his innermost thoughts spoken aloud. "I didn't—" he began confusedly.

Khardan rested his hands on the young man's shoulders. "Once again, Mat-hew, you have saved my life."

"No," said Mathew miserably. "You knew about her. You knew what she would do. You were ready for her."

"Perhaps not. All she had to do was prick the flesh once and . . ." Khardan shrugged. His eyes left the young man and stared out into the night, seeing—perhaps—the lithe figure entering once again. "Believe this, Mat-hew," he said softly. "I have faced death in many forms, but when I saw that ring on her finger, when I felt her hands touch my skin, a horror came over me that changed my bowels to water and stole the strength from my body!" He shivered and shook his head, looking back at Mathew. "It was well you came. Akhran guided you."

"I've taken a human life!" Mathew cried in a low voice, clenching his crimson-stained hand.

"We do what we must do," Khardan said offhandedly. "Come, young man," he added somewhat impatiently when Mathew shook his head, refusing to be comforted, "would you rather have let her kill me?"

"No, oh no!" Mathew looked up swiftly. "It's just—" How could he explain to this warrior the teachings of his parents that even in time of war their people refused to fight, insisting that all life was sacred. And yet, thought Mathew confusedly, there had never come a time to them when the sanctity of their home had been rent asunder, their children torn screaming from their mothers' arms.

"You are tired," said Khardan, clapping him on the shoulder and helping him rise from the cushions. "Sleep, and you will feel better in the morning. We have much to talk about tomorrow."

I am tired, Mathew said to himself. But will I sleep? Will I ever sleep again? Or will I feel the blood, hear always that horrible, dying scream?

At least, he noted thankfully when he left the tent, he wouldn't have to talk to anyone. He could make his stumbling way back in secret and alone. The tribesmen who had gathered in the initial excitement paid no attention to him. There was an amazed reaction as Auda told his story, Mathew inwardly blessing the Paladin for taking credit for the killing and leaving him out of it. The tribesmen talked volubly, a few Hrana stated that they had mistrusted the woman the first time they saw her. Since this implied criticism of the Calif—now Prophet—those few making such claims were shouted down. The Akar were speaking loudly of how all had been duped by Meryem's beauty, innocence, and charm.

"Throw her to the jackals!" cried someone.

Auda, with a procession of nomads accompanying him, carried the corpse to the outskirts of camp. The body hung limp in the Paladin's grasp. A white arm—entangled in a silken scarf—dropped suddenly down, to dangle and sway in a mockery of seduction as though she were trying, one last time, to avoid her fate. But the jackals, looking at that nubile body, would see only meat.

Shuddering, suddenly dizzy and sick, Mathew turned away. He felt eyes upon him and, glancing around, saw Zohra standing in the entrance of her tent. She said nothing, and he could not read her eyes. She made no sign, and Mathew did not go to her. She had heard Auda talking, of course. Mathew guessed she knew the truth.

He walked blindly on. Reaching his tent, more by accident than design, he started to go inside, but the thought of stepping into the smothering darkness—the darkness that no matter what he did to alleviate it always smelled strongly of goat—made him gag. Mathew drew his hand back from the flap.

He breathed in the cool night air and looked at the tents scattered around him. Many nights before he had done this same thing—stepped outside to gaze despairingly at the moon and stars, imagining them shining down upon his homeland, glinting off the water of countless streams, rivers, lakes, and pools.

Tonight he saw a new moon—a tiny wisp of a moon—balance on its tip on the horizon as if it were testing itself before rising farther. For the first time Mathew saw the moon shine—not on the castle walls of his homesickness—but on the desert. The stark and barren beauty pierced the young man's heart.

The desert is lonely, but then so are we all, wrapped in our frail husks of flesh. It is silent, vast, and empty, and it brushes away man's marks in its sand with an uncaring hand. It is eternal, everlasting, yet constantly changing—the dunes shift with the wind, sudden rain brings forth life where there was nothing but death, the sun burns it all away once more.

The past few months, I have been living only because I was afraid to die. He saw himself suddenly as the sickly brown cacti, the Rose of the Prophet, clinging to a meaningless existence among the rocks. Auda had said to him, *Your life was obviously spared for a purpose.* And all he could do with that life, apparently, was mope about whining and crying that it wasn't what he wanted. *Blossom,* Auda called him. He could either decay and rot away or blossom and give meaning not only to his life, but to his death.

Suddenly, humbly and joyfully, Mathew reveled in being alive.

He looked down at his bloodstained hand. He had taken a life. Promenthas would call him to account for it. But he had done it to save a life.

And he was no longer afraid.

CHAPTER 9

i do not trust that woman—Meryem's—story of the Imam's return to Kich," growled Majiid.

"I never trusted her," piped up Jaafar. "I didn't believe a word she said. It was you took her into your dwelling, Sheykh al Fakhar—an insult to my daughter, a woman whose virtues number as the stars in heaven."

Majiid's eyes bulged; he bristled like a cornered tiger.

"Come, come," interposed Zeid smugly. "There were three who were victims of the Emperor's whore—two of them old goats who should have known better."

"Old goats!" Jaafar shrieked, rounding on Zeid.

Khardan, rubbing his aching temples, bit back the hot words of anger and frustration that rose to his lips. Forcing himself to remain calm, his voice slid swiftly and smoothly between the combatants.

"I have sent the djinn to Kich to verify Meryem's story. They should return at any moment with word."

"Not my djinn?" Zeid glared at Khardan.

"All the djinn."

"How dare you? Raja is my personal djinn! You have no right—"

"If it hadn't been for my son, you would have no personal djinn!" laughed Majiid raucously, stabbing a bony finger into Zeid's shrunken, flabby middle. "If my son wants to use your djinn—"

"Where's Fedj?" Jaafar was on his feet. "Have you taken Fedj?"

"Silence!" Khardan roared.

The tent quieted, the Sheykhs staring at the Calif with varying looks—Zeid sly and furtive, Jaafar offended, and Majiid indignant.

"A son does not say such things to his father!" Majiid stated angrily, rising to his feet with help from a servant. "I will not sit in my son's tent and—"

"You will sit, Father," said Khardan coldly. "You will sit in patience and wait for the return of the djinn. You will sit because if you do not, our people are finished, and we might as well all go and throw ourselves at the feet of the Imam and beg for Quar's mercy." Saying thus, he cast a stern glance around at the other two Sheykhs.

"Mmmm." Zeid smoothed his beard and gazed at Khardan speculatively. Jaafar began to moan that he was cursed, mumbling that they might as well give themselves up to Quar anyway. Majiid glared at his son fiercely, then abruptly threw himself back down upon the tent floor.

Khardan sighed and wished the djinn would hurry.

It was night. The Sheykhs were meeting in Khardan's tent, holding council about their future plan of action. Crowded around the tent were the men of all three tribes, glaring suspiciously at each other but maintaining an uneasy peace.

The council had not begun auspiciously. Zeid had opened it by announcing, "We have now a Prophet. So what?"

So what? Khardan repeated to himself. He knew his predicament all too well. With the capture of the southern lands of Bas, the Amir had grown more powerful than he had been when he raided the nomad's camps. Qannadi's army numbered in the tens of thousands. His cavalry was mounted on magical horses, and Zeid had heard reports from his spies that—due to Achmed's training—the soldiers of the Amir rode and fought on horseback as well any *spahi*. Facing this army was a handful of ragged, half-starved tribesmen who could not agree on which way the wind blew.

A cloud materialized in the tent, and Khardan looked up in relief, glad to turn his gloomy thoughts to something else for the time being. Although, he told himself, this news was liable to make his problems just that much more difficult.

Four djinn appeared before him—the handsome Sond; the muscular Fedj, the giant Raja, and the rotund Usti. Each djinn bowed with the utmost respect to Khardan, hands folded over their hearts. It was an impressive sight, and Majiid cast a triumphant glance at his two cousins to make certain they did not miss it.

"What news?" Khardan asked sternly.

"Alas, master," said Sond, who was apparently spokesman since he now served Khardan. "The woman, Meryem, spoke truly. The Imam is even now on his way back to Kich, accompanied by the Amir and his troops. And he has decreed that when he reaches the city, all its inhabitants are to welcome him in the name of Quar. Any who do not will be put to death. This spear is aimed directly at our people, *sidi*, for they are the only unbelievers in the city."

"Have they been imprisoned?"

"Yes, *sidi*. Women and children and the young men—all are being held in the Zindan."

"Without food!" put in Usti. Panting from his unaccustomed exertion, fanning himself with a palm frond, the djinn was livid at the thought. The other three djinn turned on him, glaring. Usti shrank back, waving a pudgy hand. "I thought the master should know!"

"They are starving them?" Majiid shouted.

"Hush!" ordered Khardan, but it was too late.

"What? Dogs! They will die!"

An uproar started outside the tent, Majiid's voice having carried clearly to the tribesmen.

"We had not meant to tell you quite so suddenly, *sidi*." said Sond, casting Usti a vicious glance. "And that is not quite the truth. They are getting some food, but only enough to keep them barely alive."

"I don't believe it," Khardan said firmly. "I met the Amir. He is a soldier! He would not make war on women and children."

"Begging your pardon, *sidi*," said Fedj, "but it is not the Amir who issues this order. It is Feisal, the Imam and—many now say—the true ruler of Kich. "

"Quar is desperate," added Raja, his rumbling voice shaking the tent poles. "The war in heaven has turned against him, and now he dares not allow any *kafir* in his midst on earth. The people of the captured southern cities are restless, and there is talk of revolt. Feisal will make of our people a bloody example that will quiet the rebels and keep them in line."

"Then there is no help for it," Khardan said harshly.

"We must attack Kich!"

"The first to die will be our people in the prison, *sidi*," wailed

Usti. "So the Imam has threatened!"

Glaring at the fat djinn, Sond sucked in an impatient breath, his fists clenched.

Looking vastly injured and much put upon, Usti pouted. "You can threaten me all you like, Sond! But it's the truth. I went to the prison, you recall! Not you! And I saw them, master!" The djinn continued, thrusting his way forward to Khardan. "Our people are held in the prison compound, *sidi,* ringed round by the Imam's fanatic soldier-priests, who stand—day and night—with their swords drawn."

"These same soldier-priests are the ones who committed the slaughter of the *kafir* in Bastine, *sidi,*" added Sond reluctantly. "There is no doubt that they would carry through the Imam's order to murder our people. In fact, they await it eagerly."

"Our people would be dead before we got inside the city walls," Raja growled.

"And we will never get inside the walls," Sheykh Zeid pointed out gloomily. He waved a hand toward the camp, where the crowd had fallen ominously silent. A few hundred against the might of the Amir! Bah! All we could do for our people is die with them!"

"If that is all we can do, then that is what we must do!" Khardan said in bitter anger and frustration. "Can we acquire more djinn, perhaps, or 'efreets?"

"The immortals do battle on their own plane, *sidi,*" said Fedj, shaking his turbaned head. "Though Kaug is gone, the war rages still. Quar freed the immortals that he had kept bottled up, and though they are weak, they are numerous and are defending their God valiantly. *Hazrat* Akhran can spare none of his."

"At least we should be thankful that no immortals will be defending Kich," said Sond, anxious to say something hopeful.

"With a hundred thousand men, who needs immortals?" commented Usti, shrugging his fat shoulders.

Sond ground his teeth ominously. "I think I heard your mistress calling you."

"No!" Usti paled and glanced around in fear. "You didn't, did you?"

"My cousins in Akhran," said Sheykh Zeid, leaning forward and beckoning those in the tent to bring their heads nearer his. "It is true, as the djinn have reported, that the Amir despises the idea of senseless slaughter. Facing us in battle, man to man, he would kill us all without hesitation, but not the innocent, the helpless—"

"He murdered the Sultan of Kich and his family," interrupted Jaafar.

Zeid shrugged complacently. "So a wise man not only kills the scorpion in his boot but searches well for its mate, knowing that the sting of one is as painful as the other. But did he then go ahead and murder the followers of Mimrim and the other Gods whose temples—however small—were in Kich? No. It was only when this Feisal took control that we began hearing of Quar in the heart or steel in the gut. If something should happen to this Feisal . . ." Zeid made a graceful hand motion, his eyes narrowed to slits.

"No'" said Khardan abruptly, standing up and drawing his robes aside as if to remove even his clothing from the presence of such defilement. "Akhran curses the taking of a life in cold blood!"

"Perhaps now, in modern days," said Zeid. "But there was a time, when our grandfathers were young—"

"And would you go backward instead of forward?" demanded Khardan. "What honor to stab a man—a priest, at that—in the back? I will not be an assassin like a follower of Benario or of—"

"Zhakrin?" suggested a soft voice.

No one had heard Auda enter. No one knew how long be bad been there. Starting, frowning, the Sheykhs glared at him. Moving with his catlike grace, the Paladin rose to his feet to stand before Khardan.

"I remind you of your oath, brother."

"My oath was to protect your life, avenge your death! Not to commit murder!"

"I do not ask you to. I will do what must be done," said Auda coolly. "Indeed, no hand but mine may strike Feisal if I am to fulfill the oath made to my dead brother. But I would not leave my back undefended. I call upon you, therefore, to ride with me to Kich and help me win my way through gate and Temple door and—"

"—turn my head while you thrust your accursed dagger in the man? Avert my eyes like a woman?" Khardan's hand slashed through the air. "No! I say again, no!"

"A squeamish Prophet," murmured Zeid, stroking his beard.

Khardan whirled to face them. "The Imam has taken our families, our wives, our sisters, our children, our brothers, our cousins. He has destroyed our dwellings, stolen our food, left us with nothing but our honor. Now it seems that you want to hand him that as well. Then, truly, no matter what happens, we would be slaves to Quar." The Calif stood tall, his voice shook in proud anger. "I will not surrender my honor, nor the honor of my people!"

One by one the eyes of the Sheykhs dropped beneath Khardan's. Majiid's fierce stare was the last to lower before his son's, but at last even his gaze sought the carpet beneath his legs, his face flushed in chagrin, frustration, and fury.

"Then in the name of Akhran, what are we to do!" he cried suddenly, smiting his thigh with his gnarled hand.

"I will do what I would do with any other enemy who has offered me this affront," said Khardan. "I will do what I would do if this Feisal were not Feisal but were Zeid al Saban"—he gestured—"or Jaafar al Widjar. I will travel to Kich and challenge the Amir to fight us in fair combat with the understanding that if we win, we will leave his people unharmed, and that if we lose, he will do the same for us.

"Thus I will fulfill my oath to you, Auda ibn Jad," added Khardan, glancing at the Paladin, who stood listening with a lip curled in disdain. I will myself go and present our challenge to the Amir. You shall enter the gate with me, and we will face its perils together. But first you must give me your word that if the Amir agrees to our bargain you will do nothing to the Imam until my people are, safely in the desert."

"The Amir will not go along with this plan, brother! If you are lucky, he will lop off your head as you stand before him. If you are not, he will take you to the Zindan and let his executioners teach you of honor! And I will have two deaths to avenge instead of one!" Auda said in disgust.

"Most likely," replied Khardan gravely, nodding his head. The Black Paladin eyed Khardan. "I could leave you now and go forth and do this deed without you. You know that. Your sword arm is strong, but I can find those just as strong and far more willing. Why do I stay? Why do I endure this? Why did the gods mingle our blood and hear our oaths knowing them to be mismatched, spoken in mistaken belief?"

Auda ibn Jad shook his head slowly, his eyes dark with mystification. "I do not know the answer. I can only have faith. This I will promise, Khardan, Prophet of a Strange God. Should by some wild chance you prevail, I will not harm so much as a thread of the Imam's robes until the sun has risen and set upon your people three times after they leave the city. Satisfied?"

Khardan nodded. "I am satisfied."

"Then let it be also noted that your death cry absolves me from this vow," said Auda wryly.

"That, of course," agreed Khardan with a faint smile.

"So we ride to Kich," said Majiid grimly, rising to his feet.

"We ride to death," muttered Jaafar.

"Without hope," added Zeid.

"Not so!" came a clear, confident voice.

CHAPTER 10

Zohra parted the tent flap and entered, Mathew following behind her.

The Sheykhs glowered. "Begone, woman," commanded Majiid. "We have important matters to discuss."

"Don't you speak like that to my daughter!" Jaafar shook his fist. "She can make water from sand!"

"Then I wish she would make of this desert an ocean and drown you!" roared Majiid.

Worried and preoccupied, exasperated by the arguing, Khardan waved his hand at his wife. "My father is right," he began peremptorily. "This is no place for women—"

"Husband!" Zohra did not speak loudly. The clarity and firmness of her tone, however, brought the haranguing to a halt. "I ask to be heard." Politely, her eyes on Khardan alone, Zohra moved to stand before her husband. Her veiled head was held proudly; she was dressed in the plain white caftan. Mathew, clad in black, came behind her. There was a newly acquired dignity about the young man that was impressive, a calm and sureness about the woman that caused even the djinn to bow and give way to them both.

"Very well," said Khardan gruffly, trying to appear stern. "What is it you want to say, wife?" The word was tinged with its customary bitter irony. "Speak, we don't have much time."

"If you fail to persuade the Amir to fight, it is obvious to me that we must rescue our people from the prison."

"That is obvious to all of us, wife," snapped Khardan, rapidly losing patience. "We are planning—"

"Planning to die," Zohra remarked. Ignoring the Calif's scowl, she continued. "And our people will die. This is not a battle that can be won by men and their swords. She looked at Mathew, who nodded. Zohra turned her gaze back to her husband. "This is a battle that can be won by women and their magic."

"Bah!" Majiid shouted impatiently. "She wastes our time, my son. Tell her to go back to her milking of goats—"

"Two with magic can free our people where hundreds with swords cannot!" Zohra said, overriding Majiid, a glittering in her dark eyes like stars in the night sky. "Mat-hew and I have a plan."

"We will hear your plan," said Khardan, wearily.

"No." Mathew spoke up, stepping forward. He had seen the exchange of glances between the Calif and the others, the preparations made to humor the woman and then send her on her way. He knew that the Sheykhs, that Khardan himself, would never understand; that to describe his idea would bring incredulity and scoffing, and Mathew would be left behind while Khardan rode to certain death. "No, this is of Sul and therefore forbidden to be spoken. You must trust us-"

"A woman who thinks she is a man and a man who thinks he is a woman? Hah!" Majiid laughed.

"All we ask," said Mathew, ignoring the Sheykh, "is that you take us with you into Kich—"

Khardan was shaking his head, his face stern and dark. "It is too dangerous—"

Zohra thrust Mathew aside. "Akhran sent us to that terrible castle together, husband, and together he brought us forth! It was by his will we two were married, by his will we were brought *together* to save our people! Take us with you to the Amir. If he slays us as we stand before him, then that is the will of Akhran, and we die together. If he sends us to the Zindan to die with our people, then—with our magic—we will have a chance to save them!" She lifted her chin, her eyes flaring with a pride that matched the pride in the eyes intently watching her. "Or has Akhran given you the right to risk your life for our people, husband, and denied that right to me because I am a woman?"

Khardan gazed at his wife in thoughtful silence. Majiid snorted in disgust. The djinn exchanged speculative glances and raised their eyebrows. Zeid and Jaafar stirred uncomfortably, but neither said anything. There was nothing anyone could say that hadn't been said before. The Calif's face grew darker, his frown more pronounced. His gaze turned on Mathew.

"These are not your people. It is not your land, nor your God. The danger for us in Kich will be great, but the danger for you will be greater. If they capture you, they will not rest until they have discovered where you are from and what secrets you hold in your heart."

"I know this, Calif," said Mathew steadily.

"And do you also know that they will rip these secrets from you using cold iron and hot needles. They will gouge out your eyes and hack off your limbs—"

"Yes, Calif." answered Mathew softly

"We fight to save those we love. Why do you risk this peril?"

Mathew raised his eyes and looked directly into Khardan's. Silently he said, I could make the same reply, but you would not understand. Aloud he responded, "In the sight of my God, all life is sacred. I am commanded in his name and with the help of Sul to do all I can to protect the innocent and helpless."

"His danger will not be greater than ours. He can disguise himself as a woman, my husband," suggested Zohra. "The baggage of the she-devil, Meryem, is still in her tent. Mat-hew can wear her robes. It would be better so, anyway, for the guards will keep us together and put us both in with the women when we enter the prison."

Khardan was about to refuse. Mathew could see it in the man's tired eyes. The young wizard knew Zohra saw it as well, for he felt her body stiffen and heard the deep intake of breath with which to launch arguments, shout vituperation, or perhaps both, that would do nothing but cause further troubles. He was just thinking about how he could get her out of the tent, take her someplace where he could discuss this with her rationally, when suddenly Auda leaned near Khardan and whispered something to the Calif.

Khardan listened reluctantly, his eyes on his wife and on Mathew. He cut Auda off with an impatient gesture. The Paladin ceased speaking and withdrew. Khardan was silent long moments; then, "I had thought to leave you with the sick and elderly in the camp. They are in need of your skills. But very well, wife," he said dourly. "You will come, and Mat-hew as well."

Majiid, staring at his son in amazement, opened his mouth, but a swift gesture from Khardan caused him to snap it shut in seething silence.

"Thank you, husband," Zohra said. If the sun had suddenly chosen to drop from the sky and burst into flame in the center of the tent, it could not have flared more brilliantly or shone with such dazzling radiance. She bowed respectfully, her eyes lowered; but as she did so, she cast a swift, triumphant glance at her husband and a warm, thankful glance at Auda.

Khardan's brow grew darker, but he said nothing. Mathew, seeing Auda's eyes on Zohra and a slight smile on the man's lips, did not like this change of heart on Khardan's part and the sudden interest in Zohra on Auda's. He mistrusted what was behind it and would have very much liked to stay and hear what was said next, but Khardan dismissed both of them, and the young wizard had no choice but to follow the elated Zohra from the tent.

Mathew lingered outside, hoping to overhear the conversation, but Sond appeared in the tent flap, staring at him sternly. There was only silence from within, and Mathew knew that conversation would be resumed only when he and Zohra were gone.

Sighing, he trailed behind a Zohra thrilled with her victory, and the young man wondered soberly and somberly who had really won.

"Are they gone?"

Sond, standing at the tent entrance, nodded.

"Auda ibn Jad is right," said the Calif, cutting off his father's argument before Majiid could speak. "As headstrong as"—he swallowed—"my wife is, if we left her here alone, she would undoubtedly try some foolish plan of her own. Better to keep them both with us, where we may watch them."

Those had not been Auda's' words. He had reminded Khardan of what the Calif already knew—Mathew was a skilled sorcerer, Zohra an apt pupil. In this desperate situation they could not turn down any offer of hope, however small. Auda would have gone on to remind Khardan of his wife's courage, but the Calif remembered that well enough, and it was at that point he had stopped the man short. Khardan wondered why it should irritate him to hear Auda praise a wife who was not a wife, but it did; the Paladin's words of praise for her nipping at the Calif like the fiery bite of the red ant.

"Have the men ready to ride by morning," Khardan said abruptly, rising and putting an end to discussion. He wanted, needed, desperately, to be alone. "If all goes well, the Amir will face us in fair battle—"

"Fair? Ten thousand to one?" muttered Jaafar gloomily. "Fair for the Akar!" Majiid retorted. "If the Hrana are cowards, they can hide behind their sheep!"

"Cowards!" Jaafar bristled. "I never said—"

"If matters go awry," continued Khardan loudly, relentlessly riding over the impending altercation, "and I am taken, I will fight to the end. So will our people in the prison. Though ringed round by swords, they will battle for their lives with their bare hands. And you will attack the city, without hope, perhaps, but send as many of Quar's followers to their God as you can before you fall!"

Majiid—his gray cheeks regaining a measure of color, his faded eyes their old, fierce spark—clapped his son upon the back. "Akhran has chosen his Prophet wisely!" Gripping Khardan with both hands, he kissed the Calif's cheeks, then left the tent, his voice booming across the desert as he called forth his people to war.

Jaafar sidled near the Calif. The face of the small, wizened man, which seemed perpetually sad even in his happiest moments, now appeared ready to crumble into tears. Patting Khardan's arm, glancing furtively around to see that no one heard him, he whispered; "Akhran knows, I am a cursed man. Nothing has ever gone right for me. But I begin to think I have not been cursed in his choice of a son-in-law. "

Zeid said nothing, but stared at Khardan shrewdly, as through mistrusting even this and wondering what trick the Calif had in mind to play. The *mehariste* made a respectful *salaam,* then departed, taking Raja with him. Auda, too, had apparently gone, for when Khardan remembered him and turned to speak, the Black Paladin was not in the tent.

Alone, the Calif sank down despondently upon the cushions on the tent floor. He was not meant for this kind of life. He did not enjoy the taste of honey on his tongue—honey used to sweeten bitter words so that others would gulp them down. He preferred direct and honest speech. If words must be spoken, then let his tongue be as sharp and true as his blade. Unfortunately he did not possess, in this dire time, the luxury of speaking his mind.

His shoulders slumped in exhaustion, and he lay down. Tired as he was, he did not have much hope of sleeping, however. Every time he closed his eyes, he saw blond hair, smiling lips, and felt the prick of a poisoned needle. . .

"I beg your pardon, master," said a quiet voice, causing Khardan to sit up in alarm. "But I have something to say to you in private."

"Yes, Sond, what is it?" Khardan asked reluctantly, seeing in the djinn's grave expression more bad news.

"As you may have surmised, *sidi*, we djinn divided up in our search for information. Usti was sent to the prison—we thought he could cause less trouble there than anywhere else. Raja went among the people of Kich. Fedj spied upon the Imam's priests as best he could without entering the Temple, which we cannot do, of course, since it is the sacred precinct of another deity. I traveled north, *sidi*, and went among the troops of the Amir."

"You have news of Achmed," guessed Khardan.

"Yes, *sidi*." Sond bowed. "I hope I have not done wrong."

"No. I am glad to hear of him. He is my brother still. Nothing—not even my father's disavowal of him can change that."

"I thought that was how you felt, *sidi*, and so I took the liberty. I overheard some odd things spoken about him and a woman he had taken recently. A woman who has since left him under mysterious circumstances."

Khardan's face grew shadowed. He said nothing but gazed at the djinn intently.

"I waited until the young man left to perfom some duty or other, then I entered his tent. I found this, *sidi*." Sond handed to Khardan a small piece of parchment.

"What does it say?" asked the Calif, staring at the strange markings with distrust.

Sond read the message Meryem left for Achmed.

"She was with him many weeks, apparently, *sidi*," said Sond gently. "There is no doubt he was infatuated with her. That was common gossip among all the men. Since she has been gone, all note his sad face and sorrowing aspect."

"What did she mean to do with him?" Khardan asked, crushing the paper in his hand.

"One can only speculate, master. But I heard many more things about your brother while I was among the troops. He is a favorite with Qannadi, whose men, as well, have grown to respect the *Kafir*, as they call him. Achmed has proved himself, both on the field and off. Qannadi has sons, but they are far away in the Emperor's court. There is little doubt that were the Amir to die, Achmed might find himself able to rise to a position of great power and authority. My guess is that the woman, Meryem, knew of this and intended to rise with him. Perhaps even see to it that he moved somewhat faster than expected."

"What can our God mean by this?" Khardan remarked, puzzled. "In killing Meryem, we may have saved the Amir's life." He drew a deep breath, unwilling to ask the next question, unwilling to hear the answer. "Sond, will my brother come to Kich?"

"Yes, *sidi*. He is Captain of the Amir's cavalry."

"Has he— Has he converted to Quar?"

"I do not think so, *sidi*. The men say that your brother worships no God. He claims that men are on their own, responsible only to themselves and to each other."

"What will he do if his people are attacked?"

"I do not know, *sidi*. My sight reaches far, but it cannot see into the human heart."

Khardan sighed. "Thank you, Sond. You may go. You have done well."

"The blessing of Akhran upon you, master." said the djinn, bowing. "May he touch you with wisdom."

"May he indeed," Khardan murmured, and lay down to stare thoughtfully into the darkness that seemed to grow ever deeper around him.

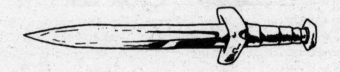

The Book
of Akhran

CHAPTER 1

rana, Akar, Aran: the tribes, united at last—if only in despair—rode for Kich swiftly and in dour silence, each man occupied with his own dark thoughts. No one—not even Khardan himself—believed the Amir would accept their challenge. The Imam had declared the *kafir* would convert or die, and he would not retreat from that stand. This was the last ride of the desert people. This was the end—of life, of future. The hope that grew in almost every heart had the taste of a bitter herb—it consisted only of being able, in death, to stand before Akhran and state, "I died in honor." Khardan was not surprised to see, as the nomads left the camp about the Tel, that the Rose of the Prophet looked nearer death than it ever had before. Still, it clung to life with stubborn persistence.

Two hearts on that grim journey, however, nurtured true hope. Zohra had never heard of this "fog" of which Mathew spoke, and which he said was common in the alien land from which he came. She found it difficult, if not impossible, to imagine clouds coming down from the sky to obey her command, surrounding and protecting and confusing the eyes of her enemies. But she had seen Mathew summon one of these clouds from water in a bowl in her tent. She had felt its cold and clammy touch on her skin, smelled its dank odor, and watched in astonishment as Mathew gradually faded from her sight and familiar objects in the tent either disappeared or looked strange and unreal.

She had thought he was gone—his body turned into the mist—until he had spoken and reached out to her. His hand had clasped hers, and then she had known disappointment.

"What use is a cloud that will not stop a hand, let alone swords or arrows?"

Patiently Mathew had explained that if each woman was

taught the magic and summoned her own "fog," it would be as the creation of a gigantic cloud that would cover them all. They could take advantage of the guards' certain confusion and panic to attack and win their way free of the prison walls before anyone caught them.

"Surely there is magic you know that can fight for us as an army!" she said persistently.

Yes, he had answered with patience, but it takes study to use it effectively. Without practice the magic is more dangerous to the spell caster than to the victim.

"The fog spell is relatively simple to cast. We can teach the women to write it easily. All we need," Mathew had added off-handedly, "is a source of water, and surely there must be a well in the prison."

"Have you done this before?" Zohra had asked.

"Of course."

"With many people?"

He had not answered, and Zohra had not pursued the matter further.

At this point, it didn't matter.

Two days hard riding on the *mehara*, and those horses that had been saved in the battle brought the men to the hills of the sheep-herding Hrana. There were few left to greet them, mostly old men and women who had been considered worthless and left behind by the Amir. They welcomed their Sheykh but regarded their Princess and her husband with sullen words and bitter looks. It was only when Fedj appeared and told the tale of Khardan the Prophet that their darting, sidelong glances widened with awe and they began to look upon the Calif with more respect—if not less suspicion.

By the time the tale was concluded, late in the night, it had been rewoven and embroidered, cut here, mended there, until, as Khardan muttered aside to Auda, he would not have known it for the same suit of clothes. The tale had its intended effect, however—or at least so Khardan supposed. The moment the people of Jaafar's tribe, who had been skulking in the hills with the remnants of their flocks, heard that Khardan was favored of Akhran, they began to pour their woes into his ears until it was a wonder his brain didn't overflow.

Their woes were the same as those of their cousins around the Tel—water was scarce, food was dear, wolves were raiding their flocks, they were worried about their families held prisoner in Kich. When was the Prophet going to make it rain? When would he give them wheat and rice? When was he going to drive off the wolves? When was he going to march on Kich and free their people?

Long after Majiid had gone to his bed, long after Zohra had retired to the empty yurt of one of her half brother's captive wives, long after Mathew had rolled himself up in a blanket on the floor of an empty hut that had been assigned for his use, Khardan remained seated with his father-in-law and the silent, watchful Auda around a sputtering fire. Blinking eyes that burned with fatigue, he stifled yawns and patiently answered either "yes" or "in Akhran's time" to everything. He did not say that "Akhran's time" was "no time," but all heard his unspoken words, saw the despair in the dark eyes and, one by one, they left him. Sond almost carried the bone-weary Calif to his dwelling where he sank into a desolate, gloom-ridden sleep.

The silence of night in the hills is not the silence of night in the desert. The silence of the hills is the weaving of many tiny sounds of tree and bird and beast into a blanket that rests lightly over the sleeper. The silence of the desert is the sibilant whisper of the wind across the sand, the snarl of a prowling lioness that sometimes jolts a sleeper to sudden wakefulness.

The silence of the hills had lulled her to sleep, but when Zohra started up, striving with every sense to determine what alarmed her, it seemed to her that she was back in the desert. There was no sound; all was too quiet. Her hand slipped beneath her pillow, fingers grasping for the hilt of her dagger, but a crushing grip closed over her wrist.

"It is Auda." His breath touched her skin. He spoke so softly, she felt his words more than heard them.

"There is not much time left to us!" breathed his voice in her ear. "Tomorrow we arrive in Kich, and my life is forfeit to the service of my God, the fulfillment of my oath. Lay with me this night! Give me a son!"

The fear surging in her slowly calmed. Her heart no longer pounded in her breast, her blood ceased to rush in her ears. That bad been her initial fright, her reaction to being taken by surprise.

Her breath came more easily; she relaxed.

"You do not cry out. I knew you would not." He released his grip on her hand and drew near her.

"No." Zohra shook her head. "There is no need. I am sure of myself."

He could not see her; the darkness was intense, impenetrable. But be could feel the movement of her head, the long, silky hair brushing against his wrist. He moved his hand to part her hair; his lips touched her cheek.

"No one but you and I will ever know."

"One other," she said. "Khardan."

"Yes." Auda considered. "You are right. He will know. But he will not begrudge me this, for I will be dead. And he will be alive. And he will have you."

He ran his bands through her tousled hair. The darkness was soft and warm and smelled of jasmine. Cupping her chin, he guided her lips to his and waited expectantly, confidently, for her answer.

The next morning the nomad army left the Hrana, taking along those old men who insisted they could ride farther and fight better than three young ones. Khardan, riding at their head, noted that Zohra seemed unusually quiet and preoccupied.

He had insisted at the beginning of their journey that she and Mathew accompany him, instead of following in the rear in the accustomed place of women. This was both a concession to his father—who never ceased to suspect Jaafar and his daughter were plotting against him—and to himself. As Zohra had said, they had traveled long and far together, faced many perils together. He came to realize, in the long hours of the ride when he had too much time to think, that he would have found it difficult, leaving her behind. It was somehow a comfort to him to look over and see her sitting her horse with the confidence of a man, a grace all her own.

Yet this day, riding out of the hills, wending their way through the tortuous paths carved into the red rock that thrust up into the blue sky of late summer, Khardan felt again the nip of fiery pincers, the unease of some nameless, nagging irritation. Zohra seemed aloof, distant. She rode by herself, instead of near Mathew, and coldly rebuffed the young man's attempts to draw her into conversation. She would look at no one who rode near—neither Mathew, Khardan, nor the ever-present, ever-watchful Paladin. Zohra kept her eyes lowered, the man's *haik* she wore during the ride drawn closely over her face.

"A fine woman," said Auda, guiding his horse up beside the Calif, his gaze following Khardan's. "She will bear some man many fine sons."

No blade that had ever struck Khardan inflicted pain as did these words. Reining in his horse with such fury that he nearly overset the beast, he stared angrily, questioningly at the Black Paladin. Khardan searched the cruel eyes. Let him see the tiniest spark and—oath or no oath, God or no God—this man would perish.

"Many fine sons," Auda repeated. The eyes were cold, impassive, except for a flicker that was not the gleam of triumph, but of admiration for the victor. "—For the man she loves."

Shrugging, his thin lips parting in a self-deprecating smile, Auda bowed to the Calif, wheeled his horse, and rode farther back to join the main body of men.

Left alone, Khardan drew a deep, shivering breath. The iron had been plucked from his heart, but the wound it had made was fresh and bled freely, flooding his body with a haunting, aching warmth. He looked over at Zohra, proud and fierce, riding by herself—riding beside him, not behind him.

"Fine sons," he said to himself bitterly. "And many fine daughters, too. But not to be. Not to us. It is too late. For us, the Rose will never bloom. "

After a week's hard journeying, the nomads came within sight of Kich. It was late afternoon. Khardan had sent scouts forward to find a safe resting place; they had returned to report the discovery of a large vineyard planted on a hillside, near enough to the city that they could see its walls and the soldiers manning them, yet far enough to remain hidden from view of those walls. At the foot of the hill, a smooth wide road ran through the plain, leading to the city walls.

Khardan appraised the thick, twisting stems of the grapevines that grew around him. The harvest had apparently been gathered, for there were few of the small, wrinkled grapes left hanging among the leaves that were slowly turning yellow, the plant going dormant following the plucking of its fruit. A tree-lined stream ran down alongside the grapevines. The ground underfoot was damp, the owner having flooded his vineyards after the grapes were gathered. Until harvest the fruit does better without water—the grapes growing sweeter and more sugary when allowed to dry in the sun.

"This will be a good place to camp," announced Khardan, agreeing with his scouts and forestalling the arguments of the Sheykhs that he could see bubbling on their lips by adding swiftly, "The fruit has been harvested. The owner will be tending to his wine, not his plants. We are hidden from sight of the road and the city walls by the vines."

To this the Sheykhs could make no reply, although there was, of course, some grumbling. Unlike many vineyard owners, this man must be a man of enterprise and forethought, for he had caused his vines to grow up stakes. Rather than straggling over the ground, the leaves were twined around a length of string that had been tied from stake to stake above the ground at about shoulder level. The foliage easily hid both man and beast from sight.

Khardan was directing the watering of the horses when Sond materialized at the Calif's stirrup.

"Would you have us go to the gate and see how many men guard it and how carefully they scrutinize those who enter, *sidi*?"

"I know how many men guard it and how carefully they guard it," Khardan answered, jumping down from his horse. "You and the other djinn stay out of the city until it is time. If the immortals of Quar should discover you, the God would be alerted to our presence. "

"Yes, *sidi*." Sond bowed and vanished.

Khardan unsaddled his horse and led the animal to drink in the stream. The other men did the same, making certain to keep the animals in the lengthening shadows, settling the beasts for the night. The camels were persuaded to kneel down near the banks of the rushing water. The men crouched on the ground below the grapevines, eating their one daily meal, talking in low voices.

Zohra began to mix flour with water, forming balls of dough that, if they had dared light a fire, could have been baked and made slightly more palatable. As it was, the nomads ate the dough raw, a few lucky ones supplementing their meager dinner with handfuls of overlooked, wrinkled grapes, stripped from the vines that sheltered them. The most that could be said for the repast was that it assuaged their hunger. Somewhere, from out of the air around them, they could hear the djinn Usti groan dismally.

Finishing his food without tasting it or even being consciously aware that he ate, Khardan rose to his feet and walked up to the top of the rise to stare at the city. The sun was setting beyond the walls of Kich, and Khardan gazed into the red sky with such intensity that the minarets and bulbous domes, tall towers and battlements seemed etched into his brain.

At length Auda rose and went to the stream to wash the sticky dough from his fingers. Removing the *haik*, he plunged his head into the water, letting it run down his neck and chest.

"The stream is cold. It must come from the mountains. You should try it," he said, rubbing his shining black hair with the sleeve of his flowing robes.

Khardan did not reply.

"I do not think it will quench the fire of your thoughts," Auda remarked wryly, "but it may cool your fever."

Glancing at him, Khardan smiled ruefully. "Perhaps later, before I sleep."

"I have been thinking long about what you said—your God forbids the taking of life in cold blood. Is that true?" Auda leaned against a tree trunk, his gaze following Khardan's to the soldiers of the city walls.

"Yes," Khardan answered. "Life taken in the hot blood of battle or the hot blood of anger—that the God understands and condones. But murder—life taken by stealth, by night, a knife in the back, poison in a cup. . ." Khardan shook his head.

"A strange man, your God," remarked Auda.

Since there could not be much comment made. Regarding this statement, Khardan smiled and kept quiet.

Auda stretched, flexing muscles stiff from the long ride. "You are worried about entering the gates, aren't you?"

"You have gone through those gates. You know what the guards are like. And that was in days of peace! Now they are at war!"

"Yes, I have entered Kich, as you well know. You made my last visit a very unpleasant one!" Auda grinned briefly, then sobered. "It was due to their strict vigilance that I was forced to entrust the enchanted fish to Blossom. And yes, you are right. They are at war; their lookout will have increased tenfold."

"And you still go along with our original plan?" Khardan cast a scowling glance at the large bundle lying on the ground—a bundle containing women's heavy robes and thick veils.

"Chances are they will not search females," Auda answered carelessly.

"Chances!" Khardan snorted.

Auda laid a hand on the Calif's arm. "Zhakrin has brought me this far. He will get me through the gate. Will your God not do as much for his Prophet?"

Was the voice mocking, or did it speak truly, from faith? Khardan stared at Auda intently but could not decide. The man's eyes, the only window to his soul, were—as usual—closed and shuttered. What was it about this man that drew Khardan near as it repelled him? Several times the Calif thought he had found the answer, only to have it flit away from him the next instant. Just as it did now.

Khardan bathed in the stream, then spread his blanket beneath the trees near where Zohra and Mathew sat talking in whispers, perhaps going over their own plans, for Mathew was repeating strange words to Zohra, who murmured them over and over to herself before she slept.

Night came and with it a gentle rain that pattered on the leaves of the grapevines. One by one the nomads sank into sleep, secure in the knowledge that their immortals guarded their rest, and leaving their ultimate fate in the hands of Akhran.

CHAPTER 2

Os Sul would have it, it was neither *Hazrat* Akhran nor Zhakrin, God of Evil, who opened the gate of the city of Kich to the nomads.

It was Quar.

"Master, wake up!"

Khardan sat bolt upright, his hand closing over the hilt of his sword.

"No, *sidi*, there is no danger. Look." Sond pointed. Khardan, blinking the sleep from his eyes, peered through the haze of early morning to where the djinn indicated. "When did this begin?" he asked, staring.

"Before it was light, *sidi*. We have been watching for over an hour and it grows."

Khardan turned to wake Auda, only to find the Paladin reclining on his arms, watching in relaxed ease. Last night, the road had been empty of all travelers. This morning it was jammed with people, camels, donkeys, horses, carts, and wagons, all coming together, jostling for position, breaking down in the center of the road, and snarling up traffic. But despite the confusion, it was clear that they were all headed in one direction—toward Kich.

Springing to his feet, Khardan shook Zohra's shoulder roughly and, grabbing Mathew's blanket, pulled it out from beneath him, dumping the young man rudely to the ground. "Hurry! Wake up! Gather your things! No, we won't need those. Only Mat-hew will dress as a woman. Ibn Jad and I won't need a disguise, thank Akhran."

"I do not think we need rush," remarked Auda coolly, his gaze on the road and the winding snake of humanity that crept along it. "This is unending, it seems."

"One of our Gods has seen fit to answer our prayers," remarked Khardan, tossing the saddle over his horse's back. "I will not offend whoever it is by seeming lax in my response."

Auda raised a thoughtful eyebrow and, without more words, prepared to saddle his own animal. By this time the camp was roused.

"What is it?" Majiid hurried over, his grizzled hair standing straight up on all sides of the small, tight-fitting cap he wore beneath his headcloth. Cinching his saddle, Khardan grunted and nodded his head at the road below, but by that time Majiid had seen and was scowling.

"I don't like this. . . this crowd coming to the city."

"Do not question the blessing of the God, father. It gets us into the gate. Surely with this mob the guards will not look too closely at four."

"Then they will not look too closely at four hundred. I'm going with you!" stated Majiid.

"And I!" cried Jaafar, hurrying up. "You'll do nothing without me!"

"Make my camel ready!" Zeid, dashing over, turned and started to dash away.

"No!" Khardan called as loudly as he dared before the entire hillside erupted into confusion. "How will it look to Qannadi if a crowd of armed *spahis* surges into his city? The Amir remembers what happened the last time we went to Kich. He would never agree to listen to me! We follow the plan, father! The only ones who enter the city are Auda, my wife, Mat-hew, Sond, and I. You and the men remain here and wait for the djinn to report back."

Sheykh Jaafar argued that the mob on the road was an ill omen and that no one should enter the city. Sheykh Majiid, suddenly siding with his son, repeated once again that Jaafar was a coward. Zeid glowered at Khardan suspiciously and insisted that the Calif take Raja with him, as well as Sond, and Jaafar shouted that if Raja went, Fedj should not be left behind.

"Very well!" Khardan lifted his hands to the heavens. "I will take all the djinn!"

"I will not be offended, master, if you leave me behind," began Usti humbly, but a glimpse at the Calif's dark and exasperated expression caused the flabby immortal to gulp and disappear into the ethers with his companions.

When all were ready, Khardan cast a stern glance at the Sheykhs. "Remember, you are to wait here for word. This you swear to me by *Hazrat* Akhran?"

"I swear," muttered the Sheykhs unwillingly.

Knowing that each of the old men was perfectly capable of deciding that this vow applied to all with the exception of himself, Khardan calculated he had no more than a few days' peace before he could look forward confidently to a chaos equivalent to that of Sul's legions breaking loose out here in the vineyard. Not at all reassured by seeing Majiid brandishing his sword in a salute that nearly decapitated Jaafar, Khardan led his horse from the grove, followed by Auda, Zohra, Mathew, and—he assumed—three invisible djinn. The thought of this procession attempting to sneak into Kich unobserved preyed on his mind. It was probably just as well, therefore, that the Calif did not know an angel of Promenthas was tagging along, as well.

Hurriedly, Khardan led the group through the vineyards, bringing them to a halt some distance from the road in the shelter of the trees along the stream.

"Either Auda or I will do the talking. Remember, it is not seemly for our women to speak to strangers."

This was said to Mathew, who was once again disguised as a female in a green caftan and a green and gold spangled veil he had taken from Meryem's tent. But Khardan could not help his glance straying to Zohra. Mathew accepted the instruction gravely and somberly. Zohra glared at Khardan in sudden fury.

"I am not a child!" she snarled, giving a rope wrapped around a bundle on the back of the horse a vicious jerk that sent the startled animal dancing sideways into the stream with a splash.

Checking an exasperated retort, the Calif turned from Zohra and, leading his horse out of the vineyards, headed for the road. He ignored the low chuckle he heard come from the Paladin, walking beside him.

Very well, he berated himself, he deserved her anger. He shouldn't have said it. Zobra knew their danger. She would do nothing to expose them. But why couldn't she understand? He was worried, nervous, afraid for her, afraid for the boy, afraid for his people. Yes, if truth be told, afraid for himself. A battle in the open air, grappling with Death face-to-face—that he understood and could meet without blenching. But a battle of duplicity and intrigue, a battle fought trapped inside city walls—this unnerved him.

It occurred to him that perhaps it was not quite fair to demand of Zohra that she honor her husband for his strength and pretend not to see his weakness, while at the same time expecting her to make allowances for the very weakness he refused to admit having. But so be it, he decided, sliding and slipping down the terraced slope. Akhran had never said that anyone's life was fair.

Leading their horses by the reins, the four stepped hesitantly, cautiously, into the road, joining the throng of people heading for Kich. They were immediately absorbed into the crowd without question or notice. Everyone appeared to be in a state of anticipatory excitement; and Khardan was wondering which of those pressing around would be safe to question when Auda, touching him gently, gestured in the direction of a rascally looking, sunburnt man clad in a well-worn *burnouse* and a small, greasy, sweat-stained cap that fit tightly over his skull.

The man held, at the end of a lead, a small monkey, who wore a cap similar to its master's and a coat made in imitation of one of the Amir's soldiers that was almost, but not quite, as filthy. The monkey scampered among the crowd, to the delight of the children and Mathew. The young man stared at it wide-eyed, having never seen an animal such as this before. Holding out its tiny hand, the monkey would run up to a person, begging for food or money or anything anyone seemed inclined to hand it. When the monkey had taken the grape or the copper piece, it would perform a head-over-heels flip at the end of its leash, then run back to its master.

Removing from his money pouch one of the last, precious coins of his tribe, Khardan considered a moment. He had no idea how long they might be forced to stay in Kich until the Amir returned. They would need food and a place to sleep. But he had to have information. Slowly Khardan held up the coin between thumb and forefinger. Catching the glint of money, the monkey ran up and hopped about in the dust at Khardan's feet, chittering wildly and beating its tiny hands together to indicate that the nomad was to toss the coin.

"No, no, little one," said Khardan, shaking his head and talking to the monkey, though his eyes were really on its master. "You must come and get it."

The monkey's master spoke a word, and to the Calif's astonishment the monkey leapt onto his robes and crawled up the nomad as deftly as if Khardan had been a species of date palm. Scampering along the Calif's arm, the monkey neatly plucked the coin from Khardan's fingers, then flipped over backwards to land on its feet in the street. Those in the crowd who had witnessed the feat applauded and laughed at the expense of the nomad.

Khardan's face flushed red, and he was of half a mind to make the monkey's master do a few flips himself when he heard an odd sound behind him. Turning, he glowered at Mathew.

"I'm sorry, Khardan," murmured the young man from behind his veil stifling his giggle, his eyes dancing in merriment. "I couldn't help myself."

"Be quiet, you'll call attention to us!" Khardan said sternly, reminding Mathew of what the Calif himself had nearly forgotten. Khardan's gaze darted to Zohra. She lowered her eyes, but not before he had seen laughter sparkling in their depths.

Khardan felt a smile tug at his lips despite himself. *I must have looked ridiculous, I'll admit that. And to hear the young man laugh—after all this time. Especially facing such danger. It is a good omen, and I accept it.*

"*Salaam aleikum*, my friend," called out Khardan to the monkey's master, who had taken the coin from the animal and, after inspecting it closely, carefully tucked it into a ragged cloth bag he carried slung over his shoulder.

The monkey's master bowed and came over to walk beside the two nomads and their wives, his sharp-eyed gaze going to the place in the Calif's flowing robes from where he had seen the money emerge. "*Aleikum salaam, Effendi*," he said humbly.

The monkey was not so polite. Riding on its master's shoulder, the creature bared its sharp little teeth at Khardan and hissed. With a deprecating smile the master stroked the creature and admonished it in a strange language. The monkey, shaking its head and making a rude noise, skipped over to the other shoulder.

"I apologize, *Effendi*," said the man. "Zar does not like to be teased. It is his one failing. Other than that he is a wonderful pet."

"He seems a very useful one," remarked Khardan, eyeing the cloth bag.

The monkey's master clapped his hand over the bag, his gaze

suddenly narrowed and scowling. But seeing the nomad walking beside him amiably, his own eyes friendly and innocent of evil intent, the man relaxed.

"Yes, *Effendi*," he admitted. "I have walked the road with starvation my only companion for many years before I came across Zar, here. His name means 'gold' and he has been worth his weight in that to me many times over. Of course," he added hastily, making a sign over the animal's head with his hand, "Zar is a foul-tempered little beast, as you have seen. Many is the time he has sunk his tiny teeth into my thumb. See?" The man exhibited a dirty finger.

Khardan expressed condolences, and knowing it would not be wise to discuss the monkey further lest the evil eye seek the animal out and destroy it, the Calif found it easy to change topics.

"You spoke words I did not understand. You are not from around here."

The man nodded. "My home—What home I have—is in Ravenchai. But I have not been back there for many years. To be quite honest, my friend"—he drew nearer Khardan and gave him a conspiratorial glance from narrowed eyelids—"there is a wife in that home who would greet me with something less than loving devotion if I returned, if you know what I mean."

"Women!" grunted Khardan sympathetically.

"It wasn't her fault," said the rascally man magnanimously. "Work is not fond of me."

"It isn't?" returned Khardan, somewhat at a loss to understand this strange statement.

"No, Work and I do not get along well at all. I take up with him on occasion, but we always end up in a dispute. Work demands that I continue pursuing him, while I am inclined to leave off and get something to eat or to take a small nap or to go around to the *arwat* for a cup of wine. Work ends up leaving me in a fit of anger, and there I am, with nothing to do except sleep, with no money to buy food to eat or wine to quench my thirst." The man shook his head over this and appeared so truly devastated at this ill fortune that Khardan had no difficulty pronouncing Work to be the most unreasonable being in existence.

"When Zar came to me— And that is a very strange story, my friend, for Zar *did* come to me, literally. I was walking the streets of—well, it does not matter to you what streets they were—when the Sultan rode out in his palanquin to take in the air. I was following along at his side, just in case the Sultan happened to drop anything that I might have the honor of restoring to him, when I saw the curtains part, and out from the bottom hopped this little fellow." He patted the monkey, who had fallen asleep on his shoulder, its tail curled tightly about its master's neck.

"He leapt straight into my arms. I was preparing to return him to the Sultan when I noticed that the guards were engaged in beating off several beggars who had crowded around the other side of the palanquin. The Sultan was watching them with interest. No one, it seemed, had noticed the creature's absence. Thinking that the monkey must have been badly treated, or he would never have left his owner, I thrust him beneath my robes and disappeared down an alley. That was several years ago, and we have been together ever since."

And he saves you from being involved with that dread fellow Work, Khardan thought with some amusement. Aloud he merely congratulated the man on his good fortune and then asked, casually, "Why is this great crowd going into Kich?"

The man looked ahead. The city walls were close enough to them now that Khardan could see clearly the heavily armed guards walking the battlements. The morning sun gleamed brightly off a golden dome—a new addition to the temple of Quar, Khardan concluded. Paid for with the wealth and blood of the conquered cities of Bas, no doubt.

The monkey's master turned his gaze to Khardan in some amazement. "Why, you must have been far out in the desert not to have heard the news, nomad. This day the Imam of Quar returns victorious to his city."

Khardan and Auda exchanged swift glances.

"This day? And the Amir?"

"Oh, he comes, too, I suppose," the man added without much interest. "It is the Imam all gather to see. That and the great slaughter of *kafir* that will be held tonight in his honor."

"*Tonight!*"

"Slaughter of *kafir*?" Auda pushed forward to ask this question, drawing attention away from the white-faced Khardan. "What do you mean, my friend? This sounds like a sight I would feign not miss. "

"Why, the *kafir* of tht desert who have been imprisoned

in Kich for many months and who have refused to convert to Quar." The man looked intently at Khardan and Auda, noting the *haik* and the flowing robes with sudden uneasiness. "These *kafir* wouldn't be relatives—"

"No, no," Khardan said gruffly, having recovered from the jolting shock. "We come from . . . from . . ." He faltered, his brain refusing to function.

"Simdari," inserted Auda, well aware that the nomad's world was encompassed within his sand dunes.

"Ah, Simdari," said the monkey's master. "I have never traveled in that land, but I am planning on journeying there when this festival is concluded. Tell me, what do you know of the *arwats* of Simdari . . ."

Auda and the rascally man who did not get along with Work entered into a discussion of various inns, of which Khardan heard not one word. So much for good omens! All their plans, running like sand from between his fingers! How could he ever hope to see the Amir, who would be busy with returning to his palace, his city? And the Imam, prepared to destroy his people this night!

It is hopeless, Khardan thought despondently. I can do nothing but stand and watch my people murdered! No, there is one thing I can do. I can die with them as I should have months ago—

A hand touched his. Thinking it was Auda, he turned swiftly only to find Zohra walking at his side. Irrationally, he felt as if this bad luck was somehow his fault and she was going to gloat over him again. He was about to order her to return to her place when she saw and forestalled his intent.

"Do not despair!" she said softly. "Akhran is with us! He brought us here in time, and his enemy opens the gates for us to enter."

The dark eyes above the veil glittered, and her fingers brushed lightly against his hand. Before he could respond or reach out to her, she was gone.

Glancing behind, he saw her talking to Mathew, their heads bent close together, whispering. The young wizard nodded his veiled head several times, emphatically. His delicate hand made gestures, graceful as a woman's. He and Zohra walked side by side, shoulders, bodies touching.

Khardan suffered a twinge of jealousy, looking at the two, seeing their obvious closeness. It wasn't the hurting, shriveling anguish he'd experienced when he'd feared Auda had . . . well, when he'd feared Auda. He couldn't be jealous of the young man in the same way. He was jealous because this gentle wizard was closer to his wife than he, Khardan, could ever come. It was a closeness of shared interests, respect, admiration. And then it occurred to Khardan, startlingly, that just as his wife was closer to Mathew than to him, so he was closer to Mathew than to his wife.

Khardan was genuinely fond of the young man. He knew his courage, for had seen it in Castle Zhakrin. The fact that he—Khardan—could relate to Mathew as a man and that Zohra could, at the same time, relate to Mathew as a woman was a phenomenon that completely baffled the Calif. He allowed it to occupy his mind, crowd out more dismal and hopeless thoughts. These returned full force, however, when Auda came to walk beside him once more.

"The situation is not quite as desperate as you first thought, if what this fellow says can be trusted. The Imam will make a speech this night in which he will exhort all *kafir* to renounce their old Gods and come to the One, True God, Quar. Those who refuse will be given the night to consider their waywardness. In the morning, at dawn, they will choose to find salvation with Quar or be considered beyond redemption in this life and considerately put to death to find it in the next. "

"So we have until dawn," muttered Khardan, not overly comforted.

"Until dawn," Auda repeated with a casual shrug. "And our Enemy opens his gate to us. "

The second time I have heard that. Khardan tried to see this as the miracle that everyone else did. Yet he was naggingly reminded of the fable of the lion who told the foolish mouse he knew of a wonderful place where the mouse could find shelter for the winter.

"Right here," said the lion, opening his mouth and pointing down his gullet. "Just walk in. Don't mind the teeth."

Khardan raised his eyes to the city walls, the great wooden gates, the soldiers massed on top of the battlements.

Don't mind the teeth. . .

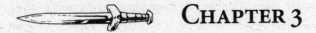 # CHAPTER 3

They swept through the gate on a tide of humanity. No guard saw them, let alone attempted to stop and question them. The nomads were in far more danger from the crowds than the soldiers. It was all Auda and Khardan could do to keep hold of their horses. Brave in battle, accustomed to blood and slashing steel, and to being accorded the highest respect by humans, the animals were angered by the rough jostling, the elbows in the flanks, the whines of the beggars, the clamoring cries, pushings, and shovings of the mob.

Just inside the gate was a large, cleared area where wagons used to haul goods to the city were stored. Slaves of every type and description were driving camels and donkeys into, out of, and around the cart-standing area; the fodder sellers were doing a literally roaring business. Khardan glanced askance at the confusion, but a momentary regret that he had chosen to bring the horses passed swiftly. They would need them in their escape . . . Akhran willing.

Catching sight of a tall, thin boy of about eleven or twelve years who was staring at them intently, Khardan motioned him near. The boy's eyes had not been on the nomads themselves, but on the horses, gazing at the magnificent animals of the desert with the hungry love and yearning of one who has grown up in the twisted streets of the city. The child never knew the freedom of the singing sands, but he could see it and feel it in the beauty and strength of the descendants of the horse of the Wandering God. At Khardan's gesture the boy shot forward as though hurled from a sling.

"What is your bidding, *Effendi*?"

Khardan's gaze scanned the cart-standing area, then turned to the boy. "Can you find food and water and rest for our horses and watch over them while we conduct our business?"

"I would be honored, *Effendi*!" breathed the boy, stretching forth trembling hands to take the reins.

Khardan fished another precious coin from the purse. "Here, this will purchase food and stable space. There will be another for you if you keep your trust."

"I would let myself be split in two by wooden stakes driven through my body, *Effendi*, before I allowed harm to come to these noble beasts!" The boy put a hand upon the neck of Khardan's steed. Feeling the gentle touch, the animal quieted, though he stared around with rolling eyes and pricking ears.

"I trust that will not be necessary," Khardan said gravely. "Watch over them and keep them company. You need not worry about theft. I do not like to think what would happen to any man who tried to ride these horses without our sanction."

The boy's face fell at this. "Yes, *Effendi*." he said wistfully, twisting the mane lovingly in his fingers.

Grinning, Khardan caught hold of the boy around the waist and tossed him up on the horse's back. The boy gasped in delight and astonishment and could barely hold the reins the nomad thrust into his eager, trembling hand.

"You may ride him, my fine *spahi*," said the Calif, handing the boy the leads for the other three animals. A word in his horse's ear and the animal suffered himself to be ridden away by the proud boy who bounced unsteadily in the saddle and wore the look of one who has ridden since birth. The other three horses followed their leader without hesitation.

"Sond," muttered Khardan beneath his breath to the air, "see that all is well with them."

"Yes, *sidi*. Shall I have Usti stand guard?"

"For the time being. We may need him later."

"Yes, *sidi*."

The Calif heard a yelped protest, "I refuse to be left in a horse stall!" that ended in a smacking sound and a blubbering whimper.

Now that the horses were settled, Khardan stared around him confusedly. His chief worry had been getting through the gate. This having been accomplished with an ease and swiftness that left him breathless, the Calif again felt a sense of disquietude about it, as if he had been given a valuable gift that he knew deep within was no gift and feared the dread payment that must be exacted later.

A shout from Auda saved Mathew from being ridden down by two donkey riders and recalled Khardan to the fact that they were standing in the center of the main road of Kich and were in danger of being trampled or separated by the mob. Though it was Zohra's first time to see the city, she was glancing about in a haughty disdain which, Khardan had come to know, masked uneasiness and awe. He knew how she felt; he could feel his own face settling into that very expression. Mathew was calm, but very pale. Above his veil, his green eyes were wide, and he kept darting swift glances at something behind Khardan. The Calif looked back, saw the slave market, and understood.

"What now, brother?" asked Auda.

What now indeed? Khardan continued to gaze around help-lessly. The Amir had once referred to the nomads—outside of their hearing, of course—as naive children. If Qannadi had been present to witness Khardan's confusion, the Amir would have been able to acknowledge himself a wise judge of men. Months ago, in the pride of his standing as Prince of the desert, Khardan had walked into the palace and demanded and received an audience with the Amir. He'd had it in mind this time to do the very same thing when—standing once again in the city streets and re-living that audience months before—he suddenly realized that he had been duped. He had been admitted purposefully, attacked purposefully, allowed to escape purposefully. He'd had a glimmer of this; Meryem's assassination attempt revealed as much, but now the light of truth shone glaringly down on him. Just why the Amir had gone to this trouble with him was still vague to Khardan, who did not know—and probably never would—of Pukah's bungling, double-dealing, mischief making.

The Calif swore bitterly, cursing himself for a fool. Would the Amir see him now? A ragged Prince whose people were imprisoned, doomed to death? Qannadi was just returned triumphant from battle. There would be supplicants and well-wishers by the hundreds who had undoubtedly been waiting weeks to see him and might possibly wait weeks longer until the Amir was at leisure to turn his attention to them. Qannadi might not even have arrived in the city.

A blare of trumpets came as answer to Khardan's thoughts. A

clattering of many hooves warned him of his peril just moments before the cavalry of the Amir swept through the city gate. Their nags whipping behind them, the soldiers' uniforms were vivid splashes of color among the drab browns and whites, grays and blacks worn by those milling about the streets. Hurrying to the side of the road just moments before they would have been stampeded into the hard-packed earth, Khardan and his companions watched the soldiers ride heedlessly through the crowd, knocking aside those who did not move out of their way, ignoring the curses and shaking fists that heralded their entry.

They were all business, these men. It was their duty to clear the way, and this they did, with ruthless efficiency. An ax through flesh, they cleaved through the masses, the well-trained horses pressing the people back against the walls of the *Kasbah* on one side, the slave market and the first stalls of the bazaar on the other. Foot soldiers, marching in ranks behind them, were swiftly deployed by their officers to keep the crowd back, taking up positions on either side of the street, holding spears out horizontally before them to form a living barricade. Those who tried to cross or who surged forward were given a swift clout with the butt-end of the weapon.

Khardan searched the faces of the riders intently, looking for Achmed, but there was too much confusion, and the soldiers, in their steel helms, looked all alike to him. He heard Auda shouting, "What is it? What is happening?" and several voices crying at once, "The Imam! The Imam is come!"

The stench, the heat, the excitement, was suffocating. Khardan felt fingers dig into his arm and turned to see Mathew clinging to him desperately so as not to be knocked off his feet by the heavings and surges of the mob. Khardan gripped the young man by the arm, holding him close, and looked to see Auda deal swiftly and silently with an overzealous believer attempting to shove Zohra out of his line of vision. A gasp, a groan, and Quar's faithful sank down into the dust where his unconscious body was immediately set upon and picked clean by the followers of Benario.

A mighty shout rose from the throats of the people, who strained forward with such force that the soldiers holding them back stumbled and fought to keep their footing. Line after line of the Imam's own soldier-priests appeared, walking proudly down the street. Unlike the Amir's men, these soldier-priests wore no armor, believing themselves to be protected from harm by the God. Clad in black silken tunics and long, billowing *pantalons*, every soldier-priest had a story about how an arrow, shot at his heart, had bounced off, how Quar's hand had turned aside a sword thrust meant for the throat. Such tales were often not far from the truth, for the soldier-priests ran into battle in a shrieking, confused knot, hacking with their naked blades, the light of fanaticism gleaming in their eyes. More than one enemy broke before them in sheer panic. The soldier-priests carried their curved blades in their hands. At the cheers of the crowd, they raised the swords above their heads and shook them in triumph.

After the arrival of the soldier-priests—and Khardan was aghast and amazed at their numbers—the roaring of the crowd reached a din impossible to believe. A hundred *mameluks*, clad in gold skirts with white headdresses made of ostrich plumes, followed. In their hands they carried baskets and tossed handfuls of coins into the clamoring crowd. Khardan caught one and Auda another—pure silver. The Calif could not hear, but he knew by the expression on Auda's face the words formed by his grinning lips.

"Our Enemy not only opens the gate but pays us to enter!"

Behind the *mameluks* two huge elephants hove into view, the sun gleaming brightly off ruby and emerald encrusted headdresses. Slaves rode their backs, guiding them through the streets. Golden, gem-studded bracelets glittered around the elephant's thundering feet. Their long tusks were tipped with gold. Khardan felt Mathew's body, pressed close against him by the crush of the crowd, tremble and sigh in awe. The young wizard from the strange land across the sea had never before seen such giant, wondrous creatures, and he gaped in staring-eyed amazement.

The elephants pulled behind them a gigantic structure built on wheels that, when it came nearer, could be seen to be a representation of a ram's head. Cunningly constructed of wood covered with parchment, the huge ram's head was painted with such skill that one might have mistaken it for a larger version of the real ram's-head altar that wavered and rocked on the swaying wooden base. Standing next to the altar, which had been hauled over the long miles traveled by the Amir's conquering army, was Feisal, the Imam.

At his coming, the cheers rose to a frenetic pitch, then

dropped to an eerie hush that resounded in the ears more loudly than the shouts. Many in the crowd sank to their knees, prostrating themselves in the dust. Those that could not move because of the masses pressing around them extended their arms, silently beseeching their priest's blessing. Feisal gave it, turning first one way, then the other, from his perch on the great wheeled wagon. Several high priests stood proudly beside him. A horde of soldier-priests marched around the wagon's wheels, glaring fiercely and suspiciously at the adoring crowd.

Glancing at Auda, Khardan saw the man's usually impassive face thoughtful and grave and guessed the Paladin was imagining how best to penetrate this ring of steel and fanaticism. He did not appear perturbed or daunted by this sight, however; he was simply speculative.

Probably leaving all the mundane details, such as getting round a thousand swords, in the hands of his God, Khardan thought bitterly, and turned his eyes back to the Imam just as the Imam's eyes turned to him.

Khardan shuddered from head to toe. It was not that he had been recognized. That must be impossible with thousands of faces surrounding the Imam. No, the shudder was from the look in the eyes—the look of one possessed body and soul by a devouring passion, the look of one who has sacrificed reason and sanity to the consuming flame of holy fervor. It was the look of an insane man who is all too sane, and it struck terror to Khardan's heart, for he knew now that his people were doomed. This man would pour their blood into his golden chalice and hand it to his God without a qualm, believing firmly that he was doing the slaughtered innocents a favor.

The Imam passed by, and the terror faded from Khardan's thoughts, only to leave despair behind. The crowd turned to follow after the procession, which was apparently meant too wind its way through the city streets before returning to bring the Imam to his Temple. The Amir's soldiers fell back once the priest was safely past, Khardan and his companions were swept along with the masses.

"We've got to get free of this!" Khardan yelled at Auda, who nodded. Linking arms, he and the Calif held firmly to each other's shoulders, forming a shield with their bodies around Zohra and Mathew. They fended off jostlers with blows and kicks and struggled to make their way down a quiet side street or into one of the nooks along the *Kasbah's* walls.

Gloom descended on Khardan like a huge bird of prey, tearing out his heart, blinding him with its black wings. Though he had repeatedly told himself he came without hope, he knew now that he had in reality been carried this far on the strong wave of that most stubborn of all human emotions. Now hope was draining from him, leaving nothing but emptiness. His arms ached, his head throbbed with the noise, he felt sickened from the stench. The desire in his heart was to sink to the ground and let the trampling feet of the mob beat him into oblivion, and it was only concern for the welfare of those dependent on him, and Auda's firm grip on his shoulder, that kept him going.

Tirelessly the Black Paladin forged a path for them, thrusting, shoving, and constantly tugging and pulling at them to follow him. Khardan marveled at the man's strength, still more at his faith that had apparently not sunk beneath the weight of impossible odds.

"Faith," muttered Khardan, stumbling, falling, feeling Mathew and Zohra clinging to him, pulling himself up again, hearing Auda's shouts driving him on. "Faith—all that is left once hope is gone. *Hazrat* Akhran! Your people are in desperate need! We do not ask you to come fight for us, for you are fighting your own battle if what we hear is true. We have the courage to act, we need a way! Show us, Holy Wanderer, a way!"

The four were swept up against a wall with a suddenness that left them bruised and scraped. A panicked moment when it seemed they must be crushed against the stone passed, and then the worst of the crowd was by them, running after the procession, leaving relative quiet behind.

"Is everyone all right?" Khardan asked. He turned to see Mathew nod breathlessly, his hands fumbling with the veil that had been torn loose from his face.

"Yes," Zohra answered, hurriedly assisting Mathew, for it would not do to let anyone catch sight of that fair skin or glimpse the fiery red hair.

A glance was sufficient to show that Auda ibn Jad was the same as always—cool and unperturbed, his gaze fixed on several soldiers who, now that the excitement had passed, appeared to be taking an undue interest in the robed nomads.

"Haste!" hissed Auda from the side of his mouth, giving elaborate attention to the arrangement of his disarrayed robes. Without seeming to hurry, he moved deftly into the shadows cast by the wall, herding Zohra and Mathew with him. Khardan, seeing this new danger, wheeled to accompany them, tripped, and nearly fell headlong over an object at his feet.

A groan answered him.

"A beggar, trampled by the mob," said Auda indifferently, one eye on the guards who were standing on the opposite side of the street, obviously watching them with interest. "Of no consequence. Keep moving!"

But Zohra was on her knees beside the old man, helping him with gentle hands to sit up. "Thank you, daughter," grunted the beggar.

"Are you injured, father? I have my healing *feisha*—"

"No, daughter, bless you!" The beggar reached a groping, frantic hand. "My basket, my coins— Stolen?"

"Leave him! We must go!" Auda said insistently, and was bending down to drag Zohra away when Khardan stopped him.

"Wait!" The Calif stared at the beggar—the milky white eyes, the basket in the lap. . . Only he wasn't seeing him now, he was seeing the beggar months ago, seeing a white hand fling a bracelet into that basket, seeing a hole in the wall—once gaping open— closed and sealed shut. Khardan looked around him. Yes, there was the milk bazaar where he had stolen the scarf for her head. Glancing up, he could see palm fronds swaying above the wall.

"Praise be to Akhran!" Khardan breathed thankfully. Kneeling beside the old man, pretending to be offering aid, he examined the wall and motioned Auda to kneel down beside him. "Guards of the Amir are pursuing us!" he whispered to the beggar. "I know about the hole in the wall. Can you get us inside?"

The milky white eyes turned their sightless gaze on Khardan, the wrinkled face was suddenly so shrewd and cunning that the Calif could have sworn the blind eyes were studying him intently.

"Are you one of the Brotherhood?" queried the old man. Khardan stared at him in puzzlement, not understanding. It was Auda who knelt near and, dropping the silver coin into the beggar's basket, said under his breath, "Benario, Lord of Snatching Hands and Swift-Running Feet."

The beggar's toothless mouth parted in a swift leer, and he

reached behind him with a dexterous hand. What hidden latch he tripped was kept concealed by his skinny body and the rags that covered it, but suddenly there was a gap in the wall behind him, large enough for a man to slip through.

"The soldiers are coming this way!" said Auda calmly. "Make no move!"

"Damn!" Khardan swore, able to see the pleasure garden of the Amir only inches from him.

"Akhran be with you, *sidi*," whispered a voice from the air. "We know what to do."

The soldiers were walking toward them, evidently wondering what the desert dwellers could find so interesting in a beggar of Kich, when two drunks—one of them a towering, muscular giant of a man with gleaming black skin, the other a well-dressed servant, obviously belonging to the royal household—rounded a corner and slammed right into them.

Startled—Khardan had completely forgotten the presence of the djinn—he stared at the soldiers grappling with the drunks and was jolted to movement only when he felt Auda shove him roughly toward the wall. Mathew and Zohra had already crept inside, Khardan followed, and Auda came hastening after. A grinding sound and the hole was gone, the wall smooth, unblemished. A covering thornbush trundled back into place with such alacrity that the Paladin had to tug his robes free of the flesh-tearing brambles before he could move.

"You realize we are in the harem, the forbidden place!" said Auda coolly, glancing around the garden. "If the eunuchs catch us, our deaths will be prolonged and most unpleasant."

"Our deaths aren't likely to be any other way no matter where we are," said Khardan, stepping cautiously onto a path and motioning for the rest to come after him, "and this at least gives us a chance of talking to the Amir."

"Also a chance of getting into the Temple," continued Auda. "When I served in the Temple at Khandar, I learned that there was, in Kich, a tunnel that ran from the Temple below the ground to the palace of the Amir."

"First we talk to Qannadi!" Khardan started to say harshly, when there came the snapping of a twig underfoot, a rustle in the trees, and a shout of joy and longing.

"Meryem!"

 # Chapter 4

Obsession sees only the object of its madness. It believes everything it wants to believe, questions nothing. Achmed grabbed hold of the slender figure clad in the well-remembered green and gold spangled veil and whirled it around to face him.

Mathew, startled, let fall his veil.

"You!" Achmed cried, and hurled the young man from him.

Looking around at the others with fevered eyes, he saw his brother, but it did not occur to him to question why Khardan was here, in the Amir's garden. For Achmed there was only one question in his heart.

"Where is she?" Achmed demanded. "Where is Meryem? This... man"—he choked on the word, pointing a shaking finger at Mathew—"is wearing her clothes..."

Too late Zohra laid restraining fingers on Khardan's arm. "Meryem's dead," said the Calif harshly, before he thought.

"Dead!" Achmed went white to the lips; he staggered where he stood. Then, in a swift motion, he yanked the sword from its scabbard at his side and jumped at Khardan. "You killed her!"

The young soldier's leap was halted by a strong arm wrapping around his neck, throttling him. A silver blade gleamed; the cruel eyes of the Paladin glittered beside him. Within another second Achmed's blood would have flowed from the slit in his throat.

"Auda, no! He's my brother!" Khardan caught hold of the Paladin's knife hand.

Auda stayed his killing stroke, but he held the young man tightly, his arm crushing the windpipe so that Achmed could neither speak nor yell. His eyes-staring at his brother-blazed with fury. He struggled impotently to escape his captor, and the Paladin tightened his grip.

"I'm sorry, Achmed," Khardan said lamely, mentally reviling

himself for his callous bungling. "'But she tried to kill me—"

"It was my hand slew her," Mathew said in low tones, "not your brother's. And it is true, she wore a poison ring."

Achmed ceased to struggle; he went limp in Auda's grasp. His eyes closed, and hot tears welled beneath the lids.

"Let him go," Khardan ordered.

"He'll alert the guards!" Auda protested.

"Let him go! He is my blood!"

Auda, with an ill grace, released Achmed. The young man, pale and shivering, opened his eyes and stared into Khardan's. "You had everything! Always!" he cried hoarsely. "Did you have to destroy the one thing that was mine?"

A sob shook him. "I hope they kill you, everyone of you!" Turning, running blindly, the young soldier plunged into the garden's sweet-smelling foliage. They could hear him crashing heedlessly among the plants.

"Don't be a fool, Khardan! You can't let him go!" Auda held his knife poised.

The Calif hesitated, then took a hurried step forward. "Achmed—"

"Leave the boy be," came a stern command.

Abul Qasim Qannadi, Amir of Kich, stepped out from the shadows of an orange tree. The perfume of late morning hung heavy in the garden-roses, gardenia, jasmine, lilies. The palm trees whispered their endless secrets, a fountain gurgled nearby. Somewhere in the darkest shadows a nightingale lifted his voice in his pulsing song—trilling a single heart-piercing note until it seemed his small chest must burst, and then holding it longer still.

The Amir was alone. He was not dressed in armor but clad in loose-fitting robes, thrown casually over one arm. One shoulder was bare, and from his wet hair and the glistening of oil upon his skin it seemed he had just come from his bath. He looked tired and older than Khardan remembered him, but that may have been because he was not king in a divan but a half-dressed man in a garden. Certainly he had not ridden with his troops this morning, nor—apparently—had he been present to watch the entrance or greet the Imam upon his arrival into the city.

"Assassins?" asked the Amir, looking coolly and unafraid at the sunlit blade of Auda's dagger.

"No," said Khardan, putting his own body between the Paladin and the Amir. "I come as Calif of my people!"

"Does the Calif of his people always sneak through holes in the wall?" Qannadi asked drily.

Khardan flushed. "It was the only way I could think of to get in to see you! I had to talk to you. My people. . . They say they're going to be slaughtered this next dawning!"

Qannadi's brown and weathered face hardened. "If you have come to beg—"

"Not beg, O King!" Khardan said proudly. "Let the women and children, the sick and the elderly, go free. We"—he gestured out past the palace walls toward the desert—"my men and I, will meet you in fair and open battle."

Qannadi's expression softened; he almost smiled. He glanced where Khardan pointed, though there was nothing to be seen but tangled, flowering vines and waxy-leafed trees. "There must be very few of you," the Amir said in a soft voice. He turned his penetrating gaze to Khardan. "And my army numbers in the thousands!"

"Nevertheless, we will fight, O King!"

"Yes, you would," said Qannadi reflectively, "and I would lose many good men before we succeeded in destroying you. But tell me, Calif, since when does the desert nomad come to issue a battle challenge with his women and"—his gaze lingered on Auda—"a Paladin of the Night God.

"Or, perhaps not women plural but woman alone." Qannadi considered Zohra gravely, speaking before Khardan could reply. "Flowers bloom in the desert as beautiful as in a king's garden. And more courageous, it would seem," he added, noting that Zohra's defiant eyes were fixed on him, not lowered in modesty as was proper.

There was no time for propriety, however. A word from Qannadi and the intruders in his garden would face the Lord High Executioner, who would see to it that they left this world in agonized slowness. Why hadn't Qannadi said that word? Khardan wondered. Was he toying with them? Hoping to find out all he could? But why bother? He would soon have everything they knew ripped from their mangled bodies.

"And you." Qannadi had been obliquely studying Mathew ever since the beginning of this strange conversation, and now his eyes finally settled on the object of their curiosity. "What are you?" the Amir asked bluntly.

"I—I am a man," Mathew said, crimson staining the smooth, translucent cheeks.

"I know that... *now*!" Qannadi said with a wry smile. "I mean what manner of man are you? Where are you from?"

"I am from the land of Aranthia on the continent of Tirish Aranth," said Mathew reluctantly, as though certain he would not be believed.

Qannadi simply nodded, however, though he raised an eyebrow.

"You know of it?" Mathew asked in wonder.

"And so does the Emperor," the Amir remarked. "If Our Imperial Majesty has his way, I might soon see this homeland of yours. Even now, Quar's Chosen readies his ships to sail the Hurn Sea. So you are the fish bone that has been sticking in Feisal's gullet."

Mathew blinked in confusion, not understanding. Qannadi smiled, but it was a smile that was not reflected in the eyes, which remained somber and sober. Khardan shifted uneasily. "The Imam received word that one of the followers of your God—I forget the name. It is not important." He waved a hand as Mathew would have spoken. "One of the followers who were presumably all struck down on the shores of Bas still lived and walked our land. And not lost and alone, but with friends, it appears."

He was quiet, thoughtful. Khardan waited nervously, not daring to speak.

"So Meryem is dead"—Qannadi's voice was smooth—"and it was you who struck her down."

The blood drained from Mathew's face, leaving it livid, but he faced the Amir bravely and with a quiet dignity. "I did what I thought right. She was going to murder—"

"I know all about Meryem," Qannadi interrupted.

"But it was not you who sent her, was it, O King?" said Khardan in sudden understanding.

"No, not I. Not that I wouldn't have slept easier nights knowing she had succeeded," the Amir admitted with a smile, which this time warmed the eyes embedded in their web of wrinkles. "You are a danger, nomad. What is worse, you are an innocent danger. You have no conception of the threat you pose. You are not ambitious. You cannot see beyond your dunes. You are honorable, trustworthy, trusting. How does one deal with a man like you in a world like this? A world gone mad."

The smile faded from the weary eyes. "I tried to insure that you left it. Oh, not through Meryem. I sent her there the first time, sent her to spy on you. And when she reported that your tribes were allying against me, I did you honor, though you did not know it. I sent you death in the form of Gasim, my best Captain. I sent you death in battle, face-to-face, blade-to-blade. Not death by night, with poison, in the guise of love."

"The Imam," said Khardan.

"Yes." Qannadi drew a deep breath. "The Imam." He paused. In the silence they could hear the murmur of the falling water. The nightingale had hushed his song. Beyond the walls, in the distance, could be heard the cheering of the crowd growing nearer. The procession was wending its way to the Temple. "So you come here to ask for the lives of your people," the Amir continued, and his voice chill. "I refuse your demand for battle. It is senseless. A waste of lives I can ill afford to spare. Let the conquered cities I control get whiff of this, and they would go for my throat.

"And now what do you do, Calif? What do you do with a woman whose eyes are the eyes of the hawk? What do you do with a man of an alien land where, they say, men possess the magical powers of women? What do you do with a Paladin of the Night, who has a blood curse to fulfill?"

Khardan, startled at these words striking so close to home, could not, at first, reply but only stare at Qannadi, trying to fathom the man's intent. He couldn't. Or if he did, it was only dimly, as a man sees through a storm of swirling sand.

"I will go to prison and die with my people, O King," the Calif said calmly.

"Of course you will," said Qannadi.

One corner of the mouth sank deep into the weathered cheeks. Raising his voice to the call that could sound over the pounding of hooves, the rattle and press of battle, the Amir shouted for his guards.

"What about Achmed?" Khardan asked hurriedly, hearing the stamp of booted feet on the garden path. Zohra stood proudly, head high, eyes flashing. Mathew watched Qannadi in silence. Auda ibn Jad thrust his dagger into some secret, hidden place and stood with his arms folded across his chest, a smile as dangerous and dark as Qannadi's on his lips. Khardan kept a wary eye on him, expecting him to fight—uncomfortable when he didn't.

"My brother should know the truth about the girl," the Calif pursued.

"He knows the truth. It festers in his heart, nomad," said Qannadi. "Would you yank out the arrow and let the barbs rip out his life? Or would you let it work its way out slowly, in its own time?"

"You love him, don't you?"

"Yes," Qannadi answered simply.

"So do I." The guards had come and taken hold of Khardan and his companions roughly, not sparing Zohra or Mathew but clasping them with firm hands and bending their arms behind their backs. "Keep him away tomorrow, O King," the Calif pleaded urgently, struggling to face the Amir as the guards tried to drag him off. "Don't let him see his people butchered!"

"Take them to the Zindan," said Qannadi.

"Promise me!"

Qannadi made a gesture. A jab to Khardan's kidney, and the Calif ceased to fight, doubling over with a groan of pain. The guards hustled them, unresisting, out of the garden.

Standing on the path, watching the strange group being led away, Qannadi spoke softly, "Your God be with you, nomad."

CHAPTER 5

Four prisoners started out for the Zindan, but only two arrived.

Zohra never heard what happened, in the confusion of the streets through which they were led, and neither, apparently, did the lieutenant responsible for delivering the nomads to the Zindan. The look upon his face when he turned around and saw that the number of his charges had been reduced by half was laughable.

Indeed, Zohra did laugh, which did not endear her to her captor. "You will not be laughing in the morning, *kafir!*" the lieutenant snapped. "Where are the men—the nomad and his friend?" he demanded of his soldiers, who were staring, dumbfounded, at each other.

"Perhaps they were stopped by the crowd," suggested the prison commandant complacently, folding his hands over his fat belly and regarding Zohra with appreciative eyes.

"Bah!" the lieutenant said, angered and more than half frightened. It would be his responsibility to report this loss to the Amir. "We weren't stopped by the crowd. Send some of your men out to search."

Shrugging, the commandant ordered several of his prison guards to retrace the lieutenant's steps from the Zindan back to the palace to see if the Amir's soldiers needed aid in bringing in their prisoners. The lieutenant took exception to the commandant's insinuation but—being in no position to vent his spleen—kept silent and aloof and stared intently out the window of the brick guardhouse into the crowded prison grounds.

"What do we do with these two beauties?" asked the commandant, his fingers twiddling.

"Put them with the others," said the lieutenant offhandedly.

"They are not to be mistreated."

"Mmmmm." The commandant ran his tongue over greasy lips. "They won't be, I can assure you. I know exactly how to . . . uh . . . handle them." Rising ponderously to his feet, he glanced out the window. "Ah, here come my men, with news from the looks of it. "

Mathew took advantage of the opportunity to creep nearer Zohra.

"What has happened? Where is Khardan? What have they done to him?"

"He is with the Paladin, of course," she whispered back. "There is nothing more we can do for them, Mat-hew, nor they for us. Our roads have separated. We are on our own."

The two prison guards arrived at the commandant's office, red-faced and breathless. "We found two of the Amir's men, sir, in a back alley. Dead. Their throats have been cut."

"Impossible! I heard nothing!" said the stunned lieutenant. "Did anyone see anything?"

The two guards shook their heads.

"I will go take a look for myself before I report to the Amir."

"You do that," said the commandant expansively. "And I'll make a special cell ready for you on your return," he muttered gleefully, watching the lieutenant walk stiffly out into the streets.

The prison chief—remembering regretfully the easy life under the Sultan—had little use for the Amir and none at all for his soldiers, a snooty lot who looked down their noses at him and were constantly interfering with what the commandant felt to be his prerogatives in the treatment of the scum assigned to his care.

"Treat you well! That I will, my flowers!" Gazing hungrily at Zohra, he rubbed his hands together. "I would have enjoyed the company of a few others of your kind if that pompous old ass in the palace hadn't kept his soldiers snooping about. But tonight everyone will be attending the Imam's ceremony. Your men have deserted you." He sidled up to Zohra with a leering grin, reaching out a flabby hand. "The cowards! But you will not miss them. Tonight I will show you *kafir* what it is to enjoy the company of a real man, one who knows how to—"

Zohra drove her foot hard into the crook of the man's knee. His leg collapsed under him, and he was forced to catch hold of a chair to keep from falling. Pain paled the heavy cheeks; his chin quivered in fury. "*Kafir* bitch!" Grabbing her veiled hair, he yanked her head back and started to kiss her. Zohra's nails flashed for his face. Mathew shoved his arm between the man's body and Zohra, endeavoring to break the embrace and drag Zohra away.

"Commandant," came a voice from the door.

"Ugh?" The prison chief, flinging Mathew from him, turned around, one hand still holding Zohra painfully by the hair.

"You are to report to the Amir," said the guard, endeavoring to look anywhere else but at his sweating chief. "Immediately. Word has already reached him about the murdered soldiers, it seems."

"Hunh!" The commandant hurled Zohra to the floor. Straightening his uniform, he mopped his face and, cursing beneath his breath, waddled out toward the palace walls.

"Take them to the compound," he ordered, waving his hand.

The guard stood over Zohra and Mathew, waiting for them to rise, not offering assistance but watching them with an unpleasant grin. The prison guards—dregs of humanity, many of whom had once been prisoners themselves—had been chosen by the commandant for their coarse and brutal natures. To be fair to the commandant, few others except men like these could be found who could stomach the work. A man sentenced to prison in this harsh land often had good cause to envy those sentenced to death. It was only through the intervention of the Imam, who never ceased to try to convert the *kafir*, that the nomads taken prisoner at the Tel had received good treatment. The guards had been forced to keep the women under their care for a month, forbidden to touch them. But that would end this night. The Amir's soldiers and the Imam's soldier-priests would be needed to help control the crowd. No one would pay any attention to the prisoners. Rapine, murder—who would know in the morning, when all were to be slaughtered anyway in the name of Quar? Who would care?

Zohra saw the hatred and lust burn in the man's animal eyes and understood clearly the doom that hung over the prisoners once darkness descended. It would be a night of horrors. Mathew's hand, as he helped her to her feet, was chill and clammy, and she knew that he understood as well. The two exchanged glances, exchanged fear.

Khardan was gone, prisoner of Auda or willing helper. He had not foreseen this danger; it had not occurred to him. Did the women in the prison realize their peril? Could they be made to fight it? Knowing her people, Zohra had no doubt that they would fight. She wondered uneasily if she could convince them to fight using this strange magic, taught by a madman.

They must, she said to herself firmly. They would. With Akhran's help. Or without it.

Khardan saw, from the corner of his eye, the guard marching behind Auda ibn Jad suddenly drop out of sight. The Calif felt a violent wrenching from behind. The hands of the guard holding his arms clenched spasmodically, then fell away from him. He was free. Turning, astonished, he saw the bodies of the two guards lying in the street, a red slit across each neck.

"This way!" hissed a voice.

"Zohra—" began Khardan, starting after the guards who, having heard nothing, were leading Zohra and Mathew away.

"No!" Auda blocked his path. "Would you ruin all?"

It was the most difficult decision the Calif had ever been forced to make, and he was forced to make it within seconds. *Do you deny me the right to die for my people because I am a woman?* Zohra's words echoed in his head.

Auda was right. Khardan might well ruin the only chance they had. He had to let her go—at least for the moment.

The Paladin and the Calif dived into a dark alley. Two shadowy shapes, blacker than night, flowed before them. A door opened suddenly. Hands yanked Khardan inside a building that was cool, lit only by the sunlight that streamed in when the door stood open. The Calif could see nothing when the door was slammed shut.

"Do you need anything else, *Effendi*?" whispered a voice that was vaguely familiar to Khardan.

"Yes, Kiber. Two robes of the soldier-priests'."

"Only two, *Effendi*?" The man sounded disappointed. "Are we not to help you in your task?"

"No, my life is forfeit for this cause. Your lives are not, and our people must not be wasted." There came a rustling sound, as of a hand clasping a shoulder. "You have been a faithful squire, Kiber. You have served both myself and the God well. My last request of my Lord is that you be knighted in the service of Zhakrin and take my place. Say to him, when you return, that this is my will."

"Thank you, *Effendi*." Kiber's voice was reverent. "The robes will be beneath the blackened stones of what used to be our mosque in this city. You will find food and drink on the floor near the center of this room. It has been my privilege to serve you these many years, Auda ibn Jad. You have taught me much. I pray that I will be a credit to you. Zhakrin's blessing!"

The door opened, the light stabbed brilliantly into the room, then the door shut and all was darkness and silence but for the breathing of the two men left behind.

"Zohra and Mat-hew." Khardan turned. "I must go—"

A hand of iron closed over his forearm. "They do what they must, brother, and so will we. I call upon you now, Khardan, Calif of your people, to fulfill the vow you made to me—of your own free will—in the dungeons of Castle Zhakrin."

"And if I do not," said Khardan, "will you strike me down?"

"No," said Auda softly. "Not I. How does your God deal with oath breakers?"

Reluctant, undecided, Khardan waited for his eyes to adjust to the darkness. He could see ibn Jad now, a vague, gray shape moving in the gloom.

"I should be with my wife, wives," he amended ironically, remembering that Mathew belonged to him. "I should be with my people. They are in danger."

"So they are. So are we. Zohra and Mathew understand how to fight it. Knowing no magic, can you help them? No, you might do them great harm. They are one hope for your people, and you are the other. And your way is with me."

"You don't give a damn about my people," said Khardan, angry, frustrated. He knew Auda was right, but he didn't like it, fought against it. "You'd slit their throats tomorrow if that God of yours ordered it."

Reaching down, he grabbed a loaf of flat, unleavened bread and bit off a great hunk, washing it down with warm, stale-tasting water from a goatskin bag.

"You are right, brother," said ibn Jad, the white teeth flashing for an instant in a grin. "But I know what drives you. That is the bond between us. We are both willing to sacrifice our lives for our people. And you see now, do you not, brother, that the only hope for the life of your tribe is the death of this priest?"

Khardan said nothing, but chewed bread.

"Surely you noticed," pursued Auda, "that the Amir himself sent you off with his blessing."

The Calif's eyes narrowed in a disbelieving scowl. Auda burst out with a laugh, then stifled it instantly, his glance darting toward the closed door. "You fool!" he lowered his voice. "Qannadi could have—should have—ordered his guards to slay us on the spot! The Amir is a traveled man. He knows the people of Zhakrin, he knows my goal. And he sends me off to prison under light guard! Nomads!" Auda shook his head. "You have the sword arms of warriors, the courage of lions, and the guileless souls of children.

"Here is this Amir, a soldier, a military man who would like very much to see the Emperor's rule spread as far as possible but would appreciate having some subjects left alive to benefit by it. Men will suffer beneath heavy taxes. They will grit their teeth and bear the lash. But touch a man's religion, and you touch his soul, his life in the hereafter, and that is something most men will willingly fight to protect. I suspect from certain words Qannadi let drop that the southern cities are rife with rebellion. He speaks of his army numbering in the thousands, but I have not seen near that many in Kich. He is spread thin to protect his holdings. The Amir was right," the Paladin added more thoughtfully. "You do not yet know how dangerous you are, nomad. When you do, I think the world will tremble."

He fell silent, eating and drinking. Khardan was quiet, too, thinking. His thoughts got him nowhere except to despair, however, and he changed the subject. "Where did those men of yours come from?" he asked irritably. "How did Kiber know we were in Kich?"

"The Black Sorceress sent them in case I needed aid. She has sent our people to all other cities where I might have gone in search of Feisal."

"And how did you contact Kiber?" Khardan pursued insistently. "I was with you the entire time! I saw no one. You spoke to no one—"

"I summoned him through my prayers, nomad. Our God sent my squire to me when I called. Never mind, you cannot understand." Auda finished the bread and stretched out comfortably on the floor, hands behind his head. "You should get some sleep, brother. The night will be long."

Khardan lay down upon the hard-packed dirt floor of the squalid hut. The heat was stifling. No hotter than the desert, perhaps, but he felt closed in, trapped, unable to breathe. Restlessly he turned and twisted and tried in vain to make himself relax.

Zohra. He feared for her, but he trusted her. That was why he had let her go. He knew her courage, none better. She had stood up to him more than once and won. He acknowledged her intelligence, though—he smiled wryly—she would never be wise. Always impetuous, with her sharp tongue and flash-fire temper, she acted and spoke before she thought. He only hoped that this fault did not lead her over the edge of the precipice she walked. But Mathew was with her. Mathew has wisdom enough for both of them, for all three of us, if it comes to that, Khardan admitted to himself. Mathew would guide her and, Akhran willing, they would be safe.

Safe. . . and then what?

Sighing bleakly, Khardan closed his eyes.

A long night.

It could be a very long night. One to last an eternity.

CHAPTER 6

There not being nearly enough cells to accommodate them, the women and children of the nomads had been herded into the central compound of the Zindan. When first captured several months ago, they had been given houses in the city and the freedom to make their livings as best they could in the *souks* of Kich. In return the Imam had hoped that a glimpse of city life—education for their children, food, shelter, safety—would cause them to renounce their wandering ways and convert to Quar. He hoped that their husbands would leave the desert and come join their families, and a few did. But when month after month passed and most did not, when it was reported to Feisal that the nomad women—though seemingly pliable and obedient—nevertheless kept their children out of the *madrasah* and never passed the Temple of Quar without crossing over to the opposite side of the street, the Imam began to lose patience.

Feisal was feeling desperate, driven. It was an irrational feeling, and he couldn't understand it. He was the most powerful priest in the known world. He had been invited to Khandar, to take over leadership of the church. It would be he, Feisal, who would lead the Emperor's troops across the sea to bring the unbelievers of that far-distant land of Tirish Aranth to the knowledge of the One, True God. Yet here were a handful of ragtag followers of a beaten-down God openly defying him, openly making him appear foolish in the eyes of the world. He, Feisal, had been merciful. He had given them their chance to redeem themselves. He would show mercy no longer.

Summarily the word had gone forth, and the nomads, mostly women and children but a few young men, fathers, and husbands, had been rounded up and sent to the Zindan.

The men were placed in cells, the women given the compound

in which to make their beds, cook their meals, tend their children. The men were beaten, surreptitiously, when the Amir's soldiers weren't around. The women and young girls were watched with hatred and lust. The soldier-priests, naked swords in hand, stood around them. The spectral figure of Death often passed by the Zindan, her hollow eyes eager, watchful.

When Zohra and Mathew entered the compound, shoved through the gate by the grinning guards, everyone was watching them. Yet no one said a word. The play of children was hushed, mothers clasping them tightly to the skirts of their robes. Conversation ceased.

Gritting her teeth, her chin held firm and high, Zohra walked among her people. Mathew—looking and feeling very uncomfortable—followed a few paces behind.

Glancing around, Zohra saw many she knew, but nowhere did she see any friends. The women of her own tribe, the Hrana, despised her for her unwomanly ways that told them plainer than words the contempt their Princess had for them. The women of the Akar hated Zohra for being a Hrana, for marrying their darling, their Calif, and then being insensible of this great honor, for refusing to cook his meals and keep his tent and weave his rugs. The women of Zeid's tribe disliked her for being a Hrana and for the gossip they had heard about her.

As for Mathew, he was crazy—a man who chose to dress as a woman to escape death. Akhran decreed that the insane were to be treated with all courtesy, and so he was treated with courtesy. Respect, friendship? Out of the question.

The women separated to let Zohra and Mathew pass. Zohra viewed them all at first with her lip curled in scorn, her own feelings of hatred and derision burning her blood with poison. Turning, she cast a sideways glance at Mathew, prepared to ask why they had bothered. The expression on his face stopped her cruel words. Compassion, mingled with growing anger, had brought a shimmer of tears to the young man's green eyes. Zohra looked at her people a second time—and saw them for the first time.

Conditions for the people were wretched—inadequate, unhealthful food, little water; they lived daily, literally beneath the sword. Each woman had a space in the crowded compound big enough for her to spread her blanket. Children whimpered in hunger or sat staring out at the world with eyes that had seen too much, too early. Here and there a woman lay on a blanket, too weak to move. There was a sound of coughing, a smell of sickness. Without their herbs and *feishas,* the women had been unable to tend the sick. In a quiet corner of the yard a blanket covered those who had died during the night.

Yet these women, like their men, had one thing that their captors could never take from them: their dignity, their honor. Looking at them, looking at the quiet calm that surrounded them, seeing the eyes that were unafraid, the eyes that held the faith in their God and in each other that sustained them, Zohra felt her own pride ooze from her. The wound in her spirit, lanced and drained of its infection, would at last begin to heal. The eyes of these women were a mirror, reflecting her to herself, and Zohra suddenly did not like what she saw.

Longing for the power of men, she had not seen—or refused to see—that women had their own power. It took both forces, acting together, to keep their people alive, to bring children into the world, to protect and shelter and nurture them. Neither was better nor more important than another; both were necessary and equal.

Respect and honor for each other. This was marriage in the eyes of the God.

Zohra could not articulate these confusing thoughts. She couldn't even begin to understand them. She knew only at that moment that she felt ashamed and unworthy of these coura- geous, quiet women who had fought a daily, grinding, hopeless battle to keep their families together and maintain their faith in their God.

Zohra's head drooped before those eyes. Her steps faltered, and she felt Mathew's arm steal around her.

"Are you sick, hurt?"

Wordlessly she shook her head, unable to speak.

"I know," he said, and his voice burned with an anger she was startled to hear. "This is heinous! I cannot believe men could do this to each other! We must, we will get them out of this place, Zohra!"

Yes! So help her, Akhran, she would! Lifting her head, Zohra blinked back her tears and searched the crowd for the one she sought. There she stood, at the end of the line of silent women, waiting. Badia—Khardan's mother.

Zohra walked up to the woman, who did not quite come to the Princess's chin. Looking at Badia, Zohra saw the wisdom in the dark eyes whose beauty seemed emphasized by the lines of age in the corners. She saw in those eyes the courage that ran in her son's veins. She saw the love for her people that had led Khardan here to give his life for them. Humbled, Zohra sank to her knees before Badia. Extending her hands, she grasped those of her mother-in-law and pressed them to her bowed forehead.

"Mother, forgive me!" she whispered.

If a leopard had come up and laid its head in her lap, Badia could not have been more astonished. Perplexed, a thousand questions in her mind, Badia reacted from her own compassionate nature and from the secret admiration she had always felt for this strong, obstreperous wife of her son. She remembered that the girl's mother was dead, had died too early, before she could impart a woman's wisdom to her daughter. Kneeling, putting her arms around Zohra, Badia drew the veiled head to her breast.

"I understand," she said softly. "Between us, daughter, there is nothing to forgive."

"My son lives!" The joy and gratitude in Badia's eyes was a gift Zohra was pleased and proud to present her mother-in-law.

"Not only lives, but lives with great honor," said Zohra, saying this more warmly than she had intended, apparently, for she saw a spark of amusement flicker in Badia's dark eyes.

The two, together with Mathew, spoke quietly during the afternoon, the other women surrounding them. Those in front passed along the news to those in the rear who could not hear. The guards glanced at this huddling of chickens—as they viewed it—without interest and without concern. Let them cackle. Small good it would do them when it came time to wring their necks.

"Khardan has been named Prophet of Akhran, for he brought the djinn back from where they had been held imprisoned by Quar." Not quite true, but true enough to speak of in this hurried time.

"And Zohra is a Prophetess of Akhran," added Mathew, "for she can make water of sand."

"Can you truly do this thing, daughter?" asked Badia, awed. A murmur swept through the women, many—not as forgiving as Badia—regarding Zohra with suspicion.

"I can," said Zohra humbly, without the pride that generally accompanied her words. "And I can teach you to do the same. Just as Mat-hew"—she reached behind for the young man's hand and held it fast—"taught me."

Badia appeared dubious at this and hastened to change the subject. "My son, where is he? Is he with his father?"

"Khardan is in the city—"

There was an excited rustle, an indrawn breath of hope among the women.

"He has come to rescue us!" Badia spoke for all.

"No," said Zohra steadily, "he cannot rescue us. Our men cannot rescue us. We must rescue ourselves." Slowly, carefully, she explained the situation, presenting the dilemma of the nomads, who dared not attack the city to free their families, knowing that their families would be put to death before they ever reached the city walls.

"But the Imam has decreed that we will die by morning!"

"And so we must be gone from this place by morning," said Zohra.

"But how?" Badia glanced helplessly at the tall walls.

"Do you propose we sprout wings and fly?"

"Or perhaps you can turn the sand to water, and we will swim out," suggested one of Zeid's wives with a sneer.

Mathew's hand tightened on Zohra's, but his warning was not necessary. The Princess's newly found coolheadedness quenched the hot words that would normally have scorched the flesh of her victim.

"We have come here with a plan to save ourselves. Sul gives magic to men in the land across the sea from which Mat-hew comes. Mat-hew is, in his own land, a powerful sorcerer."

The women exchanged glances, frowning, not quite certain how to react. One must, after all, be courteous.

"But my daughter, he is mad," said Badia cautiously, bowing to Mathew to indicate that she intended no offense.

"No, he isn't," said Zohra. "Well, maybe just a little," she was forced to add in honesty, much to Mathew's discomfiture. "But that doesn't matter. He has a magical spell that he can teach all of us, just as he taught me the spell to make water."

"And what will this spell do?" Badia asked. She glanced around sternly to enjoin silence.

"In my land," said Mathew, speaking uneasily, aware of hundreds of pairs of dark eyes turned upon him, "it is very cool, and it rains nearly every day. We have large bodies of water—lakes and streams—and because of this there is a tremendous amount of water in the air. Sometimes, in my land, this water in the air becomes thick enough that it is possible to see it, yet not so thick that one cannot breathe it." He wasn't getting very far. Most appeared more convinced now than ever before that he was crazy as a horse who eats moonweed.

"It is as if the God Akhran sent a cloud down from the skies. This cloud is known as fog in my land"—he plunged recklessly forward. Time was growing short, they still had much to do—"and when this fog covers the earth, people cannot see very clearly through it, and consequently they feel confused and disoriented. Familiar objects, seen through fog, look strange and unreal. People have lost their way walking through a wood that they have known all their lives.

"With Sul's blessing the sorcerer can create his own version of this fog and use it to protect himself. Through the power of this spell the magus surrounds himself with a magical fog that has the power of instantly creating doubt and confusion in the minds of all who look at him."

"Does he disappear?" questioned Badia, interested in spite of herself.

"No," said Mathew, "but it seems to those looking directly at the magus as if he has disappeared. He can neither be seen nor heard, for the fog deadens the sound of his movements. Thus he can escape his enemies by slipping away."

Just how he would go through locked gates was another matter, but Mathew hoped a solution to that would present itself when the time came. In his land, where people were accustomed to seeing fog, this spell was only partially efficient and was mainly used by those who found themselves set upon by robbers in the woods or dark alleys of the city. It was, as he had said, a simple spell, one of the first taught to novices and often practiced gleefully to escape their tutors at bedtime. Mathew hoped, however, that the creation of fog in this land where it had never before been imagined, let alone actually seen, would unnerve the guards sufficiently that the men could wrest the keys from them and unlock the gates.

There was one tiny, nagging doubt in Mathew's mind, but he chose to ignore it. At the very bottom of the page in the spell book, written with red ink, was the warning that the spell be used by an individual, never by a group, unless warranted by the most dire circumstances. He supposed some instructor had explained to him the reason for this warning, but-if somehow must have slept through class that day, for he could recall nothing of it. It had never seemed, important in his own safe, serene country.

But now. . . well, certainly these could be considered dire circumstances!

"The only things we need to perform the spell," he continued, seeing the quickening interest in the women's eyes and feeling himself heartened, "is the parchment upon which each of you must write it. Zohra and I carry these beneath our robes. And we need water."

"Water?" Badia appeared grave. "How much water?"

"Why. . ." Mathew faltered. "A bowlful apiece. Isn't there a well here in the prison?"

"Outside the walls, yes." Badia pointed.

Mathew cursed himself. Would he never come to accept the fact that in this land water was scarce, precious? He thought frantically. "The guards must bring you water. When? How much?"

Badia's face cleared somewhat. "They bring us water in the mornings and evenings. Not much, maybe a cup each, and that must be shared with the children."

Seeing the swollen tongues and cracked lips of the women—forced to stand or work in the hot sun of the prison compound—Mathew guessed how much they drank and how much they gave to the children. His rage startled him. If he'd had the Imam beneath his hands, he would have choked the life out of the man and never felt a qualm. With an effort he mastered himself.

"When the guards bring the water this evening, you must not drink it but keep it hidden, keep it safe. Not a drop must be wasted, for you will need every bit." And pray Promenthas that is enough!

"Will you do it?" asked Zohra eagerly.

All the women looked to Badia. As Majiid's head wife, she had the right to command a leadership role, and she had earned it during this crisis. All respected her, trusted her.

"What about the young men and some of our husbands, locked in the cells?"

"Where are the cells?" Mathew asked, looking around.

"In that building."

"Any guards?"

"Three. They keep the keys with them so that they may enter the cells when they choose to mistreat those within," Badia answered bitterly.

"Before we cast the spell, we will go first to the guardhouse, overpower the guards, and free the men." Mathew said this glibly, completely unaware of how this would be done. "The men must stay near you when the spell is cast, and the fog will surround them as well."

"They will want to fight," said a young wife knowingly. "We must see to it that they do not," countered Badia crisply, and there was the glint of steel in the eyes that had been known to bring even the mighty Majiid to his knees on occasion. The glint faded, however, and she looked at Zohra with grave earnestness. "If we do not do this thing, daughter, what chance do we have?"

"None," said Zohra softly. "We will die here, die"—she faltered, glancing at the leering guards—"most horribly. And our men will die to avenge our deaths."

Badia nodded. "An end to our people."

"Yes." There was nothing more to say, no softer way to say it.

The women in the compound waited, watching Badia, whose head was bowed in either solemn thought or perhaps prayer. At last she raised her eyes to meet those of her daughter-in-law. "I begin to see Akhran's wisdom in choosing you to marry my son. Surely the God has sent you here and perhaps sent us the madman"—she appeared none too ready to credit even Akhran with this—"to aid us."

Badia turned to Mathew. "Show us what we must do."

CHAPTER 7

night fell over parts of the city of Kich, was held at bay in others. The Temple and the grounds surrounding it shone more brightly than the sun; torches and bonfires hurled back the darkness and kept it outside the barrier that had been erected around the Temple steps from where the Imam was to speak to his people. The great golden ram's-head structure was in readiness. The golden altar having been carried inside the Temple, another altar had been constructed and made holy by the under priests, to prepare for the presentation of the faith of the living and the souls of the dead to Quar.

The Imam and his priests were due to speak to the people at midnight. Feisal intended holding them spellbound and enthralled with his words, whipping them to a fevered pitch of holy frenzy in which they would lose all thought for themselves or for others and exist only for the God. In such a state the smoke of the burning bodies of butchered women and children would not stink with the foulness of murder but would be sweetest perfume and rise like incense to the heavens.

The bright radiance of the lights around the Temple made those parts of the city left to night that much darker by contrast. The streets late in the evening were—for the most part—empty. Except for the occasional merchant who took the very last opportunity to try to wring money out of lingering customers and who was only now shutting up shop and starting to hurry toward the Temple, there were few loiterers. The soldier-priests of Feisal could sometimes be seen, looking for those who might need a little extra persuasion to receive Quar's blessing. Thus it was that two soldier-priests, walking down the street near the *Kasbah*, attracted little attention.

The street was dark and empty, the stalls across from it shuttered and closed up. The lights of house and *arwat* were extinguished, for none would sleep in their beds this night. At first glance the street seemed too empty, and Khardan cursed.

"He's not here."

"Yes, he is," returned Auda coolly.

Squinting, peering into the deep shadows, Khardan could barely make out, by the reflected light of the flaring flames that lit the sky, a huddled figure squatting next to the wall.

"The followers of Benario will not be worshiping Quar this night, but their own God, to whom these celebrations are meat and drink," said Auda with a grim smile.

True enough. More than one person in that crowd would discover his purse missing, her jewelry stolen. More than one man would return home and find his coffers empty.

Creeping down the streets, keeping a wary eye out for the Amir's soldiers, Khardan caught hold of Auda's arm and pointed.

"Look, not everyone in the palace is attending the celebration."

Far up in a tower shone a single light. There sat—although the two below could not see him—Qannadi. Alone in his room, surrounded by his maps and his dispatches, he was reading each one attentively, concentrating on each, making notes in a firm, steady hand. Yet as he listened to the silence that was breathless, hushed, and tense, the Amir felt himself poised on a dagger's edge. He had set forces in motion over which he had no control, and whether for good or for ill, Sul alone knew.

Auda shrugged. The light was far away and posed no threat. Moving softly, he and Khardan walked over to where the blind beggar sat, his back against the wall of the *Kasbah*. But though their bare feet had not made a sound that either of them could hear, they had not moved softly enough. The milky eyes flared open, the head turned toward them.

"Soldier-priests," he said, holding out his basket. "In the name of Quar, take pity."

"You smell our clothes, not the men inside," returned Auda softly, dropping several coins in the basket and motioning Khardan to do the same. The Calif handed over his purse, containing every last piece of money of his tribe.

The beggar wrinkled his nose. "You are right. You reek of incense. But I know that voice. What do you want, you who speaks the password of Benario yet is not one of the Brotherhood?"

Auda appeared discomfited by this, and the blind beggar grinned, his toothless mouth a dark, gaping hole in the flamelit night. Reaching out a groping hand, he took hold of Khardan's arm, clutching him with a grip surprising in one who appeared so feeble and infirm. "Tell me what you will do, man who smells of horse"—the other hand grabbed hold of Auda—"and man who smells of death."

"Death is my mission, old man," said Auda harshly. "And the less you know the better."

"Death is your mission," repeated the beggar, "yet you do not come to kill the Amir, for that you could have done this day. I heard you talking—my ears are very good, you may have noticed. What Benario takes away, he sometimes repays in double measure. I am thinking you might want to know how to find the tunnel that leads beneath the street to the Temple."

"Such information might be of interest," said Auda offhandedly. "If not this night, then another."

The beggar cackled and let loose his grasp of each of them. So hard had he held them, however, that Khardan continued to feel, for long minutes after, the warm pressure of the gnarled fingers on his flesh.

"We have no more money," said the Calif, thinking that this was what the old man was after.

The beggar made a gesture as if to consign money to the nether realms of Sul. "I do not want your coin. But you have something you *can* give me in exchange for my help."

"What is that?" Khardan asked reluctantly, having the uncanny impression that the unseeing eyes could see through him.

"The name of the woman who stopped to help a poor beggar when her man would have passed him by this day."

Khardan blinked, starting in surprise. "Her name?" he looked dubiously at Auda, who shrugged and indicated impatiently that they needed to make haste.

"Zohra," said Khardan, speaking it slowly and reluctantly, feeling that there was something very special about it and not liking—somehow—to share it.

"Zohra," the blind beggar whispered. "The flower. It suits her. I have it in my heart now"—the empty eyes narrowed—"and it will protect me. When you go through the wall, take four steps forward, and you will come to a flagstone path. Follow this path for a count of forty steps, and you will come to another wall with a wooden door set within. On this door is placed the mark of the golden ram's head. There is no lock, though I'll wager Qannadi has often wished there were," chuckled the old man. "The Imam and his priests have free run of the palace these days. Follow the tunnel, and it will bring you to another door that *does* have a lock. But you, man of death, should have no trouble opening it. The door will bring you out into the altar room itself."

So saying, the beggar slid his hand behind his back. They heard a click and the wall gaped open. Auda darted inside, and Khardan was about to follow when he touched the beggar's bony shoulder. "The blessing of Akhran be on you, father."

"I have the woman's name," the beggar said sharply. "That will be all I need this night."

Puzzled, not understanding, but thinking the beggar was probably touched with madness, Khardan left him and—for the second time that day—sneaked into the forbidden pleasure garden of the Amir's palace.

They had no trouble following the beggar's directions. It was well he gave them in counted steps, for the darkness beneath the trees was thick and impenetrable. They moved as blind men themselves, Khardan forced to grasp Auda's forearm so that they did not become separated. Slipping ahead cautiously, they fended off low-hanging branches, but for the most part found the pathway free of debris and easy to follow. Auda counted the steps under his breath, and they hurried over the flagstone, gliding beneath the perfumed trees, past the dancing fountains. Forty steps brought them to a part of the garden that was less overgrown than the rest. Coming out from under the tree branches, they could see by the red glow in the sky and discovered the door they sought.

The golden ram's head on the wood gleamed eerily. Khardan had the uncomfortable impression that the eyes were watching him with enmity, and he pushed forward to open the door and enter the tunnel but Auda stopped him.

"One moment," said the Paladin.

"What is it? You were the one impatient to get here," Khardan snapped nervously.

"Wait," was all ibn Jad said.

To Khardan's astonishment, the Black Paladin sank down on his knees before the golden ram's head, whose eyes seemed to flare brighter than ever. Removing something from within his robes, Auda held it forth in his right hand. Khardan saw that it was a black medallion, the image of a severed snake worked upon it in glittering silver.

"From this moment," said Auda ibn lad clearly, "my life is in your hands, Zhakrin. I walk forth to fulfill the blood curse cast by the dying Catalus on this man called Feisal, who has sought to take away not only the lives and freedom of our people, but our immortal souls as well."

Auda reached into his robes and took out an object Khardan recognized easily—the severed-snake dagger. The Paladin held it up in his left hand, level with the medallion. "The hand that holds this dagger is no longer my hand, but yours, Zhakrin. Guide it with unerring swiftness to the heart of our enemy."

Auda's face, turned toward the light, was pale and cold as marble, frozen with an unearthly calm, the cruel eyes dark and more empty than the sightless orbs of the blind man. A chill wind rose and blew through the garden. A wave of evil smote Khardan so that he could barely stand, leaving him weak and shaking and powerless, or he would have turned and fled this place that he knew was accursed.

What am I doing here? the nomad Prince thought in horror. Was it you who sent me, Akhran, or have I been deceived? Have I been yoked to this evil man by trickery, and will it end with my falling into the dark Pit of Sul and losing my soul forever? What difference is there between Auda and this Feisal? What difference between Quar and Zhakrin? Surely Zhakrin would strive to become the One, True God if he could! What is transpiring in the heavens that has led me to this path on earth?

I would take this wicked priest's life in battle, but I want no part of wrenching it from him in the dark. Yet he will not face me in battle, and how can I save my people other than by striking him down? Help me, Akhran! Help me!

And then Auda spoke, and there was a softness and wry humor in his voice. "One final prayer, Zhakrin. Absolve this man, Khardan, of his vow, as I absolve him of it. When I am dead, he will have no need to avenge my death. If my blood touches him, it will be only in blessing, not a curse. I ask this, Zhakrin, as one who goes forth with the expectation of being with you soon."

Auda bowed his head, raising both dagger and medallion higher to the night.

Khardan leaned back against the wall, shivering, yet feeling somehow that he'd received his answer, if only to understand that he was free to act of his own will. Whatever constraint—if there had truly been one—had been lifted.

Auda, prostrating himself to the ground, rose to his feet. Kissing the dagger, he slipped it into the folds of his stolen priest's tunic. Kissing the medallion, he hung it around his neck.

"It will be seen," said Khardan.

"I want it to be seen," answered the Paladin.

"When they set eyes upon it, they'll know you for what you are and strike you down."

"Very probably. I will live long enough to obtain my objective—my God will see to that—and then it does not I matter."

Auda opened the door, but Khardan barred his way.

"I would see and hear this man speak," said the Calif gruffly. "I want to give him one final chance to rescind his order regarding my people. Promise me that before you attack?"

"I am not the only one they will strike down," returned Auda with a fleeting ghost of a smile across the bearded lips.

"Swear, by your God!"

Auda shrugged. "Very well, but only because you could prove a useful diversion. I swear."

Breathing somewhat easier, Khardan moved his arm and entered the tunnel, walking beside Auda.

The door shut without sound behind them.

CHAPTER 8

Well, that's that," said Sond, staring gloomily at the tunnel door through which his master had just vanished. "We may not enter the holy place of another God."

"We could stay here and guard their way back," suggested Fedj.

"Bah! Who is there to guard against?" retorted Sond sourly. "Everyone is gathering for the ceremony, Only the Amir's bodyguards are about, and there's not many of them. From what I could gather, Qannadi has sent them to reinforce those responsible for controlling the crowd."

"We could go to the Amir's kitchens and see what they have prepared for dinner," suggested Usti, rubbing his fat hands.

"Didn't I hear your mistress calling you?" Sond scowled.

"You have played that trick on me one time too many, Sond," said Usti with lofty dignity. "It is well past dinnertime, lacking only an hour or so of being midnight. There is nothing more we can do here, and I do not think any harm would come of visiting the kit—"

"Usti!"

It was—most definitely—a feminine voice.

"Name of Akhran!" Usti went pale as the belly of dead fish.

"Hush!" ordered Sond, listening carefully. "That is no mortal tongue—"

"Usti! Sond! Fedj! Where are you?" The names were called urgently, yet reluctantly, as if the speaker vied within herself.

"I know! It is that angel of Pukah's!" Sond looked amazed and not entirely pleased. "What can she be doing—"

"You forget the madman," interrupted Fedj. "She is his guardian, after all."

"You are right. It had slipped my mind." The djinn frowned.

"She should not be calling like that. It will alert every one of Quar's immortals in the city."

"I will go to her," offered Raja, and disappeared only to return presently with the white-robed, silver-haired angel, looking small and delicate and fragile beside the powerful djinn.

"Thank Promenthas I have found you!" Asrial cried, clasping her hands. "I mean"—she flushed in confusion—"thank Akhran—"

"How may we serve you, lady!" asked Sond impatiently.

"First," interposed Fedj, with a rebuking glance at his fellow, "we want to offer our sympathy for your sorrow. "

"My sorrow?" Asrial seemed uneasy, uncertain how to respond.

"Pardon us, but we could not help but notice that our companion, Pukah, had earned—although I'm not certain how—a very special and honored place in your heart."

"It is . . . foolish of me to feel that way, I fear," said Asrial shyly. "It is not right that we immortals should care for each other. . ."

"Not right!" Touched by her sadness, Sond took her by the hand and squeezed it comfortingly. "How can it not be right, when it was your love for him that brought out the best qualities in Pukah and gave him the strength to sacrifice himself?"

"Do you truly believe that?" Asrial gazed up searchingly into the djinn's eyes.

"I do, lady, with all my heart," said Sond.

"And I, too," rumbled Raja.

"And I. And I," murmured Fedj and Usti, the latter wiping away a tear that was creeping down his fat face.

"But you were calling us," said Sond. "How is it we may serve you?"

Asrial's fears, seemingly forgotten a brief moment, returned, causing the color to leave the ethereal cheeks. "Mathew, and your mistress, Zohra! They are in the most terrible danger, or soon will be! You must come and help them."

"But we may not. We have not been summoned," said Sond, appearing worried, yet not certain what to do.

"That is because they don't know they're going to be in danger!" Asrial wrung her hands. "But Matthew is talking of overpowering guards, and he carries a dagger one of the women managed to sneak into the prison with her. He knows nothing about fighting, and the guards are strong and brutal! You must come with me! You must!"

"We are certainly useless here," prodded Fedj.

"That is true." Sond gnawed his nether lip. "Yet we have not been summoned."

"Yes, we have," said Usti unexpectedly. He pointed a jeweled, chubby finger at Asrial. "*She* summoned us!"

"An angel summoning a djinn?" Sond appeared doubtful.

"Let them argue about it at the next tribunal," said Raja. "I, for one, am going with the lady." He bowed, hand over his heart, to Asrial.

"Are all resolved?" Sond looked at Fedj, who nodded.

"My mistress is so stubborn, she would never summon me," Usti commented. "I will go."

"Not stubborn. Intelligent—knowing well if she summoned what she'd get," returned Sond. "Lady Asrial, we are yours to command. And may Akhran have mercy on us if he ever finds out we worked for an angel!" breathed the djinn, casting a worried glance toward heaven.

Inside the cell block of the Zindan, the prison guard, his face twisted in sadistic pleasure, brought his lash down on the bare back of his victim. The boy writhed in the arms that held him, but he did not cry out, though the effort it cost him drove his teeth deep into his tongue.

"Hit him a couple more times and loosen his voice," said one of the guards, holding the boy by the arms.

"Yes, his screams won't be noticed this night," said the other.

The guard did as he was requested, striking at the back that was already marked with scars from previous 'punishment' sessions. The boy flinched and gasped but swallowed his scream and managed to cast a triumphant glance at his captors, though blood ran from his mouth and he knew he would pay for that look with the next blow.

The next blow did not fall, however. The guard stared in astonishment as the whip was plucked from his grasp by a gigantic, disembodied hand and carried up to the ceiling.

The three prison guards stood near the cell block's outer door where they could keep watch and see if any of the Amir's soldiers might be snooping about. This area was their usual location for 'punishment,' as could be witnessed by the numerous splotches of dried blood upon the stone floor. Surrounded by three walls, it was not a large area and it grew smaller still when it was filled with the massive bodies of four huge djinn (Usti taking up as much room sideways as the others did lengthwise).

"Ah, you seem to have dropped this," said Raja, the huge whip dangling between his thumb and forefinger.. "Allow me to return it to you, *sidi!*" He deftly wrapped the whip around the guard's neck.

The guard fought and struggled, but he was no match for the djinn and was soon trussed up like a chicken, as Usti commented, licking his lips.

"Order them to let the boy go," said Raja.

The guard glared balefully at the djinn. "I take no orders from you, *kafir* spawn. And I'm not afraid of you, either. When Quar gets hold of you, he'll make you wish you'd never been born!"

"As intelligent as he is handsome," said Sond gravely. "Let us see if he will reconsider."

Raja, nodding, gave the lash a twist and a tug that sent the man spinning wildly across the floor, smashing headfirst into the far wall. His limp body sagged to the floor. The other two guards suddenly released their hold on the boy, who staggered and fell at their feet.

The boy was up almost at once, moving more hurriedly when he saw Sond coming toward him. The djinn stared at the boy closely. "A Hrana?" he asked.

"Yes, O Djinn," said the boy warily, staring at Sond and recognizing him as an immortal belonging to his enemy. Seeing Sond in company with Fedj—the immortal of his own tribe—the boy did not know quite what to make of it.

"You are brave, Hrana," said Sond approvingly. "What is your name?"

"Zaal." The boy's wan face glowed at the djinn's praise.

"We have need of you, if you can walk."

"There is nothing wrong with me," said the boy, though he grimaced with every move he made.

Sond concealed his smile. "Where do these dogs keep the keys to the cells, Zaal?"

"On their fat bodies, O Djinn," answered Zaal with a glance of bitter hatred.

Sond walked over to investigate. "You do seem to be carrying a monumental load in the area of your gut, *sidi*, the djinn said, speaking to the guard who was slumped against the wall. "I will relieve you of some of that weight, *sidi*, if you will but give me the keys to the cell."

The guard, coming around with a groan, retorted with a foul oath suggesting something physically impossible that Sond might do to himself.

Fedj slammed the man's head against the wall with a swift backhand. "What kind of language is this? How do you expect the boy to learn to respect his elders if you speak in that manner, *sidi?*"

"I grow tired of this," growled Raja impatiently. "Let us kill him and take the keys."

"Oh, ho!" howled the guard, glaring around them from rapidly swelling eyes. "You don't frighten me! I know that you djinn may not take a human life without the permission of your God. And where is the Wandering Akhran these I days? Dead, from what we hear!" The guard spit on the floor. "And good riddance. We'll soon make short work of his followers!"

"He has a point," said Fedj. "We cannot take a human life."

"Ah, but is he human?" Usti inquired complacently. "Is any of this. . . this"—the djinn waved a hand at the guards—"excrement?"

"An interesting technicality," commented Fedj.

The other two guards looked fearfully to their leader, who turned exceedingly red.

"What do you mean? Of course, I'm human!" he blustered. "You just try killing me and see how much trouble you'll be in!"

"Is that a command, *sidi?*" inquired Sond politely. "If so, I hasten to obey—"

"N-no!" stammered the guard, realizing what he'd said. His voice raised to a shrill shriek as the djinn loomed over him. "No!"

"The keys, *sidi*, if you please?" Raja held out a gigantic hand that would have engulfed the guard's neck without any effort at all.

With a vicious snarl the guard lifted the keys from a belt around his waist and hurled them, cursing, to the floor. At Sond's gesture, Zaal leaped to pick them up and brought them to the djinn.

At that moment there came a rattling on the door, and it burst open under the combined strength of Mathew and several nomad women, who flooded into the room, daggers flashing in their hands.

Mathew gasped and stared at the massive djinn. His face was grim. He had obviously prepared himself either to meet death or to mete it out, and this unlooked-for respite literally stole away his breath.

Walking forward, Sond bowed low before the astonished wizard and held out the keys. "These are yours to do with as you will, O Sorcerer. Have you further need of us this night?"

"I . . .I—You don't serve me," Mathew faltered.

"No, Lord Sorcerer. We serve one who serves you."

Sond looked to a point above Mathew's shoulder, to the boy's great confusion. "The Lady Asrial."

"Wait!" said Zohra. "Yes, we need you. The gates—"

"Raja, come with me! Hush!" Sond cocked his head, listening. "My master!" he cried in a hollow voice, and vanished.

Raja disappeared. Fedj and Usti remained, staring at each other uncertainly.

Then they heard the sound—a strange and eerie sound that made the hair on the neck rise and sent a shiver over the bodies of all those in the room.

The frenzied yell of a rampaging mob.

And it was coming closer.

CHAPTER 9

The tunnel ran from the palace, dipping down below the busy central street of Kich, rising up to the newly built and lavishly decorated Temple of Quar. The tunnel's floor was smooth, swept clean, and dry, its condition undoubtedly maintained by the servants of the Imam. Torches stood in wrought-iron sconces affixed to the wall, their flames smoking and wavering in the draft that came with the opening of the door from the garden. Entering the cool, dimly lit tunnel, Khardan marveled at the peace and silence below ground when all above him was noise and chaos.

Moving swiftly, neither speaking—bodies tensed and readied for danger—the Calif and the Paladin of the Night traversed the narrow tunnel. They traveled a long distance. Glancing back, Khardan could no longer see the entrance. The floor they walked began to slope upward, and they knew that they were nearing the Temple. They moved more cautiously and quietly—out of instinct more than necessity. With the praying, swaying, chanting, screaming crowd located almost directly above them, they could have held a game of *baigha* down here, complete with horses, and no one would have heard them.

Soon the two could see, glittering in the torchlight, the eyes of another golden ram's head, and they knew they had reached their destination. Auda carefully studied the door. Carved of a single, massive block of marble, it sealed shut the tunnel entrance like a plug. There were no seams that Khardan could see, no ring embedded in the rock with which to pull it open, and he was just about to suggest—in mingled relief and frustration—that their way was blocked when Auda laid his hands on either side of the golden ram's head, fingers covering the eyes, and pressed.

There was a click and a crunch, and the stone door shivered slightly, then began to turn, revolving around some unseen central post. Stepping back, Auda waited with obvious impatience for the slow-moving stone to swing into an open position. Beyond the door, Khardan could hear a voice speaking, and he tensed, thinking they had been discovered. He soon realized—from the tone and the few words he could catch—that it was the Imam, and he was apparently addressing his priests prior to going out to address the crowd.

No one had noticed them.

"How did you know how to work this?" Khardan whispered, his hand gingerly touching the locking device.

"What, the door opening?" Auda glanced at him, amused at the nomad's awe. "I have operated hundreds more intricate and complicated than this. In the palace at Khandar, one must be a mechanical genius to move from one's bedroom to the bath."

"What about the door on our way out?" Khardan asked uneasily, looking behind him again, though it had long since been lost to sight. "Will it be locked? We may be needing to get through it in a hurry!"

"There was no such device used on entering that door. I doubt if *you* will find one on your return." The Paladin coolly emphasized the singular. "This door is much newer, built more recently than the tunnel itself, which is—I should judge—probably as old as the palace. Who knows where it led before this? Some private playground of the Sultan's, I should imagine."

The stone had almost completed its rotation, moving in oiled silence.

"But why a locking device here and none at the palace?" Khardan argued.

Auda made an impatient gesture. "Undoubtedly the entryway is guarded by the Amir's guards, nomad. Except on this one night, when they were needed to help with the crowd or"—his thin lips tightened in a grim smile—"perhaps Qannadi gave the guards orders to be elsewhere."

Spend the cold winter in here, little mouse, said the lion, pointing to his throat. *It is warm inside and safe, very safe...*

Khardan shivered and, suddenly anxious to end this, pushed past Auda and slid through the crack in the stone that was barely wide enough to admit one man turned sideways.

He entered a murmuring, whispering chamber, warm with the heat of many bodies, smelling of perfumed oil and incense and melting candle wax and sweating flesh and holy zeal. It was lit by the light of many, many candles flickering somewhere on the altar at the center of the room. Khardan caught only a glimpse of that altar, his view blocked by the soldier-priests. Their backs turned to the Calif, they were staring straight ahead with rigid intensity at the Imam, who stood in their midst. No one had heard the opening of the stone door, which was not surprising, considering the reverberating voice that held them mesmerized. But they must feel the rush of cool air on their backs, and Khardan realized with a pang that it would be necessary to shut the door. Hurriedly he glanced about the candlelit altar room, trying to find something that would give him a point of recognition for the tunnel door, which—he could see—would become one with the wall once it was shut. But to his astonishment, Auda left it open. Taking the nomad by the arm, the Paladin hustled Khardan well away from the entry. They moved silently, their backs pressing against the wall, until they were almost halfway around the large room.

Of course, Khardan thought to himself, the blood beating in his ears, it doesn't matter if they discover someone has entered their sanctuary. They're going to know in a matter of moments anyhow, and this insures our way out.

"—Sul's Truth seen in Quar," the Imam was saying. "The world united in worship of the One, True God. A world freed of the vagaries and interference of the immortals. A world where all differences are smoothed out, where all think alike and believe alike—"

As long as they think and believe like Quar, added Khardan silently.

"A world where there is peace, where war becomes obsolete because there is no longer anything over which to fight. A world where each man is cared for, and no one will go hungry."

Slaves are cared for, in a manner of speaking, and rarely allowed to go hungry since that would inhibit their usefulness. A chain made of gold is a chain still, no matter how beautiful it looks upon the skin.

Khardan turned to glance at Auda, to see how the Paladin was reacting to this, and saw suddenly that ibn Jad was no longer standing beside him. The Paladin of the Night had been absorbed into the darkness that was his birthright, the darkness that watched over and guided him.

Khardan was alone.

"We will go forth!" continued Feisal, and Khardan could see above the heads of those standing in front of him the priest's thin arms upraised in exhortation. "We will go forth and bring this message to our people!"

Khardan began to move, impelled by fear that ibn Jad might strike before the Calif could speak, impelled by the need to try to bring sight to the blind eyes of these fools, impelled by his own need to make this one last attempt to save his people.

"In the eyes of Quar, all men are brothers!" Feisal lifted his voice to a shout.

"If that be so," answered Khardan, his own cry reverberating off the walls, the candles flickering in the rush of cool air that was flowing in through the open doorway, "if that be so, then prove it by freeing your brothers—my people—who are sentenced to die with the dawn."

Gasps and shouts of alarm rippled through the crowd. The soldier-priests reacted with a speed that astonished Khardan. Before those around him could have comprehended who he was, they turned on him. Rough hands grabbed his arms, steel cut into his back, a sword was at his throat, and he was a prisoner before the last words had been spoken.

"Let us slay him now, Holy One!" One of the soldier priests pleaded. "He has defiled our Temple!"

"No," said Feisal in a gentle voice. "I know him. We have spoken before, this man and I. He calls himself Calif of his people. Calif of barbarous bandits. Yet there is hope for his salvation, as there is hope for all, and I would not deny it to him. Bring him to me."

The order was obeyed with alacrity, and Khardan was thrown at the Imam's feet, where he lay on the floor, surrounded by a ring of steel.

Slowly, as his eyes raised to meet the liquid-fire eyes of the priest, Khardan rose to his knees. He would have stood face-to-face with this man, but the hands of the soldier-priests pressed on his shoulders, holding him down.

"Yes, you know me," Khardan said, breathing heavily. "You know me and you fear me. You sent a woman to try to murder me—"

A roar of outrage met these words. The hilt of a sword smashed into Khardan's mouth; pain burst in his skull. Groggily, tasting blood from a split lip, he spit it on the floor, and he raised his throbbing head to look into Feisal's eyes. "It is the truth," he said. "That is how Quar will rule. Sweet words in the daylight and poisoned rings in the night—"

He was prepared for the blow this time and took it as best he could, averting his head at the last possible moment to keep it from breaking his jaw.

"No more!" said Feisal, seeming truly distressed by the violence. He laid his delicate fingers on Khardan's bleeding head. The touch was hot and dry, and the fingers quivered on the nomad's skin like the feet of an insect. The intense, zeal-maddened eyes gazed into Khardan's, and such was the strength and power of the soul within the priest's frail body that the Calif felt himself shrinking and shriveling beneath the fiery sun blazing above him.

"This man has been sent to us, my brethren, to show us the overwhelming difficulties we will face when we go out into the world. But we will surmount them." The fingers stroked Khardan with hypnotic sensuality. The candlelight, the pain, the noise, the smell of the incense, began to cause everything in his sight to swirl around him. He found a focal point only in the eyes of the priest. "Who is the One, True God, *kafir*? Name him, bow to him, and your people are freed!"

The fingers soothed and caressed. Feisal was certain of triumph, certain of his own power and the power of his God. The soldier-priests held their breath in awe, awaiting another miracle. Had they not seen, countless times, the Imam lead one poor benighted soul after another into the light?

Khardan had only to speak Quar's name. He held the life of his God in his hands. The Calif shut his eyes, praying for courage. He knew that—by speaking the next words—he doomed himself, doomed his people. But he would save Akhran.

"I know nothing of One, True God, Imam," he gasped, the words bursting past a barrier erected by Feisal's stroking fingers. "I know only *my* God. The God of *my* people, *Hazrat* Akhran. With our dying breath, we will honor his name!"

The fingers on his face grew cold to the touch. The eyes stared down at him not with fury but with sorrow and disappointment.

"Give me a knife!" Feisal said softly, holding out his hand to his priests. "Death will close this man's mortal eyes and open those of his soul. Hold him fast, that I may do this swiftly and cause him no undue suffering." The soldier-priests gripped Khardan's arms. One tilted back his head, exposing his throat.

Khardan did not fight. It was useless. He could only pray, with his last conscious thought, that Zohra would succeed where he had failed. . .

"Give me a knife," Feisal repeated.

"Here, My Lord," said a voice, and the body of the Imam suddenly jerked and went rigid, the eyes opened wide in astonishment.

Auda yanked his blade free. He raised his hand to strike again, when Feisal wheeled and faced him. An expanding stain of blood was spreading across the back of the priest's robes.

"You would murder me?" he said, staring at Auda, not so much in anger and fear, but in true amazement.

"The first blow I struck was for Catalus," said Auda coolly. "This I strike in the name of Zhakrin." The silver dagger, the hilt decorated with a severed snake, flashed in the light of the candles on the altar of Quar and plunged into the breast of the Imam.

Feisal did not scream or try to dodge the blow. Flinging wide his arms, he received the deadly blade into his body with a kind of ecstasy. The dagger's hilt protruded from his flesh. Clutching at it, the Imam staggered and lifted his eyes to heaven. Prayerfully holding up his hands—crimson with his own blood—Feisal tried desperately to speak.

"Quar!" He choked and pitched forward across the altar, falling in his last prostration to his God.

Paralyzed with shock and horror, the soldier-priests stared at the body of their leader. It seemed impossible that he could die and they waited for him to stand, they waited for a miracle. Yanking the black medallion from around his neck, Auda tossed it upon the corpse—then, darting forward, the Paladin caught hold of Khardan. He managed to drag the nomad from his captors' nerveless grip and propel him, stumbling, toward the door in the wall before the fury hit.

"They have slain the Imam! The Imam is dead!" The wail was terrible to hear, rising to a shriek of insane rage as they realized their miracle was not forthcoming. "Kill them!" came one cry.

"No," cried others, "capture them alive! Save them for the torturer!" And still another cry, "Slay the prisoners! The blood of the *kafir* to pay for his! Slay them now! Do not wait for morning!"

A sword flashed in front of Khardan. Smashing its wielder in the face, the Calif grabbed the blade from the man's hand, drove it into the body, and ran past without looking to see his enemy fall. The door stood ajar. The path to it was clear. No one had thought to block it.

"Nomad! Behind you!" came a hollow cry.

Khardan turned, knocked aside a sword-thrust in time to see the Paladin sinking to the floor, one soldier-priest driving a sword into his back, another into his side.

Yelling wildly, Khardan slashed at the priests, killing both of them. Others, undaunted, longing to martyr themselves and die with their Imam, ignored the danger of his flashing blade and hurled themselves at him. Grabbing hold of Auda, hacking to the left and the right, Khardan dragged the wounded man to his feet.

The Calif saw out of the corner of his eye a priest raise a knife. He held it poised to throw, but it was knocked from his hand by another, who howled, "Do not kill them! The executioner must make them pay! A thousand days and nights they will live with their agony! Capture them alive!"

Savage faces loomed near Khardan. He heard blades whistle, saw them flash, and beat them off, thrusting and kicking, clawing and fighting his way inch by inch toward the tunnel door. One hand kept hold of the Paladin, and he did his best to try to protect Auda, but he could not be on all sides at once, and he heard another groan escape the man's lips, felt the body shudder.

"Sond!" cried Khardan desperately, though he knew the djinn could not enter the Temple.

"Sond!" Fire spread along Khardan' s upper arm and tore through his shoulder blade. But he was at the tunnel door, and he had made it to safety.

Then it was that he realized, in despair, that he had no idea how to shut the door. Khardan turned at the entrance, intent on forcing them to kill him or be killed, when a huge hand caught hold of him and plucked him through the opening.

Sond flung Khardan into the tunnel. Reaching back inside, the djinn grabbed Auda and dragged him into the tunnel.

"Now?" grunted Raja. "Now!" yelled Sond.

The gigantic djinn thrust the stone door shut with a shove of his powerful hands. A screech of protest and a grinding, snapping sound indicated that the mechanism had been rendered useless. They could hear heavy blows being rained on the door from the other side.

"How long can you hold it?" Khardan gasped for breath.

"Ten thousand years, if my master desires!" Raja boasted, grinning broadly.

"Ten minutes will be sufficient," breathed Khardan, and groaned in pain.

"You are hurt, *sidi*," said Sond solicitously, bending over the Calif.

"No time for that now!" Khardan shoved the djinn away from him and staggered to his feet. "They're going to murder our people! Did you hear? I must reach them and—" Do what against that raging mob? "I must reach them," he added with the sullenness of despair. "Go to the tunnel entrance and deal with any guards who come!"

"Yes, *sidi*," and Sond vanished.

Khardan turned to Auda, who was sitting where Sond had left him, his back propped up against the tunnel wall. The front of the Paladin's robes was covered with blood. He held his hand over a wound in his side, the fingers glistening wetly in the torchlight. Khardan knelt beside him. "Come, quickly! They'll be sending guards—"

Auda nodded wearily. "Yes, they will be sending guards. You must hurry."

"Come on!" said Khardan stubbornly. "You could have saved yourself. You risked your life to save me. Vow or no vow, I owe you—" Putting his arm around the Paladin's back, the Calif felt blood instantly soak his sleeve.

Understanding, Khardan slowly stood up.

"I can go no farther," Auda said. "Leave me, nomad. You owe me nothing. You must save"—he coughed, a trickle of red ran from his mouth—"your people."

Khardan hesitated.

"Go on!" The Paladin frowned. "Why do you stay? Our oath is dissolved."

"No man should die alone," Khardan said.

Auda ibn Jad looked up at him and smiled. "I am not alone. My God is with me."

His eyes closed, he sank back against the wall—whether dead or fainted, Khardan could not tell. He looked at the Paladin, his thoughts a confusion of grief and loss mixed with the knowledge that, by rights, he was doing wrong to mourn the death of this evil man. This man who had given his life for his.

The Calif turned to Raja, who stood with his back against the door, his arms folded across his chest, as unmovable and implacable as if a mountain had been dropped across the tunnel. "See to it that they do not take him alive," Khardan commanded. "Then come as soon as you judge you can safely leave. I will have need of you."

"Yes, *sidi*," said Raja, his face grim. His hand closed over the hilt of his scimitar.

Turning, with a final puzzled, unhappy glance at the seemingly unconscious Paladin, the Calif ran down the tunnel.

Auda ibn Jad opened his eyes and gazed after the nomad. "Many fine sons. . ." the Paladin said softly, and died.

CHAPTER 10

The young men of the nomad tribes came from their cells in the Zindan, blinking dazedly at their unexpected freedom. Their eyes then widened in astonishment at seeing their mothers and sisters and wives crowding into the small blockhouse. There was a moment's joy that faded at the sound of the mob—a dread baying at the silver moon, which shone brightly as the sun in the black sky, as if the Gods—unwilling to miss the sight—had turned a watch light upon this grim scene.

"Fedj, go see what has happened," Zohra commanded. The djinn fled in obedience, and the Princess of the Hrana nervously twisted and tugged at the rings upon her fingers as she waited in fear and impatience for his return. Deep within she knew the cause, she knew the reason the voices howled in fury and wailed in grief. But she waited stolidly for the djinn and prayed to Akhran with every heartbeat that she was wrong.

"Princess!" cried Fedj, appearing with a bang that shook the cell block. "The Imam is dead! Murdered!"

"Dead!" No cheers from those gathered together. Only pale faces and frightened eyes. They knew what this meant for them. Mothers clasped their arms tightly around their babes, brothers caught hold of sisters, husbands grasped their wives. Fedj spoke their fears aloud. "Feisal was assassinated in Quar's Temple, and now his soldier-priests come to wreak their vengeance upon our people."

"Those who did it," said Zohra in a thin, tight voice.

"What of them?"

"The mob will be here in moments, Princess!" Fedj said urgently, sweat glistening on his face. "We must prepare to defend–"

"What of those who murdered the Imam?" Zohra persisted coldly.

Fedj sighed and shook his head. He had not wanted to speak this news. "The priests cry to the mob that the two men responsible were captured and . . . slain."

"Ah!" The knife that slew Feisal might have entered Mathew's heart. Clutching his hands together, he stared pleadingly at the djinn as if to beg the immortal to take back his words.

Zohra felt something within her die, something she had not known lived until now, when it was too late. Her first thought was a wish to die, too, rather than face the terror that she knew was coming. So proud of her courage, the Princess of the Hrana was as frightened and lost as the newborn lamb standing, bleating, in the darkness beside the wolf-ravaged body of its protector.

Princess of Hrana.

He is dead, and now I am responsible for the people.

The knowledge rose out of the emptiness within her.

Already Zohra could hear pounding footsteps. The prison guard had been alerted to the mob's coming. There would be confusion among the guards, perhaps even panic, for a mob might not take the time to distinguish between jailed and jailer before it tore them to shreds.

"People of Akhran, hear me!" Zohra raised her voice, and its timbre of courage, darkened with grief, made her people attentive. "The mob comes to murder us in the name of Quar. There is hope, but only if we think and act as one. Men, your women hold your lives in their hands. This is a time for magic, not swords, if indeed you had swords. Listen to your women, follow their instructions. Your lives and the lives of those you hold dear rest on this!"

She caught hold of Mathew and thrust the young man forward. His veil had come loose from his head; the red hair blazed like flame in the torchlight. Clad still in women's clothes, he might have been a ludicrous sight but that his own bitter loss and sense of responsibility as great as Zohra's gave him a dignity and power that made many regard him with awed reverence.

"From this moment on, Mat-hew—a mighty sorcerer in his land—is your leader. He comes to you in"—she drew a shaking breath but spoke without faltering—"Khardan's name. Obey him as you would the Calif. Fedj, Usti." She summoned the djinn. "Go see to the opening of the gate."

The djinn bowed low to her, and this alone impressed many of the doubtful.

Fearful that she could say no more without breaking down and revealing how weak and frightened she really was, Zohra turned and walked rapidly out of the blockhouse into the compound. She had seen the men frowning with displeasure, but she had no time to spare for argument and persuasion. Behind her, she could hear the voices of the women explaining—or attempting to—in hurried, broken whispers. The men would go along with them, she hoped and prayed. At this moment they had no choice. They had no weapons except for what a few had managed to wrest from the cell-block guards. Once the magic started, Zohra hoped, they would see it work and so do what was needed.

She heard Mathew speak a few words to the women. Not many—there wasn't time for many, and they knew already what they had to do. The screams and yells of the mob were getting closer. Looking out past the tall gates, Zohra could see the lights of their torches reflected against the sky. The commandant was up on the battlements, racing first to one end, then the other, shouting conflicting orders that sent his men scurrying about in aimless confusion. Occasionally, regretting the loss of his own private plans of savagery, the commandant was seen to shake his fist at the approaching mob. But for all that, Zohra knew he would open the gates to them.

We will be ready. Pray Akhran, pray Sul, pray that strange God of Mat-hew's that this works!

The women flowed out of the prison, shapeless forms in their robes and veils, moving silently on slippered feet. Their men and boys, those few there were, came after them. Grim, defiant, doubtful, they obeyed their Princess more because they were in the habit of following those in command than because they understood or agreed with her. The nomads had survived through long centuries by granting obedience to their Sheykhs. In their Princess the people saw the authority they were accustomed to obeying.

A touch on Zohra's arm caused her to turn her head. Mathew had come up unheard to stand beside her. The young wizard was very pale, and there were smudges of darkness beneath the eyes, but he appeared calm and quietly confident. He and Zohra exchanged one eloquent look—a sharing of inner, wrenching pain, and that was all. There was time for nothing more. They separated, Zohra going to her place in the center of the women, who were separating themselves into rows as Mathew had instructed.

The sorcerer took his place at their head.

Gathering her children and her menfolk around her, each woman knelt upon the ground of the prison compound. Before each stood a precious cup of water that had been saved from the evening meal. Hands fumbled here and there, drawing out the parchments each had spent the afternoon laboriously copying, the words written crudely with the only ink they had—their own blood. The guards had been amused at this undertaking, not understanding it and making rude jokes about the *kafir* writing their death testaments.

Each women held the parchment above the cup as Mathew had taught them. All tried to concentrate, to shut out the sounds of approaching horrors, but it was difficult, and for some, impossible. A muffled sob and the soothing murmur of one woman comforting a sister and bidding her regain her courage came to Mathew's ears. He, too, heard Death—in hideous aspect—drawing near and wondered at his own lack of fear.

He knew the answer. He was sheltered, once again, in the comforting arms of Sul.

His own cup of water standing before him, Mathew began to chant the words of the spell. He chanted loudly, so that the women could hear him and remember the difficult pronunciation. He chanted loudly, so that his calm voice might help obliterate that of the shrieking soldier-priests bearing down on them.

He heard the women repeat the words after him, slowly and faltering at first, then more loudly as they gained confidence.

Mathew sang the chant three times, and at the third recitation the words on his parchment began to writhe and crawl and tumbled off into the water. He could tell, by the sudden catching in the throats of those who followed him, that the same phenomenon was happening to at least most of the women in the compound. There would be some, to be sure, who would fail; but Mathew was counting upon the likelihood that the numbers who would succeed would be such that the fog would enshroud them all and allow them to slip through their enemies unharmed.

The words tumbled into the cup, the water began to bubble and boil, and then, slowly, a sinuous cloud drifted upward. Mathew looked out across the compound. The sound of cheering and of thudding feet breaking into a run told him that the mob had come within sight of the prison. The young wizard did not turn around but continued to face his people and chant—as much to keep their minds occupied with the soothing flow of words as to continue to work the spell. For now he could see hundreds of tendrils of mist rising into the air. He heard the men's deep-voiced murmurings of awe and dread mingle with the delighted cries of small children who, not comprehending their danger, were enchanted by the magic their mothers were performing.

The fog spiraled up from Mathew's cup and encircled him, beginning at his feet and writhing and twisting about him like a friendly snake.

It was doing the same with the women, surrounding them and those who were near them, drawing them into Sul's protective coils. It muffled sound, flattened out and rendered harmless the terrifying shouts of the mob. The nomads lost their fear and gathered together, and the fog grew thicker and more dense around them.

The misty cloud was swelling and spreading with a rapidity that astonished Mathew. He had thought they would be fortunate if it enveloped each woman and those she kept near her. But the mist—shining an eerie white in the moonlight—was wafting and drifting through the compound with what Mathew could have sworn was some type of intent purpose, as though it sought something and would not be satisfied until it had gained its goal.

A sharp thorn of doubt pricked Mathew's satisfaction. He saw the warning again, printed clearly in red ink in the book. *Large numbers of magi should never resort to the use of this spell except in the most dire circumstances.* And suddenly he remembered words that followed, words that had seemed irrelevant, almost laughable, in his land:

Make certain there is a plenteous source of water.

Mathew understood. He knew what he had created, he knew why the warning had been given. He foresaw clearly and with horror what must happen, but there was no way he could stop it.

The magical mist crept over the ground—delicate white arms with thin, long, curling fingers, guided by a searching, central intelligence. Some of the prison guards had taken to their heels. Others had leapt from the wall and were striving to push open the gates that, for some reason, wouldn't budge (not with the bulk of an invisible Usti planted against them). Their commandant stood on the battlements above them, alternately berating his guards for their slowness and pompously shouting out to the mob that he was in charge here.

The mob, led by the soldier-priests, ignored him. They stormed the walls, those at the front being crushed against the stone by those surging forward in the rear, and began flinging themselves at the wooden gates in an effort to force them open.

The commandant, still shouting, was beginning to get the dim impression that no one was listening to him and that he might want to consider removing himself from this area, when a panicked cry from one of his guards caused him to turn around and stare into the compound with bulging eyes.

His prisoners were gone! Vanished in a cloud that had seemingly fallen from heaven and swallowed them up. The commandant couldn't believe it. He stared into the writhing, shifting mist, but he could neither see nor hear any signs of life. The commandant's fat body shook until his teeth rattled in his head. There was no doubt in his mind that the God of these people had come to their rescue, and all knew Akhran to be a vengeful, wrathful deity. The mob was still hurling itself against the gates; the wooden doors were starting to splinter and crack from the combined weight of hundreds pressed against them.

The guards in the compound gazed fearfully at the mist whose delicate fingers seemed to be reaching for them. Usti and Fedj, nearly as terrified of Sul's magic as the guards, had abandoned their posts and were staring at each other helplessly. Frantically the guards sought to unlatch the gates and push them open—a crowd of humans held no terrors for them compared to this accursed fog. But the pressure on the gates from the mob pushing in the opposite direction held them firmly shut. The guards could not escape and could only watch, in tongue-tied horror, the first tendrils curl about their feet.

Their screams split through the voice of the mob like a whistling sword blade, so awful that even the most fanatical of those clamoring for blood beyond the prison walls hushed and listened.

The commandant, atop the wall, saw the fog curl around the legs and trunks of his screaming men, saw them wrapped in clutching fingers of shimmering white. He saw the mist boil and writhe. The screams ended, dying to dry whispers. The fog lifted and continued on, rising thicker than before.

On the ground in front of the gates lay several piles of dust.

A plenteous source of water!

One wizard casts this spell in a land of deep wells and moist air and travels safely within his cloud, the spell drawing the water from all around it. Many wizards cast the spell together, and the same thing occurs, except that the power is so much greater, the spell so much stronger, that it demands more water to sustain it. A land of lush vegetation, of gigantic trees and green grass and thick foliage, a land of running streams and raging rivers, a land of rain and snow—the spell has all the water it needs.

But cast the spell in an arid land, a land of sand and rock, where water is measured in precious drops, and the spell thirsts and becomes desperate to maintain itself, sucking life from what sources it can find.

Mathew saw the guards fall, he heard their screams. He saw the commandant race back and forth across the wall in a frenzy of terror, trying to avoid the clutching fingers of the mist, falling victim to them at last with a frightful, gurgling wail. Mathew watched the magic drain what small amount of water there was in the wood of the gate, saw the beams wither and wilt. He heard the joyous shouts of the mob change to cries of amazement, and he heard the first wails of those tangled in the mists, the awful screams as they felt their lives being sucked from their bodies.

He, who had agonized over killing one, would now be responsible for the deaths of hundreds!

Zohra was beside him, grabbing hold of him.

"Mat-hew!" Her eyes glistened through the fog. "We have done it! They run before us!"

She didn't know. She had not seen, or if she had, she didn't comprehend. Or maybe she didn't care. After all, Mathew tried to force himself to remember, the mob had intended a death for her people as horrible as that to which they themselves were falling victim. He had to think of that, concentrate on that, or go mad.

Zohra led her people forth. Surrounded by the magic, moving slowly that they might not outrun the mist, the nomads walked calmly through the withered prison gates, trampled the dust of their enemies beneath their feet. The fog, growing stronger as it fed, billowed around them—a silvery, lethal cloud rolling down the streets of the city of Kich.

 # CHAPTER 11

earing no warning from Sond that the tunnel exit was guarded, Khardan sprang incautiously through the open door into the Amir's pleasure garden. The Calif was brought up short by a soldier clad in helm and armor, a naked sword blade gleaming brightly in the moonlight. Casting a bitter, reproachful glance at the djinn, who was standing nearby, Khardan raised his bloodstained weapon to attack.

"*Sidi*," Sond said quietly, "it is your brother." Khardan, lowering the sword, stared.

Slowly the young man removed the helm and let it fall to the paving stone, where it clattered and rolled beneath a bush. Without the helm, which had hidden the face, Khardan could recognize the features of his half brother, but that was as far as recognition went. In all other aspects, this tall, battlescarred young warrior was a stranger to the Calif.

And though Achmed had dropped his helm, he held his sword poised and ready.

"I knew it had to be you," he said in a toneless voice, his eyes dark shadows in the pale face. "I knew when I heard that the Imam had been slain that it was you who did it, and I knew where to find you. The other guards ran to the Temple, but I knew—"

"Achmed," said Khardan, attempting to moisten dry lips with a tongue nearly as dry, "the priests have gone to murder our people!"

The young soldier nodded. "Yes," he said, and no more.

Khardan could hear angry shouts and the clashing of weapons. He shot a swift glance at Sond, who shrugged his shoulders helplessly as if to beg, "I will gladly obey you, *sidi*, but what would you have me do?"

I could send the djinn against the mob, Khardan thought

frantically, but it would take an army of 'efreets to stop those fanatics. He could order Sond to transport him, take him away from this place. But what about his brother? Achmed was one of his people, no less important. Must he lose him forever, completely?

"Come with me!" Khardan held out a hand. "We will fight—"

"No!" Achmed stared at the outstretched hand, and Khardan saw that it was covered with blood. His own, Auda's, the Imam's. . . The young soldier's words echoed hollowly in his throat. "No!" he repeated, and though the night air was cool, Khardan saw sweat glisten on his brother's face. Achmed glanced behind him, toward the prison, though nothing could be seen of it beyond the tall walls of the palace. There was horror in his eyes now, and it was obvious he was seeing not the present, but the past. "There is nothing you can do! Nothing I can do! Nothing!"

"Achmed," Khardan said desperately, "your mother is in that camp!"

"Maybe." The young man tried to shrug, though his face was strained, and as the howls of the mob grew louder and more savage, the sweat trickled down his cheekbones. "Maybe she is dead already. I haven't seen her or heard from her for months. "

"Very well, then, brother," Khardan said coldly, "I am leaving. If you want to stop me, you had better be prepared to kill me, for that is the only way—"

The horror-darkened eyes turned to him, and slowly the nightmare vision receded. Once again they were cool and impassive. Achmed fell into a fighting stance. Khardan did the same, pain shooting through the wounded shoulder that was already stiffening. It would not be an even match. The Calif felt his strength flag. The only thing keeping him going was fear for his people, and that was more an impediment than a goad, for he felt his mind distracted. He could not concentrate. He could not help letting his gaze dart toward the area of the prison, and thus he nearly missed his brother's first lunge. Moonlight flashing on the blade, a timely slip of Achmed's foot on loose rock, and the reaction of the appalled djinn, who leaped between the two, saved Khardan.

"*Sidi!* You are brothers!" gasped Sond, grabbing the bare blades of both scimitar and sword in his crushing hands and holding them apart. "In the name of the God—"

"Don't preach to me of the Gods! I have seen what has been done in the name of the Gods!" Achmed cried furiously, trying to wrench his weapon free. He might as well have tried to pull the raw ore out of the mountain where it was forged. "There are no Gods. They are only an excuse for man's ambition!"

"Then how do you explain Sond? An immortal?" shouted Khardan angrily. He could tell by the sound that the mob had reached the prison.

"Sond deludes himself into believing he is mortal," Achmed returned. "Look, he bleeds!" It was true; blood rolled down the djinn's arms from where the blades bit deep into his ethereal flesh. "Just as we mortals have deluded ourselves that immortal beings exist!"

Khardan was finished. Stepping back, he released the handle of the sword, and it fell from the djinn's bloodied hand. "Sond, take me to—"

An explosion shook the ground; a blast of air whooshed from the tunnel, followed by a rumble and another blast of flying rock and debris. Coughing and choking, both brothers peered through clouds of dust to the tunnel entrance to see Raja emerge from the ruin, covered with dirt and rubbing his hands in satisfaction.

"You need not fear pursuit from that direction, *sidi*," said the djinn, bowing to Khardan. "And," Raja added, more gravely and solemnly, "it is a fitting tomb for the one who lies within. Only Death will be able to find him now."

"May his God be with him," Khardan responded, subdued. He did not look at Achmed, but—turning his back on the young man, making himself a target if his brother chose—he bent down to pick up his sword. "Sond, you and Raja come with me—"

He ceased speaking, lifting his head to hear more clearly. The sound of the mob had changed—no longer threatening, but threatened.

"What is it?" asked Khardan, puzzled.

"Great magic is being worked, *sidi*." said Sond in awe. "It is as if Sul himself had entered this city!"

Hope alive within him, Khardan ran down the pathway through the garden, heading for the opening in the wall. He had not waited for his brother, detected no footsteps behind him for long moments, and then—to his vast but unspoken relief—he heard booted feet pounding after him.

"This way," said Achmed when Khardan, in his excitement and confusion in the moonlit garden, would have taken the wrong path.

Together they reached the place where the thornbush mounted on a sliding platform could be moved aside and the sliding panel in the wall revealed. To Khardan's astonishment and consternation, the hole gaped open. He could have sworn that the blind beggar had closed it behind them when he and Auda had entered. Warily, the Calif slowed his pace. Achmed bounded ahead, however, and was out into the street, motioning Khardan to follow.

"The way is clear, *sidi*." said Sond, growing thirty feet in height and peering over the wall. "The street is empty except for the beggar."

"What of the prison?" Khardan demanded, when he had emerged to stand beside the old man, who sat cross-legged and relaxed, in the street.

"It is covered with. . . with a billowing mist, *sidi*," said Sond, his eyes huge with wonder. "I have never seen any thing like this in all my centuries!"

"Nor will you, ever again!" cackled the beggar. Khardan started off at a run, but a hand caught hold of his tunic and yanked him backward with such force that he nearly lost his footing. Turning in anger, thinking it was Achmed, the Calif found himself staring down into the milk white eyes that glistened with a terrible brilliance in the moonlight. A bony, scrawny hand, reaching upward, clutched a handful of fabric.

"It will be your death if you approach, for though the magic saves those within, it is killing those without. Look! Look! It comes!"

How the blind eyes saw it, Khardan was never to know, but at the end of the street, winding among the shuttered stalls of the bazaars, long white tendrils crept over the paving stone, licking thirstily at whatever they touched. Stalls fell with a crash, the wood sucked dry of what small moisture was within. A man, darting out into the street to see what was happening, was caught in the silvery white hands, the water of his body wrung from him as though he were a piece of clothing on wash day. The fog moved past, leaving behind a heap of dust that only moments before had been living flesh and blood.

Khardan began to back up, his eyes fixed on the approaching, curling mists with awe and horror. "We must run!"

"There is no escape," said the blind beggar with a peculiar satisfaction, "except for those sheltered behind stone walls. And for those whose hearts are one with those wielding the magic. Quick, sit beside me!" The old man tugged peremptorily on Khardan. "Sit beside me and bring to your lips the name of someone in your heart, someone who moves safely through that mist and thinks of you!"

"Sond, is he right?" questioned Khardan, unable to take his eyes from the drifting, deadly fog.

"I think it is your only hope, *sidi*," said the djinn. "I can do nothing. This is Sul's work." He glanced uneasily at a wide-eyed Raja, who gulped and nodded. "In fact, we are going to leave you for the moment, *sidi*. We will return when Sul is gone!"

"Sond!" Khardan cried in fear and exasperation, but the djinn had vanished.

"Quickly!" the old man cried, dragging the nomad down.

The fog was almost upon him. Khardan saw Achmed, squatting beside the old man. His brother's face was livid.

"The name!" the beggar insisted shrilly. "Speak a name, if one exists in your heart, and pray that she is thinking of you!"

Khardan licked his parched lips. "Zohra," he murmured. The mist, as if catching sight of the moisture-laden bodies, bounded toward him. "Zohra!" he repeated, and involuntarily shut his eyes, unable to watch. He could hear the old man muttering Zohra's name, too, and recalled—with a start—how the beggar had demanded that name in payment for opening the wall. Near him, Achmed was whispering his mother's name with a sob in his throat.

A chill as of a cavern dug deep in the earth clutched the nomad's ankles, freezing the very marrow of his bones. The pain was intense, and it was all he could do to keep from screaming. Feverishly, he repeated the name over and over and with it an image of Zohra came to his eyes, the faint smell of jasmine to his nostrils. He saw her riding her horse through the desert, the wind tearing off the headcloth, blowing the black hair behind her—a proud, triumphant banner. He saw her on their bridal bed, the knife in her hands, her eyes gleaming with triumph, and he felt the touch of her fingers, light and delicate, healing the wound in his flesh she herself had inflicted.

"It is passing," said the beggar, with a deep sigh.

Khardan opened his eyes, stared around to see the mist retreating, being sucked back down the street as if by a massive intake of breath. An ominous quiet settled over the city.

"Your people are safe, man who smells of horse *and* death," said the beggar, his toothless mouth a black slit in his skull-like head. "They have passed through the gate and are out in the plains. And there are none left alive to follow."

Despite his thankfulness, the Calif could not help but shudder. The night wind rose, and he saw with a start a cloud drifting up into the night air. It was not fog. It was a cloud of dust—a dreadful, oily kind of dust. Shivering, Khardan stood up and glanced back down at the beggar.

"I must go to them. Will it be safe?"

"Once they understand that they are free, the magic will begin to dissipate. Yes, it will be safe."

Khardan turned to Achmed. "Will you go with me, brother? Will you come home?"

"This is my home," said Achmed, standing and facing Khardan. "All I love is here."

Khardan's gaze shifted, almost as if drawn, to the solitary light in the palace. He could see the silhouette of a man—arms folded—standing at the window, staring-where? Down at them? Out over his ravaged city?

"This means war, you know that," Achmed continued, following Khardan's gaze. "The Amir can't let you get away with this."

"Yes," Khardan agreed absently, his mind too much occupied with the present to consider the future. "I suppose it does."

"We will meet on the field, then. Farewell, Calif." Achmed's voice was cold and formal. He turned to make his way back through the opening in the wall.

"Farewell, brother. May Akhran be with you," said Khardan quietly. "I will bring news of you to your mother."

The armored back stiffened, the body flinched. For a moment Achmed halted. Then, straightening his shoulders he passed through the wall without another word. The stone wall ground to a close behind him.

"You'd best hurry, nomad," said the beggar. "The soldier-priests are dead, but there are still many alive in this town who, when the shock is past, will be crying for your head."

"First I would ask who you are, father," said Khardan, staring intently at the old man.

"A humble beggar, nothing more!" Curling up like a mongrel dog, the old man lay down upon a ragged blanket, pressing his back against the stone walls to garner some of the lingering warmth left behind by the heat of the day. "Now get you gone, nomad!"

The beggar shut his eyes, wriggled his body into a more comfortable position, and a rasping snore rattled in his lungs.

His fear for his people gone, Khardan felt a great weariness come over him. His shoulder burned with pain, his arm had stiffened beyond use. Every move seemed an effort, and he dragged himself through the moonlit streets, keeping his hand over his mouth to avoid inhaling the horrid dust that stung his eyes and coated his skin with a greasy feel. The city of Kich appeared to have fallen victim to a marauding army—an army that attacked wood and water and plant and humans and left stone alone. Sick and wounded, he stared at the devastation in dazed disbelief, and his brother's words sank home. Yes, this would mean war.

Reaching the place where he had left the horses, Khardan saw only large piles of dust. The last of his strength was draining fast, and he knew he could not go far on foot. Grief for the gallant animal that had carried him to glory and ignominious defeat wrung his heart, when he heard a shrill whinny that nearly deafened him. Hastening forward, hope giving him strength, he found all four horses alive and well and dancing with impatience to leave this awful place.

Curled up in one of the stalls, shivering with fear, was the young boy the Calif had set to watch them.

"Ah, *sidi!*" He sprang to his feet when he saw Khardan.

"The cloud of death! Did you see it?"

"Yes," said Khardan, letting his horse nuzzle and sniff and snort at the strange smells, including that of his own blood. "I saw. Did it come here?"

Useless to ask, seeing the mounds of dust beneath camel blankets, smaller mounds that had once been donkeys, and even mounds that had once been—he didn't like to think.

"It came and they. . . they all died!" The boy spoke dreamily, in shock. "All but me! It was the horses, *sidi!* I swear, they saved my life!" The boy buried his head in the stallion's flank. "Thank you, noble one! Thank you!" he sobbed.

"They know in their hearts those who care for them," said Khardan, rubbing the boy's head fondly. "As do we all," he murmured with a smile. "As do we all. Now go home to whoever cares for you, young man!"

Jumping onto the animal's back, the Calif guided the horse from its stall, the others following obediently behind. And here were the djinn to help him. Together they rode out of the city of Kich, galloping through the gates that stood open, the gigantic wood posts withered and shrunken, the iron bands that had held them together fallen in a heap on the dust-covered ground.

Khardan returned to the Tel to find an army awaiting h... was not the Amir's.

It was the Calif's own.

The ride from Kich had been wild and joyous on the part of the *spahis,* reunited with their families. Singing songs of praise to Akhran, waving their banners high in the air, extolling the virtues of their Prophet and Prophetess, the horsemen of the Akar, the shepherds of the Hrana, and the *mehariste* of the Aran were united at last in glorious victory over their common foe. The only persons on that uproarious, saber-slashing ride who were not drunk with triumph were the Prophet, Prophetess, and the young man whom the nomads now called *Marabout,* a term Mathew came to understand—with a sigh—meant to them a sort of insane holy man.

Husband and wife met formally and spoke coolly when reunited, then turned and went their separate ways. Wounded and exhausted, supported by the djinn, Khardan missed seeing the flash of joy that illuminated and softened Zohra's hawk eyes. Zohra did not notice the pride and admiration in the eyes of Khardan when he praised her for her courage and her skill in saving the people. A wall stood between them that neither—it seemed—was willing or able to scale. It had been built over months. Every stone was an angry word, a demeaning remark, a bitter moment. The mortar that held the wall intact was both centuries old and newly mixed, compounded of blood, jealousy, and pride. What it would take to shatter the wall, neither knew, though each lay awake during the cool, star-filled nights and pondered the matter long and hard.

That was not all each was being forced to confront within his or her own soul. Going to war with the Amir when death was certain and the nomads had everything to gain and nothing to lose

e restored
nd little to
new he had
nished. The
at happens to
n's mind was
strike the city
rt, build up his
ight on his own
antages and dis-
raction that hung

e sudden ability to
man was, at this ear-
Thus she kept herself
le, though they made
d her as one of them-

selves and would have welco   ir group with pleasure.
A few began to remark that the   ss had not changed after all; but their disparaging words were cut short by Badia, who
alone thought she understood somewhat of the battle raging in
the breast of her daughter-in-law. The fight for self-understand-
ing is like fighting an enemy who never stands in front of you
but always attacks from the rear, who is never seen clearly, who
continually jabs away at every weakness. Only the most fortunate
get the best of him.

As for Mathew, every time he shut his eyes, he saw again the
people dying all around him. He asked himself bluntly—as Khardan had asked him when the young wizard had killed Meryem—
if he wanted to reverse the outcome and die at the hands of his
enemies. But he knew that the memory of those withering faces
seen dimly through the fog would remain with him into the next
life, and that there he would be held to account.

One by one, every fine precept in which Mathew had believed
had been hacked up, slashed open, and left to die in the sand of
this harsh land. Mathew tried to bring his old, comfortable beliefs
back to life, but it was impossible even to summon their ghosts.
He was so far changed from the boy who had walked the forested,
water-rich land of Aranthia that he seemed to have split into another being. But what amazed and truly confounded him during

the long nights, when he had nothing to do but think and stare at the stars, was that he looked back on that boy wistfully, sadly, but no longer with regret. Perhaps he wasn't a better person, but he was a wiser, more thoughtful one. He knew himself to be truly one with every other human, no matter how different in manners and appearance, and he found an abiding sense of comfort in this knowledge.

The only question remaining to him was what his future held. Mathew began to see the road he was traveling nearing its end, and he knew in his heart he must soon be called to make a choice. The Amir had mentioned ships sailing to the continent of Tirish Aranth. He could return to Aranthia, the land of his birth, or remain in Tara-kan, the land of his rebirth. Right now he had no idea what that choice would be.

The other members of the three tribes had no such besetting preoccupations. The three Sheykhs rode side by side at the front of their people and were the best of friends, the closest of cousins, the most loving of brothers. Instead of attempting to rival each other in insults, they sought to outdo each other in flattery.

"It was because of the courage of the Hrana that our people escaped the prison," said Majiid expansively, patting Jaafar on the shoulder with a friendly hand.

"But without the fortitude of the Akar, the courage of the Hrana would have been for naught," said Jaafar, leaning out—somewhat nervously—in his saddle to twitch at Majiid's robes, a sign of respect.

"I may safely say," added Zeid from the height of his swift-moving camel, "that without the courage of the Hrana and the fortitude of the Akar, the Aran would, at this moment, be feeding the jackals."

"Ah," cried both the other Sheykhs as one, "without the wisdom of the Aran it is *we* who would be feeding the jackals."

And so on and so forth until the djinn rolled their eyes and Khardan became so disgusted with all of them that he took to riding at the end of the line.

Thus it was that the Sheykhs, and practically everyone else in all three tribes, topped the crest of one of the gigantic dunes overlooking the Tel and came to a halt, staring down in loudly exclaiming wonder, and calling for their Prophet.

Fearing, irrationally, that Qannadi had somehow stolen a

march on him and was in the Tel waiting his return, Khardan rode his horse at breakneck speed, driving the animal, foundering and sliding, up to the top of the dune.

Spread out before him in such numbers that the floor of the desert now resembled a vast city were tents of every shape and description and size—ranging from small ones designed for one man to rest through the heat of the day, to others full seven poles long. In addition, there seemed to have fallen an unseasonable and unusual rain during the time they were gone, for the oasis was green and thriving. Women crowded around the well, drawing water in plentiful supply. Children played and splashed in the pools. Horses, camels, donkeys, and goats were tethered and hobbled near the water or roamed the camp. On the Tel itself the cacti known as the Rose of the Prophet was green and thriving, though as yet no blossom appeared.

Their return had evidently been expected—a group of riders were seen detaching themselves from the camp and dashing madly toward the dune. In their hands they carried *bairaq*—tribal flags—not weapons. Khardan, along with the Sheykhs, rode down to meet them on the desert floor, leaving the people on the dune to watch and speculate in tones of wonder.

"We seek one known as the Prophet of Akhran," shouted a man clad in the uniform of a soldier of some unknown army.

"I am called the Prophet of Akhran," said Khardan, riding forward, his face dark and glowering. "Who are you, and who are these who camp around the well of the Akar?"

"Those who come to do you honor, Prophet," said the soldier, dipping his flag to the ground as did those who rode with him. "We come to ride with you into battle against the Amir of Kich!"

"But where are you from?" asked Khardan, so amazed that he wouldn't have been at all surprised if the man had answered modestly that he'd dropped from the moon.

"From Bastine and Meda, from Ravenchai and the Great Steppes—everywhere the Emperor has placed the heel of his boot on a man's neck."

Seeing a familiar face, Khardan gestured to an old man seated on an aged horse—both man and beast had outlived several generations of offspring. "Abdullah, come forward."

The *aksakal*, one of the tribal elders of the Akar, rode his ancient beast up to the line of Sheykhs. Mindful of where it was and who it carried, the horse kept its neck arched proudly and lifted its rheumatic feet as high as possible.

"What is this, Abdullah?" Khardan asked the old man sternly. "You were in charge in our absence. Why have you allowed this?"

"It is as the man says, O Prophet of our God," answered the *aksakal*, speaking with dignity. "They began arriving almost the day you left, and there has been a steady flood of them ever since. I was minded at first to turn them away, but that night a storm struck such as I have never seen this time of year. The water poured from the heavens. It rained four days and four nights, and now the well is filled, the pools are deep and cool, the desert blooms, and here is an army at hand. Should I be so mad as to throw the blessings of *Hazrat* Akhran back in his face?"

"No," said Khardan, troubled and wondering why his heart was heavy when all burdens should be lifting from him. "No, you did right, Old One, and we are grateful."

"Hail, Prophet of Akhran!" shouted the soldier, and the desert resounded with the cheers that came from the throats of the multitude.

They assisted Khardan from his horse and bore him on their shoulders with boisterous ceremony to the largest, most luxurious tent in the camp. Zohra was no less honored, though she would have been, if she could have escaped. Nothing would do but that she must be led on a pure white donkey to her own tent, hardly less magnificent than Khardan's. Here she was greeted by women bearing costly silks and jewels, food and sweetmeats. Usti was in a rapturous state and refused to be parted from his "dear Prophetess" no matter what threats she issued under her breath.

Mathew, too, was given a tent, though no one offered to carry him to it or dared touch him at all but stared at him as he passed in silent, reverent awe. The Sheykhs were accorded the same honors as their children, and even Jaafar was observed to look happy for the first time that anyone, including his own elderly and infirm mother, could remember. Zeid suddenly recalled that he was uncle to both Prophet and Prophetess, though how this could be no one knew; but all were pleased at any excuse to honor anyone, and the rotund Sheykh was granted his due.

As soon as Khardan was settled in his tent and had thought wearily of going to his bed, the people began to form lines outside, demanding an audience with their Prophet. Khardan could not refuse and, one by one, they brought him their problems, their needs, their wants, their requests, their suggestions, their demands, their gifts, their offerings, their daughters, their good wishes, and their prayers. Meanwhile, in another tent, the Sheykhs and the djinn were gleefully planning to go to war.

Chapter 13

The talk and celebration lasted far into the night. The noise of shouting, drunken laughter, and tramping, dancing feet roared into a wild cacophony that drove Mathew to seek the quiet and solitude of his tent. Walking through the crowded camp, his ears battered by noise, he found himself missing the sounds of the night desert—the incessant, eerie song of the wind; the throaty growls of night animals about their business; the restless murmurings among the horses catching scent of a lion; the gentle reassurances of those who guarded the herds; the clicking of the palm fronds.

How many nights, he wondered, had he lain in his tent and listened to those noises in terror and loneliness, and hated them? Now, in place of this hubbub of humanity, he longed for them back.

He passed Zohra's tent on the way to his and decided to enter and talk to her. She had been so silent and preoccupied upon the journey, and he, too, had been taken up with his own thoughts and wonderings. They had not spoken more than a handful of words since that awful, triumphant night in Kich. Peering into the open tent, he saw Zohra surrounded by women—chattering and laughing and exclaiming over the latest gifts that came pouring in—perfume, jewelry, bolts of silk and wool, candied rose petals, slaves, brass lamps enough to light a palace. Usti—his fat face radiating warmth until it seemed they might douse the lamps and rely instead upon the djinn—hovered about the Prophetess, accepting the gifts with unctuous gratitude, casting a critical eye upon them, and then nearly driving his mistress wild by whispering in her ear how much each was really worth.

Mathew lingered, watching, unnoticed. The Princess Zohra that he knew would have fled this perfumed prison, caught her horse, and galloped away among the shifting dunes. The young wizard waited to see if this would happen. His thoughts touching her, Zohra raised her dark eyes and looked into his, and he saw there that very longing. But he saw also resignation, enforced patience, rare self-discipline. His astonishment must have been visible, for a flush deepened the rose in her complexion. She smiled a rueful, twisted smile and shrugged slightly as if to say, "What else can I do? I am Prophetess of Akhran."

Mathew smiled back, bowed to the Prophetess, and left. And just as he missed the wind and the song and the lion's growl, so did he miss the impetuous, unpredictable Princess.

Weary from the long ride, Mathew lay gratefully among his cushions. He was just wondering if it would be worth his while to douse his *chirak* and hope sleep would come to him, when the tent flap opened suddenly. A dark figure, the *haik* covering its face, darted in. Avoiding the lamplight, it sank back swiftly into the shadows. Reminded unreasonably of the Black Paladin, Mathew started up in alarm. But the figure raised an admonishing hand and, drawing aside the facecloth, let his features be seen.

"It is only Khardan," came a tired voice.

"*Only* the Prophet," returned Mathew with a gentle, mocking smile.

Khardan groaned and threw himself down among the cushions. His handsome face was lined and brooding; dark shadows could be seen beneath the eyes, and Mathew's smile gave way to true concern.

"Are you well? Does something pain you? Your wound, perhaps?"

Khardan waved it all away with a gesture. "The wound is healed. I had it attended to when I first rode into camp. How long ago was that? A week? It seems a year, a thousand years!" Sighing, he leaned back and closed his eyes. "My tent is filled with storytellers and tea drinkers, gift bearers and would-be advisers, soldiers and dancing girls—all staring at me hungrily as if I were some sort of stew that each could dip his fingers in and take away a piece! I would have ordered Sond to clear them out, but the djinn have vanished, disappeared again. So I pleaded nature's call, threw on these old clothes, and came here."

A voice called from somewhere outside. "The Prophet? Have you seen the Prophet?"

Khardan covered his face as the voice, now just outside Mathew's tent, asked permission to enter. "Pardon, *Marabout*, for disturbing your rest. Have you seen the Prophet?"

"He was walking in that direction," said Mathew, pointing straight at Khardan.

The nomad thanked him profusely and shut the tent flap. They could hear his feet running off toward the oasis.

"Thank you, Mat-hew." Khardan started to rise. "You were— as my tribesmen reminded me—going to your rest. It is the middle of the night. I am disturbing you."

"No, please!" Mathew caught hold of Khardan's arm. "I couldn't sleep, not with all the noise. Please stay."

It did not take much persuasion to convince the Calif to return to his cushions, though this time he lay sideways on them, propped up on one elbow. His dark eyes, gazing intently at Mathew, glittered in the lamplight.

"Will you do something for me . . . if you are not too tired?" Khardan asked abruptly.

"Certainly, Prophet," answered Mathew.

Khardan paused, frowning. This was obviously a difficult thing he was about to ask, and he was still mulling it over in his mind, uncertain whether or not to proceed.

His heart singing with joy, Mathew kept silent, fearing the song might come to his lips. At last Khardan nodded once, abruptly, to himself. He had, it seemed, made his decision.

"You can use your magic to"—be coughed and cleared his throat—"see into the future?"

"Yes, Prophet."

"Call me Khardan, please! I grow weary of that title." Mathew bowed.

"Then can you do so, now?' Khardan pursued.

"Yes, of course. With pleasure, Pro—Khardan."

On his arrival Mathew had carefully unpacked and hidden in a safe place the precious magical objects he had acquired during his journeys. One of these was a bowl made of polished wood he had discovered in the Hrana's camp in the foothills. Though Mathew had offered to trade a piece of jewelry for it, the owner had been more than happy to present it as a gift, following the nomadic custom of offering a guest anything in one's dwelling he admires. (Which led to being very careful what one admired.)

Mathew brought the bowl forth from its place near his pillow, handling it lovingly, delighting in the smooth feel of the wood that was a rare thing in the desert. He set it down upon the tent floor between himself and Khardan, pretending not to see the Calif's first involuntary motion to draw away from it, the stiffening of the body as he forced himself to remain where he was.

Reaching for the *girba* that hung outside the tent to keep the water cool for drinking, Mathew filled the bowl. Outside a voice had been raised in song in praise of the Prophet, reciting all his valorous acts. Mathew lowered his head, seeming to be looking into the water. But he glanced through his lashes at Khardan, who was listening with a certain amount of pleasure, yet at the same time an almost helpless irritation.

Mathew began to speak. "The visions I see in the bowl are not necessarily what will come to pass." Waiting for the ripples to fade from the water, the wizard made the standard warning as proscribed in his texts. "They will indicate only what may happen should you continue to follow the path you now trod. It might be wisdom to turn aside and try another path. It might be wisdom to keep to this one. Sul gives no answers. In many cases, Sul provides only more questions. It is up to you to ponder the vision and make your decision."

Staring almost hypnotized at the water, Khardan nodded. His face had softened into awe, fear, and eagerness. For both of them, the outside sounds had receded into the background. Mathew could hear his own breathing, the too-rapid beating of his heart. Tearing his gaze away from Khardan, he focused on the water and, commanding himself to concentrate, began the chant. He repeated it three times, and the images began to appear on the liquid's smooth surface.

"I see two falcons, almost identical in appearance. Each falcon flies at the head of a huge flock of warlike birds. The flocks meet and clash. There is fierce fighting and many of the birds fall, injured, dying."

Mathew was silent a moment, watching. "When the battle ends, one of the falcons is dead. The other rises higher and higher in the sky until he is crowned with gold and wears a golden chain about his neck and many are the numbers of birds who come and go at his command."

Raising his head, sitting back on his heels, he looked at Khardan. "Thus is the vision of Sul."

The Calif scowled, gesturing disgustedly at the water bowl. "Of what use is this?" he demanded bluntly. "That much I could have seen for myself looking into a cup of *qumiz!* There will be a battle. One side will win, the other will lose!" He sighed heavily, then—thinking he may have hurt Mathew's feelings—he cast him an apologetic glance. "I am sorry." He put a hand at his shoulder, grimacing. "I am tired. . ."

"And in pain!" said Mathew. "let me see to the wound while I interpret this vision. It is not quite the clear crystal you make of it, Khardan," he added, carefully concealing a smile.

Shaking his head, indicating a willingness to listen though obviously expecting nothing to come of it, Khardan submitted to Mathew's gentle touch. Withdrawing the Calif's robes, the young man revealed the wound, not healed, but ragged-edged and inflamed.

"You did *not* have this attended," Mathew said severely dipping a cloth into the bowl of water. "Lie down, that I may see it in the light."

"There was no time," Khardan said impatiently, but he lay down, stretching himself on his stomach full length upon the cushions, the lines of pain beginning to ease from his face at the touch of the cool cloth on his fevered skin. "The women were exhausted from their use of their magic. I have taken wounds before. My flesh is clean and knits rapidly."

"I will do what I can for it, but I am not skilled in the art of healing. You should have Zohra treat it—"

Khardan flinched. Mathew had his hands on the crude bandage he was fashioning; he was not touching the wound, there was no way he could have hurt the man, and he wondered at the Calif's reaction. Then Mathew understood. He had not touched the wound inflicted by steel, but another that had struck much nearer the heart.

Resting prone, on his stomach, Khardan stared straight ahead. Though it could not be seen, Zohra's tent stood in the direction of his frowning gaze. "Have you ever been in love, Mat-hew?" was the next, completely unexpected question.

The gentle fingers ceased their calm ministration. It was only an instant before their touch resumed, but that instant was long enough to catch Khardan's attention. He turned and cast Mathew a sharp, intense look before the young man was prepared to receive it.

In Mathew's eyes was the truth.

The young man shut his eyes, too late to hide what was there he knew, but hoping to shut out the expression of revulsion, anger, and contempt that he knew must contort Khardan's face. Or worse—pity. Anything—even hatred—must be better than pity.

"Mat-hew. . ." came the Calif's voice, hesitant, groping. A hand touched his arm, and Mathew jerked away from him, bowing his head, the red hair tumbling over his face.

"Don't say it!" He choked.' "Don't say anything! You despise me, I know! Yes, I love you! I've loved you from the moment you held the sword over my head and pleaded with me to choose life, not give myself up to death! How could I not love you? So noble, so strong, facing ridicule for my sake. And then in the castle. You were in agony, near death, and yet you thought of me and my pain that was nothing, nothing compared to what you suffered!" The words, burstling forth in a torrent, were followed by wrenching sobs. The slender body doubled over in anguish.

A hand, rough and callused, yet gentle now, reached out and rested on the quivering shoulder. "Mat-hew," said Khardan, "of all the costly gifts I have received this night, this you offer me is the most precious."

Slowly, confusedly, Mathew raised his tear-stained face. A shuddering sob shook him, but he choked it back. "You don't hate me? But your God forbids this. . ."

"*Hazrat* Akhran does not forbid love, freely offered, freely accepted. If he did, he would not be worthy of the trust and faith we put in him," said Khardan gruffly. His voice softened, and he added, "Especially love from a heart as courageous and wise as the one that beats within your breast, Mat-hew." Clasping the young man, Khardan drew him down and pressed his lips upon the burning forehead. "This love will honor me the rest of my days."

Mathew bowed as though receiving a benediction. The hands holding the wet cloth trembled, and he hid his face within them, tears of joy and relief washing away the bitter pain. His was a love that could never be returned, not precisely the way he sometimes dreamed of it. But it was a love that was respected and would be given back in trust, in turning to him for guidance, comfort, advice, in offering him protection, strength, and friendship.

Rolling over on his stomach, giving the young man the opportunity to compose himself, Khardan said with quiet casualness, "Tell me now, Mat-hew, what you make of this vision."

CHAPTER 14

Mathew wiped his eyes and drew a deep, shivering breath, thankful to be able to change the subject, grateful to Khardan for suggesting it.

"The vision, you remember, was of two falcons—"

"More birds," grumbled Khardan.

"—leading opposing armies," Mathew continued severely with a light, rebuking tap on the man's shoulder to remind him of the seriousness of their undertaking.

"Myself and the Amir."

"The falcons looked very much alike," said Mathew. He neatly wound the bandage around the man's wounded arm. "These falcons represent you and your brother."

"Achmed?" Worried, Khardan twisted his head.

"Lie still. Yes, Achmed."

"But he couldn't ride at the head of the army!" Khardan scoffed. "He's too young."

"Yet I believe from what I have gathered that he rides with the Amir, who is head of the army. The visions are not literal. remember. They are what the heart sees, not the eye. If you fought the Amir's army, your thoughts would be with the man, Qannadi, riding at the head of his troops. But your heart would be with your brother, would it not?"

Khardan grunted, settling himself in the cushions, his chin resting on his arms.

"Now then," said Mathew, adjusting the bandage. "Is that too tight? No? What else was there? Oh, yes. The battle. Both sides take heavy losses. There are many casualties. It will be a bloody, costly war." His voice grew halting. "One of the falcons dies. . ."

"Yes?" persisted Khardan, though he lay very still. "The survivor goes on to become a great hero. He will rise with the wings of eagles. All manner of people will come to his standard, and he will challenge the Emperor of Tara-kan and eventually emerge the victor, wearing a golden crown and a golden chain about his neck."

"So"—Khardan, forgetting his wound, shrugged and winced with the pain—"the victor becomes a hero."

"I did not say 'victor,'" Mathew returned gently, "I said 'survivor.'"

It took a moment for the truth to sink home. Slowly, his movements hampered by the stiffness of the bandage, Khardan sat up and faced the young wizard, who was watching him with a grave and troubled expression. "What you are saying, Mathew, is that if my brother and I meet in battle, one of us will die."

"Yes, so the vision indicates."

"And the other becomes what—Emperor?" Khardan looked at him darkly, with disbelief.

"Not immediately, of course. I have the impression that many, many years will pass before that happens. But yes, the one who lives will eventually rise to a position of great power and wealth and also tremendous responsibility. Remember, the falcon wears not only the golden crown, but the golden chain as well."

Khardan's thoughts strayed outside, to his people and to those who had come to him. Only now, when the night was well past its fullness and falling off to morning, were they beginning to think of going to their beds. With the dawn the Prophet of Akhran would be faced with yet another line of men and women, bringing to him their small griefs, their great griefs, their wants and desires, their hopes and fears.

"Perhaps he can help them," said Khardan, speaking with ashy, reluctant pride. "Perhaps, even though he is not wise or learned, he has been chosen to help them, and he cannot lightly give up that which was given him."

"It is his decision, certainly," said Mathew. "I wish I could be of more help," he added wistfully.

Khardan looked at him and smiled. "You have been, Mathew. He only wishes he were as wise as you; then he would know he was doing the right thing." The Calif rose to his feet and prepared to leave, winding the folds of the headcloth about his face so that he could move through the camp without being mobbed. "Perhaps, being so wise, you can answer me one more question."

He halted at the entryway.

"I do not know that I am wise, but I will always try to help you, Khardan."

"Auda ibn Jad. He was cruel, evil. He cast helpless men to monsters. He committed murder and worse in the name of his evil God."

Mathew answered with a shudder.

"Yet our Gods yoked us together. Auda saved our lives; without him we would have perished in the Sun's Anvil. He saved my life by giving up his own there in the Temple of Quar. I mourn his passing, Mat-hew. I grieve that he is gone. Yet I know the world is better for his death. Do you understand any of this?"

Khardan looked truly puzzled, truly searching for an answer. After a moment's thought, Mathew said earnestly, "I do not understand the ways of the gods. No man does. I do not know why there is evil in the world or why the innocent are made to suffer. I only know that a blanket made of thread running all one direction is not of much use to us as a blanket, is it, Calif?"

"No," said Khardan thoughtfully. "No, you are right." His hand clasped the young man's shoulder. "Sleep well, Mat-hew. May Akhran—No. What is the name of your God?"

"Promenthas."

"May Promenthas be with you this night."

"And Akhran with you," said Mathew.

He watched the Calif slip out of the tent, stealing across the compound of his own people with more care and caution than he ever took stealing into enemy camp. Seeing Khardan reach his tent in safety, noting several dancing girls in bells and silks being shooed out, Mathew—smiling and shaking his head—returned to his bed.

The young man was at peace. His decision was made. Closing his eyes, comforted by the sound of the wind singing in the rigging of his tent, Mathew slept.

CHAPTER 15

Though Khardan spent a restless night pondering the vision Mathew had spread before him, he was not able to reach a decision. And thus it was his people who finally swept their Calif into the whirlwind of war.

The Sheykhs were the first to enter the tent of the fatigued and bleary-eyed Prophet, half-stupefied from pain, worry, and lack of sleep. Before Khardan could open his mouth, the Sheykhs presented their plan for battle—for once agreed upon by all present—and sat back to await his glowing commendation.

The plan was viable, Khardan had to admit this much. Reports trickling in along with a seemingly endless stream of refugees, rebels, and adventurers indicated that the forces of the Amir had been considerably reduced by the magical fog that swept over Kich. Those soldiers who survived were busy rebuilding the gate and other damaged fortifications. In addition they had to quell a near riot in the city when the rumor started that the nomads were threatening to unleash the killing mist on its citizens unless Kich surrendered.

The Sheykhs hinted that summoning the fog again might be a reasonable suggestion, to which Khardan asked them grimly if they meant to send their women before them into every battle they fought. "Bah! You are right!" stated Majiid. "A stupid idea. It was his." He waved his hand at Jaafar.

"Mine!" Jaafar bounced to his feet. "You know—"

"Enough!" said Khardan, stifling a yawn. "Go on."

According to reports, Qannadi had sent messengers to the southern cities, calling for reinforcements, but it would take many weeks before they could be expected to arrive. A raid, swift and deadly, on Kich, and the Prophet could take control of the city, use it as a spearhead to launch attacks that would drive the enemy from Bas.

The plan mapped itself out further in Khardan's mind, though the Sheykhs never knew it. Bas would fall to him easily. The people, under his skilled guidance and leadership, could be counted on to revolt against the Emperor's troops.

With Bas and its wealth at his disposal, Khardan could cut the trade route to Khandar and leisurely build his strength. Letting Khandar starve, he would march north and free the oppressed people of Ravenchai from the slave traders who ravaged their lands. He would ally himself with the strong plainsmen of the Great Steppes. The Lord of the Black Paladins would undoubtedly agree to add his own forces to the battle.

Then, when he was strong, he would attack the Emperor. Yes, Khardan admitted to himself almost reluctantly, it could be done. Mathew's vision was not as wild and farfetched as it had seemed to the Calif in the early hours of the dawning. It could be done. He could be Emperor of Sardish Jardan if he wanted. He would live in a magnificent palace of splendors that he could only dimly begin to imagine. The most beautiful women in the world would be his. His sons and daughters would number in the hundreds. No luxury would be too good for him. Rare and exotic fruits would rot on his tables. Water—there would be water to waste, to squander. As for his horses, all the world would come and fight to buy them, for he could afford the finest breeding stock and raise them on lush grasses and spend all his day, if he chose, personally supervising their training.

But no, not all day. There would be audiences, and correspondence with other rulers and his military leaders. He would have to learn to read, he supposed, since he would not dare trust another to interpret his correspondence. He would make enemies—powerful enemies. There would be food tasters, for he would not dare to eat or drink anything that some poor wretch had not sampled first for fear it was poisoned. There would be bodyguards dogging his every step.

He would make friends, too, of course, but in some ways these would be worse than his enemies. Couriers fawning on him, wazirs intriguing for him, nobles protesting their great love for him. And all prepared to fall upon him and tear out his throat should he show any sign of weakness. His own sons, perhaps, growing up to plot his downfall, his daughters given away like any other beautiful object to gain some man's favor.

Zohra. He saw her as head wife of a *seraglio* teeming with women, most of whose names he would not be able to remember. He saw her grow strong in her magic, and he knew that this, too, would bring him great power. And then there was Mathew—wise counselor—always near, always helping him, yet never seeming to intrude. These would be two people near him he could trust. Perhaps the only two.

A rumbling sound interrupted his daydream. Blinking, he raised eyes that burned with fatigue and saw his father glaring at him. "Well?" demanded Majiid. "Do we ride this night for Kich? Or are you going back to your bed and your dancing girls?" From his leer, it was obvious what he suspected his son of doing in the night.

Khardan did not immediately answer. He was seeing in his mind not the glorious palace or the hundreds of wives or the wealth beyond reckoning. He was seeing his younger half brother, clad in the armor of a man with a man's face and a man's sword arm, crouched in a fog-shrouded street, whispering his mother's name in a voice choked with tears.

There could be no help for it. Achmed had chosen his path, as Khardan must now choose his.

"We ride to war," he said.

Day, a week later, dawned upon Kich. The sun's light had no more than spread a blood red glow over the horizon when the cry of a tower lookout brought a captain running to see for himself. A messenger was sent to the Amir, who did not need it, having glanced out his own window and seen for himself.

His orders had already been given.

In the *Kasbah* below there was organized confusion as the troops made ready. Panic raged in the city, but Qannadi had that, too, in as much control as possible; men, women, and older children arming themselves and preparing to fight the invading horde.

"Send for Achmed," said Qannadi to Hasid, and the old soldier left upon his errand without question or comment.

Abul Qasim Qannadi walked over to the window—the one behind which he'd been sitting the night Feisal had died—and stared out across the plains into the low hills. A line of men, some mounted on swift, fearless desert horses and some on long-legged racing camels, spread over the hilltops. They had not yet moved but were waiting patiently for the command of their Prophet to ride down and deal death to the city dwellers of Kich. Their numbers were vast, their tribal banners and banners of other allegiances were thick as trees in a forest.

Rubbing his grizzled beard, Qannadi gazed out to the highest hilltop. He could not see him, not from this distance, but he had the instinctive feeling that Khardan was there, and it was to this hilltop that he directed his words.

"You have learned much, nomad, but not enough. Hurl your head at this solid wall. You will end up with nothing but a cracked skull for your efforts. I can stay here days, a month, if need be. By that time, my troops will have arrived from the south, and if any of your people are left—assuming they have not got bored with sitting there exchanging insults and the occasional arrow with the enemy on the walls—I will catch you between this wall and my advancing troops, and I will crack you like an almond."

Satisfied with his observations, running over his plans in his head, the Amir turned back to his desk. There was always the possibility, of course, that the nomad's first onslaught would crash upon them like sea water, sweeping aside all defense and carrying the hordes of invaders into the city walls where Qannadi and his people would be cut up and fed to the buzzards. The Amir had planned for this eventuality, as well.

"You sent for me, sir," said a clear voice.

Qannadi nodded, resumed his seat, and made a show of sliding several pieces of folded and sealed parchment into a leather bag. "I am sending you, Achmed, with dispatches to Khandar. These are for the Emperor and the Commander General. You will undoubtedly find them both in the palace, making plans to attack Tirish Aranth. Here is a pass. You had best leave now, in case the nomads cut the roads."

He spoke calmly, evenly, and did not look up from his work until all was in readiness. Then he started to hand the packet to Achmed.

The young man's face was livid, the brown eyes had turned a smoky gray color in the pale light of dawn. "Why do you send me away?" Achmed asked through stiff, bloodless lips. "Do you fear that I will betray you?"

"Dear boy!" Rising to his feet, Qannadi dropped the packet

and grasped the quivering hand that clutched, white-knuckled, the hilt of a sword. "How can you ask such a thing of me?"

"How can *you* ask such a thing of me? Sending me forth like a child when danger threatens!"

"It is your people we fight, my son," Qannadi said in a low voice. "It is said that Sul inflicts demons on those who shed the blood of near kin. I do not know if that is true, but I have known men who killed those they loved and—whether the demons came from without or within—I saw them tormented to their dying day. It was in my mind only to spare you this. Think, my boy! It is your father, your brother you will meet in battle this day!"

Achmed grasped the Amir's hand in his and held it fast.

"It is my father I will ride beside in battle this day," he said steadily. "I know—I have known—no other."

Qannadi smiled and for a moment could not speak. His hand ruffled the young man's dark, curling hair until he found his voice. "If you are resolved in this—"

"I am," broke in Achmed firmly.

"—then I place the command of the cavalry in your charge. You know your brother, you know how he thinks, how your people fight. My young general," he said in a teasing tone, regarding Achmed with fond pride, "I had a strange dream last night. Shall I tell you?"

The young man nodded. Both men were alert to sounds outside, sounds that would tell them the enemy was on the move. But nothing came, so far. Khardan must be waiting until the sun rose full and bright.

"I dreamed I found a young, half-grown falcon that had been caught in a snare. I freed it and trained it, and it became the most valuable bird in my possession. Its worth was beyond measure, and I was more proud of it than certain other falcons I had raised from infancy. Time and again this falcon flew from my wrist and soared into the sky, yet it always returned to me, and I was proud to welcome it home.

"And then there came the day when the falcon returned, and the wrist it knew was still and cold." Achmed clutched Qannadi's hand and would have spoken, but the Amir silenced him and continued steadily. "The falcon spread its wings and rose into the air. Higher and higher it flew, attaining heights it had never before imagined. I looked up and saw the gold of the sun touch its head, and I closed my eyes, well content.

"I wish I could see your future, my falcon," continued Qannadi softly, "but something tells me it is not to be. If not this battle, then another will claim me." Or the assassin's dagger. There were those among Quar's priesthood—not to mention Qannadi's wife, Yamina—who blamed him for Feisal's death. But this he carefully kept to himself. "Always remember that I am proud of you and, from this moment on, I name you my son and heir."

Achmed gasped and stared, then shook his head, stammering an incoherent protest.

"My decision is firm," said Qannadi. He pointed at the leather case. "It is all in there, my will and testament, signed and witnessed in proper form, legal and correct. Of course"—he grinned wryly—"the charming sons of my loins—at least my wives claim they are of my loins—will no doubt sit back in their haunches and howl, then try their best to sink their teeth into you. Don't let that stop you! With the Imam out of the way, I think you can handle them *and* their mothers. Fight them and know that you have my blessing, boy!"

"I will, sir," murmured Achmed, half-dazed, not entirely comprehending the gift that was being bestowed upon him.

"We will send Hasid to place my will in the Temple of Khandar. He's the only one I trust with this—my life. It will be kept secret, of course. My wealth is considerable and worth the cost of a poisoned flask of wine. I know you care nothing for gold or lands now. But you will. Someday I think you will find a use for it."

Rising from his desk, Qannadi picked up his helm and the leather pouch. Achmed helped him to gird on his sword. His arm around the young man's shoulders, the Amir walked with Achmed to the door.

"And now we best prepare ourselves to face this so-called Prophet of a Ragtag, Wandering God. I must admit, son, that I sometimes miss the Imam. It might be very instructive to know what is transpiring in heaven this moment."

The Book
of Sul

CHAPTER 1

All was not well in heaven.

Once again the One and Twenty had been summoned. Once again they met at the top of the mountain at the bottom of the world. Once again each stood firm upon his own facet of the Jewel of Sul, viewing the others from the safety and complacency of his or her own familiar surroundings.

Promenthas stood in his grand cathedral, his angels and archangels, his cherubim and seraphim, gathered around him. The God was looking particularly fierce, his eyebrows bristled, his lips were drawn so tightly their usual smile was lost in the snowy beard that tumbled over his cassock. The angels were in a tense state, muttering and whispering among themselves, except for one young guardian angel who sat alone in the choir loft. She seemed nervous and abstracted and kept tugging at her wing feathers as if—though knowing she must be here—she wished herself flying somewhere else. It was rumored among the seraphim and confirmed by the cherubim that the protégé of this young angel was involved in the great conflict among the humans, the outcome of which would be determined, perhaps, by this meeting among the Gods.

Uevin was in attendance, no longer fearing to leave his wondrous palace. Evren and Zhakrin both arrived, standing at opposite ends of the Jewel, eyeing each other askance, yet now according each other a grudging respect.

As the Gods came together, they spoke together, and their words were words of worry and concern, for the Jewel was still out of balance, still wobbling chaotically through the universe, and though the balance had tipped in another direction, it continued to be an unsafe and an unhealthy balance. Yet the Gods were uncertain how to correct it.

Almost all were gathered—the exception, as usual, being Akhran the Wanderer, and in this exception some saw sinister portent—by the time Quar arrived. In his almond-eyed beauty, the God had always seemed fragile and delicate. Many noticed that the delicateness had lately melted into boniness, the olive skin had a sallow, sickly yellow cast, the almond eyes darted here and there in ill-concealed fear.

Quar did not appear to his fellows in his pleasure garden but entered—in fawning meekness and humility—the dwellings of the other Gods. Those who had caught a glimpse of the God's habitation saw that the lush foliage of the pleasure garden seemed to be suffering from a drought. The leaves of the orange trees were drying up, the fragrant gardenia had all but a few of the strongest—withered and died. No water poured from the fountains, and their pools were scum-covered and stagnant. Gazelles wandered about aimlessly, panting in thirst. Here and there lurked an emaciated immortal, peering out furtively from the parched trees and trembling whenever the dread name Pukah was pronounced (as it was, by Quar, with a curse, about twenty times an immortal day).

"Promenthas—my friend and ally," said Quar warmly, advancing down the aisle of the cathedral toward the God and, at the same time, speaking the same words to each of the other Gods, "I come to you in this time of dire peril! Heaven has gone awry! The world below totters on the brink of disaster! It is time to put aside petty differences and join together against the coming menace."

So interesting and unusual a spectacle was it to see Quar oiling his way into each God's domain that Benario hesitated a moment too long in swiping a fine emerald from Hurishta and lost his chance forever, while even Kharmani ceased, for the moment, to count his money. The God of Wealth raised a languid eye.

"I thought *you* were the coming menace," said that God to Quar carelessly. The teeterings of the Jewel never bothered Kharmani, for war meant money to somebody at least.

A nervous laughter among the younger angels greeted this remark, to be instantly squelched by the elder cherubim, whose serious faces reflected the grave concern in the eyes of their God. Quar flushed in anger but bit his tongue—and spoke in injured tones.

"I sought only to bring order to chaos, but you would not have it so and let yourselves be duped by that desert bandit! Now his hordes stand poised to attack! *Jihad!* That is what Akhran the Wanderer, now called Akhran the Terrible, will bring down upon you! *Jihad!* Holy war!"

"Yes, Quar," said Promenthas drily. "We know what the word means. We recall hearing it before from your lips, though perhaps in another context."

Staring intently at each God in turn and seeing them hostile at the worst, indifferent at the best, Quar dropped the honey-coated facade. His lips curled in a snarl. "Yes, I would have ruled you. . . you fools! But my rule in the heavens and in the world below would have been a lawful one—"

"*Your* laws," muttered Promenthas.

"A just one—"

"*Your* justice."

"I sought to rid the world of extremes, to bring peace where there was bloodshed. But in your pride and your own self-impor-tance, you refused to consider what would be best for the many and looked, instead, to the one—to yourselves.

"And now you will pay," Quar continued in grim satisfaction. "Now one comes to rule who abides by no law, not even his own. Anarchy, bloodshed, war waged for sport—this is what you have brought upon yourselves! The Jewel of Sul will crack and fall from its place in the universe, and all up here and all down below will be doomed!

"See!" Quar, hearing a sound behind him, whirled in terror and pointed a trembling finger. "See—he comes! And the storm follows!"

Galloping across the dunes on a steed luminous as moon-light, trailing stardust from its mane, rode Akhran. His black robes flowed around him, the feathers on his horse's elaborate headdress glistened a bright, blood red. The God was flanked by three tall, muscular djinn. Their golden-ringed arms clasped for-biddingly across their broad chests, they gazed down with grim and threatening faces upon the Gods.

Akhran the Wanderer guided his steed into the meeting place of the Gods, and so powerful had he grown and so commanding his presence that it seemed to the other Gods that their domains must be blown away by the southern wind called *sirocco*, and that they would soon wander lost and helpless in a vast and empty desert.

Reining in his horse, causing the animal to stand upon its hind legs and trumpet in loud triumph, Akhran slid skillfully from his saddle. The *haik* covered his nose and mouth, but the eyes of the God flared like lightning and those eyes saw no one, paid no attention to anyone except Quar. Slowly, resolutely, Akhran the Wanderer stalked across the sand, his gaze fixed upon the almond-eyed, cowering God. Putting his hand to the hilt of his scimitar, the Wandering God drew forth the sword from its ornate scabbard. Suns, moons, planets—all were reflected in the shining silver blade, and it flared with a holy light.

"There!" gasped Quar, licking his lips and casting a bitter glance around at his fellows. "There, what did I tell you? He means to murder me as his accursed followers murdered my priest! And you"—he glared around at the other Gods—"you will be next to feel his blade at your throat!"

If Quar had not been in such a frenzy of terror, he would have noted with supreme satisfaction the growing fear and concern in the eyes of Promenthas, the return of terror to the eyes of Uevin, the eager gleam in the eyes of Benario. But Quar was stumbling here and there, endeavoring to escape Akhran's wrath and noticed nothing. There was nowhere to go, however, and he found himself backed up against the lip of a deep, dark well. He was trapped. He could go no farther without tumbling into Sul's Abyss. Spitting puny curses and baring his tiny teeth like a rat caught by the lion, Quar crouched at the feet of Akhran, glaring at the God with unmitigated hatred.

Coming to stand before the shrinking, sniveling God, Akhran raised above Quar's head the sword that gleamed with the light of eternity. He held it poised for an instant during which time on earth and in the heavens stood still. Then, with all his strength and might, Akhran the Wanderer brought the sharp-edged blade slamming down.

Quar screamed. Promenthas averted his eyes. The angel in the choir loft buried her head in her hands.

And then Akhran laughed—deep, booming laughter that rolled like thunder across the heavens and the earth.

In one piece, safe, unharmed, Quar stood cringing before him. The blade of the scimitar had missed the God by the breadth of a hair split in two again and yet again. It stuck, point down, in the sand between his slippered feet.

His merriment echoing throughout the universe, Akhran turned his back upon the other Gods and whistled to his steed. Vaulting into the saddle, treating himself to a final amused look at the shivering, quivering Quar, the Wanderer caused his horse to leap into the night-black sky and dashed away amidst the stars.

One by one, sighing in vast relief, the Gods dispersed—returning each to his own facet of Sul, returning to their eternal bickering and arguing over Truth. Last to leave was Quar, who slunk back to his blighted garden, where he—noting that some of his plants continued to flourish—sat down upon a cracked marble bench and plotted revenge.

Promenthas dismissed the cherubim and the seraphim and all the rest back to their neglected duties, then wended his way up the narrow, spiraling stairs to the choir loft where the angel sat, her head hidden, afraid to look.

"Child," aid Promenthas kindly, "all is ended."

"It is?" She raised a face both fearful and hopeful.

"Yes. And here are some who have come to talk to you, my dear."

Looking up, Asrial saw two tall, handsome djinn in rich silks and jewels approach her. Walking beside one of the djinn, her small white hand clasped fast in his, was a beautiful djinniyeh.

"Lady Asrial," said Sond, bowing from the waist, "we know we can never take the place of Pukah in your heart, but we would deem it an honor if you would come with us and dwell among us both in the world of humans below and on our immortal plane above."

"Do you mean that, truly?" Asrial gazed at them in wonder. "I can stay with you and be close. . . close to . . . Pukah."

"For all eternity," said Nedjma, her eyes glistening with tears, her hand gripping Sond's more tightly.

"Who knows?" added Fedj with a smile. "Someday we may find a way to free the"—he was about to say "little nuisance" but, considering the circumstances, thought it best to change it magnanimously to—"great hero."

Asrial's eager eyes went pleadingly to Promenthas.

"Go and my blessings with you. . . and with the human you have so valiantly protected and defended. I think that your vigil over Mathew may now be relaxed, for—unless I am much mistaken—it will soon be shared by others."

"Thank you, Father!" Asrial bowed her head, received Promenthas's loving benediction, and—giving her hand timidly to Nedjma—walked with the djinn and the djinniyeh into the desert.

CHAPTER 2

igh on a ridge overlooking the walled city of Kich, Khardan
sat on his war-horse and gazed out over the plains. It was
after sunrise. The blazing orb, shining in the heavens, was reflected in the drawn and glistening blades of the *spahis,* the shepherds,
the *mehariste,* the *goums,* the refugees, the mercenaries, the rebels, and all who rode with the Prophet of Akhran.

Khardan turned his attention to the walled city. It was some
distance from where he and his army stood poised and ready to
sweep down upon it like birds of prey. But the Calif could see—or
fancied he could—the Temple of Quar. He wondered if rumors
about it were true. It was said to be abandoned. The refugees had
brought stories that it had been cursed-the deadly fog lingered
in its halls, the ghost of the Imam could sometimes be heard
preaching to priests as disembodied as himself. Whether or not
this curse was true, most of the Temple's gold and jewels had been
stripped from it, those who worship Benario having small respect
for the curses of other Gods.

His gaze wandered restlessly from the Temple to the slave
market, and his thought traveled back to the man with the cruel
eyes in the white palanquin, to a slave woman with hair the color
of flame. He glanced at the *souks,* the houses piled one on top of
the other. His eyes went to the massive palace with its walls of
thick stone that seemed to grow thicker and taller as the Prophet stared at it. He could have sworn that he saw the blind beggar seated in his accustomed place, he saw a blonde woman in
pink silk languishing in his arms. And here came Qannadi and
Achmed, armor flashing in the sunlight, to be greeted with cheers
from the soldiers, who may have momentarily lost faith in their
God, but who retained it in their honored commander.

Khardan blinked, wondering at these impossible visions.

Now he swore he could smell the city, and he wrinkled his nose in disgust. He decided he would never get used to it and supposed bleakly that Khandar—capital of an empire, a city , containing not thousands but millions of people—must smell not a thousand but a million times worse.

And he would win this treasure at the cost of his brother's life. As a child Achmed had taken his first steps from his mother's arms into Khardan's. In those arms, according to the vision, Achmed would find his death.

The Prophet's horse fidgeted beneath him. The animal smelled battle and blood and longed to surge forward, but its master did not move. Khardan understood the horse's restlessness and stroked its neck with a trembling hand. The Calif had never in his life felt fear before a battle, but now he began to pant for breath, as though suffocating. Lifting his head, Khardan looked about wildly for some means of escape.

Escape from a battle he was sure to win.

His eyes encountered the fierce eyes of Sheykh Majiid, riding at the right hand of the Prophet and glaring at his son impatiently, mutely demanding the reason for this delay. The plan had been to strike at dawn, and here it was, nearly an hour past, and the Prophet had made no move.

At the Prophet's left hand was Sheykh Jaafar, his face falling into its customary gloomy foreboding, sweating in the brightening light, the saddle rubbing sores on his bony bottom.

To the left of Jaafar was Sayah, Zohra's half-brother and the Sheykh's eldest son, who was casting looks of secret triumph at Khardan as though he had guessed all along that the Prophet was a fraud.

To the right of Majiid, Zeid towered magnificently over the horsemen on his long-legged camel, the Sheykh's shrewd, squinty eyes growing shrewder and squintier the longer they sat here, exposed to the enemy on this ridge.

Behind the Sheykhs, muttering and grumbling with impatience, the army of the Prophet began to question among themselves what was happening, and giving answers that were half truths, and untruths, and no truths at all, gradually working themselves into a state of confusion and demoralization.

Off at a distance, separate and apart from the men, Zohra and Mathew watched and waited—the heart of one wondering at

Khardan, the heart of the other knowing and pitying, yet trusting.

Suddenly out of the air appeared the three djinn, Fedj, Raja, and Sond. Bowing low before Khardan, they hailed him in the name of *Hazrat* Akhran, who sent his blessings to his people.

"About time, too," said Zeid loudly.

"Are these what we've been waiting for?" questioned Majiid of his son, waving his hand at the djinn. "Well, they've come back. Let's attack before we all faint from the heat!"

"Yes," muttered Jaafar gloomily. "Let's get this over with, take the city, steal what we want, and go back home."

"You"—thundered Majiid, pointing at Jaafar—"have no vision! We will take the city, steal what we want, and burn it to the ground. *Then* we can go home."

"Bah!" snorted Zeid. "What is this talk of taking a city? Here we sit, slowly putting down roots into this God-cursed rock! If the Prophet will not lead us, I will!"

"Ah, but who will follow?" questioned Majiid, whirling around angrily to face his other old enemy.

"We will see! Attack!" yelled Zeid. Reaching out, he yanked his *bairaq* from the hands of his standard bearer and waved it high in the air. "I, Sheykh of the Aran, say 'attack'!"

"Attack! Attack!" The Aran echoed their Sheykh. Unfortunately their eyes were not on the city but on the Akar.

"I, too, say 'attack.' " Sayah leaned across his father's horse and sneered into Khardan's face. "But it seems our Prophet is a coward!"

"Coward!" Khardan turned on the young man in a rage. Wait! Consider! said an inner voice. Consider what you will be giving up. . .

The Prophet—pausing—considered. He looked up into the blue-and-golden sky. "Thank you, *Hazrat* Akhran!" he said softly, reverently.

"Attack!" shouted Khardan, and doubling up his fist, the Prophet of the Wandering God turned in his saddle and aimed right at Sayah's jaw.

Sayah ducked. Jaafar didn't. The blow sent Khardan's father-in-law tumbling head over heels backward off his horse.

"Have you gone mad?" A shrill voice rang over the crowd. Zohra galloped into their midst, her horse rearing and plunging.

"What of Kich? What of becoming Emperor? And what do you mean by striking my fath—"

"Get out of my way, sister!" cried Sayah.

"Oh, shut up!" Twisting in her saddle, Zohra took a vicious swing at her brother that, if it had hit, would have left his ears ringing for the next year. It missed. The momentum of her swing carried the Prophetess of Akhran out of her saddle to land heavily upon her father, just as the groggy, groaning Jaafar was struggling to his feet.

"Dog!" Sayah launched himself at Khardan and the two, grappling together, went for each other's throats.

Majiid, shrieking in fury, slashed wildly with his sword at Sayah, only to hit Zeid. The sword slit open a wide gash in the sash wrapped around Sheykh's round belly.

"That was my best silk sash! It cost me ten silver *tumans!*" Zeid foamed at the mouth. Clasping his standard in both hands like a club, he swung it in a wide are, unseated two of his own men, and clouted Majiid soundly in the ribs.

"You know, Raja, my friend," said Fedj, giving the gigantic djinn a rude shove that sent him flying through the skies, clear across the border into Ravenchai, "I have always thought your body to be too big for your small-spirited soul."

"And I, Fedj, my brother, have always found your ugly nose to be an insult to immortals everywhere!" snarled Raja. Bursting back on the scene, his hands grasped hold of that particular portion of Fedj's anatomy and began twisting it painfully.

"And I"—shouted Sond, leaping suddenly and unexpectedly upon the complacent Usti—"say that you are a doughfaced lump of sheep droppings!"

"I couldn't agree with you more!' Usti gasped and disappeared with a bang.

The hills around Kich erupted in confusion. Akar leaped at Hrana. Hrana smote the Aran. The Aran battled the Akar. Remnants of all three nomadic tribes banded together to turn upon the outraged refugees of Bas.

Making his dangerous way through the flailing fists and slashing sabers, maddened horses and screaming camels, Mathew ducked and dodged and pushed and shoved, seeking always the flutter of blue silk that robed the Prophetess of Akhran. He found her at last, pummeling with the butt-end of a broken spear a hapless Akar who had knocked out, for the second time, a befuddled Jaafar.

Zohra had just laid her victim low and was looking around, panting, for her next, when Mathew appeared before her, catching hold of her arm as she took a swipe at him.

"What do you want of me? Let me go!" Zohra demanded furiously, trying her best to break free.

Mathew held onto her grimly and determinedly, however, and Zohra, struggling but too battle-weary to free herself, had no choice but to follow him, cursing and swearing at him with every step.

Hanging onto Zohra with one hand, Mathew forged their way through the melee until he reached a black-robed figure, who was hacking away with a sword at another black-robed figure, neither making the least progress, both seeming prepared to spend the day and possibly the night in combat.

"Excuse me, Sayah," said Mathew politely, shoving between the two heavy-breathing, exhausted men. "I require a word with the Prophet."

Seeing—through a bleary haze—the *Marabout* and recalling that this man was not only crazy but a powerful sorcerer as well, Sayah waved a hand toward Khardan, bowed in respect for his opponent and, gasping for breath, staggered off in search of another fight.

"Come with me," said Mathew firmly, taking hold of Khardan's arm. He led the suddenly docile Prophet and the suddenly calm Prophetess back down the ridge, as far from the fighting as possible. Here, in the quiet of the vineyard where the people had hidden only weeks before with no expectation except that of death, Mathew turned to face the two people he loved.

Neither was much to look at. Zohra's veil had been torn loose—probably by her own hand—and cast to the winds. Her black hair, shining like a raven's wing, was tangled and disheveled and streamed across her face. Her best silken *chador* had been torn to shreds, her face was smeared with blood and dirt.

Khardan's wound had reopened, a patch of crimson stained his robes. Numerous other slash marks covering his arms and chest indicated that he had not found Sayah the easy match he had once scornfully considered the herder of sheep. His cheek was bruised and one eye was swelling shut, but he kept his other—dark and watchful—upon his wife.

Zohra, in turn, cast fiery glances at him from behind the veil of hair. Mathew could almost see the acid accusations rising to Zohra's lips, he could see Khardan preparing himself to catch the venomous drops and hurl them back at her.

"I have a gift for you two," said Mathew smoothly, as calmly as if he were meeting them on their wedding day.

Reaching into the folds of his black wizard's robes, Mathew drew forth something that he kept hidden in his hand. "What is it?" asked Zohra with a sullen air.

Mathew opened his palm.

"A dead flower," said Khardan scornfully, yet with a hint of disappointment. Imperceptively, perhaps by accident since he was literally swaying with fatigue, he took a step nearer his wife.

"A dead flower," echoed Zohra. Her voice was tinged with sadness, and surely by accident as well—she took a step nearer her husband.

"No, not dead," said Mathew smiling. "Look, it lives."

Khardan, Calif of the Akar, and Zohra, Princess of the Hrana, both leaned forward to stare at the flower lying in the wizard's palm. Inadvertently, undoubtedly by accident, the hands of husband and wife touched.

The crumpled petals of the flower grew smooth and shining, its ugly brown color deepened and darkened to a majestic purple, the center bud unfolded, revealing a heart of deepest red.

"The Rose of the Prophet!" breathed Khardan in awe.

"I found it growing on the Tel the morning we rode forth to battle," said Mathew softly. "I plucked it and I brought it with me, and now"—he drew a deep breath, his eyes going from one loved face to the other—"I give it to you and I give you two to each other."

Mathew held out the Rose.

Husband and wife reached for it at the same time, fumbled, and dropped it. Neither moved to pick it up, each had eyes only for the other.

Khardan clasped his arms around his wife. "I couldn't live within walls!"

"Nor I!" cried Zohra, flinging her arms around her husband.

"A tent is better, wife," said Khardan, inhaling deeply the fragrance of jasmine. "A tent breathes with the wind."

"No, husband," answered Zohra, "the yurt such as my people build is a much more comfortable dwelling and a much more suitable place in which to raise children—"

"I say—a tent, wife!"

"And I say, husband—"

The argument ended—momentarily—when their lips met. Clinging to each other fiercely, they turned their backs on the glorious brawl that raged unchecked on the hillside. Arms around each other—still arguing—they walked farther into the vineyard until they were hidden from view by the sheltering leaves of the grapevines, whose entwining stems seemed to offer to teach, by example, the ways of love. The quarreling voices softened to murmuring sighs and, at length, could be heard no more.

Mathew watched the two go, an ache in his heart that was both joy and a sweet sorrow. Leaning down, he picked up the Rose of the Prophet that had fallen, unheeded, to the ground.

As he touched it, he felt a tear fall warm and soft upon his hand and he knew, though how or why he could not tell, that it fell from the eyes of an angel.

GLOSSARY

agal: the cord used to bind the headcloth in place
aksakal: white beard, village elder
Amir: king
Andak: Stop! Halt!
ariq: canal
arwat: an inn
aseur: after sunset

baigha: a wild game played on horseback in which the "ball" is the carcass of a sheep
bairaq: a tribal flag or banner
Bali: Yes!
Bashi: boss
bassourab: the hooped camel-tent in which women trave
batir: thief, particularly horse or cattle thief (One scholar suggests that this could be a corruption of the Turkish word "bahadur" which means "hero.")
berkouks: pellets of sweetened rice
Bilhana: Wishing you joy!
Bilshifa: Wishing you health!
burnouse: A cloaklike garment with a hood attached

Calif: prince
caftan: a long gown with sleeves, usually made of silk
chador: women's robes
chirak: lamp
couscous: a lamb stuffed with almonds and raisins and roasted whole

delhan: a monster who eats the flesh of shipwrecked sailors *dhough:* ship

divan: the council-chamber of a head of state

djinn: beings who dwell in the middle world between humans and the Gods

djinniyeh: female djinn

djemel: baggage camel

dohar: midafternoon

dutar: two-stringed guitar

Effendi: title of quality

'efreet: a powerful spirit

Emshi besselema: a farewell salutation

eucha: suppertime

eulam: post meridian

fantasia: an exhibition of horsemanship and weapons skills

fatta: a dish of eggs and carrots

fedjeur: before sunrise

feisha: an amulet or charm

ghaddar: a monster who lures men and tortures them to death

ghul: a monster that feeds on human flesh. Ghuls may take any human form, but they can always be distinguished by their tracks, which are the cloven hooves of an ass

girba: a waterskin; four usually carried on each camel of a caravan

goum: a light horseman

haik: the combined head cloth and face mask worn in the desert

harem: "the forbidden," the wives and concubines of a man or the dwelling places allotted to them

hauz: artificial pond

Hazrat: holy

henna: a thorn-shrub and the reddish stain made from it

houri: a beautiful and seductive woman

Imam: priest

jihad: holy war

kafir: unbeliever
Kasbah: a fortress or castle
kavir: salt desert
khurjin: saddlebags
kohl: a preparation of soot used by women to darken their
eyes

madrasah: a holy place of learning
Makhol: Right! (exclamation)
mamaluks: originally white slaves; warriors
marabout: a holy man
mehara: a highly bred racing camel
mehari: a plural of mehara
mehariste: a rider of a mehara
mogreb: nightfall

nesnas: a legendary, fearsome monster that takes the form of
a man divided in half vertically, with half a
face, one arm, one leg, and so on

palanquin: a curtained litter on poles, carried by hand
pantalons: loose, billowing pants worn by men
paranja: a woman's loose dress
pasha: title of rank

qarakurt: "black worm," a large species of deadly spider
quaita: a reed instrument
qumiz: fermented mare's milk

rabat-bashi: innkeeper

saksul: a tree that grows in the desert
salaam: an obeisance, a low bow with the hand on the
forehead
salaam aleikum!: Greeting to you
saluka: a swift hunting dog
satsol: a desert-growing tree

seraglio: the quarters of the women of the harem

Sheykh: the chief of a tribe or clan

shir: lion

shishlick: strips of meat grilled on a skewer

sidi: lord, sir

sirocco: the south wind, a windstorm from the south

souk: marketplace, bazaar

spahi: native cavalryman

Sultan: king

Sultana: wife of a Sultan, queen

surnai: a traditional folk reed instrument, generally conical and made of wood

tamarisk: a graceful evergreen shrub or small tree with feathery branches and minute scalelike leaves

tambour: similar to a tambourine

tel: a hill

tuman: money

wadi: river or stream

wazir: an adviser to royalty

yurt: semipermanent tent